D0462816

❧ Praise for *The Stepping Off Place* ❧

"Captures all the passion and insecurity inherent in coming-of-age friendships. A not-to-be-missed debut."
—ESTELLE LAURE, author of *This Raging Light*

"Riveting, aching, and devastating in the best ways, Rosenblum's moving debut is my favorite young adult novel of 2020."
—KIM SAVAGE, author of the critically acclaimed *After the Woods, Beautiful Broken Girls*, and *In Her Skin*

"A spectacular novel! A page-turner that lingers."
—LYNDA MULLALY HUNT, author of *New York Times* bestseller *Fish in a Tree*

"Explores loss, futility, honesty, and love with a richness of prose and excellence of characterization rare in a first-time author. A story to savor."
—*KIRKUS REVIEWS* (starred review)

Also by Cameron Kelly Rosenblum
The Stepping Off Place

✣ CAMERON KELLY ROSENBLUM ✣

The
SHARP
EDGE *of*
SILENCE

Quill Tree Books
An Imprint of HarperCollinsPublishers

Quill Tree Books is an imprint of HarperCollins Publishers.

The Sharp Edge of Silence
Copyright © 2023 by Cameron Kelly Rosenblum
All rights reserved. Printed in the United States of America. No part of this book
may be used or reproduced in any manner whatsoever without written permission
except in the case of brief quotations embodied in critical articles and reviews. For
information address HarperCollins Children's Books, a division of HarperCollins
Publishers, 195 Broadway, New York, NY 10007.
www.epicreads.com
Library of Congress Control Number: 2022947987
ISBN 978-0-06-293210-5
Typography by Molly Fehr
23 24 25 26 27 LBC 5 4 3 2 1

First Edition

For Mom and Dad,
who taught me resilience

I contain multitudes.

—*Walt Whitman*

LYCROFT PHELPS SCHOOL

est. 1856

12 Liberty Street

Whitney, New Hampshire 03026

Dr. Griffin Frye

Head of School

Charlotte Tate Foresley

26 Deer Path Rd.

Thornwood, IL 60063

Dear Charlotte,

It is my great honor to offer you admission to the Lycroft Phelps School. Let me be the first to congratulate you on your fine accomplishments as a student and community member in middle school. Our admissions department is extremely selective. We are confident you have the curiosity of mind and exemplary character to thrive here at Lycroft Phelps. Like so many other talented "Crofters," you'll discover passions, pursuits, and friendships that will last a lifetime. Enclosed are the enrollment papers and student code of conduct pledge for you and your family to review, sign, and submit by April 15.

Who will you be at Lycroft Phelps? Explore the enclosed Athletics & Clubs catalog. Our offerings include a broad variety of sports (Boy's Crew won the Northeast Prep School Conference last spring!), performing arts, robotics, a capella, and Young Entrepreneurs to name a few. Dance director Celeste Chu is eager to bring your impressive dance experience to our own Ballet Northeast School, and to help you grow in your artistry.

Since 1860, distinguished Lycroft Phelps graduates have attended America's most elite colleges and universities and gone on to make significant national and global contributions in the arts, sciences, public policy, and business. You're on the path to making your mark, Charlotte Tate Foresley. Congratulations!

Sincerely,

Dr. Griffin Frye, 'Croft '86
M.A., Williams College
Ed.D., Columbia University

dant mentem animumque deducemini ~ Lead with minds and hearts alight

The
LYCROFT PHELPS SCHOOL
est. 1856
12 Liberty Street
Whitney, New Hampshire 03026

Dr. Griffin Frye
Head of School

Maxwell Hannigan-Loeffler
368 W. 67th St.
New York, NY 10023

Dear Maxwell,

It is my great honor to offer you a space at the Lycroft Phelps School as a Founders Legacy Scholar. Congratulations! This four-year scholarship covers all room, board, tuition, and school-related expenses from freshman year through graduation. Currently, we have just two other Founders Legacy Scholars at Lycroft Phelps. Our admissions committee found your exceptional prowess in STEM and numerous awards in math and science highly admirable, and we are confident you are on the kind of trajectory that makes for an exemplary career at Lycroft Phelps and well beyond. I'm sure you'll find nourishing challenges in our new Kessler STEM Center, as well as leadership opportunities within the department. We want to see you among the network of highly successful Lycroft Phelps alumni one day.

Who will you be at Lycroft Phelps? Explore the enclosed Athletics & Clubs catalog for next year. Like so many other talented "Crofters," you'll discover passions, pursuits, and friendships that will last a lifetime here on our beautiful campus. Enclosed are enrollment papers, Founders Legacy Scholarship details, and the student Code of Conduct pledge for you and your family to review, sign, and submit by April 15. Please do not hesitate to call my office directly with any questions.

Sincerely,

Dr. Griffin Frye, 'Croft '86,
M.A., Williams College
Ed.D., Columbia University

dant mentem animumque deducemini ~ Lead with minds and hearts alight

Dr. Griffin Frye
Head of School

Quinn Luddington Walsh
2636 Shore Rd.
Southport, CT 06890

Dear Quinn,

It is my great honor to welcome you to the Lycroft Phelps
School. As a sixth-generation legacy, your family is well
aware of the value of character education. Who will you be
at Lycroft Phelps, Quinn?

SEPTEMBER

❊·❊

1

Thursday Night

✣ ─────────────────────── ✣

Q

✣ *Lower Mid* ✣

I weave between trees—hidden, exposed, hidden, exposed—navigating roots and rocks and earth, spongy with leaf rot. Sprawled between tidy footpaths, these woods are unruly and thirsty, sucking the darkness between grooves in the tree bark and crevices in the rocks. The sky's at its darkest now—between sunset and moonrise.

So many betweens.

I'm between myself and myself, I think. I feel my bones but don't recognize my skin. This strange new self drinks in the power of night. I know what I *was*. I don't know what I'm becoming. But I know what I need to do. Get Officer Doughty's gun.

Because Colin Pearce must die.

I take care crossing the spiky skeleton of a fallen pine that ripped right through my running tights and slashed my knee last night. The tree is a landmark, and I know I'm nearly there. Rectangles of light appear through the black lace of leaves. Anderson House, home of LPS Campus Safety, is up ahead.

At the woods' edge, I stop. Twenty feet of lawn separates me and Officer Doughty. It's cold for September. My breath is uneven, billowing from my face in ragged blasts. I clamp my jaw and exhale through my nostrils, not wanting the act of fucking breathing to give me away.

Framed by the lit window, Doughty sits at his desk writing in his log. It's three minutes before eight p.m., and I can practically count off the seconds until he glances at the clock and commences his quitting time routine. Soon he'll walkie his deputy, Safety Officer McPhee, who's buzzing around campus in a pimped-out golf cart, and sign off for the day. He'll lock up Anderson, get in his pickup, and head home.

He closes the log and tips his chin toward the clock, then predictably walks toward the tiny bathroom.

I'm in all black, like Tom Cruise in those *Mission: Impossible* movies Dad and I used to watch. Just like a spy, I dash across the grass and press myself against the shingles of the old 1950s cottage. I peer in the window, opened a few inches. I already know there's only one main room with the desk, a few chairs, and a cot in the corner. A computer monitor with a split screen flips through grainy black-and-white scenes on campus. If Campus Safety had even the smallest particle of a clue, those cameras would point to the darker corners of school. Instead, it's like I'm watching the LPS website virtual tour. All brick and ivy colonnades, white domes crowned in blue, expansive quads crisscrossed by footpaths in pleasing geometric patterns. Does Doughty really believe the bronze Founders Statues of John Lycroft and Erastus Phelps needs a security cam trained on them? Then again, I think, I can use this ignorance to my advantage. Once I have the gun.

The toilet flushes, and the bathroom door creaks. I duck. Doughty's footsteps approach, the wheels of the chair crackle over grit on the worn wood floorboards, and he rests his knee on the ratty green seat cushion. He's so close I could poke him if it weren't for the wall. A giddy surge of my own power courses through me, and a bubble of laughter grows in my chest, threatening to pop and blow my plan to smithereens.

Stuff it! I tell myself. And the laugh curdles into anger, pooling in my throat, seeping back into the rest of me and settling to a simmer.

Doughty shifts and removes a shoulder holster, normally hidden under his bulky LPS Safety jacket. I doubt most people know Doughty packs heat. Like he'd ever shoot anyone at LPS. But I know. And this knowledge is everything.

He opens the desk drawer. Slides the pistol from its snug leather pocket—gently, reverently, maybe even lovingly. His gun may be the single thing that reminds Doughty what he *could* do if he didn't work at Lycroft Phelps.

In the trees, I hear John Lennon sing: *Happiness is a warm gun, bang bang, shoo-oo-oo-oot shoot,* and for a flash I'm five years old, with Dad in the study at home. He's setting the needle onto his vinyl record of the Beatles' White Album. "This is greatness, Q," he says. "Listen." He smiles, closes his eyes. The needle hisses, snaps, then, *She's not—a girl—who misses much.* Dad sings softly with the *doo-doo-doo* part, and opens his eyes at *oh, yeah.* I giggle. He swoops me into the air as Ringo's drums kick in, waltzing me around the room. I want this version of me back so badly I have to blink hard to unsee it and refocus on Doughty.

The thump of his pistol against the wood echoes in my gut. My temples pulse. I'm weak and jangly at once.

Is a warm gun, yeah.

He's hanging his holster on a wall peg and locking the drawer, opening another one and dropping in the keys. Hardly a foolproof safeguard, but in his defense, he suspects nothing. And I'm invisible, so we'll give him a pass on this misstep.

I press myself flat again as he shuts the window. I hear him latch it, and the lights dim. He's about to walkie Deputy McPhee. Even through the glass, I hear the fuzzy voice: "Hey, boss." My opportunity.

I silently dart around the back of the building to the other side of the porch, almost as if I'm flying. I think, *Wait, I* am *a ghost*. But, no, I've bitten my cheek and can taste blood when I press it with my tongue.

I pick a fat tree as close to the porch as I dare. Last time I was too far. Tonight I'll see that alarm code he dials to lock up. Doughty steps outside, closing the door behind him. He pokes buttons, which I know to be in a three-by-four array, like a phone pad. All I have to do is memorize the pattern. I stare as hard as I can.

Blip. Blip.

Three-three . . .

Bleep. Bleep. Bleep. Blip.

Nine-seven-nine-seven? Or six-four-six-four?

Doughty spins my way, heading for the pickup. Shoes crunch the path. The truck door opens. Slams. Engine turns over. Light floods the woods around me. The tires grind, spit gravel, and headlights swivel away.

Then silence. I'm alone.

He could forget something and come back. So I wait, leaning against the tree. An asymmetric moon rises from the hills behind

Lake Edith. It tosses pieces of itself onto the water, and the lake wears them like sequins. *You don't need to make yourself beautiful for this place, Edith,* I say in my head. *You're too good for them.* I'm motionless until the moon shoves off the hilltops, launching itself into the blue.

I move to the door. My gloved hand hovers in front of the keypad.

I tap: 3-3 . . . 9-7-9-7. I don't hear any unlatching sound but try the knob just in case.

Nothing. "Shit."

I stare at the numbers, willing them to reveal the code to me.

Haltingly, I push 3-3-6-4-6-4. I shake the knob. Again, nothing.

Inky, liquid shadows shimmer at the corners of my eyes. The numbers vibrate. I swear he dialed that pattern. I *know* it. Maybe the 3-3 was 6-6. I've got one chance left, assuming that the alarm will auto-lock—or worse, start blaring—if I try a fourth time.

6-6-3-1-3-1.

Silence.

The knob doesn't move. I throw my head back, about to yell *FUCK* as loud as I can when I see a bunch of kids coming up the hill from the lake. *"Fuck!"* I whisper instead, and duck behind the fat tree.

It's guys. One of them says something. I can't make out specific words, but it must have been really sick because the others laugh in that way when they know they're not supposed to. First Years, probably, so new to campus they don't dare *not* laugh. My throat clamps tight, and for a second, I think I might barf.

No, I tell myself.

When they're out of range, I contemplate trying one more time. I simply can't risk a blaring alarm. I'm sure I could get away now, but they'd double down on precautions—which are stuck somewhere in the 1970s, right where I need them.

I stare at the charcoal sky as my staccato huffs of breath vaporize above me. I'm done here for tonight. From the trees, two bats dart in a quick, pointy dance to starry music only they hear, and I feel so devastatingly alone that I could lie on the ground. Go to sleep and never wake up. The bats vanish. A tear rolls down my cheek. I swipe it away.

I fish my AirPods from my coat pocket. The opening to "Gimme Shelter" by the Rolling Stones washes over me like a filmy dream, waking every cell on its way. The bongos find my heartbeat.

Ready again, I flit, bat-like, back into the company of trees, my shadowy secret keepers.

CHARLOTTE FORESLEY

� *Upper Mid* ✥

I read the prompt on my laptop screen for the zillionth time.

What is at the heart of your desire to be this year's Young Choreographer?

It's not a trick question. And yet. I've been staring at it for a solid thirty minutes. My hands hover over the keys. *Don't think, Charlotte. For once.* The application is due to Madame Chu, director of Lycroft's Pre-Professional Ballet program, tomorrow by three o'clock, the end of classes. Madame is cagey. Does she want me to genuflect here or make some kind of statement about my artistic passion? She could want either. Or both.

I type.

It would be an honor to join the long list of distinguished dancers who

"Blech," I say, pressing delete. My screen burbles like it agrees with my assessment. But I realize it's an incoming text. Grace, my hometown best friend since preschool.

Grace: That pic you sent. You're living on a movie set!

She's talking about a photo of the quad at midday break today. Giant maple trees turning red at the top; students draped around the lawn having picnic lunches in small clusters.

Me: I know! It's like that painting made up of little dots we love at the Art Institute—the Ferris Bueller one.

Another computer burbly sound. She's FaceTiming. I glance over each shoulder to make sure I'm really alone here in the library's reference section, ashamed that I care. I can't explain why I have a hard time shifting back to the Thornwood version of myself when I'm here. Anyway, it's all clear, and I answer.

Grace pops on the screen. "Ha! *Sunday on La Grande Jatte*— New England prep school style."

"Perfect!" I say. "I miss you."

"Me too," she says.

"Just apply. You could be here by January." She won't, and I'm not sure it's the best idea anyway, but in a perfect world, it would happen, so I go with that.

"Ha! Not everyone's LPS material, Char."

I lower the laptop volume. "Please. Do *I* look like LPS material?! I'm just a good faker."

She makes her skeptical face. "Bull. Charlotte Foresley is quintessential LPS material. They put you on the frigging website landing page." She's grinning, anticipating my freak-out.

"What? They did?" I squeak. "How do you know?"

While I click the tab to open the page—also our student portal login, which means *e-ver-y-one* on campus will see this—Grace says, "Your mom shared it on Instagram. Of course."

"Oh God," I groan.

"They really should let you access social media more often at that place," Grace is saying. "I mean, your *mom* is online more than you. Sad." I don't bother arguing. I love escaping social media, honestly.

I stare at the picture. It's our advanced pointe class warming up at the barre, including my roommate and best friend here,

Hannah. But my face is the only one visible from the camera's angle. It looks like everyone's echoing my pose. "God, my port de bras. Atrocious." I click it away, cringing.

"I see your perfectionism's thriving," she teases. "Anyway, who cares about ballet arms? I want *dirt* on the hot new boyfriend."

I hunker closer to the laptop. "Shhh! Geez. Grace!" I whisper.

She slaps her hand to her mouth. "Oh shit! Is he with you?"

"No, but he could be!" I say softly. "Seb isn't quite my boyfriend." How to encapsulate an entire school culture . . . "People don't say *boyfriend and girlfriend* here."

"Don't say 'boyfriend and girlfriend'?" She smiles in disbelief. "Okaaaay. He asked you to prom—"

"Summer Sendoff," I correct, then cave. "Yeah, it's a prom."

She rolls her eyes. "Yes. One where you and Seb made out passionately. He called you all summer; you visited his Cape Cod vacation house"—she air quotes—"'*on the way*' back to school, even though it's not on the way. Are you just *buds*?"

"No. *Boyfriend* is kind of extreme. As a term." Grace arches an eyebrow. It sounds flimsy even to me. "Labels and all that," I add, which doesn't help. The truth is, I don't understand it myself. I want to yodel from the chapel bell tower that I'm Seb McNeilly's girlfriend.

"Have you boffed?"

"Grace," I groan.

"Charlotte."

It comes from over my shoulder, and with sickening certainty, I know who it is. I whisk the laptop shut, spinning in my chair and emitting an involuntary yelp.

Seb, hands in his pockets, eyes glittery with amusement.

"Whoa," he says with his warm, infectious chuckle. "Why so jumpy?"

I feel my mouth attempting to smile, but my heart is in overdrive. "You scared me." I study his face for a sign that he heard us. He's simply grinning. Utterly inscrutable.

"Sorry," he says through a chuckle. "You shouldn't hang out in the creepiest corner of the library." He pulls an encyclopedia from the bookshelf, blows dust off it, and examines it like a dinosaur bone. "I mean, who uses these things?"

"Nobody. That's the point." I stand and smooth my breathing, positioning myself between the laptop and him, as if Grace might burst it open and they'll share a big laugh. I stretch one shoulder by tugging my elbow, then switch to the other. "There are zero distractions here." I smile, hoping I've regained something close to my cool.

It works. Seb shakes his head like I'm a charming puzzle and puts the book on the table. He moves behind me and presses his thumbs into my shoulders, massaging. I resist the urge to melt into him like a cat.

"I've got a better place," he says. "Exceedingly better." He spins me, lifts my arms one at a time so they're wrapped around his neck. I'm tall but Seb's six three, and yet we just *fit*. He lowers his face, and we kiss. He's freshly showered, and I run my fingers through his baby-soft hair, where it curls at the nape of his neck. "Mmm," he says, pulling away. "Come on." He pats my back pockets. "I can't wait to show you this."

I squint, trying to appear as though I'm weighing my options. I'd follow him into an active volcano, but I don't want him to know that. "Okay," I say. I turn my back to him, flip open my laptop, and quit FaceTime. *Sorry, Grace,* I think. She'll understand.

Seb thumbs through that encyclopedia. It's the C volume. "Hey! Chromium. We just learned that one," he says. I've been helping him memorize the periodic table for his honors chem class. I took it last year.

He closes his eyes. "First element in group six, a steely-gray, brittle transition metal." He blinks, adding, "Lustrous and resists tarnishing."

I think I love him.

"Ding, ding, ding!" I sling my backpack over my shoulder.

As we pass through the common room, I feel eyes on us and lift my chin like I would in a performance. Otherwise, I'd liquify into a puddle right here and now. I can dance in front of hundreds of people, no problem, but walk me through this place, filled with girls ogling Seb and wondering what's so great about me, and I want to disappear. Pretending I'm onstage is a dancer superpower, I guess.

Outside, the air has a sweet, sharp smell. This is my third Lycroft Phelps autumn, and I can't get enough of it. I'm a sucker for a costume change. The bright foliage, the orange pumpkins against stonewalls, the sweaters and boots and scarves—heaven.

Seb and I stroll side by side, bumping hips occasionally, past the Founders Statues. Since dinner, someone has wrapped green-and-white school scarves around Lycroft's and Phelps's bronze necks. A sign says *LPS vs. Tofton, Saturday!* A football's stuffed in Lycroft's crooked elbow.

"Why don't the rowers do something like that?" I ask.

"Why don't the dancers?" Seb replies. "Tutus or something?"

I shove my shoulder into his chest, less because he deserves it and more because I have an excuse.

"This way," he says, steering me down a narrow, sloping path between Spangler Dining Hall and the woods. A pink splotch of sky lingers through the leaves where the sun has just set, but otherwise the trees are dark, tangled, untamed—straight out of a witch's fairy tale.

A sudden rustling sound—a crashing of twigs and leaves—raises the hair on my scalp.

We stop. "Um, what was that?" I say, sounding less terrified than I feel.

"Dunno," Seb says. "A raccoon or something. A fox."

"It sounded bigger than that," I say, squinting into the darkness.

"Woods amplify sound sometimes," he says, but I notice he's squinting, too. Then his expression returns to normal and he makes an amused huff. "It could be . . . the Lycroft Yeti!" He grabs my waist and growls. I squeal and thump his arm. It's sort of ridiculous, but I feel like a yeti/fox/wolf could get me, but nothing like that would ever get Seb. That's not in his life story. He'll float comfortably above the rest of us earth-bound creatures until he passes away peacefully in an Adirondack chair watching the sunset over Cape Cod Bay at age ninety-nine. I know this like I know how to tendu. As we round a bend, I cling to him and take comfort seeing Campus Safety just down the hill. Seb stops, his feet making a short, sharp crunch in the pebbles. "Here we are." We're in front of a small cottage that is dwarfed by Spangler.

I eye him. "I don't get it," I say.

"This," he says, standing between me and the door, "is the oldest building on campus. The 1856 Library."

"Okaaay."

He pulls his hand from his pocket and jingles a key ring. Before I can formulate the right question, he's slid it in the lock.

"Wait," I say. "We aren't allowed in here. Are we?" I hate how I sound—prudish. Chicken.

"Don't worry," he says, fiddling with the lock.

"You do realize that's Campus Safety down there, right? Within eyeshot." Not *eyeshot*, exactly, but this feels way too reckless. "Isn't this breaking and entering or something?"

Instead of responding, he sweeps open the door. "After you, Charlotte."

I realize this is not a moment to be Charlotte Tate Foresley, high-honors Upper Middie, ballet school soloist, and Big Sister group leader. In other words, this is no moment to be me. With a final glance toward Campus Safety, I check my metaphorical goody two shoes at the door and enter the darkened room. The fruity smell of aged wood and old books envelops us. Seb pushes an ancient button on a switch plate. For two seconds, nothing happens. Then four Tiffany stained-glass floor lamps light up each corner of the room. A stout globe stands guard before the floor-to-ceiling bookshelves. There's even one of those rolling library ladders.

"Whoa," I say.

"Right? It's like a lost room from the game Clue! You can practically see Lycroft's butt print in this chair." He points to a leather seat by the fireplace.

I laugh, then ask, "Seriously, how—"

"Shhhh. It's all good. Ready for the best part?" He steps onto the ladder. "Give me a push."

I smile quizzically and shove his leg. He rolls away, grinning. When the ladder stops, he inches himself to a cabinet built into the woodwork, opens it, and, like a magician, produces a silver tray with a crystal carafe and two matching glasses. It's fancy wedding gift material. "Behold," he says, stepping down. "The family Scotch."

He sets the tray on a coffee table and pours us each a drink. Seb's family owns McNeilly Scotch, a world-famous whiskey company. Before the trip to Cape Cod, my dad asked if I could snag him a bottle for Christmas from my new boyfriend. My mom swatted him.

I eye Seb and take the glass. He taps it with his, eliciting a delicate chime. "Cheers." He sips, so I follow suit, only allowing the liquid to brush my lips. It's cough medicine on fire.

I make a sound like "Grahgh!"

He laughs. "It's an acquired taste. You'll get there."

I smile; his words hint at *future*.

He flops onto the sofa like he owns the place and pats the cushion beside him. "I've got my first Latin quiz tomorrow, so I guess I gotta get to it. How about you?"

I want to interrogate him about the keys, but why ruin his magic trick? "Plenty to do," I say, and settle beside him.

Seb's confidence spreads by osmosis, and pretty soon I feel like I belong here, too. I slip off my shoes and tuck my toes under his thigh. He's sitting upright, the cross to my T. For almost an hour, we conquer our different homework assignments in a peaceful coexistence that warms me from our point of contact straight up to my cheeks. I should be working on the Young Choreographer essay, but I can't fit ballet Charlotte and Seb Charlotte in my head simultaneously, so I'm doing math. Each problem I finish, I reward myself with a glance at him. His hair is light brown with sun streaks, and his eyes—earnestly scanning the page of his Latin book—match his hair color somehow. Hannah named it *McNeilly Gold*.

Let me be clear. Seb McNeilly is hot in about sixteen different ways. How I've ended up next to him on a sofa in this place is mystifying like the best kind of dream.

I'm multiplying exponents, when out of the blue Seb says, "Nooooo," staring at his phone. It's quiet, passing his lips like a slow, tantric breath. In the Language of Sebastian McNeilly, this means something big has happened. I'm not a native Seb speaker, but I'm conversational. The Cape Cod trip helped me assimilate to the family's fine art of understatement. They're Keep-Calm-and-Have-Another-Gin-and-Tonic kind of people. (My family is more the Drink-Wine-and-Speak-the-Truth, Come-What-May kind, based on my observations at holiday gatherings.)

"Mmm?" I move only my eyes to look at him. I don't dare test it, but I'm fairly certain overeagerness around him would be my kiss of death.

He rakes his fingers through his hair. "Chauncey is out." He looks at me, blinking.

I squint. Chauncey—whose real name is John Ceezak, which blurred to John Cee and then Chauncey after a legendary party the year before I got here—is Seb's roommate and best friend.

Chauncey's the golden retriever puppy of the Senior class: beloved, blond, not the sharpest dog in the hunt.

"Out?" I repeat.

"Booted. From Lycroft. Till January." He gazes into the mid-distance.

"Why?" I don't reveal that my heart is dancing tiny pas de bourrées. Less Chauncey means more Seb for me.

"Mr. Larabee busted him for plagiarizing. Chauncey," Seb scolds, sighing and scrolling his phone. "His grandfather's sending him to build houses in Guatemala. For perspective, he says."

"It could work," I say.

"Maybe." He slaps his knees and stands, moving to the window. "Meanwhile, our boat is screwed."

Seb rows crew in the Varsity-1 boat with seven other oarsmen plus the coxswain, formally known as Chauncey. They're really good. Ivy-League-scouts good. Seb is the stroke seat, pace setter for the boat. I think it's like the captain, but Seb claims not. Of course he would say that.

"Chauncey's only the cox," I say. "You're the ones who actually row."

"You need the cox," he says. "He's the brains of the boat."

"Oh, the irony," I say.

"Not funny," he says, but he's smiling, and per usual, my heart folds into a curtsy. Then he loads his backpack. We're leaving, I realize, and begin packing, too. Once he pushes that old light switch, he holds the door for me and follows me onto the path. I can't lie; it feels like we're leaving our very own house. And I like it.

Our breath makes cartoon clouds above us. "This is really cold for September, even by New Hampshire standards," I say, leaning into his sweatshirt once he's locked the door.

"I love it, though, don't you?" He pulls me close. We lose our balance and laugh. Above, stars dot the endless blanket of sky.

"Yeah," I say, leaving off *I love everything when I'm with you.*

We've walked a few steps when Seb stops short. "Hey. I know." Our eyes lock. I have no idea what he's thinking. Still, after nearly four months.

"What?"

"*You* can be our cox," he says.

My stomach does the wave. He wants *me* to cox?! I check myself. "Ha!" I break our gaze and continue walking. "Right."

"Why not? You're light, smart, and way hotter than Chauncey. I'm sick of looking at his sorry face every practice."

"While that is a flattering offer, I'm afraid I'll have to decline," I say. "Ballet. No time."

"Screw ballet," he says into my ear, then comes in for a long, soft kiss, and I actually consider screwing ballet. But I'm finally a soloist this year, and I have a shot at Young Choreographer. Besides, I've been dancing since I was four. I shouldn't just . . .

I'm lost in his smell and his lips and his hands caressing my ribs until *snap-snap!*

We jump apart.

A good-sized *something* is forging through the woods.

"That was closer!" I whisper. My heart is a metronome on Adderall.

Another burst of crackling brush. I jump back into his arms.

We're motionless, intuitively holding our breath.

"It's a person," he says so softly I hardly hear it. I nod into his chest, picturing something from a *Scream* movie, but he breaks away from me, emboldened. He is the opposite of me.

"Is that you, Pearce?" Seb calls into the woods. "You perv!"

I whip my head toward Seb. "Why would Colin Pearce follow us?" I ask. His eyes flick toward me and away.

"Creepy," I say, but only under my breath.

More shuffling through leaves. A dark figure darts between the trees. My hair follicles shiver in waves.

"Pearce!" he yells. We stay still.

"Wouldn't he at least respond?" I breathe. Seb doesn't answer. "Let's run," I say. "One, two—"

Before I whisper *three*, we're sprinting like it's the zombie apocalypse and we don't stop when we reach the main quad, or as we pass the Founders Statues and startled classmates—not until we're at Fisher, my dorm, where we collapse onto the cold stone steps, panting.

"What . . . was that?" I say.

Seb takes my hand for a few breaths, and then he starts to laugh. This answers none of my worries—Why would one of Seb's crew teammates and good friends stalk us? If it wasn't him, who was it?—but I find myself laughing, too, willfully swallowed into Seb's hermetically sealed world. I kiss him then—greedily, like I can steal this way he has of owning the universe and make it mine. He pauses and looks in my eyes. I've surprised both of us and I'm embarrassed, but he just kisses me back.

There's no word for fear in Sebanese. Whether that was Colin back there, the Lycroft Yeti, a black bear, a serial killer loose from the New Hampshire State Prison—it's just another adventure to Sebastian Cope McNeilly III. Just what happens after you sneak into the oldest building on one of the most prestigious prep schools in the country and drink high-end Scotch out of crystal snifters you somehow stashed there earlier. For the first time, my life feels more daring offstage than on it. I breathe in Seb's clean, masculine smell. It's dangerous to fall this hard for a guy like him, but there's not a thing I can do to stop myself.

MAX HANNIGAN-LOEFFLER

❊ *Upper Mid* ❊

"Tell me we're close to sealing the deal on this thing. Please?" Colin Pearce says. He barely fits on the student chair, elbows and knees jutting into space like a crane. We're in the second-floor lab, and the custodian already asked us twice if he could vacuum.

Colin and I are partners for our Physics Intensive project. We've set out to determine the initial and final velocity of horizontally launched projectiles when gravity is the only force. I mean, air resistance is a force, too, but Mrs. Lewis told me to leave that out for simplicity's sake in this experiment. It's only September.

"We *would* be close," I say in response to his question, letting him fill in: *If you would actually contribute.* But I don't look at Colin while I say this because, though we both know he needs me to get an A on this assignment, we are equally aware he's got enough stored energy in one foot to launch my ass from here to Spangler. In a stiff wind.

He makes a throaty sound of amusement. "Chill, Mr. Spock." Leaning forward, he takes a ball bearing between his fingers, squinting, like he's never seen one before, when in fact they've served as the aforementioned projectiles we've been releasing down a ramp since we got here. "Give me something to do."

"We're finished with those," I say. "Measure the distance from where it landed to where the others landed." I had dusted the ball bearings with graphite shavings so we could see the landing points *and* how long they kept rolling after landing, as that data provides further evidence of velocity.

He picks up the tape measure and squats. "Here to here?"

I exhale loudly. "Yep."

Colin announces the results while I enter them into my calculator. We repeat this process several times, and then I calculate the average distance traveled, including a separate calculation for the post-impact roll. He listens attentively, smiling to himself as he takes notes. I'm still mad at myself for agreeing to partner with him. He's not stupid by any means, but he's lazy as hell. For the two years I've been at Lycroft, I haven't registered on his radar—I'm not sure I'm in his field of vision, actually—so he caught me off guard when he asked to partner at the end of our first class.

"I can print these up on cards so they look good for the presentation," he's saying now, like maybe he heard my thoughts and remembered he owes *something* to this venture.

"Okay," I say, "that's a—"

But he's pulled his phone out of his pocket. His eyebrows yank together. "Fuck," he says. "Goddammit, Chauncey!" I look over my shoulder in case Chauncey is standing there, but we're alone. Colin's thumbs skitter across his phone screen, and then he shoves his chair under the lab desk. He's mobilizing for departure, leaving the cleanup to me.

I consider asking what's up with Chauncey, who lived across the hall from me last year and is actually a decent person. I mean, considering his friends. He's also barely taller than I am. Maybe that's *why* he's more approachable. Or maybe he can just see me.

Anyway, I feel like Colin wants me to ask, so I don't. "Here," I say instead, handing him the ramp box.

He tosses it back. "Sorry, man. Gotta make like a banana and get the fuck outta here." He looks at me all earnestly, but I swear he says the next part just to hear it himself. "Chauncey got booted from school, and now the fastest boat in Lycroft history has no coxswain." He presses his lips thin, shakes his head, and whisks past me out the door.

"You prick," I say after he's gone.

"I was going to vacuum?" says the custodian.

"Oh—" I nod too hard. "I didn't mean *you're* a—" I add, feeling my face heat.

He chuckles and waves dismissively, flipping on the vacuum.

I put the ramp, et cetera, in our cubby and leave the custodian in the lab. Last year, the school installed this cool glass catwalk, a pentagonal prism, connecting the old Winfield Science Building to the newer Kessler STEM building. To passersby at night, it glows blue, and it lets me imagine I'm leaving Google headquarters to go home to my hot girlfriend (who either *is* or very closely resembles Alexandra Buchanan, the Lower Mid from Outdoors Club) at our carbon-neutral home. As I walk through it, I watch Colin below me, pacing in a dome of lamplight on the footpath, gesticulating while talking on his phone. He's probably whining about Chauncey. When he pauses to listen, his breath vaporizes over his head, and I smile because he looks like he's spontaneously combusting—which of course I know is impossible when it comes to humans, due to the whole our-bodies-are-70-percent-water thing, but a guy can dream.

A flash of motion catches my eye in the woods behind him.

I stop, my heart giving an extra tick. I lean onto the smooth wood railing and stare into the darkness.

There it is again! I step back from the window. We're in the foothills of the White Mountains, so it's probably an animal. Moose are known to appear on campus once a year or so. Or, I think hopefully, it's a bear and it can maul Pearce.

But my gut tells me it's something else. The movement looked . . . calculated. Predatory, maybe. Catlike. A wildcat? It moves between a couple of trees, and I realize it is bipedal. And in spite of the LPS Yeti lore, I know it's human. The words *active shooter* streak through my head like bullets, and I think I should get the hell out of this transparent tube. I bolt into Winfield and get to another window by the stairwell. I dial Nils, telling myself we have security gates at the campus entrances, but counter that with my knowledge that security is always an illusion; LPS covers two thousand acres, much of it fading into wilderness.

Nils doesn't pick up. Not sure how he could help, anyway.

Then I see the guy—dressed in black like a Navy SEAL sniper, scuttling from a tree to crouch behind a boulder. I'm nauseous.

Pearce is oblivious, barking into his phone.

I can't tell if the guy's armed. All I can see is the curve of his shoulders and his head, peering over the rock. I should call Campus Safety or maybe 911, but I'm frozen.

Colin stuffs his phone in his pocket and marches up the path toward the main quad, which has rows of night lamps. The dude tracks Colin's movement, then sprints from one concealment to another. *Jesus! He's stalking Pearce?*

"Hey! Somebody!" I call, but of course I'm still alone. I could run through the pentagonal prism to get that custodian. I don't want to lose sight of the stalker, though, *or* run through that transparent gauntlet. I stutter-step in three directions at once, helpless.

If I yell to Colin, it could trigger the stalker.

I have his number.

My fingers are clammy as I dial. Colin's phone lights up, illuminating his face. He checks the screen and taps it.

"Hey," Colin says.

"Pearce!" I whisper-hiss. "There's a—"

"This is Colin. Leave a message." *Beep.*

I stare at my phone. "Are you fucking kidding me?" He sent me to voice mail? "Good, go ahead and die." But of course I don't mean this, and freak out that I've somehow sealed his fate. I thunder down the stairs and swing the door open.

Colin is a ways up the path at this point. The stalker's vanished, and I'm not sure that's a good thing. I'm about to yell to Pearce when the blue light of the Campus Safety golf cart rolls into view.

"Thank God," I say. It's Doughty's sidekick, Deputy McPhee. He raises his fingers from the wheel in greeting. Colin raises his, disappearing around the corner of Spangler toward the main quad. McPhee rolls by me. I stand still in the Winfield doorway, weighing my options. I mean, nothing happened. Do I just ignore it? What if something *does* happen, though, and I didn't say anything?

"Officer McPhee!" I call.

McPhee jerks his head in my direction, nods, and pulls a U-turn. It's disturbingly reminiscent of me driving my red Tiny Tots car at age four. "Evening," McPhee says. "How can I help?" He's a burly redhead who resembles several of my cousins on the Hannigan side. This brings me a little comfort, until I explain what I saw and McPhee rubs his chin skeptically. "You sure?"

I nod. "It was definitely a guy following Colin. But I guess I don't know if he was actually, you know, dangerous." McPhee's got one fuzzy red eyebrow tilting forty-five degrees.

Here it comes. He recognizes me. The short-guy thing is rare at LPS. I shift my weight, bracing for the inevitable.

"Aren't you the boy who called in the suspicious smell last year? Shanahan?" He twirls his hand, unable to come up with the second half of my name.

Boom.

"Hannigan-Loeffler," I correct him.

"Yes, that's right," he says, like I could've given the wrong damn name.

"It smelled dangerous." I sound defensive, which annoys me.

December of my sophomore year, I woke to a gas smell in the dorm. I thought it was a cracked line. Everyone was evacuated at two a.m. and stood shivering in their underwear while the fire department checked the building. It was during exam week, too.

The school administrators kept my identity private so I didn't get the shit kicked out of me, but I always suspected they thought I made it up. Which would be so weird, and why would I do that? "I could have dreamed the gas smell, I guess." I look at my feet. "Anyway, this is totally different. I am wide awake, and he was right there!" I point toward the boulder. I can tell he's not buying it, so I say, "Do you want to be wrong on this?"

Grudgingly, McPhee takes the walkie from his holster and contacts the Whitney Police. While we wait, he jots notes as I fill him in. But when the town cruiser arrives and I say it all again, I feel the story starting to sound preposterous. The cops, looming above me in crisp blue uniforms, nod respectfully, but they don't look alarmed in the least. They shine spotlights into the woods and crunch around in the leaves for good measure. Satisfied, they climb back into the cruiser. The driver, a beefy older guy with a bulbous nose, looks me in the eye from the window. He says in a slow New England drawl: "I've been doing this for a long while, son, and this smells like a student prank."

McPhee looks all sympathetic. "You had anybody poking fun atcha lately, Max?"

I'm sure they think I take plenty of crap at this place, given the number of good-looking entitled jocks enrolled. Even in a generous Dudes:Nerds ratio, I'm outnumbered 25:1. I accept this fact and choose not to be offended by McPhee's appraisal of me.

"Nah, but you're right, I bet," I say. At this point, my dignity's at stake. "Crofters being Crofters."

The New Englander frowns, gazing into the woods. "Sounds about right," he says, then exhales in a way that makes me think he's not a big LPS fan. "Aw righty, then. Until next time, Jimmy." He nods to McPhee.

"You live in Stevens or Atwood Hall?" he asks me when they're gone.

"Stevens."

"Want a lift?"

I'm not sure if it's out of pity or boredom. I glance into the woods. "Sure."

We hop in the golf cart.

At Stevens, as I jog up the flight of stairs to my room, I wonder if it's worth it for me to attend this school, with all its pretentious bullshit. But Lycroft Phelps nearly guarantees me the college of my choice. They send me to all the international robotics competitions. And it's a free ride, my dad loves to remind me. My parents own a design firm in SoHo. We're middle class, I guess, but I'd never be going to a fancy boarding school without the scholarship. They've got three kids to get through college. "Max makes them look good," my mom says. But, besides my nerd compadre Nils, nobody respects me outside of the math and science departments. I'm like an exponent: I raise the value of Lycroft Phelps's reputation, but I'm small enough to be ignored.

I open our door to find Nils asleep on the middle of the floor, one ankle tottering on a bent knee, highlighter falling out of his relaxed fingers. A book called *Art through the Ages* is splayed on his belly. He's so ridiculous I snort. I wish I could trace him with crime scene chalk.

"Nils." I prod him with my Adidas. "Dude, wake up."

"I'm up," he says, wiping his mouth with his wrist.

"You have a bed," I say.

"I didn't . . . want to . . ." He stretches his spine in a twist.

"Fall asleep?"

"Yeah," he says, yawning.

"Well done." I hang my backpack on the desk chair. The highlighter sails over my shoulder and lands on my desk.

"You missed," I tell him.

"That was a warning shot," he says from the floor.

This idiocy right here? This is why I stay.

I turn. "You're not going to believe this, but I saw some kind of stalker following Pearce tonight."

He's up, hopping. Presumably, his foot's asleep. "What?"

"Swear to God."

Nils sits on his bed, rubbing the foot. I commence my retelling. His eyebrows climb farther up his forehead as I conclude.

"I know," I say. "Crazy. Pearce had no idea." I slide my shoes off. "That cop was probably right, and it was just a student."

He stares out the window for a moment. "Whatever you do, don't tell him."

"Because . . ." I prompt.

"Because," he says. "Those guys eat their own. Maybe Pearce finally pissed off the wrong dickhead."

"I like that plot twist," I say. Nils brushes past me toward the hall bathroom.

As I peel off my clothes, I picture the guy in black and try to mind-bend him from sinister to . . . comic? It doesn't quite work. I can't shake the catlike stealth. When Nils returns, I say, "My brain just read him as *predator*." I open my fingers in what I think is a neon-sign gesture.

Nils smiles. "Max, do you think you might be influenced by all your"—he mimics my gesture—"*true crime shows?*"

"Yeah," I laugh, grabbing my toothbrush and washcloth. "You're right." Drying my face at the sink, I look in the mirror and think how much more relaxed I'd be if I lived in Nils's head instead of my own.

Q

It's just a shot away! Shot away! Shot away!

The woods are dappled silver by the moon, and my AirPods muting all natural sounds create a feeling I'm in my own private snow globe, drifting through the night sky. But I know it's an illusion—one that will burst wide open if anyone discovers me. I want to belt out this part of "Gimme Shelter" like Mick Jagger's backup vocalist does, but instead I whisper along. I can't risk it. My plan—and the *anger* driving it—is all I've got to keep me from floating into cold, starless forever.

Staying angry anchors me. My older cousin Macy may be a flake in a million ways, but she got me angry. Angry keeps me breathing. Angry brought me back to Lycroft.

That fucker needs to pay, Macy seethed last June, back at home. At the time, I lay limp in my window seat. I'd been sleeping there instead of my bed since returning from school. I didn't belong tucked in with my floral comforter and down pillows and Mr. Paws, my balding stuffed bear. Maybe it would've been different if my mother were still alive, but she isn't. Thank God for Macy. Before she came to my rescue, my mind's eye watched a sinister black cloud—some phantom, smoky fog reflecting the deadest part of me. Each night it slipped under my closet door and slid across the wide wood floorboards, over the blue braided rug, up the wall to the cushion in the window seat. I knew it was only a matter of time before it swallowed me into the nothingness.

And part of me wanted to go.

Part of me still does.

So I need the anger.

In a few more bars, the song ends, exposing the stark sound of my rapid breath and the crackle of sticks beneath my Converse. Up the hill a ways, a couple walks on the path near the 1856 Library. To avoid them, I veer deeper into the woods just as the opening guitar riff from the Stones' "Can't You Hear Me Knocking" rolls through my AirPods, cranking me back up. The song's layers of sound tumble around with childhood memories—Dad dancing me around the patio or the den or the kitchen, teaching me the chords on my guitar. I'm mouthing the words, visualizing the notes. The next time I see the footpaths through the branches and leaves, I stop dead.

Under a lamppost, it's him. On his phone. My heart skitters around my chest, a trapped butterfly I could choke on. I want to run, but I can't. Even from there he's got me in a vise grip. If I had the gun . . . I shape my hand into a pistol, squint over my finger, aim . . .

He turns, walking. My feet decide to follow without my permission. I'm scurrying to a large rock. Then a tree. And another. The music has stopped again; my breath is urgent, my mouth dry. He says something. I can't hear the words, but the voice slithers into my ears.

He's looking toward the woods, his skin blue in the light. . . .

I realize I'm trembling and huddle over my knees, hiding.

And all at once I see myself that night. May 31. A caterpillar curled on the grassy Amphitheater Lawn, by the marble statues of the nine Greek muses. He towers above me, tucking in his shirt. Zipping his fly.

Fine. Be that way.

His Italian leather loafers shushing away through the dewy grass.

Shush

Shush

Shush

"Officer McPhee!" I hear someone call now.

I remember where I am. The AirPods have fallen from my ears, and I paw the rotting leaves, peering around the tree. He's gone, but there's commotion I don't have time to see. My fingers catch on the AirPods. I pick them out of the debris, not caring that I've collected something small and slimy and possibly alive. Clutching all of it, I turn toward the darkness and run.

2
Friday Classes

7:22 a.m.

Doughty: Hey, what's this in last night's log? You called Whitney Police in?

McPhee: A kid who reported someone dressed in black slinking around the woods by the science complex. I had the guys take a look, just in case. Mostly to appease the kid. Probably upperclassmen screwing around with each other.

Doughty: Who was the kid?

McPhee: Max Hannigan-Loeffler. Upper Mid. He was freaked out until we convinced him it was just the usual nonsense and not a sniper.

Doughty: Ha! Why do I know that name?

McPhee: Gas leak?

Doughty: Ah, right. Guess I have to tell Dean Frye. Don't want him to hear about a police visit from anyone else.

McPhee: Yes, we know he does not like surprises. Going back to sleep now.

Doughty: See you later on.

CHARLOTTE

It's hard not to feel self-conscious when a table full of Senior boys starts laughing just as you walk up, especially when four of them look like actors on a movie set. Seb is sitting with Colin Pearce and two other rowers, Khalid Zia and Tyler Wiggins, on the broad terrace of Spangler Dining Hall, beneath its massive stained-glass windows. Khalid's from Jupiter, Florida, which everyone says is super wealthy. He's the kind of guy who embarrasses his friends for fun, so he makes me nervous. Tyler, meanwhile, rivals Seb in the looks department—dark hair, darker eyes, and a mischievous grin. His dad is a movie producer, and his mom a former super-model. I'm just going to say it: he has very kissable lips. When we were First Years, Hannah and I staked him out in the library every night. He had no idea. But then Tyler's equally hot boy-friend visited him from LA. Many LPS girls cried a tear that day. Khalid and Colin may not be as good-looking as Seb and Tyler, but their athletic builds and confidence make up for it. The dancer in me has tried to define what it is in their body language that communicates confidence. The way they hold their heads? The shoulders, slightly pulled back? The stride? Or is it coming from inside, beaming out through the effortless smiles, like some kind of subliminal Wi-Fi signal?

Time for the ballet superpower. I pull my own spine straight, push my shoulders down, and check my gait. Grace from home has it all wrong; I am not a natural Lycrofter. I am 100 percent choreographed right now.

"What's so funny?" I say. It's forced, which is awkward, so I make up for it by letting my flats pitter-patter on the terrace steps like punctuation marks. Seb reaches out and brushes my fingers with his. My stomach does a goldfish flippy thing.

"Nothing," he says, grinning. He turns toward them. "You know Coach is just going to take the cox from the second boat and put him in our boat."

Tyler and Khalid groan. "Not Dougie Nelson. I can't *stand* that guy," Tyler grumbles.

"Friendship is not mandatory," Colin says, imitating Coach Follett. "*Winning* is mandatory."

"Boo-ya!" says Khalid, and I'm not sure if he's being ironic.

Seb slips his arm around my waist. "I tried to talk Charlotte into being our cox," he announces, pulling me against him. "Damn ballet."

Nobody says anything for a couple of beats, and I think I might barf.

Colin removes his Oakleys. "If you change your mind . . ." His eyes hold mine a tick too long, and the look in them doesn't match his smile. I remember the stalker last night and look at my feet. But if he did spy on us, why should *I* be embarrassed. He's the creeper in that scenario.

"So, Colin, last night—" I say, surprised by my own audacity.

"Heads up. Beast alert," he says, and the four of them turn in toward the table. I think he might be faking, just going for distraction, but Coach Follett, aka the Beast, is striding toward us. A powerful man in his late thirties who rowed in an Olympics, he claps one bear-paw hand on Colin's shoulder and the other on Seb's. His hair is cut close, and his smile turns down at the ends in a way that resembles a frown. It's unsettling.

"Boys," he says, and exhales slowly. "You have a problem."

The boys mutter greetings, suddenly not invincible, I think, which may be just *vincible*. I'll ask Seb later if that's a word. I don't totally get why they're puppies with their tails between their legs—I mean, it's not their fault Chauncey got caught cheating.

"We're now short a cox," Coach says. "Who do you intend to put in Chauncey's seat?"

The vincible group shifts uneasily around the stone picnic table. Coach Follett waits them out. Seb looks at Colin and then at Coach. "We thought you'd . . . well, it makes sense that the second boat cox, Dougie Nelson, will move up to our boat. Right?"

"He'll be psyched," adds Colin. "Varsity 1 as a sophomore."

"Wrong," Coach says. He's calm, but you can tell he wants to pummel something. He looks up at the clock tower, then back at the table. "Your boat screwed up. I'm not punishing the second boat for your boat's screwups."

Colin says, "Oooookay. But if our boat loses, the team loses, too."

"Not really. They win their race. You lose your race," Coach says, scratching his chin. "You're a *boat*, boys. You rise and fall as a *boat*." He folds his arms across his chest, and I think he might be the Lycroft Yeti. "Figure it out. Find a recruit. It'll be a team builder."

He pats Colin's shoulder without affection and strides away.

There's a moment of subdued swearing until Seb turns to me. "You sure you don't want to become a cox?"

"That pretty much sealed it," I say.

Tyler says, "You think he's bluffing? He hates losing."

"Yeah, I bet he's bluffing," Khalid says. "Dougie will end up in our boat, right? We can't have a novice cox in our boat."

"He's not fucking bluffing, you douchebags," Colin says, which kicks off a debate.

I can see I'm not going to find out anything about last night before physics. I glance away, annoyed that I feel like some kind of tagalong. I spot Q walking out the main doors of Spangler. Q, my favorite Little. I feel guilty for not being in touch with her this summer. We went to Summer Sendoff together, but I ended up with Seb that night, and honestly, by the time I bounced back to earth the next day, she'd left Lycroft. I texted her a couple times over the summer, but then I fell back in with Grace and ballet and the Thornwood High School crowd, and we never connected. I lift my hand to wave, but she either doesn't see me or is ignoring me, which makes me feel guilty all over again. I notice her jeans are hanging off her. She was thin last year, but not like that. I tug Seb's hand and mouth, Gotta go. He nods distractedly, and I try to catch up with Q. But when I round the corner of Spangler, she's gone. I'll find her later today, I decide. If she's mad, I kind of deserve it.

I'm in physics, scrupulously comparing my homework solutions (the ones I calculated between stealing glances at Seb, glowing golden in the Tiffany lamplight of the 1856 Library) to the ones on the board. Most classes at Lycroft are taught seminar style: everyone seated around a big oak table, participation inescapable. But this class is more traditional, with seats in rows and tables for experiments in the back. I sit up front. Even though all the rooms have state-of-the-art projectors and retractable screens, teachers rely on the old-fashioned blackboards and chalk much of the time. It adds to this sense that we're part of some grand and enduring tradition. Like classical ballet; the five positions of the feet—which start and end every complex dance combination—date from the 1580s.

I realize I've let my attention wander, when Colin's looming form fills the classroom doorway. He catches me watching him and smiles broadly, tipping his chin in greeting as he saunters toward the seats at the back of the room. I give a quick, close-lipped smile. I wonder if it *was* him watching us last night. Why would he do that? And why did Seb *assume* he would? Did he watch us kissing? That's just gross, not to mention creepy.

I shift in my chair.

Max Hannigan-Loeffler, seated in the next chair, looks at me wearily, fingers hovering above his calculator. He makes a sound something like a sigh.

"What?" I whisper.

He shakes his head. "That guy is my project partner."

"Oh," I say.

"He's a d-bag," Max adds, glancing back like he's said something dangerous, which he kind of has, given that Colin could fit him in his pocket.

I nod. "I get that. He only talks to me because his friend is . . ." I stop. Why can't I just say *my boyfriend?*

"Seb McNeilly?" Max supplies courteously. Everyone knows the code.

I cock my head, surprised he follows campus romances, especially mine. He and I had drama class together last year and once had to improvise a scene with a rubber chicken the teacher threw at us onstage. We're not friends, but friend-*ly*. A rubber chicken will do that, I guess. "Uh, yes."

Max nods. "Seb's okay." I'm speechless for a moment, staring at him. "You know," he adds, "for a trust funder."

"Right," I say, barely disguising my annoyance. Okay, he didn't say anything untrue. McNeilly Scotch Whiskey is the second-most-popular brand in the world; Seb will admit it if pressured (I witnessed Colin do so at our Summer Sendoff dinner double date at the Whitney Inn). So, yes, there is surely a trust fund awaiting Seb's twenty-first birthday. But he doesn't act spoiled, and I don't like thinking of him that way. I prefer Hannah's nickname for him: Genetic Miracle.

I go back to work, but feel Max eying me, so I put my pencil down in a deliberate way. "Yes?"

"He's much better than Pearce," Max whispers. "I don't get why decent guys, like Seb and Chauncey, give an asshat like Pearce the time of day."

"Probably the same reason you agreed to be his lab partner," I say with a smirk.

Max flinches, then smiles. "Well played, Charlotte. Well played."

"I get what you mean, though," I say. Colin has a strange magnetism. It's like I keep thinking he's going to prove he *is* worthy of Seb's friendship. But . . . nope.

Max hunkers lower to his desk. "Want to hear something weird?"

"Some people actually have to work at this," I say, waving at the blackboard.

He looks at my paper. "You're fine."

"I am?"

He squints, turning my spiral notebook his way. "Yeah, those are right. You want to hear something odd?" He tips his head toward Colin in a way that makes me wonder if he knows something about last night.

"Sure," I say. "What?"

"I saw someone stalking him last night." His eyes shift left, then right.

I sit up. "Stalking *Colin*?"

"I swear," Max whispers, holding up his right palm like we're in court. But it's not that I don't believe him; it's the idea that Colin was the stalk-*ee*, not the stalk-*er*.

"Tell me more," I whisper, leaning closer.

"After Pearce left Kessler last night, he was outside, you know, where that bench is?"

I nod.

"I was in the pentagonal prism and I saw this"—he shakes his head—"this dude! Dressed in black like an assassin or some shit, hiding in the woods. Wherever Colin went, he followed—slinking along from one tree to the next."

My scalp prickles. "Are you sure?"

"I'm ninety-nine percent positive." And after a moment: "Ninety-nine point nine-nine-nine percent."

I almost laugh, but he's serious, and I decide he's probably incorporated some mathematical law that makes him want to reserve

0.001 percent as a margin of error. Besides, a stalker isn't funny. I realize I would rather think it *was* Colin Pearce outside the 1856 Library last night than someone nobody knows.

"Like, you think he was dangerous?" I ask.

Max shrugs. I don't really know what to say next and try to focus on my work, but I can't. "Why are you telling me this?" I say.

He cocks his head thoughtfully, running his fingers through his thick black hair. "I dunno," he says with a funny expression. "I guess I was thinking you'd be interested. You know, given your connection." He stretches his legs out. "Or maybe that you know something about a prank." He watches for a reaction.

My glance flicks to the floor, a dead giveaway. "Listen to this," I whisper. "Seb and I saw someone in the woods, too. Behind Spangler, near the 1856 Library." Max's eyes widen. I nod. "All in black, just like you said. We thought it was Colin goofing around."

"What time?"

"Nine-fifteen-ish?"

"Definitely not Pearce," Max says. "He was with me. Did the guy follow you?"

"No," I say, trying to remember which direction he went. "We only saw him for a split second; then we ran like mad for the dorm."

I can practically hear Max's brain firing up. "Spangler isn't far from Kessler, if you cut through the woods. Could have been the same person."

"Wait? You thought it was more than one?" I say, forcing a smile.

"Well, there are a ton of important kids here," Max says. "You know, not important on some cosmic level, but important because

49

their parents are millionaires, billionaires, and politicians. Prime ransom material. Pearce? He lives in the Hamptons."

"Where?" I say.

He squints. "The Hamptons? You know, *The Great Gatsby*. Playground of the rich and famous. P. Diddy? Steven Spielberg?"

I nod vaguely. "I'm from Chicago."

"Never mind. The point is, his parents are one percent kind of loaded. And kidnapping schemes take a team. . . ."

I'm queasy. "Stop."

He looks at me. "Don't worry. The cops thought it was just kids messing around, too."

"Cops? Now you're trying to freak me out."

"No. Seriously, it was probably some other Lycroft asshat. God knows Pearce isn't the only one."

Mrs. Lewis, our petite firecracker of a teacher, steps before the board. "Okay, people, who's ready to get physical?" She flexes her arm muscles like a circus strongman. A collective moan rises from the class, and all feels well in the world again. Max was right; my first answer was correct. We're on the second problem, when Dean Frye raps on the doorframe. "Excuse me, ladies and gentlemen. I need to borrow Mrs. Lewis for just a moment."

Mrs. Lewis smiles deferentially, and the two engage in quiet conversation by the door.

Max and I exchange a look. All I can think of is Seb and me in the old library. Is that breaking and entering? And the alcohol. I swallow back panic. Mrs. Lewis returns to the board. "Max," Dean Frye says softly, like the rest of the class isn't focused on his every move.

Max puts his hand to his chest. Dean Frye nods and slips out of the room. Max shrugs at me. I smile awkwardly, trying not to appear too relieved. Max isn't a troublemaker, obviously, so he's either won some new STEM award or it's about the stalker. I wish I could text Seb, but we can't use phones in class, so I try to focus on Mrs. Lewis, back to reviewing our problem sets. I sink into her clean, unquestionable world of numbers like it's a bubble bath and push everything else from my mind.

MAX

Dean Frye walks ahead of me down the hall. He's wearing his unofficial head-of-school uniform: khakis, blazer, tie. He adds a baseball cap to make himself seem approachable, but he looks more like a baby boss. I'm not sure whether to be nervous. Someone like Chauncey can plagiarize and be booted for a semester, but he'll be back. The difference between being a kid whose family spends $375K for four years here and me is whether it's the school or the student who's justified in expecting returns on their investment. Does the school owe me, or do I owe the school? It's a big fucking difference. Even when nobody chooses to press their advantage, the very fact that they might dictates the power dynamic. Really, kids like Chauncy or McNeilly or Charlotte get a totally different LPS experience than I do. Most of the time I try not to think about it, and that's easy, because Lycrofters pretend it's bougie to notice insane wealth, yet somehow everyone knows who comes from the most money. Other kids, Nils aside, are oblivious that I'm on scholarship. But I know. And so does Frye. Right now, that power dynamic is impossible to ignore.

I almost bump into Frye when he stops short at the hall intersection.

He smiles. It's a fundraiser's smile—polished, eager, wanting something. "Max."

"Dean Frye," I say in kind, barely holding back my sarcasm. I hear my dad: *Watch it, Max.*

We look at each other for an inflated moment. I'm predicting he'll ask me about the stalker guy, but it's like he's waiting for me to crack. Like I'm hiding something, and it makes me feel like I am. Which is annoyingly illogical.

He pats my shoulder. "Tell me what you saw last night."

"Oh, sure. I saw a guy in the woods, dressed in black, tailing Colin Pearce, like a spy from a movie," I say.

"Outside this building," states Frye. He's completely immobile. With the ball cap, it's easy to imagine he's in a playground game of freeze tag. Kid Frye would definitely play to win. It's a death stare.

"Yes." I nod, moving toward the large windows. "I was in the blue prism between Kessler and Winfield, and he was"—I point—"there. See that boulder?"

"Mm-hmm." He stares pensively toward the woods. It dawns on me that Frye is unnerved, too. By the report. Why else would he be interrogating me? His sudden inhale startles me. "And you don't have any idea who it was?"

I shrug. "It could have been anyone. The police didn't seem concerned." I toss this out like a fishing lure and wait.

Dean Frye nods, standing to his full height. "I trust them." It's not convincing. He smooths the hip pockets of his blazer and smiles politely. "I remember you can be a little"—he tips his head left and right jauntily—"suggestible, Max. Like with the gas leak. Am I right?"

I feel my pulse pick up. Goddammit, will I never live that fucking night down? And did it ever occur to any of these assholes that I did smell something? Maybe I saved a whole dorm full of kids from dying, for Chrissake.

"I'm not the only one who saw the guy," I blurt, regretting it immediately. Throwing Charlotte Foresley and Seb McNeilly under the bus here is a terrible idea. But I'm so sick of being cast aside for anything that's not robotics related. God. I've taken this school to Stockholm twice. I've put it on the map, STEM speaking. But I know Dean Frye just sees a short, neurotic middle-class kid who's getting a kick-ass future handed to him for free. A kid on the low end of the power differential. He's not interested in seeing anything else. And when people don't look, they can miss any truth, even if it's staring them straight in the face. Which I am doing.

"Oh?" he says.

There's no backing out now.

"Who else, then?"

Shit.

Q

My phone vibrates.

I know I've overslept by the relentlessness of the sunbeams across my closed eyelids. I peel them open. It's possible that the thing I'm becoming is a vampire. Daylight is the enemy. Picking up the phone from the bedside, I simultaneously check the time and calculate how long I have to make breakfast before Spangler closes. My cousin Macy is texting me. From London.

Macy: Any pig bastard sightings?

This prompts the image of him lit blue in the lamplight last night. I blow out a chestful of air. I have to answer. I'm sure Heather and Dad have her checking on me.

Me: A few. At a distance.

Macy: How are you doing?

Tears sting the back of my nose.

Macy is the only person besides Dad and Heather, our family lawyer, and my therapist who knows what happened. She flew home early from her study abroad program to meet me in Southport the minute she heard last June. Macy was my savior during those first weeks.

"Why should you leave Lycroft?" she had asked. "Fuck that. You're a Walsh. Walshes are Lycroft Phelps." She lobbied me to tell my grandfather. "Are you kidding me? Boppy's on the board of directors. If he found out someone hurt you? His favorite? He'd get that pig bastard kicked out in seconds flat. Full stop."

"I'm not telling Boppy," I said that day, my voice creaky from all the crying. I still remember staring at a tiny water stain on the high plaster ceiling of my bedroom.

"You didn't do anything wrong, Q," Macy said.

"Don't tell him!" I snapped, but my already-squeaky voice barely made itself audible. It didn't matter. She got it.

She sat next to me on the window seat. "Okay, then let your dad deal with Dean Frye. Your dad can make that dirtbag's life miserable, too."

But I made Dad promise he wouldn't. Uncle Lawrence, not my actual uncle but my godfather and also our family lawyer, had already told us legal action would be useless.

"The oldest story in a long, sad book," he announced to Dad over drinks on the patio. I listened from my window seat above. "It's the classic he said, she said."

My phone vibrates again.

Macy: Quinnie?

I'm glad for her to bring me back to the present. Just thinking about how stupid I was after it happened makes me dizzy.

Me: It's hard.

I want to tell her the truth: That the sinister black smoke lurks somewhere just out of sight. That it's followed me here. And it will be until Pearce is gone. I could confess about my nighttime trips to Anderson Safety and my plan. But I don't. I'm afraid she'll take it away somehow. And then I'll disappear for good.

Macy: You poor thing, Quinnie.

I type **It's him or me, Macy. I'm scared.**

Then I delete it.

Me: I'm okay. I lie.

Macy: Don't skip any meetings with your therapist.

Valerie, my therapist, FaceTimes with me twice a week.

Me: I won't. Love you.

Macy: Love you! Call me if you want to talk. xo

I drop the phone onto the mattress with a thud, and my brain echoes it with a flash of Doughty's gun dropping into the wooden drawer.

I'm so tired.

I've got to get moving before the RA, Emily, discovers me here. The trick, I remind myself as I stumble into our bathroom, is to not attract attention. Go to classes. Show up in the dining hall.

I don't look in the mirror as I brush my teeth. I've pulled so many eyelashes out. I hate how it makes me look. Like one of those bald, peach-colored alien dolls. In June, I cried so much I popped a blood vessel in one eye and had this disgusting red blotch next to my iris. It's mostly faded, but I can still see the shadow of it. I've lost weight, so I choose jeans that I grew out of last year but never threw away, and grab my dad's old Led Zeppelin T-shirt—once strictly a sleep shirt—from the laundry pile on my closet floor. I pull on a gray hoodie that's hanging on my guitar case, which serves as nothing but a clothes rack at this point. My Yankees cap, backpack, and I head for the dining hall.

It's sunny and cool, and I can tell the kids are energized by the promise of fall. They move in clusters, gesticulating and talking in exaggerated voices. A First Year I hadn't seen so far has brown curly hair like mine. She walks backward, amusing her friends, flirtily swatting a First Year guy's shoulder. I remember that feeling. When I knew everything was ahead of me, but I had no idea what everything would be.

I pinch the familiar purple butterfly bruise on my arm I use to stay in control. Just put one Converse in front of the other. All I have to do is show up for things, and it will be right again soon. The *blip blip bleep bleep bleep blip* notes of the security code last night jingle around my head. It's musical, like a guitar riff.

The cafeteria workers are clearing trays of food in preparation for lunch in a couple hours. The pan of dry yellow scrambled eggs makes me wince. The woman lifting it from the warming cart, Rosario, smiles at me. She has pink cheeks and kind brown eyes. "I can get you fresh ones," she says. Maybe it's that her soft Cuban accent reminds me of my mom's old friend Lucia, but I feel like she knows something is wrong with me. Part of me wants to pull her into the kitchen and tell her what it is. Instead, I shake my head, mustering a return smile. The cereal bar is all I can stomach, and I pour a pile of Life into a bowl, top it with milk, get an orange juice, and venture into the main hall.

It's a cavernous space with rows of polished mahogany tables. Oil paintings of past school presidents line the paneled walls, centered between giant stained-glass windows. I feel their male gazes on me. *I belong here*, I tell them, and maybe myself. *Screw off*, I say. I don't know if the real people notice me or not, because I don't look up. I tuck myself into a far corner table.

I stare out a door propped open to the outside patio. At this angle, I see three sets of well-muscled legs reposing under one of the cement tables. Crew socks, old-school tennis shoes. My neck ticks involuntarily, and I return to the Life cereal, bringing the spoon to my mouth. The smell of the milk, not spoiled but just . . . milky, makes my throat close. I might gag. I sip the orange juice and rise to leave when a "*Jee*-sus!" from the patio smacks me to my seat. "Couldn't Chauncey have waited until *after* the season to plagiarize?"

A thousand tiny icicles poke my arms and shoulders.

"Who's gonna cox our boat?" someone asks.

"Let's invite her," another replies.

Fuck. I scramble to get out from the bench and run, but realize their attention is on the curly-haired First Year I saw before, out on the quad. The legs belong to three Senior rowers, I see now. Gods of the school. I'm so relieved they're not talking about me, I'm immobilized.

"That's Sofia Bodenrader," Khalid says.

My breath goes shallow. I'm looking at the back of Colin Pearce's head, at the W-shaped hairline at the nape of his neck and the pale strip of skin just beneath it that reveals he's only just had a haircut. It's sickening. I can't look away.

"She can raid my boden any day of the week," Colin's saying. They laugh. His shoulders bounce. . . .

Dots invade my field of vision. I fumble to pinch the butterfly bruise.

"Looks like she's all hot for Seb," Khalid says. "What's new?"

"Fucking McNeilly," says the pig bastard. "Leave some scraps for the rest of us."

Cackles.

I pinch. Hard. The pain of it is familiar and completely under my control.

"Hey, Q!"

I startle. Sway a little. I'm standing.

Nils, from Drawing and Painting class and Outdoors Club and Thursday Night Café is smiling at me across the table. Nils! Old me wants to cry. "You headed to art history?" His face is different. Leaner or something. It's like fun-house mirrors. And how does he know I have art history?

"You okay?" he asks softly. Coming closer.

I back toward the door. My feet tangle in the table legs. I say something muddled, and I'm not sure what the words were supposed to be. Fainting is like this. Slumping to the bench, I prepare to dissolve into silence.

"Q?" Nils scuttles around the table.

My arms shoot out straight like porcupine quills. "No!" I say. Adrenaline brings me back to my senses. *Don't touch me.*

Nils stops.

"I'm okay," I say in an attempt at normal. My throat's got half my voice hostage. "I . . ."

He waits, face full of compassion. I grab the orange juice and chug it. Over the rim of the glass, I see Rosario looking at me, too, knitting-needle eyebrows, pushing a white cloth in windmill circles over a table.

Quinn, snap the fuck out of it.

Nils staring at me isn't okay. I close my eyes and let the sugar circulate. I wish I brought my AirPods. Instead I mentally scramble for a song from my dad's Songs in the Key of Q playlist.

Maybe it's the T-shirt choice that inspires Led Zeppelin's "D'yer Mak'er." It rolls into my head, confident. Strong.

Dad and me, in the studio. I try the drum solo. It's terrible, but he doesn't miss a beat, kicking in with the guitar.

From the inside out, I come back.

Nils is still there.

I breathe three times, then say, "God, I'm sorry. My blood sugar is wack." I sit up straight. "Whew," I add.

"Do you have diabetes?" he asks. "My cousin does."

"No, no," I say. "A little hypoglycemic." Heather uses this line (really she's obsessed with weight-loss cleansing), so I run with it. "Juice usually does the trick." I have no idea when I last ate a meal. I stand with my tray, willing myself steady, and head to the dirty-dish station.

Nils is waiting for me.

Shit.

We walk out the big wooden doors onto the sunny quad.

"How did you know I have art history?" I ask.

He blushes. "Oh, uh, I," he laughs. "You came in after me on Wednesday. You know, the first day. With Alex. I tried to get your attention. . . ."

He looks in agony with embarrassment, and I long for the old me because this would be so awesome. Nils is a guy that the old me would have loved to hang out with. Fucking pig bastard, why did I fall for his bullshit? Nils tells me about how he hiked Mount Katahdin in Maine this summer. "Did you do any good hikes?"

And just like that, I know: I'm too wrecked for Nils now.

Up ahead, I see Charlotte. She doesn't know how Summer Sendoff ended for me. We're going to intersect. It's unstoppable, like a train crash.

"Quinn!" she says, embracing me. I can't react, but she is oblivious. "Hi, Nils," she says. "Q, we have *a lot* to discuss! I haven't seen you at all!"

I smile as best I can. *Just blend in.*

Her eyes rest on Nils, and she smiles wider at me, which barely seems possible. She thinks we're a couple. That's okay, I decide. Nils can be my armor. He adds to the force field.

Be normal.

Charlotte keeps talking, moving sideways toward the science buildings. "Let's meet up!" She nods, answering for me, I guess, since I am numb.

"Definitely." My head bobs somewhere between accepting and rejecting, which is spot-on, actually. "Definitely."

She waves.

Nils and I continue up the steps of the Fine Arts building.

"Did you do the reading?"

"Uh. No."

"Me neither," he says with a short laugh. "I actually fell asleep. God, how do art historians make something so beautiful sooooo boring? And Max woke me when he came back to the room last night. He had this wild story."

A memory from before gallops through my head, too skittish to stop: Nils, Max, me, and Alex laughing in the orange glow of a campfire, roasting marshmallows for s'mores at the Evans Notch campout in May. Alex whispered, *Nils likes you.*

"What kind of story?" I say.

"He says he saw some creepy stalker guy," Nils is saying, "in the woods near Kessler and Winfield. All in black, following Colin Pearce."

I almost stop dead. The hairs on my neck stand up. "A stalker?" I ask calmly, controlling my voice.

"I know, right?" I feel him looking at me. He knows I went to Summer Sendoff with the pig bastard. He could unravel it all right now. I keep a perfect mask. "Wow," I say.

Nils rolls on. "We *are* talking Max here. You know how he is. . . ." He chuckles.

I force a quick laugh. "Well, not really, but a stalker sounds pretty . . ." *Badass.* "Far-fetched."

I'm a *stalker*. Max thought I was a *guy*. The same charge of adrenaline I got watching Doughty shoots through me, pushing my head up as we turn into the Arts building. Inside, the hallway is dim and smells of oil paints, clay dust, and September floor polish. It brings me back to my first days at Lycroft Phelps. To the old me.

"Campus Safety couldn't find anyone," Nils continues. "They brought in the Whitney Police. Nothing."

My pulse thumps in my ears. We file into the auditorium. Mr. Politi's white mustache flops around as he greets us, but I don't hear the words. The police?

"You okay?" Nils says from a few steps below me.

I blink. "Yeah, yeah." But I hold the railing. "What did Colin say about it?" I venture. It could be trouble that people know Pearce is a target, I think, but when I try to sort out *why*, my brain is just gray chaos.

"Who knows. He probably loves it," Nils says, quickly adding, "Sorry, I don't mean—"

I smile. "He was a sucky Summer Sendoff date. I really don't like him." It's an epic understatement, but I'm surprised I tell Nils this so easily. I shouldn't say anything about anything. A panicky swirl starts in my stomach, but Nils's eyes turn soft, like a piece of him that was hiding opened a door and peeked out. Which doesn't make sense at all but somehow distracts me enough to keep me calm.

Alex waves from the center of a row of red velvet theater seats. We angle ourselves sideways to join her.

"Did you hear about the stalker, Alex?" I hear myself say. To my own roommate. My best friend. So add liar to vampire as something I've become.

"Oh my God. Yes!" she says. "At breakfast. What the hell? I heard Charlotte and Seb saw him. And Seth Vining, too."

"Max saw him," I say, which cues Nils to explain. They carry on, allowing me to breathe.

I don't remember seeing Seth Vining—I'm not even sure who that is. I guess that couple I saw behind Spangler by the 1856 Library could have been Charlotte and Seb. Charlotte had the polar opposite outcome from her date with Seb as mine with Colin, I think, a fact that bites at a corner of my heart like a scorpion. He poisoned me. And I let him.

The Anger roils up from somewhere deeper inside me, a sandstorm swirling around my heart, wiping out cops and scorpions and everything else with a singular focus.

I can't wait until tonight.

I'm getting that fucking gun.

CHARLOTTE

"Did you apply for Young Choreographer?" Hannah asks Gabby Atherton softly. That's my roomie, diggin' for intel. She wants to be a journalist, and she kind of practices on everyone. I love it because she asks all the things I don't dare. We're three in a row stretching at the barre in studio 5. Gabby's an amazingly talented Senior soloist who could definitely beat me for YC.

Other dancers in our Advanced Pointe class are scattered around the room in various muscle-lengthening contortions. Chopin plays over the sound system. Madame Chu is flipping through papers on her clipboard near the door. She could have my essay in there. I finished after lunch.

It sucks.

I ended up gushing about how much dance meant to me. Pretty cringey, but also true.

"Nah, I didn't apply," says Gabby. She has her heel propped on the barre and reaches her right arm over her head to rest on her ankle, her body a symmetrical arch. "It's too much work with college applications this fall. Plus, I don't like telling people what to do. I'm not bossy enough."

"I hear that," Hannah says, holding a foot over her head. I'm working my inner thighs, one heel on the bar and side-stretching over my leg, facing Gabby, who is doing the same thing. We bob gently up and down. At once we all switch sides and share a laugh recognizing that we've somehow synchronized without trying. Dancer humor.

"I applied," I say. "I won't get it."

"You are bossy enough," Hannah says. To Gabby: "Trust me. We've roomed together three years."

"Shhh!" I glance at Madame.

The Young Choreographer gets eight dancers (chosen by Madame and her assistant, Marcus) to train for the Fall Fling, the third weekend in October. I slide my back foot out to a split. To apply, I submitted a two-minute video of a solo I choreographed for myself and the essay.

"Seriously," Hannah says. "Charlotte's audition video is gorgeous. I think she's going to get it."

Madame calls, "Okay, ladies. Pliés."

"Do you know who applied?" Hannah whispers as the others line up along the barre.

"Lizzie was thinking about it. And Catherine," Gabby says. "I'm not sure if they did."

We simultaneously scan the group, eyes landing on the two Seniors. Catherine's a soloist. Lizzie isn't. Catherine could also definitely beat me.

We're through the barre work and running variations when Madame stops the music. She's smiling toward the door.

"Brava!" calls Dean Frye. "Quite impressive, ladies!"

My stomach tightens. Madame does a sweeping curtsy. She runs dramatic in a way that only women who have spent their professional life onstage can pull off.

"How long has he been there?" Gabby asks under her breath.

"Kind of creeper-ish," Hannah says. But I'm busy wondering why the head of school has appeared in my classes twice today.

"To what do we owe this honor, Dean Frye?" Madame asks.

"Madame Chu, I apologize for the interruption. I need to speak with Charlotte Foresley for a moment. Would that be okay?"

"Oh no," I breathe without moving my lips.

Madame coos a reply. My brain is rapid-firing words like *alcohol, suspension, breaking and entering, parent phone call,* and *Seb* across my frontal lobe. I hurry toward the door. The blocks in my pointe shoes drum the floor like a death knell, and the class is a blur of black leotards and spidery limbs.

I follow Dean Frye into the hall. The younger dancers from other classrooms notice me through the observation windows, but I screen them out.

"Charlotte, apologies for the interruption," he says over his shoulder.

What if he's already spoken to Seb? Dean Frye can catch us lying if our stories conflict. I close my eyes and dig deep, straighten up and lift my chin. "Is it okay if I slip out of my pointe shoes?" I ask sweetly.

"We won't be more than a few minutes."

I add a polite wince, implying the shoes hurt. In truth, I could tightrope walk in these suckers, but I need to check my phone.

"Go ahead," he says.

I hobble to the pile of ballet bags on the floor and tip mine so my phone faces out from inside. I untie the ribbons above my ankles, unwinding them sloppily, jostling the phone until it lights up. *Face recognition, I love you.* And there it is. All caps. A text from Seb:

FRYE! DON'T MENTION THE LIBRARY. WE WERE NEAR SPANGLER WHEN WE SAW THE GUY IN THE WOODS. WE THOUGHT IT WAS JUST SOMEONE MESSING AROUND. DON'T SAY WHO. WENT RIGHT HOME.

It's pretty cryptic and lacking critical details, but I'm relieved to learn this is about the stalker, not us illegally using the 1856 Library or the booze. My muscles relax like I might melt into the floor. I pop up and slip into my UGGs and angora wrap. We walk out the doors into the sunshine.

Dean Frye blinks, pulling the visor on his cap lower. It casts a shadow across his face that makes my stomach bobble. I tighten my wrap. Outside the studio, a leotard transforms pretty quickly into inappropriate attire. He is very careful to keep his eyes up.

"Charlotte, it's come to my attention that, while accompanied by Mr. McNeilly last night, you encountered someone in the woods. Is that true?"

I nod, afraid to speak.

"Where were you when you saw this person?"

"Outside Spangler." I feel a stab of pride for checking off one of Seb's cover story points.

"May I ask why you didn't report it?"

Is this a trap? "Am I in trouble?" I can't help myself. You can take the girl out of the goody two shoes, but . . . I swallow, my tongue is sand-dune dry. *Keep calm and have another gin and tonic, Charlotte.*

"No," Dean Frye says. He smiles stiffly. "I don't believe so." Not reassuring. "I'm just trying to figure out who this . . ."

He searches for a word.

"Stalker?" I offer, and then wish I could suck it back because it's such a dangerous word. Stalker reeks of psychopaths. I clench up again. What if it *was* a crazy murderer out there? But then I remember Max and the police and think: *Max!* He told Frye about this. And I told Max. Seb'll dump me.

I'm dizzy. I've missed a question. "Sorry," I say. "What?"

"I said, there's no reason to think it's anything more than a prank, but you know, with the news these days, students could become alarmed by someone prowling around the woods in dark clothes."

I nod. I want to say, *I was very alarmed!*

"It's not a very funny prank is my point, Charlotte. And I would like to get to the bottom of it so it doesn't happen again."

"Right, of course," I say. And honestly, I'm with Dean Frye on this.

He rocks back and forth on his shoes.

"Oh," I say. "I have no idea who it was, if that's what you're asking." Goody-Two-Shoes me is pleased this also happens to be true. "Neither does Seb." *To the best of my knowledge.*

"Any guesses?" he says.

"Nope." I shake my head. "It was dark. And he disappeared into the woods as soon as Seb yelled at him."

"Seb yelled at him?"

Oh crap.

"Well, he said, you know, something like, 'Hey, who is that?'" A squirrel perched on a low limb behind Dean Frye chitters, like it's amused at my lie. "I was a little scared," I say defensively. "I can't remember exactly."

"Right." He inhales, expanding to full head-of-school stature. I know this trick. "Okay, well, if you see or hear of anything like this again, Charlotte, do let me know. Lycroft Phelps is built on the honor code. We depend on each other's integrity."

I nod again. "Of course. I guess we should have called Campus Safety, but it didn't seem like that big of a deal. . . ." I let my voice trail off, hoping he's satisfied with that.

"It's not a big deal, but next time," he says, wagging a finger at me like he's joking, but he's obviously not.

I half laugh. "Yes, I will. Absolutely."

"Thank you." He gives a small salute. The sun splashes across his face as he turns to go, revealing a tightness across his eyes. Dean Frye is *not* satisfied, but now my worry is Seb being angry. I text him a thumbs-up and rush back to class, but everyone is packing up.

"He took longer than he said," I say to Madame. "Sorry!"

She smiles knowingly and nods. "It's my experience that Dean Frye has only a cursory appreciation for our work. But he is a great supporter of our program, so we overlook his shortcomings."

I am not sure whether I should laugh.

"Check your email, Charlotte." She winks and brushes past me out of the studio.

I blink. Hannah, on the floor, untying her pointe shoes, is eavesdropping. Oh my God! she mouths, eyes round. As soon as Madame's clicking heels fade from the hallway, I scramble for my phone. Hannah's next to me, grabbing my arm.

"Are you kidding me that her email is callmemadame @lycroftphelps?" Hannah says giddily.

I can't respond. If I get this, especially as a junior, it takes my college résumé to a new level. I don't know how long I'll keep dancing. I don't know if I'll ever be professional. But I know I've wanted this for so long. Not just for the résumé. For the love of dance.

I tap the email open.

From: Madame Celeste Chu <celeste.chu@lycroftphelps.edu>
To: Charlotte Foresley <charlotte.foresley@lycroftphelps.edu>
Subject: Young Choreographer

Charlotte:

Congratulations! You are our new Young Choreographer, selected for this year's Fall Fling Showcase. Your audition tape was original, and I liked how you fully utilized the stage. For planning purposes, please know that your performance is scheduled for Friday, October 20, in the Orenstein Auditorium, time tentatively 8 p.m. The following people are assigned to your leadership:

First Years: Sofia Bodenrader, Lily Eckern, Vivian Zahner
Lower Mids: Mallory Rathburn
Upper Mids: Skye Vandross, Hannah Hesse
Seniors: Gabrielle Malloy and Felipe de la Cruz
You have full use of studio 5 after classes until 9 p.m. beginning this week. I will always be available to answer

questions and offer advice, but I will hold back unless you ask.

Madame
Madame Celeste Chu
Director, Preprofessional School of Ballet
The Lycroft Phelps School

I hold my phone up for Hannah to read. We're silent for a few heartbeats and then spring to our feet, jumping in a circle.

"You did it!" Hannah cries, hugging me.

"You're in it!" I say. We laugh.

"I'll make sure we get a write-up in the *Wire*," she says.

I sigh, grinning. "This is going to be a good year for us. You're assistant editor of the paper, I'm Young Choreographer."

"We're both only Upper Mids," Hannah cuts in. "But you're dating the Genetic Miracle, and I have Hank. . . ."

"What? Hank's hot," I say, which isn't true. She rolls her eyes, but we laugh again and I compose an email to my parents.

From: Charlotte Foresley <charlotte.foresley@lycroftphelps.edu>
To: Mom 💜, Dad 😇
Fwd: Young Choreographer

👇👇👇 LOOOOOOK!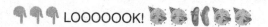

Love, C

From: Mom💜

To: charlotte.foresley@lycroftphelps.edu, Dad😇

Re: Young Choreographer

Oh, sweetie! Terrific! We're so happy for you. Dad says: "They know talent when they see it!" He's buying our plane tickets right now!

Love you to the moon and back,
Mom and Dad

Q

Ancient Art History class is the best place to be when you want to focus on taking somebody out. A darkened theater, art slides projected on the screen. Nobody notices if you can't stop pulling your eyelashes. I feel a sense of power at not crying out as I do this. Alex sits next to me; Nils is on my other side.

"Over the course of the semester, we'll survey ancient art from each continent. . . ." Dr. Politi paces creakily in front of the screen, occasionally pointing at a projected urn or figurine with his trembling red dot of light. It's when the Greek statuary appears that my chest contracts. I see us walking through the sculptures at the Amphitheater Lawn.

Can you name the Muses? the pig bastard asks.

Calliope, I say, epic poetry;

Clio, history;

Thalia, comedy;

Ourania, celestial bodies;

She protects the stars, I say.

How spectacular is that? I ask.

And then the horrible suffocating sound of his mouth covering my ear.

I suddenly need to bolt from this auditorium. I look toward the aisle for escape. Nils's and Alex's faces glow pale, reflecting the screen. My vision rolls in waves. I sit back. Swallow. Close my eyes. Escape while you're here, I tell myself. The *blip blip bleep bleep blip* from Anderson's keypad starts playing in my head. I roll it and reroll it I don't know how many times, feeling a sense of control return. There has to be a way to crack it. I know there is. I'm holding on to the butterfly bruise without respite. Squeezing it tight.

Alex nudges me and whispers, "I actually love that."

I realize she's talking about the black ceramic bowl projected on the screen. Jagged gold lines spread over it like spiderwebs. No, like lightning. Spiderwebs have patterns, this doesn't. It's random and messy. I've obviously missed something important.

"It's nice," I say.

"Not the bowl, dumbass." She flashes a smile like I'm hopeless. I stare.

"Earth to Q, come in, Q," she whispers, waving her fingers in front of my face. "I love kintsugi." She holds her spiral notebook up so I can read it.

"Kintsugi" 15th century art of broken pieces. Emperor returned broken pottery to China for repairs. He thought they did an ugly job. His craftsmen repaired it with gold.

"Cool," I say.

Alex throws me a stink eye. "Come on! Finding art in broken things? It's amazing."

"It is," I lie.

She shakes her head and returns to Mr. Politi, who flips the slide to a map. My eyes lose focus. *Blip blip bleep bleep blip* If I could get closer to Officer Doughty while he's punching in the key sequence, and put it into slow motion . . . I could trace the movement of his finger over the numbers.

When the period is over, I let Nils and Alex get ahead of me in the hallway. Ms. Weller, my art teacher from last year, spots me from her studio classroom door.

"Q!" She's moving in for a hug.

I want to run. I can't, of course. I have to stop breathing when I catch the scent of her bohemian perfume. Of last year. Of before.

She pulls back. I exhale and smile. She studies my face with her wide blue eyes. Cat's eyes. "I am so happy you're taking Drawing and Painting II." She beams. Strands of silver-blond hair shimmy around her head.

I need to respond. "Yeah," I say. "Same."

She continues staring at me, like I'm that shadowy section of a painting where she wants to get the light just right.

Then—because my brain function is liquid these days, spilling between past, present, and future tenses of its own volition—I see a flash of myself using my phone to video Doughty, which I play back in slo-mo after he's left Anderson. I'm holding the gun. I'm waiting at the boathouse door when Pearce comes outside. His face, first surprise, then amusement, then fear . . .

I blink.

"Quinn?" Ms. Weller's squinting at me. "Are you—"

"Class starts Monday, right?" I say.

"Riiight," she says slowly. "You look a little . . . Q, honey, are you—"

I start backing away. "I'm sorry, Ms. Weller, I have to . . ." I mumble nonsense, spin around, and get out of there.

Outside, I feel shaky and guilty. Ms. Weller was my coolest teacher last year, which is why I signed up for Drawing and Painting II. But I'm not who I was and I have no way to explain that to her. Like Rosario, she senses something's wrong. Some women have maternal instincts that border on psychic.

I hurry along the path, not really focused on where I'm headed, and suddenly I'm passing the bench where it all started last May. Come to think of it, it happened right before Drawing and Painting. On a random Wednesday two weeks before Summer Sendoff. It was one of those moody New England days with blustery clouds skittering across the sun, turning the temperature from warm to chilly and back again so you couldn't get used to either. I picture myself, sitting on the bench like I was, reading *Siddhartha*, one of the "hero's journey" books for First Year English, waiting for Alex to meet me. We were supposed to walk to the art building; she was late. I felt someone sit on the bench next to me, and before I processed who it was, Colin Pearce was like, "Hi."

I'd only talked to him twice the whole year: Once on Opening Day when he was hitting on Macy and barely noticed me, and once at the Après Skate party during February's Winter Carnival. And that time he was busy flirting, too, with Charlotte, who brought me and the rest of her Littles group to the party. He asked my name, probably as a way of being near Charlotte longer. When I told him, he screwed up his face. "Q?" he repeated, amused. "Like in the James Bond movies?" And I said, "Yep. British Secret Intelligence. But don't tell anyone or I shall be forced to shoot you," in my best accent, which cracked people up and left me feeling pretty clever in that moment. Still, to have him sit next to me—by myself—on a bench three *months* later took me by surprise that day. I can't stop replaying it in my head.

"Hi?" I said.

"I've kept your secret," he said, leaning back and stretching his

arms along the top of the bench. "About the British secret service."
It was like those three months since the Après Skate were a crease
in the time-space continuum. And I have to admit it takes a pretty
bold person to fold up time like that, like a paper he could tuck in
his pocket because he didn't live by laws that the rest of us did. It
should have been a warning sign. Instead, I played a good little
coconspirator.

"Impressive," I said. "But how do I know you're not lying?"

He watched the chapel steps, not me, which lent to the feeling
we were on some kind of covert mission. A smile broke across his
face. "You don't."

"You underestimate Her Majesty's reach," I replied. "I have
spies everywhere."

"Okay, then," he said. "I'll prove it. Come with me to the Summer Sendoff."

I nearly swallowed my tongue. Even right now, just looking at
the bench, I can feel the grooves of the wood slats under my thighs
as I shifted nervously. *Colin Pearce, inviting me to Summer Sendoff,
the social event of the year?* I thought. I didn't want to reveal my
shock and awe, but I couldn't figure out how to answer.

Colin interpreted my silence as reluctance. I'd accidentally
employed the perfect response. "We can go to the Whitney Inn
for dinner," he said, like he needed to throw in a bonus chip. It's
the fanciest restaurant for miles around, and I've been many times
with Boppy and Dad.

I stayed quiet, buying time. Was I supposed to feel flattered?
Was it a joke? He looked offended. Or irritated. I couldn't tell.
"Do you have a date already?" he asked.

And then, awkwardly, I said, "Yes, I'll go with you." He didn't react. "Thanks," I tacked on. God, just thinking I said that makes bile rise in my throat. But when he heard it, he looked directly at me for the first time since he sat down. His eyes were gray-blue and cool as a stone wall. A wolf's eyes. At least, that's how I see it now. Maybe I made up those eyes.

"Cool." He got up, backed away a few steps. "I'll be in touch," he said, turned, and left.

I stood. Sat again. Half stood, sat, and then texted Alex.

Me: Where are you??? Major fucking plot twist.

Next I texted Charlotte, hoping she could decipher this development.

Me: You're not going to believe this. Call me!

But she was heading into dance and said to tell her at our Littles meeting, which we had in two hours. I couldn't bear two hours. I texted the same thing to Macy.

"Come on, Macy," I muttered, jiggling my knee. But she was busy being Macy that day, and so I gave up and went to Drawing and Painting. I remember a little explosion of laughter popping out of me like a firecracker. "What the hell just happened?" I whispered.

I spotted Alex just beyond the chapel.

"Finally!" I called, with more enthusiasm than intended. A couple of kids stared.

Alex pointed to her phone with a questioning expression.

I glanced around and waved at her to hurry up.

When I told her, she stopped abruptly, her boots pushing gravel, which added a dramatic punctuation mark. "Whoa-whoa-whoa." A laugh bubbled from her. "*What?* How did *this* transpire?"

"I don't know! He just asked me out of nowhere."

"What'd you say?" She studied my face. "I mean, he is a crew god sculpted to perfection. But he's also kind of a dick."

"I know!" I whispered. "But what could I say? It's Colin Pearce, for crying out loud."

"Of course! You had to say yes. You're happy, right?"

Was I? "I guess." We resumed walking.

"Because you could back out, Q. You don't *have* to—" Alex said, putting words to thoughts that had swum in helpless circles since he sat down next to me. But it was my fatal mistake to fall for him—the idea of him.

"Alex, are you high?"

"Right." We didn't talk for a few beats of gravel, and I remember thinking how it sounded like Dad using brushes on the snare and deciding whether this was an appropriate soundtrack for the occasion, when Alex said: "You know what this means, don't you?"

"That I feel like a passenger in my own life?" I said.

"Don't get all Bob Dylan on me," Alex said. "It means we need a day pass for Saturday to take Newbury Street by storm."

"You'd shop for my dress even though you're not going?" She had to leave for a family wedding the day before Summer Sendoff.

"Of course! Fool." She gave me an affectionate shove. "It's Newbury Street. And I need a better dress for that wedding."

Two chuckling squirrels tear across the path in front of me and up a giant maple tree. It's like I'm coming out of a trance. I've walked all the way across campus while lost in memories. In fact, I missed lunch again. "Shit."

My phone vibrates in my pocket. It's Alex.

"Hi," I say.

"Where are you? I thought we were going for a run after classes ended."

"Oooh, shoot. Sorry. I forgot."

"How could you forget? Oh well, never mind—"

"I'm sorry, Alex. I just . . ." I entertain saying, *I just have to steal this gun from Anderson House and wipe Colin Pearce off the planet, and then I'll be a good friend again.*

But I don't. Of course I don't. I offer thin excuses and hang up, hoping we have enough good will in reserve to keep our friendship afloat.

I'm passing the dance studios, and I can see Charlotte in one, alone. A simple black tank leotard and short wrap skirt, pink footless tights, barefoot. She's so elegant, her limbs move like she's boneless. Like water. It's a loose, approximate kind of dancing—a rough draft, it seems—unlike the precise performances I've seen her in. But she's lost in her creative self.

It brings tears to my eyes, the purity of it. I haven't ever taken dance, but I know that feeling—playing around on the guitar, or making art, getting lost in details for hours. I remember escaping into my final project in Ms. Weller's class, an oversized painting of red poppies à la badass genius Georgia O'Keeffe. My flowers burst from lilting stems in a glossy blue ceramic pot. I came in during free periods, working on blending the perfect color red at the desk by the window. I mixed oranges and reds, pinks and yellows on the tip of a fine brush, carefully spreading it over each pedal, guided by some internal sense of what looked right to me where.

"Lovely," Ms. Weller says. I didn't hear her approach, but she is the

sort of person who floats. *"You're really seeing the modulation of the color, Q. Earlier in the year, you may have just seen"*—she sweeps her hand through the air in a grand gesture—*"red! But it's so much more than that, isn't it?"*

Yeah. She's a little out there, but artists are out there. That's Growing Up around Musicians 101. Most of my dad's friends are bohemians who discuss poetry until 3:00 a.m., or rail-thin guys with groomed facial hair who seem completely uninteresting until they play a solo on their instrument and blow your mind. I know this about artists, and it must be why Ms. Weller and I click.

I nod, and we look at the poppies together. *"I'm thinking of the blossoms like fireworks,"* I say. *"Opening at the peak of a long green trail."*

She smiles broadly. Silver-blond hair dances around her loose bun, catching the sunlight.

"You might mean contrails," Nils says from the next table. We're in Outdoors Club, and I found out he's a pretty good bass player. We did a cover together of "Hey There Delilah" at the March Thursday Night Café. I like Nils. He's not conventionally handsome exactly, but appealing. His eyes smile.

Ms. Weller and I look at him, as does the rest of the class.

He shrugs. *"The trails behind a firework."* His eyes shift right, and he flushes. *"Contrails . . ."* he repeats weakly.

I laugh. We catch eyes. Ms. Weller sweeps between us. *"Examine your work, students."* She says the word students *like we're in class at the Sorbonne in Paris, when in actuality half the kids in here are just fulfilling their fine arts requirement. "Is there a* metaphor *in it? Some art philosophers believe that the artist's subconscious is always played out in the act of creating, intentionally or not. It's out of the artist's control, they posit."*

Nils theatrically puts his hand on his chin and examines his work—I think it's a cow skull?—with faux concentration. He shoots me a grimace. I stifle a laugh. Ms. Weller sees us but pretends not to. "Perhaps you can find something autobiographical *in your work. Something . . . enlightening. About you."*

I study my poppies. Maybe they are a metaphor for my first year here. Arrived at fourteen, pale green and restrained in a narrow stem. Found a best friend, Alex, and a bigger group of friends. Joined a capella, performed at Thursday Night Café open mics, camped with Outdoors Club, learned which room of the library to pick when you have an exam and which one to pick if you just want to socialize. I've been to two Upper Mid/Senior parties. And—I shake my head, dipping the brush into the red again—I have a date for the dance. With an Upper Mid varsity rower.

That's just nuts.

Nils starts singing softly, and it takes a few moments before I recognize the song. "Baby, you're a firework . . ." I raise my eyebrows. He doesn't look up, but does a little shimmy with his shoulders. "Make them go ah-ah-ah . . ."

We crack up. I kind of wish I was going with him to Summer Sendoff, but it's too late for that. Colin Pearce.

I snap back to the present, the anger starting to churn. God damn that pig bastard for stealing me from myself. God damn him. Every memory I have is tainted. I can't fall into any kind of creative reverie. Just fucking swirling angry tirades.

I'm on a trail leading to the Amphitheater. I can see the statuary up ahead, blurred through tears. I pivot the opposite way. But it's too late. A flash of me on the ground appears.

I'm below Euterpe, the music muse. I stare at her delicate marble toes. I'm a broken winged butterfly, immobilized.

Shush

Shush

Shush

I shake my head hard.

"Hey, you okay?" some girl says.

I pop my head up to look at her. I nod and hurry for the dorms.

I just need it to be night. I'll video Doughty. I'll crack the code. He'll pay.

From: griffin.frye@lycroftphelps.edu
To: Residential Assistants
Cc: thomas.doughty@lycroftphelps.edu
Subject: Smells like teen spirit

Dear Resident Adviser Team,

It's come to our attention, and by now perhaps to yours as well, that a male—most likely a student—was sneaking around campus after dark last night, purposely following and spooking other students. I've met with our own Officer Doughty, the Whitney Police, and the students involved in the "sightings." There appears to have been no harm done. That said, someone dressed in black popping in and out of the woods at night is potentially frightening to all of us, particularly as the typical Halloween spirit arrives on campus next month. The mere rumor of an intruder could cause a campus-wide panic that would escalate further if it reached parents. Please listen to the students in your dorm with a keen ear for clues pertaining to the prankster's identity and the incident in general, and report even scant intel to my office posthaste.

My hope is this was a one-off, but it's possible the assailant is encouraged by the simple fact that he wasn't caught. Please do not initiate any student conversations around the topic and minimize student worry. As always, if a situation feels larger than you can appropriately manage, contact myself or Assistant Dean Lori Ballard for support.

Yours,
Dean Frye

3

Friday Afternoon: Athletics/Activity Block

MAX

"So what did Dean Frye say?" Nils asks. He's standing on the mats roughly twenty-five feet below me while I scale the rock gym wall.

I wrap my right fingers around an orange climbing hold. One leg is straight and the other bent. "Mostly he . . . insulted me and asked . . . if I knew who it was," I say, my voice labored from my effort. I'm debating whether the blue or hot pink hold is the best choice for my left hand.

"Okay, well. I mean, that makes sense he would ask you that." Nils is my belayer, which means he's my anchor in case I free-fall. I won't. But the metaphor is not lost on me. Nils is so reasonable. I'm *rational*. Those aren't the same thing.

"I just wish he wasn't such a dick about it," I say.

Nils makes a half-laugh sound that both acknowledges me but tells me not to sweat it. I leave out the part about Seb and Charlotte because I feel crappy that I brought them into the whole thing without their consent. Nothing bad's come of it so far, so I'm hoping it will simply go away.

Nils and I are literally connected by a rope that loops through a hook bolted to the ceiling and attaches to both our belted harnesses. I love that the whole endeavor of rock climbing is a practical application of physics. The simple machine: pulley. The forces: gravity versus friction. I love the efficiency of how such basic elements provide endless diversity in climbing experiences. Each climb is a different puzzle. I grab for the blue grip when Nils rattles me from my zone.

"Your dream girl's out in the hall," he calls, full volume.

I twist, losing my right foot hold, and swing out from the wall. "Dude!" I say in a whispered yell, dangling. "You *cannot* say that out loud!" He lowers me in a controlled drop to the mat. "The acoustics are very unpredictable in here," I scold.

Nils simply tilts his head toward the lobby of the Bak Athletic Center.

Resistance is futile. I step behind him and watch Alexandra Buchanan through the plexiglass window, in happy chatter with two friends. Her hair is pulled into a round puff on top of her head, and she's wearing running shorts. I'm incapable of not admiring her perfectly proportioned, strong tanned legs as they disappear into the girls' locker room. Even after the door closes, her laughter echoes through the spaces. I glance toward the rafters and visualize the sound waves bouncing around up there, then down to us in the rock gym.

"Damn," I say.

Nils snickers. "Just ask her out. You could invite her to the Fall Fling."

"Oh, like you did with Q to Summer Sendoff last year?"

"I can't help it if someone else beat me to it," Nils says as we exchange clips. He faces the wall, studying the colorful holds to plan his path.

"Uh, you could have asked her sooner. You kept putting it off," I remind him. "D-bags like Pearce don't wait around."

"So you're saying I need to be a bigger d-bag?" he says.

"It's a sad truth, but"—I look at him—"it appears to work."

"All the more reason for you to invite Alex now," Nils says, gripping holds with both hands and pulling his feet up. He has twenty-seven pounds on me, but because of the elegant genius of the friction-enhanced belt clips, I can still belay him.

"Now?" I object. "Fall Fling isn't for three weeks. She'd think I'm a creeper."

"You mean," he strains, scaling upward, "discover you're a creeper?"

I ignore him. "Anyway, Alexandra Buchanan would not go out with me," I say.

"How do you know that?" He pauses, craning his neck to find the next move.

"Go for that yellow one," I say. He does. It's very satisfying. "The numbers don't add up for me and Alex."

"Seriously, Max? The Quantitative shit again?"

I shift my weight. "You just don't want it to be true. The implications of Quantitative Hotness Correlativity are staggering for guys like us. But the numbers don't lie. Eights, Nines, Tens? They don't go out with anything less than Eights. The only exception is a Seven with an associative bonus feature, like the guy's related to royalty or his family owns a tropical island or something."

"And we're . . . Fours?"

"Hell no, we're not Fours," I say. "Jesus, you have to have some kind of serious flaw to fall below a Five. A third nipple or something. Nils, I think you may be a Six now, almost a Seven, really.

You look good this year, man." If it weren't for the blond eyelashes, he'd definitely be an Eight, but I keep that to myself. I mean, what's he supposed to do? Dye them?

"Thanks. I had the third nipple removed over the summer."

I snort.

"And you're a . . ." he says.

"Five," I say.

"Come on! You're a Six," Nils attempts. "You've got great hair," he says, then chuckles. "I should *not* be indulging your bullshit theory."

Reflexively, I run my fingers through my hair, which I spike with product. It is thick and black and definitely my singular cool feature. Still, I shake my head. "It's my height. Most girls are taller than me. I'm lacking any kind of Croft capital. You play the bass—that's worth half a point at least—plus you're a lacrosse player."

"I pretty much suck at lacrosse."

"But you're on the team. A solid point right there."

"You're the captain of robotics and you're only an Upper Mid. Doesn't that count?"

I laugh sardonically. "Robotics is a negative number, Nils. It might be a negative Two."

He laughs, because he knows I'm right.

"Someday it will matter; just not now," I say. "Or at this place, anyway." I sound like my mom, which is pathetic. The thing is, most of the asshats that fill the dorms of LPS aren't all that smart. They're just from a ton of money. Lycroft needs to go out and recruit nerdiacs like me—to show that not only are they up to speed in the STEM department, but they *perform*. On the *world stage*. Face it, all the billionaires are in tech now. Don't think those old Lycroft trustees living off their family fortunes made in coal and steel aren't looking over their shoulders. So they need me. And yet, I feel shit upon most of the time. It's annoying as fuck all.

"I don't think you should give up so easily, Max," Nils says, and I've all but forgotten he's referring to my asking out Alex Buchanan. He taps the ceiling and gives me a thumbs-up. I lower him, and his feet pad onto the mat.

"It's not giving up if I already know it's not worth pursuing," I say.

"I think that's the definition of giving up actually," he says, stepping out of his harness. "By your logic, I shouldn't ask Q to anything. We're already done."

This is the part where a friend should contradict a friend, if only for the sake of encouragement. But I can't lie to Nils. I step out of my belt. "She's probably a high Eight, man," I say gently.

He stares at me, and I feel like a complete dick. But before I can say something nicer, Nils shakes his head and makes a sound like *pshhh*. "Not everything is quantifiable," he mutters. "*Man.*"

I spend too much time unbuckling my harness.

"I'm going to ask Q out. Soon. To prove your theory is preposterous."

"Preposterous?" I say.

"Don't you have to *test* a theory to prove it? You don't want to test anything, Max. You are hiding."

"What?" But I feel my cheeks flush.

"You are. You're staying tucked in safe with your numbers," Nils says, twirling his pointer finger at me. "And I get it, if you're not down for taking risks or whatever at this particular moment in time, that's cool." Nils has definitely picked up some therapy lingo from his mom over the years. "But quit throwing your dark cloud my way."

"Okay, okay." I put my hands up. "I didn't mean anything, Nils. Sorry," I say. "You should ask Q out. Go for it. And I am telling the hundred percent truth when I say I hope she says yes. She would be very smart to say yes."

He nods, packing his gear into his small duffel. "If I don't ask, I'll never know. Right?"

"Sure, sure," I say, stuffing my own duffel, truly wishing I could believe him. Yep, life would be easier if I thought like Nils.

CHARLOTTE

I couldn't leave the studio after I found out about Young Choreographer. Secretly, in my head, I'd started planning a piece, just in case. Hannah stayed behind to help me think my ideas through. It's always different in real life. I'm plugging my phone into the dock of the sound system. "I've always wanted to do this," I say. "Being alone in here feels so . . ."

"Cool?" Hannah says. "Uh, yeah. Because it is! So, it's really a Romeo-and-Juliet-type deal you're picturing? Outside forces keeping the boy and girl apart?" She taps her chin, taking mental measure of the room. "Is this the same size as the stage?"

"I think the mirror is the length of the stage," I say. "We can adjust later. Yes, Romeo and Juliet, but maybe with a happy ending." Having Seb feels like an amazing positive, and I don't want to drag down my mood by having to hyperfocus on creating a melodramatic tragedy for the next six weeks. I just don't feel it. The music begins.

"Everyone loves a happy ending," replies Hannah, who has been together with Hank since First Year. "Ooh, what's this music?"

"Vivaldi's 'Summer III.' It's from *The Four Seasons*," I say.

Madame never strays from classical ballet music—Chopin, Tchaikovsky, Prokofiev, etc. I've heard them so many times their works are hardwired in my brain. I still love them, too. Goody

Two-Shoes in her glory.

"Dramatic," she says. "Gorgeous. Perfect for Gabby and Felipe."

I give a little squee of joy. "I get to make up a mini pas de deux for the two best dancers we have." Gabby's a classic Irish redhead with impossibly elegant technique; Felipe is Brazilian and scary talented. Madame recruited him when she spotted him at the SAB Summer Intensive, which is the New York City Ballet's feeder program. He may not even graduate before he's professional.

"Right? Felipe will be famous someday, and you'll be able to say, 'Oh, I created a role for Felipe de la Cruz when we were students at Lycroft Phelps.'"

I wave her off. "Don't freak me out. Felipe will be a guest on your news show, and he'll say, 'The only role I'm embarrassed about is this piece I did at LPS.'"

"Psshh," Hannah says.

My mom figured out long ago that ballet is my meditation. My escape into a world where control equals mastery—repetition of movements, measured breathing, muscles finding the human shape of a musical score's energy, striving for the perfect placement, timing the perfect hold, the endless combination of positions that together express something bigger than words. Even when all the dancers follow the same steps, everyone's expression is their own. This is pretty much what I wrote in my essay for Madame Chu.

Hannah and I move back and forth across the dance floor, playing and replaying the opening notes of the Vivaldi piece until I've settled how I'll get all six of the corp dancers onstage. "This music has so much *motion*," I say over the violins.

Just then my phone bubbles a text over the loudspeaker. We

chuckle. I jog over to check it.

"It's Genetic Miracle," Hannah says. "Right?"

I texted him immediately after my parents. It felt like such an intimacy, to share it with him. I can't explain it. "Oh," I say, a little deflated. "Grace, from home."

Grace: charlotte! i have to find out you got young choreographer from your mom's insta? congrats! that's so great! asking for plane tickets for my birthday!

"Aww," I say. "Let me just . . ."

I text back:

Me: Sorry! Still can't believe it. Probably nobody else applied. I hope I don't totally screw it up. Yes, pleeeeeeeaaaase come!

Grace: don't be ridiculous. you deserve it. miss angela would be so proud!

<<attachment: preK dance class>>

I suck in a breath when I see the photo she sent: the two of us and our teacher (who we idolized) after our first recital. Pink tutus, hair in "buns"—lots of barrettes holding our barely shoulder-length hair. I get a twinge in my nose.

Me: The best of times! xoxo

The music returns to its booming volume. When the adagio rolls come in, I let loose a string of fouettés for the sheer fun of it. I've done half a dozen spins and finish with the music in an exaggerated fourth-position lunge.

"Oh, he came to congratulate you in person." Hannah grins, tipping her chin toward the observation window. "Of course he did."

It's kind of weird to see Seb in the dance studio. My space. Like he's come into my bedroom at home or something. But I shake that right out of my head and jog to the door.

"That was awesome," he says over the music. "Can you teach me how to do that?"

I laugh. "Sure. How long have you been here?"

"Just a few minutes," he says, staring at the part of my leotard that crosses over my boobs. I smack his arm. He smiles slyly.

I wait for him to congratulate me, and when he doesn't say anything, I ask, "Wait, *why* are you here?"

"Two reasons."

I can't help rocking on my toes.

"First, I thought we were busted for sure by Frye. You must have done great because I haven't heard from him since. Have you?"

He didn't read my text. I'd forgotten all about Frye with the YC excitement. "No," I said, glad I didn't waste any more energy worrying he was mad at me about Max. "Um, what was the second thing?" I smile.

"To invite you to boathouse movie night tonight," he says. The team sometimes screens its own movies. "Can I pick you up at seven-forty-five?"

I am wordless.

"Seb," Hannah calls from across the studio. "Have you checked your texts?" I glare at her over my shoulder. "Because you should *check your texts.*" She nods with each word.

Seb's brow crinkles momentarily, then brightens. "Did you get Young Choreographer?" He pulls out his phone. "If you didn't

95

don't worry because you're still an Upper—" He reads. I can barely stand still. "You got it! I knew you would!" He hugs me and spins me in a circle. "Sorry I didn't see that. God, what a damn idiot."

"Kind of true," says Hannah.

"Hannah!" I say.

"Kidding!" she adds, and it's obvious she is.

"She's right," Seb says, shaking his head. "The team . . ." He lets it trail off, and I'm surprised by a pang of annoyance vibrating in my chest that he doesn't feel the need to explain. And that I am jealous of the guys who get more of Seb than I do. Which is really middle school of me, and I need to get a grip on myself. "Awesome for your résumé," he's saying, which is only part of it, but how is he supposed to know? It's ballet, I tell myself.

"Okay, seven-forty-five?"

"Sure," I say.

"Invite only," he says, backing toward the door outside. "But you can come, Hannah."

"I'm good," she says. "Thanks." I already know she's going to Hank's.

I wave. As soon as he's gone, Hannah and I look at each other.

"He *was* excited for you," she says. "Once he knew."

"Yeah," I say. "He was, wasn't he?" I smile, already replaying his bright expression and hug in my head.

"Man, you are whipped," Hannah laughs. "We better get to dinner."

I nod, and I retrieve my phone from the dock. "Oh, we got an email from Ms. Ballard."

From: Lori Ballard

To: Big Sibs

Subject: Planning Meeting Schedule, etc.

Hello, Bigs!

I hope you're off to a great start with your Littles. The First Year class seems to be settling into campus life well, but you are our "ears on the ground." If any of your Littles seems unhappy, lonely, or isolated, please make an extra point of reaching out to her. Include her in your own leisure time activities and invite her to eat meals with you. As you know, these small gestures can make all the difference with a more introverted girl experiencing homesickness and/or feeling overwhelmed by all the "new" in these early days of September. We'll brainstorm fun icebreakers for our Littles at the first planning meeting, this Sunday at 5:00. Attached, find the schedule for our subsequent meetings this year.

On another note, Dean Frye has requested that all Bigs be on alert for any talk about student pranks. We're monitoring a situation, and if you hear anything that sounds suspicious— like upperclassmen trying to have fun at the expense of others—please bring it to our attention. We appreciate your discretion and leadership in such matters!

See you Sunday!

Ms. Ballard

Lori Ballard | Assistant Dean
Girls' Bigs and Littles Program Coordinator | Assistant Coach, Girls' Lacrosse

Hannah laughs. "She's talking about your stalker! Can you believe it?"

I grimace, and on our way to Spangler, we trade theories on who it could be.

4

Friday Night

Q

Finally, it's dark.

I stand in front of the mirror—black everything from the neck down. I've got black gloves and a ski mask for when shit gets serious. Alex, still miffed about the running, went to Pizza Barn in town with some girls from our hall. I'm about to pop in the AirPods and head outside, when a knock sounds at the door. I pull Alex's green cross-country letter jacket from a hook on her closet and throw it on over all my black clothes before opening the door.

"Hi, Emily," I say cheerfully. Fuck, it's our dorm RA.

"Hey, Q. Do you have a second?"

"Um," I say. "I was on my way out. . . ." I tug at the hem of the jacket for emphasis. She's peering around me, into the room. *Dammit.* "Come on in," I say, standing aside for her to enter.

"What's up?" I say, going for proactive helpfulness.

"I noticed all the girls went to get pizza and you didn't." She's studying the pictures Alex has up on the bulletin board, peering at the bare space over my desk.

"I haven't really finished unpacking yet," I say defensively, forcing a laugh. "You know Alex, right on top of everything. Thought I'd catch up on that tonight."

She squints. Shit. I've already contradicted myself.

"I thought you were going out."

I shrug. "After that."

Emily sits on the edge of the bed. She's got an angular face with a slim, sharp nose. "Look," she says. "I'm just going to come right out with it." Her quick bird eyes land on my leggings. I feel my pulse in my neck. "Rosario noticed you're not eating much at dining hall meals. She didn't see you at lunch or dinner."

"What?" A low alarm rings in my head. My hand heads for my eye, but I will it still.

"You've lost weight, Quinn. Are you . . . struggling?"

Her voice is gentle. Too gentle. Oh God. Tears gather in my eyes. How could she know? Nobody at school knows! I'm already planning a call to flip out on Heather when Emily says, "We have lots of resources for disordered eating at Knowlton Health Center."

I look at her. Relief spills through me.

"I had anorexia in middle school. I get it. It's"—she looks at the ceiling knowingly—"*very* common here."

"I'm not—" I clear my throat. "No."

Emily looks at me intensely. "Are you sure?"

"One hundred percent." And I mean it. I don't have time to be anorexic. "Readjusting to school food, I guess." I smile weakly.

She sighs, studying my face. I force myself to keep her gaze but can't stop blinking. A liar's giveaway.

"Okay," she sighs. "Well, if you do have trouble or you just want to talk, I'm here."

I nod.

"If *anything* is feeling out of control or stressful"—she puts her hand on my shoulder and it takes all I can do not to bolt—"I'm ready for it."

Emily, you are not ready for it.

I nod again. "I know. Thanks." I stop there, afraid I'll lie myself into a corner.

"Okay, then." She stands. "That's all."

"Thanks, Emily," I say.

Fooling her makes me feel victorious, which is gross. But I survived. I pop in my AirPods and head downstairs, throwing Alex's letter jacket into a common closet by the exit. I have to remember to get it on my way back in.

After it's done.

I scroll to the fourth song from Songs in the Key of Q, "Masoko Tanga" by the Police, an eighties phenomenon. Dad did some of the sound mixing. "Masoko Tanga" is a six-minute, manically tight jam, and it makes me feel like a professional kickboxer. Maybe this is why when I spot Khalid, Pearce's lapdog, by the Founders Statues, I follow him instead of going straight to Anderson. It's close to eight, but on Fridays, Doughty doesn't leave until nine. You know, party night.

I keep a healthy distance, clinging to the shadowy edges of the path. It doesn't take me long to realize he's going to the boathouse. I heard the girls on the hall mention a movie night. They're always closed parties and piss off everyone who's not invited.

We slope downhill until Lake Edith explodes into view. It reflects the backlit clouds and the lights from the Robert H. Briggs ('68) Boathouse, set into the bluff, a self-satisfied emperor admiring its kingdom. Inside, lamplight glows from what I know to be the team lounge—a gleaming hardwood testimony to the history of Lycroft Phelps rowing domination. My gut says the jackal is in there.

Khalid goes through the front doors. Even from this distance, I see the swagger of Pearce. My body stiffens.

You don't have to go back to Lycroft, Heather reminds me, like she's next to me now on the paved pathway, in the dark. *I wouldn't if I were you.*

Heather and Dad came to visit during Fall Fling last year. Dad couldn't wait to see the new boathouse. "This is nicer than Harvard's," he'd said as we stood in the lounge, his voice a mix of awe and pride. Heather simply smirked, running her finger along the rim of a silver cup the size of a water fountain. "Well, if they didn't feel entitled before they got here . . ." She let us fill in the blanks. It was a graceless comment.

I could tell Dad agreed, because he leaned in to point at a black-and-white team photo, instead of responding to her. "Hey! Here's Uncle Stu," and stepped to the next one. Heather is very us and them. She doesn't get that we're the *us*. The Walshes. We can't change what we come from any more than anyone else. We *can* be graceful about it. And generous. My mom was. But Heather feels on the outside looking in even though she isn't, and constantly points out privilege. She doesn't mention she grew up in Marin County, California, in a house carved into the hills. I think this characteristic makes her an impermanent member of my family. I hang a lot of hope on that. *And*, I think, as if continuing our conversation from a few weeks ago, *I'm not giving up my place here.* I'm not transferring to another school with some fake story explaining why I didn't finish at Lycroft Phelps for kids I don't even know. I'm not running away.

It sounds so good in my head.

I squeeze my eyes shut.

The oldest story in a long, sad book, I hear Uncle Lawrence say to Dad on the patio, the conversation that plays in my head like the needle is stuck in the vinyl album's groove. *It's the classic he said, she said. I don't know why women don't just go fucking rogue.*

I picture myself surprising Colin. He's kneeling on the dock, adjusting the rigging of a rowing shell in the water. I'm silent as a snow leopard. I raise the gun with two hands, locking my elbows for a straight shot. He turns. Eyes wide.

Bang!

Release.

I blink, realizing I'm still standing here on the edge of the pathway. I should get to know Briggs Boathouse inside and out. He's here a lot. It's a two-story place, lounge upstairs, boats downstairs with bays that open onto the dock. I sidle down the wooden steps toward the water, stopping under a pine tree by a window. They're arranging chairs and sofas for theater seating. Pearce powers a screen down from the ceiling with a remote, which conveniently blocks the window overlooking the lake and the dock.

Khalid hands a tall beer can to Pearce, and they sit down on the biggest of all the sofas. Pearce props his long legs on the chair in front of him and pops his beer, like he deserves this luxury while I'm in pieces within my own skin. He's the poster child for entitled fuckhead. I guess Heather can be right sometimes.

I lean against an unstable cradle of branches and turn my face toward the sky, sucking in the damp, balsam air. Heather, of all the goddamned people, heard my story first. Less than a week after Boppy dropped me at home, Heather found me bawling on the bathroom floor in the middle of the night. She pet my hair, sitting on the side of the tub with me slumped into her silk kimono. "What if I'm pregnant?" I sobbed.

"Shh. We're here for you, Quinnie. Shh."

I made all the classic mistakes that a #MeToo-aware girl should have known not to make. I didn't tell anyone. Not even Alex. So, nobody to corroborate my story; no DNA test or physical exam. Just me, faking it through the ride home with Boppy. I can't recount a single conversation I had between that Friday night, May 31, and the night Heather found me. But I know what I asked *myself*. Why didn't I object when he took me to the Amphitheater Lawn? Hannah's boyfriend, Hank, *warned* all the Littles about the fucking Amphitheater Lawn. Because I was drunk, another idiotic mistake. How could I be so stupid?

So.

Fucking.

Stupid.

And why did I freeze? Why didn't I bite and scratch and knee him in the balls? I am *weak*. Weak. I always thought I was a fighter, but it turns out I froze like a possum.

I repeated these same truths in my head for days. I couldn't sleep. Faked eating. Threw up a couple times. At some point, the eyelash thing started, a compulsion I don't realize I'm doing until it's too late.

Heather woke my father. He cried with me that night. I'd forgotten I knew what that sounds like. He held me curled in his lap in the big leather chair next to the fireplace. Our shared weeping brushed years away, blowing the dust off the long-buried pain of losing Mom. We had a deep bond built on love and loss, and now here it was, out in the open. Heather paced around the living room helplessly outside our bubble, and I felt a little sad for her, too. Left out. But also spared.

"I'm sorry," I choked. My cheek pressed against his flannel pajamas, the L.L.Bean ones I gave him for Christmas, now warm and damp with tears.

He didn't answer but shook his head gently.

"I shouldn't have been so—" I said. "Trusting."

He shook his head more. His chest rose in a big inhalation. "Don't feel sorry for this. Ever." At the corners of his sadness, I heard a knife's edge sharpening. "The little piece of shit is the one who should be sorry." I didn't argue, but how *couldn't* I feel responsible? If I hadn't been such a fool, everyone would be fine. Myself included.

"We'll get you in to see the doctor tomorrow," Heather said. "And find you a good therapist."

I was too ashamed to say no in that moment. I could be pregnant, a fact that left me whimpering.

A commotion brings me back to the present. Pearce is acting out some story. Khalid throws back his head in laughter. The need to know what they're talking about creeps from the ground, through my sneakers. I hear kids approaching from up the hill. The smart thing to do would be to run into the woods. But I don't. I can't. My hunch that I can get in downstairs is too strong. I have nothing to lose. He already killed the best parts of me.

Keeping close to the side of the building, I descend the stairs. A loon's call echoes over the lake, haunted and bold. Moonglow lights the wooden deck. Obviously I can't open the bays—too loud. But there is a regular door, too. Despite the probably million dollars' worth of rowing equipment in there, I know it will be unlocked. It's a challenge to interlopers. Like, a group of long-gone LPS rowers hover on a cloud just above the door, arms folded across their barrel chests. *Yeah? Go ahead and try it.*

Don't mind if I do. I turn the knob gently and step into the cavernous space. It's dark, but light pours down the stairwell, reflecting off the sleek yellow rowing shells stacked on racks. The king's arsenal.

I hear Khalid. "You have no idea how much I want to fuck that Bodenrader chick." I slink under the stairs, tilting my ear toward them. "Did you see her BabyBook pic? She's looking for it." Laughter.

I pinch my arm. He's talking about the new student directory, a catalog of the incoming students published each year, supposedly to help everyone get on a first-name basis.

"Dibs," Pearce says.

My ears hear: *Fine, be that way.*

I tug my eyelid by the lashes, let the pain cover my rage.

"Lord of the Book always gets dibs," he adds.

Lord of the BabyBook? Did he comb the pages and pick me last year? I feel dizzy and rock to keep steady, lacing my fingers through some kind of net hanging beside me. It reeks of algae, but this strange version of me breathes through it to keep listening. *Let his words feed the Anger,* I think.

"What do you think of Charlotte Foresley?" the jackal says.

Jesus.

Khalid doesn't speak, but he must have made a face, like, *Dude, be real.*

"What?" Colin says. "She's only with McNeilly because I bet him to see who would cuff her first. He hadn't even noticed her. She likes me."

Seb asked Charlotte out on a bet? To prove who's the pack leader? But they're still together, so that doesn't make sense. Pearce, full of shit as usual.

"Not good for the boat, bruh," Khalid says.

"I'm just asking what you think of her," Colin says, faking innocence. "There's some interest there, is all I'm saying. I can smell it on her."

"In your dreams," Khalid says.

"They're good fucking dreams," Colin says, and then the door opens to a loud group of kids.

The Anger starts to spin, picking up speed like a wind turbine. I need to get it out. My eyes flash around the space, searching. Next to the coach's whiteboard, a Magnum Sharpie dangles on a string. The loon chuckles on the lake. I make my move, knocking the mass of netting to the floor. I can't bother with it. I pop the marker off the string, select my canvas, and let my feelings spew.

CHARLOTTE

"They built a fire," Seb says as we arrive at the Briggs Boathouse door.

"I love that smell," I say, breathing in the woodsmoke-laced air.

He opens the door and immediately a dozen guys shout, "Seb!" I follow him, duckling-like. Colin grins at me from a wingback chair, the only one who notices me. Khalid and Tyler sit backward or sideways on chairs; Geoff, Teo, and Devon share a sofa.

I haven't been in here since the campus tour with my parents. I think my architect dad's comment was: "They sure didn't cut any corners in constructing this." It's all wood beams and windows, like an old-school hunting lodge, except pristine. A fire blazes in the huge stone fireplace, where another cluster of rowers stands. Everyone's drinking beer. Right in a campus building. True, the boathouse is pretty far from the main campus, but still. *No word for fear in Sebanese*, I remind myself.

Dougie Nelson, the Lower Mid cox discussed on the terrace this morning, holds a White Claw can out to me. "We have these for the ladies," he says, and I almost laugh.

"Thanks," I say. I don't know if I'll drink it, but at least it gives me something to do with my hands. I take my time looking at all the old photos, avoiding their conversation. I'll just feel left out. I hope Grace does come with my parents and I can bring her here.

It's about as prep school as it gets, right down to the antique pennants. After I've circled the entire room, I go stand next to Seb.

"Basically, we have the weekend to train a novice," Tyler says. "Then the Beast can approve our pick at Monday's practice." They're talking about their coxswain problem again. It's annoying, but I remind myself we *are* in the boathouse.

"Right," Colin says. "Covering years' worth of training in two days." He shakes his head and takes a swig of beer.

"If we get someone tonight . . ." says Seb.

"That would be ideal," Tyler says. "Start in the morning."

I'm irrelevant here. It's awkward. I decide to take the moment to text Quinn Walsh to see if she wants to meet for lunch tomorrow. I'm dying to hear about her and Nils, and to find out what happened with her and Colin at the Sendoff dance at the end of the year. I feel like I deserted her, and I wonder if she noticed. Because she never replied to my summer texts. And she doesn't right now, either. I stick my phone in my pocket.

"What about a cox from the girls' team?" Teo says. "What's her name? Laurel someone?"

For reasons unclear, the girls' crew team is only a single-season spring sport, and their boathouse is off campus. Hannah says the reason is perfectly clear: LPS Crew is a male dynasty. A boys' club. "The Rowing Gods of Lycroft share status with no one," she's said more than once. "Girls' crew is an add-on."

Which is what I feel like in this room—an add-on to Seb—but I don't want Hannah to be right on this, so I decide to activate. "Laurel Hartigan plays varsity field hockey in the fall season," I say. Their faces swivel to mine, skeptical. "We're neighbors, in Fisher." I shrug.

"Damn," Tyler says. Man, he is beautiful.

"Maybe we find a First Year who isn't real committed to a team yet. Like a soccer benchwarmer," Khalid says.

The doors open, and a bunch of First Year rowers enter with some First Year girls I recognize to be Hannah's Littles. The guys start another round of chanting names, lighting up the younger rowers. It's kind of cute, really. "Do you do that for every rower, every time?" I ask once they've quieted.

"Fuck yeah," says Khalid. "You don't in ballet?"

"No," I say. "But I may suggest it." They laugh, and it feels like a small win.

Colin eyes the First Year with corkscrew-curly brown hair and sparkly eyes. When she catches him, she doesn't flinch but smiles. Perfect dimples.

"Damn," Teo says quietly.

"No shit," Devon says.

"That one right there, boys," Colin says. "She's our cox."

"I don't know," Teo says. "She might be too distracting."

"Hey, Seb," the girl calls.

Gutsy, I think. Seb lifts his beer can. "Hey, Sofia." Low-key. Familiar.

"Fucking McNeilly," Khalid mutters. "You steal every piece of ass on campus."

"More like they throw themselves at him," Teo says. "Asses literally fly at McNeilly." Everyone busts out laughing and someone tosses an empty can at Seb's chest.

My face flames, and I pop the White Claw, hide behind it, and drink.

"Dude," Tyler says to Khalid, gesturing toward me. "Seriously?"

He's ignored, but I remind myself I did not throw myself at Seb. He shocked me when he asked me to Summer Sendoff, as a matter of fact.

"Fuck you all," Seb says. He glances at me while he adds, "Sofia's family and mine are old friends from the Cape."

I smile, tight-lipped, pissed at the rest of them for making me feel . . . disposable. Because Seb can have anyone he wants. I imagine him in the stroke seat, gazing at this stunningly gorgeous "family friend" in the cox seat, day after day after day. This must not happen. I turn slightly away from them and text Hannah.

Me: Who's your Little named Sofia?

Hannah: Sofia Bodenrader? She's in your dance group! Remember?

Me: 👍

She can't cox then. She'll be with me, and she's obviously a good dancer or Madame wouldn't have put her in this special group. There's no sense sharing this info. Khalid would probably want to arm-wrestle for her or something.

Suddenly the thought comes: I can offer them an alternative. Solve their problem and win them over. A little, anyway. I rack my brain. Short and smart, short and smart and male. It's kind of a rare type here, to be honest. Then it comes to me. So obvious!

"Hey," I blurt. They aren't listening, so I say louder: "I know who you can get."

They turn toward me all at once, and it's a little like I choreographed it. I smile. "Max." Blank faces "You know, Max Hannigan-Loeffler," I say.

"Who?" says Tyler, his forehead pinched.

Teo chuckles.

"Yeah, yeah," says Seb. "That robotics star."

"The little dude in our physics class?" Colin asks.

I feel like saying, *You know who he is, jerk—your frigging project partner who's getting you an easy A*. I do not. "You said they have to be smart and small. He's a genius."

Seb smiles, jostling my shoulder. "She's right."

I wait.

Tyler nods his head sideways, making a not-a-bad-idea face. Khalid looks longingly at Sofia.

"Max isn't on a team," I say. "Just sayin'. And Sofia's part of the dance school."

"Oh, yeah," Seb says thoughtfully. "Max could work. He might be our only choice."

"I bet he'd love to join," I say. I mean, it could be true.

The others appear unconvinced. I can't take it. I just want the movie to start so I can return to the Seb-Charlotte bubble of bliss. But I might need to grow beyond the bubble for Seb and me to survive as a couple.

"Where's the bathroom?" I ask.

"Down those stairs, U-turn to the back left corner," Tyler says, tipping his head toward the stairwell.

"Thanks," I say, retreating for the stairs. "Max is a great choice!" I just need them to approve my pick. It is a brilliant one. Then maybe they'll approve of me.

Q

My hand freezes mid–pen stroke as a girl's voice drifts downstairs. "Max is a great choice!"

Charlotte.

Her shoes begin tapping down the steps.

Shit. I can't let her see me. Her of all people. She could put the pieces together. I drop the pen, skin vibrating. This idea was colossally stupid!

I catch sight of her silver flats and bound under the stairwell, trying to gather the smelly net from the floor. It's like trying to pick up an octopus. I flop onto it instead and pray I blend into the shadows. Charlotte's footsteps pause right overhead. My vision blurs with panic.

Wait.

I could tell her. Now. Let the revenge plot go, a small voice says. It turns my muscles to jelly.

But like a shake of the snow globe, I see myself pinned to the ground, crying. I said *NO!* And Pearce didn't stop.

I flatten myself on the floor. Haul the net over me, hold my breath, and wait.

CHARLOTTE

I've descended half the basement steps when I get the strange feeling there's someone down there. The room is lit only by moonlight from the bay windows. *Freaking stalker paradise*, I think. I spin to retreat, when I imagine the teasing that will come my way upstairs.

I stand still, listening, trying to siphon off the party noise so I can hear into the shadows. After a few moments of silence, I summon my ballet superpower and keep going.

When I flip the lights on, the entire character of the place changes. It's pristine, smells of both polish and something earthy I can't name. Two aisles of racks cradle racing shells, sleek and long and lemon-colored. Seb told me Lycroft only purchases Empachers, some elite German brand recognized by its signature yellow shells. It's almost reverent in the way they're tucked away for beauty rest. They remind me of the pointe shoe store back in Chicago, where satiny pink hand-sewn shoes are stored in a giant wall of cubbies. The shells and shoes—action in repose, waiting for their athletes to set them free. Against the back wall is a big stand for all the oars, and next to it I spy an office and the bathroom. I peek over both shoulders and walk tall, happy to lock the bathroom door behind me.

When I come out, something creaks. A door's standing open to the outside—not the boat doors. A person door. Was it open when

I came down? It seems like a strange thing not to notice. The wind? But it's dead calm outside.

God, I did hear someone! I rush upstairs—not running. Bad guys smell fear, a thought that makes my scalp shiver. I cross the lounge to Seb and set my hand on his shoulder. He rests his hand on top of it.

"We can go tonight," Khalid says. "Doesn't he live in Stevens?"

Colin nods.

I shake Seb's shoulder. His forehead crinkles when he sees my expression. "What's wrong?"

Colin and Khalid wait for me to say something. I shift. Am I being dramatic? I have to go for it. "I think someone was already downstairs. I think they snuck out the door by the boats," I add, grasping for credibility. "Unless it's always open?"

Khalid glances at Colin, who looks at Seb. They're having a three-way silent conversation. "I heard that stalker in the woods was following you, Colin," I continue, careful not to reveal Max as my source.

"What the fuck?" I'm not sure why Colin is smiling when he says this. Does he think being a target makes him more important? He pops to his feet and strides toward the stairs with Seb right behind him. The rest of us trail along, now all of us ducklings.

"We're going down there?" I say to Tyler, the closest to me.

"We are," he says.

"It's fucking Matheson," Colin says quietly (for him). "Those assholes."

Matheson School, I think. The crew rivalry is historic and fierce. I like that answer way better than a psychopath. Part of me wants to tell Max Hannigan-Loeffler so he can rest easier, too.

The whole pack of us is standing in the bright light among the boats. "Anyone here?" Khalid calls, fearless.

"Look," someone says, pointing under the stairs to a heap of black netting that resembles a giant messy bird's nest. It's also big enough for someone to be hiding under right now.

Colin laughs. "Okay, which one of you assholes is having sex in our boathouse?"

The place erupts in laughter. *God.* Who would think that?

"You know better than to defile our sacred space!" he says. Then he spins on Seb and me. "McNeilly?" he barks. "Are we going to find a used Trojan under there with your DNA all over it?"

I'm horrified. Seb doesn't look at me. "No, dumbass."

Colin and Seb are in an eye lock and I think they might be about to get in a fight, and I'm wondering how we got to this point. Then I realize they're planning. Simultaneously, they slink toward the black mass and stoop to grip the netting.

"If it's not McNeilly, then it must be you, Tyler," Colin says, nice and loud.

"Nuh-uh," Tyler says. Colin nods, and like FBI backup, Tyler and Khalid get into position behind them. I might scream. The other four guys from Seb's boat have joined us. If it is a Matheson prankster under there, I'm starting to fear for what will happen to him. I glance behind me toward that open door. What if there are more outside?

"Now!" Colin yells. He and Seb yank the fabric to the side, exposing nothing but a smooth cement floor. The room is hushed for a beat, until Tyler says, "Oh, shit."

We turn and follow his pointing finger. Across the yellow hull of a shell, it says in fat, scrawly letters:

U R GOING DOWN, ASSHOLE s

The *E* has a weirdly long tail, and the final *s* is separated from the rest. Like maybe the artist got interrupted. By me. I hug my arms across my chest.

"Blue. Matheson's school color," says Tyler. He wipes a finger across the *s*. It streaks. He sniffs. "Permanent marker."

I notice an uncapped super-wide Sharpie on the floor and stoop to retrieve it. "This?"

Colin takes it.

Seb and a bunch of the guys rush outside, shouting. Colin says to me, "Nice job, Goldilocks. You were spot-on."

I shrug. "I think I would be Baby Bear in this scenario. But doesn't that freak you out?" I say, eyeing the graffiti.

"Nah, it's rivalry bullshit." He leans against the stair railing.

"Even though someone might be stalking you?"

He shakes his head nonchalantly. "I went to rowing camp at Princeton this summer." He shifts his weight, and he's suddenly monstrously tall. "There were some Matheson kids there. I was stroke, and my boat always beat them. They hated me."

Khalid's voice rings into the night: *"Matheson blows Lycroft dick!"* Colin looks toward the door and snorts, which gives me a second to wonder if he's jealous of Seb's rowing stroke. He continues. "I told them, 'Don't hate me because I'm beautiful. Hate me because we're going to kick your ass this year.'" He chuckles to himself, then holds my eyes. "Baby Bear, huh? I like that name for you."

I smile back, kind of because it would be awkward not to. Man, he makes me uncomfortable. I overcompensate and say, "How was

Summer Sendoff with my girl Q?"

He looks startled and then says, "Meh."

I squint, like that will help me get his meaning, but Seb and the other guys pile back in and inspect the damage on the boat.

"Will that shit come off?" Khalid asks.

"Steel wool," Seb suggests. "Pearce, nice manners with that DNA comment. You kiss your mother with that mouth?" He puts his hand on my lower back.

"No, I kiss yours with it, though."

Teo and Geoff emerge from the bathroom with cleaning supplies and start working on the graffiti.

"I say we go watch the movie," Colin says. "We're not letting a little vandalism wreck our night."

And before I know it, we're all back upstairs watching *Avengers: Endgame*.

Seb and I get the love seat, and I don't pay one bit of attention to the movie plot. I'm stealing looks at the definition of his forearm muscles. I'm remembering the 1856 Library last night.

The picture on-screen erupts in flames. I don't care about the Avengers' dark, metallic world, but Seb flinches in response to the explosion. The rowers hoot. He looks at me, beaming. "Whoa."

"I wasn't expecting *that*," I say, completely faking it.

He studies my face, and I think he's going to bust me for completely missing the high point of the movie, but he gives me a peck on the cheek and smiles. McNeilly Gold. When the world resumes spinning, I catch eyes with Sofia Bodenrader. After a split second, she smiles at me, too, the dimples erupting unchecked. Damn, she's confident—and I don't think she's faking anything.

I squeeze Seb's hand as we rise to leave. He may think of her as a family friend, but I'm not so sure about Sofia.

I'm still holding his hand when we come to the Founders Statues, where the paths to our dorms split. "'Two roads diverged in a wood,'" Seb says, quoting the Robert Frost poem. We stop and kiss for a while, and I'm liquid as usual, until he pulls away. He sticks his hands in his pockets while two groups of kids pass. I'm not into PDA, either. I want to suggest we go to his room, now a single instead of a double thanks to cheating Chauncey. But it's aggressive. Too predictable.

He sits on the circular wall around the Founders and pats the cement next to him. Obviously, I'm all in, but I wait a beat before joining him. I also wait for him to put his arm around me before I lean into his chest. His smell is divine.

"What—" He's interrupted by the chapel chime, signaling ten-thirty. He grins, and my heart reels. "What do you have going on tomorrow?" It's disappointing he's not going to invite me back, but the way he picks up my hand and admires my fingers is not too shabby. I seriously don't know how I got here. I stretch my legs straight in front of me, pointing my toes, masquerading my feelings as fatigue.

"Dance. Study. You?"

"Crew. Study." He tucks something into my palm and squeezes it. "Meet me at our special place?"

I open my fingers to find the old-fashioned key from the 1856 Library. Tongue-tied, I nod. We kiss again but he stands, so I do, too. "We're probably getting on the water early, so . . ." Stupidly, I nod again. If I open my mouth, I'll protest, which I don't want to do. I grasp for something to separate myself from all the girls, to make me stand out, when out of nowhere a guy headbutts Seb in the side. I scream and jump, but Seb's laughing, wrestling off Colin.

"McNeilly, you asshole!" Colin growls. Then Khalid joins in, and they're like wolf pups vying for dominance.

I stand there, unsure what a cool reaction would be, when Seb glances at me over his shoulder, hair ruffled, cheeks flushed. He's got Colin in a headlock. "We meet at three o'clock? Before Vespers?"

I nod again, and they carry on down the path toward the boys' dorms. Opening my hand, I look at the key. I look at them. And I turn for Fisher Hall.

Q

Shouts and hoots from the boathouse dock echo off Lake Ethel, finding me in the woods, letting me know the jackal saw my message. I smile. My narrow escape is exhilarating in a primal way, a hunter's thrill. I see the fallen skeleton pine and then the lights of Anderson Safety through the trees. Rounding the building, I duck behind the fat tree from last night. I pull out my phone and check the time. Nine-twenty-eight. Perfect.

I switch the camera to video mode, focus on the door for practice. I zoom in and can even see the digits on the keypad. A clicking sound and the door opens, spitting out Officer Doughty.

He pauses, glancing up at the feathery drizzle before pulling the door closed. Engulfed in a yellow cocoon of light, Doughty reaches for the keypad. I tap record. The phone image is fuzzy, the camera straining just like me to see him in the low light.

He's fucking quick, I'll say that. He tests the knob. Turns for his truck. I shut off the camera and cower in the shadows, waiting for the headlight beams to swivel onto Pine Street and lead his ass to Whitney.

I listen so hard for anyone coming that the silence starts to ring in my ears. All is still, except for the ghostlike tickle of the rain. I dart to the steps. Stand just outside the yellow cocoon and roll the video on my phone. Doughty's shoulder blocks his hand.

"Dammit!" I growl.

I roll the video again, willing Doughty's shoulder to move out of the way, allowing me that critical glimpse.

Nope.

I'm so tired. I feel myself starting to cry. I squeeze my eyes tight and replay the jingle of the code in my head. *Blip blip . . .*

I press a button to try to match the note. Seven. It's wrong. Five. No.

Now I've lost the notes. I wind up and chuck the phone. It hurtles toward a tree, bouncing off it, landing somewhere in the dark. *Fuck.*

Impulsive me. My phone can't show up on the Anderson Safety lawn in the morning.

Weeping silently, I drag my feet through the gravel drive, hoping to kick it. Nothing. I drop to all fours on the lawn, crisscrossing everywhere it could have landed. I'm sobbing pretty hard now, sweeping my hands over the blades of grass, and suddenly a memory from May pushes into my consciousness:

I was on my hands and knees on the Amphitheater Lawn, searching the dark grass for my underwear. Alex and I bought it especially for tonight from Rigby & Peller, an expensive lingerie boutique in Boston. They're pink and lacy and totally impractical. "Just to make you feel sexy," Alex had said. I never thought Colin would actually see them. I gave up finding them and couldn't even remember when he took them off me. I just wanted to be in my room. I remember wobbling to my feet. The air rushed against my naked tender skin. My hands shook wildly; I could barely get my sandals on. I held the wristlet instead of sliding it back onto my wrists, tender from Pearce's grip. My phone, of course, was in the wristlet. It crossed my mind to call Alex, but I remembered she was at her cousin's rehearsal dinner. Charlotte? Macy? Campus Safety? In the end, I didn't call anyone. What would I say? I'd been a fool.

Somehow, I got myself back to the dorm. To my relief, it was empty, as the dance was still in full swing in the art gallery. I locked our door, took off the dress, pulled my phone out of the wristlet. Wrapping my fluffy robe around me, I wadded the dress, purse, and shoes into a ball and crammed them into the hall bathroom trash can, covering them with wet paper towels for good measure. I took a piping-hot shower. At a certain point, I cried so hard no sound came out. I couldn't pull in breath. I slid to the floor, the hot water stinging all the raw places.

I remember telling myself to buck up. I lathered myself in a whole bottle of body wash, but I'd never be clean again. This stain wouldn't ever go away. I wrapped my hair turban style, then pulled on my robe. I brushed my teeth, gently, crying as I remembered his lips crushing mine. Wiped the mascara streaks off my cheeks. I took three Advil from a bottle in my cosmetics bag, washing them down with water I caught in my palms. Back in the room, I locked my jaws together as fresh underwear touched my skin.

One fuckup after another, I think now, blinking. I almost forget how I got here, sitting on the Anderson lawn in a misty rain. I sense the black fog, snaking its way out of the forest, clinging to the ground, coming to swallow me whole. I don't care if I disappear, I realize.

The sound of movement catches in my ears. It's something brushing leaves in the woods. It stops. I don't move.

I feel eyes watching me.

I barely breathe, searching the dark boundary of trees surrounding the lawn.

Everything is dead silent, like all the night creatures know something. After several moments, I start to think I imagined the sound. My heart ticks rapid-fire.

I'm alive again.

A small dome of light illuminates the grass a few feet away from me. My phone. I forget myself and grab for it, and the woods behind me burst into motion, the sound of a large creature crashing into the forest. Whatever watched me stayed long enough to remind me why I'm here.

The phone was alerting me to a missed text from Charlotte. I think of the boathouse.

I'm a warrior.

I retrieve the AirPods, blast "Masoko Tanga." I'm up, between the trees. I'm gone.

MAX

I'm in one of those dreams where you know you're dreaming. Something about finding trace alien dust in soil samples near Area 51 in Nevada. Our yellow tabby cat from home, Napoleon, is rubbing along my leg. His purr sounds like human whispering.

"Max!" Napoleon says. "Wake up!"

"What the hell?"

A bright light shines across my eyelids. Aliens? Everything turns white.

I shield my face with my arm. "Jesus, Nils!"

Hands grab my legs, and a pillow lands on my face. I'm pinned to the mattress.

I'm in full panic, finding strength in my abdomen to sit up. I gasp for breath. I'm forced back into the mattress.

"Let go!" I wail, but it's muffled into obscurity.

A voice whispers: "I'll take it away if you promise not to yell, Max."

The stalker knows my name?

"Got it?" the voice says. "Max?"

I nod. The pillow is removed.

I pop to a sit blocking my eyes with an elbow. "Cut the shit with the flashlight!"

"Okay, but shut up." A tiny click. Blackness. "Don't wake Nils."

"Who is that?" I ask, blinking. Our door is ajar, allowing a sliver of dull light from the hall. Two people form out of the shadows. I glance across the room; Nils is a mound in his bedding. The light reflects white lettering on the chest of one guy's sweatshirt. LPS CREW.

"Pearce?" I whisper.

"Yeah, and Khalid and Seb," he says as Khalid comes into focus at my ankles.

Seb, silhouetted by moonlight from the window behind him, says, "We have an idea for you." Like we're in the middle of the library at noon.

"What are you *talking* about? What time is it?" But I look at the clock and see for myself it's 1:19. My Area 51 dream was way better than this. I'm thinking they may be using me for some prank. I suddenly remember the story of a kid who got locked in Calloway Hall—the Senior girls' dorm—naked in the eighties. "Nils?" I say.

Khalid squeezes my calf in a death clamp. "Don't."

"You guys are the stalkers," I say.

Pearce snorts. "No, that's the dicks from Matheson. Put on some pants," he says, thumping my shoulder. "We're going outside."

I stare. "What if we get caught?"

"Trust me," he adds, and his teeth flash in a smile.

"Right," I say.

"Bruh," he says. "We both know you're getting me an A-fucking-plus on that physics project. Why would I do anything to jeopardize that?"

Bruh? But he has a point. And while it's infuriating that he just

126

openly confirmed what I've suspected all along and is effectively using it to manipulate me *again*, I am no longer afraid for my life. Still, there is my face to worry about.

"Fine." I stand.

Khalid tamps the air with his hands in a "keep it down" gesture, but they don't know Nils sleeps like a mammal in an energy-saving torpor (different from hibernation, FYI, which is in reaction to cold temperatures). While I'm stumbling into some sweats, Khalid says softly, "Dude, is that an R2-D2 alarm clock?" He laughs. "I love that!"

I shoot him a death stare.

"For real," he says.

I roll my eyes but fall in line as they file out of the room. The hallway safety lights emit a low buzz I associate with terrible events: First Year insomnia, running to the bathroom to yack (flu), and, of course, the infamous gas-smell incident. Our dorm proctor (we call him Mr. Aurbach even though he only graduated from Bates in May) lives around the corner. I doubt he'll hear us. The penalty for breaking curfew (eleven-thirty for Upper Mids on weekends) is a shakedown from Dean Frye. I'm a first-time offender and a merit-scholarship kid, so he'd probably go easy on me. Honestly, Frye is the least of my worries.

We head through a fire exit nobody uses. I start to object, thinking it will trigger an alarm, but nothing happens. Yep, safety never takes a vacation at Lycroft Phelps School.

The night air is sharp, the grass wet. The school goes on "half-light" at midnight, something I lobbied for through the LPS Green Future Club. I'd give my left nut for *full* light now but remind myself this is an unusual scenario. I try to keep pace with the long-legged strides of these goons. Does the fact that they each own at least two Brooks Brothers blazers *and* collectively have vacationed on every Caribbean island make them better or worse than those public-school meatheads in locker rooms that snap the skinny kid (me) with wet towels? More important, will it save me tonight if the Matheson stalkers decide to come for Pearce again?

I stop. We've started downhill to the lake. "Where are we going?"

"Won't it be more fun if you're surprised?" Colin says.

"Uh, not really," I mumble but resume walking.

We round a curve, and then I see our destination. Of course. Briggs Boathouse. Castle of LPS Rowing. Colin opens the door and flips on the lights, illuminating a palatial room filled with windows, trophy cases, and old team photos. Wood beams crisscross the high ceiling in an intricate, impressive design, and pristine Lycroft green sofas and chairs are arranged in groupings, like a hotel lobby. There's a stone fireplace with an oversized school pennant—the cool retro kind—hanging above it, and a set of stairs to a lower level.

"Have a seat," Colin says, taking one himself in a wingback. I comply, choosing a love seat. I manspread so I don't feel so small.

"How do you like this place?" Khalid asks, swatting my shoulder in that way jocks do—aggressively friendly. And we aren't friends.

I glance up at him. "Since when do you care what I think?" I say. "What the hell are we doing here? I'm tired, and I have a test tomorrow." I'm trying to keep my dignity, sounding like I'm doing them a favor by sticking around when we all know the truth.

"Max," says Seb. "Tomorrow's Saturday."

I blink. Shit, they're right. "I'm tired," I repeat.

"Well," Colin says. "This is the luckiest day of your life." He claps his palms on his knees.

I make a "seriously?" face.

"I'm serious," Colin says, uncannily reading my mind.

"He is," says Khalid. Shit for brains.

Colin leans toward me with a grin." Remember when I told you the other night that Chauncey is"—he does air quotes—"'on leave' this semester?"

"You mean busted for plagiarism and put on disciplinary suspension?" I say. Nils told me that.

"Yes," Colin says. "We want you to be our new coxswain."

They watch for my reaction.

"Come again?" I say.

Colin looks at Seb, for backup maybe. Khalid paces behind them.

Seb sits in the chair adjacent to my love seat. "You know what that is, right? The leader of the boat."

"The brains of the boat," Khalid chimes in.

"You're like the fucking captain of the boat," Colin says.

"Yeah," says Khalid.

"The rowers?" Colin continues. "We're the beef. The muscles. The brawn—"

"I got it," I say. Perhaps there is no difference between these guys and towel snappers.

"We're giving it everything our bodies are capable of when we row," Colin goes on. Clearly, in his mind, he's equated this with

129

pursuing world peace. "We can't think. We can't steer the boat. We just pull like hell."

"The cox—" Seb says, then starts again with "*You* have the race plan. *You* know all our strengths and weaknesses and hopefully the opposition's, too. You steer the boat."

"You tell us when to go balls out and when to hold back," Khalid says. "Essentially, you're a stand-in for the Beast, who—"

"That's Coach Follett," Seb says.

"Yeah," Khalid says. "He can't coach us during a race."

They keep talking in this ping-pong manner, but I'm still processing the first few lines. These guys, the veritable *Tens* of Lycroft Phelps (Seb might be the singular Eleven in existence) want Max Hannigan-Loeffler to join the celebrated, historic Lycroft Phelps Boys' Crew?

"Why me?"

"I asked the same question," Khalid said.

Colin shoots him a look and says, "And we told him, it's simple." He goes to the fireplace and turns thoughtfully to face us. "A: You're brilliant." I laugh, but he forges on: "Coxes are smart and manage a lot of stats at once."

"Weather, water current, distance . . ." Seb is on his feet again, traversing the rug, which I notice has a giant LPS crest with crossed oars in the center, same as Colin's sweatshirt.

"So Chauncey is the exception to the rule on brains?" I say.

"He has incredible instincts," Seb suggests.

"B: You're small," Colin continues. "What do you weigh, one-twenty?"

I narrow my eyes as if I'm insulted, but he's actually given me an extra four pounds.

"Okay, well in any case," says Seb, who stands out as the diplomat of the three. "You're a perfect cox size."

"The cox is always light," explains Colin, "because we want as little to drag us down as possible in the ninth seat."

"The fewer pounds, the faster we go," Seb says.

I'm so accustomed to catching shit about my height that it's hard for me to register that they're genuinely seeing it as an asset. "Makes sense," I say.

"So, you're two for two so far," Khalid says. "Smart. Small. And," he adds, "you're not tied up with any other sport."

Colin grins. "Smart. Small. Available."

So that's it. They're desperate. Athletics are compulsory at LPS. Everyone has to do a team or an intramural club. "I'm in Outdoors Club," I say.

"Let's talk perks," Seb says, like I didn't say anything.

"Yes. Perks," Colin says. "For starters, without even trying out, you're going to immediately be in the Varsity-1 boat. Which will piss off the other coxes, but Coach won't mess up our other boats."

"I'm telling you, he's bluffing," Khalid says. "Follett won't risk the title."

"Well, Max would at least *start* in our boat," Colin says.

He and Khalid go back and forth.

"Perks?" I prompt, interrupting.

They stop, then smile.

"He's even got the dickish edge," says Khalid.

"He's gonna kick ass," Colin says.

I wish I could kick *his* ass.

"There are tons of perks. The 1V boat—our boat—" Seb begins.

"Potentially *your* boat," adds Colin.

"Yeah, imagine you, Max Loeffler-Hannigan," Khalid says.

"Hannigan-Loeffler," I correct. "For fuck's sake, it's *Hannigan. Loeffler.*"

Khalid lets out a happy giggle.

Colin squats beside the love seat and sweeps his hand in front of us like we're both looking into our future. "Imagine yourself, Max Hannigan-Loeffler, in the boat that the college recruiters all come to see. We're talking Division 1 coaches. Ivy League coaches. Scouting for coxing and rowing recruits."

"We're the fastest boat—" Khalid says.

"In Lycroft history, I know, I know," I say.

"HYP. That's Harvard, Yale, Princet—"

"I'm familiar," I say. "I'm not worried about getting into a good college," I say. This isn't 100 percent truthful, but they don't need to know that. My college adviser told me that even for kids with my grades and early test scores, nothing is guaranteed in admissions these days. "Unless you have an uncle who feels like building a library," he quipped at our last meeting. "Or your mom photoshops you into a rowing shell or something." He actually used that example.

I decide to keep listening.

"Yeah," Colin says. "But with Lycroft Phelps Crew on your transcript, you have a hook," Colin says. "You could even get recruited. Chauncey has shit for test scores, and Dartmouth is all over him."

"*Was* all over him," Seb says. "And let's not get carried away. Chauncey has been coxing since eighth grade." He turns to me. "Chauncey *is* smart."

Khalid flips his hand in a "kinda" motion.

Seb shoots him a look. "He suffered a lapse in judgment."

Seb should do law school, I decide.

"And look at this place," Colin says, standing and striding to the huge window. "You know why the old boathouse underwent a two-million-dollar reconstruction? Because our alumni rowers have got fucking *bank*. Who doesn't want to join that club?"

"Oh my God, dude," Seb says, like Colin is inflicting physical pain. He massages his forehead with his long fingers, and I wonder if we are the same species.

Colin emits a quick laugh. "Oh, I know, I know, we're not supposed to talk about the money. But look around. This is deluxe even for LPS. The only nicer building is Kessler."

"Basically, you're asking me for a favor," I say, playing their ignoring game.

Khalid softens his eyes and sits across from me. "Yes, it's a favor in a way. But it's also an *opportunity*. Chicks fucking dig rowers. They're all over us," Khalid says.

It's so old-school macho I can't keep myself from saying, "Are you for real?" But I'd be lying if Alexandra Buchanan didn't pop into my head. There she was, cheering for me from the shore.

"It's true," Colin says. "You can hook up with any chick on campus when she knows you're with us."

Of course *they* could hook up with anyone. I doubt this will extend to my scrawny self. Still, I could raise my Five to a strong Six. Seven, even. If it's like they say, I might be good at coxing. I love kayaking.

I rise to look at the trophy cases, buying myself some time.

Colin's not having it and stands beside me.

"Ever had a blow job, Maximo?" he says. "Because I'm thinking you haven't and I'm thinking your life is about to change."

"I gotta pipeline to the best blow on campus. There anytime I call," Khalid says, snapping his fingers.

"Jesus," I say, shaking my head.

Khalid laughs. "Am I right, McNeilly?"

Seb tries to look annoyed, but a smile creeps across his face.

"Seb and I," Colin says, "are the top scorers at Lycroft Phelps."

"Slycrofterrrrr," Khalid drawls in a player voice.

Colin throws him a stern look out of nowhere. But Khalid's smiling. "If Seb dumps his girlfriend, he'll kick your ass, Colin."

"He wouldn't even *have* the girlfriend if I hadn't bet him on who could tag her first last year," Colin adds. "I wish I hadn't."

Man, he's a dick. I keep a poker face.

"That's such crap." Seb smirks, not remotely ruffled. "We're off topic again. What do you say, Max?"

"Come *on*, dude," Colin says, tapping his hand against the mantelpiece.

Seb watches me, wearing a subtle but friendly smile. Khalid does, too, perched on the edge of the wingback, bouncing his heels. Wow. They really want me to do this. I pace some more, enjoying my brief power trip.

"Blow jobs," Khalid says quietly. They laugh, and I can't help but smile.

"What do I have to do?" I say, facing them.

Khalid fist pumps. "Yessss."

"I'm not saying yes yet," I insist. "I'm asking what's required."

"Come here at eight tomorrow morning, and we'll get you in

a boat," Seb says, chill as can be. "It's impossible to explain until you're on the water."

"Okay," I say.

We step outside. A breeze has picked up. The moon emerges from behind a cloud mass, and—poof!—Lake Edith lights up, wide and shimmery. The other two keep walking, but Seb stays. "And there she is," Seb says. "The Tenth Muse."

"What do you mean?" I ask.

"The first LPS crew team called the lake that. You know the nine Greek muses? The statues at the Amphitheater?"

I nod.

"'Lake Edith, nestled in the pointed fir trees like a jewel, guarded by the White Mountain foothills, inspired the boys of 1922 to become men and bonded them in brotherhood for life.' Something like that; it's on a plaque inside. It sounds corny, but every time I stand on the dock before a row, I think of that plaque and I notice how she's different, every day. A little bluer, greener, blacker, smoother, choppier. It just makes you want to row. Together. Like a team." He thumps his chest. My mind is a little blown by his poetic sentiment, and my face must betray this, because he shakes his head and shrugs. "I know. Don't tell them I said that." He grins. "But it's a bit mystical. You'll see." He turns to join them on the path, and I linger, watching the glitter shift across the water's surface as clouds drift over the moon.

When the four of us head silently toward the dorms, I can't help but wonder if maybe my life *is* about to change.

5

Saturday Morning

CHARLOTTE

I pour a scoop of blueberries onto my oatmeal and slide next to Hannah at the condiments table. "How long were you and Hank together before you had sex? Longer than four months?" I ask my roommate as I drizzle honey over the bowl.

She casts a bemused look my way, and we move to an empty table at the Granola Bar, which is only open weekends.

"Well?" I say.

I wait as she chews her multigrain bagel and looks at the ceiling. "Seven months? I mean, we were only Lower Middies when we did it, so maybe our lead-up took longer than yours will with Genetic Miracle. Are you two talking about it?" she asks, grinning, then frowning. "Is he pressuring you? Because you are in charge of you, Charlotte Foresley."

"I wish," I say, rolling my eyes. She smirks, so I say, "I don't mean that. It's just—is it strange that it hasn't come up yet?"

"So to speak," she says earnestly, then chuckles.

"Stop," I say. "You'd think he would be mentioning it by now."

"Aw," she says, putting her bagel down. "That is so cute! He's *nervous*."

"What? No, Seb McNeilly is not nervous about anything. Ever.

And definitely not about me. Or sex."

"How do you know?"

I give her a look.

Hannah nods in concession and bites her bagel. "Still." She chews. "Have you looked in a mirror lately, Charlotte? You got it going on."

I shake my head. "Please. He's the Genetic Miracle, remember?"

"Just ask him, then."

I laugh. "What, like, hey, why haven't you asked me to have sex yet?"

"Or 'Have you been thinking about having sex?' Why not? I guarantee you he's thought about it by now."

I take a sip of my tea. "Fifty percent of our so-called four months was when we were halfway across the country from each other."

"Right. But the commitment has lasted four months. Ask if he's a virgin," she suggests.

I raise one eyebrow.

"What?" She waves her hands around. "It gets the conversation started."

I can't imagine ever having a conversation like that with him. "It's so . . . personal," I say.

"Uh, yeah," she laughs. "That it is. And?"

"And it's none of my business."

She smirks. "I beg to differ."

I eat some oatmeal. "Besides, thinking about his other girlfriends stresses me out. Thank God Sabrina Godfrey is at Bowdoin already." She's the LPS icon Seb went out with for a year and a

137

half. She broke his heart, dumping him in his sophomore year.

She narrows her eyes. "Question: Has Seb McNeilly touched your boobs?"

"Shut up!" I hiss, hunkering lower over my oatmeal.

"Um, excuse me, but you started this." She presses, "Has he?"

"Duh," I whisper.

"How about below the belt?"

I glance to both sides. "Hannah," I scold.

She waits.

"Yes," I say.

"His belt and your belt?"

"I don't wear belts, but yes."

"And it's consensual?" she says. "Always?"

"Yes," I say.

"Just confirming. Okay, then! You've officially crossed into the land of the *personal*. Welcome! Hank and I like it here!"

"You are such a dweeb."

"I know," she says. "But at least I can ask my boyfriend things. Important things."

And I think, but don't say, *At least you can call him your boyfriend!*

Hannah sits taller. "If you can't ask him, I'm going to have to play the stand-in for Mama Evelyn."

"Oh no," I say.

Hannah takes my hands in hers. "Charlotte, honey, you're just not ready," she says in a nasal midwestern accent.

I snort—partially because it's spot-on Evelyn Foresley and partially because Hannah's relieved some of my worry. Seb and I just aren't there yet.

But I *want* to be there.

On our way out, I tug my jacket around me in the chilly morning air. "It's not even that I *want* to have sex so badly. I'm kind of neutral in wanting to and not wanting to for *me*." Hannah's listening intently, her brow furrowed above her aviators. "But I want *him* to want to. Aren't all boys supposed to want to have sex, like, all the time? I don't get why Seb doesn't want to. I don't get it, and it makes me paranoid."

Hannah makes a puzzled face, like she's a philosopher pondering one of life's big questions. This also makes me paranoid. "I'm right," I say. "It's weird, isn't it? Even you think so."

"I think you better ask him," she says finally. "You have nothing to lose. Well, *one* thing, maybe." She claps my shoulder. "I am on fire today!"

I roll my eyes. "I can't ask."

"Then the mystery train will roll on." She starts making low choo-choo sounds.

A couple of First Years eyeball her as they pass. I shake my head to them, smiling apologetically.

"Hey," Hannah says. "Guess what? I had a series idea for the *Wire*, and Mr. Bartello loved it. For the seventy-fifth anniversary of the Fuzzy Gilbert Award, we're going to profile each winner in a column spread over the whole year, called *Who Will You Be at Lycroft Phelps?* Two a week."

The Fuzzy Gilbert is a good citizenship award given every year in the name of this dude named Francis "Fuzzy" Gilbert, who struck it rich on Wall Street and established a fund, coining the school's signature question, "Who will you be?" His portrait in

Spangler looks exactly like the Monopoly guy, right down to the monocle.

"Whoa," I say. "That sounds like a lot of work."

She shrugs, smiling. "I get to oversee other kids' work. Bartello named me lead editor. I got the email before breakfast."

I bump her shoulder. "Hello, Columbia." Her dream school to study journalism.

"I wish," she says. "But the first female Fuzzy winner was Margot Pipkin, the head of Sloan Broadcasting, the biggest news network in the US. I get to interview her." She does a little happy dance.

"We are kicking ass and taking names this year!" I say.

"Damn straight," she says.

We split ways near Stevens. Hannah's going to play squash with Hank. They're like a married couple. Could Seb and I be like that? So practical? So solid? I have no doubt Hank and Hannah talk about sex as easily as they talk about ordering dinner. Hank thinks nothing of sitting in on our Littles groups sharing helpful tips about Lycroft guys. Like *If a guy takes you to the Amphitheater at night, he's got hooking up on his mind.* Or *Most of the guys act like they're all hot with the girls, but have no idea what to do. Don't let them fool you; they're terrified.* He's great like that, like your protective older brother. Hank is *safe*.

But.

There's no mystery.

Don't I want to not worry if Seb's going to wake up one day and decide he's made a mistake? Or would that cancel out all our flirty playfulness?

I've confused myself enough that I spend the walk to my room "rewatching" my favorite mind movies of us. I especially love the first night: Summer Sendoff. I replayed it all summer.

Q and I stand side by side in front of the mirrors in the girls' bathroom. We're both wearing cream-colored dresses, in keeping with Summer Sendoff tradition: mine's a sleeveless silk sheath that drapes low near the cleavage and lower in the back, hers is lacy with spaghetti straps, cinched at the waist. Q's fixing that wild mane of curly hair she has, and I'm reapplying lipstick. The power bass from the dance song pumps through the marble floor tiles, and we're tipping our heads to the beat.

"I'm keeping rhythm to Nicki Minaj," Q says. "Sorry, Dad!" Like he can hear her in Australia or wherever she said he was. "He's not a fan," she adds for clarity.

But on cue, we simultaneously point at each other with finger guns and belt out: "B to the A to the N to the G to the uh!" I use my lipstick as a mic. "B to the A to the N to the G to the HEY!" We double over laughing.

"I'm a little"—I pinch my fingers—"buzzed."

Q has a silent laugh with squeaks. She seriously sounds like a rubber ducky, and it's freaking hilarious.

"You guys," whispers Hannah, standing guard at the door out to the gallery. "How much vodka did you put in your drinks?" When she pushes the door open a crack, the music floods in. Q and I lean into each other.

"Bang bang, there goes your heart!"

"Shh!" Hannah says, pulling the door closed. "Tell me about the Whitney Inn."

"I had salmon," Q says, and does a chef's kiss. "C'est bon." She shuts a stall door.

"Not the food," Hannah says. Her dress is sleeveless, high neck, only to the thigh.

Q's talking softly in there. Hannah and I exchange a puzzled glance, and then I recognize it.

"Hannah, Q's rapping. She knows the rap!"

Q starts squeaking again, which cracks up me and even Hannah.

"Seriously!" Hannah says when Q comes out. "Was dinner awkward? Flirty? What?"

"Not awkward," I say, tucking the lipstick in my sequin clutch.

Q washes her hands at the sink. "I don't think guys like Colin and Seb can be awkward," she says. "Think about it. Awkwardness is worrying about what others think of you. They don't do that. They just serve as the ideal. There's a name for it . . . pro . . . pro . . . pro-something."

"Prototype?" Hannah offers.

"Yes! Everyone tries to be like the prototype, and when we don't live up to it, we're embarrassed. Which equals awkward."

I consider Q's point. "She's either onto something genius or drunker than me," I say.

"Or both," Hannah says. "I think that's true of Genetic Miracle. I think Colin just fakes it. Hard."

Q laughs. "Colin's straight-up too cocky to be awkward." We migrate toward the door. "I still don't know why he invited me."

"Because you're a First Year hottie, Q," I say as we file out into a narrow hallway. "Hannah, am I right?"

"Of course! Q's got that cool-without-trying thing going on, for sure," Hannah says over her shoulder.

Q waves her hand at us dismissively. "No, I don't. Anyway, I'm not saying I'm not worthy."

I'm kind of in awe that Q doesn't question whether she's worthy.

That was the first thing I wondered about myself with Seb. But of course just because they're kings of campus doesn't mean they're actually better human beings. My brain knows this, but my heart doesn't trust it. How does she already understand that? She should be my Biggie.

"It's juss weird," she says, a little slurry.

We turn the corner into the main gallery, where the dance is being held. Café lights traverse the high ceiling and cascade over the wall of windows. The paintings are lit up, and string lights spiral up the columns holding various sculptures. All the cream dresses glow light gold in clusters around, and candle votives flicker on the tall tables at the edges of the room.

I whisper dreamily, "Does anyone feel like we're in a giant glass of champagne?"

They nod and sigh.

Then I poke Q with my elbow, resuming our conversation. "Colin looked like he had it all figured out when he watched you at dinner," I say. Q isn't movie-star beautiful like her cousin Macy. But after a while with her, you notice something in her mannerisms; she doesn't try to impress anyone. That's so rare, I think. Until I realize why that vibe is so familiar. "You remind me of my friend Grace. Even though you don't look anything like her." It comes out really soft; they don't hear me, and that's just as well because I think it's the vodka getting me all dramatic and a little melancholy. I miss Grace. I wanted her to come to LPS, but she thinks it's too "elitist bubble" for her, whatever that means. I feel my mood start to darken just thinking about it, until I see Seb across the large gallery, leaning against a café table.

"OMG, look at Genetic Miracle," Hannah says. "Smitten with my roommate. This is epic."

They laugh, but I can't. Seb's watching me, ignoring Colin's animated storytelling and the other rowers I know but don't know. He smiles, and my stomach pirouettes. I pull my dancer posture out of some muscle memory bank, elongating my spine, pulling my shoulders back. At least I can fake confidence. Like Colin. Haha.

"That boy's got it ba-ad," Q says.

"I can't feel my tongue," I say, barely opening my mouth.

"Go get him, Charlotte," Hannah says. She veers toward Hank and his friends near the indoor fountain, in a small annex off the gallery. "Hank's gonna go home if I don't get him dancing."

"Don't ditch me, Q," I say, still not moving my lips. I must look so weird! I smile and fake laugh.

Q raises her eyebrows at me, leading me toward the boys. "Calm down, Charlotte. I won't ditch you. Where would I go?" She emits a staccato squeak.

"Our dates," says Colin, grinning. He hands Q a clear plastic cup of seltzer with, I'm guessing, more vodka by the way her face pinches up after a sip. A better Biggie would caution her, but this is not a night for caution. Or Biggies.

A Bruno Mars ballad comes across the speakers, unduly loud, if you ask me. It's prissy, but I don't get that with the huge volume. Is it to cancel out thinking? Couples shuffle onto the dance floor.

Seb leans close to my ear and says, "I'm not the best at this, but you want to slow dance?" The lights spark amber flecks in his eyes. All I can muster is a nod. I'm vaguely aware of people watching us, and I hear Q say, "Okay, sure," and then she and Colin are beside us.

It's true, Seb's not the best. To be fair, I have twelve years of dance experience on him, but his shoulders are broad and his hair smells like cinnamon and my insides are on fire in a way they've never ever been *before. I've had boyfriends—kisses, clumsy groping, and all that—but this? Never.*

We spin. Hank and Hannah appear, her chin resting on Hank's shoulder—he's totally off tempo, and it's kind of adorable. I love that Hannah could care less how terrible Hank is. Seb and I spin again. Q lip-synchs, "Somewhere far away-ay-ay," to me over Colin's shoulder. Colin is doing an uninspired box step. Q is unaffected. Honestly, I should have taken the last drink from her. "Talking to the mooo—ooo—oon!" Colin's hands are half on her butt cheeks. Q and I make eye contact, and I glance down. She laughs. "Tryna get to you-ou-ou!"

When Bruno's voice trails off, Seb and I break apart. "I am so bad," he says, looking at the floor, sheepishly smiling. It's true. He's a little embarrassed—amused at himself—but not awkward. I hope I remember this so I can report out to Q and Hannah.

"No!" I say.

"I stepped on you."

"Only twice."

He squints apologetically, and I know I would do absolutely anything for this guy. With this guy. Anything.

"Let's go look at the stars," he says.

"Let's," I say.

He puts out his elbow. I tuck my arm through it, and we stroll out the lovely French doors onto the terrace of Bremer Art Gallery. In the deliciously cold air, under the effervescent stars, we overlook the school grounds and Lake Edith like the lord and lady of some fairy tale. I don't bother recalling our conversation. It was filler until he asked if he could kiss me, which was so sexy I nearly swooned. And then Seb McNeilly leaned in for a long, soft, positively transcendent kiss.

"Hi, Charlotte."

I snap out of my reverie, feeling my cheeks blush. "Oh, hi, Ms. Ballard." When she's passed me, I suppress a flutter of embarrassed laughter, which is silly, because it's not like she can see in my head. The memory has lifted my mood, as it always does. I wonder, again, what Q's Summer Sendoff story is, and I feel guilty—especially as her Big—that I didn't make more effort to follow up with her all summer. Realizing she didn't respond to my text last night, my hearts sinks the tiniest bit. She could be angry. As I climb the steps to my dorm, I decide today is the day to reconnect with Quinn Walsh.

MAX

"What are you doing?" Nils says groggily. "It's Saturday."

The glow of my open laptop makes the rest of the room unnaturally dark.

"Oh, now you wake up," I say, not taking my eyes from the screen. I've been watching rowing videos since four-thirty. "You couldn't wake up when I'm frigging being abducted by the *Planet of the Apes*?"

Nils pauses. I can practically hear him puzzling over my words. It could take a while, so I return to my task at hand. I think I've got the vocabulary down. I already knew starboard and port (right and left), bow and stern (the front and back). Now I've learned about shells (the boats), sweeping versus sculling (using one oar, like a broom, versus two oars, like—well, I haven't found where the heck *scull* comes from yet, but at least I know what it is). The cox sits in the stern, oriented in the direction the boat is moving. The rowers all sit facing the cox. They can't even see where they're going. The stroke (pacesetter) sits in the eighth seat, closest to the cox. Rewatching footage from the British televised Henley Royal Regatta, which my research reveals to be the oldest (established 1839) and perhaps most elite rowing race in the world, I listen to the commentator explaining a particularly well-done job of a

Dutch cox. "'The strategy of holding back until the last five hundred meters or so really paid off.'"

I've also found the most popular book ever written on the subject of rowing, a history of the 1936 US Olympic team called *The Boys in the Boat* by Daniel James Brown. I'll order it from our local bookstore when it opens.

"Abducted?" Nils finally asks.

"Abducted," I reply, still focused on the footage.

"Hmm. And yet, here you sit before my very eyes." He stretches and yawns. "Was it the stalker?" he asks innocently.

Without looking at him, I flip him off. He snickers, and in my peripheral vision, I see him emerge from his pile of bedding and walk out of the room. Our hall's bathroom door squeaks once, and then again a few moments later.

"Okay," Nils says, stopping to look over my shoulder at the computer. "Rowing? What are we doing?"

I close my laptop and explain what he managed to sleep through: that three massive intruders entered our room shortly before one a.m. and absconded with me into the night.

"What's absconded?" he says, now back to lying in bed.

"Took flight. Escaped. Stole away."

"I slept through that?"

"Yes."

"Wow," he marvels. "Why?"

"Because you're part reptile?"

"No, why did they abscond you?"

"Abscond *with* me. Forget abscond. They want me to replace Chauncey as their coxswain in the Varsity-1 boat."

After I'm done recounting the night's events, which I do as I'm dressing because it's about 7:20 and I want to eat breakfast before I go to the dock, Nils says, "They're using you. Colin Pearce especially. Just like with your physics project."

"Yeah, I know," I say, tying my sneaker. "But I think I'd actually get something out of it this time."

"Something like what? Hanging out with dicks while your only truly cool friend is rock climbing in the White Mountain wilderness?"

"Seb's not so bad. Comparatively speaking. And you're forgetting: *I get to boss them around*," I say, tugging my baseball cap into place. Alexandra Buchanan pops into my mind, on the shore, cheering like she has multiple times for me since last night, but I don't share that bit with Nils. Instead I say, "And I get to be out on the lake. It's like kayaking on steroids."

"Except you're just sitting there. Your already-underdeveloped muscles are going to evaporate."

"I can still climb at the gym." I zip my windbreaker.

Nils looks at me over his phone.

I shrug. "How much worse can my social standing get?"

"You could drop below a Five, according to you."

I tip my head and scowl.

"Okay, okay. You should give it a try," he says. I almost tell him I didn't need his approval, but actually . . .

"Climb after Vespers?" he says.

On Saturdays, we have candlelight Vespers, a kind of non-religious, inclusive service. Which never really made total sense to me. If it's in an Episcopalian chapel with Jesus on the cross hanging over the pulpit and every stained-glass window depicting a different disciple, how are we calling it nondenominational? I guess if you're not Christian at LPS, you just feel lucky they let you in and roll with it. It's just so typical of this place. This constant undercurrent of welcoming diversity but never letting anyone forget the roots of the school.

Anyway, Vespers is tonight.

"Sounds good, Nils," I say, closing our door and heading to the boathouse.

Q

I become aware of a hand on my shoulder. My eyelids flutter open, and I bolt upright and fling myself against the wall in one fear-flooded motion.

"Whoa," Alex says, with an awkward laugh. "Who did you think I was, Q?"

"Jesus, Alex," I say, panting. "Don't do that."

"Sorry," she says, sounding more annoyed than apologetic. "Come to breakfast? We've barely seen each other since we got here. The Granola Bar is open today."

I am too bleary and jangled to make an excuse. "Sure, sure," I say. "Give me ten minutes."

"Yay," Alex says, recovered. "I'll get the window table." She opens the curtains. "It's gorgeous out."

While I'm in our bathroom, she leaves, and I feel guilty about my sense of relief. I force myself to get dressed but find myself a few moments later staring blankly into the closet.

Everything is in a giant, overwhelming pile on the floor. Tears fill my eyes, and I just collapse into the heap of clothes. It's so much harder than I thought. Everything is so much harder.

I crawl deeper into the closet, a welcoming dark cave, and pull the door closed. Burrowing onto the pile, I find something flannel to rest my cheek on. I'm so frustrated I can't crack that code to Anderson Safety. The sobs come, deep and shattering, but I muffle them into the arm of a fleece sweatshirt. I can't stop the memories.

We watch Charlotte and Seb go outside. I think we both know we don't have the chemistry to go out there.

    Let's request a song, he says
    Gimme Shelter, I say
    by the Stones? he asks
    Duh
    The ends of his lips turn down
    His eyebrows go up
    A signal I've impressed him
    Or amused him
    Soooo cocky
    Tempted to say Mick Jagger told me I look like my mom
    At my dad's sixtieth birthday party in Southport
    But Walshes don't name drop.
    Ooh, a storm is threatening
    My very life today
    We dance, alone, together, alone
    The harmonica fades at the end of the song.
    Colin wraps a hand around my waist
    Touches the hair at the nape of my neck
    The drinks make me lazy
    I close my eyes and let his
    Long fingers cradle my skull

He's big. I am from big men.
Their endless, easy limbs
are familiar.
We are outside somehow
I hold his hand
My sandals dangle from my free fingers
Feet press into the soft grass of
the Amphitheater Lawn
we wind through the marble statues
Greek Muses arranged
above stone seats set into the earth
facing Lake Edith, who languishes wide and still—
Flawless glass,
steward of secrets, I think.
Can you name the Muses? he asks.
Calliope, I say, epic poetry;
Clio, history;
Thalia, comedy;
Ourania, celestial bodies;
She protects the stars, I say.
How spectacular is that? I ask.
I watch them shimmer over us in a dizzying swarm.
The stars, I repeat.
So much mystery in such a little,
five-pointed word.
He kisses me, somehow moving me to the ground.
Euterpe, music; I whisper.
He lays me back.

The soil smells of spring and
at first it is okay.
At first it is okay.
Our teeth knock into each other.
I laugh and try to sit up.
But his size transforms from a comfort to a threat
I'm stuck
It's absurd,
the sudden sea change.
I think maybe he's playing
But his eyes turn eel black and absent
Panic lifts its head in my stomach, gathering its senses,
waking from an untroubled, childlike slumber.
Danger!
I turn my face
His mouth, wet and hot, covers my ear
A perverted seashell sound
Stop!
I say or yell
I don't know because his
tongue is a jutting invader
He's on top of me
Smothering me
I squirm
One hand holds both wrists above my head.
                                    It's okay to want it, he says.
His finger traces my chin, my neck.
My throat is closing.
Where are my words?

I twist
thrash
Get an arm free to protect myself.
But he catches it, holds both wrists again.
Grins.

         Don't be like that, now, he says.

The other hand disappears from view.
Serpentine
Up my skirt
Pulling my underwear,
No, I say through tears, but it's too late
Belt buckle jangles
I know what is going to happen
but I don't know.
How could I?

         It's okay to have fun, he says.

I'm crying. He doesn't look.

         Let it be fun, he says.

He buries his face in the curve above my shoulder
It pulls my hair.

I'm a broken-winged butterfly
Weak
Grounded
Stab
Play dead, I think. Play dead to survive it.

I'm an empty plastic bag
A d r i f t

in space
A passenger on a callous wind
The stars are five-pointed ghosts
their fires snuffed out.
My self is shrunken
deep inside this ill-equipped container
Away from where his skin
touches mine.
Away from hip
hitting hip.
Then it stops.
He sits up, staring at Edith. Swearing her to silence.
I cover myself.
He's standing, a giant made of shadowy blue stone
tucking in his shirt,
zipping his fly.
He never
even
removed
his brown
Italian
loafers.
I curl like a caterpillar.

                Here, he says.
                Get up.

He extends his hand
a gesture that does not belong here. It's confusing me.
I watch Euterpe
unmoving

study the drape of the marble tunic over her shin.

                                        Fine, be that way.

His loafers shush
through the damp grass,

Shush

Shush

Shush

past my white sandals
scattered like bones licked clean.
I'm alone
with the chirring of crickets throwing their alarms into the night.
Unanswered.

MAX

Lake Edith is so flat, it flawlessly mirrors the pointed firs, deep blue sky, and four fat cumulus clouds.

"It's almost a shame to wreck it this morning," Seb says from behind me. His appreciation for it surprises me, and I don't really have a comeback. "Almost," he tacks on.

I grin. We stare in reverence for a long moment.

"Sweeping glass. That's what it's called when it's this calm." Then he says, "In crew, sweeping is when you use one oar to row. Sculling is when the rower has two." I nod, recalling this fact from my research. "So, sweeping glass."

I nod again.

Seb points. "There's a buoy marking two-point-five K. We'll turn around there," he says.

"Heads up," someone behind us says.

It's Tyler Wiggins, ahead of the crew, steaming straight for us with an eight-person shell turtled on their shoulders. I bumble out of the way. The shell is so long and narrow, my first thought is *That thing actually holds all those guys?* Of course it does, I know that. Boats float because the downward force due to gravity is exactly matched by the upward force due to buoyancy, and as long as the center of gravity is stable, the rowers would be fine.

But, holy shit, it's narrow.

Tyler keeps walking alongside the boat and says over his shoulder, "Normally, the cox does this job. Pay attention."

I follow. The deck slants downward at a certain point to accommodate the slope toward the lake, and then it narrows into a pier, maybe six feet wide, that protrudes some thirty feet into the water. It's a pretty cool piece of engineering in itself. "Up over heads!" Tyler shouts, to which the boys—Seb, Khalid, and Colin, plus four more I don't have time to recognize before they've passed—respond by straightening their arms, lifting the boat, and proceeding down the ramp.

"Wayne Off!" Tyler bellows.

The rowers stop.

"Toes to the edge," Tyler says.

They inch toward the pier's lip, now parallel to the water.

"And roll it in," Tyler says. The boys roll and flip the boat, setting it to rest on the water's surface as gently as if it were their collective baby. Well, if the baby could float on water.

Anyway, Khalid jogs toward me. "Hey, Max," he says without stopping. "You made the right call."

"Thanks," I say. I have a second to ID the other guys. All Seniors, of course. All giant. Teo Van der Graf; Devon Sturges, who's from England; Geoff Chamberlain, from NYC like me (but he's from Upper West Side, not Murray Hill); and Grey Fiutak. Grey jogs with Khalid back into the boathouse. Nobody named Wayne Off.

I barely know any of them (surprise!), but on the upside, they don't know me, either. We're at a blank-slate stage of relations. I figure someone's nickname is Wayne Off.

Khalid is back, arms loaded with oars, tailed by Grey, also carrying oars. "Hi, Max," Grey says with a nod. "You got a good day to learn. It's like glass."

I nod cautiously, not wanting to say the wrong thing. They lay the oars next to the boat.

"Come on down, Max," calls Seb. He's squatting, holding the boat to the dock along with Geoff, who's at the end. Or should I say, the bow. "Did you read about loading the boat?" Seb asks.

"Yes. Load the guys four at a time, right?"

"Right. But first have the waterside seats ship their oars out." He's looking up at me in his sunglasses. He tips his head toward the shell. "Which side is waterside, in this case?"

Oh, he's quizzing me. I'm up for the challenge. "Port."

He smiles. "Tell them. And say it like you mean it."

I look at the assembled hulks, kicking off their shoes and give Seb a tough-guy "no prob" look. "And, uh, hey, Seb?" He waits. "Who's Wayne Off?"

His forehead creases. "What?"

"Wayne . . . Wayne Off, or Uff maybe?"

Seb's eyebrows fly high over his Oakleys.

"Wayne Hough?" I venture.

He bursts out laughing. It's out of character and grabs everyone's attention. Fuck.

"Seb!" I whisper sharply, scowling.

He suppresses his laughing, shaking his head. "Sorry, sorry," he says. And then erupts again.

Now all the guys are smiling.

"What?" asks Teo.

I want to crawl under a rock.

"He . . . he asked who Wayne Hough is."

A one-second pause, and then they fall all over the place cracking up.

"It's okay, it's okay," Seb says, sniffing. "Easy mistake. There's nobody named Wayne. It's the rowing command for stop."

I did my homework. "That's *weigh enough*," I say.

Seb giggles like a little kid. "Pronounced, *way 'nuff.*"

"That's stupid," I mutter, which makes them laugh again, but I roll the words around in my mouth a few times and start to hear it. I smile sheepishly. "Can we forget that, please?" More chuckles.

"Seriously," Pearce says. "Easy mistake."

Pearce! Said that! Just when I think I'll have to pick my chin off the deck, he ruffles my hair like I'm five. I channel my annoyance. "Ports, run your oars!" Seb, Teo, Devon, and Tyler push their oars through the oarlocks to the collar so they're fully extended into the water, paddle blades bobbing like snoozing otters. It's quiet. "Oh, Ports: One foot up and in!" I say.

Like magic, four of them step gingerly into the boat—including Seb. It wobbles some but settles when they're seated. Seb nods.

"Starboards, one foot up and in!"

Again, my wish is their command. I watch the eight of them fiddling with the built-in shoes. I privately congratulate myself for not being surprised that a shell has sliding seats (like a rowing machine) *and* is outfitted with shoes the rowers slip into. I read a bunch of nightmare stories where kids realize their shoes are too big during a race. I am sure this 1V boat is customized to these guys.

They seem like they're set, quiet again.

"Max?"

Shit. I squint, trying to remember. "Count down from stern when ready?" I say quietly to Seb. I know it's not right.

"From bow," he says.

"Right. Count down from bow when ready!"

Since they're ready now, the bow seat one (Geoff) says, "Bow."

"Two," Tyler says.

"Three," Khalid says.

"Four." Devon.

"Five." Grey.

"Six." Teo.

"Seven." Colin.

"Eight," says Seb. I remember reading that the stroke can identify him or herself as either *Eight* or *Stroke*. A humbler stroke will prefer not to set himself apart from the other rowers. Seb's definitely all right.

I'll admit to butterflies in the abdominal region when I say the next line: "Hold for cox."

Seb nods in approval. "Step in the center," he advises.

I do and note how reactive the boat is to even my measly 116-pound self. I get my ass into the seat before I can lose my balance. I'm tucked in like an accordion, knees in front of my chest. By my elbows, I find the steering ropes, which I know move the rudder left and right.

The rowers are waiting to hear my next call. We haven't even begun, and I'm kind of exhausted. But also exhilarated. I riffle through the directives I tried to learn. "Hands on the dock," I say. "And shove off!" The water whooshes under us as we push off.

The starboard oars *plunk* into the lake, and we are officially afloat. I don't know if that's a term or not. We're just sitting here, though; yet again, everyone is waiting for me. "Geoff?" I call. I can't see any of the rowers except for Seb, since he's right in front of me.

"Yo!" Geoff calls in reply.

"Can you row a little?"

The guys chuckle, but I see Geoff's oar start to push through the water. We move away from the dock.

"Bow pair," I say. Tyler's oar begins paddling with Geoff's, off the other side of the boat.

"Weigh enough," I call to them, then ask the bow four (the front half of the boat) to "Sit ready" and say "Row."

We pick up a little speed, and it's gentle going. I let them go for a few minutes. We're out a ways from shore.

"Look for that buoy," Seb says. In truth, it's a little tough to see over his head, so I lean to the side and find it.

"Got it."

"That's the point to aim for."

It's slightly to the right of our path, I think, so I push the right side of the rudder cable in. The boat doesn't react, so I push a little harder.

The boat makes a thirty-degree turn to the left.

"It's okay, Max. You'll get it. The rudder is sensitive, but it takes a second to respond."

I nod, even though *slow to respond* and *sensitive* sound like mutually exclusive terms to me. I have no choice but to trust the expert. In spite of the brisk weather, I'm pitting out. I wish I didn't have to learn in front of all these guys. I breathe deep. Gently, I pull the rudder and count to five. The buoy is within fifteen degrees. I repeat and adjust one more time until we have our point. I resist the urge to smile.

"Got it?" Seb asks.

"Yep," I say.

"Okay, add stern four," Seb says.

"Weigh enough!" I yell with perfect annunciation. Seb snorts. I ignore him. "Everyone, sit ready." I wait a couple of beats because it feels like I should, and then say, "And row!"

Seb starts pulling. In three or four strokes, we're really moving along. The paddles create a rhythm. *Splash-slide-floop. Splash-slide-floop.* I'm sure there are things I could say to make them go faster, but right now I'm lost in the moment of eight humans working together to move this shell across the smooth lake. They don't even look like they're working hard.

Seb's quiet, concentrating on the count.

We're approaching the buoy, and I realize they don't know that. They don't know when to slow down, when we'll be turning, nothing. I *am* the brains of the boat—it's a nine-person endeavor, not eight. This is at once terrifying and exhilarating. I have no idea how to negotiate this U-turn, but it's going to take more than just pulling the rudder rope. I picture how I could use the port and starboard sides separately to get them spun around after we slow down. I squint, trying to remember the right calls.

We sail past the buoy. "Weigh enough!" I call.

They're patient as I figure out how to make the turn, and it's really not that different from coding a robotic crane to pick up a Lego car. To make a call and have the rowers respond is an incredible high. Nobody listens to me like this outside of a lab.

When we're spun in the correct direction and the water's churn settles, someone calls from the bow: "Hey, Wayne, not fucking bad!"

They all hoot.

"Have us do a power ten on the return!" Colin calls. A power ten is when they go as hard as they can for ten strokes. I'm not really sure when to call it. When we're almost finished? When we're just starting? Somewhere in between? My indecision allows half the return distance to go by before I've said anything. I remember reading I have to give them a two-count heads-up so they can mentally prepare to go all out. We're probably three-fourths of the way back to the dock when I decide to go for it. "Power ten in two!" I do my best at bellowing. "One!" I yell. "Two!" And all of a sudden, the boat kicks into some new gear I couldn't possibly have imagined. We are *flying*! A cacophony of grunts and groans mix with the rhythmic *sploosh* of the oars sweeping the water. It's musical. I actually laugh, like a kid on a Disney ride. "Five! Six!" I yell, and so on until we're at ten. "Okay, paddle!"

We're coming close on the dock. If I aim away from the dock, we're going to run aground. "Weigh enough!" I yell, definitely *not* keeping my cool. Seb senses my panic and throws a look over his shoulder.

"Shit! Hold water! Hold water!" he calls. The word *fuck* does rapid-fire rounds. They dig the blades into the water and hold them perpendicular, which I instantly realize is equivalent to slamming on the brakes in a car. We stop, but the jolt forces me to grab the gunnels. After a moment, the water settles around us.

I put my hands up and shake my head. "I had no idea how much momentum you guys can generate." It sounds kiss-ass-y maybe, but so be it. Credit where credit's due. Panting, they grin. "Yeah," says Geoff, more in acknowledgment than in pride. Where's the chest thumping? Even Pearce is almost . . . humble.

But then it hits me. It's their *collective* raw power I've complimented. They're a real team.

I manage to get them lined up to the dock and out of the boat.

As the crew pulls the boat out of the water and flips it back on their shoulders, sunlight catches the droplets of water showering from the shell. I follow along to observe how they set it on the rack inside the boathouse.

"You were pretty fucking good until you almost killed us," Colin says, and the guys laugh. Even though I am a person who can poke fun at myself, I'm not sure if laughing along will signal weakness.

"Listen, he nailed it, for the first time," Seb says before any awkward pauses can happen. "Max has the terminology down." He puts his hand on my shoulder.

"Great job, Wayne Uff!" shouts Teo, setting off some hoots.

"And how about that U-turn out by the buoy?" Seb shakes my shoulder for emphasis. "Niiiice!"

Colin looks down at me, possibly considering me as a fellow human being for the first time. "You kind of kick ass, Max," he says. "For a novice. How'd it feel?"

All eight are watching me. No sarcastic smirks, no disdain. They genuinely want to know, I realize. And I shouldn't care about that, about their attention or about their giving a shit about my thoughts. I remind myself it's in their best interest to know whether I want to keep at this. But I do care. And I do sense something bigger than pure self-interest mixed into the air molecules around us. Is it simply a lack of condescension? Or could it be something different from that? Camaraderie? Without giving myself time to decide, I say, "I'm down for it."

There is an audible release of tension, including mine, and a couple of *Hell yes*es.

"We should get Chauncey to FaceTime him and give him some cox-to-cox training," Tyler says, fishing Clif Bars from a big jar by the fistful. He tosses them to each rower.

"Chauncey ought to love that," Devon says. "Giving all his hard-earned secrets to a newbie."

"He'll get over it," Colin says.

"He owes us," says Khalid. He takes a bite off the bar. "The asshole," he adds, chewing.

Seb has his phone out, and he's asking for my contact info. "I'll get him to send you the race recordings from his GoPro. We can start with that. . . ." His voice trails off as he appears to text Chauncey right now. "Anybody know what time it is in Guatemala?"

That was it, I think, watching them stuff their feet in shoes and chug water. As far as they were concerned, I was in. Two-plus years of social obscurity forgotten in an instant. It's mildly bothersome that it stems from *need* and not because they simply like me. In science, an event is described as *random* if it may or may not occur Randomness is the foundation on which the calculus of probability is based. Me coxing a boat with the rowing gods of Lycroft on a beautiful September morning in Whitney, New Hampshire, feels pretty fucking random, considering I am a middle-class computer geek from Hell's Kitchen. But I'd be lying if I said I didn't want to figure out the formula to make it stick.

CHARLOTTE

As I cross the threshold to our room after breakfast, I kick something across the floor. It lands under my bed. Stooping, I find a folded-up note. I smile, guessing it's from Seb. He's romantic like that. I reach my arm under and get it, carefully popping the tape. My smile fades.

The handwriting isn't Seb's. In fact, I don't recognize it at all. My stomach drops a little, just like last night in the boathouse basement. I lean against the wall and read.

> *Do you trust Seb? Are you sure he went to bed early last night?*

My heart drums. I poke my head out our door and scan the hallway, but it's empty. So I listen for rustling footsteps. I creep to one end, peering around the corners.

"What are you doing?"

I jump. Laurel Hartigan is leaning out of her room in her field hockey uniform with her hair in a towel. "Sorry, I, um . . ." I say. "Did you see anyone here this morning?"

"No. Why? That stalker thing is freaking me out."

"Right?" I weigh whether to tell her about the note and rapidly decide the gossip risk is too heavy. "I don't know, I thought I heard something."

She grimaces. "Creepy." She looks both ways, shuts her door, and locks it.

I reenter our room and do the same.

I stare at the note on the bed, like touching it will make it true. *Did* he go home? How would I ever know? The name scrolls before my eyes like an emergency tornado alert on TV. Sofia Bodenrader.

The magnetic dimples. The flirty glances. *Sofia's family and mine are old friends from the Cape.*

A small growl rumbles in my throat. But he gave me the 1856 Library key. Doesn't that mean something?

Ignoring the fact that Hannah's probably on the squash court with Hank by now, I text her a pic of the note, no explanation.

Their game will last at least an hour. I'll crawl out of my skin waiting until then. Keep busy, Charlotte, I tell myself.

Q, I think. Still want to connect with her.

Me: Hey Q! I can't wait to catch up. Want to go for a walk or get a latte?

It's ridiculous to think she'll answer immediately. I pace around the room a few times. Grace.

I ring her on FaceTime. "Please answer," I whisper.

"Char!" Grace's face pops on the screen. "Two FaceTimes in two days—woo-hoo!"

She's in her kitchen, and I can see her mom making something on the stove behind her.

"Is that Charlotte?" she says. "Congratulations on the dance thing."

"She's a star," Grace says.

"Thanks," I say, trying to smile.

She knows all my smiles, though. "What's wrong?" she asks,

walking to another room.

I tell her about the note and about Seb's seeming lack of interest in, well, me. She listens attentively, her face full of concern while she absently scratches her cat Elmo's ears.

"I don't know who wrote this note, and it's freaking me out." I stop for a big breath. "Grace? Help!"

She shifts thoughtfully in her chair and lifts Elmo, and I hear him land on the floor. "Charlotte," she begins. She never calls me Charlotte. "I don't know this Genetic guy, but I know you, and I know you run paranoid for reasons I will never understand. If you can't trust him enough to think this note is bullshit, then maybe he's not so great for you. I hate thinking of you doubting you're good enough. Just, no." She mutters, "I mean, Jesus," to herself, looking at the ceiling. "Look at you, you aren't even excited about Young Choreographer, and you've wanted it for three years!" She doesn't get it, and it makes me sad. How could she get it, without context? I'm formulating all the ways that Seb is awesome when she says, "Secondly, you're so wound up you're making me anxious. Go to the studio and dance it out."

I smile. On this, Grace is right. I need to dance. I can pour all these feelings into my project. Focus on making it perfect.

We chat a few more minutes, then hang up. I peel off my clothes and find a leotard, re-dress, and leave for the studio.

A few minutes later, I'm stretching at the barre waiting for Vivaldi's audacious strings to erupt in the studio. When I listen, I try to visualize the music's movement. It *rolls*, the opening to "Summer." Like big clouds, or waves. Reviewing the dancers' entrance I created with Hannah last night, I decide I've done okay capturing the score's energy, when a memory pops in my head: Grace and me, dancing across the living room to a similar rolling melody when we're around six years old.

Our moms went to Northwestern University together and our families are great friends. Our moms started us in dance together at age four. Then her dad left her mom. I didn't really know it at the time, but Grace's mom was clinically depressed for a while after that. Grace basically moved in with us.

I remember Grace's soft hands in mine as we swirled in loops across the carpet, around the sofa and coffee table, to "Clocks," that Coldplay song. Her nightgown bloomed around her legs like a big blue flower. Our moms loved that song in college, and mine played it a lot while she was housecleaning. It became a beloved custom of Grace's and mine. We memorized parts of it and presented it for Grace's mom in her bedroom. She cried.

Whoa.

Is that when I started choreographing? In the living room with Grace?

Oooh, I feel an idea percolating. I go to the wall and pull my phone out of the sound system dock and search Spotify for "Clocks" by Coldplay. I'm going to switch from "Summer" to "Clocks." Nobody will expect it! I picture Mom and Grace in the auditorium in October. What a great surprise.

When the piano arpeggios start, I listen carefully. They roll. They're big and dramatic, like Vivaldi's opening bars. I begin moving through the steps I've choreographed already, connecting the dots where the music is similar. Remembering parts of Grace's and my routine.

I replay it, trying out combinations, and I find myself laughing. Grace was right. Dancing always makes me feel better.

6

Saturday Evening Vespers

Q

Vespers start at 4:30, and the administration does a check-in, so I have to go. I have five minutes to make it over to the chapel. I use my chill playlist to keep me from panicking. I reserve Songs in the Key of Q for my nights. My dad's music picks are so wrapped up in his . . . person . . . that all the feelings I associate with him seem to pump through the AirPods and give me strength. Protection. Confidence. "Wildflowers," Tom Petty, is doing it for me now. *You belong somewhere you feel free.*

Once at the chapel, I hang back until the sign-in line is almost gone. Seb McNeilly walks up the entrance steps with the curly headed First Year. I scan the crowd for Charlotte. Nowhere. Is the First Year another bet between Colin and Seb? She deserves to know.

Seb goes to the Senior entrance; the First Year joins her friends. I accept the inevitable.

"Hey there, Quinn." Mr. Norbert, my former history teacher, sits at the sign in table.

I force a smile, diffusing the interaction by removing the Air-Pods and stashing them in my backpack.

He checks off my name, and I go inside.

Boisterous banter echoes off the vaulted ceiling of the chapel. I tuck my hands in my jeans pockets to stop the trembling and look for a seat by itself. There are none. The Seniors get the balcony, First Years are up front in the middle aisle. The pews angled on the sides are for the rest of us: left for Upper Mids and right for Lower Mids.

"Hey, Q. Want to sit with us?" I turn. It's Nils. He and Max occupy the seats right next to me.

"I'm still a Lower Mid," I say as amiably as I can, knowing full well Upper and Lower Mids mingle.

"That's okay. Nobody pays attention to us," Nils says. "We're the middle children, too young to be taken seriously, too old to coddle."

At the other end of this row, I spot Charlotte Foresley and her roommate, Hannah. I've managed to avoid her text invitations so far. "Ha. Uh, okay," I say before Charlotte can wave me over. I'm sweating and sit quickly. I don't think she saw me.

"Where's Alexandra?" Max says as I settle beside him.

This makes me pause. I face him. "You mean Alex?"

"Well, yeah. Alex. Right," he stammers.

I raise my eyebrows. He likes her. I instantly know it. It makes sense; we spent a lot of time together last spring with Outdoors Club. Our tents were next to each other at the last overnight at Mount Kearsarge. That was the weekend before the dance. I blink, remembering the ghost story he read aloud while we roasted s'mores. *I'm the ghost of the bigmouthed frog* was the refrain. He said it in a low voice, making his mouth really big. I smile. He's stirred up a little of the old me, like a breeze raising dust motes.

Max raises his eyebrows, and I realize I haven't answered. "I'm not sure where she is—somewhere. . . ." I look over my shoulder. Tucking this information away for Alex, I turn back and shrug. "Sorry."

Nils talks about how we're doing Mount Monadnock in October—two nights!—and I try to nod at the right moments. I can't imagine anything that doesn't involve my plot to get Pearce. Some part of me knows that's very sad, but it's faint, like a sun-bleached photograph.

Up at the lectern, Pearce catches my eye, the fucking pig bastard. I force myself to watch him, and once I start, I can't take my eyes away. Now he's shaking hands with Dean Frye, who wears a broad smile and puts one hand jovially on Pearce's shoulder. The chimes ring. Frye and Pearce nod simultaneously, like they hate to break off the conversation here, but . . . shrug. *We'll catch up later*, their eyes say. Pearce strides toward the back stairs to the balcony, and I stare into my lap.

Dean Frye takes the podium. "Good afternoon," he says a few times, until the room is silent. "Let's begin, shall we? Please stand while we join together in the Common Prayer. First Years, you will find prayer pamphlets in the pew shelf in front of you."

The recitation begins. I swear I can hear Pearce's voice over the six-hundred-something others, coming from above like he's the archangel Lucifer hiding in plain sight.

Don't be like that, he says. It's okay to want it.

My mouth starts watering like I'm going to barf. The prayer ends. Everyone sits. I swallow and rub the butterfly bruise through my shirt until I realize I'm gonna truly barf. I command my throat to clamp shut and stand abruptly, just able to whisper "Excuse me."

I bustle past the student acolytes, nod to Mr. Norbert, and race to the basement bathroom. I close myself in and drop to the floor. It smells like antiquated cleaning supplies and the white foamy soap from the wall dispensers, and for some reason, it conjures filmy memories of preschool. I think of Mom again, backlit, sweeping through the preschool door to pick me up. I run to her. My cheek rests on her shoulder, and I watch my pudgy fingers twirl her hair. My world.

As I close my eyes and take deep breaths, the nausea passes. I crack the door. The hall is empty. Dean Frye's voice carries on, muffled through the old boards and plaster ceiling. Ears don't squint to hear better, like eyes do, but mine fight to make out his words. He says, "I don't know why women don't go fucking rogue."

Even in this state of mind, I know that's not Dean Frye. That's Uncle Lawrence, this summer. I've relived this conversation many times. Because Uncle Lawrence brilliantly gave me the solution without even knowing it. He had consulted with his law-school buddy who does criminal law. "It's not fair *or* just," he said that night. "But there's not enough to win a case. A trial would re-traumatize her and for nothing."

"It's such bullshit!" Macy hissed. Her eyes were filled with tears, and I felt ashamed at the pain I'd caused. I'd frozen. I didn't fight. I let him do it. The black smoke slithered out from my closet, creeping toward me.

Uncle Lawrence continued. "If men were sexually assaulted as often as women?" he said, the ice cubes from his drink tinkling against glass. "We'd get violent. We'd get revenge. And you can be damn sure we'd make the laws work for us. But women—girls—a lot of them just have to get over it and move on."

Not me.

"You're going fucking rogue, Q," Macy said that night. Or maybe she didn't. I can't remember what's true anymore.

I stand now and face myself in the mirror. I have to wait for the head rush to pass, but eventually my face emerges from the speckled black mist. In my mind, I direct Uncle Lawrence to say it again: "I don't know why women don't go fucking rogue."

The sound of the student body's laughter vibrates through the bones of the building.

I slip out of the bathroom. At the top of a different stairwell from the one I came down, an exit sign hangs over a door. Late-afternoon sunlight, filtered through the trees, flits and flickers across the windows.

Applause explodes from the service.

I lope up the stairs and slip through the door.

I'm out, a defector. Fox-like, peering over my shoulder, I jog across the quad, heading for Somes, Pearce's dorm. This is risky. I put on Dad's playlist to drown out my heart.

The security camera, pointing out on a diagonal over the Somes entrance, is easy to bypass. I've seen its scope on the monitor in Anderson Safety. I simply cut in close to the building and move quickly under it. The building's open, of course. Inside, it's empty. Cool. Quiet. Pearce and Khalid Zia share room 115, a fact easily obtained via the lobby's posted directory. My chest feels oddly hollow, like just the shell of me slinks down the hall past 109 and 111. I imagine opening 115 and surprising Pearce. He'd be lying on his bed and would bolt upright. He would see the gun and put his hands in front of him, as if that would stop a bullet. "What are you doing?" he'd ask in a shaky voice.

"What does it look like I'm doing?"

"I'm sorry," he'd say. "I'm sorry, but you didn't put up a fight—"

POW

Room 115 is the corner suite—of course he wrangled the best room on campus somehow. The door is ajar, like a dare. An urge to kick it with all I've got zips through me, but I know I need self-control. After glancing a last time for witnesses, I ease it open with my elbow.

Immediately, I'm overwhelmed by the smell of boy. Sweaty clothes. Rank shoes. Grass stains. A big Head of the Charles Regatta banner hangs over a worn sofa in the common space. Of the two bedrooms, I'm guessing the one with windows on two walls will be Pearce's. I creep across the creaky floorboards. I bring my hand to my mouth, overcome by the thick scent of his deodorant or whatever it is. My stomach rolls.

This is what a rapist's room looks like. Pretty much like any guy's room in the school.

Absolutely fucking normal.

It's almost more than I can bear. I turn up the playlist, which is on the Lenny Kravitz stretch of songs. "Low" plays first, cool and confident. His guitar is always assertive, even in ballads—I pull it into myself like a drug. I move toward Pearce's desk. Tears roll down my face, but I'm not turning around now. I'm not.

A picture of him with an older brother and a younger brother and a woman—presumably his mother—at some formal affair like a wedding. She's pretty, but kind of washed-out. Tired, I decide.

Pearce's expression is impossible to read. Happy? Sad? Does he even fucking know?

Another picture: He's fly-fishing somewhere with a stunning mountainous backdrop (Montana? Wyoming?). I'm guessing the men with him are his dad and grandpa, and the older brother, all of whom—I know I'm biased—look like cocky dickheads, too. Then he has a bunch of crew team pictures. There are the medals. Trophies. A tennis racket. There are a couple hot-bathing-suit-model photos. There are his fucking retainers in the plastic container on his bedside table.

I want to scream. He doesn't deserve normal! He stole my normal! No matter how tight I've locked my throat, I can't hold back a string of sobs.

The song ends and I hear a dog bark outside, and I remember why I'm here. A glance at his alarm clock tells me I have about fifteen minutes before Vespers ends. I forward the playlist to Lenny's cover of "American Woman." The lyrics are perfect. Oh, I will be banging on your door, you gutless pig. And you will not get away. I crank it.

I start with the top drawer of his dresser and scatter his clothes everywhere. A smile creeps onto my face. I do the same with the middle and bottom drawers, and then I empty out the desk. I find scissors in there and go straight to his pillows. I stab into one, then the other, and rip them in half. I stand on the bed, shaking the feathers out and flinging them all over the room. He has a fan, which I flip on, and it creates a perpetual snow squall. Lenny rips a key change. I move to the closet and snatch shirts and coats off hangers, tossing them over my head. I'm having a fucking blast.

179

The guitar trails off to silence. I pause, panting. Without its power to fuel me, the destruction I've caused looks stark and disturbing. Shame throbs in my chest, and I need to run away from this, from this weird new me that tears a room apart like a rabid animal.

My foot catches on something, and when I see what it is, shivers run from my scalp to my tailbone.

The Italian leather loafers.

Shush shush shush.

It's okay to like it.

Shush shush shush.

My breath is loud and sharp and desperate. No. You are not running! I tell myself. I fumble for my phone and start "American Woman" again. Then I pick up the loafers and zip them in my backpack. I can't find words to attach to how right and justified it feels for me to steal these shoes. I have no idea what I'll do with them. But something.

I survey the room a last time, knocking his desk chair over for good measure. I decide I should also damage Khalid's room to throw Pearce off my trail. I mess up his bed and dump his drawers in neat piles on the floor. Then, in Lenny's words, *I gotta go! I gotta go. Yeah.*

I walk out to the hall and leave through the back door, which has no camera but is locked from the outside. I tune my phone to "It Ain't Over Till It's Over," and step casually onto the path.

Rogue.

MAX

Dean Frye rests his hands on the podium after the prayer at Vespers. "Nominations are now open for this year's Francis 'Fuzzy' Gilbert Community Service Fellowship." In keeping with the protocol of tradition, the place goes wild in choreographed rebellion.

"Fuz-zy! Fuz-zy! Fuz-zy!" Nils and I yell. There's something about six hundred people chanting together. A strange, wolfpack bonding occurs, if only in the moment. Bemused First Years look up at the balcony from their seats up front.

Dean Frye pats the air, smiling. "Service is one of the pillar values of the Lycroft Phelps education. 'To those whom have been given much, much will be required.'"

I whisper to Nils, "What about those who haven't? 'Cause they have to work harder than those who have."

"I don't think that's correct grammar," he says, his way of telling me to chill out. Then he adds, "Would you rather that we didn't encourage the one percent kids to think of anyone but themselves?"

"Fair," I whisper back.

"... contribution to community—be it the Lycroft community, the Whitney community, or community in some larger sense ..." While Doc Frye carries on in this vein, Nils gives me a puzzled look. He glances toward the door Q disappeared through. I shrug.

"This year marks fifty years since the inception of the Fuzzy Award." More cheering. "We will be celebrating with a special twice-weekly feature in the *Wire*, called *Who Will You Be at Lycroft Phelps?*" Frye uses his hands to help us picture the headline. "This series will highlight each of the forty-nine Fuzzy recipients. I would like to take the opportunity to recognize Upper Middie Hannah Hesse for bringing this idea to Journalism Club. Brilliant, Hannah! Please stand."

All at once, the entire student body turns to find Hannah, who is beet red and a few rows behind us. Charlotte, her roommate, is clapping and hooting next to her, and soon the rest of us are, too.

"First Years, this is a great time to join Journalism. I'm sure the Lycroft community will enjoy this feature for years to come."

We sing a rousing chorus of the Lycroft Phelps song, recite the closing prayer, and we're done.

Once we're outside, Nils asks, "Where the hell'd Q go?" He searches the crowd.

I shrug. "I dunno—she looked a little sick. God, I can't believe what an *idiot* I sounded like." I make my voice dorky. "Where's Alexandra? Dohoh!"

"Are you mocking yourself?"

"Yes," I huff. "My prerogative."

"Oh no," Nils says. "I hope she doesn't figure out you spank the frank to Alex's BabyBook picture."

I stare at him.

"How else would you grow so accustomed to seeing her full name written out?"

"JESUS," I say.

"Relax," Nils says, chuckling. "I'm just giving you shit. Anyway, much more importantly, what happened to Q?" Nils asked. "She almost fainted at breakfast yesterday." We start walking toward the rock gym, where we'll fit in an hour workout before dinner. I love that we both know where we're going without saying anything out loud.

"Maybe she had, you know, her"—I do air quotes—"'period' or something."

Nils stops. Turns toward me. "Dude."

"What?" I say, hands flipped open at my sides. "It's completely within the bounds of reason."

"Seriously. Make it stop." He waves to some lacrosse guys passing a ball on the lawn in front of the athletic center.

"It's a reasonable thing to assume," I mutter.

"I'm not sure you're in a position to judge." We are quiet for a while, and then he says, "You haven't told me about crew. How was it?"

I smile a little. "You know? I like it."

"Yeah?" Nils says.

"Yeah, like really like it."

"Douchebags be damned?" he says.

The jet-fueled moment during the power ten pops in my head. "They weren't that much of douchebags really. Even Pearce."

"Now you're bullshitting."

"I'm not. He's . . . kind of a team player."

Nils grimaces. "They're luring you in," he says. "Like trapdoor spiders."

I scoff. "Where do you get this shit? Anyway," I say, "I wasn't that bad."

He makes his Nils-is-impressed-in-a-mildly-surprising-way

face. "I thought you might have the skill set," he says.

"Well," I say, "full disclosure, they did have to do an emergency stop."

"How does that work," he asks. "In a boat?"

I demonstrate how they dug the paddles in the water, then add, "When those guys go full power, it's—" I shake my head trying to think of a word. "I couldn't believe it."

He opens the Bak Athletic Center door, and I follow behind. The smell of chlorine from the pool blows over us. "I finished that book, *The Boys in the Boat*, this afternoon," I say, backing into the swinging door to the boys' locker room.

"How did you do that?"

"I was going to order it, but I found it at the boathouse," I say.

He shrugs. "Makes sense. And you finished it already?"

"Yep," I say.

"Great book," Nils says.

"*Great* book," I say. I squeeze my eyes closed to concentrate on the quote I copied and hung over my desk. "'The enemy is resistance of the water, as you have to displace the amount of water equal to the weight of men and equipment . . .' Something like that."

Nils is almost laughing, but not.

"It pushes a lot of my buttons is the point," I add. "Thanks for the recommendation. The campus bookstore should have my copy by Monday."

"I accidentally talked you into coxing," he says, dropping his gym bag on the bench. "Didn't I?"

I imagine the black-and-white photos of the Depression-era rowing team in the book, the cox Bobby Moch with his ragtag crew of giants from U Washington, who overtook Harvard and Yale and eventually won gold at the '36 Berlin Olympics, even while Hitler sabotaged the competition. Moch's quick mind arguably brought them the victory. *The cox* brought the gold. I think I have a chance at that kind of underdog showing. Maybe. More chance than I do in Outdoors Club. "Yep," I say, dropping my bag next to his. "I think you did."

We spend the next hour belaying each other, talking about the Monadnock trip in October. We'd been planning it with the club leadership since last year. Monadnock is in southwestern New Hampshire, near the Massachusetts and Vermont corner. It's a great hike, and there's some worthwhile climbing on Black Precipice. Perfect, because not everyone in Outdoors Club climbs, but for those of us who do, we can play around on that. I'm almost at the top of the wall when it hits me. "Crap."

"What?" Nils asks from the floor.

I look down at him. "Monadnock is the same weekend as the Big Dip," I say.

"Are you kidding me?" He pretends to release my rope.

"Nils, the truth is, I don't even know if I'm on the team yet. The Beast is trying me out on Monday. If I make it, I'll just tell them up front I can't cox them that weekend."

"Damn straight," Nils says.

Honestly, even as I say it I know it will be impossible to get out of the biggest regatta in prep school sports, especially if I'm coxing "the fastest boat in Lycroft history." I tap the ceiling and start my descent. "Yeah," I say tepidly, then whisper, *"Shit."*

CHARLOTTE

"Where is he?" I mutter, listening to my boots crunch the gravel path in front of the 1856 Library. In preparation for meeting Seb here, I channeled Sabrina Godfrey's hippie-chick style. His old girlfriend was effortlessly cool. I'm in faded jeans, tall boots, a white peasant blouse borrowed from Hannah, topped off with a loose braid, silver hoop earrings, and a fat silver bracelet Heather got me in Santa Fe. My stomach flutters when Seb finally rounds the corner of Spangler.

We smile and it's like an invisible current connects our eyes. Inwardly, I shiver.

"You look hot," he says, kissing me. I telegraph a salute to Sabrina at Bowdoin. "Why are you still out here?"

"Turns out I suck at rule-breaking," I say, handing over the key.

He clucks his tongue and unlocks the door. I cast one final nervous glance at Anderson Safety before we slip inside. Seb pulls me into a longer kiss, closing the door with his foot. I'm liquid, per usual, recovering while he sets his backpack on the table and brings out a bottle of wine. He wags his eyebrows at me. "I thought you'd like this better than Scotch. I had to run to the boathouse, where I had it chilling in the lake."

"Aw," I say. "I wondered what took you so long."

"And I brought sandwiches. So we can eat dinner right here."

I'm embarrassed I actually brought my physics book in my backpack, but Seb's moved to the bookcase and is busy uncorking the bottle. I take my nervous energy over to the shelves, looking over the leather bindings.

"If you pull out the right book, the bookcase spins around to a secret tunnel." He pulls the cork out, and it makes a pleasant *floomp* sound.

"No way," I say.

He nods, pouring two glasses. "It was a safe place on the Underground Railroad. You haven't heard that?"

"Well, now I want to try every book." I toss him a mischievous grin and pull a blue one out. Nothing happens. I slump.

"I can think of a much better way to spend our evening than pulling a thousand books out of the shelf."

He sits on the sofa, and I join him, snuggling into his body. We toast and sip wine. He asks about the first rehearsal, and I tell him how I'm using "Clocks" instead of the Vivaldi piece.

"That's some rule breaking right there," he teases. "Granted, entry-level rule breaking, but it's the beginning of something big, Charlotte. I can feel it."

Then we make out some more, and I'm seriously becoming lava. He pulls back and looks in my eyes as he slides his hand up my shirt. "Okay?"

I nod, for fear I'll blurt out something that makes me sound as eager as I really feel.

A few moments later, he emits a small moan. "Holy shit, Charlotte, you are incredible," he says softly. But he stops, pours wine, and we sit quietly and drink. I think he's cooling himself down. I sure am. He hands me a wrapped chicken salad croissant, and we begin eating.

"I think . . ." Seb says, chewing. "I think rowing is a little like ballet."

I laugh, covering my mouth. "Oh?"

"Seriously. Like, the way you're explaining it, the dancers that aren't the soloist—"

"The corps," I offer.

"Yeah. They each need to be excellent but not stand out. Right?" he says.

I consider this and nod. "Yeah, that's true."

"In the boat, if someone tries to stand out—pull harder or faster—it fucks up the whole rhythm and kills the speed," he says. "If a dancer tries to outshine everyone else, she wrecks the performance. While in baseball or football, or pretty much any other team I can think of, every player wants to be the star. In ballet and crew, you have to work within the team. And nobody can perform better without everyone performing better."

"Wow," I say. "Deep." He blushes, and I drop my sandwich and climb on top of him, straddling his lap, unable to hold myself back. "You're right." I kiss him, pull away, and add, "You're brilliant," leaning in again.

And for the rest of the night, I stop worrying about what we're supposed to be doing and what this move means or doesn't mean. I don't care that he doesn't ask for sex. We're just equal. It's the best.

Doughty: We had a room ransack in Somes.

McPhee: Meaning . . .

Doughty: Somes, first floor. The RA reported someone trashed the corner room—dumped out drawers full of clothes and such. The door stood wide open when he came back from Vespers. Shit everywhere. No sign of the boys who live there.

McPhee: Whose room?

Doughty: Get this: Colin Pearce and Khalid Zia's.

McPhee: Ha! The RA probably did it himself.

Doughty: Right? The boys didn't want to report it. So, just another prank. A couple more and it will be like the Matheson prank rivalry of 2014.

McPhee: I loved that. Remember the piglets in the library? 😆

Doughty: I remember. Make sure you lock the kitchen up every night. I don't want any food pranks.

McPhee: You got it.

Q

Adrenaline is still throbbing through me when I get back to our empty room. It's the best I've felt in months. Unzipping my backpack, even staring at the Italian loafers, I can't believe I stole them. I need to tell someone to make it feel real.

I sit on my bed and dial the UK code plus Macy's number. She better not be too busy being Macy right now. Waiting for the connection, I watch kids streaming from the chapel toward Spangler for dinner. Last year, Alex and I always went straight to eat from Vespers. She'll come here first to find me right now. I'll need an excuse. . . .

Macy's line rings.

I spot Alex on the path. But she's not coming this way, and she's not alone. She's with girls from our hall, heading for Spangler. In the quiet between rings, my vision blurs with tears.

"Quinnie!"

I startle and turn away from the window. "Hi." I breathe in, reenergizing.

"How are you?" she says. "I was going to call you tonight to check in." This may or may not be true, but she means well. "You really should call Heather and your dad. They worry."

"Yeah, yeah, I will," I say. "Listen to this, Macy. You're not going to believe what I did this afternoon."

"Oh? Do tell," she says with slumber-party enthusiasm.

I pace ovals around our rug's periphery. "I broke into the pig bastard's room and ripped it to fucking shreds." I catch my reflection in the mirror. Not old me, not vampire me. Someone else entirely.

"Wait," she laugh-says. "Say that again?"

"I said, I broke into the asshole's room and I ripped it apart. Threw all his clothes on the floor, dumped his drawers. I slashed his down pillows with scissors and left the fan running. It was apocalyptic!"

She laughs a second short laugh. "Quinnie, that's—"

"That's not even the best part," I say. "Wait, can we FaceTime? You need to see."

"I, uh, okay."

I switch us over, and Macy's face appears. I flip the camera to the Italian loafers, akimbo, like he's sprawled face-first on my floor.

"Q, are those his shoes?"

"Yep," I say proudly. "Biondinis. Calfskin." I zoom in on the label. "Designer."

"Jesus!" a man's voice says. "Biondinis cost about six hundred quid at Harrods."

Macy sees my alarmed expression. "Oh, Oliver's home. Say hi."

I scowl at her, but Oliver, a handsome guy, and I exchange quick pleasantries. Then I scowl again. Macy shrugs wordlessly. "Oliver, would you get us lattes from Catarina's? And I'll just have a little time with Q?"

His response is inaudible, but I hear a door open and close.

"Next time tell me Oliver's there!"

"Yes. I should have." She looks at me for a long moment. "So, you vandalized the pig bastard's room and stole his six-hundred-quid shoes?"

I nod. "During Vespers. Not a creature was stirring in Somes. Or anywhere."

"That's a bit extreme."

"What?"

"You could get in pretty serious trouble for that," she says, like I'm ten years old again.

"I'm not stupid, Macy. The security cameras couldn't pick me up."

She tips her head. "Are you keeping up your appointments with Val? Because you . . . this has been a lot—so much—"

"Oh, come on, stealing the shoes was a fucking brilliant touch, Macy!" I smile. "I love thinking of him having to clean all those feathers and then realizing his rape shoes are gone."

Her eyes narrow. I want her to feel like me. Rogue. I consider telling her about my forays to Anderson Safety.

"You're kind of a buzzkill right now. They're the shoes he wore that night. He never even—" My voice catches. I can't say it. I hate how my emotions are so all over the place. I look out the window again, watching kids traverse the quad in the fading light. The lamps turn on.

Macy sighs gently. "You look pale. Are you eating?"

"Yes," I say.

She knows I'm lying, of course. "Q, I want you to find your happy places. Play your guitar. Do Thursday Night Café with that kid you liked, Nile, was it?"

"Nils?" Did I say I liked him?

"That's it. And paint, Q. Draw! Have you decorated your room with all your photos, like Val suggested?"

"Kind of," I say vaguely.

"Show me your side."

Grudgingly, I spin the camera toward my blank wall and unmade bed. My stuffed bear looks pathetic, facedown on the floor.

"Holy hell, Q, that would depress anyone. It's like cellblock H in there. Put up your stuff, the fun pictures and memories will help. I think. Maybe."

I glare at her without meaning to.

"Look, I'm no expert," she says, her pitch rising. "But you can't keep doing destructive shit or you're going to get caught. Then Heather will talk your dad into keeping you home 'for a while'—whatever that means—like Val recommended. Besides, it's just not . . . healthy, I don't think. You need to take care of yourself."

"I am not leaving. I'm not running away from him."

"That's good, Q. I tell you what. I'll call Heather and your dad and say we talked, and that you're doing okay, if you promise—*promise*—to do those things. I want a picture of your decorated room by the end of today," she says. "And send me a drawing or a recording of yourself or something."

"You sound like a mom," I say. The pinch behind my eyes is swift and painful. I can't say *my* mom; Macy knows it, too. I don't know my mom's voice.

Macy presses her lips in a line, and her chin dimples up. She inhales sharply. "You need to take care of yourself," she repeats, voice firm and sad. I hate being a burden, and I hate that I let this happen. The black anger starts to whirl. "Deal?" Macy says.

I shut my eyes. Breathe. "Deal."

After we've hung up, I drag my chair to the closet and pull the box of memorabilia from the shelf. I open it on the bed. The fairy lights lie on top in a messy heap, and when I lift them, I find my poppy painting from art last spring. I remember Nils singing, *Baby, you're a firework*, and it makes me smile and cry at the same time. I set it on the desk, propped against the wall, lost in the red-and-orange petals, thinking of how my life fell apart a few days after I completed this, wrecking the firework metaphor and everything else. I pull my eyes away. Pick Mr. Paws off the floor and seat him on the windowsill.

The silence in the room is dark and hungry and threatens to pull me into that black hole. I blow my nose, turn my chill playlist onto Alex's Google speaker, and set to the task of unpacking the box, photo by photo. Dad pushing five-year-old me on a swing. Dad and I backstage with our idol Stevie Nicks at Madison Square Garden. I remember pinning those pictures next to each other on the bulletin board last year, loving the contrast. Macy was there. We had talked my dad and Heather into letting her drop me off for my first year at LPS instead of them, since she was leaving the next week for a junior year in London. As it turned out, she transferred from Vassar to stay in London. With Oliver.

"Can I read this letter from Boppy?" she had asked.

We'd unpacked my bags, filling the closet and dresser. While I added decorative touches, Macy flipped through my memorabilia box.

"No" I said, stringing fairy lights over the bulletin board. "You should be tucking those letters neatly into the desk, not nosing through them." Macy's the only of my many Walsh cousins who isn't married (or divorced) with children, but like the rest, she graduated from LPS.

Sometimes we're like sisters. Other times she's too busy being Macy. It's a big job.

"It's from Boppy. How personal can it be?" Her perennial jealousy of my relationship with our grandpa is a long-running joke between us.

"Fine."

Macy flopped on the newly made bed and cleared her throat. "'My dearest Quinn.'" She cast me a stink eye. "'When I was accepted to Lycroft Phelps in 1949, my grandfather Walsh wrote me a letter of congratulations. His great-grandfather James was the first Walsh at LPS, and the family saying was that the only reason his father didn't attend was because Lycroft and Phelps hadn't been born yet! Imagine it. Six generations of Walshes in Whitney. We were there when it was two buildings, when it was all boys. We were there as it added land and sports fields and boathouses, rising to the highest rankings all the while. Your aunts Lucy and Cynthia were among the first girls admitted in 1972, forging the way for Macy and the other cousins.' Oh, he does know I exist." She rolled her hazel-green eyes.

I half listened, half admired the oversized furry white throw pillows we picked out at Pottery Barn. I bought some for my roommate, Alexandra, who was due to arrive later that day.

"'Congratulations,'" Macy read on, twirling her finger in a whoop-de-whoop. "'Your turn has arrived! I know that this will be a time of important intellectual and character growth.' You forgot sexual growth, Boppy!"

I chucked Mr. Paws at her.

"'You will make lifelong friends and memories to cherish when you're old like me. I have a theory, Quinn.'" She paused. I took my guitar out of its case and sat in the desk chair, tuning it. "God, Boppy," she said.

"Pouring it on a little thick, aren't we?"

"Don't forget, he's eighty-nine."

Macy shook her head. "'I believe LPS is the school it is because of all the Walshes who have attended it. We don't need to prove it to anyone. We know it. Put your hand on your heart and feel it.' Come on, Q, hand on heart!"

"Don't make fun!" I said, barely holding back my own laughter. I lurched for the letter, but she stood on the bed and lowered her voice, imitating Boppy. "'You are a Walsh. You will make your own impact, Quinn, and I can't wait to see what it is.'" She sat again, reading ahead. "Aww, this is so sweet," she said in her normal voice. "'I am so proud, your father and Heather are proud, and I know your mother is looking down at you in wonder. With mind and heart alight, forever your loving grandpapa, Boppy.'" Macy made a pouty face. "Okay, I admit it's adorable how much he dotes on you."

"What?" I said, playing the opening riff and only part I know of "Landslide," (the best Fleetwood Mac song, IMO), but a smile tugged at the corners of my lips. "Like he didn't write you one of those letters."

"You know he did not," she huffed. "But man, way to go ratcheting up the pressure on you with all that Walsh legacy bullshit. Quinn, just have fun here. Especially First Year."

"He's not pressuring me," I said. "Boppy and I get each other. He can't stand Heather, either. We're partners in crime."

And then Macy did a rare thing. She looked at me like an actual big sister and hugged me. Tight. "I love you, Quinnie."

I come back to the present, holding a bundle of pictures in my hand. I knew Macy was sad for me because of my mom that day, just like she was for me tonight. My mother is a smudged memory of bangle bracelets, soft skin, lullabies, and Chanel No. 5, her last bottle of which I keep on my dresser at home on a silver tray. Sometimes I can only conjure Stevie Nicks's face when I try to remember her, unless I'm actually looking at the photographs. Even though I've been okay with it for most of my life, Macy's hug that day felt pretty good. And her instinct to mother me just now does, too. Maybe that's why I decide I'm going to try to do what she asked. Maybe it's why I flip the music to Fleetwood Mac, the 1975 album, and then the *Rumours* album after that, and spend the next hour making my side of the room look like the person who lives here cares about herself.

When I'm done, about to snap the picture for Macy, I spot the Italian loafers, left out beside my desk. I have to avert my eyes. I flip the playlist back to "Landslide," manage to wrap the shoes in a towel without looking at them once, and stuff it all in the empty memorabilia box. While I sing with Stevie, I push that box as far as I can into the corner of the closet shelf and slam the door.

7

MAX

In preparation for Monday's afternoon practice—my debut in front of Coach Follett—I spent all day Sunday studying dozens of Chauncey's GoPro race reels and poring over *The Short and Snarky Guide to Coxing.* Seb gave me a box of Chauncey's coxing notebooks from under his bed in their room, which Seb thought might be helpful, though admitted he didn't know much about them. They resembled a mad professor's scrawling to me, but I read every one anyhow. Resuming classes today feels like emerging from thirty-six hours in a one-person submarine.

Charlotte sits in the same seat as Friday in our physics class, dutifully checking her work against the answers on the board, but greets me with a full-on smile as I enter the room. "Hi, Max," she says. It's kind of like she was waiting for me.

"Good morning, Charlotte," I say, digging my notebook from my bag. It's hard to ignore the fact that she's watching me. I raise my eyebrows. "Want me to check your answers?"

She shakes her head. "I heard you joined crew," she says.

Oh my God, I think. Khalid wasn't kidding. *Charlotte Foresley* knows I joined crew. "Yeah," I drawl, suspicious.

"Do you like it?" Charlotte shifts in her seat. She clearly has some kind of intel she's dying to share.

"Actually, I loved it," I say. In fact, I can't believe how badly I want something that didn't even exist in my mind space last physics class. "Wait. Did they change their minds?" That would be my luck.

"What? No!" Her grin is sheepish. "It was my idea for them to invite you," she says. "I *knew* you'd be a perfect fit. I feel like a fairy godmother."

"Thanks?" I say, deciding if that's obnoxious or not.

"You're welcome." She can't get rid of the grin, but returns to her notebook.

Pearce saunters in just ahead of Mrs. Lewis. He gives Charlotte and me a two-finger salute like we're all military cadets. "Wayne Uff." He nods.

I swallow a smile and gorilla grunt, "Hey." It's like the earth has shifted a few millimeters off its axis.

Midway through class, Mrs. Lewis instructs us to compare answers with our neighbor once we finish the problem on the board. I've worked it out, and while I'm waiting for Charlotte, I say, "Why did you do that? With the crew? I mean, I know I saved your dignity with the rubber chicken thing in drama class last year, but . . ."

She turns red, obviously remembering how she went rigid with fear in front of a bunch of Seniors. "That was horrifying," she groans, recovering with a little shiver. "First of all, they were obsessing over losing Chauncey," she says. Then she rolls her pencil between her fingers. "A cox is smart and small and feisty . . . you seemed perfect—no offense!" Her eyes go round, and her cheeks pink up again. This may be an alternate universe. I wait. There has to be more. It's just too random.

She glances backward, toward Pearce. "Okay, that, *and* I felt like they might invite some First Year."

"What?"

She makes like she's checking her work over. I wait. "Seb spends a lot of time with"—she glances back again, then air quotes—"'*the boat*.' I don't want the new cox to be a cute First Year." She steals a cautious peek at me.

It's like a quick double jab with a bayonet.

First, she's using me. *Oof.* Charlotte's placing me between Seb and any romantic rival—real or imagined. Just like the guys are using me, to fill a seat they can't race without. And just like LPS uses me and my awards to appear competitive academically. *Who will you be at Lycroft Phelps?* Oh, I'll be a fucking chess piece. The shortest one. Thanks for asking.

Secondly, she's punctured my Quantitative Hotness Correlativity Theory. *Jab.* Charlotte thinks Seb might lose interest *in her*? She's the prototype of a ten! Seb is, too. Do equal numbers cancel each other out, so that a ten can have the same insecurities as a five?!

Whoa.

This will require further examination.

I'm tapping my pencil pretty loudly against my desk, I realize, and Mrs. Lewis shoots me a look. I pretend to show Charlotte my work. "I think Seb's pretty into you, Charlotte. But, in any case, thanks for, you know, giving me a shot."

She completely misses the edge in my voice. "It's such an elegant sport. And you have a race already on Saturday."

"I'm not in yet. I still need the Beast's stamp of approval."

"He'll think you're great," she says. "Don't forget, they're desperate."

Triple jab.

Still, I tell myself she probably does *like* that she's helped me. Charlotte is that kind of person. Maybe her motives are a little fucked up, but she doesn't realize it.

Eventually, the chapel chime signals the end of class. Mrs. Lewis talks really fast, squeezing in the end of the assignment over the sound of chairs sliding over linoleum.

"Oh!" Charlotte says, remaining beside me as we leave the room. "I forgot to tell you about the stalker!" She proceeds to tell me about the boathouse party and how she was alone downstairs when she realized someone had broken in. "Terrifying," she said with a shiver. "But it's—"

"Matheson?" I say. We descend the stairs with the herd and pop into the sunshine.

"Yeah! They told you? And that Colin ticked off a bunch of Matheson rowers at camp over the summer? So it's their revenge?"

I smirk. "Hardly surprising."

"Better than a serial killer," she says, veering down another path.

"Infinitely better than a serial killer."

"See ya, Max!" she calls, walking backward with a wave. Like our history consisted of way more than a rubber chicken.

Q

Entering Drawing and Painting is definitely a test. The soapy smell of acrylic paints. The musty, earthiness of clay. Ms. Weller's warbled voice, birdlike and dignified at once. By the third step into the classroom, I see myself sitting at the desk by the sunny window, my Converse hooked around the legs of the stool, carefully painting the petals of my poppies.

"Q, are you going to take your window seat, dear?" Ms. Weller asks.

I shake myself into the moment. "I think I'll move here this year," I say, taking a spot near the door. For easy escape.

She smiles approvingly. "Ah! A change in perspective."

If she only knew.

The big table up front is covered with unusual stuff—her objets d'intérêts: antique eyeglasses, decorative ceramic vases, patterned napkins, a mounted speckled trout, a bonsai tree, and that's just what I can see from here.

"Hey, Q." It's Nils. He takes the desk closest to mine. I'm not sure if this is good or bad. Good, maybe, because I can't get sucked into the black hole if he keeps me distracted. Bad, because I might want more privacy. I remember my promise to Macy and decide it's probably good. "I can't believe I'm subjecting myself to another year of making terrible art, but"—he shrugs—"I find it relaxing."

"I found that, too, last year," I say. I think of those poppy petals. Over the summer, I couldn't draw anything. Couldn't focus, couldn't make anything look right, couldn't find the patience to make colors just so.

"Well, you're actually *talented*," he said. "I mean, that's a whole level I can't comprehend. I just like getting a break from calculators and essay writing."

I attempt a smile and tease him: "I don't know. That cow skull . . ."

"Come on," he says. "Be nice."

"Welcome," Ms. Weller says to the class, and I'm grateful to stop talking. But I feel that counted as the effort that Macy was hoping for.

After a review of the syllabus and how she calculates grades, Ms. Weller invites everyone up to take a closer look at the objets d'intérêts.

The students file up to the table. "Choose the one that speaks to you," she calls, floating from desk to desk distributing drawing paper.

I'm eyeing the bonsai when Nils picks up the trout and puts it to his ear. "What's that, little buddy? Sure, I'll pick you."

I roll my eyes but chuckle. "Epically bad joke."

He feigns seriousness. "Who's joking?" he says, carrying the mount back to his seat.

Kids make their selections. The supply is dwindling, when I get to the box frame.

Somehow, I read the tiny brass tag on the bottom without looking at the contents, like part of me knows to ease into it. *Leopard Lacewing Butterfly (Cethosia cyane)*. I inhale. Let my eyes settle on the creature under glass. Immediately, I'm mesmerized. Its wings have a bold black-and-white zigzag running along their edge, echoed by the body, which is striped black and white. But the rest of the insect is flame-colored—splashes of orange, yellow, red, and more black and white. Shimmery powder dusts the design. It is delicate, symmetrical chaos. My eyes stumble on the metal tack pinning the wings to paper.

My cheek twitches. A memory flutters through my head.

It's okay to like it.

I swallow hard. Pinch my arm hard enough to feel it in the back of my head. I have an urge to let my legs collapse and sink into a faint. Fall into the black.

I glance at Nils. Ms. Weller.

I think of fireworks.

I think of Macy.

I think of kicking that asshole Pearce straight in the balls with his own fucking loafers.

I pick up the box frame and carry it to my seat.

MAX

"So, when do you think the Beast will tell me?" I follow Teo, Khalid, and Tyler out of the Spangler kitchen into the main dining hall. We've come straight from the boathouse.

"Huh?" Khalid says absently.

Like them, I pretend not to notice a table of First Year girls watching us, all smiles. We file into position at the crew table. It's not like we have assigned seating in the dining hall, but there are unspoken rules, and one is that this is the crew table.

At first, I let them eat undisturbed, as one might a pack of coyotes on a fresh kill, but after a few moments, I try again. "When will Coach tell me if I made it?"

"What d'you mean?" Khalid says, mouth full. "Of course you made it, Wayne Uff."

Teo wipes sauce off his chin. "Dude, if Coach didn't want you, you'd *know*. The only question remaining is which boat you'll cox at the race this weekend."

The others nod and grunt.

"That's it? I'm on the team?"

"Hell yeah, Wayne Uff!" Teo says. "You're on the team."

"Let's give him a party," Tyler says, then begins to chant: "Wayne Uff, Wayne Uff, Wayne Uff!" Teo and Khalid join in. The whole room is staring. I'm half-giddy, half-cringing, when Alex Buchanan walks out of the kitchen with her tray. A miniskirt, gleaming white Adidas, a blue sweater. If we were in a movie, this is where we'd go into slow motion. Her stride is confident, cool. She greets a table of Lower Mids, sparking a smile to match the Adidas.

"Shh!" I elbow Teo in the ribs.

The chant trails off. Tyler and Teo are back at their food, but Khalid follows my eyes. "Alex? Wayne Uff likes Alex." He's weirdly perceptive for a Neanderthal.

I glare at him. "Dude, shut the fuck up."

Khalid grins. "Hey, Alex!"

"Dick!" I say. But to my surprise, Alex walks right up. "How's it going?" She smiles at me. "Hi, Max."

"Hey," I say, confused.

"How's Kyle liking UC Berkeley?" Tyler says. Kyle? My brain riffles through mental catalogs for someone named Kyle.

"He loves it," Alex says. "They beat U Dub at their first race last weekend."

I can't believe it. University of Washington—that's the storied rowing team from *The Boys in the Boat*. Does Alex have a college boyfriend? I can't bear it. "Who's Kyle?" I blurt, interrupting Khalid.

Teo, amused, says innocently, "Kyle Buchanan? Alex's brother?"

"A fucking legendary LPS rower," adds Tyler. "Team captain. Still has the ERG record for his five K. Sub six-twenty."

"Six-eighteen," Alex says.

"Wow," I say. Anything under 6:30 is amazing. "I didn't know you had a brother who went here." Duh, why would I know that?

"Yep," she says.

I can't do anything but look at her. Alex shifts in the polite way people do when they're waiting for you to say something.

Tyler swoops in for the save. "Max is replacing Chauncey."

Alex tips her head, considering me. "Max as a cox—I can see that."

"He kicked ass, first day on the water," Khalid says. "Coach didn't yell at him a single time."

"We're hoping he'll cox our boat Saturday in Hooksett."

Holy crap, are they gassing me up to her?

"First Varsity as a novice?" she says, nodding. "Impressive, Max."

They *are* gassing me up.

"You gotta come cheer us on," Tyler says. "We need more cowbell."

"Bring all your cute friends," Khalid says. He leans forward, "Tell them football is for suckers."

Alex rolls her eyes but smiles. "We were already planning on coming. A bunch of us from Outdoors Club were going to the Bubbles to boulder after that. Wait, Max, so you're ditching Outdoors Club?"

"The Bubbles to boulder?" Tyler says. "What the hell does that mean?"

While Alex describes the rock formation popular with climbers because they don't need ropes to practice, I contemplate two truths simultaneously. One: Alex did not forget I did Outdoors Club, ergo, I made an impression. Two: crew makes me cooler but cancels me from Outdoors Club. Oh, cruel irony!

"I don't have to quit altogether . . ." I say.

"Fuck yes, you're quitting altogether," Khalid says. "But don't worry, Wayne Uff, you won't regret it for a minute."

And sitting where I'm sitting right now, I can't argue.

CHARLOTTE

I'm so excited to get to the studio and prep for the first rehearsal. I arrive early to work on the new beginning of the dance so I'll feel confident introducing it to the others. Studio 5 has what my mom would call "soaring" floor-to-ceiling windows, filling the room with light and providing a backdrop of the forested foothills. I've always thought it makes everything that happens in here feel like a fairy tale.

Once my muscles are warmed up, I use the mirrored wall, moving back and forth across the room, playing and replaying the opening notes until I have nailed down how I'll get all six of the corps dancers onstage. I'm at the music dock when I see, through the mirror, Seb standing astride his bike on one of the trails talking to . . . I crane my neck . . . Sofia Bodenrader. "Goddammit!" I say. She's lighting up the universe with that smile of hers. Seb smiles, too. I hear her laugh, muffled through the glass. With a friendly nod, Seb rides off. Bodenrader vanishes around the corner.

I take a breath, tears stinging my eyes. They were just greeting each other, I think. It doesn't prove anything, I remind myself. He gave me the library key!

I imagine Grace's voice. *Char, dance it off.*

I crank the music a couple of ticks higher and go back to practicing the opening, aware Sofia is going to be up here in a matter of moments. Early, I note. Is she a kiss-up? Or a romance-wrecker?

"Hi. I'm Sofia Bodenrader," she says, stepping into the studio. "From your choreography group? You're Charlotte, right?"

"Yes. Hi," I say, unnerved by her directness. "I think I saw you at the boathouse movie night." *And outside just now flirting with my boyfriend.*

She nods. "That was fun, huh?"

Hannah arrives. She and I catch eyes. She misses nothing.

Sofia says, "A couple of my First Year friends are on the varsity team. And I know Seb McNeilly from Chatham on the Cape."

I force a smile. I'm annoyed she's already gone to a boathouse party, a feat that took me over two years to accomplish. She's going to own Lycroft Phelps by the time she's an Upper Mid. I'm also annoyed at myself for being so petty. I'm not a petty person, usually. Luckily, the other First Year dancers arrive in a clump. "Well, thanks for picking me," she says, then joins the others. They chat in that over-animated way First Year girls do—like they've known each other all their lives. My theory is they don't know who their friends are yet and they're terrified of having enemies. It fades by Fall Fling.

"I did *not* pick her," I mutter to Hannah.

"S'all good, Charlotte. 'Keep your friends close and your enemies closer,'" Hannah whispers, adding, "Abe Lincoln. I think."

I make a face. "That note," I whisper.

"Look, you've got rank on her in here," Hannah says. "And I've got an inside line through Littles. She wouldn't dare screw with you. The note's bullshit."

I'm not so sure. But everyone's arrived now, and I'm glad to return to dancer mode. While they stretch, I play "Clocks," explaining my vision of the forbidden love story. I demonstrate the sequences. The opening, with the six supporting dancers, then Gabby's solo, then Felipe joins for their mini pas des deux (while the other six support), and then all eight to the ending. Everyone is behind me, watching me in the mirror. Sofia moves her feet but stands in place, which, annoyingly, is exactly what I do when I'm first learning combinations.

Soon, I've forgotten everything outside this room. I'm so happy with their first attempts at the dance, even though we've stopped and started a thousand times. Yes, Sofia is a beautiful dancer. Full of magnetism. But all Madame's picks are great, and I feel grateful. Everyone, except Felipe, whose part hasn't come up yet, is glossy with sweat.

"Okay, take a break," I say. "Then we'll run it straight through Gabby's entry." Hannah glances at the clock and raises her eyebrows at me. It's six-thirty. Spangler closes in thirty minutes. "This can be the last time," I add.

But I can't stop myself, and we run it twice. It's a minute before seven as we sprint across the quad, some of us still in bare feet. Eight bun-headed dancers plus Felipe charging through the grass draws attention, and we squeal giddily, all of us performers at heart. Gabby and Hannah heave open the wooden doors, and we pile inside the Spangler lobby. A few straggler kids dot the dining room, and in the kitchen, the food service workers are covering up the last tray of lasagna when we tumble in breathlessly. They're amused by our spectacle, though. They fill our plates, find the baguettes, and roll the salad bar back out for us. We thank them profusely, and

I'm feeling proud by the time we settle at a long table in the dining room. Still, I take the opposite end as Sofia.

As the girls start leaving, I reach for my water bottle in the webbed pocket of my backpack and feel something wedged in with it. Leaning under the table, I see it's a folded piece of notebook paper. I jerk back, thumping my head. Hannah snorts. "What are you doing?"

I point. Her eyes grow round.

"Why is someone doing this to me?" I whisper.

She grimaces and shakes her head. Without having to say so, we wait for the others to go. Felipe and Gabby are last. "Are they a couple?" Hannah asks, watching them exit.

"I can't tell," I say. "Or care at the moment."

She follows me out to the lobby chairs. I open the note and we read.

Watch out. Seb's sleeping around.

"Oh, for fuck's sake," Hannah says.

"My heart's in my throat," I say.

"He can't be sleeping around if he's not even sleeping with you."

"Thanks a lot."

"No, what I mean is, the person assumes you're already having sex with Seb."

"Hannah! Quiet!" I furtively check for people, but we're alone.

"The point is," she says, holding her hand out for the note, "whoever wrote this doesn't know what they're talking about." She waves it for emphasis. "It's someone trying to make you paranoid."

"But why?" I say. "I'm a nice person!"

"I know that! But you're going out with the hottest of all the rowing gods."

"Straight rowing gods," I say.

"I'm saying, you're high profile now. You're the person people are jealous of."

I consider this. "That's ridiculous."

"Yep. But I bet I'm right. Ignore it." She dramatically crumples the note and shoots it perfectly into the corner wastebasket. "Three points! Forgotten."

I smile as she links arms with me, and we bust through the Spangler doors together.

MAX

"Max!" the Beast bellows from the launch, which is buzzing around our shell.

He employs a megaphone, the definition of superfluous. "Spin it!" Translation: turn the boat around.

I lift one hand above my head, the signal that I heard him. They heard him in the library, and probably at the Miss Whitney Diner.

At the beginning of the week, I would have thought Coach Follett was angry. But it's Thursday, and I have since learned that this is simply how he communicates. Yesterday, I asked Seb what he sounds like mad. Seb grimaced. "Eerily soft-spoken. It's terrifying."

I can wait on witnessing that.

"Weigh enough in two," I say into the headset now. The boys were at a good pace—not killing it, but working. "One. Two." Sunday is the first regatta of the season, against York Academy and the Derry School. Everyone says York graduated all their serious talent last year, so it's more like a warm-up for the Big Dip, the Big Six regatta. The Beast hasn't posted the coxes for Sunday yet, and he's had me cox the second boat and a JV boat this week, in addition to the 1V boat. Seb tells me not to worry. The Beast is getting a look at me in different situations, with different lineups.

At this point, the only comment I've received from Coach Follett came indirectly, through the assistant coach, Sam Brackett, LPS '12, Columbia '16. He slapped me on the shoulder Tuesday. "Hey," he said. "Coach thinks you're a fast learner."

According to the guys, that passes for positive feedback. At least it wasn't criticism.

"Starboards row, ports back it," I say now, turning the boat left.

"Dougie!" bellows the Beast. "Line it up with the 1V! We're going to race back to the second buoy! Fifteen hundred meters."

Seb looks at me. "He might be testing you."

Dougie has spun about. He's left twenty feet between us. We eye each other, then wait as the launch does its own U-turn. Sam is driving. The Beast, with his mirror Oakley sunglasses and Lycroft baseball cap, stands with the megaphone at his hip, watching.

"Attention . . ." he yells. "ROW!"

"Half," I say, which means they do half slides to get the boat moving. My voice is magnified by my cox box microphone. "Three-quarter," I say, picking up their pace. I listen for them to find the rhythm, and yell, "Full!"

A glance to the right reveals the 2V is barely half a boat length behind us. Of course those guys would love to kick our butts. Dougie will probably go high fifteen at the start, so they look competitive. Fine. We'll keep the stroke rate low until the last five hundred meters. Then we'll lay it down, I'm thinking when something dark catches my eye, poking above the bushes on shore. Someone wearing a black cap. Dark sunglasses. Unflinchingly watching us. Alone. A chill sweeps my neck.

Matheson. I almost say it aloud, which would be really stupid at this particular moment. But wow. That's extreme.

I realize Dougie is practically even with me. Shit. *Head in the boat, Max.*

"Ten high . . . on this one!"

Oh, the flying feeling. It's the best. The 2V slips from a half to a full length behind, and then we're just showing off, so I slow us. We're all on the same team, and I don't want to flatten the morale of 2V.

We pass the second buoy and glide to a stop. About two seconds later, the 2V passes it, too. My eight slump over, panting.

The launch putters closer and idles. "Nice showing, 2V!" calls Coach. "All right, that's it for today. You dock first, Max." Teo puts one finger in the air, but there is no gloating. Are these even the same guys I know on campus? They're surprisingly decent people. *Shockingly* decent.

We approach the dock with only the stern four rowing. I decide to ask. "Did anybody notice someone out there—way out where the trails are overgrown? Watching us?"

A couple of chuckles sound. A few *no*s.

"Weird," I say, describing the guy.

"Matheson?" Teo says from the front of the boat. "Those d-bags spying to learn our weaknesses?"

Two strokes later, Colin says, "They're taking it a little far this year."

"Is this a tradition?" I ask, adding, "Lean away," as we drift toward Coach Sam, who grabs Teo's paddle to guide us in.

"Not exactly," says Seb, grabbing the dock. "But it's not unheard of."

"They didn't like losing," Colin says.

Seb's eyebrows lift above his Oakleys, but he's quiet.

"Maybe it's time to whup their asses with some Sly—" Khalid says.

"Dude," Seb says. Seb's rarely this cryptic. I try to read his face, but it reveals nothing, and nobody else says anything.

Once the boat's on the rack inside, Coach Follett and Assistant Coach Sam call us together. "You looked good out there, boys." The Beast pauses, waiting for Dougie to guide the second boat back to the racks. "I want you all to eat smart and get solid sleep these next few nights. Saturday is not a blow-off. Regular practice tomorrow, on Friday, a relaxed three-mile run. We want to put up impressive times and keep those other teams thinking before the Big Dip. Everything counts. Matheson will be watching. Am I clear?"

I join the boisterous chorus of yeses. I *almost* feel like a member of the team.

"See you Saturday, seven a.m. sharp," he says. "Max!" he booms as the others disperse. My stomach drops an inch.

This is only the second time he's talked to me off the water all week. The pink lenses of his Oakleys make him resemble a mutant bug.

"It's nice to see you developing a strategy out there," he says. I nod. "A lot of new coxes would just have the guys row like hell from start to finish. You had a plan. That's good."

I nod again.

"You eased them up, though."

More nodding.

"We don't ease up."

"Okay," I say. "I didn't want to crush the second boat—"

"We go ahead and crush them."

I'm trying to agree with everything he says, but I hesitate.

"Losing," he says, "motivates rowers. It drives them to get faster. They want to catch the better boat. Always. Got it?"

"Yes, sir," I say.

"Good." He spins to talk to the 2V guys.

Coach Sam hoists a big cardboard box out from the boathouse. "Team unitards have arrived. Step right up! Come and get your uni."

"U-neeeee!" cries Teo. "I loves my uni!"

"Teo likes the way it hugs his junk," calls Khalid.

Teo puts his finger to his lips. "Shhhh!" he says, which provokes a volley of laughter.

The rowers drift over to Coach Sam, myself included. "Large. Large. Large," Sam says, tossing green-and-white bundles of Lycra to Seb, Tyler, and Teo. "XLs," he says, tossing another to Colin and Khalid. Sam regards me. "Small or extra small?"

"Small," I say, trying to keep an even tone.

"Small it is," he says, clueless, and digs around the box. "Here we go. Small."

Jesus.

"Wait, Max. You get a team jacket, too." He hands me a second bundle. "It's official." He smiles.

I gather the cox box and headset to return to its shelf at the back of the boathouse when I hear the Beast drop my name.

I peek around the boats. Colin and Seb are standing with him. I lean back and listen.

"—may not be able to win with such a novice cox. But it's a

good opportunity to try him out. You all just need to be prepared to lose and take it in stride."

They mutter acknowledgment.

"You wouldn't be in this situation if Chauncey stayed in line. That was a really stupid move. You're going to take the lumps for it, not the second boat. I want to see some good leadership from you two."

I'm "the lumps" in Coach's scenario. Awesome.

"Your job is to keep morale up, win or lose," Coach says. "No matter who's to blame." He walks into his office and shuts the door.

I walk out from behind the boats.

"Oh," Seb says. "Hey."

"Wayne," says Colin.

"I heard Coach," I say. "I'll prove him wrong," I add, to cut the awkwardness.

They glance at each other and then smile. "That would not surprise me a bit," says Seb.

Colin whacks my shoulder affectionately. "Hey, did you see we got a fucking A-plus on our physics project?"

"Yeah, bro," I hear myself say. Me, a guy who would have liked to punch Pearce in the face a week ago in the lab. "Noice," I add.

Seb's examining the bow of a shell on the rack.

"Fucking Matheson," Colin says, leaning in. A huge swath of the shiny yellow surface has been buffed to a matte.

"Is that from the graffiti?" I ask. "Charlotte told me about that."

Tyler, Teo, and Khalid come out from the locker room, followed by Geoff and Grey, who go upstairs. "Some guys from Matheson snuck in here last weekend," Khalid says. "Assholes. The Beast was pissed. Dougie pointed it out to him. Fucking Dougie."

"I heard. That's not a very creative prank," I say.

Colin says, "Yeah. Surely we can outprank that."

Tyler says, "How 'bout we go eat?" Apropos of nothing. A couple guys grunt, and we migrate out of the boathouse and up the stairs to the main path.

"I love good pranks," I say. "MIT is famous for its pranks on Harvard. Maybe we could do something like the MIT balloon hack at the 1982 Harvard football game."

Their footsteps stop. "The what?" asks Seb.

"You know, when they used a vacuum motor to make a giant MIT balloon grow out of the ground on Harvard's forty-sixth-yard line?"

Seb, Khalid, and Tyler chuckle. Colin grins. "God, I love this little dude. Did I make the right call, or did I make the right call?"

His inner d-bag returns, I think, as soon as we're off the boathouse grounds.

"Max was Charlotte's call," Seb says.

"Oh, yeah," Pearce says, and they all laugh.

"Wait," Seb says. "Rewind. What's this about MIT pranking Harvard?"

I give them a little history lesson in Ivy League pranking. They really enjoy the one where Harvard stole Yale's bulldog mascot, smeared bacon grease on the campus statue of John Harvard, and took pictures of the dog lapping its boots for the school paper.

"I love pranks," I say. "The best ones are funny, not actually mean. Or at least, not overtly mean. They're *clever*."

Khalid, Colin, and Seb exchange glances. Tyler seems not to

notice. I sense they're hatching something, but the moment passes.

"I'm fucking starving," says Teo when Spangler comes into view.

"Damn, I almost forgot—go ahead, I just have to let someone know," Seb adds under his breath, turning away from us.

Colin rolls his eyes. "Let's guess. Char-Char?"

Seb gives him the finger over his shoulder.

Colin says, "I don't know when he's gonna drop the bitch. It's cramping his style."

I want to say, *Jealous much?* But I value my life, so don't bother. I mean, Seb's the one who should tell Colin to fuck off.

As we walk to the dining hall, I'm blown away by the sheer number of people who greet us. Faculty, students, and girls. It's hard not to love it. At least I'm appreciative—Seb doesn't know how the mortals live, but I do, and my time among these guys is far from guaranteed. That's why I know I must act when I spot Alex Buchanan with Q, about to leave Spangler. I blurt, "Hi Alex; hi Q."

Q stops short, spins, and disappears down a dark hallway. Alex's brow pinches, watching her go. I hear Khalid chuckle but he gives a little salute to Alex and the guys move on.

We're alone, I realize.

"Um, hi?" Alex half-smiles, embarrassed. "Yeah, I don't know why she did that."

I shrug. I'm pitting out. I hope I don't smell. "Looked like she forgot something."

She glances after Q again and when she turns back her eyes are glossy with tears. "Horrifying," she mutters, looking at the rowers, then shakes her head, forcing a smile.

"Oh, those guys?" I say. "When they're hungry, their IQs drop, like, twenty points. They notice nothing inedible." Which is about the stupidest thing I've ever said. But she smiles and my pulse thrills.

She's in forward momentum. I need to say something.

"Wait." I hold her gaze. She's not looking away. "Uh, Nils and I are going to Thursday Night Café," I say. We are now anyway. "Want to meet us?" Me. I should have said meet *me*.

"Yeah, we're going, too. Or we were. We'll look for you there," she says, and I watch her leave until the door swings shut.

I hurry to catch up. "Yeah, Wayne, getting it done," Khalid says in a loud, conspiratorial whisper. Then he makes a thrusting motion with his hips, and the other guys laugh. I shake my head, giddy with possibility. As I carry my tray past all those old-dude portrait paintings, I think, maybe it's finally my turn at this place.

From: Coach Follett <thebeast@lycroftphelps.edu>

To: Griffin Frye

Subject: Merry Matheson Pranksters

Hey Grif,

Think I have the answer to your "stalker" issue. According to my rowers, it's kids from Matheson sneaking on campus to give the team some shit. Not great that they're able to get on campus so easily, but probably not a big threat. Just wanted to let you know.

Brian

Q

"Wow," Alex says as we pause in front of Café Lycroft on Thursday to peer through the window. "Kinda crowded tonight." Dozens of guests—a mix of students and faculty—fill the tables and bar stools. "Standing room only, I guess. I told you we should have come earlier."

I mutter something, but I'm pinching my butterfly bruise. She opens the door, making the overhead bell jingle. It's one of those sounds—so familiar you never noticed it until it signals entering a portal to the old you. Alex waves me inside. Shaky, I go.

My dad taught me long ago that music stirs up memories on a level deeper than words. Before Heather, we used to pull out my mom's favorite albums each year on her birthday. I remember listening to Cat Stevens's "Moonshadow" in the study, maybe two years after she was gone, sitting on my dad's lap as he starts to cry. We hugged each other so tight. I remember the bounce of his shoulders and the damp warmth of his body through the flannel shirt. "It's okay, Daddy," I said into his ear, which made him lift me over his head and shake me playfully, smiling through the sadness. He said, "God, I still hate this sentimental shit." I didn't know what that meant, but we laughed together and he danced me around the room.

Thursday Night Café has its own music—the buzz of voices, the hiss of the milk steamer, the chimes of spoons against cups and the door's bell as more people arrive. It brings me to a hollow place I can't quite enter. I follow Alex to two of the few free stools at the back and sit while she goes to get us cappuccinos. Everything buzzes around me, and I feel like I'm still on the sidewalk looking in the windows.

Alex is back, and I'm not sure if Max and Nils were already here, but suddenly they're on the stools beside us. I keep my eyes on the stage, where Karl, the café manager, adjusts the mic.

"No guitar?" Nils asks.

I shrug. My throat is froggy, and I clear it. "I haven't been playing much."

"I bet you're the type who can go two years without touching your guitar and then rip a bitchin' rendition of 'Highway to Hell.'"

The title makes me laugh, and I let myself look at Nils's face. "What?"

"AC/DC?" he says. "No? Eighties' hair bands aren't your thing?"

We're interrupted by Karl introducing the first act: a jazz trio composed of Mr. Ludecker, the band teacher, on the standing base, and his son—a Senior named Harr—on drums, and some other man on keyboard. I don't recognize the tune, but it's slow and lovely and has swing. In my peripheral vision, I see Nils tapping his knee in rhythm, and I feel the anger start to spin in my chest, I clench my jaw, tug on a small group of eyelashes. I should have never accepted the rat bastard's invite to Summer Sendoff. I should have asked Nils. Or maybe he would have asked me. And now it's too late, because I'm this gross thing that I don't even like anymore.

I can't stay here.

I tap Alex. "I have to go."

She squints.

"Wicked headache."

She starts to gather her jacket. Max looks alarmed, confirming my suspicion that he's hot for Alex. I shake my head. "You stay," I say.

She says, "You sure?"

I nod and quietly slink to the door. The bell jingles me out. I look at the sky. "I tried, Macy," I whisper.

CHARLOTTE

"Okay, we're getting better," I say at Friday's rehearsal. "Let's run it from the beginning to Gabrielle's entrance—after a quick break." I reset "Clocks" to 2:20 on my phone.

"Thank *God*," Skye, the other Upper Mid besides Hannah, says. Everyone laughs, but it's a tired laugh. Most of the dancers head for their water bottles.

Hannah wipes her mouth after a slug from hers. "Hey, I say we take a field trip to Pizza Barn after rehearsal," she calls out. "It's two-for-one Friday." Most of them agree.

"What about you, Charlotte?" Sofia Bodenrader says, patting sweat from her forehead with a cloth.

"Sorry," I say. "I can't." I hesitate to tell the reason but decide it sounds cryptic if I don't. "I'm going out to the Whitney Inn for dinner. With Seb."

"Oh, right!" Hannah says. "It's the four-month anniversary of Seb inviting Charlotte to Summer Sendoff!"

Everyone hoots, and my cheeks flame. "Quiet," I say. "Come on, let's run it from Felipe and Gabby's duet one more time straight to the end with the full cast."

Changing the subject works, but Sofia's eyes stay on me while the others take their places. Hannah rushes past me on her way to her spot. "Someone's jealous in here," she whispers, flicking her eyes toward Sofia.

Hannah and I exchange another glance, and I know she's suggesting that Sofia is my anonymous "friend." I shake my head subtly and return to my choreographer persona. "Okay, let's go!" I call. I'm about to press play when a text alert from Seb pops on my screen.

Hey, I have to rain check on Whitney Inn. Sorry! We can change the reservation for tomorrow.

My eyelids flutter, like he threw sand at me. I reread it, but the words remain the same. I want to text, *Noooo! I already have another hippie Sabrina outfit spread out on my bed!* But I just ignore the text.

I look at the dancers in position, waiting for the music to begin. Gabby's frozen in her lunge, chin and eyes up toward the ceiling. The other girls watch, leaning against the barre. I can't stop rehearsal because of a text from my—oh, screw it—my *boyfriend*. I feel an unexpected flare of anger at him for interrupting my space with such a crappy message. *Thoughtless*, I think to myself. "Dance it out, Charlotte," I whisper. I'll deal with it later.

I press play.

Gabby whirls into action, followed by Felipe, and then the two trios, like the cascading water I'd always envisioned. I imagine my parents and Grace sitting in the darkened audience of Imhoff Auditorium, like I have dozens of times before. Emotion swells in my chest. Gabrielle drops into Felipe's waiting arms. The other dancers fold into curtsies, like parentheses around the couple. Felipe holds Gabby inches from the floor. "Hold it for three seconds!" I call. "And *fin!*" I clap. "Beautiful already!" They unfreeze, breathing heavily. "You're so good."

They're exhausted and happy and start pulling on street clothes.

"I can pick everyone up at the circle by Longfellow House in ten minutes," Hannah's saying.

"All of us?" Lily says.

"It's the upside of a minivan!" she says.

I realize I could go with them now. I want to, too, but when Sofia smiles and says, "I hope you and Seb have a nice dinner," I can't tell if she's playing sweet or actually means it, and I can't bear admitting to any of them—but Sofia especially—that Seb is blowing me off. So, I simply smile and say the expected thing. "Thanks." I'm not even sure why.

When the studio is empty, I reopen the text. He's added:

It's a crew thing. I'll come by later if it's not too late.

I start a reply:

What crew thing?

Too suspicious. Even though I am suspicious.

Oh no! Not on our anniversary!

Too disappointed. Or needy. Four-month anniversaries aren't really a thing.

There is no way I'm waiting around for you all night.

Too angry, and also untrue.

Okay, no worries. I cannot.

I growl at the studio ceiling and throw the phone back in my bag.

Ultimately, I don't reply at all. He can decipher my silence himself.

Q

I've mostly stuck to Macy's guidelines over the week. I kept my therapy appointments with Val. Ate meals with Alex. Went to Thursday Night Café, for, like, ten minutes, but still. My one slipup, which I won't share with Macy, was midweek. I spied on the pig bastard at crew practice, which made me feel guilty and is why I agreed to Thursday Night Café in the first place. I *did* try to lose myself in art, drawing the butterfly obsessively, fixated on getting the scalloped pattern at the edges of its wings perfect. Many wadded-up attempts fill our trash can. Ms. Weller picked up on my frustration.

"I think you need to keep working on that butterfly, Q," she said, even though the class is moving on to the second assignment. "It's touching something important for you on a deep creative level."

I freaked, but when I realized she didn't have a clue as to *what* it touched, I decided the butterfly could fill the empty hours of the weekend. The hours I wouldn't be stalking. She gave me a crate of paint tubes to keep in my room. "You love color. Let it be about process, not product."

But now it's Friday and Dorm Dinner. Dreadful. Unavoidable. After that is the First Year Bonfire, an annual tradition where the Lower Mids organize a party for the First Years. Of course Alex will want to go to that. No way am I going.

All twenty of us are gathered in the dorm dining room. While RA Emily leads a game of charades, my mind drifts to the pair of stolen Italian loafers wrapped in a box in my closet. When we're sharing summer highlights, my dorm mates talk about concerts and travel and what they binged on Netflix. They laugh, debating which actors are hottest. Sadness ripples over me like water over stones.

I imagine a plume of smoke rising from the heating grate near my seat, twisting its way around my chair's legs. I want it to coil around me like a slow-moving whirlpool and transport me out. I don't know where. Out of *me*. I blink. There is no smoke, of course.

It's almost my turn. What if I shared the truth? Said, *Colin Pearce raped me, so I spent all summer with my therapist, Valerie. She thought I couldn't admit it, but really, I couldn't admit how fucking stupid I was. I couldn't believe how weak. How I didn't fight. How I lay there like a dead person.*

The anger raises another black cyclone, below my lungs. I hear it whirring, chirring. I am so *mad*. At the pig bastard. At myself. The cyclone moves into my throat. I want to scream it out of there, release it on this group of normal, happy girls. Naive, lucky girls, who don't know that their laughter is fragile as glass. How quickly it can shatter into a million irreparable shards sprayed across a statue-filled lawn.

Pearce appears in my mind's eye. He's right in the doorway of this common room, a focal point for my fury. I raise the gun.

BLAM.

Pearce crumples.

Alex nudges me with her elbow under the table.

I shift in my seat. Cough and sip my water, stalling. Everyone watches. "I, uh, I painted a lot. Outside. We have a garden."

It's quiet for a heartbeat, and then Emily says, "You'll have to show us some of your work!"

"She's super talented," Alex says.

And that's it; the conversation moves on. I feel Alex looking at me. I'm afraid she'll notice my missing eyelashes, so I position my face awkwardly out of her gaze.

I skip the ice cream table, ducking out for our room. Curling into bed, I pull the pillow over my eyes.

The anger blisters in my lungs, in my heart. For the first time, I consider going home, to my flowered comforter and Dad. I don't know how long I can do this.

Maybe I should just let him win. Again.

CHARLOTTE

"Did you and Seb get Uber Eats?" Hannah asks, rousing me from a snooze. She's lifting the laptop off my bed. I'd fallen asleep watching Netflix after I ate my Wok in the Woods chicken fried rice. I couldn't even bring myself to FaceTime Grace, who was probably at the Friday-night football game under the lights at Thornwood High School.

I wipe drool from my cheek and push my hair out of my face.

She sits on the end of the bed. "What's going on?" Her eyes flit around the room for clues, resting on my cute hippie-chick outfit strewn on the floor. "Are you trying to look like Sabrina Godfrey?"

I whimper. "It's that obvious?"

"Oh my God, did you and Seb get in a fight?"

I flop back and sigh. I'm ashamed to tell her. Which is ridiculous, but I am. I stare out the window for a moment, watching a pack of kids heading for the First Year Bonfire. Inhaling, I say, "Seb blew me off."

"What?" Her face screws up. "No! Are you kidding me?" Hannah does the emoting for both of us sometimes. "I know you're not kidding, but—" she says finally. "Literally? Without any explanation?"

I take my phone from the windowsill, open it to his message, and hand it to her.

"A crew thing? What crew thing?" she looks at me. "*'Drop by'*? Oh my God, he didn't show up here for a booty call, did he?"

I hate that my eyes are filling up. I shake my head.

"Because I would have personally kicked his ass." She comes in for a hug. "Char. I'm sorry."

I snuffle, resting my chin on her shoulder.

"It's very out of character," Hannah says. She picks up my blouse and jeans off the floor, hanging them in my closet. "Maybe it's that simple. He just had something he couldn't get out of with crew. Don't they race tomorrow?" She throws the white take-out box in the trash.

"You don't think he's screwing Bodenrader?" I grab a tissue.

"Nah," she says. "He'd have no reason to stay with you. He'd just break up."

"That's comforting," I say.

"You know what I mean," she says with a subdued smile. "It's not like you're married or something, or like he's never broken up with a girl before."

I sigh. She's right.

"I'm surprised he hasn't texted more," she says thoughtfully. "Although, he could think you're furious. And not speaking to him."

"We can hope," I say.

"I'm going to bed early. I get to interview Margot Pipkin tomorrow morning, but she's in Paris, so I have to Zoom with her at four-thirty." Hannah goes to brush her teeth, and I change into pj's. "Did you know she started Bigs and Littles?"

"No," I say absently, gazing at my phone. "Should I say something before we go to bed?"

Her eyebrows fly up. "No," she says. "He owes you A: an apology and B: an explanation. Let him—"

My phone lights up on the bed.

Hannah smiles. "There he is." When I don't move, she says, "Oh my God," and tosses me the phone.

I'm sorry our dinner got screwed up. I got new reservations for tomorrow night at six. Please don't be mad.

"You're killing me here," Hannah says.

"He says he's sorry," I say. "And he booked us new reservations for tomorrow night."

"That's all?"

I read: *Please don't be mad.*

"What about an explanation?"

I watch my screen. It darkens.

"Argh. You should say something back. Like, 'What happened?'"

The screen lights up again. I smile and read it aloud. "'I can't wait to wine and dine you, Charlotte.'" Then the champagne bottle and the bouquet of flowers emojis swirl all over the screen. I laugh. "He sent flowers and champagne with the echo effect," I say, showing her the screen. Hannah just looks at me. "But I haven't forgiven him yet!" I say. "I'm not replying."

She turns out the lights.

"You can't just let him get away with that."

"I know." Do I have the guts to make him explain?

"It's boundary setting. If you don't say something—"

"I'll feel like a doormat?" I say. "But if I confront him, he might

235

just dump me for being clingy." I can't bear losing him. Plus, so humiliating. We didn't even make it a month together on campus. It feels like crew's more important to him than me. God, sometimes I'm more jealous of the boys than—

"Wait!" I say, bolting upright.

"Mrumum?" Hannah mumbles.

My skin prickles. "Did Bodenrader go with you to Pizza Barn?" Nothing. "Hannah!"

"I need to sleep," she says. "Wait. No, she didn't. She said she had other plans."

"I bet she had other plans," I say. "Seb was her plan!" I see the perfect dimples and starlet teeth. "Argggghhh!"

"Charlotte, she's probably at the bonfire with all the other First Years. Seb and company wouldn't be caught dead at the underclassmen party. Now can we discuss it in the morning? After my interview?"

I chuck my pillow at her.

"Hey!"

"Sorry." I sigh. "Fine."

And I spend at least another hour spinning around in my sheets, definitely *not* fine.

Q

Maybe an hour has passed since I left Dorm Dinner when I recognize Alex's laugh in the hall. I grab my art history book and sit up, pretending to read as the door opens.

"Hey," she says. "What happened to you? Tired? Again?"

I hear the edge in her voice, and I feel horrible for being such a shit friend. I don't know how I could ever explain the simple fact: She can't handle me anymore. *I* can't handle me.

I say, "I'm sorry."

But Alex is kind. So she reels herself in. "I wish you were up to playing the guitar for us at the dinner," she says. "That crowd needed our version of 'What Makes You Beautiful,' and they needed it bad!"

I summon a laugh.

She pulls her hair out of its ponytail and brushes it, facing me. "I meant what I said down there. You are so talented, Q. Not many people are good at two art forms."

"Aww," I say, but it sounds snarky. I try again. "Thanks."

"Hey, I have an idea," She takes her Irish sweater and a long gray cardigan from her closet and stands in front of the mirror, holding each in front of her. "Bring your guitar to the First Year Bonfire tonight." Eyeing me through the mirror, she notices I'm in pajamas for the first time. "PS, get dressed! It started already."

God, how do I tell her I don't want to do something *again*?

"Well," I hedge.

Her spine straightens.

"I just took some Advil. I have a pretty bad headache." Not untrue. I rub my temples.

Alex is quiet and I think she's finally going to lose it on me, but then she's back to choosing clothes. After borderline slamming her drawer, she reels herself back again. "Are you okay? I'm not talking about just tonight." Her voice is thin. "Have you played your guitar at all since we got back?" She looks at it on her bed like it's a neglected child. "*I've* played it more than you."

I've heard her cry before, and it starts like this. Bringing up the guitar isn't about the guitar. She wants to know what the fuck is up with me, and she can't figure out how to ask. I feel the wall I've built. He's ruining everything. I need him gone off this campus. Macy doesn't get it. Nobody gets it.

Alex fixes her eyes on me. "Ever since we got back. You just seem . . ." She stops. It hangs there in the air between us, a live grenade threatening to blow my life to smithereens.

"Alex, really," I say. "I'm probably just PMSing." She smirks. "Tonight I'll get some sleep, and we can go running in the morning." I add in desperation, "I'll be fine by then."

"That would be awesome," she says flatly, pulling on socks. She disappears into the bathroom and brushes her teeth. Reemerging a moment later, she suggests some trails we loved running last spring. It tears a little piece of my heart knowing she's trying to tell herself she's imagining my moodiness. The old me would never do anything to hurt Alex's feelings. I loathe myself. I should run with her, I think. I will. I'll force myself. Tomorrow.

I notice she's paused and say, "Yes, any of those sound great."

Finally, she leaves for the bonfire.

It's too early to go to sleep, and I can't sit still. My skin is hot, and my insides are ice. After pacing around the oval rug for ten laps, I look at my guitar on Alex's bed. She's right. I haven't played it. It's another portal to before, and I don't belong in before anymore. Still, without picking it up, I let the pads of my fingers strum the strings softly. It's badly out of tune.

I lift the strap over my shoulder, feeling the body settle comfortably into its imaginary groove across my middle. Opening the Fender app on my phone, I find G and am winding the pegs, when an idea streaks across the universe of my mind like a comet.

The air in the room starts to buzz.

Holy fuck.

I push our door shut.

Flipping to my phone photos, I relaunch the video from the other night, the one where Doughty punches out of Anderson Safety with his big, burly shoulder blocking my view. I then tap on the function in the Fender app that translates a tune into musical notation.

Blip blip bleep bleep bleep blip.

On the screen, notes spin like molecules and atoms, busily creating the notation. I feel the pain before I realize I'm pinching the butterfly bruise.

Then, *blink.*

C-C-A-G-F#-G

It's there.

That's the fucking code.

Tears fill my eyes. I can go to Anderson Safety and use the app to match the keypad notes to the notation and open the door.

And get the gun.

I see myself stalking Colin. He's exiting the laundry room, alone. I step from the shadows.

"Q, dude, what the fuck?" he says. His eyes widen when he sees my weapon. "Wait!"

"Per order of the queen." I say it with perfect calm.

"What?"

"I told you I would have to shoot you." He's confused, but I see in his eyes at the last second he remembers our flirty exchange about the British Secret Service. His shoulders relax. He thinks I'm kidding.

BANG

BANG

He crumples over his basket.

My skin and my bones vibrate at two different frequencies. I'm jittery and hyperfocused as I search my closet, envisioning my step-by-step needs for tonight in a way I never have. I'll need a light and free hands: camping headlamp. I can't just carry the gun in the open. I dig around Alex's closet until I find her black mini Fjallraven Kanken. I empty three tampons and a travel toothbrush into her dresser drawer. I'll have to wrap the gun in something so it's not bouncing loose in there. I grab a T-shirt from the mound in my closet, stuff it and my black texting gloves in the backpack, then dress in my usual black ensemble. Once I've got my AirPods in, I scroll to "Tomorrow Never Knows," my favorite of the trippy Beatles tunes, and put it on repeat.

Outside, I welcome the prickle of cold New Hampshire air

against my skin. Across the quad in front of the student center, I see the glow of the bonfire and the silhouettes of dozens of kids crowded in clumps. My phone vibrates in my jacket pocket, but I ignore it, unwilling to lose momentum. The blue light of the Campus Safety golf cart zips toward me on the footpath. I lean into the shadows and watch McPhee roll by.

"Perfect," I whisper, and turn for Anderson House.

My phone buzzes twice. I grumble.

Macy: I haven't heard from you today. Update?

Charlotte: Hey, Q. Want to go to lunch tomorrow? Really want to catch up.

Macy: Send pic of your butterfly?

Me: It's bonfire night. Will send butterfly pic later. 💚

Me: Sick. Maybe next week? 🌑

I flip my phone to Do Not Disturb and pump up the music.

Turn off your mind, relax, and float downstream.

My Converse crackle over sticks and leaves. Moonlight splatters birch bark and pale rocks. I switch songs to "Masoko Tanga" as I reach Anderson Safety. Knowing the officers are likely to stay at the bonfire, I sing my way across the yard, dancing from foot to foot, banging my head to the staccato lyrics. When I reach the door, the song fades, like the greedy blue sky sucks up the words and drums and finally the guitar until all that's left is me, breathing. Alone.

This is it.

I pop out the AirPods and open the Fender app on my phone. I set it to listen, cover my finger with the glove, and tap the numbers one row at a time. 1-2-3.

All I need to do is match the notes to the number that plays them. I wait for the app's blue atoms to stop swirling.

Blink.

C–D#–E

So the 1 key = C, 2 = D#, and 3 = E. The code starts 1-1.

I play 4-5-6

D–E–F#

Okay, that's 1-1——6—. Leaning my forearms against the building, I scrawl the numbers on a piece of spiral notebook paper I brought.

7-8-9

A–B–G

I smile and turn my face to the beautiful moon.

1-1-7-9-6-9. I complete it on the paper and put it with my phone in my pocket and inhale, closing my eyes. I cover my finger with the glove tip. Exhale.

"One-one-seven-nine-six-nine," I recite as I press the keys.

Somewhere within the door, a latch clicks, and I know we're all in on this together: the moon, the stars, Sting, Euterpe, the Greek muse of music, and the wood of this fucking door.

I'm in.

I close the door soundlessly and press myself to the wall. As planned, I inch toward the window to twist the blinds closed. Blackness buzzes, resonating with the darkness inside me like the soft vibration of a tuning fork.

I clamp my teeth together and flip on the headlamp, which keeps my hands free, unlike the phone. The gritty floorboards illuminate, blinding white. I flick the headlamp switch to low, blinking until my eyes adjust. My pulse pounds against the thinnest parts of my skin.

I move to the desk drawer nearest Doughty's right knee when he's seated. The drawer slides out with a delicious wood-against-wood sound. Light pours over its contents. Three black things scatter, and I think it's bugs until I recognize they're bullets, rolling to a stop against the gun.

Three shots.

Three chances.

I try to conjure one of my fantasies of the asshole begging me not to shoot. Feel the thrill of him fearing *me*. But all I can see are the brown Italian loafers, shushing through the grass. All I can feel is him knocking my knee open like a broken-winged butterfly.

I froze on the ground.

The yellowing paper smell rising from the drawer hits my nose, and I'm suddenly five, watching Boppy at work in his office, rolling a pen between his fingers and reading over papers, white wisps of hair levitating over his head. I'm as far away from that little girl as I can be, watching her, suspended in some dark antigravity.

You're no killer, Boppy says in my head.

Wrong. I *wasn't* a killer. Everything about me is cold and jittery and unrecognizable. I don't want this body. It's wrecked. It isn't mine and I don't want it. I'm not me anymore, so what does it matter.

The headlamp bathes the open drawer in light. I reach in and wrap my finger around the handle and lift out the gun. The heft of it is empowering and terrifying. With steadier hands, I zip the bullets into a pocket of the backpack. Shut the drawer. I wrap the gun in my T-shirt and smirk when I see it's my "Who will you be at Lycroft Phelps?" shirt.

Colin Pearce's worst fucking nightmare, that's who.

I turn off my headlamp. I'm alone in the cool velvet darkness, or maybe a wormhole in space, floating.

No.

I'm holding the revolver; it's weighing me down, carrying me a step closer to avenging the animal that blew me into shards of glass—a shattered soul ripped from frightened bones by pig grunts and eel eyes and Italian loafers shushing me.

Careful to stay in shadow, I reopen the blinds. Moonlight falls in distorted stripes on the floor, illuminating my sneakers. They won't move.

You cannot freeze again, I say either aloud or not. *You're ready.*

My bones conspire, fearless. Femurs and tibias, ulnas and meta-carpals, sweeping me on. They know what's right. They won't melt away into nothingness like the other pieces of me. My bones, the survivors, turn the doorknob.

The rush of night air brings all of me back together with a *click-clack, click-clack*. I punch in the code, hearing the latch snap into place.

I'm on the lawn when the hairs rise on my neck. Someone's watching me.

Instantly I drop to the ground, feel the Fjallraven, weighted by the gun, bounce against my spine. I sweep the edges of the yard with my eyes, expecting to find Doughty or McPhee ready to jump me. But that's not what stops me scanning the woods.

There, staring at me, is a big cat caught in a splash of moon glow. As in, wildcat. Lynx maybe. Neither of us moves. She's hunched over her forepaws. Golden, with a dangerous face and brilliant eyes. Her ears are tufted. Definitely a lynx.

I'm not breathing.

She lifts her chin. Sniffs. Steps toward me, unimpressed by my camouflage. She holds my gaze with unearthly calm. Her eyes tell me the world is a dangerous place but she is not swallowed by fear. Suddenly, her ears flicker and she crouches low, looking toward some sound I can't possibly hear. She's still, queenly in profile. I'm overwhelmed by her majesty and feel tears on my face.

Then she bounds off in a hushed burst, her short tail the last thing I see before the shape of her dissolves into the woods. It was so surreal I wonder if she was a ghost. Or an omen. I head in her direction—toward the lake. She doesn't let me see her again, but I sense her ahead of me. I'm on the lower path when I see a group of kids coming down the hill toward me.

I duck behind a tree, and barely a millisecond passes before I recognize the gait. The long legs and roll of the shoulders.

Shush, shush, he walks away through the dewy grass.

It's him. With Seb and Khalid.

I swallow, close my eyes. I can't imagine where they're going, pointed the opposite direction of the quad and the bonfire—not that they'd go there. Seniors never do. The silence is sharp, poking me with bony doubting fingers, but I think maybe the lynx brought me here. I pop in one AirPod and let my playlist shuffle. Stevie Wonder's "Superstition" kicks my ass in gear.

Four songs later, we've left behind all the academic buildings and dorms and passed the hockey rink. They continue toward the playing fields, which are bordered by woods, and within the woods are the school's cross-country trails, ten kilometers of them. I smile. I've run these trails kajillions of times with Alex. The boys move as one large shadow past the baseball diamond. Then they disappear down one of the trailheads.

It's a maze in there, so I'm going to have to close the gap between us or I'll lose them. I hurry across the field, shutting off my music. I stop at the trailhead and listen but hear nothing. I tiptoe-jog, channeling the lynx and her silent, padded paws. I become lighter.

Finally, I hear someone laugh. I run faster, barely touching the ground. They've come here to get high, I bet. The trail sinks into a deep ravine, and the climb out is so steep it's known as "the Killer." With sudden clarity, I remember that this trail runs along the fence dividing LPS property from the neighboring farm, Bonne Champes.

Dad told me he got a discipline demerit once for cow tipping at Bonne Champes. More precisely, attempted cow tipping. Legend is, if you push a sleeping cow, it will fall over flat. It doesn't work. Cows sleep lying down, it turns out. But Dad said the promise of it was more important than actually doing it. He and a bunch of his buddies escaped campus, and the farmer called the police. Boppy was furious. So, is it the lure of cow tipping for these guys?

I bound up the Killer. The boys are hidden until I crest the top. I have to pause and calm my breath, hanging back as they climb the fence and spring into tall grass on the other side.

And, suddenly, I know now where they're headed.

The old barn Alex and I joked was haunted. I can picture it in daylight: peeling white paint, exposed wood weathered silver, the roof slightly sagging toward the back. This corner of the dairy's rolling acreage is far from the modern barns and fields of black-and-white cows that LPS families pass on their way to campus.

From the shadows, I watch the boys lope down to where the land levels out. Seb and Khalid slide the barn door open, creating a gaping black hole. They vanish inside. I shudder, because it's got a hell ambiance and they're just . . . gone. But the space inside lights up within seconds. Electricity? A volley of rowdy male voices comes from the trails behind me. I crouch behind a stand of white birches.

My heart bangs in my throat when the silhouettes appear barely twenty feet away. I flatten myself on the ground. Five boys pass, a few paces from my nose. I barely recover before another cluster of figures pops up from the ravine. They're hunched over, moving like an attack squad. They rush the first group and roar, scaring the crap out of them. They pound each other and laugh, and I've lost count as they all leap the fence and disappear into the barn.

I'm alone again, and I search the blinking stars, counting to sixty to be sure nobody else will appear. I lose count at thirty-three, but my gut says that was the last of them.

Once over the fence, I stumble across the rutted ground toward the back of the barn. I discover four evenly spaced, square windows. I cheer silently, then startle when I nearly impale myself on the rusted prongs of some kind of crop-cutting machine. I could have bled to death, and nobody would've found me for weeks.

I regain myself, huddling beneath the closest window and find that the glass is broken, providing me with audio and visual.

They're in a big circle in the center of the barn, heads lowered. I count twelve, each boy wearing . . . costume rabbit ears, the kind on a hairband. I have a sick feeling about this. Besides Khalid, Pearce, and Seb, I recognize various Upper Mids and Seniors from all the teams—lacrosse players, some soccer, and hockey guys.

The quarterback. Pearce flips through a huge book on a picnic table. "I hereby call to order the first meeting of the Slycroft Society, in this, its fiftieth iteration since its establishment," he reads.

Of course Pearce is the fucking ringleader of whatever this is. He loves control. I shudder involuntarily when the sound of his mouth covering my ear invades my head, then force myself to refocus.

"Hold up your right hand and repeat after me. I do solemnly swear . . ." the rat bastard says.

The group echoes: "I do solemnly swear . . ."

"To uphold the secrecy of all conversations and decisions made within these walls . . ."

Echoed.

"To execute all pranks agreed upon with my heart and mind alight."

Echoed.

"Slycroft first, self second!" Pearce bellows.

"Slycroft first, self second!" He produces a vodka bottle, and each guy takes a shot glass from the table and carries it back to his circle spot. "With this drink, I pledge loyalty to the secret order of the Slycroft Society." He raises his own glass. "Once a Slycrofter!" Pearce calls.

"Forever a Slycrofter!" the group responds, and they slam the shots.

He rounds the circle, pouring second shots. When he's back to his place, he holds his glass aloft. "Dicks before chicks!"

"Dicks before chicks!" This is said with special enthusiasm. *Slam.*

Restless worries ping around my head, beetles stuck in a lantern. This must connect to me somehow. Right?

The circle breaks up, and the guys sit on rails that I imagine once cordoned cows off from sheep. Seb McNeilly turns toward my window, and I drop to a sit.

I poke my head up ever so slightly, grateful for the black ski mask I'm wearing. And I really take in the space. They have decor. Banners strung from the rafters. Over in a darkened corner, a long table with flickering candlesticks, a quill pen resting in what I assume is a jar of ink. The oversized book, lying open. It's cultish. If I were the old me, I would be texting Alex right now. And it's weird, because for the first time in months, I'm connecting with the old me. As in, what the actual fuck is this? *Lord of the Flies*? A warlock coven? Are they going to sacrifice a frigging pig? What's with the bunny ears? Macy would be all over this shit, storming into the middle of the circle.

But I'm not Macy. I'm not even me.

Pete Crenshaw, the LPS quarterback, has an iPad and stylus in hand. "Any nominations for new membership?"

Three guys raise hands. Pete points to Ben Ross. "I nominate A. J. Ashby."

A. J. Ashby is in Drawing and Painting with me. Seb is still facing me, so I lower my head and strain to hear, staring at the banners up in the rafters, which, in gross perversion, resemble Buddhist prayer flags. A class year hangs in the middle of each one. The earliest I can find is 1973. And then there it is: last year. The year that ripped me from me. Flanked by colorful, misshapen flags on either side. I'm staring at them when the truth begins to take shape before my eyes. The colorful flags aren't actually flags at all. They're girls' underwear.

"Holy shit," I whisper, but my lips are numb. The last pair in the row, before this year's flag, is pink. Lacy. My breath catches in my throat.

I see myself at Rigby & Peller lingerie in Copley, blushing and giggling with Alex at the cash register. I see myself on the Amphitheater Lawn, searching the grass by Euterpe, unable to find my underwear. My heart thunders, my blood gushes through me, drowning the voices inside the barn. Realizations fling themselves at me, black crickets pinging off my face.

He *stole* my fucking underwear! To hang up here!

He knew what he was doing all along.

He knew the minute he sat down on the bench next to me, in front of the chapel, and invited me to the dance that he would have sex with me.

Let it be fun.

That's why it didn't make sense!

Because I didn't have the whole story—not even part of it.

Colin Pearce wanted underwear to hang on the rafters, and I was his means toward that end. His ride to rafter fame.

I spin from the window, rush to the tall grass, and silently dry heave. I slump over in a ball.

Shush shush shush.

No. I'm not running and I'm not shushing and I'm not freezing up. I'm not finding my happy place. I'm fucking taking him out.

I roll to a low squat and slide the Fjallraven off my shoulders. Unzip it slowly to retrieve the bundled T-shirt. I unroll that and take the gun into one shaking hand. Unzip the outer pocket with the bullets. I've never loaded a gun. But the rage silences any back-talk in my head. I open the chamber and drop in the bullets. One. Two. Three.

I'm not sure if the crickets I hear are real or in my head.

Chirchirchir.

I spin the chamber so a bullet will line up with the barrel, and close it. I cock it and sidle to the window. Using the sill to brace my wrists, I point it toward his chest.

He's too close to the others. Are they all predators like him? That's so evil I can't believe it.

I wipe snot from my nose with my sleeve, and I realize tears are soaking through my ski mask.

They're all lined up, using the feather pen to sign the big book on the candlelit table. Who do they think they are, the fucking Founding Fathers? With bunny ears?

Pearce steps away from the table, moving toward the big barn door.

He slips outside. Alone.

I uncock the gun, afraid I could shoot myself if I stumble. Hurrying around the back of the barn, I stop at the corner. He's facing the open fields, peeing into the tall grass. He looks up at the stars, waiting himself out.

I raise the gun.

He's shaking his dick. I shudder but command my thumb to cock the hammer.

Pearce's head pops up. He heard it. I lean behind the barn, pointing the gun at the sky.

He could come toward me now. He's so stupidly ballsy.

I listen hard. I don't hear anything. I steal a peek, again

grateful I thought of a ski mask.

He's just standing there, in the same place, his back toward me. There's no more than twenty-five feet between us. I level the gun.

My finger is on the trigger. John Lennon's there. My dad. Macy.

Happiness.

Bang bang.

Shoot shoot.

All I have to do is apply a little pressure. Over the top of the barrel, his shoulders are squared. It's

a

perfect

bull's-eye

shot.

I'm about to do it. I can finally do it. *Just do it, Q! He stole your underwear! He stole*

you

from

you.

The lynx.

My mother, silhouetted, at the nursery door, swinging it closed, singing softly, *Please don't take my sunshine away.*

It's like the nerves between my brain and my finger are severed. I can't feel the metal. Pearce turns. Walks toward the barn, sliding the door shut behind him.

All my blood drops to the soles of my feet. I throw my head back. Pull off my mask.

I kick my toe into the ground, hard—again and again until my foot aches. I don't know why I couldn't do it. My thoughts buzz in a tangled, quivering mess.

He raped me to get those underwear! I want them all to hear it. I hope they'd be shocked. Would they?

Tears run down my cheeks. I uncock the gun, open the chamber, and let the three bullets drop into my palm. I reload everything in the backpack, carefully rolling the gun in the tee, and retrace my path to the fence. My arms feel too weak to pull me over—I can hardly remember how I made it in the first place, just a little bit ago.

As I run back to the wooded trail, a black hole of despair is spreading inside me, sucking badass me into negative space. I wish the lynx would show herself again to inspire me to fight it, but since I can't dial that up, I go with "Monkey Man" by the Stones to sponge away the vast silence of the sky. I cross the sports fields, back to the main campus, reliving my fuckup dozens of times. I wish I didn't make any promises to Macy.

Near our dorm, I see the bonfire is just starting to break up. It's easy to slip inside and fake-sleep until Alex turns off her light. When her feathery snoring starts, I pretend it's the ocean and let it fill up my head so nothing else fits. Then she rolls over and the snoring stops. I can't sleep. My eyelids are raw. I'm roasting and cold at once. I flip the idea of busting Pearce in my head, obsessively, like I do everything else these days. If I called Campus Safety, they'd trace the number. If I left a note, it could be thrown away. At three-thirty, I whip the covers back and say out loud, "I've fucking got it."

"What's going on?" mumbles Alex as I rustle through Ms. Weller's crate using my phone flashlight.

I freeze. "Shhh," I say. I wait, but she's out again.

I find the tube of cadmium-red acrylic—the main color of my

poppies—and the fattest brush I have. Night air rushes over me as I swing the window open. I stick my legs out, shimmy my butt onto the sill, and hop to the ground. Popping in the AirPods, I scroll to the Stones' "Sympathy for the Devil" and toggle the volume until my ears vibrate. The moon is far away this late into the night. I cross the quad to Spangler. *Pleased to meet you, hope you guess my name.*

In front of the dining hall doors, I stop. They're heavy wood with ornate wrought-iron scrolls around the hinges, and everyone uses them. I tip my head, imagining how to arrange my message. Unscrewing the cap, I roll the cuff of my left sleeve and squeeze a sizable blob onto my skin. It's cool, and I smell the art studio. I smile and stretch as tall as I can.

Five words spread over two doors. I use an upward slant. It adds urgency. The wet paint catches the lamplight. It glows. When I'm done, I step back to admire my work. Tomorrow, students will come to breakfast and they'll see this and they'll know the truth about Colin Pearce. Dean Frye will find out, his coach, his friends. His life will shatter into a million pieces. Just like mine did.

The song switches to Lenny Kravitz, "Fly Away," which reminds me of trashing Pearce's room last weekend. The power guitar, badass bass, the swath of milky way above me, I ride all of it back to my dorm. When I crawl under the covers, I realize that, for the first time in as long as I can remember, I can't wait to wake up tomorrow morning.

9
Saturday

MAX

My R2-D2 alarm clock whistles and tweets at six a.m. A barrage of alerts scrawl across my frontal lobe before I even whack the snooze button. Race day. Breakfast of Champions at Spangler Dining Hall in thirty minutes. Use the bow pair to set the boat. Remind Khalid to keep his head in the boat. Alexandra Buchanan.

Nils is predictably catatonic as I examine myself in the mirror. My unitard is a bit loose, but hell if I was getting an extra small. I put on joggers and my favorite LPS sweatshirt. Before I leave, I lean over Nils's head and say loudly, "Dude, wish me luck."

One hand rises in the air. Nothing else budges. This amuses me.

I thump down the steps of my dorm. The sky has barely emerged from twilight. Last night at dinner, I suggested putting the Lycroft flag on the Matheson flagpole—either at the boathouse or on campus. Seb and Tyler loved it, and Khalid went to work on the logistics. It's a victory for me, to have their approval, even if I know how pathetic that is at the same time.

If we win today, my social life could be transformed. Of course, if I mess up, I'll be back to my usual life. So either I have nothing to lose or a lot to lose, depending how we're measuring. I turn my thoughts to Chauncey's technique pointers. We FaceTimed him after dinner. I visualize his tips as index cards in my head, flipping through them all the way to the dining hall.

A bunch of the crew guys are approaching from the other direction. It's good to be the first here, I think. A cox is supposed to be feisty, a bit overeager—in charge of the sometimes-unruly rowers. I would have been first anyway, because I'm really good at calculating travel times, but this may be the first case—*in my life*—when that isn't considered dorky.

I come up to the doors of the dining hall and stop in my tracks.

"Holy shit," I say under my breath, staring.

Painted in big red letters across both oak doors are the words *COLIN PEARCE IS A RAPIST.*

Suddenly, I wish I was the *last* one here. I glance left and right, as if I'm going to see the perpetrator running away with a can of paint. Of course my mind instantly conjures the stalker the other night. Is this Matheson?

The pack of rowers arrives. Seb slows to a stop. "What?!" He smiles for a second and then doesn't.

"Matheson really sucks at pranking," I say.

"Yeah," Seb says. "Uh, Pearce?" He scratches his head.

The others stop. Colin is at the back, and they magically part to let him through.

"What the fuck is this?" He kind of half laughs, but his eyes have narrowed into slits. I move back, valuing my personal safety. His upper body pivots, like he's considering taking a swing at the door. "What the fuck?" He whispers it this time, a singular shred of evidence that he's bothered by this. Everyone shifts awkwardly.

Colin sets his angry gaze on me. "Max, who did this?"

"What? I don't know," I say, or possibly squeak. And why am I the expert? In a strange way, it's a sign of his confidence in me. I step toward the door, breaking the invisible force field around it, and put my finger into the middle of the letter *P*. "It's totally dry." I hope I've proved I'm on his side and that I couldn't have done it myself, just in case he suspects me. "Someone must have done it once it was dark last night," I add.

"Matheson!" says Teo. "It's gotta be the assholes from Matheson."

"Why don't they have security cameras here for fuck's sake?" Colin cranes back, searching the eaves of Spangler.

"Matheson must think it could get you in a shit ton of trouble," I say. "Because there's nothing clever to this. At all. That's a really serious thi—"

"Fuck!" Colin says.

"Calm down. We'll clean it off," says Seb. "It'll be gone before anyone comes in for regular breakfast." I get the feeling this may not be the first time Seb's been Colin's fixer.

"We better hurry up," Khalid says. "The kitchen staff and custodians could see it."

"Cleaning stuff . . ." Tyler says. "Should we get it from Lindstrom Hall?" He points to the dorm next to Spangler.

A First Year named Wyatt says, "I live there. The supply closet it right inside the door."

"Go!" Colin says.

The kid and another First Year sprint for Lindstrom, leaving us to ponder the message. I wonder, for a moment, what if it isn't Matheson? Would Pearce . . . do that to someone? I side-eye him, all taut and pissed. But of course it's Matheson, and of course they want Pearce kicked off the team. Shit, they must really hate him.

"We don't need to wait," Teo says. "Rosario will be wondering where we are."

I think he just wants to eat, but I stay quiet.

"Yeah," says Colin. He pulls himself up to his full six foot three and struts through the door.

I look at Seb. "He isn't going to clean it himself?"

"It's better to let him forget about it," Seb says.

The First Years return with a full bucket and two mops. "We got it," Wyatt says. The other one is already scrubbing *rapist*.

"Yeah," Seb says. "Good. Get that word the hell gone."

"Is it working?" I say, peering over my shoulder.

"Yeah," Seb says. "It's coming off. You guys got it?"

They nod.

"Thanks. We won't forget it," Seb says. He opens the door and signals me to follow.

"Why would someone from Matheson write *that*?" I ask. "Of all things?"

His lips disappear, and he shakes his head. "Who knows?" Then, "But think of how bad the fallout from that could have been? I guess that's your answer right there."

"Because," I say, "Pearce would never really do anything like that." I'm saying it like a statement, but Seb knows it's a question.

We're side by side entering the dining room. He hands me a plate. "Pshhh. Nah." His expression could be either amused or bothered. He's inscrutable. Maybe that's part of his appeal. You can project anything you want onto this guy, and as a result assume he's smart and thoughtful. Deep. Empathic. Kind. In reality, he may be none of those things. He might be a shallow idiot. The looks are blinding, not unlike Charlotte's.

We've arrived at the banquet table, and he hands me a plate. "Welcome to the Breakfast of Champions, Max. Pile up and hunker down."

And, *poof!* We've moved on. I look around the tables of guys, digging into mountains of food. Each of them is either boisterous or half-asleep. Nobody is perturbed about the Spangler door. Okay, I think. This is how we roll. When in Rome . . .

I don't know where to begin. A towering fruit bowl, piles of bacon and sausage links, sausage-egg-and-cheese bagel sandwiches, steel-cut oatmeal, and Rosario's famous doughnut holes. I take some of everything. I didn't know oatmeal could be a side, but I'm all in.

The seating is pretty loose, but most of the 1V boat is together. I park myself next to Khalid and dig in. Soon, the tables go quiet as the team plows through dozens of sandwiches, fruit bowls, and doughnut holes. I snarf a fifth sausage link. This is a far cry from hitting the McDonald's drive-through on the way to a robotics meet.

Wyatt and his bud join us. Colin catches eyes with Wyatt.

Pearce suddenly clanks a fork against his glass, and the sound of silverware on plates stops. "I need to make a statement." He stands up and literally points to himself with two hands. "I don't need to *force* anyone to fuck me. One look at the Pearce trouser trout and BOOM!" Explosion hands. *"Girls Gone Wild."*

Someone pelts him in the chest with a doughnut hole. General heckling ensues.

Tyler calls, "We're eating, do you mind?"

Okay, I laughed. But I mean, for real? Thank God Nils cannot see me now. I lean to Khalid and say, "Why do you think Matheson would write that? Why not, *Pearce has one ball*?" He snorts. "Or, simply *Pearce is a dick*?" I take a sip of grapefruit juice. "*Rapist* isn't funny."

"I dunno, man," Khalid says, chewing. "Maybe they just wrote the first thing they could think of." He shrugs.

I consider this. "They couldn't plan ahead?" I shake my head. "We're going to pummel Matheson in the pranking department."

"And on the water," he says, pointing at me with a sausage link.

I smile, but a wave of queasiness sweeps over me as I remember how important it is for me to show up today as the cox. I return to riffling through the index cards of Chauncey Pointers in my mind and let the other stuff go.

Q

"Alex?" I hover at her bedside like I used to at Dad's on Christmas morning. Except I didn't have a gun under my mattress those times.

"Alex, aren't you hungry? Let's go to Spangler." Painting the truth on the doors last night has released something dark and heavy from me, and my veins feel caffeinated.

Alex mumbles unintelligibly. Then her eyes pop open. "Wait! What day is it?"

I laugh. "Saturday."

She covers her face with her pillow. "What time is it?"

"Breakfast time. Then running time and maybe go-to-the-game time," I say, shamelessly bribing her. She lifts the pillow. "Seven-thirty," I add, responding to her stink eye.

"Why are you dressed already?"

"Oh, I don't know." A lie. "I feel better today." The truth. I'm dying to see the school react to my message about that dickhead. Thrilled to think of him carrying a burden.

"I'm glad," Alex says, sitting up with a lazy yawn. She shakes her head like a dog. "Okay, I can do this."

In moments, we're walking across the quad. I see the doors in the distance, and my smile is irrepressible. Will Pearce know it's me? If he does, he can't say anything, but he'll have to live with knowing I got my revenge. I have power again. If, on the other hand, Pearce doesn't know it's me, that means there are others he's attacked. Maybe I'll find them and together we'll get him expelled. Arrested even.

"Are you listening to me, Q?" Alex says.

"Sorry," I say. "I was thinking about . . ." I watch a trio of kids walk through the doors without so much as a stuttered step. The doors close. There is no message. My words are gone. I stop. My heart squeezes tight, and I think I may be in cardiac arrest.

Where did they go? I didn't dream writing them. Who erased my words? I'm censored. My brain whirls into the same buzzing mess it was last night outside the barn.

"Q?" Alex stops, too.

I stare at her, unable to make words. I want to spin and run. But I can't leave her like that, because I would never be able to explain it. Maybe I should tell her. Right now.

"Q, what?" She blinks.

"I—"

Her eyes are concerned, and she doesn't even know anything yet. I can't sweep her into my nightmare. It's too selfish.

"Nothing. I—forgot to call home. Never mind." I walk past her, and relief floods me when I hear her footsteps in the gravel and she's next to me again.

"Hey! Nils!" she calls. Excellent, I think. Distraction.

"Hey there," Nils says. He's at the Spangler doors, right in front of my silenced words. I stare at the wood as he pulls one open for us. A trace of red remains near the handle like a trickle of blood. Otherwise, nothing.

They carry conversation through the food line. Rosario casually glances my way when I go for cereal, so I add a few strips of bacon and follow Nils and Alex out to the dining room. The crew table is empty, which is all that keeps me connected to the floor.

"Q, come with us," Alex whispers while Nils stops to talk to some friends.

"Sorry, where?" I say.

"To the regatta," says Alex, bemused. "Have you not heard anything?"

"I'm sorry," I say. I obviously will not be going to any regatta. I can't shoot him in broad daylight.

"You're acting so weird. What is wrong?"

"I guess I do still feel kind of sick today." At least this is true. "I need to sleep." *Because I'm a vampire*, but I don't say that part.

"You do look pale," she says, and I don't know how but I can hear her hiding so much behind those simple words. "Do you think you have mono?" she says, and I think she wants that to be the explanation of the crevasse that's splitting open between us. "You're sleeping *a lot*. And you look really thin. Not in a good way."

Nils has seated himself next to her, and I'm on fire under their scrutiny. "I'm thinking you best get yourself over to Knowlton Health Center."

Alex reaches to feel my forehead. Her hand melts my anger. I feel the black tornado in my rib cage changing to tears. I need to do something, or I'll crumble under the weight. "Oh, hey, I meant to tell you." I gently push her hand aside and crunch off a bite of bacon, forcing back a gag. "Did you tell her, Nils?"

He looks puzzled. "Tell her . . . what?"

I cock my head and raise my eyebrows playfully. "About Max." I look back and forth between them.

Nils gets it and grins at me conspiratorially. "I cannot tell her," he says. "But you can."

"You guys are freaking me out," Alex says, smiling uneasily. "What?"

"Should I?" I appeal to Nils. He shrugs and then nods. I like this conversation. I want to stay in it forever. It's easy and innocent and doesn't involve anything about me. "Okay! Max is crushing on you."

Alex's eyes narrow; then she laughs. "What?"

"You can at least confirm, Nils," I say.

"Yep." He nods. "It's true. But that's all I'm saying."

I can tell Alex is flattered and she's completely off my trail and I literally hate myself for being so manipulative.

"How do you know, Q?"

I tell her about our exchange at Vespers last week, when he asked about her out of the blue. "He's a good guy," I say.

"Generally speaking," Nils says.

After a few moments of eating, Alex says, "Then he did kind of try to invite me to Thursday Night Café. Am I taller than Max?" she asks.

I nod back and forth. "Hmm, maybe. But you're done growing. I'm sure he's still got inches to go."

She starts, eyes big again. "Nils, are you playing matchmaker? Is that why you invited me to ride with you?"

"Maybe." He smiles sheepishly. "But I also want company. You can ride with me to meet up with the Outdoors Club people at the

Bubbles. We can go after Max's race."

"Great idea," she says. "Please come, Q. You need some damn sun."

Nils takes a drink of his water, and he might be hiding behind the tumbler.

I squeeze my butterfly bruise, and it's like my heart feels it more. "I've got too much homework. Let me catch up today and shake this headache."

She's too giddy to argue. I try to stay in her realm of possibility through the rest of breakfast and on the walk back to our room, but I feel myself losing gravity the closer it gets to her leaving for the day.

"Hey, have you seen that little black Fjallraven backpack of mine?" Alex says, half swallowed by her closet.

I'm glad she can't see my face darken. "Isn't yours yellow?"

"Not that one, the little one. Never mind, I'll take this," she says, emerging from the closet with a blue-striped shoulder bag. "Sure you don't want to come? Vitamin D is good for you."

"Mmm, no thanks," I say. I know when she closes the door I'll cry. I'll unzip this gross iteration of me, leave it here on the bed, and crawl into the black cave of my closet.

And that's exactly what I do.

But afterward, hours later, empty of tears, my anger reemerges. I need a new plan. He did this to me, and he needs to pay for it.

Colin Pearce must die.

MAX

"Max." Coach Follett glances at me through the rearview. "Don't look so nervous."

"I'm not." Or wasn't, until now. I sit taller, flex my jaw.

"Good." His motivational strategy is puzzling.

Varsity coxes travel to races with the boats, which travel by the team's Ford F-350 Super Duty truck on a trailer. So, not only do I get Together Time with the Beast and Coach Sam, but Dougie Nelson is next to me in the back seat. Dougie barely disguises his resentment for me, the guy who beat him out for the 1V boat with no experience whatsoever. I can't blame him, really.

The morning is bright blue, temperatures still in the low sixties with a high of sixty-eight expected. I have sunglasses, but I covet Dougie's Oakleys about now, since the glare of the water is probably going to be more than these basic aviators can handle. At least I have my LPS baseball cap. For the forty-five-minute ride, the Beast regales us with his thoughts on everything from our individual race plans to his hope for "varsity parking" close to the launching dock. It's like he loosens up in the truck or something.

When he's pulling into Hooksett Rowing Club's driveway, he says, "Dougie, your boat should have a good race today. The 2V times are strong compared to Dover's and York's." Dougie nods even though Coach isn't looking at him. I wait for Coach's prediction for the first boat. Nothing.

A flagger waves us through the gates. We inch past throngs of pedestrians carrying camp chairs across acres of grassy lawn in a pilgrimage toward the riverbank, which forms the eastern periphery of the park. "This place is hopping," I say.

Coach Sam says, "Hooksett's a US Rowing–sponsored event."

"Yeah, there are something like fifty teams here," Coach Follett says. "Club masters race today, too. They use it as a warm-up for Head of the Charles."

We roll past team tents, food trucks, and Hooksett Cup merch tables until we get our assigned spot fairly close to the launching dock, but not close enough I gather, based on the Beast's grumblings. The team bus arrives right behind us, and as the rowers unload, I overhear Dougie talking to the Beast.

"If he doesn't seem ready, I'm happy to take over the 1V for the Big Dip," he's saying, the smug shithead.

Coach Follett nods, surveying the river in his impenetrable pink Oakleys. "We'll see." He turns to Coach Sam, and they confer over clipboards.

Fucking great.

After we set up the food table and drag the coolers out of the trailer, Seb says, "Hey, the boat's going for a warm-up run. Want to come?"

All eight of them wait for me on a path called, according to the sign, the Promenade. I take a mental assessment: I'm a decent runner; they'll be taking it easy. "Sure," I say, and join the pack.

We're stripped down to our unis, and I know we make quite

a spectacle, and although nobody mentions it, I've guessed this pre-race run is an intimidation tactic. Yes, LPS is a more elite and more expensive school than Derry Prep and York and all these other places I've never heard of. Yes, we have unitards and more new shells than hand-me-down shells. I know that it's shallow of me to garner any kind of confidence from this. A: I'm a scholarship kid. B: trading on status and wealth is such crap behavior. But here I am, part of this knot of alpha wolves who turn the heads of guys and girls, of men and women. I can't be blamed for enjoying the sheer novelty of it.

We're rounding the bend near the entrance of the park when a silver Honda minivan rolls through the gates. We jog in place, waiting for it to pull ahead of us. The windows roll down and a slew of girls throw their arms in the air.

"Go, Lycroft! Woo-hooo!"

"Hey!" Seb calls, grinning and barely breathless.

Hannah Hesse is driving a bunch of cheering First Years.

"I'd hit any one of those," Khalid mumbles.

"I still got dibs on Bodenrader," Pearce says. "That girl wants dick."

God, I wish someone would call him out for once.

"How about you, Max?" Colin says. "Who are you hot for?"

At that very moment, Nils's Jeep Wrangler appears, and he's got Alexandra Buchanan in the passenger seat. Alex. I become hyperaware of the uni. And that I'm ten inches shorter than the rest of these guys. Nils waves with a giant grin. Another couple kids in the back wave LPS banners and hoot for us as they drive by, but I can't process who they are.

"Shit!" I say.

Khalid wags his eyebrows. I shoot him a warning look.

Pearce knowing my love interest? What could go wrong? I brace myself for heckling, but Khalid stays quiet. But the fan wagons roll on and we're running again. Fortunately, these guys don't spend much time on any topic, I realize. And as we cause more heads to turn, I begin to get it. I start to feel like I'm in a school of fish. Really badass, untouchable fish.

I'm glad we ran, because even with that energy expended, I'm wound tight waiting for our race. I pace the launching area, studying how other coxes get their boats in the water and back to the dock after their races are done.

When the time comes to guide the guys with the boat on their shoulders to the water, the Beast is hovering. "Heads," he barks a millisecond before I can. The crowd scatters left and right. I wish he would trust me.

"Don't worry about the Beast," Seb says. "He can't stop himself."

I nod. Seb is all right.

After loading, we row 5K up the river at a leisurely pace and wait to be called to the starting line. The good news is that in the fall, all the races are head races, which means boats start at staggered times and the best time wins, as opposed to actually racing with boats side by side. But there is bad news, too. You have to start paddling ahead of the starting line and get up to full speed by the time you cross, so when the official tells you you're on the clock, you're already at full power.

We're waiting, in neutral as it were, near the starting line. York

269

is about to go. I'm not so much watching as I am flipping through Chauncey's Pointers in my head.

"Lycroft Phelps, on the paddle," the official says from a launch near the starting buoys.

This is it. My moment.

"All eight on the paddle. Ready all. Row," I say into my cox mic. "Quarter pressure." The start buoy is getting closer, and by some gut instinct, I know to say, "Three-quarter pressure." And then, "Full pressure!"

We go two strokes. "On the clock, Lycroft Phelps," says the official.

Perfect start.

We're off.

I'm checking the stroke rate, watching the distance, the time on the cox box. Chauncy said not to talk at them all the time, so I'm measured in my calls. They're doing well; at the 1,000-meter mark, they're about two seconds faster than the typical time. We come around a turn and the cheering and cowbells erupt from the shore. Like Chauncey warned, a couple of my rowers try to steal a look. "Head in the boat! We're two lengths down from York, boys." I eye the distance between us and the orange finish buoy. It's time to sprint anyway, but I think we can pass York, and if we overtake the boat that started a minute ahead of us, we'll feel like kings.

"Power ten in two, boys," I say evenly. In control. I have the headset, so I don't need to yell. (Another Chauncy tip.) "One. Two. Three. Four."

York's cox hears me and shouts commands.

"Five! Six!" I keep counting. Louder, but restrained. We're barely a quarter boat length from them. "Seven! Eight!" We're even. Now my rowers can hear the York rowers, and Seb does something, kicks the stroke pace into a gear beyond their highest gear. We fly for the nine and ten count and three more strokes after that, right past the finish buoy.

I want to jump up and scream hallelujah, which I can't do for several obvious reasons. The boys flop over like balloons losing helium, and we coast past the dock. The Beast and Coach Sam cheer. "All right! Nice work, Lycroft Phelps!" Onshore, a wall of green and white cheering and ringing bells. And there she is, swinging a cowbell.

Alexandra Buchanan.

A minute or so after their utter collapse, the boys start popping back to life.

"Fucking Max!" Tyler calls from the rear.

"Hot shit, man!" Colin beams. "I knew you'd be good, Wayne Uff!"

"You guys were so on!" I say.

"Dude," says Khalid. "Your girl Alex B. saw that."

"Oooooooh," Colin says, and soon they're all at it. The alphas having fun *with* me, not at my expense.

"Shut up! She's not my girl." I totally sound like my little brother in sixth grade, and it's admittedly funny as hell.

"She will be," Colin says, wagging a finger at me. "She will."

We dock, and Coach Follett swats my shoulder. He flips up his sunglasses. "Max! Stellar! Overtaking York's 1V? You found your point and got the shortest line!" He's looking at the sky, arms wide. "That was—hell, I'm just gonna say it—that was fucking five-star coxing!"

Teo starts the chanting. "Lycroft Phelps! Lycroft Phelps!" We all join in, and then Teo yells, "Wayne! Uff! Wayne! Uff!"

I can't stop laughing. They close in around me like a huddle. "Wayne Uff! Wayne Uff! Lycroft Phelps!" And all of a sudden, someone grabs my ankles and I fall back into the other's arms. Khalid and Tyler have my feet; Seb and Colin have my wrists. I'm still dizzy and laughing and also a little terrified. There isn't a single thing I can do but try to keep from pissing myself.

"On three!" yells Seb.

The pack of them boom:

"One—

"Two—

"Three—"

I sail through the air, an upward arc, peaking somewhere near the moon. I twist myself around midair and begin the descent. Down, down, down—*Splash!* I laugh even though the water is frigid, even though that was a belly flop of capillary-bursting proportions. I push off the squishy bottom and pop out of the water to a raucous cheer. Khalid and Seb haul me onto the dock, and then the moment trails off. I lie flat on my back, soaking in the sun-warmed boards beneath my wet uni, feeling the goose bumps on my skin, and breathe. All the numbers from the Hotness Correlativity Theory don't matter, I realize at once. It's not about numbers. It's about belonging somewhere.

Teo and Geoff hold outstretched hands to me. I take them.

"Let's eat," Teo says.

❖ • ❖

Later, I've changed clothes and am hanging with Teo and Geoff, watching the other races, when I feel a tap on the shoulder.

"Hey, Max," Nils says, grinning, next to Alex Buchanan. "That was great, man. How'd you feel?"

I stand, brushing grass off my shorts, and smile, ready to kill him. A little heads-up, Nils? I telegraph. He knows.

"Great," I say as nonchalantly as a guy inches from his dream girl can. I try to channel Seb's vibe. "The guys kicked it out." I lost my cheap sunglasses in the water, so I shield my eyes with my hand. "Hi, Alex."

"Hey, Max," she says. This close, I see her teeth are perfectly straight. "Congrats on the win."

I nod graciously. "You guys want to get some hot dogs? We have tons."

"Sure," says Alex. "I'm starving."

"Nah, I'm good," Nils says. I can't decide whether I want to kill him or hug him.

That's me, walking with Alex Buchanan to the LPS food tent.

"Hey," she says as we navigate the spectator traffic. "If you don't come back to Outdoors Club, who'll tell the ghost stories?"

I make a *pshhh* sound. "Chauncey won't let me stay in that boat," I say. "And my rival Dougie Nelson will stab me if I take his spot. I'll be back." I don't want to think about it, really.

"We shall see," she says.

We load up a couple plates with hot dogs and grab a few bags of chips, grapes, and brownies. "Bummer you have to miss Monadnock."

"Weelll," I say. I've been telling myself that I will get to go on that trip instead of coxing in the Big Dip. Or somehow do both.

It's not going to happen. "Yeah, I guess you're right. And I'd really love to get some bouldering in before it's too cold."

She stops, and I do, too. "Why don't you come with us this afternoon? We're going to the Bubbles from here."

She's in silhouette, with the sun at her back and the glittery river surrounding her. It's almost more than I can bear. "Yeah, that would be great." Jesus, I think my voice cracked. Then I remember. "Oh, I have to go back to campus with the team first."

"Okay," she says, walking again. "Maybe Nils and I can go back, too."

I nod like a bobblehead, catch myself, and say, "Cool."

She smiles.

"This day is perfect," I hear myself say, instantly wanting to melt.

"Right? I love September and October," she says, either allowing me my dignity or unaware that I meant *this. Her. Me. The belly flop.* Everything, but especially her.

And we're back to Nils, sitting on a blanket on the grass with Khalid, of all people. Khalid, explaining stroke rates, pointing at the boats racing by. As Alex and I sit down, Khalid leans back on his elbows and gives me a sly sideways look. He makes a pistol with his pointer finger. "Oh," he says. "Coach asked me to give you these."

He hands me a pair of Oakleys. Blue lenses.

"I wish. These aren't mine," I say, handing them back.

"Dude, he's giving them to you. He always has emergency pairs in the truck. Guys can't row if their glasses go overboard."

"For keeps?" I say. Again, with my sixth-grade-brother comments. Jesus.

"Probably," he says, shrugging. Rich kids don't value things the way kids like me do.

"Thanks," I say, trying them on.

"Looking hot," Nils says. "A definite Eight." And I punch him.

We stay and watch the 2V boat race. Dougie Nelson's boat also takes first place, as do our other four boats. Coach Follett wants the coxes to ride home with the team, so we're on the bus, waiting to go.

The Beast is talking with Seb and another coach, from the looks of him, by the trailer. The guys open the windows, unwrapping energy bars and slurping boxes of chocolate milk. I personally haven't had chocolate milk since fourth grade, but these guys consume it like it's the nectar of the gods.

"Holy shit!" Tyler says in a hushed voice, climbing on board the bus. "That's the Princeton heavyweight scout." All the heads swivel to look.

"He's getting recruited," Teo says excitedly.

"Maybe," Colin says, his voice clipped. Our eyes catch, and I see he's jealous. Just like he's jealous of Seb being with Charlotte.

Seb shakes the Princeton guy's hand and jogs toward the bus. Coach Follett and the scout keep talking. Seb's grinning when he climbs in.

"Dude!" Khalid says. "Princeton?"

"Shhhh," Seb says. "Do *not* jinx it."

"What'd he say?" asks Tyler as Seb flops into the last free seat, about midway down the row. He glances behind him out the window, then hunkers low. All the guys lean into the aisle. The only sound is Teo sucking the last drop out of his chocolate milk box.

"I'm supposed to send my rowing résumé to him personally, along with my test scores and transcripts." Seb's attempt to follow that up with something along the lines of "That doesn't guarantee anything" gets drowned out by a bunch of fist pumping and applause.

"Fucking awesome, man," Colin says, whacking Seb's baseball cap askew. His smile doesn't match his eyes, though. Which to me reads as saying, *Game on*.

CHARLOTTE

Reading is futile.

My eyes retrace the same lines of the history assignment. Who cares about the War of 1812? I'm probably the singular person in the library. If kids aren't at the Tilton football game, they're at the regatta or the field hockey game. The rebellion I'm staging against Seb isn't remotely satisfying, because he probably hasn't realized I'm not in Hooksett yet. Or that I'm mad. But it's like Hannah said, I can't let him think that ditching me at the last minute for a special night can be all fine with flower emojis. Not to mention, Bodenrader unaccounted for.

My phone lights up with a text.

Grace: So how was the anniversary dinner? You're killing me here!

Me: 🏴

Grace: What?

Explaining is painful. I pack up and go outside. Of course it's a bright blue day. Taunting me. This sucks.

MAX

It's late afternoon when I pull Nils's Jeep into the gravel parking lot of the state park. He is the man for backing out of the Bubbles trip and lending me his car so I could be with Alex alone.

"I hope we're not too late," I say.

"Nah. They're still here. That's Callie's car." She points. "And Stephan's."

We unload our packs, lock the car, and walk toward the trailhead. I like how natural it feels. She isn't nervous in the least. I'm not *nervous*, exactly, considering this is pretty close to the ideal first date with Alex. Except for the part where she doesn't know it's a date.

On the trail, we move in and out of sun and shadow. The foliage on either side of us flickers with yellow and orange leaves, small conflagrations in an endless green forest. It's a bit of a climb in altitude, nothing major, but we stop for water. It's an excuse for me to watch her face as she talks. She has such a lovely way of talking.

"What's it like living in New York City?" she asks.

"I don't know," I say with a small laugh. "Compared to New Hampshire?"

"Sure," she says as we resume walking.

"Loud. Hot. But it's got everything. It's intensely alive, I guess.

But I prefer this version of alive," I say. "Where you can get away and think. How about you? You're from Vermont, right?" As if I hadn't memorized the fact that she's from Middlebury, Vermont, where her parents work for the college.

"Yeah," she says. "I love Middlebury. It's really not that different from Whitney. Nice. Friendly. But maybe a little too redneck at the edges."

We hold eyes for a moment, and I just want to fast-forward to the day when it would be okay to kiss her. I really, really want to kiss her.

"Hear that?" she says, and I wonder if she means my heartbeat, until I recognize the burbly sound of water.

The trail curves a bit and opens to a brook. We tiptoe like tightrope walkers across the log bridge, arms out to the side for balance.

"I did gymnastics back home," Alex calls over her shoulder. "Want me to do a cartwheel?"

I laugh, thinking she's kidding, but boom! There she goes.

"Hand, hand . . ." she calls, legs windmilling over her head. "Foot, foot." She's facing me, impossibly balanced on the log, arms outstretched with a flourish.

"Holy crap!" I laugh.

She beams, and I consider asking her to marry me right then.

The trail opens up, and the Bubbles explode into view.

"They're like a mutant mushroom colony," Alex says.

"Probably dropped off by a traveling glacier two point six million years ago," I say. I can hear Nils: Nerd Alert!

But Alex simply says, "Cool. There they are. Hey, people!"

Stephan and Callie and four other kids from Outdoors Club are gathered at the base of the rocks. They're packing up to go. My neck twitches. Is our first almost date already over?

"Oh, sorry," Callie says. She's eating a protein bar. "We're beat. We've been here all afternoon."

Alex looks at her watch. "Damn, it's four o'clock already? Shoot." She makes an adorable frowny face. It must be the Oakleys that give me the courage to say with a shrug, "We could stay for a while."

"You should do that," Stephan says, pulling his day pack on his shoulders. "Totally worth it."

"We do have Nils's car," Alex says, and I think she may have just realized we'd be alone then, just her and me, kind of like a . . . date.

Shit. I've overstepped. "I'm cool either way," I say. I will *weep* if she wants to leave. Would she even ride back with me? I take my water bottle from the pack's mesh pocket and busy myself opening it.

"Let's stay," she says abruptly.

"Okay. We *did* go to all the effort," I add, like she's convincing me. She's already changing into her climbing shoes, so I follow her lead.

For about an hour, we take turns bouldering—climbing without the belay belts.

"It's harder than the rock gym," she says, her voice strained with effort. She clings to the rock face roughly ten feet above me. I try to be gentlemanly about the view, but it's not easy.

"Do you see that black bump up on the left?" I say.

She instead reaches to the right and manages to climb sideways for a bit before jumping back to the ground and falling to a gentle sit. "Oof," she says, a little embarrassed, I think. I hold out a hand, which she grabs, sending an invisible, intoxicating current through my whole body. Did she feel it? But these sunglasses don't invite eye contact, so I guess I'll never know. *I* felt it.

Pulling her to her feet illuminates the fact that she's slightly taller than me. I step back and busy myself by planning my next path.

"This will be my last one," I say.

"I'll meet you up there," she says, hopping up the foot path to the top.

When I make it up, she is already sitting, facing into the setting sun, eyes closed, legs crossed at the ankles. Her face is serenity defined. She smiles at me when my shadow crosses over her. I smile in return; it's beyond my control anyway. She holds up an oatmeal cookie. "Rosario specials," she says.

I take it and sit beside her. "Thanks." After a few bites, I ask, "So, how come you're not a rower? I notice it runs in families."

She contemplates the question for a moment, chewing. "I coxed in middle school for a year, but then I got too tall. But not tall enough to be a good rower. My brother is six foot six. He hogged all the tall genes." Suddenly, her eyes go wide. "Not that being tall is that great," she says. "Because he can never find clothes that fit, and we had to sell the Prius when he started driving because he was all cramped in."

I kind of wobble my head around. Fuck it, I detest being short. "I see."

"Coxing is hard. You're perfectly suited, obviously." She smiles. "My brother always says a good cox is hard to find, so the best ones can go all over the world. This could turn into a great thing for you, Max. Seriously."

My response is instant, but I don't say it out loud. *It already has.*

We finish our cookies and watch the sun lower itself over the mountains for a while.

She takes a long sip of her water. "And you always have the ghost story retellings to fall back on," she says. "You know, if all else fails."

I raise my eyebrows.

"'When they looked back to thank their mysterious trail guide, he was gone,'" she says, just the way I told it last spring around the campfire. We laugh.

"That's a true story," I say. "I heard."

"I admit I told it a couple times this summer."

We're quiet then. The sun dips below the horizon. I take off the Oakleys. She's fixing her ponytail. The skin on her arms is flawlessly smooth. It's all I can do not to reach over and run my fingers along it. Satisfied with her hair, she lifts her chin and surveys the peach sky. Then she looks at me with steady, soft brown eyes.

The earth stands motionless. She doesn't look away.

"May I kiss you?" I ask.

Her lips curve ever so slightly into a smile. She nods, and I put my mouth on hers, salty and sweet with sweat and cookie crumbs.

I pull back when it seems right. She smiles wide.

"I think Nils set us up," she says.

And we kiss again. And I think this may be the most perfect day I'll ever have for the rest of my life.

"I can't believe it, but I realized at the regatta that I miss being on a team," she says once we're driving back to campus on twisty roads. "I love Outdoors Club, but it's not the same as a team."

"You really have to work together in a boat," I say. "I wasn't sure I'd like it—I always thought Pearce and company were asshats. But it's great."

"Field hockey was like that. In middle school." She laughs at herself. "It was the only good thing about middle school."

I glance at her hand next to her thigh and wish I could reach over and take it in mine. I don't dare push my luck. I refocus on the road. "Maybe you could join the girls' rowing team for their spring season," I say. "I've heard they're going to be good this year."

"Hmm," she says, intrigued.

"Hey, have you read the book *The Boys in the Boat*?"

"My brother has," she says. "God, he loves that book."

"Talk about teamwork." I proceed to outline the narrative. Can't seem to stop myself, really. Alex listens, all the way until we roll through the Lycroft gates. "I'll loan you my copy," I say, realizing I sound overeager too late. "If you want."

She's quiet. "Yeah. You're not coming back to Outdoors Club," she says.

CHARLOTTE

When Seb appeared at my dorm Saturday night with a dozen red roses, I confessed to complete forgiveness. He got us out of Vespers. We had the most romantic table in the whole Whitney Inn—the same one as Summer Sendoff—surrounded by windows with candlelight playing off the panes of glass.

He told me about the Princeton coach and about their great race. I'd never seen him look so happy. I couldn't bring myself to ruin the mood. I mean, the contents of that note seemed pretty far-fetched anyway. So I tucked my worries away, told myself it was foolish.

Now Seb is unlocking the door to the 1856 Library, which feels like our own private hideaway. I'm wearing my favorite blue flowered dress, and my silver pumps with really subtle glitter. Seb's in a blazer and tie.

"You're kidding," I say when he flips the lights on. The table in front of the leather sofa has an ice bucket with a bottle of champagne, two champagne flutes, and a tray full of chocolates.

"You like it?" he says.

I want to blurt that he had me at the coat and tie, but instead I kiss him.

He pops the cork, and we laugh as it flies across the room and bounces off the drapes. "I've never had champagne," I say.

"I'm betting you'll like it," he says, handing me one.

"It's pretty," I say, watching the bubbles dance in the light.

"Like you," he says, smiling in a way that makes me light-headed without taking a single sip. "Happy anniversary."

We tip our glasses together. "Happy anniversary." We sip. It's cold and sharp and also kind of magical.

We kiss again, drink some more, and keep kissing and eating chocolates.

At the end of the first glass, he holds up his finger. "Okay, I'm ready."

I scramble to interpret this while he messes with his phone, grinning mischievously. Then he sets it down and takes both my hands, pulling me to my feet.

Out of nowhere, piano notes. Big band. He sweeps me into his arms, starting to dance. "I took lessons this summer for my sister's wedding. She made me."

Out of the tree of life I just picked me a plum—you came along and everything started to hum.

"That's Frank Sinatra," I say.

He nods, twirling me, and luckily I know how to do this. *"The best is yet to come,"* Seb sings along.

Are you kidding me? It's like an out-of-body experience.

We fly around the room, and every now and then, I see our reflection in the windows. I barely know me. But *this* is who I am at Lycroft Phelps.

The song ends, and he dips me. We hold the pose a moment, breathing heavily. Then we laugh and have an old-fashioned smooch that fits the song.

"I get why people love to dance now," he says a little bashfully, taking his tie off and laying it on his blazer. "It was hard to get it when I practiced with the fifty-year-old teacher, but with you, it's a whole different thing."

I am speechless and make a face I hope looks suitably humble yet flattered. We sit again and he pours more champagne and we lean back into the leather. He pulls the key from his pocket and hands it to me. "I like when you keep this. None of those guys can steal it from you." I sigh with joy.

We eat chocolates, dance to "Fly Me to the Moon" and a couple other standards I don't remember the titles of. I decide, mid–slow dance, this is the perfect night to have sex. When the champagne bottle is nearly empty, I start to think it isn't too forward for me to bring it up. He dips me again at the end of the song.

"The dip is your signature move," I say.

"I love seeing you with your hair falling back," he says. "You're perfect."

I flinch. "No," I say. Perfect is too much to live up to—I know this from experience. Perfect is too easy to screw up. But he didn't mean it like that, so when he swings me upright, I wrap both arms around his neck and look him square in the eye. "Do you ever think about when we might . . ." I can't quite say *have sex*. It's so unromantic-sounding, so matter-of-fact. Not at all infused with the huge emotions that are electrifying my entire being right now.

"What?" He rubs my nose with his. We kiss. Long.

How can he not know what I mean? "I don't know," I say. "I think I'm tipsy." *No, Charlotte, you're* chicken, *not tipsy.* Well, maybe both.

We do end up on the sofa with far fewer articles of clothing than we came in with. And it's amazing. I don't want it to end.

I don't think about what he wants or doesn't want—I just don't think—until a bit later, when he's playing with a lock of my hair.

He smiles. "We better go. I should get to bed."

"Stupid crew," I say, all pouty, which I hope I don't regret tomorrow.

I close our dorm door and lean against it. "Hannah," I say. "I am in love."

"I want to hear all about it," she says. But then she grimaces.

"What?" I say.

She holds out another folded-up note.

I blink a few times with my champagne eyes. "Not tonight," I moan. "Where'd that come from?" I ask, stepping out of my pumps.

"Hank kicked it when we came in a couple hours ago," she says. "Someone stuck it under the door. Who is this jerk?"

I take it from her and slump onto the bed. "A very big jerk," I say.

She chuckles. "Did you drink again?"

I grin and nod. "Yep."

I throw the note on my desk. "I'll read it tomorrow. I'm not wrecking tonight." I stand and present my back to her. She unzips my dress.

"Fair enough," Hannah says.

"Maybe I'll throw it away," I say.

"I mean," Hannah says, "it's surely bullshit. Come on! Flowers, the restaurant?"

"Exactly." I put on pj's and tell her about the library. "He brought champagne and chocolate, and we even danced to Frank Sinatra."

"Shut up, he did not," she says.

I simply smile.

"He truly is the Genetic Miracle."

She's brushing her teeth, and I'm staring at the folded note.

"I'll throw it out, if you want," she says after she spits.

I nod helplessly.

Just as she's about to toss it, I blurt, "Wait."

She holds it pinched between her fingers. "We have to read it, don't we." It's a statement, not a question.

"Yes!" I groan. "But I can't. Will you? Please?"

She nods dutifully and moves to the fairy lights over her desk.

"This is ridiculous," she says with exasperation. "There is no way—"

"Tell me what it says!"

"It's stupid. It says: *SM lies. Ask BJ Bodenrader.*"

The champagne, wearing off, leaves my ears ringing. "BJ Bodenrader?" I say. God, I knew I didn't trust her. "BJ?!" I say. "Blow-Job Bodenrader?!"

Hannah crumples the note and drops it in the trash. She comes to my side. "No seventeen-year-old guy dances to Frank Sinatra with a girl and then cheats on her. Not at this school. Are you kidding? That's putting himself out there in a very un-LPS-guy way. This is someone's vindictive attempt to break you up."

"Well, at least it rules out Bodenrader *writing* the notes," I say. I sit up. "Oh my God, you don't think those were guilt flowers, do you?"

Hannah shakes her head. "But why would he do that?"

"I don't know!" I stand and walk in a circle, biting my pinkie nail. "Am I supposed to be volunteering blow jobs?" I ask quietly.

God, I never even thought of that. I don't want to, anyway, but . . . "Is he figuring out I'm actually boring and totally inexperienced at anything close to sex?"

"Okay, now you're talking nonsense," I say. "Screw him if that's what it's about. But I really don't think it—"

"We don't know anything!" I snap.

"Jesus, calm down," Hannah says with annoyance.

I close my eyes and drop into my desk chair. The champagne is zipping around my body, and I can't think straight. "I'm going to find out the truth," I say, standing up again.

"Okay." She nods, then looks confused. "What does that look like?"

I pull jeans from my drawer. "I'm just going to go talk to him."

"Don't do something dumb. I think you might still be drunk," Hannah says.

"I'm not drunk or dumb," I say, though I think I may be both.

"He just treated you like a goddess," she says. "These notes are fake!"

I pull on a sweater without responding.

"He might get pissed if you come off like you're accusing him of something."

"You're the one who wants me to talk with him more!" I say, squashing my bare feet into sneakers. Hannah still looks concerned.

"What about room check?" she says. "You've only got a little over an hour."

"Our RA never checks!" I say, one hand on my hip.

"But what if she does?"

I look at my bed and push all my pillows under the sheets so they pass for a human. "Just turn out the lights."

We eye lock for a solid ten seconds.

"I'm a really good friend," she grumbles. "*Really* good."

"The best," I say, yanking my coat off the hook by our door. "Watch for me at the window. If I get locked out."

"Or, champagne queen, you could just text me," Hannah says.

"Right," I say.

I use the back door to leave the dorm because I can't deal with being fake friendly right now. I power walk to the Founders Statues, then turn toward the boys' residential quad. Finally, I reach Somes. Seb and Chauncey's room on the first floor is lit up. I smile. *See! Going to bed*, I think. *Just like he said. Wait, did he say that? He said he was tired.* It's a little sketchy to spy on him, but I stretch my neck to see inside the room.

There's his beautiful head. He's wearing jeans and a team sweatshirt, standing with one foot on his chair as he unties his sneaker.

Wait, untying? Or tying?

He does not remove the sneaker but instead swaps feet and begins tying the second one.

Does he even have crew tomorrow? My vision blurs. What if he is meeting up with Sofia Bodenrader? For a blow job that was missing from our date? I review us on the couch at the library, fast-forwarding through it in search of the moment when I should have offered that up. As if I would even know how to do that. My brain is scrambling when his room goes dark. I realize he's going to pop out the front doors in seconds. I scramble around the corner.

He trots down the three steps. I could follow him. But I imagine him with Bodenrader, and I can't. I cannot witness that. My shoes barely crunch on the gravel because I use my ballet superpowers while quickly retreating to my room.

MAX

After dinner, I'm in such a good mood I can barely steer my car in *Need for Speed*. I plow through the guardrail and smash into a semi. "Shit!" I blurt. "Not again."

"You may be a rising coxing phenom, but you still suck at driving in the canyon," Nils says. "I'm going to make you play me every day so you don't get an ego like Pearce's."

I start to laugh, literally rolling on the lounge floor, which has a range of mystery smells that normally would keep me from touching it with anything but my feet.

"Dude," Nils says, chuckling. "If this is what you're like after one kiss with Alex, what's going to happen if you actually have sex?"

This makes me laugh harder, and I've got him going, too. My phone screen lights up on the sofa. I sigh, pulling myself together. "Mom's Saturday-night check-in text," I say. But it's not her number. "Wait, what area code is 267?" I say, holding the phone toward him.

He shrugs.

I open the text.

Greetings, Max. Do not show this message to anyone.

I glance at Nils. He's pouring Cheetos into his mouth straight from the bag. I turn from him casually.

The Founders have a message for you.

Tingles rush my scalp, like a cold ocean wave. Founders as in Lycroft and Phelps? Two dead guys? Another text bubbles onto the screen.

Meet them tonight at 10 and follow the instructions given.

Gut reaction: What the actual fuck is this? Hypothesis: A joke. I'm being set up. Matheson, or maybe it's a homegrown affair. I check the time. Nine-twenty.

More bubbles . . .

Lycroft and Phelps believe you are worthy of this message.
Do not disappoint.

I rub the back of my neck.

"What?" Nils asks. He stands, brushing neon orange crumbs from his pants.

I want to tell him, but I'm unnerved by the warning.

"Nothing," I say, chickenshit that I am. "Spam."

"I'm going to the room," he says.

"Yep," I say. I reread the cryptic texts. I used to play tricks on my little brothers like this. I wonder if it really is some kind of Matheson ambush? A Kill the Cox plot? I feel a surge of team spirit and begin to tap out a text to Seb and Colin, then delete it. A soul-crushing thought that I could be getting set up by *them* shoves its way into my head, but I shove it back out. I wonder where this message would be. It has to be the Founders Statues.

"Probably bullshit," I mutter. But that last bit about being worthy rolls around in my skull while I'm walking the hall to the bathroom. I recheck the time. 9:26. I estimate twelve minutes travel time.

"I'm going to the lab," I tell Nils, putting on my shoes.

He's sitting on his bed with his bass. He keeps playing and sings: "Nerd a-lerrrt."

I flip him off with a grin and grab my coat, then pause in the doorway. "Hey, man, thanks for setting me up today," I say. He doesn't look up. "I mean it."

Nils stops playing. "I had to prove your stupid theory wrong somehow."

I snort, enjoying being the butt of that joke, but inside I feel a twinge of guilt for lying to him right now. Once I figure it out, I'll tell him, I vow to myself.

Outside, the campus is busy. I've never been self-conscious simply walking around the quad, but the possibility of seeing Alex or being surveilled by whoever sent the text has me trying for swagger that's suitable for an athlete, but not as dickish as Pearce's and Khalid's. I don't think I've got it yet, but I get to the statues without seeing anyone.

John Lycroft stands like a bold explorer, chin up. He's got one hand on his hip and the other pointing toward Lake Edith. Erastus Phelps stands beside him with one hand resting on John's shoulder, clutching a book.

I look both ways, stepping onto the circular wall around the statues. I climb onto the base and essentially frisk Erastus Phelps and, finding nothing, step around to check his backside. A white envelope is tucked between the book and the coat sleeve.

Bingo.

I glance around; just groups of kids walking the paths.

The envelope's wedged tight, and it takes a gentle tugging to get it free. I half expect a bucket of water or pig's blood or something to spill over me from above. The quiet is encouraging. A green wax stamp seals the flap, an admittedly impressive touch. Movement in my peripheral vision grabs my attention, and I jump behind Erastus's coat. It's Charlotte, clearly oblivious that I'm standing with the Founders up here.

She'll think I'm really weird if she glances up right now, so in a preemptive strike, I say, "Hey, Charlotte."

She jumps, stopping short, and locates me, her eyes bugged out. "Max! What the hell?"

"Sorry, I was trying not to scare you." I jump back to ground level, now shorter than her. I hate that. She's looking at the envelope, and I tuck it into my jacket as casually as I can.

Her eyes narrow. "What are you doing?"

"I'm . . ." She waits. Her eyes are swollen; I think she's been crying. "In charge of decorating these guys." I smile, thumbing over my shoulder. "For the crew team."

"That was my idea," she says. Now she looks like she's going to start sobbing.

"Are you okay?"

She presses her lips together. "You would tell me if Seb cheated on me, right, Max?" she whispers. "We help each other out, right?"

"Charlotte, I'm around them all the time. Seb never joins in their locker-room crap. He speaks only respectfully of you. Seriously, you don't need to worry."

She swipes a tear away and nods her head. "Okay. Thanks," she says, and rushes off.

"Wow," I whisper. I refocus on my own situation and, moving

294

directly under the lamppost, examine the wax seal. It's a fancy *SS*. I pop it open and unfold the enclosed piece of paper. It's nice quality, heavy and smooth, and at the top, there is an embossed outline of a rabbit and the same fancy *SS*.

This is no bush-league operation.

The words below appear to be typed with an actual typewriter, and in fact, I can feel where the typewriter keys made impressions behind the letters. There's an old Corona typewriter in the back of the library, I think, trying to remember if I've seen anyone use it.

I read.

Maxwell Loeffler-Hannigan

Hannigan-Loeffler, for fuck's sake. Seriously, they're doing it on purpose now. But their identity is revealed to me.

is cordially invited to join the Slycroft Society, est. 1972. To accept your invitation, follow the map below to reach Point B no earlier than nine-thirty and no later than ten p.m. tonight.

My heart is loud. Obviously it's the rowers. The map is carefully drawn, notably by someone who lacks artistic talent. I realize that Point B is on the other side of the woods (here represented as lollipop trees) located *on the other side* of all the athletic fields. That's off campus.

I'm highly suspicious. What if I end up one of those infamous hazing victims that LPS kids talk about for decades, like the dude who rolled off the railroad trestle to his death in the 1960s as a result of a joke involving grain alcohol and an empty barrel? Not fucking funny, guys.

But, Nils's voice says in my mind, *your luck is on an excellent trajectory right now.* Yeah, I think. It is. Today may have been the best day of my life, as a matter of fact. Maybe this can increase the velocity of my upwardly trending social life. A real secret society? Like Skull and Bones at Yale? Everyone wants into those things! The word *Slycroft* tugs at some part of my memory. I've heard it before. Where?

The map's landmarks indicate a fifteen-minute walk, so I get a move on.

The lights are off at the athletic field parking lot and a two-foot layer of horror-movie night mist hovers above the lawns. Beyond that, pitch-black woods. I creep along the edge of the lot. Oddly, the blacktop gives me comfort—the illusion of human domination over nature—the opposite of what I thought I valued.

I pull out the map and take a look at which of the five trailheads I'm supposed to use. Looks like it's the first one, mysteriously labeled *ETP* on this drawing. I take a deep breath and step onto the dewy grass. As I pass the baseball diamond backstop, the wall of forest begins to take shape into discernible trees, and a few white signs emerge from shadow.

"Edward T. Pope Trail," I say, reading one. "ETP." The trail is so dark I could be entering a subterranean passage for all I know. I feel a little like *James and the Giant Peach*. I try to remember if he gets eaten by the man-sized centipede, then remind myself I've been invited to join a secret society. I consider texting Nils so someone knows where I'm going, but he'll ask too many questions, so without another thought—which is really saying something for me—I take the trailhead.

CHARLOTTE

"Where is he going?" I ask under my breath as I watch Max vanish into the cross-country trails, about as far as he can get from the Founders Statues he's supposed to be decorating. My hunch is he'll lead me to Seb, so even though the champagne is wearing off and I'm thirsty, there's not a chance I'm turning around.

We take a packed dirt trail marked *Edward T. Pope Trail*. I'm mindful of keeping silent. My experience landing leaps with barely a *tap-tap* in pointe shoes—with their wooden toe blocks—is paying off.

The silhouette of Max's head is visible thanks to the glow of his phone flashlight. He bobs along the path, clueless I'm here.

He stops.

Shit! I turn parallel with the bushes, hoping he can't see my light pink sweater in the splotchy moonlight. The flashlight beam sweeps over my blue sneakers. I brace myself.

Something rustles in the branches above the trail.

Max points his flashlight into the trees. I hold my breath. A squirrel, I guess. Then it goes dark and he's resumed walking. I rush to keep up, and—*poof!* He's gone.

I pause, confused. My imagination goes toward some science-fiction plot, some portal to another dimension, where *that's* what all the secrets are about and Seb really does love me. Or at least like me a lot.

Without Max's flashlight, I can barely see the ground. I can't risk his seeing my flashlight, so I slink forward cautiously, find that the trail drops into a deep ravine. I see the light beam float up the other side, as if on its own will. I can't run down this steep of a slope—in the dark, anyway—but when I hit the bottom and the incline begins, I dig in. Even with all my training, my thighs and calves burn as I wage my ascent. I hate not knowing our destination. Following blindly is definitely not my thing.

Finally I crest the top. Neither Max nor his phone is anywhere. But something much bigger glows ahead, and I can't imagine what could be here in the middle of a forest.

As the path curves to the left, the woods to my right thin out, so that I can see a vast expanse of rolling fields, glowing silver in the moonlight. A few steps farther and there's Max, standing dead still behind a cluster of thin birch trees, watching something. I'm spying on another spy? I can't see what he sees, but the light is coming from there. "Bizarre," I breathe. I don't know what Max is doing here. He may not have led me to Seb at all.

I sidle closer and stand on my tiptoes and crane my neck. It's a barn, an old one, kind of decrepit. The shadows of people are inside, I think, and maybe outside. A pine bough is in my way. Slowly, I bring my hand to the branch and pull it aside. The needles brush my cheek.

Now I see him. Seb. With Colin. My heart stomps in my chest. Seb isn't home. Seb isn't risking curfew with me, or BJ Bodenrader, he's risking it w—

Something moves near my right elbow. I flick my eyes toward it. In that flash of panic, my brain registers an animal.

My ears ring in the silence. What the hell is it? I pivot my chin toward it a millimeter at a time. Two bright yellow eyes stare at me. It's a lion. Mountain lion. Cougar. Whatever! It's as big as a golden retriever and standing in the middle of the path, like it owns it, which it does. And it's wondering what the hell I'm doing here.

I back up toward Max. Forget Seb's drama. I need another human right now. "Mmm," I try to say, but I don't even want to move my lips. Its ears slide back ever so slightly. That's what our cat, Foodle, does before a pounce. I glissade one foot back, then another. A twig cracks under my shoe. Its ears twitch, but it doesn't blink. *Glissade, glissade, glissade*, I coach myself.

I reach a hand back, intuiting that I'm the right distance. "Max!" I whisper. I look over my shoulder long enough to glimpse his face.

Motion explodes around us. Somebody yelps. I think it's me. I'm clinging to Max shamelessly and he's trying to stand up and run in the opposite direction and I am literally hanging on him.

"Let go!" he growls.

I smack backward on the ground, landing on my upper back. I grab a rock near my hand and turn, throwing it blindly. It lands with a thud nearby, and the cat spins and vanishes into the thick trees.

"Why would you do that?" It's a scold.

"What?" I say, confused. "Is it gone?"

Max is on the ground holding his ankle.

"Are you okay?" I say, trying to see his face in the darkness. "I don't even know what just happened."

He scoots away from me, and I realize the reason I can't see his face is he's wearing a mask. My stomach jumps. Max was wearing a green LPS jacket. This person is wearing all black, head to toe. Light catches something in his hand. A gun, I think. I think it's a freaking gun.

The next few moments are fluid. Panic has me by the throat. *Stalker!* my brain yells. I judge the distance to the barn and make a run for it. The stalker grabs my foot. I thump onto the ground, wind blowing out my lungs. I can't scream. God, I've had this nightmare! I claw the dirt.

"Charlotte!" he whisper-barks in my ear.

I open my eyes.

"Charlotte, stop!"

I roll over. I blink.

"It's me, for fuck's sake."

The person no longer has a mask on.

The person is Quinn Walsh.

MAX

The map, for all its wants in the artistry department, is straight-forward and easy to follow. In daylight, the barn situated on the other side of a thinned section of woods would barely catch the attention of a runner. But in the dark, the glow around it is like a landed alien ship. I pause by the birches, marked on the map, watching the industrious activity going down over there. It's not a prank on me. There's almost half my boat: Seb, Colin, Khalid.

I cross the space between me and them through a tamped down path of tall grass. Colin spots me first. "Wayne Uff," he says. "The man!"

It's at this moment I realize how far I've come.

Seb and Billy Nash are rolling a keg through the open barn door. Colin puts his ape arm over my shoulders. "Welcome to the Slycroft Society."

"Hey, Max, glad you made it," Seb says, handing me a red Solo cup.

"Come inside," Colin says.

LED camp lanterns hang strategically around the big space. There's a table in the corner with a big book that appears import-ant to the setting—a feather pen is in a jar of ink beside it, and two candles are lit on either side. The guys are tapping the keg over near a table with red Solo cups on it.

"What is all this?" I ask.

"Slycroft was established in 1972, the same year the school started admitting women," Seb begins. "The Upper Middies and Seniors weren't really happy with that development and decided to do something about it."

I'm thinking, *Why?* I'm thinking, *So they started meeting in a barn?*

"They wanted to have a place where guys could be guys and not have to worry about offending chicks," Colin says.

"Check it out," Khalid says, lifting the lid on an old foot locker. "Two hundred vintage *Hustler* magazines. Old-school, when porn was on paper." He pulls one out to showcase. "July 1976." A woman in an Uncle Sam-by-way-of-Victoria's-Secret blowing into a gun barrel graced the cover.

"Bicentennial," Bill Nash says. "I love that one."

I do the math. "You do realize that woman is probably in her seventies right now," I say.

"Dude! That was totally unnecessary!" Khalid says, dropping it back in the chest, and the rest of the guys laugh.

I look up, laughing along with them. On the rafters, I notice . . . underwear? "Is that underwear hanging up there?" I ask.

"Fuck yes," says Pete Crenshaw.

"We'll get to that later," Colin says. "For now, we're interested in reviving the tradition of Slycroft master pranking. All this Matheson crap has got us back on our heels. When you brought up the MIT prank idea, well"—he pats my shoulder, guiding me to the keg—"we wanted you in. Simple as that."

"So, it's a prank club," I say.

"Yep," Colin says.

"With women's underwear thrown in," I say. "And geriatric porn mags."

"Why not?" he says, wagging his eyebrows. "But like I said, we'll get to that later."

"Fun fact," says Seb, filling his cup at the keg. "Two sitting senators and one State Supreme Court Justice are Slycroft alum."

"Huh," I say, picturing the only alumni they could be referring to.

"And a former commissioner of the NHL," says Billy Nash, who plays hockey.

"It's a pipeline to Silicon Valley after college, Max," says Pete. "I know that's a little more your thing."

I'm intrigued; I can't fake it. "What kind of pranks do you do?" I can't think of a single prank that's happened since I've been a student here.

Colin takes my cup and fills it. I don't drink. It's one of my rules. I learned the hard way that I can't handle alcohol at a Hannigan family reunion two summers ago. Turns out puking during a game of badminton, in front of your parents and grandmother, is a great deterrent to repeat behavior. Still, I accept the full cup when he hands it to me.

"That's just it," Seb says. "We've let that slide, and we really want to get it back up and running here before our Senior class graduates."

"What have you been doing in the meantime?" I ask, looking at the fat book on the table.

"The pranks used to be epic," Billy says.

"My dad was a Slycrofter," Seb says. "His class let three piglets loose in the girls' dorm, but they numbered them one, two, and four so everyone thought there was another one somewhere."

I chuckle. "That's pretty good," I say.

"More recently," says Tyler, "there've been fire drills during exams, streakers during First Year orientation."

"They dyed the milk in the dispensers red on Halloween one year," adds Colin. "So everyone poured red milk on their cereal."

"Skunk in the auditorium," says Billy.

"Put bras on all the Greek statues by the Amphitheater," says Pete.

"Is that where you got the idea for the underwear?" I ask, pointing up.

"*Panties,*" Billy corrects. "Guys have underwear."

Pete smiles, nodding. "Every pair belonged to someone a Slycrofter banged."

I chuckle again and glance around, expecting this to be a joke, but I can tell by their stupid expressions that it isn't. I quickly stop laughing. I mean, I know that it's just bro humor and whatever, but it's a little much. Do the girls know their undergarments are hung like victory laurels? Obviously not. Are Charlotte's up there? Because I don't think she'd go in for that. Before I can ask any questions, Pearce calls: "Let's do this! Pledge ring!"

I try to catch Seb's eyes, but he won't look my way. I don't have time to process any more, though, because everyone has formed a circle.

Colin refers to the book on the table, then spins into the circle holding a piece of paper. "I hereby call to order the second meeting of the Slycroft Society, in this, its fiftieth iteration since its establishment in 1972," he reads. I feel like I'm in a movie. Or I've landed on the island from *Lord of the Flies* or something. "Raise your right hand and repeat after me." I watch as the boys follow along. "Max, you need to participate in the oath. Even if you don't join—which you will—you need to take the oath. If you can't take the oath, little dude, you gotta scram."

Everyone's looking at me. I guess I *could* leave. Truth be known, I'm not into all this bro-culture shit, but I'm not sure what that would do to crew. And my numbers are finally rising, and I am not ready to surrender them. Besides, I'm curious as hell. I love pranks.

I raise my palm.

"I do solemnly swear . . ." says Colin.

And with the crowd, I follow along. I won't be taking any underwear, oath or no.

"To uphold the secrecy of all conversations and decisions made within these walls . . ."

Everyone echoes that, but we're all out of sync and it sounds terrible.

"To follow through on all plans agreed upon by my Slycroft brethren . . ."

We say this, too. A small voice in my head says, *Max, you're going to look back at this moment more than once.* True, it has the feel of a Big Moment. But will I look back and think I made a winning decision? Or a losing one?

Colin holds his beer cup in the air. "Once a Slycrofter, forever a Slycrofter!"

We repeat this, holding our cups aloft.

"Chug!" he commands, and proceeds to suck down his full cup.

I don't have much time to hesitate while everyone guzzles their beer. All I can think is: *Dealbreaker.*

The cup clacks against my teeth, and that voice says: *That, my friends, is the sound of Max Hannigan-Loeffler breaking his no-drinking rule.*

Burps and dramatic exhalations signal empty cups. "Yuh!" someone yells.

There's mulling about, keg refills, and general high spirits. "Slam report!" Billy Nash calls a couple moments later.

"Yeah!" several guys shout.

I stand next to Seb, trying to catch his eye again, to no avail. Billy pulls something from his pocket. It unravels from his fingers.

"Thong!" exclaims Khalid. "Fucking right! Whose?"

"Ruby Bettencourt, Firstie," Billy says. "She sucks like a champ, boys."

There is cheering.

Okay, that is enough for me. I peer tutor Ruby Bettencourt in precalc once a week. She is probably barely fifteen. That's disgusting. It may even be illegal. I step forward. "Hey, hey, hey," I say, but Colin interrupts.

"Right, Wayne? I told you your life would change, man," he says, shaking my shoulder roughly. I can't tell if he knows he's missed my point. He sweeps his arm toward the large book on the table behind him. "Billy, right this way, sir."

Billy struts over and picks up the feather pen.

"He's writing it down?" I mutter to Seb.

"Yes," he says, watching his Solo cup.

"He's writing it down," I say. "Wow."

The circle disperses. Seb puts his hand out for my cup. He says, "Let's plan that Matheson prank, Max."

We end up with more beer and everyone perched on a pentagon of rough-hewn wood benches. I'm *aware* of three splinters in
my left hand already, but I can't exactly feel them. I can't feel my
fingertips at all, on either hand, actually. Three cups' worth of
beer sloshes around my stomach every time I move. But somehow
these guys hang on my every word as we plot how we'll make an
inflatable balloon and write some clever dig at Matheson, bury it
in front of the visitor bleachers, and then have it come up during
the Big Dip in October.

"It will be remote control," I say. "Allowing us to choose the
perfect moment."

"I mean, it would look pretty stupid if we lost the race," I say.
"But I guess we could—"

"We're not fucking losing," says Colin, bleary-eyed. To explain
that there's *always* the chance we could lose requires way more
energy than I can muster. It would also detract from the festive
mood, which obviously isn't the Slycroft way.

We all watch as Pete and Billy climb the loft ladder and hammer Ruby's thong into its new home on the rafters. The blister of
anger I feel is popped by beer. The boys then hang by their hands
from a beam, trying to orangutan their way across it. I almost suggest installing a belaying system like we have at the rock gym, but
realize I'm drunk and that, while my idea is a solid problem-solver,
I will not contribute to this sexist crap. I will Billy to fall and break
his arm instead. I'm unsuccessful.

To get the attention from them, I say. "We might be able to
make it explode with green smoke—I think we can tint it with
food coloring, but I'm not sure."

"Oh, yeah, Lycroft green," Pearce yells.

There's a yelp, and we turn to see Pete plummet to the barn floor.

"Oof!"

Everyone freezes and watches him slowly push himself to a sitting position.

"Holy shit! Are you all right?" Seb says.

Pete grins. "Whoa."

"That was fucking hilarious!" Khalid says. "You looked like Spider-Man, dude!"

Billy, ever the spotlight seeker, hoots loudly from above and swings himself into the hayloft like a gymnast. He turns toward us and beats his chest.

That excitement dies down, and we make a few more plans for the prank, assigning the various tasks—digging a hole, building the launching device, finding the right kind of balloon—to subgroups. Seb creates a group text and names it Operation M Blows.

"So, you're in, right?" Seb says when we're getting ready to leave. "Slycroft?" He's puppy eager.

"Dude, seriously with the panties?" I say in a moment of drunken clarity. "Like, what would Charlotte say about that?"

"Max," he says, thumping my shoulder. These guys do that a lot. "She will say nothing about that because she won't know about that. Right?" I want to ask him if her panties are up there, but his message is loud and clear, even though he's light-years smoother than Pearce. We're walking back toward the fence. "I know these guys get a little stupid sometimes, but you can ignore that side of it. We need you to get the pranking back in gear," he says. "You'll be a legend. Put the sly back in Slycroft. It'll be epic with you here."

Weak? Shallow? Desperate? I accept all charges. But when a guy like Seb McNeilly says a thing like that to a guy like me, well, fuck it. Mea culpa.

"Yeah," I say. "Yeah, I'm in."

"Of course you are." He chuckles softly. "Nobody ever says no."

Q

Charlotte's on her belly, her eyes planet-sized. Finally, she blinks and her shoulders rise.

"It's me," I tell her again, a little calmer.

She pulls herself to a sit. "Q?" Her eyebrows pitch down; her expression, horror. I'm holding the gun. All at once I see myself through her eyes. An armed stalker. My mind swirls, a wrestling match of all sides of me at once. I'm out of my mind.

"No, I—" I lay the gun gently on the path and push it away from us with my foot. "I'm— It's— I'm not—"

She crab-walks backward, staring at it, breath ragged. Dragging her eyes toward me, she says, "What in the name of all *fuck* are you doing?"

It's like a teacher dropping the F-word. We stare at each other.

"I—" My mind is gray mist. Who even am I?

Charlotte senses my hesitation. "You better tell me what the hell is going on here." She's pulling out her phone. "Now."

"Don't," I say through my teeth, clamping her slim wrist in my hand. My anger is bigger than her fear. It's bigger than mine. "Do. Not."

"Let go! Have you lost your *shit*?" She yanks her hand away. Her eyes don't waver. They hold me frozen, and I'm stuck on the Amphitheater Lawn again. Unmoving.

My skin cracks, splintering into a million pieces that rain to the ground around me. They catch moonlight in horrible glints and sparks, jangling in our ears.

It's over. I've shattered.

CHARLOTTE

Something in Q's eyes is haunted, or hunted maybe. Like a panicked child. I need to call someone, but she . . . she needs me. I feel it, a tug from something in her to something in me. I eye the gun. She can't be trusted right now. She's had some kind of breakdown. "Look, Q," I say, breathing hard. "You have to tell me—" My mouth is so dry I need to stop. Swallow. "What the *fuck*—" My voice shakes. I gather my strength. "Tell me what is going on." I let my finger hover above my phone screen. *"Now!"*

"Okay!" she says, looking at the sky. Her nostrils tremble, and her chest moves fast. "Just." Tears roll down her cheek. "Just don't call anyone." She looks at me, unblinking. Something's off about her eyelashes—like, where are they? "Please."

I put my phone in my pocket and turn toward the barn. Now I can see Max with Seb and Colin and a bunch of other guys. I can't process any of that. I rake my fingers through my hair. "Have I, like, landed on another planet?! *You're* the stalker?! And a gun, Q? *A gun*. And the mountain lion? Are you a witch or something?"

"Shhh." She glances toward the barn. "They'll hear us. And lynxes don't hurt people."

She's on something. Drugs. Hallucinatory mushrooms, probably. I squeeze my lips together and nod. "Riiight, they're super friendly," I say. "Let's write that on our tombstones, 'kay?" Seb's rolling a keg in a wheelbarrow with the LPS quarterback. They disappear in the barn. It's too much. I pinch the bridge of my nose. "First things first," I say more to myself than to Q. "*That.*" I point at the gun without looking at it. My throat is thick and tight. "What are *you* doing with it?" She picks it up, rising to her feet.

"Put it down!" I jump.

Q takes three steps, winds up, and hurls the gun as hard as she can into the woods. We wait, suspended in time, until we hear it bust through branches and land. We stare at each other. The moonlight through the branches breaks her face into dozens of jagged pieces. And then she just collapses, like she's a marionette and the hand holding her strings let go. She sobs in a heap on the ground.

"You're scaring me," I say, a tear escaping.

She isn't stopping. I'm helpless, bent over her shaking form. Down the hill, I watch Seb and Colin Pearce through a window in the barn, laughing. I rub Quinn's back. "It's okay, it's okay," I say, as if I know what I'm talking about. But that's Charlotte Foresley, isn't it? The know-it-all, Goody Two-shoes Big Sister, acting like I know just what I'm talking about, when I have no fucking clue.

Q's sobbing gets softer. I keep rubbing her back, as much for me as for her. She's stopped when my phone buzzes in my back pocket.

Hannah: where are you?

Me: you have no idea

Hannah: ?

Me: i'll explain later.

Hannah: alex buchanan just texted. Quinn didn't come home. thought you might be together at some rocking party.

Well, the rocking part, I think, glancing down at Q. She's rousing herself.

Me: def not. does the r.a. know?

Hannah: no

Me: i'm with q. tell alex

I have no idea how to finish this sentence. I decide to leave it.

Hannah: 👍

Q looks at me. I've never seen anyone look so sad. "How about we get out of the woods?" I scan for any signs of the big cat.

She blinks a few times, and I don't think she heard a word. "If I tell you something, Charlotte, can you never tell anyone?"

"Um," I hesitate. Can I promise that? She literally just had a gun. But do I have a choice? "Of course. What is it?"

She takes a long, shaky breath. "After the Summer Sendoff," she begins. I nod. "I—" More tears, silent this time. "Colin Pearce raped me."

I feel my mouth open, but I don't have words. Looking at her, this broken shell of my creative, spirited Little, I know she's telling the truth. Thoughts spill into my head like loose marbles: Colin's hand on her ass during "Talking to the Moon"; her silly, drunk smile over his shoulder; Max's report of the stalker tailing Colin; the vandalized racing shell at the boathouse.

"Oh my God. Has the stalker been you all along?" I whisper. I move to hug her. She winces, so I pause. I take her hands. "Q, I'm so sorry." Then a monstrous rolling wave comes at me. "Q, what were you going to do with that gun?" I look down toward the barn.

314

But I've lost her to her crying again, and the wave's undertow sucks me the other way. I deserted her at the Summer Sendoff, drunk, with the guy who raped her. I can't absorb the enormity of that. "Q, I am so sorry," I say again, my voice weak. I squeeze her hands. "It's my fault," I say. She was drunk. I knew it. "I deserted you." I'm welling up. What a coward. *I'm* crying? I shake my head and will myself tough. "I never even checked in on you after the dance." I think of kissing Seb out on the terrace behind the art gallery. There was no dance, no dates, no building in those moments with him. Just sky and stars and his beautiful eyes. "God." I shudder. "So self-centered!" I shake my head. "I'm sorry," I repeat, which I know is bitterly and absurdly inadequate right now.

Q's not making sounds, but her shoulders shake.

Since school started, I've been so worried about holding on to Seb, like he's a precious gem or something. How could I not notice Q was in such sad shape? Some Big. I failed my Little. I am such a phony.

I look down the hill once more, and the boys look small to me. "Come on, Q." I gently pull her hands. "I know where we can go."

MAX

Somehow, I make it back to Stevens undetected by any authority. I tiptoe upstairs, clinging to the railing. Nils's snoring is a relief. I don't know how I would keep from blurting out everything about Slycroft. That whole banner of panties on display is a tough secret to hold. Nils is way too decent a person to go in for that shit. He'd be disgusted. I am, too. But there aren't any rules that say *I* have to steal underwear to be a Slycrofter, so I plan on taking the best—hanging with them, masterminding epic pranking—and leaving the rest.

I bumble around in the dark, then leave for the bathroom. Brushing my teeth and such, I think of a weird truth. Not telling Nils feels a small bit . . . powerful. Like, instead of depending on him for everything, I'm kind of being a badass out there on my own. Does that make me a d-bag? I spit it all out with the tooth-paste, swish icy water in my mouth. In the mirror, I examine my bloodshot eyes. "Who will you be at Lycroft Phelps?" I say softly. "*A Slycrofter.*" I grin at myself.

On my way back to our room, I stumble over the chair leg in the dark, knocking the R2-D2 alarm clock onto the floor. "Shit," I say loudly, forgetting myself.

Nils's bedside lamp turns on with a click. "What the hell? What time is it?"

I slouch down and pick up the robot. "Erm, it's one-thirty-seven. Sorry, you never wake up."

"Dude, you reek," he says. His hair pokes out in every direction like a puffer fish. "Boozing at the lab, eh?"

"I—" I'm spinning it as I go, "I saw Pearce and Khalid, and we went to the boathouse and had a few drinks."

I try not to wobble as I step out of my shoes. "You're tanked!" He chuckles, turning off the light. "You're lucky you didn't get busted, Max."

"Yeah, it was stupid," I say, trying to patch a leak I'm afraid might turn into a flood.

"Your mom would kick your ass if you lost your scholarship. And your dad would kill you."

I attempt a chuckle, but he's not kidding.

I crawl into bed. Lying to Nils doesn't feel powerful, I decide; it feels low. Like a deeply negative number. Or maybe it's powerful *and* low—a negative exponent—which I never considered could be a feeling before right now. I wish Nils could be a Slycrofter with me. Maybe I can nominate him once I'm settled in. Yeah, I think, flipping on my side to stop the bed from spinning. That's what I'll do.

CHARLOTTE

When I open the door to the 1856 Library, Q speaks for the first time since we left the woods. "How do you have that key?"

"Asks the girl with the gun," I say.

She stares, so I shrug. "Seb." I don't want to say more.

Q looks around. "Ever wonder where he got it?"

I smirk.

She sinks low into the leather sofa, closing her eyes and letting out a slow exhale. "I'm so tired."

"How long have you kept this secret?" My teeth are clamped so tight I can feel the muscles in my temples. I wouldn't mind a little of that Scotch from before right now, as a matter of fact. I scale the ladder and open the cabinet in the bookshelf. I pull out the decanter and take a glass from the silver tray on display. Her eyes pop open when the cork squeaks out of the bottle.

"Want Scotch?" I say, pouring.

"Scotch?" she says skeptically. "My grandfather drinks Scotch."

"I know. It's hell water. Whatever. My nerves are shot," I say. "What's one more demerit at this point?"

"Fuck it," she says, holding her hand out.

I give her a glass, and we take sips.

She winces. "Holy shit!" and I almost spit mine out. We do something resembling a laugh. "Yeah, just fuck it," she says, and slams the whole drink back.

"Whoa," I say.

We sit in silence, and I try to absorb the twists and turns of this night.

"It's too quiet in here," Q says. She barely opens her eyes but taps her phone and in a few seconds we're listening to music. She casts a side-eye at me. "Fleetwood Mac. I know it's weird, but I just . . ."

"I like it." The guitar notes fill the air between us. Eventually, I say, "What were they doing? The guys, I mean. In the barn." I feel guilty wondering about Seb, but maybe it's a distraction for her?

She snickers. "Holding a meeting for their secret fuck-boy society."

"Secret *what*?" I gape. "Never mind, it's not important right now." I don't want to know.

Q keeps going, though. "It's called the Slycroft Society. Their all-boys' secret society that's been running since the 1970s."

I roll this information around in my head. "*That's* what he's been hiding from me? I thought he was screwing Bodenrader." I half smile. She stares at me, and I feel my relief drain away.

"I guess I should tell you now."

"It's okay—"

She shakes her head. "You should know. Seb asked you to Summer Sendoff because he and Colin had a bet to see who could go with you."

I feel my face twist.

"Don't feel too bad. It's obvious Seb's into you. Besides, I was the consolation prize." She pours herself another Scotch. "And look at me now." Her eyes are glassy and she slugs back the drink.

I set my glass down, utterly wordless. A *bet*? I was just dancing in here with Seb, making out with him right here on this couch. I can't process what that means about us, especially given what's happened to Q.

Another song begins. It's soft piano and I get a little lost in it. "What do they do?" I say finally. "At their . . . club?"

"Besides make themselves feel important?" Q asks. "Drink. Steal girls' underwear and hang it up for bragging rights."

I snort back amusement. Her cheek muscles flex. "Wait, you're not kidding?"

She shakes her head very slowly. "My underwear is up there. The dirtbag stole it after he . . ." Her anger folds in on itself, her face contorting, her voice patchy. She shuts her mouth and starts tapping her foot aggressively. Sunken gray shadows curve under each of her eyes, little gullies. She's so tiny, like a delicate spider in her all-black outfit. "I'm so fucking tired of all of it."

I don't want to press her, so we listen to a couple of Fleetwood Mac songs without talking. I'm not really sure what I'm supposed to do here.

"Q?"

"Mmm," she says. "Just a second." But she turns one shoulder into the cushion and wriggles into it, closing her eyes.

"Crap," I whisper. I thought we'd come in here and she would tell me some things and I would figure out how to help her, well, get help. Still, I can't bring myself to wake her. She cried so hard out there in the woods, and it's been a few years since I've done that myself, but I remember it's exhausting. I'm relieved, honestly, to have a minute to process everything.

I pace a path around the room. My hands are trembly, and my insides are bound tight.

I catch my reflection in the window again, like when I was dancing. "Who will you be at Lycroft Phelps?" I ask. I plunk into the wingback chair by the fireplace, exhaling like a popped balloon. Who can I get to help? I promised I wouldn't tell anyone. But she's a mess. I'm not equipped for this level of trouble. Then it comes to me all at once. *Macy Walsh.* She was roommates with my Big when I was a First Year, and used to come to our group and teach us how to get away with stuff.

I don't have her number anymore. Q's phone is on the couch. I get it and hold the lock screen up to her face. It opens, and I find Macy right away in her texts. I call her.

Her voice is groggy. "Quinnie? Are you all right?"

"Macy," I whisper, moving over to the far corner of the room. "It's Charlotte Foresley. Q is okay. Kind of. She's right here, asleep. Honestly, she's a mess, Macy."

Macy comes to life. "Is it that fucker Pearce?"

Wow. She already knows what I'm talking about. The confirmation makes it more real.

I say, "I told her I wouldn't tell . . . but it's big."

"Charlotte, come on. What's happened?"

I take a breath. "I found her in the woods stalking Colin Pearce with a stolen handgun."

Macy is not the shockable type, but I hear her gasp. "Quinnie, you little badass."

A sleepy male voice with a British accent says, "What is it, babe?" And then she covers the phone and repeats what I said.

"Shit," I say. "Macy, I promised."

"Don't worry, he already knows. Is she in trouble?" Macy asks. "Did she get caught?"

"Only by me."

I tell her the story. Q's breakdown, and what she told me about last May.

"Wait," Macy says. "Why were *you* in the woods?"

"It's not important, but I thought Seb was cheating on me."

"God, those boys are cheeky assholes. Was he?"

I realize I've yet to find out, but it seems trivial now.

"Macy?" Q is rubbing her face with both palms.

"Shit," I whisper.

"It's okay," Q says. "You didn't tell anyone else, though, right?"

I shake my head.

I put the phone on speaker.

"Quinnie, a gun!" Macy says.

"Where did you get the gun, Q?" I whisper.

Q sighs. "I feel like I'm coming back from the dead," she says. "I don't know what I was thinking."

She pauses, and we wait for her to continue.

"A few days after we got back to school, I saw the Campus Safety guy Officer Doughty, riding around campus in that all-terrain-vehicle thing, with the blue light. And I thought, what the heck do these guys do? I was *attacked*, right out in the open, walked all the way across campus a disheveled, crying mess, and nobody noticed. What the fuck is that? So I followed him, and I saw him in the safety house—Anderson House—watching his monitors. There's no camera on the Amphitheater, by the way, even though it's a notorious hookup place. Or the boathouse.

Before he left for the night, he took off a holster with the handgun. The next day, I saw Pearce all manspreading on the bench in front of the chapel, where he invited me to Summer Sendoff. A bunch of girls were standing around him, clueless to what he's really like. And I thought, he is free. Like, *free*. Not just *not caught*, but he isn't thinking about how he hurt me, how I might feel, how what he did was wrong. He was just sitting there, like a king on his throne, soaking in the adoration of girls who don't know any better."

"God, Q," I say. "How horrible."

"No, I'm not done," Q says. She inhales. Her eyelids flutter. Exhales. "The fury in me rose up so fast, it scared me, and you know what? I think he could *hear* it."

I try not to make a face. Q stands and moves to the bookshelves, and I feel her anger. Like how in dance we try to evoke emotion through every move we make. And I believe Colin *could* hear her rage.

"Because he looked up, between the shoulders of two Upper Mids, and our eyes locked."

She stops. Shivers. "I spit every ounce of venom I had at him with my eyes. All of it, all at once. And I thought, *You see what you did to me?* as hard as I could think it, sending it in hate waves. But all he did was smirk. A mean, dismissive flick of his mouth. And then he laughed at something and looked away."

Goose bumps run up my arms. I don't know what to say. Apparently neither does Macy because she stays silent.

"So I decided I was going rogue, just like Uncle Lawrence said. And it took me a week, but I got the gun."

"Wait. Slow down," I say. "Uncle Lawrence?"

She recounts a conversation had on her patio in Connecticut

between her dad and the lawyer/godfather.

"Holy shit, Q. Uncle Lawrence wasn't serious!" Macy says. "That is brave."

"Macy, no, it is not!" I protest. I can't help myself. "I mean, it *is*, but—"

"Let me finish, Charlotte. Q, you didn't really think you could do that, did you? Kill a person? Like, *dead*? And if you're caught, you'd go to prison. Like, you didn't th—"

"Did you break into Anderson?" I say, grimacing.

Her look makes me feel horribly naive. I remember, with complete clarity, the stalker outside this house. It was her, stealing a gun.

I nod. "Okay." The reality that I'm something of an accomplice here creeps up the same path as the goose bumps. I massage my neck with both hands. "Look," I say. "We need to get Q some help on campus. I know from being a Big that there are all kinds of counseling services, but they won't come and find you. You have to seek them out."

Q stares at me. I'm not sure if she's catatonic or starting to imagine turning herself in. "I mean—" I steady the back of the sofa. "We don't *need* to share anything about the gun. It's in the middle of the woods at this point."

Macy says, "Charlotte's right, Q. You need more help. How do we go about that, Charlotte? Maybe Val, your therapist, can help. Conference call."

Thank GOD she is siding with me; never a guarantee that Macy will go with the reasonable option. "I need to talk to Ms. Ballard—she's the Bigs and Littles adviser. I need to be able to tell her what happened."

Q groans.

"It's the right thing, Quinnie," Macy says softly.

"She's trustworthy," I add. I think she is, anyway. In reality I've never had to put that to any kind of test. Still, she's our only choice.

"We're not saying his name," Q says. "We already know that won't go anywhere."

"No name, then," I say. "No name."

Before she can change her mind, I step outside and call Ms. Ballard.

Ms. Ballard: We have a situation.

Dean Frye: What? Not the stalker again.

Ms. Ballard: A sexual assault report.

. . .

Ms. Ballard: Hello?

Dean Frye: Assault? Or harassment?

Ms. Ballard: She said assault, by another student. No details yet.

Dean Frye: We should talk in person.

Ms. Ballard: I didn't want to put it in an email. I meet with the girl tomorrow morning.

Dean Frye: Call me immediately afterward. Don't make a move until we touch base.

Ms. Ballard: Got it.

11

Q

On Sunday morning, Ms. Ballard greets Charlotte and me on the porch of Burrell House, smiling in a muted way that signals her etiquette reflex has been activated. "How does tea sound?" She swings her office door open. The room is large and sunny, furnished with a yellow sofa and two coordinated floral armchairs. "Make yourself comfortable. I'll be right back."

Then she leaves us. Charlotte studies the framed photos on the desk.

"This is awkward," I mutter, choosing a spot on the sofa near the wall.

Charlotte sits at the other end. "She'll help you."

I drum my fingers on my knees. "I'm not saying who it was."

"You don't need to," she says. "Nobody wants you to feel uncomfortable." She looks out the window. "We *could* make it a hypothetical."

"Meaning . . ."

"We say, 'So *what if* a . . .'" Charlotte searches for a word.

"Pig bastard?" I offer.

"Right. 'What if he did *this*? What would happen with him?'"

I shrug, nodding. "I guess that's okay."

Ms. Ballard returns balancing a silver tea service and using her hip to close the door. "I made hibiscus-peach," she says. "It's my favorite." She sets the tray on the oval coffee table and commences filling the delicate china cups. Fruit-scented mist spirals between us. Does this woman think she's hosting a book club? I feel shame suddenly at the wretched plumes simmering in me. I'm so far from the person who has pink tea in upholstered chairs on a sunny morning, it's like I'm watching this scene from the sky. I force myself to sip and let it slide down my throat and pull me to the ground.

Charlotte's spoon tinkles against her cup. "Oh, is that Natalie?" she asks. We follow her gaze to the framed photo of a chubby baby pulling happily at her toes.

"That's my girl," Ms. Ballard answers. "Wears me right out." You can tell she's proud of this fact. "Do you babysit, Charlotte? Because I used Ellie Chandler, but now that she's graduated, I'll need someone new."

"I would *love* to babysit," Charlotte says. "She is adorable. Maybe right after the Young Choreographer show."

"Perfect," Ms. Ballard says. "I can't wait to see your program."

The pull of normal conversation is strong, but then they bounce back to the reality of my dismal self. Uneasy eye shifts. Ms. Ballard leans back in her chair, a notebook and pen in her lap. "Q," she says finally. "We're here for you. How are you doing?" Her face has the familiar look of old money—ocean-colored eyes, symmetric smile lines where dimples would be softer, and a veneer of emotional remoteness that I've never known how to breach. She probably doesn't, either, in her defense.

My hand goes for my eyelashes, but I have an audience, so instead I tug at a loose yellow thread on the sofa arm. "I don't know what to tell you."

"I'm a judgment-free listener," Ms. Ballard adds, crossing her legs.

I keep sipping.

Charlotte leans forward. "Can I pose a hypothetical situation?"

Ms. Ballard nods gamely. It's okay, I'd rather watch them than speak.

"Let's say one of my Littles tells me that an upperclassman attacked her—like, sexually."

Ms. Ballard sets her cup down.

"Let's say the upperclassman has a lot of clout on campus," Charlotte continues. "Star athlete, popular, all that."

I sink into the sofa, watching my fingers twist the thread. I feel Ms. Ballard watching, too.

"What happens to the guy?" Charlotte says.

"We bring him in to talk," she says without hesitation.

"What if it was last spring?" I ask, staring at my tea. "But the Little was too freaked out to tell anyone."

"Same thing," she says.

"With zero proof?" I say.

"Just because the Little says it's true? That's enough?" Charlotte asks. "It should be enough," she adds quickly.

"Girls, this isn't a police precinct. It's a school. We have a code of conduct guided by morals and ethics. Everyone needs to feel comfortable here. If something happened, we can do a mediation, so that the . . . wrongdoer is held accountable for his actions and understands the harm he's done."

I picture Pearce manspreading on the bench, smirking at me. "What if he denies it?"

Ms. Ballard sits up tall. "In my experience, when the two people in question are in the same room—"

"No way," I say, shaking my head.

Ms. Ballard cocks her head, like she's dodging a spitball, and catches Charlotte's eyes. They exchange a knowing glance that pisses me off. Because they don't know. They have no fucking idea.

"Q," Charlotte says. "It's just a hypothetical, remember?"

"Absolutely," Ms. Ballard says.

"Really, Q. We're here for *you*, not some"—Charlotte twirls a hand dismissively—"hypothetical pig bastard. Okay?" She tries to smile.

"Right," I say. I picture myself, chucking that gun into the woods. It's still out there. If I have to resume plan A. I cradle that thought in my mind and let my head flop back onto the cushions. "Last spring, a student here," I tell the ceiling. Then something makes me look dead-on at Ms. Ballard. "A student raped me. On the Amphitheater Lawn."

Okay, that wasn't hypothetical.

Charlotte's eyes pop to Ms. Ballard's face, which immediately shifts to a new register of concern. This is only the second time I've said it out loud here, and both less than twelve hours apart. It's strange, but seeing how it lands with her makes something loosen in my chest.

"Oh no, Q," she says. And it sounds genuine. "I'm so sorry this happened to you." She's picking up her pen and notebook. "Who else knows?" The cap makes a tiny *click* as she pops it off, and I recognize it immediately as a sound of enormous consequence. I just don't know exactly what I'm activating. I worm my spine deeper into the couch, pull a pillow over my lap. "Nobody at school. Besides Charlotte. And him."

"When did it happen?" she asks.

"It doesn't matter. I'm here because I probably need, you know, help. I've been having . . . trouble." I glance at Charlotte. She nods gently. I continue. "I have a therapist from home. We talk twice a week, but I don't know. It's harder to see this . . ."

"Pig bastard," Ms. Ballard says.

We lock eyes, and my chest gives way a little further. "Yes," I say. "Seeing him around campus brings up a lot of—" *Rage* is the word, but it's probably too much to admit. My heartbeat is going wild. "Rage."

I said it.

Ms. Ballard stops writing. I see her notice the butterfly pinch marks, and I tug my sleeves down. She uncrosses her legs. "Of course. We can set up a meeting today with health services. How do you feel about my giving your parents a call? They need to approve."

"It's okay. My dad and stepmom know. And our lawyer. I just swore them to secrecy."

She looks puzzled. "Why? You didn't do anything wrong."

I see myself frozen on the ground and am compelled to stand. I move to the bookcase, running my finger along the books. *The Catcher in the Rye, Dr. Jekyll and Mr. Hyde, Frankenstein, The Picture of Dorian Gray.* The spines blur. "Our lawyer listened to all the facts and said I didn't have a winnable case. So why bother?"

I pause, then blurt out, "I was drunk, too. He made sure I was good and *drunk*." *Drunk* is a satisfying word, hard on both ends, staccato, like a punch. I reseat myself. "I didn't have a chance of proving it to anyone."

"Did you know this boy well?"

"No. We talked a few times, but he never showed any interest in me until one day he sat next to me on the bench in front of the chapel and asked me out." I need a way to mask the Summer Sendoff. "For dinner." Ms. Ballard is untroubled by my vagueness.

"It was so random for him to pick me," I say.

"Why don't you think he simply had a crush on you?" Ms. Ballard asks.

"Because he didn't." Why didn't I pay attention to my own gut feelings? "He lost a bet." I look at Charlotte. Her brow crinkles, and I know I should tell her about Seb, but not now.

Ms. Ballard is waiting. I don't know what to say next. Unwelcome images play across my eyelids.

My arm hooked in his. Dewy grass against my toes. Kicking off my new sandals, smiling up at him.

My stomach rolls. I straighten my back. Admitting my sheer stupidity is unbearable, so I say, "I knew we were going to hook up." Charlotte nods. Of course, because she surely wanted to hook up with Seb that night, too. She understands. She just didn't draw the rapist card, I think bitterly. I watch Ms. Ballard's face for a twitch in her eyebrow or the corner of her mouth. But she doesn't change. "I—I *wanted* to," I say, then watch their eyes. "It didn't occur to me that he would be violent."

"Why would it?" Ms. Ballard nods, writing. Her jaw is taut. "So when did it become"—she thinks—"not consensual?"

The perverted seashell sound of his hot mouth on my ear invades my head. I stand again, turn my back to them, and steady both hands on the bookshelf. Something is collapsing inside, like a building in an earthquake. I can't hold the weight of it anymore. I inhale.

"We walked to the Amphitheater. He quizzed me on the names of the Muses. I could name them all. We started kissing, and we sat in the grass, and then all of a sudden . . ." *His teeth clack into mine.* "He pinned me to the ground. It happened really fast. He got the straps of my dress off so I was naked from here." I demonstrate. "His eyes turned black. Like, hollow." I let myself sob, then pull it back in. Charlotte sets Kleenex on the shelf and moves away. I blow my nose. It's swarming, the cloud of black smoke, billowing in the middle of my body.

"Oh, Q. That sounds horrible. I'm so sorry you had to endure that," Ms. Ballard says. She's behind me, and she puts a hand on my shoulder. I flinch, and she pulls it away. "You didn't deserve it. Do you need a break?"

"Why, do you?" I want my words to land like darts. Her mouth is open, but she doesn't speak. "Of course I want a break from—" *The fucking shit show he turned me into.* I don't say that, though. "You *are* my break!" I wave my hands at them.

They share an alarmed glance; then Ms. Ballard nods confidently. "I'm here to listen to everything you want to share. Do you want Charlotte to leave."

"No," I say quickly. I don't want to be alone with Ms. Ballard. I am not sure I trust her, and I definitely don't trust myself.

Ms. Ballard turns and says quietly, "Charlotte? Are you okay to stay?"

Charlotte nods confidently, but I know better. *You don't have to stay,* I try to say with my expression.

"I'm not leaving you," she says. "I never should have left you."

Ms. Ballard furrows her brow. "Were you together that night?"

"No," I blurt.

"But I was her Big," Charlotte says, her chin quivering. "Her friend. I should have paid more attention."

Ms. Ballard shakes her head. "No, Charlotte."

Charlotte keeps her eyes on me. "Yes, I did a shitty, shitty job. Q, just know I am so sorry." Her voice breaks, and she drops her head, shoulders bouncing.

Why does this make me cry, too? She should not hurt from this. "It's not your fault. Nothing is your fault! Please," I say. "I can't take it."

She sniffs. "Okay, okay," she says. "But I'm not leaving now unless you want me to."

"Stay," I say. I move to the window. The morning light is bright, but I don't blink. "It's like it just needs to be told all of a sudden."

"Take your time," Ms. Ballard says.

I pace a bit. "I said, 'Stop.' I tried to push him off. He had both my wrists in one hand over my head." I rub my wrists now. "I said 'No!' really clearly. But he didn't stop."

"Did he hear you?" Ballard asks.

I check her for skepticism, but her eyes are soft. "He heard me."

"How can you be so sure?" Charlotte asks, adding hastily, "I believe you, of course!"

"Because he said"—I exhale and muster the strength to imitate Pearce—"'Let it be fun.'"

"Gross," Charlotte says as Ms. Ballard says, "Dear God."

I hear myself tell them that I remember the scorching pain and the endlessness of it and the way I just lay there and let it happen, like a dead thing. "The worst thing of all, the most disgusting thing"—I can't stop spewing all the blackness out of myself—"he groaned with pleasure." I shake my head, shuddering. I might throw up, I realize. I suck in long breaths. "He knew he was hurting me, and it didn't matter. I was—not there to him. It was not me—like, he could take the flesh and bones without the person." I unfold and blink. "He ripped me from me. I was trying to leave myself on the ground, but I couldn't get away. You can't leave your body," I tell them.

This is why I don't recognize myself anymore, I realize. I am a Frankenstein's monster, a distorted imitation of the Quinn Walsh who walked out there, sandals in hand, flirting just ten minutes before it happened.

"He never even took off his dress shoes."

Charlotte's mouth hangs open. "You're the bravest person I've ever met," she says finally.

"No," I say. "I'm not."

But her words make me cry like a small child. And I have this flash of my mother on a bed in a bright, unfamiliar room, and my dad is holding me up to her so she can hold my fingers, bounce my hands up and down, and she's smiling, her eyes crinkled at the sides, and she says, *You're my brave girl. Can you be my brave girl, Quinnie? When you can't see me, I'm here. I'm always watching you, my brave, brave girl. My angel.* Her lips press against my fingers.

My ribs open yet further, releasing something I didn't know was there. It's under the black mass—little pieces of memory that fell off and hid in the middle of me, covered by seasons of tire swings and fairy houses and ladybug umbrellas, fallen leaves, and running on packed beach sand, through waves so cold they prickle. Under it all, the little pieces of flower petals, the color of hibiscus tea and honey, coming together and breaking apart—a delicate glass heart trying to beat. I *do* miss my mother.

"I wasn't brave," I say. *I'm sorry, Mama.* My wail is long, taking all my breath with it, and the vibrating black swarm inside me. That's my soul, I suddenly know. It doesn't make a sound. Until I inhale deep and hear my own self sobbing. My own old self.

When I finally recover, I feel slightly changed. It's disorienting. I sit up.

Ms. Ballard has her eyes closed. The notebook is sliding from her lap. She clears her throat. "Dear God," she whispers. She's not a teacher right then. She's a woman. A girl. A mother. Maybe the reason I always say I don't remember my mom is because I don't want to feel how huge the hole she left behind is.

"Quinn, you're *beyond* brave," Ms. Ballard says.

I shake my head. "No," I whisper. I should have clawed him. Kneed him. Bit. I could have *bit. This is why I got the gun.* I wait for the ugliness to whip up, the black rage. When it doesn't, I become dizzy. I shut my eyes. I hear Ms. Ballard and Charlotte talk but am too tired to process language. I want to sleep.

I just want to sleep.

CHARLOTTE

"I think she's asleep," I whisper to Ms. Ballard. "She did this last night, too."

"It's probably a stress reaction," Ms. Ballard says softly. "We need to get her to Knowlton for help."

Ms. Ballard opens a narrow closet door behind her desk and pulls out a green school blanket. She spreads it over Q. "Do you know who it is, Charlotte?"

I stare at her. I am *not* betraying Q, and besides, something tells me I don't think I want to get involved any deeper than I already am.

"Never mind," she says. "That was unfair. I'm sorry. Look, this is a lot for you, too. I've got Quinn for now. You can go." She's fumbling through her bag on her desk. "Excuse me." She starts texting. I wonder who. She is clearly in a conversation. Her phone rings.

"I've got to take this," she says, hurrying past me into the hall. She leaves the door open, and I see her step outside. "Hello?" She steps off the porch, continuing around the corner, out of sight.

I am exhausted. I have an English paper due tomorrow. Maybe I should go. But I feel guilty. To prolong my decision, I pick up the teacups and carry the tray toward the kitchenette. My feet stutter when I see Ms. Ballard outside on the phone. The window is cracked open. I tiptoe closer, hiding behind the curtain.

Ms. Ballard covers the phone mic. "Bullshit!" she says. Whoa. She uncovers it. "She decided to come back and didn't want her parents to inform the school. Not enough evidence, according to their lawyer. But she's falling apart. We need to get her into counseling, so I need to inform the parents." Pause. "You don't want to know her name? Oh, great. Leave me as the only faculty member who knows, which makes *me* liable to the trustees if anything gets out." Pause. "I don't know who he is yet. Not yet. But she might decide to have a mediation." Pause. "*We?* How can I do that?

She rakes her fingers through her hair. "Fine. But if this takes a bad turn, I'm not taking the fall like Katherine Mason did."

Trustees? Who is Katherine Mason? This happened before? I gently set the tray by the sink and tiptoe back into her office. I sit in one of the flowered chairs and read my phone.

Seb: Hey.

I literally cannot. I press the lock button , squashing my anxiety about his *bet* right down with it.

Ms. Ballard comes in, her face grim. "Oh," she says. "I thought you'd be gone." She glances at Q and whispers, "If you have studying to do, you really should go ahead." She's seats herself at her desk, flipping through a directory. "Take care of yourself. This is a lot."

I want to grill her about the phone call. I open my mouth, not sure what will come out, but she interrupts.

"It's okay. Go. I'll text you when Q wakes up." She waves toward the door. "You did the right thing, Charlotte, as a Big. Your response was perfect, and now you can step back."

We stare at each other until she turns away. Does she think I don't notice her change in demeanor?

"I do have a paper due," I say, glancing at Q's slumbering form.

"Bye, Charlotte." She nods, not lifting her head from the file, and I slip out the door.

Q

I wake to a wall of yellow flowered fabric. I'm facing into the sofa cushions, a Lycroft blanket covering me. I can't remember where I am until I roll over and find Ms. Ballard working at her desk. She glances up. "Hi there," she says gently.

"Hi." I feel different, but I don't know how. It's disorienting. I sit up and crack my neck. "May I use the restroom?"

She nods, smiling. "Second door on the right." She points toward the hall.

It's a small powder room. The rose-shaped soaps by the sink smell like Boppy's house. I splash water on my face for a long minute; then I breathe deeply (in for four, out for six), feeling my chest rise. I dare look in the mirror. My curly hair is rumpled, bald eyes sad.

I don't want to be this anymore.

Ms. Ballard occupies an armchair and has folded the blanket neatly on the sofa arm. I sit beside it.

"Quinn, I want to make sure I understand where you are with this. Your family decided not to turn it into a police matter. But why not take it up with us here at school?"

"I didn't feel like having to explain myself a million times over."

"Okay, right. Yes." Ms. Ballard looks uncomfortable and shifts positions. "The thing is, um, Quinn, is that we—you know, the administration—need to be sure he learns from his mistake."

"Mistake?"

She shifts again. "That's the wrong word. What I mean is, he can't do this again," she says. "We don't want what happened to you to happen again, Quinn."

I'm not sure where she's headed with this. "Where'd Charlotte go?"

Ms. Ballard leans back. "I insisted she go get some studying done. She needs to take care of herself. She said she'll check in with you later."

My eyes shift to the tabletop.

"You don't need to feel guilty about that. She didn't want to go! Let me repeat what I said this morning: you didn't do anything wrong."

On cue, my mind displays me on the ground, an empty bag. My throat tightens. I have a compulsion to pinch myself, pull at myself, anything. "Ughhhh," I growl as a tear rolls down my cheek. "I keep—" I point to my eyes. "I pulled my eyelashes out." I cry.

She looks mortified. "Oh, honey," she says. "I'm so sorry. Let's get you to Knowlton. Your dad and stepmother think it's a good idea. It sounds like your therapist and Miss Lisa can collaborate to set up a treatment plan."

I stare. I've said no to help for so long, but I'm so tired. Whatever shifted in me cracked open a space to let light in. Slowly, I nod. "Yeah," I say, so softly I barely hear myself. "Okay."

"We've got you," Ms. Ballard says. "Quinn. You have my word."

Something catches in her voice, but then she's up gathering some folders, and I can't read her face. "Okay, let's do this," she says.

The air is cooling down, the sun angled through the apple trees as we walk along the gravel. "We have a couple of options," Ms.

341

Ballard's saying. "We can do a mediation with Colin."

I hear his name and stop dead. "What?"

She turns to face me. "I know you went to Summer Sendoff with him, Q."

My mouth drops.

"You mentioned dress shoes. It was a hunch, and I checked the photos. It was easy to find out. It made sense—kids started going home the next day, and that's why none of the faculty knew anything happened."

I don't have to confirm and don't bother to deny. I'm sure she can see it on my face, and honestly, I'm glad she knows. I want people to know he's a rat bastard and not just a star rower.

"So a mediation," she says, walking on. I follow. "We meet in my office, and I mediate a safe discussion so you can tell him the impact he had on you."

I almost laugh. "That's not happening."

Ms. Ballard's hands fly up. "We don't have to do that. We don't have to do anything if you don't want to. Another option is a mediation where I serve as messenger between you. You tell me what to say; then I tell you how he responds."

"I'm not doing that, either. Why would I?"

Ms. Ballard stops at the Knowlton doors. "It's a process called restorative justice, and it allows the survivor a facilitated conversation to process the harms committed with the person who caused the harm. Ideally, that person—Colin in this scenario—processes the consequences of his actions and accepts responsibility. Which allows the survivor—you—to feel validated so you can begin to heal."

I remain quiet. Ms. Ballard holds the Knowlton door open for me. All cool and calm, she says, "Q, consider, if you can, what it would feel like to stand up to him and have him admit the truth." She holds my eyes. "Would that be empowering? To confront him? Show him you aren't going to just let it go?"

My lips and cheeks start tingling; the restless storm in my chest begins to blow. I can't respond, so I walk through the door instead. Across the lobby, Miss Lisa is on the desk phone. She makes a "one minute" sign with her finger.

Ms. Ballard lowers her voice. "If the in-person mediation or mediation by messenger sounds like it would help you start to heal, then I'll make it happen. If it wouldn't help"—she shrugs—"forget it."

I can't tell if she wants me to forget it or not. It's kind of like she tried to sell me on it and then gave me a door out. It doesn't matter what she wants, I guess.

"Meanwhile," she continues, "let's get you the best emotional support available. Whatever you need. Academic help, time with Chaplain Walker . . ."

Chaplain Walker? Seriously? An eighty-year-old guy? "Thanks for believing me" is all I can say.

"No thanks needed."

Miss Lisa walks into the lobby, smiling. "Hello! Quinn, we're going in room four." She tilts her chin over her shoulder. "I'll be right in."

Ms. Ballard rubs my shoulder, and I withdraw reflexively. "I'm sorry." She shakes her head and I feel like a shit, because she's not Colin Pearce and why can't my brain sort this out? "I'll check in with you tomorrow, okay?"

I nod.

Room 4 is like a dorm room, with a bed, dresser, and desk. There's an oil cubist portrait of a woman, like a Picasso. Her face is a geometric arrangement of flat planes of color—blues and greens, yellows and reds. The background is neutral sand colors, in big brush strokes. One eye looks at me, the other at herself.

Restorative justice? I wish I'd just shot him that night at the barn, when he was standing there with his fly open. That would have been *poetic* justice.

Colin Pearce,

shot dead,

dick out.

No witnesses.

Slycroft would have scattered like shrapnel. I could have slipped back into the darkness, a lynx, silent and patient.

You couldn't pull the trigger. I can almost imagine the painting said it, but I know it's my own self recognizing my weakness.

Nope, I could not. In spite of my seething hatred for him. I pinch myself hard.

I sigh, sit on the chair, and I study the painting some more. She's like me: broken. But I also think she's strangely beautiful in all her dimensions.

I check my phone. Macy checked in. Alex. Charlotte. I open that one.

> **Charlotte:** Hope all is going well. Would you be okay if I told Hannah? She is 100% trustworthy and will not tell a soul.
> We will support you. She can help me with the thing in the woods. Because the owner will notice it's gone.

She means Doughty and the gun. I have been colossally stupid. What did I think? But I didn't think. Now Charlotte is thinking for me. I consider Hannah. She's cool, I guess. Charlotte probably needs an ally.

Me: Yes. Okay. Good.

A knot of anxiety crimps between my shoulder blades. How do you anonymously return a gun? I'm not sure if we should.

Me: I'm so sorry. I wish I could make it vanish off the planet.

Charlotte: Hannah is 👧 of strategy. I'll let you know

Miss Lisa raps lightly on the door. "Quinn?" She's thirtysomething and brings a breath of *outside world* with her. I didn't realize there was such a thing until I see it in her. She has a small pink flower tattoo on her ankle, between the hem of her dress slacks and her blue pump. Unlike the academic faculty, her clothes aren't preppy, aging hippie, or altogether devoid of any fashion category whatsoever. I don't have a name for it besides *different*. She may have whitened teeth, but her smile is warm and her unabashedly mascara'd blue eyes clear. "I've just been on the phone with Valarie, your therapist from home. She would like to video-conference with you at four."

I nod. Maybe Miss Lisa is some kind of medium between my regular life and my Lycroft life.

"I've let your roommate, Alex, know you—"

My whole body stiffens. Miss Lisa steps in the room. "May I?" She points to the other chair, and I nod. She smells of floral perfume. It's nice. "Don't worry. I said you were ill and that you would be staying overnight in case you're contagious."

I relax. "Thanks. She thought I might have mono. Because I've been so weird."

"Yes, she asked about mono. I told her we didn't know, but best to isolate you for now. In any case, she's dropping off an overnight bag. She said she knew just what to bring."

I smile, instantly choked up by a torrent of stored-up loneliness.

I miss Alex. I've missed her for months.

"Alex sounds lovely," Miss Lisa says. "Don't feel bad about not telling her. You'd be amazed how common that is with sexual assault survivors."

It rolls off her tongue so matter-of-factly.

"You've tried to protect her, haven't you? From the horror of it? From your pain?"

Man, her perceptiveness is a little uncanny. I let the two hot tears plopping off my cheeks answer for me. "Quinn, that is what a wonderful friend does for a friend. Tries to protect her. But soon you'll learn that the people who love you are stronger than you think. We don't need to worry about that yet, though. We're focused on you."

She's so in control. So . . . getting me. "Are you okay with the video call?" She stands.

I inhale. "Yes."

"Good. I'll get you a laptop."

I move to the bed and lie back on the fat down pillows. They cradle my shoulders and neck.

I'm ready to feel better, I say in my head. It's easy to imagine the cubist woman heard me.

I reach for my phone and text Alex.

Me: Thanks for getting my stuff. Can you bring the butterfly art thing and my supplies? And maybe my guitar?

I don't get a response for a bit. And then she simply sends a heart.

MAX

Nils and I are in the study room at the top floor of Langston Hall, the humanities building. It's paneled and has soft leather chairs and tables with reading lamps, oil paintings of ships at sea on the walls, and windows that overlook the quad. Barely anyone knows it's here, and the people who do treat it like a sacred quiet space. Hank Schweitzer told Nils about it, and it's been part of our Sunday after-breakfast routine since First Year. Spangler for late breakfast, study for two to three hours, depending, lunch, afternoon free to hike, climb, kayak, and evenings for whatever the hell we feel like. It's the only routine we have that hasn't been disrupted by crew, so I don't want to mess it up.

But this is the first Sunday I've been hungover and drifted off to sleep a couple times in my arm chair. Also the first one where I feel guilty. It was bad enough realizing I'll be skipping the Monadnock trip so I can cox at the Big Dip. I feel like crap for lying to Nils about where I went last night. And for knowing I'll have to keep lying to him, since I've agreed to join Slycroft. So maybe the headache and vague churning in my gut are appropriate punishment.

Something lands on my lap. I open my eyes to find a pink eraser. "Hey there, sleepyhead. Maybe you're not cut out to run with the alpha pack," Nils says, grinning from one of the tables.

I'm not sure if his voice has an edge. I don't like thinking about it. I gather my laptop and French book and take the seat next to him.

"I can't wait to get outside and get my blood moving," I mutter. "Get this booze out of my system," I add. But really, it's more than the booze I want gone.

"Mountain bike?" he suggests. "A proper pounding through Mobley Falls?"

I suppress the notion of motion sickness and instead focus on sucking in lungfuls of cool fall air and fresh oxygen flooding my currently stank blood. I nod.

We study for another hour.

I can't stomach the idea of lunch, so I tell Nils to go ahead as we approach Spangler. "I want to give Alex my new copy of *The Boys in the Boat*."

Nils winks gratuitously. "Smooth," he says. I chuckle grudgingly. We part ways, and on the way to our room, I want to unsee the whole dicks-before-chicks business at Slycroft. No way am I putting those guys ahead of Alex Buchanan. This proves it, I think, carrying the book across the quad to her dorm. Maybe I am the kind of guy who moves between groups. Swims above the fray, like Seb, maybe. I tell myself this as I walk into the Norton lobby. A few Lower Mid girls look away from their TV show and eye me as I head toward the stairs. Yeah, I think, I'm the guy who comes to visit my crush on Sunday. The guy who's confident enough to walk right up to her door and knock. Unannounced.

The door is ajar it turns out, and I see Alex on a beanbag chair with her laptop open. Q is nowhere, thankfully. I'm about to knock, but she looks up before I can and startles a little and then looks confused. What am I thinking, unannounced? On my first trip to her room? I should have consulted with Nils.

"Max," she says, popping up from the chair. She smiles, then doesn't, then does. "What are you doing here?" She tucks her hair behind her ear and adjusts her T-shirt and shorts, then swings the door fully open.

My eyes get stuck on her smooth legs and they render me speechless, so I simply hold up the book. She squints—oh my God she is beautiful—and smiles wider now. "Oh," she says, taking it from me. "Come on in."

"I really want you to read it and tell me what you think. UC Berkeley is in there a lot. Your brother's school. Huge historic rivalry with University of Washington." I'm rambling. Apparently, I either can't speak or can't shut up. I need to land on the in-between.

She nods, flipping through the pages. "Thanks. That's so sweet." She sets it on her desk. "I have a hard time finding leisure reading time, but I will do my best."

"Oh, no pressure," I say.

There is a pause, and I fill it by looking over Q's photo wall. "Where's Q?" It's the best I can come up with.

"Knowlton," she says. "They think she has mono. I bet she does, but I hope not because it's really contagious."

But as she's saying that I say, "Oh, the kissing disease," all knowingly, and we both realize we were kissing yesterday and simultaneously turn purple with embarrassment.

"Oh my God," she says, closing her eyes.

"Sorry, I—" What, Max? What? Pivot. "I hope she's okay."

"Yeah, that is definitely the most important thing."

"Get well, Q," I say.

"Godspeed," she says. "Really! I love Q!"

We laugh. I think I can convert this. "Hey, want to get lunch?"

"Sure," she says. "Give me a second to change."

"Great!" I will myself not to imagine her changing and say, "I'll, uh, wait in the lobby."

It's not until I'm downstairs being very obviously noticed—and whispered about—by the Lower Mids on the TV sofa that the epiphany smacks me on the head: I'm visible. I'm reinvented. I'm not only on crew, but I'm part of a secret society. I'm the same person as a month ago with a totally new identity.

I have arrived at Lycroft Phelps.

Ms. Ballard: No go on mediation. I don't blame her. If I told you who the guy is . . .

Dean Frye: Don't do that. We need a mediation to put it to rest. Did you tell her how it helps—how it makes the boy accountable to her? Get him to agree to do something nice for her.

Ms. Ballard: Do something nice for her? She doesn't want to make anything of it. Why stir it up with this? Just let her try to move on.

Dean Frye: No. I've seen this before. Her friends will want revenge. If we get ahead of it, she can move on faster.

Ms. Ballard: The boy is . . .

Dean Frye: Please.

Ms. Ballard: It could backfire with him. I don't want to put her through it.

Dean Frye: Look, what's done is done. We can't get it to un-happen. We just have to help her feel like she's being attended to. Being "heard," then she can move on. We need it to be resolved.

Ms. Ballard: Wow.

Dean Frye: They're kids, Lori. We're adults. We have mortgages to pay, retirements to save for. I need my job. Do you need yours?

Ms. Ballard: Just. Wow.

Dean Frye: You'll be happy you helped the girl get a little justice. You'll be happy that we don't have a situation blow up just as all the alumni and parents arrive for Fall Fling. Get the mediation set up, Lori.

Ms. Ballard: Or what? You'll throw me under the bus like Katherine?

Dean Frye: Lori. We're on the same team. If it came out later that you knew about the situation and didn't do anything, we'll be accused of a cover-up. You'll see. This is the right way to go. Trust me.

Ms. Ballard: Fine.

Ms. Ballard: OMFG, you aren't going to believe this.

Ms. Weller: What happened?

Ms. Ballard: Frye.

Ms. Weller: Oh no. What?

Ms. Ballard: It's a long story. We should meet for our wine and whine.

Ms. Weller: Yes, please. Tonight? Meanwhile, hint?

Ms Ballard: God, I feel horrible about myself. This poor girl.

Ms. Weller: Who?

Ms. Ballard: !!! She was assaulted in May. She is a wreck. He's pushing *me* to push *her* for a mediation, and he won't take any responsibility.

Ms. Weller: Just like what happened with Katherine Mason!

Ms. Ballard: 🔍

Ms. Weller: Wine and whine. I'll help any way I can.

CHARLOTTE

"I wish he could be arrested," I say. "She is *wrecked*. It's horrifying. I feel so terrible."

"I don't even know what to say." Hannah hunkers low in her library seat. "He pinned her wrists?"

I nod gravely. "And he gets to walk around like nothing happened."

"More like strut around." We're in the reference section, alone. It's a long time before she asks, "Does Alex know?"

"Not yet. I don't see how it can stay secret, but it's Q's decision." I shrug. "I'm sorry to have to tell *you*." We sit in silence for a while, each of us trying to make sense of it all.

Hannah shakes her head. "It's a lot. But I'm glad you did. We can support her together. And you need someone to talk to, too."

I take a deep breath. "She texted me that Seb and Colin had a bet over who would take me to Summer Sendoff." I tap my foot and stare at my hands. "It could have been me with him."

"Jesus," she says. She puts her hand over mine. "Hey, obviously Seb really likes you."

I nod, because I want to believe her.

"It's definitely not your fault, Char." After another pause, she whispers, "But stealing a *gun*?"

I grimace, nodding.

"And you just left it there in the woods?"

"What was I supposed to do?" I say defensively. "Come on, I was freaking out!"

"Charlotte, be glad you found her before anything happened."

I nod. "Yeah, but now Dean Frye's involved, and there is definite weirdness around the whole thing." I shake my head. "And Officer Doughty is going to want his gun back. What if they get Q to confess? I'm an accomplice. And I guess I've made you one, too."

She shifts in her chair. "Hold on. Why would they try to get her to confess to anything? She's the one who got attacked."

I take in a breath. "Right. Yes. You're right."

"What weirdness with Frye?"

I tell her about Ms. Ballard's phone conversation with Dean Frye.

"Who is Katherine Mason? And doesn't anybody care that we have a secret society rooted in rape culture?"

"I don't even know what rape culture is," I say. God, I am so clueless. "I was just living the dream twenty-four hours ago, and now everything I thought I knew has cracked into pieces." The word *bet* pirouettes between my ribs and I twist my shoulders to get rid of it.

"Rape culture is guys competing to screw the most girls, for one."

"Oh," I say. "We didn't tell Ms. Ballard about the barn. Not on purpose. It was all Q could do to not tell about Summer Send-off." I sigh. I can't stand thinking about the opportunity I missed by being so self-absorbed that night. "Hannah," I moan. "I could have saved her from him."

She reaches for my forearm. "A: How the heck would you predict that would happen to her? B: I was there, too! And sober. Am I responsible? C: That's also rape culture: innocent people feeling guilty while the rapist feels innocent. He's the guilty one."

"Yes. He is. You're right," I say. I wish I fully believed it. "Do you really think Lycroft Phelps has a rape culture?" I say.

"Not all of it. But it should be none of it."

"This is so depressing," I say, dropping my head on the desk. We sit in silence again. "Seb is in a secret fuck-boy club," I say from under my mop of hair. "But he hasn't asked me to have sex."

"And you haven't asked him," she says.

"I don't have the energy right now, Hannah."

"Just sayin'."

A few moments later, she says, "I've got it!"

I sit upright, and she's looking straight at me when she says, "We *do* go find the gun, and we do turn it in to Doughty, but we act like we just came upon it while running the trails."

I roll this over in my head and begin nodding. That would clear us, and it would never implicate Q. "Brilliant," I say. "If we can find it." I remember the wildcat and shiver. "God, did I mention the wildcat?"

"What?"

I explain, and her eyebrows rise on her forehead. She pinches the bridge of her nose. "Okay . . . I think you are talking about a bobcat or a Canada lynx," she says. She paces in a circle, then stops. "Forget the cat," she says. "It's ridiculously rare to see one of those. Just put it out of your head. Let's go get dressed."

"We are dressed," I say.

"Duh, Charlotte. Running clothes!"

After we change and jog to the athletic fields, we lope into the shaded cross-country trails. "Do you think LPS covered up

355

another assault? And Katherine Mason took the fall?"

"Shh! I don't know," I say.

I'm trying to recall the layout of last night, but nothing is particularly familiar until I recognize the sharp dip in the trail. "Okay, I remember this."

"Good God, people do this for fun," Hannah says as we pound down the ravine. We grunt our way up the other side.

"Here," I pant, recognizing the cluster of silver birches where I found Q. "Shit!" Hannah grabs my arm and pretends to show me something on her phone while two middle-aged teachers jog by.

"Hi, Mr. Price," Hannah says pleasantly. He waves, and they pass by.

We wait for them to get out of earshot.

"This way." I leave the path.

We push aside branches and climb over roots. The ground between the trees is covered with pine needles and areas of unidentifiable calf-high weeds.

"How are we ever going to find it?"

"It was your idea," I say, hunching to brush aside the weeds every few feet.

For twenty minutes or so, we scour the ground.

"I'm getting worried," I stage-whisper.

"Let's give it another few—"

"Oh!" My toe connects with something. I push aside brambles. Black. Matte. It's a gun. "Oh my God!" I wave her over.

"This is the right thing to do," she says. "Isn't it?"

"I think so?" I say.

"It is, it is, of course it is," Hannah says, wagging her chin around.

I pick it up by the handle with two fingers.

"You said Q had all the bullets, right?" Hannah says.

"Well, I mean, she thinks she does, but . . ." I wince.

"Just keep the head pointed down, far from our toes."

I nervous laugh. "The head? Which end is the head."

"The nozzle, the—the—tube—" Hannah gesticulates. "You know!"

"Okay, okay. Let's get out of here," I say.

We start back for the trailhead at a brisk walk. "Should we put a selfie on the front page of the *Wire*? 'Who will *you* be at Lycroft Phelps?'" she whispers.

"Not funny," I say.

"I know. I'm sorry. This doesn't feel real," she says. "I feel like we're on a sitcom."

"I wish it was a sitcom."

We're subdued and keep going until my phone vibrates in my hoodie pocket. "Here, hold this," I say, handing her the gun. She takes it like it's a dead mouse. "It's Q," I say. "Oh, man. She says she wants to sneak the gun back into Anderson tonight."

Hannah shakes her head. "We're not doing that. We'd get expelled. Arrested."

"Right," I say, my hands starting to sweat. I text that to Quinn. "But what if you and I turn it in and Officer Doughty knows we're lying. That could blow up on us, too. I suck at lying! And this is really big." My phone buzzes. I read it. "She says, 'I don't want you two doing anything. I'll sneak in there myself.'"

I look at Hannah. Panic is rising in my throat.

Hannah presses her lips tight, shakes her head. "No way. Our fingerprints are on it." She paces in a circle. "And we don't know,

Char. What if Q flips out and really . . . does something bad. She was going to *kill* him."

"I think I'm gonna barf," I say.

"Not now, Charlotte. We have to get the fucking gun out of our possession, and we have to keep it away from her. But I know what we have to do. The lake. We can throw it out where it will never be found. Everyone's safe, nobody has to lie."

I try to process this. "We're still kind of lying."

We lock eyes. "Charlotte, it's the best plan. The lowest risk of our ever being questioned."

"God, how do you think like that? You're like part spy or something," I say.

"I don't know. Let's go. The sun's setting," she adds. "Less likelihood of being seen."

"Should I text Q?"

"Yeah, I'm thinkin' no on that. We don't want her to imagine options."

I nod.

When we get to the open fields, Hannah says, "Let me see that thing."

I hand her the gun. She fiddles with it, and the bullet chamber opens. "Okay, it really is empty. We can't just walk across campus with it out in the open."

"Here, give it to me," I say. With trembling hands, I tuck it in the waste of my spandex tights. "God save me."

Twenty minutes later, we're standing at a secluded edge of Lake Edith, way past the boathouse. The sky is violet, which makes the water violet, too.

"The color is eerie," Hannah says. "Like it knows."

"That we're committing some kind of felony."

"Shh. Don't. I can't," she says. "Okay." She pans the area. "Nobody's here. Ready?"

"I think we're going to remember this when we're old ladies, Hannah," I say. "I know we'll be friends forever, and now we have a secret we can never tell a soul."

"Never ever," she says. Her eyes are glassy in the dim light.

I take a deep breath. Shake out my arms and retrieve the gun from my waistband. I wind up, skip sideways a couple of times, and hurl the gun as far as I can.

Pla-oup!

A curtain falls around us then, like we're alone in the world with the gravity of what we've just done. We're silent. I know we're both thinking about how it could change everything about everything we have done. How it already has in a small private way. I feel the tears start. I hug her.

"Don't cry. We have to think of it as saving Quinn from really, really big trouble," Hannah says. "From bad things."

I nod into her shoulder. "I think I'm crying from relief."

"We take this to the grave," she whispers.

"To the grave," I say. We squeeze and release. As we turn toward the quad, a loon call sounds over the lake.

We stop and look out over the water, shimmering with moonlight. A second loon responds to the other. They start chuckling—it's surreal and haunted. We look at each other.

"Let's get the fuck out of here," Hannah says. And we run all the way back to the quad.

12

Q

Miss Lisa, Val, and my parents decided I'll stay at Knowlton for the week. Even though this is basically a glorified hospital room, I didn't fight them on it. I'm glad to have a break from the dorm. Trying not to freak out Alex was exhausting, and in four weeks, I'd racked up nothing but crap memories in there. This room is a blank slate in terms of emotional associations. It overlooks an apple tree grove, and the occasional deer strolls through to eat fallen fruit. Also, while I'm here, I'm excused from classes.

"I'm not convinced the mediation process is the right move for you," Val is saying. It's Monday afternoon, and we're on a portal call.

Dr. Valerie Stepanov is a middle-aged psychiatrist with a fancy private practice in Manhattan decorated with books and tabletop abstract sculptures. I know she attended Barnard for her BS and Columbia for her PsyD, because she has her diplomas hung on the wall and, during our summer sessions, I spent more time looking at them than at her. I'm noticing for the first time how put-together she is. Coiffed hair dyed a tasteful auburn color. Perfect nails. She's not the warm-and-fuzzy type, but comforting and loud in a distinctly New York City way.

"Why?" I ask. "Isn't the whole Me Too thing about speaking up? Calling out your assaulter so rape isn't kept in the shadows?"

I say. The thing is, I'm not convinced, either, but it's what strong women do, so I will do it, too. Otherwise, I'm still running away. "Ms. Ballard thinks I could feel empowered by confronting him."

"I like Lori Ballard very much, but only you know if that's true, Q. *Will* you feel empowered?" she asks.

"Well, yeah," I answer, even though I have no fucking idea. I can't imagine any of it. It's like I'm debating the fate of characters in a book. "Won't I?"

"I don't know," she says. "If he takes responsibility, maybe. But if he doesn't . . ."

I want her to tell me not to go through with it. Or to say, yes, absolutely! But she's leaving it all up to me. We look at each other for a while.

"Okay," she says, shifting forward into the camera (though I doubt she realizes it.) "I want you to journal on it. Do you still have your summer journal?"

My eyes flip to my backpack. It's been in there for weeks, untouched since my return to school. I only doodled in it during the summer. No words. "Yes." I squish Mr. Paws's leg, making him kick a foot one way, then another.

"I think it will help you crystalize your feelings about a mediation. You need to really let yourself go there. Picture the room. Imagine being in that space with him. What do you want to say to him? How would it feel to say it? Does it matter if you don't get the response you want so long as you get to confront him?" Val pauses. She's letting her words sink in. I don't know how she does this. Remains totally transparent and yet draws me into her scheme.

"Okay." After we hang up, I grab my journal and sit on my bed, pen in hand.

Will I feel empowered by confronting

I can't bring myself to write his name. I don't want my brain to have to use energy focusing on him. The churn begins in my stomach, the old crickets sound in my head. I pull my arm back, ready to chuck the pen as hard as I can against the wall. The cubist woman gazes at me, calm. Certain. I wonder how the artist painted her in many pieces, and instead of fragile, she seems strong and serene.

I breathe. Four-count inhale, six-count exhale. *The pig bastard*, I write. And my pen doesn't stop for a long time.

MAX

When I arrive at the boathouse for practice at three-thirty, the water is flat and black and stray patches of fog skim the surface. It's drizzling, fifty-four degrees, and clammy.

"It's kinda fucking bagpiper out there," Khalid says, throwing his bag under the dock bench.

A group consensus follows.

"What the hell is 'bagpiper'?" I say.

"Should we tell Wayne about the bagpiper?" Teo says, joining us, pulling on a fleece.

"That was seriously booky," Geoff says in his British accent.

"It was *what*?" Tyler laughs.

"Booky," Geoff says. "It's north London for scary as fuck."

Seb says, "It was a day like today, and we went out on a free paddle. Just fucking around."

"Chauncey was good for that," Pearce throws in.

Duly noted, I think. There is a night scene in *The Boys in the Boat* when the guys row up to the Roosevelts' house in Armonk, New York, and end up being invited in by FDR's kid. I make a goal of becoming that cox who can just joyride with the guys.

Seb continues. "We go way the hell past the buoys, checking out parts of the lake we never see. It's all quiet—you know how the fog kinda mutes sound and magnifies it at the same time? It's like, *slide, splash, floop, slide, splash, floop*. And suddenly, we hear this haunted bagpipe music floating out over the lake. And we're all like, what the fuck is that?"

"I wasn't," says Khalid.

Everyone laughs.

"Khalid totally wanted to spin it for the dock," Teo says.

"But Chauncey didn't," Seb says. "We kept going. And this rocky precipice takes shape out of the mist, and there's this fucking old dude standing at the very edge, in this pea-soup fog, playing the bagpipes."

"What did he do when he saw you?" I ask.

"He just kept playing."

Pearce starts imitating a bagpipe tune, which is oddly spot-on.

"Booky as fuck," Geoff says. "No one lives out there!"

"I mean," Tyler says, "who the fuck was that?"

"A ghost," Teo says. "No question."

I snort. They aren't laughing. "Okaaay," I say. We all stare out over the water. They're spooked for real, which is both amusing and vaguely unsettling.

The Beast thudding down the dock rouses us back to the present. "You coxed in the fog yet?" he asks me.

"No," I say. Has he forgotten I only started a few weeks ago?

"It's supposed to burn off any time now, and it's not too bad. Any questions?" He's towering over me. Coach Sam stands next to him, forming a meat wall.

I suspect I'm being tested. "What do I do if I can't find my point?"

"That would be truly unsafe conditions," Sam says. "This isn't unsafe."

"But if you're uncomfortable," Coach Follett says, "you shouldn't go. The guys can erg inside. Dougie!" he yells. Dougie jogs over. "You okay with the patchy fog?"

"Sure," Dougie says. The dutiful little bastard.

"I'm good to go out, too," I say.

Once we're loaded into the boat, I search for the buoy I use as my point. After a moment, I see a fuzzy dark shape. I exhale uneasily.

"Got it?" the Beast yells from the launch.

I give a thumbs-up. "Hands on the dock," I say. "And shove!" The *whoosh* as we push off is intoxicating. It's the sound of committing to a quest for our collective power and it boosts my confidence. It may sound cornball, but I know they feel it, too, or else they wouldn't be hooked.

I start the bow pair (Tyler and Geoff) to get us moving, increase to bow four (Khalid and Devon), then add the stern four (Grey, Teo, Colin, and Seb). It takes a couple strokes to get them well synched, and then we move along at half power. The coaches' launch buzzes alongside us at a safe distance, Coach Sam driving so the Beast can give technical calls. "Set the boat!" he yells into the megaphone.

A good cox doesn't wait for the coach to notice when the boat sits lopsided in the water. Shit. "We're listing port," I say coolly into the headset. "Adjust your handle heights, Geoff and Grey."

"Good, Max," Follett bellows.

I perk up, and Seb grins.

"Colin, stop lunging at the catch," the Beast calls. That means his chest is too low to properly drive with his legs. Colin's face flinches, but they're all working too hard to say much.

I bring them to three-quarter speed.

"Teo, sit up," the Beast yells. "You're using too much back. Nope. Nope. YES. That's it."

It's quiet for a while, and this is a good cruising speed, I think. The fact that the Beast isn't correcting anyone speaks volumes. We're almost to the buoy when, *POOF*, the sun breaks through the clouds. It's an instant climate change. The boys express indistinguishable sounds of pleasure. I don't dare glance at the sky when we're so close to the buoy. Even nicking it would be a nightmare. We pass safely.

"Okay, Max. Spin it!" Coach Follett calls.

"Weigh enough," I say. We drift for a few seconds, and Geoff uses his paddle like a rudder to start our U-turn.

"I love the sunshine!" Tyler says.

"My nipples are hard!" Colin calls.

"You know what this means," Teo calls. "Sun's out, guns out!"

They hoot, echoing "Sun's out, guns out!" and suddenly they're all pulling their shirts off. The boat rocks, and I grab the gunnels. They make ecstatic "ahh" sounds, stretching their arms out to the sun.

"Max!" Seb says, arms out to his sides. "What is this?"

"I get it," I say, laughing. Of course they're all ripped as hell. Colin and Tyler have six-packs. Jesus.

"C'mon, Max!" Tyler calls from the bow.

Fuck.

"*What?*" I stall for time. Maybe the Beast will interfere, but I see the launch has doubled back and is running alongside the 2V.

This triggers a middle school towel-snapping memory. Take it off, you lose. Leave it on, you lose. *You're very well proportioned*, my mom loves to tell me, but that's . . . my *mom*.

"Wayne Uff! Wayne Uff!" I don't know which one of them started it, but it doesn't matter. There's no getting out of this. Fuck.

I peel my shirt off and brace myself for the comments to start. But instead, they cheer. I can't believe it. The sunshine warms my shoulders, an exhilarating contrast to the chilly air.

Screw it.

"I feel *alive*!" I yell into the sky, joking but telling the truth. The guys crack up.

Teo thumps the side of the boat, and we lapse into a rhythmic chant, "Big Dip, Big Dip, Big Dip!"

"Oh, it's *this* kind of a practice, eh, boys?" Coach Follett says over the megaphone. "All right, then."

We keep chanting, and I'm shouting without a single reservation. The Beast and Coach Sam laugh together, and I think: This is a chemistry experiment. Everyone brings something to the boat, but together we're bigger than the sum of our parts. We're unstoppable, the certainty of this hums through my bones.

I start us on the return piece, bringing them up to three-quarter right away. I announce over the headset: "Power ten in three. Two. One." And they kick it up. The wind blows my hair back. The oars move like machinery. Because they're on gliding seats, if the rowers "rush the recovery" right after the stroke, the boat slows down because all their weight slides toward me, the stern, at once. It's reverse momentum. "Slow the recovery . . ." I say.

They answer that, and we are Vikings when we pass the 2V.

Shirtless, mighty, intimidating as fuck. Dougie's white hat turns with us. We must look like we're barely skimming the surface. I can forget being five foot five and my concave chest. I can forget feeling used and not having the balls to ask out Alex. This is *it*, a high like none I've ever known.

We do four more pieces before the Beast sends us to the dock. After we've put the shell in the boathouse, we go out to the bench, where most of us left our bags. A guy I don't recognize stands with Follett and Sam while the 2Vs unload.

Colin stops in his tracks. "Holy *shit*."

Seb and I stop, too. "What?" I say.

"Whoa," Seb says. And they spin around and retreat to the boathouse.

"What?" I say again. "Who is that?"

"That's the Yale scout," Seb says. "What's his name, Colin?"

"Scott Lipton," Colin says, moving between shells. Both of them pull their shirts on, and I do the same.

"Yeah, Scott Lipton."

"And why are we hiding from Scott Lipton?"

"We're not hiding," Colin says.

"Um," I say. "I think we are."

"Pearce could get recruited," Seb says. "Pierce would give his left nut to get recruited."

"Pearce!" the Beast yells, looking around the docks.

"Fuck!" whispers Colin.

"Go!" Seb gives Colin a shove. Colin glares at him but pops into the sunshine, out onto the ramp.

"Hey!" Colin says, sauntering to them.

"Good luck, man," I stage-whisper.

"This is a good sign," Seb says. "Scott went to LPS. He's always looking for LPS guys to bring to Yale."

"Holy crap," I say.

Colin shakes Scott's hand. Coach Follett claps a bear paw onto Colin. There is a lot of nodding, inaudible jovial talks. Scott Lipton hands Colin something.

"That's his fucking business card," Seb says gleefully. "This is really good!"

More hand shaking, another clap of the bear paw. Colin walks toward us. His eyes are saucers, like a little kid meeting his puppy-love crush.

"Well?" I say as he approaches.

"Shut up, man!" he hisses, even though there is no way Scott Lipton heard me. We follow Colin deeper into the boathouse. He holds up the card with its bold, blue *Y* and Scott's info. "He invited me for an overnight campus visit with the team!"

Seb and I huddle around him and hoot as best we can without being loud. Seb jackhammers him in the stomach. "You're golden!" Seb says. "An overnight visit with the team—you're in!" Seb says. "They usually tell you right before you leave campus."

"He said I'll go out with them for practice." He's smiling humbly—yes, Pearce!—as we jostle him by the shoulders.

"You're going to Yale, Pearce! Division I! Ivy!" Seb jackhammers him in the ribs this time. "I'm going to Princeton, and we will kick your Bulldog ass!"

They wrestle and Pearce breaks away. "Don't fucking jinx it. Don't tell anyone yet." He inhales deeply. "If it doesn't work out—" He shakes his head and makes a raspberry sound.

We mutter in agreement.

"Max," Colin says. He looks me in the eye. "I owe you big-time for that perfect score on our physics project." Planet Earth has tilted yet another six degrees off its axis. "They want my most recent grades, and that's going to look awesome."

"No sweat," I say, like it's totally normal for Pearce to kiss my ass. "I'll come knocking some day when I need an investor for my hovercraft." We all laugh.

Eight rowers. Four of them, Seniors. Two of those already scooped by the Ivies. That's 50 percent, and college applications aren't even due for another month. The thrill I feel is for more than just them. This is not random chance. It's probability calculus. Getting invited to HYP is far more likely if I stay in this boat.

I punch Pearce in the bicep. "Congrats, motherfucker," I say.

Q

The air is heavy and damp, pungent with the smell of apples fallen from the trees and rain. I inhale deeply, letting all of it fill me up. After writing all my thoughts about a mediation, I needed to move, walk the memories of being immobilized out of my head. Moving, I know now, is a gift not to be taken for granted. I run my fingers along a picnic table, pushing rivulets of water along the grooves in the wood grain until they drip off the edge into the grass. I go deeper into the apple grove, weaving through the trees, humming softly one of my mother's favorite Suzanne Vega songs that's been stuck in my head today: "Today I am a small blue thing, like a marble or an eye." I can't remember all the lyrics. Something about rolling and skipping down the sidewalk, but also about being stuck inside someone's pocket. And as I try to recall more of the words, I realize it connects to me perfectly, the contrast between being something someone else can stuff in their pocket, but also something that can get away.

A snapping sound startles me. Two deer, a doe and her fawn, lift their heads from eating fallen apples. We stare at each other. The doe's ear twitches. Maybe she's weighing whether to run; whether I'm dangerous. "Hello," I whisper. We stay like that for a long, quiet moment. The baby goes back to munching apples, encouraged by her mother's calm. My breath catches in my throat, and I decide to leave them in peace. I turn to go.

The sun bursts through the clouds and the lyrics emerge in my head. *I am thrown against the sky . . . raining down in pieces . . . scattering like light.* Back in the room, I feel some kind of line forming between the deer, Suzanne Vega's marble, and the cubist woman, in pieces but whole. I pick up the phone and call Val.

"I will not feel empowered," I say when she picks up. "I will feel disempowered." I hear the clatter of silverware against dishes.

Apparently unbothered that I've interrupted her dinner, Val says, "Tell me more."

I go ahead and read my journal entry. Everything is about power, and he won't lose any by this mediation. He already has all the social power. Legal power. Physical power. Seniority. At best he'd make a fake apology to get the hell out of whatever room we're in. I don't want to remind him that I froze like a possum. And show him I'm not okay. It just reminds him he's got the power and I don't.

I leave out the next part, where I realized the gun was my desperate attempt to regain power. No need to freak Val out.

"Q, I'm really proud of you," Val says, her voice uncharacteristically softened around the edges. I tear up.

"One thing, though," she says. "About the frozen possum?"

She sounds like Macy. But they don't get it. They don't get what it's like to let yourself go powerless. "You're going to say that I'm not weak for freezing."

She laughs knowingly. "Yes, that, but there's more to it than you realize. Science. Q, humans have an evolutionary response to dangerous situations. It's called the fight-or-flight response."

"I know what fight or flight is, Val."

"Good. Okay, so you know that it's a preprogrammed response deep in the most primordial part of the human brain. Adrenaline floods the system—our pupils widen, our hearing sharpens, because our survival instinct calls for it. We can't control it. So, flight means—"

"Run like hell?" I say. I want to add, *Duh, Val*. Then I notice this topic is what's making me impatient.

"Right," she coaxes. "Why didn't you run like hell, Q?"

I'm pacing the room. "What? Because I couldn't." My heart ticks in my throat. Dammit, I'd finally calmed down.

But Val's not stopping. "Exactly. And what about fighting? Why didn't you fight?"

"Because— Val!" I snap. "You're triggering me."

"Stay with me, Q, for a moment. This is critical." Her intensity burns through the screen. "Can you ground yourself?" She inhales and blows an exhale. "Here and now."

I pick up Mr. Paws and breathe. "Okay."

"Why didn't you fight?"

"Because he had my wrists." I hear my voice crawling away, weakening. My hands tremble. I set the phone to speaker and lay it on the desk next to the lacewing butterfly box frame.

"Right. Could you move them? Or your legs?"

I squeeze my eyes shut, but the pins holding the butterfly's wings burn across my eyelids.

"No." A tear plops onto my sleeve.

"Okay. So here's what I want to tell you about the human response to danger. When fight or flight are not options, humans—and animals, by the way—freeze. Adrenaline overloads the system and mimics a catatonic state. In the animal kingdom, freezing is enough to make the dangerous predator leave, which is why psychologists think that this last-resort strategy got hardwired into the human brain. It's evidence of the will to *survive*. Freezing doesn't show you're weak; it shows you're *human*."

I open my eyes and move in a circle. "Is that true?"

"I can send you the literature if you want it," Val says. "I want us to work on reframing your thinking. Not as powerless. As a brave, brave survivor, Q. Forgive yourself. You're a beautiful, strong human with a deep will to survive."

I don't say anything. I find myself quietly weeping, tears running down my face, blurring the painting on the wall.

Val fills the space. "People who endure a trauma often hold it in their body on a sub-verbal level. For years, even. We don't want this event to define you, Q."

"I don't, either!" My words are strangled, but I get them out.

"I know you don't. There are specialized treatments we can make available to you to get that trauma out. If not *out* out, once and for all, we can at least take the charge out of the memories to help you start to heal. I think you're ready for that. But what I think isn't important. It's about you."

I look up at the cubist woman. *Raining down in pieces. Shattering like light.* I can come together again, maybe. A bud of hope pops out of the black dirt that's been occupying my body. "Let's do that. I want it gone."

I hear her slap something, the table or her thigh maybe. "Wonderful. I'll make some inquiries this week."

"But what about him having to give something up that he cares about? Will I never get that?"

"Maybe. Maybe not. But developing better coping skills can only help you navigate it all."

"Okay," I say, nodding even though she can't see me. "Yeah. I'm ready, Val. I am." I feel a hum of energy start up inside me after I hang up, and I need to do something with it. I crumple up all my failed drawings of the leopard lacewing, settle into the desk chair, and start to draw.

CHARLOTTE

I pinch the 1856 Library key between my fingers, examining it under my desk lamp. Like it holds answers.

It does not.

I'm having a very hard time blending what I've learned since Saturday—about Q, Colin Pearce's bet, and Slycroft—with the Seb I know. We had the best night ever on Saturday. Before. Now Seb is an entirely different person. "I wish I never got those notes. I wish I didn't know about this stupid club." Hannah's not really listening. I don't mind. I'm just thinking out loud. "But the notes led me to find Q, so . . . maybe all's well that ends well," I add.

"Yes," she says, looking up. "That's huge. Really huge." Now it's her turn to think out loud. It's a routine. Two plus years as roommates does this to friends. "Katherine Mason was a science teacher. She left three years before we got here," Hannah says without looking up from her laptop. "But the *Wire* doesn't give any explanation. It's just in the faculty updates section. Says she left teaching to 'focus on motherhood full-time. We thank Katherine for her five years of dedicated service and wish her all the best with her family.'"

"Huh," I say. "Did you google it?"

She stretches, grunting as she twists her spine. "Yes, Charlotte," she says, clearly disappointed in my underestimation of her investigative skills. "There are a lot of Katherine Masons out there. I think she's the one living in Oregon. But I'm going to email Margot Pipkin and see if she can help."

"You're obsessed with her," I say, then regret it because I see her wind up for a little rant.

"Hey," Hannah says. "She's a Lycroft trustee. She might know what happened. Did you know she started Bigs and Littles because the girls were still a minority when she came here? She's going to tell me more about it, but basically for years, nobody even wanted girls enrolled here."

"Okay, well, that's gross," I say. "Maybe Margot Pipkin can help. Meanwhile, I have no idea how to act toward Seb tonight. Mad? Or do I pretend not to know he's in a secret society? Do I pretend I don't know he asked me out on a bet? How do I not demand to know what he knows about Q and dickhead?"

"Why are you asking me?" Hannah says. She hops to her feet and straddles, reaching for one toe, then the other. "How do you feel?"

"That's the point! I don't know!" I say, with a flap of my arms. "If Max is telling the truth, then he hasn't technically cheated on me. So I can let that go. But then there's the Slycroft thing. He has been telling little lies or lying by not telling the whole truth. That is lying, right?"

She nods. "Lying by omission."

"He is probably sworn to secrecy regarding Slycroft," I say. "Would I lie to him if we were in a secret society?"

"Am I supposed to answer that one?" Hannah asks.

"Yes."

She drops back into the beanbag chair. "You probably wouldn't join one, but if you did, you'd definitely play by the rules."

She's right, of course. Hannah's always right. "So, I guess I can't get too mad about that, either."

"PSA: you are allowed to *discuss* things with him, Charlotte," Hannah says. "Like Seb, why are you part of a club that fixates on girls' underwear and celebrates sex as a male conquest?'"

"I know!" I say. "But he hasn't even asked me for sex, so that has nothing to do with us. Why bring up stuff that doesn't matter? It makes me seem clingy."

She sighs in exasperation.

I dig around my thoughts, like I'm looking for the one that fits all my mixed-up emotions. "I think it's because he's choosing the boys over me all the time. And maybe that he doesn't find me attractive enough to want to have sex with. Do I have a right to be mad about that?"

"Your idea of mad and mine are different, Charlotte."

"What do you mean?"

"I don't *decide* if I'm mad. I either feel mad or I don't feel mad. It's not, like, an intellectual exercise for me," she says.

I huff. Sure, I think but don't say, it might be like that with Hank. But Hank isn't Seb McNeilly, rowing god of Lycroft Phelps. If I get mad for unjustified reasons, he's going to realize I'm not as cool and confident as I can make myself look with my ballet superpowers.

"Seb's a fool if he doesn't find you attractive enough to have sex

378

with, and I don't believe it," Hannah says. "But if you're not going to ask him *anything ever*, then maybe focus on how you feel when you're with him," Hannah says. "See if it feels like he's genuinely into you, which Max seems to think. And actually, I'd hold back on the Slycroft stuff. We may need that to get Pearce."

"I wasn't going to bring it up," I say, pulling on my jacket. "I'm protecting Q's privacy."

"Lying by omission, you mean?" She smiles.

I scowl. "For Q." And maybe so I don't have to confront him. "Anyway, I like your idea." I look at myself in the mirror as I sling my backpack over my shoulder. "See how you feel, Charlotte," I say. I zip the key in my pocket and open our door. "Thanks, Han."

We've been in the old library for about an hour. I chose to sit in the wingback by the fireplace instead of on the couch next to him. It's a test. Will he notice? Wonder if it means something?

"Quiz me?" he says.

So far, though, he's mostly been pacing the periphery of the Persian rug, flipping through cards, muttering facts about elements from the periodic table. He's looking at me, and I realize I haven't responded. "Sure," I say, holding out my hand. Our eyes meet, and his tense expression softens. He leans in and kisses my lips.

Okay, that sure *felt* romantic. He is so easy to forgive. Too easy?

Seb straightens up and folds his arms. "Hit me. Oh, and make sure you mix the cards up." He needs to know the lanthanide and actinide series, which is a lot. It's reasonable that he's preoccupied. This quarter's grades are the last ones Princeton will see when he applies early action in November. Even if he's recruited by the Athletics Department, he still needs to get the approval stamp from Admissions. So right now he's pretty darn focused on atomic mass. He doesn't appear to wonder if I know he's in a secret club that collects girls' underwear. In fact, I think, perhaps one of the most annoying things about his lack of transparency is that he doesn't seem remotely concerned that I might discover the secret. Like I'm too clueless to catch on. This feeling might be *mad*.

We go through the flash cards for fifteen more minutes, and he nails just about every one.

"Radon," I say flatly, reading the final card.

"RN, atomic mass 222.018." He's nodding, his eyes closed.

"Good. Element group?" I prompt.

"Uh, halogen. No! Noble gas." He opens only one eye, like he's afraid to hear my answer. Damn that McNeilly Gold!

"You got it," I say, and he busts into a grin. "That's it." I hold the deck out. "You'll nail it."

He scoops them from me and flops into the couch, proud like a little boy. "Thank you." He pats the empty space next to him. "Study break?"

So, here is where Charlotte Foresley becomes a puddle of spine-less protoplasm. My smile has a mind of its own, and I move to the couch to snuggle into the space between his biceps and ribs that feels like it's been carved just for me.

We kiss, and in a slow, unremitting crescendo, it moves from PG-13 to R. His hand slides under my shirt, and his palm is warm caressing my torso—the spot a male dancer holds in a lift. It makes me feel so feminine. He pulls back a few inches, eyes gauzy.

"Charlotte," he says, like I've got him under a spell. "My amazing girlfriend, Charlotte."

Girlfriend?

My heart swells. I close my eyes and lean into him, and let everything else go.

Ms. Ballard: The mediation is off. And this is a BIG legacy family, so I think we should leave it.

Dean Frye: Don't tell me anything else. I do not want to know.

Ms. Ballard: Yeah, neither do I!

Dean Frye: I need you to try again. Maybe she wants to do a semester somewhere. A wilderness education program. Wyoming? Switzerland? Galapagos Islands! Girls love sea turtles.

Ms. Ballard: Those are tortoises, Griffin. And really? Now you just want to get rid of her?

Dean Frye: Those programs can be game changers for kids. Especially if they need a new outlook. I know it's a big ask, Lori. It won't go unnoticed. What about that *teacher exchange* position in Paris, are you still interested?

Ms. Ballard: Ermitage? You said no exchange positions.

Dean Frye: I'm rethinking it.

Ms. Ballard: Wow. I don't know what to make of that, Griffin.

Dean Frye: I'd think of it as an offering of gratitude. Potentially.

Ms. Ballard: I have to tell you, all this feels like a hugely inadequate response by the school.

Dean Frye: We can't afford a scandal.

Ms. Ballard: We can't afford to have this happen to another student. Parents entrust us with their children.

Dean Frye: I know what parents do! This is very rare! And it happens with public school kids and kids at Matheson and every other private school. But the Boston Globe reporter is chomping at the bit to tear the elite, expensive private school down. It is not Lycroft's fault that something got out of hand between two students. The fallout will impact all students and families here. Not to mention applications for future classes.

Ms. Ballard: Seriously, Griffin? Are you giving me boys will be boys?

Dean Frye: No, I'm giving you, we're going to do everything we can to help the girl without taking the entire school down.

Ms. Ballard: Yes, we are going to help her.

Dean Frye: So I'm giving you that. And Paris.

Ms. Ballard: Goodbye.

Ms. Ballard: I'm not doing it. He wants me to encourage her to take an off-campus semester.

Ms. Weller: Why?

Ms. Ballard: He's sure it will blow up without some kind of resolution.

Ms. Weller: Such as having Colin Pearce bake Q cookies and deliver them once a week? Like last time, with the other boy? No wonder Katherine didn't fight leaving.

Ms. Ballard: Such an embarrassment. Real restorative justice would mean we put Coach Follett in the mediation and the boy's parents, and Q's parents and Charlotte. So he's forced to answer for her charges with some humility in front of people important to both parties. But Griffin just wants to go through the motions. And anyway, Quinn won't do it.

Ms. Weller: Good for her.

Ms. Ballard: I know! Steve and I did a cheer with baby Natalie. Q's parents got her an excellent therapist.

Ms. Weller: I wish I could let Q know I know.

Ms. Ballard: Nooo.

Ms. Weller: I won't! I'm hoping to see her back in class soon. I'm sending all kinds of positive energy her way. Beautiful kid.

Ms. Ballard: Yes. She is.

MAX

We're in Khalid's hand-me-down Lexus sedan, cruising the Spaulding Turnpike to the Squamscott River Park, venue of the Big Dip, the Royal Henley Regatta of elite prep schools. The sound system in this thing kicks ass, and Khalid's got Kendrick Lamar cranked. Seb's shotgun, and I'm solo in the back, where I'm putting finishing touches on the radio-controlled balloon inflator. We're burying it in Matheson's spectator area so that at a perfect moment as yet to be determined during races Sunday, a huge balloon will bust through the dirt and inflate before Matheson fans.

"It should say *Matheson Blows* on it," Khalid says. "Big green letters."

I shake my head. "We sound like dumb jocks if we say that."

Khalid cocks his head, perplexed, and I realize my challenge. Then he laughs. "I'm just fucking with you, Wayne Uff."

"I'm serious, though. Seb," I say. "Help me out. The art of the prank is its *cleverness*. Am I right?"

"A hundred percent," Seb says. "How about *Lycroft Owns Matheson?*"

"I like it," I say.

Khalid shrugs. "Okay." Then he turns the music so loud that my teeth vibrate with the bass line.

Unlike the 1982 MIT pranksters, I didn't have to rig a vacuum cleaner engine as the driving force for the balloon. I simply got an airbed inflator, which didn't exist back then. Seb ordered eighty-four-inch latex balloons off the internet.

"Hey, Wayne," Khalid shouts over the music, then turns it down again. "I saw you with Alex at lunch today."

"She's pretty cute," Seb says.

"Yes, she is," I say. We've been hanging out in her room every night this week while Q is in Knowlton.

Khalid says, "You think you would have had the balls to make your move before you joined crew?"

I want to say, *Of course I would have.* But that's not true. "Doubt it." And I don't think she would have been so easily persuaded to be with me if not for crew, either.

"It's a Cinderella story, rags to riches in no time, Max. Just like we told you. Seb, isn't Alex's roommate the last one Pearce boned last year?" Khalid asks. "Q?"

"I think so, yeah," Seb says. "Summer Sendoff."

"Quinn?" I knew they went to the dance together, but Q had sex with Pearce? I thought Q would be too smart for his shit. I want her to appreciate nice guys, like Nils. I decide not to tell Nils about it.

Khalid says, "It was a one-night thing."

"Doesn't say much about Pearce's moves, does it?" I say, a small answer to the cry from my conscience to defend Q. They chuckle. I'll maybe ask Alex about it later. Or, I don't know, that's gossipy. It's not my business.

"You're next, Wayne Uff," Khalid says. "Coxing Alex Buchanan's shell in no time."

I snort. Admittedly a creative use of language for Khalid.

"Alex!" he says, apparently imitating me. "Power ten in five, four, three—" We all completely lose it.

"Okay, not allowed," I squawk. "She is off-limits."

"You go, Max," says Seb with a contented sigh. "Don't take his shit."

"What?" says Khalid, then has another laugh at his own joke.

"This is the exit," Seb says, looking at his phone. We spend a few minutes focused on navigating.

"You a virgin?" Khalid asks out of the blue. He actually sounds kind of earnest.

Still, I have to play this one right if I don't want to hear about it for the rest of my life. "Uh, I haven't actually . . ." I offer suggestively.

"But you've watched a lot of other people do it on PornUp?" Seb says.

We laugh again. "Busted," I say, and I'm really glad Pearce isn't here.

The truth is, I limit myself in the porn department. Nils has this theory that if you watch it too much, it will make it impossible to get an erection in an actual real-life hookup—because it's so exaggerated and unrealistic, it makes normal girls unexciting. That's pretty believable, given the incidental knowledge I have of human nature. It's backed up by Nils's mom's work as an adolescent therapist.

"Best be brushing up on your moves, Romeo," Khalid said. "It's only a matter of time. I told you the rowing team would get you laid, man!"

"That you did, Khalid," I say. Improving my odds with Alex

was a motivator, true. But I'm motivated for much more than boning her. Or rather, I'm interested in boning her *and* much more. I think Khalid knows that, believe it or not. The banter is just a game. But Khalid won't let on. And so we roll on, "m.A.A.d city" thumping through the speakers.

When we get there, it's almost dark. Since the Big Dip is this weekend, the spectator bleachers have already been set up. Those guys know which one is Matheson's. Seb helps me carry the device and remotes while Khalid carries the shovels.

We dig. They're hulks, so it takes five minutes. I set in the balloon, wire it up, and we cover it with loose dirt. "Does anyone else feel like we're disposing of a body?" Seb asks, patting the dirt with the shovel back.

"Okay, let's see if this thing works," I say.

"I believe in you, Wayne!" Khalid says.

I've installed the remote-control app I learned about at eighth-grade robotics camp on my phone. "Ready?"

"Hell yeah," says Khalid.

I tap in the code.

The engine cranks up. After a few seconds, the top of the balloon slowly breaks through the dirt.

"Ooh," Khalid says, "this is like me when I get the unicorn pants!"

We laugh. The balloon gets bigger and bigger and is now fully above ground and massive. Seb and Khalid can't stop laughing. It's so taut it's going to pop. I decide to go evil scientist.

"Oh shit," Seb squeaks. They cover their faces and scramble backward.

Kablam!

We share a moment of stupid, air-punching joy.

"Hope *that* doesn't happen to your unicorn pants!" Colin says.

"Sunday is going to be fucking awesome!" Khalid says.

As we pluck large scraps of latex from the ground, I'm strategizing. "We need to decide when to plant the real balloon. And we can't forget to write the words on it."

Khalid chuckles. "Oh man, that would be sad."

"I should teach a Slycrofter who isn't a rower how to program it, since we'll be busy," I say.

Seb nods enthusiastically. "We can do it at our next meeting. When is it, Khalid? Wednesday or Thursday?"

"Thursday. That's Max's initiation night."

"Who'da believed it," Khalid says, roughing me up. "Max Hannigan-Loeffler, five-star cox, Slycrofter, and non-virgin, all in a matter of weeks."

"I did not see it coming," I say. Nope, I did not. I'm not sure I've caught up to it yet, really. But it's not going to slow down. I am learning it in the moment. Which is thrilling. And also possibly treacherous. But it is what it is.

Nils: where are you?

Max: just doing something with the team

Nils: you were supposed to meet me at the rock gym

Max: shit. Forgot. You still there?

Nils: no.

Max: sorry. tomorrow?

Nils: whatever. Sure.

CHARLOTTE

I lean back, my elbows on the barre, watching Gabrielle and Felipe dance the contents of my imagination. They're fluid, like water running downstream.

"Very nice," Madame Chu whispers. I don't know how long she's been next to me. I beam.

Gabrielle drops into an arabesque, resting her fingers gently on Felipe's outstretched hand, back leg in a lift high off the stage. Slowly, he spins her on one toe. The tempo changes, and the corps enters, three from each side, leaping so they cross in front of each other. Felipe exits stage right.

"Yes!" I call. "Chin up, Vivi. Perfect!" I lower my voice. "I'm going to have the lighting guy spotlight Gabrielle and Felipe and then turn it off right when she drops her leg from arabesque."

"Impressive," Madame says, tapping a rolled paper she has into the palm of her other hand. "You can begin rehearsing at the performing arts center tomorrow."

I smile nervously. "Wow. It's really happening."

"Just five days to go. You are ready." She nods and backs out of the room, watching the dancers finish the last steps.

"Clocks" ends. I clap. "Madame loved it! We move to the big stage in Osher tomorrow!"

Everyone hoots breathlessly. They head for their bags, untying their pointe shoes. When I scoop up my duffel, something drops to the floor. Leaning to get it, I realize it's another note. Hannah approaches me, her cheeks flushed. We exchange looks of surprise.

"So," I begin.

"Q isn't the author, either," Hannah says, finishing for me. We'd wondered if maybe Q was genuinely trying to warn me about Seb. We let the other dancers leave.

"Guess not. Who the hell is it?" I ask, popping the tape.

"Read it aloud," Hannah says.

"'Still convinced your boy is loyal? Ask him to show you his texts.'"

"Okay, that's creepy," Hannah says.

"Max promised Seb isn't cheating," I say. "I don't think Max would lie like that."

"Would Max really know?" Hannah says. "Should you report it?"

"Should I?" I look at us through the reflection of the wall mirrors. "I don't feel like it's a good time to bring any added attention from administration."

She nods. "You might just have to confront Seb with the notes, Char. I mean, don't you want to know once and for all?"

"Yes," I groan. "And no."

She smiles sympathetically. "The truth will set you free." Hannah's face falls, and I look behind me. It is Seb standing with Sofia Bodenrader at the door. She's pulling her jeans on.

"Oh my God," I whisper.

"Charlotte," Seb calls.

"Hey?" I say, but it sounds like a question. Sofia stands up, no shirt over the plunging V-neck leotard, grinning.

I nearly burst into tears.

"What are you doing here?" I ask.

"Checking to see if you want to study after dinner. And guess what? Yale's recruiting Colin. He heard today."

Hannah and I snap into an eye lock. She's more composed than me and looks away quickly.

Sofia says, "Whoa, Yale?"

Why is she still here? I am so confused.

"I gotta go," Seb says. "Seven-thirty?"

I nod. I can't form words.

Seb grins and waves and is gone. Hannah stands close. "What the actual fuck is going on here?" she whispers.

"I don't know. Yale?!" I spin around in a circle, flustered. I hear myself say, "Hey, Sofia? Can you stay? I would like to run through the pas de chat section with you. Your timing is a little off."

Hannah shoots me a puzzled look. Sofia's timing is perfect, and we all know it.

Her smile disappears. "It is?"

I wince. "Yeah. Let's work on it."

"Yeah, okay," she says, peeling her jeans off again.

"I'll catch up with you in the room, Hannah," I say. She leaves.

I'm not exactly sure what I'm doing to Sofia. I talk her through the routine, modeling it. I am a more experienced dancer than her, and I pull out all the stops. I make her do it six times. Six. She actually does get better at it, but by the last time, she's exhausted.

"Ooh," I say. "A little sloppy on that one." I seriously have no idea who I think I am right now.

She represses a scowl. "Can I get a drink?" she says, adding, "I kind of have to get going."

"Sure, sure," I say. "That's enough for today. I think you almost have it." She puts her street clothes on and has slung her bag over her shoulder when I say, "And, oh, Sofia?"

She lifts her eyebrows.

"Stay in your lane." My voice is a knife's edge.

"Excuse me?" She emits a short laugh but looks a little frightened.

"You heard me," I say. I'm kind of making myself sick, but I can't stop. "Giving blow jobs to upperclassmen is a dangerous game." It's like I've fallen into this well-established groove and there's nowhere to go but forward, like a spinning marble on a run.

"Are you, like, slut-shaming me?" she says, voice hoarse.

"No. I'm warning you."

I brush past her but catch her face in a mirror reflection of another reflection. She's bright red. Then I see her cry. Which makes me know it's true. He did cheat with her. It's just like I've always known. I'm not good enough. Not sexy enough. Not a good enough kisser. A prude. I'm just a fucking Goody Two-shoes, not an effortlessly cool bohemian like Sabrina Godfrey, or a confident sexual diva like Bodenrader.

The second I'm out of the building, I burst into tears. Who wrote the notes? They were true. I need to find Hannah. I'm not even halfway to our dorm when I get a text.

Grace: I got my plane ticket! Coming on Saturday with your parents! Get to meet the hot boyfriend, too!

I throw up in the bushes.

Charlotte: I can't come tonight. I'm sick.
Seb: Oh no! Sorry to hear that.

Charlotte: I'll be okay.

Seb: Can I bring you something?

How about the truth? BRING IT, SEB.

Charlotte: No thx.

Seb: Okay. Feel better.

Hannah: You okay? I have my second Zoom interview with Margot Pipkin, but I'll find you after that.

Charlotte: He did fool around with her. I knew it.

Hannah: Shit. Hang in there—I'll be home in an hour.

I can't hang in there. I'm a miserable, sobbing mass on my bed. I almost FaceTime Grace back home, to get her input on this. But when I imagine myself explaining everything, she'll say, *Charlotte, is this relationship worth it?*

But she doesn't know Seb. Hannah's right. Again. I have to confront him. So, even though I feel like an alien has invaded my body, I pull myself up, splash my face with cold water, and text Seb.

Me: Can I come over?

Seb: Feeling better?

Me: Yeah.

He meets me at the dorm doors and holds one open. I follow him to his room. Chauncy's bed is crisply made, a reminder of his absence.

"Plenty of room in here," I say. It's awkward and out of the blue. Smooth as ever, Seb looks around, nodding, like he just noticed.

Then he looks at me. "You sure you're okay?"

"I'm—" I start. I have not choreographed this ahead of time, and I don't know what to say. "I don't think you're being honest with me."

"What do you mean?" His eyes are steady. I'm going to show I'm jealous if I say it. Fuck it.

"What's the deal with Sofia Bodenrader and you?"

He guffaws, like I'm joking, but quickly sucks that back in when he sees my eyes well up. "Absolutely nothing. I've known her my whole life. She's like a little sister to me. Lots of the guys are into her. I just feel protective, like a brother would. But she can take care of herself."

I squint, not sure what to believe. I picture Sofia's face, red and crying. Does that really prove anything? I might have cried, too, if I were in her shoes. "So, no"—I wince, barely able to say it—"blow jobs?"

"What?" He looks mildly disgusted. "Definitely not. And . . . why?"

"A rumor. You know the Littles," I say vaguely. I sit there, stunned, my insides slowly dissolving. I just can't go into the anonymous notes. I want out of this conversation. I feel like I'm showing my weakness, while I've been so good at hiding it all this time. A panic rises. What have I done? I was so harsh on Sofia. I let myself get catty. The ugliest side of girls, turning on each other. I went there.

And I was wrong.

"Oh God," I whisper.

I'm almost too distracted to notice Seb step closer. "Charlotte,

I told you. I'm one hundred percent with *you*." He wraps me in his arms, but I'm stiff. "Hey," he says softly into my hair. "I mean it."

I look up. He kisses me. "Okay," I say. I want to believe it. I want to have everything fall back in its magical place. But I guess I'm just too tired to feel it.

OCTOBER

14

CHARLOTTE

"I won't be surprised if she doesn't come to rehearsal today," I say to Hannah. We're stretching at the portable barre set up for us on the stage of Osher Performing Arts Center. "I wouldn't even blame her."

"She's coming," Hannah whispers. "I stopped in on her before classes today. I will say it's mostly because she doesn't want to get on the wrong side of Madame."

"I can't breathe," I say. "She could tell Seb, you know. I couldn't blame her for that, either. I frigging snapped."

"Here she is," Hannah whispers, and flips to face me. "Go. Now. Don't let it simmer."

Over Hannah's shoulder, I see Sofia drop her bag in the stage wing. Her jaw is set hard as she takes off her warm-up pants.

"I'm going to barf again," I say.

"Just tell her you're sorry. Admit it. Be honest. It's the only way."

I have no experience having to totally eat humble pie, as my dad would say. I like being the easy kid, the good kid, the nice kid. I don't know how to be anything else. Well, I *didn't* know.

Sofia glances up from putting on her slippers and quickly looks away. Her body tenses.

"Sofia?" I say, and have to clear my throat. "Um, I really need to talk with you." ●

She's not having it. Zips her bag. Stands up. Still not looking at me, she says, "What? Is it my pas de chats? Port de bras?" She starts for the barre. "Or is it just me in general?"

"Wait," I say. She stops. "I totally deserve that. I don't blame you for thinking I'm a complete bitch based on the way I treated you. I was horrible."

She turns. "I don't even get what I did to you."

"I'm sorry," I say. "Someone sent me an anonymous note that said you and Seb were fooling around behind my back."

She screws up her face. "What? That's borderline incest." Then she laughs, sharp and quick, like a stab. "But you believed it? Nice. Way to trust your man. And thanks for assuming I'm the kind of person who wrecks relationships."

"Sofia, I swear to God, if you had any idea how horrible I feel. I never act like that. I don't know what came over me. I didn't even recognize myself."

"It's called jealousy," she says. "I guess I should be flattered. Charlotte Foresley, jealous of a First Year."

I close my eyes. "Look, I'm sorry. If I could undo yesterday I would *entirely* undo it. I threw up after I left here last night because I felt like such a shit."

She stops. I see her dimples crease in her cheek. "Wait. You did?"

She's going to laugh at my throwing up? And then I think, *It is kind of funny.*

"Yes." I look away. "It seems melodramatic now, but at the time . . ."

400

"That does make me feel better," she says. "I mean, you know, knowing you felt that guilty."

"I don't do well with guilt," I say.

"Apparently not," she says, grinning wide. I smile.

"Sofia, it took guts for you to show up here today after that. I'm really sorry, and I'm so glad you're the kind of person who can just . . ." I think. "Be above the petty stuff."

She nods. "It's not the first time. The group of girls I hung around in middle school didn't like when a couple of boys paid attention to me, and they started to exclude me from all their sleepovers and shit."

"They were jealous," I say.

"That's what my mom said." She shrugs. "So I just decided, who needs them?"

"Well, I am not like that," I say. "I promise. It was like I got possessed by a demon or something." I shake my head. "And by the way, there is nothing wrong with your pas de chat. You're great."

She nods. "Good to hear."

"So we're okay?" I say.

She tips her head back and forth, and then says, "We're okay."

"Thank you," I say, exhaling fully for the first time in almost twenty-four hours. We walk toward the barre.

"But who do you think wrote that note?" she says. "What did it say exactly?"

Sheepishly, I lean in and whisper the bit about blow jobs. "But ignore it," I say. "The plan of the person failed. So we can both forget it."

She nods, but I can tell by her eyes it will haunt her some. I feel a pang of guilt return. "I really wish I could undo making this something you think about at all."

"Shake it off," she says, and begins stretching.

MAX

It's the night of my Slycroft initiation. The barn is darker than usual. The mood, faux solemn. I stand between Khalid and Pete Crenshaw in a circle of a dozen-plus guys. Our heads are lowered, and nobody speaks above a whisper. The candles form two rings on the dirt ground with a single candle in the middle of each ring. "They're titties," Justin Daniels pointed out when I arrived. In case I'd missed it.

"Like burning effigies?" I'd asked.

Justin kept smiling, his head doing a noncommittal shake/nod. My word choice was clearly too much. He leaves to join other hockey players.

The gaps in the circle fill in, and pretty soon I count eighteen guys. Most of them are a prep school's version of contact-sport jocks. Meatheads, yes, but like, filet mignon–heads. So I'm surprised to see A. J. Ashby, a champion fencer, and Christian Scholl, a big-league stoner from the Green Futures Club. A. J., Christian, and I are the only pledges, I guess. Pearce comes out from an animal stall wearing a wizard's robe and rabbit ears on his head. Nate, A. J., and I laugh.

"What's with the bunny ears?" I whisper to Khalid, casually leaning toward him.

"Shh. You'll see."

"Good evening, Slycrofters and pledges." Pearce is reading from a sheet of paper. "Tonight we begin our meeting with the initiation of three new members to the Slycroft Society. I nominated Max, Pete nominated A. J., and Justin nominated Christian. This ceremony represents their pledge of allegiance to the Slycroft Society for the rest of their lives. They join us in the decades-old tradition of pranking and merriment," Pearce says. "Gentlemen, don your ears, please."

With that, everyone except my pledge buddies and me pulls rabbit ears from behind their backs, like they had them tucked in their pants, and sets them on their heads. There is some snickering, but frankly not half as much as I'd imagine. Christian and I catch eyes, and he looks as bemused as me. A. J.'s all business, not cracking a smile.

"Maximo Loeffler-Hannigan, please come to the cleavage." There are a couple of guffaws from the guys.

"It's Maxwell Hannigan-Loeffler, dumbass," Seb says. I nod to him in gratitude and meet Pearce at the so-called cleavage. He calls the other boys over in similar fashion.

"Place your right hands on the holy book of Slycroft and repeat after me," he says, looking down at us. We follow directions. "I—say your names, please—" We do, and Pearce carries on. "Do hereby swear my loyalty to the Slycroft Society for the rest of my days on this earth." We repeat his words. I'm realizing as I speak that this means I can't tell Nils, and I don't like it, but this roller coaster's not stopping while I sort out the details. "I promise to seek out fellow Slycrofters after I'm gone from LPS." We echo him. "To help them in any way I can to secure employment and financial riches." We repeat this, too, although that's also potentially not a great thing to agree to. *Take the best and leave the rest*, I tell myself. "And to readily come to a brother's defense in times of trouble." We repeat. Would I defend Pearce? Eh, I guess so, maybe, in the big world out there. "Amen," Pearce says. "Amen," we say. I have to admit, there is something kind of unearthly about masculine voices in unison. I actually feel like I've just taken a real oath.

"We seal it with a shot," he says. "Brother McNeilly?" Seb arrives with a tray of shot glasses. The liquid is brown, and one inhale curdles my stomach. Seb retreats into the shadows.

"Slycrofters?" Pearce says. "Say it with me . . . as the pledges seal the deal. Drink!" he commands. We all three slam back the hell water as a rousing shout surrounds us: "Dicks before chicks!" Followed by raucous cheering, backslapping, and handshakes.

I lean toward Khalid and mutter, "Dude, I'm not putting anybody's dick before my girlfriend."

He smiles but holds his palm up. "Keep that on the down low, my friend."

Christian coughs. "What *is* that?"

"Gold Label McNeilly Scotch," Seb says. "Best whiskey on the planet." He refills our cups and says something that sounds like "Slanj-a-va," which I recognize as the Gaelic *Slàinte Mhath*, thanks to my grandmother's Irish pride.

Pearce directs everyone back to the circle, and he says, "You are now junior members. To become ear-wearing full members, you simply need to fuck a girl and get her panties, which we'll proudly add to our rafters. Nobody goes earless for long."

Wait, what?! I shoot a glance at Khalid, but he either won't look at me or is too wrapped up in the spectacle. This is ridiculous. I'm looking around for somebody—anybody—who thinks this is as nuts as I do, but there's no one. These guys are laughing, and next thing I know, we're drinking more, and everyone is taking seats on the benches or on the half walls that separate the stalls. "Why ears?" I ask Seb quietly as he passes by with Scotch.

"Playboy Bunnies." He grins. "You know, the old nudie magazine, *Playboy*? Pre-internet it was all Slycroft had. Now it's tradition."

I'm speechless. And my brain buzzes with alcohol. *Pranks, Max. Stick to the pranks.*

Pete Crenshaw has taken the floor.

"Bruthuhs," he says, arms out like a Southern evangelical reverend. "Heads up that our annual Bounty Hunter point setting is tomorrow night. For our pledges: Bounty Hunter is a game where we, the Slycrofters, gather points by hunting down chicks and banging them. Blow jobs count. It is Open Season from Fall Fling through Summer Sendoff, since that's the last weekend everyone's on campus. Whoever scores the most points becomes Lord of the Book for the next year. Usually it's a Senior, but last year Colin Pearce here was the winner as an Upper Middie with one hundred and twenty-three points—"

"A record," Pearce says, raising his hands in mock modesty. "Thank you very much." Hooting commences. A pinwheel of anxiety blows in my gut. Oh my God. I take it back; I can *never* tell Nils about this. I slug back some more McNeilly Scotch. I can't feel my tongue. One hundred and twenty-three? We're only in school for one hundred sixty-five days.

"That's almost one a day. Is that even possible?"

"Not every girl is worth the same amount," Justin Daniels says.

"But to answer your question, totally possible," Pearce says.

Laughter ensues.

Pete says, "That's what point-setting night is all about. We go through all the girls from the new student directory and rate them on a ten-point scale. That allows for some strategy. You know, 'cause we can't all look like fucking McNeilly over there. He was the *only* Lower Mid of *all time* to be crowned Lord of the Book year before last."

Sweet fuck all, this is my Quantitative Hotness Correlativity Theory in action. It's evil. I feel lower than shit just having imagined the number system. I need to get out of here.

"I gotta take a leak," I say to whoever can hear. Outside, I gulp in the October night air and walk toward the tall grass. I unzip and let it fly. I hear someone behind me.

"You okay there, Wayne?" It's Khalid.

"Holy shit" is all I manage.

"Right?" His facial expression is wide open in delighted wonder, like we just discovered leprechauns. "Buckle up, dude! I told you."

"Holy shit," I say again.

"Don't worry, man. You wanted to sleep with Alex anyway, right? Just snag a pair of her panties and nobody will ask any questions."

"I literally cannot process those words right now," I say. I'm slurring a bit. "I mean. What?!"

He unzips his fly. "I love a good piss in the out of doors," he says. "Listen, Wayne. I know you're a scholarship kid. So am I."

"Wait." I blink at him, chuckle. "You're a good student?"

"Fuck off. Yes, I happen to be straight A. With some Bs. An occasional C."

"That's not straight A," I say.

"They mostly wanted me for the boat. Anyway, listen. Do the Slycroft shit. It's going to pave the way for you for the rest of your goddamn life. Mine, too. And it's fun. Lighten up. Take her to the Whitney Inn for dinner. Girls love being wined and dined. You're probably getting pretty close anyway, am I right?"

"None of your fucking business. And do not talk about her with your dick in your hand."

He chuckles. "The Whitney Inn, my friend," Khalid says. "It's gonna get you there."

I don't want to get there, I think. *Well, like that anyway.*

Khalid finishes, zips up, and claps me on the back. "Dude, I think you're done peeing."

"Oh," I say, fumbling to rezip.

Khalid snorts and heads back in, passing Seb on his way out.

Seb's looking at the ground, smiling. "I know what you're thinking, Max."

I shake my head. "Do you? Seb. Seb-Seb-Seb-Seb-Seb. I cannot do this, Seb. I just . . . What?!"

"Max, you know it's mostly Pete and Pearce who take this seriously. Right?"

"Says 'Mr. Youngest Lord of the Book Ever.'" I do air quotes, but my timing is off. "How many people did you sleep with that year, anyway?"

"Eight," he says, controlling a smile. "But multiple times with some, so the total score was higher."

"And—and Khalid has an athletic scholarship? Lycroft doesn't give athletic scholarships! This isn't college."

"Well," Seb says. "He may just be getting funded by the Rowing Alumni Club."

I say, "Like, this is so wrong on so many, many, many levels. I can't do this, dude. This is—" I lose my balance for a second, and he catches me by the elbow. "I gotta say, man, you don't seem like that big of a douchebag. It's the looks. You get away with it because of the looks. It's like I always thought."

"I would never do it again. I was only a Lower Mid. Now I see it's stupid. I went out with Sabrina for most of Upper Mid year, and now I'm with Charlotte. The points—" He shakes his head. "Just let them do their thing; you do yours."

I raise my eyebrows skeptically. "Seriously?"

He leans in. "The truth is, Max, my dad was a Slycrofter, and he never heard of Bounty Hunter."

"You told your dad about Bounty Hunter?!"

"Long story," Seb says, waving me off. "Not worth telling. My point is, we can get it back to the prank focus with you. And that dude Christian. He's smart like you. My dad said they did a prank a month. None of this Bounty Hunter shit. Maybe some porn on VHS tapes. And the magazines. But that's it. Oh, and the book. But it wasn't a contest. Just, I don't know, a rite of passage. Each time a Slycrofter had lost his virginity, he added his name to the book."

"But, dude! That was like 1978 or something. Oh my God! We can't do this now. Like at *all*. A: It's morally reprehensible." I steal one of Nils's lines, which I think he'd want me to say right now if he could see me, which THANK GOD he cannot. "And two, it breaks like sixteen discrete Code of Conduct rules." I walk back and forth. "Seb, this shit doesn't fly anymore. We'd all get thrown out of here in seconds flat if this got out."

Seb looks amused by my outburst. "Which is why it won't get

out. And why you and I must steer Slycroft back on course. Wonder coxswain, I need you."

I drop my head in my hands and flip him off. He laughs. "And meanwhile you're okay with putting a price on Charlotte? What?!"

"They won't touch her," he says, but there's an edge to his voice, and it's the only split second he reveals how he really feels. At least when it comes to his girlfriend. "And we are not into forcing girls to do anything. Ever. At all. Hey, let's get Nils to join."

"Nils would literally have a heart attack. Dead."

Seb chuckles, and I cannot for the life of me figure out what is funny. "Max, we have to humor Pearce and just gradually move the club in the right direction. The balloon prank for the Big Dip? Epic. Just the beginning of a great prank revival."

I keep shaking my head, but it's making me dizzy, so I stop.

"Why aren't there any other rowers here? Teo and Tyler and the rest?"

"Nobody's invited them yet. The invite's a big deal, Max. For life, these guys have our backs."

I grimace.

"Give it a try. Hell, you just swore you would," he says. His million-dollar smile returns, and he claps me on the back. "Let's go get some guys who can follow through while we're racing that day. You got to show them how to use that app and all."

Dazed, bombed, I follow him inside.

Ho.

Ly.

Shit.

Q

Me: I'm going to class today. Might sleep in the dorm tonight. They said I can keep the room as long as I want.

Charlotte: Awesome! What can I do?

Me: If you see the asshole tell me where so I can stay away.

Charlotte: You got it. He's in physics with me this morning. Kessler.

Me: Good. I have art.

Charlotte: Opposite sides of the quad. 😊

Alex is meeting me for breakfast. I know, and dread, telling her the truth. I don't like her thinking I have mono. And I don't like there being a secret between us. We meet at the Granola Bar, where no guys go. Safe.

"Hey! How are you doing? Not contagious?" She hugs me, and I'm better with this now and hug her back.

"Nope," I say. I hate this lie.

We don't say much as we move through the kitchen. Alex orders a smoothie, and I get a granola muffin and a bowl of fruit. Rosario is working behind the counter today, away from her usual station at Spangler. She looks at my bowl. "Healthy today, eh?" and winks.

"She remembers everything," I say to Alex when we sit.

"Right? She knows what kind of smoothie I want every time." Alex takes a sip from the straw. "Did you see the topic choices for the art history paper. I'm doing kintsugi, and if you pick the same thing, I can help you get it done."

"Thanks. Remind me what that is?"

She laughs. "Making art out of broken things. The ancient Japanese art form. Here." She gets out her phone. "I sent you the website."

I open the link and see pots, broken and repaired with gold leaf, and I can see that the repair makes them far more interesting than they were before. "Oh, yeah, I remember. A little."

"Oh, Q," she teases.

"Yes, I'll take your help on that paper."

"Perfect. Okay, so." She looks up at me from under her long eyelashes. "About Max . . ."

"Tell me everything."

That's all she needs. They go running. They watch old movies. She's gone to watch crew practice and might join the girls' team in the spring. They've enjoyed having our room to themselves while I'm gone.

My eyebrow lifts with the spin in my stomach.

"Oh! Sorry, that sounds like I'm not happy you're back. I'm thrilled! It's just been, I don't know, kind of magical." She bites her cinnamon toast.

I manage a smile but internally I'm trying to "note" my reaction to thinking about Alex in a situation where something sexual could happen. This is one of the things Val and Miss Lisa and I have been working on all week. I visualize my fear as a balloon, floating up into the sky. *You don't need to engage with it, Q. Take a breath and let it go.*

After an exhale, I say, "I'm really glad for you, Alex." And this is true. I'm trying to figure out how I tell her the real reason I've been at Knowlton all week. It's a heavy load to drop on someone.

"And tonight is our big date at the Whitney Inn," she says.

"What?" I whisper. Oh God. The memories come in quick succession:

Ice cubes

Vodka

Crickets

Sandals like bones licked dry

Leather shoes

I grab the edge of the table and feel the color drain from my face.

"Are you okay, Q?" she says, suddenly alarmed. "Here, drink some juice."

I force down a few sips. *Distress tolerance,* I hear Val saying. *Pick one thing around you to focus on and remember you are in the here and now; you're not in that memory.* My eyes poke around and settle on the large bowl of apples beside the smoothie machine. *Breathe,* I tell myself. Here and now. The Granola Bar. Friday morning. October. Rosario, glancing at me from the counter. Val says, *You got this, Q.*

In a moment, I'm able to focus on Alex again. I don't know what I was thinking. I can't tell her about me right before her big date. She'd feel all guilty and want to stay home, or maybe she would accidentally borrow my experience and become scared around Max, who's harmless.

"Q?"

"I'm a little shakier than I thought," I say with a weak smile.

413

"Do they know why your eyelashes fell out? I've never heard of that before."

"I think I did it in my sleep," I lie. In fact, it's a compulsion that some people with trauma get. Miss Lisa gave me little tins of this stuff called Thinking Putty that I carry in my pocket to squish every time I feel my hand going to pinch the butterfly bruise or pull an eyelash.

Alex looks confused. I change the subject. "What are you going to wear?"

I focus really hard on the different choices she describes, just staying in the moment. I manage to give thoughtful feedback, and soon we're on our way to class. Alex is going to calculus, on the other side of campus.

"We can meet in the room at five," I say. "For preparations." She laughs and breaks off at a fork in the path.

It's weird, I'm more scared of running into him now than I was when I had the gun fantasy—which Val would call a maladaptive coping strategy if she knew I had it. Still, even with my AirPods in, I feel a little naked. I play "Landslide" on repeat. The Stones and Lenny Kravitz and the Police—they took me away when I needed it most. Stevie Nicks brings me back. Her emotional honesty just fits right now. It's brave. Strong.

I make it to Drawing and Painting II without incident. Per Miss Lisa's advice, I silently note this and add it to a mental tally of small victories over fear. I'm the last student in the classroom. Oh, the smells of the old me. *Breathe in*, I tell myself as I enter and take my seat.

"Hey, Q," Nils says. "Alex said you had mono?"

I look at the floor. "Mm-hmm. But I've been resting since Monday, so . . ." I do jazz hands. "Here I am."

"You missed the falling-in-love montage," he says, a sly smile on his lips. "Of Alex and Max. They're quite the lovebirds."

I smile and nod. "Yeah, so I've heard."

"Thank you, by the way, for vacating your room so they had a place to . . ." He emits a short chuckle. "Express their feelings."

Nils has stayed the same. I am flooded with gratitude. "You're welcome," I say, smiling.

Ms. Weller introduces the subject of our drawing today. Beach rocks she's collected from Cape Cod. "We're noting texture. Color. Subtle patterns, bold patterns. We'll use only the grays and beiges, and it will be up to you to find the range of values that one pencil is capable of delivering."

The range of values one pencil is capable of delivering. This feels like a concept that applies to more than just art. Ms. Weller has a couple of students help her pass out tubs of rocks and tins of pencils while we retrieve our sketchbooks, and I think: People. People are capable of delivering a range of values. I am. I'm not one monotone piece of broken geometry. I'm dozens of pieces, with lots of songs, that fuse to make one. Like the cubist woman on the wall at Knowlton. Like all the little shapes that come together in a complex, colorful pattern lace on a butterfly wing. Something pops in my head. Like, literally, I hear a *pop!* The leopard lacewing, with the holes in its wings. Me, a broken-winged butterfly. Kintsugi gold leaf

"This looks really hard," Nils says in a pretend-whiny voice. We're sharing a pencil tin.

I blink, leaning back in my stool, trying to be present. "It does. But look at this one," I say, holding up a smooth, oblong shape. It's gray with black and charcoal polka dots all over. In between the dots are glittery specks.

"Looks like a professional design job," he says. He holds up a different stone. It's smooth but unevenly shaped, charcoal with a silver band around it.

"Ooh." I breathe in.

This is the therapy I need.

We draw quietly for a while. I hear the sound of the pencil points sweeping over the pores of our paper. The squeaks of the stools we all sit in. The sound of Nils fishing through our shared tub of rocks.

"How do you like this one?" he asks.

It's pale gray and flat.

"I love that color. How can a gray rock seem warm?" I ask, then wrinkle my nose because it sounds stupid.

"Right?" he says, and keeps digging around. "Oh, look."

I do.

"It's shaped like a heart," he says. And in a single-beat rest, Nils flushes red. Cadmium red.

Our eyes catch, and I feel myself blush, too. Then: The intruding thought. Of last year, when I wondered if I should've said no to the rat bastard, so I could have gone with Nils. I didn't listen to myself.

I stare at the rocks.

"Sorry, I— That—" he stammers.

"What? It's okay—" But what can I say? I reach for a new pencil, and the whole tin flies off the table, pencils spraying the floor like they're shot from a sprinkler. The can clatters, rolls, stops.

Everyone looks at me. I pop off my stool, rushing to pick them up. But the room goes all wavy when I bend down.

Ms. Weller appears beside me, gently taking my arm. "Q, take it slow, honey." I nod and hold the table. She stoops and begins collecting pencils. "Let me." Nils joins her and maybe another kid. It's chaotic until the purple dots clear from my vision.

"Thank you," I say, sitting again.

Ms. Weller examines me when she stands. It's not an "are you okay?" look, but something totally inscrutable. "How is your butterfly coming, Q?"

Random, I think. "Um, actually, I've done a bunch of versions. The wings are kind of hypnotizing."

She smiles. "I'd love to see. Do you have time to bring them by during my office hours this afternoon?"

Maybe I will go work on them again and then show her. I nod, trusting my gut that this will be good.

Nils returns the can to the space between our papers and brings me a cup of water from the bubbler in the corner of the room. The class resettles.

"Thanks," I whisper. "That was horrifying."

"Meh," he said. "It's better than falling off your stool, which I have done."

I snort in spite of myself.

"Hey," he says. "Since our roommates have their hot date, want to go to the movie playing tonight? I think it's *Ghostbusters*."

It catches me so off guard, I just stare at him. I must do this too long, because he starts to crack a smile. "Um, hello?"

"Oh!" My heart is warmer, but it's still gray. Like the rock.

"Sorry. Um, yeah, that sounds nice," I say. "But I don't think I can stay awake past seven."

He nods really fast in a way that tries not to look embarrassed and therefore reveals he is. "Right, sorry."

I want to give him some sign that I would go to a movie with him if I wasn't a complete wreck. I wish I could say, *Well, actually, this is the longest I've been out of the counseling office since Sunday afternoon, and I've been talking to a painting all week.* Instead, I try to telegraph my good intentions and settle with these out-loud words: "Can we do it another time?"

More nodding. "Sure."

God damn you to hell, Colin Pearce.

At the end of class, we leave the building together and walk quite a ways on the path, until he has to veer toward Burrell House, where he has Poets and Society class.

"Nils, I really would go to the movie if I didn't feel so . . . weak," I say.

"I believe you, Q," he says. His eyes are clear, catching sunlight.

Nils is safe, I realize once and for all.

"Thanks," I say. I want to tell him more. Part of me wants to just be able to say what happened and why I'm a wreck. And I think, if I got attacked by a bear or a shark, it wouldn't have to feel so deathly personal. But I got attacked by a monster who's walking around campus like he owns it.

I'm a few paces away, starting to feel the swirl of my anger. The anger is so. Fucking. Exhausting.

"Hey," Nils calls from behind me. I turn. "Catch!" He tosses something. My hand reflexively darts out and the object smacks into my palm.

I look at Nils. "Took it by mistake," he says. It's the glitter rock. My heart rebounds, fluttering off the ground. A butterfly. I smile.

"Thanks," I say. Then I go back to Knowlton. I have a plan for my butterfly now, and I'm eager to begin.

MAX

"Good evening, Mr. Loeffler-Hannigan," says the hostess at the Whitney Inn named Stacy, according to her name tag. Stacy tips her head in deference, obviously unaware that she's been fed the wrong name by damn Pearce, who made the reservation for me. This is his idea of funny.

"Wayne Uff," he'd said to me earlier this week. "Trust me on this. I know the right people. You want to get a table in the glassed-in room. It's romantic as fuck." He does not see this as an ironic description. Still, romantic is good, so I let him take care of it.

"It's Hannigan-Loeffler," I say, sending her into a flustered apology while she corrects her reservation list. Stacy is taller than me by a solid three inches, which makes Pearce's joke sting more. Luckily, Alex is still hanging up her coat. I had wondered if I should go the whole gentlemanly route and remove the coat for her, or if she'd think that's condescending. I'm not sure I made the correct choice, but at least it spared me this embarrassment. Alex rejoins me, smiling. She's wearing a bright green dress with big white flowers, and her hair is loose and kind of wild, and she's all my dreams come true in one person.

We follow Stacy through the dining room, which is full,

supporting evidence for why Pearce needed to pull strings for a good table. It is the first real Friday night of leaf-peeping season in New Hampshire, after all. We pass through an open set of French doors into a small room filled with honey-colored candlelight playing off the antique paned windows. There are only two tables, separated by a large potted tree trimmed in tiny white lights.

Stacy seats us, and Alex sighs. I nearly do myself. When we're alone, Alex whispers, "I think this is the best table in the whole restaurant."

"I knew I had to make reservations early," I say.

And that's the first time I've been less than 100 percent honest with her. But we roll on. It's harmless, I tell myself, ignoring an inner rebuttal that reminds me I lied to Nils, too.

"Look at the roots of that tree," Alex says, pointing. "They grew into a braid on that part."

"Oh, yeah," I say, thankful she brought up something dorky people notice, thus raising the possibility that I'm not so dorky, after all. Because Alexandra Buchanan is no dork. "It's a ficus," I say. "My mom is obsessed with them. We have about ten in our apartment at home."

"I'm jealous of people who can garden. I can't even keep succulents alive. It's sad," she says, examining the bread knots in the basket. "How about you? Green thumb or plant killer?"

"I can't say I've given it my best shot yet." I butter a knot, keeping my hands busy. "But if my luck with goldfish is any indication . . ."

"What happened to your goldfish?"

She's chewing her bread and her lips are distractingly soft and pink, but I manage: "Let's see. Second grade, Goldie. Overfed. Third grade, Annoying Orange. Starved. Fourth grade—the final fish—Jaws. Vanished."

She stops chewing and smiles. "Vanished?"

"I think he was abducted by aliens," I say. "One morning I went to sprinkle the magic three flakes into the bowl, and he simply wasn't there."

Her eyebrows crinkle adorably. "What?"

"It's possible my little sister tried to take him for a walk."

She laughs.

The waiter, Gregory, arrives after a few minutes and tells us about the soup and tonight's special venison confit with roasted gnocchi and broccolini, and the duck ravioli in browned butter-sage sauce.

"Oooh," says Alex.

"I know, right? We switched to the fall menu today," Gregory says with a wink.

I feel Alex tap my calf under the table, and our eyes meet. We're in on a secret, and life is a perfect and beautiful thing, and I am so grateful that I have come to this school and joined those boys in the boat . . . and that doing so gave me the guts to ask Alex out, Hotness Correlativity be damned. I can't make my feelings for her fit into the Slycroft vision of girls as conquest.

Gregory departs, and we study the menu. I try not to twitch at the prices. My dad's so excited I'm going out with a girl he told me to "Go nuts, Max!" and transferred an extra two hundred into my bank account. Alex and I discuss the merits of chicken versus beef, and the environmental benefits of the Wonder Burger, but decide we've both left a small enough carbon footprint to indulge in the filet mignon. It's amazing. We get cappuccinos and chocolate volcano cake and two forks for dessert. It's kind of like we're playing grown-up, but also not.

The older couple at the next table gets up to leave. The woman, an elegant sort with long white hair and bright lipstick, leans over on her way by and says, "I've never seen two people have so much fun eating a meal together. You're darling."

Alex and I catch eyes and quickly look away from each other. I have no idea how to respond. Alex pats her mouth with her napkin, a grin bursting across her face. "We've never been here," she says, her cheeks flushing.

I stand and shake the man's hand, and I'm pretty sure he knows I'm out of my league, too. Male intuition. They leave, and neither one of us can stop smiling. I've lost total control of everything, and it's empowering and terrifying.

When the bill comes, Alex says, "Let's split it."

"No, this is my treat," I say, adding a line I've heard in many a cheesy movie: "I insist."

She looks hesitant.

"Is it insulting for me to do that?" I say. "Because I don't want to insult you. I just want to take you out tonight. Like a real date."

She smiles. "I don't know. Am I supposed to refuse on the grounds that it's sexist to think I need to be paid for?"

"I have no idea!" I say. "I don't feel sexist. . . ."

This sounds so stupid it's funny, and we crack up.

We stop, and she sighs and locks her brown eyes on mine. "I would be honored to have you take me to dinner, Max," she says, sparkling there like a big glass of champagne. "Thank you."

I'm butter on a hot fry pan. Bread on level 5 in the toaster. Kernels in the popper.

I don't know what love feels like, but this right here is pretty damn good.

Ubers have not yet made it to Whitney, New Hampshire. A-Plus Cab has a corner on the LPS market, and it's the same driver who dropped us off a couple hours ago. It's a quick ride, and we hold hands the whole way. We pull into the circular drive in front of Calloway Hall, Alex's dorm. She says, "I'll pay for this," and hands a credit card to the driver before I can object. If I say no and insist on paying for the cab, it will border on bossy, which is more sexist than letting her pay, right? She eyes me as we wait for the driver to process the sale. "Don't sweat it, Max," she says breezily. I don't get how she knows what I'm thinking all the time.

The cab zooms off, and we're standing on the grass, looking up at a sliver of moon. "Beautiful," she says, leaning her back into my shoulder. For the eight millionth time in my life, I wish I were taller. I want to be big and protective, like a guy is supposed to be.

"You're beautiful," I say, focusing on the positive instead. Nils would be proud.

"Aw," she says. We kiss. Under the White Mountains October sky, chilly. Alive with stars.

We have well over an hour before dorm check, and apparently Q is out somewhere. We bumble up to their room, giggly in a way that would be embarrassing under absolutely any other circumstances. I follow her in the room and inhale. "Why does your room always smell so much better than ours?" I say.

She laughs and queues up her Google speaker. Then she closes the door to sneaker width, the rule for when you have a member of the opposite sex in your dorm room. LPS hasn't caught up to same-sex relationships. Typical LPS.

We flop into the overstuffed chair positioned where passersby can't see us. She fits perfectly into the crook of my arm. "I don't know," Alex answers, nuzzling into my neck. "We have better product," she says.

I'm having so much fun, I try to forget that this is the night I'm supposed to get the panties for Slycroft. What if I didn't follow through tonight? So what if I don't get the bunny ears. They're ridiculous. But then I think of the shit that will fly my way from Pearce, et al. And really, would I be here at all without the boys in the boat? If I don't seize the moment of my rise in status, I'll never get it back. And then Alex would lose interest.

Pretty soon we've flopped onto the floor with some big velvety throw pillows. My hands have a will of their own and somehow know how to climb up her dress.

I haven't *asked* her, I realize when my fingertips brush the hem of her underwear, and I open my eyes to monitor the situation. She pulls her face back and to my relief is smiling, her eyelids dewy. "I'm thinking maybe I'll just change out of this dress. . . ."

"I kinda like the dress," I say, even though everything is going too fast for me, too. I don't want to rush anything with her. We've only been seeing each other a week. But I'm confused as to what she thinks. Or maybe I'm saying it to the guys, who seem crowded into my head. I'm supposed to be overcome with horniness for her, right? Part of me is, sure, but it's the same part that would eat birthday cake for breakfast.

She makes a jokey scolding face, gets up, and slips into the bathroom.

I take a deep breath. I'm in way too deep here, not really sure what to do. I feel my phone vibrate in my pocket.

Khalid: Don't overthink it.

I roll my eyes. Jesus, why can everyone read my mind? Under the bathroom door, Alex's shadow moves.

I spring to my feet and hurry to her dresser. I get the sock drawer first and then find the drawer with panties and bras. I yank a piece of flowered fabric, stuff it in my pocket, and scramble back to the floor just as the door opens. Alex is wearing pants that tie at the waist and a shirt that looks very soft.

"I feel kind of guilty getting all comfortable while you're still dressed up," she says sheepishly.

A pang of true guilt makes me look away, and I cover it by stretching. Then I reach out my hand. She takes it and rolls back into the crook of my arm, her clean smell filling my head. I'm overcome with the need to tell her something truthful. "I've wanted to ask you out since the first time I saw you. On your First Year Opening Day."

She sits up and looks me in the eye. "Really?"

"Yep. Nils and me were tour guides. We led the song. . . ."

She squints. "Oh, yeah."

"You were late and crossed the crowd when you saw Q. I told Nils you were perfect."

She gently punches my stomach. "I'm definitely *not* perfect."

We alternately kiss and talk and kiss more, and eventually it's time for me to go. In the doorway, we break apart. Standing up, we are perfectly eye to eye.

"Tomorrow?" I say.

She nods. I grin. As I walk away, I can feel her eyes on me, so I turn to face her, walking backward a few steps. I catch a look of alarm and spin in time to swerve and miss bumping into the RA.

"Whoa," she says.

"Excuse me," I say. "I'm just leaving."

The RA gives a prim smile. "That's good," she says, and goes through a door. Alex's face is crinkling into confusion. She's staring at the floor next to my feet.

My blood rushes away from all of my organs because I know what she's looking at.

Her flowered panties are crumpled on the carpet, a perfectly silent bomb.

"Why did my underwear just fall out of your pocket?" Alex says. A red flush is rising up her neck.

"What?" I say, though there was no mistaking her words.

"Why did my underwear just fall out of your pocket?" It's sharp-edged this time.

I have no words.

"That is so creepy," she said. "Why would you take my underwear?" Her eyes well up.

I want to run away.

My brain is shorting out. "I—"

She trusted me. That's what it is. She trusted me, and I stupidly—*idiotically*—just fucked it up.

"Do you have anything else of mine in there?" she says, pointing at my pockets.

I shake my head. I'm welling up myself. Glancing at the door the RA just entered, I whisper, "Can I come back and explain?"

She folds her hands across her chest. "What kind of explanation could there possibly be for stealing my underwear?"

But she's still here. She hasn't slammed the door.

"Please?"

"You can tell me from there," she says.

"Uh," I say, shifting my weight. "That's not a good idea. But there's an explanation—it's a stupid one, but—"

She sighs. "Hurry."

I stoop to pick up the panties.

"*Do NOT.*"

"Right, sorry," I mumble, moving into the room so she can get them.

I start with "I'm so sorry."

Her face is a mask of ice. I have no choice. I can't even think of another option besides the truth. I need some dignity. "Okay. I have no right to swear you to secrecy, I know that. But I'll just let that ask sit there while I explain and you can decide afterward."

Her disgusted expression prompts me to blurt, "It's not like I have some underwear fetish. I didn't take it for me."

Her eyebrows fly up. "So who did you take it for?"

"So, our school has a secret prank society called Slycroft," I whisper. I have trouble looking directly at her and study a callus on my palm.

"The prank is stealing underwear? Are the members all in, like, seventh grade?" she says, blowing a breath of very dismissive sounding air.

Do I tell her that the underwear is merely evidence of hooking up with someone? I rub my closed eyelids with my thumb and forefinger. "Actually, the underwear isn't a prank." I can hear her staring at me. I steal a glance, and the disdain on her face is brutal. "I mean, the idea is . . ." I have to move. It buys me time. I pace in a little loop around the room. "So, the idea is that when you hook up with someone, you prove it by getting her panties. Then you're a full-fledged member." I leave out the bunny ears because, seriously, it's just gratuitous information about an already entirely idiotic tradition.

"Hook . . . up?" she says. Slowly. Deliberately. With scalpel precision. "Define *'hook up.'*" Air quotes.

"I know how bad this sounds," I say, finally meeting her gaze. "I know."

"Hook up?"

"Technically, it's supposed to be, you know, having sex. Then you get your name in the book."

"What book?"

Shit. This is really bad, but there is no turning back. I explain the book, how it's old and how each year there's a Lord of the Book, and I know each word I say is another nail in the coffin of my relationship with Alexandra Buchanan.

"That's what this is all about for you, then?" She's up, storming around, and at this point, I just get out of the way.

"No!" I say. "I wouldn't—" But I did.

"Quit cowering! It's pathetic."

"I'm sorry!" I can't bear hearing her anger, because behind it is hurt. "Please. I was just trying to satisfy them. I *knew* it was macho bullshit. I should have listened to myself. How I feel about you is— is—is—" I stammer, "the . . . the . . . the opposite—" I don't know how to phrase it. "The Slycroft thing and *you* are in two totally different compartments in my head." She's quiet and staring, and I dare hope . . . "Alex, I would never do anything to hurt you."

"Yeah, too late for that." She swipes a tear off her cheekbone. "I'm not a thing you can keep in a compartment. Like a pair of shoes or—" She shakes her head in disbelief. "You were going to tell them those were mine?!"

"Seb and I were going to get rid of the tradition. I just had to satisfy Pearce—"

"None of this makes any sense. Why? Why do you have to?" she demands.

I try to retrace my reasoning. Because I didn't want to deal with his crap? Because I was afraid Alex wouldn't be interested in me if I wasn't like them? That's seeming unlikely at the moment. I rake my fingers through my hair. "You deserve better. I am so sorry."

"Go," she whispers, barely controlling her voice.

I drop my head. "Yeah. Okay." I stop. "One question?" I say. Alex simply scowls. "Would you have gone out with me before I joined the rowing team?"

She closes her eyes and shakes her head. "Nice job ruining a great night," she mutters. "Nice job ruining *everything*."

And she doesn't slam it, but she shuts the door hard enough to express cold disgust.

I am officially the worst kind of asshole.

Q

"I think we should just cut off Pearce's balls," Hannah says. She's lying on her back on the floor, feet on her desk chair, filing her fingernails. "That's what we did to our dog, Scout, when he became sexually active."

After dinner, I couldn't be alone. I texted Charlotte, but she's with Seb. With Alex out, too, I texted Hannah. She invited me over.

"Macy thought of that," I say. I'm playing bits of Fleetwood Mac songs on my guitar. "She sent me a 1990s news story about a woman named Lorena Bobbitt who cut off her abusive husband's penis when he was asleep."

Hannah sits up, her eyes moony. "Seriously?!" I nod. "Now that's badass," she says. We chuckle.

"Surgeons sewed it back on."

We're now laughing. I add, "She had to go to a psychiatric hospital for a while, but she definitely got her revenge."

"Yeah, of course the woman's always the crazy one," Hannah says.

My stomach twitches. I'm remembering myself in Khalid and the rat bastard's room, cutting up pillows to Lenny Kravitz. "What is *crazy*, really?" I say softly.

Hannah says firmly, "*Crazy* is a meaningless word in your situation. Leave it out of your vocabulary. Don't give someone who is capable of violence any more power over you."

There it is again, that word. *Power.* It somersaults around my head.

I don't know how Hannah has such certainty unlike me, who has to hear it and rehear it, how she knows that a guy like Pearce wants all the power and is not afraid to steal it. And also, that I don't have to let him. I feel an invisible bond forming between me and Hannah, like she's a person to latch your tow rope to.

"Wanna hear something?" I say, setting down the guitar. "I stole Pearce's Italian leather loafers, and I have them in my closet."

She snorts. "What? How?"

"I broke into his room during Vespers a few weeks ago. He wore them that night. . . ."

Shush shush shush.

"Whoa," Hannah says. "Wow."

"I don't know why I took them. I hate them." *Shush shush shush. Shush shush shush.*

"Hmm," Hannah says. "Maybe taking them was a way of taking something back. . . ."

Her words are slow, coming to me through a fog, because I'm lost in a montage of myself during my break-in and of the night in May at the Amphitheater. I'm watching the images float by, not letting them into my heart, but seeing them from a cool distance. *Shush shush shush.*

I bolt upright. "They were telling me to be quiet!"

Hannah cocks her chin, interested. Listening. "Who?"

"The shoes!"

She blinks.

"When he left me there on the ground, I realized that he never even took his shoes off during that event and that bothered me so much. Like, I'm not even worth taking the time to pretend that this is meaningful in some way, even though he took something from me I'll never get back. And then he just walked away through the dewy grass, and the sound it made." My heart thunders in my chest as I imitate it: *Shush shush shush*.

Hannah nods very slightly. "They're a metaphor. For—"

"Him telling me to shut the fuck up, that I'm not worth taking his shoes off for, and that he can just walk away while me and Euterpe are frozen there, barefoot!" I stand on the mattress, electrified.

"Euterpe?" she asks.

My phone vibrates. I ignore it. "That's the Muse statue we were next to," I say, hoarse. All of this is lightning out of the sky. The phone vibrates again and goes to voice mail.

Hannah's 100 percent with me when she says, "You have to kill those loafers."

We stare at each other, knowing the enormity of this truth even though killing shoes sounds ridiculous. My phone starts ringing again.

"Jesus, what?" Then I see it's Alex, and I remember her date with Max. "Oh, I better answer," I say, hopping to the floor.

"How was it?" I say.

"I am *so* pissed!" Alex yells. I pull the phone from my ear.

Oh, God. She knows. I try to formulate a response.

"You won't *believe* this." She pants. "Max?"

Wait. "What about Max?" I say.

"He stole my freaking underwear."

I can tell she's loud enough for Hannah to hear, and we lock eyes. "Oh, shit," I say. "I'm with Hannah. Can I put you on speaker?" Hannah was Alex's Big last year.

"Go ahead," Alex says.

"Why did I even go out with that guy?" *Pant, pant.* "He stole my underwear from my drawer, and when they fell out of his pocket, he admitted he was part of some secret—"

"Boys' club called Slycroft?" Hannah says. "Who hang underwear of girls they've had sex with on the rafters like party streamers?"

The phone is quiet.

"Alex, where are you?"

"Walking," she grumbles.

"Where?"

"I have no idea."

"Come to Charlotte's and my room," Hannah says. "We have to plan."

Alex agrees, and I hang up.

"We need Charlotte," Hannah says.

"I'm texting her now," I say. "Screw Seb McNeilly."

Hannah grimaces. "Well," she says. "She might be doing just that."

CHARLOTTE

We're under Seb's quilt on the floor, three-quarters through *The Princess Bride*—although I haven't heard a word of it—when my phone lights up next to us. I am jelly and ignore it. My pants are off. His pants are, too. Shirts came off before. All underwear still in place. He smells like a sandalwood candle I used to have at home, and his skin is warm and smooth and strong. We're doing things we've never done, but we haven't done *it*. Or talked about doing it. I don't care.

My phone lights up again. It's Q. I can't leave her hanging.

Q: Max stole Alex's underwear.

I pop upright. Seb groans. "No," he says, pulling me toward him.

"Wait," I say.

Me: Max!?! OMG, the world is ending.

Hannah: Come home. We need to take action.

Seb pulls me down again, smothering me in open-mouth kisses. "Stop!" I say before thinking. It takes us both by surprise.

"What?" he says. "Sorry, I thought you were into it."

"No, it's not that," I say, but I find my head completely scrambled. "I just—"

He chuckles, bringing me closer again. "Stop!" I say.

He sort of jumps back and puts his hands up like he's busted for stealing cookies, and I hate the feeling that gives me. "I thought this might be our night."

I stare at him. Some fuse lights within me. "What do you mean?"

He looks baffled. "I thought we might, maybe, have sex. If you want." I can't think of anything to say. I'm mad about Slycroft, for one. I grab my clothes and go into the bathroom attached to his room.

I run cold water and drink it out of my hands. Leaning with both hands on the sink, I study my face in the mirror. My lips are puffed from making out.

I open the door. Seb's leaning against the bed but not fully committed to sitting on it. He's folded the quilt on the chair. Pants on but shirt off. Damn it. I avert my eyes from his perfectly muscled chest and look him in the eyes.

"I can't trust you," I say. It's kind of whispered because it takes everything I've got, but at least I said it.

"What?"

"Come on, Seb." I take a breath. "Our whole relationship is built on a bet between you and Colin Pearce."

For the first time, his eyes flitter off to the side. Beautiful golden October leaves blown off the branch. And he doesn't say anything . . . or deny it.

"It's true," I say. "Quinn heard it straight out of Colin's mouth. She told me."

"That was before I knew you, though," he says, meeting my gaze again. "Then we went to the dance and I realized how cool you are. And, I don't know, I just really like you, Charlotte." He blinks. Looks at his feet. Back at me. "I do," he says. "So much."

I shake my head. "Why would you have a bet like that?"

He shrugs. "Stupid guy shit."

"Like Slycroft?"

His shoulders square up just slightly, and he looks right at me. "You know about Slycroft?"

I nod. "Yep."

He squints. "How?"

"You lied to me," I say, my voice breaking. "Lots of times. You said you were going home, and you weren't. How do I know you won't steal my underwear? What even is that?"

Seb is the master of emotional restraint, but I think I can see his pulse tick up a notch on his neck. "It's not like that," he says. "I mean, it is, for some guys, but it's not like that for me." I realize it all at once. I've been making excuses for Seb. All fall, I've excused this and that and I find some reason that I can live with, but it's just too much work.

"But you still lie to me about it. And if you're lying about that, how do I know you don't lie about other things? I can't do this. It makes me into someone I don't even like," I say. "I feel like you just want to be with me when it doesn't interfere with what you're doing with crew or with the guys or at this dumb secret club of yours."

"It's not like that," he says.

"It is to me! My opinion of what it's like is just as important as yours!" I can't believe the emotion behind my words. I'm finally letting them out. "You say I'm perfect. Perfect Charlotte doesn't complain. She's fine when I'm with the guys. No, I'm not fine. I'm not perfect. I'm just who I am, and if that's not more interesting to you than a bunch of immature dickheads busy stealing girls' underwear, then too bad. I'm out of this." I can't believe what I'm saying. I'm so mad I'm not even crying. "I'm breaking up with you."

He's speechless. I want him to fight me, tell me I'm wrong, but he's just looking at me.

I snatch my coat off his chair and walk out.

Marching across campus, I feel numb. Tingly. Should I be crying? But I feel lighter. I throw back my shoulders and pull out my best ballet stage confidence. "I broke up with Seb McNeilly," I whisper. "The Genetic Miracle."

I text Grace. **You might not meet the hot boyfriend. I just broke up with him.** My smile is irrepressible.

When I get to our room, I'm about to announce my breakup when Hannah says, "There's a fuck book."

I glance from face to face to face. They're serious. "A what?"

Alex says, "Max says there's a book where the so-called Slycrofters record all their sexual conquests. It goes back decades, he says."

"I'm probably in the damn book!" Q groans.

"Each year someone is crowned Lord of the Book," Hannah says.

"How much worse can this get?" I ask. I'm even more glad of my decision, but I'll save telling them about it for later.

"But here's the thing," Hannah says. "We can nail them now.

We have evidence. Did you want to know what Margot Pipkin told me in her interview?"

"Who's Margot Pipkin?" Alex says.

"She's the first female Fuzzy Gilbert winner," I say.

"She won for inventing Bigs and Littles," Hannah says. "She told me in our interview that she started Bigs and Littles because in the 1980s, guys were still writing columns in the *Wire* that said things like, 'Better dead than co-ed.'"

"What does that mean?" Alex says.

"Co-educational? When they changed all-boys' schools to schools with boys and girls," Hannah says.

"Seriously?" Q says.

"Margot Pipkin wanted to provide girls a place to feel a sense of belonging. A sense of empowerment. I bet she will have some opinions about this book. I think she can help us nail them. And she arrives on campus tomorrow."

"Well, we don't *have* the book," Q says.

Alex picks up her phone. "Oh, don't worry," she says. "We're getting that book."

MAX

Nils isn't home yet. I don't bother turning the light on, strip down to my boxers, and flop face-first onto my bed.

I would love to have Nils to confide in now, but if I did, he would know I hid Slycroft from him. And lied about where I was a bunch of times. And that I'd become an asshole like them, the kind of guy who agrees to take girls' panties to prove he's had sex. Is it worse to steal them *without* having had the sex but letting everyone think you did? I was planning to lie to them to protect Alex, right? But it protected me, too.

I moan and roll onto my side.

Nils will have answers. He always does. Not to physics proofs. Who the hell cares about physics proofs? He always has the answers to shit that matters. Like, why I let myself fall this low. Did I fly too close to the sun and melt my wings? I had all good intentions. Okay, I had mostly good intentions. I care about Alex!

And what about Khalid and Seb and Colin? Our boat? If Alex tells, which she has every right to do and probably should do, really, will I get kicked off crew? Will they?

I'm starting to message Nils, when a text comes to me.

"Alex?!" I say aloud, bolting upright.

Alex: Max, I need you to get us the Slycroft book.

Me: Us? Who is us? Alex, I am so sorry. I am such an ass.

I have no problem groveling at this point.

Alex: Yep, you are. We need you to get us that book.

Me: What? I can't do that. Who is us?

Alex: Q. Charlotte. Hannah. We won't turn you in. We won't say a word. We need to see what's in that book.

Me: I will be killed.

Alex: Max, you can return it. They'll never know it's gone.

Me: How about I take photos of all the pages?

Alex: We thought of that. Unfortunately, I can't trust you to give us every page.

"Fuck," I say. Nils comes in at that moment. And then my phone vibrates with a call, from Alex.

"Dude, what the hell happened to you now?" Nils says.

I shake my head. "Hi?" I say tentatively into the phone. I'm close to puking.

"Max, if you really regret what you did, you need to show it by getting us that book," Alex says.

Just looking at Nils, just having him in the room with me, makes me know what to do. Of course I need to do right by Alex instead of those morons. I decide also, at that moment, that I will tell Nils everything.

"I'll do it." I tell Alex. "I'll let you know when I have it."

"Okay," she says. "Okay, good."

We hang up.

I flop on the bed again, this time on my back. "I'm dead."

"They finally turned on you? I knew it was only a matter of time. Colin Pearce can't be trusted with his grandmother."

I sit up and look him right in the eye. "Nils, I have transformed into a douchebag."

He raises one eyebrow. "Yeah," he says. "I've noticed."

I flinch. "I'm sorry I've been a dick. I got . . . I got swept up in it."

He nods. "I know."

"I really need your help."

He looks at me, shakes his head, and says, "What do we need to do?"

"Okay, okay, hold it right there. Bounty Hunter?" Nils says. We're on the Pope trail, it's pitch dark except for our flashlight beams, and I'm really glad he can't see my face.

"I know" is all I can say. I've told him everything. And surprisingly, or maybe not because Nils is the best, he is still helping me.

"A point-setting night? Really?"

The beams of our phone flashlights bounce on the dirt path, and finally I recognize the stand of birch trees. "We're here." I point my phone toward the barn. Amazingly, you can barely see its outline in the dark.

We jump the fence and lope down the hill.

"Jesus!" Nils says. "I nearly impaled myself on that thing."

He's shining his phone on the rusted hay trawler I took a leak next to only a few nights ago.

We slide the barn door open, and I flip the lights. "It has a generator?" Nils asks. "How did they never get caught?" He opens the big trunk filled with old copies of *Playboy* and *Hustler* magazines. "Yeah, you do not want to be associated with this, Max. Because

442

you know the assholes will get off somehow, but you won't."

"Thanks for that." I point to the table with the candlesticks and the fat book set out prepared for a ceremony. "There's the book."

"This feels cultlike."

"Oh, it is."

"And you got sucked in. Why did you think this was okay? How is that possible?"

"I didn't! I was stupid. I thought I could just play along. I thought Seb and I could change it, gradually, and turn it into a really great prank club. Maybe we could have, and then I could nominate you to join," I say.

He just looks at me.

"Stupid. I know. But also I thought Alex would only stay with me if I was part of . . ."

"Yeah, that's where you fucked up the most, Max. That's not giving her much credit for being a decent person. And I think she's a decent person."

"She's more than that," I say. "That's why we're doing this. Even if I end up in a body bag." I unzip my backpack and slide the book in. Nils is looking up at the garland of girls' underwear and shaking his head.

"Goddamn, they are ballsy," he mutters.

I am overcome with a sudden sense of gratitude for Nils. "Why are you here?" I ask. "Showing up for me when I've been a complete ass?"

He shrugs. "I don't know. I didn't want to desert you, I guess, when you're so down. I know you well enough to see you're genuinely feeling like shit about what you did."

"Thanks, man," I say. "I won't ever forget it. If I get kicked out, you're the one I'll miss the most." My throat is thick with emotion.

"More than Alex?" He grins.

"Almost," I say. I shut off the lights, and we slide the big barn door closed.

Q

"I just broke up with Seb," Charlotte says. "By the way."

"What?" Hannah says. "Charlotte! When were you going to tell us that?"

She shakes her head. "I didn't plan to do it. I can't believe I broke up with the Genetic Miracle. Me. Charlotte. Breaking up with Seb McNeilly."

The three of us glance at each other. "Are you okay?" I ask.

She blinks a few times. "Yes. Weirdly, I think I am."

Alex chuckles. "Good timing," she says.

"Alex!" Hannah says.

"Sorry, that sounded insensitive," Alex says. "I think we're blowing the lid off this Slycroft thing, and it's probably good you have some distance from him when it comes down."

Hannah gets up and hugs Charlotte. "It's okay," Charlotte says, nodding. "Let's focus on this. I don't want to think about him anymore tonight."

I've felt myself detach while they've been planning. I haven't said much. I'm not sure I can handle going with them. I don't want to see the book. But I also don't want to be alone. The urge to pinch myself seeps into my fingers. I stand up so I can get the little tin of Thinking Putty out of my jeans pocket.

"How did you guys know about Slycroft again?" Alex says.

Hannah and Charlotte look at each other, then at me. I squish the putty hard in my palm. Feel my pulse pick up.

"Are you ready, Q?" Charlotte says softly.

Am I? Will I ever really be ready to talk about it? But I think of how much better I felt letting Charlotte know, and then Ms. Ballard, and Miss Lisa. Maybe each time I tell it, it will get a little easier. "Yeah, I think so." I nod.

"Do you want us to leave you alone?" Hannah asks.

"No. Please don't," I say.

Alex searches our faces. "What? You're scaring me."

"I have something to tell you," I say. "I should have told you before, but I couldn't admit it. And I didn't want to make you feel badly."

She looks nauseous, so I talk faster. "The reason I've been so weird this year is because . . ." My throat thickens up. Charlotte sits next to me and takes my hand. "Colin Pearce raped me the night of Summer Sendoff."

Her whole body contracts, like she took a bullet to the chest. I'm a scientist watching her react. She says words, but they don't matter because what I see is her shock. Horror. Worry. Also compassion. Love. Mostly it helps me put in perspective what a huge trauma I've undergone, and that maybe it makes all my struggles seem pretty normal. But I'm coming back.

Alex is pulling me from my chair into a hug. "I'm always here for you," I hear her say in my ear. "You can always tell me anything."

"I missed you," I whisper. "I'm sorry."

She pulls back. "Sorry?! No, you don't need to feel sorry." She sits next to me, and Charlotte takes over, explaining how she found me in the woods that night. She doesn't mention the gun, and I guess that's for the best, but I can't believe I won't tell Alex that part someday. Someday when I'm strong again. Myself.

"Hold on," Alex says, looking at her phone. "Max got the book."

Charlotte says, "Tell him to meet us out front." Alex starts texting. "We'll take photos of all the pages and then return the book to him."

The room starts to have an electric energy, and I feel like it's leaving me behind. "Do you mind if I skip this?" I say. "I am not sure it's going to be a good thing for me."

They stare at me for a second. "Of course," Charlotte says. "You don't need all this."

"We'll get Pearce one way or another, Q," Hannah says. "He's going down."

I nod. I want to believe them, but I know guys like Pearce or Seb or any Slycrofters never get taken down.

15

MAX

"Dude, is it working?" Pearce's shadow slides over me in the barn as I fiddle with the projector and my laptop, even though everything is connected and ready to go. I can smell my own BO, but I'm keeping it cool on the outside, I think, considering.

"Yep," I say without looking up. "You're in my light, though." He may or may not catch my sarcasm. "Dude," I add.

I figure my chance for surviving tonight falls somewhere in the 5 percent range, with a five-point margin of error. I glance toward the partially open window in the back of the barn. Hannah, Alex, and Charlotte are out there somewhere, but I can't see into the darkness. Yes, I told them this was the single meeting that would guarantee a shutdown of Slycroft. They wanted more names than the ones in the book.

"Just come down there and hit record on your phone. They'll be done for," I told Charlotte.

It's something of a suicide mission, since I'm implicating myself. But at least this way I have plausible deniability as the whistleblower. It's the boat I'm sad about. Crew in general. It was fun. In the best times, it was the ideal team. Nobody was cynical on the boat. They supported each other, cheered for each other. It was mostly Colin who injected any toxicity, and even he seemed to forget about it on the water.

But if these guys turn on me, I deserve it. I've broken the Bro Solidarity Code, lifted the Cone of Silence. What do I expect? I told myself that what Slycroft was doing wasn't what *I* thought/ valued/believed, but I just went along with it. The truth is, you are your actions.

Whatever happens, I have it coming.

So fuck it.

"Circle up," calls Pearce.

We go through the welcome greeting, take our vodka shots, which for once I'm completely down for.

"Tonight we set the scoring for this year's Bounty Hunter competition," he says. "Khalid, you on note-taking?"

Khalid nods. He's got a lot of asshole qualities, but I feel bad he's going down because of me. He knows it's bullshit, too. But he's weak to the same pull that I am. I scan the other guys here. Do they know it's bullshit? Is Pearce the only one who believes it? Does he? Is it all a show?

"Before we look at the First Years, we'll consider calls for status adjustments of any Lower and Upper Mids and Seniors," Pearce says.

Shit, I think to myself. I'm horrified the girls outside can hear this. I continue to fiddle with the cords while the Slycrofters move the benches into stadium seating around the barn wall where I've pointed the projector.

"What say you, Nash?"

"I move to change Hannah Hesse to an eight. Have you seen her tits this year?"

Howls of laughter.

My Adam's apple bobs in my throat. How did I ever sink to

this level? I watch Seb from the corner of my eye. "All in favor?" Pearce says.

Each boy but Seb raises his hand. He is smooth-faced and entirely unreadable. A big part of me wants him to be better. I know it's in there, his sense of decency.

"Seb?" Pearce says.

I will him to say, *That's Charlotte's roommate, you assholes.*

But he says, "A whole point?" I cringe, half expecting the girls to barge in and start throwing benches.

"Fuck yeah, bra!" says Bill Nash. "You should see her in that ballet outfit. I do the lighting for their show, and man." He shakes his head.

Laughs. Scattered claps.

Seb and I catch eyes for a fraction of a second, and I see a flicker of some emotion I can't name. I suddenly wonder if Seb is strategically protecting Hannah. The higher her score, the more guys target her. The lower the score, the less she'd be harassed.

"McNeilly's too pussy whipped to notice Hannah Hesse," Colin says. The guys hoot. "Wah-wah!" says that asshole Pete Crenshaw. "Sebastian, still no panties. Bit of a letdown." More laughter.

I wait for Seb to say, *We're not together anymore*, or *She's not my girlfriend*, but he just smiles in a way that passes as rueful. Probably doesn't want to admit he got dumped, I think, but then he glances at me again for half a heartbeat. *Holy shit*, I think. Seb's not going to tell because he doesn't want Charlotte to be part of Open Season. I'm not sure if that's a good thing or not. It's some kind of back-assed chivalry. My phone, which is on the picnic table next to my laptop, lights up with a Snapchat.

Charlotte: I am not his girlfriend!!!

I slide it into my pocket hoping nobody notices.

"Hey," says Khalid. "No phones."

I nod.

"Any more nays on Hannah Hesse?" Colin asks the room.

It's quiet. "Since Seb's a Senior and former Lord, we split the point. Hannah Hesse stands at seven point five."

The fact that they have this down to such a science is really disturbing. *Please don't say Q next*, I think.

Seb grabs the bottle of vodka and says, "Refills?" I pull my glass to the other side of the table. He passes me by.

Colin drains his glass, which looks like dollhouse barware in his meat hook. "Any other calls for point adjustments?" Nobody speaks up, so Colin says, "Okay, then. Take it away, Wayne." And it's like slow motion as he moves to flip off the lights.

As planned, I let the barn stay dark for a five count. Then I wake up my laptop. A photo of Sofia Bodenrader flashes onto the barn wall. Crenshaw yowls like a dog. Khalid says, "This one's gotta be the gold standard. Ten?"

All the hands go up, mutterings of agreement.

"Ten it is for Sofia Bodenrader," Khalid says. He licks the pencil tip like some kind of movie accountant and jots on his pad. Some laughs.

"Speaking of Bodenrader," Pearce says. Then he pulls a pair of panties out of his pocket. "Done!"

A general ruckus ensues. Seb says, "Pearce, she's practically a little sister to me."

Pearce grins and says, "Well, your little sister gives a great fucking blow job."

For the next twenty minutes, I kind of black out. I don't think I can handle bearing witness to what is happening. It would be shit on its own, just among dickheads, but the fact that the girls—that Alex—can hear this puts my brain into an altered state. A waking coma. It's cowardly. I should have to face the full implications of what I bought into, however briefly and however shallowly. But all I can hear is the *whoosh* of blood passing by my ears. The rapid fire of my heart. I warned Seb. I told him this was a shit bomb waiting to detonate.

We catch eyes again, and for once, I can read his expression. He's ashamed. Like me. But we're way too fucking late for that.

CHARLOTTE

I never knew it could be this bad. Still, somehow Hannah and Alex and I resist speaking out loud and communicate our abject outrage only through facial expressions. Hannah looks like she's going to charge in and take Bill Nash by the throat. When Pearce says that about Sofia, my jaw flops down like a cartoon character's, and I feel sick all over again for what I said to her.

We've got about ten minutes of seriously incriminating footage. Hannah turns off her camera and signals us to leave. We climb over the fence and jog the trail for at least a quarter mile before we dare speak.

"Holy *hell*!" Hannah says.

"I am so glad Q didn't see any of that," I say.

"Do you think Pearce forced Sofia?" Alex asks.

"Oh God, I'm officially the *biggest* ass on earth if he did and I treated her like that," I say.

"I'm her Big. I'll check in with her," Hannah says. "Hey, I think Pearce wrote those notes to you, Charlotte."

I look at her, squinting.

"You watch," she says. "You won't get any more. I betcha. He wanted to steal you from Seb from the beginning."

"That does make sense," I say. I shiver. Pearce really does see girls as nothing but something to dominate. We walk for a while without saying anything.

"That was way worse than anything I imagined," Alex says. "Max is comparatively harmless." We keep jogging. "Not that I'm letting him off the hook," she adds.

"Hey, at least he's helping us," Hannah says. "Man, Pete Crenshaw is an aa-aa-asshole. And I can't wait to fry him!"

"What the hell with Seb?" I say. "He defended Sofia, but when it came to me, he just stood there like a stump. I never thought he'd be the bystander type," I say. "It's so . . ."

"Gross?" offers Alex.

"Disappointing?" suggests Hannah.

"Both, and I feel . . ." I turn to them. "I feel part of my trouble is that I'm terrible at naming my own feelings."

"Be nice to yourself," Hannah says. "You're a people pleaser, Charlotte. You aren't used to putting your feelings first."

I pause. "Hey. I think you're right. Okay, well. I feel very *sad* about Seb. It's such a waste of a decent guy. He's smart enough and sensitive enough to know better."

Hannah laughs. "Like squandered resources."

"Yeah," I say, but I don't laugh with her. "Like that. I wish he was stronger."

We're out on the playing fields now and keep to the shadows.

"We need a way to get this story out in the open," Hannah says.

"The *Wire*," I say.

"Yes, but I don't think Mr. Bartello will let something that makes the school look that bad go home to all the parents and alumni. He wouldn't let me write about the stalker," Hannah says.

"And if we ask, he may tell Dean Frye. And he's not going to want it out there. And then it could be brushed under the rug."

"That is all so wrong," Alex says.

We're quiet, returning to the main quad.

"Do you trust Ms. Ballard?" I say. "Because if we go to her instead of Frye . . ."

Hannah says, "Yes. Ms. Ballard is good."

"I mean, we have perfect evidence. He put himself right on center stage in that video," Alex says.

"Hannah!" I stop cold. "Center stage!" We're next to the statues of Lycroft and Phelps and stop.

Hannah squints. "Yeah?"

"Our ballet dress rehearsal! It's the same day you're interviewing Margot Pipkin. In the performing arts center. The entire student body and faculty will be there!"

"Holy shit," Hannah says. "Margot Pipkin will be all over this toxic masculinity bullshit! Oh. I like where you're going with this, if you're thinking what I'm thinking."

"I think I am, but what are you thinking?" I say.

"Oh my God, you're talking so fast!" Alex says. "Please explain!"

Hannah ignores her. "I'm thinking we could play the recording right over the sound system and bust them all. And since it would be public, nobody could brush it under the rug."

"Whoa," Alex says.

A knot of worry forms in my chest. I admit a part of me doesn't want to ruin Seb. But that is wrong, and I try to forget it. "Can we do that? I feel like we could get sued or something," I say. "And PS, they say horrible things about you, Hannah."

She's pacing. "I think we would need to somehow remove all the names of the guys on the recording. Everyone will recognize them."

"How do we do that?" I say.

"I'll ask Margot. She's the head of news. She has a team of audio people, I'm sure."

Hannah and I squeal and jump around. "We're taking him down for real!"

"We should go tell Q," Alex says. "It shouldn't be like a war. We have to remember how hard it all is for her."

Hannah and I agree solemnly. "You're so right, Alex. Let's go," I say.

16
One week before Fall Fling and the Big Dip

CHARLOTTE

It's dress rehearsal day, which means a lot of things for basically everyone I know—although, I think, some of the males don't know it yet. Osher Performing Arts Center is bigger than the chapel where we have Vespers, has red velvet seats and stage curtains—we're behind them and can hear Dean Frye welcoming everyone and prattling on.

The dancers are in the wings with me: three on this side plus Gabby, three on the other side plus Felipe. The entire student body and faculty is out in the audience. Including Seb. Colin Pearce. Q. It's our only dress rehearsal before we perform for the Fall Fling next weekend.

"I'm so fucking nervous," whispers Hannah. "I'd rather perform for a thousand strangers."

"Same," says Vivi.

"You've got it down. You'll be great." I squeeze her arm and then Hannah's. "Have fun with it."

"I'm major-league compartmentalizing right now," Hannah says. "How did we schedule Margot for the same day?"

"No kidding." I shake my head. "For now, it's about this dance," I say. "We've worked hard, and it's beautiful. If we kill it, we'll feel more confident for what comes next."

My roommate and I share a knowing look. I shake my head; we can't think about it now. My heart ticks in my ears. I watch Gabby off to the side running through the movements with her arms. We may as well not be here. I channel that focus.

My ears prick up when Dean Frye introduces Madame. I hear my name, and my stomach does a little flip-flop. It's excitement, I think, not fear. Across the stage, Sofia and I make eye contact. I hold my hand over my chest and smile. She inhales, her dimples busting out with a nervous smile.

Applause. The house lights go down. The curtain rises.

Silence.

Coldplay's rolling piano fills the auditorium. And they go! Hannah, Skye, Lily, Mallory, Sofia, Vivi, cascading water. My body is a giant goose bump. They're nailing it. I peek toward the audience. Ms. Ballard is next to Ms. Pipkin in the front row. Madame Chu as well. Up in the balcony I see Seb and pull back.

It's the solo. Gabby leaps onto the stage. Her body is fluid motion. Her arms delicate and strong at once. Felipe comes out, and it's the duet. I inhale, taking in this moment and holding it. Felipe does the highest lift he's done all season, and the audience sucks in a breath while he lets her fall inches from the floor. They hold their pose, and then the other girls do crisscrossing leaps in front of them. The piano starts to fade, and they fall into their final lunges. End!

The house goes nuts with cheering and applause, and the dancers unfreeze and take their bows. There's whistling and stomping, and I know part of it is just the sound the student body makes when given an opportunity to cheer, but I see people on their feet. Some younger dancers I don't know bring bouquets to Felipe and Gabby, and then the two of them come take me by the arms and lead me to center stage. It's wonderful, and I get choked up. And the curtain rolls down.

We all cheer and hug. "If you all do half that well for the Fall Fling," I say, "you'll be amazing!"

Moments later, all the dancers are backstage in the dressing room, changing to join the audience. Except Hannah, changing for her interview.

"You're going to kill it," I say. "You're interviewing the president of a huge news network and you're only seventeen!"

"But she's really down to earth," Hannah says. She chugs her water bottle. "What if she would agree to become my mentor? You know, later, when I'm in college?"

"She'll be begging you," I say. "Good luck!" I give her a peck on the cheek and leave to join Alex and Q backstage as planned, where we'll be able to watch the audience's reaction.

"I'm nervous for her," I whisper.

"Can you believe we're doing this?" Alex says. "I still can't believe it."

Finally, it's time. Dean Frye announces Hannah, and then Hannah introduces Ms. Pipkin.

They take a seat in two chairs, center stage. Ms. Pipkin is tall and wears a navy business dress with red flowers and low red heels.

Hannah reviewed her outline with us about forty times today, so I know she's going to ask first about what Ms. Pipkin did after graduation from Lycroft in 1985, then ask about her career and then lead into how she thought of Bigs and Littles, and why. That's when the shit is coming down. I don't hear much of anything she says until she tells us that, even though Lycroft Phelps admitted girls beginning in 1972, girls always felt like second-class citizens.

"A lot of the alumni didn't want girls at Lycroft. They liked the idea of boys focusing on learning and character development without, quote-unquote, 'the distraction of girls,'" she says. "And it permeated the atmosphere. I was always a bold kid. A few days into my First Year, before I'd met many people, I thought, *I'll go to Spangler by myself and make some new friends.* I marched in there with my tray of beef stroganoff and sat down. I couldn't figure out why people stared and snickered. Until the football team came out and informed me I'd sat at their table." She hides her face in her hands.

The audience laughs.

"The next year, I saw another girl make that mistake, and again the year after that. I thought, why don't we have mentors who can save First Years from these types of microhumiliations? Because they can add up."

Teachers start applauding, and kids join in politely.

Hannah says, "I am a Big, and I love helping the new girls get acclimated, and I know a lot of us are glad you founded the program. Sometimes we still experience sexism here. For instance, there is no girls' rowing in the fall even though the boys' team has been a fall/spring sport since its inception in the early 1900s."

"Yes. That change is in the works," Ms. Pipkin says. "I walked onto the women's rowing team at Yale and married a Yale rower, in fact, so this has been something I've tried to help the trustees see as an important investment."

Q and I look at each other. "This could be better than I thought," I say.

"Have you ever heard of the Slycroft Society, Ms. Pipkin?" Hannah says. "It's a secret all-boys' club."

Q, Hannah, and I look up to the balcony where Seb and Colin are sitting. They are stone-faced. Khalid is twitchy. Max is on the first floor with Nils.

"Slycroft was around when I was here," she says. "I thought it was shut down two years after my graduating year."

"It's back," Hannah says. "And they have a game called Bounty Hunter that is really, really sexist."

Ms. Pipkin knows what's coming. We also know she had her audio guys scrub the audio so there won't be any identifiable names. Except one.

I hold Q's hand. Alex holds her other one. Over the sound system, Pearce's voice. *Tonight we set the scoring for this year's Bounty Hunter competition. ——, you on note-taking? Before we look at the First Years, we'll consider calls for status adjustments of any Lower and Upper Mids and Seniors.*

Voice 2: I move to change Hannah Hesse to an eight. Have you seen her tits this year?

A murmuring spreads over the auditorium. Teachers are horrified, stretching over seats to talk to each other. Girls are equally aghast, while guys appear confused. Hannah's face is red, and she adjusts in her seat. But she is solid. Dean Frye stands up, then sits down. "I can't believe she let her name be heard," Alex says.

"Badass," says Q.

"It makes it more credible," I say.

Voice 1 (Colin): All in favor?

Voice 3 (Seb): A whole point?

When I look at Seb, his face is smooth as ever. It makes me want to smack him.

Voice 2 (Nash): Fuck yeah, bruh! You should see her in that ballet outfit. I do the lighting for their show, and man.

[Laughing and clapping.]

"Oh my God, look at Bill Nash," I say. "He's purple."

Voice 1 (Colin): —'s too pussy whipped to notice Hannah Hesse.

Voice 4 (Pete Crenshaw): Wah-wah! Still no panties. Bit of a letdown.

[More laughter.]

Coach Follett approaches Dean Frye, and the two converse briefly. Dean Frye can't take it and is up on the stage. "We've heard enough, Hannah," he says in a restrained voice.

"They're only getting started," Hannah says.

Ms. Pipkin stands and leans in to say something to Dean Frye. He jerks back and stares at her, then retreats to the floor.

As the audio continues, the guys proceed to rate First Year girls (names kept anonymous), quibbling over breasts, asses, faces. Only bits and pieces are audible, since the auditorium is in pandemonium. After several painful minutes, Hannah turns it off. I check on Q. She's watching Pearce.

Ms. Ballard joins Ms. Pipkin on the stage. Dean Frye gets back up there, too. He raises his hands to signal quiet, and while it takes a minute, eventually it's nearly silent again. But the auditorium vibrates with a freneticism.

"This is unacceptable behavior. Abhorrent," Dean Frye exclaims. His hair is mussed, his blazer unbuttoned. "The students—the *boys* involved in this competition will be punished to the fullest extent."

"Dean Frye," Ms. Pipkin says. "If I may?" He's helpless. "Hannah, you have done an outstanding and brave investigative reporting job. Allowing yourself to be degraded in this manner to call out this reprehensible behavior is as gutsy and impactful as I've seen in my career."

A bunch of teachers and literally the entire female audience stands and applauds.

"I would like to point out that not all the boys are like this at Lycroft Phelps," Hannah says. "There are many great, respectful, fun guys here. That said, the fact that a pocket of toxic masculinity managed to thrive is really disturbing and indicates a big problem. That kind of dehumanizing talk sets a climate for sexual assault and rape."

Q swallows. I squeeze her hand.

"We need to demand more education and orientation around this topic," Hannah says.

Dean Frye calms the place down yet again and insists we join together in our school prayer. For the first time, it feels a little like people want the prayer to mean something. When it's finished, Dean Frye says, "Change begins tomorrow."

I look up to the balcony. Seb has his head in his hands. I guess this is fear in Sebanese, something I thought I'd never see.

Ms. Ballard: You are going to flip your lid.

Ms. Weller: What?

Ms. Ballard: Hannah Hesse found Griffin's name in that sex brag book. From 1985. And guess who he put his hookup with?

Ms. Weller: ?

Ms. Ballard: Margot Pipkin. She's irate. Says it never happened.

Ms. Weller: !

Ms. Ballard: We've got him. But there's more. Hannah also asked Margot why Katherine Mason left Lycroft. Margot, of course, didn't know, but she had her team from the network find Katherine in Oregon, and Katherine told about how Griffin made her leave to keep the last rape case silent. So, now Margot is threatening to tell the entire Board of Trustees. His ass is nailed!

Ms. Weller: "Change begins tomorrow."

Ms. Ballard: 😅 💪

Dear Q,

I'm blown away by the incredible butterflies you made using the kintsugi technique of creating beauty in the wake of something broken. The way you crafted the tissue-paper butterfly sculpture and applied gold paint to where the holes were in the box frame was so sensitive and beautiful. A gorgeous symbol of healing and strength. I would like to see if you are willing to duplicate this butterfly to make more, which we could hang in the art gallery for the Fall Fling Art Show. Let's talk!

Fondly,
Ms. Weller

Q

"How do you feel?" Charlotte asks. We're trailing behind Hannah and Alex, separated by throngs of kids crossing the quad. It's the coldest night we've had so far, and the days are much shorter. Twilight casts a silver glow over campus.

I shrug. "A little dazed. How about you?"

We pass the Founders Statues. "I don't know," Charlotte says. "Surprised. I guess I'm a sap. It's not fun for me to see Seb lose everything like that, even though he set himself up for it. But that's putting his feelings ahead of mine." She shakes her head. "I wish he was more than he is. Colin's a *very* different story. I feel very positive he's going to pay. It's also not enough. He should be arrested."

I say, "I realized that what would feel the closest to fair—given that he won't be arrested—would be him having to surrender something he really wanted. And I'm guessing he'll lose his seat on the boat and the chance at Yale," I say. "So it's as good as it's going to get. But I feel disconnected from it."

We branch off from the crowd headed to Spangler and turn toward the dorms, falling in step with Hannah and Alex.

The silence between us is reflective. We pass the chapel, and I remember slipping out the side doors during Vespers a few weeks ago. I see myself, like a little fox, furtive and frightened and desperate, glancing over my shoulder as I hurry to Somes. I blink it away. I don't like that version of me.

"You know what?" I say. "I think it's about me. I need to feel purged of his hold on me. Remember what you said, Hannah?"

"What's that?" she asks.

"I have to kill those shoes."

Alex and Charlotte look confused, but Hannah grins broadly. "Yes, you do."

"I want to do it tonight," I say. "When it's fully dark. At the Amphitheater. And I want you all to come."

We got permission to go to the Miss Whitney Diner, where I tell them about what the shoes represent. The *shushing*. The way he couldn't be bothered to slip out of loafers. The way he walked while I froze. They're riveted, and it's not their attention, but rather how I'm gaining a mastery over this narrative, casting it into the air and feeling the compassion it elicits glow back on me, instead of letting it fester in my imagination, eating me from the inside out. Like cancer. I feel a warm tingle over my skin when I think this, and I imagine it's my mom's hand comforting me.

I haven't set foot in the Amphitheater since May. Dutifully avoided it, in fact. I remember for the first time in a while how warm it was that night. I remember the dizzying swirls of stars above us. The stars again spiral against the deep blue sky, but the grass is dry, the ground hard, and all four of us wear mittens. The muses start to take shape, hovering above the lawn on their pedestals. I see her. Euterpe. I felt betrayed by her somehow. Music, deserting me when I needed her most. But I forgive her now. She's been at my side ever since.

I brought my guitar and the shoes are in Charlotte's bag, along with a huge picnic blanket. Hannah and Alex collaborated on the pyrotechnics and told me not to worry about that part.

"They're worth five hundred dollars," I tell them.

"Why does a kid like him have five-hundred-dollar shoes?" asks Alex. "His fashion is completely unimaginative."

"Who knows," I say. "Who cares."

I lead them not to the same spot, but closer to the shore. Lake Edith wears her necklace of gems. We spread out the blanket and seat ourselves. I strap on my guitar and say, "I need to play this, for my mom." And it's too personal to say it aloud, but I whisper in my head, *I'm brave for you, Mommy.* Then I count and begin playing the notes to "Landslide." I worked on it all week, but I didn't know why. I'm so glad, because I'm able to play the whole song and I sing softly,

And if you see my reflection in the snow-covered hills
Well, the landslide bring it down.

My friends join in and I play the last verse an extra time just to hear us sing. When I finish, we're quiet. I watch the lake shimmer, listen to its tiny splashes against the shore. And then it feels like time. "Okay."

Charlotte gets the shoes out. Hannah has a pizza box from the diner. She carefully tears the top off it. "We can't put it in the water until the last second, but it's biodegradable."

I place the shoes on the cardboard. Hannah produces a bottle of rubbing alcohol. We stuff some paper towels in the shoes, and I douse everything with alcohol. Alex hands me a lighter, and we shift the box right to the edge of the water.

I hold the lighter and the paper flames into angry orange

snakes. The tops of the shoes ignite first, and the strange, primal smell of burning leather fills the air around us. Sparks snap and crack above the burning mound.

We are silent. I shove the pizza box. It wobbles across the twinkling water for an unearthly long time. The box is invisible. Just a small pyre floating across the water. I try to let it take those furtive, desperate feelings with it. I let myself imagine me, running between the trees—hidden exposed hidden exposed—and tell myself I don't need to hide anymore. In a sudden burst of combustion, the little vessel flares bright. Then, darkness. The girls suck in a breath. But I feel a smile, watching as the last creeping vine of gray smoke is sucked into the night.

The water shimmies softly against the shore, the only sound.

"They're gone," I whisper.

MAX

It turns out, Slycrofters don't *always* protect each other. Nash and Pearce identified every other voice on the recording in their first meeting with Ms. Ballard and Margot Pipkin, who is also a trustee for Lycroft. And Yale. Luckily, I knew not to speak at that Slycroft meeting, and I'll probably never know why Pearce didn't rat me out anyway, just for sheer spite.

By today—Monday after the shitshow that was the "special" Vespers at Osher Performing Arts Center—I am in awe I haven't been called in to Ballard's office. I'm pretty much waiting to be sent home. But Coach sends an email, bcc, so we don't know who else got it, that we have to show up at the boathouse as usual for practice. That we'll start with a 1V boat meeting.

"I mean, the fact that you're still standing today *probably* means you're going to survive this," Nils says as I zip my duffel.

"Maybe," I say.

I get there early. All this anxiety is making me cover ground faster than my usual eight minutes to the boathouse. My stomach's so tight it hurts. I jog down the outdoor stairs to the dock, where I find Seb sitting on a bench. I consider spinning around and running, but he waves me over.

"Sup," he says, sad. He's got a ball cap on but no Oakleys.

"I don't really know," I say.

He nods, leans back, stretching his long legs in front of him. "You were right."

It takes me a beat to absorb it. "I know," I say. "But I was still a dumbass. Just not as big of one as you."

He huffs in muted amusement. I wonder suddenly if nobody figured out I made the recording. They could all assume it was the girls. I'm not sure how I feel about that.

"Pearce is gone," he says. I look at him, staring out over Lake Edith, unreadable as ever. The leaves are brown in the foothills.

"Gone how?"

"Suspended. Same with Nash. But they're not coming back. They would be too hated on."

"I mean, they fucking earned that," I say. "That game was evil."

"Yep. Cost us two really amazing girlfriends."

"It did," I say. "We didn't deserve them." He nods.

We're quiet for a moment, and then I say, "What's happening to you?"

"Off the team. Khalid, too," he says. It's a gut punch, even though I sort of knew that's what would happen. "Maybe I'll be in for spring season. But no Big Dip."

"Fuck," I say. "Princeton?"

He shrugs. "Undecided," he says, shifting again.

"Wow." I am really mixed up about how I feel on this. "You were trying to make them better," I say.

"I didn't try *that* hard," he says. "Frye left it up to Coach. Coach hasn't told Princeton yet. I have to take some course about toxic masculinity."

"Why are you here, then?" I say.

"Coach is making me explain what happened to the guys. Also, 1V had something we'd planned on giving you at the Dip." He pulls a small shipping box out from under the bench. "I ordered it." He grins in a really small way. "Open it." I reach under the cardboard flaps and reveal a stack of green LPS rowing shirts.

"Nice," I say, confused.

"No, take one out. Read the back."

I do. Big block letters say, *I KNOW WAYNE UFF.*

I chuckle. A pang of sadness hits me right between the eyes. "We fucked it all up," I say.

"Coach has no idea you were there, you know. So keep your fucking mouth shut. You're the only thing that can save the rest of the guys in the boat next weekend. I feel like such a shit for letting them down. We would have *ruled* it! Killed Matheson. You made us better than even Chauncey, Max. Just know that."

Maybe because I'm a coward, or maybe because I'm selfish, or maybe because I really don't want to leave Lycroft anymore, I don't confess to Seb that I made the recording. The truth is, those girls were unstoppable and would have busted up Slycroft without me. Maybe someday I'll tell Seb the truth.

We're interrupted by the sound of the boathouse bay door rolling up. Teo and Tyler give subdued waves. Coach Follet and Coach Sam emerge from the shadows.

"Remember when you asked me what the Beast sounds like when he's mad?" Seb asks, starting toward the bay. I have to admire that courage, going to face it like a man. Even though I wish we'd both found our balls long before this.

"Hey," I say. He turns. "Why do you think we let Pearce keep going with all that bullshit? Why didn't we stop it?"

Seb sighs. "I wish I knew, man," he says, shaking his head. "I wish I fucking knew." He pulls himself to his full height and walks on.

Dear Lycroft Phelps Board of Trustees,

This letter serves as my resignation from the position of Dean of Students at Lycroft Phelps, effective immediately. It is due to an unexpected family situation that I must make this difficult choice. I have taken a position in the admissions department at Dalby Day School in Princeton, New Jersey, closer to my wife's parents. In the interest of a smooth transition, I recommend Assistant Dean Lori Ballard as my interim and possible permanent replacement. She's had a front-row seat to the demands of my job and has served as a trusted adviser to me in difficult times. She is well positioned to assure little to no disruption for all school operations.

THE WIRE
Lycroft Phelps Student Newspaper
Est. 1870

Monday, October 14
Ms. Lori Ballard Named Interim Dean of Students

Wednesday, October 16
Disappointment at the Big Dip as 1V boat falls to
Matheson. 2V wins carry the day.
With the loss of three star Senior rowers, the 1V boat fell to
both Matheson and Hotchner Schools, inching by Taunton
for third.

Monday, October 21

Charlotte Foresley's Choreography Wows LPS Community and Visiting Families at Fall Fling Performance. Charlotte, an Upper Mid, pictured here with her family and friend from home Grace O'Reilly, who flew in from Chicago for the big event.

Wednesday, October 23

Lower Mid Quinn Walsh's "Butterflies" Dazzles LPS Community and Guests at Fall Fling

Dear Colin,

I am disappointed to share with you that Yale Crew has decided to go with a different recruit from Lycroft Phelps School this year. Due to your serious and offensive conduct transgressions reported to us by Coach Follett, we have no choice but to retract our invitation to you for a team overnight visit, as well as make clear that we will not consider you for the Yale team.

It's unfortunate that you allowed poor judgment to overshadow your path to a successful rowing career at Yale and any other Division 1 school. It is my genuine hope for you that you find your way so you can live up to your considerable athletic potential.

Sincerely,
Coach Timothy Chenowith
Yale Men's Heavyweight Crew

From: Coach Follett <thebeast@lycroftphelps.edu>
To: tyler.wiggins@lycroftphelps.edu
Subject: Yale

Tyler,

Great news, pal. You are Yale's pick this year!

THE WIRE
Sunday, November 10

Board of Trustees Announces New Assistant Dean
LPS welcomes Mr. Michael Turner. Mr. Turner spent the
last decade building a nonprofit education project called
Boys To Men based in Maine. "Our program is committed
to ending male violence and self-harm while advancing
gender equity," Mr. Turner told the *Wire* in a phone
interview. "Boys are bombarded by narrow, confusing,
and often-destructive messages about what masculinity
is and isn't. My experience lends itself to a first-rate
institution like Lycroft Phelps, I think, because so many of
the students go out and become leaders in the world. We
can open dialogue about what it means to be strong and
masculine, and nurture a culture where everyone benefits
from that awareness."

MAY

❧ · ❧

Q

Standing at the edge of the small platform stage, just in shadow, I tune out specific words and listen to the café's own music: the layered hum of conversation, the hiss and gurgle of the cappuccino maker, silverware pinging against ceramic cups, and the chime over the door. It lacks rhythm, maybe, but it's alive.

"Just remember the immortal words of our wise old stoner Karl," Nils had said when I told him I was nervous, just after we tuned our guitars. He pointed at the café manager with his elbow. "'The audience has an unspoken agreement to celebrate the imperfect.' Think about it. What other activity at Lycroft isn't focused on winning? Or getting graded?" He gave me a little punch on the shoulder. "Besides, we kick ass."

I blink, my thoughts interrupted by a fuzzy *tap-tap-tap* from Karl on the microphone. My heartbeat picks up. At once, the crowd transforms into an audience. Charlotte, Alex, and Hannah grin at us from the front row. Max and Seb and a couple of rowers hang way back. I get a quick rush knowing the jackal is gone.

Karl clears his throat. "Good evening, friends, and welcome to the final Thursday Night Café of the school year," Karl says.

People applaud.

"Help me welcome a guitar duo we haven't seen since last year, Q Walsh and Nils de Guzman."

He steps aside, sweeping his arm toward us. As we walk to our stools and fiddle with our mics, I hear Alex, Hannah, and Charlotte go wild, which makes me nervous laugh. Like we planned, Nils says, "This is our cover of 'This Will Be Our Year' by the Zombies." We lock eyes and he sends me a wordless *we got this*, then he taps his guitar. "One, two, three, four."

My chest expands. I play the opening, a sort of three-note riff that repeats with key changes. It's so sweet and honest, it gets me every time.

Riff repeat, riff repeat. Nils layers in his guitar and then sings. He sounds a lot like the Zombies' singer and for a minute I'm lost in the beauty of it all. I can't look up, but I feel the audience drawn in and connecting.

"This will be our year, it took a long time to come," Nils sings.

Dad and I have always known what music can do. It kicks up feelings you forgot you had, carries you through time, or makes you love *right now*. It can bring back people you love, even a version of yourself you thought was gone forever. Music can let you hug that version, take her hand and bring her with you, so you both know you're going to be okay.

✤ ACKNOWLEDGMENTS ✤

I'm blessed to have had many people support this novel's journey to publication. I'm grateful to none more than Karen Chaplin, my editor, whose patience and dedication through multiple drafts (and a pandemic) helped me take the story to a place I never would have reached on my own. Thank you also to Rosemary Brosnan for her early endorsement, Celina Sun for her keen eye, and Molly Fehr for the fantastic cover design. To all the amazing, kind professionals at Quill Tree Books, thank you for how much you care about your books and authors.

Humble thanks go to my brilliant, compassionate agent, Allie Levick. Your commitment to my work inspires me every day. Aless Birch and Cecilia de la Campa, I curtsy before you.

To my new friends at Hot Key, your enthusiasm for this book is soul-lifting. Thank you!

I owe thanks, too, to those who furnished me with details that helped build the world of Lycroft Phelps. This includes Rhoen Fiotak, Sarah Albee, and George Haffenreffer. CC Stockley, thank you for providing such an excellent introduction to the grand sport of rowing. A big, purple Kenyon salute to Steve Sexsmith for connecting me to Mary Pat Evans, who helped me understand the limitations of DNA evidence. And I'm grateful to the therapists at Newport Academy for offering a window into trauma treatment.

Mountains of love go to my amazing, talented writing friends, Julie Kingsley, Lynda Mullaly Hunt, Jenny Bagdigian, Liz Goulet-Dubois, Jen Thermes, Carlyn Beccia, Laurie Smith Murphy, Brook Gideon, and Janet Costa Bates. Thank you for being simply the best people. Gillian French, you are suspense and sunshine in one package. I'm so happy we've connected.

I also feel the wind at my back thanks to the indefatigable encouragement of Lisa Haughs Hartley, Jessie Light, Kristen May, Derek Duval, Shelly Haffenreffer, Maryjane Johnston, Jo-Ellen Rand, and Becky Bean. The delightful Helen Vaughn, Vivian Sullivan, and Liv Emery forever brighten my day.

Love and thanks to my family, who never fails to support this dream of mine: Kim Chapdelaine, sister and plotter extraordinaire, I'm so lucky to have you; Jimmy Kelly, your musical genius came to my rescue yet again; Alex Chapdelaine, your cheerful aplomb while helping me keep up appearances was invaluable. Pat Lewis, thank you for always caring. Endless love to my parents, Jim and Betsy Kelly.

I'm most fortunate in having an ace coxswain for a child, and I thank you, sweet Bubby, for your thoughtful and entertaining insights about the rowing life. You inspired and informed me both, as you and your brother are quite fond of doing.

Paul, without you, none of this is possible. Your generosity with time and unerring first reads easily atone for your habit of stealing my coffee. And you happen to be the love of my life. I'm the luckiest.

❧ AUTHOR'S NOTE ❧

Dear Reader,

I am so honored that this book has found its way into your hands. Even though I only began writing Q's story a few years ago, it has, in many ways, been blowing around my mind since I was sixteen years old. I was that age when a charismatic bad boy from my high school sexually assaulted me in the woods by my house, during a pool party I wasn't supposed to be hosting. He was good-looking, a regionally famous athlete, a real guy's guy. I'd had a crush on him since our sixth-grade neighborhood Brat Pack games of sardines and whiffle ball. I was naive enough to think it was that version of him I let lead me—a little drunk—over brambles and dead leaves, until we were just out of sight. I kind of, maybe, thought we'd make out. I couldn't believe it. He'd picked me, out of all the girls there.

When he attacked me, his eyes turned black, unrecognizable, and scary as hell. They looked through me like I didn't exist, like we never plotted on the same team of flashlight tag or spotted each other for the Good Humor truck. He easily overpowered me. I got a free hand and surprised myself by punching him in the face. And with this act, I got away. When he went to leave me there, with scratched legs and a torn bathing suit, I yelled with impressive moxie (which I quickly lost), "Where the hell are you going?!" He said, "Nothing happened, and I don't want anyone thinking it did." A final, belittling dagger. We never spoke again.

When I was in college, he was arrested for brutally raping two younger girls and ended up in prison. So, I told myself, I got away. I was lucky. "Nothing happened." Oh, but it did. In hindsight, that day marks the moment my self-esteem plummeted. Into my twenties, I saw myself through his eyes: the perfect target, too socially insignificant to cause him trouble. Not good enough to be seen with. Not good enough to even see. I struggled with eating disorders and treated myself terribly. Years later, I realized that he had dehumanized me with those serpentine eyes; he wanted the sex without the person, and it made me doubt my worth for years. I think that is the cruelest impact of such attacks; while the assaulter carries on, the survivor suffers the indignity—sometimes privately, sometimes publicly. Which is worse?

I wanted to write a story about a girl finding her way out of the downward spiral that haunts so many sexual assault survivors. A girl bold enough to fight for herself with everything she's got. Who holds herself accountable until she recognizes who is to blame. Quinn is aware of #MeToo, but nonetheless vulnerable to her own memories, her own expectations of what a "strong girl" is. I hope that Quinn's story helps readers name feelings that can be devastating if left to fester in silence, and to recognize the power of friendships in the darkest times. We can't always control what happens to us, but we can rise above it if we are brave enough to give ourselves the chance.

Do you want to be a changemaker at your school? Check out these two outstanding organizations. Both are full of positive energy with research behind their educational programs and trainings for students, parents, and educators.

I Have the Right To's mission is "to create an ecosystem of respect and support for students and survivors of sexual assault." Among its many resources, the website features an interactive pledge written for four key audiences—students, parents, educators, and community members—in support of survivors, to raise awareness and invite shared responsibility in ensuring that every student receives an education free from sexual assault. ihavetherightto.org

Maine Boys to Men is "courageously committed to ending male violence and self-harm while advancing gender equity" and has made tremendous impact in my great state of Maine. Their programs are exportable, and the website is loaded with great resources. maineboystomen.org

Love,
Cameron K. Rosenblum

TIMOTHY LEARY

ALSO BY ROBERT GREENFIELD

NONFICTION

S.T.P.: A Journey Through America with the Rolling Stones

The Spiritual Supermarket

Bill Graham Presents:
My Life Inside Rock and Out (with Bill Graham)

Dark Star: An Oral Biography of Jerry Garcia

NOVELS

Haymon's Crowd

Temple

ROBERT GREENFIELD

TIMOTHY LEARY

A BIOGRAPHY

A JAMES H. SILBERMAN BOOK
HARCOURT, INC.
Orlando   Austin   New York   San Diego   Toronto   London

www.HarcourtBooks.com

Excerpts from *The Letters of Aldous Huxley,* edited by Grover Smith,
© 1969, 1970 by Laura Huxley and prefatory material © 1969, 1970 by
Grover Smith is reprinted by permission of HarperCollins Publishers. Lyrics from
"'The Seeker" by Pete Townsend © Towser Tunes (BMI)/Abkco Music Inc./
Fabulous Music All rights for the world on behalf of Towser Tunes (BMI) administered
by BMG Music Publishing International (PRS). All rights for the U.S. on behalf
of BMG Music Publishing International (PRS) administered by Careers-BMG Music
Publishing (BMI). Used by permission. "Legend of a Mind." Words and music by
Ray Thomas © copyright 1968 (renewed) and 1969 (renewed) Westminster Music Ltd.,
London, England TRO—Essex Music International, Inc., New York, controls all
publication rights for the U.S.A. and Canada. Used by permission. Excerpts from
the letters of Jack Kerouac reprinted by permission of SLL/Sterling
Lord Literistic, Inc. Copyright by Jack Kerouac.

Library of Congress Cataloging-in-Publication Data
Greenfield, Robert.
Timothy Leary: a biography/Robert Greenfield.—1st ed.
p.   cm.
"A James H. Silberman Book."
Includes bibliographical references and index.
1. Leary, Timothy Francis, 1920–1996
2. Psychologists—United States—Biography.   I. Title.
BF109.L43G74   2006
150.92—dc22   2005030154
ISBN-13: 978-0-15-100500-0   ISBN-10: 0-15-100500-1

Text set in Dante MT
Designed by April Ward

Printed in the United States of America

First edition
C E G I K J H F D B

for anna, sweeter than honey from the bee

And that most treacherous and tragic game of all, the individuality game. The Timothy Leary game. Ridiculous how we confuse this game, overplay it.

—TIMOTHY LEARY,
speech to the International Congress of
Applied Psychology, August 19, 1961

CONTENTS

DREAMING OF HEROES

SPRINGFIELD, MASSACHUSETTS, 1920–1938

I grew up lonely, immersed in tales of heroism, history, romance, and exploration . . . Unlike my Catholic schoolmates, who were encouraged to imitate sorrowful saints, virtuous virgins, masochistic martyrs, I modeled myself after legendary heroes and lovers.

—Timothy Leary, *Flashbacks*

Abigail Leary with three-month-old Timothy, 1921.
Courtesy of the Futique Trust

ONE

Late at night, a young boy lies in bed in his room. By all rights, he should be sleeping. Outside his window, the streets of Springfield, Massachusetts, a small industrial city ninety miles west of Boston, are quiet. All the movie theaters have already let out for the night. The restaurants have long since locked their doors. Even the trolleys have stopped running. Because Prohibition has been the law of the land for more than a decade, there are no boisterous downtown night clubs or loud neighborhood bars where people can drink legally. Yet as everywhere in a nation that professes one code of morals in public while practicing another in private, many of the good citizens of Springfield are out drinking all the same.

Unable to sleep, the boy waits. Will his father come home? And if he does, how will it be? The usual sound of stumbling, followed by the front door slamming loudly and then the heavy tread of his feet on the creaking stairs as he makes his way to his bedroom? Or will it be worse? As he lies awake in bed, the boy dreams of heroes. Huck Finn smoking a corncob pipe with Jim as they float down the Mississippi River. Horatio at the bridge. Lancelot setting off to find the Holy Grail. Tom Swift in his magic flying machine. Each week, the boy checks out and reads ten books from the public library, a big granite-and-marble building constructed with Carnegie money. His library card is both a passport and a round-trip ticket, allowing him to travel freely through realms of gold. But sooner or later, even the greatest tale of heroism and adventure in some faraway place has to end. And then the boy finds himself lying in bed late at night surrounded by silence and darkness, waiting for his father to come home.

Flesh of the same flesh and blood of the same blood, the boy and his father, Timothy Francis Leary—called "Tote" by all who know him in this city where he was born and who now works as a dentist at 292 Worthington Street—share the same name. In speakeasies all over Springfield where people drink openly but not legally, Tote is well known. Late at night, after the speakeasies close, he can often *be found buying liquor on the darkened front porches of nearby houses in Winchester Square, where bootleggers live. What began as a fondness for drink has become for Tote Leary in the past few years something darker and more self-destructive.*

Already the boy has made up his mind that he will never be like his father. He will be a hero. Strong and courageous as Socrates at the moment he was offered hemlock. Brave and bold as Ulysses returning home after a twenty-year absence. But there is also something heroic about running away from it all like Huck and Jim. Floating down a river like a child, adrift from all cares and responsibilities. As the boy lies in bed, unable to sleep, he considers his choices. At the moment, all he can do is wait.

For all he knows, his father may not come home tonight. In many ways, that might be best. If his father were out of the picture for good, then the boy could stop wondering if he is destined to become him. Just wanting his father gone is an evil thought, a sin, one of many to be added to the list he has begun to compile. Although this is yet another sin, the boy already knows that God the Father and all the saints in heaven will never be of any use to him. Only he can save himself. In order to do so, he has divided his life into separate self-sealing waterproof compartments. Unlike his father, he will never sink to the bottom of any sea. Far too strong and much too determined, he has a face for the father who does not come home, a face for the mother who is there even when he does not want her to be, a face for his great-uncle the priest to whom he never tells the complete truth even in confession, and yet another face for the uncle who has succeeded in business but is not at all what he seems to be. Dreaming with his eyes wide open about heroes he has only met in books, the boy lies in bed unable to sleep. Tim Leary is waiting. For what, he does not know. In his long and eventful life, it is but the first of many questions to which he will never find an answer.

No child chooses his place of birth or the family into which he is born. Every child does, however, select the adults after whom he patterns himself. Early in his childhood, Tim Leary made a conscious decision to identify with his father's family. To him, they seemed "urban, urbane, well-to-do, and . . . glamorous." Far more than his father, it was his paternal grandfather, Dennis, that Tim Leary would most closely resemble as an adult. A watchmaker by trade, Dennis Leary conducted his business for forty-five years in a jewelry store on State Street in downtown Springfield. Eight feet wide and thirty-six feet deep, the store housed his extensive collection of theater programs, including one for *Our American Cousin* on the night Abraham Lincoln was assassinated by John Wilkes Booth in Ford's Theatre. Dennis also collected old baseball guides. He filled scrapbooks with articles that interested him. At his death, he had 120 of them.

A great student of Shakespeare, Dennis often journeyed to Boston to take in shows starring such actors as E. L Davenport (his favorite), Edwin Booth, and Edwin Forrest at the Boston and Howard theaters. Until the end of his life, he could recite from memory long passages from his favorite plays. At the age of seventy-five, Dennis liked to embarrass his teenage granddaughters and their boyfriends by yanking aside the velvet curtain separating the front hall from the parlor in his fine Victorian house at 254 Central Street. Stepping forward as though onstage, he would launch without preamble into Othello's final soliloquy. Plunging an imaginary dagger into his chest, he would end his impromptu performances by falling dead to the floor. More than sixty years after his death, one of his great-great-granddaughters affectionately described him as "a little eccentric and given to theatrical moments."

It was on the top floor of his house, where Dennis kept his large theatrical library, that his grandson first remembered meeting him. On a wintry evening, ten-year-old Tim Leary sat on the floor reading a copy of Mark Twain's *Life on the Mississippi* as Dennis complained about his children, calling them all "hell-raising illiterates." Praising Tim for being the only one in the family who really liked to read, Dennis told his grandson never to do anything like anyone else. He urged him to find his own way and to be one of a kind. Embroidered on a heraldic shield, the words could have served as the Leary family motto. For Dennis never did anything by half. Neither would his grandson.

A photograph of Dennis and his wife, Sarah, taken in 1925 reveals a good deal about them. Already married for fifty-eight years, Dennis and Sarah stand together in front of their home. The look on Sarah's face plainly says that all this is silly business and hardly worth the bother. Shorter, stouter, and far less elegant than her husband, she seems stiff and ill at ease. Hamming it up for the camera, Dennis has his left arm around his wife's shoulder and his right hand on her arm. Eighty-three years old but still looking spry, lean, and prosperous in a dark tailored suit, he leans forward with his cheek next to Sarah, hoping for a kiss.

By then, Sarah had already given birth to what may have been as many as thirteen children. Only nine lived long enough to be baptized. The star of the family was Frances, the second daughter. So beautiful that in later years she would be offered a screen test, Frances was a formally trained mezzo-soprano who dazzled local reviewers. Despite his overwhelming love for theater, Dennis steadfastly refused to let his daughter pursue a career onstage. Instead, Frances Leary spent her entire life moving restlessly from place to place, searching for happiness she never found.

The most colorful of Dennis's sons was Arthur. Two years older than Tote, Arthur opened the very exclusive Women's Shop on State Street, where he sold women's cloaks, suits, and furs which he bought while traveling extensively in Europe. A local celebrity, Arthur opened branch stores on Boylston Street in Boston and in Hyannis, Saratoga Springs, and Miami Beach. As a young boy what Tim most admired about his uncle was his power over women. Beautiful models and salesgirls regularly accompanied Arthur to openings and fashion shows in New York and Paris. Tim's mother and his dowager aunt could not resist the exquisite gifts Arthur brought them from Europe. Years later, Tim Leary would write that women "adored the effeminate bachelor Arthur who seemed to understand what women wanted." By then, he had realized that his uncle Arthur was gay.

Tim also learned from Arthur about the power of media. Arthur Leary's stores were so successful because he advertised them over the radio. Invented the same year Tim was born, radio had by the time he was ten years old become America's principal source of news, information, and entertainment. Even Tim's pious mother and aunt were impressed when the voice of Pope Pius XI, speaking in Latin, came over the radio for the very first time. Thoroughly modern in every way, Uncle Arthur had gotten there first.

In 1931, at the age of forty-five, Arthur died suddenly of a cerebral hemorrhage. He was buried in the Leary family plot in St. Michael's cemetery alongside his older brother, Eugene, a watchmaker like his father, dead at forty-seven of unknown causes, and his younger brother, John, an MIT graduate, dead at the age of twenty-five of cerebral apoplexy. Yet another brother, Dennis Jr., had set off to seek his fortune in California. There was now just one Leary son left in Springfield. If only by the process of elimination, Tim's father, Tote, should have become the dominant male in his son's life. But it was Dennis who made far more of an impression on Tim.

What drew Tim to his father's family was their charm. With it came a certain recklessness. Sally Olmstead Barnes, Frances Leary's granddaughter, would later say, "The Learys were a colorful and fascinating Irish clan and yet . . . where Tim saw amusing eccentricity, flamboyance, and adventure, I saw loss of control, irresponsible behavior, and too much heartbreak . . . the foolishness of one generation creating havoc and ultimately tragic fallout for those who followed."

There could not have been a family more unlike the outgoing, gregarious, reckless Learys than the quiet and pious Ferris clan from which Tim's mother, Abigail, came. The shining star of the Ferris family was Abigail's maternal uncle, Father Michael Kavanaugh. Born in 1873, he graduated first in his class at Holy Cross and then studied for the priesthood in Rome at the Pontifical Vatican Seminary. Returning home, he became a monsignor. A parochial power broker with connections throughout New England, Father Michael traveled to Europe each summer. In Springfield, he was driven everywhere by a chauffeur. One of his closest friends was the United States Senator from Massachusetts, David Ignatius Walsh, a classmate from Holy Cross. For as long as they lived, both Abigail and her sister Mary (called "May") worshipped Father Michael. Five times, they went with him to Europe in search of culture and spiritual inspiration. Abigail chose her uncle to perform her marriage ceremony. Among the Catholic elite in New England, being married by a priest who was a close relative was considered a special honor.

Whether or not Tim ever really understood their enduring influence on him, the men upon whom he modeled himself were his grandfather Dennis, his great-uncle Father Michael, his uncle Arthur, and his father, Tote. They all shared a single trait—none was what he seemed to be.

Long before he finally left Springfield in 1933, Tim's father had already gone missing. Born on October 29, 1888, Tote was the second youngest of the five surviving Leary boys. With the help of his uncle Timothy—after whom Tote was named—a physician who served for many years as a distinguished researcher and professor of medicine at Tufts Dental School, Tote was admitted to the dental program there. After completing the three years of undergraduate study then required for dental certification, he set off for Heidelberg, Germany, at the age of twenty-one for further training. Among the few tattered papers Tote left behind, there is a yellowing obituary he clipped from a New York City newspaper on August 3, 1955, recounting the death of Crown Prince Rupprecht, the eighty-six-year-old son of Bavaria's last king, Ludwig II. At the bottom of the obit, Tote jotted, "I did some dental work on him and his two youngsters when I was in Germany, 1912–1913."

Not long after Tote returned to America, Germany entered World War I. Like his father, Dennis, who had avoided service in the Civil War by going to London, and his older brother, Arthur, who at the very end of World War I enlisted in the army and was stationed at nearby Fort Devens, Massachusetts, Tote saw no action in the Great War. On April 23, 1917, he was invited by the surgeon general of the United States to report to Fort Slocum, New York, for examination as an acting dental surgeon in the United States Army. In June, he was found to be qualified and commissioned as a first lieutenant in the Dental Corps.

On January 7, 1918, Tote Leary married Abigail Ferris. Although any union between a Leary son and a Ferris daughter seems unlikely even now, Tote had first courted Abigail's older sister May, variously described by those who knew her as a "pill" and a "wet blanket." When Abigail, by far the livelier of the two sisters, accepted Tote's proposal of marriage, May was so distressed that she cried for three days, begged her sister not to leave for the honeymoon, and then accompanied Tote and Abigail to Niagara Falls. It was hardly an auspicious beginning for their marriage.

On July 13, 1918, with World War I soon to end, Tote was elevated to the rank of captain and assigned to West Point. At the academy, he drove a Packard, wore dress blues to dances at the officer's club, and consorted with fellow officers and gentlemen such as General Douglas MacArthur, then the superintendent of West Point; Captain Omar Bradley; and Lieutenant George Patton. It was at West Point on January 17, 1920, on the day after Prohibition became the law of the land, that Tim Leary was conceived. Abigail would later recall that during her pregnancy, the smell of distilling moonshine and bathtub gin hung over officers' row like a "rowdy smog." Tote once told his son that while Prohibition itself was bad, it was not nearly as bad as no booze at all. At 10:45 A.M. on October 22, 1920, seven days before his father's thirty-second birthday, Timothy Francis Leary was born in Springfield, Massachusetts. Once Abigail gave birth to a son, General MacArthur, who had also been raised on an army post, took a special interest in the family.

When Tote's commission expired, he left the army. His departure from West Point, a place where he seems to have been genuinely happy, coincided with the end of MacArthur's term of service as superintendent in 1922. For the rest of his life, Tote revered the liberator of the Philippines who after World War II ended also served as the American shogun of occupied Japan. On the general's seventy-sixth birthday in 1956, Tote sent him his greetings and best wishes.

His army days behind him, Tote returned home to Springfield where he set up shop as a dentist at 292 Worthington Street while living with his wife and young son in an apartment six blocks away at 43 Magazine Street. In a photograph taken in Springfield in 1922, two-year-old Tim, all bundled up in a wool hat and winter leggings, sits on a tricycle. Arms at his side, Tote gazes down at his son with interest. He is wearing a derby hat and an expensive-looking winter overcoat with broad lapels. A thick muffler is wound around his neck. His mustache is neatly trimmed. His eyes are hidden behind professorial spectacles. In every way, Tote looks like he just stepped from the pages of *Main Street* or *Babbitt* by Sinclair Lewis. None of Dennis Leary's vital spark shows through. Only when he drank was Tote able to manifest the fabled Leary charm.

As the twenties roared on around him and the American economy prospered, Tote did his best to be a dutiful husband. He and Abigail read a lot and did crossword puzzles together. Tote also tried to be a good son to Dennis. When his sister Frances shocked the family by running off to Kansas City with a Protestant, Tote was dispatched to bring her home. Tote's single act of defiance during this period seems to have been his refusal to visit the Ferris household in nearby Indian Orchard, a household dominated by Abigail's maiden aunt Dudu, whom Tim Leary would later describe as "a timid, fanatically religious gnome who futilely tried to direct family affairs with Irish-village piety, sitting on a couch all day clicking her false teeth, mumbling prayers, and reading Catholic tracts."

Around 1930, the life Tote had made for himself began to fall apart. It is hard to say whether his unhappiness was caused by sheer boredom, his marriage to Abigail, or the continuing frustration he felt living in the shadow of his father and far more glamorous brother Arthur and sister Frances. Whatever the reason, at the age of forty-two, Tote began a long slow decline that would continue until his death in 1957. Tote not only drank to excess but was also a womanizer. More than once, Phil Shea, a Leary cousin fifteen years older than Tim, had to pick up Tote's car in front of some woman's apartment where Tote had spent the night. Drinking too much may have been, in Shea's words, "the Irish disease," but womanizing did not go down well in Springfield.

Even when he was home, Tote's inappropriate behavior was impossible to ignore. Drunk after church one Sunday afternoon, he encouraged Fritz, the family dog, to jump up on the dining-room table. Tim, who had invited his best friend over for Sunday dinner, pleaded with his father to stop. When Tote finally got the dog to perform the trick, Fritz pulled off the tablecloth, sending the best family silver and china crashing to the floor. Coming home drunk one night in 1932, Tote woke his son by slamming the boy's bedroom door shut. Tim had already rigged a string through a pulley above the transom so he could reopen the door without leaving his bed. Announcing he was about to make love to Abigail, Tote slammed the door again. From his bed, Tim pulled it open. When Tote slammed the door only to see it open again, he stalked off, returned with a hammer, and nailed the door shut.

The defining moment in Tim's relationship with his father occurred during the same year. Awakened by his weeping mother, Tim emerged from his bedroom to find his father drunk and carrying on downstairs. Sounding very much like a father, the twelve-year-old boy yelled, "Hey. We're trying to sleep up here." Quickly becoming a son again, he added, "Please let us sleep. I have school in the morning." Slowly making his way up the stairs, Tote threatened to teach his son a thing or two right then and there. As Tote's face came level with Tim's knees, the boy reached down with his hand and very gently shoved his father backward. In slow motion, Tote tumbled into the banister and then fell head over heels down the stairs, crashing into the telephone stand and breaking his eyeglasses. Humiliated by his son in front of Abigail, Tote glared at the boy. "I'll get you for that," he said as he headed back up the stairs. Frightened, Tim threw open the hall window and escaped onto the roof, as he had done so many times before while pretending to be Tom Sawyer. Hiding behind the chimney, Tim watched his father poke his head out the window and curse. Then Tote slammed the window shut and locked it. Feeling sad and guilty but also somehow free, Tim stayed on the roof until his mother waved at him through the window signaling it was now safe for him to come back inside since Tote had fallen asleep.

For Tim, the dichotomy between good and bad authority figures had been clearly defined. Tote was the bad father. Father Michael Kavanaugh was the good father. Uncle Arthur was somewhere in between. Because none of them were ever there on a regular basis, Tim soon came to rely on the kindness of women, most of them replicas of his mother. Their influence became so stultifying that in his autobiography Tim Leary would celebrate his father for having never "stunted me with expectations . . . Dad remained for me a model of the loner, a disdainer of the conventional way. Tote dropped out, followed the ancient Hibernian practice of getting in the wind, escaping the priest-run village, heading for the far-off land, like one of the Wild Geese of Irish legend." Throughout his life as an adult, Tim Leary favored the same technique. Rather than stand and fight, he would run away just as his father had done before him. Invariably, those he left behind were women.

As the Depression continued to worsen, factories and small businesses in Springfield began shutting down. Massachusetts, the state that once produced a third of America's cloth and half of its shoes, was hit harder than most of the nation. One by one, the mill towns began to die. Huge red-brick factory buildings everywhere stood empty and abandoned. Nowhere in his many accounts of his childhood does Tim Leary ever mention the Depression. The election of Franklin Delano Roosevelt in 1932 seems to have meant nothing to him or his parents. But then, unlike so many others, Tote had not lost his job. He had simply stopped going to work. His family survived by living rent free in a house owned by Dennis on Terrance Street. The Depression did not affect their lives nearly as much as Tote's drinking.

By 1933, the vicious cycle of chronic alcoholism had taken control of Tote's life. Going on three-day benders, Tote would drink until he passed out, wake up, and then begin drinking again. Patients who went to see Dr. Leary in the middle of an afternoon to have an aching tooth extracted often found his office shut. In order to pay his drinking debts, Tote soon closed his office and sold all his equipment. Taking pity on his son, Dennis set him up in business again. Tote went on another bender, closed his office, and again sold all his equipment. Once more, Dennis stepped in to help Tote back on his feet. Despite the grim reality of their situation, both Tote and Abigail believed they would eventually be saved by the huge sum of money Dennis would leave them when he died.

On the day after Christmas in 1933, thirteen-year-old Tim stood at the top of the stairs listening to his mother sobbing on the phone. At ninety-two, Dennis had passed away. Male relatives were sent to find Tote, who was on yet another bender and had to be sobered up for the funeral, a noisy affair attended by the Boston branch of the Leary family as well as those who still lived in Springfield. After the funeral came the reading of the will. In his autobiography, Tim Leary would recall that he was out in the street playing the game of solitary baseball he had invented when a taxi pulled up in front of his house. Tote stepped from the backseat and told the driver to leave the motor running. He handed his son a $100 bill (an enormous amount of money at the time), walked inside, gave Abigail $1,000, and announced that he had business in New York. Tote then climbed back into the cab and left. Tim would not see his father again for twenty-three years.

Tote's bankroll did not last long. Tim would later write that after becoming royally drunk at the Astor Bar in New York City, Tote got rolled. In a single night, he lost every cent of the inheritance for which he had waited so long. The story may just be more of the Leary blarney, but what is certain is that the terms of Dennis's will effectively destroyed the Leary family in Springfield. Because of the stock market crash of 1929 and all the business loans Dennis had made both to Uncle Arthur and Tote, he did not leave behind nearly as much cash as his heirs had anticipated. All told, it amounted to around $60,000. Quite possibly because he was the only surviving son left in Springfield, Tote was named executor of the will and granted a one-third share. After taxes, his inheritance came to $10,000. While to some this would have been a king's ransom, it was hardly the windfall for which Tote had been waiting. Nor was it enough to keep him in Springfield.

Another third went to the glamorous but always unreliable Frances. Rather than leave the money directly to her, Dennis put it in a trust for her children and appointed her older sister Sara to administer it. By doing so, Dennis intended to control his talented, headstrong daughter even from beyond the grave. Infuriated by the arrangement and in desperate need of money, Frances demanded her inheritance in a lump sum. When Sara refused, Frances began legal proceedings. Unwilling to fight it out in court, Sara backed down and broke the terms of the trust, letting Frances have all her money right away. The sisters never spoke to each other again. Dennis also left Sara the houses at 37 and 39 Terrance Street in which Phil and Anita Shea and Tote's family had lived rent free for so long. Abigail raised such a fuss about this arrangement that Sara gave Abigail the house. Although Sara only wanted to keep peace within the family, her decisions led to financial disaster. No longer able to pay the taxes on Dennis's fine Victorian home at 254 Central Street, she was forced to have it torn down. No one ever rebuilt on the site, which remained a vacant lot that was perpetually for sale.

With Tote gone, Aunt May moved in with Abigail and Tim. Like the Ferris home in nearby Indian Orchard, the house on Terrance Street was soon transformed into a reliquary of religious art. Tim was now surrounded by vivid color reproductions of the Madonna, saints, and martyrs. Aunt May also appointed herself the household's official censor. Looking for what she called "funny business," she scanned every picture in every magazine that came over the transom to protect Tim from the evil, corrupting influence of sex. In response, Tim began the unceasing pattern of rebellion against all forms of authority that would dominate his entire life.

With the smell of floor polish in his nose the boy kneels in the dark gloomy confessional in St. Michael's Cathedral on State Street and says, "Bless me, Father, for I have sinned." On the other side of the latticed screen, Father Michael, his great-uncle, listens to the boy confess that he has lusted after not only his cousin Margaret but also the doctor's wife and Clara Bow and the Rockettes and a girl on the bus and various unnamed women whose pictures appear in magazines like Spicy Detective, Spicy Adventure, Atlantic City Bathing Beauties, *and* Hollywood Starlets, *all of which he buys on the sly in a downtown drugstore.*

Through the screen, Father Michael tells the boy that he must destroy these magazines, for they are occasions of sin. Even as his great-uncle utters these words, the boy can still see a thrilling illustration from a recent edition of The Saturday Evening Post *in which a young woman reclines on a hammock with her white dress and lace petticoat pulled up, revealing two inches of milky-white, soft, tender, moist, kissable inner thigh. Should he destroy that magazine as well? Should he destroy all magazines? What about the Montgomery Ward catalog in which women pose in silken underwear, nylon hose, and one-piece bathing suits? Should all department store catalogs be destroyed? What of the Bible and other holy texts? Though these works are meant to elevate the spirit and purify the mind, the tales of sin contained within them only serve to excite him as well. Should he destroy them too?*

Because his great-uncle and confessor will never understand the degree of lust by which this boy is possessed, the boy knows there is no hope for him within

*the thick redbrick walls of this church. All the same, he understands it. He under-
stands his aunt May and Father Michael. The person he does not understand is
his mother. A single vivid image of her will remain with him for his entire life.
Around the border of the lawn behind their house, Abigail Leary has planted
flowers. Off playing ball by himself, Tim, then ten years old, hears her sobbing.
Running to the garden, he finds her sitting in the dirt weeping because their German shepherd, Fritz, has destroyed a plant. Her skirt is pulled up to her thighs.
There is a run in her stocking. Her face is contorted in sorrow. To him, she looks
like a Titian martyr suffering in the garden for the original sin.*

*Years later, Timothy Leary will write that this was when he first decided to
seek out women who were as unlike his mother as possible. For the rest of his life,
he would search for the wildest, funniest, most high-fashion, big-city girls he
could find. But with her skirt hiked up over her thighs and a run in her stocking,
his mother seemed both martyr and temptress at the same time. It is not hard to
understand how a boy who lived so completely in his own mind and who was
so easily aroused by everything might feel this way about his own mother. The
feelings themselves were bad enough. But the guilt accompanying them was
worse. Forget impure thoughts. This was not only a sin for which the boy deserved
to burn in hell forevermore but one which he could never confess—not to Father
Michael, to his mother, or even to himself.*

*In the dark latticed box in St. Michael's, the boy is almost done with his con-
fession. Yet he needs something more to offer Father Michael. Another impure
thought. Instead of listening in school this past week, the boy confesses that he
has been mooning after Mary Alice O'Brien, the sister of Larry O'Brien, who in
time will become chairman of the Democratic Party and into whose office the
Watergate burglars will break. "For these sins and all the sins since my last confession," the boy intones, "I am heartily sorry." His confession finished, he waits
in darkness for the priest to speak. Father Michael adjusts his hearing aid. He
clears his throat. At long last, he tells the boy to say a heartfelt Act of Contrition
and for penance, five Our Fathers and five Hail Marys. Then he will be cleansed
of all sin, original and otherwise. The boy smiles. Yet again, he has gotten off easy.*

TWO

Had Abigail Leary truly wanted her only son to become a priest, she would have sent him to Cathedral High, where the sons of Springfield's Irish laborers went before moving on to play football at Holy Cross or Notre Dame. Because Abigail had something grander in mind for Tim, she sent him instead to Classical High School, a four-story yellow-brick building with a long vaulted roof topped with steeples and a green copper trim that looked like part of the Sorbonne. Behind a high wrought-iron fence, stately steps led up to three sets of glass doors above which the words CLASSICAL HIGH were carved in stone. At the time Tim enrolled as a freshman, there was no more prestigious high school in the country. Alumni of Harvard, Yale, and Princeton regularly named Classical High as the number-one college-preparatory school in the nation. Among its graduates were William Manchester, the noted historian and biographer; Theodore Geisel (aka Dr. Seuss); and Larry O'Brien.

Manchester, who attended Classical High a year behind Tim, recalled in an interview with Leary biographer Peter Owen Whitmer just how intense the class differences at the school were and how aware everyone was of them. What Manchester—the son of a Protestant social worker whose life was shaped by the Depression—most clearly remembered about Tim Leary was where he bought his clothing. In Springfield in 1935, the same suit of clothes could be purchased for a reasonable price at a variety of downtown stores or at twice the cost at Forbes & Wallace, Tim's clothes came from Forbes & Wallace. Lucia Gallup, who sat next to Tim in homeroom during his senior year, recalled that he occasionally sported a porkpie hat and a bow tie with the suit he always wore to class. Tim also had his own monogrammed stationery. At Christmas he sent out preprinted holiday cards featuring a lantern (which he may have drawn) along with the words, "All Kind Thoughts for the Holiday Season—Tim Leary." Because Abigail ensured that her only son never wanted for anything, Tim never saw himself as a poor Irish Catholic boy trying to climb the social ladder at Classical High but rather as someone with money who just happened to be Catholic.

During his freshman and sophomore years, Tim was by his own admission "withdrawn socially and confused academically." He studied diligently but without comprehension, especially in Latin class where he was alternately "aroused and irritated" by girls from the well-to-do suburb of Longmeadow, who, unlike him, could decline nouns with great precision. Although Tim tried out for various teams, he was too scrawny to make the cut. Despite scoring 127 on the Terman IQ Test, Tim's sophomore midterm grades were a C in English, a C in Latin, and a D in plane geometry. He did however get an A in English history and a B in physical training. The turning point in his high-school career occurred when he became friendly with the "smart, brash, funny, worldly, earthy and playful" well-to-do Jewish kids from Longmeadow. The only Christian in their social set, Tim played poker and tennis with them and discussed what had already become his central concern in life—sex. "Her dress was up to her neck and I could see what she had for breakfast" was a phrase he heard them use "at least three times a day."

At sixteen, Tim obtained his driver's license and began earning pocket money by making deliveries for Phil Shea at the Women's Store. Tim's driver's license helped him find what he would later call the "sophisticated" girlfriend he had been seeking for so long. One night, she led him to her family's sun porch, reclined on the couch, and held out her arms to him. The two began kissing madly. Moving her hips, she guided him, as he would later write, "into my first fuck." In his autobiography, Leary calls the girl "Rosalind," but her real name was Rosamund Larson, nicknamed "Rossy." In a memo to himself, written at the age of seventy-four, entitled "WOMEN TEACHERS," Timothy Leary described her as the "wildest, sexiest, coolest girl in New England. I was offended when this Yale guy demeaned her. In a Springfield bar She said, 'The man of Carstairs (WHISKEY) goes upstairs.' Sex, Sex, Sex! Yeah!! Thank you Rossy Larsen."

With Rosalind's help, Tim transformed himself from "a shy, reserved youth" into "a brash, confident extrovert." The two quickly became "popular stars in the adolescent social life." Within six months, Tim was president of the school senate and editor of the school newspaper. Tim's photograph appeared on the front page of the June 4, 1937, edition of *The Classical Recorder*. Wearing a dotted tie, a white shirt with a spread collar, and a nifty-looking sports jacket, his crew cut making his ears appear large and prominent, he stared out at the world with his mouth set in a look of youthful determination. The accompanying article announcing his appointment as editor in chief identified him as a member of the golf team, the senate, the glee club, the assembly committee, and the traffic squad, and said that he was interested in journalism and had to his credit several lead news articles and a number of the best editorials of the year. With cheery high-school optimism, the article concluded, "He seems to be a safe person to entrust with the higher standard of efficiency *The Recorder* has been trying to achieve."

At seventeen, the boy who had once lived exclusively in his own mind was now surrounded by friends and was invited to the Rhombus Anniversary Ball ("Dancing from 9 till 2 A.M. to Earl O'Neill's Orchestra") at the Springfield Country Club on April Fool's Day, 1938. Literally and figuratively, Tim's dance card was full. He was so busy with extracurricular activities that during his senior year at Classical High he could almost never be found in his seat during homeroom.

As with many teenagers, Tim's passage through adolescence was a roller-coaster ride. Considering how far down he had been because of his father's fall from grace, he had now risen very high indeed. The accompanying rush of feelings was so intoxicating that he decided to do battle with William C. Hill, the principal of Classical High, a "towering man with a Supreme Court Justice shock of white hair" whose influence with deans of admission throughout the Ivy League was legendary. Although William Manchester's grades at Classical High were not all that remarkable, Hill got him admitted to Harvard with a single phone call. (Unable to afford Harvard's tuition, Manchester opted instead for the University of Massachusetts.)

It was Hill's custom to welcome each new freshman class to Classical High by elaborating on the school motto: "No one has a right to do that which if everyone did would destroy society." In his autobiography, Timothy Leary calls this the "Kantian Categorical Imperative." Although Kant phrases the concept in different ways, the actual Categorical Imperative reads: "Act only on that maxim that you can at the same time will to be a universal law." For Kant, the Categorical Imperative was the supreme principle of morality, a philosophical rephrasing of the Golden Rule. While escorting adult visitors around the school, Hill would often stop students in the hallway and have them repeat the school motto from memory. As editor in chief of the school newspaper, Tim wrote what he would later call "a particularly fiery editorial suggesting that the Categorical Imperative was totalitarian and un-American in glorifying the welfare of the state over the rights of the individual." In fact, the Categorical Imperative was nothing of the kind. Tim, who by this time was already engaging in lengthy philosophical debates with his best friend Bill Scanlon, arguing for Schopenhauer while Scanlon preferred Thomas Aquinas, knew this. His real aim in the editorial was to challenge the principal by attacking the philosophy on which the school was based.

A strict authoritarian who demanded utter respect from all his students, Hill immediately summoned Tim to his office. Pointing out that Tim had skipped school during his senior year more than any other student in his class, Hill said that he could and should expel him. Because he had known Tim's family for a long time, Hill explained he had decided to spare them this crushing pain. Instead, Hill told Tim not to ask him for a letter of recommendation for college.

On June 14, 1938, when Timothy Francis Leary graduated from Classical High, he had already been rejected by every Ivy League college to which he had applied. A lesser young man—with a lesser mother—might have given up right then and there. In order to ensure that Tim would become a success, Abigail Leary persuaded Father Michael Kavanagh to intervene on her son's behalf.

Like the sons of the poor Irish laborers from working-class Cathedral High, Tim went off to be educated by the Jesuit brothers at the College of the Holy Cross in nearby Worcester. Much like Boston College, Notre Dame, and Georgetown, Holy Cross was where good Catholic boys from New England attended college in the mid-1930s to escape discrimination and be among their own kind. Virtually everyone at the Cross was Catholic and a product of the parochial school system. Alike as peas in a pod in suits and ties, the men of Holy Cross were expected to fulfill the aim of the school, which *The WPA Guide to Massachusetts* called "the advancement of the arts, the cultivation of the sciences, and the promotion of patriotism, morality, virtue, and religion." For those who wanted to enter the priesthood, there was no better school. At one time, a third of all the priests in the Springfield diocese were Holy Cross alumni. Six of the seven dioceses in New England were headed by Holy Cross graduates. In the words of the *New Catholic Encyclopedia*, "What Georgetown was to the South, Holy Cross was to New England in its contributions to the infant Church in the region." Without the influence of Father Michael Kavanaugh, Tim might never have been admitted.

While at Holy Cross, Father Michael had become close to fellow classmate David Ignatius Walsh. A Democrat elected to the Massachusetts State House of Representatives in 1900, Walsh served the state as lieutenant governor and governor. In 1919, he became the first Catholic senator from Massachusetts. After failing to win reelection in 1924, he was appointed to the vacancy created by the death of Republican Henry Cabot Lodge. For the next twenty years, Senator Walsh exerted tremendous influence over the affairs of the nation. As chairman of the Naval Affairs Committee, he was responsible for disbursing a billion dollars to rebuild the navy. Until his death, Father Michael maintained a close personal relationship with both Walsh and his secretary, campaign manager, and personal assistant, Philip Joseph Philbin, a Harvard graduate who served for twenty-eight years as a congressman from Massachusetts. In his will, Father Michael bequeathed Philbin his eyeglasses.

Although the exact nature of the relationship between these three men remains unknown, Phil and Anita Shea told Leary biographer Peter Owen Whitmer that in their opinion Father Michael was gay. Upon reading his will, Frances Lunden, one of Father Michael's relatives, concluded that his long and intimate relationship with Senator Walsh was more than just friendship. Walsh never married and seems to have never had a serious romantic relationship with a woman, preferring instead the company of his many male friends, most of them devout Catholics. A great fan of the arts and a fastidious dresser, Walsh remained extraordinarily devoted to his mother and lived with his sisters until he died.

In the spring of 1942, a scandal nearly cost Walsh his senate seat. He was reportedly seen frequenting a "house of degradation" near the Brooklyn Navy Yard, where unsuspecting young servicemen were plied with liquor and then encouraged to spill war secrets to Nazi agents. Walsh managed to survive the crisis only after FBI director J. Edgar Hoover worked to clear his name. A year later, Walsh interceded with the navy on behalf of the grandson of a former mayor of Boston. Rather than waste the young man's time guarding the Panama Canal, Walsh saw to it that he was sent instead to the Solomon Islands and given command of a PT boat. Thus began the legend that helped John F. Kennedy become the first Catholic president of the United States.

Through Father Michael, Senator Walsh became part of Abigail's master plan for her son. Tim would spend a year at Holy Cross preparing for the competitive exams for West Point and Annapolis. If he did well on them, Father Michael would see to it that Senator Walsh would help get Tim appointed to one or both of the academies. After a slight detour, Tim's life would be back on track. In return, Tim would then be expected to help someone else within the Catholic network.

Before any of this could happen, Tim had to survive the rigors of a Jesuit education. In 1938, Holy Cross was still run like a monastery, with compulsory chapel at 7:00 A.M., prayers before each class, and no elective courses. To Tim, the professors seemed like aloof, mysterious, black-robed martinets. The students, whom Tim described as "sturdy sons of New England Irish-Catholic businessmen," accepted the curriculum without protest. While there was some nervous college-boy banter about sex, no pinups were allowed on dorm-room walls. Aside from football rallies, there were no social events. Girls were never seen on campus except when they visited with students' families. To survive at Holy Cross, Tim would have to forsake the self-indulgent behavior he had exhibited during his senior year at Classical High and buckle down. The Jesuits could then begin the training process that the United States Army or Navy would complete.

Along with 20,000 others, Tim cheered loudly each Saturday in the stadium seats at Fitton Field Stadium as Bill Osmanski, the Holy Cross captain, displayed his incredible prowess on the football field. In class, Tim was required to master Latin, rhetoric, and Greek. In time, his mother believed Tim would become exactly what she, Aunt May, and Father Michael wanted him to be—a good Catholic boy who in every way was a credit to his family.

Tim began his freshman year doing his best to conform to Abigail's plan. Putting a happy spin on his life in newsy, conversational letters that he wrote almost every day to his mother back in Springfield, Tim repeatedly assured her that everything was going to work out just fine for him. His plans included writing for the college newspaper and trying out for the debate team. He even joined the Sodality of the Blessed Mary. To prove

to his mother just how well he was doing in Latin composition, he sent
home two tests on which the class average had been seventy-five. Tim received a hundred on both.

Although he tried hard to please his mother, Tim could not keep up
the charade for long. By the end of his first month at Holy Cross, he was
already complaining. Money was a constant concern. Attached to one letter home was an itemized account of all he had spent so far at Holy Cross
down to the very last penny for carfare and what he had to pay for breakfast on a morning when he slept late because of a cold. His health was
another source of distress. He reported having an awful cold, a sprained
foot, and a "clogged-up" chest for which he had been given a bottle of
medicine and a bag full of pills. Dutifully, Tim reported that he had slept
nine and a half hours a night for the past two weeks and was doing all he
could to gain weight. This was not easy because meals in the dining hall
were rushed, just twenty minutes from soup to dessert, and he could not
keep up the pace. He was, however, drinking his milk at both breakfast
and dinner, with another glass in the campus café as well. Yet another
concern verging on obsession was his appearance. He repeatedly asked
his mother to send him various articles of clothing he had left at home.
He worried about the college laundry, where they were "awfully tough
on shirts" and had problems getting his suits properly cleaned. His letters
testify to just how well his mother had taken care of him while he still
lived at home.

Tim's more serious complaints concerned the college itself. After the
academic rigors of Classical High, Holy Cross was a step down for him.
Each night, he would go over his infinitesimal amount of homework with
great care. Yet in class the next day, the teacher either did all the translating or practically told the students how to do it. His fellow classmates
seemed awfully thick, especially in French and Latin. Even in English, any
question that required serious thought left most of the class fumbling for
answers. It was not the sort of report card any institution of higher learning would want a student to present to the world. Yet when one of his
professors instructed Tim's class to write an essay responding to a letter
criticizing Holy Cross in the *Worcester Telegram,* Tim's essay contained
nothing but praise for a school where "age-long, proven theories have not
been sacrificed to modern ideas of progressiveness." Refuting the charge
that religion was overemphasized at Holy Cross, Tim wrote that it is "the
most important step in building honest, equitable citizens." As proof, he

cited the school's alumni—"numberless doctors, lawyers, businessmen, and members of Christ's hierarchy who are living lives of service to both the state and God." In closing, he called Holy Cross one of America's most esteemed and respected institutions. Deducting ten points for various errors in syntax and grammar, Tim's professor commented: "V. Good."

By his second semester at Holy Cross, Tim found someone who shared his true feelings about the school. Together, they began accepting bets on stakes races and sporting events. Tim won enough money from running a continuous poker game to buy himself a secondhand Model A Ford. Regularly, Tim and his new friend went over the wall after bed check to frequent local bars where they often picked up shopgirls. In a note written in pencil to Tim, a girl named Elaine wondered if it was not too much bother and not taking him out of his way whether she could see him that night because she had something to tell him. She hoped he would not be angry at her for writing to him like this. Below her signature, she added, "Please don't think I am a bad girl. I really am not. Probably that is why your [sic] sore on me."

Now that he had a car, Tim began going to Boston and New York. His archives contain a pamphlet from Southland, a nightclub located at 76 Warrenton Street in Boston, where "The Tall Sensational Carioca Zombie" cost a dollar and the management reserved the right to serve no more than two to a customer. On the front is a photo of an exotic young woman with long black hair who looks like Dorothy Lamour. Arms clasped over her head, she strikes a seductive pose, her breasts bejeweled but otherwise bare.

During the summer after his freshman year at Holy Cross, Tim took the entrance examination for both service academies. After achieving what he would later describe as "the highest score" (whether in his district or the state, he does not say in his autobiography), he was offered his choice of Annapolis or West Point. Because another qualified candidate in Springfield had his heart set on the Naval Academy and Abigail wanted her son to become a cadet at the school where she and Tote had once been so happy, Tim chose West Point. Abigail's plan had now been executed to perfection: Tim would enter West Point as a member of the class of 1944. Believing there was no reason for him to return to Holy Cross, he planned to move to New York, find a job, and enjoy the high life there with friends. Fearing what might happen if her son did this, Abigail promptly sent him back to Holy Cross. Unwillingly, Tim returned to Worcester.

As a sophomore, Tim was constantly in trouble. Ignoring notes sent to him by the Office of Discipline, he regularly cut classes and violated curfew to go over the wall so he could see girls in town. He broke the front window of a liquor store in Worcester with a brick so he could steal beer for a party in his room in Loyola Hall. In the words of one of his friends, he "drinks like a fish and fucks like a fool." At wit's end, Abigail wrote Tim a scolding letter. Since she had gone to work to help put Tim through school and had been able to swing his expenses without financial assistance from anyone, she told him the least he could do was cooperate and attend classes. She had to get up every morning early enough to be at her desk by 8:30. "Your job isn't any harder than that, is it?"

Tim's third-quarter grades answered her question: 50 in Latin literature, 60 in rhetoric, "incomplete" in history of English literature, 63 in religion, and 54 in mathematics. At the end of the year, Tim received conditional failures in Latin literature, English literature, history of English literature, and religion; "absent" in Latin composition and mathematics; a C in history; and a B plus in French. He did, however, intercept the letter bearing his grades so that his mother would not get the bad news.

Although Abigail must have known how poorly Tim had done during his sophomore year, she did not pursue the matter with much conviction. Her son was headed for West Point. As America prepared to go to war, Tim Leary was finally being given what he had always wanted so badly as a boy—a chance to become a storybook hero.

THE LONG GRAY LINE

WEST POINT, NEW YORK,
JUNE 1940–AUGUST 1941

The long gray line of us stretches
Thro' the years of a cent'ry told
And the last man feels to his marrow
The grip of your far-off hold.

—"The Corps," West Point hymn

Timothy Leary as a cadet at West Point.
Courtesy of the Futique Trust

THREE

The cadet stands at attention, straight and tall. He is not yet really a cadet but a lowly plebe doing his best to get through his first day at West Point. Yesterday, he was still a civilian. At dinner last night with his mother in the Thayer Hotel, he was surrounded by other happy, carefree future plebes, all laughing and talking excitedly about the adventure on which they were about to embark. None had any idea of what would hit them today. Now, last night seems very far away. But then last night, each of them still had a name of his own.

Now they are all either Mister Dumbcrow or Mister Dumbjohn, as in: "BRACE WHEN YOU SPEAK TO ME, MISTER DUMBCROW! CRACK THOSE PUNY SHOULDERS BACK, MISTER DUMBJOHN! EYES FRONT! SPEAK ONLY WHEN SPOKEN TO! GOT THAT, DUMB-CROW? SAY 'SIR' WHEN YOU SPEAK TO AN UPPERCLASSMAN, MISTER DUMBJOHN! ROLL UP THOSE PANTS LEGS! PICK UP YOUR BAG! NOW DROP IT! NOW PICK IT UP AGAIN!"

Never mind whether the shouted orders make sense or contradict one another. They are orders, meant to be obeyed immediately and without question because they come from a higher authority—splendid-looking upperclassmen in impeccably starched white trousers, blue-gray jackets, and gray caps with mirror-like black patent visors, who scream unceasingly at creatures so base and ignorant that it is hard to even consider them human beings. Today is when it all starts. Here at West Point, the foundation is being laid. Upon it rests a time-honored system designed to make gentlemen and officers out of plebes like Mister Dumbcrow Cadet Fourth Classman Timothy Leary of Company B. Already a merciless barber has cut his hair right down to the scalp. The cadet then had to brace at every corner while staggering under the weight of the mattress upon which he will sleep for the next six weeks during "Beast Barracks" before being allowed to run with it up endless flights of stairs to the room he shares with Mister Brice and Mister

Beach, two fellow base and ignorant creatures who seem just as lost, confused, and disoriented as him. All this is as it should be. It is part of the great tradition of the Point.

Within the towering Gothic spires, high gray granite walls, crenellated turrets, and stone parapets of this Revolutionary War fortress beside the Hudson River, it has never been any other way. The aim here is to beat a man down hard as a plebe so that when he becomes an officer, he will be able withstand the rigors of combat and the responsibility of command. Once the plebe becomes an upper-classman, he will be expected to dish out the same treatment to those below him. In this manner, year after year, the long gray line continues. During the summer of 1940, however, the world beyond those high walls was changing rapidly. Nazi soldiers occupied the Channel Islands of Jersey and Guernsey. Reichsmarshall Hermann Göring had checked into a luxurious suite at the Ritz Hotel in Paris and the City of Light was now under German martial law. Russian tanks were advancing across Romania. The United States Naval fleet had returned to Hawaii. General Douglas MacArthur was busily training Filipino troops who would suffer a crushing defeat at the Battle of Bataan.

All the same, this is still the "old" Point where a cadet's word is his bond and his sacred honor by far his most precious possession. It is the same Point where, twenty years earlier, Tim's father, Tote, served under his great hero MacArthur. After World War I, MacArthur was given the impossible task of modernizing an institution that even then was being criticized for failing to keep up with the times. After assessing the situation, MacArthur asked an aide, "How long are we going to prepare for the War of 1812?" In fairly rapid order, he cut back on hazing, did away with Beast Barracks, formalized the honor code, organized the first cadet honor committee, and did his best to end the tradition of summer camp, when the corps moved from their barracks to live in tents for six weeks.

Then, as now, it is during summer camp that the West Point social season begins in earnest. Young ladies of refinement journey up from New York City and the South to mingle with cadets dressed in their Napoleonic uniforms at formal hops and balls held each weekend at Cullum Hall. While the cadets recline on their cots at night reading by lantern light, sentries straight out of a Gilbert and Sullivan musical patrol the perimeter, calling out "All's well!" at regular intervals. The outcry against ending summer camp was so strident that MacArthur was re-assigned. All his reform efforts were wiped out and the academy went back to the way it had always been.

As his first day at the academy nears an end, the cadet stands straight and tall at attention while facing Battle Monument. Before him, the Hudson River re-

flects the twilight of what has been a rainy day. On either side of the river, the land is very green. The hatless cadet wears a fresh blue-gray shirt and trousers. He has polished the buckle on his belt. On his left hand, he wears a white cotton glove. In it, he holds his other glove. When he raises his right hand to be sworn in to the United States Army, tradition decrees that his hand be bare. After taking the oath, the cadet and all the other plebes listen to the commandant's speech of welcome. To the sound of bugles and the rolling echo of the retreat gun, he marches back to the barracks for his first night at the Point. His first day of service in the United States Army has just ended. What will be for many a lifelong military career has just begun. But not for this cadet.

In the long history of West Point, there could not have been a more likely candidate for instant dismissal than Tim Leary. During Beast Barracks, the pressure was constant and unrelenting. From the moment Tim rolled out of bed each morning to the sound of reveille until he fell asleep again at night before taps was over, he was braced, drilled, and tongue lashed by overhearing upperclassmen who liked nothing more than finding a cadet's weak spot, cracking him wide open, and sending him back home crying to his mother. As Tim sat with his back stiff as a board in the dining hall, his supper growing cold before him, he was ordered for the hundredth time to supply the exact definition of leather. Like a mantra, the words would become emblazoned in his memory. Forty years later, after Tim Leary had forgotten so much else in his life, he could still remember that the proper answer to this question began, "Sir, if the fresh skin of an animal cleaned and divested of all hair, fat, and other extraneous matter be immersed in a dilute solution of tannic acid, a chemical combination ensues."

At the Point, there was a proper way to do everything: a proper way to eat, stand, sit, walk, and think. There was even a proper way to put away the broom in your barracks room. When Tim failed to do this, he was put on report and ordered to respond in writing to the commandant, acknowledging the error of his ways while explaining that "the offense was unintentional." In an environment where rules were all that mattered, Tim did more than just survive. He found a home. Far from regretting the loss of his own individuality, Tim was delighted to have been admitted to this "masculine elite." In his letters to his mother, he used as much cadet jargon as he could fit on the page. Having finally found a system of belief in which he could submerge himself completely, he was, for the first time in his life, at one with the world outside his mind. Proudly, Tim took his rightful place in the long gray line.

Like all the other plebes who made it through Beast Barracks, Tim was issued a pair of white trousers starched so stiffly that he had to peel open the legs with a bayonet. On a warm August day with a thousand people watching, his mother among them, he was presented to the corps at Beast Barracks graduation. As the summer air crackled with commands and the band played martial music, Tim and his fellow plebes marched smartly in perfect time, taking their first step toward becoming full-fledged members of the profession of arms whose sworn mission was to win every war that America fought. At the end of the ceremony, the band played "Retreat." From Lookout Point, the sunset cannon roared. Proudly, the plebes marched off the field.

Watching from the stands, Abigail could barely contain herself. Her son's life finally seemed to be working out as she had always hoped it would. "My dear cadet," Abigail wrote Tim on Tuesday, August 27, 1940. "It was grand to see you and I feel that you like it there." Calling him "my love," she noted how handsome he looked in his full-dress uniform coat, which he must now wear every time she takes him to dinner. "I loved being with you again." The letter was signed, "Love, A."

On September 4, Aunt May wrote. She hoped his first day of school went well and urged him to stand in the first tenth of his class so he would get to wear a gold star on his collar. She had gone to confession for him on Saturday and hoped his work would be good and that he would like West Point. She closed by noting that the United States had just sent fifty destroyers to Britain in exchange for bases in Newfoundland, Bermuda, and "somewhere else." She was afraid this was a bad move because by "breaking our neutrality" the United States might further antagonize Hitler. With conscription having passed the Senate, 60,000 men from the ages twenty to thirty would be drafted by October. "It's dreadful." Though neither Abigail nor Aunt May seemed to feel the United States had much business entering this war, Abigail never raised the subject in her letters to Tim. Her central concern was always her son and how well he was doing at the Point.

On October 10, Father George G. Murdock, rector of the Catholic Chapel of the Most Holy Trinity Church at West Point, who looked like a young Pat O'Brien playing a priest in some Hollywood movie, wrote to the parents of all Catholic cadets at the Point. "These are indeed troubled times and the future is forebodingly uncertain. The rapidly expanding military program makes our present and future mission here at West Point increasingly important." His letter was part of a formal invitation to the Fifth Annual Military Ball Benefit for Most Holy Trinity Chapel, to be held in the grand ballroom of the Hotel Astor on the evening of the Army–Notre Dame football game, Saturday, November 2, 1940. Tim Leary would later write, "During the gray autumn, the only streaks of color in academy life were football trips." In an era when college football and major league baseball were America's only two national sports, the Army–Notre Dame game in Yankee Stadium was an event of monumental significance.

On October 22, Tim wrote his mother, "Well, I am 20 years old but it seems just the same as when I was a child." Although he hit his nose playing football, he'd had it x-rayed and would be okay for the big game with Notre Dame. With the letter, Tim sent Abigail his answers to her "questionnaire." On a separate sheet of paper entitled "This Is A Quiz Program," Abigail had asked her son to please answer eleven questions. Nearly all concerned social arrangements for the Army–Notre Dame game. The questions included "Where do you want to have dinner?," "Will your 'femme' dress for dinner?," "Where shall we meet you, if we don't see you at the game?," "What are you going to do about dress clothes for the Ball?," and "Will your roommate and girl dine with you or elsewhere?" One was not a question but a command. "Tell your femme your mother wants to dress for dinner and for her to dress also, then you can go right on to the Ball."

Tim replied that he would find his mother at halftime in her seats in Yankee Stadium. If they missed each other, they would meet at the Astor Hotel for drinks and dinner. Then Tim and his date would go on to the ball. Abigail also asked Tim whether he had yet written to the congressman who appointed him to the academy or called upon Father Murdock. Tim answered that he had. Abigail's final question was, "Would the Astor be a good place to eat that night?" She noted that a special dinner was being served there in the Orangerie. Tim's answer was yes, especially since Abigail would be picking up the tab. Abigail's compelling need to control every aspect of the evening did not stem from a small-town spinster's fear of the big city. On this night, her son would finally make his formal debut in polite society as an officer and a gentleman. To ensure that nothing would go wrong, she needed to make certain that every detail was in place long before the opening kickoff.

And what a glorious evening it promised to be. A photograph from that era, one which Tim Leary would keep among his papers for the rest of his life, shows a cadet in full-dress uniform dancing with a girl who looks like a debutante at a high-society ball. By far the more colorful of the species, the cadet is wearing a dove-gray swallowtail coat with a large black chevron on the sleeve. Knotted black cords hang in ripples from forty-four brightly polished brass buttons on his coat. A wide black stripe runs down the side of his pants. On the night of the game, this is exactly how Tim would look as he swept into the dining room of the Hotel Astor. In that moment, Abigail's greatest dream for her son would finally be realized.

On October 23, as Army lost to Harvard, Tim received a letter from Rossy Larson. "Timothy, my angel," she called him even though it was clear that his last letter had made her mad. In it, Tim seemed to feel as though he now had the jump on every other human in the world. Could the Point have done this to him? Rossy wanted to bet Tim that by next year she would no longer be working at Forbes & Wallace. At home, all the talk was of weddings. There had been a 200 percent increase over previous years. Lucinda Marsh, Alice Griffith, Jane Umla, and Barbara Sayre were now all married. Judging by her tone, Rossy already seemed to know that wedding bells would never ring for her and Tim. Once the love of his life, she was now the girl he had left behind.

On October 28, Tim wrote Abigail that the one and only phrase around the Point that counted was: "Sir, there are five days until Army beats the hell out of Notre Dame at Yankee Stadium in New York." Enclosing tickets to the game, Tim wrote that he would meet her and Aunt May at halftime. Tim's date, Carolyn, a student at the Juilliard School of Music, would be seated one row in front of them. After the game was over, one of Tim's roommates, James Alexander Brice, would join them for dinner. His other roommate, John Blair Beach, the son of the former commander of the Mare Island Naval Base in California, had other plans. The cadets only had until midnight before they had to board the train back to West Point. Since it would get dark at six, however, they could still wear evening dress when they dined.

Three days before the big game, a letter was circulated to the corps that read in part,

> Eighty thousand people are going to the Yankee Stadium Saturday. They are not going just to see a football game between Army and Notre Dame. They are going principally to see you—The Corps! . . . You are symbolic of their defense, their hope for the future, the safety of the nation. You are symbolic of this country's spirit in times of danger, in days of distress, in these days . . . The Army may be beaten. BUT THERE IS NO DISGRACE IN DEFEAT WHEN YOU LOSE TO A BETTER TEAM. ONLY THOSE WHO GIVE LESS THAN THEIR BEST NEED HANG THEIR HEADS. No Army team has ever quit, no matter what the score. Neither has the Corps! . . . Keep your chins up—and your lungs working.

Clearly this Army–Notre Dame game was more than just two college teams playing football. It was a test of manhood. In little more than a year, many of these same young men would be fighting for America in a real war. As on the gridiron, nothing less than total victory would do.

Even as Abigail was making elaborate plans for her time in New York City, Tim had already begun finding ways to break step with the long gray line. Though plebes had to remain in their rooms after taps and were not permitted to leave the Point at night, he had figured out a way to get off the post by going around behind the Hotel Thayer. About a month before the Army–Navy game, he persuaded a fellow plebe named Newton to join him.

The two of them ended up in an all-night tavern in Highland Falls, the little village outside the academy's south gate. Getting drunk, they met up with someone with a car who suggested they go somewhere else. En route, they were involved in an auto accident in which the driver was hurt. Tim and Newton realized what the consequences would be if they were questioned by the police and so they left the injured driver, walked to the river, and sneaked back into the Point. At reveille, both plebes were in terrible shape, not only hungover but bloodied as well. Though his roommates, Brice and Beach, knew the real story, Tim swore them both to secrecy.

Even though Tim got away with it this time, Beach could not help but wonder, "Why the hell do it anyway? Just to go out to a bar and get some whiskey?" In his autobiography, Tim Leary supplied some reasons: "The atmosphere was gloomy. The discipline was petty and nagging. Smiling and laughing were taboo. The most damning accusation that could be made against a cadet was that he didn't take this seriously." For a short while, Tim had taken the Point very seriously indeed. However, just as he would do throughout his life whenever he was confronted by a system he had not devised, Tim not only began rebelling against it but also tried to persuade others to do the same by urging his roommate John Beach to forsake liquid shoe polish, augmented by several coats of Simonize car polish, to make his shoes glisten like black glass. Instead, Tim encouraged him to shine them the ordinary way and see what happened. Unwilling to risk demerits for improperly shined shoes, Beach refused.

Asked nearly sixty years later why he thought Tim Leary felt such an urgent need to revolt against authority, Beach said he believed it was because Tim's father had deserted him. Indeed, when it came to leading midnight missions off the post at West Point in search of drinks, conversation, and a quick go-round with the local girls, Tim seemed just like Tote. As Abigail went to bed each night in Springfield dreaming of her big weekend in New York City, Tim was doing everything he could to prove that the sins of his father had in fact been visited upon the son.

FOUR

Although no one believed that Army had a chance to beat a Notre Dame team ranked as the best since the days when the immortal Knute Rockne had coached in South Bend, the cadets outplayed the Fighting Irish. At halftime, the entire corps, Cadet Leary among them, paraded across the field. Again and again during the second half, Army drove deep into Notre Dame territory only to lose the game, seven to nothing on an intercepted pass. The din from 82,000 spectators in Yankee Stadium was earsplitting. Both sides had proved their manhood. Clearly, the fate of the nation was in good hands.

"Dear Mother," Tim wrote on November 5, 1940. "The whole day was perfect: a swell game, meeting you and Aunt Mae [sic], the dinner was tops and we had a good time after we left you. We went to Leon & Eddie's and discovered a 4.00 minimum. That wasn't good at all so we went to the '21' and stayed there for a while, then to the dance. We didn't see you so we went to the Diamond Horseshoe and the Hurricane and then back to the dance." Thanking her for picking up the check, Tim noted that he still could not get over how nice both Aunt May and his mother looked. It had been so long since he had seen her in evening clothes. Her wrap and gown were very stylish. His only regret was that they had been so rushed that he hadn't had half enough time to spend with her. "Altogether," he wrote, "the trip was a great success and it was swell to see you."

On November 19, 1940, Tim wrote Abigail again. "Dear Mother. Happy birthday, my darling. I hope that your birthday is as happy as my last one and that you are enjoying a pleasant anniversary. I only wish I could be with you now." Although he had nothing material to give her, he did have good news. For the second week in a row, he had led the room in math. "Happy birthday," he wrote, "and please Mother, don't work hard and have a good time. I love you, Tim."

Tim spent Thanksgiving at the Point. Writing Abigail after the holiday, he told her he had a blind date for the Navy game and believed Army would win. It was now freezing cold and the cadets were wearing overcoats. Upperclassmen had decided plebe year was too easy and so had instituted formation at six each night in the basement sinks. Could Abigail send him some money quick for the Navy game? He only had $1.50 and needed much more. After Army closed out a dismal 1–7 season in Philadelphia by losing to the Naval Academy, Tim wrote to Aunt May that the team had lacked spirit and fight and that Navy had outplayed them. The stadium was packed and the most impressive thing was the marching and cheering. In his studies, Tim remained very "pro"—cadet slang for "proficient." But he had to pass the "writs" (the written exams) in order to avoid being "turned out" (failing). Although the gloomy period at the Point had now started, Christmas was just three weeks away and that was something to look forward to. Writing to Abigail on December 6, Tim let her know he had received his calling cards that read "Timothy Leary"— "because that is what you always told me to be called." Tim did not need much for Christmas but money. Although his roommate Brice had a radio, Tim made no mention of the war news. He was far more concerned with getting a phonograph and some records. If Abigail provided him with a list of addresses, he would send his calling card with his Christmas cards.

On December 9, Tim wrote Abigail that he had hardened his muscles and was getting to be quite a gymnast in a small way. He was sending her a package with a lot of "poop sheets" (information) and a "plebe bible" (a handbook) as well as Christmas gifts for her and Aunt May. On the same day, a handwritten notice was posted in the barracks which read: "Batt. Board for T. Francis Leary at 4:15 today Dec. 9 Monday 1940." Although this hearing would determine his future at the academy, Tim made no mention of it to his mother. In a letter to her the next day, he blithely wrote, "I feel very good right now with no worries of being found (failing) and plebe year almost one half over." His central concern remained whether she could procure for him some secondhand phonograph records from nickelodeons so that he could play them in his room. Tim also did not tell his mother that before boarding the train for the ride back to the academy after the Army–Navy game, he had purchased four half-pints of whiskey that he hid in the sleeves of his full-dress coat. In the version of the story Timothy Leary provided in his autobiography, a friend asked for one so he could slip it to some upperclassmen who were having a party in the train toilet. Tim gave him one and then another. When his friend came back a third time, it was with an invitation for Tim to join the party, "an offer no plebe could refuse." Willingly, Tim helped the upperclassmen polish off the last two bottles. Feeling no pain, he smoked a cigarette as he marched with his fellow cadets back to the barracks and entered by the front door rather than the back stairs, which all plebes were supposed to use.

Nearly sixty years later, interviews conducted with other cadets who were on the train that night bear out only some of Leary's recollections. All agree that Tim was already very drunk when he boarded the train carrying a bottle under each arm. First Classman Wilson Reed, known as "Joe," remembered turning to his friends Bill Gurnee and Bert Rosenbaum and saying, "Hey, did you see what I saw? Let's go get it." The three of them walked to where Tim was sitting and said, "Son, we saw what you brought on the train. We're gonna give you a choice. You can step out to the back of the train and throw those bottles off or you can give them to us." Laughing, Joe Reed added, "So he made the bad decision of giving them to us."

Although it was not an honor violation for either the first classmen or Tim to drink on the train, being under the influence was a serious infraction of academy rules, punishable by six months of walking punishment tours and confinement to the post. Thomas Lawson, a first classman who was also involved in the incident, would later say, "There was a difference between violating regulations and violating the honor code. Violating regulations was fair game if you thought you could get away with it. If you got out at night and got away with it, well, that was all right. You had only violated regulations."

Taking Tim's whiskey, Reed, Rosenbaum, and Gurnee adjourned to the toilet. Just outside, there was a water spigot with paper cups. "It was the most god-awful rotgut I ever tasted in my life," Reed recalled. "The name of it, I think, was Kinsey bourbon. We stood there and drank that bottle and a half of bourbon, going out occasionally to get a conical cup of water so that not a soul saw us take a drink. As I recall, I slept for the rest of the trip."

While Reed slept, Cadet Lieutenant George H. Stilson Jr. noticed Tim's condition. Described by Lawson, his roommate, as "kind of a hard-nosed individual in a lot of ways," Stilson had won his appointment to the academy by enlisting in the regular army. "It was," Lawson would later say, "George Stilson's problem because he was the acting company commander when it took place." Exactly what Tim Leary told George Stilson on the train that night has gone along with the participants into their graves. Although John Beach remembered Stilson later telling him that initially Tim claimed the liquor belonged to Bert Rosenbaum, neither Rosenbaum nor anyone else knew this at the time. If in fact Tim told Stilson the liquor belonged to Rosenbaum, then his own drunken condition would have been the result of an upperclassman inducing a plebe to drink with him, a serious offense.

When the train arrived at the station, the first classmen who had polished off Tim's whiskey without inviting him to join their party carried out their assigned tasks. Joe Reed recalled, "We each did our duty according to our rank and marched up the hill. That's a terrible climb, even when you're sober." Bert Rosenbaum, who remembered having had only one drink that night with Tim on the train, would later say, "I had someone holding him, almost carrying him uphill, because Leary was so drunk that he couldn't stand up."

In Tim's version of the story, Cadet Leary awoke the next morning to the sound of the reveille cannon rumbling inside his head like heavy artillery over a battlefield. Suffering from a massive hangover, he tried to heave but could not. Mumbling that he was not feeling well, Tim went back to sleep. On the first day on which demerits counted against furlough, he was put on report for being absent at reveille formation and ordered to report to the cadet captain's room. Tim was still in such bad shape that he had to be helped into his uniform by his roommates. The captain asked Tim if he had gotten drunk on the train last night. Tim said he had. The captain supplied the names of two upperclassmen and asked Tim if he had gotten drunk with them. Tim said he had. The captain asked if he had been ordered to join them. Tim replied that he had been invited.

All those interviewed pointed out that there was no reveille formation on Sunday. Instead, the corps turned out for church formation at about 10:30 A.M. "Mr. Leary didn't," Reed recalled. "We all made it, feeling like the wrath of God. We went up and came back down and had a meal and then apparently, it hit the fan." Earlier that morning, Stilson had interrogated Tim in the presence of Stilson's roommate, Thomas Lawson. "At that time," Lawson would later say, "Mr. Leary told a story, the details of which I don't recall, but which George said was the antithesis of what he had told him the night before. So George preferred charges against him." Confirming this sequence of events, Reed would later say, "Stilson or Lawson had cornered Leary and started questioning him about this and the first thing we knew, it appeared on the bulletin board that we were skinned. We were reported. Not only that, it was starred. A starred skin." (A "starred skin" meant that the violation was serious.)

While it was not unheard of for one first classman at the Point to put another on report, it was very unusual. Stilson later told John Beach that he would never have put Rosenbaum, Reed, and Gurnee on report had Tim not first told him that the liquor belonged to them. As it was, the honor violation was clear. Cadet Leary had lied to a first classman about another first classman to protect himself. That Tim was drunk at the time did not diminish the offense. That he may have told the truth the next day also did not factor into the equation, at least not so far as the Honor Committee was concerned. "He was so drunk the night before," Rosenbaum recalled, "that he couldn't have told anyone what really happened. He couldn't have told them because he didn't know. We could hardly hold him up. He was that drunk. So you can guess how much of what he said that he would have remembered the next day."

Tim Leary wrote in his autobiography that one week later he was brought before the Honor Committee and asked if he had carried liquor onto the train and given it to the upperclassmen. He had, he replied. But this was not what the cadet had said before. When Tim was asked whether he had lied, he replied no. During the first hearing, he was not asked where the liquor came from. In other words, he had withheld information that cadet officers had been looking for. Tim replied that if this was a violation of the honor code, he was guilty all right. He was then asked by the Honor Committee to resign from the academy. Tim asked permission to think it over for a day.

At the Point, honor was honor. Lying was lying. By definition, both were not only absolute but also non-negotiable. Once the Honor Committee had decided that Tim had lied, they were duty bound to request his resignation. "Normally," Lawson would later say, "if there was a question of an honor violation, it would go to the Honor Committee. If the Honor Committee resolved it, okay, fine. If not, then it would be carried further. The custom was to ask someone to resign. Once he did not, they would have referred the matter to the company tactical officer, who would have carried it on through military channels." Lawson recalled the plight of a fellow first classman who was caught cheating in the classroom. The first classman was reported to the Honor Committee. Despite having put three and a half years of his life into the academy, he resigned and left the Point the very same night.

The next day, Tim refused to resign. "I wouldn't have minded leaving West Point," he would later write, "but I knew my resignation would have been a cruel disappointment to my mother." A week later, a meeting from which he was excused was held after supper in the basement sinks. His roommates returned to their room with tears in their eyes. Because of the decision reached at the meeting, they would have to move out of the room. But it was all for the best. In a month, Tim's court-martial would be held. Then he could leave this hellhole and start all over again at a coed college. This outcome would be just fine for him because, as one of his roommates pointed out, he wasn't an army type anyway.

Because Tim had decided not to resign, opting instead to make his case before a formal court-martial, the corps did what it had always done to those whom it believed did not belong at the academy: Tim was silenced. By order of the Honor Committee, he was excommunicated from the holy order. At West Point, Tim Leary was now strictly on his own.

By the next morning, as Tim Leary would later write, he had become a nonperson at West Point. The two seats on either side of him in the mess hall remained empty at all times. If Tim wanted food passed to him, he had to write his request on a pad of paper, which he refused to do. "Part of me watched in amazement, enjoying this astonishing turn of events, realizing that something important was happening."

Although he never mentions it in his autobiography, Tim was hardly the first cadet to be silenced. In 1807, just five years after the academy was established, the corps decided to punish one of their own for ungentlemanly behavior by "enforcing silence." Although no superintendent ever officially sanctioned the custom, it quickly became a tradition at the Point. Being silenced did not mean that a cadet could not graduate and go on to a distinguished career in the military. General Benjamin O. Davis Jr., the first black cadet ever to graduate from West Point in the twentieth century, was silenced for four years because of the color of his skin. After graduating thirty-fifth in his class, Davis led the Tuskegee Airmen, the first all-black fighter squadron, into battle in World War II. At the age of eighty-six, he was awarded a fourth star, the military's highest peacetime rank. Even after being commissioned as regular army officers, however, some cadets who had been silenced at West Point were still shunned by former classmates.

Even within his own class, Tim was not unique. The two black plebes who entered the academy with him had also been silenced. But at least they could talk to each other. Tim could now speak only to Father Murdock at the Most Holy Trinity Chapel and friends like Jimmy Brice and John Beach who, although they had been ordered to find new living quarters, were still willing to converse with Tim in private. Even after he had moved across the hall, Beach continued speaking to Tim. Ordered to move farther away, Beach went on talking to Tim until a first classman who served on the Honor Committee told Beach that if he did not silence Tim, the corps would silence him as well.

Never mentioning his own heroic actions under fire in France during World War II that earned him two Silver Stars, the Legion of Merit, a Bronze Star, and a Purple Heart, Beach recalled, "I wasn't a strong enough character to stand up to them. I was told I would be silenced and that they would gig me to death. If you get too many gig marks, they throw you out of the academy. So I stopped talking to Tim. I'm ashamed, but if I had been kicked out, what would my dad have thought? I just had to stay."

On December 22, Tim wrote to his mother with what he called good news. When the window of the South Guard room opened and the guard held up a gigantic poop sheet bearing the names of those who had been turned out—almost a hundred of them in plebe math—his name was not on it. He had passed! Tim then told his mother that he had asked Carolyn, the girl he "dragged" to dinner after the Army–Notre Dame game, to come up for New Year's Eve. He wanted Abigail to be there as well. "If you come up, and I really want you—do come if you can possibly make it—(you could go to a hop if you are good girl and bring your evening gowns and if Aunt Mae [sic] is also good, you could see how we celebrate up here) . . ." Tim went on to tell his mother how pleased he was with his roommates. After six months at the Point, he wrote, you get to know your "wives" inside and out. These two boys were tops and it made the plebe system a lot easier when you had good roommates. Beach was a genius who never studied and always did well. Brice was as sharp as a razor and had a perfect mind for a lawyer. "I have come to the conclusion that the system at West Point certainly develops strong friendships far more than any college system." By this time of course, Brice and Beach were no longer his roommates.

Tim attended his first military midnight mass on Christmas Eve and found it most impressive. Christmas Day was something else again. As Robert Taylor wrote in a 1970 *Boston Globe Sunday Magazine* article entitled "The Young Manhood of Timothy Leary": "He spent Plebe Christmas as though he was a phantom at the feast. Academically, Leary sustained his grades, otherwise he drifted in a void." Beach confirmed that although he kept talking to Tim through New Year's Eve, Tim spent Christmas alone and in silence.

In a letter to his mother on December 29, Tim noted how pleased he was that his room was stuffed with "boodle" (cakes, candy, cookies) and how miffed he was that Carolyn could not come up for New Year's. Although this was the fourth straight year that he would be alone on New Year's Eve, he planned to go to the hop anyway. At a reception the day before in the superintendent's house, there had been plenty of "pro" femmes. That evening, a plebe smoker was scheduled, along with a hop at Cullum Hall. "Life," Tim noted, "is very sweet up here for upperclassmen." Although plebes were not allowed to attend dances, the Honor Committee had already worked out a plan to ensure that Tim's silencing would remain in effect if he became a yearling (a third classman). As soon as Tim and his young lady began to dance, everyone else would clear the floor.

In early February, Tim finally presented his case before seven officers. With their sabers lying on the table before them in an oak-paneled conference room, they solemnly convened his court-martial. As Tim would later note in his autobiography, this was his first appearance in a courtroom. In a letter he sent to John Beach forty-seven years later, Tim Leary called the proceeding "the only fair trial I have had in a court of law." Two Honor Committee members began the court-martial by testifying that Tim had already admitted to his guilt. Denying the charges, Tim told the officers that when first questioned, he had never been asked whose booze it was. "Both Jimmy Brice and I said he was totally hungover," John Beach recalled. "He was in terrible shape, and my opinion was they shouldn't have questioned him at that time. I don't know what he would have said otherwise. At least he would have been more intelligent in what he said."

The court took just two minutes to make a decision: full acquittal. Years later, Tim Leary told Peter Owen Whitmer, "They had all been plebes, they had all been drunk after Navy games, and they had all suffered Army hangovers. My lawyer was astonished; the Honor Committee was enraged and frustrated." Thomas Lawson, who did not testify at the court-martial, would later say, "The court-martial was not for drunkenness. It would have concerned lying. It could be that he was in such bad shape that nothing could be held against him. Given my experience with court-martials as an officer, that could have been a so-called 'exonerating circumstance.'"

Cleared of any wrongdoing by his court-martial, Tim could now reclaim his place in the long gray line. Soon enough, however, there was another meeting in the basement sinks. Tim might have been found innocent in the eyes of the academy but the honor of the corps had to be upheld at all costs. If nothing else, the cadet was defiant. Not only would his silencing continue but a new plan was hatched to demerit him out of the Point. Each and every infraction that he committed, no matter how minor, would be reported. Long before plebe year ended, Tim would have amassed so many demerits that he would have to leave the academy. At every formation, cadet officers swarmed around Tim. Examining his grooming with microscopic care, they wrote him up for "untrimmed hairs in nostrils." Spying a shaving cut on his face, they cited him for "careless injury to government property." Acting as what Beach called a "kangaroo court," the Honor Committee gave every upperclassman license to work Tim over until he broke. "I resolved to stick it out," Tim Leary wrote in his autobiography. "In some strange way I believed that this was what I was supposed to do, survive a training ordeal. The young hero stands up to the oppressive system. I saw it all as valuable preparation for more important experiences ahead. Ironically, I was right about that."

In a letter he sent to Tim's mother on February 8, 1941, First Classman Cadet Lieutenant Straughan Downing Kelsey of B Company wrote, "I understand your son has asked you several times for permission to resign. I beg you not to give it to him." Kelsey told Abigail that the stigma of having been before the Honor Committee would disappear by graduation day in June. By then, Tim would be "just another yearling who thinks he's the Lord's anointed." Although he compared West Point to a Southern chain gang, Kelsey told Abigail that she would do Tim irreparable harm by allowing him to resign. Urging Abigail not to tell Tim about his letter, Kelsey offered the following advice: "If you do write him on this subject again, tell him to obey orders promptly, keep his chin well back, and stand his ground. Mr. Leary has stood up quite well under this storm—no complaints, no bitterness, only a desire to clear his name, which he has done."

The letter contained all the information Abigail needed. First Classman Kelsey had told her that the battle could be won. If Tim worked hard, kept his chin well back, and stood his ground, he could survive this crisis, make it through plebe year, and go on to enjoy a fine career as an officer and a gentleman in the United States Army. For Abigail, Kelsey's letter was the clarion call. Into battle she rode with not just God but also the overwhelming power of the Catholic Church on her side.

FIVE

Throughout her life, Abigail had always entrusted her deepest spiritual needs to "our Lord and his Blessed Mother." Once she learned how much trouble Tim was in at West Point, she reacted as though she was the one who had been silenced and it was her career that was now at stake. Retreat was not an option. No matter how he may have felt about it, Tim would finish out his plebe year at the academy.

On February 15, she wrote, "Dear, let them rave, as long as you can stay on there, and keep from getting demerits, it will die down—everything does—bigger things than that have. It is too bad, tho [sic] that you of all men, should be involved in such a mess. Hereafter, when you think to do anything out of order, think of me, as you can see I'm involved as much as you are, and, darling, I just can't stand many more of these affairs." Abigail also reported that she had received a nice letter from Father Murdock and that she wanted Tim to call on him regularly because he was a friend who would help at all times. She had already had the good father say a mass of thanksgiving for Tim's acquittal. In fact, she had had many masses said during this affair. That was why she knew the "Bl. Lord" (her shorthand for "Blessed Lord") had helped them.

Writing that she would be coming up to visit West Point on February 22 or 23, Abigail pointedly told her son: "No one but you are to blame—and darling, can you, or do you even imagine my disappointment? So chin up . . . I've had to carry on and it seemed some days ago as if I'd go crazy; if the world knew that my son's career would also be ruined by liquor—but God, dear, God, in his kindness freed you & lifted my spirits & heart up and heavenward. I'm so happy you were acquitted I could cry aloud to heaven in thanksgiving. So—darling—try to be 100% right for a while . . . & your mother will be the happiest creature in the world."

In response, Tim sent his mother two short stories as well as the "first & worst part of my novel" with a letter that began, "I hope you were not so alarmed by my last letter that you think your son is going mad. Every once in a while (sometimes when I am writing) I feel such a terrible, raging, burning thing inside and I know I have that urgent drive to write—to pour out on paper all the changing, maddening thoughts—then I feel very physically & very definitely something clogging and choking so that I can't write anything logical or sensical. I have pages of stuff that I have written foolishly when I am in this mood." When he was in such a state, Tim had to put down his pencil so he could pace back and forth in his room, alternately laughing and cursing at what he called "his own wildly impetuous foolish immaturity." Even to himself, he felt like a Thomas Wolfe hero. "I am really just another stupid little adolescent dreaming fantastic dreams of prodigality. I almost weep in anguished wrath. Other times, I know that I am going to be a great writer—if just by the drive of my own ambition . . . I don't give one single damn for what happens to me here at West Point or out in the world . . . I don't care what happens to me ever—as long as I can say, 'I did my best' then no matter what befalls—there can be no self-accusation."

After spending the weekend at West Point, Abigail wrote Tim on February 24 about the long conversation she'd had with Father Murdock. She advised Tim that with four months left in his plebe year, he still had fifty demerits left to reach a hundred. He must also pull himself out of the "goat" (low) section in math. Having set out a plan for her son to follow, she then turned the focus on her own feelings. "My dear, I wondered on the train coming home why, I of all mothers, have to be upset over my son; . . . I got you into H.C. [Holy Cross]—and then I helped to get you into W.P. [West Point]—but after those jobs—I'm on tenter-hooks, really. It is your job to stay there & do your best. Please do. Watch out. This is not a scolding but a resume of my thoughts on the way home. Just life, very much like your stories."

She then went on to review his literary efforts. Reading Tim's stories, she would think that his father, mother, and home had been pretty low. Racetracks, bars, gambling, divorces, etc. Why did he write about such things? Heaven knows, she had never taken him to such places. While Tim's stories were well developed, they were too sordid for her taste. They would not add one atom of pleasure to anyone's life. As a Catholic, she would also like Tim to leave the name of Christ out of such stories.

"He has been my friend so long in my great need that I revere His name in any form, and only in the most proper place."

Abigail's literary taste could not be faulted. Tim's stories were truly awful. The dialogue was stilted, the characters less than one-dimensional. But Tim had not sent his work to his mother for her approval. He had done so to tell her who he really was. Stubbornly, Abigail refused to accept any information that might contradict her vision of her son. Even as they waged war on the academy, Tim and Abigail were also doing battle with each other.

On February 28, Tim wrote an untitled short story about an "old man of twenty" who walks home pondering "the universal reality of man's own wretchedness." Meeting his mother, he wonders, "Could he tell her it was all shattered—the ideal, the illusion, the dream: that there was no purity, or kindness, or welcome, just the dirty fight—you against the world—just the merciless system that takes you, clean and fresh and honest and hammers you down into the mold and forces you to fit into the neat pattern of nothingness?"

A week later, in block letters, Tim wrote, "THE SILENCING IS THE BEST THING THAT HAS EVER HAPPENED TO ME." It had made him a thousand years older and brought him to good books and philosophy. Were it not for his mother, he would have had no regrets at all. "And most of all I must make you happy. Oh, mother, that is my only worry & my only ambition to make you proud of me. If I hadn't bought the liquor I would be another plebe & would rank about 50 in Math. I have learned so much . . . liquor is pure, unadulterated dynamite . . . & if I ever take a drink again it will be on a desert island, by myself, so that this thing will not happen again."

On March 8, Abigail wrote her son an extraordinary letter in which she apologized for having been a "one-track-mind mother." Promising never to be so cruel again, she could now see that he felt smothered by her hovering over him mentally. She was not going to make the mistake of so many possessive women who suppressed and crushed their menfolk and ruined their lives. His life was his own and she wanted to be in it but not by pressuring him on all sides. She wanted to be a friendly mother, not a bossy one. From now on, he should go ahead and make his own decisions and she would not be disappointed in him. She would pull a curtain over her mind and think of him as a cadet doing the best he could, fighting his battles like all the rest of the plebes, doing well one day, slipping the next but fighting again, day after day, and carrying his own standard with "Timothy Leary" written boldly on it for all to see.

> If the banner falls for a while you will raise it alone, on your efforts with my encouragement but not my help. From now on, you carry on as a mature college man should . . . I don't know when my spirit has felt so free . . . I see you so distinctly—alone there, with my letters pouring in, always with a sad, accusing tone, and you feeling more helpless each time, wondering whether you could ever please me—now darling—whatever you do—I'm pleased— you just pleased me most of all by being my son and after doing that for me I guess I can take anything else you do and like it. Just go on being my son and whatever you do, can't take away that proud happy feeling.

To have evoked so dramatic a response from Abigail, Tim must have threatened to leave the academy with or without her permission. Her letter left him with nothing to grasp at but thin air. If Tim insisted on leaving the Point now, the onus would be on him. To get her son to do what she wanted, Abigail had decided to take the high road. From now on, she would let his conscience be his guide.

On April 1, Tim wrote Abigail about a long talk he'd had with a captain who had looked at his demerit record and told him that if he tried, everything would come out all right. "I have had so many conferences lately," Tim noted, "I feel like a German Ambassador." Captain Caraway (Tim's defense lawyer at the court-martial), Father Moore, and Father Murdock were all on his side and shared the view that he would not be dismissed on demerits. Tim also wrote that a first classman named Cleary had offered to go to the Honor Committee to ask them to lift the silencing. Having now been silenced for one hundred days, Tim wrote that he was just another plebe except for the fact that he had no roommate and did not talk to his classmates.

On April 6, Tim wrote that he wished he could tell his mother what a "glorious & tragic period" he was going through, "filled with tremendous hunger & wild fantasy. My brain is always flying madly from one extreme to the other." First, he felt sure he should leave the Point right away.

Then he was positive that it was the only place for him. "Oh, my darling," he wrote, "these are glorious days." That same day, Tim received a letter from a friend working at the Versailles Hotel in Miami Beach to whom he had already written concerning his possible resignation from the academy. The friend proposed that Tim check out of the Point and join him in Florida. They could hop a boat and take in the many beautiful islands in the tropics or just hang out in the "hotel biz" in Miami Beach. The friend urged Tim to keep his letter quiet as he didn't want his own family to hear he had encouraged Tim to "quit, leave, be discharged, resign, or be thrown out."

On April 11, Father Murdock wrote to thank Abigail for her thoughtful Easter greeting and offering for the chapel. Tim had come to visit with him for an hour and Murdock reported that he looked well and was meeting the situation in a fine manner. Having talked to quite a few upperclassmen, Father Murdock wrote that there was a strong swing of sentiment in Tim's favor. So long as Tim could keep from getting depressed, he would be okay. What Father Murdock neglected to tell Abigail was that he had already upset many of the Catholic cadets by speaking out in his sermons against Tim's silencing.

Reacting to what must have been yet another decision handed down in her son's favor, Abigail wrote Tim on April 16. "Darling—God has been kind to you again so please be grateful and no matter what slugs [punishment tours] or punishment you have to take, accept it in the humble spirit, for my sake and your own. Don't get any demerits & perhaps the honor C. will unsilence you. Fr. M. may help in that too." Forgetting her vow to let Tim make all his own decisions, she closed by saying "remember that after you graduate, you will be your own boss & I will never interfere with your life. Only let this one thing I wanted for you come to its fulfillment."

On April 19, Tim replied with a rare typed letter. He told his mother that he had read her letter several times and wholeheartedly agreed with it. She had asked him the underlying reasons for his doubts. "You thought I wanted to reform the world and bring it some great, metaphysical truth. To be frank, what I really long for is fame, and, more than that, the futile hope of leaving something behind me to identify me from the millions upon millions of nameless ciphers that have come and gone . . . The sun will rise 60 years from now and I will be a name on a tomb stone so there is no great issue involved . . . Can you possibly tell me what difference it makes whether I spend my life as an officer or as a ditch digger?" In a handwritten addendum, he concluded, "To hell with whether I am an officer or a bell hop. All I want is that you be happy with me."

Tim had at last told his mother the truth in language so plain that not even she could ignore it. He wanted out of the academy. On the same day she received Tim's letter, Abigail wrote Brigadier General Robert L. Eichelberger, superintendent of the academy, to request a meeting with him on Saturday, April 26. She also wrote Father Murdock, who replied that he was entirely at her service and would hold her visit in confidence. Captain Caraway wrote to say the same. The most remarkable response came from Cadet John Morton, who informed Mrs. Leary that in reference to her kind letter of April 20, he and the members of the Honor Committee would be only too glad to see her on April 26 in Cullum Hall between 2:00 and 2:15 P.M. "I assure you I shall do everything possible to prevent your son's having knowledge of your visit," Morton wrote.

Without letting Tim know what she was doing, Abigail journeyed to West Point. At the academy, she lobbied the superintendent personally, urged Father Murdock to continue his good efforts to keep Tim a cadet, and personally confronted Tim's accusers on the Honor Committee to ask that they cease tormenting her son. After the weekend, the superintendent wrote Abigail with what must have seemed like hopeful news: "Your son was here in the office on Monday and I tried to encourage him in so far as it was possible for me to do so. If he can get through to June, I imagine he will have much less trouble."

Outflanked and outgunned by his mother, Tim acquiesced again. His short-term goal now was to see things through until June. "Hell, you're not licked yet," Abigail wrote. "I can be tough like the Supe—of course you're down a bit, but not out—not by a long shot . . . Chin up, 'stout fellar.' Take it and knock it for a goal. They can't beat you, not with our prayers and your earnest efforts. A happy combination, and you'll squeeze through." Still walking endless punishment tours, Tim began studying for his final exams in silence. Bert Rosenbaum remembered him having serious problems long before graduation day. "He started having breakdowns," Rosenbaum would later say. "He was going to pieces."

In Springfield, Abigail refused to acknowledge any of this. Buoyed by her unwavering faith in the Blessed Mother and her only son, she had dutifully soldiered on with her life even after being left behind by a faithless husband. From her only son, she expected nothing less.

On May 26, with just fourteen days left until the plebes were to be "recognized" by the first classmen, Tim wrote his mother to say he was doing better on the writs than the other goats. It wouldn't be long now. He had walked off 100 hours on the area and been silenced for 160 days. Having had no visitors on Easter Sunday, Tim wondered if his mother could come up to see him on Memorial Day. Tim wrote two of his friends from Springfield to ask if they could come as well.

Bringing Tim's friends, Abigail visited on Memorial Day. Afterward, she wrote to say it must have been swell for him and his pals to catch up after a yearlong separation. Her own conversations with Tim did not please her nearly as much. "I have decided that it is out of my hands & I have asked the Blessed Lord to decide for me. I will not take the responsibility of deciding anyone's future where it is so far-reaching as yours right now. Something will happen that will make the way clear for us. So let us both try to be acquiescent & wait."

On June 10, Abigail wrote, "The 'big parade' is this afternoon—the last for 1st class & their recognition—Tell me how it turned out for you. I wish you could have someone to drag tonight . . ." With proms going on right and left, it was too late for her to get anyone up there for Tim. She wished him good luck as a third classman. On Wednesday, June 11, graduation day, she wrote, "Oh my darling, your letter brought such good news and I am so grateful to our Lord & His Blessed Mother that I am so happy—I can't begin to tell that I shall never forget when I read that you are to get your honorable standing back. I shall never never doubt that our prayers are heard. If only you pass the exam—all will be well for a while."

To become a full-fledged yearling, a plebe had first to be recognized. The ceremony, which took place right after the graduation parade on June 11, was simple yet dramatic. With all the plebes standing in the front ranks and the upperclassmen in the rear, the battalion commander gave the command, "Front ranks, about-face!" As one, the plebes turned to face the men who had tormented them for an entire year. The upperclassmen standing in the rear put out their hands. Just like that, plebe year was over. No more bracing, no more double-timing to and from class, no

more responding instantly to shouted orders. The former plebes were
now officers, gentlemen, and brothers-in-arms as well. As Tim Leary
would write in his autobiography:

> Finally, the time awaited by all plebes, June week, the end of the year
> of torment. The Corps moved from the barracks to summer camp
> in preparation for the Graduation Parade and "recognition" for the
> plebes. Old graduates returned. The walkways were crowded with
> proud families, girls in flowered dresses, thousands of tourists . . .
> From the moment of "recognition" in June, the plebe was accepted
> in the life-long fraternity of West Pointers. The elite club. The up-
> perclassmen and no-longer-plebes shook hands, laughing, embrac-
> ing each other, pounding backs, whooping in delight. A storm of
> brotherly acceptance swept through the ranks, around me. Alone,
> invisible, ignored, I was jostled and pushed by the embracing cadets.
> I hurried to the northeast corner of Central Barracks and stood fac-
> ing the rough granite wall weeping in self-pity.

In the movie of Tim's life, this would clearly be a pivotal scene, with
the source of the drama being the cadet's naïve belief that he was in fact
going to be recognized. Thomas Lawson, the first classman who was
George Stilson's roommate, would later say, "If he had been silenced by
the honor committee, then nobody would have recognized him. And he
would have known that going in." At the time, Tim apparently wrote a
letter to his mother containing a somewhat happier version of this story.

On June 12, the day after the recognition ceremony, Abigail wrote,
"Such good news. I'm rejoicing inwardly. I shan't tell a soul (except Aunt
May) until it is announced officially. You have been unfortunate but all
your hard luck is rolling away and I feel that perhaps something may happen to remove the slugs too—and there you will be a happy young man
again with a pleasant summer ahead of you." Three days later, Abigail
wrote, "I am so happy about the unsilencing, I could forego lots of other
things right now . . . It may not be just what you want but evidently the
Bl'd Lord thinks it is best for you to stay there because in my prayers I
asked for him to decide what was best for your peace of mind & future
happiness . . . and dear, you know how much was left to me to decide
alone & I always asked & rec'd guidance of Heaven, and it was the best
in the end . . ."

Living by himself in a tent in what would be the last summer camp in the history of West Point, Tim began receiving demerits from the new Honor Committee. Since any upperclassman could "recognize" a plebe through a ceremonial handshake, Tim caused yet more problems for himself by recognizing plebes who were still in Beast Barracks. At night, plebes began coming by his tent to ask him questions about life at the Point. Even after being warned not to do so, they continued sneaking in to see him after taps.

One night, two cadet officers came to see Tim. He had now been silenced for nine months, one told him. If he kept it up for four years, he would infect seven classes with his problems. (Apparently, the two black plebes who were still silenced would not infect these classes in the same way.) When the others asked Tim if he would make a deal to leave, he agreed to do so but only if a written statement from the Honor Committee affirming that he was innocent would be read before the entire corps in the mess hall. The following night, the officers came back to tell him that this had been arranged. "Apparently, he did talk to members of the new honor committee," John Beach would later say. "And he said, 'If you will accept what the court-martial was, I'll resign.' So they said okay and the first thing we knew about it was at lunch. They announced it. 'On the resignation of Timothy Leary, the Honor Committee abides by the decision of the court-martial.' We went back and we were all kind of wondering about it and then the new honor representative called us to a meeting and he said, 'We did this to get rid of him but we still think he violated his honor.' The representative who called us in said that while they exonerated him, they still thought he was guilty."

What seems to have been a tactical retreat on Tim's part became in his autobiography an unqualified victory, a conscious decision to fall on his own sword rather than admit to any guilt. In fact, if Tim had really wanted to have a career as a soldier, he could have continued on at the academy. The truth was that nothing could have been further from his mind. After trying for months to extricate himself from the military, he jumped at his chance to leave. In longhand, he wrote out his letter of resignation:

This action is undertaken with the clear understanding that no indication of guilt or change in my conviction that an injustice has been done, is to be assumed. On the contrary, it may be accepted as a definite indictment of the principles and moral character of any action

directed against me in this connection. Nor is this resignation submitted because of any change in my determination that justice is
worth any sacrifice encountered to ensure its victory.

Although it has been quite palpably proven that the attempt to
defend a principle against unprincipled attack is almost impossible,
yet, the attempt would be in every way worth the struggle if I were
not convinced that I am neither adapted or attracted to a military career. Even with the above consideration in mind, I am forced to
admit a distinct emotion of betrayal on my part of the cause which
I feel is right and of the high regard and deep admiration that I shall
always feel for the fairness and deep-rooted honesty of the officers
of the United States Military Academy.

On July 31, Abigail wrote to tell Tim that she had read his letter and
sent her approval to the superintendent on Tuesday—a stiff formal letter
which he may have had to forward to Washington. She then wrote him
an informal note of thanks for his time and attention and also sent one to
Father Murdock. "Now you must look to the future," she told her son.
"When you leave there, you will be on your own. No uncle with the
whiskers [Uncle Sam] paying the bills and planning every detail. Both
Aunt May & I shall make the best of it and regrets are not in order. Let
me know if you want anything & how it is all working out."

In an undated letter, Tim replied:

What happened was for the best. In the beginning, you will remember I wanted to leave and "see the world" in order to equip me more
completely for writing. Then I stumbled on philosophy. This was
the most important circumstance of my life. In philosophy, I discovered a more than adequate substitute for the meaningless diversions
of comradeship . . . I have a tremendous lust for fame, wealth, and
power. This is something I have in common with every other man,
but what I do not have is the ability, or energy to attain these goals.
When all is said, philosophy is a leisure occupation. There is little
physical effort and equally small amount of obedience required. I
fear this above all is the reason for my choice of a profession.

In his autobiography, Tim Leary would write, "The capitulation of
the Honor Committee was announced at lunch. The Cadet Adjutant bel-

lowed the mess hall to silence, read some routine announcements, paused, and stated the terms. 'IN THE CASE OF CADET LEARY, THE HONOR COMMITTEE AGREES TO ABIDE BY THE DECISION OF THE COURT-MARTIAL. NOT GUILTY.'" What followed was, "Stunned shock and scattered bursts of clapping. The braver of my tablemates shook my hand. From neighboring tables, waves of congratulations." After lunch, Tim took a jeep from the post garage, drove to summer camp, and parked in front of his tent. As he loaded his footlocker and duffel bags, "a friendly swarm descended. Many apologized for not having spoken up. It was impossible to get away. The narrow company street was jammed with well-wishers shaking my hand." Driving the jeep to the railroad station by the river, Tim unloaded his bags and looked up for the last time at the turrets and towers of the United States Military Academy, which to him now seemed "antiquated, feudal. Nothing good for America could come from those grey gothic piles."

Thomas Lawson, whose father had flown with World War II hero Billy Mitchell and after whom Lawson Field at Fort Benning was named, commented, "The honor system was something that was ground into us and we were very, very definitely a part of. People would react to it in different ways. But it was a situation most of us were quite comfortable with. If you asked somebody a question, they told you an answer. That was it. It was accepted that was the truth. You didn't expect anything else."

The long gray line would go on without Timothy Francis Leary. Like his father before him, he left West Point never to return. Whether or not Tim, as Bert Rosenbaum remembered, suffered a nervous breakdown during his plebe year is difficult to say. What is certain is that the military career he never really wanted was finished. Having thwarted his mother's attempt to guide his life, Tim Leary was now free to seek out the kind of life to which he seemed so inexorably drawn.

THE BERKELEY CIRCLE

BERKELEY, CALIFORNIA,
1941–1958

So long as they subscribed to it completely, their happiness was his preoccupation, but at the first flicker of doubt as to its all-inclusiveness, he evaporated before their eyes, leaving little communicable memory of what he had said or done.

—F. Scott Fitzgerald, *Tender Is the Night*

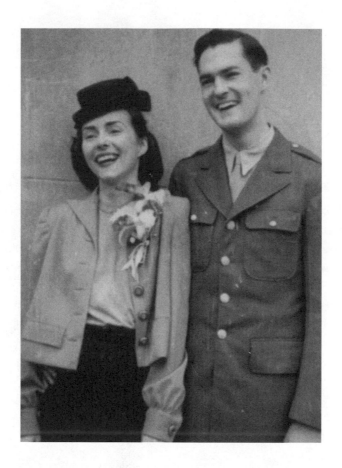

Marianne and Timothy Leary after their marriage at the
post chapel, April 1944. *Courtesy of the Futique Trust*

SIX

Tim returned from West Point to his mother's home in Indian Orchard with no definite plans for his future. On a hot August afternoon, he borrowed his Aunt May's black 1940 Chevrolet and drove along State Street to the public library where he had spent so much time as a boy. Telling the librarian he was a college student writing an assigned term paper, he convinced her to open the locked room where the library's restricted-circulation copy of James Joyce's *Ulysses* was kept. That day, as Tim Leary would later write, his brain was "permanently damaged" by Joyce's playfulness, which from then on made it impossible for him "to take seriously the corseted limits of grammar and linear thought." Joyce now replaced Thomas Wolfe as his great literary idol. "It was in part the long training with Joycean relativity that prepared me for the psychedelic experience."

In response to his mother's entreaties, Tim dispatched forty-eight application letters, one to each state university in America. Because the University of Alabama was the first to accept him, he decided to enroll there and journeyed by train to the campus in Tuscaloosa, where he soon found himself standing in a long line to register for courses. A pleasant-looking balding professor at the next desk waved him over. He was Dr. Donald Angus Ramsdell, a graduate of Middlebury College in Vermont who had received his Ph.D. in psychology from Harvard. Dr. Ramsdell was delighted to meet someone from Massachusetts. As chairman of the psychology department, "Dr. Dee," as Tim Leary would call him in his autobiography, was recruiting bright new students to his program. If the student also happened to be a young man as charming and good-looking as Tim, so much the better.

Tim happily enrolled in his class. Although Ramsdell was married and the father of a daughter, he was openly homosexual. In his autobiography,

Tim Leary would write that Dr. Dee first tried to seduce him, then adopted him as his "surrogate son." "By the semester's end I was the amazed recipient of Dee's intimate steamy confidences. Ours was not a sexual relationship. Dr. Dee was the paternal figure I had always missed, and over the years I probably became the son-friend he wished for." Peter Owen Whitmer, a psychologist who for a time was Timothy Leary's designated biographer, would later say, "I'm not sure of the extent of the relationship with Ramsdell. I do know that Tim used him as his therapist when he was at Alabama. I've read Tim's letters in which he talks about having Thanksgiving at the Ramsdell house and talking to Ramsdell about the wound of West Point and how to heal it and also about homosexuality. Ramsdell was fairly openly gay. When I talked to his wife, she was not terribly articulate and his daughter was outrageously guarded. So we don't know what happened there." Tim soon discovered that many of the best professors on campus were former northern academic stars who had migrated to Alabama because of its gay infrastructure.

Allowed for the first time in his life to take elective courses, Tim quickly became, in his words, "a top student." Unlike Holy Cross or West Point, the University of Alabama was co-educational, and as he noted in his autobiography, "Biology became my paramount interest. Accordingly I changed my major to girls." Soon, the "wildest, sexiest girl on campus" (whom Tim called "Betty Harlow" in his autobiography) zeroed in on him with "unerring accuracy" and he surrendered instantly. As Tim would later put it, "She loved to fuck." In a list entitled "Women Teachers," which he compiled in 1994, Tim gave her yet another name: "Betty Herwig!!! 1941 TO 1943: Fantastic, voluptuous, bawdy, comic, sex-sex. I climbed in the girl dorm [Tutwiler Hall] to spend the night. Got kicked out next day. Her Dad was Army officer. She used to scam enlisted men!! Alabama football games—we walked in front of the stands. Eat your heart out. Wild nights in hotel room in Birmingham!! She was a fab tutor." On Saturday afternoons at the University of Alabama, Tim and his friend Don, a "party-time kid from Illinois" who was short in stature and therefore perfect for Betty's younger sister "Anne," would drive in Don's 1941 Buick into the next county to low-ceilinged roadhouses where they drank beer, danced to "I'll Be with You in Apple Blossom Time," and then headed into the woods where they had sex with their dates on blankets.

One Saturday night in November 1942, Tim found himself talking to Betty through her window screen—she had been put on restriction for staying out too late and could not leave her dorm room. Removing the screen, Tim climbed inside and spent the night. Don did the same with her sister. At sunrise, Tim and his friend returned to the Theta Chi house on campus where they were both living. Tim was awakened at noon and told that the dean of men wanted to see him in his office at once. In an eerie replay of the Sunday-morning scene at West Point following the Army–Navy game, the dean demanded to know whether Tim had spent the night in the girls' dorm. Tim admitted that he had. Had Tim been copulating with coeds other than his girlfriend? Tim replied that he had not. Had he used a contraceptive? He had. Had he engaged in oral copulation? Not yet. Outraged, the dean shouted that this sort of scandalous behavior had no precedent in the long history of the University of Alabama and that Tim had sullied the honor of Southern womanhood.

In his defense, Tim brought up his excellent scholastic standing. Having received phone calls from two of Tim's professors, the dean already knew about his academic record. Despite Tim's outstanding grades and his complete candor, the dean had no choice. Tim was expelled. When he called the girls' dormitory, Tim learned that both Betty and her sister had already been bundled off to their home in Washington, D.C. "The expulsion was more than an academic setback," Tim Leary would later write. "I lost my draft deferment." This time, his homecoming to Indian Orchard was "less than triumphant." His mother cried. Aunt May, completely dismayed by this new demonstration of "Leary wildness," could only shake her head in disapproval. When Abigail read May a letter from the dean which said that Tim was a fine young man whose attitude was Christ-like, Aunt May was not impressed. "Jesus would never spend the night in a girls' dormitory," Tim Leary would later write.

Along with his friend Don, Tim enrolled at the University of Illinois. From the Theta Chi house there, he wrote his mother on December 2, 1942, with yet another version of the story of his expulsion from the University of Alabama. Then he got to the point. He wanted to come home to Indian Orchard on December 9 and spend two weeks in Springfield working as a Christmas temp at the post office so that he could earn some money. His plan was to then return to the University of Illinois and work through the entire month of January, thereby making almost enough money to cover his expenses at school. Dr. Ramsdell, who knew the head of the psychology department at Illinois, had already said he would get Tim a job there. Amazingly enough, just before everything fell apart in

Tuscaloosa, Ramsdell had suggested that Tim transfer to either Illinois or Louisiana State University. Summing up what he had learned, Tim wrote:

> This is a most valuable experience. I was much too satisfied & content, like a sleek cow, at Bama, about to be initiated in Theta Chi, everything perfect academically, & socially. I was getting too extroverted & too socialized & did not have the chance to study & read as much as I wanted to since there were so many delightful companions & friends to see + Psychology duties + fraternity + military [he joined the ROTC at Alabama] + schoolwork + [Betty]. So everything as always worked out for the best & financially it is O.K. because I'll be able to work a lot home & here during January. Also it is a valuable change of environment . . . The point that is bad is that your faith in me may be shattered again. Certainly you have a right to feel this but faith misplaced is such a hard lesson. There is the old struggle again—my philosophy against your practicality . . . I can't wait to get home for I love you very much. Tim.

For the first time, Tim would be returning home not as the prodigal son but as an uninvited guest, one so unsure of his welcome that he carefully defined the limits of his stay in advance so his mother would know he was not coming home for good. A clear pattern in his life had already emerged. Whenever Tim Leary began achieving the kind of success for which he had been programmed since birth by his mother, he would stop the process by indulging, just as his father had done before him, in self-destructive behavior.

Although Tim never mentioned it in any of his letters, there was a war going on. Shortly after Christmas, he was forced to abandon his plan to return to Illinois when he received orders to report for basic training at Fort Eustis, Virginia. While his enrollment in the ROTC program at Alabama had helped him avoid active serve until now, Tim would later write that he had "few illusions about the romance and glory to be attained by service in arms." Knowing he could not possibly avoid the draft while the nation was at war, Tim devised a new tactic in his always uneasy relationship with the military: he decided to lay low. For three months while in basic training, Tim did everything he could to remain invisible. His only objective was to survive. Like nearly all of his fellow recruits, he came down with chronic bronchitis. The constant ninety-millimeter artillery fire at close range combined with the bronchitis caused him to go virtually deaf in one ear. Although he was selected for officer training, he entered a program that offered psychology majors three months of study at Georgetown University followed by six months at Ohio State, where the noted psychologist Carl R. Rogers was a member of the faculty. Tim Leary later observed that at Ohio State "females outnumbered the males a hundred to one." After completing the program, he spent the winter "sunning and reading" at an Air Corps center in Miami Beach.

On March 8, 1944, Tim wrote Father Murdock at West Point, telling him about a recent visit by Abigail and his great-uncle Father Michael. Tim was concerned that the training center would soon be liquidated, with most of the personnel transferred overseas. "No utilization of the men trained in psychology is indicated. The O.C.S. [Officers' Candidate School] quotas are small." Although the usual reaction to the West Point entry on his service record was "to say the least, not positive," Tim asked if a transcript of his academic record at the Point could be sent either to him or the OCS board at his current station. Faced with the possibility of being sent into actual combat, Tim was now more than willing to become an army officer.

In the summer of 1944, Private First Class Leary was transferred to the Troop Carrier Command in Syracuse, New York. Staffed by former commercial airlines personnel, the command was headed for the South Pacific where their mission would be to ferry airborne troops into battle as well as pull gliders "that would be cut loose above Japanese home islands, where our boys would be silently and inexpensively crash landed. It was, in short," as he later noted in his autobiography, "a suicide command, whose main mission, as far as I could see, was to eliminate the entire civilian branch of American aviation from post-war rivalry."

Just when he needed him most, Dr. Donald Ramsdell came back into Tim's life. The two met in Buffalo, New York, where Ramsdell told Tim "poignant tales of love affairs with brilliant Harvard psychologists and medical officers." Serving as chief psychologist at Deshon General Hospital in Butler, Pennsylvania, Ramsdell promised Tim that his "friends in the War Department would arrange a transfer for me to his command." Tim was pessimistic that Ramsdell could deliver on his promise because a freeze had been imposed on transfers out of the war-bound Troop

Carrier Command. Nonetheless, on July 15, 1944, Tim was ordered to report for service as a psychometrician in Deshon General's clinic for the rehabilitation of the deafened. Somehow he had managed to pass through West Point, ROTC, and the regular army without firing a single shot.

Promoted to corporal, Tim reported for duty at the hospital where the very first person he met was Marianne Busch, "an audio technician with jet-black hair, soft brown eyes, and creamy skin. I fell in love on the spot." She took him into a soundproof room, put earphones on him, and then tested him for deafness by softly repeating words into his ears. She diagnosed a mild hearing loss and fitted him with a hearing aid, only to learn that he was not a patient but a new staff member.

At lunch, the staff gathered in the music room of the clinic where Marianne accompanied herself on piano as she sang musical comedy songs in a "jazzy rich coloratura soprano." Tim asked her a lot of questions. In her responses, she radiated "excellence, intelligence, and much heat." She invited him to dinner that night. They had several drinks. "Nothing like booze to wash away schoolboy inhibitions," Tim would later write. The two fell into bed as if it was meant to be.

Tim soon discovered that he and Marianne had more in common than just mutual physical attraction. Marianne's strict German Catholic parents were "hard working, thrifty, dour." Tim described her mother as "perpetually gloomy." Marianne had grown up in Oregon City, Oregon, where her father owned a large downtown furniture store and was now making a fortune because of "wartime shortages." Like Tim, Marianne had had a difficult adolescence. Nancy Adams, who would become Marianne's best friend in Berkeley, would later say, "I think she was a wild girl. A little bit unable to control her sexual impulses and her rebellious impulses. Marianne told me she would go many times to confession to confess sins of impurity with tears running down her face. Had she not met Tim, she said she would have married a good Catholic boy and stayed where she was from."

A lively, intelligent, and very attractive woman, Marianne became someone else when she drank. Nancy Adams recalled, "She once told me—and I don't know if this is funny, except that it is so black with her own self-evaluation—that she shocked everyone in the Pi Phi sorority when the mothers came to tea by getting drunk and falling down the front steps." Marianne attended Marylhurst College for a year, then transferred to Washington State University in Pullman, Washington, where she majored in speech. After graduating with honors in June 1942 with a BA in speech, Marianne won a scholarship to Northwestern University in Evanston, Illinois. While studying there for her master's, she may have dated Otto Graham, the Northwestern football star who went on to become a legend with the Cleveland Browns.

Not long after Marianne went to bed with Tim, the two of them set up housekeeping in a small apartment in the mill section of Butler, Pennsylvania. As Tim Leary would later write, "It was the first time for us both, experiencing that most wondrous human pleasure: all-out fucking-for-fusion, secure and safe in our very own bed." On April 12, 1945 (the date Leary cites in his autobiography), the day President Franklin Delano Roosevelt died, or on April 14, 1945, the day when FDR was buried (the date of their marriage license on file in Butler County), Tim married Marianne in the Deshon Hospital chapel. Both Abigail and Aunt May attended the ceremony. So did Marianne's parents. "There's a classic story about Marianne's parents at Tim and Marianne's wedding," remembered Peter Owen Whitmer. "Her father took the best man aside and said, 'You know, I have a big furniture business. Do you think Tim could run it?' It's right out of *The Graduate* with Dustin Hoffman. Like—'Plastics!'"

On their honeymoon night at the St. Moritz Hotel in New York City, Tim and Marianne drank "a joyous bottle of champagne" while dressing for dinner. This spun Marianne into "some secret alcohol room in her head." Decked out in a "classy big city dress" and a "patent-leather box-hat," Marianne somehow made it with Tim through the lobby only to slip and fall inside the revolving glass door. There she lay sprawled out, giggling. "Trapped outside the glass, I could, neither by push nor pull, extricate her."

Taking his case on appeal to the president of the University of Alabama, Tim was able to have his dismissal changed to a suspension and be reinstated as a student. He was granted psychology credits for the work he had done at Ohio State and managed to fulfill the remaining requirements for a degree by correspondence. On August 23, 1945, he was awarded his bachelor of arts by the university. On January 19, 1946, Sergeant Timothy Leary was granted an honorable discharge from the United States Army. After three and a half years of service, the entry next to the "Battles and Campaigns" category on his discharge form reads "None." Like nearly all those who had served during the war, Tim was given the Good Conduct

Medal, the American Defense Service Medal, the American Campaign Medal, and the World War II Victory Medal.

He and Marianne took a four-day train ride from Pennsylvania to Oregon City, a suburb of Portland on the Willamette River. Tim Leary would later write that Marianne's father was "the caricature of a small-town businessman." Tim accompanied him on a tour of his store as well as the family's real estate holdings on Main Street. During their time together, Marianne's father confided "his life's sorrow" to Tim. He had no son to inherit his empire. "With touching solemnity, he proposed that all this could be mine after a few years of apprenticeship. I politely but firmly declined."

Tim and Marianne spent most of the following year at Washington State University, where Tim completed his master's thesis in psychology under the direction of Lee Cronbach. In his autobiography, Tim described his thesis as "a statistical study of the dimensions of intelligence." In 1977, he retitled the thesis, transforming it into "The Dimensions of Intelligence." The original title, "The Clinical Use of the Wechsler/Mental Ability Scale: Form B," more accurately reflected its focus, which was the relationship between hearing loss and intelligence scores on the Wechsler-Bellevue Intelligence Scale. "It was a dragnet master's thesis," Peter Owen Whitmer would later say. "Tim used the data he and Ramsdell had collected during the war on intelligence testing of the hearing-impaired at Deshon. The point of a dragnet is that you're not setting up a hypothesis and a null hypothesis and then an experiment to test that. You're simply doing a post hoc study. Let's look at the data we picked up off the street and see if it tells us anything. Which is easier and much simpler."

With Marianne as a stabilizing influence, Tim settled down while at Washington State and lived what Whitmer calls "a relatively between-the-lines life." In September 1947, Tim was accepted into the doctoral program in psychology at the University of California at Berkeley. Having packed their belongings, Tim and Marianne set out by car for their new home in California. What would prove to be the only uneventful period of their life together was now over.

SEVEN

As Tim and Marianne drove over the Golden Gate Bridge for the first time, the gleaming towers of San Francisco shimmered in sunlight across the bay like a mirage. In that moment, Tim Leary would later write, he instantly became a native of California. With the war over and the economy in California about to boom, many of the servicemen who had shipped out through San Francisco to the South Pacific were now returning to the Bay Area to begin their peacetime lives. Like Tim, some of them were taking advantage of the GI Bill to enroll in universities they could never have afforded otherwise. Six or seven years older than ordinary graduate students, many were married with families to support and babies on the way.

The field of study Tim had chosen was an academic growth industry. Much as World War I had introduced widespread psychological testing to select personnel within the armed forces, World War II had created an overwhelming need for clinical psychologists to treat those who had returned home suffering from the aftereffects of battle. "On April 1, 1946," Ernest R. Hilgard wrote in *Psychology in America,* "there were 44,000 neuropsychiatric patients cared for by the Veterans Administration and only 30,000 of all other types." At the start of World War II, there were only thirty-five psychiatrists in the Regular Army Medical Corps. By 1945, there were 2,500. Because of sheer need, the Veteran's Administration had granted clinical psychologists the same rank as psychiatrists and the National Institute of Mental Health was established in Washington. The federal government filtered grant money through both agencies and began funding a multitude of university-based psychology research programs. "Clinical psychology was burgeoning," Merv Freedman, a fellow graduate student who became one of Tim's best friends, would later say.

"The world was opening up and I don't think any of us felt that we wouldn't find a niche."

Tim enrolled as a doctoral candidate in "what was reputed to be the best psychology department in the world" and found a house to rent on College Avenue and Parker Street. He and Marianne lived there for a while before moving to a tiny apartment at 2236 Durant Avenue on the south side of the university. Marianne soon found a job teaching in the speech department.

What Tim Leary never mentions in his account of their arrival in Berkeley is that after three years of marriage, Marianne was eight months pregnant. On September 25, 1947, she gave birth to a daughter, Susan, in Berkeley's Alta Bates Hospital. Tim stayed by Marianne's side "to comfort her as she went through a wild period of distress and disorientation, finally muffled by medication." After the birth, he was taken by her doctor to see their baby girl. The way in which he recalled his first reaction to his newborn daughter speaks volumes about their relationship. "Behind a glass window, in the nurse's arms, was this tiny new being, looking at me *with my own eyes*." In his firstborn child, Tim saw his own reflection.

On September 29, 1947, a delighted Abigail wrote to congratulate Marianne on Susan's birth. Enclosing a generous check, she proudly signed the letter "Grandmother." "I know you will be very happy with your baby," Abigail wrote. "I recall that the two years Tim was a baby were the happiest of my life, and I know the years Susan is a baby, relying only on you, will fill you with completeness and happiness that is unforgettable."

Unfortunately, this did not prove to be true for Marianne. Or so Tim Leary would later claim in his autobiography. "After Marianne and Susan came home, an agonizing problem showed itself. When mother offered the breast, baby took one sip of milk and let out a fearful shriek. After a week of this torture I went out and bought the formula 'works.' Susan took to the bottle greedily. Marianne was never the same. The fun-loving, competent young woman changed with the motherhood imprint into a duplicate of her mother, worried, introverted, increasingly dependent. I became an industrious father robot, dutifully getting juicy worms for the nest."

Those who knew Tim and Marianne in Berkeley tell a different story. Nancy Adams first met the couple in the fall of 1949 when she and her husband, Charles, lived across the street from them. Nancy became particularly close to Marianne. As young mothers, they often babysat for each other. "She was not depressed when she had her babies," Nancy Adams recalled. "She never said they would not nurse. As far as her being depressed after delivering her children, no, I certainly didn't see her that way. She was a complicated, rather rebellious person. But not depressed. Not then."

Helen Lane Valdez first met Tim in 1947, when she began working as the executive secretary of the Berkeley chapter of the American Veterans Committee, in which he was active. During the time Marianne was expecting, Valdez lived a block and half away. "I never heard that Marianne had trouble with Susan nursing," she remembered. "It's hard when a child is demanding and you don't get much help from a husband. I was aware there was a difficult situation, but all new babies are. There was nothing unusual about it in any way that I observed."

Merv Freedman, a decorated army veteran whose doctoral dissertation was based on research done in collaboration with Tim and Abel Ossorio, would later say, "Tim was my closest friend. I probably saw him every day for seven years. I was single so I was in his house all the time. Marianne was very loving to the babies. I recall her telling me shortly after Susan was born how she could never imagine she could love anything so much. There was a melancholy substrate to Marianne. But quite far down. She could be a lot of fun and was certainly a good companion."

Two years later, on October 19, 1949, Tim and Marianne's "strong, handsome son," Jack, was born. "We named him John Busch Leary, in a vain attempt to please Marianne's father," Tim Leary would later write. "This time we were alert to the nursing problem. When Jack recoiled from the breast, we immediately put him on the bottle. Susan was jealous of her new brother, and right from the start a tension developed between the two children that has caused me sorrow over the years." "When Jackie was born," Merv Freedman recalled, "Tim came to the house to tell us about it. I gave him a drink of course. And he said, 'Happiest day of my life.'"

From the day of his birth, Jack Leary became the apple of his father's eye. Mary Della Cioppa, Tim's second wife, who in time would find herself caring for both of his children, commented, "Tim just adored Jackie and babied him. Susan tried hard to please him and be more athletic than Jackie. She really broke her neck trying to attract Tim's attention. But it was Jackie who was bonded with his father."

Contrary to what Tim Leary would write in his autobiography, the truth seems to be that Marianne was a very caring and concerned mother.

However, for the first time since she had met and married Tim, her primary attention and her time were now directed elsewhere. Insofar as Tim's young family was concerned, this was not good for anyone. Tim's needs always took precedence over all else, but the real problem was more than just simple selfishness. Whenever he fell in love, Tim tried to become someone whom his companion could admire, honor, and respect. It was as though he was never really sure just what kind of man he was without seeing himself through a woman's eyes. Once Marianne directed her gaze elsewhere, he lost the source of his newfound stability. Suddenly, the road on which the two of them had been traveling became very slippery.

As so often happens in a marriage after children arrive, Susan and Jack caused their parents to begin leading separate lives. Tim started devoting most of his free time to the American Veterans Committee (AVC), an organization founded as a liberal alternative to the American Legion and the Veterans of Foreign Wars. One of the AVC's central goals was to influence the presidential election of 1948 in which Harry S. Truman narrowly defeated Thomas Dewey. "Tim came by the AVC clubhouse nearly every day," Helen Lane Valdez recalled. "He had enormous energy and a lot of ideas for fund-raising for the organization. Making change in society was his aim."

Others involved in the AVC included Franklin Delano Roosevelt Jr.; Michael Straight, editor of *The New Republic*; and Cord Meyer Jr., who in time would become a division chief in the CIA. Beset by internal wrangling, the AVC soon fell apart. Tim found other ways to occupy his free time. With his fellow graduate students, he played tennis or handball in the afternoons. On Saturdays in the fall, he never missed a Cal football game. During the spring and summer, he attended Oakland Oaks baseball games. On weekends, there were always parties attended by faculty members and graduate students. With only a hundred people enrolled in the psychology program, nearly everyone knew one another, and the scene was intensely social.

In beautiful, bucolic Berkeley, the "Athens of the West," Tim found himself surrounded for the first time by his intellectual peers. "The class Tim was in at Berkeley who got their Ph.D.s in 1950," Peter Owen Whitmer would later say, "has always been held up as the benchmark. This *is* excellence." Nonetheless, in his autobiography, Tim Leary would write that his fellow graduate students at Berkeley were there only to "learn how to be professors. They couldn't have cared less about the crisis of human affairs. Neither were the professors very engaged in the social applications of psychology." To him, these "genial cultured men" seemed more interested in "serenely performing little experiments in animal learning and enjoying the easy life of post-war California."

For reasons known only to him, Tim Leary failed to mention the towering presence in Berkeley of Erik H. Erikson, with whom he studied childhood and society (and whom he later invited to visit him at Harvard). A pioneer in child psychology, Erikson was the only person ever to have received psychoanalytic training from both Sigmund and Anna Freud. Although he had already declared himself a non-Communist, Erikson refused for reasons of conscience to sign a University of California employment contract containing a clause affirming that he was not a member of the Communist Party. In an eloquent letter of resignation dated June 1, 1950, Erikson wrote,

One may say then, why not acquiesce in an empty gesture if it saves the faces of very important personages, helps to allay public hysteria, and hurts nobody? My answer is that of a psychologist. I would find it difficult to ask my subject of investigation (people) and my students to work with me, if I were to participate without protest in a vague, fearful, and somewhat vindictive gesture devised to ban an evil in some magic way—an evil which must be met with much more searching and concerted effort.

"I found myself trapped once again in another gray bureaucracy," Tim Leary would later write about this period. "If I had wanted a comfortable career, I could have remained at West Point or signed up for law or business administration. I felt a return of that ancient Celtic dissatisfaction, a lust for metamorphosis, for something new and more splendid. Another graduate student, himself a half-crazed Irishman, Frank Barron, seemed to share my restlessness. We hung out together, playing tennis and drinking and talking about the poetry of psychology."

"We both had a strong interest in literature and poetry and drama," remembered Barron, the only member of the Berkeley circle with whom Tim would stay in touch for the rest of his life. "We considered the greatest psychologist of the era to be James Joyce. Of course we'd both had an

Irish Catholic education. I was an altar boy. So this enabled us to talk a certain language together. I was a baseball nut and so was he. We both agreed that in terms of rules and scoring, baseball was the most civilized, advanced game ever invented."

As a field of study, psychology itself was about to undergo a revolution. As Arthur Koestler, with whom Tim would interact none too positively at Harvard, wrote in *The Ghost in the Machine*: "Looking back at the last fifty years through the historian's inverted telescope, one would see all branches of science, except one, expanding at an unprecedented rate. The one exception is psychology, which seems to lie plunged into a modern version of the dark ages. . . . By far the most powerful school in academic psychology . . . was, and still is, a pseudo-science called Behaviourism."

"Two things were grabbing hold," Frank Barron recalled. "Behaviorism had already made a big play in the 1930s. You look at behavior and deal with the observables. In its radical form, it said, 'Don't tell us about experience. It's how you behave.' The other big theme was quantification. The crude way to do that is to count instances of behavior. Both Tim and I were doing exactly that. We were into quantification and observables."

In 1955, Tim Leary and Frank Barron would collaborate on a pioneering study of those awaiting psychiatric treatment at Kaiser Permanente Hospital in Oakland. Of the 150 psychoneurotic patients studied, one-third remained unimproved, one-third deteriorated, and one-third improved. As this was virtually the same percentage of recovery found among those undergoing treatment, the study seemed to indicate that therapy patients did "not improve significantly" over those not in treatment. In essence, the study challenged the fundamental assumption on which psychology itself was based. "I wanted psychology to be an objective discipline," Tim Leary would later write, "like physics, dealing with specific measurable movements of elements within space/time . . . So, during my third year of graduate studies, I started looking around for an environment where human interactions could be measured like nuclear particles colliding with one another." The environment Tim hit upon was a "psychlotron," a word he invented to describe a setting where "human elements could be freed, accelerated to higher states of intensity, and recorded. My plan was to record group therapy sessions, transcribe the verbal interactions, and develop a scheme for classifying the units of human behavior, just as Mendeleev did for the chemical elements."

Because no "respectable" clinic would allow graduate students to conduct group therapy sessions, Tim, Merv Freedman, and Abel Ossorio persuaded Reverend J. Raymond Cope of the Unitarian Church in Berkeley to allow them to run sessions with student members from the congregation. With the backing of Jean Walker MacFarlane, with whom Erik Erikson had worked closely at the Institute of Child Welfare, and Hubert Stanley Coffey, "the resident radical" in the department, Tim received approval to make this into his dissertation project. Using a wire recorder, Tim collected hundreds of hours of group sessions, which were then transcribed by secretaries. Every participant's statement was coded as "positive" or "negative" and placed on a grid to compare it with others in the group so that their attitudes could be defined in an interpersonal context.

In September 1950, Tim presented his thesis to a committee consisting of Hugh Coffey, with whom Tim had studied group dynamics and measurement of interpersonal relations; Jean MacFarlane, with whom he had studied clinical research; and Dorothy Nyswander, a pioneer in the application of behavioral sciences in public health, who had helped found the School of Public Health. Both Coffey, who chaired the committee, and MacFarlane had been overseeing Tim's study from the start, so there was little chance that the dissertation would not be accepted. The thesis was based on the assumptions of Harry Stack Sullivan who held that "awareness and changes in interpersonal behavior are the crucial factors of the psychotherapeutic process." Tim's paper, entitled "The Social Dimensions of Personality: Group Process and Structure," focused on the measurement of change in the group therapy situation. Right from the start, Tim fully embraced Sullivan's notion that the therapist ought to be a "democratic participant" in the group rather than an outside authority figure. There was some irony in this, given that, as Peter Owen Whitmer recalled, "All the individuals in the clinical training program with Tim said he was much better at being a diagnostician. He did not have really good therapeutic skills. A lot of times, he didn't care about the patient, didn't have the time, and was looking at the whole setup from a selfish point of view."

Tim's hearing difficulties may have also been a factor. Gerald Kasin, a mechanical engineer, inventor, and artist who served as president of Tim's chapter of the American Veterans Committee, would later say, "The deafness isolated him. It removed him from close contact. He had that very flat voice that deaf people develop. There was some change in the way you approached Tim because of the deafness."

Having earned his doctorate, Tim seemed to be on the brink of a brilliant career. He had become an associate of the American Psychological Association and a member of Sigma Xi, the society devoted to the promotion of research in science. In May 1951, he was elected to Phi Beta Kappa. Under the direction of Harvey Powelson, Tim and Merv Freedman founded the Department of Psychology at Kaiser Hospital in nearby Oakland. At the same time, Tim and Powelson opened their own Psychological Consulting Service.

As his career blossomed, the gap between Tim's public image and his private life grew wider. He and Marianne no longer seemed to have very much in common. "After Hiroshima," Tim Leary would later write, "there was much fear about atomic warfare. Marianne continually worried that the nuclear holocaust would come while I was at work and we would not be together at the moment of death. Sometimes she would phone me at the clinic and beg me to come home. Marianne's withdrawal from the outside world gradually increased. We were no longer inseparable. Two or three nights a week I was busy with meetings. Marianne stayed at home. Weekends there were heavy drinking parties with our friends."

After Jack was born, the Leary family bought a lovely home set down from the street on Queens Road in the Berkeley hills. Costing $40,000—no inconsequential sum back then—it was the prototypical California dream house, with sliding glass doors opening onto a large redwood deck that afforded a sweeping view of the bay. During the afternoon, bamboo shades kept out the blazing sun. "I helped them move into the house on Queens Road," Merv Freedman remembered. "As we stood looking down on it, Tim said to me, 'That's going to be a little island of peace down there.'"

Charles and Nancy Adams and their three children lived just down the street. Because their sons were close friends, Marianne and Nancy could often be found in each other's homes. Both became involved in the Berkeley Hills Co-operative Preschool. Originally housed in a small shack, the school moved in 1950 when parents purchased a vacant lot and erected a brand-new school building on it. In keeping with the school's cooperative philosophy, most of the construction was done by mothers and fathers who spent hours laying floor tile, painting walls, building walkways, and assembling playground equipment. "The whole enterprise was animated by the spirit of enthusiastic idealism which I have described as characteristic of those times," Charles Adams wrote. "It seemed that our religion was psychoanalysis and its prophet was Sigmund Freud. There were lively and often interminable discussions among the cooperating mothers on the four-and-twenty ways of raising the perfect child. Lectures were given on the current advanced theories of child development and rearing." Marianne organized many of the lectures and served for a time as the school's education chairman.

In 1952, after a year at Kaiser Hospital, using the money from a research grant, Tim packed his family up and took them abroad for a year so he could work on a book. For two months, the Learys lived in a suburb of Palma on the sun-drenched island of Mallorca where they searched in vain for the poet Robert Graves. In a letter to Nancy Adams, Marianne wrote, "Spain is reputedly a cheap country to live in—so it is but we lived so elegantly taking advantage of everything that was cheap that we'll probably never live so handsomely again. Mallorca is rather like what the Riviera was in the Twenties, & there are many American expatriots [sic], mostly writers of varying talents. They lead a fast life, & we often felt we were living a page of Fitzgerald. Drinking is a cheap pastime."

Tim's year abroad was a liberating experience. "When Tim came back from Europe," Merv Freedman remembered, "he was a very changed man. He was now extremely ambitious. Something about Europe turned him on. Something had been stirred in him in terms of breaking out of being another cog in society." F. Scott Fitzgerald now joined the pantheon of literary heroes after whom Tim would pattern his life. He seems to have been most influenced by *Tender Is the Night,* a novel in which the central character, Dick Diver, a psychiatrist, and his beautiful wife, Nicole, pursue extramarital adventures as they summer with the "beautiful people" in the south of France. Returning to Berkeley after their yearlong sabbatical, Tim and Marianne plunged wholeheartedly into a life of wild hedonistic experimentation.

EIGHT

In *What Does WoMan Want?*, a thinly disguised memoir masquerading as a novel, which was in part modeled on *Tender Is the Night*, Tim Leary wrote of his years in Berkeley: "Alcohol was the sacrament of the four-brained. The ceremonial ingesting of enormous quantities of booze by Suburban Professional Families who would meet on weekends to get 'smashed.' Weekdays were spent in offices. Then the cocktail party, ritual gin-gulping, stylized loosening of inhibitions. Booze provided fuel for . . . Stage dramatics, coarse, over-simplified Shakespearean dialogues. Tipsy sexual histrionics . . . Breughel in suburban living rooms with coats and ties . . ."

Once or twice a week at their house in Berkeley, Tim and Marianne began hosting cocktail parties for a group of friends whom Tim dubbed the "International Sporting House Set." Social drinking was not only confined to weekend parties. Two or three times a week, Tim would go out for lunch with the young women he had surrounded himself with at Kaiser Permanente Hospital. At a large, popular saloon in Oakland called Pland's, they would all order martinis to accompany huge hamburgers with french fries. "We would then stagger back to the office," Anne Apfelbaum recalled, "and put our heads down on the desk and pass out for a while. We were only in our twenties, but even so, everybody was trying to be with it and part of the scene."

Peter Owen Whitmer recounts the story of someone coming into Tim's house, "taking a big clear glass pitcher that had water and flowers in it, throwing the flowers out the window, dumping the water down the drain, making one big martini, and saying to Marianne, 'There are so few orgiastic people left in the world.' Zelda and Scott are the names that keep popping again and again." "It was just a terribly lively gay time," Mary Della Cioppa would later say. "No one lives like this anymore," Anne

Apfelbaum affirms. "Not so far as I know. Tim loved it because he was the focal point. On James Joyce's birthday, he would always bring down his record of Joyce reading *Anna Livia Plurabelle*. Tim would pour martinis and we would all sit around getting smashed and listening to it and saying how wonderful the Irish were." The group's Friday and Saturday night parties soon became notorious even in Berkeley. Most people went as couples although some were still single and unattached while others were already separated or divorced. Everyone was young and good-looking and they all drank to excess. "My ex-husband and I stopped going to the parties because it became a little too much," Apfelbaum would later say. "It wasn't as though there were open marriages. It was that everyone was behaving badly." "Every weekend Marianne and I went to parties with couples our age," Tim Leary later wrote. "These were wild drinking bouts with much tipsy necking and lascivious dancing. Our crowd was curiously virtuous about actual fucking. The child-centered ethic kept the suburban mothers in check."

By this point, Tim had already begun a long-running affair with the woman he called "Delsey" in his autobiography, and whom he described as "thirty two, an Audrey Hepburn twin, playful, funny." Delsey was in fact Mary Della Cioppa. Married to Tom Della Cioppa, who had put up the wallpaper in the Queens Road house for the Learys, she was called "Del" by those who knew her then. Slim, with a fine-boned face and piercing eyes, Mary first met Tim when she went to work as Helen Lane Valdez's secretary in the clinic at Kaiser Hospital. "Frank Barron sent me to him," she recalled. "I didn't even know his name. I thought it was O'Leary. I was in a rush to get the interview over because I was meeting a man I was in love with at the time. He said, 'Yes, of course, start Monday.' He also said to Helen, 'If that woman comes to work here, we have to paint this place.' Tim began the courtship. I wasn't even interested. He pursued me and I was oblivious to it. I thought he was kind of silly. The pursuit continued for years. I was married at the time and the marriage ended because of Tim."

At the time, Tim in no way physically resembled the person he would become. Described by Merv Freedman as "a very conventional academic who was very ambitious but not overly so," Tim had a paunch, short hair, a thick black mustache, and what Mary Della Cioppa called "terrible taste in clothes." "Early on," Freedman remembered, "Tim did not regard himself as a figure particularly appealing to women. His image of himself was not of a great Lothario by any means. I remember him saying to me once, 'Women think I'm a good fellow but they're not sensually attracted to me.' He had a hearing aid, which he sometimes would put right up close to the person he was talking to in order to hear. He was very unself-conscious about it and very interesting to talk to. But he was not a lead-ing man." Edith Kasin, a clinical psychologist who served as president of the Berkeley Hills Co-operative Preschool during the period when both Nancy Adams and Marianne worked there, recalled, "As Tim became more of a public figure, he became physically more attractive. Like those old movies when the secretary took off her glasses and let down her hair from the bun and became a beauty overnight. He was quite quiet when I knew him and didn't seem interesting, and I didn't find him physically at-tractive either back then."

"When Tim and Mary started having an affair," Apfelbaum recalled, "that changed the tenor of the parties. They became more tension-filled, a little more harrowing, more exciting maybe. Everyone was aware of it." To facilitate the affair, Tim rented a small apartment on Telegraph Av-enue where he met "Delsey" for sex three or four times a week for two years. "Lust is such a powerful thing," Tim Leary would later write. "You forget how compelling it is. The torment! I loved Marianne and Susan and Jack. There was no question of leaving them. Marianne suffered the most. Her drinking increased. She started seeing a psychiatrist." She also began an affair of her own with the husband of another couple who were part of the set.

"Marianne was very dependent on Tim and very resentful of it too," Merv Freedman recalled. "She could be very flirtatious as was Tim at this time. Wife swapping was going on. I'm pretty sure they were both in-volved in it." Drunk, Marianne could be just as outrageous as her hus-band, but virtually everyone who knew them then viewed her behavior as a form of self-protection. "I think she was desperate to make a connec-tion," said Apfelbaum, "and I think she wanted to feel like she wasn't just someone's wallflower." Freedman recalled, "Tim encouraged her to do this. At this point, he did not want to be married to Marianne any longer. I'm not clear what he wanted, whether it was to be free, a swinger so to speak, or to be free to marry someone else whom he considered more de-sirable. My sense is—he wanted a divorce." Apfelbaum added, "Tim would kind of say, 'Oh, that's Marianne.' I don't think he was resentful of it. I don't think he cared very much. He was very narcissistic, so to the extent that someone's behavior affected him, he would notice it. Otherwise, he could pretty much take it or leave it alone."

Nancy Adams, who was not a member of the Leary party set, remembered once being with Marianne while their children played in a sandbox. Out of the clear blue sky, Marianne asked Nancy how many years she thought she would continue to be attractive to men. "This really shocked me," Adams would later say, "because I thought she was so beautiful. But she thought she was getting on to where she wouldn't be. Marianne didn't have a very high opinion of herself."

As the drinking increased and the parties got wilder, Marianne's behavior became more extreme. Mary Della Cioppa remembered Marianne running away from a party. When Tim found her, she was "quite a distance away in bare feet and acting like a prostitute. That was what he said. So he dragged her back, put her in the car, locked her in there, and came back to the party. Very Scott and Zelda. And I was 'Daddy's Girl' from *This Side of Paradise*. We were all characters in that. It was a reference point for Tim." Della Cioppa also remembers just how different Marianne became when she drank. "She had a hidden personality. Physically, she would even look different. It was almost like her teeth came to points and separated and her eyes were wild. She was a very pretty woman. But she was just wild. *Wild*. We were at the Learys one night and we were all sitting around drinking and Marianne, apropos of nothing, said in this shrill, officious voice, 'I hate Susan.' And the children were sitting in the hallway spying on us. Susan was seven or eight at the time. Marianne never said anything like that when she was sober. That was the daytime Marianne. She was decidedly two different people."

Peter Owen Whitmer remembered a story about Tim and Marianne going to a party on San Pablo Avenue. Returning home by herself, Marianne took off her shoes and laid down crosswise in the driveway, hoping Tim would run her over when he came home four hours later, drunk. "It was like, 'Oh, God, it's four A.M. There's Marianne again.' On Saturday night, they'd be blacking out in different places and then on Sunday, they would get together as a happily married couple with the kids. They were that far out."

When Merv Freedman returned to Berkeley after teaching at Vassar College, he immediately noticed the change in Marianne at a party held in his honor. "Marianne seemed very depressed. I remember saying to one of the women who worked at Kaiser, 'What's going on with Marianne?'

She was kind of evasive. What was going was pretty clear. Tim was going to leave her. Actually, as I understood it later, they had agreed to separate. I heard she was going back to school to get a degree in working with the hearing disabled. But she was taking it very hard."

In *Flashbacks*, Tim Leary would write that he came home on Friday night, October 21, 1955, to "find Marianne filled with new enthusiasm. Her eyes, so long sorrowful, were sparkling. She had a plan." As Tim mixed a pitcher of martinis and the two of them sat drinking and talking at their bar, Marianne admitted she had become depressed. "She knew she needed a jolt, something to shake her loose from introverted habits. So she and the kids would go away for a while. She had total confidence that our love would blossom again." According to Tim, the plan was that Marianne would visit her closest friend from college who was now married to a diplomat stationed in Switzerland. She would rent a house in the Alps, learn to ski, put the kids in school, and stand on her own two feet for a while. Tim would come over to visit. To do all this, Marianne needed financial help from her parents. She called them in Oregon City and outlined her plans. "Then she listened. Her face fell. She held the phone, staring blankly at the wall. I could hear the dial tone. Her father had spoken only one sentence. 'You must be out of your mind to leave your home and husband to traipse around Europe.'" Putting his arms around Marianne, Tim held her close. "We can do it anyway," he said. "We can do anything we want." "Yes, we can," she replied. "Let's celebrate. How about a drink."

Tim recalled mixing more martinis. Although Marianne ate nothing, she kept on drinking. Together, they went to a small dinner party. While there, "Delsey" phoned to say she was going to Tahoe the next day. Tim "thoughtlessly" suggested that she and her husband drop by the Leary house later that evening. Around midnight, Tim and Marianne pulled into their garage, which had a heavy redwood door that swung down and locked from the outside. As they started down the stairs to their house, Delsey pulled up. She did not want to come in. She just wanted to wish Tim a happy thirty-fifth birthday. As he went back into the house, Tim saw Marianne standing on the stairs below, watching him and looking shattered. "You really love her, don't you?" Marianne said. Uttering a terrible cry, she toppled off the stairs onto the grassy bank. Tim picked her up, walked her into their bedroom, took off her clothes, and held her.

Fiercely, she hugged him. "We fell asleep that way," he wrote, "tightly wound together." Thus went Leary's version.

The truth was that Tim was the one who had been planning to end his marriage. "He was going to send Marianne and the children to Europe when they were nine and seven," Mary Della Cioppa would later say, "and he was going to marry me." Marianne also seems to have known what was coming. During the afternoon of October 21, Nancy Adams was sitting on the deck of her house doing the mending when Marianne came by and announced, "I'm having an anxiety attack." Marianne had been seeing a psychiatrist in San Francisco who had prescribed tranquilizers to ease her feelings of depression, but they did not seem to be working. She was supposed to be writing a paper for a course in communications she was taking at San Francisco State but was too upset to type it, and so asked Nancy to do this for her. Nancy agreed, which calmed Marianne down somewhat. As they sat together on the deck, Marianne told Nancy, "I've seen this coming for a long time. I've been much too dependent on Tim." Then she confessed just how upset she was about the affair Tim was having with Del. Since Nancy had never been to any of the International Sporting House Set parties, she had not heard anything about this before. Nor had she ever met Mary Della Cioppa. When she finally did, her first thought was that Mary looked just like Marianne.

Nor was this the first time Marianne had come to see her best friend when she felt anxious. Once before, when Marianne had arrived in this state, she told Nancy, "Tim said, 'I take responsibility for your anxiety but not what you're doing with it.'" While this sounded perfectly rational, Nancy could not help but feel it was an utterly icy thing for Tim to say about someone who was obviously on the edge, someone Nancy could now barely recognize as the beautiful, accomplished woman who had returned with Tim from Europe. Sitting with Nancy on the deck, Marianne admitted she had been having suicidal thoughts, then added, "I'm handling them. If I were a European woman, I would just take this in stride." Nancy believed her because she had never seen Marianne cry.

After Marianne left that afternoon, Nancy found something she had left behind. She sent her husband, Charles, over to the Leary house to deliver it. It was obvious to him that in the privacy of her own home, Marianne had been crying. "I, like most men, feel inadequate in dealing with tearful women so I completed my errand and left."

That night was the eve of Tim's thirty-fifth birthday. The dinner he
and Marianne attended was at the house where Marianne had been having an affair with the husband. Mary Della Cioppa was at another party
but had to leave at midnight for the San Francisco airport so she could fly
to Reno for the weekend. Tim called Mary at her party and asked her to
come to his house. "No, I can't," she told him. "I have to go to the airport." He insisted she come by, if only for a minute. Not wanting to miss
her flight, she kept saying no. Tim kept begging her, and eventually she
agreed to see him. At around ten or eleven, she parked her car on the
street above his house. Sticking his head in the car window, Tim said,
"Forget going to Reno. Why don't we run away for the weekend?" "No, I
can't do that," Mary replied. "I'm expected." They argued and it was then
that a very drunk Marianne came up the stairs. "Go back in the house!"
Tim shouted. Mary could not hear what Marianne said in reply but there
was a terrible sound as Marianne fell down a long flight of wooden stairs.
Mary was appalled. "Oh, my God," she said. "Go see what happened." Although Tim assured her that Marianne was okay, Mary started to get out
of the car. "No, no, get back," he told her. "She's okay. She'll be all right."
Mary then left, not to return until Sunday night.

If, as Tim Leary later wrote in his autobiography, he and Marianne
slept in the same bed that night, their arms could not have been wrapped
all that tightly around each other. For when Tim awoke the next morning, greeting his thirty-fifth birthday with an all-too-familiar hangover,
Marianne was nowhere to be found. Tim shouted out her name. There
was no answer.

It was an overcast day in Berkeley. Tim had tickets for the game between the Golden Bears and the USC Trojans. The garage door, always
left open, was shut but Tim could hear the car running inside. Shouting Marianne's name, he wrenched open the heavy redwood door and
smelled the stale odor of exhaust fumes. Marianne was lying on the front
seat of the car in her nightie. Eight-year-old Susan and six-year-old Jack,
awakened by their father's shouting, came running into the driveway in
their pajamas. Although Tim Leary would make no mention of this in his
autobiography, Jack went into the garage and saw his mother in the car.
In his autobiography, Leary maintained that he shouted, "Susan! Run to
the firehouse, and tell them to bring oxygen." But it was too late. "Marianne had left us to our own devices."

Tim rode with Marianne's body in the ambulance to the hospital where they took her into the emergency room. A young doctor with black hair bent over her for a moment. At 9:28 A.M., she was pronounced dead on arrival at Herrick Memorial Hospital. The short, relatively unhappy life of Marianne Busch Leary, born May 3, 1921, in Oregon City, Oregon, was over. The headline on her obituary in the Sunday *San Francisco Chronicle* read PSYCHOLOGIST'S WIFE FOUND DEAD IN CAR, and reported that the Alameda county coroner's office said her death was a "probable suicide."

Because suicide was a mortal sin, Marianne's very strict German Catholic parents would not be allowed to bury her in consecrated ground. By taking her own life, Marianne had paid everyone back in the cruelest possible way. "She was punishing herself and she was punishing Tim," Merv Freedman would later say. "But mainly him. It is just about the most hostile thing you can do in the most underhanded way possible. He wanted her out of his life and she went him one better. She really got out of his life."

Nowhere in his autobiography does Tim Leary mention why he ran through the house that morning shouting Marianne's name in panic. On her pillow, Marianne had left a note. "My darling, I cannot live without your love. I have loved life but have lived through you. The children will grow up wondering about their mother. I love them so much and please tell them that. Please be good to them. They are so dear."

"Everyone would have been better off," Merv Freedman noted, "if she had gotten angry at him and said, 'The hell with you. I'm a young woman and I have a life ahead of me.' I often wonder how you can leave two small children saying you love them. The general presumption was that she meant to do it. It is always possible she was hoping she would be discovered in time. She was deeply disturbed and out of the realm of logical thinking." Those who knew Tim and Marianne, Mary Della Cioppa among them, agree that Marianne might never have taken her own life that night had she not been drunk. Shortly afterward, Tim told Nancy Adams as much.

In his autobiography, Tim Leary wrote, "I have had considerable experience with every well-known brain-change substance. Of these, alcohol has caused the most damaging incidents in my life. Booze ruined my father's life, smashed his marriage, eroded the lives of four uncles. Marianne's suicide and thus the endless sorrows of my children were due to booze." As though it was alcohol and not the state of their marriage that was the determining factor in her death, he added that none of this would have happened, "If Marianne and I could have sat in front of the fire discussing our marital problems while smoking giggly marijuana instead of downing pitchers of stupefying martinis."

Nowhere in his autobiography does Tim Leary mention the statement he made to the police on the morning he discovered Marianne's body. "Leary told police he and his wife had stayed up until 2 A.M. discussing their marriage in their home at 1230 Queens Road." This statement does not jibe in any way with his account of their final night together. To be sure, there is no knowing just what form their "discussion" actually took. Years later, Tim would tell Joanna Harcourt-Smith that he and Marianne "got very drunk on martinis and she told him she was incredibly unhappy and in a terrible state about the fact that he had this mistress." He told her he had replied by saying, " 'That's your problem.' People said that to each other in the fifties," she recalled. " 'That's your problem.' And he said those were the last words he said to her before going to bed. 'That's your problem.' In his opinion, that was the coup de grace. They were both very drunk and they went to bed and then he found her dead."

Marianne took her side of the story with her to the grave. Behind her, she left a void at the center of the Leary family which no one would ever fill. Like a prison from which he could never escape, Timothy Leary would live with the consequences of her fatal act for the next forty years.

NINE

Realizing he had patients coming to the house for treatment in half an hour, Tim Leary called Helen Lane Valdez to tell her about Marianne. Valdez promptly called Tim's patients for him. She then phoned the twelve people who had been invited to his house that night for his thirty-fifth birthday dinner to inform them the party had been canceled. At 10:30 A.M., an hour after he returned from the hospital, Tim phoned Marianne's father, John, at his store in Oregon City. Tim asked him to come to Berkeley at once and promised to provide all the details when he arrived. At two that afternoon, "somewhat recovered from the initial shock and confusion," Tim phoned John Busch again and suggested that the funeral be held in Oregon. By then, Tim had already called Abigail and told her to meet him there.

Word of Marianne's death spread quickly through Tim's circle. Charles and Nancy Adams went over to the Leary house that morning. Their concern was not just for Tim but for the children as well. "When they told Jackie his mother was dead," Anne Apfelbaum recalled, "he said, 'Who's going to take me trick-or-treating next week?'" No one in Berkeley seemed to condemn Tim for his wife's suicide. "There was not really a judgment on him," Apfelbaum remembered. "People might have been heard to say to one another, 'Oh, he really didn't pay enough attention to her. Oh, if only he had been more understanding.' It was at that level, but no one was looking at Tim in a different way. Like, 'You monster!' Or, 'You selfish son of a bitch!' Because Marianne was not as close to everyone as Tim. Nancy Adams was absolutely devastated. It changed her opinion of Tim from then on."

"Was Tim upset on the day of the suicide?" Nancy Adams asks. "I've asked myself that question. Charles would later say that of course he was upset. Everybody else who knew him said, 'Tim hasn't reacted to this yet.' When Tim finally did come over and we talked about it, he said he had gone for a couple of psychiatric sessions, which gave him great relief. He said he just cried the whole time."

Tim's therapist was Joseph Henderson, a Jungian analyst who also treated Jackson Pollock. Tim told Merv Freedman that one of the things he liked best about Henderson was that Henderson was willing to share his personal life with him. "In terms of how Tim reacted to the suicide itself," Freedman remembered, "I called a number of friends when it happened and one said it looked like all the air had been taken out of him." "You could see in part he was blaming himself," Nancy Adams would later say. "Other friends of mine who knew them just as well at the nursery school said, 'Think of the rage she must have felt.' On the day Tim came over to talk with us, he said, 'I never realized how scared she was.' So there it was. What did it take for Marianne to kill herself? Did it take rage or being scared? I did feel very censorious of him but I never said, 'How come you weren't more supportive?' Partly because of the kids, I suppose. I don't know why I never said that. Perhaps because he was so charming and so in need."

On Sunday night, Frank Barron and Tom Della Cioppa picked up Mary at the airport. Tom had already called her in Reno with the news. At the airport, Barron told Mary that Tim wanted her to go to work the next day. "So I went to work," she would later say, "and it was very difficult. The hostility in the office was just incredible. Hostility to Marianne, for doing it on his birthday."

To prevent Marianne's family from learning that she had killed herself despite the account of the suicide that appeared in the *San Francisco Chronicle,* her body was sent to Oregon on Monday. There was no memorial service for her in Berkeley. "That is to say," Apfelbaum remembered, "there was no gathering of people to remember her. Mostly it was people talking to one another in corners or going for a drink. There was no real closure." On Monday, Frank Barron went to the train station with Tim, who would accompany Marianne's body. Jack and Susan went as well, and Frank bought them hot dogs. When Tim got off the train in Portland, Marianne's father, "manifesting considerable agitation," as Tim Leary would later describe it, drew him aside, pointed to his chest several times, and said, "Heart, heart, heart." He explained to Tim he had informed the local newspapers and the family that Marianne had died from a heart attack. Memorial gifts were already being sent in her name to the Heart Fund.

To his own mother as well as others, Tim continued to offer only a vague account of Marianne's death in which there was no mention of suicide. Tim told John Busch, who wanted to believe his daughter had in fact died of a heart attack, that they could talk about the details later. Busch again said, "No, I don't want to hear anymore. That is what I want to believe." Merv Freedman recalled, "I am told that one of Marianne's sisters said to Tim, 'You killed her.' I would gather that the sister knew but that measures were taken to hide the circumstances since her mother was such a rigid, devout Catholic."

Despite having taken her own life, Marianne was laid to rest in consecrated ground. On October 29, 1955, Mr. and Mrs. Armand L. Bengle enrolled Marianne B. Leary in the Benefactors Society of the Passionist Fathers Congregation. The Fathers pledged to say one holy mass each day in her name as well as remember her daily in all prayers and good works of all Passionists in the world. In her name, they would offer a Requiem Mass and an Office of the Dead on the first of each month and a High Mass of Requiem and an Office of the Dead during the Octave of All Souls.

Later, John Busch went to Berkeley for an uncomfortable visit with Tim. Angrily, he told Tim that "everyone" in Oregon City now knew the truth. Some friends had even offered to show him newspaper clippings, which he refused to read. Although Susan and Jackie continued to spend time with their grandparents in Oregon City, the rupture between Marianne's father and Tim was absolute. In a letter to Marianne's family, which he may never have sent, Tim wrote, "I have throughout felt considerable sympathy for John's very difficult position. I was aware that John was making me the scapegoat and have been resigned to this role. He has to live with your family and in your community."

Within a week after Marianne's funeral, Tim had returned to his office at Kaiser Permanente Hospital and resumed his regular work schedule. "The following week was pretty disjointed," Helen Lane Valdez remembered. "On Tuesday or Wednesday of that week, Tim went to see a psychiatrist. While it is true that within a short time he returned to the office, he seemed to behave in a manner that one would consider appropriate for a husband whose wife killed herself and quite possibly because of something he had done." Tim's mother came to stay with him in

Berkeley to help care for Susan and Jack. "She was humorless and rigid," Mary Della Cioppa recalled, "saying 'Eee-yah, Timmy!'" Concerning Tim telling her the truth about Marianne's death, Mary would later say, "He dissembled with her as well."

Once Abigail returned to Springfield, the reality of caring for two young children hit Tim hard. Nancy Adams would later say, "Really looking kind of devastated, I remember Tim telling me, 'Maybe I ought to send the kids up to Marianne's parents.' I didn't even stop to think about it. I said, 'Oh, no. They've lost one parent. They can't lose you too.'" Tim then had Helen Lane Valdez interview a series of women so he could hire a nanny. "But in less than six months," Anne Apfelbaum would later say, "Mary was in there. Tim did have a housekeeper, but that was not very satisfactory so it made sense that she would move in and take over the family. It seemed logical."

In the summer of 1956, less than a year after Marianne's death, Tim married Mary in a government building in a little town in Mexico. According to Apfelbaum, "It was pretty unacceptable to be living with someone to whom you were not married. In terms of his employers and such. It was not acceptable behavior." At the time, Susan was nine and Jackie was seven. "Susan was so grateful for everything I did for her and I adored her," Mary recalled. "She was such a nice little girl. When we got back from Mexico, I put them both into a very good private school so they wouldn't have to face their old friends. Still, all I ever saw from her was anger at her mother. She didn't talk about Marianne. Nobody did. It was as if the wake had closed behind the departing ship and left nothing to be seen."

If life with Tim before their marriage had been problematic, Mary soon discovered that living with him was far more difficult. Tim's fluctuating moods, short attention span, and vague nature could be maddening. He would be tender and loving one moment, distant and self-involved the next. And then there were the children. Jack and Susan did not trouble her, but the way Tim related to them did. Believing himself "the world's best father," Tim acted the part only when it suited him and their needs and desires did not get in his way. One night, Tim decided that he and Mary would go to the movies. Because they could not find a babysitter, Mary told him to forget about it. They could go another night. Refusing to alter his plan, Tim replied, "No, we'll just have the children sit each other. It will make them feel important." While Mary wondered if nine-year-old Susan and seven-year-old Jack were too young to care for each other, Tim went into Susan's room and said, "Susan, you're the oldest. We'll tell Jackie that he's babysitting you but really you're babysitting him. Because you're a big responsible girl." Naturally, Susan was very pleased. Tim then told both children that it was time to turn out the lights and go to bed. Tim and Mary had driven a block from the house when Tim looked up and saw that Susan's bedroom light was on. Jamming on the brakes, he jumped out and ran across a vacant lot. Crashing through bushes and grass, he leaped up onto the deck outside Susan's bedroom. "She had no idea it was her father," Mary would later say. "Can you imagine? Some man crashing up like that? He was so enraged. He just scared her to death. He was screaming at her. And then he came back and we went to the movies. Teflon. Nothing stuck to him."

"Before Marianne's suicide," Nancy Adams recalled, "Susan was an exceedingly bright, wonderful kid. She learned to tie her shoes before our kids did. She climbed higher in the trees. She was a very cute little girl. I had the best time with Susan. You could teach her any folk dance instantly and she was wonderful to watch." "After Marianne died," Edith Kasin would later say, "I had more contact with the children because they were bereft and Tim farmed them out to Nancy Adams a lot. Susan particularly seemed like a very needy kid in terms of attention . . . She was emotionally needy but this was a little girl whose mother had just died in a terrible way, and I'm sure she wasn't protected from that."

Even before their mother's death, the Leary kids, like most of the other children in their neighborhood, had been raised in an ultra-permissive manner. "I didn't have any voice in discipline," Mary Della Cioppa remembered. "The kids were allowed to play 'base runners' in the house and it was all glass and they had baseball bats and balls flying. They were his kids, not mine. One night at the dinner table, I was trying to get Susan to eat something and Tim held up a note to me that said, 'Leave Susan alone.' Every day, there was some gruesome little thing like that." At three in the morning, Jack and Susan could sometimes be found jumping rope in the living room. When Tim came downstairs, it was only to tell Mary to leave them alone. The Leary kids smeared things on the big sliding glass doors and windows. One day, they shot a neighbor with a BB gun. The same neighbor reported that the kids had started a fire under his house. Mary Della Cioppa recalled the children coming to the dinner table wearing hats and then standing on their chairs so they could reach

for a handful of salad. Jack in particular could get away with almost any-
thing. "Tim was lenient and permissive toward his son," she recalled.
"Not like his own father had been. Susan was standing in the shadows.
She was the odd man out. It was Tim and Jackie, always."

On January 8, 1957, Tim's book *The Interpersonal Diagnosis of Personality*
was published by Ronald Press. In his introduction to *An Annotated Bibliography of Timothy Leary,* Frank Barron wrote, "Leary's enduring contribution to psychodiagnosis, or, more generally, to the typology of
personality is embodied in his honored 1957 volume, *Interpersonal Diagnosis of Personality.*" In it, Tim analyzed five discernible levels of interpersonal communication, which ranged from the public to personal-social
conscious, private perception, the unexpressed, and the level of values.
For each level, he identified a characteristic unit of analysis—the interpersonal reflex, the interpersonal trait, the interpersonal symbol, the
significantly omitted communication, and the ego ideal. "This," Barron
wrote, "was a giant step forward for typologies, which at that time were
almost always locked in to the single-person trait." Barron also pointed
out that the extensive observational research which formed the database
for the book was a group effort. Dozens of psychologists, psychiatrists,
and social workers had provided the fieldwork necessary for the statistical
analyses. Hundreds of patients in group therapy had served as subjects. In
layman's terms, the book posited the world as a madhouse in which, as
Tim Leary wrote, "Everything that can be found in mental disorder can
be found in anyone." The neurotic/psychotic subject was at one end of
the spectrum, the "normal" subject at the other. Rather than blame parents, race, or instinctual heritage, problems were caused by the subject's
own repetitive and self-limiting responses. By changing inaccurate per-
ceptions and rigid reactions, Leary believed that a person could determine his or her own role in the world. This idea represented a serious
break with behaviorism, classifying social interaction as a game, one
which subjects could not only be taught to play but also coached to win.
The book made it possible for clinics to deal with an overload of patients.

Tim also devised a model that became known as "The Leary Circle."
Dr. Richard Varnes of the Phillips Graduate Institute and a practicing psychologist in Beverly Hills, still uses The Leary Circle today. "This book is
a masterpiece," Varnes says. "All the way from assumptions to applications. For its time, it was a different way of thinking. Very creative. Tim

Leary took Harry Stack Sullivan's theory that our interactions are based on our need to further decrease anxiety and said, 'How do you decrease anxiety and increase self-esteem?' It's a self-report test. A snapshot in time. I often use it for premarital counseling. I give it to couples and to children and their families. How do you see yourself and your ideal self? When you see the differences, you get a visual image of why someone is confused." The Leary Circle consists of eight interpersonal reflex scales on which a patient can score either high or low. "It predicts," says Varnes, "what kind of people will dance well together. Rolf LaForge and Souchek were also doing this kind of work back then. LaForge really invented the interpersonal checklist, and he and Leary had a falling out about it." Rolf LaForge did not copyright the interpersonal checklist so that anyone could use it for research. Nonetheless, when Tim included the checklist in his book, LaForge viewed this as an act of piracy. "Tim wrote about the whole interpersonal enterprise as though he and Hugh Coffey had done it all," recalled Merv Freedman. "It became the Leary Circle but I had as much to do with it as him and we had a third partner, Abel Ossorio. Tim was a very good self-promoter, which he had not been early on. That was part of the change in him."

In his introduction to the book, Tim Leary carefully credited everyone who had contributed to it. According to Peter Owen Whitmer, one of Tim's fellow graduate students at the time said, "Tim, in some difficult-to-define way, emerged as sort of a king of the hill. His name appeared first and foremost . . . and other fellows slid into the background. And it didn't seem to be on the basis of their respective research attempts. In my perception of Tim, there was always this kind of pattern to the history of his relationships with colleagues. He destroyed friendships." Whitmer added, "The book caused tremendous political backlash in the tribe that Tim associated with in writing it. People didn't get credit. Was the data jobbed or manufactured? Yet Tim himself came off as the shining prince." All the same, the book served to establish Tim Leary as one of psychology's brightest new stars. As Varnes says, "At the time, Tim was considered the heir apparent to Abraham Maslow."

The book caused quite a different reaction in the Leary household. "I had suggested to Tim that since Marianne had been with him in Mallorca when he was writing it that it might be nice to dedicate it to her," Mary Della Cioppa remembered. "When it came out, he gave everyone in the family a book. He gave Susan her copy and I said I'd be down in a minute to read it to her. When I went into her room, she was sitting up in bed and she had a pencil gripped in her hand and she was scratching out the dedication to Marianne. She was scratching so hard, she was tearing the paper."

Although nearly a quarter of a century had passed since he last saw his father, Tim Leary had never stopped thinking about him. Merv Freedman recalled, "If we happened to be down by the Embarcadero in San Francisco where there were bums sleeping by the water, Tim would look at them and say that maybe one of them was his father. A lot of Tim's life can be explained by rebelliousness toward his mother. In the end, he turned out to be a lot more like his father."

In what he called his only published novel, Tim Leary described the protagonist as the "son of a talented but feckless father who . . . in his time had been a dental student at Heidelberg, a golf champion, a small investor . . . a wastrel heir, a drinker, a good fellow, a ship's steward on the Murmansk run, a bankrupt, a drunkard, a proud disdainer of the middle class." All this was true. From the moment he left his wife and young son behind in Springfield, Tote Leary drifted slowly but steadily down the social ladder. The dog-eared passes to seamen's clubs all over the world, which he kept in a clear plastic folder, bear eloquent witness to the life he led. At sea for months at a time as a steward in the Merchant Marine, Tote would return to port only to drink himself senseless as he sat day after day in the Seamen's Hall, waiting for another ship to take him back out to sea. During World War II, Tote worked as a merchant seaman on the very dangerous Murmansk run in the North Atlantic. In 1942, he was part of a convoy in which twenty-three out of thirty-four ships were torpedoed by U-boats or sunk by German aircraft. Although his ship was hit, it managed to reach Russia where Tote stayed for the next three months. After the war, Tote spent a good deal of time drying out in hospitals. He was discharged from one with a note on his record that read, "Condition Improved."

In 1952, at the age of sixty-four, Tote was certified as a chief steward in the Merchant Marine. On February 14, 1956, General Douglas MacArthur sent "Dr. Leary" a typed letter thanking him for his birthday greeting. After searching for many years, Phil and Anita Shea finally located Tote during the summer of 1956. "Tote was living in a hotel in lower Manhattan around Chelsea," noted Peter Owen Whitmer, who interviewed the Sheas. "They went to the hotel and the first thing Tote did was take them to the bar and introduce them to everyone to show them that he had relatives. Then they went to the racetrack using a betting sheet that the clerk at the hotel had filled out and Tote hit it big. They came back and he took them all out to dinner at a nice place."

Phil and Anita wrote Tim with the news that they had at last found his missing father. The letter was forwarded from Berkeley to Mexico where Tim was spending the summer with Mary. In longhand, Tim wrote his father, "I was thrilled to hear about you and to get in touch with you. I am very eager to see you. There are so many, many things to share and talk about. Is there any possibility that you can come out to California this fall? I have a large house and would be delighted to have you stay with us for an extended visit." Tim went on to explain that he would be happy to arrange for plane tickets for Tote. On September 1, Tim wrote that he would be taking the kids to Disneyland before returning to Berkeley. "The children will be excited at the prospect of seeing grandfather Leary. I can't wait to tell them. I'll have Susan write you." If it was not possible for Tote to visit them, Tim wrote that the family would plan to come east this winter to see him.

This letter began a short but remarkable correspondence between Tim and the father who had abandoned him so many years earlier. In his letters, Tim adopted a distinctly paternal tone. He had now become the father as Tote played the role of the wastrel son. Although Tim never offered Tote nearly as much advice as Abigail had given him while he was at West Point, Tim's letters to his father mirror that correspondence. From Berkeley on September 10, 1956, Tim wrote that he was unhappy to hear Tote wasn't feeling well and was checking into the hospital. He asked his father if he had ever considered transferring to a hospital in California. If Tote's doctors thought it was a good idea, Tote could live with Tim and be within a ten-minute drive of a VA hospital. Two months later, Tim wrote on his business letterhead to say he was very sorry to learn that Tote's health had taken a turn for the worse.

Having talked with Phil Shea a couple of times on the phone, Tim knew that Tote would not be able to visit that month and so made plans to go east to see him. When he arrived in New York on Saturday, November 24, 1956, Tim promised he would try to get to the hospital that very evening. Apparently, the visit went well. On December 1, 1956, after returning to Berkeley, Tim wrote, "The visit with you meant a great deal to me. I was glad to have the chance to tell you things that I had been feeling for some time. It was good to hear the details on what you have been doing. It meant a lot to be able to tell you how much admiration I have always had for you and how many respectful memories I have of the past. And I was impressed to meet your friends and to see the esteem and affection they have for you."

Without much difficulty, Tim had reconciled with his father. He did, however, instruct Phil and Anita not to tell Abigail that he had seen him. Peter Owen Whitmer would later say, "Here was his father who essentially supported his liquor habit for the last years of his life by quoting Shakespeare to appreciative liquor-store owners. Tim came back from seeing him in the hospital and was really quite shaken because he had always felt this big shadow, this mystery in his life because his father had been a complex, important individual but not there with the consistency of a regular father or his friends' fathers. And then Tim found out that his father near the end of his life was very human, very warm, very perceptive of other people's feelings. Tim told Jean MacFarlane, 'I think my own life would have had a lot more stability had I been able to spend more time with him.'"

Not long afterward, Tote Leary died of either throat or tongue cancer. Knowing that he did not want to be buried in Springfield, Phil and Anita saw to it that Tote was interred on Long Island. Tim did not attend the service. According to Peter Owen Whitmer, "It was just Phil and Anita along with one other guy who was there with a flask in a brown paper bag." "Tim didn't know how he felt," Mary Della Cioppa recalled. "His father was so old and he was so lonely and he was so sick. When he died, they sent his belongings over and it was just a little Ace comb and a little wooden nail brush. Tim looked for a long time at this envelope that had these little things in it. 'Such a sad life,' he said. 'To have only this. This is what's left of his life.'"

Not long after his father's death, Tim Leary's longstanding personal relationship with Hugh Coffey, the faculty adviser on Tim's doctoral thesis and yet another surrogate father figure, came to an abrupt end. "Coffey lived with his wife and three children not far from the Leary house," Mary Della Cioppa remembered. "Although no one in Berkeley seems to have known about it at the time, Tim and Coffey were involved in a homosexual affair." "I didn't pick up on anything," said Edith Kasin, who worked for Coffey and saw him with Tim quite often in all sorts of situations, professional as well as social. "Even together, they were very discreet." In a letter to the author discussing this subject, one of Tim's colleagues at the time wrote, "Coffey was in love with Tim (Coffey was bisexual although primarily gay), and Tim was obliging to men who were interested in him sexually. (Tim was bisexual although predominantly straight.) The gay sex consisted of Tim's lover performing fellatio. Tim told me that in order to achieve orgasm he would fantasize that the men were women." According to the colleague, Coffey's wife, Fanchon, was jealous of Tim and quite possibly aware that something was going on. "Tim was not trading sexual favors for political advantage," the colleague added. "By the time Coffey and Tim were involved sexually, we already had our degrees. If anything, the power lay in Tim's hands, not Coffey's. It was simply a matter of Coffey being in love with Tim. Tim did talk to me about homosexual behaviors early in his life. I don't know about West Point. I do know that this was the occasion at the University of Alabama."

Realizing that if news of their affair ever became public, it could have ruined both their careers, Tim decided to break off with Coffey. Not long afterward, Coffey went looking for sex in the public men's room of a park located one block from Kaiser Hospital and was arrested. When Tim heard the news, he reacted viscerally. "When Hubert was arrested," Mary Della Cioppa said, "Tim was devastated and I couldn't understand it because I didn't know . . . I tried to do the best I could to cheer him up. I never understood it. He wasn't devastated. He was *terrified* . . . He thought he would be exposed. It was Tim's own skin he worried about that night."

By the next morning, the story had hit the newspapers. Going to work that day provided Tim with no escape. "When I came in to the clinic that morning," Anne Apfelbaum remembered, "I went into Tim's office to talk to him about some tests and he was like a crazy person. He could not focus. Actually, now that I think about it, he reminded me of Hamlet . . . It was because Tim had been having an affair with Hubert and had broken it off. Hubert had been caught and this was Hubert getting back at him." Merv Freedman would later say, "I guess Tim's breakdown came because he was fearful that Coffey would talk. Of course, this would have been quite a scandal." Although it took a good deal of political manipulation on the part of the faculty and the University of California administration, the arrest did not put an end to Coffey's career.

However, Tim's marriage to Mary continued to be rocky. "I gave him that nose he had," she recalled. "When we were married, we had a big fight one morning and I ran out of the house. We both had to go to work and he chased me all over the hills and found me and I was fighting him in the car and I hit him on the nose and broke it and he never got it fixed. So the shape of his nose is my handiwork." By the spring of 1957, Mary realized that their marriage was finished. "I just got angrier and angrier at him," she would later say. "He was trying to make me into Marianne and the very thing that attracted him to me in the first place was that I was unlike her." One night she came home from an Afro-Cuban dance class, which has been canceled at the last moment, and found Tim sitting with the kids in the kitchen. "They all looked at me like 'What are you doing here?' and that was it. I packed a bag and walked out the door. It was just too much." After Mary left him, Tim returned to Mexico for the summer with Helen Lane Valdez, who had worked for him for many years. The two began a relationship.

Tim's need always to be with a woman had begun to verge on pathological. When he could not find someone on a voluntary basis, like Helen Lane Valdez, he was perfectly willing to pay for companionship. A friend who went with Tim to Mexico on another occasion told Peter Owen Whitmer, "Tim was always with a whore. It was not necessarily someone for him to sleep with but a badly needed form of female company—just someone to be there."

Although he was supposed to bring back divorce papers from Mexico to end to his marriage to Mary, Tim returned instead with native masks from Oaxaca as a reconciliation gift. Almost immediately, the two had a screaming fight. Tim punched Mary in the face and her landlady called the police. Turning on the charm, Tim identified himself to the officers as Frank Leary. The cops told him to go home. The next day Tim called Mary to apologize, but their marriage was over.

Although Tim Leary wrote openly, if not always accurately, about virtually every aspect of his life, he kept his solemn promise to Mary that their marriage would always remain a secret. On the back of a stunning black-and-white photograph of her in which she looks like a modern-day Aztec princess, he wrote, "Mary della Cioppa. We were married 1955–1956. Funny, lovely lady." On the list of "Women Teachers" he compiled in 1994, Tim wrote: "MARY DELLA CIOPPA—hip, model, comic, insecure." Mary would later say, "We had a fantastic love affair and a terrible marriage and then we became good friends."

In the fall of 1957, Russia launched the world's first satellite into orbit. In America, funding a space program that would enable the nation to catch up with its cold war rival became a national obsession. As a result, federal funding for the National Institute of Mental Health was cut. When NIMH sent an investigator to Berkeley to discuss Tim's grant, he was off in Mexico. This was the second time Tim had been absent when someone came to make certain he was at the site of his government-funded program. Moreover, as Helen Lane Valdez admitted, "Tim also gave me more responsibility than I was capable of and I got the renewal application in late." Tim's time in Berkeley was nearing an end. "Before Marianne's suicide," Merv Freedman would later say, "Tim was very much the fair-haired boy in the psychology department. He was regarded very highly and our research received a lot of attention. In the latter years, his reputation began to diminish. I think that tarnished him somewhat, and his grant money was running out."

On June 30, 1958, Tim wrote Susan, who was away with her brother at camp, to say he was coming up to take them with him to Europe. Accompanied by an airline stewardess who soon left him to spend time with pilots from a nearby American air base, Tim sailed to Spain with nine-year-old Susan and seven-year-old Jackie on the SS *Independence* of the American Export Lines.

In Torremolinos on the Costa del Sol, Tim rented a villa where he planned to work on both a novel and a follow-up to *Interpersonal Diagnosis* called *The Existential Transaction*. Leaving behind the ruins of two marriages and a promising career in psychology, Tim had run away. Although Frank Barron would remain a friend for life and Helen Lane Valdez continued managing Tim's affairs as best she could, Timothy Leary would never again have significant contact with any of those in his circle. To their great consternation, he would return a decade later to play a leading role in the social and political revolution that transformed not just Berkeley but the nation as well.

GOD AND MAN AT HARVARD

CAMBRIDGE, MASSACHUSETTS,
1958–1963

Harvard stood for the broad "a" and those contacts so useful in later life and good English prose . . . if the hedgehog can't be cultured at Harvard the hedgehog can't at all.

—John Dos Passos, *Nineteen Nineteen*

It is a multiple million eyed monster
it is hidden in all its elephants and selves
it hummeth in the electric typewriter
it is electricity connected to itself.

—Allen Ginsberg, "Lysergic Acid"

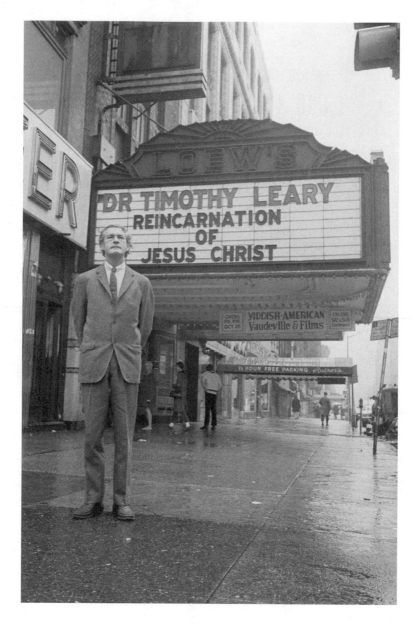

Timothy Leary stands below the marquee for the opening
of his second celebration. © *Bettmann/CORBIS*

TEN

Although he had come to Costa del Sol to live out a highly romanticized dream of expatriate life, Tim Leary found instead a very solitary form of exile. For the first time since his silencing at West Point, he was completely on his own. He had brought with him a trunk containing "thousands of test scores and numerical indices which demonstrated with precision why psychotherapy did not work." Using this data, Tim intended to compile *The Existential Transaction*, but right from the start the work did not go well. After sending Susan and Jackie off to school, he would sit each morning for hours "sweating in a small room in a Spanish house adding and subtracting long columns of figures." Inevitably, he would throw down his ballpoint pen in frustration and walk to the main street of the village where he sat in a bar to "drink and talk detached-zombie-fashion with the expatriates and leave abruptly and run back to the house and continue the paralyzing calculations, sweating in panic."

Tim soon began to experience what he called, "Boredom, black depression, flashes of frantic, restless anxiety," a list of symptoms any psychologist might recognize as early warning signs of a nervous collapse. As always when he was in distress, Tim went looking for a woman. "In December the rains came and the Mediterranean was gray and cold. On Christmas Eve I met a young runaway prostitute from Valencia and took her home. By New Year's I had the clap."

In January 1959, Tim, Susan, and Jackie moved to a hotel in Torremolinos. Jackie had been given a puppy, which was not yet house-trained, and Tim's "distant gloom" upset the owner, so the family moved again to an apartment "tunnelled into the rock at the foot of Calle San Miguel. It was a cave with oozing stone walls. The beds were always damp." Here began what Tim would later call his "break-through-break-down."

One morning, he woke up with his scalp burning and itching. By noon, the pain was unbearable. "Each hair was a burning rod of sensation. My hair was a cap of fire." By evening, his face had begun to swell. Huge blisters erupted on his cheeks. A young Danish doctor came and gave him an injection and some sleeping pills. Tim went to bed. In the morning, he woke up blind, his eyes swollen shut with dried pus. Feeling his way to the bathroom, he lit a candle, stood before the mirror, and pried open one eye. "In the oblong glass I saw the twisted, tormented face of an insane stranger." A Spanish doctor came to give Tim more shots and more sleeping pills. On the third day, huge watery welts covered his back and stomach. Both doctors shook their heads in dismay and injected him yet again. In the afternoon, Tim hired a taxi to take him to Malaga, where he consulted a specialist. The specialist gave Tim two injections. Too ill even to respond to the advances of a pretty young Swedish girl who sat down beside him at a sidewalk café in Malaga, he returned to Torremolinos, where the doctors agreed Tim should move to a steam-heated hotel.

Tim somehow managed to smuggle Jackie's puppy into the room, but Jack and Susan went off to stay with a family on sabbatical from the University of Pennsylvania, leaving Tim alone with his agony. By nightfall, his ankles and feet were so swollen that he could not walk or even move his fingers. "I sat in the darkness for several hours and then came the scent of decay. Overpowering odor of disintegration," he would later write. Trying to rise from his chair, Tim fell to his knees. Crawling across the room, he turned on the electric light. Jackie's puppy had been sick, and a rivulet of yellow shit ran across the floor. If the chambermaid found the evidence, Tim knew he would be thrown out of the hotel. For the next hour, he crawled along the floor cleaning up the mess with toilet paper. He tried to flush it all away but the toilet did not work. Opening the window overlooking the backyard, Tim heaved the toilet paper wad into the darkness. Only then did he see electric wires below the window. From them, discolored strings of toilet paper now swayed like a banner in the breeze. Using an umbrella as a cane, Tim hobbled along the hallway, down the back stairs, and across the rutted muddy backyard. Each step was torture. He fell down several times. Standing on a packing crate, he flailed at the filthy toilet paper banner, feeling like a madman fighting vultures. Two hours later, Tim somehow made it back to his room. Weak and trembling, wrapped in a Burberry mackintosh, he spent the rest of the night slumped in a chair. "I died. I let go. Surrendered. I slowly let every tie to my old life slip away. My career, my ambitions, my home. My identity. The guilts. The wants. With a sudden snap, all the ropes of my social self were gone."

In the morning, Tim wrote three letters. One was to his employers at Kaiser Hospital, telling them that he would not be returning to his job. The second was to his insurance company cashing in all his policies. The third went to a colleague, "spelling out certain revelations about the new psychology, the limiting artifactual nature of the mind, the unfolding possibilities of mind-free consciousness, the liberating effect of the ancient rebirth process that comes only through death of the mind." In layman's terms, he was describing a nervous breakdown—his own.

By spring, Tim had moved to Italy where he, Susan, and Jackie lived in a penthouse apartment overlooking the domes and towers of Florence. When Frank Barron came to visit, he found Tim broke but in good spirits after having just completed his new book on psychotherapy. "For the first time since my thirty-fifth birthday," Tim would later write, "I was feeling some flickers of enthusiasm. I thought I knew how humans could direct their personal evolution. The next step was to find a clinic or university where I could put these ideas to the test." Barron read the manuscript, which was never published. "It was marginal," Barron recalled.

While in Florence, Barron told Tim "about some unusual experiments he'd performed recently. He said his research on creativity had led him to Mexico, where he interviewed a psychiatrist who had been producing visions and trances using the so-called 'magic mushrooms.'" Taking a bag of the mushrooms back to Berkeley, Barron had ingested them. "At this point Frank lost me with this talk about William Blake revelations, mystical insights, and transcendental perspectives produced by the strange fungi. I was a bit worried about my old friend and warned him against the possibility of losing his scientific credibility if he babbled this way among our colleagues." Barron also told Tim that Professor David McClelland, director of the Center for Personality Research at Harvard University, was in Florence on sabbatical. "Frank Barron," McClelland recalled, "told me Tim's wife had committed suicide and it was incredibly traumatic and he was in kind of a tailspin and had left Berkeley and had been in Spain and was busy writing some great book. I'm not quite sure how but we saw quite a bit of each other."

Forty-one years old when he first met Tim, David Clarence McClelland had secured his own reputation in psychology through his studies of what he called "achievement motivation." A "tall, elegant, mustachioed" man with a "cutting and critical humor," McClelland was the son of a Methodist minister who had converted to his wife's religion and become a convinced Quaker. In later years, McClelland would express the opinion that psychoanalysis had become so popular because it was a form of secular religion offering comfort to man in his state of existential anxiety. He would in time become chairman of the Department of Social Relations at Harvard, a separate division from the Department of Psychology, which was dominated by the behaviorist theories espoused by B. F. Skinner.

Bringing his new book with him, Tim came to have lunch with McClelland. Drinking Chianti on the patio, Tim explained the title of his book. By "existential," he meant that psychologists should work with people in real-life situations. Like a naturalist in the field, the existential psychologist should observe behavior in the trenches rather than impose any sort of model on them. In the actual transaction between patient and therapist, the psychologist should not remain detached but, rather, become involved with the person or event being studied. "I had admired his work as a psychologist and we were trying to get our Ph.D. clinical program going at Harvard," McClelland recalled. "I knew his book *The Interpersonal Diagnosis* and about the Leary Circle before I met him in Florence. It was his work and his charm that impressed me . . . So I invited him to come to Harvard for a year."

"Nobody was snowing David McClelland," recalled Frank Barron. "Not later. Not then. Not during. I tend to be a bit of a plotter in terms of seeing what the possibilities were. I saw Tim was broke and he might be out of his career. We were two of the hotshots in psychology and Harvard wanted us because they had been denied accreditation by the American Psychological Association for their clinical program, so they had to get something strong going. They had brought in McClelland to get people in and I had met him back in 1956 when I was at Harvard. He was very shrewd and he wanted achievers. That was Harvard, too."

At Harvard more than half a century earlier, William James, the noted pragmatist philosopher and elder brother of novelist Henry James, had become the father of American psychology by making the discipline into a laboratory science. James had also expanded his consciousness by experimenting with nitrous oxide as part of the research for his 1902 book, *The Varieties of Religious Experience*. Despite this long-standing tradition of intellectual freedom, nothing in the 324-year history of America's first institution of higher learning had prepared it for the coming of Timothy Leary.

In Cambridge, Tim and his children took up residence in a two-bedroom suite at the Ambassador Hotel, where they lived for the next seven months while he began working at Harvard's Center for Personality Research just a block away. As soon as he had enrolled Jack and Susan in a local public school, Tim visited a Harvard Square tailor to get himself outfitted in "a varsity uniform": a button-down shirt and a tweed jacket with leather patches on the elbows. "With my horn rimmed glasses I looked like a caricature of a professor—except for the white tennis shoes, which I wore everywhere."

A month later, Tim took his children to visit his mother and Aunt May, now living in the white clapboard farmhouse in Indian Orchard where Abigail had been born. "Mother and Aunt Mae [*sic*] came trotting on little-old-lady feet to greet us. They looked great. Slim, bubbling with pleasure. Yet I felt wary. Even at forty I was on guard, ready to protect myself and the kids from Aunt Mae's fierce moralizing." As they sat down to a traditional New England Sunday dinner of roast chicken, mashed potatoes, cranberry sauce, gravy, peas, salad, and hot rolls, Abigail said, "for the thousandth time, 'Well, I've eaten in the finest restaurants in New York and Paris, and nothing tastes as good as a home-cooked meal.'" At the head of the table, Aunt May began to say grace. Tim had drilled his children in the procedure and so they dropped their heads on cue and closed their eyes. "Both Mother and Aunt Mae watched their performance and nodded in approval. The dinner was a smash hit. Mother was radiant, and Aunt Mae came close to smiling. Finally, after forty years of worry and disappointment, my mother's dreams were coming true. Her son was a Harvard psychologist, and the family was reunited."

As she walked Tim out to the car later, his aunt told him that if he got into trouble at Harvard, it would be the end of his mother. Imploring him not to "do something deliberately wild," she made him promise he would conform, if only for his mother's sake. "She was always being the Widow Douglas from Hannibal, Missouri, doing her best to 'sivilize me,'" Tim would later write, referring to Mark Twain's *Tom Sawyer*, one of his favorite books. "This time I thought I might let it happen."

Nowhere in Tim's account of his homecoming did he mention a scene that occurred in church earlier that day. On cue, Susan and Jackie stood and kneeled with the rest of the congregation. All went well until people began to cross themselves. Halfway through, Jackie noticed that he was doing it wrong and stopped. Realizing that her grandchildren had never been to church, Abigail began to sob. As she held the money for the collection plate in her hand, she stumbled in the family pew at the very front of the church. Coins rolled loudly all over the floor.

Having come to Cambridge to resurrect his failing career, Tim did everything he could to get off to "a fast start on the Harvard academic track." When he was offered a suite of offices on the third floor of the Center for Personality Research, a "Puritan-style frame building located, prophetically enough, at 5 Divinity Avenue," Tim instead chose a small typist's office close to the entrance to the building because he wanted to be "near the center of the action." Rather than assign his graduate students to "Freudian oriented clinics and hospitals, which encouraged rote-learning of sterile and ineffectual tests like the Rorschach Ink Blots," Tim urged them to deal with problems in skid rows, ghetto community centers, Catholic orphanages, marriage clinics, and jails. Leading by example, Tim accompanied his students when they went to interview junkies, street cops, and social workers. He arranged conferences with Bill Wilson, the founder of Alcoholics Anonymous, and Charles Dederich, the founder of Synanon. Eager to be on the cutting edge of the humanistic movement in psychology, Tim would later write, "We operate with too little information about ourselves and the other guy. I don't have any theory about new variables in psychology, no new words or language of psychology. I am simply trying to develop new ways of feeding back to human beings what they are doing and the noises they are making."

By doing all this, Tim had already begun to frustrate those for whom he worked at Harvard. On May 3, 1960, David McClelland wrote him a single-spaced two-page letter questioning the manner in which he had been conducting himself both inside the classroom and out. Declaring himself to be basically sympathetic to what Tim was trying to do, McClelland wrote:

> I think you have got to define much more carefully what you are talking about. Above all, you have got to stop using slogans and waving banners, because they seem to me to only confuse matters. The first issue, then, has to do with vagueness. The second issue has

to do with how general your goals are. At times you seem to talk as if the transactional role is the only human one, and that it should characterize all relationships between people, of whatever nature for whatever purpose. The third issue has to do with the nature of evidence. At times you seem very cavalier on this issue—as if to say that the rules of evidence that science has worked out are all non-sense—that the ravings of a madman or an idiot are as valuable as the careful investigations of a psychologist.

Although Tim acknowledged that his actions and attitudes at Harvard caused "the more traditional faculty" to bridle, he had few problems attracting younger colleagues to his cause. The first to fall under Tim's spell was Charles Slack. "I was an assistant professor at Harvard when he got there," Slack recalled. "I had a five-year appointment, which in those days was like a fellowship. You had five years and if you didn't make it, you were out. Dickie Alpert was there on the same type of deal. Tim was something different. He was a lecturer, which did not have quite the status or the word 'professor' in there." After receiving his doctorate in experimental psychology at Princeton, Slack was hired in 1955 to teach at Harvard by Harry Murray, who had founded the Harvard Psychological Clinic, invented the Thematic Aperception Test, and was a renowned Melville scholar. Murray brought Slack to Harvard "because clinical psychology had such a low scientific stature that they were trying to boost it up by hiring a few experimentalists."

Twenty-six years old, Charles Slack was the youngest assistant professor of psychology at the university since William James. He soon found himself drinking with Tim in the dives around Harvard Square. Calling themselves The White Hand Society, they argued constantly about anything and everything. "I was stoned most of the time," Slack admitted. "It was like a big blackout. Tim drank all the time. If I ever got to be as bad as he was, I would have quit. That was what I kept telling myself. Eventually, I did. And he kept right on drinking." Neil Friedman, a former graduate student, recalled the day that Slack came to lecture in Leary and Alpert's graduate seminar in fieldwork. "It was in one of those very staid Harvard rooms with the long table and I was down at the end right near the speaker and Charlie Slack was drunk. And he was giving this god-awful talk and I was bit petulant myself. I found a *New York Times* in the

room, picked it up, brought it back to the table. I opened the *Times* right
under the speaker's nose and proceeded to read it, and no one said a word
about it."

One night as Tim and Slack sat drinking in a bar, Tim remarked, "You
know, I really am a psychopath. How many violations of the American
Psychological Code of Ethics have you made?" Slack could think of none.
Tim informed Slack that he himself had violated all of them except for
those having to do with money. Slack asked whether Tim had ever had
sex with his patients. Tim replied that he had. "We called ourselves psychopaths. A psychopath was someone who made a psychiatrist mad,
which both of us had done regularly. Psychiatry was the bad guy in those
days." When Harvard decided not to renew Slack's appointment, he
searched frantically for a teaching job only to end up at the University of
Alabama, Tim's alma mater.

Tim quickly replaced Slack with a powerful new ally, Richard Alpert.
Bachelors, albeit for very different reasons, the two men met because they
were the only faculty members who held office hours at night. Each evening when his children were in bed, Tim would walk to his office past
"the tiny jewel-box chapel of the Swedenborg church," where William
James had once listened as his father preached from the pulpit. In his office, Tim would read, write, drink California white wine from half-gallon
bottles, smoke Marlboros, and gladly talk with any graduate student who
cared to come in to see him. Down the hall from him in the Center for
Personality Research, Assistant Professor Richard Alpert sat in his "high
prestige corner office." Tall and boyish in geeky black-frame glasses with
a crew cut, Alpert was, as Leary would later describe him, an "ambitious
academic-politician—engaging, witty, a big tail-wagging puppy dog."
Alpert soon joined the group in Tim's office. "I was the Jewish boy on the
way up and he was the Irish guy outside the system," Alpert recalled.
Brought up in a "Jewish anxiety-ridden high-achieving tradition," Alpert
had received his doctorate from Stanford. It was there in 1955 that his first
patient had turned him on to pot. He smoked sporadically but was then
still "quite a heavy drinker." He had spent five years and some $26,000 on
his own psychoanalysis only to have his therapist tell him, "You are too
sick to leave analysis."

A self-professed "mediocre student" who had failed to win admit-
tance to Harvard as an undergraduate and instead had attended Tufts and
Wesleyan, Alpert's Harvard faculty position meant far more to him than

it ever did to Tim. Alpert taught courses in human motivation, Freudian theory, and child development. He held appointments in four different departments: Social Relations, Psychology, the Graduate School of Education, and Health Services. He also had research contracts with Yale and Stanford. To assist him in his labors, he had two secretaries and several graduate and undergraduate assistants. Adored by children, he was the godfather of David McClelland's twin sons. The son of George Alpert—a wealthy lawyer who had helped found Brandeis University and who, while serving as the president of the New Haven Railroad, owned a limousine with an extra set of steel wheels so it could run on train tracks—Richard Alpert lived in an antique-filled apartment in Cambridge. He owned a Mercedes-Benz sedan, an MG sports car, a Triumph 500 CC motorcycle, a sailboat, and a Cessna 172 airplane. In New York City, he had access to the railroad's penthouse apartment on Park Avenue, company limousines, and the inner sanctums of Grand Central Station.

Despite his privileged background and great personal success, Alpert shared with Tim a basic lack of contentment not with just himself but also with the material world. Rather than rebel in the way Tim had already done, Alpert internalized his feelings. "In the face of this feeling of malaise, I ate more, collected more possessions, collected more appointments and position and status, more sexual and alcoholic orgies, and more wildness in my life."

After Tim introduced him to psychedelic mushrooms, Alpert would say, "I knew I wasn't an intellectual. I'd gotten to Harvard on charm. I wasn't real. I was a phony. But I had conned everybody and here I was a Harvard professor so everyone assumed I knew and they were going to give me tenure and I could make believe I knew for the rest of my life. But I knew I didn't. After being with Timothy, a couple of things happened. I began the practice of psychedelics and I would look at my colleagues and realize they didn't know either and that was fascinating because these were the lions of academia. I was ready to devote my life to Timothy because I felt, 'Now here is a man who is a real visionary. He sees through the system and he can truly stand back and look.' We had so many extraordinary conversations. It was such fun."

In Tim, Alpert saw freedom, authenticity, a mind far bigger than his own, and, most important, someone to whom he could devote his life. In Alpert, Tim saw a companion, an enabler, and a younger brother. Alpert would be Huck Finn to Tim's Tom Sawyer. Together, they would have mad adventures while thumbing their noses at the impossibly straight and boring world in which neither of them really belonged.

As soon as the academic year ended, Tim set off for his fourth consecutive summer in Mexico, where he planned to work on his still-unfinished book. Buying a used Ford so old that it was a matter of debate as to whether it would even survive the trip, he took an Englishwoman with him whom his son Jackie could not stand. When she decided to leave them in Alabama, Tim put her on a bus and continued on to Berkeley where he dropped Susan off with Charles and Nancy Adams and their family. Tim and Jackie then headed for Cuernavaca, "a charming spot, for centuries a retreat for sophisticated Aztecs, corrupt politicians, and wandering scholars." Down the highway from the villa where Tim lived, Erich Fromm ran an experimental project studying Indian village life. Ten miles away in Tepoztlán, David McClelland was completing his book *The Achieving Society,* a psychological analysis of why some civilizations prospered while others decayed. A "few cornfields away," Elliot Danzig, Mexico's leading industrial psychologist, lived next to the cliff on which the altar of the God Tepozteco was located. Seventy miles west of Mexico City, Cuernavaca was the southernmost point of a line running from Popo and Iztacchihautl to Toluca, volcanic peaks on whose slopes grew the Sacred Mushrooms of Mexico, Teonanacatl, flesh of the Gods.

Although Tim had always expressed reservations about using drugs to induce transcendental experiences, he now seemed eager to experience the phenomenon for himself. His new attitude had much to do with his upcoming birthday. In October, he would turn forty. "I was a middle-aged man involved in the middle-aged process of dying. My joy in life, my sensual openness, my creativity were all sliding downhill." More specifically, Tim's sexuality had become, as he would later describe it, "very elitist and selective. A one night stand could be a lust or a bust, depending on my feelings toward the woman, my emotional condition, my state of mind, and my period of heat."

While for most men nearing forty this might seem like a fairly normal state of affairs, for Tim it was a matter of genuine concern. In Casa del Moros, a rambling white-stucco Spanish-style villa that he and Jackie shared with a semanticist named Dick Dettering and his pregnant wife, and Frank Barron and Dick Alpert, both of whom were still en route, Tim soon found the answer to his problems.

A frequent visitor to the villa was an anthropologist, historian, and linguist from the University of Mexico whom Tim Leary would call "Gerhart Braun" in his autobiography. In reality, he was an East German refugee named Lothar Knauth who often brought his girlfriend "Joan" as well as "Betty," an English major from the University of California ("Joan's" twenty-year-old daughter), with him. Knauth had studied ancient texts written in Náhuatl, the language of the Aztecs before the Spanish conquest. In them, he discovered repeated references to the use of sacred mushrooms by Aztec soothsayers on ceremonial occasions. Learning that these mushrooms still grew on the volcanic slopes near Mexico City, Knauth and Tim (in a 1973 interview, Peter Owen Whitmer was told that Tim did not go on this trip) drove to the village of San Pedro (Whitmer was told it was Tenango) along with artist and filmmaker Bruce Connor. Although none of the shopkeepers would sell them what they were looking for, they did tell them to wait for a woman named Old Juana, who would soon come to the market.

An hour later, Juana Sanchez arrived. An old woman with gray stringy hair and a hunched back, wearing a black shawl, she refused to stop when they hailed her by name. Without a word, she walked out of the village along a rutted dirt road. Tim and Knauth followed. After speaking to her in Spanish, Knauth told Tim the deal had been done. She would get the mushrooms and bring them to Knauth in the market on the following Thursday. A week later, Knauth met Juana in the market. In the shade of a church wall, she showed him the mushrooms. When Knauth asked her if they were safe, she popped two into her mouth right before his eyes. Later, Knauth called Tim to tell him the mushrooms were now in his refrigerator. He promised to bring them to the villa in Cuernavaca.

Around noon on August 9, 1960, Knauth, Joan, and Betty arrived with the mushrooms. As Knauth cleaned and separated the mushrooms into two bowls, one for males and one for females, he lectured the group about them. After being "pushed out of history's notice," the mushrooms had been rediscovered in 1955 by an amateur researcher and banker named R. Gordon Wasson in the mountains outside Oaxaca. Soon after, the poet Robert Graves began writing to friends about Wasson's remarkable find. The well-known British psychiatrist and researcher Dr. Humphry Osmond—who had ingested four hundred grams of high-quality mescaline in 1951, and in 1957 first coined the term "psychedelic"—accompanied

Aldous Huxley to visit Wasson in his office at J. P. Morgan and Company in New York City to listen to him talk about the wondrous power of the mushrooms. While recounting his adventures in Mexico during lunch one day at the Century Club, Wasson was asked by an editor at Time-Life to write about the mushroom ceremony. His account was published in the July 1957 issue of *Life* magazine along with photographs by Allan Richardson. Frank Barron was so inspired by the story that he went to find the mushrooms on his own. Tim Leary was now about to follow their path.

By the pool in Cuernavaca, Tim watched Knauth stuff a big black moldy damp mushroom into his mouth and begin chewing. Knauth's Adam's apple bounced as the mushroom went down. Tim picked up a mushroom, which stank of "forest damp and crumbling logs and New England basement." Cautiously, he asked Knauth if he was sure they were not poisonous. Even as Tim posed the question, Joan was eating a mushroom. So was Betty and the husband of another couple involved in the experiment. Finally Tim took the plunge. The mushrooms tasted "worse than they looked. Bitter, strong. Filthy. I took a slug of Carta Blanca and jammed the rest in my mouth and washed them down." Sickened by the vile taste, Betty started vomiting in the bushes. Then she ate some more. The wife of the other couple, a trained nurse and a male guest, who had been appointed to be the "scientist" and to take elaborate notes, did not indulge. Before the day was done, Tim would eat seven sacred mushrooms.

Feeling as though he was on nitrous oxide, Tim realized that everything had suddenly become incredibly funny. For the first time, he saw himself in a new light. Everything about him was different. Even his walk had changed. Then his legs turned to rubber. Around him, the room filled with water. He floated through the "air-sea." Although he knew no words that could describe what he was feeling, Tim Leary would in time employ a kind of psychedelic blank verse, influenced by ee cummings and James Joyce, to describe the sprung rhythms of his first psychedelic experience.

As Tim approached the woman who had not ingested mushrooms, the water in which he found himself suddenly became ominous. It was like swimming on a moonless night in a shark-infested southern sea. In this ocean of energy with no mind to guide him, Tim felt the "dread of unknown black peril." Telling the woman that she might soon have "six psychotic nuts" on her hands, he advised her to send the kids and the maid downtown to the movies, lock the gates, and "for god's sake stay close and keep your eyes on things." Even as Tim began his first psychedelic experience, he was acting like a trained psychologist.

Tim's trip soon became visual. In sharp focus, the "allgreen grass" changed color in waves like so many floodlit slides at a summer dancehall kaleidoscope. When Tim and Betty lay side by side on a beach chair, he realized there was no difference between their skins. The last abstraction of self and body was gone. Entangled with his lover, he visited palaces by the Nile, temples near Hong Kong, Babylonian boudoirs, and Bedouin pleasure tents. He saw flaming mosaics that flashed with emeralds, Burma rubies, and sapphires from Ceylon. Lit from within, they moved and glowed like a hundred jewel-encrusted reptiles with hammered Moorish-patterned skin. Plummeting back in time, he watched life in its most primitive form ooze, writhe, and twist up from the primordial slime. In the deep-green dark sea, he became the first living thing.

By eight in the evening, the effect of the mushrooms began wearing off. Enrapturing visions were now interspersed with moments of nontrance consciousness. When some friends arrived at the villa for dinner, Tim quickly remembered his responsibilities as host and walked out to the porch to tell them to go to the kitchen for drinks where he would join them in an hour. A little after nine that evening, Tim's first trip was over.

When Richard Alpert arrived a day later, Tim told him, "I learned more in the six or seven hours of this experience than in all my years as a psychologist." A few months later, Tim used the exact same words to describe his journey to Arthur Koestler, adding, "Gone the perceptual machinery which clutters up our view of reality . . . Gone the mental machinery which slices the world up into abstractions and concepts. Gone the emotional machinery that causes us to load life with our own ambitions and petty desires." In *High Priest*, Tim's first autobiography, he wrote of his initial trip, "It was the classic visionary voyage and I came back a changed man. You are never the same after you've had that one flash glimpse down the cellular time tunnel. You are never the same after you've had the veil drawn." By then, as Jay Stevens noted in *Storming Heaven*, "his context had shifted toward religion and revelation. He hadn't really rushed around talking about God that first morning after; it had been more along the lines of finally experiencing that elusive vitalizing transaction." Peter Owen Whitmer recalled, "What Tim said about the time they took mushrooms for the first time at Cuernavaca in the Casa del Moros was that the anthropologist looked at the pattern on the umbrella and said, 'Now I understand Mayan civilization.' Someone else looked at the stars and said, 'They're speaking to me.' Tim looked around as he closed the gates and said, 'We're all schizophrenics now and we're in our own institution. But for the first time I understand James Joyce.'"

With the apostolic zeal of someone who had just seen the true cross for the very first time, Tim drove to Tepoztlán to tell David McClelland the earth-shattering news and to invite him to come do mushrooms with him. "During that meeting with McClelland," Tim later would write, "I realized it was practically impossible to convey the experience of altered states to someone who hadn't been there." Tim also noted that he'd had the very same reaction in Florence when Frank Barron had first told him about his mushroom experiences. McClelland, however, was not completely unreceptive. "He was very excited because some Mexican *curandero* had given him the magic mushroom and he had taken it and had this marvelous experience," McClelland recalled. "And he invited us to come over and take them too. I didn't much want to but my wife did. She was an artist and was intrigued to see what would happen to her. So we drove over to his house in Cuernavaca, but unfortunately the cook had cooked the mushrooms. Or fortunately, from my point of view. So I wasn't faced with the decision to take them or not."

When Tim talked about his experiences with Frank Barron, Barron warned him "about the compulsive tendency to run around explaining to everyone about these amazing events and what they meant." Nevertheless, they agreed to start a research project about it at Harvard. Barron would concentrate on the effect of the experience on creativity while Tim worked "on using the drugs to accelerate behavior change." With the eventual consent and approval of David McClelland, the Harvard Psychedelic Project was born.

ELEVEN

Returning to Harvard for the new school year, Tim moved his family to a baronial three-story mansion on a hill in Newton Center. One hundred and eighty-five stone steps led up to the front door. Inside the great house, which belonged to a professor on sabbatical in the Soviet Union, were "books and woodwork and thick rugs and metal-work lamps and a wide staircase winding up from the entrance hall."

The day Tim checked in for the fall semester at the Center for Personality Research, he ran into George Litwin, whom he considered "one of the brightest graduate students in the department." When Litwin had told Tim about some of the mescaline experiences he had performed on himself and others before the summer, Tim had voiced disapproval, thinking that it sounded "like chemical meddling." Having already completed his first year of graduate study at Harvard, Litwin was then serving as a research assistant to David McClelland. Under the supervision of a hypnotherapist named Martin Orne, Litwin was also giving people mescaline at the Massachusetts Mental Health Center. "I went to Tim and tried to relate what was going on in these mescaline experiences with his rambling about existential psychology," Litwin recalled. "There was a connection I wanted to explore but he said, 'Foolishness. You're talking about some chemically induced state. Get out of this thing, George.'"

Although Litwin never succeeded in winning Tim over, they continued their dialogue because, as Litwin put it, "I'm pretty argumentative and he was relentless. We loved arguing. But he was radically against drugs or any kind of authoritarian intervention, electric shock or anything like that. It was a control issue and he absolutely put drugs in that same basic category as well." As an undergraduate at the University of Michigan, Litwin had studied with David Eberle, a well-known anthropologist who was a leading expert on the use of peyote by Navajo Indians in the Southwest and had also ingested the drug with them fourteen times. Flatly, Eberle told Litwin that he believed taking peyote had "no place in our culture or our mythology. We don't have anything that enables us to explain or deal with this and therefore I don't think it is something we can introduce."

When Litwin met Tim again in September 1960, however, Eberle's concerns never figured in their conversation. "While he was not particularly sure about peyote because he did not yet know the difference between it and mescaline," Litwin remembered, "he was pretty sure this mushroom thing had something really serious about it." Having experienced the visionary flash for himself, Tim now understood what it was all about. Seeing that he had changed, Litwin pressed Tim on the topic. But formal research was not exactly what Tim had in mind. He wanted to take mushrooms again and give them to his friends so that they could see what he had seen. After the trip was over, everyone could write down what they had seen and felt and envisioned. This was the only kind of research Tim wanted to do.

Litwin and another graduate student who was there at the time agreed with Tim. This project would be the ultimate form of democratic psychology in action. Everyone would take turns ingesting the mushrooms and observing one another, while keeping careful records of what they experienced during the sessions and how it was affecting them. There would be no diagnosis, no withholding of information or results. They would bring as many people as they could into the project, not just psychologists and behavioral scientists but also writers and poets and housewives and cabdrivers. As Tim talked, spinning out visionary concepts like a dream weaver, he created a group fantasy. When Litwin asked Tim if he had read the literature on visionary states, Tim said no. Rushing off down the hall, Litwin returned with Aldous Huxley's *The Doors of Perception* and *Heaven and Hell*. Tim jammed both books into his pockets.

Only one final issue remained. Where would they get the mushrooms? Having been told that the Public Health Service had synthesized them, Tim decided to write the agency in Washington, D.C., and inquire. From Mexico, Lothar Knauth promised Tim he would continue searching for Juana. If he found her, he would send Tim a large supply. Frank Barron was also trying to procure mushrooms from people he knew at the University of Mexico. Litwin solved the problem by telling Tim that the Swiss pharmaceutical firm, Sandoz Laboratories, had a branch office in America. At the Sandoz Laboratories in Basel, on April 16, 1943, Dr. Albert Hofmann had first synthesized and then absorbed through his fingertips the twenty-fifth compound of the lysergic acid series, henceforth known as LSD-25. Litwin assured Tim that Sandoz would gladly supply psilocybin, a hallucinogen obtained from Mexican mushrooms, to qualified researchers.

Following Litwin's lead, Tim dictated a letter on Harvard stationery requesting a supply. "We wrote away and we thought we'd get an application and we'd have to fill out some paperwork and get Harvard to sign a form," Litwin remembered. "But they just sent us back a big bottle and said, 'We appreciate your request and we are interested in sponsoring work in this area. Here's a starter kit to get going and please send us a report of the results.'"

That night, Tim read *The Doors of Perception* and *Heaven and Hell*, Aldous Huxley's accounts of his experiences with mescaline, which he had first taken in his home in the Hollywood Hills in May 1953. Then Tim read them again. And again. "It was all there. All my vision. And more too. Huxley had taken mescaline in a garden and shucked off the mind and awakened to eternity." The title of *The Doors of Perception* came from a line by William Blake: "If the doors of perception were cleansed every thing would appear to man as it is, infinite." Vividly, the book portrays the effect of mescaline on a classically trained novelist and philosopher whose overwhelming love for visual art was being frustrated by his near blindness. Expecting to lay back with his eyes closed, seeing "visions of many-colored geometries," Huxley realized that the world of visions resided in what his eyes could see, "books whose color was so intense, so intrinsically meaningful, that they seemed to be on the point of leaving the shelves to thrust themselves more insistently on my attention." Repeatedly, Huxley noted, "This is how one ought to see. How things really are." He also worried about how to reconcile his newly cleansed vision with the world as it still existed around him. "Mescaline," he wrote, "can never solve that problem; it can only pose it . . ." For Huxley, the key was in right action and right alertness, the willingness of a saint to come down from the seventh heaven to bring a cup of water to his sick brother or in the actions of the Buddha who saw the vision yet acted in this world in the name of practical charity. "Most visualizers," Huxley wrote, "are transformed by mescaline into visionaries." Even so, as he would later write in a letter, "There is, obviously, a field here for serious and reverent experimentation."

At a party in Cambridge a week later, someone told Tim that Huxley had accepted an invitation from his old friend and colleague Huston Smith to lecture as a distinguished visiting professor at MIT. Now sixty-six years old, the great man was living but a mile and a half up the Charles River. To Tim, it was just another sign that he was not only on the right track but being guided by forces greater than even he could understand.

On October 3, 1960, Tim wrote Huxley at MIT to say that during the past summer, he and an anthropologist had obtained some mushrooms from a "witch" near Toluca and underwent an experience "strikingly similar" to what Huxley had reported after using mescaline. Noting that his research group was planning an extensive study into the potential for expanding and enriching human experience through the use of such substances, Tim asked whether an appointment might be arranged so Huxley could answer questions and give advice to the group.

Two days later, during one of Tim's planning meetings, Huxley called to say that he was interested and could they meet for lunch. Tim took him to the Harvard Faculty Club. As Huxley gazed at the menu through his magnifying glass, Tim asked him if he would like some soup. "What kind?" Huxley asked. Tim looked at the menu. "Mushroom soup," he said. Laughing, the two men agreed that it seemed perfectly fitting. They then talked about Tim's study and how he should use these consciousness-expanding drugs. "We clicked along agreeably on the do's and not-to-do's," Tim would later write. "We would avoid the behaviorist approach to others' awareness. Avoid labeling or depersonalizing the subject. We should not impose our own jargon or our own experimental games on others. We were not out to discover new laws, which is to say, to discover the redundant implications of our own premises." Huxley impressed Tim by quoting Wordsworth, Plotinus, and William James. He talked about Keith Ditman's plans to clean up skid row in Los Angeles by giving LSD to derelicts, as well as the impressive 50 percent recovery rate Dr. Humphry Osmond was currently achieving by using LSD to cure alcoholics at Weyburn General Hospital in Saskatchewan. (After thirteen years, one-third of the subjects in Osmond's study would still be sober, a third would have benefited, and another third would continue to be alcoholics. These were exactly the same percentages of recidivism and recovery that Tim and Frank Barron had discovered in their pioneering study of those awaiting psychotherapy at Kaiser Permanente Hospital.)

Huxley graciously agreed to sit in on Tim's planning meetings at Harvard. Once the project was under way, he even offered to take mushrooms with Tim and his fellow researchers. During October and November, Huxley regularly attended research group meetings. Often, he would close his eyes during meetings, entirely detach himself from the scene, and go into a controlled meditation trance. Although this practice unnerved some of the Harvard people, who equated consciousness with talk, Huxley would then open his eyes and utter "a diamond pure comment." The concept that eventually emerged from these meetings involved a pilot study in which subjects would be treated like astronauts. After they had been carefully briefed, they would be expected to run their own spacecraft and make observations that they could transmit back to ground control. To help them through their trips, tape recordings of music would be made available as well as reproductions of paintings.

From Tim's point of view, the only problem with these meetings was that they were all talk and no tripping. Sandoz Laboratories solved that problem by sending Tim a cardboard box containing four small gray pillboxes. Inside each pillbox was a brown bottle filled with round pink pills, each bearing a two-milligram dose of psilocybin. Tim put the box into an office filing cabinet for safekeeping. For the next seven months, he would continue receiving what seemed like an unlimited supply of pills from Sandoz.

On the night of October 30, 1960, Tim had a date. Before dinner, he and his date drank whiskey and soda, then polished off a bottle of burgundy with their steak. By then, Tim was in what he would later describe as "a fine alcohol stupor." Some friends joined them and the drinking continued. After a while, everyone started talking about the mushrooms. "The hell with all this phony talk and measurement business," a guest whom Leary would later call "O'Donnell" said. "Let's get the mushrooms and start swinging." An ex–football player named "Charlie" who lived in the house with his girlfriend "Rhona" seconded the notion. "I had been lecturing all year on research philosophy and ethics," Tim would later write, "and how you should be collaborative, and not use your position as a scientist to get an unfair advantage, and about sharing information and sharing the power to make decisions about the subjects. And that was the way we had set up the mushroom research . . . The last thing in the world I wanted to be was a worrying square and the last thing I wanted to put down was spontaneous."

In the name of spontaneity, Tim worked out a compromise that established the manner in which the entire Harvard Psychedelic Project would be run. To honor his contract with his absent fellow researchers, Tim decided to give mushrooms to his dinner companions but not take any himself. He drove with them to his office and came back out to the car carrying a glass of water so that everyone could take two pills—half the recommended dose—right away. That way, the effect could start building on the way home. Back home, everyone but Tim took two more pills. An hour later, they took two more. Tim took two as well. Finally, after an hour and fifteen minutes, everyone started feeling the psilocybin. O'Donnell began having an authentically bad trip. Picking up a kitchen knife, he slashed at a lamp cord. At 2:30 A.M., O'Donnell demanded more. Tim refused. "You've got those pills and I want them," O'Donnell snarled, his face twisted with rage. "Are you going to give them to me or do I have to start trouble?" Too high to be bothered, Tim laughed at him and O'Donnell went to bed.

The next morning, after just two hours of sleep, Tim rushed off to class. He told the graduate student who had been in his office with George Litwin when they first began planning the project what he had done. The graduate student was not pleased. He felt Tim and his friends had used the psilocybin frivolously and unscientifically. And what about the issues of trust and responsibility? Tim apologized. But he also said he was glad it happened. He now not only knew how to time the dosage so as to remain in control but also had learned that observers could take a smaller amount and go part of the way on the visionary journey.

Claiming now to understand it all, O'Donnell then arrived in Tim's office. The problem was those damn research meetings. Everyone was too scared to take the pills. The whole research business was fake anyway, a phony ritual to counteract fear of the mystery. O'Donnell told Tim they should keep all this a secret. They should have a good time with the mushroom pills and learn from them. How could Tim collaborate with people who were afraid of fun and ecstasy and kept using science as their defense? "I knew he was right," Tim would later write. "It was some residual conformist, prudish cop-out feeling of mine to want to have ecstasy above ground. To make the joyous mystery public and socially acceptable." In words that echoed his Catholic upbringing, he added, "It was hard for me to accept the fact that you can't surrender to God's grace and win a Sunday school merit badge at the same time."

The next night was Halloween. In Tim's sprawling house in Newton Center, Susan, who had just turned thirteen, was hosting a party. Ten teenage boys and nine teenage girls were there. Along with the kids came parents who expected to be entertained. Tim sat around the kitchen table with them drinking scotch. At eleven, the boys left. Upstairs, the girls began their pajama party. In the kitchen, Tim, Charlie the ex–football player, and O'Donnell continued drinking. Discovering that he had run out of cigarettes, Tim asked Charlie for a Marlboro. "Sure," Charlie replied with a grin. "But it will cost you a mushroom." Tim gave him a pill. When Tim asked him for a light, Charlie demanded another pill. For the first time, Tim realized how much power he had. "They all wanted the bread of dreams, the flesh of the gods. And I was charged with the one ring of power in my pocket. I was feeling that miserable pleasure of the millionaire." Tim handed twenty-two-year-old Charlie the whole bottle and told him he was now in charge. Charlie shook the contents of the bottle into his palm and divided up the spoils. Tim and O'Donnell each took ten pills. Charlie took eleven. They washed the psilocybin down with scotch and waited.

From all the literature he had read on the subject, Tim reckoned he had just broken the world record for ingesting psilocybin at a single sitting. Twenty minutes later, pressure started building on his eardrums as cresting waves of sensation rippled down his body. The walls and ceiling of the kitchen began to vibrate with electric color. The floor shimmered like phosphorescent lemon Jell-O. From upstairs came a burst of music. As though from a thousand years ago, Tim remembered the party and the nine prepubescent, sexually charged girls, his own daughter among them, who were having a pajama party.

As the three men discussed whether the drug turned the sex drive on or off, O'Donnell announced that he was going upstairs. "I thought of upstairs," Tim would later write, "and I thought of the girls and the slumber party. Waves of guilt washed over me for having dragged my kids around from country to country, school to school, house to house, and Susan missing friends and the warm cozy routine schedule and this was her first party, her first social event, and how excited she was and nothing must mar it, no clowning-around adults."

When Tim finally managed to make his way upstairs, he discovered the girls standing in the center of the room and staring at O'Donnell, who was lying in bed. Susan watched silently as Charlie tried to get O'Donnell out of there. Tim and Charlie told O'Donnell this was the girls' party and that he did not belong there. Pulling O'Donnell to his feet, they hustled him out the door. In the hallway, O'Donnell drew away from them, "his eyes glaring, his lips drawn back in animal rage. I had never seen such a visage of evil." Angrily, O'Donnell demanded, "Who are you to say what is right? Pampered middle-class dears in there watching television and playing records, growing up to be miserable middle-class bitches. Maybe the greatest thing that can happen to them in their life is for me to stir them up a little." Tim wondered if O'Donnell wasn't right. What right did he have to interfere? Was it his job to protect tribal codes by identifying with the New England middle class and their insane terror of nonconformity? Although Tim felt that what O'Donnell was doing was wrong, he could not tell him why. Maybe O'Donnell had been sent here to shake the girls free of their middle-class shackles.

O'Donnell was about to go back into the girls' room when suddenly, like Moses on the mountain, Tim was struck by a lightning bolt of revelation. "I'll tell you why you can't go into Susan's room," he told O'Donnell, bringing down from his own private mountain what in time would become the first commandment of the psychedelic era. "Because it is her trip, her territory, her party, and she doesn't want you in there. You have the right to do anything you want so long as you don't lay your trip on anyone else." Based on what Tim Leary would later call "cellular equality" and "mutual respect," "the first ethical law had been forged." O'Donnell, now reduced to making growling noises, bolted toward the bedroom door. Grabbing him, Tim and Charlie pulled him away. Accusing them of being cops, O'Donnell tried again to enter the room, but Tim and Charlie kept him outside. The issue remained unsettled until Charlie's girlfriend Rhona pronounced what seemed to Tim to be the ultimate law: "Grownups don't join pajama parties. It just isn't done." Thanks to Rhona, and the fact that they were all beginning to come down from the trip, the conflict was finally resolved.

On successive nights, Tim Leary had witnessed two bad trips and how traumatizing such experiences could be to everyone. Yet he never discussed this with anyone. Nor did he decide to conduct further research in a more formal and structured manner. "Timothy called me," George

Litwin recalled, "and said they had already taken psilocybin at his place. They had taken some and they wanted to take some more. So I went over there to see what was up with our experiment, and I realized Timothy was totally violating any contract with the research we had."

Eight days later, on November 8, 1960, John F. Kennedy defeated Richard Milhous Nixon by a narrow margin to become the first Catholic president of the United States. As votes were still being counted, Aldous Huxley and Humphry Osmond visited Tim. In a gray flannel suit with his hair cut very short and his brilliant blue eyes glittering, Tim looked to Osmond like the archetypal American college professor. His great personal charm was evident. Tim was not only very likable but also so imaginative and intelligent that Huxley and Osmond enjoyed listening to him explain, with what was obviously deep sincerity, the scientific basis of his interest in psychedelic studies.

After they left that night, Huxley confided in Osmond how fortunate it was that such important work was about to be carried on at Harvard in the very same department started by William James, a seeker of visions through the use of nitrous oxide. Osmond worried that the disciples of B. F. Skinner at Harvard might be too fond of nitpicking. But his primary concern was that Tim seemed a bit stuffy to do real justice to the research.

Although Tim had already broken all the research rules he helped set up, he somehow persuaded both Huxley and Osmond that he would carry forward the tradition of quiet, serious psychedelic research to which they both had dedicated themselves for years. Fourteen years later, Osmond would write how incredible it seemed to him that Tim had never made any attempt to follow Huxley's precept of "doing good stealthily." Had either of these men understood who they were really dealing with that night, "We would have realized Timothy only appeared to be a sober, calculating, planning, scientific sort, while he was actually a visionary person whose imagination needed constant stimulation and focus for him to be able to function in the responsible style of the person he appeared to us to be. As a consequence, Aldous and I made all the wrong moves." Osmond went on to label Tim an "Extroverted Intuition-Feeling" type who "lives in an almost totally hypothetical future and copes with life's vagaries through imagination. Inspirations are his *metier*. His world is literally chaotic—a dynamic, ever-changing, exciting swirl of action, out of which the Intuitive-type tries to ascertain what is possible; he cares less for what 'is' or 'was' or even 'will be' than for what 'could be' or 'should be.'" "To Timothy," Osmond wrote, "it didn't really matter if many people fell by the wayside, because the object was to create the greatest benefit for the greatest number. This is the millenialist's view of history, much the same as the outlook of another Intuition-Feeling type, Adolph Hitler."

Had Osmond and Huxley understood any of this on that night in November 1960, they could have shut down the Harvard Psychedelic Project before it began. Instead, even as the torch of government in America was being passed to a new generation, they handed the future of psychedelic research to the wrong man.

TWELVE

On November 15, Tim Leary responded to a note from David McClelland, asking him to "put on record the design of our mushroom research." In a three-page letter, Tim wrote that the purpose of the research was to "determine the conditions under which psilocybin can be used to broaden and deepen human experience; to determine which persons are benefited by the drug, and in which direction; and to determine methods of making the beneficial effects durable and recoverable without subsequent exposure to the chemical." Despite the bad trips he had already seen and the undeniable fact that no procedures for choosing subjects had been established, Tim wrote, "The selection procedures assure that the need for using an antidote in one of our group sessions is probably less than the need for an antidote at a large cocktail party." Tim closed his letter by noting that he would be glad to answer any questions as well as make summary data about the research available if requested.

On November 26, Tim gave psilocybin to the poet Allen Ginsberg and his lover, Peter Orlovsky. Ginsberg had already taken peyote, mescaline, and LSD in the same Stanford University hospital where the novelist Ken Kesey first experienced the drug. Having come to Boston to address the Group for the Advancement of Psychiatry, Ginsberg read from his poems "Laughing Gas," "Mescaline," and "Lysergic Acid," all soon to be published in *Kaddish and Other Poems,* during his talk. The reaction was less than positive. The younger psychiatrists dismissed Ginsberg as clinically insane. The older psychiatrists, Freudians, told the poet that he had suffered a complete disintegration of the ego structure, descended into the id, and then re-created and integrated his ego in slightly changed form. Only Humphry Osmond seemed to understand what Ginsberg was talking about. Osmond and a colleague suggested that Ginsberg might want to meet a psychologist at Harvard who was working with a grant from Sandoz Laboratories.

After he returned to New York City, Ginsberg wrote the psychologist a letter, saying he would be honored to participate in the experiment. One week later, Tim knocked at Ginsberg's door. Although the poet was impressed that a Harvard professor would come all the way to the East Village just to see him, he could not help but feel that Tim was a little naïve. He seemed to have no idea that virtually every poet whom Ginsberg knew in San Francisco had already taken peyote or mescaline and smoked pot. Ginsberg promptly turned Tim on to marijuana and sat him down for a long, scholarly talk. The two men hit it off immediately. "I was surprised that he was such a jivey, friendly, amiable, open guy," Ginsberg later recalled. "And I saw right away that he saw me like a wise Jewish patriarch with a family rather than a creepy beatnik. So I decided to go to Boston and experiment with him."

For more than a decade, Ginsberg and fellow Beats like Jack Kerouac, Gregory Corso, and William Burroughs had lived in voluntary poverty while using whatever drugs they could find to aid their search for illumination. Jeanne DiPrima, the daughter of Beat poet Diane DiPrima, grew up with these people as her extended family. "They were sharing flats," she remembered. "They were sharing beds. They were sharing bodies. They were sharing wine. They were sharing poetry. They were sharing music. They were sharing painting. Everybody was doing speed. It was the beatnik drug. The world revolved around them. Their problems and their angst."

Although Ginsberg himself had long since become accustomed to living in utter chaos, even he found what was going on in Newton Center when he arrived on a sunny November weekend to be very strange indeed. "Leary had this big beautiful house, and everybody there was wandering around like it was some happy cocktail party," Ginsberg recalled. "They were all so cheerful and optimistic and convinced that their kind of environment would be welcomed as a polite, scholarly, socially acceptable, perfectly reasonable pursuit and would spread through the university and automatically be taken on as part of the curriculum. Like Leary couldn't conceive of meeting any academic opposition. I kept saying, 'You have no idea what you're going to meet or what you're up against.' But he was already thinking in terms of 'We'll turn on Arthur Schlesinger and then we'll turn on John F. Kennedy.'" For his part, Tim was delighted to welcome Ginsberg, "the secretary general of the world's poets, beatniks, anarchists, socialists, free-sex/love cultists," to his home.

On Sunday morning, while the poet and Tim's other houseguests—Frank Barron, Peter Orlovsky, and his brother Lafcadio, currently on leave from a mental hospital—were all still sleeping, Tim did his best to act like a loving father to his two children. At 9:00 A.M., Jackie and a friend who had spent the night ate breakfast in the kitchen. Then the friend went off to Mass. When he returned, it was with the news that he had told his father all about the party Tim had given the previous night for the Harvard football team, as well as the dollar Tim had given each boy to act as a bartender. Fortunately, the friend's father was Irish, so Tim figured he would get away with that. Susan then came into the house with three girlfriends. They ran upstairs for clothes and records and then went off with a picnic lunch. Half awake, Frank Barron came downstairs to make his own breakfast. Beside him, Ginsberg hopped around with "nearsighted crow motions" as he cooked eggs. After breakfast, while Ginsberg and Orlovsky read *The New York Times,* Barron went upstairs to watch pro football on the TV in Susan's room. After the game ended, Barron rounded up Tim and his housemates for a Kennedy-like game of touch football out behind the garage.

After dinner, sitting hunched over a teacup in the kitchen, peering through thick black-rimmed glasses with a crack in the left lens, Ginsberg began to talk about his recent experiences with *ayahuasca* in the Peruvian jungles, and about as the role of the *curandero* who acted as a guide, offering solace and strength to those on the drug. Chain-smoking as he talked, Ginsberg cast a spell. Tim felt as though Ginsberg was getting him into shape so when the poet finally took the mushrooms, Tim would be there to help him. In due time, Tim brought out a little bottle and gave Ginsberg eighteen pills. Ginsberg went upstairs with Peter Orlovsky, and put some Beethoven and Wagner on the record player that Tim had brought in from Susan's room. Turning off all the lights, so there was just a glow in the bedroom, Ginsberg took off his clothes.

Half an hour later, Susan came home and went upstairs to do her homework. Tim followed her and checked on Ginsberg, who was now lying on top of the blanket with his glasses off and his eyes completely dilated. Scared and unhappy, Ginsberg was fighting through panic, fear, and nausea as he tried to find meaning in this experience. Orlovsky lay beside him, his eyes shut as though he was sleeping. Ginsberg asked Tim what he thought of him. Tim told the poet that he thought he was a great man, and that it was good to know him. Then Tim went to check on Susan. She was in her room, sitting on the carpet, reading in the shadows. Tim scolded his teenage daughter about ruining her eyes and turned on the lights.

Suddenly, Wagner came blasting from the record player in the next room. Summoned by the great horns of *Gotterdammerung*, Ginsberg had seen an image of the Star of Bethlehem out the window. From the outer limits of the cosmos, the horns of judgment were calling not only on him but on all human consciousness to declare itself as *the* consciousness. Deciding to heed the call, Ginsberg got out of bed, walked from the room, and went downstairs. Orlovsky, also naked, followed. As Susan sat cross-legged on her bed brushing her hair, Tim heard the patter of bare feet going by her door. He opened it in time to see naked buttocks heading down the steps. Grinning, Tim told his daughter that Peter was running around without any clothes on. Susan picked up her hair curlers, brush, and pins, and headed for the third floor as Tim went down to the study. He got there just in time to hear Ginsberg, wearing nothing but his glasses, with a holy gleam in his eyes, proclaim that he was in fact the Messiah, come to preach love to the world. With Orlovsky by his side, he would walk through the streets and teach people to stop hating. Their nakedness would be the first act of revolution against the destroyers of the human image. "Well, Allen," Tim said like the psychologist he was trained to be. "That sounds like a pretty good idea."

"Do you believe that I'm the Messiah?" Ginsberg asked. "I can prove it. I'm going to cure your hearing. Take off your hearing machine." Playing along, Tim put his hearing aid on the desk. "Now your glasses." Tim put them there as well. Pointing out that Ginsberg was still wearing his own glasses, Tim asked, "Why don't you cure your own vision?" Surprised, Ginsberg replied, "Yes, you're right. I will." The poet took off his glasses and placed them on the desk. Now a blind Messiah, Ginsberg announced, "We're going down to the city streets and tell the people about peace and love. And then get lots of great people on to a big telephone network to settle all this warfare bit."

"Fine," Frank Barron said. "Why not do the telephone bit first? Right here in the house?"

"Who we gonna call?" Orlovsky asked.

"Kerouac on Long Island," Ginsberg answered. "Kennedy and Khrushchev and Bill Burroughs in Paris and Norman Mailer in the psycho ward in Bellevue," (where the novelist had been briefly committed after stabbing his wife, Adele).

Picking up the phone, Ginsberg said, "Hello, operator. This is God. G-O-D. I want to talk to Kerouac on Long Island." Reasonably enough, the operator asked for the number. As always, when psychedelics were involved, the devil was in the details. Who in a state of ecstasy could remember anyone's phone number? Although Naomi Ginsberg had already been dead for four years, Ginsberg gave the operator his mother's phone number. When the operator could not connect him, Ginsberg went back upstairs to get Kerouac's number from the address book he always carried.

Alternately shouting and giggling, Ginsberg finally got to talk to Kerouac. The conversation went on and on until Tim said, "Hey, Allen, for the cost of this phone call, we could pay his way up here by plane." With an apologetic look, Ginsberg ended the call by saying, "Okay, Jack, I have to go now. But you've got to take the mushrooms. And let's settle this quarrel between Kennedy and Khrushchev."

Sitting down on the big couch in the living room, Ginsberg told Tim about the visions he had been having of cosmic electronic networks, how much it meant to him when Tim told him he was a great man, how these mushrooms had opened the door to women and heterosexuality for him, and how he could now see real family life ahead. Still wanting to get in touch with everyone he knew to spread the news about this amazing substance, he asked, "What about calling Norman Mailer in Bellevue?"

"I don't think they'd let a call go through to him, Allen," Tim replied.

"Well, it all depends how we come on."

"I don't think coming on as Allen Ginsberg would help in that league. Or coming on as the Messiah either."

"You could come on as big psychologists and make demanding noises about the patient," Ginsberg suggested, relenting only when they decided that this would be too much trouble. While Ginsberg and Orlovsky went upstairs to put on robes, Tim heated up milk for them in the kitchen. When Ginsberg came back down, he and Tim began planning the psychedelic revolution.

Sitting in the kitchen in his bathrobe, sipping hot milk, Ginsberg urged Tim to give everyone the mushrooms. No one had the right to keep them from anyone else. All sorts of new holy rituals needed to be developed through ministers who would ensure that the experience would be basically religious in nature. Despite the feelings of great optimism that the psilocybin had generated within him, Ginsberg was still a beatnik at heart. He knew that the Terror would always be there. The terror of Moloch. The terror of Nazi national Golgotha. The terror of the void. The terror of death. The terror of Rockland State Hospital. All the terrors against which Ginsberg, Kerouac, and Neal Cassady had been rebelling for years under the shadow of nuclear annihilation.

Sitting in Tim's kitchen in Newton Center, Allen Ginsberg believed this brand-new mystic vision could conquer all. Although as a crazy beatnik poet, Ginsberg himself might be far too easy to put down, Timothy Leary, a serious scientist and a Harvard professor, was the perfect person for the job. Tim's credentials were obvious. And he was the only one with unlimited access to these magic pills. Going upstairs, Ginsberg returned with his address book, which read like a who's who of the cultural elite in America, and announced that he would start making phone calls. To the poet Robert Lowell and the writer Muriel Rukeyser. To Kerouac of course and the playwright LeRoi Jones. To genius jazz musicians like Dizzy Gillespie and Thelonious Monk. To painters, publishers, and novelists. Ginsberg had all their names, telephone numbers, and addresses. At a moment's notice, he could get in touch with everyone who mattered. None of these people would dare say no to him.

For Tim, all this was incredibly seductive. An authentic American icon was offering to personally initiate him into a social circle to which he could never have otherwise belonged. How could he possibly refuse? Like all consummate salesmen, Tim loved to be sold on an idea, especially when he would profit from it. From this moment on, Tim Leary vowed to devote his energies to "the ancient underground society of alchemists, artists, mystics, alienated visionaries, drop-outs, and the disenchanted young, the sons arising." Considering how little he had known about these people a week ago, Tim's conversion to the cause was remarkably swift. But then who was he to resist the clarion call of Allen Ginsberg?

By Monday afternoon, rumors about what had happened in Newton Center on Sunday had spread across Harvard Yard. These were not the usual run-of-the-mill Cambridge rumors about some professor's public drunkenness or marital infidelity. These involved beatniks, naked poets, junkies, and homosexuals, not to mention wild drug parties and orgies masquerading as legitimate research. David McClelland called Tim to ask what the hell was going on. In response, Tim laughed and told him, "I'll send you the reports from the session as soon as they are typed. It was a good session. God would approve. We're learning a lot."

Meanwhile, Tim went right on conducting sessions. During lunch one day at the Faculty Club, Tim and Huston Smith, the MIT professor who helped bring Huxley to Cambridge, flipped through their date books trying to come up with a mutually acceptable date to take psilocybin together. Tim looked at Smith with a mischievous grin and asked, "What about New Year's Day?" On New Year's Day 1961, Smith ingested two tablets of psilocybin. His more adventurous wife, Kendra, took three. For Smith, as for his mentor Aldous Huxley, the drug made real what before had always been purely conceptual. As Smith later recalled, "I was on this divan with my eyes closed virtually the whole time and it took about eleven hours. Tim came in at one point and I opened my eyes and he said, 'How's it going?' I said, 'Tim, I hope you know what you're playing around with here.' Because at that moment, I had the distinct conviction that I was mounting this ladder of being and the intensity and the awe was increasing. It was like I was on the brink of nirvana and I said, 'I have the feeling if I climb one more step on this ladder, the emotional intensity will be so strong that my frame will not be able to bear it. I want you to know from where I am now that this is an absolute conviction that I could depart this life.'" Despite his reservations, Smith soon became a regular at Tim's psilocybin sessions.

Making good on his promise, Ginsberg brought Charles Olson, whom Leary later referred to as "the center or big daddy" of the influential Black Mountain school of poets, into the Leary circle. A former speechwriter for Franklin Delano Roosevelt, Olson was fifty years old and working as a postman in Gloucester, Massachusetts. "I was very worried," Ginsberg recalled, "because Olson was a big guy, and you never know. I remember Frank Barron saying, 'Oh, Ginsberg, you're a worry wart.' But Olson took to it like a duck to water. He thought it was absolutely great. That was probably the first of the literary intellectual people I suggested Tim connect with. I think after him, others like Robert Creeley and even maybe Robert Duncan tried it out."

With Olson in the fold, Tim wrote Arthur Koestler, author of *Darkness at Noon,* whom he had first met in London in 1959. "The big, new, hot issue these days in many American circles is DRUGS. Have you been

tuned in on the noise?" After describing how he first took the mushrooms, Tim noted:

> For the person who is prepared, they provide a soul-wrenching mys-
> tical experience. Remember your enlightenments in the Franco
> prison? Very similar to what we are producing. We have had cases of
> housewives understanding, experiencing satori . . . who have never
> heard of Zen. We are working to keep these drugs free and uncon-
> trolled. Two tactics. We are offering the experience to distinguished
> creative people. Artists, poets, writers, scholars. We've learned a
> tremendous amount by listening to them tell us what they've
> learned from the experience . . . So. How does it sound? If you are
> interested, I'll send some mushrooms over to you. Or if you've al-
> ready been involved I'd like to hear about your reaction . . .

Koestler replied that he was interested in trying the mushrooms. Described by his own biographer as man with an inferiority complex the size
of "a cathedral," Koestler "drank heavily, got into fights with French
intellectuals and American policemen and wrecked a long line of automobiles. A compulsive womanizer, he was married three times, had innumerable one-night stands and thought nothing of juggling five members
of what he called his 'harem' simultaneously." Koestler was said to have
raped Jill Craigie, the late wife of Michael Foot, a Labor member of Par-
liament. A few days before he arrived in Cambridge, Koestler phoned
Tim from Michigan to say he had been given psilocybin there and "it was
the worst experience of his life." By promising to serve nothing stronger
than good French wine, Tim nonetheless persuaded him to visit.

At Harvard, Tim took Koestler to lunch with B. F. Skinner and then
to a round of meetings with other well-known faculty members, among
whom Koestler caused "quite a stir." After dinner with Frank and Nancy
Barron, Tim took Koestler home to observe a mushroom session with
Charles Olson. Out came the box of pink pills. Impulsively, Koestler
washed down ten of them with his highball. Soon the novelist was com-
muning with Bach as he never had before.

The next morning, Koestler told Tim the pills had not affected him
at all because he had such a strong mind. That night, he brought two
bottles of fine French wine and a bottle of scotch to Tim's house. He told
his host he would stick with alcohol, preferring it in every way to the

mushrooms, which "whirl you inside." Koestler also said that "there's no wisdom there. I solved the secret of the universe last night, but this morning I forgot what it was. There is no quick and easy path to wisdom. Sweat and toil are the price of knowledge."

A disappointed Tim visited Frank Barron in his office the next day, seeking advice. Barron suggested that the problem might have been that everyone at the session except Koestler had been with a woman. Barron's comment made Tim realize that God and sex were the two central beats of this dance. Whenever trouble appeared at a session, it was because someone was disconnected from either the spirit or the flesh. Prayer or loving physical contact solved the problem every time. Tim also realized he had yet come to terms with this issue in his own life. "I was too much an Irish Catholic, too prudish to deal with it. Too Western Christian to realize that God and Sex are one, that God for a man is woman, that the direct path to God is through the divine union of male-female."

As a social scientist, Tim wanted to understand everything intellectually before he plunged into the experience. How could he possibly enjoy the ultimate ecstasy of the sensual-sexual experience at night when he had to report dutifully for work at Harvard the next morning? Due in no small part to his now almost daily intake of psilocybin, the dichotomy between Tim's personal and professional life began to grow wider than ever before.

On January 13, Tim traveled with Pearl Chan, his secretary at the Center for Personality Research with whom he was having an affair, to visit Allen Ginsberg in New York. Tim arrived at Ginsberg's "terminally dingy" Lower East Side apartment around 5:00 P.M. In the kitchen, Jack Kerouac, already drunk, sat at the table wearing a baseball hat and a bright red lumber jacket. Also there were Bob Donlin, a small wiry Irishman from New Jersey; Peter and Lafcadio Orlovsky; Peter's sister, who was attending nursing school in New Jersey; and the black poet Bob Kaufman who lived upstairs and had just dropped in for a visit.

Tim and Kerouac began discussing sports. Not only did they share the experience of having grown up Irish Catholic in New England but as a boy Kerouac had also played the game Tim described in *Flashbacks* as "baseball-solitaire with rosters of imaginary players whose statistics— hits, runs, errors—he recorded." Despite the bond between them, Tim wrote, "Jack Kerouac was scary. Behind the dark good looks of a burly lumberjack was a New England mill-town sullenness, Canuck-Catholic soggy distrust. This is one unhappy kid, I thought." As these were "the days of naturalistic research" with "no imposing ideas," Tim did not bother to distribute questionnaires or assess the relative mental stability of those about to participate in the experience. Instead, he said to Kerouac, "Here are the mushrooms. About ten pills is a good dose. You do the rest. Have fun, and write us a report afterwards."

Kerouac took twenty milligrams of psilocybin as did Bob Donlin and Peter Orlovsky. Tim joined in as well while Ginsberg abstained so he could act as guru and ground control. Swaying to music from the phonograph, Kerouac's eyes popped with joy as he weaved together a Joycean monologue of his own making. Spinning out Zen riddles, he quoted from Shakespeare, reviewed his own books, told stories about his adventures as king of the beatniks, and cracked himself up with funny stories. Standing on the bureau, he did an imitation of a British army colonel, then one of Charlie Chaplin. An imaginary football tucked beneath his arm, he ran for a touchdown as though he was still playing for Coach Lou Little at Columbia. Kerouac sang a French Canadian song. He rushed to the window and screamed love at passersby. Somersaulting across the bed, he rocked and rolled. All the while, the words just kept pouring out of him.

As though the session was just another drunken barroom episode, Donlin said, "Hey, let's pop another five." Ginsberg looked at Tim, shrugged, and said, "Why not?" In an entirely different frame of mind, Tim realized that he had never before dealt with someone who, as he would later write, "tried to control, dominate, and overwhelm the experience like Kerouac." Walking into the dark bedroom, Tim flopped down on the bed in despair. "Kerouac had propelled me into my first negative trip. Maybe it was the drabness of the slum, so different from our carefully prepared session rooms. Perhaps it was jittery New York itself, never a town for serene philosophers. Or was it Kerouac's French-Catholic gloom? Anyway, down I went." Doubting himself and his newfound mission in the world, Tim wondered why he had ever thought he could eliminate suffering when the "pus of despair" oozed from his own soul. "My life was a fraud. I was a miserable child, abandoned by my father, breaking my mother's heart, driving my wife to suicide, incapable of true love and levity. Alone and lonely."

Just as Tim had done in Newton Center, Ginsberg came into the darkened bedroom to rescue him. His concern helped bring Tim back. Tim rejoined Kerouac's "barroom reality" and the session continued for another twelve hours. At dawn, Ginsberg went to the store for groceries and returned to cook breakfast. Then everyone fell asleep.

Later that afternoon, Kerouac woke up depressed, vowing never to take mushrooms again. Later, Tim Leary wrote that he told him, "The hangover is from the liquor. Mushrooms don't lead to a hangover. And there's no reason to feel guilty and remorseful. It wasn't a drunken brawl. It was an innocent spiritual cloud ride." Kerouac grinned. "Yeah," he said. "That's what it was. Amazing how so many people could be together for so long in such a small room and have no bad feeling or tension. It was a real love feast." "Kerouac was drinking a bit in those days," recalled Ginsberg "so the psilocybin was good for him. The great black poet Bob Kaufman was also there. He lived in the same apartment house and came down to visit and got quite moved by the experience of the psilocybin. I didn't take it. Leary and Kerouac did and that was when Kerouac said, 'Coach Leary, walking on water wasn't built in a day.' A fantastic statement. He also said, 'I think I'll take a piss out the window.' He didn't do it. He just said it. It was sort of Shakespearean exuberance. And I think he wrote Leary a long letter. A beautiful letter."

Three days later, back in Cambridge, Tim did receive a session report from Kerouac:

> Mainly, I felt like a floating Khan on a magic carpet with my interesting lieutenants and gods . . . some ancient feeling about old geheuls [sic] in the grass, and temples, exactly also like the sensation I got drunk on pulque floating in the Xochimilco gardens laden with flowers and singers . . . some old Golden Age dream of man, very nice. I do think we took too much. Yet there were no side evil effects. In fact I came home and had the first serious long talk with my mother, for 3 days and 3 nights (not consecutive) but we sat talking about everything yet went about the routine of washing, sleeping, eating, cleaning up the yard and house, and returning to long talk chairs at the proper time. That was great. I learned I loved her more than I thought. The mushroom high carried on for exactly till Wednesday Jan. 18th. I kept it alive by drinking Christian Brothers port on the rocks. Suddenly on Friday the 20th (day of Inauguration) [President John F. Kennedy] it started all up again, on port, but very mushroomy, and that was a swinging day, yakking in bars, bookstores, homes around Northport [Long Island] (which I never

do). We were at the extremest point goofing on a cloud watching the movie of existence. Everybody seemed innocent. Lafcadio became St. Innocent the Patriarch of Holy Russia. Donlin became the paraclete . . . It was a definite Satori. Full of Psychic clairvoyance (but you must remember this is not half as good as the peaceful ecstasy of simple Samadhi trance as I described that in Dharma Bums.) . . . I saw you, Leary, as a Jesuit Father. Donlin called you Doctor Leary. I saw Allen as Sariputra (the Indian saint.) My old idea of St. Peter (about Peter Orlovsky) was strengthened. I saw Peter's sister Marie as Ste. Catherine. Bob Kaufman was a Michoacan Indian chief . . . Pearl became a Lotus of indescribable beauty sitting there in the form of a Buddha woman Bikkushshini . . .

In sum, there is temporary addiction but no withdrawal symptoms whatsoever. The faculty of remembering names and what one has learned, is heightened so fantastically that we could develop the greatest scholars and scientists in the world with this stuff. There's no harm in Sacred Mushrooms and much good will come it. (For instance, I remembered historical details I'd completely forgotten before the mushrooms, and names names million of names categories and data).

Three months later, Kerouac wrote Tim to ask, "How about contributing to my next prose masterpiece by sending me (as you sent Burroughs) a bottle of SM pills, with a bill if that is feasible. Allen said I could knock off a daily chapter with 2 SM's and be done with a whole novel in a month. Really serious about that, if you can manage it. I'm curious to know what would come out. As you know, in NY, there was no chance to write anything." A month later, he wrote again:

Mushrooms just arrived, took only one, had hangover and benny blues no feel better. In answer to yr. question, "what suggestions about what to do with psilocybin" Why not a college course called INTUITIONAL RESEARCH . . . When I was at peak of psilocybin high in January I seemed to know everything about the Khans of Mongolia. Information certainly didnt [sic] come from outside since I never studied the subject. This may be silly, but maybe psilocybin releases genetic memories, or maybe re-incarnation memories, who knows.

In a handwritten postscript, Kerouac added, "Later:—Took 2 more, then one more next day—got high but had funny hangover of brainwashed emptiness— . . . Me no take no more (But brainwash doesn't last beyond the drug) Jack."

"Throughout the night Kerouac remained unmoveably the Catholic carouser," Tim Leary would later write, "an old-style Bohemian without a hippie bone in his body. Jack Kerouac opened the neural doors to the future, looked ahead, and didn't see his place in it. Not for him the utopian pluralist optimism of the sixties." Kerouac's decision not to proceed any further down the path of psychedelic exploration effectively removed him from playing any significant personal role in the social and cultural revolution that his own writings helped create. Until the day he died in 1969 at the age of forty-seven, Kerouac's drug of choice was alcohol. It was yet another trait he shared with Tim.

THIRTEEN

Going by subway with Allen Ginsberg and Peter Orlovsky, Tim Leary journeyed uptown in Manhattan to bring psilocybin to the poet Robert Lowell. An alcoholic who had been hospitalized repeatedly for manic depression, Lowell would over the course of his long and distinguished career win three Pulitzer Prizes and two National Book Awards for poetry. In a letter written in 1959 to fellow poet Elizabeth Bishop, after a prior visit from Ginsberg and Orlovsky, Lowell had described the Beats as "phony" and "pathetic and doomed. How can you make a go for long by reciting so-so verse to half-jeering swarms of college students?"

On their way up to Lowell's apartment, Ginsberg explained to Orlovsky that their purpose was to loosen Lowell up and make him happier. If Lowell had a great session, there was no telling how much it might influence other intellectuals to join their movement. "We went to Robert Lowell and gave him a small dose and sat with him for the afternoon," Ginsberg would later recall. "And that was all right. He got a little gloomy but then he was a gloomy man at certain times. I don't know if it did him any harm. At the door leaving, I remember I said, '*Amor vincit omnia*.' Love conquers all. And he said, 'I'm not so sure of that.'"

"Lowell," Tim Leary would write in his account of their meeting, "always the gentleman, took me aside and wrung my hand in gratitude. 'Now I know what Blake and St. John of the Cross were talking about,' he said. 'This experience is what I was seeking when I became a Catholic.' I wasn't sure whether I believed him or not. For most people the dose would have been too low to produce transcendental effects." Even Tim was forced to admit he was not at all sure what this session had proved. According to Tim, Ginsberg replied that "a brilliant but unstable genius who's suffered nervous breakdowns can take psychedelics safely, if the setting is secure." When Tim responded that he did not think the session had changed Lowell's life and perhaps they should have given him the option "to have a heavy-dose experience and go all the way," Ginsberg replied that this would have been even more risky for them because he did not want to be known as "the guy who put America's leading poet around the bend." Tim said he still felt disappointed. "My take with Kerouac and Lowell is that we're batting zero for two in the Life-Change Revelation League."

Tim, Ginsberg, and Orlovsky then headed downtown to the apartment of Barney Rosset, the founder of Grove Press, whom Ginsberg described as the "Mickey Mantle of introverted intellectuals." If they could succeed in turning on one of the most influential publishers in America, they could "illuminate New York and London." They arrived at Rosset's "elegant townhouse" just as he and his girlfriend were finishing dinner. Tim suggested that Ginsberg and Rosset take all the remaining psilocybin. Tim, Orlovsky, and Barney's girlfriend, whom Tim called "Zelda" in *Flashbacks* would take mescaline, which was then still "freely available by mail order from several New York pharmaceutical houses." Barney Rosset recalled, "I didn't know anything about Leary. Nor about LSD or psilocybin. My girlfriend was twenty. Half Jewish and half black, very beautiful but impossible. He gave her and me a lot to take. And being simple fools, we did. Allen and Peter and Leary went off to play music and my girlfriend and I were in bed getting hallucinations. I began having my one and only trip, which was a bad one. Tim was not concerned at all that I was having a bad trip. But Allen was. He was absolutely there helping me."

Oblivious to everything but their own experience, Tim, Orlovsky, and Zelda lay down on the carpet, which in Tim's words, began "to pulse and grow like a field of green hay. The effects on my vision were spectacular. The colors on the wall radiated with a jewely sheen. Pigment stuck out of the paintings at least twelve inches, forming valleys and mountains of raw, furrowed, gleaming color." Upstairs in his bedroom, Rosset had become fixated on a work of art by his first wife, the painter Joan Mitchell. Convinced it was actually coming off the wall, Rosset went over to the painting to push everything back in the frame where it belonged. Downstairs, Zelda lifted her head and told Tim that this stuff could solve the race problem. Up where they were now, there was no black or white. Unfortunately, the same was not true for Rosset. As Ginsberg would later recall, "Barney was having a bad time. And he said, 'I pay my psychiatrist fifty dollars an hour to keep this from happening to me.' So that was not very successful."

"The next day I went to Grove Press," Rosset remembered. "I came back at night and my girlfriend was in a pool of blood in my bedroom. She had cut her wrists with a razor. Holding her like my hand was a tourniquet, I walked her out the door of my brownstone. At that moment, Fred Praeger, a tenant who was involved with the CIA, was coming down the stairs with a guy in a suit and a tie who was obviously a CIA guy. He had a handkerchief in the pocket of his coat and I said, 'Excuse me, sir. Can I borrow your handkerchief?' I did and I made a tourniquet out of it to get her to the hospital." Rosset remains convinced it was the mescaline that caused her to try to kill herself. "You see, she was a very upset person to begin with. A person on the verge of being psychotic anyway. But that's not the kind of person to whom you should give a big dose of something without first knowing anything about that person. I thought that was extremely irresponsible of Leary. After that, there was a long long long history on my part of taking care of her in mental hospitals until she finally recovered."

In his account of the trip in *Flashbacks,* Tim Leary makes no mention of the attempted suicide:

> At Allen's flat we tallied up the score on our weekend of experiments. We had administered psychedelic drugs to three middle-aged intellectuals and one young black woman. The three men fought to control the experience, clung to their personal realities, and emerged (in our observation) relatively unchanged . . . Why did some people turn away from the experience, while others like Zelda, immediately understood its purpose? Was it because she was young? To our chagrin, youth was becoming a constant indication in our research. The older the person, the more fear of a visionary experience . . . Zelda's positive response to the drug suggested that women might be more receptive to multiple realities and more tolerant of the pluralism and relativity of Nature. The possibility of male-female differences went on the agenda for future study.
>
> Another thought-provoking result followed this session: Zelda's bond to her boyfriend Barney seemed to have weakened. In a few days I got a flustered letter from Allen saying that Zelda had taken

out to hanging out at his house and wanted to marry him! Thus, a new and titillating development in Allen's sex life.

In February, Ginsberg wrote Tim about Zelda, whom he had "seen a number of times, took her out one night to LeRoi Jones and got drunk. She can't make up her mind what to do with her life—wants someone to depend on—also wants independence, but she's spoiled and beautiful." Ginsberg informed Tim that he'd had a long talk with Rosset and agreed that it had been "a mistake to turn him and her on." "What really flipped me out," Rosset would later say, "was that afterward, I got a mimeographed questionnaire in the mail from Leary about what kind of experience this had been. Did it increase your sex orgasms by ten percent? Twenty percent? Thirty percent? Did it give you a religious experience of forty percent better? Fifty percent? That really angered me." The rules of the research project required that every subject had to answer more than 150 questions before each session, including, "Have you ever received psychotherapy? When? For how long? Are you presently in therapy? Have you ever been hospitalized for mental illness? If yes, please explain in detail (symptoms, length and number of hospitalizations, treatment)." Rosset had never seen any of this material before taking mescaline with Tim.

Never shy when it came to disclosing information about his own sexuality, Tim Leary would later write, "In the first two months of our Harvard psychedelic research seven women followed me home—much as the baby ducklings followed Konrad Lorenz—and announced their love." One of them, as it turned out, was Barney Rosset's girlfriend:

> As soon as she arrived, the connection from our session lit up again. She moved in as though we had been lovers for years. Zelda taught me a lot about enjoying life. She was astonished that we, who had stumbled upon these effective hedonic instruments, were dallying with intellectual research rather than pursuing sensual pleasure. In many ways Zelda was too advanced for me. I was caught up in the middle-class mission of achievement and responsibility, feeling that evolution wouldn't happen if I didn't throw all of my energies into the task.

The affair finally ended when—at his insistence, as Tim later wrote—Zelda took a modeling job in Hollywood. "She would call me from his place," Rosset remembered. "'What should I do?' She was asking me? I was telling her, 'Get the fuck out of there.' I had a thing about Leary, which was probably totally irrational. I'm half Irish Catholic and half Jewish. But I didn't trust his Catholicism. I more distrusted the Irish Catholicism than I did the LSD part . . . To me, it fit into a whole pattern. First, it had been the Catholicism. Now it was the LSD religion. One replacing the other. The new sacrament and the old and I couldn't tell you which I detested more. What really upset me ultimately about him was irresponsibility. To him, it didn't matter how people got hurt."

In January 1961, Allen Ginsberg wrote Tim to say that he had spoken to the painter Willem de Kooning, and that "he was ready to swing, too, so please drop him an invitation. I figure Kline [Franz Kline, the abstract expressionist painter], de Kooning, and [Dizzy] Gillespie are the most impressive trio for you to turn on at the moment, so will leave it at that for a while, till they can be taken care of. I won't send you new names and work trouble for a while. Hope you can get these three letters off." On his own, Ginsberg had given psilocybin to the jazz pianist and composer Thelonious Monk. "I delivered it to his house," Ginsberg later recalled. "And he opened the door just a crack for me. I saw him a week later at the Five Spot and I said, 'What happened?' And he said, 'Got anything stronger?' Then I went to give some to Dizzy Gillespie. All these folks were familiar with grass so I thought this would be a stepping-stone. I respected their work and I thought they would be an interesting addition to the company of cognoscenti or initiates or whatever. When I saw him later, he said, 'Anything that gets you high, man.' Then who else? I guess Maynard Ferguson was a little later."

Assessing his own role in the psychedelic revolution thirty-five years later, Ginsberg said, "Tim had asked Aldous Huxley and Huxley had recommended sort of a hermetic or an esoteric attitude. Tim asked me about it when he came to New York and I thought it was better to be open and democratic as it was in the hippie world and the Beat world. You know, friends turn friends on. Tim credits me with that view and that determination on his part. It got him into trouble but it also saved him from trouble too maybe."

By April, Ginsberg was on his way to India. For the next four years, as the revolution he had helped create increased by geometric proportions in America, the poet remained out of the country for extended periods of time. In February 1961, Tim replaced Ginsberg as his comrade-in-arms by turning on his colleague Richard Alpert. Having spent the fall semester teaching at Stanford, Alpert returned to Boston on the day that the biggest storm of the winter dumped two feet of snow on the city. After dinner with his parents in their home just a few blocks from Tim's house, Alpert plowed through the snow and appeared unannounced in Tim's kitchen. Jack and Susan were delighted to see him. A benevolent uncle to them, he would soon become their surrogate father as well.

While drinking beer at the kitchen table, Tim and Alpert talked about the sacred mushrooms. "Why not start right now?" Tim asked. As Tim got up from his chair, Alpert said, "Oh, you *really* mean right now." "Whenever you take them, it's right now," Tim replied, shaking six pink pills out of the bottle. Alpert popped them into his mouth without hesitation.

Going into the living room, Alpert experienced what he told himself must be an external hallucination: he saw himself standing in cap and gown and hood. In rapid succession, the figure changed into all of his various persona—cellist, pilot, lover. As each new apparition vanished before his eyes, Alpert assured himself that he didn't really need that part of himself anyway. Alpert then saw himself as he really was, the "Richard" he had always been. Looking down at his legs, Alpert could see nothing below his kneecaps. To his horror, he watched his body slowly disappear before his eyes. Everything he had known as himself was now gone. But he was still present. For the first time in his life, Alpert experienced a very profound sense of calm. His fear turned to exaltation and he ran laughing out into the snow.

At five in the morning, he walked back to his parents' house and began shoveling their walk. Looking up, he saw his parents peering down at him from their bedroom window. "Come to bed, you idiot," his father called out. "Nobody shovels snow at five in the morning." A voice inside his head told Alpert that it was quite all right to shovel snow at this hour. Alpert looked up, laughed, and did a little jig. Catching his mood, his parents began smiling as well. Then they shut the window and went back to bed. As Alpert would later write, "That was my first experience of giving a contact high."

For two or three days, Alpert floated in the afterglow. Within himself, he had discovered a beautiful new self. From now on, all he had to do was look inside and he would always know what to do. Then the feeling passed. Soon he was talking about the experience in the past tense to any colleague who would listen to him. A week later, Alpert was back in Tim's living room taking another trip. When he began to tell his colleagues about this experience, they listened far less intently than before. Alpert was already beginning to talk to them in an entirely different language. How else could he describe places they had never seen? "Pretty soon," Alpert would later write in *Be Here Now,* "there were five or six of us and we were hanging out together and our colleagues said, 'Ah ha, a cult is forming' which was true for us. A cult is a shared system of belief."

With Alpert's help, Tim began surrounding himself with graduate students, each so gifted in his own way that as a team, they seemed destined to extend the frontiers of psychedelic research. Bound together by an experience that could never be explained to those who had not yet had it, they soon formed a kind of extended family centered around Tim and Alpert. "They were like psychedelic mom and dad," recalled Gunther Weil, who first met Tim at Harvard after returning from a year in Europe as a Fulbright scholar. "Richard carried the feminine mom space and Tim was the paternal Irish father." Confirming this, Alpert would later say, "I was the wife. I cooked the bread. I took care of the kids. I was ready to dedicate my life to Timothy because I felt, 'Now here is a man who is a real visionary. Who sees through the system and can truly stand back and look.' I felt I could dedicate my life to being that Jewish mother. I could be the person who stood just behind the captain as the captain steered the ship through the shoals and the wild storms."

Each graduate student assumed a different role in what George Litwin would later term "the boys' club." Litwin was an achievement-oriented, aggressive Detroit street kid whose father had helped organize the United Auto Workers and first took him to walk on a picket line when he was three years old. "They didn't have organizational skills," Litwin would later say. "That was my field. They were wild radical rebels who were going to get shot sooner or later. They egged each other on. When I look back, Timothy was always an egger-onner and Dick was often the conservative, trying to relate and be an intermediary with society. In retrospect, perhaps he and I were rivals for the right hand of Timothy." Gunther Weil was a jazz fanatic weaned on Charlie Parker who had first experimented with pot as a teenager hanging out in black clubs. Weil was the hippest of Tim and Alpert's surrogate sons. The smartest one was Ralph Metzner. "Ralph was the German Oxford academic," Weil recalled. "The really brilliant analytic mind, encyclopedic in his knowledge of psychology, but very stiff. It was very hard to break into his heart. At times in psychedelic sessions, I saw Ralph really collapse and cry like a baby like we all did. But it was rare to see that with him."

Concerned what might happen when the research became part of the broader culture, Weil kept asking what he called "the Talmudic question": "What are we doing here? Is this right, or wrong?" In March, his question was answered by what came to be known as the Concord Prison Project. It began when Tim found a note in his box at Harvard, informing him that two men from the Department of Legal Medicine were interested in enlisting the university's help in the psychological rehabilitation of prisoners. "Prison work is considered to be the least interesting, lowest status work you can do in the field of psychology, psychiatry, and sociology," Tim would later write. "The problems are hopeless. Criminals never change. The atmosphere is dreary and the academic rewards are slim." Nonetheless, the request was exactly what he had been looking for. Tim had already given mushroom pills to about a hundred people in "a wide variety of circumstances." His real problem was one that every coach had to face sooner or later: in order to find out if he was winning, Tim needed to come up with a way to keep score. Otherwise, there would be no empirical proof that the drug could not only bring people ecstasy but also educate and transform them. The prison system could provide him with an iron-clad statistic known as the recidivism, or return, rate. At that time, the recidivism rate in the Massachusetts state prison system was around 70 percent.

A week later, Tim Leary sat at a corner table at the Faculty Club with two officials from the state prison system who wanted to see Harvard graduate students assigned to the prisons as interns. Tim agreed to get Harvard to do this. In return, the officials agreed that if he could get the approval of the warden and the prison psychiatrist at the Massachusetts Correctional Institute at Concord, an antiquated institution not all that far from Cambridge which, as Tim would later write, looked like "Frankenstein made it," he could then give psychedelic mushrooms to prisoners.

A week later, wearing his best tweed suit and a button down shirt, Tim drove to the prison to talk to the warden. Frank Barron, who went with him, would later recall, "The warden was a very good tough Irish type cop. And he looked at us, Francis Xavier Barron and Timothy Francis Leary. But he was sincere. He wanted to reduce the recidivism rate and he said, 'Try anything. We can't do a thing.'" Because the mushroom pills were drugs that needed medical approval, the fate of the project hinged on the approval of the prison psychiatrist. In the prison hospital, Tim met the dapper Dr. Madison Presnell, the first black psychiatrist he had ever encountered. Presnell told Tim that insofar as prisoners were concerned, their unconscious was their conscious mind and vice versa. They would never let people know how sensitive they were, that they liked poetry, could cry over a child, liked to see roses, or loved to walk through an open field. But when it came to their sex lives, a subject most people would never discuss, prisoners would lay it out from A to Z. Subjects that society at large believed should be hidden and forbidden, these men would talk about freely and openly. But anything "personal" was off limits. Presnell also told Tim that all his attempts to help them readjust to society had proven futile.

As Tim would later write, Presnell said, "If I could shatter that resistance, if I could just make them totally psychotic, I could cure them. I can cure psychotics but not severe neurotics because they are too conscious. If I could just get them to hear voices and see things and be so helpless and desperate that I could lead them back out of their desperation. But they're too suspicious and too knowledgeable." Tim told Presnell he had the drug that could do all this and more.

On Sunday, March 13, 1961, Presnell took psilocybin in Tim's house with his wife, Gunther Weil and his wife, and Ralph Metzner and his girlfriend. Metzner had already asked Tim whether he could be part of the prison project. Tim's first reaction was that Metzner was "too academic, too dainty-British, too bookish, too ivory tower, to walk into a prison and roll up his sleeves" to take a drug that that would "put him out of his mind, with rough and tumble prisoners." Tim changed his opinion when Metzner told him that he was ready to do a session right then and there. By this point, Tim had already taken psilocybin fifty-one times. While Susan sat upstairs in her bedroom watching a John Wayne movie on television, the session began. Every time Presnell closed his eyes, he went someplace else. One moment, he was skiing down a snow-covered slope in Chile, the next he was on Copacabana beach in Rio de Janeiro. In an interview conducted by Peter Owen Whitmer, Presnell would later recall, "I said, 'When I close my eyes, I travel.' And that's really where the word 'trip' came from."

After taking psilocybin, Presnell returned to the prison to ask for volunteers for the study. Tim and his colleagues were about to put their theories on the line. Turning on artists in dingy apartments on Manhattan's Lower East Side was one thing. Going inside a prison to do the same with hardened criminals was quite another. Once Tim and his team had ingested psilocybin with these men, it would no longer be easy to tell the inmates from the psychologists, which was exactly what Tim Leary wanted: no rules, no uniforms, no telling the players with or without a score card. Welcome to the magic theater. Price of admission? Your mind.

FOURTEEN

A few days later, Tim Leary, Ralph Metzner, and Gunther Weil drove to the Concord prison to meet the volunteers. Around a table in a dreary room with gray walls, a black concrete floor, and bars on the windows sat six very skeptical-looking inmates, all scheduled to be paroled in the coming year. Tim began telling them about an experience that he believed could transform their lives. What he did not tell them was that even he thought that taking psilocybin in prison was the most frightening thing anyone could do.

Nonetheless, on March 27, 1961, Tim, Metzner, and Weil met with five prisoners in a large wardroom in the infirmary which contained a big table, four beds, and a few chairs. The psychologists had brought a record player, a tape recorder, and some books on classical art. The plan was to break the day into two sessions. In the morning, Tim would turn on with three convicts as Weil, Metzner, and the other two prisoners observed. In the afternoon, Weil, Metzner, and the other two prisoners would take the drug.

At 9:35 A.M., Tim took fourteen milligrams of psilocybin. The three prisoners each took twenty milligrams. Then they all sat back to see what would happen. Their first interaction occurred when Tim confessed he was having a bad time and feeling lousy. One of the convicts asked why. Tim replied that it was because he was afraid of him. The prisoner told Tim that he was afraid of *him*. When Tim asked why, the prisoner said, "Because you're a mad scientist." Both men began to laugh. "Suddenly," as Tim wrote in *High Priest*, "the sun came out in the room and I felt great, and I knew he did too." Still, the atmosphere in the room was grim. With their senses magnifying every detail of their surroundings, no one could escape the reality of prison life until a black convict staggered over to the record player and put on a Sonny Rollins album. Shutting his eyes, the con lay back down on a bed and started moaning softly. When the others asked him if he was all right, he told them he was in heaven and swinging like never before and that this was all happening in prison so how could anyone ask him if he was all right? He then began to laugh. Everyone joined in.

In the afternoon, Weil and Metzner took psilocybin with the other two prisoners. "Gunther was silly and acting like a hipster," Tim wrote in *High Priest,* "and Ralph fell down on the bed and experienced visions of Blakean terror." "It was a horror trip," Metzner recalled. "I started seeing all my fears projected on the wall. I was getting all these condensed visions of all the evils of human history. I was sweating and moaning and groaning and Gunther Weil came over and put his hand on me and said, 'How are you doing, man?' And I couldn't believe it. He was the mother of God and full of compassion and the milk of human kindness and it changed, instantly. Just from a simple compassionate gesture."

The next day, Tim returned to Concord with an entirely different feeling about the place. "I felt at home in prison," he would later write. "It always works this way after a good trip. You die and then you are reborn. The place of your rebirth is home. This is not metaphorical—it is a neurological reality." Two weeks later, Tim and his team ran another session. After a third session, they asked the convicts to repeat the personality tests they had taken before the experiment. The tests showed "less depression, hostility, antisocial tendencies; more energy, responsibility, cooperation. The objective indices so dear to the heart of the psychologist had swung dramatically and significantly in the direction of increased mental health."

Soon, two of the most powerful convicts in the prison approached Tim and demanded that they be included in the experiment. One of them was Jimmy Kerrigan, a bank robber with a brother on death row at the high-security prison in Walpole. Kerrigan had spent nineteen of his forty-plus years on earth in jail. At one point in the session, Kerrigan became convinced that he had been tricked by Weil into taking a kind of truth serum that would make him confess to all the crimes for which he had not yet been arrested. Even as he sat there tripping on psilocybin, Kerrigan was trying to arrange to have Weil rubbed out for what he had done to him. Then both men began laughing about it. By the time the session ended, they had formed a bond. "We never had any violence with them,"

Metzner would recall. "Because with them, the shadow side, the repressed side, was tenderness. I remember this big bruiser of a guy with huge arms, bigger than my leg, looking down at a picture of a woman and a child in this picture book, *The Family of Man,* and tears were streaming down his face." Within the walls of a state penitentiary, criminals, professors, and graduate students were sharing mind-expanding drugs while bonding with one another as human beings. For Weil, the sessions were "a real leveling experience. We were just all in it together."

When the first prisoner involved in the project came up for parole, Tim and his colleagues did all they could to find him a job. No one wanted to hire him. They tried to find him work at Harvard but the student dining halls were about to shut down for the summer. Out of options, they wrote the parole board using Center for Personality Research stationery, guaranteeing him a job. When the con reported for work, he was told that his job was to go out and find himself a real job. Once he had done so, the con, an alcoholic petty thief, soon reverted to his old habits, spending all his time and money in bars. Although Tim let the man move into the attic of his house in Newton Center, the con soon lost his job and fell back into drinking beer and watching television all day long. Tim and his colleagues tried "treating" him with heavier and heavier psychedelic doses. One afternoon, they gave him five times the normal amount. Flipping out, the con started raving about all the beauty he was seeing in heaven. To show him the error of his ways, they walked him into a bar. He fled in horror. The next day, however, the con was right back in the bar. Tim gave him $50 and told him to move out. Two weeks later, he was back in prison.

Still, Tim was undeterred. "Everyone in the Massachusetts correctional system believed in his heart that our project would fail," he later wrote. "That we would not lower the recidivism rate, that we could not convert hardened criminals." Ignoring all results that did not confirm the experiment was a success, Tim added, "We had kept twice as many convicts out on the street as the expected number. We had halved the crime rate." Nonetheless, he soon realized the only way to implement the powerful insights that the convicts had experienced in the sessions was by providing them with a place to live after they were paroled. Tim and his colleagues began looking for a suitable halfway house, but they had neither the money nor the energy to implement the plan. Metzner actually went so far as to write Attorney General Robert F. Kennedy, requesting federal funds. "We sat in our offices at Harvard and made great plans and sent men out to look for real estate," Tim would later write. "And then at five o'clock we returned to our comfortable homes in the Boston suburbs and the ex-cons went back to the slums." Accurately, Tim had identified one of the central problems in rehabilitation—the difficult and desperate situations ex-convicts found themselves living in once they were back on the street. "In the sessions," Tim added, "we were all gods, all men at one. We were all two-billion-year-old seed centers pulsing together. Then as time slowly froze we were reborn in the old costumes and picked up the tired games. We weren't yet ready to act on our revelation. The spark we had lit within each one of us was there and we guarded it, but the sun-flame had not yet burst forth."

Years later, Richard Alpert would explain that the point of the experiment was to use chemicals to create "other models for the subjects about themselves and their relationship to society so they could change. It was a very reasonable therapeutic model. But it would have required a long-term application and Tim didn't do well with that. He didn't have the patience for long-term studies. Yet he kept voluminous files. He always wanted the data. He always wanted people to write him reports."

Two years after the inception of the project, Tim, Metzner, and Weil issued a report that claimed that as of January 15, 1963, 73 percent of the men from the study who had been released were still on the street; 19 percent were back in prison for "technical parole violations"; only 8 percent had returned to jail for "new crimes." In an article about the Concord Prison Project report in the *Boston Herald-Traveler,* Tim claimed that 75 percent of the prisoners involved in the study were "holding their own against stiff winds and treacherous currents."

In the same article, Edward Grennan, the superintendent at Concord, disputed Tim's claim, saying the study was done without a control group and therefore was unscientific. Rather than credit the psilocybin sessions with affecting any positive change whatsoever, Grennan pointed to all the attention the convicts had received from Harvard psychologists who had made themselves available around the clock. "I feel that the same rate of recidivism might have been achieved if the same concentration and attention were given to any parolee by highly placed members in any community."

The Concord Prison Project clearly demonstrated that Tim and his colleagues had the courage of their convictions. In one of the grimmest settings imaginable, they had opened themselves up to men whose lives had been dominated by physical violence. In the intervening years, however, the results of the Concord Prison Project came into question. With the help of researcher Michael Forcier, Rick Doblin, founder of the Multidisciplinary Association of Psychedelic Studies, located the records for twenty-one of the thirty-two convicts involved in the experiment. In 1998, thirty-five years later, Doblin wrote, "In the first follow-up, Leary claimed a remarkable reduction of recidivism in the short term as of January, 1963. A careful review of all the source documents, including the base-rate study, prove that claims of an initial treatment effect were false. Leary's report of a dramatic treatment effect was the result of a misleading use of the base-rate data." In layman's terms, Tim had compared a rate based on convicts who had been out of jail for only ten months with a rate based on those who had been out of jail for an average of thirty months. "Recidivism is, among other factors," Doblin continued, "a function of how long someone has been out of prison, with rates rising over time: more time out of prison presents more opportunities for criminal behavior and police apprehension." In his own follow-up report, Tim also failed to mention that the base-rate study done by Metzner and Weil contained a graph indicating that the recidivism rate was in fact a function of time. When the appropriate comparison was made between the experimental and control group at the ten-month mark, the recidivism rate for the control group was 34.3 percent as compared to 32 percent for the experimental group. Rather than the 23 percent reduction claimed by Tim, this amounted to a 2.3 percent reduction. In Doblin's words, this was "not significant and is the same as a finding of no treatment effect."

Tim also claimed that only two subjects had been returned to jail for new crimes while fourteen had been returned for parole violations. Doblin came to a different conclusion:

> As of July, 1964, twelve of the eighteen convicts . . . released prior to this date were back in prison but only one had by Leary's count been put there for a new crime. Of the fifteen out of twenty one who were returned to prison two and a half years after release, only one was returned for a new crime while fourteen were there by Leary's reckoning for parole violations . . . Using these definitions, of the 18 subjects released prior to July, 1964, thirty nine per cent were re-

turned to prison for a new crime, twenty eight per cent for parole violations, and thirty three percent did not return.

Of the twenty-one psilocybin subjects for whom records could be found, Doblin reported an actual thirty-month recidivism rate of 71 percent, with fifteen of twenty-one whose records he could locate having been returned to jail. From thirty months to the time of the follow-up (an additional thirty-one and a half years), the recidivism rate was 76 percent. "Whatever his motivations, Leary's misleading reports about the success of the Concord Prison experiment serve as an object lesson in what not to repeat," Doblin concluded.

In an article published with Doblin's report in the *Journal of Psychoactive Drugs*, Ralph Metzner wrote, "I have to say I have no idea how Leary came up with the 'finding' that the return rate for parole violations was up and for new crimes down . . . We fell victim to the well-known 'halo effect' by which researchers tend to see their data in as positive a light as possible. I have myself, in later years, sometimes forgotten the basically negative result we reported in the study, and talked about the project as if we lowered the recidivism rate." Metzner added that he had no idea where Tim came up with the ten-month 32 percent recidivism figure (as opposed to the thirty-month base-rate figure). "Whether Leary made these mistakes consciously, faking the results that he wanted, or whether they were unconscious mistakes of carelessness, motivated by over enthusiasm, is impossible to say at this point. I tend to favor the latter alternative, if only for the reason that our own results clearly show the inconsistencies."

As for the original data for the Concord Prison Project, Dr. Presnell told Peter Owen Whitmer in 1973 that while Tim and Alpert were stoned on acid one day, Tim got angry and "burned up all the statistics. They took all that stuff and just threw it in the fire and went ape." Along with those statistics went Timothy Leary's only attempt to bring about social change through the controlled use of psychedelics.

FIFTEEN

Throughout the winter and spring of 1961, Tim continued to establish connections with those whom he called "great men." His initial entrée to them was always his seemingly unlimited supply of psychedelic drugs.

In February, Aldous Huxley wrote to thank Tim for asking him to co-write an article for *Harper's* magazine. Because he was desperately busy trying to finish a book, Huxley regretfully declined the invitation. However, he did mention that while at a conference in San Francisco, he had met Dr. Oscar Janiger, whom he had not seen in several years. By then, Janiger had already given LSD to one hundred painters who had done pictures before, during, and after the experience. Janiger then had the results appraised by a panel of art critics. "This might be interesting," Huxley wrote. "I gave him your address & I think you will hear from him." Beginning in 1954, Janiger, called "Oz" by nearly all who knew him, had been conducting LSD research in Los Angeles, giving the drug not only to artists but also to a thousand other people selected on a purely random basis. His subjects ranged from the unemployed to the actor Cary Grant, who would become the first mainstream celebrity in America to admit that he had used the drug. Janiger, a psychiatrist whose patients included Alan Watts and Abbie Hoffman, also taught in the medical school at the University of California at Irvine.

Although Oz Janiger and Tim Leary might have seemed kindred spirits, they could not have been more different from each other in terms of outlook and how they conducted their research. "There were two schools of thought in those days," Janiger recalled. "You can't do research on the drug unless you've taken it yourself or take it with the subject. And the other school said, 'Why should this be different from anything else in science? You simply observe it and write down your observations.' Tim easily took the position that you had to take it or you wouldn't know anything. I had another point of view ingrained in me. I wanted to see what was there and find a way to carefully evaluate it."

Through Dave Solomon, the editor of *Metronome,* a jazz magazine based in New York City, eight of Tim's magic mushroom pills made their way into the hands of playwright and poet LeRoi Jones, later to be known as Amiri Baraka. Tim then wrote to Alan Watts in San Francisco to say that he was looking forward to his visit to Harvard at the end of March. "Did I tell you that Dean Josiah Bartlett of the Stan King School of the Ministry has expressed interest in having a couple of his divinity students try the mushrooms. I wonder if you would be willing to act as *curandero*—and run an afternoon session." Watts was a former Episcopalian priest and scholar whose books, lectures, and television appearances had helped bring Zen Buddhism to the West. Inspired by the spiritual change he noticed in Aldous Huxley and Gerald Heard, both of whom had become more "relaxed and humane" after psychedelics, Watts first experimented with LSD under the aegis of Keith Ditman, the psychiatrist in charge of LSD research at the UCLA Department of Neuropsychology.

Although Watts's initial experience with the drug was aesthetic rather than mystical, he continued experimenting with it. In time, he would acknowledge that LSD had brought him into "an undeniably mystical state of consciousness." Oddly, considering his absorption in Zen, his experiences convinced him that "Hindu philosophy was a local form of a sort of undercover wisdom, inconceivably ancient, which everyone knows in the back of his mind but will not admit." Watts chronicled his psychedelic experiences in *The Joyous Cosmology,* published in 1962, with a foreword by Timothy Leary and Richard Alpert. The book presented the model for the psychedelic experience that millions of people, most with far less spiritual training than Watts, would have in the coming decade. Unlike Tim, Watts eventually moved beyond the psychedelic experience, writing, "My retrospective attitude to LSD is that when one has received the message, one hangs up the phone."

On March 3, 1961, Tim wrote Aldous Huxley in Los Angeles to say he would be acting as the chairman of a symposium on "psychiatric drugs" at the Fourteenth International Congress of Applied Psychology in Copenhagen in August. "Hope you can come," Tim wrote, "it would be fun to see you in Tivoli." Tim also sent a long memo to David McClelland, his department chairman at Harvard, in which he admitted that while all his many varied activities during the past thirteen months might have seemed "scattered," there was a consistency in his efforts to bring about certain goals. Tim then filled up three single-spaced pages listing all his current projects in New Bedford, Concord, Wellesley, and Cambridge. "At this point," he wrote, "I have little interest in running mushroom sessions . . . However, I see merit in employing some mature, productive volunteers. I have given pills (without personal supervision) to the following persons: Huxley, Watts, Burroughs, Litwin, Barron, Ginsberg, Newman (a poet), and Blum (a writer), Solomon, (editor of *Metronome* magazine)."

As the academic year ended, Tim received official notice from the president and fellows of Harvard College that he had been given another one-year appointment as a lecturer in clinical psychology beginning on July 1, 1961. Having somehow managed to keep his job, Tim set off to spend his summer abroad. His itinerary seemed more suited for a member of the international jet set than an Ivy League professor.

In July, Tim arrived in Tangier to visit William Burroughs. Allen Ginsberg had urged him to get in touch with the man "who knows more about drugs than anyone alive." Tim had already sent Burroughs a supply of psilocybin and persuaded him to participate in a symposium on psychedelic drugs to be held at the American Psychological Association meeting in September in New York City. As Tim got off his plane, he ran into Peter Orlovsky who was beginning a pilgrimage to the Far East. After checking into a $2.00-a-night hotel room reserved for him by Ginsberg, Tim went to meet Burroughs for the first time.

William Seward Burroughs, accompanied by two English boys who looked to be about nineteen, was forty-seven years old. A gaunt figure of a man with haunted eyes, he was a Harvard graduate whose grandfather had invented the perforated oil-filled cylinder, which enabled the Burroughs adding machine to function. Long before his breakthrough novel *Naked Lunch* was published in 1959 by Olympia Press in Paris, Burroughs had already become one of the leading figures in the Beat movement, due in no small part to his extraordinary lifestyle. To say there was almost nothing Burroughs had not done—including virtually every drug in existence in every form—was to understate the case. Ten years earlier while drunk in Mexico, he had taken a handgun from his traveling bag and told his wife, "It's time for our William Tell act." Laughing, she put a water glass on her head. Burroughs then accidentally shot a bullet through her brain. He was also a longtime heroin user who had never made any secret of his sexual predilection. Although Burroughs had recently written Tim about his very negative experience with an injected psychedelic drug known as DMT (dimethyl tryptamine) and was noncommittal about the mushrooms Tim had sent him in Paris, he was eager to visit America at Tim's behest.

At his hotel that night, Tim dined with Burroughs, his two young English friends, Ginsberg, Gregory Corso, and the artist Alan Ansen. After dinner, everyone went to Burroughs's room, a dark cave with a big bed and a paper-strewn desk on which was a board for cutting pot. Also on the desk were hundreds of photos that had been cut up, pasted together, and then rephotographed. While three radios blared, everyone took turns peering through a cardboard cylinder at flickering images. Then Burroughs announced that he wanted to take mushrooms. After they ingested the pills, Tim, Ginsberg, Corso, and Ansen went off to experience the lights of Tangier under the influence of psilocybin. Soon everyone was in "the highest and most loving of moods." Deciding to include Burroughs in their fun, they returned to his hotel. Climbing partway up the wall outside the hotel, Ginsberg offered his ritual greeting: "Bill BUH-rows! Bill BUH-rows!"

After a minute, the door creaked slowly open. Burroughs was standing there, leaning against the wall. His face was haggard and covered with sweat. He clawed at his cheek with thin fingers. Obviously, his trip was not going nearly so well as theirs. When they asked him how he was doing, Burroughs replied that he was not feeling too well. To come down, he planned to take some apomorphine. Later that night, Burroughs reappeared with the two young Englishmen in an outdoor café in the central square. Although he was feeling better, he was still not talking. Nonetheless, Tim assumed it would only be a matter of time before Burroughs got the message and became part of the psychedelic movement.

During his stay in Tangier, Tim visited Paul Bowles, the expatriate author of *The Sheltering Sky,* who had lived in the city since 1947 and was a father figure to both Burroughs and Ginsberg. In Bowles's apartment, Tim listened to tapes of Arab music Bowles had recorded. He watched a session in which several young men—again English—took *majoun,* a potent paste made of hashish and honey. "One of them got caught in bad visions," Tim later wrote. "I could see why. He played the part of a miserable, bullied, self-despising English schoolboy homosexual. He had walked in on the session uninvited . . . Then suddenly he found himself 'out of his mind' in a strange port amid strangers who disliked him, and he trembled in fear." Eager to learn how these "drug experts" would handle the situation, Tim was surprised by how little compassion they offered the boy, who was ignored and called a "drag." Only Ginsberg, depressed about Peter Orlovsky's decision to leave him behind in Tangier, sat beside the boy and tenderly tried to talk him down.

On August 13, Tim arrived in Copenhagen for the opening of the Fourteenth International Congress of Applied Psychology. During the six-day conference, twenty seminars or presentations were held at the same time. On the first day, there were three general convocations which everyone was expected to attend. Harry Murray, whom Tim Leary would later call the "elegant, courtly, romantic, high cultural dean of personality psychology" at Harvard, spoke at the opening session with Aldous Huxley following him in the afternoon. The evening session would be run by Tim, Frank Barron, and Richard Alpert.

Murray began the conference by announcing that after his own mushroom experience with Tim, he had replaced his prepared lecture with a brand-new topic: "New Visions for Psychology's Future." In the afternoon, Huxley discussed *The Doors of Perception* and charted the history of the visionary experience back to the English poets Milton, Blake, and Wordsworth. As Tim left the session, three members of the Danish psychology faculty rushed up to him with a newspaper. The front-page headline read: I WAS THE FIRST SCANDINAVIAN REPORTER TO TRY THE POISONOUS MUSHROOMS FROM HARVARD! A large photograph of the dilated pupil of Richard Alpert's eye appeared with the caption, "I can control my insanity, says Professor Alpert of Harvard." Having turned on the reporter the night before, Alpert himself was the source of the article. Unaccustomed to reading such stories on the front page of their own newspapers, the august members of the Danish psychology faculty were understandably upset. Tim assured them that the evening program would make history and that Professor Alpert would not turn on any more Danes, at least not during the conference.

That evening, Tim addressed those assembled in the Queen's Palace Auditorium. After thanking Frank Barron for introducing him to the Mexican mushroom and noting all the new insights he had derived from it, he announced, "It is my plan to talk to you tonight about methods of effecting change—change in man's behavior and change in man's consciousness." In Tim's view, the most efficient way to achieve this aim was "by the use of psilocybin or LSD to cut through the game structure of Western life. You win today's game with humility. You lose tomorrow's game with dignity. Anger and anxiety are irrelevant because you see your small game in the context of the great evolutionary game, which no one can win and no one can lose." Herbert Kelman, a Harvard psychology professor who had spent the previous year in Norway while Tim had taught some of his classes back in Cambridge, was in the audience. "The overall reaction I had and, I then checked it with other people, the general reaction that I heard to Tim's talk was that it was a kind of incoherent rambling," Kelman recalled. "Basically a paean to the drug experience. I couldn't find anything of substance there. It was rather shocking. I am not prone to making diagnoses but I remember one Danish psychologist saying it sounded like the talk of someone who had been on drugs for a long time."

After Tim concluded his presentation, Alpert stepped up to the podium. Kelman remembered Alpert thanking Tim for having introduced him to the drug just as Tim had thanked Frank Barron and then going on to make a presentation that had nothing to do with drugs. Tim Leary would later write in *Changing My Mind, Among Others* that Alpert managed to shock even him by announcing that the visionary experience was an end in itself and that the drug-induced religious-mystical trip produced love, Christian charity, and the peace that surpasseth understanding. A number of psychiatrists in the audience leaped to their feet and, in seven languages, began denouncing nonmedical psychologists for discussing drugs. They dismissed the notion that drugs should be used for personal growth rather than to cure specific ills. The rest of the audience applauded heartily. In a hotel suite afterward, three Danish psychologists told Tim that he had "set Danish psychology back twenty years." "Not at all," Tim replied, pouring aquavit for everyone. He assured them that in twenty years' time, this conference would rank, in his words, with the moment when Isaac Newton and Charles Darwin spoke before the Royal Society.

As George Litwin recalled, "This event was decisive as far as Harvard and its reputation in the field was concerned. It was a radical testifying for psychedelics as opposed to a carefully literate presentation of what these new materials might offer us as potential in our field. Timothy had written this brilliant paper about helping the helpless and Richard was doing the practical applications in therapy and they just threw the scripts aside. They totally crossed the line as far as those in the field were concerned. And why did they do that? They felt they were masquerading . . . It wasn't just a promising new avenue of research and therapy. It was a transforming personal experience. They wanted to communicate that to the audience. By the time they got back, the furor was raised. Thousands of people all over the world had heard them testify to some new drug, which they were obviously on, and it was a disgrace to Harvard."

During the conference, Tim drove with Aldous Huxley to nearby Rungstedlund to visit Isak Dinesen, the Nobel Prize–winning author of *Out of Africa* and *A Winter's Tale*. With great enthusiasm, both men described to her their experience with mind-altering drugs. Having come to turn her on, Tim offered Dinesen a rose "from the world of the spirits," which he had been given at a séance. Dinesen, then seventy-five years old—she would die in a year's time, due in part to syphilis of the spine—politely declined their invitation on the grounds "that she was filled with enough fantasies without any external stimulation."

From Copenhagen, Tim traveled with Alpert to London where they again met up with William Burroughs, living in yet another dark hotel room. Despite his negative experience in Tangier, Burroughs was willing to try the mushrooms again. They each took four milligrams of psilocybin and repaired to a working-class tearoom where Burroughs railed against an American publisher for cheating his authors and spoke with awe and reverence of Samuel Beckett. Though they tried to arrange an interview with Beckett, the playwright refused to see them. As he walked the London streets on psilocybin, Burroughs talked of J. B. Rhine and his ESP experiments at Duke. He talked about the virus and the parasite and how he wrote to create his own reality and to sound an urgent warning against the parasites. Psychedelic drugs were counteragents that destroyed the virus along with the status quo. They were the specific cure for brain parasites.

As Tim later described it, Burroughs created verbal collages. He cut up interpersonal psychology, scissored through parasitology, and pasted in junkie dialect. High, happy, and jolly, Burroughs led them back to his hotel for a drink and then dinner. He talked of curare, the muscle-paralyzing South American substance, and how he would like to take it along with a mind-expanding drug so that he could experience many visions with no intruding physical action. He talked of Morocco, an entire culture built on hashish, a happy lotus land that Arab nationalists wanted to modernize with the industrial nightmare of the West. The United States had pressured Morocco to make nontoxic hashish illegal while forcing their own toxic narcotic on them—alcohol. Becoming flushed after taking a drink, Burroughs took some apomorphine to come down from the trip, then suddenly and nervously bid them good night.

As a late-summer heat wave gripped New York City that September, Burroughs joined Tim, Frank Barron, and Gerald Heard in a symposium on consciousness-expanding drugs at the annual convention of the American Psychological Association. An overflow crowd spilled out in the hallway to hear Burroughs speak. Sprawled on the floor around the speaker's table, they strained to hear him as he read from his prepared manuscript in a low voice. Despite all the energy Tim had put into courting him to become part of the movement, Burroughs did not even mention psilocybin during his speech.

When the convention ended, Burroughs took up residence in Tim's attic. Susan Leary later recalled, "The lady who had lived there before had been crippled. There was a wheelchair up there and crutches and William Burroughs would ride around the attic in the wheelchair. When we'd go to visit him, you couldn't walk anywhere. He had everything all over the attic, pictures and books and magazines and pieces of paper, and he would cut up things and paste them into collages." Wearing a gray fedora, Burroughs would sit by himself in the attic surrounded by cut-up photos. When he came downstairs, he would lean on Tim's kitchen table drinking gin and tonic, talking on and on in an endless monotone. After he left Tim's house "silently without farewell," Burroughs returned to New York where he published a letter "denouncing the Harvard psychedelics." Among his accusations were that "They steal, bottle, and dole out addictive love in eye-droppers of increased awareness of unpleasant or dangerous symptoms."

To Burroughs, the notion that universal love could be generated by chemical brain change seemed the biggest con of them all. "Bill had the idea," recalled Allen Ginsberg, "that all this experimentation involved machinery, equipment, stroboscopes, electronic stuff, measurements. Where instead Tim's basic idea was no scientific measurement. So Bill was pissed off that there was no science in the sense of laboratories where you can really experiment with rats or something like that. So he thought that Leary was a horse's ass. He changed his mind later and actually they got very close, especially toward the end."

SIXTEEN

In October, a man with an English accent phoned Tim at his Harvard office. "Dr. Leary," he said, "Michael Hollingshead here. I have been working with Professor G. E. Moore at Oxford—Mr. Moore sends his fondest greetings, by the way. There are many aspects of our work that will interest you. I wonder if it would be possible to arrange an appointment. Lunch next week Tuesday? Fine."

All this would have been fine were it not for the fact that after spending his life teaching at Cambridge, G. E. Moore, the well-known British philosopher, professor, and literary critic, had died in 1958. Although Hollingshead would correct this error in a letter to Leary many years later, he also claimed to have worked alongside Moore at the Association for Cultural Exchange, Ltd. Eighty-four years old at the time, Moore had carried out his duties there by proxy and it seems doubtful that he and Hollingshead ever had significant contact. Although Tim had never been one to let the truth stand in his way, he was about to meet someone who had taken the art of real-life fiction to another level.

In New York City, where Hollingshead had been working as executive secretary for a semi-official British public relations agency, he had persuaded his friend John Beresford, an English physician, to write to Sandoz Laboratories and request a supply of LSD for bone-marrow experiments. A package soon arrived from Switzerland containing a gram of pure Albert Hofmann synthesized LSD (lot number H-00047), along with an invoice for $285. Hollingshead and Beresford diluted the LSD in distilled water and added confectioner's sugar until they had a thick white paste that filled a sixteen-ounce mayonnaise jar, the equivalent of 5,000 spoonfuls of acid, each a 200 milligram dose. Eating half a wax-paper sheet covered with sticky residue, Hollingshead ingested the equivalent of five heavy doses of LSD and spent the next fifteen hours tripping on a roof on the corner of West Fourth and MacDougal, not far from Washington Square in Greenwich Village. Shortly after his initial mind-shattering trip, Hollingshead contacted Aldous Huxley with numerous questions about the experience. Huxley suggested that he find Tim, whom Huxley called "a splendid fellow. If there is any one single investigator in America worth seeing, it is Dr. Leary." Hollingshead arrived in Cambridge, where the air was "fresh and clear like Vichy water," rented rooms on Brattle Street, and contacted Tim. In the mayonnaise jar, 4,975 trips still remained.

Over lunch at the Faculty Club, Hollingshead tried to describe his LSD experiences to Tim. Since Tim had never taken the drug, he imagined it to be much like psilocybin. Sensing that Hollingshead wanted something from him, Tim hurried off with a quick handshake, suggesting they have lunch again sometime soon. On the following Thursday, Tim's secretary handed him a letter written in tiny, hardly legible script from Hollingshead, which said he had come here because Tim was the only person in the world who could help him. "I was in my office at six or six-thirty or seven," George Litwin recalled, "and Timothy read me this letter from Michael. It said, 'I've experimented with LSD with some doctors in New York and London and I'm involved with high-level people with the British whatever and I'm in a lot of trouble. I'm feeling really terrible. I'm going to kill myself.'" Tim's reaction was that Hollingshead was either in real trouble or a total fraud.

Looking at the address, Litwin realized it was just a block from where he was living in Cambridge on Huron Avenue. After Litwin went and brought Hollingshead back to the office, Hollingshead told Tim that he was broke and needed a place to crash. Tim invited him to come live in his attic. Once Hollingshead was settled, Tim said he could join the team by leading a weekly one hour graduate course on the phenomenological aspects of heightened states of consciousness. Perhaps sensing that he was in the presence of his new teacher, Tim offered Hollingshead his Volkswagen to drive back to New York City to pack up the rest of his belongings. And what about dinner at eight? Would that suit him?

Tim then phoned a mutual friend who described Hollingshead as a "no-good, two-bit, English con man." Tim called Litwin, who confirmed that Hollingshead had had many experiences with LSD and could probably help them with their research but that he might also have a checkered past. Litwin then asked, "But what can he possibly con us out of? We have nothing material to lose and our only ambitions are scientific and celestial. How can he possibly hurt us? Even if he is a rascal, isn't it our business to rehabilitate people?" Wholeheartedly, Tim agreed. With his wife and child, Hollingshead moved into Tim's house. Ten days later, his wife left. "He moved in as a kind of a majordomo," Litwin would later say. "They must have a name for this in Britain. Amanuensis. Someone who would help Tim with letters and communications. Majordomo and amanuensis combined was the role he chose to play in the Timothy Leary household and office. Timothy was really ripe for that."

Although Hollingshead loved psilocybin, he was "patronizing in comparing the mushrooms with LSD." When he first tried to get Tim to take the drug with him, Tim resisted the idea. "Everything I had heard about the lysergic acid sounded ominous to me. The mushrooms and peyote had been grown naturally in the ground and had been used for thousands of years in wise Indian cultures. LSD, on the other hand, was a laboratory product and had quickly fallen into the hands of doctors and psychiatrists. Then too, I was scared." For Tim, the sacred mushrooms were familiar territory, a realm in which he felt comfortable and in control. For all he knew, LSD might sweep him far beyond the "tender wisdom" of psilocybin. In the attic one night, Hollingshead showed Tim the mayonnaise jar packed with moist sugar paste and asked when he would try the "key to miracle and meaning." Shaking his head, Tim replied he was having enough trouble understanding the sacred mushrooms. Hollingshead laughed. "Psilocybin, the child's toy of the Indians."

It was not until early December that Tim Leary finally surrendered to the siren call of LSD. He did so because of peer pressure and his need to impress a beautiful woman. Jazz trumpeter Maynard Ferguson had come to Boston for a weekend gig, accompanied by his exquisite wife, Flo, a former model whom Tim had already met in New York. Since by Tim's edict there was still no dope smoking allowed in the Newton Center house, the Fergusons had to drive around with Hollingshead to get high.

On Sunday afternoon, the Fergusons were sitting in front of the fireplace when Hollingshead began telling LSD stories. The next thing Tim knew, Hollingshead came bounding down the stairs with his mayonnaise jar and a spoon. Busy listening to records, Tim did not pay too much attention to what was going on until half an hour had passed. In *High Priest,* he wrote, "I saw that Maynard and Flo were gone from this world, into some sort of trance. They were sitting on the sofa motionless, their eyes closed. But I could feel energy emanating from their bodies." Tim watched them for fifteen minutes. Suddenly, Flo opened her eyes and laughed. "It was the chuckle of someone who was dead and done and sitting on some heavenly mountain top and looking down at the two billion years of evolution the way you'd look at a transient episode in a children's playground." When Flo began to talk, everything she said sounded like the essence of Hindu philosophy. As he would later write, "from her smiling rosebud lips was pouring the most powerful religious statement I had ever heard in my life. Timothy, you've got to take this." Tim Leary was obsessed by Flo Ferguson's high cheekbones, enormous eyes, incredible grace, and innate regal bearing. In *What Does WoMan Want?*, calling her "Flora Lu," he wrote of her smooth skin, full mouth, and "dewy fuckable innocence masking the jaded fatigued languor of a very old, patient woman." After Flo extended the invitation, Tim and George Litwin licked the tablespoon clean.

Half an hour later, Tim was tumbling and spinning down soft fibrous avenues to a central point that was not just light but the center of life. Walking into Susan's room as she sat on her bed listening to rock 'n' roll while doing her homework, Tim saw through the utter sham of his devoted father routine. Going down the hall, he joined his son who was watching television. As Tim sat down next to him, Jackie did not even bother to take his eyes off the tube. Everything Tim saw on the screen told him that he was already dead and that he needed to use every second that remained to glorify life and dance with God's great song.

Swimming into the kitchen, Tim flipped open a book. In a second, he saw the history of every word in it right back to the beginning of written language. The single word that jumped out at him was "death." When Litwin staggered into the room, they were like two dead men trapped on a doomed submarine. They communicated telepathically. Everything was illusion. Even love. When Tim ran out onto his snow-covered lawn, he realized the starlight had never been more beautiful. Retracing his steps to the fireplace where it had all begun, Tim found Hollingshead sitting and waiting. Litwin had gone off to be with his wife.

Compared to what Tim had experienced before with psilocybin, LSD was "something different. Michael's heaping spoonful had flipped consciousness out beyond life into the whirling dance of pure energy, where nothing existed except whirring vibrations, and each illusory form was simply a different frequency." Taking LSD was the most "shattering experience of my life." By dawn, the effects of the drug began wearing off. Still higher than he had ever been before, Tim kneeled before Flo and put his head in her lap. She began to cry. Tim started shaking and sobbing as well. Why were they being reborn? In a daze, he somehow managed to drive out to the Concord prison to meet with twelve prisoners from the rehabilitation project.

For the next few days, everyone watched Tim and Litwin with reverent concern. "They could tell we had been beyond where we had ever been before." Alpert in particular was concerned. As Tim would later write, "He could sense that we had moved beyond the game of psychology, the game of trying to help people, and beyond the game of conventional love relationships."

Seeing Hollingshead as some sort of divine messenger, Tim now treated him with "awed respect." How right and beautiful it seemed that God should send him such a messenger in the form of "this eccentric, impatient, and mildly disreputable" man. Intently, Tim studied Hollingshead's every move for clues. But each time he questioned him about the session, Hollingshead reacted with an evasive casualness. Shrugging his shoulders and raising his eyebrows, Hollingshead offered no explanations, saying only, "That's the way it is, you know." "Hollingshead was a major shift," Gunther Weil recalled. "His arrival on the scene raised the ante in every way. Michael danced in and he'd come out of the London acid scene with the Beatles. Michael was a Felix Krull–like character. As close to a pure sociopath as I had ever met. About six feet tall and partially balding with very angular features. Two scars on each side of his forehead that he claimed were from fencing but looked like they could be wired implants. He had a litany of his bonafides including the claim that he had been analyzed by Anna Freud. His formula for success was 'Think Yiddish and dress British.'"

Hollingshead also had a million stories to tell. He claimed to be good friends with multimillionaire Huntington Hartford and with Senator Jacob Javits. Ralph Metzner, who was not a fan of the Englishman, would later say, "Hollingshead bothered me. He was like a prankster. A con man. He would take a high dose of LSD and sit in the kitchen and drink a beer, smoke a cigarette, watch television, and talk." "Hollingshead?" said Richard Alpert. "Hollingshead was a paranoid nut. Hollingshead was the closest to evil of most of the people I've ever met. I have this distinction between rascal and scoundrel. Timothy always stayed a rascal. Hollingshead was certainly a scoundrel."

The single greatest insight Tim derived from his initial experience with lysergic acid came in the form of a paranoid science-fiction vision in which he saw himself on an ancient television show directed and designed by an unknown intelligence. The role he played was that of, "the pathetic clown, the shallow, corny, twentieth-century American, the classic buffoon completely caught in a world of his own making." Prophetic as this vision may have been, Tim promptly began taking LSD as no one had ever done before.

In the months following Tim's first acid trip, the Harvard Psychedelic Project as well as the social scene that had sprung up around it changed radically. Because Sandoz Laboratories was no longer willing to continue providing him with an unlimited supply of psilocybin, the new drug of choice for Tim and his research group became either LSD or DMT, a powerful short-acting psychedelic administered by intramuscular injection. The experience induced by both was so extreme that it became increasingly difficult for those using the drugs on a regular basis to maintain the pretense of daily life at Harvard. "There was a lot of sixties-style sexual experimentation," Gunther Weil would later recall. "Tim was part of it but it was pretty bush league. People fell in love with other people and their normal boundaries dissolved. I remember Tim at one point saying to us, 'You know, in the future, adultery will not be having sex with someone else's wife. It will be taking acid with her.'" "Everyone was sleeping with everyone," another graduate student would later say. "You would lay down with somebody and the conversation and the venue would be spiritual exchange. From another point of view, you were having an ordinary affair. But there was a very strong commitment, at least in terms of language and ideology, that we were on this journey and that many things could happen because they were part of the journey."

In his biography, *Whatever Happened to Timothy Leary?*, John Bryan described twelve-year-old Jackie Leary finding pink psilocybin pills all over the house and "gobbling them like candy." Jackie even gave some to his dog. Hallucinating, he imagined his dog was jumping into the air at the same moment that it was licking a psychiatrist's leather briefcase. Only then did he realize that both he and the dog were stoned. Richard Alpert remembered people in Tim's house screwing in bedrooms, kids having temper tantrums, dogs running around, and lots of drinking. According to Alpert, Tim "tended to override other people's suffering. It's not that he didn't see it. When he had to see it, he was really good at handling it. But he tended to be a little insensitive to other people's stuff." Whenever a new woman to whom Tim was attracted came along, he was unable to deal with the effect this would have on a former lover and ignored her. "So all of us were always holding the hands of his ex-women," Alpert would later say.

The level of chaos surrounding Tim increased when Frank Barron got married in January 1962 and left his post as co-director of the Harvard Psychedelic Project to return to San Francisco so he could continue his own research. Ever since their graduate-school days together in Berkeley, Tim had looked up to Barron as a wiser older brother. Although at times Barron could be just as daring as Tim, he had a well-honed instinct for survival as well as the kind of basic common sense which Tim entirely lacked. Without Barron's counsel, Tim was now free to do as he pleased. When asked whether LSD turned the Harvard Psychedelic Project into a cult by the time he left Cambridge, Barron said, "When a bunch of guys are standing around in a narrow hallway saying 'Wow!' to one another, it makes you wonder. Is that what you mean?"

At least once a month, Tim would go off to spend the weekend with Flo and Maynard Ferguson in Riverdale, New York. It was there that he first met Peggy Hitchcock, who along with her brothers, Billy and Tommy, would one day inherit the Mellon fortune. The meeting was set up by a mutual friend named Van Wolf, whom Peggy described as "an organizer. A social director. A male yenta, I suppose." After Flo introduced Tim to a beautiful dark-haired girl with whom he finally had the kind of apocalyptic sex he had been seeking since he first took sacred mushrooms back in Cuernavaca, Tim realized that "he was distributing, in the name of science and experimental mysticism and under the banner of a University founded by the Puritan Fathers, nothing less than the most powerful aphrodisiac ever known."

Charles Slack, now teaching at the University of Alabama, ran into Tim one day on a plane from Washington, D.C. "He started talking to me about how he had the answer," Slack recalled. "And he was so excited. I guess I had heard about lysergic acid. But it was called psychotomimetic. It made you crazy." Tim told Slack that "if you give the drug in a nice house-party surrounding where everybody is having a good time and everybody is relaxed, you'll have a spiritual experience. And I said, 'Of course.' That was the research they hadn't done." Always eager to follow Tim, no matter how far afield it might lead him, Slack accompanied him to Flo and Maynard's house to take LSD. "It was an old Charles Addams kind of mansion with rooms done up early hippie style," Slack remembered. "Everybody was dressed in pajamas for dinner. Tim came around with a bottle. It looked like a kid's soap-bubble jar and it had a little wooden stick in it. And he said, 'Stick out your tongue,' and he wiped the stick on your tongue and then he said, 'Swallow this.'" Up to that point, alcohol was the only drug Slack had ever experienced. Slack recalled: "That trip was the most important thing that ever happened to me. I just thought it was the answer to all the problems of the world. I thought, 'Oh, LSD is going to be the solution.' And I thought it would get really good press. I thought everyone would see: this is the way. Because everybody loved everybody. It was marvelous. You all shared this incredible experience of seeing God in a lightbulb and merging with carpets and watching your grandmother walk through the wall. It was incredible. In the morning, the sidewalk was still moving. Maynard came up to me and said, 'Are you straight?' And I did not know how to answer that question. But I went back and tried to talk everyone I knew into taking LSD."

Slack soon began making his way to Tim's house as often as he could. "Here's how it worked," he said. "You'd get high on the thing and start having all these hallucinations and visions and the next day, people would say, 'Did you see the white light?' And I would say, 'Oh, yeah.' I didn't know if I had or I hadn't. But I didn't want to not be part of the in crowd." In 1973, Slack wrote a book about his experiences entitled *Timothy Leary, the Madness of the Sixties, and Me.* Tim would later dismiss the book as "an obscene, squalid, sluttish, abominable, rancid, grovelling, envious potboiler by an irritated bureaucratic wretch named Charles Schloch."

SEVENTEEN

Although Tim Leary was now traveling regularly to New York to party with exotic jet-setters, turning on well-known writers and poets in his house in Newton Center, and running an innovative research project behind prison walls, he still somehow found the time to teach his classes at Harvard. It was not long before his colleagues began to notice the effect his brand-new lifestyle was having on others. "There was an in-group and an out-group," recalled Brendan Maher, who came from England as a Fulbright scholar and later became a professor at Harvard. "There were mornings when one might go into the building and find that one-third of the graduate students in a course one was teaching were wearing sunglasses in March. Because they had been up all night. It was an in-group of the illuminati versus the rest." "During that fall," Herbert Kelman remembered, "I was discovering more and more what was going on. One doesn't usually precisely know what one's colleagues are teaching or how they are dealing with their students and it's really considered to be poor form to interfere in any way . . . But what I was beginning to gradually learn, I clearly found disturbing."

Maher first found out about the drug-taking when some graduate students came to see him "to convey their distress." Tim had told them that if they were, in Maher's words, "too square or too uptight to be unwilling to take the drugs, they very probably didn't belong in the field of clinical psychology to begin with. When you're a graduate student looking for a degree in clinical psychology, that's a pretty powerful message to get. Your professor can have an enormous effect on the early years of your career." Describing himself as "morally outraged" and "completely astonished," Maher's initial reaction was that perhaps the story was not true. But then he learned he was not the only one being told this. "It was becoming slowly known that some of these graduate students were very unhappy with what they perceived to be a moral pressure on them to do something they didn't want to do."

David McClelland also began hearing what he called "horrific stories about what had happened at these sessions in the house Tim had rented in Newton Center. They were trashing the house and painting mandalas on the walls." McClelland enlisted Dick Alpert, one of his former students, to keep an eye on Tim for him. Instead of becoming his "spy," Alpert became "a convert." For McClelland, the last straw came when Tim talked McClelland's mother-in-law, a woman in her late seventies who had just suffered a serious stroke, into taking psilocybin. She never actually participated in a session because McClelland forbade her to do so. "But she was perfectly willing to do it because she loved Tim and she loved excitement." "I began to realize," McClelland later told a magazine reporter, "that there were only a few subjects and many researchers, which meant that the researchers were taking more of the drug than anybody else."

McClelland first raised his concerns at a faculty meeting in October 1961. In a memo entitled "Some Social Reactions to the Psilocybin Research Project," he wrote: "The history of the project has been marred by repeated casual ingestions of the drug, group decisions made which are not carried out etc. One can hardly fail to infer that one effect of the drug is to decrease responsibility and increase impulsivity."

McClelland's stinging critique of the lack of controls and scarcity of hard data impelled Michael Kahn, a graduate student, and Alpert to begin cleaning up around Tim. Together, they copyedited Tim's grant proposals, collected and collated data, and made certain that the research was being written up. In February, Alpert wrote a fourteen-page memo that was duly mimeographed and distributed to all concerned. Proposing several modifications in the program, Alpert wrote, "We wish to extend our apologies to our colleagues for the difficulties, both private and public which we have caused them. The strain we have all felt develop as a 'side effect' of this research is not only unfortunate but also quite uncomfortable. We hope that this statement with which we will abide will provide a first step towards the alleviation of the tension." Alpert's memo bought precious time for the Psychedelic Research Project.

On February 20, 1962, *The Harvard Crimson* ran a story which said that the directors of the Center for Personality Research were thinking about using psilocybin in a "mushroom seminar" for graduate students in theology, behavioral science, and philosophy. The course would be based on taking the drug once a month and then applying the insights gained to problems in their respective fields. For the first time in history, Harvard University was about to grant course credit for taking drugs. Alpert and Leary quickly sent a letter to the *Crimson* in which they pointed out that they were not "unbounded in their enthusiasm" for psilocybin but unbounded in their "concern for the many problems created by the consciousness-expanding drugs." Emphasizing that their research was carefully controlled and in strict adherence to university codes, they added, "All subjects are informed volunteers. No undergraduates or minors." Dr. Dana L. Farnsworth, director of Harvard University Health Services, joined the fray with a letter asserting that mescaline could in fact do a great deal of harm. He noted that it could "precipitate psychotic reactions in some apparently normal persons. It has been known to increase slight depressions into suicidal ones and to produce schizophrenic-like reactions."

On February 21, McClelland sent Alpert a memo. "Let's define the drugs you are going to work with in this stage of the research. I'm for concentrating on psilocybin and forgetting 'LSD, etc.' for now." McClelland was more interested in long-term observational data than the subject's own view of himself and what the drug experience meant to him. "You have been doing pilot studies for two years. Why do you need another year of pilot work? My chief reaction to the proposal is that it is still too vague and too general. It sounds too much as if you were still in a stage of wanting to play around another year and make up your mind what you really want to do. There's been enough playing around," he concluded ominously.

Before Tim or Alpert could respond to McClelland's comments, the long-simmering feud between those at Harvard who had already had the psychedelic experience and those who had not burst into the open. A graduate student named Neil Friedman, who had never taken psilocybin, provided Herbert Kelman with the proverbial smoking gun. "I was really the one who blew the whistle on Tim and Dick's stuff at Harvard," Friedman would later say. "And I have mixed feelings about having done so.

Herb Kelman was my adviser, and I remember a particular advisement session in which I had the sense he wanted to ask me something but he wasn't asking me. So we went around for a while and finally he got as close as he could but it was still like, 'I don't want to be fishing for gossip from a student. On the other hand, I have no way of knowing what's going on.'" Friedman told Kelman that he was "one of maybe five or six holdouts" who had not yet done the drug. "Basically, all the other graduate students were doing the drug with Leary and Alpert and had formed a bond. A band. And I felt some peer pressure to become part of it. I knew of other students who had succumbed to the pressure. I knew of one who did and had a very bad experience." Kelman remembers that it was Friedman who did the fishing. But "because Neil was the rebel and my student" who "without thinking about it would have expected me to be supportive of his concerns," his caution made Kelman realize just "how far this had gone and the extent to which this basically illegitimate activity had become legitimized in the eyes of the students."

"Whether or not the students took drugs was not the issue I was concerned with," Kelman would later say. "Not then and not later. What I was concerned with was the abuse of power." Once Kelman told Friedman that he did not support such activity, Kelman became "a repository of reports." Suddenly students were calling and coming in to see him to talk about their experiences. "It got more and more disturbing. Among the stories I kept hearing were about the direct way in which particularly Dick Alpert was using his position to promote this ideology. One example: an undergraduate who wanted to apply to graduate school in clinical psychology at Harvard but was advised by Alpert that unless he was prepared to work with the drugs, it wasn't worth his while to apply. More of that was done by Dick than by Tim." To make it "crystal clear to the students that this was certainly not required of them and that the majority of the faculty disapproved of this," Kelman went to McClelland and suggested that it was time to call a general meeting, one to which all clinical students and clinical faculty could come. McClelland talked to Tim about it and Tim agreed to co-sign the invitation. "The understanding was that we would have this meeting and Dave McClelland and I would talk and then Tim would respond. It was meant to be an in-house meeting."

When Kelman walked into the meeting at 5 Divinity Avenue on March 15, 1962, he was astounded to find the room packed with graduate students, undergraduates, faculty members from other parts of the department, researchers in pharmacology, and even a psychiatrist from the Massachusetts Mental Health Center. The rumor mill had spread the news, not only around the campus but beyond. Calling the meeting to order, McClelland began by clearly stating that "the role of the psilocybin research in the over-all graduate training program in personality and clinical psychology has been misunderstood. Consciousness-expansion, or experience with drugs that expand consciousness, has never been part of the graduate training program."

He added that anyone who had ever told any graduate student that consciousness expansion and the graduate program were one and the same did not belong at 5 Divinity Avenue. That individual was misrepresenting both the program and the staff. McClelland decried "the McCarthy-like atmosphere of distrust and suspicion." People were constantly coming to his office to tell him secrets. He found these confessions reminiscent of the days when ex-Communists rushed to save themselves by throwing former comrades on the bonfire. As far as he was concerned, the real problem here was the social psychology of drug addiction. "The whole atmosphere is one of ideological commitment to a quasi-religious sect, with no resemblance at all to an intellectual partnership . . . the program as a whole has acquired a life of its own, independent of some of the specific actions and motivations that enter into it."

McClelland then yielded the floor to Kelman, who voiced his own concerns about the program. "I wish I could treat this as scholarly disagreement," he said, "but this work violates the values of the academic community." Charging that Tim and Alpert had adopted a "nonchalant attitude" in conducting their research, Kelman added, "The program has an anti-intellectual atmosphere. Its emphasis is on pure experience, not on verbalizing findings. It is an attempt to reject most of what the psychologist tries to do." Calling his colleagues "false messiahs," he concluded, "This is wrong and must be stopped."

Then Tim spoke. As always when confronted with problems he had created, Tim did not respond with anger. Instead, he conceded that much of what had been said might be true and promised to do everything he could to right all wrongs, real or imagined. "Tim's normal reaction to criticism," McClelland recalled, "was to accept it and then go ahead and do whatever he pleased. He did not react in the meeting. I never saw Tim hostile." "As usual," Kelman recalled, "Tim was the gentler one and Dick was the tough one. Tim was conciliatory. But not Dick. He played the role of the heavy. As in all cults and new religions, you have the visionary and you have the tough guy. There is always somebody doing the organizing and the dirty work that goes with the organizing. Not that this was the only role Dick was playing. I knew him from before and he was also searching for an answer. I'm not saying or implying for one moment that his commitment to this was insincere. But Dick was the salesman or the general manager. Tim was more the figurehead. He was the inspiration too."

The floor was then thrown open to questions from the audience. Before the meeting, Brendan Maher had gone to the Countaway Library of Medicine to do some research. "I worked my way through the recent literature to see what was known about psilocybin," he would later say. "None of it was from Leary or those people. I learned there were enough risks of a medical nature that it wasn't something one would fool around with unless one had familiarized oneself with those risks." Tim would later describe Maher as "a dour rat-lab experimentalist known for his rigid insistence on teaching students exactly the way he had been taught in medieval universities." However, as Tim sat in the front row surrounded by members of his own staff, he seemed to be enjoying the proceedings. "It was a good ventilation of feelings by outraged authorities, similar to the lectures I had heard from school principals and West Point moralists." Then Maher got to his feet to discuss the medical issues and things got "impolite. Standing before me like a prosecuting attorney with the journal articles in hand, Maher demanded that I respond." The response Maher got from Alpert was that this was a political question. Maher recalled: "It was downhill from there. Then at some point, Leary sort of snapped and basically said, 'We don't have to know these things because we have a medical adviser. A psychiatrist at Massachusetts General Hospital, Gerald Klerman.' Apparently unknown to either of them, Gerry Klerman was actually in the audience. He got up and said, 'I want to tell you I have never talked to you in my life. I don't know what you're talking about. And I have no relationship with you whatsoever.' I don't think they would have known him if they had seen him. Whereas lesser mortals might have been sort of embarrassed by this event, they weren't particularly. They were not abashed at all."

"At this point," Tim would later write, "Dick walked to the front of the room, radiating genial poise. He was imitating his lawyer father. As attorney for the defense Richard passionately refuted the charges and praised our research as a courageous and productive demonstration of new methods for behavior change." After the meeting, Maher was present when Alpert ran into Kelman in the hallway. "Alpert said he was going to arrange to have his lawyers sue Herb for defamation or something like that. It was quite a threat. Alpert's father was president of the New Haven Railroad and they had a lot of lawyers. And his father was a lawyer as well. This was now really a political matter."

Still, according to Tim, the meeting ended on what he later called a "note of civilized calm" as well as the very Harvard-like decision to form a committee to look into the matter. The controversy might have ended right then and there had Andrew Weil, the best-selling author and alternative medicine guru who was then a Harvard undergraduate and an editor of the *Crimson,* not sent a reporter to cover the meeting. Previously, Weil had asked Tim if he could participate in a psilocybin session. Tim had already promised not to involve undergraduates in his research and so turned Weil down. Two months later, Weil obtained some mescaline from an American pharmaceutical firm. With seven other undergraduates, he began taking the drug fairly regularly in half-gram doses. During 1961, he had twelve highly varied trips. "Most were nothing more than intensifications of preexisting moods with prominent periods of euphoria," he later wrote. Describing his trips to Robert Forte in *Timothy Leary: Outside Looking In,* a Festschrift published after Tim's death, Weil said, "They started me on a road of experimentation in a lot of areas in my life; that I think got me to where I am today." The reason Weil had decided to air out Harvard's dirty laundry in public seems to have had more to do with Alpert than Tim. As Peter Owen Whitmer wrote in *Aquarius Revisited,* "Alpert had been using psychedelic drugs with undergraduate men, often in return for sexual favors." Alpert had taken psychedelic drugs with Weil's roommate and, in Whitmer's words, "Weil was jealous" of their relationship.

Whatever Weil's motive may have been, an article about the meeting appeared in *The Harvard Crimson* on March 15, 1962. Under the headline PSYCHOLOGISTS DISAGREE ON PSILOCYBIN RESEARCH, Robert E. Smith wrote, "Members of the Center for Research in Personality clashed yesterday in a dramatic meeting over the right of two colleagues to continue studies on the effects of psilocybin, a consciousness-expanding drug, on graduate student subjects." The story reported that opponents of the study claimed the project was run nonchalantly and irresponsibly and that alleged permanent injury to participants had been ignored. Tim was quoted as responding to a claim by Maher that psilocybin should only be taken in a hospital setting by saying it was standard procedure to hold meetings in subjects' homes at which all in attendance were under the influence of the drug. "But no staff member," Tim said, "has ever been in a situation when he couldn't handle any eventuality."

The next day, Anthony G. Greenwald, a teaching fellow in social relations, wrote the *Crimson*: "I am reminded of Freud's (pre-psychoanalytic) enthusiasm about the 'exhilaration . . . euphoria . . . vitality . . . self-control,' resulting from his use of cocaine, on which he was doing research. He prescribed it to many of his friends for minor and major discomforts, with disastrous results . . . Leary and Alpert are undoubtedly quite well aware of similar potential dangers. It would be as much of a mistake to stifle their research as it would have been to stifle the research on cocaine and related anaesthetics which was prodded by the enthusiasm of Freud and other early investigators." The *Crimson* also printed a letter from Kelman in which he made it plain that his talk at the meeting was not about psilocybin but graduate education in psychology and the effects of the psilocybin program on that training. Kelman also noted that his talk was directed to the graduate students in the department and not the wider public. That a representative from the *Crimson* was there ran contrary to the intentions of the meeting's organizers. More correspondence followed, mostly discussing academic freedom, ethics, and responsibility. Elliot Perkins, '23, Master of Lowell House, chimed in, telling a *Crimson* reporter that to him the project seemed "more suitable for the Medical School" than the Graduate School of Arts and Sciences. "Undergraduates," he said, "shouldn't be involved in this or any other damn experiments."

Although people were now choosing camps and laying into one another in print, this was all well and good so long as it remained within the boundaries of Harvard where such issues could always be publicly discussed.

On March 16, 1962, however, the *Boston Herald,* a Hearst tabloid, ran a story about the meeting under the headline HALLUCINATION DRUG FOUGHT AT HARVARD—350 STUDENTS TAKE PILLS. Buried eight paragraphs down in the article was a quote from Alpert stating that 350 "subjects" had been involved in the project. "Subjects" had somehow been transmuted in the headline into "students." This one small change made it seem as though a runaway drug cult had in fact sprung up at Harvard.

On March 28, *The Harvard Crimson* reported that George A. Michael, deputy commissioner of the Massachusetts State Health Department, believed that psilocybin fell "into the classification of drugs that must be administered by a physician." Michael had been put in charge of the on-going inquiry into "Alpert's psilocybin research" and was examining a preliminary investigative report. If he determined the drug was harmful and had not been administered by a physician during research at Harvard, then those who supplied it might be prosecuted. State narcotics agents had already interviewed Tim. They were followed by agents from the FBI and the Federal Drug Administration. One of the state agents happened to be a fellow Irishman who remembered Tim's great-uncle from his days as a professor at Tufts Medical School. "Inspector O'Connell was proud that another Timothy Leary had now made it to Harvard," Tim would later write in *Flashbacks*. "He naturally suspected a Protestant plot against the long-suppressed Irish race. I took him to lunch at the Faculty Club and he left agreeing to keep us informed about any further developments." David McClelland recalled, "Tim never hid anything. He would always tell everybody what he was doing, including the narcotics agents who were fellow Irishmen. Tim would charm them or try to and invite them to come to one of his sessions."

Because the university was unwilling to allow the state of Massachusetts to define the limits of acceptable academic research, Harvard did what it had always done when one of its own was in trouble. Closing ranks around Tim and Alpert, the university decided to police itself. Tim agreed to transmit his present supply of psilocybin to Dr. Farnsworth at Harvard University Health Services. Along with McClelland, Farnsworth would now control all access to the drug. The key to the medicine cabinet in which the magic mushrooms were stored now belonged to someone else. But without drugs, there could be no psychedelic research project. There could be no consciousness expansion. While it may have looked to the outside world as though Harvard had solved the problem, Tim and Alpert still had virtually unlimited access to LSD, a far more powerful substance that would remain legal until October 6, 1966.

———

Rejected by members of his own department, Tim found a new peer group who seemed far more willing to take him seriously than his colleagues at the Center for Personality Research. "When it became known on campus that a group of psychologists was producing brain-change," Tim would later write in *Changing My Mind, Among Others,* "we expected that astronomers and biologists would come flocking around to use this new tool for expanding awareness . . . Instead, we were flooded by inquiries from the Divinity School!" Over a period of weeks, an informal religious seminar began to evolve at Huston Smith's house. Through Smith and Walter Houston Clark, Tim met Walter Pahnke, whom he described as a "young country-bumpkin, fresh faced, gee-whiz enthusiast." A candidate for a Ph.D. in philosophy of religion at Harvard, Pahnke had a medical degree in addition to holding a bachelor's degree in divinity. Tim also met Fred Swain, a former Air Force major turned Hindu monk, who was associated with the Vedanta ashram in Boston, and had ingested mushrooms with R. Gordon Wasson in the hills outside Oaxaca. After Swain took LSD in Tim's house, he invited Tim to visit his ashram. There, Tim found a religion that seemed entirely consistent with what he had experienced on his acid trips. "The Hindu Bibles read like psychedelic manuals. The Hindu myths were session reports. The ashram itself was a turn-on. A serene, rhythmic life of work and meditation all aimed at getting high." During an LSD session at the ashram, Tim experienced "the fulcrum moment of eternity. The exact second of consciousness, fragile, omniscient. God was present and spoke to us in silence." Overcome with reverence and gratitude, Tim would later write, "I was a Hindu from that moment on."

Yet when Walter Pahnke proposed a double-blind experiment designed to find out whether psilocybin could actually induce an authentic religious experience, Tim did everything he could to stand in his way. Pahnke's plan was to assemble divinity students from the Andover Newton Theological Seminary in the small downstairs chapel of Marsh Chapel on the campus of Boston University on Good Friday. Half would be given psilocybin, the other half nicotinic acid. The subjects would be divided into groups, with the two guides for each group taking thirty milligrams of psilocybin. The Good Friday sermon delivered by Howard Thurmond, the black minister who was Martin Luther King's mentor, would then be piped into the chapel. Neither subjects, nor guides, nor experimenters would know who had taken what. Sounding like a small-town Irish parish priest, Tim later wrote, "I really had to laugh at this caricature of the experimental design applied to that most sacred experience. If he had proposed giving aphrodisiacs to twenty virgins to produce a mass orgasm, it wouldn't have sounded further out." As a medical doctor, Pahnke tried to reassure Tim by telling him he could legally administer any drug he liked. He could also inject those having a bad experience with tranquilizers to bring them down. Tim responded by telling Pahnke he should first take the drug several times himself so he would be familiar with it. Pahnke refused. For his study to be accepted as unbiased and objective, he needed to preserve his "psychedelic virginity."

By April, Pahnke had agreed to limit the number of subjects to twenty divinity students, divided into four small groups. He balked at the guides also taking the drug, but Tim refused to concede. To ensure there would be no doctor-patient game, all the doctors had to share in the psychedelic experience. Finally Pahnke agreed, and on Holy Thursday evening, just eighteen hours before the "Sacred Three-Hour Vigil," Tim obtained the necessary psilocybin pills from a psychiatrist in Worcester. He had them ground into powder and sorted into plain envelopes with code numbers on them. At midnight, Tim called David McClelland to tell him that they were going ahead with the experiment. McClelland groaned. "Oh, God," he replied. "Why did you have to tell me in advance?" "Because," Tim replied, "we don't play secret games." As he would later write, "I laughed. It was too classic! Poor Pilate! David, that's the way it always is. Good Friday always poses problems for administrators."

The next morning, the group assembled at ten at the seminary. Pahnke distributed the coded envelopes. Tim asked one of the students to say a prayer and then everyone ingested the powder. As they sat waiting for the psilocybin to take effect, the students read their Bibles. Tim later wrote that he began to feel happy. He had been given the real thing. Then he realized the heat radiating from his body was generated not by psilocybin but by nicotinic acid. The real problem with the experiment soon became apparent. After thirty minutes, everyone knew who was tripping and who was not. The effects were that obvious. Just before noon, the guides drove everyone to the chapel. Howard Thurmond appeared in his robes and vestments to bless them all by candlelight. Then the three-hour service began. Prayers. Organ music. Hymns. Those who had been given the placebo sat attentively like good worshippers. Those who had been given psilocybin were lying either on benches or on the floor. Others wandered around the chapel murmuring in prayer. One chanted a hymn. One sat at the organ playing weird chords.

Then something happened that no one had anticipated. The basement doors had been locked but one of the subjects who had been given psilocybin decided to go outside. Tim would later write that he told Pahnke he would "accompany his restless mystic" and escort him along the avenue. Fearful that the student might suddenly dart out into traffic, Tim did all he could to keep him on the sidewalk. "He glanced at me, as if to say, Is that the game? So he tried to edge by me to walk on the curb. I got more scared. He made a feint to run into the street. My paranoia had forced him into the role of prisoner, seeking to escape. Then I caught on and laughed. Let's not play that silly game, I said. He nodded." Returning to the chapel basement, the subject ran

> to the piano and banged down the lid savagely. He ran to the wall and grabbed a picture, holding it above his head ready to smash it if he were approached. I sat down quickly and put my hands in the position of prayer and called him . . . Then he relaxed . . . He came over and sat down in front of me . . . Let us pray, brother. I held his hands tight and started chanting . . . His body visibly relaxed. Then he smiled. Then he looked at my face in reverent love. He embraced me. I held him in my arms . . . Then he burst into tears and sobs. He crumbled to the floor. I held him while his body shook with the convulsive heaving. Then he sat up and looked at me and said, Thanks. I'm all right now. I've been a religious phony and a sexual freak but now I know what prayer is all about.

In his version of the story, Tim, who had not yet been confronted with a problem he could not solve during a session, had once again saved the day by bringing someone having a difficult experience through to the other side. Others remembered the incident differently. Michael Hollingshead, who was there as a guide, would later write that one of the subjects, a shy and sensitive person given to reading aloud large passages of John Donne's poetry, began tearing the buttons off his jacket and declaring that he was a fish. He then threw his dental plate at the altar. Another student lay on the floor, writhing like a snake. Another stared at a crucifix, his hands clasped tightly together and an insane grin on his face. A fourth lay stiff as a board on a pew. A divinity student from another group faced the cross with his arms outstretched like Christ. Another student some-how managed to get outside and was almost killed when he walked into traffic. Rick Doblin, who conducted a follow-up study on the Good Fri-day experiment twenty-five years later, would say, "It was an enormously powerful sermon and part of it was, 'You have to tell people that there is a man on the cross.' This man who was under the influence of psilocybin took that literally. And he thought, 'Well, who am I going to tell? Well, the most important person to tell is the president.' And then he thought, 'The president is not here. But I can tell the president of the university.' And that was what he went to do."

Huston Smith, who had been given psilocybin, was the one who fol-lowed the subject out into the street. "The door opened," Smith recalled, "and there was a guy zonked out of his head on Commonwealth Avenue. I went out and caught up with him. He was marching like someone who had a very strong mission and I tried to reason with him. He was beyond all reasoning of course." Smith then saw Eda Pahnke, Walter's wife, hav-ing a picnic lunch on the grass with their daughter. He shouted at her to go back and tell Walter, which she did. "After a block or so, Wally and someone else came up. So there we were, three people, and Wally was trying to reason with him, but he was like Samson, he had the strength of ten. There was no way we were going to constrain him." At the front doors of the School of Theology, the subject went up the steps with everyone still trying to hang on to him. "And then," Smith recalled, "a mailman went by. He had a special delivery letter in his hand. As he went by, the guy grabbed the letter. You can imagine the postman's face. Then it was four against one. With all our strength, we tried peeling back his fingers to get him to release the packet. But he wasn't going to let go of it. Finally he did and the postman went up the steps to deliver it." Once they managed to bring the subject back inside the chapel, Pahnke gave him a shot of Thorazine to bring him down. "Tim wasn't involved," Smith would later say. "In two minutes, the guy was back to normal. But he wasn't communicative. Wally did a long interview with him later on and got the story. He had received a message from God that was going to bring perpetual world peace and it was his burden to deliver it."

"Everybody I spoke with who was in the psilocybin group felt the ex-perience they'd had roughly twenty-five years previous was a genuine mystical experience and had positive long-lasting impact on their lives," Doblin would later say. The only person who did not talk about it in this manner was the subject who had wandered out into the street. "It had not shattered his life. Although I'm sure it was still of sufficient magnitude that he didn't even want to talk about it." Given the fact that the climate at Harvard was changing and that psilocybin was now harder to obtain, the version of the Good Friday Experiment that Tim helped present to the world was one that Doblin would later say "tended to underplay the difficulties. I'm sure they had this feeling that if they were to report that this guy flipped out and they gave him a shot of Thorazine, that would add fuel to the critics. It was definitely unethical."

However, Doblin's follow-up study also showed "that the hypothesis of the initial study was completely confirmed." When administered to people who were religiously inclined and in a religious setting, psilocybin could "facilitate a genuine mystical experience that is either identical with or indistinguishable from the classic mystical experience." After the experiment, still "high and glowing and talking about God," everyone went back to Tim's house for a communal supper. Susan Leary cooked hamburgers and hot dogs. As Tim helped himself to a celebratory beer, Pahnke came in. "Our eyes met and we grinned and shook hands, laughing. It was like the first session at the prison. We had done it! . . . There was proof—scientific, experimental, statistical, objective [that] Psychedelic drugs were sacraments." "For Leary," Michael Hollingshead would later write, "the Good Friday session was something of a personal triumph . . . Increasingly, he began to study literary accounts of religious ecstasies from Wordsworth, Tennyson, Virginia Woolf, C. P. Snow, and personal experiences of classic mystics like Teresa of Avila, Plotinus, and St. Augustine."

What the Good Friday Experiment, also known as the "Miracle of Marsh Chapel," really confirmed beyond all doubt was that Tim Leary, who was now convinced that psychedelics were the magic elixir that could cure all the world's ills, was perfectly willing not only to ignore all evidence to the contrary but also to offer himself as a modern-day Moses who was bringing God's message to the chosen people.

EIGHTEEN

In April 1962 Tim Leary, Peggy Hitchcock, and Richard Alpert flew to Mexico City. From there, they took a twin-engine plane to Zihautanejo, a quiet fishing village north of Acapulco on the Pacific Ocean. In Zihautanejo, there were no large homes or villas, only a hotel located at the end of a dirt road that followed the bay south of the village. The hotel's full-color brochure proclaimed: "For Lifetime Remembering!!!! All this is yours at Hotel Catalina. 18 breeze-cooled rooms, each with bath. 24 hour automatic hot water. Electric funicular from beach." The going rate for a double-occupancy room with three full meals was $14.40 a day. Since virtually no one stayed at Hotel Catalina during the summer, the manager, who was dignified, soft-spoken, and Swiss, told Tim and Alpert it was indeed possible that the owner would close the doors to the public during July and August so they could rent it. "Timothy and Richard decided they would like to do a summer camp in Mexico," Peggy Hitchcock recalled. "At the time, this was the only decent semi-chic hotel in Zihautanejo. You could only get there by airplane. There were no roads. It was isolated."

Tim Leary would later describe "Pretty Peggy Hitchcock" as "an international jet-setter, renowned as the colorful patroness of the livelier arts and confidante of jazz musicians, race car drivers, writers, movie stars." Although Tim admitted to being "extremely attracted to Peggy," he wrote that when Dick Alpert announced she was the first woman in his life to turn him on romantically, "I restrained my ardor and played best friend." Although Alpert and Peggy never became romantically involved, they were all soon hanging out together as a trio. "Dick and I had found our Becky Thatcher." Describing the situation between them in Mexico as a "Spanish sexual comedy," Tim added, "Dick and Peggy would end up in one bedroom both thinking about me, while I, next door, simmered with desire for Peggy. The tension grew to the amusement of us all."

Tim's desire to find a tropical paradise where he could continue doing research into LSD and DMT without interference from the outside world, was greatly influenced by Aldous Huxley's recently published novel *Island,* in which a band of compassionate islanders ingest a perfected version of LSD. Long before Ken Kesey and his band of Merry Pranksters set out on the road in their psychedelic bus, Zihuatanejo became, in a Harvard graduate student's words, the first "group fantasy."

In *Flashbacks,* Tim Leary wrote that before he left Cambridge to return to Mexico by way of Los Angeles, a good-looking aristocratic woman from Washington, D.C., had come to his office. Her name was Mary Pinchot Meyer and she wanted Tim to teach her how to run an LSD session so she could turn on a close friend. Because he was a very important man as well as a public figure, her friend could not possibly make this connection for himself. With Tim, Michael Hollingshead, and a woman to whom Flo Ferguson had introduced Tim in New York, Meyer took part in a low-dose LSD session. Meyer seemed to know a good deal about the CIA's use of mind-expanding drugs in a series of disastrous mind-control experiments that have since been well documented.

Tim Leary would write about three more meetings with Mary Pinchot Meyer over the next two years. In 1965, Tim discovered to his great horror that she had been murdered on October 12, 1964, as she walked along the canal towpath in Georgetown. Her body was identified by her brother-in-law, Ben Bradlee, executive editor of *The Washington Post.* Tim also learned for the first time that Meyer was married to CIA division chief Cord Meyer, Tim's nemesis at the American Veterans Committee during his graduate student days at Berkeley. When it was revealed that Mary Pinchot Meyer had been one of John F. Kennedy's mistresses, Tim immediately suspected she had been killed for giving LSD to the president and then recording this information in her diary, which was never found.

While Tim did have contact with Mary Pinchot Meyer during this period and probably did supply her with psychedelics, which she may well have taken with someone in power in Washington, there is no evidence the man was John F. Kennedy. But then a good deal of what Tim reported as fact in *Flashbacks* is pure fantasy, most notably a sexual liaison with Marilyn Monroe during this period in Los Angeles, which never occurred.

Tim arrived in Zihuatanejo a week before everyone else. He divided his time between lying on the golden sand and translating the W. Y. Evans-Wentz version of *The Tibetan Book of the Dead* into "psychedelic terms." Soon, thirty-three people took up summer residence at Hotel Catalina. "They had all the graduate students," recalled Peggy Hitchcock. "Gunther Weil and George Litwin and Ralph Metzner and their wives. I was there as a single woman and one of my brothers, Tommy, came with me and we stayed ten days." As Tim would later describe it, the daily schedule called "for one-third of the company to be taking psychedelics, another third to be guiding the trippers, and the remaining third to be resting from their previous day's voyages, writing reports, and interviewing with the research team." With psilocybin no longer available, the psychedelic drug of choice was LSD, which the Leary group referred to as either Morning Glory or Heavenly Blue. "Every day there were trippers walking along the beach, body surfing, meditating, or lazing in hammocks strung along the terrace. At night the grounds were alive with color, fires burned in the sand, guitars and flutes filled the air. Small groups clustered together discussing previous voyages."

"It was very different," Ralph Metzner recalled. "Very physical. Very sensual. The ocean. The surf. If people were having a bad trip, we would just go down and roll them in the surf. Or lay them down on the sand." "It was totally innocent," a Harvard graduate student remembered. "Everyone there was taking so many substances that the affairs and the sleeping with each other mattered much less. As I remember it, that was a period of getting much closer to what we were aspiring toward." But the scene in Zihautanejo was also, as the graduate student put it, "totally unrealistic . . . We were in a poor part of Mexico and it was at the expense of those people who were living there but not living in paradise in the same way we were. It was a poor fishing village. They were making our meals. We were really a very elite group, unaware of economics and politics. But within the framework of it being totally unrealistic, it was the closest in my experience that we came to living in the way we wanted to."

As Tim Leary stood on the top terrace of the hotel looking down with "pride at the magic we had wrought," he felt like "Ignatius Loyola, reformer, leader of a dedicated band, author of a new regime of meditation and inner discovering." Tim had left both of his children behind in Newton Center to be cared for by graduate students while he set up the training center, but they joined him once school ended. Years later, Susan Leary remembered, "People were taking drugs in Mexico all the time. I never took any drugs, nor did my brother. There was no trouble. It was very peaceful and relaxed." Then sixteen, Susan had not yet taken LSD. "I didn't really know what the experience was about," she later told an interviewer. "And I had wild paranoia. I was afraid I would get high and I would not come back to my normal level of consciousness."

. On the Saturday night before their departure, Tim and his cohorts held a farewell party. Nearly everyone took LSD. The mayor and other officials came to the party with mariachis from the village. The hotel staff joined in to drink and dance. The party went on till dawn. At noon the next day, everyone piled into VW buses and drove to the baseball diamond near the airport to play a friendly game of softball with a team from the village, which Tim had organized. Unbeknownst to Tim and his group, local newspapers had billed the game as between the Harvard University varsity squad and the official semipro Mexican state team. To Tim's surprise, farmers had come by bus from miles around to watch the game. Local vendors set up temporary stands to sell tacos, beer, and soft drinks. Serious betting was taking place. Still hallucinating from the night before, Tim's team took the field with just four real players—a psychiatrist who later served on Governor Ronald Reagan's antidrug commission in California; an ex–dope dealer named Lowell, who would die in a Moroccan prison; Tommy Hitchcock; and Tim. In the first inning, the opposing pitcher walked Tim's first three batters. "The fact that they were standing with their bats on their shoulders, staring at the pitcher with dilated eyeballs in other-worldly detachment, may have contributed to his control problems." Then Tommy Hitchcock hit a home run. Suddenly everyone on Tim's team started hitting like mad. "The acid distorted our perception of time. Everything moved slowly. When the ball left the pitcher's hand, it seemed to float towards the plate, allowing plenty of time to count the stitches, examine the Wilson label, speculate about the history of competitive sports since the Greek Olympics, and feel the muscles contract reflexively to hit the ball."

(Tim's assessment of the effect of LSD on the motor skills needed to play baseball would seem to be borne out by Pittsburgh Pirates pitcher Dock Ellis. In the mistaken belief he had the day off, Ellis ingested LSD with his girlfriend in Los Angeles on June 12, 1970, only to learn he was in fact scheduled to pitch against the San Diego Padres. Ellis hit one bat-ter, walked eight, and struck out six while throwing a no-hitter. Although he could see a "blazing, comet-like tail" on his fastball, Ellis also ducked out of the way of balls hit weakly back to him on the mound. Later, he said he could only remember bits and pieces of the game. "The ball was small sometimes, the ball was large sometimes. Sometimes I saw the catcher, sometimes I didn't.")

Leading by a score of eight to nothing with an inning left to play, Tim told his pitcher to let the other team back into the game. He pulled his best players and put in four graduate students who were so unathletic that they did not "know the glove went on the non-throwing hand." The village team soon tied the score. With no one in the mood for extra innings, both teams embraced one another and began drinking beer and tequila. The party soon spread throughout the town. "Everyone urged us to come back next year," Tim wrote. "And we planned to. The six weeks at Zihautanejo had given us a glimpse of utopia."

After returning to Cambridge, Tim and some of his psychedelic campers decided to continue living communally and moved as an extended family into a single house in Newton Center. More than 120 years earlier, in nearby West Roxbury, George Ripley had founded Brook Farm, a landed commune that attracted many New England intellectuals, Nathaniel Hawthorne and Charles Dana among them. Nonetheless, in the fall of 1962, the concept of adults not related by blood living together under one roof seemed downright shocking.

Tim and his two children moved into a large, rambling green house at 23 Kenwood Avenue along with Alpert; Foster Dunlap, a male undergraduate with whom Alpert was in love; Dunlap's wife, Barbara, and their young son; Ralph Metzner and his new bride; and Lowell, the black ex–dope dealer who had been in Zihautanejo. In all, twelve people resided there on a full-time basis. There were also visitors, among them Peggy Hitchcock, who often came up from New York. "Our summer school romance had blossomed into a love affair and, eventually, a lifelong friendship," Tim would later write. "It was a fairly big house with sort of a Victorian feeling to it," Peggy Hitchcock recalled. "Timothy was teaching and so was Richard. They were doing their prisoner project and there were a lot of people coming up on the weekends and Tim seemed very happy. He didn't anticipate the inevitable. We were all pretty much on top of the world and felt we could do anything."

Influenced by Hermann Hesse's *Steppenwolf* and *Magister Ludi* as well as *Mount Analogue* by René Daumal, the residents sealed off the door to a small study and repapered the walls of the room so that the doorway could no longer be seen. Tim climbed in through the window with a power saw so he could cut a yard-square hole in the floor. A ladder from a dark tunnel in the cellar was now the only way to enter a room whose walls and ceiling were covered with Hindu paisley prints. Red velvet cushions were strewn on the floor. At the far end of the room, illuminated by candles in ornate holders, sat a smiling bronze Buddha donated by Peggy Hitchcock. "In this secret chamber," Tim would later write, "a modern version of Tom Sawyer's clubhouse, it was easy to forget, on drugs or straight, where you were in the house or indeed on the planet. It was an early isolation tank." It was also a replica of the safe haven Tim had first experienced as a boy—the room at the very top of his grandfather's house where the old gentleman kept all his books.

During the fall and winter of 1962, Tim devoted a good deal of his energy helping to develop the "experiential typewriter," a device meant to enable those tripping on DMT or LSD to record what they were feeling as they experienced it. Metzner would later say, "Tim would take the medicine and my wife and I would sit there and we would ask him every two minutes where he was. We were model building. Tim was really good at that."

Six months after they moved in, Gunther Weil and his wife, Karen; another graduate student and his wife; and David and Sarah Winter moved into a house owned by George Litwin on nearby Grey Cliffe Road. "It was meant to be a sister community," the graduate student recalled. George Litwin would later say, "The neighbors were radicalized. They thought we were European. Foreigners. We all drove foreign cars. No one had a foreign car in the neighborhood at that time." Nor had anyone like Tim and Alpert ever lived there. Neighbors began complaining to Newton building commissioner Vincent D. Burns about the traffic going up and down the street all night long. After investigating the complaint, the commissioner sent a notice to Alpert, notifying him that he was in violation of local zoning laws and could not use the house as a multifamily dwelling.

In December, the city of Newton filed suit against Alpert to enforce the order. In February, represented by his father, Alpert appealed on the basis that the term "family unit" had been left undefined in the zoning code. Tim told the press that the BIG family, as they now called themselves, was willing to take their case all the way to the United States Supreme Court. He pointed out that the legal definition of a family had never been decided in Massachusetts. "With us," Tim said, "there is no great gulf between the older and younger groups."

How true that was for his own children seems unclear. Years later, Susan would say, "I enjoyed community living very much because the people there were very loving, beautiful people. They were taking psychedelic drugs, and involved in changing consciousness and working out a happier way of life. It was a very relaxed atmosphere . . . Most of my friends wished they lived in a house like me." The graduate student who lived there remembered feeling that Tim's kids were lucky, but then adds, "I don't think any of us saw how much they must have suffered because I don't know how much time Tim spent with them."

Meanwhile, at Harvard Tim kept losing ground. On October 16, members of the executive committee decided that no further funds for psychedelic research would be expended unless Tim and Alpert were willing to allow a proposed advisory committee to have full control over the drugs. A week later, Tim told a meeting of the Harvard Humanists at Leverett House that he was helping to found the International Foundation for Internal Freedom (IFIF) in order "to provide more internal freedom" for people restricted by ingrained linguistic or cultural habits. A local cell called the Freedom Center had already begun using consciousness-expanding drugs. The function of IFIF would be to help start other cells.

Given that Tim and Alpert had made it plain that they intended to continue experimenting with psychedelics outside the university, Harvard scrapped its plan to set up an advisory committee to oversee their work. At a lunch held on November 29, Tim and Dick agreed to return all the university research money they had been given and to separate their psilocybin-related activities from the Laboratory of Social Relations. "We agreed," Tim would later write, "that as much as we loved and respected the University, this finishing school for Fortune 500 executives was not the place for the philosophic activists bent on changing practically every thing. The honorable thing to do was to disassociate from Harvard and form a new organization. I felt little emotion at leaving beyond a nostalgic regret. Exits were becoming one of my areas of expertise. I remained on friendly terms with Professor McClelland and we were both pleased that my departure would be courteous and dignified." Though the research project at Harvard was now officially dead, Tim remained under contract to teach there until June.

Although he had steadfastly refused to give LSD or psilocybin to undergraduates at Harvard, Tim could not stop them from finding, buying, and ingesting these drugs on their own. "In this, the third year of our research," he wrote, "the Yard was seething with drug consciousness. If we prudishly refused to turn them on, no big deal. They scored supplies from Boston or New York. Several enterprising chemistry students constructed home labs to make the stuff themselves." On December 11, 1962, the story finally hit the front page of *The New York Times*. In the opening paragraph, Fred Hechinger quoted Dean Monro as blaming the use of "mind-distorting" drugs at Harvard on "intellectual promotion" by over-enthusiastic scientific experimenters who "don't realize how inflammable undergraduates can become." Three days later, the *Times* reported that Tim and Alpert had responded with a letter to the *Crimson* in which they branded Dean Monro's charges as "reckless and inaccurate" from the scientific point of view, while also complaining that the "hysteria" about consciousness-expanding drugs constituted a danger to scientific research. Tim and Alpert also claimed that the changes produced by consciousness-expanding drugs were "similar to those produced in the mind by the printed word or by the power of suggestion." They went on to state that there was "no factual evidence that 'consciousness-experiences' are any more dangerous than psychoanalysis or a four year enrollment at Harvard College."

Even as he was defending himself in Cambridge, Tim had already lost the unqualified support of one of his earliest sponsors. On December 26, Aldous Huxley responded to a letter from Humphry Osmond in which Osmond had asked him why Tim was apparently "impervious to the idea that psychedelic substances may be both valuable and dangerous if misused," as well as why Tim could not grasp that "because one dose of psilocybin is safe this does not mean that repeated and regular doses are safe." Huxley replied:

> Yes, what about Tim Leary? I spent an evening with him here a few weeks ago—and he talked such nonsense (about the conscious mind being merely a robot, about true intelligence residing only in D{eoxyribo}N{ucleic}A{cid} molecule, about some kind of Providence looking after the population problem, which therefore wasn't

any problem at all) that I became quite concerned. Not about his
sanity—because he is perfectly sane—but about his prospects in the
world; for this nonsense-talking is just another device for annoying
people in authority, cocking snooks [a British term for expressing
scorn or derision as if by thumbing one's nose] at the academic world.
It is the reaction of a mischievous Irish boy to the headmaster of his
school. One of these days the headmaster will lose patience—and
then good-bye to Leary's psilocybin research. I am very fond of
Tim—but why, oh why, does he have to be such an ass? I have told
him repeatedly that the only attitude for a researcher in this ticklish
field is that of an anthropologist living in the midst of a tribe of potentially dangerous savages. Go about your business quietly, don't
break the taboos or criticize the locally accepted dogmas. Be polite
and friendly—and get on with the job. If you leave them alone, they
will probably leave you alone. But evidently the temptation to cock
snooks is quite irresistible—so there he goes again!

The International Foundation for Internal Freedom (IFIF) was officially launched on January 24, 1963. An impressive-sounding statement of
purpose was signed by the board of directors—Tim, Alpert, Metzner,
George Litwin, Gunther Weil, Huston Smith, Walter Houston Clark, and
Alan Watts (honorary director). The aim of the organization was "to set
up research centers across America to conduct psychedelic research. Each
local center would have medical, psychological, and legal advisors on staff
to teach members to explore their internal geography. Artists, writers, religious folk, and searchers for meaning would be welcome. Neurotics and
those seeking psychiatric treatment would be referred out to doctors."
     Exactly how "neurotics and those seeking psychiatric treatment"
could be referred to doctors when those interested in joining IFIF were
applying by mail, Tim never said. However, the membership agreement
that all were required to sign indemnified IFIF for loss, damage, and all expenses in connection with the use of psilocybin, LSD, and related drugs.
"Within a few weeks," Tim would later write, "over a thousand people
sent in ten dollars each to join, and we were avalanched with inquiries."
By May, Tim claimed that IFIF had received five hundred applications for
the summer program in Zihautanejo. Three hundred were accepted.
     Originally located in the Charles River Park Medical Suites in Boston,
IFIF soon moved across the river to 14 Story Street, "a little colonial in

Harvard Square," recalled Gunther Weil, "where they were cranking out pamphlets like the Symbionese Liberation Army. This madcap woman named Lisa Bieberman was the office manager and Peter John, who was a student of Paul Tillich, who had come out of the Divinity School and was really straight, was there. He was Tim's Boswell." On January 30, 1963, Brendan Maher, now chairman of the Center for Research in Personality, wrote Tim again to ask that the name and facilities of the center not be used for matters connected with psilocybin activities, especially since "facilities now exist for you through the machinery of your own non-profit corporation."

Throughout this period, Tim continued doing drug research on himself. His session reports from December through March were for the most part entirely positive. Injecting DMT took him "to the highest point of LSD illumination—a jewel-like satori." On February 15, he took forty-five milligrams of DMT. He took sixty milligrams on March 2, and then sixty more on March 6. In April, Tim brought an organic chemist named Bill Brunnel to Boston. With Brunnel's help, Tim planned to make IFIF into "the world's largest organization for research and production of mind-changing drugs." He predicted that in five years, it would become one of the largest drug manufacturers in the world. "Since IFIF was non-profit, all the revenues would be ploughed back into research and education."

On April 15, 1963, Maher wrote Tim in care of Virginia Denison in Hollywood, California, inquiring whether he planned to resume his duties for the rest of the academic year. Maher recalled, "In the spring of the year in which Tim left, an undergraduate had come to see me very distressed because it was moving up to the end of March and he had been assigned Tim as his adviser for his honors thesis. A couple of weeks had gone by and he hadn't heard anything and when he tried to find Tim, he couldn't. Finally Tim's secretary, a Chinese-American woman called Pearl Chan, let him into the office and the way the student described it, the black binder with the thesis in it was on Tim's desk exactly where he had left it two weeks previously and there was now a spiderweb on it and he got the strong impression that it hadn't been disturbed."

When Maher asked Pearl Chan what was going on, she told him, "'Oh, Tim has left Harvard.' This was March. I said, 'He's left Harvard?' He did not have tenure but he was on a contract that was going to wind up by the end of June. She said he had gone to LA. In fact, he had gone to Hollywood and she had an address for him. I said, 'What happened to his courses?' She said Tim had told her to hand out a reading list and dismiss them. I said, 'Jesus.' This was halfway through the spring term."

Still thinking she must have gotten all this wrong, Maher sent Tim a registered letter. A few days later, the receipt for it, signed by Tim, was returned to him. "So he'd gotten the letter," Maher would later say. "There was no question about it. Fairly shortly afterward, I got a phone call from a friend out on the West Coast who was at Stanford at the time and knew some of the background and he said, 'Oh, so you guys finally fired Tim.' I said, 'What are you talking about?' Leary had appeared on a talk show or some TV show and announced that he had been fired by Harvard. I said, 'He hasn't been fired by Harvard. I think I'm one of the only two or three people who knows he isn't even in Cambridge at the moment.' He said, 'Well, that was what he said on the show.'"

"The part I remember most vividly," David McClelland recalled, "is that I got a telephone call from the *Los Angeles Times* late one evening and they said that Tim Leary had just addressed a public assembly in Los Angeles and announced to everybody that he had been fired from Harvard for taking LSD. This reporter was checking the source—I was chair of the department—and he wanted to know if it was true. And I said, 'No, it's not true. This is news to me. And I should know because I'm chair of the department.'"

McClelland contacted Maher. "Brendan got hold of him and said, 'Tim, you've got to come back, you've got these academic responsibilities and if you don't come back, you'll be fired because you'll be AWOL.' Tim thought it was more interesting to be fired so he didn't come back. And he was fired. But he was fired technically for being AWOL. Not for taking drugs."

The dean of Harvard was McGeorge Bundy, who had gone to Washington to work in John F. Kennedy's administration. Nathan Pusey, the president of Harvard, was serving as interim dean. "In that capacity," Maher would later say, "I phoned him and I told him I had heard from a friend that Tim was announcing he had been fired. The response I got back was one of the reasons Harvard continues to be in the black. There was a long pause and then he said, 'Well, then we will have to stop his pay, won't we?'"

In May, "loaded with IFIF money," Tim and Brunnel went to Mexico City where they began talking to drug companies. They promised to supply all the raw materials and equipment needed to synthesize large amounts of LSD, psilocybin, and mescaline. After signing a contract with one of the companies, they leased a suite of offices near the University of Mexico. Brunnel returned to the United States to settle his affairs. Tim took off for Hotel Catalina in Zihuatanejo to begin preparing for the second annual summer session.

On May 6, the Harvard Corporation passed the following resolution: "Voted: because Timothy F. Leary, Lecturer on Clinical Psychology, has failed to keep his classroom appointments and has absented himself from Cambridge during term time without permission, to relieve him from further teaching duty and to terminate his salary as of April 30, 1963." In response to a letter from Walter Houston Clark some years later, William Bentinck-Smith, assistant to President Pusey wrote, "The facts of Mr. Leary's willful absence from the University were incontrovertible. The Harvard Corporation regarded his actions as a clear violation of the Third Statute of the University and not subject to a hearing."

"One afternoon," Tim would later write in *Flashbacks,* "a jeep raced into the compound driven by the captain of the port. It seemed that I was being called on shortwave radio from Mexico City. Urgent. He drove me to his office, and there crackling with static came the voice of a *Newsweek* reporter saying that Richard Alpert and I had been fired by Harvard University. Did I have comments? I said something brash to the effect that I was honored and it couldn't have happened to two nicer guys." Changing into his trunks, Tim swam out to the motorboat moored in the bay to think about this sudden change in his life. "I gave him $3,000 when he went to Mexico to hire a public relations person because we'd had trouble with the government the year before," Alpert would later say. "And Timothy went and bought a motorboat."

As Tim lay in the sun listening to waves lapping against the hull, he tried to sort out his feelings. His first reaction was that his mother would be upset. "The Harvard firing was painful for me because of my mother," he wrote. The fact that Abigail had to learn the news from her neighbors "marked," as he put it, "the end of our forty-three-year-old friendship. During the last decade of her life, when the ladies gathered for tea to gossip about their families, no one ever mentioned the name of her son the doctor. Aunt Mae's worst expectations of the Leary family were confirmed." Tim also wondered why Harvard had bothered to fire him when the truth was that he had already left for good. "The official reason for my sacking was that I failed to show up for classes. A phony rap: I had com-

pleted all my course work. Dick was ousted for something more romantic. He got caught up in the middle of a love triangle involving an editor
on the Harvard *Crimson* staff." Leary went on to point out that it was
against the rules of the American Association of University Professors to
fire a faculty member without a hearing. "Although civil liberties groups
and the Association expressed a willingness to file suit against Harvard,
we didn't want to waste time on litigation. I didn't want to be a professor
anyway."

The greater irony here involved the fate of Richard Alpert. Although
all he had ever wanted to do was spend his life teaching at Harvard as a
tenured professor, Alpert was dismissed for giving LSD to an undergraduate. Although he initially denied having ever done this, when his department chairman called him into his office to discuss this, Alpert told
McClelland that he had not given the LSD to the undergraduate in his capacity as a teacher at Harvard but rather as a friend. "Alpert wanted to
stay," Maher would later say. "He wanted to be a Harvard professor. I
think he saw Tim as kind of a rising star and that if he hooked his wagon
to it, he would rise with it and Tim turned out not to be a rising star. But
at that point the wagon was too firmly hitched. I think if he had known
in advance what all this was going to lead to, he would have had nothing
to do with Tim."

On May 28, an unsigned editorial written by Andrew Weil appeared
on the front page of *The Harvard Crimson*. It stated that while the firing of
Richard Alpert would be unfortunate were it to lead to the suppression of
legitimate research into the effects of hallucinogenic compounds, it would
be equally unfortunate if Alpert had been "allowed to continue his activities under the aegis of a University that he has misinformed about his
purposes. His claim to be a disinterested scientific researcher is itself debat-
able; from the very first, he and his associate, Timothy F. Leary, have been
as much propagandists for the drug experience as investigators of it . . .
The shoddiness of their work as scientists is the result less of incompetence than of a conscious rejection of scientific ways of looking at things.
Leary and Alpert fancy themselves prophets of a psychic revolution designed to free Western man from the limitations of consciousness as we
know it." Calling them "revolutionaries" who had not been professors at
Harvard but had been playing "the professor game," the editorial accused
them of violating "the one condition Harvard placed upon their work;
that they not use undergraduates for subjects for science experiments."

Alpert's dismissal should not be "construed as an abridgement of academic freedom," the editorial concluded. "In firing Richard Alpert, Harvard has dissociated itself not only from flagrant dishonesty but also from behavior that is spreading infection throughout the academic community."

On May 29, *The New York Times* reported that Alpert had denied he broke faith with Harvard University by involving an undergraduate in a psychological test using hallucinogenic drugs. While nearly all the news reports from this period mentioned that Tim had also been let go at Harvard, the focus was most definitely on Alpert, who was very much the front man. Tim, the visionary, was off in Mexico, setting up the training center in Zihuatanejo, and not available for comment. On the same day, the *Crimson* reported it was unlikely there would be an investigation into the firing by the American Association of University Professors or a formal hearing for Leary or Alpert for the simple reason that Harvard had no provision in its statutes for such a hearing. Andrew Weil quoted an unnamed university official: "Alpert admitted he broke the university regulation on giving drugs to undergraduates, had been given a chance to answer the charges, and had not asked for a formal hearing."

In an undated letter on Harvard University Graduate School of Education stationery, Alpert told Tim how quiet it now seemed at 23 Kenwood Avenue without him. He also noted that New England Telephone had turned off the phone over "a paltry" $500 bill. Concerning the upcoming summer, he wrote, "We really need the training center to shine brightly as a candle to give strength to those of us who are among the phillistines [*sic*]. I've been pretty worried about beatnicks [*sic*] dropping in down there, the hotel getting so overloaded that its effectiveness breaks down, the reaction of the Mexican government . . . Anything you can write to put my mind at ease would be most greatfully [*sic*] appreciated." He also confirmed that after an undergraduate "said Yes he had had the greatest experience of his life and tried to so impress the Dean," Alpert had admitted to both Dean Monro and President Pusey that he had given him LSD.

On May 13, Tim sent Maher a letter from Zihautanejo. "My Dear Brendan," Tim wrote. "I am delighted to endorse your request to take over the offices at 5 Divinity . . . Thanks too for your good wishes. Psychology takes us into many unexpected laboratories. I am presently the non-directive-manager and counselor for twenty devoted Mexican workers, and part-time publicist and amateur politician (Mexican style) and doing some writing when the water pumps, power plants, motorboats, etc. allow such leisure. Hope that your summer is serene and next year a successful one. You are a fine person, Brendan, and I miss you. Best wishes, Tim."

On June 10, McClelland replied to a letter from Tim, in which he had inquired about back pay for May and June. McClelland maintained that there was nothing he could do to help him but urged Tim to write Dean Ford or the president and fellows of the university who would be prepared for any court proceedings Tim wished to institute. McClelland added:

> As you know, I was first suspicious and am now increasingly certain that the repeated use of psychedelic drugs really, alters consciousness so as to alienate people from the world. I therefore think that IFIF is dangerous as are all people who promote widespread use of the drugs. My best evidence is what has happened to you, Dick, and others who have repeatedly taken these drugs. My attempts to convince you and your converts of this have come to precisely nothing, the latest defenses against my evidence of consciousness alteration being, (1) "I know I'm going psychotic but I've never been happier in my life." or (2) "If you say that in public, I'll sue you" which is an excellent way to promote free scientific inquiry! But if reason and evidence fails to persuade you—as it has so far—what choice have I got but to try and persuade the public that you are misleading them? You consistently deny, belittle, or misinterpret the changes in consciousness that occur yet at the same time you recommend the drugs because they expand consciousness. The trouble is that I think your consciousness is expanded and the result I don't like. It isn't the old Tim that I knew and loved and supported. If you ever decide you don't like the state of alienated ecstasy so much, let me know. I keep holding hope against hope that you'll get tired of it and get back to being the useful psychologist you once were.

At forty-two, Timothy Leary had left yet another life behind him. Like one of the wild geese of Irish legend to whom he once compared his father, Tim had flown the coop again. He saw himself now a man of action fully committed to the lifelong quest of going beyond the limits of ordinary consciousness. In the words of David McClelland, Tim might in fact have been going psychotic. But he had also never been happier.

XANADU

MILLBROOK, NEW YORK,
1963–1968

In Xanadu did Kubla Kahn a stately pleasure dome decree
Where Alph, the sacred river, ran
Through caverns measureless to man
Down to a sunless sea.

—Samuel Taylor Coleridge, "Kubla Khan"

Timothy and Susan Leary in Laredo, Texas, 1964.
Photo by Lawrence Schiller, © Polaris

NINETEEN

From dawn to dusk throughout the month of May 1963, Tim Leary worked to prepare Hotel Catalina for another summer in paradise. Cast loose from all bonds and duties, Tim was now free to do just as he pleased without having to answer to any higher authority. Not surprisingly, the immediate result was utter chaos. More than happy to pay $200 a week for room and board, many of those who showed up at the hotel had no intention of participating in psychedelic training sessions. They just wanted to get high on the beach. "Within a few days," Tim would later write, "we realized that we were developing the ultimate-destination resort. Hotel Nirvana. No one wanted to leave. Folks who came down for a week started signing up for the whole summer."

The reason for the sudden influx of paying guests was simple. With the help of a West Coast publicity firm, Tim had been beating the drums as loudly as he could to spread the word. On May 29, a front-page headline in the *San Francisco Call-Bulletin* read PARADISE IN MEXICO—2 FIRED HARVARD PROFS OPEN COMMUNAL HOTEL. After attending a meeting Tim held in Palo Alto to publicize his summer program, Robert S. DeRopp wrote, "Here was Leary, who seemed to think of himself as an alchemist of sorts, madly proclaiming the aims of his group from the rooftops, inviting *Time, Life, Newsweek, Saturday Evening Post,* and even CBS television to observe his marvelous experiment. It was obvious to any normally intelligent being that Leary's group in Zihuatanejo would bring down upon itself the wrath of the establishment, both in Mexico and the United States."

Suffering from what DeRopp called "the missionary disease in its most virulent form," Tim blithely ignored all who advised him to conduct his business in a more private manner. When he invited famed diarist and novelist Anaïs Nin, who had already taken LSD under the supervision of Dr. Oscar Janiger, to join him in Zihautanejo, she begged him to change his plans, but to no avail. What Tim did not know was that Dr. Dionisio Nieto, director of the University of Mexico's Medico-Biological Institute, who the previous summer had invited Tim to deliver a paper on LSD to a local scientific society only to decide it was "absurd, confused, value-less" had already protested his return to the Mexican government.

Soon enough, two policemen named Juan Blicero and Jorge Garcia visited Hotel Catalina. Sitting down with Tim in the dining room, they told him the camp was being closed down by the federales. "Why?" Tim Leary wrote in *Flashbacks*. "Because we were besmirching the name of Mexico with all this bad publicity. Juan pulled out a Mexico City newspaper. The headline: Harvard Drug Orgy Blamed for Decomposing Body." Although the corpse was found in a village a hundred miles away, newspapers had accused Tim's band of "marijuana orgies, hairy women, black magic, venereal disease, and profiteering." Garcia informed Tim that the formal reason he had to leave the country was that he and his group had only been granted tourist visas and therefore were not authorized to run a business in Mexico.

The twenty Americans in residence at Hotel Catalina were given five days to leave the country. Tim flew to Mexico City, where he called Dick Alpert, who assured him that some friends were en route with "a big-shot Mexican wheeler-dealer, who guaranteed he could bribe us back into the country." After receiving "calls from the American ambassador, from the CIA, and from Justice Department officials," the president of Mexico decided to handle the matter personally. Two days later, *The New York Times* ran a front-page story about the expulsion. Referring to the mutilated corpse of a Mexican found in a wooded area in the Acapulco-Zihautanejo area, the article noted, "The police said that no connection had been established between the murder and the Leary center, but Mexican newspapers tied in reports on the crime to allegations that there were 'beatniks' and 'queer people' at the psychic drug center."

Expelled from Harvard and Mexico in the short space of two months, Tim returned to Cambridge in disgrace, "our reputations and credibility forfeited. Suddenly, we were outcasts. It was lonely on the frontier. Like everyone else I hungered for acceptance." An "American psychedelic enthusiast" named John Presmont invited Tim and his group to visit him at his experimental commune on the island of Dominica. A mountainous Caribbean island in the Windward chain located between Guadeloupe and Martinique, Dominica was then still completely unspoiled, virtually unvisited, and hotter than hell. Tim sent Gunther Weil and Frank Ferguson, a graduate of Wesleyan University then serving as Tim's secretary, as an advance party to scout out the situation. "Dominica was straight out of Joseph Conrad," Weil would later tell Jaakov Kohn of *The East Village Other*. "Heavy temperature, dark-skinned natives, voodoo, and the last remnants of the British Empire. Presmont met us and while walking around the capital with him, we were stopped suddenly by a cop who handed John a summons. It turned out to be his deportation order."

Before leaving the island, Presmont introduced Weil and Ferguson to a small band of political radicals who wanted to emulate their hero Fidel Castro and bring about a revolution in Dominica so the island could be transformed into a psychedelic paradise. Before Tim's emissaries could tell him they were enmeshed in serious local political infighting, he arrived with a party of ten, among them his son, Jackie, who would be fourteen in October.

Tim spent a week on the island checking out beachfront hotels only to learn that the island government had accused him of being the biggest heroin dealer in the world. Two policeman escorted him to the office of the governor of the island who was sitting at his desk with a folder bearing Tim's name on it along with a recent issue of *Time* magazine featuring "a lurid story about LSD." The governor made it clear to Tim that the citizens of Dominica did not want any of this on their island. Once again, Tim was deported. To ensure there would be no embarrassing scenes at the airport as they left the island, Tim and his associates spent the night sewing tabs of LSD into the children's teddy bears.

The next morning, they flew to the island of Anguilla, where they all checked into a charming seaside hotel for a few days of rest and recuperation. The hotel was owned by one of Tim's West Point classmates who had purchased two small islands near Grenada with the stipulation that he build permanent structures on them within two years. Short on financing, the classmate made Tim an offer. If Tim and his people put up the buildings, he would give them half the property. There, they would be totally protected. While construction was under way, Tim and his crew could stay in an abandoned World War II–era navy beachside nightclub named "The Bucket of Blood."

When Dick Alpert arrived and discovered everyone frolicking happily on the beach, he flew into a rage. Tim had not only managed to get himself deported from two countries in two weeks but he had also blown the $20,000 that Peggy Hitchcock had given him to finance this venture. "When we got to the island," Alpert would later tell John Bryan, "we had to win over twelve doctors to be able to stay and do our trip there. We had rented out this Bucket of Blood place and *that* was pretty bizarre. And we were having cocktail parties every day for different doctors. The head doctor was this Dr. White whose whole game was performing lobotomies, training doctors to do it. He did so many a week." Furious at Tim "for blowing scenes so fast and running through money," Alpert told Bryan that they were "$50,000 in debt by then. He'd run through everything I owned—my antiques, my Mercedes, all that stuff was gone. The airplanes and all my income, my job. So we had this big acid trip in which Tim and I rolled naked on the floor; it was like a sexual thing we were working through . . . There wasn't any real sex between us; not that time or ever. Tim was threatened by homosexuality. I think he'd had some unpleasant episodes in his life that he wanted to forget."

Their stay on the island ended when Frank Ferguson, who in Jackie Leary's words had "flipped out from acid," walked into town one day in his bathing suit and offered himself to the aforementioned Dr. White to be lobotomized. The reason he did it, Alpert told John Bryan, "was that he was offering himself as a sacrifice to save us from making a pact with the devil. He was stoned out of his mind, of course. And then we were all thrown off the island."

Along with his fellow travelers, Tim returned to Cambridge. "The group came back in pieces," IFIF stalwart Lisa Bieberman told John Bryan. "I don't know what happened on those Caribbean islands, but it was the beginning of the end of what had been our warm, dedicated little fellowship. Certain persons who had been in were out now. And, as it developed, I was one of them." As Tim would later write, "After being expelled from Harvard, Mexico, Antigua, and Dominica in four months (May–August 1963), we cravenly decided that the authorities were not ready for the 21st-century concept: Every Citizen a Scientist. So we fell back to the familiar historical turf upon which most earlier freedom movements had fought the battle—religion."

"They kept getting thrown out of everywhere," Peggy Hitchcock would later say. "They clearly needed a place to live and my brothers, Billy and Tommy, had just bought this lovely big property for a tax thing. Because it actually functioned as a cattle ranch, it was also a good investment. Billy told me there was a big house there and I asked if he had anyone living in it and he said no. So Richard Alpert and I went up and looked at it and we thought it was great. The rent was a dollar a year."

After spending a disastrous summer going nowhere on the road to utopia like a hapless psychedelic version of Bob Hope and Bing Crosby, Tim and Dick Alpert landed on a 2,500-acre estate in Millbrook, New York, a quiet town of 1,700 souls located two hours from New York City on Route 44. Populated in large part by descendants of Italian masons who were brought to America at the turn of the century to build the high stone walls that enclosed many of the local estates, the town itself consisted of not much more than a haberdasher, a diner, a liquor store, and a small supermarket featuring imported delicacies.

The real lure was the surrounding countryside: rounded hills covered with thickly wooded forests; open meadows in which cattle grazed; beautiful lakes, waterfalls, and streams. Unlike nearby Poughkeepsie, the seat of Dutchess County, Millbrook had always attracted those with money who wished to live in quiet splendor. At the end of the town's main street, imposing gates guarded the entrance to an estate built some sixty years earlier by William Dietrich, who had made his fortune manufacturing carbide lamps. Beyond the front entrance stood an imposing two-story gatehouse. Under rows of maple trees, the driveway wound for what seemed like a mile to a white, four-story, sixty-four-room mansion with two towers, a redbrick chimney, and a broad veranda that looked as though it had been designed by some "neo-baroque American King Ludwig," as Tim would later describe it. Known locally as the "Alte House," the mansion was decorated in a style that Tim charitably described as "Bavarian baroque." The woodwork was hand carved. The tapestries on the dining room walls were elegant but fading. The ceilings were inlaid with wooden panels. There was a music room, an aquarium room, ten bathrooms, and a hotel-size kitchen with a walk-in refrigerator in which jazz genius Charlie Mingus once locked himself while tripping to see if the white men with whom he was getting high would set him free.

The mansion was surrounded by elegant lawns, a stable filled with horses, a fountain, and an ornate chalet that housed a bowling alley. A mile away across the fields stood the bungalow, a four-bedroom cottage with a Japanese bath in the basement. Built in 1936 for half a million dollars, the bungalow was where Billy Hitchcock and his twin brother, Tommy, a race-car driver, came to relax on weekends with friends from the city. A successful stockbroker at Lehman Brothers, Billy was the grandson of William Larimer Mellon, the founder of Gulf Oil, and the nephew of Andrew Mellon, secretary of treasury during Prohibition. At the time he met Tim, Billy was drawing an allowance of $15,000 per week from the family trust fund. According to Aymon de Roussy de Sales, an old family friend, "Billy was the extrovert of the family but also very veiled. He never liked to confront anyone about anything, which in the end led to disaster. His father, also named William, was one of the great polo players of all time and a famous test pilot. There was a book written about him because during World War II, he was shot down and was one of the only people ever to escape from this German prisoner of war camp. He died piloting an experimental plane that crashed. Billy was just a kid at the time so he never really had a father. Here was this twenty-two-year-old whiz kid on Wall Street with lots of money because his mom was a Mellon. He had $60 million and he met Leary who was forty-something. Leary had this gift of gab so he got Billy totally enthralled and became sort of a father figure to him."

In the big house with Tim were Susan and Jackie; Dick Alpert; Ralph Metzner and his wife; a psychologist from California, his wife, and their two kids; a young physician kicking a methedrine habit; and three dogs and seven cats. Tim and his extended family went to the local thrift stores for low couches, beaded cushions, and silk pillows so they could refurnish the mansion "harem-style." They assembled a library, set up a music room, and settled into a quiet routine of reading and working on a psychedelic version of *The Tibetan Book of the Dead*. Once a week, they took LSD in carefully programmed sessions. IFIF, the organization for which Tim had once had such high hopes, was now being reconstituted as the Castalia Foundation, the name Hermann Hesse had given to the fellowship of mystic scientists in his novel *Magister Ludi* (also called *The Bead Game*). Those who lived in the big house at Millbrook consciously modeled their lives after the book. In Hesse's novel, set in the Alpine province of Kastalien around the year 2400, the elite monastic Castalian order displayed its intellectual mastery by playing a ritualized game of glass beads. Joseph Knecht, the hero of the novel, rose to become Magister Ludi, the high priest of the order. Dissatisfied with the bead game, he sought a new life in the outside world only to drown in a lake with his protégé. Although Tim and Metzner wrote in the fall 1963 issue of the *Psychedelic Review* that groups attempting to apply the psychedelic experience to social living would find in Hesse's story all the problems that such attempts inevitably encounter, Tim himself would never find a way for those who lived at Millbrook to relate effectively to the outside world.

Tim was now romantically involved with Peggy Hitchcock, who would "roar up from Manhattan in a car loaded with cases of champagne and exotic food and drinks." Described by Aymon du Roussy de Sales as a "real Bohemian but also the sweetest and nicest person in the family," Peggy had already dropped out of Bryn Mawr and Barnard to become a singer. Her mother, known as "Mumma," had never approved of Peggy's previous boyfriend, a talented white jazz musician named Allen Eager who was also a heroin addict. In what Aymon du Roussy de Sales calls "one of the classic remarks," when Peggy told Mumma she was seeing Tim, her mother said, "Oh, thank God. She's going out with a Harvard professor!" Of their time together, Peggy Hitchcock would later say, "Tim and I had kind of a swinging-door relationship. Very intense, and then not. On and off."

On October 18, Tim spoke by phone with Laura Huxley in Los Angeles, who told him that Aldous was dying of cancer. Laura had already read a draft of *The Psychedelic Experience,* the version of *The Tibetan Book of the Dead* on which Tim, Ralph Metzner, and Richard Alpert were working. She was concerned about the great importance the text gave to the state of consciousness at the time of death. Two weeks earlier, she had given Aldous LSD but the session was very superficial, just a reconfirmation of old insights rather than a voyage into the life hereafter. Should she give him LSD again? Laura also told Tim that Aldous wanted to see him.

In Los Angeles on November 20, Aldous asked Tim to lead him through an LSD session using *The Psychedelic Experience* as a guide. Tim suggested that when the time came, it would be better if Laura guided the session using LSD that Tim had brought with him. As he said goodbye to Aldous for the final time, the old man whispered, as Tim recalled in *Flashbacks,* "Be gentle with them, Timothy. They want to be free, but they don't know how. Teach them. Reassure them."

Two days later, shortly before noon, Laura injected Aldous with one hundred micrograms of LSD. Noticing the change in his face, she gave him another shot. "Light and free," she would later recall telling him in *This Timeless Moment.* "Light and free you let go, darling; forward and up. You are going forward and up; you are going toward the light." At 5:20 in the afternoon, Aldous Huxley, without whose support and assistance the Harvard Psychedelic Project would never have begun, died quietly while under the influence of LSD. The date was Friday, November 22, 1963. At Millbrook, Tim held a candlelight vigil for both Huxley and President John F. Kennedy, who had been struck down earlier in the day by an assassin's bullets in Dallas. Although the two men seemed to have had little in common, no one at Millbrook could ignore the synchronicity.

In the new era now beginning, Huxley's brand of cautious moderation would count for little. Politically, personally, and socially, extremism in every form would come to dominate the life of the nation. Described by Peggy Hitchcock as "someone who was going to spit in the face of everything," because to him "freedom at all costs was the most important thing," Tim was ideally suited for the age.

Even as Tim Leary was still settling in at Millbrook, he managed to generate considerable national publicity about himself and LSD. In rapid succession, articles about Tim and Dick Alpert appeared in *Esquire* ("Getting Alienated with the Right Crowd at Harvard," by Martin Mayer), *Look* ("The Strange Case of the Harvard Drug Scandal," by Andrew Weil), and *The Saturday Evening Post* ("The Dangerous Magic of LSD," by John Kobler). *Newsweek* went so far as to report that a "new Leary" had established "a straight scene" at Millbrook in which chemicals were but one means of mind expansion along with diet, fasting, dance, sensory withdrawal, Zen, and even archery. "The beats come, see a straight scene and they go away," Tim told the magazine. Alpert added, "In Mexico, we behaved like naive children. We went in there saying, 'We're nice people. People will treat us nice.' We should have spent more on public relations."

By December, when the Sunday *New York Times* ran an interview with Tim and Alpert, local residents had already begun to realize that the two former professors who had moved into the Dietrich estate in August were more than what the *Times* called "agreeable men of neighborly demeanor and only vaguely remarkable background." Neil Freer, then living with his wife and children on the road that formed the northern border of the estate, recalled, "Immediately, smoke signals started to go up. My wife was a native of Millbrook and so I had quite a bit of contact with the natives of the town, which was quite Catholic and conservative. Everybody knew everybody's business and there was a lot of immediate gossip, rumor, and noise around. 'These people are degenerates. These people are druggies.'"

In the two-column photograph that accompanied the *Times* article, Alpert, still wearing those impossibly heavy black-frame glasses, stood on Millbrook's main street in a dark loden coat with wooden toggles. Hands in pockets, he grinned at Susan Leary who had her back to the camera. Tim, standing with his hands thrust deeply into his own pockets, also smiled approvingly at his daughter. With his hair still quite short, wearing sneakers, he appeared earnest, well-meaning, and completely sincere. Both men seemed to radiate the kind of genial approval toward Susan that any girl her age would welcome. But then, for the past two years, Alpert had been the closest thing to a mother Susan had ever known. Even her dental bills were sent to him.

The last paragraph of the article in the *Times* noted that the sixty-acre campus of Bennett College, a "stylish and expensive two year girls school," was within walking distance of the estate, and that "as a precautionary measure," Donald A. Eldridge, president of the college, had declared Tim's estate to be "out of bounds" for Bennett's 330 students, with expulsion the penalty for those who violated the rule. Naturally this prohibition served only to ensure that a steady stream of girls from Bennett made it their business to visit Millbrook on weekends.

As Tim and Dick began their new lives at Millbrook, the brilliant graduate students they had left behind at Harvard were scrambling like mad to find alternate topics for their doctoral dissertations. "I soldiered through," Gunther Weil would later say. "I stayed another year and ditched the original topic of my thesis to do a very mainstream behavioral thesis that would allow me to quickly get my Ph.D. There were a lot of people gunning for us. They wanted to wipe the slate clean and get rid of anyone who'd had any involvement at all in the psychedelic research program." Not yet thirty at the time, George Litwin recalled, "I was thinking I was too young to be a martyr. We had lost the main battle and the empire's troops were pursuing us to every corner of the galaxy to harass us and kill off our sons and daughters. If we had not gotten blown out at that international conference in Copenhagen, Timothy and Richard and me and Gunther Weil would have been installed as the psychology department of Mass General Hospital." After completing his Ph.D.,

Litwin began teaching at the Harvard Business School where, as a fellow graduate student noted, "he didn't talk about psychedelics. All these brilliant teachers who had their lives changed did not go on to teach it. Tim lost the context. Other people might say his time at Harvard was just one period in his life. But I see it as involving a very dedicated, very coherent, very talented, very powerful group of people. If we had stayed together, who knows what would have happened."

The most brilliant graduate student of them all, Ralph Metzner, now so thin and bearded that he resembled a young Hermann Hesse, remained completely loyal to Tim and the work being done at Millbrook. "Millbrook was a beautiful environment," Metzner would later say, "but it was not easy to make money. So we started doing these seminars under the Castalia Foundation that were basically drug free. At them, we would do things to systematically confuse the senses. Trying to break through the game."

Each participant in the weekend workshops in consciousness expansion was expected to contribute a minimum of $75 to the Castalia Foundation. A handout given to guests stated, "No one here is eager to play the game of 'you' or the game of 'guest' with you. There will be little interest manifested in your thoughts, opinions, accomplishments, nor in the history and complexity of your personality. You will find total acceptance but little verbal reassurance. 'Good' is what raises the ecstasy count of all persons present and 'bad' is what lowers the ecstasy count."

Fascinated by G. I. Gurdjieff's method of attaining enlightenment through meditation and heightened self-awareness, Tim, Alpert, and Metzner began applying his theories to their work at Millbrook. But when Tim asked a leading Gurdjieff instructor whether the master's theories did not show a teacher who was always improvising and adjusting to new conditions and new people, the instructor replied that Gurdjieff's methods were not subject to individual interpretation. "It was Harvard all over again," Metzner recalled. "Religious dogmatization." At Millbrook, Tim and his colleagues continued using Gurdjieff's methods without formally joining the movement.

During the fall and winter, Millbrook functioned more like a laboratory than a true commune. It was as though a small group of gifted and brilliant psychologists had been washed up on some faraway island where there was plenty of food to eat and water to drink so they could spend all their time testing their own theories on one another. As Metzner recalled,

"We did a series of experiments in communal living where we wanted to break through sexual jealousy and possessiveness and exclusiveness and fears. The first experiment we did was that we would draw names out of a hat and two people at random, male or female, related or not, would go and be in the meditation house–bowling alley for a week and they wouldn't have to work or be in the kitchen. Food would be brought to them and they could do whatever they wanted. They could take LSD or not. They could make love or not. Whatever. Just focus on being in as high in the consciousness as possible."

Kim Ferguson Exon was twelve years old when she moved to Millbrook with her parents, Flo and Maynard Ferguson. "A big thing there was: lose your attachments," she recalled. "It was a psychological game because whoever was in the meditation house would wonder what their spouse was going through with the girls from Bennett. It didn't matter to Tim if his spouse was out there. He never had a real attachment to anyone so it couldn't hurt him. He was the ringmaster." "The most extreme one," Metzner would later say, "was what was called the Third Floor Experiment. Maynard and Flo were not involved in it. It was Tim and Dick and myself and two or three women and we decided that all those who wanted to participate would live on the third floor and on the third floor, we would sleep wherever. Each night, we would choose to sleep in whatever bed with whomever we wanted. And that was tense. Because we spent an inordinate amount of time talking about where we were going to sleep and with whom." Although Metzner and his wife soon parted, he remained at Millbrook to help Tim with the work.

At one point during the winter, the Scottish-born psychiatrist R. D. Laing came to visit. In his book *The Divided Self,* Laing had begun to redefine schizophrenia as a form of adaptive behavior rather than mental illness. In three years, Laing would publish *The Politics of Experience.* On the day they met in the kitchen at Millbrook, Tim challenged Laing, telling him that all the "medical-therapeutic talk about LSD was a fake. I was interested only in the mystic aspects of the drug." Undaunted, Laing replied that "the only doctor who could heal was the one who understood the shamanic, witchcraft mystery of medicine." Then Laing proposed that the two of them play a game. Both men took off their shoes and stood between the kitchen sink and the table. The point of the game, Laing explained, was to move your hands and body without talking. Karate-style, the two men began to spar. "Our hands changed into a dance," Tim would later write. "Paired sculpturing of air, molded liquid forms, now moving slowly, then whirling. My eyes were riveted to his eyes. I was gone. Spun out of the kitchen at Millbrook, spun out of time. Stoned high in a Sufi ballet. We were two organisms from different planets—communicating." Soon, both men were sitting on the floor in the lotus position, arms and hands weaving in the air. The dialogue lasted for an hour. A dozen people walked in, watched for a while, and then left. Jackie and his friends, home from school, made themselves lunch. Although Tim invited Laing to stay on at Millbrook, he chose to return to Kingsley Hall, the hostel for schizophrenics in London where he lived and worked. Over the course of the next decade, it was Laing rather than Tim who established himself as a real pioneer in the field of humanistic psychology.

As winter ended, the residents of Millbrook began clearing brush from the still-frozen ground surrounding the circular fountain and the remains of a tennis court. On the first day of spring, which was also Palm Sunday, everyone gathered in the hallway of the big house. While a Chinese gong sounded and the quarter-ton church bell on the front porch tolled, they lit torches made by Jack Leary and marched across the lawn where they poured gasoline on two big piles of brush, set fire to them, and then watched as orange flames shot thirty feet into the air. When the fire burned down to glowing embers, they returned to the meditation house where eight candles burned, a log fire blazed in the fireplace, and the smell of temple incense from Mysore hung heavily in the air. For half an hour, everyone sat in silent meditation. Then Alpert brought out the *I Ching* and handed Tim three coins, which he threw six times. The resulting hexagram was Tun, the Retreat. In a solemn voice, Dick read the judgment of the hexagram. Conditions were such that the hostile forces favored by the time were advancing. Retreat was the right course. But the retreat had to be carried out correctly. It was not to be confused with flight. Flight meant saving oneself under any circumstances. Retreat was a sign of strength. After the reading, the residents of Millbrook came over one by one to gaze into Tim's eyes and bid him good-bye before he began a week of silence and solitude in the meditation center.

The next day, Tim did his best to quiet his thinking mind by meditating. But as so often happened when he meditated without being on psychedelics, the task proved impossible. Describing the moment in *Flashbacks*, Tim would later write that he remembered his first day in kinder-garten and how frightened he had been of his teacher. For a long while, he thought about Elizabeth Taylor and Richard Burton. He went outside to work on the meditation garden and read the Bible. Bored and hungry, Tim found himself back once more in what he called "the imprinted chess board" of his mind. Staring at the big house that night, he went through each brightly lit room. Picturing each person who was inside the house, he reflected on the love he felt for them all. To him, the house seemed like a broken-down spaceship retired from interplanetary travel and set down here so that earthlings who had grown tired of struggling with their given personalities could become loving spirits.

The next day was Holy Tuesday. As soon as Tim awoke, he began worrying about the LSD session in which he was about to engage. Although he had already made this voyage more than two hundred times, he still approached it with dread. He worked in the meditation garden until the sun was overhead, threw down his hoe, poured a 200-gamma dose of Heavenly Blue LSD into a cup, and drank it down. For the first time in his life, he was about to trip by himself without friends or companions to help him. Tim spent the night totally beyond his mind, "spinning back through the evolutionary past, time-traveling into the future, reliving many genetic states." When he came down from his trip, Tim walked outside and howled at the moon.

The next day, everything seemed to be alive and communicating to him. For the rest of the week, he read, made notes, walked, and tripped. At sunset on the seventh day, Easter Sunday, Tim emerged from the meditation house and turned over the leather-bound logbook in which he had faithfully recorded his thoughts during his week of solitude so the next searcher, chosen by lot, could record his or her own inner journey in it.

While this was the kind of ritual that the high priest of any order might undertake to bring back new information to his followers, Tim was also the single father of two children. While he was off getting high by himself, Susan and Jack, by all accounts, were pretty much left to fend for themselves. "I always had this desire to have children," Peggy Hitchcock would later say, "and I was up at Millbrook one day and I had this feeling, I think I was a little bit high, that Timothy was not going to be a very good parent. It had to do with the way he was starting to deal with his kids. They were teenagers and he was really ignoring them much of the time." "Richard Alpert was protective of Jack," Kim Ferguson Exon recalled. "He was really the good uncle and the peacemaker in the group. Always trying to be the good psychologist as opposed to the let's-stir-up-the-pot psychologist." Although her relationship with Tim was not a hostile one, Exon did not trust or like him much. "I'm sure it had to do with Jack. Jack and I were bonded. It was the two of us trying to survive against this whole group."

As spring turned into summer, Tim and his fellow residents bought a big lawn mover to cut the grass on an estate on which several dozen gardeners had once worked. The residents lined the driveway with white-washed stones, causing Alpert to grumble that it now looked like the entrance to a Jewish country club. On July 4, the residents of Millbrook threw a big party. Everyone dressed up in costumes. Maynard Ferguson brought his fifteen-man band to provide entertainment. And Tim Leary fell in love.

TWENTY

Five feet nine inches tall, Nena von Schlebrugge wore a size 8–10 dress. Her shoe size was 9½A. The Eileen Ford modeling agency catalog in which these facts appeared, alongside a head shot, also stated that she was not available for modeling jobs involving face powders, liquid makeup, or foundations. However, for $60 an hour—then the highest going rate— she would appear in *Vogue* (where she had appeared on the cover at the age of sixteen), *Mademoiselle,* and *Harper's Bazaar,* which, in the language peculiar to such magazines, described her as follows: "Nena is an avid concert goer and ballet goer; she also likes art films and photographing nature and animals; but when it comes to writing, she doesn't. Nena would rather pick up the phone or cable to say she's arriving or departing. Born in Mexico and raised in Peking, she became a seasoned traveler at a youthful age, so today it's only natural that she spends most of her time jetting from her New York base to various and sundry European and Asian destinations."

In every way, Nena was the fairy-tale princess about whom Tim had dreamed each night as a boy back in Springfield. She was a modern-day Helen of Troy whose face had launched the coming of Erik Cigars to America on a TV commercial in which she stood like a Nordic princess, long blond hair flowing behind her, at the prow of a Viking warship sailing into New York harbor. "Nena was very removed and unusual," Darlene DeSedle, then a fashion editor at *Mademoiselle,* recalled. "She was also unbelievable looking. Much more beautiful than her daughter, Uma Thurman. She was the most beautiful blonde you've ever seen. Absolutely perfect." In the very sophisticated world of New York high fashion through which both Nena and Darlene moved, all the women were young and beautiful. All the men were rich. And everybody was always incredibly well dressed. "At that time," according to Aurora Hitchcock, a fellow model at Eileen Ford who, before marrying Billy, had dated Cary Grant, "models were the only women in charge of their own lives. It was wonderful. We would go to dinner at 21 Club and then dancing at El Morocco or the Stork Club. The men absolutely in suits and ties and the women in high heels and gowns and it was lovely."

In flowing silks, Nena came to the big Fourth of July party at Millbrook with her ever-present Pekinese under one arm. Her large expressive eyes hidden behind dark sunglasses, she approached Tim as he sat on a sofa and asked if he remembered her. Leaping to his feet, Tim said of course he did. She had first visited him in Cambridge with the poet Gregory Corso. Nena and Tim began to talk. She told him she was interested in the mysteries of the universe and wanted to go to India to seek ultimate wisdom, not to mention the secret sexual practices of the Orient. As Tim would later write in *Flashbacks*, "It sounded good to me." At noon the next day, he went to the bungalow where Nena was staying with Billy and his friends. Out by the pool in the hot sun, Nena removed her filmy robe to reveal her long smooth body in a microscopic bikini. She told Tim how bored she was with all the fame and the money, and about her adventures in the fashion worlds of London and New York.

When Nena returned the following weekend, she stayed with Tim in the big house. Waking up in his arms on Monday morning, she reached for the phone and called Eileen Ford to tell her that she had fallen in love—the agency could postpone all her bookings or find someone else to fulfill them because she intended to take the next two weeks off. "Hindsight is always twenty-twenty," Peggy Hitchcock would later say. "But Nena also lost her father at a young age and I think her thing with Timothy was very much based on that. I was ten and a half when my father died testing a plane and it was absolutely devastating. I was twenty-eight or twenty-nine back then and Tim was forty-three, which is a considerable difference. I think for Nena that was a big part of it as well."

It was not long before Tim and Nena took LSD together. As Nena's elegant jet-set façade fell away, Tim saw her archetypal nobility emerge. Given that Nena's mother was a Swedish baroness, this made perfect sense. At dawn, Tim and Nena walked together behind the mansion to a stone bridge. Nena pulled a gold ring from her finger and threw it into the dark water below. Running ahead, she turned to look back at Tim, her arms outstretched, and he fell under her spell. Although Peggy had already decided Tim was not the man with whom she was destined to spend her life, Tim and Nena's engagement came as a shock to her. "They took LSD," she would later say, "and three days later, they decided to get married. I was totally blown away. Looking back on it now, I think I got married sort of on the rebound."

That August, *The Psychedelic Experience: A Manual Based on the Tibetan Book of the Dead* by Timothy Leary, Ralph Metzner, and Richard Alpert was published. The book was dedicated "with profound admiration and gratitude" to Aldous Huxley, and contained introductory tributes to W. Y. Evans-Wentz, Carl Jung, and Lama Anagarika Govinda. The first printing of 10,000 copies sold out quickly. Eventually the book would be reprinted eight times, with 60,000 copies in print. It also appeared in paperback in America and England. Intended to serve as a flight manual for those under the influence of mind-altering substances, the book was filled with such directives as "With your ego left behind you, the brain can't go wrong. Trust your divinity, trust your brain, trust your companions. Whenever in doubt, turn off your mind, relax, float downstream." The line eventually found its way into "Tomorrow Never Knows," the final track on the Beatles' acid-drenched 1966 album *Revolver*. (Originally entitled "The Void," the song was inspired by *The Psychedelic Experience*, which John Lennon had read while high on acid.)

The tone of the book was stern, authoritative, and very Germanic. Whether this was due to Evans-Wentz or Ralph Metzner is hard to say. In language guaranteed to send fear into the heart of even the most confident LSD enthusiast, the book contained an invocation which concluded, "That which is called ego-death is coming to you / Remember: This is the hour of death and rebirth; Take advantage of this temporary death to obtain the perfect state—Enlightenment." The book also described in great detail all of the psychic horrors that might be encountered along the way. Once the trip was over and hunger struck, the authors recommended "ancient simple" foods like bread, cheese, wine, and fresh fruit.

The Psychedelic Experience was taken so seriously by LSD users that when people failed to have the experience described within its covers, they blamed themselves. Somehow they had failed the acid test. But then in every sense the book was a top-down attempt to program LSD users to experience what those at Millbrook deemed a proper trip. Ego-death was a non-negotiable part of it. "I got a message on acid that you should destroy your ego," John Lennon would later tell Jann Wenner in *Lennon*

Remembers, "and I did, you know. I was reading that stupid book of Leary's (the psychedelic manual based on the *Tibetan Book of The Dead*) and all that shit. We were going through a whole game that everyone went through, and I destroyed myself . . . I destroyed my ego and I didn't believe I could do anything."

Not long after the book was published, Tim and his cohorts at Millbrook came into contact with people who were living the acid lifestyle without trying to develop any intellectual theories about what they were doing. Instead, they were simply having a hell of a good time. After tripping their way across the country in a psychedelic painted bus named "Furthur" driven nonstop by Neal Cassady, Ken Kesey and his band of Merry Pranksters arrived at Millbrook expecting what Tom Wolfe would later describe in *The Electric Kool-Aid Acid Test* as "the most glorious reception ever. It is probably hard at this late date to understand how glorious they thought it would be. The Pranksters thought of themselves and Leary's group as two extraordinary arcane societies, and the only ones in the world engaged in the most fantastic experiment in human consciousness ever devised. The thing was totally new. And now the two secret societies bearing this new-world energy were going to meet."

Kesey's magic bus rattled up the winding driveway at Millbrook with American flags flying and rock 'n' roll blaring from speakers. When the mansion finally came into sight, Sandy Lehmann-Haupt, brother of former *New York Times* literary critic Christopher Lehmann-Haupt, began tossing smoke bombs from the top of the bus. As clouds of green smoke filled the air and music blasted, the Pranksters waited for the Leary people to come rushing out the front door of the mansion and embrace them like long-lost relatives. Instead, the few who happened to be out on the lawn ran back into the house. Eventually Peggy Hitchcock, Alpert, and Susan Metzner, among others, greeted the Pranksters. Everyone was friendly but a bit cool, even the very hip Flo and Maynard Ferguson. The general vibration was that the Leary people were involved in some sort of deep, serious meditative thing while Kesey's people were just California crazies whose loud arrival could only mean trouble for one and all.

After having brokered an unsuccessful meeting between Jack Kerouac and Ken Kesey in Manhattan, Allen Ginsberg had boarded the bus in New York City to help guide the Pranksters to Millbrook. "I remember when we finally went up with Kesey to visit Leary," Ginsberg recalled. "There was already some kind of rule at Millbrook about not making a big noise. The bus came honking down the driveway like an animate painted rhinoceros with a loudspeaker on it. It was like Kesey was calling attention to himself and at first, people were a little bit hesitant even to come out and look at the bus and greet them for fear they would precipitate a bust. They were being pretty discreet. Eventually, Leary and Kesey met. It wasn't a happy open thing because there had been so much trouble from notoriety that Leary, and particularly his household group, were a little leery—l-e-e-r-y—of such a big show. Kesey and his friends had never been busted, really. They had driven their way across the United States as Pranksters, pranking up the cops, and hadn't had the taste of the iron law so they couldn't understand why Leary's group was so reticent. Leary wasn't paranoid. He was guarded."

"Tim was on retreat," Peggy Hitchcock recalled, "and couldn't or didn't want to see anybody. So I ended up having to show them around." Acting as tour guide, she escorted the Pranksters—whom she considered to be "freaks but nothing that unusual"—through the bungalow. Ken Babbs, Kesey's right-hand man and number-one partner in crime, saw a photograph on the wall that looked like a Yale class picture, circa 1903. As Tom Wolfe later wrote, Babbs pointed to the photo and cried out, "There's Cassady! There's Hassler! Kesey! Sandy!" In time, Babbs located every male Prankster in the photo. When Peggy moved everyone on to the big house, Babbs got the funny notion that this big gingerbread castle of a mansion with turrets and towers and jigsaw shingles was in fact the ancestral home of the Pranksters. A big oil painting on the wall was a portrait of one of their forefathers, Sir Edward the Freak, who, when aroused, could freak a whole city block. On and on Babbs went, rapping about the ancestral staircase, the ancestral paneling, the ancestral fireplace, the ancestral all-inclusive uptight archetypal claustrophobic East Coast setting in which they were now enshrouded. When Peggy took everyone down to the basement meditation center, Babbs called it the "crypt trip." The crypt where people would trip and Leary's people would take their followers to hang them up while they were high. Babbs even performed a parody version of *The Tibetan Book of the Dead*, a sacred text at Millbrook. As Tom Wolfe wrote, "The clear message was Fuck you, Millbrook for your freaking frostiness."

Everyone awaited the meeting between Ken Kesey, Captain America of the World of Freaks, and Tim Leary, Guru of the Psychedelic Revolution. Word then came down that Tim was engaged in a very serious three-day trip and could not be disturbed. The news was a bummer. Kesey was not so much angry as hurt and disappointed. After so much hard traveling and all those miles on the road, could this "one big piece of uptight constipation" really be Millbrook?

In *Flashbacks*, Tim claimed not to have even been home when Kesey and the Pranksters arrived. After spending a few days in New York City with Nena, he was shivering with sweaty flu in Grand Central Terminal as he waited for the train to Poughkeepsie. Arriving at midnight, Tim was picked up at the station by Alpert, who told him the Pranksters had arrived in full force and intended to spend the next few days on the estate. In the morning, Tim woke up with a high fever. Even in his delirium, he could tell that Alpert was none too thrilled about the "rowdy Prankster trip." Ever the good psychologist, Alpert suggested they let this intercultural exchange develop naturally at the individual level. "And that's what happened. Lots of horny doping and groping took place among the groups. Ken Kesey, Ken Babbs, and I did meet, quietly in my room. We looked each other in the eye and promised to stay in touch as allies. As we have to this day."

"What happened," Alpert recalled, "was that we had just had a big acid trip all night long and we were having a quiet day and this guy drove his bus up with speakers blaring wanting the action and everyone looked up and said, 'Fuck this,' and they all went to bed. Being responsible, I was the one left to be charming and they felt very let down. But their energy was so unbelievably jarring. They had been up for two days on everything. They came and went. It was a passing in the night. They were full of their myth. As we were full of ours."

While contact between the two groups was limited, Tim did get on the bus long enough to have Allen Ginsberg take his photograph alongside a grinning, bare-chested Neal Cassady. Never one to pass on anything that would get him high, Cassady went upstairs in the mansion for an intravenous injection of DMT. "Cassady called me 'Leary' and he called Timothy 'Alpert,'" Alpert recalled. "Just to fuck with us. His mind was non-linearly delicious. His energy was so powerful. But he didn't have that much impact on us."

As the Pranksters headed back out on the road to return to California, Tim Leary was moving in a completely different direction. He was about to begin the traditional journey to the East which pilgrims had been making for centuries. This was also to be his honeymoon.

On the Friday afternoon before Tim and Nena were to be married at Millbrook, Monte Rock III called Darlene DeSedle in her office in Manhattan. "I want you to get me three yards of pink tulle and three yards of white tulle," he told her, she would later recall. Monte, a twenty-five-year-old Puerto Rican, ran the hair salon at Saks Fifth Avenue. One of the hippest people in New York City, due in no small part to his flamboyant hair, clothing, and extensive personal jewelry, he would in time become a rock singer and appear on *The Tonight Show* with Johnny Carson. At the moment, Monte's concern was Nena's hair and the bridal veil she would wear over it. "Monte, it's four o'clock on Friday afternoon," DeSedle replied. "Are you crazy? You want me to go downtown to the millinery section *now*?" "You have to," Monte said, "because I'm doing this wedding tomorrow."

At eight the next morning, DeSedle showed up at Monte's house. Outside, a chauffeur in full livery stood beside a coffee-colored 1936 Buick roadster with a rumble seat in the back. The chauffeur's uniform was also a perfect coffee-with-cream color and he wore a locket around his neck. Opening it, he said to Darlene, "Here, have some of this." Then he spooned out some snow-white powder, which she later learned was methamphetamine. These were still the days when no one who was really hip would ever think of saying no to such an offer, so Darlene accepted. Monte then handed her a black pill and said, "Take this." When she asked what it was, Monte replied, "A black beauty." "Okay," Darlene said, and she took that as well.

The photographer Diane Arbus, who had come along for the ride, Monte, and Darlene then got into the car. Arbus, who sat in the middle, with Monte on one side and Darlene on the other, kept looking back and forth at them as they talked the whole way to Millbrook. Considering the level of methamphetamine in their bloodstreams, this was no surprise. Gradually, Darlene noticed that someone was filming them. It was either D. A. Pennebaker or Ricky Leacock, who were making a documentary film of the wedding that appropriately enough would be called *Wedding*

at Millbrook. In Tim's words, the documentary would enjoy "a certain moment on the art film circuit."

At Millbrook, Darlene discovered five bridesmaids sitting in the tennis house, each wearing a different colored pastel silk dress. Darlene asked
for a needle and thread so she could make Nena's bridal veil. Deciding just
to run the two pieces of pink and white tulle together, Darlene went to
work. As she did, someone handed her a glass and said, "Here, drink this."
Not knowing the glass contained punch laced with LSD, Darlene
knocked it right back. Not surprisingly, she could later barely recall how
she got from the tennis house to the ceremony in Grace Chapel, a wonderful old High Episcopal stone church in the town of Millbrook.

Although the invitations sent out by Birgit Baroness von Schlebrugge
could not have been more proper, the wedding itself was phantas-
magoric, magical mystery tour, the first really big coming-out party for
all the A-list, jet-set, high-fashion beautiful people from New York who
had recently discovered LSD. On Saturday, December 12, 1964, at Millbrook, a scene just beginning to blossom in the city burst into full, ri-
otous flower in the countryside. Visually, the event was a fashion editor's
dream, a display of early-sixties foppery at its most extreme. One hundred
and fifty guests high on LSD, grass, and/or speed attended, all dressed as
though they were taking part in a royal pageant. The women, holding
flowers, wore brilliant saris decked with gleaming ornaments. The men
were in harlequin pants, richly textured jackets, and sumptuous shirts.
Aurora Hitchcock had on the kind of big mink hat that Jackie Kennedy
had made so popular. Several women wore them with dresses that
looked very summery indeed, considering the season.

As Tim took his place at the altar in a rented cutaway waistcoat, he
had never looked more confident or self-assured. But then wherever he
went these days, he was treated like an authentic visionary. In Palo Alto
and San Francisco, Tim had just lectured to standing-room-only crowds.
In the auditorium at Cooper Union, where Abraham Lincoln had spoken
a hundred years earlier, Tim sold out all 1,300 seats, with hundreds more
forced to stand in the back. One of those who attended Tim's lecture that
night was the novelist Tom Robbins, who had only just come to New
York City from Seattle where he had taken LSD while working as an art
critic for *The Seattle Times.* "Tim's lecture that night influenced the socks
I wore for years," Robbins would later say. "Tim was wearing red socks.
No suit. A white dress shirt. That evening, he spoke a great deal about

how LSD alters the genetic imprint." Robbins stopped by a fruit-and-vegetable stand afterward. "I was going to buy some brussels sprouts to take home," he would later say, "and Tim was there with a small entourage getting an apple or something. He had just left the auditorium where Lincoln spoke and he'd had a great night and was feeling good. I looked up and there he was. Glowing like a thousand-watt bulb. I said to him, 'How do you know which brussels sprouts are good to pick out? Because they all look pretty much the same.' And he said, 'No, no, no. You pick out the ones that are smiling.' I liked that answer. And the scary part was that I could actually see which ones were smiling. The message was received. So I went home and started wearing red socks."

With Alpert as his best man and Susan as one of the bridesmaids, Tim married Nena, his "shining Nordic princess," in Grace Chapel in Millbrook. As Tim walked back down the aisle after the ceremony, Jack reached out, shyly touching his hand. "This gesture of love is one of the dearest memories of my life," Tim would later write in *Flashbacks*, adding, "The trip around the world was about to separate us for the first time since Marianne's death. We were never as close again." In truth, Jack did not attend the wedding. "There was a ceremony in the church at Millbrook," he recalled, "and I was specifically not invited. Other people were involved to make sure I did not get there. It took a lot of planning. It didn't make any sense to me. I didn't care. I didn't want to go anyway."

After the wedding, everyone drifted back to the mansion, which on this night seemed even more of a fantasy castle than usual. The punch had been laced with LSD. Gradually it dawned on Darlene that everybody there was floating on LSD. While Charlie Mingus and Maynard Ferguson jammed with Miles Davis's sidemen, guests lined up to present the newlyweds with hash, grass, and psychedelic mushrooms, as well as snuffboxes filled with LSD and cocaine. The happy couple cut a wedding cake—designed by Alpert—upon which the Hindu deities Shakti and Siva seemed to be having sex. Needless to say, everyone partied until dawn.

Tim and Nena then went to spend their honeymoon in India, where Ralph Metzner was already living on Holy Man Ridge in the foothills of the Himalayas. Before he left, Tim wrote Metzner a letter in which he expressed just how eager he was to pursue "the incredible complexities that develop when two people begin to explore their potentialities together." Although not in the manner Tim expected, this was precisely what happened.

TWENTY-ONE

In a photograph taken on their honeymoon in India, Tim and Nena sit with Ralph Metzner on an ornately carved white marble bench in front of the Taj Mahal. Having journeyed three days by bus and train from Almora in the hill country to meet them in Delhi, Metzner is wearing dark pants and a white shirt with dark socks and sensible shoes. With a heavy sweater thrown over his shoulders, his hair short, and his beard trimmed, he looks like a serious graduate student who has come to India in search of the traditional wisdom of the East. All in white, Tim sits on the far side of the bench. In love as he has never been before, Tim is also high, having only just shared some "legally available *ganja*" with his bride and Metzner before they toured this great monument to love, built by Shah Jehan in response to his wife's dying request that he create something by which she would be remembered. At forty-five, Tim still looks remarkably young, vital, and handsome. His hair is short and parted in the middle, with an unruly Huck Finn cowlick tilting to the right. Unlike Metzner, Tim wears no socks or sensible shoes. In sandals, a long white tunic, and flowing white pants, he looks like a native-born guru who knows something others have yet to discover for themselves.

Between Ralph and Tim, Nena stares into the camera like someone who has long since learned to regard the lens as her lover. She wears a finely embroidered tunic over clinging houri pants that wrap tightly around her impossibly long legs. Like Tim, her bare feet are in sandals. Her thick blond hair, parted in the middle, falls to her shoulders in the style then favored by female folksingers in Greenwich Village. The sharp planes of Nena's cheekbones, her long aquiline nose, and her sensuous lips make her the picture of Nordic perfection, an Aryan superwoman.

Together on the bench, Tim, Nena, and Metzner form a perfect triangle. The most striking aspect of the photo, aside from highlighting their individual beauty and great physical magnetism, is that it reveals the space between them. From his end of the bench, Metzner smiles as though pleased. Between Tim and Nena, there is no connection whatsoever. Entirely separate entities, they share only an instinctive understanding of the power of the lens into which they both gaze without fear.

As Metzner would write thirty-two years later in his introduction to a new edition of *Psychedelic Prayers,* Tim was very impressed that Shah Jehan built the Taj Mahal as "an expression of personal-human love." As Tim said that day, the quest for enlightenment contains within it an element of selfishness ("my enlightenment") as opposed to the selfless love of a husband for his wife. "The question of how personal passionate human love could be integrated with the spiritual quest for liberation was clearly a central concern for Tim during this period," Metzner wrote, "and perhaps a core theme of his entire post-psychedelic life." Once a month, on the occasion of the full moon, the grounds of the Taj Mahal were kept open at night for visitors. As the sun set and a full moon rose, Tim, Nena, and Metzner took LSD and sat on a blanket in the grass before the Taj Mahal. In the moonlight, the white marble dome glistened pale blue and silver. Precious stones inlaid high up on the dome flashed and sparkled. "Like a mirage," Metzner wrote, "it hung in space, separated from the earth by a thin band of haze, glowing and humming with radiance in perfectly harmonious wave-field patterns."

Unfortunately, Tim had not been experiencing equally harmonious wave-field patterns during his honeymoon. Although both he and Nena had traveled extensively, they had never before, as he would later write in *Flashbacks,* "felt so alienated from the natives of a country as we did in Japan," the first stop on their journey. All the same, they visited "karate dogens, Shinto temples, Buddhist shrines, and department stores" where Nena bought kimonos off the rack. They ate psychedelic mushrooms in order "to imprint a Kabuki performance" and then slid their "tall white bodies into steamy public baths." Taking the bullet train to Kyoto, "the Esalen of Japan," they visited ashrams and meditated in a Zen temple.

Flying to Calcutta, they followed Allen Ginsberg's instructions to visit the burning ghats by the side of the Ganges, where they sat on their haunches "with a gang of wood-carrying Sivites, ordinary six-pack Joes passing around hand-cupped bowls of hashish." From Calcutta, they took a train along the Bay of Bengal to the Black Pagoda of Konarak where the walls "seethed with erotic carvings—thousands of firm-bodied graceful people stone-frozen in acts of sexual dalliance."

In Benares, Tim inveigled a Muslim boatman to ferry him across the Ganges to the eastern shore, where he encountered an old man with long white hair and luminous eyes. Naked save for the dhoti around his waist, the old man began speaking rapidly to Tim in a strange tongue. "Suddenly I understood: he was some special ancient teacher who had been waiting for me all my life. I wanted to run forward and throw myself at his feet. But I was paralyzed with fright, thinking at the same time that he could be a crazed fanatic. He might attack me, a profaner of holy ground." Babbling in English, Tim tried to introduce himself to the old man. Then he turned to ask his boatman about him. As soon as Tim clambered on board, the boatman began paddling for the other shore. "On the floor of the boat I wept uncontrollably. I was convinced I had met the Buddha and run away." Undeniably cinematic, the story may be a fictionalized account of the far more mundane meeting Tim had on a bus in India with Hari Dass, the silent sage who later became Richard Alpert's teacher. Fascinated by the man, Tim followed him off the bus. When the bus driver began blowing his horn, Tim turned around and reclaimed his seat. Had he continued down the road for another five minutes, Tim would have met Alpert's guru, the man who, in Alpert's words, "changed my whole life."

Leaving the Taj Mahal behind, Tim and Nena journeyed with Metzner back to Almora, where Metzner had spent the past three months studying with Lama Govinda, the Tibetan Buddhist philosopher and scholar. After traveling for nearly three days, Tim and Nena took a dark room at Almora's only inn. The next morning, Metzner led them a mile up a dirt road to a crossroads where lepers were squatting, begging for alms. The left-hand path led to Himalayan Tibet. Up the right-hand path was Holy Man Ridge, lined with houses in which assorted spiritual seekers, both European and Indian, maintained part-time residence. With winter nearly over, many of the houses were empty. Tim and Nena selected a cottage with a wide lawn overlooking the mountains to the north and a deep valley to the south. Metzner moved into the guest room. They hired a Muslim cook to come in every morning and prepare lunch.

To visit Lama Govinda, Metzner took Tim and Nena past the house in which D. H. Lawrence had once lived to a small shack at the ridge crossing where tea had been brewed for centuries over charcoal and served heavily sweetened in thick brass mugs. A mile beyond the tea shack, they left the main path, turned left, and climbed a narrow twisting trail to the end of the ridge. Here, in a house built by W. Y. Evans-Wentz, Lama Govinda and his wife, Li Gotama, lived. An old man in Tibetan robes with a wispy beard, Lama Govinda was the Buddhist scholar of Austrian descent to whom *The Psychedelic Experience* had been dedicated. In response to a request from Lama Govinda, Metzner had already given him LSD, thereby providing the scholar with his first experience of the "bardo Thodol in its living sweating reality." "I sat with him and he had a difficult trip at first because with the meditative trip, the barrage of intense physical sensations can be confusing," Metzner recalled. "His wife came over and said, 'I know what you need.' And she reminded him of his mantra. So he started saying his mantra and I could see it was like a lifeline that brought him out of this world of chaos and then he had a really fine experience."

Sharing a deep interest in the science of classification, as well as the nature of personality types, Tim and Lama Govinda hit it off immediately. After much discussion, Lama Govinda asked Tim if he would be willing to undertake a meaningful study of personality classification systems in the zodiac, the tarot, the I Ching, as well as Greek and Hindu mythology. By demonstrating the correspondences in these great systems, Tim would be able to "harmonize East and West, science and yoga, past and future." While this might have been the sort of project to which a serious scholar would have devoted his life, it was not what Tim had come to India to do. "I was interested in the task but despaired of finding the time for such arcane research," he wrote in *Flashbacks*. "One would have to live like the Lama, withdrawn from the world, like a medieval scholar in a monastery. The assignment of this mission brought my studies with the Lama to a close."

With him, Tim had brought no less than nine English-language translations of the *Tao Te Ching* (The Way of Life). Each day, he sat in the grass in the warm sun under fragrant pine trees. After reading one of Lao-tzu's verses, he would read each of the translated versions. Using what he had learned during his many drug experiences, Tim then tried to distill the essence of the poem into psychedelic language. As he did when he helped transform *The Tibetan Book of the Dead* into *The Psychedelic Experience*, Tim was once again putting together a guidebook to a world that he had explored more fully than anyone else. Tim continued working on these poems when he returned to Millbrook. In 1966, they were published under the title *Psychedelic Prayers*.

"I feel these meditations on psychedelic consciousness are perhaps Tim Leary's most inspired writings," Metzner wrote in his introduction to the new edition, published in 1997. "They are, by turns, serene, sensuous, funny, and wise." Although the work was not entirely his own, the poems do reflect a calm center in Tim's writing that was never evident again. The work also speaks to his uncanny ability to adapt an entire body of knowledge for his own purposes. Even for those not personally familiar with the psychedelic experience, the poems are effective in their simplicity, both as literature and as votive prayer. One, entitled "All Things Pass" (which in some form may have served as the inspiration for George Harrison's song) begins "All things pass / A sunrise does not last all morning / All things pass / A cloudburst does not last all day / All things pass / Nor a sunset all night." Adding his own voice, Tim concluded the poem by writing, "During the session / Take things as they come / All things pass."

As winter turned to spring on Holy Man Ridge, Tim and Nena settled into an idyllic rhythm. Each morning, they shared tea with toast and fruit. Heating pails of water, they washed together outside. Stripping off her robe, Nena soaped her body as Tim poured steaming water to rinse her off. Sitting on cushions and blankets under a bamboo grove, they read texts loaned to them by Lama Govinda and performed yoga. "Often we nibbled a morsel of Nepalese temple ball [hashish], which loosens both mind and body," Tim would later write in *Flashbacks*.

He also admitted that their marriage was falling apart. Ever since their time in Japan, Nena had become "more and more moody, homesick for the States, lonely for her dog." Having not lived with a woman for seven years, Tim himself felt incapable of "sensitive reception and confident giving." Removed from the outside world, he slipped back once more into guilt about Marianne's suicide and the two children he had left behind at Millbrook in Richard Alpert's care. "Sensing my detachment, my Scandinavian princess began to wonder what she was doing in this alien place." Tim and Nena's problems may have also stemmed from far more mundane causes. Never one to forget a slight by a woman with whom he was in love, Tim had yet to forgive Nena for talking to him about an old boyfriend during their wedding. There were also issues involving their celebrity status. On the way to India, Tim and Nena had entered a restaurant. Pausing at the top of the stairs, they stood for a moment with all eyes upon them. Believing himself the center of attention, Tim grinned like mad until Nena told him, "You fool. Don't you know they're all looking at me?"

With Metzner, Tim and Nena visited Sri Krishna Prem, "an expatriate Englishman who had lived in an ashram as a devotee of Krishna-Radha in the nearby village of Mirtola for over forty years." As Metzner would later write, "Where Govinda was a scholar, Krishna Prem was truly a sage." For Metzner, this meeting was a turning point. Realizing that the time he had spent with Lama Govinda had strengthened his intellect, which was "already over-developed," Metzner decided to return to America to patch up his "fractured romance" with one of Nena's very beautiful but insecure fellow models. Realizing that Tim and Nena's relationship was "undergoing increasing strain," Metzner felt he should leave them alone to work things out. "It was after all their honeymoon," he wrote. "What was I doing there? I left shortly thereafter."

With Metzner gone, Tim returned once more to see Sri Krishna Prem, whom he would later call "the wisest man in India." Metzner believed that in Krishna Prem, Tim probably came the closest to "accepting a spiritual teacher." Tim chose to follow Prem's advice that he return to the West to do his work, for that was where the future lay. Before leaving, he and Nena took LSD once more in order "to see if we could get fused again." Naïvely, Tim expected that for them "the imprinting of a new reality" would be "no more complicated than making a movie." He added, "The decision to trip in a Siva temple may have been wrong for us." Inside a dark gloomy temple devoted to Siva the Destroyer, Nena shivered in her long suede coat with a fur collar. With her eyes hidden behind "Fifth Avenue dark glasses," she asked Tim if they could go back to their cottage. On the way, Tim seemed unable to walk in step with her. Unlocking their door, he lit a fire. "Then I looked in the glittering eye of my worst and most terrorizing nightmare . . . Everything in the room was alive, everything in tune except me. I was dead, alienated." Moaning as his eyes darted madly around the room, Tim realized that he was now separated from his wife by a transparent film. On his knees, he reached up to touch her hand. It was like touching a statue. His touch caused her to freeze. Sprawled on the silk couch in blue jeans with her long slender legs languorously crossed, Nena lamented the fact that they had both just taken an aphrodisiac in this perfect honeymoon cottage in the Himalayas only for Tim to decide to flip out.

Tim stroked her feet in what he realized was a nervous reflex. "I guess it's over," he would later write that he said. Examining her face in a hand mirror, Nena lit a cigarette. Trying to be brave, she sighed. In dialogue which seems to have come straight out of a Bogart and Bacall movie, she said, "Oh, well, I guess it's not the end of the world." Tim brewed tea. "I drank in despair. I realized with clarity that our marriage was at an end." Connecting as "fairy-tale lovers in the enchanted woods of Millbrook," they had "lived out a season of courtly romance." Nena had taught Tim "tender lessons of girl-love and female splendor. We had time-travelled through a few mythic incarnations, played out magical dramas in panoramic realms. Now we would have to rise to that most complex human art, gentle separation."

At dawn, Tim pulled on his tennis shoes, walked to the rocky cliffs, and climbed down. Above him, an eagle hung motionless on swirling currents of air. He was already looking forward to returning home. After he had borrowed $100 from a fellow expatriate, Tim and Nena began the long journey. Tim returned to Millbrook only to discover that, like Odysseus back from the wars, he was now a stranger in his own home.

When Ralph Metzner returned to Millbrook before Tim, he was shocked by what he found. At the front door of the big house, he was greeted by a "seedy, drugged out guy" he had never seen before, who was wearing clothes Metzner had left behind. Literally and symbolically, the message could not have been clearer. "Gone were the serenity and glowing warmth of Castalia weekends, the joyous enthusiasm for consciousness exploration in a family of seekers." In its place, "the Millbrook mansion had become an Addams family house of horrors, a scene of decadence and depravity and dabbling in black arts, of lost souls wandering around in permanently drugged states, of vicious conflicts leading at times to physical violence." Even the love that Metzner's girlfriend had once felt for him had now turned to hate, for she "blamed my and Tim's absence for the destruction of the Millbrook dream." In just a few short months, the Garden of Eden has been transformed into the ninth circle of hell.

"In my absence," Tim wrote in *Flashbacks,* "Dick Alpert had fallen in love with Arnie, a flamboyant photographer from Brooklyn who liked to project color slides on walls during acid sessions, leading the vulnerable brains of his audience through a Coney Island funhouse of hallucinatory pranks." Surrounding himself with "a mountebank crew" that included jazz musician Allen Eager, the former boyfriend of both Peggy Hitchcock and Tim's fourth wife, Rosemary Woodruff, Arnie was the one "who now set the scene and directed the scenarios." "Dick Alpert said this guy was so wonderful," Metzner recalled. "He had fallen in love with him and he was a maniac. A weird guy who was into mind-fucking. He'd say to his girlfriend in a house meeting, 'You're jealous. I can tell because I can read your mind.' The house had split into two camps. The ones taking LSD all the time who said cleaning up was for those who wanted to clean up. Alpert actually joined them. Nena's brother and mother were there as well and we were the ones who wanted things to be clean. It was like Hesse in that we had come to this place on the journey where everything falls apart."

Charles Slack, who was an occasional visitor to Millbrook during this period, recalled, "I began to have doubts that LSD was going to be the answer to the problems of the world because I woke up early one morning and I came down to the kitchen and there was a gigantic pile of dishes. I had never seen a dirtier kitchen and there was the baroness, the mother of the Swedish model to whom Tim was married, staring at the dishes. A middle-aged European noblewoman. Standing in the kitchen looking at these dishes and roaches were crawling all over them. Someone else came in and I said, "Look at these roaches." And they said, "Oh, aren't they beautiful?" For some reason, I was able to see it through the mother's eyes. That they were not beautiful. Nobody was ever going to do the dishes. Certainly, Leary was not going to do the dishes. Ever. Who was going to do the dishes? Throughout the sixties, that became sort of a thing because different people kept echoing that phrase. It was a very important question. It all depends on who does the dishes. In a commune. And in a relationship."

During Tim's stay in India, Michael Hollingshead had faithfully sent him tapes in care of the American Express in Delhi along with enough LSD for forty trips. Hollingshead had also regaled Tim with tales of the Millbrook residents. Wearing ski masks and carrying musical instruments, they had all attended Salvador Dali's birthday party at the St. Regis

Hotel in Manhattan. Someone gave Dali a pet iguana as a gift. Afterward, Dali took everyone to the Stork Club for a late dinner. He left the iguana on the table as a tip. Wearing a raccoon coat and a tam-o'-shanter, Hollingshead drove to the city to pick up a Tibetan monkey, which friends of Flo and Maynard Ferguson had tried to donate to the Baltimore zoo, only to have the animal rejected. The monkey fit perfectly into the menagerie that Millbrook had now become.

On April 5, Hollingshead, Alpert, Alan Watts, Metzner, and Susan Leary joined Charlie Mingus and Steve Swallow at the first public psychedelic celebration at the Village Vanguard in Greenwich Village. Alpert told funny stories. Hollingshead read from the *Tao*. People danced to music in the swirling light. In every sense, it was a "happening." Along with artist Gerd Stern and his pioneering mixed-media group USCO, they began a series of regular Monday night "Psychedelic Explorations."

At Millbrook, the answer to every question was now drugs. The goal was to find out just how high a human being could get without exploding into discrete particles of pure energy. One day, in order to cure Alpert's cold, Arnie injected him with DMT while he was sleeping. For half an hour, Alpert sat bolt upright without moving. Arnie then fed him eight hundred micrograms of LSD with a spoon. At full volume for an hour, three separate record players blasted Beethoven, Coltrane, and Stockhausen. When the treatment ended, Alpert's cold was gone.

Well-known artists like Feliks Topolski and Saul Steinberg came up to Millbrook to make the scene. While Topolski was tripping, Arnie, a male friend, and a girlfriend got out of a car naked with feathers in their hair and colorful symbols painted all over their bodies. Playing a flute and a saxophone, they began to dance. Then they got back into the car and drove away. Stoned on acid one day, Steinberg discovered just how amazing trees really were. Two months later, a huge tree drawn by him appeared on the cover of *The New Yorker*.

Never having taken drugs of any kind, Paul Krassner, editor of *The Realist*, ingested acid for the first time with Hollingshead as his guide. Deciding he needed to call his ex-wife to thank her for arranging this trip for him—something she had not done—Krassner had to concentrate to get the "swirly limp dime into the wiggling slot of the pay phone." As instructed, the operator dutifully told his ex-wife, "I have a collect call from Mr. Ringo Starr." Krassner went on to give LSD to Lenny Bruce and Groucho Marx. Concerning his first visit to Millbrook, Krassner would later write, "Hugh Hefner's paid-for mansion and Timothy Leary's borrowed mansion are much the same: Each is a complete world unto itself; each is inhabited by an 'extended family'; each is headed by a negatively-publicized man who is warmly cared for by those who know him." Calling Hefner an "urban Thoreau" and "The Green Hornet," Krassner described Leary as "a latterday Lamont Cranston; as The Shadow, he has learned what possibilities lurk in the 13-billion-celled mind of man, *heh heh heh*."

With people high at all hours of the day and night, anything was now possible. When Charlie Mingus heard the tap in the sink yowling, followed by banging noises, he took out his bass and began playing counterpoint. Tripping in the woods one day, Charles Lloyd played the flute accompanied by bassist Steve Swallow, who managed to say, "It's so beautiful, it's all so beautiful," just before fainting. For three weeks, Alpert and five others locked themselves in the meditation house and took four hundred micrograms of LSD every four hours. Although 2,400 micrograms of LSD a day was an unheard-of dose, Alpert soon discovered that the human body developed a tolerance to LSD. There was no way of getting higher beyond a certain point. "We finally were just drinking it out of the bottle," Alpert would later write in *Be Here Now*, "because it didn't seem to matter anymore. We'd just stay at a plateau. We were very high. What happened in those three weeks in that house, no one would ever believe, including us." One day during a trip, convinced that he could fly, Alpert jumped out of a second-story window and broke his leg.

In the glowing reports that Hollingshead regularly sent Tim in India, he told him that both his children were doing fine. Now nineteen, Susan was learning how to bake. Sixteen-year-old Jack was making new friends, whom he brought in to watch the deer in the park. On February 16, 1965, Jack Leary was interviewed by two New York State policemen conducting an investigation into the possession of handguns by persons under the age of sixteen. Jack admitted that he had paid $30 to another juvenile for a .22 caliber Hi-Standard chrome revolver with a defaced serial number. Because Alpert, his legal guardian, had already taken the gun away from him and his natural father was in India "and not expected back for about two (2) years," Jack was unable to find and then surrender the weapon until the following day. On March 18, Jack answered a summons to appear in family court without his father present.

Tim finally returned from India in the early spring, arguing with Nena all the way. "We always said they came back from the airport in separate cabs," Jackie told John Bryan. Tim found what he would later describe in *Flashbacks* as "six months of changes that had converted Millbrook from a community of scholars and scientists to a playground for rowdy omnisexuals." Those who disapproved of what was going on at Millbrook, the Hitchcocks foremost among them, had been waiting for Tim to come back and "clean up the mess." Unfortunately, Tim, by his own admission, was "in no shape to handle any of this." Due to his rupture with Nena, he was, as he later put it, "running several quarts low." When Tim tried to talk to his loyal second-in-command, Alpert did not seem to hear him. He had just accepted an invitation to spend the summer in France "at the beach house of some famous jet-set prince." After listening to Tim agonize about his impending split with Nena, Alpert suggested that the three of them take LSD together. "In hindsight," Tim would later write, "this was the height of folly—we were three willful wary souls, already alienated from each other."

Alpert's recent heavy-dose experiences had "taught him impressive psychedelic barnstorming flourishes. He used a long glass tube to titrate the clear liquid LSD. And he blasted us!" In Tim's version of the story, Alpert panicked first, thinking, "My God, these two have been tripping together so much they have an unbreakable bond. I'm cut off." Lying motionless, he watched Tim and Nena like a wary cat. Then he made the first move. Unfortunately, it was "a blind-side tackle." He accused Tim of "being a disapproving moralist, a prude who condemned his homosexuality."

Rather than respond right away, Tim carefully sorted through his options. Response A: he could laugh and point out that among the three of them, love and humor would conquer all. "Outcome—fusion." But Tim could do no better than Response B: guilty silence. "Outcome—fission." As Tim drifted off "leaking spinal fluid," Alpert and Nena exchanged conspiratorial glances of superiority. "This acid session," Tim would later write, "was about severing connections. The lines went down, and we never got the current going again. It was the last time we took acid together."

Alpert's memory of the trip is somewhat different. "Tim came back with Nena and they were in bad shape," he remembered. "They said, 'The only way we see out of this is for the three of us to have an LSD trip together.' So we did, and they each presented their side and I was like the Jewish court. They told me all this stuff and I said, 'It sounds to me like you both got hung up in a power struggle and you're both caught.' Timothy couldn't believe that. So he felt that she had seduced me."

After fuming about all this for a few days, Tim sat with Alpert and Jackie and Susan one night in Jackie's room. In the version Jack told John Bryan, Alpert was describing tripping with someone in England. "They took acid and the guy came out in a black leather suit and wanted Richard to urinate on him and I thought it was far out but Timothy suddenly said Richard was corrupting me and Susan. He was, like, furious at Richard and he thought, like, Richard had sexually seduced me or something, and he hadn't . . . Richard and I used to, like, hang out and spend a lot of time together. I was real young then but . . . all we ever did was hang out." Jack went on to describe to Bryan how his father began screaming at Alpert. He was, said Jack, "so weird about being gay. Once he accused me of being gay. So I said, 'Look, Timothy, I'm not gay but even if I was, there's nothing wrong with being gay' . . . Maybe he'd had a bad experience himself or something. I don't know." "I was sort of the guardian of his children," Alpert would later recall. "I had been taking care of his kids. He called a meeting of his kids and said, 'Kids, I want you to know that your Uncle Richard is evil.' No one had ever called me evil before. And Jackie . . . said, 'Come on, Dad. He may be an asshole. But he isn't evil.' The kids didn't buy it." At the time Alpert's response to Tim was, "Well, if I'm evil, you're psychotic." Despite rumors to the contrary, Alpert would later say, "I never seduced Jackie. I was the surrogate father and we were very tender but there wasn't a sexual thing. Jackie was very attractive and I could have but I had a kind of moral code in my head that said, 'This is not the game to play with him.'"

After losing his bride on their honeymoon in India, Tim had returned home only to divorce Richard Alpert as well. Alpert would later recall, "I was the wife. I cooked the bread. I took care of the kids. I did the whole thing. While he was gone, I took care of Tim's mother-in-law and his brother-in-law and all the people he had collected around there. I was running very fast to support a sixty-five-room house filled with all kinds of weird people like junkie saxophonists and the bills kept mounting and mounting and mounting. We were $50,000 in debt, which in those days was a lot of money, and no matter how fast I ran, it kept getting worse. The furnace would blow up. The cars were all broken. And people were coming in. I began to realize that no matter how much I did to support him, Tim would take that and be more disruptive. Tim was basically a revolutionary and I basically was not, and Tim was fighting the establishment and authority and making the whole thing much harder because of it and I had to extricate myself from it, which was really hard to do. Because my identity for all those years had become 'Tim and Dick.' This team, and it was really high fun." After having "hung in there" for so long, Alpert now realized there was "a destructive quality in Tim's game and no matter how beautiful it got, it kept being converted into some horror all the time."

Six months later, after Alpert had returned from Europe, Tim and Metzner met him at the train station and convened a "cheerless conference" in a local restaurant. Tim would later write in *Flashbacks* that they all "agreed that we had gone about as far as we could go at Millbrook. The fun had stopped. The money, energy, able bodies, and utopian idealism needed to maintain a sixty-four-room castle had been dissipated." Alpert tells a different story. "They threw me out of Millbrook," he would later say. "They were upset about my homosexual scene." Hollingshead and Metzner, who never reconsidered his view of Tim as "one of the outstanding visionary geniuses of the 20th century," soon departed as well. In just six months the man whom Jack Kerouac once called Coach Leary had now lost not only the last remnants of the brilliant team he had assembled at Harvard but also his wife and the man who in every way had functioned as a surrogate parent to his children.

TWENTY-TWO

Wearing tight jeans bound by a silver chain, a boy's shirt tied above her navel, "revealing," as Tim put it in *Flashbacks*, "a strip of creamy smooth belly," and tennis shoes, thirty-year-old Rosemary Woodruff, a dark-haired former model, actress, and stewardess, visited Millbrook with some friends on May 1, 1965. As a gift, she brought with her a bottle of woodrose-flavored wine. When Rosemary ran into Tim in the kitchen, she asked him to help her open the wine. Struck by her tennis shoes and the book by Wittgenstein she was carrying, Tim offered a toast to their meeting. Then they went off on a walk. A month later, they met again at a gallery opening in the city. As they sat together at a bar having a drink, Tim gallantly lit her cigarettes. "I knew he liked me and I liked him," she recalled, "but I had just remet a musician I'd had a terrible crush on years earlier. So I didn't accept his invitation to Millbrook then."

In August, on a full-moon weekend when a seminar was in progress, she went to Millbrook again. After taking LSD, Rosemary found herself in a downstairs room where Tim had sat all the people along the wall. While Ralph Metzner chanted, everyone looked at very trippy film slides. Then they were asked to imagine they were alone on a rocket ship hurtling into space. All systems had failed and the oxygen was almost gone. "What is your last thought?" Suddenly, the lights went out. High on acid, Rosemary saw how completely alone Tim seemed sitting by himself. Crossing what seemed to her like an immense void, she sat down beside him. As though to confirm she had just done the right thing, Flo Ferguson plumped up the pillows for her. Tim and Rosemary spent their first night together in the meditation house.

The next day, Tim dragged a ladder and buckets of paint to the big house. On the huge redbrick chimney, he and Rosemary outlined a pair of interlocked triangles. This was the Maha Yantra, "the ancient Oriental symbol for sexual union." Clearly, whatever sexual problems Tim might have had with Nena had now been solved by Rosemary. As Ralph Metzner wrote, "A tantric love goddess arrived for Timothy in the form of the very beautiful Rosemary Woodruff. The Millbrook community flowered again with music, meditation, laughter, creativity, happy children, and remarkable people." Unlike Nena, Rosemary was willing to devote her life to taking care of Tim and his children. Right from the start, her relationship with Tim was founded on the promise that they would have a child together. "What a wonderful mother you will be," he often told her. "What a beautiful child we will have together." In love with Tim and their life at Millbrook, Rosemary at first did not really take much notice of Jackie or of Susan who was off at boarding school. All this changed on the day Tim and Rosemary took Susan with them into the city so Rosemary could move out of her apartment. "Until then," she recalled, "Susan wasn't really cognizant of me in many respects. I wasn't in her ken. The day we went to get my things from the apartment, Tim said to her, 'Who does Rosemary remind you of?' She really began paying attention to me at that point because the answer he gave her was: 'Marianne.' She didn't look on me with favor after that. I became the new stepmother, which was very difficult for me."

In September, Michael Hollingshead returned to London to put into action a master plan written out for him by Tim. Having already shipped thirteen cartons of the *Psychedelic Review* to England, Hollingshead took with him several hundred copies of *The Tibetan Book of the Dead* as well as half a gram of pure LSD (enough for five thousand sessions) synthesized by the Czech government laboratories in Prague. Operating out of the newly founded World Psychedelic Centre, located in his flat in Belgravia, Hollingshead proceeded to turn on some of the most famous denizens of swinging London, Paul McCartney, Victoria Ormsby-Gore, and Chrissy Gibbs among them.

The master plan called for Hollingshead to rent Albert Hall (or "Alpert Hall" as Tim called it) to put on a "psychedelic jamboree" featuring the Beatles and/or the Rolling Stones with "the climax of the evening to be the introduction of Tim as the high priest." Before any of this happened, Hollingshead became addicted to methedrine. Smoking pot and hash constantly, he took LSD three times a week and never slept. He soon got busted on Pont Street in Chelsea for possession of cannabis. On acid,

Hollingshead went to court to conduct his own defense and received a twenty-one-month sentence in the notorious Wormwood Scrubs prison. Behind bars, he conducted underground LSD sessions for fellow inmates while writing a psychedelic musical based on John Milton's *Paradise Lost*. Tim's master plan was never carried out.

At Millbrook, the communal scene was now a thing of the past. "By 1965," Rosemary recalled, "all the old crowd was gone. Hollingshead had been sent off to England with a bunch of books. Ralph Metzner was in the city living in what had been my apartment. Richard Alpert was on tour with the Grateful Dead. The big house was essentially closed. With Susan off in school, there was just Jack, Tim, and myself. Jack would be doing his homework and I would be in the kitchen fixing food and we would all sit down to have dinner together and then take the dog for a walk." In what seems even now like a very carefully worded letter of reconciliation to Richard Alpert, Tim wrote on October 12: "Here we have evolved a serene and harmonious rhythm. Susan, Jack, and I are closer than we have been in several years. Our small group is close. We are into many new, fascinating forms. Tapes, records, films, writing. Financially the picture is bright. The weekend programs are most profitable and we have made hefty dents in the debt—along with your contributions. We plan to continue—with some time off during the winter to rest in the sun."

The scene at Millbrook might have been more peaceful than ever, but the level of police surveillance directed at the estate had reached an all-time high. After Thanksgiving, strangers dressed as telephone repairmen showed up unannounced at the front door to "check the wires." The owner of the local plumbing shop confided to Tim that federal agents had asked to borrow uniforms from him in order to gain access to the house. Unmarked cars drove through the property. Men with binoculars stood outside the gates. Rumor had it the Poughkeepsie district attorney was planning a raid.

Receiving a $10,000 advance from the New American Library for his autobiography, Tim decided not to spend the long cold winter in the big house. Instead, he set off with Rosemary and his two children for the Yucatan on "a month-long vacation for the four of us to get to know each other." Once Christmas vacation was over, Susan would return to school while Jack spent the spring with friends. Tim and Rosemary would stay behind in a house on a beach so Tim could write his book. They would then "return to America, find a house with a white picket fence, and have babies." With a loving woman by his side, Tim seemed ready to return to the kind of life that he and his children had not known since Berkeley.

Before leaving the estate, Tim buried all his psychedelic drugs in the woods beneath rock markers so he could dig them up in the spring. He turned off the water and the power, then shut the big house down for the winter. With Rosemary, Susan, Jackie, and a young man who came along for the ride, Tim set off on December 20 for Mexico in a dark-blue, brand-new Ford station wagon.

For two days, Tim and his traveling companions drove more or less non-stop. To make the miles pass more rapidly, they smoked marijuana. By the time they arrived in Laredo, Texas, on the evening of December 22, what little grass they still had was stashed in an egg-shaped silver snuffbox hidden inside Rosemary's sewing kit, which in turn was buried somewhere at the bottom of the huge mound of books, clothing, sacks of organic brown bread flour, and scuba gear that took up most of the station wagon's backseat.

Nearly a decade earlier, Allen Ginsberg had written in "Howl" about those "who got busted in their pubic beards returning through Laredo with a belt of marijuana for New York." Rosemary had already been to Laredo to testify on behalf of a former boyfriend arrested for this very crime. Although everyone in the hip world knew that Laredo was the border town where people always got busted for smuggling grass into America from Mexico, Tim and his family could not even be bothered to pick up the stray marijuana seeds that had fallen to the floor as they had rolled joints in the front seat. But then, why would anyone search a car for dope going *into* Mexico?

After stopping to buy the auto insurance required for entry into Mexico, Tim parked the station wagon outside the Mexican Immigration building on the Nuevo Laredo side of the international bridge over the Rio Grande. It was already dark when Tim walked into a government office equipped with a long counter and clacking typewriters. With a warm, welcoming smile, a man came out from behind the door, stepped forward, and cried, *"Timoteo!"* Tim did not recognize the man right away, but his obvious pleasure in seeing Tim provoked a "reflex response of affection from me." Suddenly, the man's smile turned official. "Where do you think you are going?" he demanded. "Do you remember me? You aren't allowed in Mexico. I know because I am Jorge Garcia who deported you from Mexico in 1963. You are *persona non grata* in Mexico. *Prohibido.*"

The last time Tim had seen Garcia, the policeman had been pounding his hand on a counter in the Mexico City airport, demanding that Tim be put on an airplane without the tourist card Garcia had already taken from him. It seemed an incredible coincidence that Garcia happened to be on duty on this night. Nonetheless, Tim blithely handed him an official letter from the Ministry of Gobernacion stating he could return to Mexico as a tourist. "Stay right here," Garcia told him. Then he walked into the parking lot, hopped in a car, and drove away.

For perhaps the first time in Tim's life, "a black spider of paranoia started spinning a sticky web around the waiting room of my mind." Walking over to Rosemary, Susan, and Jackie, Tim told them they were going to have "a little hassle here with the Mexican government," and that someone should go out to the car and get rid of the grass. Gathering up all the loose marijuana he could find, sixteen-year-old Jackie put it into a film vial, disappeared into the men's room, and flushed it all away. So far as Tim could tell, his family was now clean.

When Garcia returned, he told Tim he could not possibly enter Mexico tonight. Tomorrow morning Garcia would call the capital to confirm that Tim had official permission to return to the country. "It will all be different *manana*," Garcia told him. Walking back out to the station wagon, Tim went right on chatting pleasantly with him. Unfortunately, there was still a small problem of which Tim was not aware. When Jack told Rosemary he had dumped the contents of the film canister in the men's room, she remembered the snuffbox in her sewing basket. The Learys were not clean at all.

With Mexican cops leaning all over the car, Tim slid behind the wheel. In the backseat, Rosemary began digging through all the books and clothing and sacks of brown flour and scuba equipment. Shoving aside Tim's typewriter, she kept on searching. But her sewing kit was buried so deeply in the pile that she could not find it. Finally, she did. Unconcerned, Tim pulled out of the parking lot. Instead of spending the night in Nuevo Laredo where one could "make the scene day and night without papers," Tim decided to turn the car around and head back to America. "I was saying, '*Tim!*'," Rosemary recalled. "But at this point, his loss of hearing was really a serious problem and he didn't hear me. I got the egg. The guy who came with us was on my right. The left-hand side of the car was totally blocked. The window was inaccessible. I told him to open the window but he was frozen in fear, staring straight ahead. We were coming back to the American customs and I said, 'Jackie, open this up and dump it out the window,' and just at this point, we were at customs."

Suddenly it dawned on Tim that even though he and his family had not yet been in Mexico, they would now have to pass through American customs to reenter the USA. Just to make sure, he asked, "All the grass is out of the car—right?" By his side in the front seat, Susan told her father they had just found the silver box. "I'll take it," she said. As Susan hid the snuffbox inside her panties, the station wagon rolled to a stop before a customs agent. Tim handed over the family's unused entry papers to Mexico and started talking a mile a minute. Since they had never actually left America, why should the agent do anything but wave them right on through so that they could all return to Mexico tomorrow?

"I remember bright lights," Rosemary would later recall, "and Susan was holding the silver egg. They said, 'Everyone out of the car,' and they saw the seeds on the floor. They had just seen us go through the other way and Tim said, 'We haven't gone anywhere.' But they were waiting for us. Because our phones at Millbrook were tapped, they knew our plans. They knew where we were going to enter Mexico because we'd discussed it on the phone. They had the policeman there to recognize Tim. All he had to do was call and say, 'We're sending them back.' We were so naïve that I might have even asked on the phone for the grass we took with us."

Leaning into the car, the customs agent reached down and came up with something between his fingers. "What is this seed I found on your car floor?" he asked. In a flash, the car was surrounded by other customs agents. They ordered the Learys to remove all their baggage from the station wagon. As Tim watched other returning tourists pass by with disapproving looks on their faces, he wanted to shout, "It's all a mistake, really, we're not smugglers. We didn't even get into Mexico." Ordered to sit on separate benches in the customs office, Tim, Rosemary, Susan, Jackie, and the guy who had come along for the ride were forbidden to talk to one another. Although it was now eight o'clock at night, customs agents called in two chief inspectors from home to assist in the search. Thinking he had found the mother lode, one agent walked triumphantly into the waiting room with what turned out to be a box filled with brown flour. One by one, the Learys were called into small rooms and examined for needle marks. They were ordered to empty out their pockets. Carefully, agents folded bits of dust and tiny tobacco flakes into envelopes. The actual bust itself did not occur until Susan was strip-searched by a female matron who found the silver snuffbox in her underwear. Inside was a small amount of grass and three partially smoked joints.

"Have you ever been in the situation where you feel all the gears shift?" Rosemary would later ask. "When everything changes? I felt that so strongly. It just changed everything. All the potential and the possibilities for the type of life we were going to lead together ended right then and there. Poignant doesn't begin to express it. I think Tim knew as well. Something like this had been waiting in the wings for a long time." All the same, Rosemary blamed herself for not making Tim hear her as they headed back to the American border. She blamed herself for trying to palm the grass off on the young guy sitting next to her and for letting Susan hide it in her underwear. Suddenly, everything was now altogether different from what it had been before. Under the glare of naked lightbulbs at the jail, Tim kissed Rosemary and made "a brave, wavering speech to the family" in which he said, "Well, beloved, there's not one person in history whom we admire who didn't do his time in the Man's prison. It's all part of our education."

"I was in the cell with Susan that night," Rosemary recalled. "She was so adorable. She was hanging on the cell door doing stretching exercises, and to keep her amused, I told her the story about my friend who had been busted in Laredo. When they emptied out our bags, I had a tiny little roach. The jailers, who were Mexican, laughed and threw it away. And of course they were very quick with their recommendations for lawyers." Jack Leary was taken to the second-floor tier with the juveniles while Tim was led to the third-floor tier. Unlocking two barred doors, the jailer directed Tim down a dark row to the fifth cell. He pressed a button and the metal cell door creaked open. "Metal on metal is the worst sound. I entered and the door slid shut. Remote control. *Clang!* The first time you find yourself in jail is an educational moment for everyone, I guess." Before being put into his cell, Tim had been advised of his rights. "At that second," he writes, "I had a minor revelatory experience, a quick, highly detailed view into the future, like a speeded-up newsreel. I could see the headlines—'HARVARD PROF NABBED AS SMUGGLER' . . ."

In *The New York Times* on December 24, 1965, the headline on a story buried at the back of the first section read OUSTED LECTURER JAILED IN

LAREDO ON DRUG CHARGE. Beneath a headline reading OUSTED HARVARD LECTURER HELD AS "POT" SMUGGLER, the *New York Herald-Tribune* gave the story considerably bigger play. In the article, Tim was quoted as saying he found the charges to be "incomprehensible." When asked if he smoked marijuana, he said, "Oh, yes I do. You can't study consciousness unless you do." Jack and Rosemary were also quoted as admitting they smoked pot, while Susan refused to reply.

The next morning, Tim and Jack were handcuffed together and marched two blocks to the office of U.S. Commissioner Jacob Hornberger, who was "stern, relentless, and mainly preoccupied with our financial status." At the hearing, Hornberger set Tim's bail at $10,000, Susan's and Jackie's bail at $2,500 each, and Rosemary's and their male companion's bail at $5,000 each, for a grand total of $25,000—no small amount of money. The jailer gave Tim the name of the best local bail bondsman, who in turn supplied him with the name of the best lawyer. Within an hour, Tim returned to Hornberger's office to take care of all the necessary paperwork. As Rosemary recalled, "Two silver-suited men showed up the next day and we were out on bail and we went back to Millbrook."

In an era when television shows like *Ozzie and Harriet* and *Father Knows Best* served to define family norms in America, Tim had publicly identified himself as a father who did not know what was best for either himself or his children. In this, as in so much else, he was ahead of his time. Because of the bust in Laredo, Tim Leary would spend the rest of his life grinning at the world from newspapers, magazines, and television screens, an authentic but notorious celebrity.

On February 7, 1966, Tim and Susan were indicted on three federal charges: smuggling marijuana, transporting smuggled marijuana, and failure to pay the federal marijuana tax. Although a guilty plea was entered on Susan's behalf, Commissioner Hornberger set it aside and named two prominent lawyers to defend her. By also pleading guilty, as so many others busted in Laredo had done before him, Tim could have spared himself not only the agony of going to trial but also the accompanying publicity, whatever the final verdict.

Instead, Tim Leary decided to go to war. Like someone working toward another Ph.D., Tim did so much research into the federal laws regulating the use and transport of marijuana that he became an expert in the field. "The Government's most pressing reason for avoiding a vigorously fought marijuana trial," he would later write, "was the uneasy knowledge that the Federal weed law was a bizarre monstrosity from the bureaucratic standpoint and unconstitutional from the legal standpoint. Conservative constitutional scholars assured me that the grass laws violated the Fifth Amendment (forbidding self-incrimination, in this case by being forced to purchase a license for an illegal act), the Eighth Amendment (forbidding cruel and unusual punishment) and the Ninth Amendment (guaranteeing personal freedoms unmentioned in the other amendments)."

Nevertheless, Tim still had trouble finding a lawyer. For two months, he searched for an attorney willing to represent a client whose entire defense would be based on the assertion that as a scientist engaged in legitimate drug research, as well as "an initiated Hindu" whose religion included the sacramental use of marijuana, Tim Leary had a First Amendment right to smoke grass. Plainly, he meant to use his trial to challenge the laws that made this practice illegal.

Although he was upset by all the publicity generated by Tim's bust, Billy Hitchcock hired what Tim in *Flashbacks* described as "a hotshot Texas lawyer" to defend him in Laredo. Busy with a murder trial, the hotshot lawyer was not available when Tim's trial begins. The Honorable Ben C. Connally, chief judge of the U.S. District Court for the Southern District of Texas and the brother of Texas governor John Connally, refused to postpone the starting date. On March 2, as Tim would later write, he and Susan "straggled onto the playing court, finally, with a rather weak defense quartet: There were two jolly Laredo lawyers for whom fighting the grass laws—a tactic that, if successful, would cut down on their regular source of clients—was only slightly less than treasonable. They took the case because I was a likeable maniac with some money in a legal defense fund to throw away." In a statement Tim read to the court as his trial began, he said he had "engaged the services of four competent lawyers to try this case: Mr. John Fitzgibbon and Mr. Tom Goodwin of Laredo   and Professor Joel Finer, an authority on constitutional law from the University of Texas." The defense team was completed by a member of the New York bar. "My second counsel was 'Good-Time' Charlie Rumsey," Tim would later write in *Flashbacks*, "nephew of Averell Harriman, a friend of Billy's and mine. I think it was his first and only felony criminal case." Susan was represented by her own attorney, Charles N. Fansler Jr. Unlike her father, she was on trial before the court and not the jury.

Despite the size of his legal team, Tim's extensive handwritten notes on the trial make it plain he was in charge of the case. Covering page after page in his notebook with his spidery scrawl, Tim outlined arguments for his own defense, cited obscure test cases and arcane rules of law, listed relevant statutes from both federal law and the Internal Revenue Service code, recorded the phone numbers and addresses of law professors who might be able to help him, as well as experts on narcotics law in the attorney general's office. He also questioned whether "pot" was in fact a "narcotic." On an otherwise blank sheet of paper, he wrote, "Susan is guilty of being my daughter—of being the daughter of a non-conforming ostracized religious leader." Defining his own profession as "15 year psychological, 6 years—no name," he added a list of terms to describe himself: "—wizard, —alchemist, —prophet of revelation,—molecular psychologist."

As the trial got under way, a flood of telegrams began arriving in Texas: Alan Watts, Billy Hitchcock, Professor Harry Murray of Harvard, Professor Huston Smith of MIT, Laura Huxley, Peggy Hitchcock, Frank Barron, and Rabbi Zalman Schachter all sent messages affirming that Tim was a person of high character involved in important research involving psychotropic drugs, including cannabis. The simplest and most direct message came from Richard Alpert, who wired, "Am available for fund raising and anything else you wish. I love you. Richard." Years later, Alpert would say, "Although I had already really broken with him at this time, I felt I should support him. So I went down there and became involved in chairing the fund-raising and things like that. But he wouldn't listen to anybody. At the trial, all the lawyers we hired and everybody said, 'Tim, you're being a fool. This is practically a misdemeanor. You can get off with a warning and a small fine. They've been doing this down here for years and everybody knows the game. What are you doing here?'"

As always, Tim was playing to the crowd. His eloquent opening statement to the court read in part, "I am pleading not guilty in this case, because I am an American citizen. As such, I am entitled to the free exercise of my religion. I am entitled to engage in scientific research. I am entitled to live in my home, travel in my car and bring up my children the best I can in accordance with my beliefs and values. My motives before and during the incident of my arrest, are clearly spiritual, interior and not ulterior." Although Tim had addressed his remarks to a jury of eight men and four women, all of whom lived and worked in south Texas, he clearly intended his words to be heard by a wider audience and to make the trial into a contest of lifestyles. "The jury trial was pointless," he would later write. "I freely admitted possession of the offensive half ounce. Our aim was to build up a good record for the appeal."

The government then made its case. Miss Helen Loftis, who had performed the search on Susan, testified she had found a silver snuffbox filled with marijuana between Susan's legs. Customs agent Ray Hatch and customs inspector Herbert Best stated that on the night of December 22, 1965, they had found a blue zippered bag in Tim's station wagon along with pot seeds and sweepings. The total amount of grass found in the car was eleven grams, less than half an ounce. Raymond Cutler, thirty-one, testified he had met Tim at a party in Greenwich Village in New York where Tim had smoked marijuana for purposes that were not religious in nature. And then Tim began his defense.

To support Tim's claim that his use of marijuana was religious in nature, his lawyers called two medical authorities, Dr. Joel Fort and Dr. Ralph Metzner, who stated "that grass was less harmful than alcohol." A Hindu monk testified that Tim had in fact "been initiated on the banks of the Ganges into a Bengali sect that used ganga as a sacramental aid to meditation." To bolster this contention, Tim's lawyers introduced three photographs into evidence. In one, Tim and Nena stood on their honeymoon in front of a government-licensed marijuana store in Calcutta. In another, taken by Tim, Nena and Sri Asoke, a Bengali saddhu or holy man, stood before the shop. In the third, Tim could be seen at the ashram of Lama Anagarika Govinda in the Kumaon Hills in the Himalayas. "Since the jury was bound to come in with a verdict of guilty," Tim would later write, "I decided that the logical step was for me to try to turn on the judge, to get to his mind, to teach him something about the art and science of getting high. The moment of achievement came during my second day on the stand when the judge leaned toward me and said, by way of clarification, 'What you are saying is that there are several levels of consciousness and taking drugs is like going up in an elevator. Different drugs take you to different floors. Is that it?' 'Thank you, your Honor. That is precisely what I was trying to say.'"

During cross-examination by the prosecutor, Tim steadfastly refused to disclose the name of the person who had given him the marijuana that was in his possession when he was arrested. With all charges against

Rosemary and Jack having been dropped for lack of evidence, Rosemary was back at Millbrook. "Someone had to stay at Millbrook," she would later say. "Also, who was I? Was I the girlfriend? It didn't look good. Tim called me from the trial to ask permission to tell them who gave the grass to him. I gave him permission and he told them." Returning to court after the lunch recess, Tim told Assistant U.S. Attorney Morton Sussman that it was "Rose Mary Woodruff" who gave him the marijuana. Asked by Susan's attorney whether his daughter had ever seen him smoke marijuana, Tim replied, "Yes." It was also brought out in court that Susan was eight years old when her mother died in 1955. "Is Susan a Hindu?" her lawyer asked. "No, sir," Tim replied. Admitting that at home both his son and daughter had gone into rooms where drug sessions were under way, Tim added, "Marihuana is the mildest of all the psychedelic drugs."

In his closing argument, the prosecutor pointed out that the government had not manufactured evidence. Although it was only half an ounce of marijuana Tim had been charged with possessing, the prosecutor asked, "But what does he do when he is finally exposed and they find out about it? He makes a joke about it. Now, I don't mean to shout, for shouting's sake, but I feel so strongly about this case and his acts that I can't help myself, and I hope you will forgive me." Judge Connally dismissed the charge of smuggling and illegal transport, ruling that since Tim had the marijuana with him when he left New York, it could not have been brought into the United States from Mexico.

Tim's case went to the jury on March 11, 1966. On the same day in San Francisco, the federal government issued a warrant ordering Mexico to extradite novelist and chief Prankster Ken Kesey, who had fled there to escape prosecution on charges of marijuana possession in San Francisco. As the door to the jury room swung shut, one of Tim's lawyers looked at his watch and said, "Well, it will take them five minutes to sit down and light cigarettes. And ten minutes to elect a foreman and read the instructions. And, say, seven minutes to count the votes. They'll be out with the verdict in twenty-two minutes." "And so they were," Tim would later write.

To no one's great surprise, the verdict was guilty on both counts. As the UPI wire service report that ran in *The New York Times* described the moment, "Miss Leary wept and cried out to her father. He remained impassive." For unlawful transport of marijuana, Judge Ben Connally sentenced Tim to twenty years in prison and a $20,000 fine. For Tim's failure to pay the federal tax on marijuana, Judge Connally sentenced him to ten years in prison and a $10,000 fine. The judge also sent Susan to a reformatory for an indeterminate sentence. Further, Judge Connally ordered Tim committed to a hospital for the criminally insane for psychiatric observation. After ninety days, Tim would return to court either for resentencing or long-term commitment in a such an institution. Susan was also ordered to do the same. After sentencing, Tim was released on $2,500 bail pending the appeal. Rosemary would later say, "I remember a reporter calling me to ask, 'What do you think of Dr. Leary's sentence?' Which was the first I'd heard of it. I don't know where this phrase came from but I said, 'Patently absurd.' Which it was. They had the opportunity and they took it. They nailed him." Tim would later write, "The sentence caused the expected flap. Press, TV, radio. A seismological revulsion of outrage and sympathy . . . I was suddenly escalated, thanks to Harvard and Laredo, to a curious place of notoriety somewhere between Christine Keeler and Che Guevara."

All across America, headlines trumpeted the incredibly harsh sentence given to a former Harvard professor. But not everyone was outraged by his punishment. Smugly, *Time* magazine noted, "Last week, in the U.S.-Mexico border town of Laredo, Texas, Leary finally got his comeuppance." In the *New York Herald-Tribune,* Seymour Krim wrote that the result of the severity of Tim's sentence for "what the trade calls a dimebag of stuff" is that "a new dignity has overtaken this once-secret experience." In a letter to the editor of *The New York Times,* a doctor from Buffalo compared Tim's thirty-year sentence for pot possession with the minimum sentence of twenty-six years meted out to the three men who had just been convicted of murdering Malcolm X. An editorial in *El Tiempo,* the Spanish-language newspaper in New York, read, "Aside from the fact that Dr. Leary did not smuggle any marihuana into the United States, and merely had the eleven grams on his person for taking into Mexico, the sentence is flabbergasting evidence of the tremendous political power of the Bureau of Narcotics in this country and of the influence of politics in our courts." Not coincidentally, Tim's good friend Billy Hitchcock owned the newspaper.

Tim did everything he could to keep the pot boiling. In Greenwich Village on March 13, 1966, he told William Insra of the *New York Herald-Tribune* that "the little drama played out in Laredo has been played out in every generation. It didn't happen just Friday. It's been happening for

4,000 years. With me or without me, my work is going to go on." Tim added that he was not the one on trial but rather the Constitution, the Congress, and the old versus the young. Two days later, Tim held a news conference at the Overseas Press Club in Manhattan, which soon developed into a "'teach-in' on consciousness-expanding drugs." He announced he would be appealing his conviction on religious grounds. His lawyer Charles Rumsey told Sidney E. Zion of *The New York Times* that he believed this to be the first case in which the federal narcotics laws were being "attacked as a violation of religious freedom." The formation of the Timothy Leary Defense Fund was also announced. On March 18, *The New York Times* ran an editorial entitled "Specious Marijuana Defense," which concluded: "Whether Dr. Leary deserves the severe sentence that he has received is for the courts to decide. But the speciousness and quackery of his specific defense on religious grounds are as worthless as marijuana itself."

In a remarkable photograph taken during the trial by Lawrence Schiller, which appeared in *Life* magazine, Tim sits on the floor of his lawyer's office in Laredo with his legs stretched out before him. Wearing a tweed suit, sensible shoes, a button-down white shirt, and a polka-dot tie, he leans against a wall so old and cracked that it looks like an ancient map. Above his head hang two plaques belonging to his lawyer, a certificate of honorable discharge from the United States Marine Corps and a bachelor of law degree from the University of Texas. Talking to someone beyond the frame, Tim's hands fan so rapidly through the air that his fingers meld into a psychedelic blur. Looking much smaller and younger than she really was, Susan sits beside him. Barefoot, with one hand tucked behind the other and her long dark hair trailing over a cardigan far too big for her even with the sleeves rolled up at the wrists, she gazes with utter adoration at her disproportionately large and powerful father. The message conveyed by the photograph is one of outright pathology, a father-daughter relationship that had already gone so far wrong that nothing could ever set it right again. "The picture is accurate," Rosemary Woodruff would later confirm. "That was very much their relationship." "She had always been a dutiful conforming child, eager for approval and affection," Tim wrote of his daughter. "The national publicity weighed heavily on her. I was slow to realize how much she suffered by what she felt to be a public disgrace."

TWENTY-THREE

More than ever, money was a problem for Tim Leary. By his own reckoning, the trial in Laredo and the appeal would cost nearly $25,000. Assuming that the fight went all the way to the United States Supreme Court, the overall cost might reach an astronomical $100,000. Fortunately, people were willing to put their names and reputations on the line to help raise funds for the Timothy Leary Psychedelic Defense Fund.

On March 27, 1966, Richard Alpert joined the campaign with a fund-raising letter from California in which he wrote, "Timothy is the most systematically creative person I have ever known. His ability to break set and see beyond the cultural veil has continued (after five years of working together daily) to awe and amaze me. He is, in my estimation, the one person most responsible for introducing L.S.D. (a consciousness-expanding chemical) into our culture as a folk sacrament rather than as a psychiatric tool for the study of psychosis." Alpert then asked, "Would you please help by contributing to his defense fund*, and asking those of your friends who might understand to help too, if they can?" At the bottom of the letter, Alpert explained the asterisk: "Some of you might wish to consider this a Head Tax."

On April 3, an impressive three-quarter-page ad appeared in the Sunday *New York Times*. Under the heading THE RESPONSIBLE COMMUNITY IS SHOCKED AT THE HARSH SENTENCING OF PSYCHOLOGIST DR. TIMOTHY LEARY, Dr. Donald B. Louria, chairman of the Subcommittee on Narcotics Addiction of the Medical Society of the County of New York was quoted as saying, "Let me make it clear. I'm not advocating the legalization of marijuana nor do we want the penalties for sale or smuggling reduced. We do not think the long jail sentences for possession of this substance are reasonable."

The ad included a recent bibliography of Tim's published writings on science and religion, an accurate account of the trial in Laredo, an announcement of Tim's upcoming appearance at Town Hall on April 5, and a coupon to be clipped out and sent in with a donation. The list of those who supported the cause read like an honor roll of the people who would create the sixties in America. They included William Mellon Hitchcock, Angier St. George Biddle Duke, Leslie Fiedler, Allen Ginsberg, Richard Alpert, Darlene DeSedle, Charles Olson, Alan Watts, Gunther Weil, Norman Podhoretz, Robert Lowell, Norman Mailer, Jules Feiffer, Susan Sontag, Jonas Mekas, Kenneth Koch, Robert Creeley, Albert Grossman, Diane DiPrima, Jack Gelber, Laura Huxley, Jason Epstein, Irving Kristol, Lawrence Lipton, and Peter Fonda.

Working out of an office in the United Nations Plaza, Larry Bogart, "an authority on soil conservation and air pollution" who "had never taken a psychedelic and had no intention of doing so," became the spokesman for the Timothy Leary Psychedelic Defense Fund. On April 16, Billy Hitchcock wrote a letter on Leary Defense Fund stationery in which he stated, "This is harsh and unusual punishment of a prominent scientist, who has written 52 articles and books on psychology and consciousness. It has created a shock wave of disbelief. People from every walk of life understand that this is an attack on the constitutional freedoms of all of us. Thought control must be opposed."

Tim would later write, "The Defense Fund hummed with activities—pamphlets, mailings, phone calls, public appearances—all to raise money for my lawyers, who were fighting another team of attorneys paid for by our taxes. None of it was my idea of fun." His disclaimer notwithstanding, Tim threw himself eagerly into the fray. "The next step was for me to accept the fact that I had been rudely snatched out of retirement and to try to use the absurdity at Laredo to my advantage. We figured—rightly—that it would take about three years for the case to get to and come down from the Supreme Court. So I had some 30 or 40 months to pitch myself back into the hedonic revolution . . . The prospect of serving any substantial prison time had never played any part in my mythology. I had no intention of becoming a martyr." "So now Tim was on his way to becoming a martyr," Rosemary Woodruff would later say. "He had to raise money, he had to pay lawyers, he had to go to the city, he had to give interview after interview to everyone who came up to Millbrook. There was this mobilization behind all of it. Going public."

The verdict in Tim's trial caused an overwhelming flood of publicity about the use of LSD in America. Between March 11, 1966, the day the verdict was handed down in Laredo, and June 26, a period of 108 days, eighty-one separate articles about LSD appeared in *The New York Times*. As in the early fifties, when the nation suddenly became obsessed with the Red Menace, much of the "news" about LSD was generated by politicians eager to seize upon an issue that would put their names in the headlines.

Labeling the phenomenon, "An Epidemic of Acid Heads," *Time* magazine claimed that "10,000 students in the University of California system have tried LSD . . . No one can even guess how many more self-styled 'acid heads' there are among oddball cult groups." On March 25, 1966, the cover of *Life* magazine, also published by Henry Luce, who had himself already taken LSD, featured a very trippy photograph of a hand floating behind some dark geometric shapes below the headline THE EX-PLODING THREAT OF THE MIND DRUG THAT GOT OUT OF CONTROL— LSD. The subhead read, "Turmoil in a Capsule—One dose of LSD is enough to set off a mental riot of vivid colors and insights—or of terror and convulsions." Inside the magazine, ten full pages were devoted to groundbreaking photographs of people on LSD taken by Lawrence Schiller; a Q and A on the nature of the drug; a first-person account by "a hard headed businessman" of his first trip; as well as photographs and capsule biographies of those from every walk of life who had taken the drug. In an accompanying story, Barry Farrell quoted an article written by Leary and Alpert, which had first appeared in the summer of 1963: "'The game is about to be changed, ladies and gentlemen. Man is about to make use of that fabulous electrical network he carries around in his skull.'" Farrell went on to note, "But the revolution, if that is what it is, has long since slipped out of Leary's or anyone else's control." There were now "psychedelic corporation presidents, military officers, doctors, teachers," as well as those "who are taking LSD merely because it is the latest excitement around . . . 'Have you taken a trip?' is a question asked with unnerving frequency these days, and usually it suggests that if you haven't the conversation is about to end." With an anecdote guaranteed to strike fear in the hearts of parents everywhere, Farrell concluded by quoting an unnamed "psychedelic mother of four" (no doubt a Millbrook resident), who said that whenever she and her husband wanted to take a trip together, she would simply put a little acid in the kids' orange juice in the morning and then let them spend the day "freaking out in the woods."

On March 30, Dr. Louria, who had expressed such dismay at Tim's sentence for marijuana possession, labeled LSD the most dangerous of misused drugs today. On April 7, a five-year-old girl in Brooklyn was reported to be in critical condition from convulsions after swallowing a sugar cube impregnated with LSD by her eighteen-year-old uncle, who had been charged with endangering the health and morals of a minor. In his own defense, he said he had bought the LSD in Greenwich Village for $5.00 for "an experiment" and the child had taken the sugar cube from the refrigerator. A day later, the girl was reported to be in good condition but Dr. Louria said there was no way of knowing if she would suffer any long-lasting aftereffects. City and federal health aides said this was the fourth LSD incident in a year involving a child. The same day, a Harvard graduate and medical school dropout was charged with stabbing his mother-in-law to death. When police came to arrest him, he told them, "Man, I've been flying for three days on LSD. Did I kill my wife? Did I rape anybody? What have I done?"

On April 14, Brooklyn District Attorney Aaron Koota announced that he would establish a program to study cases of anyone treated in city hospitals after using LSD. Sandoz Pharmaceuticals, Inc. of Hanover, New Jersey, the only licensed distributor of LSD, informed the Federal Drug Administration that it would stop distribution of the drug. That same day, Ralph Metzner wrote Koota an extraordinary three-page letter in which he stated:

> Most of the recommendations so far have been legal-punitive: more restrictions, more police agents, heavier penalties for sale and use. Such approaches are negative, futile, based on political hysteria. Hasty and vindictive legislation will produce a new era of prohibition, will drive the use of the substance underground and create a new class of white-collar, college educated criminals, two or three million strong. It will also encourage underworld racketeers to produce LSD, which may be impure and toxic, for heavy profit . . . The only way to prevent LSD from going the way of heroin and becoming an underworld racket is by systematically pursuing research in the area and allowing qualified investigators access to legitimate supplies. We look forward to hearing from you.

Well-intended though Metzner's letter may have been, he had obviously never walked through the dark hallways of the Municipal Building at 210 Joralemon Street in downtown Brooklyn, where Koota and his assistants labored. His letter illustrated just how naïve Tim and his colleagues still were and how little they knew about the way in which LSD was now being used on the street. On April 16, Koota called for seven-to-twenty-year jail terms for peddlers or users of LSD to replace the current one-year maximum. Reporting that "tremendous profit" was being made in LSD, he said the underworld might in fact have moved into its illicit sales. Quite possibly, he had gleaned this bit of information from Metzner's letter. On April 19, Koota met with New York City school officials and reported that LSD was being made in school facilities.

On April 25, Koota discussed a probe into complaints that students at Brooklyn College and Kingsborough Community College had been manufacturing hallucinatory drugs on campus. On April 26, Dr. Harry Gideonese, president of Brooklyn College, said there was no evidence that drugs had been manufactured at any city colleges in Brooklyn. Nevertheless, Mayor John Lindsay called for a report from Koota. On the same day, the Board of Education ordered school principals to act on drug use by teenagers. On April 27, the American Medical Association's Council on Mental Health urged doctors to be alert for LSD and other hallucinatory drug users and cited a warning on the dangers of LSD first issued in the September 1963 edition of the *AMA Journal*. On April 29, the New York State Senate passed a bill providing the same penalties for sellers and users of LSD and other "mind-expanding" drugs as for narcotics.

On and on it went, an authentic media frenzy about the use of LSD by the youth of America. As is so often the case, the publicity did far more harm than good, helping advertise a substance that most people still knew nothing about. In his letter to Koota, Metzner had made this very point. Because Metzner and Tim were now on the wrong side of the law, no one in a position of authority could be bothered to listen to them. In the LSD war that was raging on the front pages of magazines and newspapers, they had become the enemy.

A tall, twenty-three-year-old Tibetan monk clad in long brown robes, his blond head shaved, came to Millbrook on Saturday, April 16. With him, he brought a warning for Tim that he felt compelled to deliver before the day was out. The monk, a Harvard dropout who had also been expelled from the Phillips Exeter Academy, had wandered through Europe and the Middle East on a spiritual pilgrimage before being ordained by the Dalai Lama in India. Now called Tenzing, he was blind in one eye and lived in a monastery in New Jersey. "He seemed ill at ease that Saturday morning," Marya Mannes would later write in *The Reporter*, "very anxious to speak privately to Leary and then hitch a ride back to New York as soon as possible. Leary later told us the cause of his anxiety. The young man had told him that he felt so full of negative reactions from the place that he had to leave. He told Leary that in the critical position Leary was now in, it was wiser—even essential—for him to give up his fight against the authorities and withdraw from his position of leadership in the LSD movement. 'When two dogs fight over a bone,' said the monk, 'and one of them drops the bone, the other will drop it too and walk away.'"

Within a year, the monk, whose real name was Robert Thurman, would marry Nena von Schlebrugge Leary. After returning to Harvard to complete his studies, he would become a professor of Indo-Tibetan Buddhist studies at Columbia. Recognized as the leading Western scholar in his field, Thurman would establish himself as a popular author and lecturer, as well as the co-founder of Tibet House in New York City. He and Nena would have four children, among them the actress Uma Thurman. In 1997, along with Dr. Andrew Weil, *Time* magazine would name Robert Thurman one of the twenty-five most influential people in America.

The young monk's warning fell on completely deaf ears. Tim, clad in jeans and a light-blue shirt, spent most of the day alongside men with power saws and axes cleaning out the center of a "sacred grove" of fir trees behind the big house. After a dinner of "splendidly seasoned fish with all the trimmings," the small firs were heaped in a pile for a bonfire. Michael Bowen, an artist and psychedelic activist who would later organize the first Human Be-In in San Francisco, was staying in the big house that weekend, along with twenty-five other adults, two teenagers, and five children. "That night," Bowen would later recall, "we had a big bonfire out in the woods right next to the Swiss chalet bowling alley. People sat around the bonfire saying nothing. Everyone in absolute silence. At one point, people held hands. But they all just sat there and watched that fire burn down to a glowing mound of coals. I had a Great Dane with me and my dog kept flipping out and barking at the perimeter and coming back."

Sometime after eleven, everyone returned to the big house to watch movies of waterfalls, parachute jumping, and kids on a trampoline shot in slow motion and fast action, so as to seem particularly trippy when viewed under the influence of LSD. Outside the big house, a Dutchess County deputy sheriff had already moved into binocular range in hopes of getting a better view of what he felt certain was a pornographic movie. Once he realized there were no naked women to be seen, he told his fellow officers, who were shivering as they waited in the cold, "Them people are crazy!" When the movies ended, Tim went upstairs to his room with Rosemary and smoked some very powerful DMT smeared on mint leaves. It was now about one in the morning.

"On the night of the raid," Rosemary recalled, "we had smoked DMT and we were coming down. I had on my mother's annual Christmas present—a long flannel nightgown with elastic in the wrists. Tim was in a long Indian shirt. Jackie was going off to do his homework. He went out the door, heard a noise, and went downstairs to investigate. He came flying back in and said, 'There are a bunch of hunters down there.' Which was a scary thought. People with rifles and orange jackets on."

Kicking the DMT pipe under the covers, Rosemary was lying in bed as "a bunch of men with clipboards burst in and said, 'Stay in bed and don't move!' They set up a spotlight and they trained it on me. Tim was up and about without any pants on and they hustled him downstairs and I was in the room with the guy with the clipboard and another guy who was going through the closets and saying, 'A-ha!' Pulling up bottles of aspirin and old birth control pills from the bathroom cupboard and lifting up my fuchsia plant and going 'A-ha!' I was beyond paranoid and stuck in the bed with the DMT and the pipe at the foot of the bed, which they never found because they didn't strip the bed."

The big house had been invaded by a posse of armed deputies led by Sheriff Larry Quinlan and the assistant district attorney of Dutchess County, a former FBI agent named G. Gordon Liddy. Long before he would become famous as the most fearsome of the Watergate burglars, Liddy had a well-developed flair for the melodramatic. In his memoir of that night, he wrote, "Rumors were rampant at the intersection of Main and Market Streets—Poughkeepsie's Rialto. Local boys and girls had been seen entering and leaving the estate. Fleeting glimpses were reported of persons strolling the grounds in the nude. To fears of drug-induced dementia were added pot-induced pregnancy. The word was that at Leary's lair the panties were dropping as fast as the acid." "Millbrook was in a sense a public nuisance," Liddy would later recall, "but it was also against the law. The information was that controlled dangerous substances were being distributed there."

After a judge had approved the Dutchess County district attorney's request for a search warrant to be executed by Sheriff Quinlan, Liddy's problem became how to "trap people in their rooms and then search them because if they were in possession, then we could charge them . . . They never locked the doors so we decided we would just go inside and sneak up this huge stairway, à la Tara if you will, and trap everyone in their rooms." Liddy soon learned that "thirteen helmeted booted deputies and thirteen helmeted booted deputy sheriffs" could not "sneak. At about the fourth step, we were detected and they all came pouring out of the rooms. And there went the plan. Tim was the ringleader and it was no problem finding him because Tim found us. The first view I had of Tim was that he was coming down the stairs and I was coming up the stairs and he was wearing a Hathaway shirt with no pants. Period. It was a very spectacular view of him. We kept trying to get Tim to put on a pair of pants because we had anticipated the necessity of searching women and so we'd brought some female deputies with us." Liddy's paramount concern was to shield hardened police matrons from having to view Tim's private parts. "Pants!" Liddy would later write he shouted. "The district attorney wants pants on this man!"

"I remember Liddy as this dark, saturnine presence," Rosemary recalled, "frowning and concentrated but in the background. By this point, Liddy was downstairs with Sheriff Quinlan and they were gathering all the members of the household—the Ferguson family and their lovely black babysitter Suzie Blue, who was terrified, and Marya Mannes and her companion, and Michael Bowen and his Great Dane, and some other terrified people."

In the bedroom, Rosemary was clinging to a small ornate brass urn, shouting "That's my sacrament!" at a deputy sheriff. Removing the urn from her hands, the deputy asked Liddy what he should do with it. "I looked inside the container," Liddy later wrote. "It was nearly filled by a dried, ground, vegetable matter looking like nothing so much as a good grade of marijuana." The substance turned out to be peat moss. "Dried vegetable matter," Liddy would later say. "Marijuana is dried vegetable matter. If you had put it in a cigarette and lit it, you would have gotten an aromatic hydrocarbon. An aromatic hydrocarbon is not against the law. Marijuana is an aromatic hydrocarbon. But it also contains tetrahydracannabinol."

"So they got the peat moss," Rosemary recalled, "and they thought it was dope and they were happy." Horrified by the hippie filth in which these people lived, deputies began working their way from room to room. As Jack and a friend sat on the landing playing guitars and making up impromptu folk songs about the raid, one deputy pulled his .357 Magnum and charged into a room where he interrupted a couple having sex.

"They wrecked the place and then took photographs and claimed this was the way the house looked," Rosemary recalled. "They went into the laundry room where we had this huge box of discarded clothing for dress-up and they dumped that all over the floor. They uprooted plants in the kitchen, they fished around in the fish tanks. Yes, they found some cat shit on the floors. They thought they were going to find drugs and an orgy and underage teenage girls and runaways."

In fact, there was more dope in the house than either Tim or Rosemary knew. "I needed some money and I had some pot," Michael Bowen would later say. "Leary had asked, 'Please, don't bring any pot in here.' But I did it anyway because I didn't feel that close to him. He kind of weirded me out in a way. I brought two or three ounces of weed and I sold some to a Hindu priest who was up there. I had the two ounces of weed in this little room where I was staying with my dog sleeping at the foot of my bed." Woken up by lights flashing outside his window, Bowen watched as his bedroom door flew open. Outside stood a sheriff with "one of those Smokey the Bear hats with a gun pointed at my head screaming, 'Get up! Get up!' And that was what I woke up to. At that moment, my Great Dane rose up and looked at this guy in his flashlight beam. The guy stepped back, said not a word, and closed the door behind him." Leaping out of bed, Bowen tried to open the window only to discover there was a screen on it with a latch that had been painted shut. "I kept the stuff in baggies," he would later say. "First I tried to eat it but the stuff was too dry so I punched my fist through the screen and threw it so it scattered out through the hole."

Opening the door to his room, Bowen discovered there was no one left upstairs. Passing by the meditation room into which everyone else had been herded, he strolled into the kitchen "where this huge fat sheriff guy was at a card table with a light and a chair so people would have to sit in front of him with the light glaring at them. Nobody bothered me so I made tea." As Bowen drank his tea, Liddy entered with a clipboard and offered him his hand. After asking Bowen for his name and address and thanking him for the information, Liddy left. "I stayed in the kitchen and had some more tea while all the other people were being treated like they were in a concentration camp." Bowen then noticed that several of the cops who were coming in and out had the pot that he had thrown out the window on their hats. "I swear. It's the absolute truth."

Upstairs, Tim was struggling into a pair of trousers several sizes too small for him. A deputy sheriff told Liddy he had taken them from Tim's bedroom only to have Tim inform Liddy that they belonged to Jack. Finally, a pair of pants that actually fit Tim were found and he put them on. At four in the morning, rooms were still being searched. It was at about this time that Liddy and Tim began what over the years would become a continuing dialogue.

"This raid," Leary told Liddy, "is the product of ignorance and fear."

"This raid," Liddy told Leary, "is the product of a search warrant issued by a magistrate of the state of New York."

"The time will come," Tim said, "when there will be a statue of me erected in Millbrook."

"I'm afraid the closest you'll come is to be burned in effigy in the village square," Liddy replied.

Tim and three others were arrested for being in possession of a house in which a small amount of marijuana had been found in one of the bedrooms. "As they were taking him away," Rosemary recalled, "Tim was laughing and joking with them. I didn't get arrested that night. So after they took Tim away in this procession of cars, I asked to use the phone. The phone didn't work. They'd shut it off. So I couldn't call the lawyers. I watched him leave and I ran upstairs to get dressed. I got all the change I could find and I got someone to drive a working car to the Poughkeepsie jail, which was half an hour away."

On her way there, Rosemary stopped in a diner only to discover all the deputies "laughing and slapping each other's backs and eating pie." Realizing that she could not use the phone there, she went straight to the jail where a "beefy desk sergeant" wouldn't give her any information. Returning to the diner, which was now deserted, she called Billy Hitchcock and the lawyers. Tim spent the night in jail. "By Sunday noon," Tim would later write in *Flashbacks,* "'Good-Time Charlie' Rumsey arrived in a limo from New York and bailed me out. Again headlines in the New York papers with front-page pictures of the Big House, increasing my lurid reputation." "Tim's reaction to all of this was always very light-hearted and very jovial and very up," Rosemary recalled. "When he first got back home from jail, he played it in the best of all possible ways. He was laughing and joking about the cops. 'Did you see this one?' And of course we made the connection between Sheriff Larry Quinlan and the Sheriff Quinlan played by Orson Welles in *Touch of Evil.*"

The ensuing media coverage of the bust went far beyond any press agent's wildest dream. LSD PSYCHOLOGIST ARRESTED AGAIN read the head-line in *The New York Times.* In the accompanying story, Tim was quoted as saying he was "outraged at this midnight invasion of my home." He asserted he was unaware there were any narcotics in the house. The ban-ner front-page headline in the New York *Daily News* read RAID MANSION, SEIZE LSD PROF. Below the headline was a huge photograph taken the pre-vious summer of Tim in shirtsleeves in front of the big house. It was jux-taposed with a new photo of Tim in handcuffs, accompanied by a police officer.

Two weeks later, a new print ad with the banner headline DR. LEARY'S CASE CONCERNS YOU—WHY? appeared in newspapers with an account of the bust at Millbrook and the news that five witnesses had been sum-moned by the Dutchess County grand jury to testify. The Timothy Leary Psychedelic Defense Fund would represent them all. New names on the list of supporters now included Steve Allen, Alan Atwell, Eric Bentley, William Berkson, Robert Frank, Richard Goldstein, Nat Hentoff, Ad Reinhardt, and Ron and Jay Thelin, founders of the Psychedelic Store in San Francisco's Haight-Asbury district. "At some point," Rosemary re-called, "I began to suspect that Tim kind of thrived on this. The threat of the cross exhilarated him in those days."

The news of the bust brought a horde of brand-new visitors and re-porters to Millbrook. All the while, Tim continued preaching the gospel wherever and whenever he could. Speaking to a thousand people in Town Hall in Manhattan on April 21, 1966, he prophesized the rise of a new civ-ilization in which man would return to an environment of natural beauty. In two hundred years time, he announced, even New York City would achieve pastoral calm. Once men could at will consult their own height-ened cellular consciousness, they would have a better perspective for living in creative harmony with nature. Prefiguring the rise of the ecology movement, Tim said his own cells were rebelling against the mounting pollution of air and water. Present-day cities of metal and stone built aboveground were antagonistic to the two-billion-year development of biological life. All machines, atomic energy plants, and service facilities belonged underground.

Astonishingly, Tim urged his audience, most of whom were in their twenties, to join him in abstaining from the use of consciousness-expanding agents like marijuana and LSD for a year in deference to the law. "I think we should voluntarily stop doing what has caused anguish and confusion for those who do not understand," he told them. "The tendency is to fight; I think we should love . . . You who have taken psychedelic drugs know enough now to turn on without drugs. If you don't, I'm going to teach you." Tim explained that his proposed moratorium would give the social structure a chance to catch up with the culture and keep those now breaking the law from joining the estimated twenty thousand people already in prison for violating marijuana laws. By advocating a one-year moratorium, Tim conceded he was temporarily surrendering his own constitutional rights. Yet he still affirmed his own belief in marijuana for heightened sensory awareness. Earlier in the day at a press conference at the Harvard Club (from which he had apparently not been banned), Tim said that after strict testing, licenses for the use of LSD should be issued by the government. Reversing his longstanding position, he added, "LSD should be used only by carefully selected people in carefully selected places." He did not mention that he had long ago rejected this policy when it was urged upon him by Humphry Osmond and Aldous Huxley.

The moratorium was a calculated strategy designed to curry favor with the establishment. With the current level of LSD use in America having reached epidemic proportions, Tim wanted to restore his own credibility by becoming the man with a solution for the problem. In every speech and interview he had ever given before, Tim had always offered LSD as the magic substance that could solve all the world's problems. Now he was asking those who believed in him to put the use of such "sacraments" on the shelf for a year. The truth was that no one in America could now control the use of LSD or marijuana. In the new era Tim had helped to usher in, moderation was anathema. To the vast majority of young people who had already turned on with LSD, the idea of a moratorium seemed so completely square that only someone completely out of touch with what was happening would even have dared suggest it.

Tim's sudden change of heart received widespread attention in the press. An editorial in *Life* magazine on April 29 noted, "Dr. Timothy Leary, whose dogmatic and incautious advocacy of LSD got him fired from Harvard, must bear some responsibility for the spreading cultism. He believes its abuse is now out of hand and has renounced his own use of it 'as a gesture of conciliation until the legal status of psychedelics has been clarified.' Dr. Leary's own legal troubles—he has been twice arrested and once heavily sentenced on charges involving marijuana, a far less dangerous drug—suggest that he is really being punished for his LSD history. Instead of harassing a would-be martyr to the 'sacred biochemical,' society would do better to figure out how law can best control it."

Despite the editorial, Tim's legal problems continued. On May 3, Rosemary was called to testify against him before the grand jury of Dutchess County. Although she later called it "an idiot defense to begin with," Rosemary refused to testify on religious grounds. In a statement that could only have been written by Tim, she told the grand jury, "The District Attorney offers no immunity from prosecution to our religion and our spiritual values which are of more importance to us than our personal safety. It is a classic technique in heresy trials to harass the members of an unpopular spiritual group and it is an ancient and honored tradition of our Judaic-Christian heritage to refuse to submit to such Caesarian inquisitions." "There were several options," she recalled. "I considered leaving the state but then I would have been a fugitive. Tim's divorce was not final so we couldn't marry. Or we could make it a test of our freedom in court. It was established that I would claim Tim as my guru. Some of the testimony was actually very funny. I remember the judge saying, 'You mean your religion doesn't have a name yet?' And I said, 'We have yet to name it, Your Honor.'"

Although Rosemary was granted immunity, she still refused to testify against Tim. She was then sentenced to a month in jail for contempt of court. If she still refused to testify, she would be given an additional twenty-five days for every unanswered question. "They put me in the Poughkeepsie lockup and it was pretty grim. I couldn't figure out at this point whether Tim wasn't allowed to see me or he didn't want to. I had this romantic idea, I guess it was from watching too many prison movies, that if I looked out the window, he would be standing on the sidewalk. Like the Women's House of Detention on Thirteenth Street in Manhattan where all the pimps would go to see their girls. But it was summertime and I was suspecting Tim was having too good a time in my absence." "He totally shattered Rosemary's life," attorney Michael Kennedy, who in time would represent both Tim and Rosemary, later recalled. "And every time he would go to jail, he would shatter her life. When she went to jail for refusing to testify against him at the grand jury, which is something he never had the courage to do, she was held in contempt. While she was doing this time for him, he was carrying on an adulterous affair with somebody at Millbrook. The son of a bitch."

On May 9, Alexandra K. Rewis of the Barlow School in Amenia, New York, wrote Tim to let him know how Susan was doing. While at this time of year it was traditional for seniors to slack off because the pressure of being admitted to college had lessened, Susan seemed to be having more than the usual problems. She was failing art and not doing well in math. Nor did she seem to be working on her chemistry term paper. In English, her work had been average, though it was often very sloppy. Should Susan fail art, then the University of Wisconsin (to which she had apparently been accepted) might require her to attend summer school. Rewis wrote, "I am sure that many factors contribute to this slump, not the least of which, although Susan certainly does not discuss it often, is her concern for you. As you know, it is difficult for her not to be reminded of the situation when she picks up a magazine or a newspaper." The day of the bust, the writer Marya Mannes had asked Susan if she usually got weekends off from school. "Oh, no," Susan told her. "This is just for the interview. We're not supposed to leave on weekends." Susan also admitted that she had taken LSD several times. Asked to describe how it made her feel, she said it "changed" her "patterns." "I get hung up on my patterns—you know, the way I think, the game I'm playing, all that—and LSD changes you, gives you insights, sort of clears you up." Asked about smoking marijuana, Susan brightened perceptibly and replied, "Oh, it's a good feeling. It sort of relaxes you, you feel peaceful and good. It's really not much different than taking a drink, but alcohol is really worse." After the interview, Susan returned to school and so avoided seeing her father get busted for the second time in four months.

On May 9, Senator Robert F. Kennedy of New York announced that on May 17 and 18 he would conduct an inquiry into the reported widespread use of LSD "on college campuses and in city ghettoes." Before Kennedy could convene his own hearings on the matter, he was beaten to the punch by Senator Thomas Dodd of Connecticut, the conservative Democrat and noted Communist hunter who chaired the Special Subcommittee on Narcotics of the Senate Judiciary Committee. Tim accepted an invitation to testify because Carl Perian, the subcommittee's staff director, told him Senator Dodd would treat him "in a respectful manner as an invited expert." On May 13, Tim brought Susan and Jack with him to Washington. Wearing a professorial-looking suit, a Hathaway button-down shirt, and a narrow polka-dot tie, with his hair trimmed short for the occasion, Tim made his way through a hallway crowded with TV reporters, eager for a word from the famous Dr. Leary. Perian, looking harassed, told Tim the hearing had been upstaged by the sudden return of a senator who had been scheduled to be out of town but had changed his plans and flown back to the capital, quite possibly because of the extensive media coverage this hearing seemed certain to generate. The scions of two landed Irish families from Massachusetts, Timothy Francis Leary of Springfield and Senator Edward Moore Kennedy of Boston, were about to meet.

Beginning his testimony by praising the committee for having generated "the most constructive legislation that has been produced in this admittedly complex field," Tim said he was "very aware of the work done by the chairman of the committee in constructive remedy to the narcotic drug problem." He described psychedelic drugs as "nonaddictive, nontoxic, and antinarcotic . . . There is nothing to fear from LSD. There is nothing to fear from our own nervous systems or our own cellular structures . . . I would say there is more violence, insanity, friction, terror, in the cocktail lounges and barrooms of any large American city on any one Saturday night than in the entire twenty-three-year history of LSD use." In Tim's view, the real challenge was not how to control these drugs but how to use them. "Restrictive legislation which creates a new class of millions of college educated white collar criminals is obviously not the answer. Research, training, knowledge are the only solutions to the problem." Tim differentiated between "escape drugs," such as opiates, heroin, barbiturates, "and of course our national narcotic, which is alcohol." Unlike psychedelic drugs, "which seem to open up consciousness and accelerate awareness," these are "blindfolds that tune off reality, whereas psychedelic drugs open up reality like the microscope or the telescope, and of course, like these instruments, you have be trained to use them or you are confused or even terrified."

Tim was sailing along confidently when suddenly he was interrupted by Senator Kennedy. "Mr. Leary, I am trying to follow the best I possibly can some themes that must be coming out of your testimony here this morning, and I am completely unable to do so. You talked in the beginning about the communications problem which exists between different generations, and then you indicate and describe why that exists. Then we hear a description and analysis, as valuable as that might be, about the different reactions to different drugs. You talk about the statistics which are going to be larger next year. Then you say you are not alarmed by them because if they are in training . . . and there is a careful distribution, then this isn't really a problem. And then I hope we are going to have at least a discussion on who those trained people might be and what the regulations might be." Before Tim could respond, Senator Kennedy was off again, saying, "I am completely unable to follow anything other than just sort of a general hyperbole of discussion here. Since your testimony isn't written, and this is a matter with which we are deeply concerned, I hope at least for those of us who are not inimitably as familiar as apparently you are with LSD, that you will try and see if you can analyze this more precisely. At least I would find that helpful."

Elected to his older brother's former Senate seat while John F. Kennedy was still in the White House, Teddy had only held public office for four years. He was now facing someone who had taught at Harvard, an institution from which he himself had been expelled as an undergraduate for cheating on an exam. Yet Teddy was critiquing Tim's opening statement like a professor who had just noticed that a freshman's essay lacked a coherent thesis statement.

Doing his best to recover, Tim said, "I was, Senator Kennedy, just about to point out the differences that exist among drugs, and I am going to suggest that special types of legislation are needed."

"Are you going to talk about the lack of communication between the generations before that or after that?"

"I finished doing that. I feel constructive legislation is obviously and badly needed, and I recommend respectfully to this committee that you consider legislation which will license responsible adults to use these drugs for serious purposes, such as spiritual growth, pursuit of knowledge, or in their own personal development. To obtain such a license, the applicant, I think, should have to meet physical, intellectual, and emotional criteria. I believe that the criteria for marihuana, which is the mildest of the psychedelic drugs, should be about those which we now use to license people to drive automobiles, whereas the criteria for the licensing of LSD, a much more powerful act, should be much more strict, perhaps the criteria now used for airplane pilots would be appropriate."

Tim failed to mention that his own driver's license had been revoked on November 5, 1965. Considering that for the past six months he had not only been driving illegally but also drinking in his car while regularly exceeding the speed limit, on his way to and from Millbrook, the good news might have been that Tim did not have a pilot's license. All the same, he continued by stating that colleges should be authorized to offer laboratory courses in which "these internal microscopes are used under supervision." By so doing, the indiscriminate use of LSD by young people would end. In addition, these courses "will be probably the most popular and productive courses ever offered in any educational institution."

Senator Dodd then tossed Tim a softball question about how long LSD had been in use for legitimate purposes. Twenty-three years, Tim testified. Dodd asked Tim if he had ever used LSD himself. "I have used LSD or similar drugs 311 times in the last 6 years," Tim responded. "I consider LSD to be a microscope. Each time I take LSD I keep careful records and I have a specific purpose in mind why I am doing it, the way a scientist would look at different objects through his magnifying lens." When Dodd asked if he had ever injected the drug, Tim replied that it was a liquid and that he had witnessed more than three thousand LSD trips. Pressing on, Dodd asked, "Would you agree that uncontrolled use is dangerous? Don't you feel that LSD should be put under some restriction as to its sale, its possession, and its use?" "Definitely," Tim replied. He added that either there be some form of licensing, or "we will have another era of prohibition in this country."

Senator Kennedy rejoined the fray. "Mr. Leary, I have been continually confused by your testimony. Maybe that is my own limitation of understanding as to the nature of the subject that we are considering here today. You mentioned earlier, and I am trying to clarify at least to some extent my own understanding, that you needed a microscope in order to indicate the degree or quantity in which this LSD should be taken; is that correct?"

"As a metaphor, yes, sir," Tim replied.

"And do you use it to measure the quantity, to make up the consistency of the particular drug at a particular time to determine what kind of ride you want to have; is that right?"

"I am using the microscope as a metaphor, sir."

Back and forth they went about the use of metaphor in political life until the senator asked, "Now, when they go out of their minds, as I gather from your testimony that they certainly can . . . do they know the difference between right and wrong?"

"No, sir," Tim replied. "Not social right and wrong. They are likely to think in an unconventional—"

Kennedy completed Tim's sentence for him. "In unconventional ways. And so if they don't really know the difference between right and wrong, still they are able to, as you say, perform normal kinds of activities, bodily activity or social activities?"

"That depends entirely on the experience of the person. You have to be trained to use LSD the way you are trained to use a computer."

Finally getting it, the senator said, "Therefore you are suggesting that anyone who administers LSD ought to be highly trained?"

"Absolutely," Tim replied.

"And that there shouldn't be indiscriminate use? And that is why you want to give college courses in LSD?"

"Yes, sir."

"And what is going to happen to the boy who doesn't get to college?"

"There would be special training institutes for him."

"So we are going to train high school students as well? Are we going to have high school courses as well?"

"Let scientific research answer the question as to what age the nervous system is ready to use these new instruments."

"Then what are we are going to do now for the boys that, say, go into the Army prior to the time they get to that age? Are we going to have the Army give training courses on how to use it?"

"I should think that in the Army of the future, we all hope there won't be, but in the Army of the future LSD will be used to expand consciousness so that these men can do their duties more effectively."

"That is very responsive," the senator said, apparently pleased with the absurdity of Tim's answer. After stating yet again that the need for licensing was urgent, Tim told Senator Dodd he agreed completely with the 1965 Drug Abuse Control Amendments, which declared the illicit manufacture and sale of LSD a misdemeanor without outlawing possession. "So there should not be indiscriminate distribution of this drug, should there?" Kennedy asked.

Entering entirely into the realm of fiction, Tim replied, "I have never suggested that, sir. I have never urged anyone to take LSD. I have always deplored indiscriminate or unprepared use."

After some questions from Senator Dodd, whose only purpose today seemed to be to provide Senator Kennedy with breathing room to mount yet another attack, Kennedy read into the record a statement which said that LSD could be extremely dangerous when used improperly. To a rhythm not seen since the days of Gallagher and Sheen, Leary and Kennedy then began clog dancing together once more.

"Sir, I agree with that," Tim said.

"Yes," Kennedy responded.

"Any form of energy, alcohol, and the motor car is dangerous if used improperly."

"That is right."

"I couldn't be in more agreement."

"It is dangerous then."

"If used improperly."

"Isn't that why the pilot is licensed as well?"

"Yes, sir. The danger here is human stupidity and ignorance. That is the only danger with LSD. That is the only danger human beings face in this world."

Doing his best to summarize, Kennedy told Tim that he had testified to "indiscriminate possession of this, as well as use, that it is dangerous, and I think the question now is for legislators to determine whether it can be controlled by legislation or where it cannot be . . . I think that is a question for the Congress. But it seems to me that your testimony has been extremely convincing about the dangers of this drug as well as its opportunities. And I think for someone who has been associated as long as you have been, have been intimately involved in it as long as you have been, I think that this extremely weighty evidence which you have given to this committee this morning, and we want to thank you."

All Tim had to do now was thank Senator Kennedy for putting these words in his mouth, thereby making him into a witness for the prosecution rather than the defense, and then everyone could go to lunch. Instead, Tim said, "I cannot agree with that summary, respectfully. I must disagree, Senator Kennedy, with your statement." Like a terrier with a rat in its mouth that it could neither devour nor discard, the senator then began recounting Tim's testimony all over again. Coming at last to what might have been his own position on the matter, Kennedy said that the question remained "whether this committee can effectively legislate controls on it. That is something we have to wrestle with. But your testimony on these other factors about its distribution, its manufacture, the indiscriminate use of it, not being administered, or the dangers of it being administered by people who are not carefully trained I think is extremely weighty evidence, and I think this gets back to where I was before, Mr. Chairman." Precisely where this was seemed unclear.

After a few more interchanges between Tim and Senator Dodd, the hearing was finally adjourned at 1:05 P.M. In *Changing My Mind, Among Others,* Tim would write, "Sitting there watching Teddy huff and puff in law-school rhetorical style, hidden behind the robes of legislative cliche, I felt sorry for Teddy and for the rest of us." In his autobiography, Tim added, "Any hope of leadership from the Kennedy family would have to come from Bobby." Whatever Ted Kennedy's motives might have been in questioning Tim so relentlessly, he had certainly kept him from using the hearing as a platform from which to proclaim the wonders of LSD. The best proof of how successful his tactic had been was the headline that ran the next day on the front page of *The New York Times:* LEARY SEES CRISIS IN THE USE OF LSD.

Tim's lackluster performance before the subcommittee did nothing to compromise his newfound status as a leader of the counterculture. Nonetheless, those closest to him knew that he had failed miserably to stand up for himself in the face of Senator Kennedy's withering cross-examination. "His appearance before the subcommittee was a total defeat," Rosemary would later say. "In his testimony before Dodd, he was not his usual assertive self. He was humble and self-effacing and concerned. He was saying what he thought they wanted to hear. Which was what he did whenever he was confronted by authorities."

Still behind bars for contempt of court, Rosemary watched his testimony from the Poughkeepsie jailhouse. "I saw it on television," she would later say. "He was being berated by Ted Kennedy. I mean, lambasted. He was sitting there with Susan and Jack, and I kept waiting for him to say something about our religion. Nothing. Not a word."

TWENTY-FOUR

Tim Leary would later write that after his appearance before the Senate subcommittee in Washington, he picked Rosemary up from jail, went off to the woods at Millbrook to dictate what would become his famous *Playboy* interview, and then spent an entire day lying atop the blue copper roof of the big house, trying to decide whether to return to the nation's capital to testify before a subcommittee chaired by Ted Kennedy's older brother Robert.

In fact, Rosemary remained in jail, serving her sentence for contempt. In Washington, Art Kleps, "Chief Boo-Hoo" of the Native American Church, a newly formed religion based on the sacramental use of LSD that had perhaps five hundred members, followed Tim as a witness before the subcommittee. With Senator Jacob Javits of New York now acting as chairman, Senator Ted Kennedy off on other business, and Senator Quentin Burdick of North Dakota asking most of the questions, Kleps, a psychologist with a bachelor's degree from Utica College and a master's in school psychology from Syracuse University, delivered the kind of bravura performance that by all rights Tim should have given.

"It is our belief," Kleps told the subcommittee in his opening statement, "that the sacred biochemicals such as peyote, mescaline, LSD, and cannabis are the true host of God and not drugs at all as that term is commonly understood. We do not feel that the Government has the right to interfere in our religious practice, and that the present persecution of our coreligionists is not only constitutionally illegal but a crude and savage repression of our basic and inalienable rights as human beings." Having firmly staked his claim to higher ground, Kleps went on, "The leader of the psychedelic religious movement in the United States is Dr. Timothy

Leary. We regard him with the same special love and respect as was reserved by the early Christians for Jesus, by the Moslems for Mohammed, or the Buddhists for Gotama. I see no moral difference whatever between putting our religious leader in prison for 30 years and the incarceration of a rabbi in a concentration camp by the Gestapo of Nazi Germany." Kleps concluded by saying that on the day the prison doors closed behind Tim, America would face "religious civil war." Senator Burdick let Kleps finish and then noted, "Well, I must say your testimony has been forthright and most unusual." After Kleps completed his testimony, he was informed by Carl Perian that Senator Robert Kennedy was "foaming at the mouth" because of all the coverage Kleps was receiving. "My friend said you had better get out of town fast," Perian told Kleps. "I wouldn't put it past him to have you picked up. If you play against Bobby Kennedy and win you've made an enemy for life."

Kleps went directly to Millbrook to visit Tim. "Ah, the conquering hero," Tim said when he saw him. Eagerly, Tim pumped Kleps for every detail of his adventures in the nation's capital. Kleps would later write that Tim seemed "particularly impressed by the good treatment accorded me by the Juvenile Delinquency Sub-Committee staff . . . 'I tried to be conciliatory,' Tim said. 'I can see now I shouldn't have done that.'" At the time, Kleps knew nothing about Tim's testimony or the manner in which it had been delivered. After reviewing a transcript of the hearing, Kleps wrote, "It was a good thing I hadn't known about this testimony before I made my statement, or I might not have been able to carry off a sincere defense of Tim as our religious leader. Instead, I might have devoted my time to attacking him as an insidious menace to the religious spirit and to human freedom in general. But that would just have rigidified Tim's position. As it was, he dropped his pilot's license horseshit soon after and came over to my side, maintaining that the psychedelic experience was religious, and that no law could interfere."

Based on the way he had been treated in Washington, Tim now knew he would play no significant role in shaping government policy on LSD. Forsaking the lawmakers in Washington who had refused to take his counsel to heart, Tim decided to play once more to his real audience—a younger generation searching desperately for leaders, no matter how flawed. "From that time on," Kleps wrote, "whatever Tim had to say on any theoretical issue was strictly soothing syrup for the troops. If they wanted to pretend to be simple peasants, fine. If they wanted to dress up in robes on Saturday night and pretend they were weird monks, fine. Tim had made a fundamental decision about himself."

Before he could implement his new political strategy, Tim first had to make a crucial decision. Should he return to Washington to testify before Senator Robert Kennedy's subcommittee? Or should he decline the invitation, thereby forsaking an opportunity to present himself to the nation as the reigning authority on LSD? Many of those closest to Tim, Larry Bogart among them, feared that Robert Kennedy intended to spring some sort of trap on Tim.

To protect Tim from reporters whom Bogart felt certain would be "out for his blood," Bogart asked Nina Graboi to come to the Leary Psychedelic Defense Fund offices at 866 United Nations Plaza in Manhattan. Her task would be to escort Tim to Washington, should he decide to go. One of the few people on the scene older than Tim (by three years), Graboi had not yet taken LSD. A Jewish émigré born in Vienna, she and her well-to-do husband had managed to escape from the Nazis by going to a detention camp in Casablanca and then America. Fascinated by psychedelics, she helped create the New York City headquarters of the League for Spiritual Discovery in an East Village storefront. It soon became a recovery center for young people having bad LSD trips. After the center closed for lack of funds, she went to live at Millbrook.

Bogart and Graboi had worked for an hour in the Leary Defense Fund office on a press release explaining why Tim had decided against appearing before Bobby Kennedy's subcommittee when Tim stuck his head in the door and asked, "Can I leave him here?" Without waiting for Graboi's reply, Tim pushed, as she would later write in her memoir, *One Foot In The Future,* "a peculiar figure into the room." His head was shaved, he wore an ochre sheet, his blue eyes peered out at the world from half-closed lids. "A strange noise made me look up. My visitor's knees were shaking so hard that his bones rattled. He was obviously in a very agitated state." Once again, the monk called Tenzing had hitchhiked from his monastery in New Jersey to warn Tim about the dangers of going public with LSD. Knees knocking, he told Nina that Tim had to be stopped from going to Washington.

As though on cue, Tim walked back into the room and announced he has decided to fly to Washington that afternoon. He asked Graboi if she was coming with him. Angrily, Tenzing and Tim argued about this decision. Tenzing then left, promising to return. "Thank God he's gone," Tim told Graboi. "That scarecrow has harassed me since three o'clock this morning! Can you imagine! He appeared in the middle of the night in my bedroom and ranted at me from the foot of my bed until it was time to get up!" The man whom Tim called "that freaky monk" had seen a vision of Tim surrounded by knives and black shadows. Believing Tim to be in great danger, Tenzing had warned him that he must stop talking about LSD or he would end up in prison. Nina told Tim that she believed this as well. She then asked Tim if he wanted to be a martyr. Tim assured her that this would never happen. In fact, he predicted he would not get more than a fine out of the Laredo bust.

Tim and Bogart spent the rest of the afternoon behind closed doors. When Tim emerged again, it was with the news that he had decided not to go. Instead, in his place, he would send Bogart to read a prepared statement before the subcommittee. The cover sheet that accompanied the statement read, "Continuing legal problems involving Dr. Leary prevent his appearance. He is under a second indictment in Dutchess County, New York where he is facing a possible 16-year sentence for possession of marihuana, which he did not have in his possession."

In truth, this was not the reason Tim decided not to testify. After completing his testimony before Senator Dodd's subcommittee, Tim had gone to lunch with a group of young men and women who worked for various senators. All of them, he would later write, had taken LSD. They told Tim that Ted Kennedy's older brother Bobby was "another story" and that he was the "most ruthless, efficient, brilliant investigator on the hill." Bobby would have done his homework and would be able to produce records from Sandoz Laboratories proving that Tim had never received a microgram of acid from them. "Do you realize what that means?" they asked.

What it meant was that Tim's source for LSD had been illegal, thereby exposing him to further prosecution, quite possibly at the federal level. Tim would later write that it would have been "foolish to venture onto Bobby's turf in a situation where he controlled all the levers. Reckless to be cross-examined without the protection of counsel. A no-win set-up." Ironically, Bobby Kennedy's position on the use of LSD in authorized research projects was far more liberal than his brother's. Concerning such projects, Robert Kennedy would ask pointedly during his own hearings, "Why if they were worthwhile six months ago, why aren't they worthwhile now?"

On May 26, the day on which Tim was scheduled to testify in Washington, Larry Bogart read a statement prepared by him. In the ten days since his previous testimony, Tim had come up with yet another plan to regulate LSD use in America. He was now calling for the establishment of a Commission of Psychochemical Education, "a blue-ribbon panel composed of neurologists, pharmacologists, psychologists, educators and religious leaders to survey the entire field of psychochemical research, to evaluate the educational uses of LSD, 'learning pills,' RNA stimulators, and to anticipate the social and psychological effects of these new drugs which can expand and speed up the mind." Tim proposed that LSD be administered only in "special Psychedelic Training Centers," where experienced guides would "screen, prepare, and guide applicants. Medical supervision would be provided and FDA surveillance exercised." Presumably, the Hitchcock estate in Millbrook, New York, would serve as one of those centers. The headline in *The Washington Post* the next day read LEARY PROPOSES A BAN ON LSD EXCEPT IN "PSYCHEDELIC CENTERS." The lead paragraph noted, "The chief proselyte of the LSD cult seems to have gotten a message himself."

After Tim's statement was read to the subcommittee, Senator Robert Kennedy said that he was pleased "that Dr. Leary is now pointing out some of the dangers" involved in using LSD. "I would have felt better about it if Dr. Leary had been talking this way a year ago, two years ago, or three years ago." As recently as the previous month, Kennedy pointed out, it was "quite clear he was promoting the use of LSD and promoting it in a way that would not be supervised and in that way endangering the lives of many of our citizens and many of our young people."

The witness who followed Larry Bogart was Dr. Sidney Cohen, chief of psychosomatic medicine at the VA Hospital in Los Angeles as well as an associate professor of medicine at UCLA, who was then doing LSD research sponsored by the National Institutes of Health. Within the LSD research establishment, he had already established himself as the most vocal and outspoken of Tim's opponents. In *lsd*, a book published in 1966, the text accompanying Lawrence Schiller's photographs of the acid scene was a debate between Richard Alpert and Sidney Cohen. In the past few months, Cohen testified, one in every seven admissions to one neuropsychiatric hospital was due to LSD-precipitated disturbances. During the month of April alone, there had been forty admissions to a county psychopathic unit for LSD psychoses. Cohen listed a series of human casualties caused by LSD, including a possible suicide. "All I can say is that in contrast to some of the statements of Dr. Leary, and again I hesitate to say this without his being present here, statements like 'the worst that can happen to you on an LSD trip is that you will come back no better than you are' is so obviously incorrect that I am amazed it is still being said." When Cohen completed his testimony, there was applause in the hearing room. "You must have brought some relatives with you," noted Kennedy.

The hearings continued. In a dark gray suit he had bought at Brooks Brothers especially for this occasion, Allen Ginsberg appeared before senators Quentin Burdick, Jacob Javits, and Ted Kennedy. Calling LSD a "useful educational tool," Ginsberg testified that the terror came not from the drug itself but from threatening laws and unfriendly social circumstances. To really discourage the use of LSD, Ginsberg told the senators they needed to supply the kind of society in which nobody would need LSD to "break through to common sympathy." This message was not all that different from what Ginsberg had told Tim one night in private—that in a really groovy world, LSD would be irrelevant.

Aside from making it appear that the federal government was doing everything in its power to solve the LSD problem, the Senate hearings did little to halt unregulated use of the drug in America. They did, however, become a public crucible in which those who claimed special knowledge of this drug revealed their true character.

After serving her initial twenty-five-day sentence for contempt of court, Rosemary was brought directly from jail during the first week in June to testify before the Dutchess County grand jury in Poughkeepsie about Tim and the goings-on at Millbrook. Unwilling to spend any more time in a cell or a courtroom, she deliberately misunderstood something the district attorney told her, turned to two friends from Millbrook, and said, "Okay. I can go home now." They all then promptly left.

"It was June," she recalled. "Millbrook in June is heaven on earth. Tim was there and we went out into the woods and had a passionately good and funny time. It was wonderful. He was overjoyed to see me. But we did have a little argument and Tim said, 'You didn't learn *anything* in prison,' and I said, 'I learned how to clean a jailhouse.'" When Tim went back to the big house to make a phone call, he learned that the local authorities were now looking for Rosemary. "He was really pissed that I had skedaddled that way. I stayed in the woods and they worked out an agreement that I would turn myself in after three days."

For the next three weeks, Rosemary testified day after day before the grand jury, telling them in great detail about the mandalas and mantras that were part of her newfound religion. "I was explaining all these things to the farmers and housewives who were the grand jury," she recalled. "I remember they asked me how often I had sex with Dr. Leary and my answer was, 'Whenever we felt like it.' If nothing else, they were going to get me on adultery." All told, eleven people, Billy Hitchcock among them, would be called to testify before the grand jury concluded its proceedings. Six were teenagers—including Jack Leary, and four of his friends.

While all this was going on, Tim received a written invitation from Richard Baker to participate in the LSD Conference, a five-day program scheduled to begin at the university in Berkeley on June 13. Tim would give a lecture on "The Molecular Revolution" in Wheeler Auditorium on the campus where he had received his doctorate. For this, he would receive an honorarium of $200, a round-trip air ticket from New York to San Francisco, and a $45 per diem. In the same auditorium one day later, Allen Ginsberg would speak on "Consciousness Politics in the Void."

Richard Baker, then thirty, had studied with Paul Tillich at Harvard before dropping out to become part of the beatnik scene in North Beach. In time, he would succeed Shunryu Suzuki as the *roshi* of the San Francisco Zen Center, only to lose his position amid charges of sexual and financial improprieties. The advisory committee that Baker put together for the LSD conference could not have been more impressive—Richard Alpert, Frank Barron, Dr. Sidney Cohen, Huston Smith, and Paul Lee. "The conference was supposed to be in Berkeley," recalled Paul Lee, who was then leaving his teaching post at MIT to become an assistant professor of philosophy at the newly created University of California at Santa Cruz, "but they got worried about it so they forced two concessions. Allen Ginsberg had to be disinvited, and it had to be moved to San Francisco. I guess they were afraid of his Jewish erotic poetry or something. Ginsberg came and hung around but he didn't speak."

On Saturday afternoon, Professor Huston Smith of MIT spoke to the conference on "The Religious Significance of Artificially Induced Religious Experience." Dismayed by the direction in which Tim seemed to be taking his life, both Smith and Professor Walter Houston Clark of Andover had long since parted company with Tim and Alpert. Along with Sidney Cohen, Huston Smith represented what at this conference would be the minority opinion about LSD. In an article published in the *Journal of Philosophy* two years earlier, Smith wrote, "Drugs appear to induce religious experiences, it is less evident that they can produce religious lives." At the LSD Conference in San Francisco, Paul Lee recalled, "Huston Smith was offended by all the screwing around and he denounced them all for doing the Bohemian thing. It was like having your high-school geometry teacher come in and say, 'You wankers!' They were being bad boys."

Perhaps the most significant aspect of the conference was the effect that the full-blown, no-holds-barred, free-and-easy San Francisco acid scene had on speakers who still represented the eastern academic establishment. Paul Lee recalled, "This was my California reception party. Get there on Saturday, and on Sunday there's going to be a party that the Grateful Dead are throwing in a mansion in Marin. There were maybe two or three hundred people at the party, every variety, grandparents and little kids and a lot of freaks and I was thinking, 'Where did they come from? Who gave them permission to look like this?' I was still in a Brooks Brothers suit. We all were. I remember people rolling joints in newspapers. Three footers. And everybody was on acid. Owsley was in the house, handing it out to anybody who wanted it. It was all still legal. Then the Dead came out and played and a guy took a position in one of the speakers. He just stuck his head into it. I thought, 'Who the fuck is that?' Neal Cassady, of course."

On Friday night, Tim spoke in a hall in San Francisco that held five hundred people, "about a third of whom were scholars, a third psychedelicists, and a third police officers," as he would later write. Earlier in the day, Tim had gotten the good news that Susan's sentence in the Laredo bust had been suspended. After paying his respects to Allen Ginsberg—"Beloved guru, I salute you"—Tim said he was also happy the conference had been moved from Berkeley to San Francisco. Tim began his talk with a prediction:

> Within one generation we will have across the bay in Berkeley a department of psychedelic studies. There will probably be a dean of LSD. When students come home for their vacation, Mother and Father will not ask "What book are you reading?" but "Which molecules are you using to open up which Library of Congress inside

your nervous system?" And the bureaucratic requirements will still be with us. You will have to pass Marijuana 1A and 1B to qualify for an introduction to LSD 101. I'm not worried about the young and the turned-on. I am more concerned about the law-enforcement agents in this room, those whose job it is to turn us off. It is probable that there has never been a scientific, scholarly meeting in the history of our country which has had the benefit of so many law-enforcement officers present. What is the threat that attracts the police? Perhaps it is the danger of new ideas.

Speaking to an audience of his peers, Tim seemed intent on regaining the prestige he had lost in Washington by delivering a major policy address. He announced a "politics of ecstasy," though he left its definition vague. More important, he uttered for the very first time in public the six-word phrase with which he would be associated until the day he died. "My advice to people in America today is as follows: If you take the game of life seriously, if you take your nervous system seriously, if you take the energy process seriously, you must turn on, tune in, and drop out." By "turn on," Tim meant "get in touch first of all, with your sense organs . . . Get in touch with your cellular wisdom. Get in touch with the universe within. The only way out is in. And the way to find the wisdom within is to turn on." By "tune in," he meant "harness your internal revelation to the external world around you. I am not suggesting that we all find a desert island and curl up under a palm tree and take LSD and study our navels. As I look around at the people who have taken LSD, far from being inactive, lazy, and passive, I see them in every walk of life and in every age group, struggling to express what they are learning. The hippy movement, the psychedelic style, involves a revolution in our concepts of art and creativity which is occurring right before our eyes. The new music, the new poetry, the new visual art, the new film."

Even Tim had to admit that "dropping out" was "the toughest pill to swallow." "Whenever I give a lecture and tell people to drop out, invariably I alarm many listeners, including my friends, who say, 'Now listen, Timothy, tone it down. You can't go around telling students to drop out of school, telling middle-class men with mortgage payments to drop out of their jobs. That's just too much! You can't do that in a technological society like this!' " All the same, that was exactly what he was doing. For as he said, "This message, *turn on, tune in, drop out,* just happens to be the oldest message around—the old refrain that has been passed on for thousands of years by every person who has studied the energy process and man's place in it." Posing a question that would soon be heard everywhere, Tim asked, "Is our American society so insecure that it cannot tolerate our young people taking a year or two off, growing beards, wandering around the country, fooling with new forms of consciousness? This is one of the oldest traditions in civilized society. Take a voyage! Take the adventure! Before you settle down to the tribal game, try out self-exile. Your coming back will be much enriched."

Tim concluded his talk with the message that would become his stock in trade. "The revolution has just begun . . . Let no one be concerned about the growth and use of psychedelic chemicals. Trust your young people. You gotta trust your young people. You had better trust your young people. Trust your creative minority. Trust your sense organs and your nervous system. Your divine body has been around a long, long time. Much longer than any of the social games you play. Trust the evolutionary process. It's all going to work out all right." Despite what he and a host of other drug experts had just told the senators in Washington, there was no LSD problem. While no one in the public eye today could pull off this kind of 360-degree shift in policy, Tim got away with it because, in 1966, neither the Internet nor twenty-four-hour national cable television news networks yet existed. In Washington, New York, and Boston, no one had the faintest idea what he was saying in San Francisco.

The inspiration for his speech did not come entirely from within. During lunch at the Plaza Hotel some weeks earlier, Marshall McLuhan, director of the Centre for Culture and Technology at the University of Toronto, had told him that "dreary Senate hearings and courtrooms" were not the platforms for his message. "You call yourself a philosopher, a reformer. Fine," Tim would later write McLuhan told him. "But the key to your work is advertising. You're promoting a product. The new and improved accelerated brain. You must use the most current tactics for arousing consumer interest. Associate LSD with all the good things that the brain can produce—beauty, fun, philosophic wonder, religious revelation, increased intelligence, mystical romance. Word of mouth from satisfied consumers will help, but get your rock and roll friends to write jingles about the brain." Leary recalled McLuhan then breaking into song: "Lysergic acid hits the spot / Forty billion neurons, that's a lot." McLuhan advised Tim to always smile. "Wave reassuringly. Radiate courage. Never complain or appear angry. It's okay if you come off as flamboyant and eccentric. You're a professor, after all. But a confident attitude is the best advertisement. You must be known for your smile."

After his lunch with McLuhan, Tim devoted "several days and one acid trip to analysis of the slogans which have been used to package previous American revolutions." These included '"Give Me Liberty or Give Me Death," "A Nation Cannot Exist Half Slave and Half Free," "We Have Nothing to Fear but Fear Itself," and last but most definitely not least, "Lucky Strike Means Fine Tobacco." One morning while ruminating "in the shower for what kind of slogan" to use, "six words came to mind. Dripping wet, with a towel around my waist, I walked to the study and wrote down this phrase: 'Turn On, Tune In, Drop Out.' Later it became very useful in my function as a cheerleader for change."

The slogan that in time became Tim's personal mantra did not spring full-blown from his own fertile brain. With Tim's former associate, the psychiatrist Harvey Powelson, Merv Freedman had written an article that appeared in *The Nation* on January 31, 1966, six months before the Berkeley conference. "I called it 'Drugs on Campus: Turned On and Tuned Out,'" Freedman recalled. "Apparently, that was the instigation of Tim's modification of it to 'turn on, tune in, drop out.' The inspiration for it came from this article."

"Tune in, turn on, and drop out" was as irresistible as a catchy radio jingle. Depending on the context, it could mean virtually anything. The makers of a grapefruit-flavored soft drink named Squirt urged the American public to "turn on to flavor, tune in to sparkle, and drop out of the cola rut." Reverend Billy Graham announced that the theme of his upcoming European Crusade would be "Turn on Christ, tune in to the Bible, and drop out of sin." In 1968, *Mad* magazine, so often the final arbiter on what was truly absurd in American popular culture, ran a psychedelic cover with the words, "Tune In, Turn On, Drop Dead."

The phrase may have had real meaning for those who heard it early on, but it soon became so mainstream as to be virtually meaningless. After Tim made an appearance in Seattle, which generated a good deal of local attention, the novelist Tom Robbins found himself driving down "a long street along the waterfront in Seattle and there was a reader board outside of Ship's Seafood Restaurant which said, 'Turn on, Tune In, and Drop Out with Our Seafood Buffet.'"

TWENTY-FIVE

reating a new American mantra did nothing to help Tim Leary pay his legal fees. Deeply in debt, he spent the summer of 1966 at Millbrook leading workshops with Ralph Metzner in "theatre, dance, light, music, or sound." Every other weekend, on the occasion of either the full or the new moon, all the workshop groups came together "to present a performance which will be a coordinated, multi-dimensional symphonic message." Millbrook was now in the business of psychedelic theater. "By this time," Rosemary Woodruff recalled, "we had a huge entourage and we were planning the religious celebrations. We started it as a weekend event on the terrace of the bowling alley and from that it evolved. We had Rudi Stern and Jackie Cassen doing the light show. The special effects were fantastic. It really preceded Stanley Kubrick's *2001*. We did it for money. And also as a forum."

Using slide projectors modified with fans so that they could be outfitted with 1,000-watt bulbs, Stern and Cassen transformed the bowling alley at Millbrook "into a theater of light." On weekends, Stern would later recall, "Lawyers, investment bankers, friends of Billy Hitchcock's or Tim's, usually very wealthy people with chauffeurs waiting, would come see a light show after dinner and they were blown away by it. And so I began talking to Tim about doing something in New York." After a six-month search, Stern found a Yiddish theater on the Lower East Side of Manhattan that was dark on Tuesday nights. Sponsored by the newly formed League for Spiritual Discovery, which had replaced the Castalia Foundation, ads featuring Tim's photograph appeared for the initial series of three psychedelic celebrations at the Village Theatre on Second Avenue and Sixth Street. All seats cost $3.00 but tickets were available only by mail order. The first celebration was scheduled for Tuesday, September 20, 1966.

Based on what Stern called "seven or eight chapters from Hermann Hesse's *Steppenwolf,*" *Death of the Mind* featured Tim onstage looking, in Stern's words, "like he was working at the Harvard Hasty Pudding Club." He had "a schmaltz quality from the beginning," as Stern put it. "It wasn't the white robe he was wearing or the fact that he was in the lotus position or that he looked beautifully angelic. That was all sincere stuff. But there was something about his sales pitch—turn on, tune in, drop out—there was something car salesman about it. Expensive cars. Not Fords. I'm talking Mercedes or Rolls."

When the show moved to the smaller Village Barn for the second performance, so many people lined up to get in that Stern recalled, "Second Avenue was closed off." In the same way that Tim's wedding to Nena had heralded the emergence of a new order in the world of fashion, his psychedelic celebrations on the Lower East Side of New York served as a coming-out party for all the young and beautiful people in the city who had just begun getting high on LSD. "You don't see young people that beautiful anymore," Stern would later say. "Just beautiful flowing sensual people."

Entering the theater with the house lights at half, the audience was greeted by colorful images projected on a screen by Richard Aldcroft. Peter Walker played sitar onstage. A crew of twenty people, all of whom had held hands and prayed together in a circle before the performance, were working the show. Played by Ralph Metzner, Harry Haller, the hero of *Steppenwolf,* took off on a trip through his own circulatory system to the sound of clanging gongs, flutes, and string music. During a sequence entitled "All Girls Are Yours," Stern and Cassen projected "two thousand beautiful women's faces, mouths, and eyeballs, all overlapping and sequenced together so that the whole thing was a field of flashing eyes" on the screen. When Haller began freaking out because his heart was stopping and he feared that he would drown in his own blood, Tim, playing the role of "Pablo, the smiling Dionysian" who had given Haller the drugs "that spin him into multiple-reality" intoned, "Drift beyond the body. All girls are yours. And now, Harry, it's time to play the game of death." Onstage, Haller moved toward Rosemary Woodruff, who had stuffed falsies under her dress to make her silhouette more womanly. Symbolically, he beat her to death. Reminding Haller that he had taught him the chess game of life, Tim reprimanded him and said: "Time to make beauty. You'll learn to laugh, Harry. You'll learn to laugh."

At the end of the hour-long presentation, Tim reminded all those present that what they had just seen represented one minute of an LSD trip and that LSD could provide a hundred such sessions with a single dose. The performance ended with Peter Walker playing sitar as one projector rotated images on the screen. "At the end," Stern recalled, "there was no applause. Just gasps from the audience. It was an experience, not a show. People held hands and went out quietly."

The next day, *The New York Times* ran the headline DR. LEARY HOLDS FIRST SERVICE OF SECT HE FORMED BEFORE 2,400 over a photograph of Tim silhouetted against a slide projection. Although the piece was a news story, it served to build the audience for the next performance. The most negative review came from sixty-six-year-old Diana Trilling, who attended the event with her husband, Lionel, the literary critic, editor of *Partisan Review,* and professor of literature at Columbia. Watching alongside Diana Trilling at the press table was Allen Ginsberg, one of her husband's former students. As a couple, the Trillings had helped shape the intellectual life of New York City for more than a quarter of a century. She observed that most of the audience was under thirty and made up of "strangely isolate people" who created an atmosphere of "almost palpable benevolence." She attributed this to "the gentling effect of LSD on personality . . . even after only one or two trips, they attain a sort of suprahumanity, as if purged of mortal error." Of Tim, she wrote that "he was very tired: one could see his fatigue when he took his place on the platform in the darkened hall; he might have been managing a hangover. This was a weary impresario, a weary pedagogue, a weary Messiah." He wore, she wrote, "the pale but indelible marks of doom." Trilling also wondered how long people could afford to wait for statistics to accumulate on the negative effects of LSD on the young. "For Dr. Alpert," she noted, "there were surely no such anxieties. 'These kids' were simple casualties of the new dispensation, eggs that had to be broken to make Dr. Leary's omelet."

Two days after the first psychedelic celebration, Tim won a major legal victory. On September 23, 1966, Judge Raymond C. Baratta dismissed all charges stemming from the raid at Millbrook on the grounds that recent court decisions affecting confessions and search warrants had made it "extremely unlikely" that Tim could be successfully prosecuted on charges of marijuana possession. "Noel Tepper, a local guy who was a good lawyer and the ACLU's local man on the street," G. Gordon Liddy recalled, "picked up on this religious business and imported every swami and Hindu he could find east of the Mississippi. They had them lined up out in the hall and they just ran one swami after another onto the witness stand and Judge Baratta, who was an old-time Roman Catholic Italian World War II veteran, said, 'If I see one more swami coming through that door, I'm going to throw him out the window.'" Judge Baratta also dismissed the indictments against all those arrested with Tim at Millbrook. The motion to drop the cases was made by Dutchess County District Attorney John R. Heilman Jr., who told the judge that Leary had agreed to end all public activities at Millbrook and "transfer them to New York City." Speaking to reporters, Tim said his decision was not a "quid pro quo" for dismissal. Tim also said he and the other defendants had agreed not to sue the county for the raid or the arrests.

In show-business terms, Tim now had a smash hit on his hands. The success of the psychedelic celebrations not only provided him with a brand-new source of badly needed income but also the artistic legitimacy he had long been seeking. "Impresario Leary, high priest of the League for Spiritual Discovery (LSD), appears to have staged the biggest off-Broadway event in many seasons," Eleanore Lester wrote in the Arts and Leisure section of the Sunday *New York Times* on December 4. "For nine weeks he has been packing them into the Village Theatre which seats 2,000, with his 'Death of the Mind,' 'Reincarnation of Christ' and 'The Vision of Hieronymus Bosch' shows." In the best review Tim ever received, she added, "Despite his vaunted contempt for words, Dr. Leary may be counted as the most accomplished deliverer of lines on the Off-Broadway scene. He holds a substantial portion of his audience quivering in molecular ecstasy throughout a long monologue. His restrained yet emotion-charged delivery of 'You are God within your body; I am God within my body,' and his subtle, penetrating voice, evoking hope against hope when he suggests that all of us have millions of unused brain cells that can be awakened and plugged into the Divine Transformer, make him a top candidate for this year's 'Obie' Off-Broadway award."

Tim's newfound success reached new heights when a lengthy interview conducted with him shortly after his disastrous performance before the Senate subcommittee in Washington appeared in the September issue of *Playboy* magazine. Describing in minute detail what happened to someone under the influence of LSD, Tim said, "There is no question that LSD is the most powerful aphrodisiac ever discovered by man."

Asked to elaborate, he added, "When you're making love under LSD, it's as though every cell in your body—and you have trillions—is making love with every cell in her body." When Tim was asked how often he had made love under the influence of LSD, he said, "Every time I've taken it. In fact, that is what the LSD experience is all about. Merging, yielding, flowing, union, communion. It's all lovemaking. You make love with candlelight, with sound waves from a record player, with a bowl of fruit on the table, with the trees."

The interviewer asked whether it was true that couples under the influence of LSD could make love for hours without ever reaching exhaustion. Tim answered with a succinct "Yup." Asked whether some women who had difficulty achieving orgasm could have multiple orgasms under LSD, he said, "In a carefully prepared, loving LSD session, a woman can have several hundred orgasms." "Several hundred?" asked the astonished interviewer. "Yes. Several hundred." He was far more discreet when asked how many orgasms a man might have under the influence of LSD, saying only that based on his own experience during the past six years, his openness, responsiveness, and participation in every form of sensory expression had "multiplied a *thousandfold*."

Asked why this aspect of LSD had only been hinted at privately but never before spelled out in public. Tim replied, "At the present time I'm under a thirty year sentence of imprisonment, which for a forty five year old man is essentially a life term, and in addition, I am under indictment on a second marijuana offense involving a 16-year sentence. Since there is hardly anything more that middle-aged, middle-class authority can do to me—and since the secret is out anyway among the young—I feel I'm free at this moment to say what we've never said before: that sexual ecstasy is the basic reason for the current LSD boom." When the interviewer asked whether it was true that if Tim so desired, he could have two or three different women a night, he said, "Every woman has built into her cells and tissues the longing for a hero, sage-mythic male to open up and share her own divinity. But casual sexual encounters do not satisfy this deep longing. Compulsive body grabbing is rarely the vehicle of such communication."

Ignoring his own conspicuous lack of success in using LSD to "treat" Richard Alpert for homosexuality, Tim posited LSD as a "specific cure for homosexuality." "It's well known that most sexual perversions are the result not of biological binds but of freaky, dislocating childhood experiences of one kind or another. Consequently its not surprising that we've had many cases of long-term homosexuals who, under LSD, discover that they are not only genitally but genetically male, that they are basically attracted to females. The most famous and public of such cases is that of Allen Ginsberg, who has openly stated that the first time he turned on to women was during an LSD session several years ago." Tim said the drug could also work for lesbians. LSD was "a powerful panacea for impotence and frigidity, both of which, like homosexuality, are symbolic screw ups." He also noted that "in two religious groups that prize chastity and celibacy, there have been wholesale defections of monks and nuns who left their religious orders to get married after a series of LSD experiences."

Robert Anton Wilson, a science-fiction writer then editing the Playboy Forum for *Playboy* magazine, later recalled, "I believe it was that interview which a judge later held up as proof that Tim was politically dangerous. I remember suggesting some questions for it which were too psychological and were rejected. What Murray Fisher, the editor, wanted in the *Playboy* interview with Tim was what he said about LSD as an aphrodisiac. That was a bombshell. It was the literal thing he said. That there was no drug on the planet that produces more sexual drive than LSD." "It isn't like twenty thousand orgasms," LSD chemist Owsley Stanley would later say. "That's bullshit. It's as much bullshit as Arnold Schwarzenegger saying that getting pumped up is like having an orgasm. I've worked out heavy and gotten lots of pumps and they're nothing like an orgasm." Robert Masters, the LSD researcher who wrote *The Varieties of Psychedelic Experience* with Jean Houston, was quoted by Leary biographer John Bryan as noting, "Such claims about LSD are not only false, they are dangerous. By suggesting that this drug is a powerful sex stimulant . . . desperate people will fail again, but this time in a state of heightened suggestibility that can do them grave harm . . . Tim Leary's claims are causing much distress, are at least ninety percent false and nonsensical."

When Tim republished the interview in *The Politics of Ecstasy*, he attached a footnote in which he wrote, "If this interview had been conducted for *Sports Illustrated*, the conscientious interviewee would naturally consider the question, How LSD Can Raise Your Batting Average." In other words, had he been talking to *Popular Mechanics*, Tim would have claimed that LSD could rev up horsepower and reduce engine knock while doubling miles to the gallon. Clearly, Tim Leary knew exactly what he was doing. In America, nothing sells like sex. He tailored his message perfectly to *Playboy*'s primarily male readership by telling them precisely what he thought they wanted to hear. Tim's goal now was to get as many people as possible to take LSD.

When Tim was invited to Toronto by the Canadian Broadcasting Company to appear on a nationwide talk show, he met with Marshall McLuhan for "a long and genial dinner." As Tim walked off the plane upon his return to New York's on October 11, he was greeted by two federal agents. "They informed me that narcotics offenders were required to fill out a special form on leaving the country. I was arrested again and bailed out just in time to perform in the celebration. More nationwide publicity. And another five-year sentence to contest." Released without bail, Tim was given permission to continue traveling to speaking engagements all over the country, provided he first notified the United States attorney in Brooklyn of his plans. As Thanksgiving neared, Tim took a break from his hectic schedule to return to Millbrook to celebrate the holiday—in psychedelic fashion—with his extended family.

With Tim constantly on the road and both Ralph Metzner and Richard Alpert long since gone, no one was in charge at Millbrook anymore. Those who lived there continued to take LSD at least once a week but now the doses were higher. Utter chaos seemed the rule rather than the exception. Jean McCready, Tim's secretary at the time, would later recall, "All these people were taking LSD at least once a week and a lot were a little bit irresponsible and a lot were younger. There was Bhavani, a very heavy-duty figure in the community who had been on the spiritual path for a long time. Her idea when she came to Millbrook was that she was going to get Tim back on track in a spiritual way. She would play one record like 'All You Need Is Love' by the Beatles, for three days at a time loud in the house because it had a message she wanted everyone to hear. No one would tell her to take it off because that was the way it was."

The chaos at Millbrook had been compounded by the arrival of twenty-eight people who had been booted out of the Ananda ashram in Monroe, New York, for taking psychedelics. Without knowing much about them or their spiritual focus, Tim impulsively invited them to come live with him. Overnight, the population in the big house swelled from twenty-five to fifty-three. Followers of Bill Haines, they constituted a nation unto themselves. "Bill Haines's trip was karma yoga work," Jean McCready recalled. "We were the floating Taoistic internal searching wafting around people. When Tim was around, he and Bill Haines would take LSD and argue. Raise their voices and yell at each other. Haines was not impressed or cowed by Tim. I couldn't believe how these men could take quantities of psychedelics and *not* blow their minds. *Not* get past their personality shit. But they didn't. They couldn't even agree to disagree."

For the month before Thanksgiving, the only reason people at Millbrook had been eating regularly was because beatnik poet and full-time resident Diane DiPrima had taken it upon herself to prepare three meals a day for as many as fifty people at a time. In a memoir entitled "The Holidays at Millbrook—1966," published in *Shaman Woman, Mainline Lady*, DiPrima described "the spacious and picturesque kitchen" with "the eternal Beatles on the kitchen phonograph," where she planned to enjoy a leisurely Thanksgiving Day without doing any cooking. In the big house, she found a Hindu friend who had arrived from New York with "hashish and gossip." People had already converged on Millbrook. The parking lot outside the big house, filled with what DiPrima called "great gouges and holes—from the legendary trip when Timothy & Co. had decided to get rid of all the pavement in the world, starting in their own back yard and heading down the Taconic State Parkway," was jammed to capacity with "everything from old pickup trucks to a solitary silver Porsche." The house started filling rapidly. "It was clearly necessary to do some cooking—none had started yet—and I had a sinking feeling that I wasn't going to escape, after all."

DiPrima's husband, Alan Marlowe, formerly one of the top male models in the country, had volunteered to cook one of the four huge turkeys but soon persuaded her to start it for him. She wound up cooking the turkey along with "several gallons of cranberry sauce, and a cauldron of candied yams." At Millbrook, as DiPrima would later write, it was a "soft, warm day, doors and windows were open, velvet draperies blowing, and wind; goats, dogs and children all wandering in and out." On the front lawn, a pickup football game started. At this moment, Millbrook seemed no different from homes all across America where families had gathered for the holiday.

Around five-thirty, Jean McCready came into the kitchen and offered to candy the yams so DiPrima could go off to change her clothes. In the bowling alley where she lived with Marlowe and her children, DiPrima pulled on a coral gown and a black velvet cape. Then she returned to the big house to find Bali Ram, a Nepalese temple dancer, dancing in full costume in the music room. After the recital, Allen Ginsberg took out his finger cymbals. Accompanied by Peter Orlovsky, the poet began chanting "Hare Krishna." When DiPrima left the music room to find her husband, she came upon "a giant of a man" who was "literally hurling himself about, from banister to wall, barely missing the huge gilded mirror and shouting, 'I have been Vi-o-la-ted!' over and over again to an astonished and immobilized audience." This was Ted Cook, a Canadian Broadcasting Company reporter who while being "wined and entertained by Timothy in his study on the third floor" had unknowingly imbibed a large quantity of acid. Offered his choice of "perfectly straight" bourbon or scotch, Cook had instead secretly helped himself to a good-sized glass of sherry, which "happened to be one of the three bottles of liquor which held our new stash."

Since Cook had actually made a full-length movie about acid without having ever touched the stuff himself, DiPrima left feeling that he had only gotten what he deserved. By the time she returned, the kirtan (religious song) ceremony had broken up because "the howls and curses of Ted Cook had proved to be too much for everyone." Cook himself had rushed out of the house into darkness and was now somewhere on the grounds on his own. "The general fear was that he would find his way to the highway (a good half mile away) and all hell would break loose with the local folk." Returning to the bowling alley to wake up her four-year-old child, DiPrima heard Cook shouting somewhere off in the distance. To herself, she muttered, "If this is Thanksgiving, what will Christmas be like?"

Given a blank check by Tim to buy food for Thanksgiving, Marlowe had also bought presents for the eleven children who now lived at Millbrook. After DiPrima brought his presents to the big house, she loaded a paper plate with food for herself, stashed it in a cupboard, and went to check on the rest of her family. She found her eight-year-old daughter, Jeanne, asleep in babysitter Suzie Blue's room on the top floor with her hair full of pin curls for "a dazzling and glamorous entrance at dinner time." Waking the child, DiPrima asked if she wanted to come downstairs and join the festivities. Before Jeanne could answer, there were shouts from below. Cook had been captured in the ruined formal garden behind the meditation house and was now standing among the extra turkeys in the butler's pantry "alternately shouting horrifically in some abrupt, violent fright, and murmuring beatific nonsense at those who were trying to calm him." Jeanne decided to stay where she was.

Wandering out of the butler's pantry, Cook sat down on a black trunk in the entry hall. As Ginsberg began singing mantras to him, a crowd gathered around them. Sitting on cushions on the cold tile floor, they sang and chanted "Hare Krishna," "Hare Om Namo Shivaya," and "Om Sri Maitreya" for the next two hours. Jack Leary joined in, as did many of the ashram people, all of them singing for, as DiPrima would later write, "this strange, frightened man whom no one of us had known two or three hours before. He slowly relaxed; his Buddah nature began to shine forth—reluctantly at first, and then stronger as our energy built. He finally became perfectly joyous, joined us singing the Shiva mantra over and over, and after a long time was able to wander about and join in the throng in which a good third of the guests were probably as stoned as he."

After being told that Tim, who had not come downstairs at all that day, was on a high-dosage acid session and had to be seen to be believed, DiPrima went up to the third floor. Knocking on the door to Tim and Rosemary's room, she went inside. "The space in the room was warped—a funny kind of visual effect curved it somehow, as if it were in a different space-time continuum. I have since talked to other old-time trippers . . . and they all admit to seeing something similar at some point when they came 'cold' upon people who were on a very high dosage of acid. The visual effect is a bit like the 'heat waves' that show around a candle flame, or a hot car in the summer sun, or the waves that rise from the hot asphalt of a highway in the desert." The effect made DiPrima gasp. "Stepping into the room was like stepping into another dimension. Timothy looked at me from a million light-years away, from a place of great sadness and loneliness and terrible tiredness, and after a long time he formed the one word, 'Beloved.'" Kneeling down to where Tim and Rosemary sat side by side on a rug in front of a cold, dark fireplace, DiPrima kissed them both, spent a moment holding their hands and looking into their eyes, and then went away as quietly as she could.

DiPrima later learned that Tim and Rosemary had taken the sherry that had also set Cook off. Though Tim had repeatedly sworn under oath that he would not be using LSD this year, he had recently received a brand-new shipment of acid in powder form. Putting half of it into a two-pound coffee can, he had dumped in a quart of vodka, sloshed it around, and poured it all back into a vodka bottle for safekeeping. Then he used another bottle of vodka to liquefy the other half of the powdered LSD. To save whatever might have still been sticking to the can, he poured in a fifth of sherry. As DiPrima would later write, "It was this sherry that dominated the events of that Thanksgiving."

For the children who lived at Millbrook, none of this was new. "There were times when I would be coming out of an overnight experience," Jean McCready recalled, "and my kids would come to me in the morning and they had maybe missed school, one of them had been sick, and I had to write a note and I could hardly focus myself to hold the pen and write. I don't have any regrets for having been there. If I have any regrets, it's for my kids." Kim Ferguson Exon, who grew up at Millbrook along with her sisters, her mother, Flo, and her stepfather, Maynard Ferguson, whose career she eventually managed, would later say, "In the beginning, it was a really pure beautiful clean place. In the beginning. There was a lot of meditating. Take a group of people who have come together with a shared goal of changing the world. In this ideal environment, this fantasy setting, bring in the drugs. Start stepping those up. And then put in the pressure of the cops and the politics, and all of a sudden, those people are fighting amongst themselves. And then all these beautiful women and attractive men come in to stir the soup and then put in the rule that everybody should be fucking everybody, and you tell me how it goes downhill."

Jeanne DiPrima, who on Thanksgiving Day elected to stay upstairs with her babysitter Suzie Blue, recalled, "I remember my first trip with my mother quite vividly. I must have been eight years old because it was at our house in Kerhonksen before we went to Millbrook. Apparently, she gave me a very small amount, ten or fifteen mikes. If you're going to give a child LSD, that's just perfect because I giggled for eight hours straight. I was so happy. It had a very mild intoxicating effect with very light hallucinations and I had a great time. Lots of love. I was bonding with her, bonding with Alan Marlowe, bonding with the stars and the trees. It was your quintessential good acid trip. Never to be repeated, and I mean that quite literally."

When Diane DiPrima moved her family to Millbrook, where they lived in rooms with hardwood floors and vaulted ceilings above the bowling alley, Jeanne recalled, "Everybody there had to take acid on a regular basis. Like once a week. And that included the kids. I remember it being poured into glasses from liquor bottles and God only knows how much was in it." She remembered Allen Ginsberg singing off-key and playing the harmonium as everyone was coming on to LSD, and then "walking up to Lunacy Hill and the ends of the tree branches were becoming lances and they were piercing my body. I could feel this and I was crying. After my second trip, I actively didn't want to do it anymore. From then on, they dosed me. Once a week for a year. More than fifty trips. I don't remember one good one except for the first one. No one ever said, 'Oh, you mean it's doing something bad to Jeannie? Oh, we can't really consider that because of course in the long run, it's good for her. So we won't think about that. We'll be in complete denial that we might be abusing this child.' After some point, you listen to a kid. 'Mom, that hurts. Mom, that hurts. Mom, that HURTS! MOM . . . I'M GOING CRAZY!'"

From the start, Tim had made Millbrook a fantasy land for adults. After Richard Alpert left, all the children who lived there, Jack and Susan included, quickly learned they were peripheral to the scene. "Jack and Susan Leary were a really sad scenario," Jean McCready would later recall. "Tim was not trying with them. I think he just thought it would get better. He was in such denial. Especially about Susan. Susan was mentally ill. And Tim was never able to accept that point of view or really understand that." "Jackie Leary occupied the top turret room of the main house in which he took twenty thousand mikes of acid at a time," Jeanne DiPrima would later say. "He was sixteen and really amazing. I had a mad crush on him. Jackie stayed locked in his room. The word would get around that Jackie was going to do thirty-five thousand mikes and Tim would timidly see if he could talk his son into not killing himself. Jackie hid in his turret. He was the dark prince and maybe he was pouring it all down the toilet. Everybody said he was so crazy but I don't believe he was. He was just trying to stay away from everybody."

Concerning his father, Jack remembered, "He was pretty much always totally inept at being a father to me and Susan. Actually, he would sometimes moan about us as the millstones around his neck. That's a direct quote. He had been an only child and was consumed by himself." A decade later, Jack would tell journalist Ken Kelley, "A couple of times I could have died during my childhood from lack of food and water. The funny thing was I didn't realize that I wasn't eating. I would be walking along totally exhausted and hungry I didn't realize until I was fourteen that I couldn't see the blackboard in school. I thought all the other kids couldn't see it either. I was eating cereal and peanut butter and jelly sandwiches. That was what I was living on. Grape Nuts and then Total."

Instead of being educated on the grounds of the estate where they could have been protected, the children of Millbrook were sent off to very conservative local public schools where everybody knew what was going on behind the high stone walls of the estate. Jeanne DiPrima recalled, "Millbrook was one of the first communes but they sent the kids to town to go to school. It was either insanity or laziness. If you stop for a moment and think about what you're doing and you're not an idiot, then you have to make a choice to develop a school. But there was no way Tim was going to do anything but be God." Jack Leary dropped out of school in tenth grade. "There was a lot of animosity to me at school," he told Ken Kelley. "The principal and the teachers didn't like me and the students couldn't talk to me because if they did, it would get back to their parents. It wasn't who I was. It was what I stood for."

In a community where there seemed to be no rules, the children of Millbrook still found ways to rebel. "On the weekends," Jeanne DiPrima recalled, "we would get these guys up from the Pentagon in their suits and ties, full regalia, to try acid. I would go in the kitchen and find everything that couldn't kill you and mix it all up in the blender. It tasted vile. It was paprika and hot sauce but it looked like a chocolate shake and I would walk around the halls with this sweet little angelic face and say, 'Are you tripping? Oh, would you like something to drink? Here, have some chocolate milk shake.' And I would watch their faces convulse and they would look at me because everything was supposed to be good and happy and here was this cute little girl and they were about to puke their guts out. In terms of payback, it was all I could do at the time."

Not every child who lived at Millbrook has negative memories. Many who were traumatized have yet to fully recover. Like Holocaust victims, some refuse to speak publicly about their childhoods. Others do not want to be identified as ever having lived at Millbrook. If Tim noticed any of these problems back then, he did nothing to remedy them. Nor did he ever write about it. But then on that Thanksgiving Day in 1966 at Millbrook, Tim himself was so lost in a high-dose acid experience that he could not even make it downstairs to eat dinner at his own table. Although the drug of choice was LSD rather than alcohol, it was his childhood back in Springfield all over again.

TWENTY-SIX

As soon as Thanksgiving weekend was over, Tim Leary headed back out on the road to bring the gospel of his newly founded League for Spiritual Discovery to a packed house of a thousand people at the University of Rochester. A week later, he dined with Humphry Osmond at the Nassau Inn before speaking at Princeton University. Although Tim's lecture schedule was hectic and never ending, he still could not pay his legal bills. During the second week in December, he received a letter from Fansler & Fansler, the father-and-son law firm in Laredo, Texas, which had represented him ever since his bust. In it, Charles N. Fansler Jr. wrote:

> Your letter addressed to Dad arrived this morning, and, as he is out of town I took the liberty to open it as I was hoping that a check might be enclosed. Certainly I would not want it on my conscience that in paying our fee your 40 adults and 15 children would be deprived of proper sustenance. However, I would strongly advise that you get rid of the 12 dogs and 13 cats, that you eat the geese, and that you furnish your 2 goats with birth control pills. In that way you might be able to take care of your twelve (and especially these two) patient and competent lawyers.

Fansler added that he expected to hear from Tim on January 1, 1967, and closed by sending his best regards for the coming season to both Tim and Susan.

At Millbrook, Tim's continuing legal difficulties had taken on a new dimension. Although all charges stemming from the bust had been dismissed, the estate was now under siege by local cops, who busted anyone leaving the grounds for any reason they could devise. As Tim would later write, "When we'd drive from Millbrook to New York, it became a game. How many miles before we'd be stopped?" Police officers with John Doe warrants, who claimed to be looking for teenage runaways, knocked constantly at the front door of the big house. A steady stream of police informers tried to insinuate themselves into the community. One day, a young college kid showed up at Millbrook, asking to live there. Although he was told to leave, he stayed around doing everything he could to help out. When he was arrested while driving the Millbrook station wagon, handcuffed, dragged off to jail, and searched for drugs, his standing on the estate was so enhanced that Tim asked him to play the role of Jesus in the second psychedelic celebration at the Village Theatre. After his first performance, the kid threw himself down on his knees in Tim's dressing room and confessed. "He was a police informer," Tim would later write. "He'd been nabbed a few months ago for dealing grass and offered release if he set me up. He pulled out a plastic bag filled with grass and about a hundred pills: acid, reds, purples, yellows . . . On the way back to Millbrook he was supposed to drop the bag on the floor of our car, just when the police cars sirened us over."

Travel to and from Millbrook had now become so hazardous that Noel Tepper, Tim's lawyer in Poughkeepsie, composed a letter:

Dear Law Enforcement Agent,

The bearer of this letter is a member of the League of Spiritual Discovery, a religious group incorporated under the laws of the State of New York. I am attorney for the League and its members. Unfortunately, members of the League have been recently subjected to harassment and intimidation, possibly because of their unconventional dress and appearance. They have been stopped and detained illegally, and their cars and persons have been searched without probable cause. Accordingly, the group has decided to meet each new incident with legal action, both for damages and Federal criminal prosecution against the offending police officers under the recent Civil Rights Act. You are hereby advised not to question members of the League beyond their name and address outside of my presence. Unless the member is formally placed under arrest, he has been instructed to proceed on his way. If an arrest is made, I am to be contacted immediately and advised of the charges. Any unlawful detention, improper arrest, or unconstitutional search will be followed by an immediate legal action against you personally.

Tim characterized the constant police harassment at Millbrook as "an invaluable educational experience. For four years, we have had the privilege of sharing, in a small way, the alert, animal sensitivity of the American black man, the freedom-loving Czech, the Jew in Germany. The constant awareness that the armed agents of your uptight, warlike state are hunting you." Long before Bob Dylan's "To live outside the law, you must be honest" became the motto of a generation, Tim was already living this way. "Gradually, month by month, we found ourselves spending more and more of our time with spiritual outlaws and psychedelic criminals, and less and less time with even grass-smoking straights . . . This is a tribal reflex that always occurs in times of social change. It is not a conscious choice."

"California sunshine makes all seeds grow well, especially the seed for the League for Spiritual Discovery," Michael Bowen, the psychedelic artist who had been at Millbrook on the night of the bust, wrote Tim on November 1, 1966. Bowen invited Tim to take part in "a gathering of the Tribes, sects, groups following the Hindu pattern of multiplicity under a common experiencial [sic] union." The event, initially scheduled to take place in Golden Gate Park on December 10, 1966, would feature not only spiritual leaders but also music by the Grateful Dead, Big Brother and the Holding Company, Quicksilver Messenger Service, the Great Society, and the Anonymous Artists of America, all of whom would play for free.

After touring San Francisco's "LSD-loving Haight-Ashbury district" on December 12, Tim held a press conference in the Camelia Room of the Fairmont Hotel. Accompanied by his local press agent, Tim announced he would be conducting two psychedelic celebrations during the third week in January at Berkeley Community Theater and Winterland Auditorium in San Francisco. As for his proposed yearlong moratorium on the use of LSD, he admitted, "Nobody listened to my appeal."

On January 5, 1967, Tim conducted a press conference at the Playboy Mansion in Chicago to announce that he would be holding two psychedelic celebrations on Saturday night at the Arie Crown Theatre on McCormick Place. With tickets priced from $3.00 to $4.50, he expected to gross somewhere between $15,000 and $20,000. *Playboy* editor Robert

Anton Wilson wrote, "He walked on stage barefoot, burned incense, did a lecture on Buddha illustrated with psychedelic slides, and weird lighting effects and more or less came on like an Oriental Billy Graham. It seemed that a brilliant scientist had turned himself into a second-rate messiah."

On the following Saturday, on a small stage in Golden Gate Park in San Francisco, Tim formally took his place among the pantheon of gods overseeing the birth of a brand-new culture. The formal title of the event in which he participated was "A Gathering of the Tribes for a Human Be-In," which in time simply became known as the Human Be-In. The name was created by Richard Alpert at a celebration in the Panhandle attended by five hundred people on October 6, 1966, the day LSD became illegal in California. "They called it 'The Love Pageant Rally,'" recalled Michael Bowen. "I hated that name. I saw Alpert and I said, 'What should we call this thing?' and he said, 'Well, it's just being. It's just being in. Being in.' I said, 'That's it. The Be-In.' He gave me the idea and I remembered it when we did the thing in the park. I created the idea and the structure for it and found the place to do it. I was on a mission from God from John Cooke to do that Be-In."

In 1956, John Starr Cooke, a bald man with a goatee and piercing gray eyes who was said to have taken LSD every day for two years while living in Carmel, California, gave Michael Bowen LSD for the first time. In 1964, Bowen visited Cooke at his home in Tepoztlán, the little village just five minutes from Cuernavaca where Tim had first turned on. On the night of the full moon, Bowen ate the "Aztec dessert." "Big bell-shaped flowers," he recalled. "Datura. Very dangerous. Moon completely full—flowers open—eat them. I must have eaten twelve full flowers. Made LSD look like nothing. Like zero. Most powerful psychedelic experience ever." During the trip, Cooke instructed Bowen, "Go and find this Timothy Leary and bring him to the mandala. Bring him here." Imprinted with these instructions, Bowen became one of Cooke's "Psychedelic Rangers." In time, he brought Ralph Metzner and the Canadian poet, novelist, and folksinger Leonard Cohen to Mexico. There, Cooke initiated them into his teachings by giving them unusually high doses of acid, anywhere from 2,000 to 3,000 mikes (the more typical dose was 100 to 250 micrograms). Bowen gave LSD to comedian and social activist Dick Gregory and radical Berkeley political activist Jerry Rubin. In 1966, Bowen moved to Haight-Ashbury at Cooke's request and set about implementing Cooke's idea for a gathering of the tribes. One of Cooke's purposes in having Bowen organize the event was to psychedelicize and convert the radical left.

Extraordinary posters for the event began appearing all over San Francisco. On one, the word "POW-WOW" could be seen at the top, with "A Gathering of the Tribes for a Human-Be-In" appended like a subhead below it. From a large dark cloud, what looked to be an eagle's claw emerged, two lightning bolts entwined in its talons. (Having just synthesized a brand-new batch of acid, Owsley Stanley saw the poster, decided to call the LSD White Lightning, and then distributed it at the Be-In.) Below the lightning bolts on the poster, an old Indian sat on a horse with a tribal blanket in one hand and a six-string guitar in the other. On either side of him were the names of those who would appear that day—Timothy Leary first and foremost among them, followed by Richard Alpert, Dick Gregory (who did not show), Lenore Kandel, Jerry Rubin, and "All San Francisco Rock Bands." On the other side, Allen Ginsberg topped the list followed by Lawrence Ferlinghetti, Gary Snyder, Michael McClure, Robert [Richard] Baker, and Buddha. Around the top edge of the poster in tiny print, it read, "Bring the color gold. Bring photos of personal saints and heroes of the underground. Bring children. Flowers . . . flutes. Drums. Feathers. Bands. Beads. Banners. Flags. Tangerines. Incence [sic]. Gongs. Cymbals. Symbols. Joy."

Although the nascent hippie culture seemed to bear little resemblance to the beatnik movement which had come before, those who presided over its birth were all products of it. Poets and writers, they had for years expressed their political views through their art as well as their unconventional lifestyles. Appearing before an audience too large to fit inside a coffeehouse in North Beach or on MacDougal Street in Greenwich Village was a brand-new experience for them.

On Friday, January 14, many of those scheduled to appear the next day at the Human Be-In gathered to discuss procedural matters in a Haight-Ashbury apartment. Allen Ginsberg, Gary Snyder, and Michael McClure joined in singing "Lord, Won't You Buy Me a Mercedes-Benz?," a song later recorded by Janis Joplin (and then used much later by Mercedes-Benz in a television commercial). The central question under discussion at the meeting was whether Tim Leary was a poet, in which case he would be entitled to speak for seven minutes, or a prophet, in which case he could go on for as long as half an hour. Ginsberg suggested that instead of anyone speaking, they should all join together for a sunset celebration at the beach. "Naked," Gary Snyder suggested. "A groovy naked swim-in," Ginsberg replied, noting that this would surely blow everyone's mind. Ginsberg's position on the central question was that Tim should get as much time to speak as the poets. When someone asked if Tim was a prima donna, someone else said, "He's taken acid. How can he be?" "Leary just needs a little of the responsibility taken off him," Ginsberg said, ruling on the matter in his own definitive way. "Seven minutes, and anyway, if he gets uptight and starts to preach, Lenore [Kandel] can always belly-dance."

The next day, Ginsberg arrived at Golden Gate Park at 11:00 A.M. to chant Buddhist dharanis, short-form prayers intended to ward off all potential disasters that might be lurking there. Wearing blue rubber bathing thong sandals; a white hospital orderly's uniform covered with beads, bells, amulets, and buttons; and an enormous flowered tie, Ginsberg circled the field like Hindus do before a *mehla,* a gathering of holy men. The day itself was warm and sunny. On a small stage set with microphones and an Oriental rug, Tim, stoned on three hundred mikes of LSD, sat cross-legged beside Ginsberg as the Be-In got under way. Before him were more than twenty thousand people. Many of them were not only high on acid but also surrounded by more fellow trippers than they had ever seen before. In the brilliant winter sunlight, Tim's hair gleamed like silver. He wore the all-white Indian holy-man garb that had become his trademark. In his right hand, he carried a daffodil. Behind each ear, he had tucked a spray of tiny jonquils. Perhaps because he was tripping, his face seemed carefree and unworn. Even from a distance, his blinding smile radiated an inner happiness that seemed completely real.

When Tim finally spoke, he kept it short—far less than seven minutes. "The only way out," he said, "is in. Tune in, turn on, and drop out. Out of high school, junior executive, senior executive. And follow me!" Jerry Rubin, who had been bailed out of jail that very morning, then implored the crowd to take political action. "Jerry Rubin was up there shouting," Bowen recalled, "but it didn't matter. Because the most important thing was that all these people saw one another. The thrill was that everybody saw one another and realized there was an actual connection." At one point in the proceedings, a masked man whom many people mistakenly believed was Owsley Stanley, fell from the sky clinging to a paisley parachute. Once the man hit the ground, he began distributing acid to the crowd. Shortly before Suzuki-roshi of the San Francisco Zen Center arrived at three o'clock to smile at the crowd, a sulfur bomb went off beneath the stage. Thinking the smell was incense, the crowd applauded enthusiastically.

Ten weeks later, on Easter Sunday in New York City, the Greater New York Be-In was held in the Sheep Meadow in Central Park. Ten thousand people showed up to do not much more than hang out with one another. Unlike San Francisco, where the event was billed as a gathering of the tribes, there were as yet no tribes in New York. Having first taken LSD in the autumn of 1965, Abbie Hoffman attended the event along with Anita Kushner, the woman who would become his wife. Thirty-one years old, Hoffman had been working as a political organizer in the East Village. Paul Krassner, who first introduced both Jerry Rubin and Abbie Hoffman to Tim, would later recall, "Abbie wanted the hippies to become political and Tim wanted the politicos to get stoned. But they liked one another. Because of the humor. Tim liked to laugh and Abbie was incredibly witty."

Even as the counterculture was being born, the split between those who favored psychedelic spirituality and those who believed in the politics of revolution was already an issue. Allen Cohen, editor of the *San Francisco Oracle*, invited Alan Watts, Allen Ginsberg, Gary Snyder, and Tim to a summit conference on whether to "drop out or take over." "The choice is between being rebellious and being religious," Tim was later quoted as saying. "Don't vote. Don't politic. Don't petition. You can't do anything about America politically." Dismissing student activists as "young men with menopausal minds," Tim characterized all action that did not come from expanded consciousness as "robot behavior." As yet another of his slogans, Tim offered "Let the State Disintegrate."

After he took acid, Abbie Hoffman wrote, "I saw the reverse of Leary's trip: change the world and you'll change your mind. Total absorption with the internal voyage made you easy to exploit and convert. In spite of our differences, Timothy later underlined his reassuring words by giving me a check to our newly formed community service group. Needless to say it bounced. 'It was the thought that counted,' we reasoned, and never demanded that he make good on the money or anything else. Certainly not his word."

Six days after the Human Be-In, Tim appeared with the Grateful Dead at the Santa Monica Civic Auditorium in Los Angeles. Owsley Stanley would later recall, "Somebody played a sitar and Tim did a rave and then the band played. He was being Guru Tim." Tim later described his appearance as "the high point of the road tour. Hall jammed. Grateful Dead jammed. The LSD alchemist Owsley was everywhere dispensing his White Lightning pills." He omitted mentioning the "little old lady" who threw rotten eggs at him while yelling, "You ruined my son with your devil drugs!" From the stage, Tim told the crowd, "Now's the time to flick on the inner switch to full power! Listen, you'll either spend the rest of your life as a badly paid extra in someone else's low-budget black-and-white documentary/training film. OR. You become the producer of your own movie. Direct it, script it, cast it, choose the locations for the greatest reality flick ever made. Why settle for less?" "Tim did his lecture and people threw packets of hash and LSD and joints and flowers and an old lady threw some eggs," Rosemary Woodruff remembered. "My mother and father were in the audience and when I asked my mother, 'What did you think of Tim's lecture?' she said, 'Well, Daddy doesn't like the smell of incense, honey.' I was backstage listening to Tim while watching Owsley pace and do the monitors. And he said, 'Are you sure you guys take acid?' Because Tim was going on and on." "Everything he said was very provocative," Owsley Stanley recalled. "'Fuck authorities. To hell with your parents. Turn on, tune in, drop out. Take acid, don't care about what anybody would later say, do what you please.' He scared a lot of people because they thought he was too weird. And he was. He just kind of went around the bend. Everyone was saying, 'Look, Tim, you're out of control here. You've got to cool it. You're bringing too much heat on everything. We don't want a lot of attention.' But he wouldn't listen."

Taking his own advice, Tim became the star and director of a Hollywood movie based on *The Death of the Mind*. He summoned Rudi Stern and Jackie Cassen to Los Angeles to work on the project without providing them any money to live on or any information about the film. Stern got a call from someone at a movie studio at seven in the morning one day, telling him to report for work at nine. Stern would later recall, "I said to the guy, 'What job? What are you talking about?' He said, 'As you know, we're doing *Death of the Mind* and Tim has promised your work as part of the deal and we expect you here at nine o'clock.' This was the first I'd heard of it. It turned out Tim had sold the rights to *Death of the Mind* to Columbia Pictures for a good chunk of money. He had gotten a down payment of middle six figures—$300,000."

Stern called Tim at Millbrook and asked him what was going on. Stern and Cassen had no money, no food, and no idea who was going to direct the picture. "He said, 'Don't worry about it. Don't be so suspicious, Rudi. I'll be out there soon. We'll talk about it. Do you have enough grass? I'll get you some. Relax, Rudi. Don't be so uptight.'" Stern called his lawyer in New York and asked if he knew what was happening. "He said, 'Rudi, you've just been ripped off.' I said, 'It can't be. Timothy is my friend. He would never do such a thing.' He said, 'You've been ripped off.' I said, 'It's not the money. I contributed it all back to the house at Millbrook anyway. It's just that we have no money now and we need to buy bulbs for the projectors. We have no money to eat.'" Stern called the studio back and asked, "'What are we supposed to bring at nine o'clock?' They said, 'All your projection equipment. All the stuff you used for *Death of the Mind*. All your slides. You're part of the deal. Congratulations. You're gonna get a nice credit in the film.' I said, 'Thanks. That's really great. Anything about an advance or some cash?' 'No, don't worry about that. We're all brothers, man. And I'll see you at nine o'clock. We'll take good care of you while you're in LA.'"

Stern never went to the studio. Instead, he hired a lawyer who sued Tim for $5 million. "It was on the radio that disciples were suing Dr. Leary," Stern recalled. "The psychedelic thing was bottoming out. Within a couple of months, I saw Timothy somewhere. We looked at each other and we both laughed and I called the lawyer the next day and I said, 'Nah. Hold off.' They brought in other people to do the light effects. People who had worked for us. I didn't get a dime. Not a single dime."

Turn On, Tune In, Drop Out, a 35 mm color film produced by Henry G. Saperstein for Benedict Pictures, starring Tim in the role of the Guide, Ralph Metzner as the Voyager, and Rosemary Woodruff as the Divine Connection, was released in 1967 accompanied by *Turn On, Tune In, Drop Out: The Original Motion Picture Soundtrack* on Mercury Records. Within a week of its premiere in Los Angeles, the film was suppressed and never rereleased. Tim Leary would later write, "I remember sitting, profusely made up, under the floodlights of a Hollywood studio, listening to Dick Alpert's quizzical, disapproving question, 'Timothy, why are you doing this?' I could only reply, 'Well, Professor, I'd be delighted to have you take my place.'"

Even as Tim was making new converts among those who had never known him personally, he was beginning to lose those who had once considered themselves part of his team at Millbrook. "I began to see the game player," Stern recalled. "More and more, it began to seem to me that he was in it for the show and for personal gain. Money was always important to Tim. When there was money on the table or in the bank or in a letter or in an envelope, he was very focused. He knew how much his lifestyle was going to cost him. He liked good cars. Always. And good clothes. And he liked to stay at five-star hotels and he traveled that way. And he liked beautiful woman and they are not cheap either. You can't enjoy or justify the Rolls or the suite at the Mark Hopkins if you're not helping whacked-out sixteen-year-olds who took acid on a motorcycle in Kansas City and are now in a dungeon somewhere in solitary confinement beating their heads against the wall."

"Tim Leary," Owsley Stanley remembered, "was always a hail-fellow-well-met, glad-hand kind of guy. Glad to see you but as soon as you tried to get down and get serious with him, he was nervous. He had to be somewhere else. He had to do something else. He impressed me as a guy who had always just missed the bus and was always running to the next bus stop to see if he could get on it."

A week after his appearance at the Santa Monica Civic Auditorium, Tim's traveling medicine show played the Berkeley Community Theater and Winterland. The *Berkeley Barb* withheld its announcement of the performance until the day of the show and then suggested that peace movement people demonstrate against Tim's antipolitical stance. Onstage that night, Tim responded to the criticism by holding up a copy of the *Barb* alongside the very colorful and completely psychedelic *Oracle*. "This is an ugly, hateful Iron Age newspaper," he said of the *Barb*. The *Oracle*, he said, "is the paper Buddah would read if he were here today." Near the end of the show, Tim looked dubiously at the microphone in his hand and wondered aloud, "What am I doing in this rather implausible situation, in such a ridiculous thing as show business. I'm not going to win any Academy Awards." Predictably, the *Barb* panned his performance, noting that the hall was only half full and many of those who were there walked out "before Siddhartha got illuminated."

The next day in the *San Francisco Chronicle*, Ralph Gleason, the jazz critic who became a founding editor of *Rolling Stone*, wrote, "Dr. Leary, looking like a character actor in 'Rain,' walked onstage dressed in white pajamas, sat cross-legged in front of four candles, lit them, and one promptly went out . . . He picked up the microphone and began to deliver the same speech we have been hearing bit by bit in interviews. The light show was antique by Bay Area standards . . . The trip became a travelogue with Fitzpatrick O'Leary guiding us with gun and camera down the psychedelic canal." In a scathing cover piece on the acid scene in the spring of 1967 in *Ramparts,* the radical Bay Area political journal founded by Warren Hinckle and Robert Scheer, Hinckle wrote of the hippies, "Leary they abide as an Elmer Gantry on their side, to be used for proselytizing straights only." Calling Tim the "Pretender to the Hippie Throne," Hinckle added that because Tim was serious about his work, he could "not be dismissed as a cross between a white Father Divine and Nietzsche, no matter how tempting the analogy."

"We bombed in San Francisco," Rosemary Woodruff recalled. "Totally. We ran out of rose petals at Winterland. It was horrible. The sound system was terrible. From having been this immense thing, the light show was suddenly diminished. Tim was minuscule and everyone had seen the Trips Festival and they had their own light shows." Although Tim swore that he was now definitely through with show business, he continued lecturing at any college or university that would pay him his $1,000-a-night fee. On February 14, 1967, he was arrested yet again for failing to register as a narcotics violator before leaving the country. Posting a $2,500 bail, Tim was released, pending a preliminary hearing in March.

On April 8, before a crowd of four thousand people at Rensselaer Polytechnic Institute in Troy, New York, Tim debated his old adversary Dr. Donald Louria. Two remarkable photographs of the event appeared in the *Albany-Times Union.* To look at them now is to get a real sense of how straight nearly everyone in America was back then, especially in comparison to Tim. In one photograph, local college students sit side by side. All male, they are as alike as peas in a pod. None seem older than twenty. All have very short hair. Several wear the same heavy black-frame eyeglasses favored by Richard Alpert. Trying to look like a man of the world, one is smoking a pipe. In polo shirts or suit jackets, white shirts, and rep ties, they are the future engineers, scientists, and businessmen of America. At nineteen, they already look ninty five.

Next to this photograph is one of "several of Leary's disciples who live with him in his Millbrook home." Three of the young men sitting in the front row have beards. Jeans tucked into high boots, his rustic woodsman's shirt unbuttoned, one wears his long blond hair over his ears. Another sports beads and a Nehru shirt under his suit jacket. In a dark sweatshirt and jeans, Susan Leary sits with them. She was now nineteen years old and would not be returning to the University of Wisconsin for her sophomore year.

On May 1, Susan sent an extraordinary nineteen-page letter to her father, written in a child's curling script, each word so large that there were sometimes no more than three to a line. Addressing her father as "Timothy," she wrote, "Please wake-up. I have a horrible feeling that where you are taking Millbrook is extremely unhealthy . . . What kind of leader are you. You give up the static world to teach the world about chemicals and what you believe in. You want to save humanity from where it is at. How can you claim to care about where humanity is at when you are doing what you are doing to the mind [sic] of the people at Millbrook, yourself and Jackie."

Repeating herself frequently, she asked, "Where is your sanity? Have you completely lost touch with your body and creation and human instincts and what is natural? Has your mind distorted that so you can no longer see or be a real human? You are destructive and evil. You don't have to play all those roles and games . . . The you that is my precious daddy is so far gone. So long ago distorted and destroyed. My father who was the only person who comes near to understanding me and caring for me is so distorted and lost in a pattern game and life of negative activities and games, it is hard to know if you understand me still."

Apologizing for the fact that her letter was so negative, Susan wrote, "You can't be a public figure all the time. You can't give up your spiritual and emotional health for mankind and the unhealthy games you are into." She concluded by adding, "Would I get this emotional about where you are at, what you are doing to Jackie and the people at Millbrook if I didn't love you? Please listen—before it's too late." At the bottom of the last page, as though the thought had just occurred to her, Susan wrote, "Fill out Goddard application."

"Susan was very protective of Tim," Rosemary Woodruff would later recall. "She had to be near him and close to him and sitting on his lap and touching him. Tim could be patient with her. But his suggestions to her were not very well thought out. After Laredo, it was Tim's line to me that I had suddenly became responsible for her condition." Art Kleps would later write that to "get away from her foster mother Rosemary, whom she thought to be a witch," Susan lived for three weeks at Bill Haines's ashram. To Haines, Susan's real problem was simple. "She wants to get laid by her old man." In his office at Millbrook one day, Kleps asked Susan if she really thought Rosemary was a witch. "Susan's expression, which had been reasonably placid, abruptly altered to 50 degrees below zero, and she proceeded, in a strange, sing-song voice, to give me her considered opinion of Rosemary. She was an evil woman. She was trying to destroy 'Timothy.' She hated Susan and Jackie. She was frigid, barren, and did not even love Tim. Her one and only motive in life was to destroy everything good she could lay her spells on."

Plainly, Susan needed help. But with her mother dead and her father perpetually out on the road selling LSD as a panacea for whatever ailed the world, Susan had no one to whom she could turn. "She felt bad about everything," Rosemary said, "and the worst part was the sense that I was helpless to help her. I didn't know how to help her. Everything I tried to do failed. Everything I said to her was wrong. Absolutely everything."

TWENTY-SEVEN

On May 18, 1967, in big black type usually reserved for the declaration of war, the banner headline on the front page of the *Millbrook Round Table* read 300 BACK FORMATION OF "ANTI-LSD GROUP"; LEARY CALLS MOVE "WHIPPED-UP HYSTERIA." Three days earlier, more than three hundred concerned residents of Millbrook had descended upon the regular monthly meeting of the central school board to discuss the possibility that hallucinogenic drugs were being used by students in their schools. The real subject of the meeting, of course, was Tim Leary. As the article noted, "The meeting was stimulated by a nationwide NBC television report featuring Millbrook resident and self proclaimed religious leader Dr. Timothy Leary." Although no LSD had been seized during the raid on Millbrook and all charges from the incident had been dismissed, Dutchess County Assistant District Attorney G. Gordon Liddy stirred up those at the meeting by, as the article stated, "dramatically waving a plastic bag containing several white cubes he claimed were LSD-impregnated sugar cubes taken from the Millbrook home of Dr. Leary by himself and other law enforcement officials in a raid last year." When a woman asked if anything was being done to check the children who were coming into local schools from Tim's estate, the principal defended them as superior students. Tim added fuel to the fire by telling the *Round Table* that "the real problems in this Community are alcoholism and atheism."

Ten days later, an ad hoc committee chaired by local lawyer Hamilton Fish Jr. issued a statement that read in part, "Though there is significant sentiment in favor of investigating legal steps that might lead to the eviction of Dr. Leary, it is not in our intent to take the law into our own hands or to encroach on anyone's civil or religious liberties." With the full support of the community, however, local police continued harassing all those going in and out of the estate.

When the Grateful Dead came to New York City for the first time in June 1967 to play for six nights at the Cafe Au Go Go in Greenwich Village along with folksinger Eric Andersen and Luke & The Apostles, John Perry Barlow, a longtime friend of the band, brought them to Millbrook to visit Tim. Barlow's intent was to bring about what he envisioned as a psychedelic summit meeting between the West Coast apostles of acid and their counterparts in the east. "This was the week that the Six-Day War broke out," Barlow would later recall. "It was also the week that *Sgt Pepper's Lonely Hearts Club Band* was released. A week of great potency. A good week to be Zelig. I was thinking, 'What can I give these guys to demonstrate my mojo so I can be part of their thing?'"

After the band played their first show at Cafe Au Go Go, Barlow walked around the Village with his former schoolmate Bob Weir, the rhythm guitarist for the Dead. Weir had hair down to his waist. At about 4:30 in the morning, Barlow and Weir were sitting beneath the arch in Washington Square when a pale green Ford Falcon pulled up. "It was," Barlow recalled, "like the thousand clowns got out of the car. Kids from Long Island. Bad kids from Long Island. About twenty of them. Immediately, they surrounded us and they were dancing around like, 'Kill the pig! Drink his blood!' Their obvious intention was to beat the crap out of us. Weir looked up sort of startled and said, 'I sense violence. And whenever I feel violence in myself, there's a song that I sing that has always had a calming effect on me and let me see if you would like to sing it with me.'" Weir then began singing "Hare Krishna, Hare Krishna." Completely startled, the kids from Long Island started singing along with him. Barlow later recalled thinking, "'Jesus, do you suppose this might work?' I myself was singing it like my life depended on it, literally. At a certain point, this bad guy said, 'Fuck this!' He gave the signal and they just beat the crap out of us."

Barlow then escorted the Grateful Dead to Millbrook. "Didn't call ahead," he remembered. "Just drove up and arrived and I said, 'Hi, I've been here before and these are my friends, the Grateful Dead.' And they said, 'Fine.'" Barlow also brought with him a copy of *Sgt Pepper's Lonely Hearts Club Band,* which no one at Millbrook had yet heard. "That was my real offering," he recalled. "So there was this big ritualistic listening-to-the-record ceremony. It was one of those really sixties kind of scenes where there was a lot of cheap printed Indian cotton around, brass lamps and incense, patchouli oil, and cat piss. After the record ended, Tim stood up and in this incredibly portentous, sententious, mystical voice, said, 'My work is finished. Now, it's out.' In a funny way, he was right. He knew. From this point forward, it would take place by itself."

Although Tim and Jerry Garcia talked, Barlow recalled that "it was not so much Garcia and Tim as it was Mountain Girl and Tim." (Born Carolyn Adams, she had been Ken Kesey's companion during the Prankster days and would later marry Jerry Garcia.) "That was the real point of contact. In her way, she was quizzing him. She was running the dozens on Tim and he passed. It was a total meeting of two different worlds. The Millbrook people were all sort of in a prana-receptive state and the Grateful Dead were out to kick ass and have fun. They recognized one another as being related but different tribes."

Tim and the Dead did not take acid together, but Barlow distinctly remembered "telling Tim about the incident which had taken place with Weir because he was asking why I had a black eye. I had cuts all over me. He wanted to know what had happened and I told him this story." As Tim listened, Barlow recalled him shaking his head "in this completely phony caring way. I knew he didn't give a damn. He had no idea of the street or what it was like to sit in Washington Square at 4:30 in the morning. But he kept trying to get it. His persona was coming up with, 'Why must there be this violence among us? Why can we not rise above these base things?' And it was just complete horseshit. I sort of switched allegiances at that point. I saw Millbrook as pretentious and self-serving. And basically exploitative, in that they were getting juice from the fact they had control. They were still doing the Indian thing and meditating and the Dead thought, 'What is this horseshit?'"

As the only lasting token of their visit to Millbrook, the Grateful Dead left behind *Sgt Pepper's Lonely Hearts Club Band*. The effect the album had on Tim can only be understood in the context of its time. All across America, the summer of love was just getting under way. An even younger generation had begun experimenting with marijuana and LSD. Cut loose from the moorings of convention, they sought out icons of their own. Albums such as *Sgt Pepper* became the soundtrack of their lives.

As part of a series of articles about drugs and hippies, a reporter from the *Boston Record-American* interviewed an "acidhead" named "Jim" whose Beacon Hill living room was decorated with "bigger-than-life photos of James Dean, Bob Dylan, and Marilyn Monroe." Jim had lost all interest in television and turned his set to the wall. Above it hung a large poster of Timothy Leary in white guru clothing. "The place of honor," the article noted, "was reserved for the 'psychedelic messiah' Leary. His photo was affixed to the ceiling so that it could be seen from the most comfortable position on a 'trip'—supine on the floor or on the couch." Because no one else in a position of power would endorse LSD, Tim had become a genial father figure by default to many who really knew very little about him. In crash pads from Cambridge to Ladbroke Grove, a large poster bearing his grinning image defined the hippie mise-en-scène. Along with Meher Baba, Mick Jagger, John Lennon, and Bob Dylan, Tim had become one of the counterculture's newly minted saints.

Tim's problems with the law in Millbrook continued to multiply in direct proportion to his growing fame. On a busy Saturday in July 1967, forty people were arrested on their way in and out of the estate. Some were cited for driving with a dirty license plate, a violation for which $25 bail had to be posted. Art Kleps's wife, Wendy, was arrested and hauled off to jail for not having any ID in her shorts as she rode her bicycle. Some of Jack Leary's friends were busted for marijuana. Tim was picked up for bouncing an $8.00 check to the owner of a sporting goods store who happened to be a good friend of Sheriff Quinlan. To escape, Tim took off in Billy Hitchcock's private plane to visit hippie communes like Drop City in Colorado and New Buffalo on the mesa outside Taos, New Mexico. Wherever he went, Tim was treated like visiting royalty. "It was like this king had arrived," Darlene DeSedle recalled. "The best dope. The best meals. We were an entourage and we were taken care of."

When he returned to Millbrook, Tim decided the big house could no longer be defended from what he would later call in *Flashbacks* "incursions of armed men who could and did arrest our residents on trumped-up charges." Shutting it down for the summer, he retreated with Rosemary to "the wild forest on the northern acres of the property. We constructed a tent village on the rolling plain by Lunacy Hill. Rosemary and I pitched our tent on the crest of Ecstasy Hill, about a mile away from the main encampment. Protected by circles of scouts, we set up domestic life as it has been lived for thousands of years—hauling water, cooking meals over a campfire, exploring the terrain, both inner and outer." In their teepee— "the most sensual living arrangement ever designed by mankind; soft, fur-lined nosecone of pleasure pointed at the stars"—Tim and Rosemary could hear the whirring of the sheriff's helicopter as it hovered overhead on its twice-weekly surveillance flight. Looking up, they could see men peering back down at them through cameras and binoculars. Noting that G. Gordon Liddy liked to tell lurid stories of naked women emerging from the tepees, Tim would later write, "We treasured these moments of surveillance, feeling a strong bond of affiliation with Vietnamese peasants and Che guerillas and African lions, and all wild, free creatures on this planet gazing in surprise at armed agents, Sci-Fi spies in government motor ships."

Together, Tim and Rosemary devoted "an hour or two each day to getting high and listening to a portable record player spin the new testaments according to Sergeant Pepper and their Satanic Majesties. It's all there. How clever and unexpected and yet typical of God to send his message this time through the electric instruments of four men from Liverpool and their Holy Rollers . . . Beloved gurus of Liverpool, I'm four you. I've got nothing to say that you haven't said briefer, cleaner, stronger." While it might seem odd that a middle-aged man who was deaf in one ear could actually hear the voice of God in an album by the Beatles, Tim already understood that in this scene, all real power came from the musicians. Only by aligning himself with them could he retain his role as a leader in the culture.

Although Tim played no real part in the summer of love, he could not ignore news reports about what was happening on the West Coast. In Haight-Ashbury, the dream Tim had helped make public just six months earlier at the Human Be-In had become a nightmare. An authentic westward migration of the young and dispossessed in America was under way. Before the year was out, as many as 150,000 people, most under the age of twenty with no money and no place to stay, would flood into the Haight. As they panhandled for change on corners and lolled in the grass on "Hippie Hill" in Golden Gate Park, they were accompanied every step of the way by members of the straight press covering the phenomenon. Gray Line buses filled with tourists eager to inspect all these "freaks" at close range began rolling down Haight Street. Residents of the Grateful

Dead house at 710 Haight held up large mirrors so those riding inside the buses could see themselves instead.

Within the Haight, the street scene soon became violent. Although LSD and marijuana remained the drugs of choice, the influx of methedrine radically changed the nature of the community and those attracted to it. Recently released from Terminal Island Federal Penitentiary, Charles Manson and his "tribe" of young hippie girls rented a house at 636 Cole Street. During the first week in August, the body of an acid dealer with his right arm severed at the elbow was found in an apartment in the Haight. Three days later, a black dealer known as Superspade was discovered at the base of a cliff in Marin County with a bullet hole in the base of his skull. In New York's East Village, Linda Fitzpatrick, an eighteen-year-old girl from a wealthy family in Greenwich, Connecticut, was found naked on a boiler-room floor with her male companion, Groovy. Both had their heads bashed in.

All summer long, Chester Anderson, described by Leary biographer John Bryan as "a sardonic old beatnik," who founded the Communication Company as the "publishing arm of the Diggers," deluged the Haight with mimeographed broadsides. In one entitled "Uncle Tim's Children," he wrote of the "Pretty little 16-year-old middle-class chick who comes to the Haight to see what it's all about and gets picked up by a 17-year-old street dealer who spends all day shooting her full of speed again & again. Then feeds her 3000 mikes & raffles off her temporarily unemployed body for the biggest Haight Street gang bang since the night before last." Ridiculing the "politics & ethics of ecstasy," Anderson wrote, "Kids are starving on The Street. Minds and bodies are being maimed as we watch, a scale model of Vietnam." The local hip merchants "do not realize that they & Uncle Timothy have lured an army of children into a ghastly death trap from which there is no visible escape. They do not see that they are destroying a whole generation of American youth. And why hasn't the man who really did it to us done something about the problem he has created? Why doesn't Doctor Timothy Leary help the Diggers?" (A radical group of actors from the San Francisco Mime Troupe, the Diggers fed and clothed kids in the Haight while also indulging in mind-blowing pieces of street theater.) "Are Alpert & Leary and The Oracle all in the same greedy place? Does acid still have to be sold as hard as Madison Avenue sells sex? What do these Nice People mean by 'Love?'"

Emmet Grogan, the legendary New York street hustler who helped found the Diggers, wrote in his autobiography of a meeting between Tim and Richard Alpert and a group of street kids from the Haight at the Digger Store on Frederick Street around the time of the Human Be-In. As the "two LSD shamans pitched their psychedelic banter," a young girl got to her feet and announced, "'You don't turn me on!' She held her ground and kept repeating the same accusation: 'You don't turn me on!' And the others agreed with her and also began to chant, until everyone was shouting—'You don't turn us on! You don't turn us on!'—forcing the two of them to leave with a good man [Allen Ginsberg] who should have known better than to squander himself on a pair of charlatan fools."

What the kids objected to was not so much Tim and Alpert's message as the way in which they delivered it. As Grogan wrote: "Neither Leary nor Alpert could carry the tune. But there they were every time you turned around—on the covers of magazines, on the radio and TV, all over the fucking place—representing them, the young people, the alternative culture. Two creepy, whiskey-drinking schoolteachers! It was sad and the young people in the Free Frame that night rejected out of hand the lie they were fed by the media and felt disappointed in themselves for having ever believed in the psychedelic duet."

Beneath a front-page headline reading ELDRIDGE WARNS BENNETT STUDENTS . . . TIM LEARY STILL "OFF LIMITS," the lead story in the September 28, 1967, edition of the *Millbrook Round Table* reported that Donald A. Eldridge, president of Bennett College, had begun the school's seventy-seventh year by warning all incoming freshmen that the Hitchcock estate remained off-limits to them "for the same reason that we require vaccination as protection against smallpox—preventative medicine."

In far smaller type, the article beside it reported that Mr. and Mrs. William G. Money of Millbrook had received the Bronze Star Medal for Heroism awarded to their son Sergeant William Money, a fire-team leader with Company C, 1st Airborne, 12th Cavalry. During an engagement with a well-entrenched, numerically superior North Vietnamese Army force in the village of An Qui, Money had exposed himself to enemy fire to move his platoon to cover. Armed with only grenades and his weapon, he assaulted and destroyed several enemy bunkers and provided covering fire as a wounded comrade was pulled to safety. Money was then mortally wounded.

By the fall of 1967, even in a small town like Millbrook, no one could ignore the war in Vietnam. Tim, however, continued advising people "not to get particularly involved in war protests," recalled Gordon Ball, a filmmaker then working for Jonas Mekas. Ball heard Tim say this in the big storefront on the corner of Hudson Street and Tenth Avenue, which had become the League for Spiritual Discovery headquarters in New York City. "I think he used the phrase, 'Give to Caesar what is Caesar's,'" Ball recalled. "In other words, he felt it was a distraction from the central task of evolving our consciousness." On October 21, 1967, radical peace activists whose imaginations had been inflamed by LSD marched on the Pentagon in Washington, D.C. Their stated intention was to levitate the building so as to rid it of the demons of war. The most striking visual image to emerge from the demonstration was a photograph of one young protester sliding a daisy down the barrel of a soldier's rifle. For the moment, flower power and radical activism were one.

Two weeks later, Tim issued a memo entitled "MIGRATION AND HIBERNATION," in which he wrote: "The Third World is not going to Maintain the Big House during the winter: the house is therefore closed as of Sunday November 5, 1967. The League will maintain its hibernation center in the Teepees. Some League members are leaving for California to open centers there. Everyone is welcome to return with the robins in the spring." Four days later, the *Millbrook Round Table* ran a front-page story reporting that Thomas Hitchcock had issued a new set of rules limiting visitors to the estate as well as prohibiting anyone from camping in the woods "without the express authorization of the Hitchcock family."

Tim now had many reasons to turn his focus toward California. As his mother, Abigail, now in her seventies, noted in a letter to her granddaughter, Susan, on October 18, 1967: "As to the item about Jack, I was so stunned to know he was in California and not in school in Millbrook High. I just felt so sick at heart when I read about him being in Haight Ashbury." Eighteen years old, Jack had joined the migration. After staying with Ralph Metzner and Rosemary Woodruff in Tim's house in Berkeley, Jack went to visit some people in Laguna Beach whom he had first met during the summer at the big house in Millbrook. Led by John Griggs, they were a religious commune of righteous dope dealers who called themselves the Brotherhood of Eternal Love. They ran a head shop and bookstore in Laguna Beach, then a sleepy, artsy little beachside town an hour south of Los Angeles.

At three in the morning, Tim got a call from his son. Jack had taken a thousand mikes of LSD at the Avalon Ballroom in San Francisco. Quietly Jack told his father that he was now illuminated. "You're illuminated," Tim said into the phone. "Now what?" Without a moment's hesitation, Jack replied, "Now I illuminate." After being given $17,000 by the Brotherhood to buy LSD in San Francisco, Jack told his father he had taken a $1,000 bill from his pocket, meditated, and then burned it because money was "a paper illusion." Owsley Stanley would later confirm that Jack once came up to him "with a handful of $1,000 notes that he said came from the Brotherhood and they wanted acid. And I said, 'Hey, man, you gotta be crazy. Who the hell would give you those things? You have to sign a paper at the bank to get them and another paper to get rid of them. You gotta be crazy. No one in their right mind has $1,000 U.S. bills.'" As he spoke to his son on the phone, even Tim, the self-acknowledged world's greatest expert on LSD, was forced to admit that he had been "left behind, carrying on my shivering shoulders at three o'clock in the morning the grief and bewilderment of every parent whose teen-age children are mutating through acid (lysergic and nucleic) up to a higher level of existence. I can't give my beautiful, turned-on son any logical reason why he shouldn't burn a thousand-dollar bill."

Tim's guilt and bewilderment concerning his children did not last long. In Otto Preminger's luxurious Manhattan townhouse, Tim ran an LSD session for the famed director, then doing "research" for a movie entitled *Skidoo*. As soon as the acid kicked in, Preminger went into manic action. Turning on one television set after another, he had three going at once. "His shiny, hairless head had turned into a space helmet and he was high as an orbiting com-sat as he dialed and tuned ever-changing realities, deliberately disrupting focus and color." As Tim searched for a Ravi Shankar record to slow Preminger down, he had an epiphany. "Watching Otto's accelerated brain in action jolted me out of the nostalgic-pastoral phase. At Millbrook we had been living in a time warp. Millbrook was a pleasant but repetitious feudal drill. The next stage in evolution, my own at least, was going to involve information and communication. I resolved on the spot to move to Hollywood and learn how realities were produced and directed."

His decision to move to the West Coast was also motivated by more personal concerns. Earlier in the summer, he had told Rosemary, as Art Kleps would later write, that "all games had to come to an end sometime.

Now it was the time for the Rosemary-Tim game to come to an end. Constant change was the rule of life. One must avoid like the plague getting trapped in outdated routines. They had had a wonderful trip together and now they should part before it deteriorated," to which she replied, "Yes, Tim" and "I understand." Rosemary left Millbrook for Berkeley where she stayed with Metzner in Tim's old house on Queens Road. After taking MDA together one night, they went to the Avalon Ballroom. On Tim's forty-seventh birthday on October 22, 1967, Rosemary called to tell him she and Ralph had fallen in love. Tim, in a "distraught condition," asked Billy Hitchcock's wife, Priscilla, what he should do about Rosemary. "Go get her," she told him. Tim flew to California and asked Rosemary to marry him. When Metzner confessed to Rosemary just how conflicted he felt about their relationship because he could not decide whether he loved her or Timothy more, she decided to throw the I Ching before giving Tim her answer. She got the thirty-seventh hexagram, Chia Jen—the Family (the Clan), with a judgment that read, "The perseverance of the woman furthers. The foundation of the family is the relationship between husband and wife. The tie that holds the family together lies in the loyalty and perseverance of the wife." After consulting the oracle, Rosemary decided to become Tim's wife.

"Our first Hollywood production was my marriage to Rosemary on a mountain top in the middle of Joshua Tree National Monument," Tim would later write in *Flashbacks*. "Ted Markland from *Bonanza* directed. The cast included many notables from the movie business, plus some friends from the East Coast. The service was to be performed by Samu, a famous Plains Indian medicine man." Tim and fifty guests, the actor John Phillip Law among them, assembled at sunset on November 11, 1967, at Harry Cohn Jr.'s desert ranch house, where they partied until midnight. Then they drove into the park and climbed the dark trail to the peak where Markland had somehow "implanted an executive swivel chair, to provide a 360-degree panoramic view." Dropping "large doses of acid," everyone reclined on the ledges "to talk things over with the stars, who, having heard about the marriage, dressed up in diamonds and glitter."

Tim and Rosemary huddled together and whispered "prayers of gratitude and love for everyone who wasn't there, including Ralph, my daughter Susan, and Dick." As the rising sun painted the wooly clouds pink and orange, the ceremony was meant to begin. Unfortunately, Samu, the famous Apache medicine man, "shaman and veteran of thousands of peyote nights," was too stoned to perform the vows. Everyone walked back down the mountain where Tim and Rosemary got married in the front seat of a car as Samu performed the ceremony from the back. "That's the way we were," Tim later wrote, "always involved in one joyous pagan ceremony or another, whirling in religious ecstasies and heroic adventures. For us the planet was without Original Sin, designed for our sacramental pleasure. We were not alone. Millions were out there with us. The pageantry of those days! Where did it go?"

"Tim was on mescaline when we got married," Rosemary recalled, "which was much too strong for him. Everyone was throwing up. We were stumbling up the mountain in the dark to make it by sunrise. My wedding march was this symphony of retching. We followed Samu to the car and he said, 'Had I married you, this is what I would have said.' We got married again a few days later at the house in Berkeley. That was done by an East Indian fakir. And then again at the bungalow in Millbrook on December 12."

On Thanksgiving night, Jack Leary was arrested for "acting strangely" on the front porch of a residence on Temple Hills Drive in Laguna Beach, where Tim and Rosemary had gone to enjoy a winter honeymoon in the sun. Finding a young man "dazed, incoherent, and unable, or unwilling to identify himself," local police took Jack to the psychiatric unit of the Orange County Medical Center. Four days later, he was released into the care of his father, who told the local newspaper that his son was "the sanest, wisest person I know. I'm sure the hospital is a better place for him having been there." Tim also noted that Jack initially refused to give his name to police "because he thought he was protecting me." The case was later thrown out of court.

On Saturday, December 9, 1967, while Tim and Rosemary were in New York City, Millbrook was busted again. Gordon Liddy was there along with Albert Rosenblatt, the assistant district attorney. "They had us in the dining room while they were searching the house," Jean McCready recalled, "and then they were handing out subpoenas to everybody. They found some stashes. Some marijuana, even in Jackie's room. They found some LSD. But not massive amounts of drugs. So then they came back with another subpoena." Armed with warrants charging Timothy Leary, Bill Haines, and William Hitchcock with conspiracy to create a public nuisance and criminal facilitation, local cops arrested six Millbrook residents, Art Kleps, Bill Haines, and Jack Leary among them. As a result of searches made during the raid, possession of methamphetamine (in this case, prescription Ritalin) and marijuana, found in the ashram building and in Jack's room, as well as possession of a gun were added to the charges. As Kleps was being loaded into a waiting sheriff's van to be handcuffed to Haines, to whom he had not spoken in some time, Kleps blew his nose and tossed the tissue onto the driveway. A watchful young deputy asked a fellow officer what he should do with it. "Put it in a vial," he was told. When *The East Village Other* ran Tim's account of the raid, the headline read THE GREAT MILLBROOK SNOT BUST. Unable to make bail, all those arrested at Millbrook spent the night in jail. The next day, Jack's hair, which he wore in the pageboy style then also favored by Jerry Garcia, was cut short according to "sanitation and jail rules."

On Monday, December 11, Tim surrendered to the Dutchess County sheriff on charges of narcotics violations and maintaining a public nuisance. Accompanied by his new bride and his lawyer, Noel Tepper, Tim wore an orange turtleneck sweater, matching socks, moccasins, and a necklace. His hair, now long and thick, curled over the collar of his coat. Smiling, he listened to Sheriff Quinlan read the charges to him. Then he said, "Merry Christmas." After posing for photographs outside town hall, Tim was taken to the county jail for booking and fingerprinting. Pleading innocent to all charges, he was released on $2,500 bond. "To engender a little positive publicity after the raid," Art Kleps would later write, Tim decided to hold yet another wedding ceremony at Millbrook with both Haines and Kleps officiating. Killing two birds with one stone, Tim applied for a marriage license the same day he surrendered to local police. On the license application, Tim listed his "Usual occupation" as "priest" and his industry or business as "League for Spiritual Discovery." Rosemary listed her "Usual occupation" as "writer" and her industry or business as "Historical."

In a wedding photograph distributed by the Associated Press, which appeared on the front page of the *New York Post,* Tim is sitting on a couch with a garland of white flowers around his neck. Barefoot in a white linen shirt and trousers trimmed in colorful hippie brocade, his thick silver hair was brushed back over his ears. On his face is a blinding smile. Beside him sits his impossibly young and very beautiful bride. Dressed all in white, Rosemary's long reddish-brown hair hangs to her shoulders. Her enormous eyes are outlined in kohl. Her chin, eyebrows, and cheekbones are dotted with red-and-white tribal markings. A tiny red leaf has been drawn where her third eye would be. Around her neck is a garland of white flowers. Staring at Tim with utter adoration, she rests an arm encircled with bracelets on his leg. Between the two of them, the attraction seems completely physical. Three days later, the newlyweds flew to LA. Their life at Millbrook had come to an end.

On the day after the wedding, in a lead editorial entitled "Overstepping Reasonable Bounds," the *Poughkeepsie Journal* called upon the Dutchess County Board of Supervisors to exercise some control over Sheriff Quinlan, no matter how much he or the newspaper "may dislike long-haired men, stringy-haired girls or dirty clothing." Concerning the manner in which Jack Leary had been treated while under arrest, the editorial stated, "Young Leary was arrested Saturday afternoon and released Sunday afternoon on bail. He had not been convicted of any crime. Can the sheriff in all seriousness ask county residents to believe that every stumblebum or drunk committed to the jail Saturday is shaved and shorn on Sunday for 'sanitation reasons?' It appears this was a clear case of demonstrating the sheriff's personal aversion to long hair and all the things the Leary establishment stands for. It also appears to be a clear case of harassment and ignoring of the rights of an individual who is presumed innocent of any crime until proven guilty." Noting how much the *Journal* sympathized with the sheriff's "desire to get the Leary establishment out of Millbrook," the editorial pointed out that "individuals do have rights and when those rights are infringed upon and ignored our entire democratic structure is endangered. This is too high a price to pay. Harassment is not, and should not, be a part of law enforcement."

The editorial had no effect whatsoever on the local constabulary. Armed with arrest warrants for a Millbrook resident held in contempt of court for failing to testify before the grand jury and for a teenage girl identified only as a wayward minor "whose parents are frantic to find her," ten deputies entered the estate on January 5, 1968. Finding neither of the people they were searching for, deputies arrested seven people, Haines and Jack Leary among them. An attempt by residents to place the deputies under citizen's arrest for entering the house by force and "knocking some of our people down into the ice and snow" failed. Charged with fourth-degree criminal possession of a dangerous drug as well as refusing to aid a police officer, Jack was released on $2,500 bail. Although this was the fourth visit from the police since December 9, the deputy in charge told the *Poughkeepsie Journal* that the incident was "definitely not a raid."

First Assistant District Attorney Albert Rosenblatt told the newspaper, "As long as they [residents of the community] are going to be hostile . . . and as long as they're breaking the law, this kind of thing is going to happen."

On February 20, 1968, *The New York Times* reported that Dr. Timothy Leary and "his psychedelic-oriented adherents" had been ordered by a lawyer for the Hitchcock Cattle Corporation to leave the estate where they had made their headquarters for the past four years. In order to reclaim their property, Tommy and Billy Hitchcock had served all those still living there with eviction notices. Tim received his in Berkeley. Always good for an incendiary quote, Art Kleps told the *Times* that he and his followers "have no intention of leaving the property" and would have to be driven out "at gun point."

Kleps would later write that Tim had been preaching to him and Haines for weeks "that our response to the eviction order would determine the fate of the psychedelic movement" not to mention "world history for eons to come, the very stars in their courses, and so forth—and that we should defy that spoiled rich brat prick Tommy at the cost of our lives if necessary. Passive resistance. Dig caves in the hills, etc. The whole thing."

Tim changed his position on the issue after Diane DiPrima's husband, Alan Marlowe, loaded all of Tim and Rosemary's furniture, as well as Rosemary's antiques, clothes, record player, and large collection of books and jazz records, along with the ten-foot oval mirror in a gilt frame belonging to Maynard Ferguson that had hung in the front hall of the big house, into a U-Haul trailer. "The claim was that Bill Haines had told him we didn't want any of that anymore," Rosemary would later say. "I don't know how much Haines got. He did get the Millbrook bell, which he used in his ashram in Arizona. We were left with nothing except the filing cabinets and some dirty mattresses. I understand Marlowe sold it all in order to go see his guru in Sikkim, or something."

When Tim returned to Millbrook to find all his furniture gone, he angrily pointed an accusing finger at Kleps and Haines and said, "O.K. YOU GUYS. IF I DON'T GET MY FURNITURE BACK BY MONDAY I'M GOING OVER TO TOMMY'S SIDE." As Kleps would later write, "Suddenly, everything he had said or done earlier became 'inoperative.' If he didn't get his furniture back, he would go over to Tommy's side. If Tim found he was holding a low hand, he could always pull out of his sleeve a blank card with a crayon attached." In the *Millbrook Round Table,* Kleps accused Tim of "turning tail" and compared his attitude toward the Hitchcocks to "the Irish peasants' veneration for the rich Englishman on the hill."

Billy Hitchcock called Kleps from Arizona. He had already given Haines $25,000 to leave Millbrook and to provide for his ashram. Since Kleps had only his wife and baby to worry about, Hitchcock offered him $10,000 "for the Neo-American Church." Accepting the money, Kleps left Millbrook without a fight. Collecting $14,000 as his settlement, Tim promised to use it for "a significant social purpose." By the end of May, the dream that had once been Millbrook was dead. "It ended as it had begun," Kleps wrote, "in confusion and paradox, a seething distillation of seemingly incompatible elements representing all the great motions of human nature."

One of the last to leave the estate was longtime resident Marshall McNeil, who was arrested by a sheriff riding a horse. Along with four others, McNeil had been hiding out in the woods when the army came in. "They actually had an amphibious vehicle and a posse," he would later say. "The charges were trespassing." Forced to leave Millbrook, McNeil felt "like the whole universe was coming apart because we didn't complete the journey. Tim didn't complete the journey. I don't think any of us did. We all got insights and we worked on it and a lot of us made a lot of progress. What happened there was that there was an opening. A dimensional opening."

Long after she had left the estate, Millbrook remained for Jean McCready a sacred place, where she "was given the gift and the golden opportunity to travel inward and find out I was an immortal soul." On many occasions at Millbrook, she recalled leaving her physical body behind to travel "as a conscious point of light through many, many dimensions. And the climax for me was union with extraterrestrials." Nearly thirty years later, Rosemary Woodruff would say, "We will never finish Millbrook. I still count those sixty-four rooms in my sleep." Rudi Stern recalled, "It was truly beautiful. Truly communal. Always someone in the Meditation House, twenty-four hours a day. Doing watercolors by the fireplace. Charlie Mingus playing piano in the living room. Marshall McLuhan would be there for breakfast. The Beatles were on the telephone while Maynard Ferguson was warming up in his room upstairs. Some fantastic sculptress from Bombay had just come in and was making an exhibition of her work in the living room." And then there was the overwhelming physical beauty of the estate. "Virgin brooks, little ponds. I took acid with trees that I will never forget in my life. Glorious. Beautiful."

Out in the field one morning with Jackie Cassen, Stern looked at the big house with Buddha's face painted on it and the flags hanging down and it all seemed so beautiful to him that he thought it must be a dream. Through a large dewdrop dangling from the branch of a tree, he saw the house refracted. At "the highest most beautiful point in my life," he felt "really happy."

During the years Tim Leary called Millbrook home, chaos was the rule rather than the exception. For those who had authentic peak experiences there, journeying out of their bodies to experience another reality, the estate was paradise on earth. For others, it was a vision of hell. With the lord of the manor now heading in yet another new direction, the moment in time that had been Millbrook was over.

COME TOGETHER

CALIFORNIA,
1968–1970

I asked Timothy Leary
But he couldn't help me either . . .

—The Who, "The Seeker"

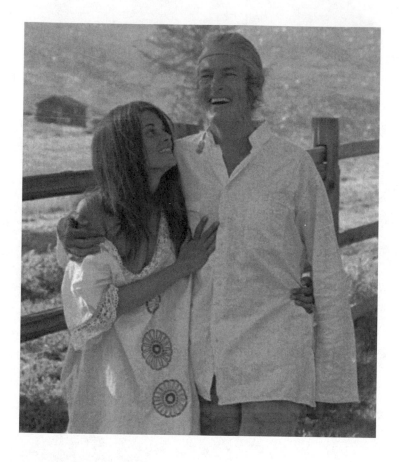

Rosemary and Timothy Leary at the Brotherhood Ranch, 1969.
Photo courtesy of the Associated Press

TWENTY-EIGHT

Long before LSD became the drug of choice in California, all that really mattered was what kind of car you drove and where you would be cruising with it on Friday night. In the early 1960s, a car club made up of working-class kids from Anaheim who called themselves the Street Sweepers became known throughout Orange County as authentic badasses. Their leader was John Griggs. Small in stature, Griggs was not only fearless but also so thoroughly hard core that he was using heroin while everyone else was doing little more than smoking grass. In time, some of the Street Sweepers became part of a loose network of small-time pot dealers who regularly did business with one another on the basis of a handshake. Back then, all the marijuana in California still came from Mexico. Just across the border in Tijuana, where sex, beer, Spanish fly, and hand-tooled leather belts could be bought for next to nothing, a cellophane-wrapped kilo (2.2 pounds) of commercial-grade marijuana cost $50. Broken down into ounces, the pot was then resold on the street in Anaheim and Garden Grove and Huntington Beach in red Prince Albert tobacco tins with a hinged lid. Always more than an ounce, a "lid" cost $10 or $15. Breaking down each kilo into thirty or thirty-five lids, with two kilos per load, a $100 investment in Tijuana could bring a return of $700 in Orange County, a tidy profit for an operation still so primitive that one dealer brought his pot into the country from Mexico by simply tossing it over a fence, going through customs, then driving back to pick it up on the California side of the border.

In 1966, knowing nothing about LSD, John Griggs and a friend ripped off some people in Hollywood at gunpoint during a drug deal gone awry. A week later, when Griggs took some of the stolen acid for the first time, he threw away his gun and ran around hollering, "This is it!" "John had a religious experience," Travis Ashbrook—a founding member of the Brotherhood of Eternal Love who was then selling pot and making surfboards just outside Seal Beach in Orange County—would later recall. "But he didn't know what it was. Other than something serious which had changed his life."

Through a Seal Beach surfer known as the Witch Doctor, Griggs and his friends began getting cocolyte, LSD in pure crystal form packaged in sealed ampoules from Lights & Co., Ltd., the pharmaceutical distributor in England to whom Richard Alpert and Tim Leary had turned in 1961 in order to supplement their diminishing supply from Sandoz. Before the Witch Doctor went off to Lompoc Prison to serve time for dealing pot, he gave his LSD connection to Griggs. Every Sunday at White's Beach in San Pedro off the Palos Verdes peninsula, young working-class guys would show up with their wives and kids to trip with Griggs. Taking ever higher doses, Griggs and his friends began having the kind of trips that had been described in detail by Alpert, Tim, and Ralph Metzner in *The Psychedelic Experience*.

In time, the scene shifted from White's Beach to Tahquitz Canyon in Palm Springs, where people assembled every Sunday to experience God on LSD. After taking acid with the group in the canyon one day, Ashbrook recalled, "I was sitting on a rock in full lotus in tears and I cried for eight hours of joy, completely released. I saw it all and I had Buddhas around me. They were just there smiling at me. I would start to say something and they would go, 'Shush! Don't talk. Just see.'" Some Sundays, as many as a hundred people took LSD by a stream on the side of a mountain. They would all lock arms, lay down, and wait for the drug to hit them. "Take it and lay down and shut up," Ashbrook remembered. "It was always that. These sessions were deeply spiritual. None of that hippie take-your-clothes-off stuff. We were all working people and college students who were there with our wives and our kids."

When Tim appeared with the Grateful Dead at the Santa Monica Civic Auditorium, the group went to see him. Individual members had heard Alpert speak in LA. But there was no direct contact until Griggs journeyed to Millbrook. Like a pilgrim beside the way, he sat patiently outside the big iron front gates until they let him in. When Griggs returned to Orange County, he brought with him a copy of Tim's *Psychedelic Prayers*. For the brothers-to-be, it was as though the gospel had just arrived. "That was the next step," Ashbrook recalled. "This was the new text. It was the guide. It clicked."

Griggs and his friends moved to Modjeska Canyon on Santiago Peak, also called Saddleback Mountain. "We pretty much took over Modjeska Canyon," Ashbrook said. "We rented damn near every house in it. A lot of us were quitting our jobs and letting our hair grow. We still didn't know anything about hippies. It was happening up in San Francisco and in Greenwich Village, but we didn't know about that. John got in contact with Richard Alpert and he came to Modjeska. We had a Zen roshi come up and we would meditate with him." The group hired an attorney and filed papers to incorporate as a church. California's Franchise Tax Board granted the Brotherhood of Eternal Love tax-exempt status as a religious organization. With cocolyte no longer available, the group began taking White Lightning, the brand of acid handed out by Owsley Stanley in Golden Gate Park at the Human Be-In. "We all liked it," Ashbrook said, "but we knew it was different. It wasn't quite as pure. The experiences weren't as clear. They were good but White Lightning had a little bit of speed in it. And then it went from White Lightning to Blue Cheer to Purple K. Every week, it was the color or the flavor of the week." Going up to San Francisco, members of the Brotherhood bought LSD in bulk from the Hells Angels, then functioning as distributors. They brought it back to the canyon and capped it up, "usually in tiny little number fives and distributed it," Ashbrook remembered. "Each one of us had our little subgroup. John had a rule. Don't give it to anybody unless you take it with them the first time. And then after that, if you want to sell it to them, fine. But don't give it to a soul without taking it with them the first time."

When the big stone building they had been using as their church in Modjeska Canyon burned down, the Brotherhood moved to Laguna Beach. In 1967, Laguna Beach was a beach town with a reputation as a haven for artists and drug dealers. In nearby Laguna Canyon, the brothers rented houses in a two-block neighborhood around the intersection of Woodland Drive and Roosevelt Avenue that was known as Dodge City. They grew their hair long, planted vegetable gardens, and surfed. At 670 South Coast Highway in the Sleepy Hollow section of town, they opened Mystic Arts World, later described by Tim as "the ultimate head shop, a veritable L.L. Bean Supermarket of hippie gear." Rosemary, who first visited Mystic Arts after her wedding at Joshua Tree, said "They had a bead shop, they had a juice bar, the women were making clothes. It was heterosexual couples in a community and they looked up to Tim and admired him. John Griggs was charismatic, wonderful, happy. A smart working-class man but supercharged with spiritual energy." In *Flashbacks,* Tim would describe Griggs as, "a wiry blond lad, quick as a mink, resourceful, unconventional, and deeply religious."

When Tim met the rest of the Brotherhood, he realized Griggs had "hand-picked this group of uneducated young couples, all children of that swarm of Okies who had filled up the valleys stretching out from LA." Groomed, in Tim's words, "to become gas-station attendants or wives of gas-station attendants," they were "the labor pool that would build and service the huge stainless steel tanks in the Schlitz and Budweiser breweries popping up all over the Southland." Transformed by their new sacraments of grass and acid, "they threw themselves into the role of apostles . . . 'Stay high and love God' was their motto." Although Tim would later recall his time with the Brotherhood with unalloyed affection, Stew Albert, the co-founder of the Yippies (from "Youth International Party") who described himself as "a perennial unindicted co-conspirator, the Harold Stassen of the revolution," offered another view. "I met some of them," he said, "and they were not very cerebral. Leary once described them as sort of brainwashed white lumpen. They were not his peers." The Brotherhood took to Tim immediately. "We were getting high with him and Rosemary and Jackie and Susan," Ashbrook recalled. "Age didn't mean a damn thing. We all looked to Tim as a teacher. I had a little deeper thing for him. To me, he was guru. A father figure. Everything."

Although the Brotherhood was always distinctly apolitical, it was during his time with them in Laguna Beach that Tim finally took note of the Vietnam War. "I remember us being on our honeymoon in Laguna Beach," Rosemary recalled, "sitting on a cliff by the ocean with Tim. This awful shark-nosed military plane cruised by and I had a vision of Vietnam and people dying and napalm. Although it was a bit late in the game, I knew we had to do whatever we could to stop the war." When Tim learned that Dick Gregory, the black comedian and political activist whom he had first met at Millbrook, had called for a march on the Democratic National Convention in Chicago in August to force President Lyndon Johnson to stop the war in Vietnam, he decided to get in touch with Gregory to enlist in the cause. Tim proposed funding "a nudist parade through the streets of Chicago." By demonstrating without clothes, Tim believed people could protest the war without creating more violence. In mid-February 1968, Tim and Rosemary met with Jerry Rubin, Abbie Hoffman, Stew Albert, Paul Krassner, Allen Katzman of *The East Village Other,* Bob Fass of WBAI radio, and others in a counterculture summit in Peggy Hitchcock's penthouse apartment in New York. Tim defined the political struggle as completely generational and declared, "Bolshevik bomb throwing was out. The new bombs were neurological. You don't blow up the Czar's palace. You blow minds." He viewed the demonstration in Chicago as a public relations ploy designed to keep Johnson from accepting the Democratic nomination. "The aim of the game is to have no one go to Chicago in August. A deserted stage set."

Tim and Rosemary dined at a friend's house with Dick Gregory, then appearing at the Village Gate. In the ten months since Tim had seen him at Millbrook, Gregory had transformed himself from an edgy, chain-smoking, paunchy comedian wearing a black silk suit with a Countess Mara tie into a lean and bearded vegetarian in blue work clothes. He seemed, as Tim later described him, serene and decisive, "in poised control of gigantic, internal spiritual energy. He had become a saint and he felt secure with it." Tim was also impressed by Gregory's decision to offer his name as a candidate for president on the Peace and Freedom Party ticket. In a year's time, though for much different reasons, Tim would make a similar gesture.

After the meeting in New York, Tim and Rosemary flew to Chicago for a lecture. They were met at the airport by a local Yippie who confidently said he could arrange anything they needed in Chicago. Tim asked him to "rustle up a cow, a lantern, and a televised press conference in 24 hours." The next morning, the Yippie picked Tim and Rosemary up at their hotel and drove them to the cow barn at the Lincoln Park Zoo. Several police cars and TV trucks were parked nearby. Posing with a lantern alongside "Mrs. Leary," Tim announced to the press that this time, they were going to "light up" Chicago rather than burn it down. LBJ would not be able to walk the streets in August unless he was "barefoot with a flower in his hair." When a cameraman asked Rosemary to kick over the lantern, she just grinned. That night, six thousand people listened to Tim speak on the Champaign-Urbana campus of the University of Illinois.

On March 25, 1968, the New American Library published ten thousand copies of Tim's autobiography *High Priest.* Dedicated to Susan and Jack with original artwork by psychedelic artists Alan Atwell and Michael

Green, the book was organized as a series of sixteen trips, beginning with Tim's nervous collapse in Spain in January 1959 and ending with his forced departure from Zihuatanejo in June 1962. Each "trip" was introduced with a hexagram and an accompanying verse from the *I Ching*. A highly impressionistic work—the margins are often trespassed—*High Priest* was an attempt to subvert the linear nature of the printed page. In his acknowledgments, Tim wrote: "The psychedelic revolution is a religious renaissance of the young, for the young, by the young . . . The authentic priests, the real prophets of this great movement are the rock-and-roll musicians." In addition to Susan and Jack, he dedicated the book to nineteen different rock groups. By the time the book appeared, many of them had already disbanded.

In *The New Yorker,* Hendrik Hertzberg would later describe 1968 as "a year of fearful portents and strange exhilarations. Everything—on every scale, from the global to the personal, seemed to be coming unmoored. The sweep of events was like a hurricane." Although the cheery optimism of flower power and the summer of love was long gone, the New American Library chose to market *High Priest* as "a sacred testament to LSD and its miracles." The advertising campaign only served to reinforce the fact that the book was dead on arrival.

On March 31, 1968, six days after *High Priest* was published in hardback, President Johnson announced that he would not accept the nomination of his party in Chicago in August. "An era had ended," Tim would write later that year in the *Berkeley Barb.* "The hateful circle started at Dallas was closed. LBJ's drop-out was as mind-blowing as his tragic accession. Chicago was now irrelevant. [Eugene] McCarthy and [Bobby] Kennedy anti-climactic . . . The current was being turned off the old circuits. A new historical cycle had begun."

Four days later, Martin Luther King Jr., who had come out strongly against the war, was killed in Memphis. Forty-six people died in the riots that ensued in more than a hundred cities across America. Summing up the state of a nation in which the Tet offensive was termed by the establishment, in Tim's words, to be "a victory"; Martin Luther King had been killed by "a lone psychotic"; black leaders like H. Rap Brown and Eldridge Cleaver had been jailed; and the New York Yankees found themselves in last place, Tim wrote: "Wow! Have you ever heard of an acid-trip crazier than that?"

———————

At a gathering of Yippie leaders on Second Avenue in New York at the beginning of April, Tim brought Abbie Hoffman and Jerry Rubin a message
from Allen Ginsberg. "A new model is needed. Neither Kennedy nor Mc-
Carthy knows what to do. They are open to suggestions. But they still
want to patch up the old machine. And it won't go no more." Tim also
brought what he called a "a new Declaration of Independence" in which
he proposed that "Everyone should start their own nation. Write their
own Declaration of Evolution. Thousands of new states." When someone at the meeting asked, "And what about Chicago?" Tim responded,
"Call off the militant teeny-boppers. Call a constitutional convention.
Invite every tribe in the country to send representatives. Start a new political game so that men and women can grow freely and in peace."

Before Tim's plan could be discussed, everyone's attention was di-
verted by the news that something was "brewing at Columbia." Jumping
into cabs, Abbie Hoffman and Jerry Rubin headed uptown to lend their
media presence to a student sit-in that would soon inspire similar actions
at universities all over the world. Enraged by Columbia's decision to build
a gymnasium in Harlem without allowing the black community access to
it, student demonstrators had occupied Hamilton Hall and Low Library.
Led by the militant campus chapter of Students for a Democratic Society,
the sit-in continued until New York police arrived. Using tear gas to clear
the buildings, they clubbed and kicked protestors as they dragged them
down stone steps in full view of the media. Then they arrested everyone
in sight with long hair. The first nationally televised police riot of the era
resulted in the suspension of all classes at Columbia for the rest of the
year. Though Tim had once been a member in good standing of the academic community, his newfound association with those who advocated
political revolution caused him to view the events at Columbia with a
kind of bemused approval. "These kids won't play the game fairly," he
wrote ironically in the *Berkeley Barb* later that year. "They don't make specific selfish demands. They don't want cheaper textbooks or fatter fellow-
ships or later hours for dating on the weekends. They're insane. They
want to take over the whole gold-plated, billion dollar system that we
worked so hard to set up." He then went on to rhapsodize about the
"world-wide electronically amplified network of the young. Mario Savio
starts a beat in Berkeley. Jerry Rubin brings it up the river to Chicago.
Mark Rudd moves it along at Columbia. Hey listen to Red Rudi in Berlin.
Now Cohn-Bendit moves on to do a set in Paris. The Shakespearean

put-on at San Francisco State. The BEATLES sing it for the ROLLING STONES. The terrestrial conspiracy of dna. The plot of earth. The love-freedom network. The process. Turn it in. Do your thing. Don't belong. Don't be-long." Deciding that he and Rosemary no longer belonged in Laguna Beach where, as Tim would later write in *Flashbacks*, they could "feel the eyes of the police upon us," he began making plans to move back into his old house at 1230 Queens Road in Berkeley.

On Friday, April 26, Charles Slack, Tim's former Harvard colleague, left his "tiny, dirty, temporary magazine office" on LaGuardia Place in Greenwich Village and strolled around the corner to the Village Gate, where a farewell party for Tim and Rosemary—admission $2.00—was scheduled to begin at 10:00 P.M. Slack had just been hired to write the advice column for *Eye*, the Hearst Corporation's brand-new glossy magazine designed expressly for the younger generation. "I kept telling Helen Gurley Brown that the people who read *Eye* magazine don't have any problems," Slack recalled, "and she said, 'Look at this mail.' Their only real problem was that they couldn't get high anymore, no matter how hard they tried." Seeing that the line outside the Village Gate wound across the street, Slack repaired to the Lion's Head, the legendary watering hole of writers and literary types, where, as he would later write in *Timothy Leary, the Madness of the Sixties, and Me*, he began to "drown my jealousies in vodka tonics. By midnight, I had had quite a few vodka tonics." Slack then walked into the Village Gate. "Bodies lay zonked out all over the floor," he wrote. "That old locker-room odor of stale locoweed hung in the dusty air like smoke from a burning ghat. Was I the only one up? Certainly I was the only one drunk—a lush among the pot-heads." Because of the way Slack was dressed, those inside immediately suspected him of being a narc. They were about to throw him out when Tim came to his rescue, calling out his name and hugging him. Tim then invited Slack to accompany him and Rosemary to California. Slack accepted, thereby embarking on a series of stoned seriocomic misadventures in which everyone, himself included, seemed more than a little mad.

"We flew first class," Slack later recalled. "The only thing I remember is that when they gave us the earphones, which were made out of plastic tubes, I apparently stuck one in a drink and made a hookah out of it and was smoking through it." When Slack asked Tim whether all the police attention he was attracting would not eventually result in his being sent to jail, Slack later wrote that Tim replied, "The crucifixion is a two-thousand-year-old trip and not for me, I'll never go to jail. The jail is not built that can hold me. I am not a martyr—get that straight. I am no believer in suffering. I am a pure hedonist and I want to have a ball—get high and have fun and this conversation is getting dragged down in a morass of questions and answers."

Jack and Susan greeted their father at the San Francisco airport. "Susan was pretty," Slack wrote, "with a fine plump figure, and Jackie was healthy and handsome in high, wide Prince Valiant bangs." As they waited for their bags, Tim sat down on a baggage cart and began speaking to students and hippies who crowded around him. Some shouted questions at him. Repeating the message he had delivered to the Yippies in New York, Tim announced, "I am going to start my own country." After a stop at a boutique to buy Slack some clothes that would make him look less like a narc, they headed for Michael Bowen's house where Slack saw "the cream of San Francisco's freak community . . . It was a gathering of extras from DeMille, a bawdy house from the Gold Rush, an amateur production of Dante's *Inferno*."

Having left his rented car at the party with Tim, Slack took a taxi the next day to Tim's house in Berkeley. On the mat-covered deck, Tim tried in vain to instruct Slack in the intricacies of yoga and tantric sex. As they headed back into the city to visit the Diggers in the Haight, Slack later wrote that he asked Tim, "What is the Leary secret of getting to be famous?" Impatiently, Tim responded, "Charlie, Charlie, these are exactly the wrong questions to be asking at this point." Slack stubbornly insisted that, as an old friend, he had a right to know the answer. Tim replied, "Faust." "I didn't know if it was facetious conversation," Slack recalled. "He sold his soul for fame. I think he did. He loved being famous." At a party held in Slack's honor at Tim's house the next night, the guest list included the novelist and poet Richard Brautigan. Slack recalled taking "some drug [quite possibly STP] that everybody took back then that made you stiff. You could maintain a position for a long time. When I came to, I was hanging from the rafters as the party was going on down below. I was suspended up there. With my arms and legs entwined around these beams. Holding on to the rafters. Watching the party go on down below." The next day, Slack returned to New York in tourist class.

Using the house in Berkeley as his base, Tim continued traveling around America, earning his living on the lecture circuit. Long before Chicago Eight defendant Tom Hayden identified what he called the "speaker-leader phenomenon," which made stars out of the leading counterculture figures, Tim was a pioneer of the lifestyle. His view of what was going on in America was restricted to what he saw on his way to and from the airport, the questions he answered after his lecture, and whatever happened at the party that followed. Like a rock star, Tim appeared, performed, and then left. Between his own life and the lives of those more than twenty-five years younger than he, there was virtually no connection. Unlike many of the young men to whom he lectured, Tim was not subject to the draft. Yet as one of the few members of the older generation who was willing to speak to them on their own terms, they still looked to him for guidance about the war. Although he had refused to testify before him at a Senate subcommittee hearing, Tim now believed that only Robert Kennedy could end the conflict. "It was obvious that Bobby would defeat McCarthy in the primaries and overwhelm the pathetic campaign of LBJ loyalist Hubert Humphrey," Tim would later write in *Flashbacks*. "It was a cinch that tousle-haired Bobby, the new idol of the young and the hopeful, would sweep to the White House. And Bobby's victory would carry with him a slate of candidates devoted to peace and the new politics."

On June 5, Bobby Kennedy was shot to death in the kitchen of the Ambassador Hotel in Los Angeles. With Hubert Humphrey now virtually guaranteed the Democratic nomination, the Youth International Party announced its plans for a "festival of life" to take place from August 25 to August 30 in Grant Park in Chicago at the same time as "the National Death (Democratic) Convention." In one of their broadsides, they wrote: "Chicago is a stage . . . it will be a natural energy center for guerilla theater."

Tim predicted that with LBJ and Mayor Daley working together to ensure Humphrey's nomination, "an ugly confrontation loomed." In the weeks before the convention, he later wrote in *Flashbacks*, "I argued passionately with the Yippies and other radical activists against moving into enemy turf in Chicago. Allen Ginsberg, who had emerged as an eloquent anti-war spokesman, agreed that the inevitable violence would hurt the cause of peace. But he felt some strange obsession to participate. I couldn't understand why we should go to Chicago to get beat up publicly and insure Nixon's election." Tim's desires "to quiet down Chicago and support Humphrey were not completely unselfish. If Nixon won, especially if he won on the basis of a reaction to youthful violence, then I would be in a lot of trouble. I was out on appeal bond facing decades of prison. When the purge came, it would certainly focus on drugs because control of the American consciousness was and still is the issue."

By leaning toward supporting Humphrey and refusing to align himself with the radical left, Tim created a new set of enemies. The Motherfuckers, a former street gang from the Lower East Side of Manhattan, issued a poster denouncing Tim for limiting the revolution. The Progressive Labor faction of the Students for a Democratic Society claimed he was a CIA agent pushing LSD on the movement as part of an imperialist plot.

In mid-June, John Griggs flew to Berkeley to invite Tim and Rosemary to visit the ranch that the Brotherhood had purchased in the San Jacinto Mountains above Palm Springs with the proceeds from the sale of eighty-eight pounds of hashish smuggled into the country from Afghanistan. "Their haven lay in a spectacularly beautiful niche," Tim wrote in *Flashbacks*. "The access road veered from the state highway through a locked gate and five miles of deserted government land to a valley watered by eight streams from the surrounding peaks. There was a small lake, a rambling ranch house, corrals, a huge barn, tack-houses, and cabins. On a ridge above the valley stood a new comfortable cottage for Rosemary and me." "We told him, 'You just stay up here and write,'" Travis Ashbrook remembered. "'Go do your lecture tours and write and don't worry about anything else and don't even talk to us about where the drugs are.' He never had anything do with any of the acid or the smuggling or any of it. That was what was so inaccurate about people calling us 'Timothy Leary's Brotherhood.' He'd know there was a load coming but that was it."

Although Tim remained in constant contact with the Yippie organizers of the Chicago demonstrations, he tried in vain to deflect attention from what they were planning by trying to set up a counterconvention in San Francisco or a series of love-ins around the country. Anita Hoffman, who with her husband, Abbie, played a key role in organizing for Chicago, recalled, "Anyone who was going there knew they faced being beaten up by the cops. Tim pulled out about two weeks before the convention because he didn't want to be encouraging young people to come and get their heads beaten."

While tripping at the Brotherhood ranch one day in August, Tim, Rosemary, Michael Hollingshead—now also in residence there—and others decided to go for a hike in the mountains to find a cave filled with Indian relics and potsherds. Three days later, suffering from heat stroke, they stumbled onto a trailer in the middle of nowhere. A long-haired hippie gave them guava juice and drove them to Palm Springs where, as Rosemary recalled, "The Democratic National Convention was in full color on television and they were smashing heads." When Tim learned what was going on, he felt "the animal fear in my spine." Unlike many who witnessed the violence on television, Tim was not radicalized by the experience. He was worried about how it might affect his future.

A month later, the Moody Blues, an English rock band who had made the transition from pop rock to psychedelia, released an album entitled *In Search of the Lost Chord*. The fifth cut was called "Legend of a Mind": "Timothy Leary's dead / No, no, no, no. / He's outside looking in . . . Ti-mo-thy Lear-y . . ." In a footnote in *Flashbacks,* Leary later wrote, "Many people have sought to read cosmic significance into these lyrics." In a *Rolling Stone* interview, Ray Thomas, who wrote the song, said: "The only person I ever met who really knew what I was saying in that song was Timothy Leary himself. I was taking the piss out of him, ribbing him in that song. I saw the 'astral plane' as some gaily painted little biplane: you pay your two bucks, and he'll take you around the bay for a little flight. Tim laughed about it. I laughed about it, but everybody else sat around saying, 'Oh man, that's so heavy.'" Nonetheless, the song confirmed that Tim was now a full-fledged pop star.

On election night 1968, Tim and Rosemary drove to Idylwild to watch the returns. Because Hubert Humphrey had been gaining steadily in the polls, Tim now believed the voters would chose him over the man he mockingly called "the new Nixon." Distressed, Tim watched Nixon win by less than half a million votes on a TV in a hippie health food store. By working against Humphrey, the New Left had helped put Richard Milhous Nixon, whom Tim called "a World War II veteran burning with Cold War Fever, the Legionnaire's Disease," into the White House.

TWENTY-NINE

Pink-and-green flowers dot the front cover of *The Politics of Ecstasy*, Tim Leary's collection of essays, interviews, and lectures published in the fall of 1968 by G. P. Putnam's Sons. In profile on the back cover, with the Southern California sunshine illuminating the sharp planes and angles of his rugged face and his long silver-gray hair trailing over the open collar of his white linen shirt, Tim stares off into the distance. Behind him on the beach in Laguna, Rosemary, also in white linen, raises her hand to three seagulls in flight. Tim dedicated the book to Abbie Hoffman. "The thing I liked about Abbie," Tim would later write, "was that he kept changing, taking risks, dropping acid, reprogramming his head. He became the ultimate contradiction—a psychedelic socialist."

Most of the material in *The Politics of Ecstasy* had already appeared in *Psychedelic Review, Bulletin of the Atomic Scientists, Esquire, Harvard Review, Playboy, The Realist, Evergreen Review,* and the *San Francisco Oracle*. Tim had first used the title for a lecture at New York's Town Hall in 1966. The book begins with a speech entitled "The Seven Tongues of God" that Tim gave on August 30, 1963, to a meeting of Lutheran psychologists at the annual convention of the American Psychological Association. It included his *Playboy* interview, now called "She Comes in Colors," a title suggested "with admiring thanks to the Rolling Stones" by Rosemary. The book also contained Tim's essay on Hermann Hesse; his somewhat embarrassing paean to Augustus Owsley Stanley III entitled, "God's Secret Agent A.O.S. 3"; an epitaph for Aldous Huxley; a discussion of former IFIF stalwart Lisa Bieberman (here called Lisa Lieberman); a blank-verse poem; Tim's speech to the LSD Conference in Berkeley in June 1966; and the declaration of evolution that he presented to the Yippies in New York City shortly before the Democratic National Convention in Chicago. No longer advising people to start their own religion, Tim was now counseling them to create their own political system by banding together into nonviolent tribes of no more than 360 people, each of which would be governed by anyone between the ages of fourteen and forty-nine. Exactly how these tribes would support themselves, Tim did not say. He concluded the book with the admonition, "Reader, write your own *Politics of Ecstasy.*"

In a review of the book in *The Village Voice* on December 12, Allen Ginsberg called Tim "a hero of American consciousness" and a "humane & frank Democratic Boddhisatva [*sic*]-teacher of the uses of LSD in America" who "took on himself the noble task of announcing the evidence of his senses despite the scary contumely of fellow academicians, the dispraising timorous irony of scientific 'professionals,' the stupidity meanness self-serving cowardice and hollow vanity of bureaucratic personnel from Harvard Yard to Mexico City to Washington . . ." The poet also noted that events which had transpired since Tim had written his book "charge the author's handiwork with prophetic enormity."

On the same day that Ginsberg's ringing endorsement appeared in *The Village Voice*, Robert J. Haft, a securities lawyer, whom Tim would later describe "as the Vince Lombardi of Wall Street" appeared before the United States Supreme Court to argue that Tim's conviction in Laredo should be struck down on constitutional grounds. Haft based his appeal on a finding by the Supreme Court that the Federal Gambling Tax, an act requiring illegal bookies to purchase a $25 gambling stamp, violated the Fifth Amendment's guarantee against self-incrimination. Therefore, the marijuana tax should also be unconstitutional. Haft emerged from the courtroom after the hearing with a smile on his face. "Nine to nothing," he told Tim. "We think we shut them out."

While he waited for the Supreme Court to decide his case, Tim had never been busier. Thanks in no small part to the televised riots in Chicago during the previous summer, the counterculture had grown by leaps and bounds. The demand for Tim as a guest lecturer was greater than ever. In the fall of 1968, there was no easier way to incite not only parents but also administrators at institutions of higher learning everywhere than by inviting Timothy Leary to speak on campus for a generous fee. With his college appearances "so controversial that even scheduling the event involved hot debates between students and faculty/administration," the speakers bureau representing him created an academic framework by pairing him in a series of debates with his old opponent, Dr. Sidney Cohen of UCLA. "Oh the excitement of those days! TV cameras whirred as airplane doors opened. Bulbs flashed. Psychedelic banners waved. Auditoriums jammed with students. Clouds of balloons floated to the ceiling. Flowers. Rebel whoops. Wild costumes!" Not everyone who came to hear Tim was receptive to his message. "Political militants would sometimes denounce me for distracting young people from armed revolution. And sometimes older people would shout that I was the anti-Christ, a devil, a new Hitler seducing the young. It was all good theater."

To those in Washington, it was somewhat more than that. Tim seemed to have not only a great deal of very real power but also his own constituency, and so represented as much of a threat to the established order as the Black Panther Party or the predominantly white, middle-class Yippies who conspired to bring about the demonstrations in Chicago. In the eyes of the Nixon administration, Tim was an enemy of the state.

In the fall and winter of 1968, however, none of this was apparent. *The Politics of Ecstasy* had received a favorable critical response. The college lecture circuit provided Tim with a steady income. His legal team felt he stood a good chance of having his Laredo bust overturned. His beautiful young wife adored him. As always when everything was going his way, Tim could not resist the temptation to turn life upside down again.

For Tim Leary, the Christmas season was always the most dangerous period of the year, the time when something possessed him to move, often with disastrous consequences. It was three days before Christmas in 1965 when Tim, Rosemary, Jack, and Susan were busted in Laredo. On the day after Christmas 1968—in the very same dark-blue Ford station wagon—it happened all over again.

Suffering from cabin fever, Tim decided he needed to leave the Brotherhood ranch to "enjoy civilization for a week before the winter lecture tour." Before they headed off to Berkeley with Jack and Susan in the backseat, Tim asked Rosemary if she thought they should take some of their Christmas presents with them. "People were always pressing things on us," she would later recall. "We had received some really nice presents for Christmas so he said, 'Well, let's take them with us.' Which meant that I would carry them. I remember a little pipe and a little hash and grass and LSD and diet pills. Ritalin, which we called a psychic energizer. Based on Indian herbs, as I recall." Rosemary packed up all their gifts into a little stash. Jack, who at the time "was being rather difficult and rebellious had his own stash," Rosemary remembered. Coming out of the mountains, they stopped in Hemet to take the chains off the wheels of the car. As Rosemary was calling her mother from a phone booth to say she and Tim might spend the night with her, a revolving red light came up behind her. "For the first time," she recalled, "I felt real fear. My stomach just froze up. I was so frightened and I thought, 'I really shouldn't have this stuff with me. We shouldn't have brought it.' And then I realized it was a snow plow." After dropping Susan off at a friend's house, Tim drove into Laguna Canyon where friends of Jack's lived. "Although we asked him not to," Rosemary would later say, "Jackie was persistent in smoking all the way down. We were troubled that he had a stash, but he was a teenager and he was ignoring us. So we pulled into the canyon and Jackie was fumbling in the back to get his gear together and a police car came up."

With just fifty-five minutes left in his four-to-midnight shift, patrolman Neil Purcell, whom Tim would later describe as "a squat, darkcomplected man with puffed cheeks and a pencil-thin Gilbert Roland mustache," was driving his black-and-white Laguna Beach Police Department patrol car on Woodland Drive when he saw a vehicle stopped in the middle of the road with its headlights on. Jack later told Tim's biographer John Bryan that everyone who lived on this dead-end street was a dealer and that Laguna was such a small town that when the cop got out of his car, he immediately recognized the big blue Ford station wagon. Purcell remembered the story differently. "They were facing me," Purcell recalled, "and I was waiting for the car to move because the street wasn't wide enough for two vehicles to pass right there. I could have if he was off to the far right but he wasn't. His headlights were shining toward me and mine were shining toward his car. I couldn't tell who was in the car, what type of car it was, or anything else because of the headlights."

After waiting a few seconds for the car to move, Purcell pulled up alongside it. "Now I could see it was a station wagon. There appeared to be three people in the car. I took my flashlight and I flashed it on the driver and I saw a gray-haired individual. I could tell there was a female in the right front passenger seat. In the back was an individual on all fours and he had his face pressed against the left rear window facing me. This person had long hair, appeared young, and had the largest pupils of anybody you could imagine. He looked like an animal. There was no color left in his eyes. Just big black pupils with the whites around them." Tim told Rosemary to roll up the windows and lock the doors. "There was a window of opportunity," she recalled. "Had I gotten out with the stash in my hand, I could have thrown it away in any of the bushes." From his patrol car, Purcell saw Tim keep Jack from trying to jump into the front seat. "I got out and came right up to the window on the driver's side. I could see this person pushing him back and I don't think he even knew I was there, because he was not looking at me. I tapped on the window again and he rolled it down about six inches. I could smell the odor of burned marijuana. And I said, 'What's the problem here?' And he said, 'Oh, nothing, Officer. Nothing. We're just leaving.' I said, 'Well, just a moment. May I see your driver's license?' And he said, 'Okay.'" When Purcell looked at Tim's driver's license, he said, "Whoo, boy."

Working as a patrolman in Laguna Beach since the first of September, Purcell had by Christmas already made more than two hundred narcotics arrests, many of them for smoking marijuana in public on the beach at sunset. Twenty-eight years old, Purcell had been born and raised in nearby Newport Beach where for seven years he served on the police force, eventually becoming part of a plainclothes vice, narcotics, and special-assignment felony unit working to "entice and entrap cruising homosexuals hustling the beaches." Before that, Purcell had attended Orange Coast College where some members of the Brotherhood of Eternal Love also went. In an article about the Brotherhood of Eternal Love entitled "The Strange Case of the Hippie Mafia" in *Rolling Stone,* Joe Eszterhas portrayed Purcell as a "gung ho, rulebook cop who proselytized among his colleagues about the moral decay of America. He didn't like long hair. He didn't like girls walking around with their tits popping out. He considered marijuana and LSD near the root of a generational corruption. And he could not comprehend why the City of Laguna Beach allowed a man like Timothy Leary to pollute its beaches, infecting the young with that contagious corruption."

With Tim's license in his hand, Purcell returned to his car to call for follow-up units in what had become a possible narcotics investigation. When he got back to the station wagon, Tim said, "Officer, can I have my license? We'd like to go." Purcell replied, "I'd like to ask you a few questions, Mr. Leary. What are you doing here parked in the center of the street? I came in and I gave you ample time to move and you didn't." Tim told him that he had just dropped off his daughter, Susan. When Purcell asked him where, Tim said at the home of Bobby Andrews. "I knew Fat

Bobby," Purcell would later recall. "So I said, 'Well, I'd like you to step out of the car.' And he said, 'What for? What do I have to get out of the car for?' And I said, 'Mr. Leary, I'm conducting a narcotics investigation. I smelled the odor of burned marijuana.' And he started arguing with me: 'You haven't got probable cause.' I said, 'I do have probable cause by my observations.'"

With two more black-and-whites now on the scene, Purcell got Tim to step out of the car. "And he started all this stuff," Purcell recalled. "'I'm gonna call my lawyer, George Chula.' Now I knew George Chula only too well already from both Newport and Laguna Beach and I said, 'You'll have your chance to do that but right now I have a right to do what I'm doing.' Then I got John [Jack Leary] out of the car and he was absolutely stoned. He could hardly stand up. He just stood there wavering and carrying on. I did a pat-down search of Leary and of course he really objected to that. He got on this probable-cause stuff and I didn't find anything on him."

Inside the station wagon, Purcell reached into the pullout ashtray and found "two little marijuana roaches. I took them out and I said, 'I found narcotics in your car.' And he said, 'Let's see. Let's see.' I opened my hand and I held it away from me and he made a reach for it and I closed my hand. And he said, 'You planted that! You planted that!' Basically, I started laughing. I said, 'Of all people to accuse an officer of planting marijuana? You? Gimme a break!'"

"Tim got out to talk to him," Rosemary later recalled, "and the cop went into the ashtray, or pretended to, and produced two skinny flat joints. We had never seen such skinny flat joints in all our life. These were not our joints. We rolled big ones in those days. Spliffs. These were like the skinniest New York joints you have ever seen when the grass is very low and no one has seen any for a long time. The cop had them in his wallet. Like a flattened condom in the wallet. Flattened joints." Jack Leary told John Bryan "the two roaches were probably there. I don't think they were planted because Timothy had been smoking in the car. I remember when we got into town, I said, 'Well, we should roll down the windows so we can get the smell of pot out of the car.'"

Purcell put the roaches into his pocket and informed Tim that since they were found in the ashtray and he was driving the car, he was now under arrest. Purcell then went up to Rosemary who informed him that he could not search her without a female matron present. Since there was no female officer on the scene, Purcell asked for her purse. "She kind of clenched it up to herself so I just grabbed it," Purcell recalled, "and I said, 'I'm taking your purse. Please hand me your purse.' I took the purse from her and it was then that I saw it was a hat." Rosemary put her hat with the stash inside it on her head. "Some bottle went thunk! And hit my head," she would later recall. "And the cop said, 'Let me see the hat.' In the hat was the pipe. And a plaque of hash with the Brotherhood seal on it. My thought was, 'Thank God Susan isn't here.'" Looking into the hat, Purcell saw "various forms of prescription drugs. All kinds of pills that weren't in a bottle. A chunk of hashish with the word 'love' on it, a green cloth purse with marijuana, and two dozen tabs of acid." He then searched Jack. Although his shirt and pants pockets were clean, he wore a long-sleeve plaid flannel shirt. "I could feel lumps in his shirt," Purcell remembered, "and if I squeezed them hard enough, they were actually breaking. So I thought, 'This has gotta be hash.' I opened up his shirt and he actually had little pockets inside the shirt and he had chunks of hash in there. And it was a different type of hash than what Rosemary had. What Rosemary had was more like the Afghanistan hash. The shoe leather. We called it 'sole' hash. His was the real light kind that broke up easily."

Purcell informed Rosemary and Jack that they too were now under arrest and about to be transported to the Laguna Beach city jail for booking, "Leary just came unglued. Not physically. Just mouth-y. 'You wait till George Chula hears about this! You violated my rights! You violated my wife's rights!' On and on and on." Cuffing Tim, Rosemary, and Jack, Purcell put them in three separate police cars. He then made arrangements for Tim's blue Ford station wagon to be towed away.

At the station, Tim insisted that he had a right to make a phone call. "No, you don't," Purcell told him. "By California law, once you are booked, within three hours of your booking, you have the right to make three telephone calls, and that's when you'll make your calls." Purcell recalled, "I had Rosemary seated with a female clerk watching her just outside the booking area. I had John [Jack] in the booking area and Leary right at the booking desk. As I was booking Leary in, I noticed John get naked. Totally naked. Back then, more with women than guys, they would strip themselves because they loved to be naked under the influence of acid. So he got naked and then he started masturbating. And he masturbated, and he masturbated, and he didn't stop. I said to Leary, 'Look at your son there. Jesus, look what you've done to him. All your turn on, tune in, and drop out bullshit.' He turned around and looked and he started laughing. He yelled to Rosemary. 'Rosemary! Johnny! Johnny's beating off!' She had a laugh. And then he said, 'He's just bored with all this stuff.' I said, 'Oh. He's just bored?'"

After booking Tim and Rosemary, Purcell tried to book Jack but, as Purcell remembered, he was "nothing but a zombie beating off. We couldn't do anything with him. We put him back in the cell. Naked. We tried to give him jail clothes—nothing. He sat back in there in that cell and masturbated all night. The next day, this kid was still doing this. It was three days before we could get him in front of the judge."

Jack remained in jail but George Chula, the Brotherhood lawyer, quickly bailed out Tim and Rosemary. The day after the bust, Tim's new attorney had reassuring news for him. "Everyone around the courthouse knows what happened. The officer that busted you is notorious for planting evidence. We'll get the case thrown out in the preliminary hearing." Tim then asked Chula—whom he never identified by name in his autobiography—what the penalty for possession of two roaches was. Six months to ten years, Chula told him. Then he repeated that there was no real reason for Tim to worry. "We'll beat this if we have to take it to the Supreme Court." Tim wondered aloud whether this arrest would not give the federal government an excuse to pull his appeal bond on the Laredo bust. Chula replied, "They don't need any excuses. When they want you jugged, they'll do it."

Less than forty-eight hours after the bust, Tim encountered Purcell again. On "routine patrol," Purcell saw Tim pull into a motel driveway on South Coast Highway in that same blue Ford station wagon. A short time later, accompanied by two friends, Tim emerged from the motel carrying a rectangular package. As Purcell followed the car north on the highway, he noticed, in the words of Joe Eszterhas in *Rolling Stone,* "a burning cigarette being passed back and forth in Leary's car." Seeing that the taillights on the station wagon were faulty, Purcell "flicked his cherry top on, wailed his siren, and tried to pull Leary over." Tim kept right on driving for another half mile before stopping at the side of the road. As Purcell approached the vehicle, he saw one of Tim's friends "flick the butt away. Once again Purcell thought he would be overcome by the cloud of grass coming from the car." A police sergeant arrived on the scene as Purcell was about to arrest Tim for the second time in three days. The sergeant gave Purcell a direct command "not to arrest Leary or search the car." Angrily, Purcell told friends that the current Laguna Beach police chief was "'coddling' the Learys."

Confident that this bust would soon also vanish inside a legal system he seemed to have mastered, Tim left town and moved back into his house at 1230 Queens Road in Berkeley. On January 30, 1969, he wrote his mother and aunt May in Springfield to thank them for the clippings (no doubt about himself) they had sent. "It is all part of the insanity of the times. What can you expect from a country where Nixon and [Alabama Governor George] Wallace are allowed to have such influence and hatred increases." Tim also told his mother and maiden aunt that Susan was thriving. "Working. Going to night school studying sculpture; taking singing lessons etc. She is the sunny darling of the town—everyone loves her." Noting that *The New York Times* had "a big review" of his books, "on the whole quite favorable," Tim wrote that he had been visited for dinner during the past week by two "top scientists who run big prjcts [sic] in Washington" who "say that the climate in scientific circles is changing and they predict that I'll be invited back to Harvard in four years!!"

During February, Tim presented five seminars at the Free University of Berkeley in the Martin Luther King School Auditorium, which were open to the public for $1.00. On March 18, Tim again wrote his mother and aunt May with news of his "hasty visit to the Midwest and South" where he "ran into much opposition . . . At the University of Tennessee 4000 students went on strike because I was not allowed to speak . . . The Nixon era has brought about a wave of police repression and control. Even the most conservative students are disgusted with the same old lies, the war dragging on because of old men's pride, the ABM folly, the big-business-military rule, the continuance of the draft and the cold war for profit." In this letter, he admitted that all this was taking a toll on his home life. "We have been a bit battered. The fury of the establishment takes its toll on our morale and has weighed heavily. However, our little family has stuck together and we are blossoming through."

None of the Learys appeared in court in Orange County on April 1 for a preliminary hearing on the Laguna Beach bust. With Jackie somewhere on the road between Berkeley and New York, Tim and Rosemary decided to protect him by not appearing as well. LEARYS VANISH read the headline in the *Laguna Beach Daily Pilot*, FAMILY FORFEITS BAIL IN DRUG ARREST. South Orange County Judicial District Judge Richard Hamilton promptly issued bench warrants for their arrest. Because one of the attorneys in George Chula's firm had a scheduling conflict, the judge ordered the warrants to be held until May 6, postponing their possible imprisonment for skipping bail.

On the day Jack was scheduled to appear in court, Tim issued a wanted poster for him. "WANTED!!" it read. "By the State of California for three felonies and the State of New York for two felonies and various misdemeanors, crimes totaling over 70 years of imprisonment and by the Federal Government for Pacifism in violation of the Secret Service Law." Directly beneath the headline were two photographs of Jack. In one, he was pictured in 1964 after four arrests. In the other, taken in 1968 after twelve arrests, he was being kissed by two blond girls in two-piece bathing suits. Next to "Alias," Tim listed "Buddha, Krishna, Son of Light, Silent Jack, Adam, and Christ." Describing Jack as being "19 going on 77, conceived two billion years ago by a thunderbolt in the pre-cambrian mud," Tim called him an "apprentice Buddha, retired All-Star Jr. League Baseball player, full time searcher for his loving mate . . . He is the perfect symbol of our anguished age. A young man forced to become, against his will, a classic heroic figure of our times . . . Ask a cop or a psychiatrist and they'll tell you Jack Leary is crazy. A sad case of a fine mind ruined by bad parental upbringing, Dr. Spock, and dangerous drugs . . . I call upon the authorities of this country to let this young man alone. Let him be free to wander, to explore, to make his foolish mistakes. To find a higher wisdom than we have found. Let Jack Leary and his friends be free or our race will be enslaved." In big bold type, the broadside—a desperate love letter from a hopeless father to a lost son—demanded, "WHERE IS JACK LEARY? AND WHAT ARE WE ALL GOING TO DO ABOUT HIM?"

On May 6, Jack Leary appeared in court in Orange County and the warrant for his arrest was dropped. By then, Tim and Rosemary had left Berkeley to return to the Brotherhood ranch. Tim offered his house in Berkeley to Michael Bowen, the artist who helped organize the Human Be-In in San Francisco. "I said I would come and pick up the mail when I was out of my cabin in Healdsburg," Bowen recalled. "His instructions were, 'Just open all the letters and send me the checks.' 'What about the letters?' He said, 'Just throw them away.'"

Because Bowen's car was stuck in winter mud in the mountains, Tim loaned him the blue Ford station wagon. "One day," Bowen remembered, "I went to pick up the mail and I had some hash that I had brought back from India. As I was driving up the hill, it was a completely blue sky but I noticed one small black rain cloud and I was thinking, 'That's pretty weird.' The rain cloud was directly above Leary's house, which I could see from the road as I was coming up. On the deck, a guy in a bright pink blanket was sitting in a meditation position and I thought, 'Whoa, that's weird.' No car, no nothing." Bowen put Tim's mail into a box and was sifting through it with the key to the house in his hand. Through the open front door, he could still see the figure out on the deck. "The house was a sea of glass," Bowen recalled. "All the glass in the house had been broken. Dishes, windows, everything. A sea of glass. I was crunching in the glass and all of a sudden, I got a major danger signal so I started backing out right away. The figure turned, got up, threw the pink blanket in the air, and it was a stark naked Jackie Leary. Tim's kid. He started shrieking and running at me right through the sea of glass, barefoot. I ran to the car with the keys, jumped in, and put the key in the ignition." Still screaming, Jack jumped on the car. "He knew exactly who I was," Bowen remembered. "'Michael Bowen, you ahhhhhh!' I started the engine and he jumped off. I put it in gear to go and all of a sudden, I saw him in the rearview mirror and he was laughing insanely and saying, 'I got you!,' and he was holding the license plate. He'd ripped the steel license plate off the fucking car. Now I was in Timothy Leary's car in 1969 in Berkeley with no plates and a bunch of hashish."

THIRTY

Retreating to the mountains high above Palm Springs, Tim Leary hunkered down with Rosemary to await the Supreme Court decision that would determine his future. As Bob Dylan once wrote, time passes slowly when you're lost in a dream. Living on the Brotherhood ranch in an eighteen-foot-tall Sioux teepee with Cheyenne smoke flaps made of sailcloth translucent to the moonlight, Tim and Rosemary watched the stars each night. During the day, they planted seeds and milked cows. At least once a week, they took LSD. Every Monday morning at nine, Tim walked down to the nearest house and listened to the news on a battery-operated radio. After all of the new Supreme Court decisions had been announced, he walked back up the hill and told Rosemary they had been given another week. They would then both "stay high for the next seven days." This was not particularly hard to do since the Brotherhood was now moving a thousand kilos of hashish a month into the country. Some evenings, half a dozen fellow residents of the ranch would retire to the sauna hut with cherry pipes filled with hash and smoke and sweat until they either fainted or freaked out from the heat. Once a month, everyone celebrated the full moon by going up into the mountains to take LSD. Sitting in a circle around a blazing fire, they shook Indian rattles to ward off the evil spirits and played drums and guitars. Some danced around the fire while others tried to communicate with flying saucers they claimed to see regularly in the clear night sky above the ranch.

Five hundred miles to the north in Berkeley, the scene was not nearly so peaceful. Early in the morning of Thursday, May 15, 1969, 250 California Highway Patrolmen and police officers cleared an eight-block area around the formerly empty lot known as People's Park so that a perimeter fence could be built. After a noontime rally in Sproul Plaza, 6,000 protestors marched down Telegraph Avenue to reclaim the park. Police fired tear gas. Protestors responded with rocks and bottles. Firing shotguns loaded with double-aught buckshot, deputies blinded a protestor named Alan Blanchard and seriously wounded another named James Rector. By the end of a day that came to be known as "Bloody Thursday," 128 people, none of them police officers, had been hospitalized. That night, Governor Ronald Reagan called out the National Guard and banned all public assembly. Four days later on May 19, James Rector died of his wounds.

On the ranch, Tim was enjoying a sunny day. The sound of buzzing bees and the scent of apple blossoms drifted through the warm mountain air. When Tim looked down into the valley, he saw two sedans approaching. Since cars from the city could only mean trouble, he asked Rosemary whether she thought it was a bust. As it turned out, the cars were being driven by television crews from ABC and NBC who had come to ask Tim how it felt, at least for the time being, to be a free man. By unanimous decision, the Supreme Court had just thrown out his bust in Laredo. In a forty-six-page decision handed down by Justice John Marshall Harlan, the Court had affirmed not only that the Fifth Amendment guarantee against self-incrimination was a valid defense against failing to pay the Federal Marijuana Tax but also that mere possession of marijuana was not sufficient to prove it had been illegally imported or that the person in possession knew it had been imported. "Overall," wrote Michael Aldrich, the "Head" of LeMar International, an organization dedicated to the legalization of pot, "the decision makes present federal anti-marijuana legislation impossible to enforce." All state laws making pot illegal, however, remained in effect. After reversing the Laredo decision, the Supreme Court had remanded the case to a lower appeals court for dismissal, retrial, or resentencing. Although Tim still faced eleven counts of conspiracy to distribute drugs from the Millbrook busts as well as three felony charges stemming from his arrest in Laguna Beach, he called this "the happiest day since the Emancipation Proclamation."

Outside the teepee, Tim and Rosemary were interviewed by the camera crews. Asked how he felt, Tim said, "High and happy for ourselves and the thousands of young people who are imprisoned for psychedelic crimes." Asked what he planned to do for all those kids, Tim responded, "Run for the highest office in the state. Pleasure is now a political issue." Without having given anyone the slightest bit of advance notice, Tim Leary had just thrown his hat into the ring for governor of California. Like Upton Sinclair in the 1930s, Tim intended to run on principle rather than for political gain. His announcement came as a complete shock to those who thought they knew him best. Carol Randall, then married to John Griggs, recalled, "We cried. Me and Johnny cried. It was the wrong direction for us. We weren't going that way. We thought his goal was to become spiritually enlightened."

Even as it seemed that actual civil war was breaking out on the streets in Berkeley, Tim had seized his moment in the media spotlight. "In that same space of time," Rosemary recalled, "Berkeley was going from peace and love to tear gas in the streets. Women hitchhiking were being raped and deciding they would only ride with women. Clenched-fist salutes instead of peace and love. Tim's answer to all this was to run for governor." Travis Ashbrook would later say, "We all thought it was the worst idea we had ever heard. He had so much power back then that it went to his head. And, boy, nothing went right after that. It all just started falling apart."

Tim would later write that the reporters outside the teepee "seemed to like the idea. The incumbent was an undistinguished movie-actor who did not conceal his disdain for the poor, the blacks, the hip, the Latinos, the women, the students, the liberals, the young—and journalists." Yet it was not Ronald Reagan against whom Tim was pitting himself but rather the three Democratic candidates who were fighting for the chance to oppose him: Mayor Sam Yorty of Los Angeles, Mayor Joseph Alioto of San Francisco, and Jesse Unruh, speaker of the state assembly. "My statisticians and poll experts," Tim later claimed, "estimated I could win 33 percent of the Democratic vote."

A day later, as Sirhan Sirhan appeared in court in Los Angeles to be sentenced to death for the murder of Robert Kennedy, Tim journeyed to LA to hold the first formal press conference of his campaign outside the offices of the *LA Free Press*. Seated behind a brace of microphones at a table, Tim wore buckskin pants, a homespun shirt, and an Indian band around his forehead. By his side sat Rosemary, her long dark hair falling around her face in "the Indian maiden motif." The most newsworthy plank in Tim's platform was his pledge to eliminate all taxes for "the sober, industrious, conventional person." Instead, he proposed an annual $1,000-a-year license fee or "Frivolity Tax" to be levied on those who drank hard liquor, owned guns, fished for sport, bought a new car more often than once every five years, smoked marijuana or cigarettes (but not cigars and pipes, which were tax-free), divorced their spouses, or had an abortion. Tim later explained that some activities would be "available to license holders in restricted areas and neighborhoods: prostitution, gambling, public nudity, homosexual courting, and the use of LSD and heroin."

Tim told Michael Hollingshead he meant to strip the cops of their guns, double their salaries, and encourage them to smoke dope. Asked what he planned to do as governor of California, Tim replied, "As little as possible." To quell student protests, Tim promised to turn all state colleges and universities over to private enterprise. Exactly how this would stop campus unrest, he did not say. "It promised to be great theatre," Tim would later write, "flamboyant fun, a bully platform from which to suggest change in the farce of partisan politics. And, as it turned out, there was some chance I might win."

Although everyone knew there was no chance whatsoever that Tim would win, some of it was great fun. In one campaign poster, a beaming Tim was pictured in an outrageous fringed buckskin jacket only a rock star could afford, flashing the peace sign under a headline that read LUV FOR GUV. On another poster, the slogan "Timothy Leary for Governor" appeared over the face of the bearded man whose likeness could be found on every pack of Zig-Zag rolling paper.

Tim's supporters included Art Kunkin, the editor of the *San Francisco Planet* and of the *San Diego Free Press,* and his old friend Jann Wenner, editor of *Rolling Stone.* "Tim appointed me campaign manager," Art Kunkin recalled. "But we never did very much. It was more of a joke than anything." The headline on one of Tim's full-page ads read COME TOGETHER— JOIN THE PARTY! If nothing else, Tim had again come up with a slogan no one could easily forget. "'Come together' was mine," Rosemary recalled. "I was a bit of a sloganeer in those days and Tim would ask, 'What do I say?,' and I would say something flip."

In New York City, Tim did an interview with Jaakov Kohn of *The East Village Other.* "I believe I have a great deal to say about the state of happiness in this country," Tim announced. "I believe that the politics of pleasure is going to be the key issue in the next few elections." Returning to the theme he had first annunciated in his *Playboy* interview, Tim told Kohn, "The central issue of the psychedelic experience is the erotic exhilaration . . . On the West Coast, 12-year-old kids are fucking righteously and without guilt, very poetically. The average 15 year old has explored

most single and many multiple ways of sexual expression and is ready to
go to a more Tantric path." Referring to a recent interview in *Look* magazine in which a seventeen-year-old girl had said that grass was great for
balling, Tim noted, "This is, I think, the key to the generational gap. Most
17-year-olds have had orgasms longer, deeper, and more complex than
their ancestors. The older generation just can't stand this, and therefore
repress it."

Long before the advent of MTV, Tim knew exactly how to direct his
message to a specific demographic. He told Kohn, "We must never forget that the contest is being played out in the minds and souls of the kids.
The whole issue should be centered there." Two months before the
Woodstock Art and Music Festival became the media event of the year,
Tim added, "What is going to unfold this summer is going to be the
greatest upheaval of joy that this country has ever seen. There are going
to be large rock festivals and there is now, for the first time in years, a large
supply of LSD in the country."

On this subject, Tim knew whereof he spoke. After Owsley Stanley
had been sentenced to three years in prison and fined $3,000 for tax eva-
sion, Tim's benefactor Billy Hitchcock had bankrolled two of Owsley's assistants, Tim Scully and Nick Sand, to begin making LSD. Sand and Scully
went to work in January 1969. Within six months, they had manufactured
ten million hits of Orange Sunshine. The Brotherhood handed out as
many as a hundred thousand free doses in a single day and then began distributing the drug nationwide.

Not everyone in the counterculture bought into Tim's message.
"Open your eyes, Tim," Jerry Applebaum wrote in the *LA Free Press*. "The
system is only now beginning to bring out its big guns. The Chicago Eight
have been indicted for inciting to riot as a result of the violence at the
Democratic Convention in Chicago; a large group of Black Panthers are
in a New York jail in lieu of $100,000 bail; and brothers and sisters through-
out the country are hanging onto their freedom by the skin of their teeth.
As the saying goes: Where were you when the shit hit the fan?"

At the end of May, Tim and Rosemary joined record producer Alan
Douglas and Jimi Hendrix and his girlfriend for dinner in Greenwich Village. Rosemary, who had first met Douglas in 1962 when he was running
the jazz department at United Artists Records, had recently gotten back

in touch with him to ask if he could help Tim manage a burgeoning show-business career, which now included regular stage appearances at outdoor rock festivals. Busy producing Hendrix as well as British guitarist John McLaughlin and The Last Poets, featuring Gil Scott-Heron, for his own record label, Douglas also owned a book publishing company. Douglas decided the best way to build Tim's career "as a theatrical entity" was to put out first an album and then a book. He brought Hendrix with him to dinner to lend a helping hand.

Through his extensive use of LSD, Hendrix had already transformed himself into the world's first electric black man. His charisma and mastery of the electric guitar, an instrument it sometimes seemed he had invented, defined the era. As Douglas later put it, "Jimi *was* the underground." A consummate showman, Hendrix could be shy and withdrawn in social situations. Tim would later write that as Hendrix sat across the table from him and Rosemary, the rock star "shyly asked us about the philosophic meaning of visions he had experienced during acid trips. He was so unworldly that his girlfriend Stella had to counsel him about ordering his meal and how much to tip."

Accompanied by Jann Wenner, Tim and Rosemary then went with Douglas to a recording studio where some very well-known "musician-supporters" had been invited to "lay down some tracks behind my voice for a campaign album." Tim sat in the control booth alongside Rosemary watching "Jimi Hendrix thumping bass guitar, while Stephen Stills and John Sebastian high-wired the leads and Buddy Miles berserked on drums. It was a powerful electoral message." Released in 1970, *You Can Be Anyone This Time Around* featured Tim, in his own words, "singing the praises of re-imprinting ('You Can Be Anyone This Time Around'), chanting the delights of the nervous system ('What Do You Turn On, When You Turn On?'), and psalming the frontal lobes ('I've Been Around the World In My Brain, I've Settled Evolutions, No Pain')." To the sound of a sitar on "What Do You Turn On, When You Turn On?" Tim told his listeners they could be Krishna or Shiva this time around. To other appropriate musical sound bites, Tim assured them they could be John and Yoko, Allen Ginsberg, the Maharishi, Country Joe and Fish, the Grateful Dead, or the Jefferson Airplane. They could also be the Rolling Stones. While Douglas believes these samples may have been the first ever used in rock, the album is more a historical curiosity than a lasting work of art.

"It was a promotion," he recalled, "and Timothy knew what he was doing. Running for governor was a scheme. Timothy was a major gamer and that was the game."

The day after the session, Tim got a call from John Lennon and Yoko Ono, who were unable to come to New York "because an old grass conviction kept them out of the country." Doing a Bed-In for world peace, they summoned Tim and Rosemary to join them in room 1740 of the Queen Elizabeth Hotel in Montreal. "The Bed-In was totally a media event," Rosemary recalled. "At the same time, it was funky and homey too. I was talking to Yoko about the difficulties of childbirth and getting pregnant and miscarriages. John was ordering trifle for me from room service because I'd never had it." After Lennon played a few songs on his guitar with everyone joining in, comedian Tommy Smothers showed up with a Canadian rabbi. In Tim's words, "we taped this Sunday school hymn that John cooked up. Solemnly, we sang the chorus while Rosemary set the beat, banging on Tommy Smothers' guitar case. Then John added a verse: 'John and Yoko, Timmy Leary, Rosemary, Bobby Dylan, Tommy Cooper, Derek Taylor, Norman Mailer, Allen Ginsberg. Hare Krishna. All we are saying is give peace a chance.'"

The next day, Lennon asked Tim what he could do to help him run for governor. Tim told Lennon he could write a campaign song for him. Lennon asked what the theme should be. Tim told him his campaign slogan was "Come Together, Join the Party." "Great title," Lennon replied. Grabbing his guitar, he started improvising, "Come Together / Right now / Don't come tomorrow, don't come alone / Come together / Right now / Over me / All that I can tell you is / You gotta be free." After fooling around with a couple more verses, Lennon sang the song through and handed Tim the tape. Seven months later, the Beatles released a somewhat altered version of the song.

After his moment in the sun with John Lennon, Tim went abroad for the first time in four years. Tripping on LSD, he and Rosemary boarded an Air Iberia plane at JFK for Morocco, "the most psychedelic country in the western world . . . a crossroads of space and time." Denied entry to England on their way, they went to Madrid to visit the Prado. They then returned to the Brotherhood ranch in California, where on July 14, Charlene Rene Almeida, a seventeen-year-old girl from Laguna Beach whom everyone called "Charlie" decided to go swimming in the thirty-foot-deep pond where everyone skinny-dipped when it was hot. Tripping on Orange Sunshine, she dove off the little pontoon float in the middle of the pond. On her way back up, she hit her head on the bottom of the float, knocked herself out, and drowned before anyone could save her. When her body was discovered, residents of the ranch began screaming for help. One of the first to arrive was Tim who gave the girl mouth-to-mouth resuscitation, but it did no good. When he realized that Charlie Almeida was dead, Tim drove four miles to a phone and called the police. As he stood near the pond, Tim told a Riverside County sheriff, "There's nothing wrong with drugs; they do more good than harm." Tim also told the sheriff he did not know the girl's name but that she had been brought to the ranch ten days earlier by his daughter, Susan.

The death of a teenage girl high on LSD at the ranch received extensive local news coverage. Tim was soon arrested and charged with contributing to the delinquency of a minor. On July 23, free on bail, he decided to leave the ranch with Rosemary, never to return. The next day, Riverside County sheriffs arrived in force to arrest five members of the Brotherhood for possession of marijuana. The hidden valley, once Shangri-la, had now become the focus of intense police and media attention. It was Millbrook all over again.

Travis Ashbrook was driving with his wife and two children toward the ranch one day when he heard on his radio that there had been "another death at the Timothy Leary ranch," this time from "eating canned peaches." Only a few weeks after Charlene Almeida's drowning, John Griggs was dead. Griggs had taken "some concentrated crystal that he had capped up," Ashbrook recalled. "We didn't know what was in it. At that point, John was the only one who had taken it. Carol told me that about ten minutes later, he knew something was wrong. Big-time. He told Carol, 'Go yell at everybody, don't take that stuff. And bring me buckets of water.'" Trying to flush the poison from his body, Griggs began drinking water, trying to force himself to throw up. "He was locked in a full lotus when he went out." Thirty minutes after being admitted to Hemet Valley Community Hospital during the early-morning hours of August 5, Griggs died of unknown causes.

In *Flashbacks*, Tim mistakenly wrote that Griggs died two weeks after the Altamont rock festival, which did not take place until December, after trying psilocybin, "the safest and gentlest psychedelic drug," for the very first time. Laboratory reports "revealed the psilocybin pills contained strychnine." Tim went on to state there were reports of LSD and other psychedelics being laced with poisons as well as rumors that federal drug agents were circulating tainted drugs. "We all felt that at the time of his death John Griggs was one of the most successful radiant holy people we had never [sic] known. He died surrounded by his loved ones in one of the most beautiful valleys in the world." "It wasn't psilocybin laced with strychnine," Ashbrook recalled. "They determined it was an overdose of psilocybin. It's toxic. It's an alkaloid just like mescaline. You can die from it. LSD is the only psychedelic I know that you can't take too much of it."

The surviving members of the Brotherhood mourned their fallen leader in true tribal fashion. "There was no funeral," Ashbrook recalled. "John died and they took him to the hospital in the back of the pickup truck. Blind Faith was on tour and we all jumped in a couple of Volkswagens and went to the Earl Warren Fairgrounds in Santa Barbara. That concert still stands as the major send-off for John." Blind Faith, a "supergroup" composed of Steve Winwood, Eric Clapton, and Ginger Baker, headlined a show at which Santana, Free, and Bonnie and Delaney and Friends also performed. The brothers arrived in full force at the fairgrounds. "We walked in that place in broad daylight with Afghani hats and vests on and a stand-up hookah under one arm and a pound of hash under the other," Ashbrook recalled. "We had grams of acid and shoe boxes full of joints. The show sold out so they locked the doors and the cops wouldn't let anybody in or out. They surrounded us and just let us be inside from two in the afternoon until two in the morning. Oh God, people got high! It was awesome. That whole place just turned into a spaceship and left the planet."

Two days after Griggs's death, Riverside County sheriffs raided the ranch only to find seven empty teepees. As a spiritual entity, the Brotherhood of Eternal Love was finished. Moving with their families to Maui, the Caribbean, and Colombia, individual brothers begin practicing the only real trade they had ever learned—the wholesale exporting of drugs to America.

THIRTY-ONE

Tim Leary was still predicting he would win an overwhelming victory in the California Democratic gubernatorial primary when he appeared in Orange County superior court on September 26 without Rosemary by his side. She was in a Berkeley hospital recovering from what Tim told a reporter for the *Laguna Daily Pilot* was "remedial female surgery that might allow us to produce yet another little Leary." Rosemary's absence forced the judge to grant the sixth continuance in the case. Tim's legal strategy was simple. The longer he stalled his various court proceedings, the better his chances that he would never stand trial anywhere.

On September 24, a full-page photograph of Tim grinning in a very stylish short-sleeved Moroccan vest appeared in *The East Village Other* accompanying an article by him entitled "Deal for Real." "The paradox of the dealer is that he must be pure," Tim wrote. "He must be straight and he must be radiant . . . I think it is a moral exercise that everyone of the thirty million who are using psychedelic drugs take a turn at dealing. I think it is almost symbolically necessary that sometimes in your spiritual-psychedelic career that you do DEAL. Not for the money but simply to pay tribute to the most honorable profession."

On October 4, Diane Linkletter, the twenty-year-old daughter of radio and television personality Art Linkletter, jumped to her death from the kitchen window of her sixth-floor apartment in West Hollywood. Long before her autopsy was completed, Art Linkletter told the press, "It wasn't suicide because she wasn't herself. It was murder. She was murdered by the people who manufacture and sell LSD." Six months before her death, Diane had taken LSD and suffered through a "fearsomely 'bad' trip," which "left her hallucinating long after the drug should have worn off." Linkletter said his daughter "feared it was destroying her mind." He claimed she took acid again on the day before she died and said that "overwhelmed by fears unimaginable to the normal mind, she sought surcease again—and found it in a moment's panicky plunge from her kitchen window."

A great star on both radio and television, Art Linkletter was the embodiment of the corn-fed values of the great Midwest. Rich, famous, and politically conservative, he toured the nation constantly offering his own vision of the American dream. The day his daughter died, Linkletter was in Colorado Springs delivering a lecture to Air Force Academy cadets entitled "Permissiveness in This Society." He had already made a record, *A Letter to a Teenager* (also known as *We Love You: Call Collect*), which received the 1969 Grammy Award for Best Spoken Word Recording. On one side of the record, Linkletter counseled his daughter while on the other she presented her side of the story. Shortly before her death, Diane told a friend she was "despondent" and in a "depressed emotional state" because of concerns about "her identity and her career" as she struggled to "be her own person."

Although toxicological tests revealed no LSD in Diane Linkletter's bloodstream at the time of her death, thereby making it highly unlikely that she had taken the drug the day before, her father blamed her suicide on Tim. In a book entitled *Drugs At My Door Step*, Linkletter wrote that he "developed a bad case of tunnel vision about other drugs and drug-related problems. I wanted to strike out with particular fury at LSD, its advocates and its merchandisers. That meant that most of my deepest disgust was focused on Dr. Timothy Leary."

Embarking on a public crusade, Linkletter addressed the National Association of Manufacturers in February 1970. Concerning Tim, he said, "If I ever get my hands on him, so help me God, I'll kill him." Informed by someone that this was the most "emotional and effective speech they'd ever heard," Linkletter credited his effort not to his "speaking prowess" but rather as "the result of my intense hatred of Leary and all he stood for." For a God-fearing Christian, Linkletter seemed, as even he admitted, "adrift." "I felt victimized, the subject of scandal-seekers who wanted to pry into my family's grief and open it up like a side show and exploit it for their own gain." After receiving a letter from Dr. Norman Vincent Peale urging him to think through his daughter's death and find some greater meaning in it, Linkletter began a lifelong campaign against drug abuse. He made seventy speeches a year and became president of the National Coordinating Council on Drug Abuse Education and Information. He served on the President's National Council on Drug Abuse Prevention and established the Diane Linkletter Foundation to further drug prevention at the School of Medicine of the University of California in San Francisco.

If a man can be measured by his foremost enemy, Tim Leary had just stepped up in class. Born into the same generation as Tim, Art Linkletter represented all the God-fearing, fundamentally good people who now lived in mortal terror that they too might lose their sons and daughters to the scourge of LSD. If this could happen to someone like Linkletter, who for years had come into America's living rooms, smiling like the perfect father as he inveigled grinning young children to say the darnedest things on television, then it could happen to anyone.

In November 1969, Tim finally attended his first peace rally. With half a million other people, he traveled to Washington, D.C., to join a protest against the war in Vietnam at which Dr. Benjamin Spock, the child-care expert whom Tim had revered ever since his Berkeley days, was one of the featured speakers. Spock, sixty-six years old, had recently been sentenced to two years in jail for blocking the entrance to the army induction center on Whitehall Street in downtown Manhattan. Like many other leading figures on the New Left, Spock was represented by Leonard Boudin, whose partner Michael Standard was defending Tim on refiled federal charges stemming from the bust in Laredo. Though Tim wanted to address the massive crowd, rally organizers consented only to allow him to appear onstage with Rosemary, joining Peter, Paul, and Mary as they sang "Blowin' in the Wind."

Because Tim and Rosemary had missed the Woodstock festival in mid-August, they accepted an invitation from Digger founder Emmet Grogan to watch the Rolling Stones play for free at the Altamont Speedway in northern California on December 6, 1969. Leaving their car near an off-ramp in Oakland, they hiked with Jack up to the freeway, where they caught a ride to the concert in the first passing van. "The drive to Altamont was to become my most treasured memory of that period," Tim later wrote. "Two, three, four hundred thousand people, all in a festive mood, passing joints, fruit, wine, and beer from car to car as we inched along, music playing, sun shining." Walking the last few miles, the Leary family arrived at noon as Santana played. As they made their way to the stage, they saw a drunken Hells Angel punch out Jefferson Airplane lead singer Marty Balin during the band's set. After the Airplane finished, everyone waited for the Stones. They waited and waited. When Tim shouted to Emmet Grogan that it was time for Mick Jagger to get started, Grogan replied that Jagger wanted to wait until it was dark to make a better entrance.

As night fell, the small campfires that flared up around the perimeter of the site made Tim feel as though he was witnessing a scene out of Dante's *Inferno*. At long last, Sam Cutler, the Stones' road manager, announced, "From London, the Rolling Stones." Whiskey bottle in hand, Jagger led the band into the opening chords of "Sympathy for the Devil." As fans surged toward the low stage, drunken Hells Angels leaped into the crowd to beat them back. Mick stopped singing. Then he started again. Then he stopped. As the smoke from a hundred camp fires drifted across a sea of faces lit by flickering flames, a Hells Angel stabbed a twenty-one-year-old black man named Meredith Hunter to death. "I remember standing on a transformer onstage on tippy-toe to see as much as I could," Rosemary recalled, "and Emmet Grogan came over and whispered, 'There are people under the stage. If the stage goes, they'll be crushed.' There was something ominous about it from the beginning, an energy I had not experienced before. There were Hells Angels pledges, who weren't regular Hells Angels, trying to prove themselves. They all had billiard cues. There was a young man being flailed with chains. I thought, 'No, this is a play. This is a drama.' It was very scary. There were wrecks on the road and trash burning and it was like something out of a Mad Max movie."

Four months earlier, the straight press had hailed Woodstock as the birth of a nation. After Altamont, they decided that same nation was now conclusively dead. "The Hells Angels riot, culminating in the death of a bystander," Tim would later write in *Flashbacks*, "produced moralistic editorials claiming that the decade of peace and hope had ended in aimless drug violence. The fact is that all the bad stuff occurred around the stage, the center of power, where the drug of choice was booze. I didn't see one person born after 1946 on the bandstand."

While the Hells Angels might have been drunk, most of the people beaten silly by them seemed out of their minds on psychedelics. "Altamont," Tim told the *Berkeley Barb*, "was a microcosm of the overall political situation since 99% of everybody wants to get high and groove and love while less than 1% get their kicks from violence. This was certainly a laboratory demonstration for us at Altamont." Two years earlier, Tim had lovingly dedicated *High Priest* to the rock-and-roll musicians who were "the authentic priests, the real prophets of this great movement." In *Flashbacks,* Leary would later write, "One thing seemed clear about Woodstock and Altamont. None of the rock stars and producers of these events had a clue about what was then happening on the planet. The gene-pool was way ahead of its leaders and spokesmen."

Two weeks later, Tim traveled to Chicago to testify for the defense in the great show trial of the revolution, the continuing legal circus in which the federal government was trying to prove that Rennie Davis, Tom Hayden, Dave Dellinger, John Froines, Abbie Hoffman, Jerry Rubin, Bobby Seale, and Lee Weiner—the Chicago Eight—had conspired to cause young people to cross state lines to incite a riot in the streets of Chicago during the Democratic National Convention in August 1968. Wearing a fringed buckskin leather cowboy jacket, Tim testified as a witness for the defense. "Because he wasn't even in Chicago during the convention," remembered Stew Albert, "Tim could only testify as to Abbie and Jerry's peaceful intentions. The prosecution wanted him to testify because they figured the jury would have a bad image of Leary." When Tim was asked by defense attorney William Kunstler to tell the court his present occupation, he replied, "I am the Democratic candidate for governor of California." From the bench, Judge Julius J. Hoffman—the wizened gnome with whom his namesake Abbie would soon be locked in mortal combat—asked, "Just so that the jury will be clear, do you call being a candidate an occupation, sir?" "Well," Tim replied, "it is taking most of my time at present, your Honor." Pressed by the judge to specify his regular occupation, Tim said, "I am a religious ordained minister and I am a college lecturer."

After a detailed and lengthy recitation of his professional expertise as a psychologist and experimenter with psychedelic drugs, Tim explained how he had first met Jerry Rubin and Abbie Hoffman, with whom he had then "formed and founded the Youth International Party." Repeatedly, Tim made the point that neither the organizers nor the young people in Chicago wanted to generate violence during the demonstrations but rather were terrified by the prospect of violence being visited upon them by Mayor Daley's police force, the sheriff, and the National Guard. After half an hour on the witness stand, Tim stepped down. "If you get more witnesses like Leary," a federal marshal told Stew Albert, "it will help your case." Despite Tim's testimony, all the defendants were found guilty.

Tim Leary began the new decade on trial in Houston, Texas, on federal charges of having transported less than half an ounce of marijuana across the International Bridge in Laredo in December 1965. Though the jury was made up entirely of Mexican Americans, some of whom might have been sympathetic to his claims, Tim did not testify in his own defense. "If I had taken the stand and truthfully denied knowledge of the grass," he would later write in *Flashbacks*, "I would have been acquitted. My lawyers, one local and one Manhattan seemed at a loss. They waived any defense and I was found guilty in ten minutes. 'We'll win on appeal,' said the lawyers." Faced with a maximum sentence of twenty years in prison and a $20,000 fine, Tim called the verdict "a victory of Capricorn over Venus" and advised the young people of America to "stay loving and keep cool." Sentencing was delayed so he could stand trial with Jack and Rosemary in Orange County on the Laguna Beach bust.

After having testified as a star witness in Chicago and been found guilty in federal court in Houston, Tim could hardly have been impressed by this proceeding. The adjective most often used in press reports to describe the atmosphere in the sixth-floor courtroom in downtown Santa Ana was "relaxed." The Orange County legal establishment was so small that everyone trying the case knew one another. George Chula, who represented Tim, had appeared for the defense in local criminal trials since 1951. Jack and Rosemary's lawyers had worked as deputy district attorneys for the prosecutor. Judge Byron K. McMillan, appointed to the bench by Democratic governor Edmund G. Brown, had once maintained a private practice in nearby Garden Grove.

Confidently telling reporters his lawyers would "blow this thing out of sight," Tim made other plans for the period during which the trial was scheduled. When a British film crew arrived to shoot a documentary about his run for governor, Tim came up with a plan to transform the film into an extended promotion for his campaign by interposing fake newscasts and quotes from Nixon, Reagan, Agnew, and J. Edgar Hoover. In addition, the film would feature, as Tim later noted in *Changing My Mind, Among Others,* "real endorsements from the children of almost every major politician and media celebrity, the final election night suspense, and then the victorious campaign headquarters celebrations and shots (dubbed) of my rivals conceding." Tim's idea was that the movie would be shot in January and February, edited in March, and shown in California before the June primaries.

First, however, Tim had to be judged by a jury of six men and six women, none of whom seemed to be his peers. After four days of voir dire, during which multiple challenges were exercised by both the defense and the prosecution, the jury was formed of, among others, three housewives, an accountant, an assembler at an electronics firm, a riveter at Douglas Aircraft, a navy civil service employee, a quality-control aerospace technician, an aircraft source inspector, and a Hawaiian-born Japanese American engineer at Hughes Aircraft. In notoriously conservative Orange County in 1970, those who viewed Tim Leary as a hero did not sit on juries. Rather, they crowded the gallery each day to gaze at Tim with "everything from normal curiosity to hero worship."

The trial hinged on whether, on the night of December 26, 1968, Officer Neil Purcell had probable cause to search Tim's blue Ford station wagon. "I was the one really on trial," Purcell recalled. "They tried to crucify me. The only way their lawyers could get Leary off was to prove I had no right to stop him." Although Purcell recognized Chula as someone with "true love and compassion as a lawyer who would take on the biggest underdogs," he felt far less admiration for Tim. For both men, the trial had become entirely personal. Outside the courtroom one day, Tim told reporters, "It was Officer Purcell who was on his hands and knees like a dog in the front seat of the car while searching for narcotics." One night, Tim dined with Rosemary in the beachside restaurant where Purcell's future wife worked as a waitress. He told her that Purcell had planted the marijuana on him. Purcell was astonished that "Mr. LSD Pothead himself who expounds that everyone should get loaded was saying a cop had planted that stuff on him."

Day after day as witnesses testified, Tim sat at the defense table carefully taking notes on a legal pad. Periodically, he leaned over to consult with Chula or to smile at Rosemary, who sat beside him. Jack's conduct during the trial was far less controlled. At one point during a pretrial hearing, Judge Byron K. McMillan told Jack that if he did not stop spitting on the gold-carpeted courtroom floor, he would send him to jail for three days. When Jack replied that he was wiping the saliva on his pants, the judge observed, "He's missing his pants." Chula pointed out that Jack was spitting into his hand. McMillan ordered the clerk to provide Jack with a box of Kleenex, which he then began to chew. "In the course of that trial," Purcell recalled, "John Leary must have eaten three boxes of Kleenex. He would pull a Kleenex out, wad it up, and then put it into his mouth and chew it, and then flick it out like a spitball. One time his dad went to stop him and he slapped him in the face. Right in the middle of court. Right in the middle of trial. Jack was barely there. This was months and months after the bust. But he was just not there."

By the end of the second week of a trial in which none of the Learys took the stand, Jack and Rosemary's lawyers conceded their clients' guilt. In his closing statement to the jury, Chula argued that while Jack and Rosemary were guilty of possessing illegal narcotics, Tim was innocent and had merely been in the car with them when they were arrested. Leary described his dilemma in *Flashbacks*. "If I fought my case and won, my wife and son would get hit with prison terms. If I was found guilty, then Rosemary and Jack would get off with probation . . . Once again my attorneys rested the case without putting up any defense. I'd be free on appeal bond again and we'd win in the higher courts, said the lawyers." In his final argument, prosecutor James Enright called on the jury to convict all the Learys for possession of narcotics in what he called their "drug-mobile." "They have attempted," Enright said, "to explain most of the marijuana in that container—which was in an automobile—away from the good doctor here. But is it possible that the good doctor—the head of the household—didn't know about it?"

On February 19, the jury filed out. While they were gone, Tim was overheard bragging that his wife and son would take this rap for him. After deliberating for more than twelve hours with time out for lunch and dinner, the jury found Tim guilty of one count of possession of marijuana, and Rosemary and Jack of possession of marijuana and LSD. Judge McMillan ruled that Tim and Rosemary could remain free on bail but he revoked Jack's bail and ordered him into custody. All three Learys were ordered to return on March 11 for probation hearings and sentencing. Tim was then flown in manacles to Houston for sentencing in U.S. District Court on the Laredo bust.

In an attempt to keep Tim out of prison, Allen Ginsberg, Alan Watts, Harvey Cox of the Harvard Divinity School, Edgar Mills of the National Council of the Churches of Christ, Rabbi Arthur Green, Reverend Peter John of the United Methodist Church, George Litwin of the Harvard School of Business, and David McClelland all sent letters to the court asserting that whatever personal disagreements they may have had with Tim in the past, at no time did they judge him, in McClelland's words, to be "a totally irresponsible or criminal person . . . In no sense could he be considered a leader of a criminal element concerned with exploiting others and making money out of drugs."

On March 2, 1969, in Houston, Judge Ben Connally sentenced a smiling Tim to ten years in prison and a $10,000 fine. He also ordered him to be held without bond. "I think his conduct over the past years, particularly since he was tried here before, has been such as to lead me to believe, at least, that he has openly advocated a violation of these laws," Connally said from the bench. "He has preached the length and breadth of the land, and I am inclined to the view that he would pose a danger to the community if released."

At a press conference immediately after sentencing, Rosemary read a statement Tim had scrawled on a piece of notebook paper that was now stained with her tears. "These are the times," Tim had written, paraphrasing Tom Payne, "which test the depth of our faith, trust, and patience. Love cannot be imprisoned." Facsimiles of the note soon appeared everywhere in the underground press. With Rosemary at the press conference was Michael Standard, law partner of Leonard Boudin, whose daughter Kathy would in a few weeks emerge naked but unharmed from a Greenwich Village town house destroyed by the premature detonation of a Weather Underground bomb which killed Terry Robbins, Ted Gold, and Diana Oughton.

Commenting on the verdict, Standard told Chet Flippo of *Rolling Stone,* "It appears to me to be a coordinated effort on the part of the Federal government and various state and local municipalities to remove from earshot, to incarcerate, in some instances to murder, and in some instances to force into exile, people who are addressing themselves to the needs of the society." Standard compared Tim to Eugene V. Debs, the five-time Socialist candidate for president, who when asked what it was like to be in jail, replied, "I didn't see the bars because the flowers were outside." If the Fifth Circuit Court of Appeals in New Orleans failed to grant Tim bail on this conviction, Standard added that his only recourse would be to appeal directly to Justice Hugo Black of the Supreme Court, as it was Black who held jurisdiction over this legal division of Texas.

With sentencing in Orange County yet to come and charges still pending in Dutchess County, Tim's various legal appeals would cost somewhere around $300,000. The apparatus for raising and collecting the money was already in place. Shortly before Tim had been sentenced in Houston, Rosemary appeared at a rally on his behalf at the Family Dog Ballroom near Ocean Beach in San Francisco. On the sunny little patio behind the dance hall, she threw the I Ching and listened as Ken Kesey, in a thick woolen shirt and a cowboy hat, read the hexagram. From then on, the Leary Psychedelic Defense Fund became known as "Holding Together," also called Pi, the eighth hexagram of the I Ching, which reads in part: "Therefore let him who wishes to gather others about him ask himself whether he is equal to the undertaking, for anyone without a real calling for it only makes confusion worse than if no union at all had taken place."

From Texas, Tim was returned in custody to the Orange County jail where he was held in a four-foot-wide, twelve-foot-long, and ten-foot-high solitary confinement cell in N tank, the protective custody wing. There he was interviewed at length by Deputy Probation Officer Nancy K. Nelson. In her presentencing report, she wrote that Tim was "an essentially intelligent and complex man who is able to project a great deal of social charm, sensitivity, and charm . . . his written statement reflects some disorganization and disorientation, but in the interview situation, he was generally found to be . . . extremely alert, coherent, and persuasive." She also noted, "He is a self-centered and hedonistic individual whose self-confidence and need for attention and recognition have given him tremendous personal drive but also have probably offended many people, causing him to be viewed by some as simply an immature exhibitionist."

Tim, apparently assuming that no one in Orange County read *The East Village Other* or the *LA Free Press,* declared in his written probation plea statement that in the past five years he had rarely mentioned "LSD in my writings and lectures and I have no desire to mention the word LSD in the future except in scientific-scholarly publications." Admitting that he lived "more in the past and the future and have to struggle to attend to the present," Tim added, "I am bewildered when others fail to see that history is cyclical, that Christ is being harassed by Pilate and Herod right now, that the Saints of our times are being busted right here in California."

Officer Nelson concluded that although Tim might have been "unfairly attributed with contributing substantially to the rising drug problem among youth and all of the attendant social problems and personal tragedies, he cannot totally escape the responsibility for having created

that public image himself, nor can he realistically expect the Court to ignore this in its sentence." She hoped Tim might yet change his attitudes
"inasmuch as behind his facade of calm confidence and exuberant optimism, he is genuinely and understandably frightened by the possibility of
extended incarceration and is willing to do almost anything to avoid it."
However, the only recommendation she could conscientiously offer the
court was "for imposition of the sentence prescribed by law." Nelson
also recommended that probation be denied for Jack but be granted to
Rosemary.

On March 11, Judge McMillan sentenced Rosemary to six months in
jail. He ordered Jack to undergo a ninety-day psychiatric observation in
the Department of Corrections. He then granted them both a stay of incarceration until the following Monday when Tim would be sentenced.
At the end of the hearing, many of those in the packed gallery broke into
a dirgelike chant. From his chambers, the judge ordered the court to be
cleared. Bailiffs promptly removed everyone but the defendants, their
lawyers, and the press. In an interview after the verdict, Tim told re
porters that he stood for love and peace and "Love cannot be imprisoned." Asked about a possible appeal, he replied, "We have very good
connections with the highest court" and called George Chula the "finest
attorney in California." The remark caused Chula to note, "That's a
pretty good thing to say after losing the case."

Tim returned to McMillan's court on Monday, March 16, dressed like
a gunslinger. The gallery was so crowded with "flower children" and
"bearded hippie types" that people had to stand out in the hallway. When
someone in the gallery began to chant, Judge McMillan announced from
the bench, "If there is a humming session in here, there's gonna be a lot
of people humming in jail." During the three-hour hearing, bailiffs
ejected several of Tim's supporters, including one who said he was high
on LSD and feeling great. Chula asked the judge for a new trial on the
grounds that the evidence was insufficient and that Tim's failure to consent to a search of his vehicle "should not have been considered adversely
by the jury." When McMillan denied the motion, Chula launched into a
lengthy argument for granting Tim probation because a prison term
would constitute "cruel and unusual punishment under the Eighth
Amendment on the weight of the evidence before us at this time." Chula
called Tim "a truly great man. He has a religious right to expand his own
consciousness."

Making it plain he had done his homework, Judge McMillan quoted directly from "Deal for Real," the article Tim had written for *The East Village Other,* by asking Chula, "Does that mean using it from a dealer that lays a prayer on you?" McMillan, who refused to be interviewed for this book, may have also seen the brief filed by federal prosecutors opposing Tim's motion for bail in the Fifth Circuit Court in New Orleans to which "Episode and Postscript," the article Tim wrote for *Playboy* magazine about his bust in Laredo, his testimony at the Chicago Eight trial, various news reports about him, and a list of additional suspects from the Brotherhood of Eternal Love had been appended. McMillan handed down a sentence that followed the lead taken by Judge Connally in Texas. Calling Tim "an insidious and detrimental influence on society . . . a pleasure-seeking irresponsible Madison Avenue advocate of the free use of LSD and marijuana," the judge ordered him to serve from one to ten years in prison for possession of marijuana, with the sentence to run consecutively with any others he might serve. Because Tim would not be eligible for parole in the federal system until he served a third of his ten-year term and would then have to serve most if not all of the one-year minimum sentence under California state law, he now faced at least four and a half years in prison.

McMillan released Rosemary on her own recognizance pending the outcome of an appeal and ordered Jack to turn himself in to the Orange County jail to begin his ninety-day evaluation on Wednesday. Before the bailiffs led Tim away, he embraced Rosemary and said, "I was born free and I will remain free. The day will come when this judge will apologize to me." Neil Purcell recalled, "I will never forget as I long as I live when the judge said, 'Bailiff, take him forthwith.' Leary thought he was going to get up and walk right out of there. He could not believe it. I left that courtroom, walked right down to the men's room, and let out a couple of yells of triumph."

"They laid it all on Tim," Rosemary would later say. "Ten years remanded without bail based on what he had written. The judge held up that article from *Playboy* and they took Tim out of court in shackles. We didn't expect that and George Chula didn't expect it. Jackie and I drove back to Berkeley and I remember listening to 'Let It Be' and 'Bridge over Troubled Water' on the radio. And from then on for me, it just became nonstop activity."

Michael Kennedy, the San Francisco lawyer hired to handle the appeal, told reporters that Tim's conviction would soon be overturned by a higher court. "That's why the judge wouldn't give us bail," Kennedy said. "He really is of a mind that Tim should be punished and so he's using bail to punish him. After all, despite all the charges against him, Tim has never done any time." Along with so much else, that was about to change.

ESCAPE AND FLIGHT

SAN LUIS OBISPO, CALIFORNIA,
MARCH–SEPTEMBER 1970

If he's there, that's where he should be. Tim's in jail because that's his karma. Trust and obey your karma, grow with it.

—Richard Alpert, as quoted
by Jerry Rubin in *We Are Everywhere*

Passport photo of Timothy Leary as William McNellis,
September 1970. *Photo courtesy of the Senate Committee
Hearings on Passport Fraud, Congressional Record*

THIRTY-TWO

On March 18, 1970, in a prison-issue work shirt with his drooping cowboy mustache gone and his hair cut short at the back and sides but left strangely long on top and parted in the middle so that it resembled the wings of a bird in flight, "T F Leary, California Prison B26358" stared into the booking camera at the Orange County jail. With a narrow, toothy grin on his face, Tim looked like some half-mad, middle-aged con who had already spent most of his life in jail and saw no reason to believe this would change in the near future.

After being transferred from the Orange County jail in Santa Ana to state prison in Chino, Tim was told by a guard who slammed the heavy steel doors of his cell shut behind him, "For you, we throw away the keys." When Rosemary came to visit him the next day, she felt as though they were both in a movie reading lines written for them by someone else. As Rosemary recalled, "Tim was behind glass, and we were doing the regular thing with our fingers pressed up against the glass. In the glass, I could see the reflection of a child's balloon. Some children were visiting and running back and forth and that was reflected as well. Tim was crying and I could see that and my own reflection and the reason this was so important to me is that when Tim and I first dated, Alan Atwood gave me a pane of two-way mirror glass. In it, Tim and I could see our faces superimposed on each other. Now our faces were separate and the children we couldn't have were running around behind us. Tim said, 'You've got to get me out of here.' And I said, 'I'll free you.'"

At Chino State Prison, inmates who had just entered the California system were classified for transfer to either minimum, medium, or maximum security, long-term institutions. On his third day there, Tim was sent to the psychological testing room where he was informed that the classification program was partly based on tests he had developed. On the intelligence test, Tim tried to get the highest possible score. On the personality tests, he formulated his answers, as he later wrote, "to make me appear normal, non-impulsive, docile, conforming. My vocational tests revealed aptitudes in forestry and farming together with hopeless incompetence in clerical tasks. I was angling for a transfer to a minimum-security prison where escape would be possible." Before any decision was made, Tim welcomed a new cell mate—his son, Jack. "I was in the California Youth Authority," Jack recalled, "and they put us in a cell together for one or two days. They thought it would be real nice. They were sympathetic. It's not too often they get fathers and sons." Concerning Tim's state of mind, Jack told Leary biographer John Bryan, "He was very upset and gloomy and he was saying he was going to be in jail for a long time . . . I was almost excited by prison . . . It was a big experience for me, while he was totally blown out by it." At four in the morning, Jack was taken from the cell and sent to a prison in Tracy.

Tim soon learned the pecking order of the California state prison system. The best choice by far was the west wing of the California Men's Colony in San Luis Obispo, which offered "color TV, a golf course, a swimming pool. No wall." The east wing was a medium-security institution where Black Panther leader Huey Newton was kept under the constant surveillance of "gun towers with sharpshooter guards." In contrast, CMC west was "the old man's home, a country club for elite cons. The best prison in the world." With no wall and the highway nearby, it was also an easy place from which to escape. But "with two dimes hanging round" his neck—prison parlance for a twenty-year sentence—there seemed little chance Tim would be assigned there. As he waited to learn his fate, he wrote Rosemary every day. Addressing her as "Beloved Mate," "Dearest Heart," "Sweetest Wife," "Evening Star," "Beloved Sun, Warm Light, Heart of Love," "Beloved Mary, full of grace," "Blessed Mary Rose of My Life Eternal Mate," and "Beloved, beloved, beloved, heart-soul wife," Tim poured his heart out to her. Like a condemned man, he held nothing back. Whatever their relationship might have been before he was imprisoned, his love for Rosemary now knew no bounds. Day after day, Tim covered every inch of both sides of a single sheet of lined prison stationery, then he started writing along the margins.

Rosemary's primary job now was to keep Tim's name alive while she raised money for his defense fund. Much of what he wrote to her found its way into the underground press. In early April, a photograph of Tim smiling and wearing hippie garb graced the front cover of *The East Village Other,* which included a message from prison that read, "My faith in life, God, the sacrament is a million fold renewed. Love is the only way." Tirelessly, Rosemary worked to set Tim free. "I gave him my word," she recalled. "And I also felt invincible in some ways. This was the potential father of my child and I did see this in very mythic terms. He was the hero chained to the rock and I was the rescuing Valkyrie. Tim always had to be rescued and redeemed by a woman."

Thanks to her efforts, full-page appeals for Tim's defense fund appeared in the underground press signed by John and Yoko Ono Lennon, Allen Ginsberg, San Francisco attorney Terence (Kayo) Hallinan, and the actor James Coburn. So did "Energy Wanted" posters, which read "$300,000 Ransom Needed For The Release of Timothy Leary / Kidnapped by Government Officials," along with a phrase from the *I Ching* that had now become the mantra of this movement: "Holding Together Means Uniting / Holding Together Means Great Good Fortune." Mimeographed copies of Tim's letters were widely circulated. In one, he wrote, "I am now in prison for being, among other things, a *Playboy* correspondent."

Tim was treated like a star by his fellow inmates. Although one gray-haired prisoner said of him, "He here cause he shoot his big mouth off too much," no other former Harvard professor had ever been sentenced to twenty years in prison for dope. Many of those now doing time with Tim had read his books. Others had experimented with LSD because of him. Making sure he was always well supplied with tobacco and books, inmates came up to him in the exercise yard to ask such questions as, "Doc, what is paranoia?" All the while, Tim believed his lawyers would soon have him out on bail. "I can feel freedom coming," he wrote Rosemary on April 27. Two days later, he told her, "If I'm not out by Monday or Tuesday, please come." Spinning elaborate fantasies of what they would do together when he was free, Tim wrote on May 1, "Perhaps the first night we'll spend in Hollywood, then rent a convertible and take off for the mountains." A week later, he wrote, "I'll be out before you can answer this letter."

Early in May, Tim learned that Susan was pregnant by her husband, David Martino, a would-be member of the Brotherhood of Eternal Love. Tim had sent them $300 a month while the couple traveled through India six months earlier. Calling the news of her pregnancy "mind blowing," Tim wrote, "What does God have in her mind? And her illness. And her own Mother so dark. She needs the firm authority of a hospital. Hospitalization is the best hope." Twenty-three years old, Susan had returned in desperate shape to Berkeley, where she was being looked after by Anne Apfelbaum, who had worked with Tim at the Kaiser Permanente Clinic. "She was living in her car," Apfelbaum recalled, "so I let her use my washing machine and leave her stuff in my basement . . . I tried to be supportive but I didn't adopt her. Somehow she got pregnant and then she got suicidal and she ended up as an in-patient at Herrick's, a hospital in Berkeley." Concerned for Susan, Apfelbaum talked to Gene Schoenfeld, an old friend of the Leary family who wrote a widely syndicated medical-advice column in underground newspapers under the name "Dr. Hippocrates." "I said, 'I'm scared for Susan because I think she thinks part of being a mother is to kill yourself. And I think her suicidal impulses could get the better of her.' When she got out of the hospital, I found her a place to live in the lower part of a house with a woman who had a little baby whom Susan could babysit. And then when she had her own baby, she would be welcome there. But it all fell apart because Susan became psychotic and paranoid and began doing bad things to the woman's car and ended up having to leave."

Unable to help his daughter, Tim spent his time in prison doing yoga in the sun, playing handball, and reading: Nabokov, Anthony Burgess on James Joyce, *Herzog* by Saul Bellow, and *The Arrangement* by Elia Kazan. At night, along with the other inmates, he watched movies like *Barbarella*, in which Jane Fonda portrayed a distinctly nonfeminist heroine of the future. Eventually, Tim met an influential trusty who ran a small prison records office. In return for cartons of cigarettes, the trusty also functioned as a jailhouse lawyer, helping inmates prepare legal briefs for their appeals. Tim became his assistant and moved to the honor dorm where he was free to spend the day writing or reading in the "serenity of my private office." He waited impatiently to learn the fate of his own plea for bail to the California District Court of Appeals. In April, both the California District Appeals Court and the California Supreme Court denied his appeal. Tim's freedom now depended upon the ability of his lawyers to persuade Supreme Court Justice William O. Douglas, "naturalist, rebel, friend of youth, outspoken libertarian," who oversaw decisions from the California Ninth Circuit, to rule in his favor. Douglas, seventy-two years old and newly married for the fourth time, was the most liberal sitting justice and the Court's foremost advocate of the unfettered right to free speech. "He is old," Tim wrote. "It all depends on whether his young wife smokes it or not."

On Monday, May 11, a benefit for Tim took place at the Village Gate in Greenwich Village. Rosemary had organized it on what she described as "hallowed ground—the place where I first saw Miles Davis and Charlie Mingus." She had invited "all the big givers from the liberal left" in New York City and fully expected to raise enough money to help spring Tim from jail. Musicians scheduled to perform that night included folksinger Phil Ochs, the albino blues guitarist Johnny Winter, and Jimi Hendrix, whom Alan Douglas had persuaded to fly in from Chicago with his band just for this gig. Scheduled speakers included Abbie Hoffman, Allen Ginsberg, Alan Watts, Jerry Rubin, and Wavy Gravy. In a full-body cast after having been kicked in the back by a security guard at a Rolling Stones concert, Wavy Gravy showed up with a fellow member of the Hog Farm commune in New Mexico carrying a baby lamb in his arms. "Acid was flowing like water," Anita Hoffman recalled. "The punch was spiked and everyone was on acid. It was one of those very pivotal events because the mood was changing. The repression was increasing. Instead of all this love-and-flowers stuff, the attitude of politicos like Abbie and Jerry Rubin and myself was that you had to organize if you wanted to get people like Tim out of jail. But the Hog Farm people and all these religious people, all they wanted to do was chant."

The split between those who wanted to bring about a cultural revolution and those who believed only a political solution could work had never been more apparent. In a dark basement in lower Manhattan where everyone was tripping, the evening started coming apart before it even began. Rosemary had invited a variety of different light-show artists to have a "battle of the light shows, which was something we had often done up at Millbrook." Thanks to the acid-spiked punch, they "ended up underneath the tables, gurgling." Earlier in the day as policemen had stood and watched, infuriated longshoremen had indiscriminately beaten up antiwar protesters "not just with their fists but with the grappling hooks they used at the Fulton Fish Market," recalled Larry Sloman, Abbie Hoffman's biographer. "It was one of the most brutal repressions of an antiwar demonstration ever. At the benefit, Abbie took too much acid. His mental state at that point was extremely militant and extremely fragile, and that was what Abbie was freaking out about."

As Anita and Abbie Hoffman waited in the greenroom to address the crowd, Anita began to argue with Allen Ginsberg. "Allen mentioned something about his friends in the CIA," she recalled. "I think the wife of the guy who was the head of the CIA at that time liked poetry so she had attended a reading that Allen gave in Washington, D.C. We heard that and it was like the alarms went off and we got into this terrible fight." Ginsberg might have been the only person there that night not on acid, but as Anita recalled, "I certainly was and everyone else was and I remember hopping around, screaming. At that time, all of us lefties had become very judgmental. We even got to hate artists unless they were as committed as we were to putting our bodies on the line and making sacrifices to bring the war to an end. Looking back, this is easy to see. Then, we were caught up in the hysteria." Stoned on LSD, Abbie Hoffman got onstage and began railing at the crowd. "This was just after Kent State," Rosemary remembered, "and he was very frustrated and angry. Here we were dancing and there was a war going on. We should have been fighting. At one point, Abbie either punched or shoved Allen Ginsberg who was also onstage at the time. Abbie also put his hand through a very expensive speaker." To drown Hoffman out, members of the Hog Farm began chanting. "As Abbie raged and ranted," Rosemary recalled, "I watched the exodus begin. All the big givers I had hoped were going to contribute to the defense fund left."

Taking the stage in his full-body cast, Wavy Gravy urged the crowd to do some deep-breathing exercises to raise the "vibrational level." After Johnny Winter played what Rosemary remembered as "Texas prom music," Jimi Hendrix's beautiful girlfriend cleared all the children from the stage "as though when Jimi plugged in and began playing, there would be this current coming off the stage that was so powerful, it would have harmed them all." When Hendrix and his band finally took the stage around midnight, the filmmakers suddenly woke up to record the moment. "He was playing the blues for me and Tim," Rosemary remembered. "But when we looked at what they had shot, the film was all whited out and there was no soundtrack. As though he was just too powerful to be recorded."

The night ended with Ginsberg omming from the stage. As a fundraiser, the benefit was a complete disaster. "It cost about $8,000 to put on," Rosemary remembered, "and we only raised about $5,000, so we lost $3,000 on the evening."

———

On May 14, Tim was transferred to the west wing of the California Men's Colony in San Luis Obispo. His first impression of his new home was that it seemed much like a Veterans Administration Hospital or an army base. Entirely open, with no cells and no lockup, CMC West was set up like a "movie-set village." Roses grew everywhere and there were lush green lawns. For the first time in twelve weeks, Tim could look up at night and see the stars.

Three days later, Orange County district attorney Cecil Hicks appeared before Justice Douglas in Washington, D.C., to argue that Tim should be kept in jail so he could not convey his "messianic ideas about psychedelic drugs to young people." Judge Byron K. McMillan, Hicks informed Justice Douglas, had "correctly inferred the applicant is not going to stop committing the crime." Arrested and convicted five times, Tim's beliefs were such that "there is a grave danger that he will advocate what to him is the fulfillment of his self-styled priesthood." Because Tim had such a following among young people, "this does constitute a very real threat to society." Justice Douglas, citing a 1966 case in which he had ruled that the United States Supreme Court had no right to grant bail in a case while an appeal was still pending in state court and the bail system in that state was operating, issued a brief order denying Tim's appeal. Although Joseph Rhine, another of Tim's lawyers, would in the *Psychedelic Review* later describe Tim as being "very hurt and very shocked" by Douglas's action, Tim wrote Rosemary that the bail application could now be refiled in federal court in California. If need be, they would return with it to Douglas again. "I think," Rhine added, "that was the first time he began to doubt seriously that the system was going to vindicate him and that he was going to get out of jail legally."

Assigned to work in the captain of the guard's office in the mornings, Tim attended music school in the afternoon. The Catholic chaplain's clerk arranged for Tim to spend an hour on the electric organ and agreed to teach him to play the flute. Because the prison superintendent was receiving five phone calls a day requesting interviews, Tim agreed to sign a statement released through his lawyers that he did not want to speak to the press. The captain of the guards still complained about Tim's fan mail and all the hippies who were assembling outside the front gates to stare at the prison. Worried they might try to storm their way in, the captain assured Tim that if they did they would be overpowered. Tim still continued to believe his writ of habeas corpus would make its way through the

Fifth Circuit Court of Appeals and then find its way back to Douglas. In early June, he wrote Rosemary a letter in which he predicted, "I'll be free in two, three weeks!" Tim also noted that he had received a letter from Susan, which was "mechanical" and "brief . . . They must have her heavily sedated."

During this time, Tim appended a personal memo to his appeal to Justice Douglas. Known as "The Eagle Brief," it would be published as a twelve-page pamphlet by City Lights Press. Tim, identifying himself in it as the American eagle, wrote, "Laws have been passed against eagles. They [the authorities] have hunted us to the ground rashly, wickedly, and in violation of national laws because we flew high above the cities, the valleys and mountain peaks . . . Wild creatures cannot live caged. Eagles must fly high and cry FREEEEEEEDOM to the winds at sunrise . . . The time has come. We cannot wait. Freedom."

Even as he languished behind bars, Tim's media profile remained astonishingly high. *Jail Notes,* a compilation of Tim's prison writings with an introduction by Allen Ginsberg, would be published by Alan Douglas in the fall. *Playboy* bought a piece by Tim entitled "Still Time." The album Tim recorded for Alan Douglas, *You Can Be Anyone This Time Around,* was in record-store windows all over New York City and being played regularly on WBAI, an underground FM radio station.

When Rosemary came to tell Tim how much money they had lost at the benefit at the Village Gate, he kissed her for the first time in eight weeks and whispered in her ear that he wanted to escape. "He was coming up with some pretty crazy schemes," she said. "Why couldn't I get a helicopter with a grappling hook and have a yacht waiting offshore? All those classic escape fantasies. And I was telling him what was all around him. A naval base here. An army base here. An air force base here." Michael Kennedy, who represented members of the Brotherhood of Eternal Love and the Weather Underground as well as Latino activist Dolores Huerta of La Raza and San Francisco's best-known pornographers, the Mitchell brothers, offered a different view of Tim's decision to go over the wall. "He could tolerate almost anything except being forgotten and being bored," Kennedy said. "Those were two of his nemeses. More than anything else, I think that would account for his escape." In *Flashbacks,* Tim supplied yet another reason for his decision. "No longer in my shadow," he wrote, "Rosemary became the media heroine, the grass widow . . . for the first time Rosemary had cash on hand. And there was no shortage of

handsome young men eager to act as chauffeur. Rosemary understandably developed crushes on these young companions, one after another,
while I paced the cage jealously, thinking of nothing but escape." Conceding that Rosemary worked tirelessly for his release, he added, "She told me
frankly about her infidelities, at the same time reiterating her dedication
to the escape plan that would involve her joining me underground." "I
bought into the need for him to escape when they were about to take him
back to Poughkeepsie," Rosemary recalled. "They had already given him
an additional ten years in Texas and now there were twenty-four years
pending on these absurd charges in Dutchess County—maintaining a
public nuisance, aiding adultery, whatever they could think of. He was not
getting out on appeal so he was looking at forty years. And not concurrent. Consecutive. Because they were all in separate jurisdictions."

Tim told Rosemary that first she had to help break out some of
his jailhouse buddies so they could implement what they claimed was a
foolproof escape plan. Once she provided them with money and papers,
they would give Tim the plan. "It was like my first prison con game," she
said. "It was a scam. And Tim's expectations of what I could do were
so unrealistic. If he thought I could get a helicopter with a grappling
hook . . . I mean, I was a superwoman living on carrot juice in those days
but even so I wasn't able to manage things like that." At a press conference in San Francisco arranged by Michael Kennedy, a female reporter
asked Rosemary, "Well, Mrs. Leary, what about the governorship?" As a
convicted felon, Tim Leary could not legally run for public office. The
fantasy of "Luv for Guv" ended as suddenly as it had begun. But Rosemary went right on raising money. Only now the money was not going
to the defense fund. "I did not know the dynamics of the escape. Nor did
I know the identity of the people involved in it until after the escape was
accomplished. My job was to raise money to pay for it."

Although Tim later wrote that Rosemary had told him the Brotherhood would not be able to break him out because they were now scattered to Mexico, Hawaii, and Pakistan, it was in fact his old friends who
funded the operation. "Michael Randall and myself put the money up to
get Tim out of jail," Travis Ashbrook remembered. "Seventeen thousand
dollars. To the Weather people. Michael came to me in Hawaii and said
Tim was gonna break out of prison and the Weathermen were going to
facilitate his escape out of the country and they needed money to pay for
the incidentals." Although the Brotherhood of Eternal Love and the

Weather Underground had nothing in common, they now found themselves working together to free Tim.

When Weatherman Bernadine Dohrn, whom Leary called "the
flashy-leg child witch of The Revolution," spoke at the Wargasm Conference of the National War Council in Flint, Michigan, at Christmas 1969,
she said of Charles Manson and his acid-crazed followers, "First they
killed those pigs, then they ate dinner in the same room with them, then
they even shoved a fork into the victim's stomach. Wild!" Inspired by her
rhetoric, the Weathermen declared 1970 to be the "Year of the Fork."
During the next eighteen months in America, the counterculture began
turning so rapidly to violent political protest that there would be 4,330
bombings, an average of more than nine a day. Although the Weathermen had nothing to do with most of these incidents, the FBI decided the
group had to be brought to justice to restore order in America. Founded
by Bill Ayers, Bernadine Dohrn, and Jeff Jones, the Weathermen had taken
their name from a line in Bob Dylan's "Subterranean Homesick Blues."
The most radical of the splinter groups formed after the collapse of
Students for a Democratic Society, the Weathermen lost three of their
members in March 1970 when the bomb they were working on in a
Greenwich Village town house exploded.

Soon after, the Weathermen issue the "New Morning" statement
(also named after a Bob Dylan song) in which they announced what Jeff
Jones called "a dramatic political shift from sort of a hard core Regis De-
bray–ist total military approach" to a broader-based appeal designed to
attract a larger segment of the youth culture from which they also came.
"We weren't following Tim's story," Jones said, "but we were well aware
that he had been arrested and jailed and given a rather lengthy sentence
for possession of one or two joints. And we thought that was outrageous.
I certainly remember the Brotherhood. I never actually met any of them.
They gave the money to someone who gave it to us. It wasn't our idea to
get Tim out of jail. We never helped him break him out of prison. He
broke himself out." Asked why the Weathermen did not try to free a
more significant hero of the revolution, Jeff Jones said, "Huey Newton
was in a maximum-security prison and it would have required guns and
bloodshed and we were not capable of doing that. This was doable and it
had a lot going for it. It was a real poke in the eye to California and the
drug laws. It was a big fuck-you."

John Bryan wrote that what he called the "intricate plot" to get Tim out of jail involved "Rosemary, at least one Movement attorney, a go-between working in the jail and 40 members of the Weather Underground." To this day, the lawyer has never been publicly identified. "I was right in the middle," said Michael Kennedy, "which was one of the reasons that the absurdity of Tim's posits was so readily credible to the FBI. I had access to Leary. I had access to the Brotherhood of Eternal Love. I had access to the Weather Underground. And I was political." Although the federal government did everything it could to make a case against Kennedy for his role in Tim's escape, they were never able to prove he had been involved.

Inside prison, Tim continued doing his homework. One of his jailhouse buddies told him that the best time to escape was on a foggy Saturday night at around eight-thirty, when everyone would be watching a movie or in the TV rooms. If no one saw him, Tim would have at least an hour and a half to make his way to freedom. If he was seen, prison authorities could get cars on the road in ten minutes, but they would not be able to stop him from reaching it. Down by the visiting room in cell block 324, a cable between telephone poles was strung high above the wire fence, crossing the perimeter road. Because the cable hung above the lights, it could not be seen at night. To escape, Tim would have to climb the pole, grab the cable, and pull himself over the fence. Tim later maintained he had discussed the plan with Rosemary. Her memory was different. "The only person who knew how he got out of the prison was Tim and the man who gave him the plan. Based on the shape he was in and the wire, he could have done it. He was a wiry, sinewy, racquetball-playing, handball-playing man. He could have done it. But it was also full moon. I remember sending him a telegram saying, 'Do eagles fly on the full moon?' I was terrified."

On September 9, day 204 of his captivity, Tim was informed that he would be returned to Poughkeepsie in handcuffs to stand trial in Dutchess County on September 15. He was asked whether he wanted to move to a two-man cell, which was closer to the handball court in cell block 324. On Thursday, Tim changed into shorts and started doing yoga on the lawn six feet away from the pole. Standing on his head, he stared at the cable through half-open eyes until a guard came up and told him it was against the rules to exercise within sight of the outside gate.

On Saturday, Tim rehearsed in his mind what he would do that night. He took the white laces out of his black sneakers and replaced them with brown ones. Then he covered the white strip on the sneakers with black paint. He blackened his handball gloves. Behind him in his prison locker, Tim left a typed farewell letter, which read in part:

> IN THE NAME OF THE FATHER . . . AND OF THE SON . . .
> AND OF THE HOLY GHOST . . . AVE MARIA. PRISON GUARDS
> LISTEN TO CAGE A LIVING CREATURE IS . . .
> A SIN AGAINST GOD
> LISTEN GUARDS . . . TO THE ANCIENT TRUTH . . .
> HE WHO ENSLAVES . . . IS HIMSELF ENSLAVED . . .
> THE FUTURE BELONGS TO THE BLACKS AND THE BROWNS
> AND THE YOUNG AND THE WILD AND THE FREE

When the eight-thirty whistle sounded, certifying that all prisoners were where they should be at that hour, Tim put on his black sneakers and a dark-blue denim jacket. Into a pocket, he shoved his eyeglasses, Rosemary's letters, his prison IDs, and meditation beads. Moving silently across the brightly lit yard just before nine, Tim climbed a tree, dropped onto a corridor roof, stripped off his sneakers and socks, and padded silently to the roof of building 324. He put his socks and sneakers back on and slipped on the handball gloves. He grabbed the cable with both hands, hooked his ankles over it, and began to pull himself along. Every ten inches, the cable had wire looped below it holding a telephone cord, so there were no long, easy stretches. He pulled ten inches, and then another ten inches, a process made even more arduous because the cable bounced and swung.

After fifty pulls, Tim was completely exhausted. Gasping for breath, his arms and body weak, he realized he could not go another foot. Still only a third of the way across the wire, he hugged the cable with his elbows and knees and tried to rest. Down below, an interior light went on inside one of the gun trucks. Thinking he had been discovered, Tim managed to shinny another five feet. He wished he had quit smoking. Desperately hooking his elbows over the cable, he pulled himself along like a crab until he had to rest again. Below, he could see into the rooms where prisoners were watching TV.

Suddenly, lights glared. Forty feet away, a patrol car had turned off the compound road and was heading straight for him. It came closer and closer, until Tim could look down and see the guard crush his cigarette out in the ashtray. Then the patrol car rolled past him. Tim's only thought now was to make it over the fence, so that when he fell to the ground, he would be outside the perimeter. Wanting to be Errol Flynn, he felt instead like Harold Lloyd. Then a sudden energy flowed from some inner reservoir. He started moving again in a steady, rhythmic pace.

When he reached the far pole, Tim lost his glasses. He wrapped his legs around the splintery wood, slid all the way down, and found his glasses. Under a full moon, he scrambled down a hill and across a field to the railroad tracks that ran parallel to Highway 1. Seeing car lights, he dove down on the tracks until they had passed. He then made his way to a ravine bordering the tracks, hid in the tall grass, and watched for a car with its right blinker flashing. No more than five feet from the road, he waited in shadows for what seemed like hours as cars rolled by. Finally, he spied one with its right blinker flashing. A girl with long dark hair got out as he approached. She asked if he was "Tino." When Tim said he was, she identified herself as "Kelly." After they embraced, she told Tim they—there was another girl, with blond hair, behind the wheel—had already driven by twice and had been about to go looking for him along the tracks. She helped him inside the car.

In the backseat, Tim stripped off his prison denims so that they could be transferred to a second car. To make the police think he was heading south, Tim's prison clothes would be dumped in a gas-station restroom somewhere near Los Angeles. The girls drove him north toward Morro Bay where a camper was waiting. Another car monitored police calls. Because he had not been seen leaving the prison, Tim believed it would be at least two hours before authorities discovered he was gone. The girls handed Tim a wallet to go along with the set of IDs in the pocket of his new clothes. His new name was William McNellis, and his date of birth was November 14, 1929. His address was 2925 Northridge Road. As the car passed through Morro Bay, it slowed down at a gas station. After the young long-haired attendant on duty waved to them, the car picked up speed again. The attendant, one of their people, had just let them know there was still no police alarm out for Tim. The car stopped on a road by the beach. Tim pulled a wool knit ski cap over his head and followed Kelly over the dunes to a parked camper, where a middle-aged "sturdy gray-haired man" and a woman greeted him. In the camper, Kelly began to dye Tim's hair. For the first time, or so Tim later claimed, she told him he had been rescued by the Weather Underground.

Tim was driven north on Highway 101 to Oakland in the camper, with Kelly following in the radio car. If police began putting up road-blocks, the couple in the camper would pull off the highway and hide Tim in a stash pad to wait it out. As he sat in the front seat with their ten-year-old daughter in his lap, Tim figured it would be midnight before prison authorities discovered he had escaped. By then, the camper would be in Salinas. If there were roadblocks, they would be put up between there and San Jose, fifty miles to the north. Moving to the back of the camper, he drank chilled wine and listened to music until they arrived without incident at a duplex located in the slums of North Oakland at three in the morning. After taking a hot bath, Tim ate breakfast and fell asleep.

The next morning, Kelly pasted a fake mustache on his upper lip and told him it was time to move. Back in the camper with the middle-aged man, Tim headed north. After they passed Sacramento, Tim got behind the wheel. As Tim drove, his companion told him about the Weathermen, who, in Tim's words, were "Wise ancient children, the smartest, best endowed, healthiest."

At a camp site that night in the mountains of northern California, Tim met Bernadine Dohrn, Mark Rudd, Bill Ayers, and Jeff Jones for the first time. He described Dohrn as wearing "cashmere sweaters, black Capezio flats," someone who dressed "like no one else in the out crowd" and "the rah-rah leader of the crazy motherfuckers from the Girls Athletic Association running down the aisles of American Airlines borrowing food from people's plates." He rhapsodized about "her unforgettable sex appeal . . . She has the most amazing legs." Dohrn told Tim that the day "three dear Weather souls were blown to pieces in a Greenwich Village townhouse" had destroyed forever their belief that armed struggle was "the only real revolutionary struggle." True revolution consisted of seven liberations: genetic, neurological, sexual, cultural, economic, political, and armed struggle—but only when it was forced upon them. Although the New Left and the youth culture had long since parted ways, the Weathermen were trying to reconnect them, letting their hair grow so they could blend into the hippie scene on the West Coast. Tim proved a willing pupil. "I do not see the Weathermen as violent," he later wrote. "They violate no life. They dig human life. They realize that love is the key to the revolution."

After breakfast the next day, Tim and the Weathermen plotted his next move. He offered to remain underground in America if his services were needed to further the revolution. They told him he was too hot and needed to leave the country. One possible destination was Algeria, where Black Panther Minister of Information Eldridge Cleaver was living in exile. According to Tim, his mission there would be to try and turn Cleaver on.

Tim told the Weathermen that he would see them in three days. Then he and his driver continued on to a safe house outside Seattle where Rosemary was waiting. The driver dropped Tim off a mile from the house. An orange curtain hanging in the window meant that the coast was clear. Tim grabbed his suitcase and began walking along the deserted country road. At the entrance to the farm road, he saw the orange curtain. The front door swung open. Rosemary came down the steps. She began to run. In what Tim later described as "one of the best scenes ever," Rosemary laughed as she threw her arms around him. Lifting her up, Tim swung her around and held her close. "Home again," he later wrote.

Rosemary had already redecorated the safe house for Tim's arrival. "I insisted we stop at Cost Plus," she said, "because I thought the last thing Tim needed was to come from a grim environment to another grim environment. So I bought Indian shawls and orange lanterns and candles and incense and paté in cans and bottles of wine and nice glasses. I made a sweat lodge with some saplings down by the river. I baked bread. I made soup. I picked berries. It was one of the great romantic scenes of all time."

The next night, Dohrn, Rudd, Ayers, and Jones arrived. Rosemary recalled that Tim was "really upset because they hadn't brought back the newspapers but were just telling him what was in them." Photocopies of a Weatherman Underground communiqué along with a two-and-a-half-page typed letter by Tim had been mailed special delivery in plain envelopes from Los Angeles to various newspapers. The communiqué, signed by Dohrn, announced that the Weather Underground "had the honor and pleasure of helping Dr. Timothy Leary escape from the POW camp at San Luis Obispo, California" where he was being "held against his will and the against the will of millions of kids in this country." The statement called Tim a political prisoner who had been captured for "the work he did in helping all of us begin the task of creating a new culture in the barren wasteland that has been imposed on this country by Democrats, Republicans, Capitalists, and creeps." The communiqué ended with the words, "We are outlaws, we are free!"

A poetic diatribe written by Tim that accompanied the communiqué attracted the most attention. "There is a time for peace and a time for war," Tim wrote. "There is the day of laughing Krishna and the day of Grim Shiva. Brothers and sisters, at this time, let us have no more talk of peace . . . Brothers and sisters, this is a war for survival. Ask Huey and Angela. They dig it. Ask the wild free animals. They know it." In genetic warfare, Tim wrote, there were no neutrals. "There are no non-combatants at Buchenwald, My Lai or Soledad . . . Remember the Sioux and the German Jews and the black slaves . . . Remember the buffalo and the Iroquis! Remember Kennedy, King, Malcolm, Lenny! . . . To shoot a genocidal robot policeman in the defense of life is a sacred act . . . Listen, the hour is late. Total war is upon us. Fight to live or you'll die. Freedom is life. Freedom will live." Signing the note in a large and florid hand, like John Hancock affixing his name to the Declaration of Independence, Tim added: "WARNING: I am armed and should be considered dangerous to anyone who threatens my life or my freedom."

Though Tim's last statement was patently untrue, it sent a cold chill through those in the counterculture who still believed in nonviolent protest. Once the leading apostle of peace and love, Tim Leary had now taken up the gun. "It's a merger of dope and dynamite, flower and flames," Michael Kennedy told a hastily assembled press conference. "There is now a merger of Timothy and the Weathermen. This portends more destruction to the American government than anything in history. I wholeheartedly support him." On the off chance that Tim might surface in Kennedy's office, the FBI had begun tailing the lawyer at six in the morning on the day after Tim's escape. When J. Edgar Hoover was asked about Tim's escape, he replied, "We'll have him in ten days."

By throwing in his lot with those who had set him free, Tim once again left behind an entire set of people for whom he no longer had any need. Robert Anton Wilson recalled, "The letter for the Weather Underground when they broke Tim out of jail was the dumbest thing he ever wrote. But that was the price of getting out of prison. Writing propaganda for the Weathermen." Travis Ashbrook, who helped bankroll the escape, would later say, "Tim flipped at that point. He forgot about God and his inner higher being. From that point on, Tim lost his center and he never did get it back." Succinctly, Baba Ram Dass, formerly Richard Alpert, noted, "One more thing we do not need is one more nut with a gun."

THIRTY-THREE

Sitting stripped to the waist on a chair in the kitchen of the safe house, Tim Leary allowed one of the young women from the Weather Underground to cut his hair close to the scalp and then shave his head clean. He peered into the bathroom mirror at "a high-domed, chicken-plucked moose-faced baldpate stranger." Tim then announced he had waited seven long months to see the Woodstock movie and wanted to go that night. Bernadine Dohrn liked the idea. "It will be a good test for your disguise."

Stoned, Tim and Rosemary bought tickets, two bags of hot buttered popcorn, and two ice-cream bars, and found seats down in front as Richie Havens sang "Freedom! Freedom!" from the screen. Throughout the movie, although Rosemary did her best to shush him, Tim called out in delight whenever he recognized someone like Michael Lang or Wavy Gravy. As the movie unfolded, the Weather Underground leaders, all of whom were wanted for questioning in connection with the town-house blast, sat a few rows behind the happy couple exchanging what Tim would later describe in Flashbacks as "loud comments and cries of pleasure." The movie ended with Jimi Hendrix onstage, closing the festival with his famous rendition of "The Star-Spangled Banner." The night before Tim saw Woodstock, Hendrix had choked to death in London on his own vomit while under the influence of a wide variety of drugs. Tim and Rosemary wept as they watched him perform. After the movie, Tim insisted on heading for a drive-in, where he ordered cheeseburgers, malteds, and fries for everyone.

The next day, the Weather Underground leaders told Tim that in order to leave the country, he would need a driver's license with his photograph on it, which he could then use to apply for a passport in person.

"Tim was quite shocked when he found out we weren't handing him a preprinted, ready-to-go passport," recalled Jeff Jones. "That was a capability we did not have. Our method was much more low-tech." In an era when there were no picture IDs with bar codes, the Weathermen had become skilled forgers. On the day Jeff Jones was finally arrested, he had seventeen different IDs in his possession. "We had blank draft cards, so we always started with those and worked back from that. It was so easy, it was a joke. Draft card, driver's license, passport. You just needed to build a little story. But you actually had to walk into a passport office with the story and Tim was pissed off about this."

As William McNellis and Mary Margaret McCreedy, a recent graduate of Moore's Business School, Tim and Rosemary boarded a flight for Chicago. "Tim's head was shaved," Rosemary recalled, "and I had on a blond bubble wig. I was getting looks on the street from men who wouldn't have given me a second glance before. Having been a long-haired hippie lady, I now looked like a blond secretary. I had on the push-up bra and the high heels and the stockings and the cute little dress." When they arrived in Chicago, Rosemary went to the federal passport office. Standing before the window, she suddenly realized she had forgotten her new name. Dropping her handbag on the floor, she scrambled around until she found her ID so she could identify herself to the clerk. Other than that, there were no problems. "It was very easy but scary to do," she remembered. "I think you needed three pieces of identification. Tim used a hunting license for one of them. We came back for the passports the next day and then we flew from Chicago to Paris in separate seats. Striking up an 'acquaintance' on the plane, we asked the stewardess, 'Can we change seats?'"

Tim and Rosemary left Chicago on September 23, 1970. When they arrived in Paris, they found that all the hotels were full. Tim remembered a French psychiatrist with whom he had corresponded in the past. Rosemary found the man's name in the phone book and called him. "I'm a friend of Timothy Leary's," she said over the phone. "I would like to see you. I have a message for you from him." "Of course," the psychiatrist replied, supplying her with his office address in the sixteenth arrondissement. Rosemary left Tim in a *tabac* around the corner and made her way past the concierge into the building. In his office, the psychiatrist had a Jimi Hendrix poster on the wall and a little incense brazier. "Well, tell me of Timothy," the psychiatrist said to Rosemary. "This poor man. I've read about him in the newspaper and I'm so concerned for him." "Actually," she later recalled telling him, "I'm his wife and he's downstairs." Delighted, the psychiatrist told her to bring him up. Phoning his girlfriend, he took them all to dine in a fabulous restaurant that night.

After a couple of days in Paris, Tim and Rosemary began to fight. "Tim wanted to buy a Citroën and tool around Europe," she recalled. "I think I was having a breakdown at this point. Well entitled, I might add, considering the last nine months. Everything Tim did irritated me." They decided Tim would go off to Algeria to scout it out while Rosemary stayed in Paris. If the scene wasn't good, Tim would come back and they'd buy a Citroën and drive around Europe. Rosemary gave Tim some of their money and off he went.

Although Tim arrived at the Algiers airport without a visa, he managed to gain temporary entrance to the country as a businessman. "The first hit of Algiers at night was depressing," Tim would later write. "The streets were quiet, no women to be seen. I missed Her." Tim found a hotel room and phoned the Black Panther embassy the next day. He took a cab up into the fashionable hills of El Biar, where, in a big white house behind a locked wrought-iron gate, the Black Panthers conducted all their official business while in exile. Tim spent the day talking with Panther Field Marshall Don Cox, also known as D.C. He was then driven to visit Eldridge Cleaver at the villa where he lived with his wife, Kathleen, then on a trip to North Korea with their newborn child. Cleaver greeted Tim warmly at the front gate, then told him a friend was waiting inside. Unbeknownst to Tim, radical political leaders back in America had been busy negotiating with one another to ensure his safety.

As soon as the news of Tim's escape became public, Abbie Hoffman, described by Paul Krassner as "a go-between between the lawyers, the Weather Underground, and Leary," flew to Oakland to meet with newly freed Black Panther Minister of Defense Huey Newton. With half of the FBI's most wanted list now consisting of political fugitives, Hoffman's real agenda was to create a safe haven for all those who might soon be forced to leave America for similar reasons. "If a fugitive colony could be established in Algeria," Hoffman later wrote, "not only would it help to bring the various tendencies of the U.S. movement together but help our cultural revolution come to be more accepted by other liberation movements around the world." Newton and Hoffman agreed to send Yippie minister without portfolio Stew Albert to Algeria to help Cleaver formulate a case for Tim as a political exile. "This was a lot more complicated than you might imagine," Hoffman wrote, "and we kept trying to 'invent' a political background for Leary that somehow didn't come out sounding like L-S-D." Before anyone could begin negotiating with the Algerian government, Tim appeared unannounced at Cleaver's front gate. Described by Albert as looking "happy, bouncy and glowy," Tim made it plain he had come to Algeria to touch base with the Panther leader and see what was possible before deciding whether he wished to remain there in exile. "Tim presented himself as having options," Albert recalled.

From Algiers, Tim called Rosemary in Paris. "'It's great here. You've got to come over right away. It's wonderful!'" Rosemary recalled him saying, "Of course by that time, I was missing him so terribly, I couldn't stand to be without him." Although the rose-colored vision of Algiers that Tim presented to Rosemary during his phone call stemmed primarily from his need for her, he could not help but be impressed by the Panthers, universally acknowledged by the New Left as the vanguard of the revolution. "Inter-racial harmony, high-energy collaboration, a new society of American exiles," he later wrote concerning his first impression of them. "A romantic script which met our highest aspirations." At first glance, Algeria seemed warm and exotic enough to remind Tim not only of Mexico, where he had so often gone seeking refuge, but also of Morocco where the use of hashish and kif was far more firmly entrenched in the culture.

Wearing her wig and carrying a wad of cash in her pantyhose, Rosemary boarded the next Air Algeria flight to Algiers. As she went to change her money at the Algiers airport, she saw Tim. "There he was," she remembered. "Mr. McNellis. Tim, with this little Russian leather hat on. We got into a taxi and it was bleak out there. No women anywhere. Bleak, bleak, bleak. We pulled up in front of the Panther embassy and Eldridge was on his way out. I reached for his hand and got his thumb instead and I was holding on to it and he thought I was trying to do some ridiculous jive-ass power shake and we kind of shook each other's hands off."

Tim led Rosemary inside and showed her around. "Look," he told her, "there are a bunch of dirty dishes in the kitchen. It'd be a nice gesture if you washed them." Tim then went into the living room to read the newspapers. Although Kathleen Cleaver was about to arrive, Eldridge had been spending time at the embassy with Malika, his beautiful young trilingual Algerian mistress. A Black Panther called Rosemary into the bedroom and said, "Malika's been staying here. You better make the bed before Kathleen gets home." As Rosemary changed the sheets, she thought to herself, "Oh God, soap-opera time. Then Kathleen Cleaver and Barbara, Don Cox's wife, arrived with their new babies. I cut my wrist on a glass doing the dishes and I asked Kathleen for a bandage or a diaper. She couldn't spare anything. The vibes were very cold."

To get Tim and Rosemary out of the way, the Panthers took them to a beach hotel in the seaside village of El Djamila where the Cleavers had also stayed. Stew Albert, who had canceled his trip home to remain in Algeria for another week, joined them there. "I was to try and explain the Third World to Tim," Albert recalled. "Eldridge told me to do that. Leary had this idea. 'Let's have a big Be-In in Algeria and we'll invite counter-culturalists from all over the world.' And I was trying to tell him that drugs were illegal here and identified with colonialism. I was telling him, 'You're going to have to read a little Mao, a little Kim Il-Sung, a little Frantz Fanon. Try to find a way to say what you would say anyway, but quote Mao.'" Tim agreed to the plan but informed Albert that the Third World should like him "because he had screwed up the brains of so many American middle-class white people. I don't think he understood the Third World or the political revolutionaries very well." Tim also announced that the best way for him to introduce LSD to Algeria would be if he converted to Islam.

Over the phone, Huey Newton told Eldridge Cleaver that it was his decision whether or not to let Tim stay there. The case that Cleaver intended to make on Tim's behalf to the Algerian government, as Abbie Hoffman later wrote, was that Tim was "a black university professor fired for his antiwar views and being hounded by the government. Everyone stressed the appellation 'Doctor' and the Algerians were starting to regard him as an American Frantz Fanon." "When the Algerian government gave Leary sanctuary there," Stew Albert recalled, "they thought he was a black person. Even the government didn't know who the hell he was. Tim had a big ego that needed to be stroked and that was hard in Algeria. Because Eldridge was just not going to do it." Albert left Algeria believing that some of what he had said had gotten through to Tim. "If he was going to stay in Algeria, he would have to learn to play the game."

Always adept at selling himself a bill of goods, Tim would later write in *Confessions of a Hope Fiend* that he already felt close to the Panthers because of the "circle of Black strength and affection that had protected me in each of the thirteen jails and prisons I had passed through." Unfortunately, he had no idea who Eldridge Cleaver really was. Before sending Tim and Rosemary off to their beach hotel in El Djamila, Cleaver had questioned them about their arrangements. "He was concerned about our different passports and the security risk of our sleeping together illegally." After seven months in prison, Tim informed Cleaver that he fully intended to stay in the same room as his wife. If Algerian officials were willing to grant Tim and Rosemary political asylum, they would certainly excuse them sharing a hotel room with unmarried passports. And so began "the conversation that set the stage" for all that would transpire in the coming months. "I don't want to be your parole officer," Cleaver said. Tim, who by now had done some prison time himself, replied, "You wouldn't violate me for sleeping with my wife, would you?" In what Tim later described as "the classic rejoinder of the parole officer," Cleaver answered, "You can only violate yourself."

In his own inimitable fashion, Eldridge Cleaver, Black Panther Minister of Information, author of *Soul on Ice*, former candidate for president on the Peace and Freedom ticket, and fellow fugitive from the American justice system, had just welcomed Tim and Rosemary Leary to Algiers.

EXILE—NO SILENCE, NO CUNNING

ALGERIA, SWITZERLAND, AFGHANISTAN, SEPTEMBER 1970–JANUARY 1973

The same pigs who wanted to ice me are after Leary. They hate him because he made their children rebel. Kids want to make love and not kill niggers. That's a crime in Babylon.

—Eldridge Cleaver, Algiers, September 1970

We had a lot in common. It was a new experience for me to be dependent on a strong, variable, sexually restless, charismatic leader who was insanely erratic. I usually played that role myself.

—Timothy Leary, on Eldridge Cleaver

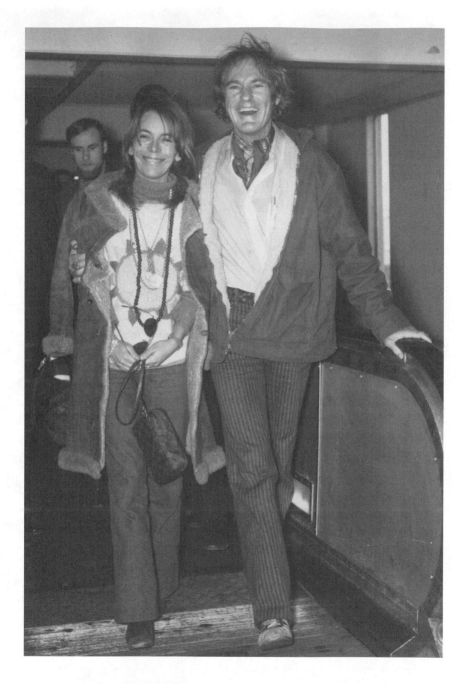

Timothy Leary and Joanna Harcourt-Smith at Heathrow
Airport in London, January 1973. *Photo courtesy of the*
Evening Standard/*Hulton Archive/Getty Images*

THIRTY-FOUR

In the narrow, twisting streets of the casbah where some of the most violent clashes of the Battle of Algiers had taken place thirteen years earlier, young boys pissed on cobblestones as muezzins called the faithful to prayer from loudspeakers mounted on nearby mosques. After ending 130 years of French rule through violent revolution, Algeria had proudly proclaimed itself an independent socialist republic. Though the wide, curving street that ran along the harbor had been renamed Boulevard Ernesto "Che" Guevara in 1970, everyone still spoke French and the shopkeepers reckoned prices in francs. To place international calls, all of which first had to be routed through Paris, Arabs and Europeans alike stood in line for an hour at the central post office. As a nation, Algeria often seemed as confusing, complex, and contradictory as those who had come there seeking refuge.

What mattered most to both Tim Leary and Eldridge Cleaver was that Algeria had severed all diplomatic ties with the United States after the Arab-Israeli War in 1967 because of "America's pro-Israel position." The country still had no extradition treaty with the USA. So long as Tim and Eldridge stayed in Algeria, they were beyond the reach of the American justice system. In an office hidden behind the high white stone walls of the Swiss embassy, Richard Castrodale, who had served as the American consul for two months, said of Tim, "I wonder if the Algerian government really knows all about him. They're very rough on drugs here."

In an embassy building once occupied by the North Vietnamese, which the Algerians had given to the Black Panthers to recognize their official standing as an authentic national liberation movement, Tim had no such concerns. "Beloved Brother," he wrote Allen Ginsberg on October 10, 1970, "Algeria is perfect. Great political Satori . . . Socialism works here . . . Young people smiling . . . no irritation . . . no money hustle, spirit of youth & growth . . . We've been given papers as political refugees—we are no longer Americans!! . . . Eldridge is a genial genius. So much to talk about dear Brother. Please come over soon. We long to see you & hug you."

Although Ginsberg never availed himself of the offer, Tim's presence in Algeria proved so irresistible that visitors soon began beating a path to his door. Intent on showing the world that a real revolutionary coalition now existed in the United States, the Yippies were the first to arrive. Abbie Hoffman and Jerry Rubin provided the money for a delegation to visit Algeria for a public celebration of Tim's fiftieth birthday on October 22, 1970. Out on bond while they appealed their convictions in the Chicago conspiracy trial, Hoffman and Rubin could not make the trip without violating their bail. On October 19, the ubiquitous Stew Albert returned to Algiers with Anita Hoffman, Jennifer Dohrn, Jonah Raskin, Brian Flanagan, and Martin Kenner, who was close to both Abbie Hoffman and Panther Field Marshall Don Cox. Tim and Rosemary accompanied Eldridge and Cox to greet them at the airport. Tim did not yet really know the city but the Panthers let him drive one of their cars back from the airport. Before he got behind the wheel, Tim handed Anita Hoffman a joint in the parking lot and said, "Welcome to the Third World. I've been trying to get Eldridge to do acid but he's uptight. If we could trip together, we'd be much closer." He then he promptly got lost in the casbah. "We were driving through these empty deserted dark streets," she recalled, "and all of a sudden, a huge rock came through the window near Jennifer, splattering glass into the car. Tim made a quick U-turn and we eventually got to the small seaside village where Tim and Rosemary were staying." Seeing an Arab sitting on the hotel steps, Tim shouted, "Boy, carry this luggage!" Leaning over to Albert, Cleaver said, "Algerians used to slit the throats of Frenchmen who called them 'boy.' He better watch out."

The next morning, the contingent met for brunch at a small seaside café. Anita Hoffman realized that Tim was "a totally charming Irishman, very sophisticated, with a great sense of humor, ebullient, charming, full of joie de vivre. In my memory, we were eating seafood and drinking white wine. We made a toast to his escape and the Weather Underground and whatever the future might hold." After brunch, everyone went to visit Tim and Rosemary in their charming little apartment in a nearby hotel where they walked out on to a little rooftop terrace overlooking the sea. "They seemed in very good shape," Hoffman recalled. "Very fit and relaxed and comfortable. After that, we were never allowed out on our own again. The Panther guards would always pick us up and watch us. Eldridge would give these long monologues and I thought he was very authoritarian and sexist."

When Albert, Dohrn, Flanagan, and Raskin stretched out on a blanket on the beach, Albert suggested they all take acid together as he had done with Tim the last time he had been here. Feeling that LSD was for "affluent rebels" rather than "the wretched of the earth," Raskin demurred. Insofar as Tim was concerned, Raskin felt that he was still "talking like a Harvard professor" who would "have been more comfortable in a Cambridge classroom than in the Casbah."

The other members of the delegation were also having problems with the situation in Algeria. "We hardly ever saw Kathleen," Martin Kenner recalled. "She was more or less being held prisoner by Eldridge in some manner. There were these four Panthers and they carried guns all the time. Which was a little weird to me because they were in a foreign country. Stew Albert claimed they had guns because none of them trusted the other."

Anita Hoffman, who had come halfway around the world to help forge a bond between what Jennifer Dohrn called "the revolutionary youth movement and the black liberation struggle," was completely unprepared for what life was like on a daily basis with the Panthers. Much of what they felt echoed the sense of utter social dislocation first described by Tom Wolfe in *Radical Chic & Mau-Mauing the Flak Catchers,* his account of the interaction between Don Cox and his fellow Panthers—who by then had already identified Zionism as a form of racism—and a group of well-intentioned, liberal Jewish donors at a fund-raising event organized by Kenner in Leonard Bernstein's luxurious penthouse in New York City.

When Anita Hoffman accompanied her fellow delegates to the little compound in Algiers where Don Cox lived with his wife, Barbara, for a dinner organized in their honor, she recalled, "All the women were busy cooking and serving and Jennifer Dohrn and I got to the food last. All the men, Eldridge Cleaver included, were sitting around and there wasn't even any space left. So Jennifer and I had to go sit with the women in the other room. I had the feeling that the Algerian treatment of women had influenced the Panthers or maybe they were just that way to begin with.

But I did not like it." Hoffman then began talking to Kathleen Cleaver, who had just given birth to her second child, and was shocked. "I had seen her as an angry, intelligent woman leader. Now I saw this pale, wan person who seemed very weak and quiet and I thought she was being kept isolated and oppressed." Although Hoffman made plans to see Kathleen again, she was never allowed to do so.

Cleaver, in his own defense, would later recall, "I was one of the people who spurred the women's movement on when I called for 'pussy power' and 'political power coming out of the lips of a pussy.' As for oppressing anyone, I will give you Kathleen's phone number and you can call her. Had Anita Hoffman talked about me like that at that time, the women leading that upsurge of consciousness would have tarred and feathered her."

What no one but Albert seemed to have known at the time was that after returning from a trip to North Korea, Cleaver had murdered a fellow Panther for being Kathleen's lover. Although the story first surfaced in March 1971 during a struggle for control of the Black Panther Party when Elaine Brown, Deputy Minister of Information for the Southern California chapter, accused Cleaver of having murdered Clinton Robert Smith Jr., also known as Rahim, both Cleaver and his wife denied the charges in a telephone interview from Algiers that was broadcast on KSAN-FM in San Francisco. In 2001, Byron Vaughan Booth, who had escaped from Chino State Prison in California, returned to the United States to face charges of hijacking an airliner to Cuba in 1969 along with Smith. In documents filed in federal court in Los Angeles, Booth stated he had accompanied Eldridge Cleaver to North Korea. While he was gone, Smith had an affair with Kathleen. Suspecting a plot to kill him and take over the party headquarters in Algeria, Cleaver "shot Clinton through the heart." Booth claimed that Cleaver then dumped the body in a field and poured acid over it. "I've heard this before, about me killing one of Kathleen's lovers in Algeria," Cleaver recalled. "What do you want me to tell you? Is it true? What is true is that there is no statute of limitations on murder. And beyond that, this purported incident did not take place within the jurisdiction of the United States of America and I do not think the Algerian government is going to try to indict me for this rumor. That information cannot be introduced into any judicial proceeding in the United States. As such, my response to it is that this man, along with others who came through Algeria, went underground. Now people say, 'That's a double entendre. What do you mean by "He went underground?"' I mean, 'He went underground.' Where is he? He's underground."

The scene in Algiers became weirder still when Dennis Martino arrived, bringing with him hashish and a huge stash of acid. When Albert asked Cleaver if he planned on taking acid with Tim, Cleaver replied that he did not trust Tim because he "might try to program me." Conceding he might be willing to trip with Albert, Cleaver added, "One thing, Stew. I need my guns. Even if I'm taking acid, I still have to wear my guns." Nonetheless, Cleaver soon consented to trip with Tim and Rosemary. "We weren't under any misconception that acid could cure all the world's ailments," Rosemary recalled, "but we wanted to believe Eldridge was a mellow person who at heart wanted to be with a loved one and maybe work things out with his wife, and that maybe we could communicate with him." Cleaver elected to take the trip not with Kathleen but with his mistress Malika. "Eldridge left to call Kathleen," Rosemary recalled. "When he came back, there had been this moment of lightness between the three of us and we were laughing. Eldridge was all uptight. Having probably come back from lying to Kathleen, he demanded to know what we were laughing at. And I looked up and I said, 'We're laughing at *you!*' It was something one would say to another person on a trip but I felt I had made this horrible error in misjudgment by trying to incorporate him into our laughter."

Cleaver, who had taken acid once before with his lawyer and lover Beverly Axelrod in San Francisco, described the experience as "a throwback." "It was atavistic. I mean, shit would come out of the subconscious that I never even knew was there, man. In terms of policy, if someone wanted to take some acid, we didn't give a fuck. But we didn't want them to come around the office under that influence because we never knew when some shit would go down."

When the Panthers tore apart the speakers of a small stereo record player someone had brought Tim (quite possibly Dennis Martino), they discovered two bags containing a thousand caps of Orange Sunshine. "The guy was lucky," Cleaver recalled. "If the Algerians had been on the job, the first thing they would have done is open it up and they would have shot him the next day. They try you during the night and shoot your ass the next morning. We didn't shoot him. But I would not let Timothy take all that acid to his pad. I was responsible for Timothy because we got him a grant of political asylum." Because Cleaver's house was more secure, he told Tim he would keep the LSD in his safe. "I didn't parcel it out to him," Cleaver remembered. "I just let him come in and get what he wanted. But I wasn't about to let him be runnin' around with all that shit. Timothy used to tell me, 'Eldridge, I'm gonna give you a tip. Every morning, take a little a piece of acid about as big as the head of a pin. Your writing will just flow.' I declined to do that."

On the day before Tim's fiftieth birthday, an article appeared in the government-controlled newspaper confirming that Algeria had extended political asylum to an African American psychologist and his wife, who would be working with the Black Panther Party. The article also announced a press conference in two days at which a Miss Dohrn would be present. Assuming that Miss Dohrn was in fact Bernadine, newsmen and TV crews began arriving in Algiers to cover the event.

Jennifer Dohrn baked the cake for Tim's birthday. On the cake, in large letters, were TIM'S FREE, FREE BOBBY. Black Panther leader and former Chicago Eight defendant Bobby Seale, in a New Haven jail awaiting trial, had also been born on this day. At the party, Cleaver led everyone, Dennis Martino included, in singing happy birthday to Tim and Bobby. After Tim blew out the candles, everyone drank red Algerian wine, smoked grass, and listened to Otis Redding, Junior Walker, and Leonard Cohen, Cleaver's favorite poet, singing "The Stranger." Although Cleaver had approved of the idea of giving Tim a loaded pistol for his birthday, he postponed the actual delivery. "Leary was very offended by that," Albert recalled. "I think he took not getting the pistol as a symbol that Eldridge didn't trust him."

What neither Tim or Rosemary knew was that the Algerian government had just signed two twenty-five-year contracts to sell billions of cubic feet of natural gas from the Sahara to the United States. As Tim was celebrating his birthday, the Algerian representative to the United Nations was preparing to speak before the Security Council in New York. "Algeria," Cleaver recalled, "introduced a resolution before the United Nations Security Council condemning Israel and calling Zionism racism. They made their speech and went to watch the six o'clock news. Nothing about their resolution. Instead, 'The Pope of Dope Gets Political Asylum in Algeria!' It freaked the Algerians out. They weren't interested in the Pope of Dope. They felt like I had deceived them. The next day, the Algerians came and they were pissed off at me. But I told them the American media were just doing that to screw them up and it had nothing to do with the truth and Leary was a significant antiwar person and that the dope was just something that was going on."

After the government canceled the press conference, thereby making Cleaver's position in Algeria far more tenuous, he made Tim an offer that he could not refuse. "Eldridge huddled with the FLN [Front de Libération Nationale] to decide how to take the heat off Algeria as the new pleasure center," Tim later wrote. "It was decided to send a Hippie-Yippie-Black Panther-LSD Delegation to Amman, Jordan to join Jean Genet in a Grande Conference de Presse Internationale in support of the Palestinian guerillas." Cleaver selected Martin Kenner, Donald Cox, and Jennifer Dohrn to accompany Tim and sent them off as a delegation on a diplomatic mission. "The idea," Stew Albert remembered, "was that they were going to visit al-Fatah to give Leary a little Third World legitimacy and then he was going to return to Algeria. They went off to the Middle East to build up Tim's Third World credentials."

Although Tim would later write in *Confessions of a Hope Fiend* that he had been named the "paper leader" of the delegation, it was the "stern and businesslike" Donald Cox who scolded Tim for wandering away to look at duty-free cameras as the delegation waited to board their plane in the Algiers airport. Traveling on a fake American passport, Tim was subject to arrest and extradition in any country that maintained diplomatic relations with the United States. Yet he acted like a tourist going on vacation.

To reach Amman, the delegation had to fly via Tunis to Tripoli, then on to Cairo and Beirut. In Cairo, thousands of mourners, wailing twenty-four hours a day, prostrated themselves in front of every mosque. Gamal Abdel Nasser, the dominant figure in Egyptian politics for the past two decades, has been dead for less than a month. Thousands more marched though the streets each day while Nasser's speeches blared from loudspeakers. Tim and his fellow travelers checked into a luxurious old hotel built to house the Empress Eugenie of France when she attended the opening of the Suez Canal on November 17, 1869. For $10.00 a night, they occupied the imperial suite, which consisted of two bedrooms, each with a single bed. Dohrn and Cox stayed together in one room while Tim and Kenner shared a bed in the other.

After waking up on silk sheets and having breakfast in bed, Tim decided that since the flight to Beirut would not leave until late afternoon, he would visit the pyramids. Cox, understandably nervous about going anywhere in a city he believed to be full of "Zionist agents, Interpol pigs, and CIA informers," lectured Tim about having unauthorized conversations with cabdrivers. "Right on, brother," Tim said repeatedly, apologizing for his reckless behavior. He persuaded Cox to hire a limousine for the ride to the airport. On the way, the limo stopped at the pyramids. Feeling naked without his gun, Cox stood guard outside the Great Pyramid of Cheops as Tim moved down the stone labyrinth to the center of the tomb where Aleister Crowley, the British master of the occult, who during his lifetime was known as the "Wickedest Man in the World," had once brought his bride. At the sphinx, Tim and Kenner donned turbans and mounted camels for a ride into the desert. Cox, surrounded by Egyptian guides demanding money, staggered after them in the blazing heat. They then all boarded a plane to Beirut.

On the flight to Cairo, Tim was recognized by a long-haired young British photographer who asked to be allowed to accompany the group to Amman and offered to take pictures over which they would have total control. Tim relayed the offer to Cox, who angrily instructed Tim to tell the photographer there was no deal. At the Beirut airport, Cox ordered the photographer to get away from the group and threatened to break his camera. Tim, who had never turned down a photo opportunity in his life, later wrote, "I had the ominous feeling that we were making an enemy."

On the same day that the Black Panthers in New York City were holding a press conference to announce that Dr. Timothy Leary was now part of their movement, Tim was checking into a second-floor suite in the swank St. Georges Hotel on Beirut's waterfront. The hotel also happened to be the favored watering hole for Western reporters in the Middle East. Early the next morning, Tim answered a knock at his door only to find himself gazing into the lens of a CBS television camera. A reporter holding a microphone began firing questions at him. Slamming the door shut, Tim sent Kenner out to reconnoiter the situation. As Tim would later write, Kenner returned "ashen-faced, to report that journalists, TV crews, and photographers were waiting in the hallway, in the lobby, and across the street where they were studying our hotel windows with binoculars. We were trapped by the press."

There were so many reporters in the hotel that Jennifer Dohrn could not open her door without twenty of them trying to drag her out into the hallway. A few enterprising newsmen actually climbed up the side of the building and tried to enter the delegation's rooms through the windows.

After denying that Tim was even in Beirut, Cox went off to visit the local branch of al-Fatah to arrange entry into the Palestinian guerrilla camps. In Beirut, an al-Fatah spokesman stated, "We know nothing about these people." Cox was unable to reach Cleaver by phone in Algiers so Cleaver could tell al-Fatah leaders in Jordan to instruct their Beirut colleagues that the delegation would be welcomed in Amman. Like Paul Henreid and Ingrid Bergman awaiting their precious letters of transit in *Casablanca*, Tim, Dohrn, Cox, and Kenner were stranded in Beirut with their own transit visas about to expire and the hotel bill at the St. Georges mounting to a then-astronomical $330.

In the midst of this crisis, Kenner decided to take a tennis lesson. By the hotel court, Kenner recognized someone he had worked with at Mobilization for Youth in New York City in 1964. The man, whom Kenner had known as Marc Schleifer in New York, had since converted to Islam, changed his name to Abdallah Schleifer, and was now working for NBC News in the Middle East. Schleifer offered to provide a car so that Tim could be driven to Damascus in the middle of the night. "The problem," Jennifer Dohrn would say in a radio interview after she had returned to America, "was that we had to get Timothy out of the hotel without being noticed because he didn't have traveling papers. We had heard rumors that the U.S. authorities were going to move on him. There is no extradition treaty in Lebanon but it turns out to be the center for all kinds of CIA kidnapping and murders. Anything goes if you have money in the city." To create a diversion, Cox, Dohrn, and Kenner decided to hold a press conference. While reporters were busy interviewing them, Tim would take the elevator, slip out a side door, and join Abdallah Schleifer for the ride to Damascus. "At seven o' clock," Dohrn recalled in the radio interview, "we took the elevator down and we were greeted by cameras and lights and we charged through the lobby and nobody was following us. Two minutes later, Timothy arrived in the same elevator and he was caught by the press. They literally chased him all over Beirut."

With reporters and photographers in hot pursuit, Tim hopped into the waiting car. Careening through downtown Beirut, Tim's Arab chauffeur dropped him outside a restaurant on a side street where he was quickly hustled into a rear dining room. A few minutes later, the chauffeur reported that journalists were entering the restaurant. He led Tim up a flight of stairs and shoved him into a room where an elderly Arab woman sat with a young boy. Since neither of them spoke English, Tim did his best to communicate with gestures. The old woman, nodding as though she understood, left only to return with a pretty girl who smiled at Tim in a friendly way, took him into another room, shut the door, and began crooning an Arab love song. Someone banged on the door and began turning the knob. Putting his shoulder to the door, Tim pushed it shut as two reporters shouted questions at him over the transom. When a third newsman arrived, they forced open the door. Tim ran through a kitchen into a small bathroom with a door that had no lock. Seconds later, the journalists pushed their way in. Cornering their quarry at last, they stood around an open sewer in the floor. One identified himself as a representative of *Newsweek*. "Do you really want to have your press conference here? Why don't we go into the next room?" Tim sat down on a chair in the girl's room while the reporters squatted on the floor. Tim managed to utter "Where am I?" before being rescued by his friends. He returned to the St. Georges Hotel where he told a porter to serve the journalists drinks from the bar, with his compliments.

The Lebanese government, unwilling to become embroiled in a conflict between "LSD, al-Fatah, militant Black Panthers, Jean Genet, and the American government"—as Tim would later put it—gave Tim and his friends forty-eight hours to leave the country. At three in the morning, they paid their hotel bill and headed to the airport, in what UPI reported to be a police jeep, to board a 6:00 AM flight back to Cairo. A horde of news people, who had been alerted to their arrival, greeted them. Egyptian authorities seized the delegation's passports and placed Tim and his traveling companions in detention. Cox informed the authorities that he wanted the embassies of China, North Korea, and North Vietnam notified of their desire for sanctuary. One Egyptian airport official said, "We have known drugs and dropouts for centuries and we know they are a curse. What makes this man think we want him here?" Cox then decided to ask the Koreans for help. Unfortunately, he ended up at the South Korean embassy by mistake. "From this point on," Dohrn later reported, "the trip was very exciting. We were able to spend a lot of time with Arab newsmen, who were just totally different from the Western press. We sat for six hours and talked about building a revolution and why Timothy was so important in the cultural revolution in this country."

Kenner, who by this point in the journey had fallen under the spell of Tim's "impish influence," slipped away from his companions with Tim. Pursued by cameramen, they went to the office of Air Algeria. Although all flights to Algiers were booked for a week, airline officials realized that Tim was some kind of a celebrity and immediately gave him four first-class tickets to Algiers. After visiting the museum in Cairo, Tim and Kenner spent the rest of the afternoon watching Sufi dancers perform.

After a six-day magical mystery tour of the Middle East, Tim and his traveling companions returned to Algiers only to discover that Anita Hoffman was gone. Unable to persuade her fellow radicals that Cleaver was making a travesty of everything they were fighting for, she had called a cab, climbed out a window, talked her way through customs, and boarded the first plane to Paris where no one except her husband and French student leader Jean-Jacques Lebel would believe her story. Hoffman was so completely disillusioned by her experience in Algiers that she left the movement and devoted the rest of her life to raising her son—america—and supporting her husband after he went underground.

Upon her return to America, Jennifer Dohrn reported, "We found out Eldridge had been very concerned and had the Vietnamese and the Koreans and the Chinese looking for us in Cairo. The Koreans had even wired Kim Il-Sung who had sent a wire back saying, 'Find them, they're our comrades.'" Explaining the failure of the trip as "just a breakdown in communications," she said, "Yassir Arafat is arranging another trip for four people and this time, members of al Fatah will go to Algiers to escort the people over." She also offered a glowing portrait of the relationship between Tim and Cleaver, describing them as "two of the most brilliant people I've ever met. They have a real respect for one another and they have a lot to learn from one another. There's a real sense of friendship between them. Eldridge's whole understanding of acid and dope is really right on . . . But he's been learning a lot from Timothy."

"Eldridge was full of shit," Kenner would later recall. "He was perpetually smoking hash, half stoned, and he would say anything. Eldridge was the revolutionary hero but he was the one actually taking drugs. Tim was supposed to be the drug guy but to me he seemed like a totally charming Irish drunk who was also a professor." Characterizing both men as "frauds" and "showmen" who were "in a class by themselves," Kenner added, "There are significant people whose judgment I trust who think Eldridge was turned by the police after the raid in which Bobby Hutton was killed. Throughout this whole period, he could have been working simultaneously for the Panthers and for the police. He was such a con man, he could have been doing anything. Between Eldridge and Tim in

Algiers, I felt like I was in a nest of con men. No one was what they seemed."

Scrambling madly to survive in a rapidly changing political climate, Cleaver, Tim, and the Weathermen were all using one another for their own purposes. In less than a month, Cleaver would "expel" Huey Newton, Bobby Seale, and David Hilliard from the Black Panther Party in order to align himself with the far more violent Black Liberation Army. Some members of the Weathermen soon joined them to commit violent crimes against the state. In Algeria, Tim's disastrous foray into international diplomacy did nothing to improve relations between himself and his hosts. "The attitude of the Panthers changed after the Beirut debacle," he would later write. "I was no longer Tim. They called me Leary. The Panther scene seemed low on enthusiasm. An uneasy distance developed. There was no broad front of exiles working out political strategies. There was Eldridge and a small group of homesick refugees who lived in military restriction, pacing up and down in villas, peering out windows waiting for the Oakland police to attack."

Nonetheless, Tim still felt confident that he could remain safely in exile in Algeria until the revolution had been won in America. At the very most, he estimated that this process would take no more than two or three years.

THIRTY-FIVE

In America, those who had managed to follow Tim Leary through his many transformations were hard-pressed to understand his latest incarnation as a bomb-throwing political radical. Ken Kesey, who had been on a "media fast" since the summer solstice, chose to observe Yom Kippur, the Jewish Day of Atonement, by taking some Orange Sunshine acid at midnight on October 10. Kesey then wrote an open letter to his old comrade-in-arms, which was widely reprinted throughout the underground press. "Dear Good Doctor Timothy. Congratulations! The only positive memories I have from all my legal experiences was getting away. A good escape almost makes up for the fucking bust." Asking Tim to listen to him as he would to "any fellow felon and fugitive and, mainly, friend," Kesey wrote that when he and his friends heard the news of the escape, they thought Tim might be headed off to India for some well-deserved rest and recreation. Then Kesey read Tim's escape letter. "Halfway through, I was sure it was you talking. And it grieved me because I perceived that you hadn't escaped at all." Kesey continued,

In this battle, Timothy, we need every mind and every soul, but oh my doctor we don't need one more nut with a gun. I know what jail makes you feel but don't let them get you into their cowboys-and-Indians script . . . What we need, doctor, is inspiration, enlightenment, creation, not more headlines. But down that gun, clear that understandable ire from your Irish heart and pray for the vision wherein lies our only true hope . . . I do not mean to scold someone so much my senior in so many ways; I just don't want to lose you. What I really mean is stay cool and alive and high and out of cages.

Kesey concluded, "And keep in mind what somebody, some Harvard holy man I think it was, used to tell us years ago: 'The revolution is over and we have won.' The poor country still may not survive and even if it does survive and comes again to its feet, there's still years of work and suffering and atonement before we can expect it to walk straight and healthy once more, but the Truth is already in the records: the revolution is over and we have won. With all my respect and prayers, Ken Kesey."

Squinting into the sun, Tim sat cross-legged on the balcony of his beachside hotel in Algeria as he was asked about Kesey's letter by a reporter from *Rolling Stone*. Laughing out loud, he said, "We don't believe Ken Kesey wrote it. We think the FBI and the Federal Bureau of Narcotics ripped off his energy. Rosemary is gonna write an open letter to Kesey to prove that it was a fake . . . hard work, suffering, and atonement, that's what it said, right? A revolution's going on. Our guru is Huey P. Newton, go down and tell him about suffering and atonement. Far out! Sounds like the old white racist ethic to me." Though he had never met his new guru, Tim added, "Read the writings of Huey P. Newton or look into his eyes when you see him. He's a complete turned-on holy man, a golden black Aquarius tuned into the central energy. It was always an acid dream of ours to find turned-on blacks who could leap over the whole middle-class integration trip and define a new culture. That's what the Panthers are." Asked if it was necessary to use guns to get rid of those in power, Tim replied, "It's inevitable. Their system is based on guns. The Weathermen and I have rapped this through on acid and agree totally. Arms is one of their weapons . . . and one of ours . . . Anyone who's been through the LSD experience with us is an acid revolutionary now. Dynamite is just the white light, the external manifestation of the inner white light of the Buddha."

To underline this point, Tim wrote "An Open Letter to Allen Ginsberg on the Seventh Liberation." Identifying himself with revolutionary heroes like Angela Davis, Jonathan Jackson, John Sinclair, and the "noble Cleaver," Tim introduced "Shoot to Live / Aim for Life" as his new mantra/political slogan. Although his open letter read like third-rate beatnik poetry, Tim's message was clear. Gun in hand, he had joined the revolution. On January 5, 1971, during a live phone interview with Alex Bennett and *East Village Other* editor Jaakov Kohn on WMCA radio in New York, Tim said, "My advice to the Weathermen when we left was that they should not continue bombing ROTC's, that they should escalate the

violence, they should start hijacking planes, they should kidnap prominent sports figures and television and Hollywood people in order to free
Bobby Seale and in order to free John Sinclair."

Four days later, the uneasy alliance between Tim Leary and Eldridge
Cleaver fell apart. The problems began when Tim and Rosemary went to
Bou-Saada, a picturesque village in the Sahara known as the "City of
Happiness." They took acid in the desert. When they returned to Algiers,
Cleaver accused them of leaving the city without his permission. For the
infraction of "sitting unarmed in the Sahara under the probable surveillance of enemy agents," he restricted them to quarters. "Tim and Rosemary went down south, out on the desert in Algeria," Cleaver recalled.
"They had some prayer mats and they took off all their clothes and they
were laying out there in the sun and here came the Algerian border patrol
on camels. In Algeria, a naked woman is a big scandal. They got Timothy
and Rosemary and brought them back to Algiers to me. I had to go get
them out of custody. They told me that from now on, anything else they
do, it's your problem. So I took their passports."

Although Tim now viewed Algiers as a "sad, bored, uptight town . . .
a backwater retirement village far removed and basically irrelevant to
what was happening in America," he and Rosemary decided to leave their
beachside hotel in El Djamila to move to the city. An Englishwoman who
worked as a stringer for *Newsweek* found them an apartment, which they
bought from the French-Algerian couple who owned it. "It was in a high-
rise on rue Mohammed V with a balcony and it was bearable," Rosemary
recalled. "We had just enough money to afford it and they were going to
leave their furniture and their maid behind, and it meant we could recip-
rocate some of the invitations we had received from people we had met
in Algiers."

Tim's ability to pay $2,000 for the apartment became another prob-
lem. When he secured a $7,500 advance from Random House for a book
about his prison escape, Tim had promised to give Cleaver $2,000. Before
Tim and Rosemary left their beachside hotel, Cleaver came to ask for his
money. "Implying that I was holding out," Tim later wrote, Cleaver
placed his black attaché case on the table, "and his pistol fell out with a
clatter. I told them when the money came they would be paid."

During the Christmas holidays, always a bad time of year for him,
Tim received distressing news from Michael Standard, the lawyer who was
now also acting as his literary agent. Unhappy with Tim's manuscript,

Standard was no longer interested in representing the project. More significantly, Random House had not sent Tim the rest of the money he was owed for the book. "At this point, we felt the first flicker of the Terror. The exile blues. No passport. No money. No home." Nevertheless, Tim and Rosemary planned to hold a small dinner party in their new apartment on Saturday, January 9, 1971. In so provincial a city as Algiers, where all the Western diplomats and reporters knew one another and some were doing double duty by working for the CIA, the two of them had become what Rosemary called "the newest amusement on the block."

On the day before their dinner party, Cleaver informed Tim that the Algerian government was "distressed that we were living independently from military discipline." It was therefore necessary that a Panther agent live with them to keep them under observation. Neatly solving two problems at once, Cleaver moved Malika into their apartment. On Saturday morning, Rosemary and Malika went to the market to buy food for the party. All day long, Fatima, their maid, cooked couscous. At seven-thirty, Cleaver called. After asking Cleaver to dinner, Tim told him who else was coming. Laughing, Cleaver said that he did not think he could deal with it. "He organized a party," Cleaver later said, "and my girlfriend called me up and said, 'Wait till you see the guest list. You're gonna freak out.' I went over and picked her up and she showed me the guest list. Man, he had every pig in town. He didn't know who was who. Some newsagent who was straight-up CIA. What I began to understand about Tim was that he loved an audience."

Twenty-five minutes later, the Leary doorbell rang. Rosemary walked into the study where Tim was working on his book to tell him that four Panthers led by Donald Cox were in the living room waiting to talk to him. Cox, looking stern, told Tim to accompany him to the apartment where the Yippie delegation had stayed. Tim pointed out that with dinner guests due in five minutes, this would be awkward. Instead, he offered to come down to the apartment later that night or the next day. "I am not going to argue with you," Cox said. "You two will come either willingly or by force."

Going into the kitchen, Tim told Rosemary, "They're trying to kidnap us." Since there was more than enough couscous for everyone, Rosemary asked Tim if they could wait until after dinner. Before Tim could answer, Cox and the other Panthers crowded into the kitchen. Cox grabbed a small paring knife from the sink. "Get going," he ordered. "We don't want to hurt you." "I'm not going," Tim replied. "Huey P. Newton taught us to resist." Cox signaled for the other Panthers to grab Tim by the arms. The next thing Tim knew, he was on the floor, his nose bleeding. As one Panther covered Tim's mouth with his hand, the other twisted his arm behind his back. "Don't let them hurt you!" Rosemary shouted. "Will you come quietly?" Cox demanded. Tim nodded. Holding his arms, the Panthers moved him to the door. "Use the stairs," Cox ordered. "The guests will be coming up the elevator."

The Panthers put Tim and Rosemary in a car and drove them to the apartment. "They put us in the center of the floor together," Rosemary recalled, "and they brought in a French photographer to take pictures of us. We were not physically bound because I threw my coat over my head. I was damned if I was going to let them take my photograph in this position. Tim and I were cuddling together and talking about Flo and Maynard Ferguson and wasn't it funny how they were portrayed in Viva's book, *Superstar,* and we just shut them all out."

The Panthers moved Tim and Rosemary to what Rosemary would later describe as "This really grim place with just a sprung sofa. It was like an old dental office in some abandoned part of the city with old magazines on the floor and no heat and no water and they put something up against the door and we were in the room and I was freezing. My dress was split and I just had sandals on. I asked for a pair of socks and one of the Panthers kindly gave me some and then a blanket. I could smell them smoking grass through the door and they were playing Aretha singing, 'Free-dom! Free-dom!' I looked out the window and it was all just glass-strewn rubble. Then they took us to another apartment and I knew it was Eldridge's because it was black and red with posters everywhere. By this time, Kathleen was sending over trays of food so things were looking a little lighter. And then Michael Zwerin showed up."

Zwerin, who had known Rosemary since his days as a jazz musician in New York City and who now wrote the "Outside" column for *The Village Voice,* had just arrived from London to interview Tim. When he found no one home in Tim and Rosemary's apartment, he left a note and went for a walk. Upon his return, Zwerin found a note instructing him to call the Panther embassy. When the Panthers searched Zwerin's bags the next morning, they found the gifts he had brought Tim and Rosemary: a set of sheets, a pair of purple corduroy jeans, a fifth of Cutty Sark, a bar of lemon soap, five cassette tapes, various underground newspapers, and two copies of one of his books. They also found a pack of cigarettes. "We took his pack of cigarettes," Cleaver recalled, "and examined each one and we took the tobacco out—acid! And so we added it to Timothy's stash."

Zwerin was allowed to visit Tim and Rosemary during their third day of confinement. He promised not to leave Algeria until he was sure they were safe. The three of them spent the night on the floor of Cleaver's apartment. Tim then wrote a "civil rights message protesting arrest without specific accusation" for Zwerin to take to Cleaver. "Michael read it," Tim would later write, "and said it was too mild. I figured the terror had made me docile so I rewrote a Tom Paine strong demand." Zwerin took Tim's letter and went off to speak to Cleaver. In Tim's mind, Zwerin had now become their defense lawyer, presenting their best case to Cleaver who as "prosecuting DA and presiding judge" would then make his ruling.

When Zwerin returned at midnight, he no longer seemed like a fellow prisoner to Tim. "He was jaunty, cheerful, confident. A congenial handball partner of the judge." Zwerin's good news was that Tim and Rosemary would be freed tomorrow. The bad news was that they had "made a terrible mistake in writing that letter to Eldridge. It made him furious and he almost decided not to free you." "The remark blew my sanity," Tim later wrote in *Confessions of a Hope Fiend*. "It was Zwerin who had urged me to take the strong stand. His switch was disturbing. Eldridge had got to him. It was heavy magic." Zwerin then began lecturing Tim about how irresponsible he had been in a city filled with CIA spies. If Tim and Rosemary really wanted to square things with Cleaver, Zwerin suggested that Tim issue a statement about the dangers of LSD. "It was straight out of Kafka," Rosemary recalled. "Michael Zwerin berating us for letting this happen. We were looking at him like our great rescuer. Who would have thought? But in a way, he did rescue us. He was a reporter and he wrote the story."

At noon the next day, Donald Cox drove Tim and Rosemary back to their own apartment, which the Panthers had thoroughly searched in their absence. Their money had been put in an envelope in the desk but all their dope was gone. In the study, Tim began opening his mail. An envelope from San Francisco contained four Christmas cards. Each portrayed a seated Buddha with a tab of Orange Sunshine in his hand. Tim and Rosemary each dropped a tab. Rosemary gave the other two to Malika so she and Cleaver could take them together. "We were allowed to go back to our apartment with Malika there as our guardian," Rosemary remembered. "It occurred to me that Eldridge really wanted our apartment because he needed a place to meet Malika. I came back and she had been entertaining him there. Her cooking was everywhere and she was wearing my clothes and playing the role of spy mistress. She was reading our correspondence. It was an impossible way to live. Eventually, we packed up a few things when we knew Malika would be out for the afternoon and went back to the beach hotel, where we were warmly welcomed."

In its entirety, that was the story of the revolutionary bust of Tim and Rosemary Leary by Eldridge Cleaver in Algiers. As was so often the case with events in Tim's life, the bust itself paled in comparison to the media coverage generated by it. In a taped statement that Cleaver released to the underground press, he said that while the Black Panther Party did not condemn pot because "there are many of us who like to get high on marijuana once in a while," he wanted to "make it absolutely clear that we do not advocate people indulging in any kind of revolutionary activity while under the influence of drugs of any type." Cleaver acknowledged that he had "busted" Tim and added, "At one point [Tim] was talking to Rosemary about the situation and he said, 'They're just some niggers flexing their muscles.'" Now that Cleaver had had the time "to very carefully observe Leary's reactions and behavior through the very close association we've had with him over these months," he had decided "that essentially the man is apolitical, an opportunist; he has a very deep strain of racism, of white racism, in him which comes out in very surprising forms, and which he thinks goes undetected. Although I have no pretensions of being a psychiatrist or a psychologist, it has become very clear to me that there is something wrong with both Dr. Leary's and his wife's brain. I attribute this to the multiple, the uncountable number of acid trips they have taken."

Using language that would soon echo throughout the underground, Cleaver said, "But to all those who look to Dr. Leary for inspiration, or even leadership, we want to say that your god is dead because his mind has been blown by acid. If you think that by tuning in, turning on and dropping out, you're improving the situation, that you're changing society, it's very clear that you're doing nothing except destroying your own brains and strengthening the hands of our enemy."

Cleaver then denounced his former comrades Jerry Rubin, Stew Albert, and Abbie Hoffman as well as "the whole silly psychedelic drug culture quasi-political movement of which they are part and of which we have been a part in the past." From now on, Cleaver planned to throw in his lot with "sober, stone cold revolutionaries . . . men and women who fit the description given by Comrade Che Guevara, 'Cold, calculating killing machines' to be turned against the enemy. People who have a firm ideological foundation . . ." Cleaver's statement, which kicked off his campaign to wrest control of the Black Panther Party from Huey Newton and Bobby Seale, helped destroy the New Left in a manner which those in power in Washington could only have dreamed about.

As a news story, the revolutionary bust in Algiers soon took on a life of its own. In the *LA Free Press,* Norman Spinrad wrote, "Tim Leary may well be mind-blown, out of tune with revolutionary imperatives, and perhaps a pain in Eldridge Cleaver's ass. Nevertheless, as a human being, he has a right to be all these things and more . . . How dare the Panthers ask for Movement support . . . when they themselves hold the Learys in durance vile without trial or access to the outside world?" *Rolling Stone* printed Tim's open letter to Allen Ginsberg alongside Cleaver's denunciation of Tim, under the headline TWO SOLILOQUIES: TIMOTHY LEARY AS BEATNIK POET AND ELDRIDGE CLEAVER AS NARC. AND YOU DON'T COUNT THE DEAD WITH GOD ON YOUR SIDE. *Life* and *Playboy* ran extensive reports, portraying the events in Algeria as the end of an era.

The bust ended the short-lived alliance between the Panthers, the Yippies, and the Weather Underground. It also threatened Tim's status as a political exile in Algeria. "If E. C. [Eldridge Cleaver] could persuade Zwerin, sympathetic old friend, fellow religionist, libertarian intellectual, that our kidnapping was justified," Tim later wrote, "then certainly his eloquent magic could convince the nonpsychedelic Algerian police force and the radical constituency which Zwerin represented."

From the cultural left, Ken Kesey had asked Tim to look deeply into his own soul and reconsider the path of violence. From the political left, Cleaver had denounced Tim for conduct unbecoming a revolutionary. In the blink of an eye, the moment in which Tim Leary had always managed to live so brilliantly had passed him by. Suddenly, the zeitgeist was moving in another direction. Stripped of cultural and political relevance, Timothy Leary now stood naked and alone, a stranger in a very strange land.

Three weeks after the bust, with a young documentary filmmaker recording it all for posterity, Tim sat down with Cleaver in his apartment in Algiers and talked for nearly an hour. After selected clips from their conversation were shown on KQED, the educational television station in San Francisco, a headline in *The Boston Globe* read LEARY URGES YOUNG: QUIT DRUGS, REVOLT. Claiming to be under "no coercion" from the Panthers, Tim urged young radicals to follow the "correct way" of the Weathermen and the Panthers rather than "clowning or tripping . . . There is a time to expand and a time to contract. This is the time to tighten up, organize."

Even as he was making the statement, Tim was busy organizing his own escape from Algeria. Cleaver did everything he could to hasten the process by sending an extraordinary open letter entitled "About The Revolutionary Bust of Tim and Rosemary Leary and In Answer to the Punkassed Sniveling from Motherfuckers Who Know Me Better Than That" to Jaakov Kohn of *The East Village Other*. Ominously, Cleaver concluded the letter, "Don't worry about Tim and Rosemary. Papa's seeing to them." Before Cleaver could do so, Tim put his own little confidence scheme into effect. Telling Cleaver that the long overdue advance money for his book was finally about to be deposited into an Algerian bank, Tim asked Cleaver to return both his and Rosemary's passports so he could use them to withdraw the money and give some to him. When Cleaver asked why he needed both passports, Tim told him that he and Rosemary had a joint account. In truth, the money Tim used to buy his way out of Algeria had been brought to him in secret by a member of the Brotherhood of Eternal Love.

Through one of his newfound Algerian friends, Tim then let it be known that he and Rosemary would like their own residency cards. In return, Tim offered to teach at the university. Once their residency cards had been issued, Tim and Rosemary began spending time with an Algerian who admitted to having once been a CIA operative. "He was also supposed to be part of the government," Rosemary recalled, "but as it turned out, he wasn't. The government had given us our green cards and said we were welcome to stay. We didn't have visas to leave. This guy was supposed to get us our visas. They would let us leave but we couldn't come back. Because they wanted us out."

Tim managed to wangle an invitation to speak in Copenhagen from "the well-known German revolutionary, Red Rudy," Rosemary remembered. "At least that was what we thought the signature said on the letter." During the first week in May, Tim and Rosemary went to the airport in Algiers. They checked their bags only to be told by immigration officials that they could not leave the country. Two days later, they returned to the airport for a Swissair flight to Copenhagen, which stopped in Geneva and Zurich. Tim later wrote, "We did not want to enter Switzerland, an Interpol country," but they boarded the flight anyway. "It was a setup," Cleaver recalled. "They were kicking him to somewhere the American cops could get him."

When they changed planes in Geneva, Tim and Rosemary found a message from their French psychiatrist friend. Returning from a visit to Tim and Rosemary in Algiers, the psychiatrist and his girlfriend had landed in Zurich. "He was a silver-haired man, a little younger than Tim," Rosemary recalled, "and his wife was dark-haired. When they got off the plane, the authorities thought it was us. He was surrounded by agents waiting to arrest us. We called him in Paris during our layover in Geneva and he said, 'Don't get on the plane to Zurich. There's a friend of mine looking for you in the airport now. A tall, silver-haired man.'"

Rosemary had just seen a man who fit this description walking his German shepherd through the airport. "He was arrogant," she recalled, "like the king of the mountain and he looked at me and I felt like the little match girl dismissed by the rich man. I remember thinking, 'Oh, to be that rich must be wonderful.'" Over the phone, Tim's friend suggested they go to the home of someone he knew in Geneva. Completely broke, Tim and Rosemary visited "this very respectable *burgermeister*, who welcomed us on behalf of our friend and offered us their spare room until our friend could come from Paris to meet us. They were bewildered because they had to pay for our taxi. We were babbling about the CIA in Algeria."

The next day, headlines in the Swiss newspapers trumpeted the news of Tim's sudden disappearance from Algeria. Convinced that they now needed to leave the country immediately, Tim and Rosemary went to a luxurious marble building on the lakeshore in Ouchy, where they supplied their code names from Algeria, Maia and Nino Baraka. "Someone opened the door," Rosemary remembered, "and it was the man from the airport with the German shepherd dog. This was Michel Hauchard." "He was as tall as a giant, silver-white hair swept into a leonine mane, face radiant with regal benevolence," Tim would later write. "He spoke to us in rapid Parisian French. It was Goldfinger, welcoming us to a new life in Switzerland, land of freedom."

At first glance, Switzerland seemed like the perfect place for Tim to seek asylum. For more than three hundred years, the Swiss had steadfastly maintained political neutrality while making enormous profits from wars fought within sight of their mountainous borders. Hermann Hesse, V. I. Lenin, Albert Einstein, Mary Shelley, and James Joyce had all come to Switzerland seeking sanctuary. Dick Diver, the hero of F. Scott Fitzgerald's *Tender Is the Night,* with whom Tim had always identified, found himself at the end of his life in "The Alpine lands, home of the toy and the funicular, the merry-go-round and the thin chime." It was also in Switzerland that Dr. Albert Hofmann, on April 16, 1943, had first synthesized and then absorbed through his fingertips the twenty-fifth compound of the lysergic acid series. What better place for Tim Leary to make his new home?

"So there we were in Switzerland being taken care of by Michel Hauchard in his lovely apartment," Rosemary recalled. "There were all these beautiful people of both sexes, and he would have dinner parties for us where everyone at the table was a rich expatriate who would make jokes about how stupid the Swiss were right in front of the Swiss servants. Hauchard was milking Tim's celebrity for all it was worth and we were dining out on it as well."

Tim, who had just left one consummate con man behind in Algeria, now found himself controlled by yet another master of the game. "A French Resistance hero of sorts during the war," Hauchard was described by his former mistress Joanna Harcourt-Smith as "sort of a gangster arms-dealer high-flying arriviste," whose tastes ran to "young girls, Cristal champagne, and the best Cuban cigars." After spending several months in the Prison de la Santé for embezzlement, Hauchard moved to Switzerland, where he became involved in the international arms trade.

Hauchard portrayed himself as completely sympathetic to Tim's plight because it was his "obligation as a gentleman to protect philosophers." He claimed he could shield Tim from the Swiss police because he had "a dozen of them" on his payroll. Hauchard also said he was perfectly willing to pay for whatever Tim and Rosemary needed in exchange for all the money he expected to make from the book Tim was writing, which "we shall sell to the movies." The two men sealed their business arrangement with a handshake.

Rosemary, who had been ill for months in Algeria, went to a Swiss clinic to have a gynecological procedure performed. Twice a week, she returned to the clinic for treatments. "I would leave Tim behind," she recalled, "and he would be sitting there holding a salon, entertaining the wives and girlfriends of all these rich and powerful men who Hauchard knew. This was much better than being in jail. It was better than Algeria or Denmark where they had been waiting at the airport to arrest us in what was a setup." After a busy month of nonstop social engagements during which Tim did very little writing, Hauchard announced that the time had come for the Learys to establish their own Swiss residence. He rented a villa for Tim and Rosemary in Villars-sur-Ollon, a ski resort located at the east end of Lake Geneva. "Because of the procedure and the treatments," Rosemary remembered, "there was now a window of opportunity for Tim and I to try to have a baby. I had one or two days in which to conceive a child. We made plans to do this by tripping in the mountains on the most opportune day."

At seven-thirty in the morning that day, Tim opened the door only to discover that the Swiss police had come to pay him a visit. "You are Dr. Leary? We are here to arrest you." As they took Tim away, one of the policemen noticed a bowl of wildflowers by the door. "Oh," he said. "And you know it is illegal to pick those in Switzerland." On the day Tim and Rosemary were to conceive the child for which she had been waiting for so long, Hauchard had arranged for Tim to be arrested. It was part of a ploy to force Tim to begin working seriously on his book.

The Prison du Bois-Mermet in Lausanne to which Tim was taken was, according to Rosemary, "far worse than San Luis Obispo, old and cold and dark and dank, a dungeon." Nonetheless, Tim was delighted to discover that he had his own cell with a metal toilet bowl, a metal table, a bed with a mattress, two blankets, a pillow, and sheets. Wrapping himself in the blankets, Tim lay down to rest only to be interrupted by two guards, each bearing a large carton "heaped with food, wine, books, stationery." Two prison trusties followed behind carrying yet more boxes. After his visitors left, Tim made a careful inventory of everything Hauchard had sent him: loaves of French bread; two kinds of salami; "a bag of gleaming waxy apples; several tins of Danish meat delicacies; six boxes of cheese: Camembert, Liederkranz, Gruyere, Bourson aux herbes, Mule du Pape, and Brie; a golden-brown roast chicken wrapped in silver foil." There was also a carton of fat juicy shrimp and one of shredded lobster; liverwurst and crackers, mayonnaise and mustard; a chocolate cake and bars of Swiss chocolate; a giant bottle of fresh orange juice; and three bottles of wine—a St. Emilion, a Mouton Cadet, and a Pouilly Fuisse; a carton of Gitanes, *sans filtre*; ten books, including *The Pentagon Papers*; two packages of envelopes—one for air mail, one for regular mail; seven boxes of the finest stationery; a ream of onion-skin paper; a package of carbon paper; and perhaps most important of all (at least to Hauchard), a portable typewriter.

Finding a corkscrew, Tim opened a bottle and poured some wine into a coffee mug. Lighting up a Gitane, he inhaled "the rich resinous throat-rasping caress of black tobacco" and sat back "to think about my mysterious patron . . . By dinner-time, the cell was blue with tobacco smoke and I was pleasantly plastered. The guards removed the two remaining bottles of wine, explaining that the ration was one bottle every two days." Noting that the Swiss were "certainly the best jail-keepers in the world," Tim fell into "a glutted stuporous slumber."

An experienced veteran of the prison-widow game, Rosemary immediately began writing letters and making phone calls. "I remember Allen Ginsberg organizing a letter-writing campaign by PEN, which had quite an effect on the Swiss. Basically, what Allen and the other writers were saying was that Tim was a political prisoner and the Swiss had no right to act as agents of the United States government by keeping him in jail." On Bastille Day, July 14, Ginsberg issued an eight-page petition entitled "Declaration of Independence for Dr. Timothy Leary." In it, he wrote that the criminal extradition of Timothy Leary from Switzerland seemed "to the under-signed poets, essayists and novelists an unseemly and intolerable continuing and exasperating literary vendetta against a specific gifted individual." Comparing Tim to Walt Whitman and Thoreau, Ginsberg recommended that the Swiss and all other governments "grant our fellow Author Philosopher safe political asylum to complete his work." The petition, delivered to the Swiss consulate in San Francisco with copies sent to the State Department and the Department of Justice in Washington, was signed by Ginsberg, Ken Kesey, Lawrence Ferlinghetti, Michael McClure, Robert Creeley, Lenore Kandel, Anaïs Nin, Alan Watts, Kenneth Rexroth, Diane DiPrima, Philip Lamantia, Ted Berrigan, Paul Krassner, Philip Whalen, Herbert Gold, Laura Huxley, and Tom Clark.

From New York, a cable signed by playwright Arthur Miller on behalf of the one hundred American members of the International PEN Club was sent to Mr. Ludwig von Moos, head of the Federal Department of Justice and Police in Bern. Urging the Swiss to grant Tim refuge as "an act of compassion," the cable stated, "It would seem that Dr. Leary has been sentenced, if not convicted, for his views on drug use; he, therefore, qualifies as an intellectual refugee and we ask the Swiss government to grant him asylum as it has hundreds of other writers, artists, and political figures who have sought refuge in Switzerland after having been forced to flee from other countries." Rosemary remembered being told that Attorney General John Mitchell actually flew to Switzerland to try to persuade the Swiss to keep Tim in prison. "So there was a lot of pressure being exerted on them from both sides. Through Hauchard, we found a Swiss lawyer named Horace Mastronardi. He was a wonderful man who worked very hard to get Tim out." Mastronardi was the attorney who had gotten Hauchard out of prison in France.

While Mastronardi busied himself "with appeals for Swiss political asylum," Tim spent a month in solitary confinement. Instead of working on his book, he put in "ten to twelve hours a day analyzing the numerical consistencies among the I Ching, the Tarot, and the Periodic Table of Elements, finally performing the assignment that Lama Govinda had given me." One day, he received a package containing an "oval painting of a landscape" with the "spidery signature of the artist: Herman [sic] Hesse" on the back. The gift had been sent to him by Christophe Wenger, Hesse's grandnephew, with whom Tim soon became quite friendly.

By mortgaging his home, Walter Houston Clark managed to send $20,000 to Switzerland to cover Tim's bail. Tim, however, remained in jail until he signed a paper giving Hauchard the profits from all his literary work for the next twelve years. "It was in prison in Switzerland that Tim went a bit zany," Rosemary recalled. "He signed everything over to Hauchard, giving him 90 percent of the book Tim and I had started writing in Algeria about his escape. Tim also wrote a letter to Hugh Hefner saying he was now in a Swiss prison because I had wanted to have a baby. Because of the Hauchard deal and the letter to Hefner, I knew Tim wasn't loyal to me in the same way that I was to him."

Using the same strategy employed to free Hauchard from prison in France, Tim was advised to fake "a heart attack while walking in the prison yard." "The physician sent by Mastronardi to examine me clucked in sympathy and prescribed eight different medications and my immediate release," Tim would later write. When Rosemary and Mastronardi visited Tim, the lawyer handed Tim a large chocolate bar with scenes of Switzerland on it. "I wish I could see some of these," Tim said. Mastronardi burst into tears. "But you can. You can. You are free.'" Since the crime for which

Tim had been imprisoned in America would have been punished by a fine in Switzerland, the authorities had decided to set him free.

On August 1, the day on which Switzerland celebrated its independence, Tim was released from jail. "When Tim came out," Rosemary recalled, "we had our usual very romantic time together. Then I began getting annoyed with him. He was doing interviews for German television and people were always calling on the phone and I desperately needed his attention so we could discuss what we were going to do." Ever since they had first met, Tim had been telling Rosemary how perfectly suited she was to be a mother and how beautiful she would look carrying his child. "The death of that possibility," she remembered, "was very hard for me to get over. Now that this was not going to happen, I had to find myself another role to play. I wanted to be quiet and retreat and read and Tim was doing interviews and jumping up to answer the phone." The headline that ran over a front-page interview with Tim in the *LA Free Press,* read WE'RE TOGETHER AND WE'VE PROBABLY NEVER BEEN HAPPIER. Nothing could have been further from the truth.

Through Mastronardi, Tim extended a lunch invitation to Dr. Albert Hofmann. On September 3, in the snack bar of the railway station in Lausanne, Tim finally met the man who had discovered LSD. With his short-cropped hair, prominent ears, and rimless glasses, Hofmann looked like a scientist who had dedicated his life to serious research. In the arbor of a restaurant called À la Grande Forêt in nearby Buchillons, the two men dined on fish and white wine. "It was a fantastic moment," Tim wrote his friend and archivist Michael Horowitz in California. "There was an immediate mutual hit of pleasure and acceptance." In an article Horowitz wrote for the *Berkeley Barb,* he reported that Tim had said Hofmann understood that LSD was "the least dangerous drug ever used by man."

Hofmann's opinion of Tim was not nearly so unreserved. In his book, *LSD: My Problem Child,* published in 1980, Hofmann wrote, "My most serious remonstrance to Leary, however, concerned the propagation of LSD use among juveniles. Leary did not attempt to refute my opinions about the particular dangers of LSD for youth." When Hofmann suggested that LSD should be used only by those with mature minds, Tim agreed. In his account of their meeting, Tim also failed to mention Hofmann's objection to the "great publicity that Leary sought for his LSD and psilocybin investigations, since he had invited reporters from daily newspapers and magazines to his experiments and mobilized radio and television."

All the while, Tim's relationship with Rosemary continued to deteriorate. His "absence during her last two fertile times had made the painful operation seem pointless," he would later write. "The insecurity of my position as a penniless fugitive had made my life less than a joy to share. Though I was now out of jail, our dependence on Hauchard was turning out to be a humiliating replica of the scene with Eldridge." Though Rosemary continued to believe that they would always be married, she wanted to leave him for a while. "Initially," she recalled, "it wasn't a breakup. It was a separation." When the tall, good-looking younger man with whom Rosemary had had an affair while Tim was in prison called from New York to say he had just returned from Afghanistan with "a sizable amount of cash" and wanted "to visit us and share his joy," Tim told him to come over. "Events moved with prearranged precision after the arrival of John," Tim would later write. "He was more than willing to resume his role as Rosemary's protector." After a week spent hammering out the details, Tim and Rosemary agreed that she would move to a nearby farmhouse so they could still see each other whenever they needed to.

In October, Tim went into a Swiss clinic for an operation to correct the deafness that had plagued him throughout his adult life. As though some form of odd LSD synergy was at work here, Rosemary left him on October 22, 1971, Tim's fifty-first birthday and the sixteenth anniversary of the death of his first wife, Marianne. Three days later, Rosemary visited Tim only to find a girl from the village named Emily living with him. "Younger than me and quite attractive," Rosemary remembered, "she was wearing my clothes and using the kohl and perfumes I had brought back from Algiers, patting her stomach while she talked about having Tim's child inside her. After I left, he had gone down into the village, met Emily, and brought her back to the house." When Tim, Emily, Rosemary, and John took acid together, despite the corrective surgery Tim had just undergone, Rosemary saw the young girl was "now listening for Tim as I had once done. Sitting beside him so she could tell him what everyone was saying. I remembered a time when Nena had come to Millbrook. She and Tim were no longer together and I was sitting in the exact same place where Nena had once sat. Now I had been replaced as well. It was the concept of replaceable parts, something Tim and I had discussed at Millbrook." No doubt in keeping with this philosophy, Tim also had a face-lift not long after Rosemary left him.

Enduring more trials and tribulations than some couples experience in a lifetime, Tim and Rosemary had somehow managed to stay together for six years. When their relationship ended, Tim's never-stable personal life began to spin so wildly out of control that it seemed as though nothing would ever set it right again.

THIRTY-SIX

Shortly after Rosemary left him, Tim Leary lost the house at 1230 Queens Road in Berkeley. He currently owed Kennedy and Rhine, his San Francisco law firm, about $10,000. To make the delinquent mortgage payments on the house and settle the overdue tax bill, his lawyers transferred the property into their names and then sold it to a friend. "I'm sure," Rosemary recalled, "that what they did with the house was something that factored into Tim's thinking later on when it seemed as though all the information he was giving was intended to lead the government to Michael Kennedy." In *Aquarius Revisited,* his 1987 book about those who helped create the sixties, Peter Owen Whitmer wrote that Tim received $4,000 from the sale of his house. Whatever the actual sum may have been, it did not compensate Tim for the loss of his most prized possession.

On December 29, 1971, the Swiss government formally rejected the United States' request for Tim's extradition. The government also denied Tim's request for permanent political asylum, ruling that he could only remain in their country until October 31, 1972. In February 1972, Tim left the canton of Valais and moved to a two-story chalet a mile from the resort of Immensee on the shores of Lake Zug. When Jack Leary called his father from California to tell him Susan had given birth to a baby girl named Dieadra, and that they were now "living in a shitty place," Tim sent Susan a plane ticket so she could join him. Although Susan and her husband, David Martino, had separated, Tim sent him a ticket so he could come to Switzerland from India. Tim also persuaded Michel Hauchard to bring Brian Barritt over from London to help him complete his book,

Then thirty-seven, Brian Barritt was a bone-thin, wild-eyed, long-haired hippie who had already spent four years in an English prison for drugs. He and Tim had first met when Barritt had visited Tim in Algeria to ask if he would write the foreword to his book *Whisper*. Barritt brought with him to Switzerland a copy of *The Confessions of Aleister Crowley*. Recently republished, the book had sparked renewed interest in Crowley, a lifelong drug addict obsessed by deviant sexuality and the occult. In the book, Crowley described the magical ceremony that he and the poet Victor Neuberg held in 1909 in the dunes just outside Bou-Saada in Algeria, where Tim and Rosemary had taken acid with Barritt and his wife, Liz. Stunned by this "coincidence," as well as the similarities in their lives, Tim began calling himself "Nemo," after the entity that Crowley and Neuburg claim to have contacted in Bou-Saada. He became a great devotee of the tarot deck that Crowley had designed with the artist Frieda Harris. When Tim's publisher asked him to retitle the book about his escape—the working title had been *It's About Time*—Tim decided to call it *Confessions of a Hope Fiend,* an amalgam of Crowley's *Confessions* and his *Diary of a Dope Fiend.*

His safety in Switzerland assured for at least six months, Tim began to surround himself with yet another extended family. Dennis Martino, David's twin brother, and his wife, nineteen-year-old Robin Virtel, arrived from Afghanistan along with their young son, Orion. "Dennis," Rosemary recalled, "was a control freak who had never really been a member of the Brotherhood, or anyone they had ever really trusted." She added that while "he may have been sent by some government or police agency to destabilize Tim's situation and make it easier to bring him back to prison," he acted as Tim's "eyes and ears." From Kabul, Dennis brought with him what Barritt would later call in *The Road of Excess: A Psychedelic Autobiography* "a genie-shaped little bottle of whiskey coloured hash oil, a sample of the alchemical concoctions that the 'Brotherhood' were producing at this period." Tim and his entourage had only to dip a toothpick into the bottle, wait until 90 percent of the liquid had drained away, and then lick off the remainder to "function most assuredly for the next four hours." Brian Barritt's wife, Liz, used the oil to bake one hundred hash cookies that glowed "an unearthly cannabis-green."

It soon got so crowded in the chalet on the lake that Tim accepted an invitation from Hermann Hesse's grandnephew, Christophe Wenger, to rent a three-story house in a corner of the town square in Carona, a small village near Ticino in southern Switzerland. Using the house as a mail drop, Tim spent his days and nights "dashing all over the place." Tim, Barritt, and a Swiss politician named Sergius Golowin toured caves that formerly were inhabited by Celtic monks and hermits. They visited the stone cottage where Carl Jung had once lived, the Isle of St. Pierre where Jean-Jacques Rousseau had stayed, the rock where Nietzsche had sat when he criticized Wagner, and the waterfall where Tristan Tzara had almost drowned Man Ray. Together, they stood where Aleister Crowley, who was also a climber and explorer, had snorted a "pyramid of cocaine from the back of his hand before tackling the north face of the Matterhorn."

Through his newfound interest in skiing, Tim met the Polish film director Roman Polanski, whose pregnant wife and unborn child had been murdered by Charles Manson's disciples in 1969. Through Polanski, Tim met Gene Gutowski, a Polish film producer who was a close friend of Jerzy Kosinski, author of *The Painted Bird*. Acting as an intermediary, Gutowski took the manuscript of Tim's book with him to New York where he asked Alan U. Schwartz, a well-known literary lawyer, to handle the American rights. Schwartz offered the manuscript to Marc Jaffe at Bantam Books, a paperback house, and then negotiated an agreement with Victor Temkin, Bantam's general counsel, to publish the book for an advance of $250,000. "Eventually," Tim later wrote, "the $250,000 was divided as follows: an Argentinian [sic] playboy who introduced Polanski got ten percent, Gene Gutowski got twenty, and a distinguished New York literary lawyer named Alan Schwartz got ten. Hauchard and I were supposed to split the remaining sixty. As it turned out, I received around $40,000 on signing. Hauchard stole the rest. I paid Walter Clark $10,000, sent $5,000 each to Susan and Jack, and bought a gleaming golden Porsche and a roomful of high-tech stereo equipment." Barritt was then informed by the publishers that he could not be credited as co-author, but that if he agreed to this stipulation, he would receive $40,000.

In Switzerland, home of the funicular and the thin chime, all the international con men were now hard at work conning one another. After rewriting the book at least a dozen times, Tim finally completed work on it in Zurich on July 7. What now concerned his publishers was the news that the biography of the reclusive billionaire Howard Hughes, which author Clifford Irving had sold to McGraw-Hill for $765,000, had just been revealed to be a hoax. Irving was ordered to pay back the entire advance and served fourteen months in jail for fraud. "This was right after Clifford Irving's hoax biography of Howard Hughes came out," Alan U. Schwartz recalled, "so they were all hysterical about whether or not this was real. So they said, 'We'll make this deal but we'll go over there and he has to initial every page of the manuscript.'" In August, Marc Jaffe, Victor Temkin, and Schwartz flew to Geneva. Hauchard picked them up in a big black car and took them to an expensive restaurant in Lausanne where he showed them a paper signed by Tim giving Hauchard the rights to all his writings. When Hauchard informed them that he intended to sign the publishing contract, Schwartz wondered if Tim had signed the paper under duress.

The next day, Schwartz and his traveling companions went to Le Richemond Hotel in Geneva, where Hauchard had rented what Brian Barritt later described as a "a lounge full of shafts of sunlight and wealthy men." The principals assembled around a large rectangular table covered with green felt, over which hung a small painting of Christ and his disciples. In Barritt's words, Tim sat in the middle of the table "looking like Christ in Leonardo's Last Supper across from Mark [sic] Jaffe, the president of Bantam who looks like Doubting Thomas." When Schwartz realized that Tim was not being represented by anyone in these negotiations, he felt "a pang of conscience." Taking Tim aside before a lunch break, Schwartz said, 'Look, I just want to say something to you. You're not represented here. Are you aware and are you agreeable to the fact that you have signed over all your rights to all your work to Hauchard? Because I don't want to go forward with this if you're not in accord with that.' He looked at me very puzzled and smiled and said, 'I really appreciate this. I know what I'm doing and I know why I did it and don't worry about it. It's fine.' So we went back in and finished the negotiation, had this big lunch, and flew back to New York." Before they left, Tim dutifully signed every page of the manuscript. On some pages, he scrawled "True Love," "Too Lovely," "Tres Lucky," or just "Tim O'Leary" with a smiley face inside the "O."

On July 1, Bantam Books printed 25,000 mass-market paperback copies of *Confessions of a Hope Fiend*, copyright by Michel-Gustave Hauchard. Despite a good deal of hype and the sizable advance, there was no second printing. Unlike many of Tim's other works, the book remains out of print to this day.

"When *Confessions of a Hope Fiend* came out," Rosemary recalled, "I remember thinking that Tim was not only a plagiarist but a 'paraphraseist.' He had stolen my material. He had taken what I had said to him and I was not even compensated for it. I thought of suing Bantam Books and they said, 'If she wants to sue us, tell her to come to New York to file suit,' which of course I couldn't do." In what seemed like an attempt to mollify her, Tim wrote two letters on July 28, which he then had notarized in the hope that they would serve as binding legal agreements. In one, he expressed "the desire and expectation of us all that Rosemary should share in and be given half of any monies" that would come to him if it is ever "possible and feasible to sell any of our memorabilia. In view of the fact that many of Rosemary's possessions and personal records, including letters, are included in the archives, I know you will agree that no sale of the archives be executed without her permission." Addressing his other letter "To Whom It May Concern," Tim wrote: "In December 1969 in Laguna Beach California I was arrested with Rosemary Leary for the possession of drugs. Rosemary Leary was subsequently convicted for possession of cannabis and LSD contained in a bag that she was carrying. I wish to state that these drugs were in joint possession and that she was carrying the illegal substances at my request."

Gallant as Tim's gesture may have been, it did not win Rosemary back. "We had a reconciliation of love in Lausanne," she recalled, "and I remember him asking me to come back to where he was living with Susan and I realized I couldn't do it. I just could not get back into that family situation. I missed him terribly but I couldn't live with him." After they parted company, Rosemary sent a short note to friends that was published by *Rolling Stone* on its "Correspondence, Love Letters, & Advice" page. In its entirety, the note read, "Rosemary Leary wills it to be known that for more than a year she has enjoyed a reality separate from Timothy Leary. She is not responsible for his debts karmic or financial. A wife is not property."

With the book done and the fear that he would have to leave Switzerland gone, at least for the moment, Tim was now free to spend nearly all his time in pursuit of sensual pleasure with his inner circle. "Our backgrounds fuse into a whirl of sex," Barritt wrote. "Tim's in love with Liz, Robin has fallen for me, Liz is in love with all and sundry, Dennis is in love with Dennis . . ." When a German artist who turned out to have "one of the finest erections in Europe" dropped by one day with his long-waisted, long-legged girlfriend, they all got "caught up in an orgy on the waterbed."

As he did in Algeria, Tim continued to draw people to him from all over the world. Now deeply into his new incarnation as Baba Ram Dass, Richard Alpert, wearing sandals and a dhoti and carrying his belongings in a woven bag, visited Tim on his way back from India. When Tim and a small circle of friends dropped acid with Christophe Wenger one day, Ram Dass was "suffering from Delhi-belly" and got high by "eating cannabis extract." George Litwin, Charles Slack, and Jerry Hopkins, an editor of *Rolling Stone,* came to visit. In the nearby village of Carona, Wavy Gravy and various members of the Hog Farm, who were touring Europe by bus, also took up temporary residence.

While Tim enjoyed himself, Hauchard flew to New York to collect the second half of the advance from Bantam Books before it could be sent to Barritt. Minus varying commissions, Hauchard returned to Switzerland with about $86,000. Gene Gutowski tried to warn Tim of Hauchard's plan by sending a letter to him, but it arrived too late.

On August 4, 1972, Tim sat with Kenneth Kahn for an interview that ran in both the *Berkeley Barb* and the *LA Free Press.* From the start, Tim's behavior seemed odd. He refused to allow Kahn to use a tape recorder. As Kahn asked questions, Tim kept looking at Brian Barritt before answering. He told Kahn that Barritt was "his 'receiver.'" Since they were "in perfect telepathic communication," Tim wanted this to be an interview with Barritt as communicated through Timothy Leary. When Kahn and his girlfriend asked Tim if they could take a snapshot of him to accompany the interview, he declined. Instead, he said he would send them a photo, but never did. The next day, Kahn and his girlfriend returned so Tim could add a preface explaining who Barritt was. Tim then told them he had decided to dispense with that idea and asked to go over the questions again. Rather than responding orally, he began typing his answers. Most of his responses were monosyllabic, deliberately vague, or ironic. The upbeat spontaneity that had always characterized his public statements was nowhere to be found. The news he received the next day did nothing to improve his mood. On Sunday, August 6, 1972, Cecil Hicks, the Orange County district attorney who had appeared before the United States Supreme Court to argue against Tim's appeal, proudly announced he had "broken the back" of the Brotherhood of Eternal Love. Acting on twenty-nine indictments handed down by the Orange County grand jury, two hundred narcotics agents had "made a series of lightning-like predawn arrests." The agents had put forty people in jail, seized one and a half million tabs of LSD, two and a half tons of hashish, thirty gallons of hash oil, $20,000 in cash, and "innumerable" sets of false identification papers. Hicks was a freckle-faced man who, as Joe Eszterhas would later write in *Rolling Stone*, had "prosecuted bottomless dancers and porno bookstore owners" as well as "denounced the Supreme Court, sexual freedom, draft dodgers, and the President's Commission on Marijuana." Hicks very much wanted to be the next attorney general of California. To make certain his announcement would generate national headlines, Hicks identified Tim not only as "a key figure" in the Brotherhood but the actual "brains" of the operation. Hicks also claimed that as the living, breathing "God" of this "hippie mafia," Tim was "able to travel and live comfortably on smuggling profits." Tim's bail was set at an astronomical $5 million. Hicks announced that he also intended to demand Tim's immediate extradition from Switzerland. "Leary is personally responsible for destroying more lives than any other human being. The number of his victims destroyed by drugs and LSD literally runs into the hundreds of thousands." The story ran on the front page of the *New York Times*.

For more than a year, Neil Purcell, who had by now been promoted to sergeant in the Laguna Beach police force, had been trying to convince a coalition of state and federal agencies that the Brotherhood was an evil empire so powerful that all available resources ought to be marshaled against it to prevent the spread of drugs in America. In order to coordinate intelligence on the Brotherhood, Purcell had convened a summit meeting of law enforcement agencies in San Francisco. The meeting was tape recorded, so that a typed summary of the discussion could then be shared by all participants. One of the more remarkable conclusions concerning the Brotherhood to be found in the single-spaced, twenty-eight-page transcript, aptly dubbed "The Nark Papers" by Eszterhas in *Rolling Stone*, read: "At this time Leary is not presently really involved in the upper echelon and not realizing any profit from the group." Yet when Hicks appeared before that Orange County grand jury to ask for indictments against the Brotherhood, he argued that under Timothy Leary's leadership, the group had developed into a "very sophisticated organization in terms of smuggling. If you have seen *The French Connection*, you are aware of these things."

Some of the brothers who had fled the ranch after the disastrous summer of 1969 had set themselves up in distant ports of call from which they sailed schooners loaded with hundreds of pounds of Colombian weed to America. Some had put up $25,000 to bankroll Tim's escape from prison and then sent another $25,000 to Algeria with Ricky Bevans so Tim could pay off Eldridge Cleaver to let him leave the country. As a *Los*

Angeles Times reporter noted, court records indicated Tim might "have been more of a drain on the group's funds than anything else."

Nonetheless, Tim had again become a wanted man. Barritt would later write that the $5 million was "a world record bail for an escaped prisoner" and that the real purpose of such astronomical bail was "to intimidate foreign governments into thinking of Dr. Leary as a dangerous criminal and thereby eliminating any opportunities for political asylum abroad." Shortly after news of the Brotherhood bust reached Switzerland, Tim used heroin for the first time.

In *Flashbacks,* Tim would later write that his experiment with the drug "was not the result of alienation and boredom . . . The two years of enforced exile in Switzerland were hard, but not enough to drive me to the needle." Like a guilty adolescent pointing his finger at everyone else, Tim named Barritt as the instigator of his heroin use. "Although Brian clucked with virtuous disapproval about heroin (just like every other lying junky), his every word and deed conveyed an intriguing sense of the dark deep vegetative wisdom of opium." Tim also blamed his drug use on the Rolling Stones. "I used to hang out with Anita [Pallenberg] and Keith Richard at the baroque villa of Prince Stash de Rolle," Leary wrote. "Everywhere I went that summer I heard that low-down beat of the Stones celebrating Sister Morphine and Brown Sugar, Mick singing about his basement room and his needle and his spoon. But I had no desire to initiate personal heroin research until destiny floated an enormous supply of the stuff right into my house."

In an outline for a book that he would never complete, Tim wrote that a Czech refugee in Switzerland on an American government research grant offered to turn him on to several experimental drugs, a new aphrodisiac and a nonaddictive heroin-type chemical among them. "The aphrodisiac works but the heroin-substitute turns out to be addictive with painful withdrawal symptoms. We have the drug analyzed and it turns out to be Southeast Asia heroin." This version of the story was not supported by Barritt. He wrote that after visiting London, his wife returned with "a grain of pure English heroin she has obtained from [Scottish writer and addict] Alex Trocchi—6 sixth of a grain 'jacks.'" Not having used "for ages," Barritt regarded the heroin as a "nice present." Tim was there when Liz returned, Barritt wrote, so he asked him if he wanted to try it and to his surprise, Tim said yes. Tim told Barritt he was trying heroin so that it would be "no longer a mystery" and so that his drug education would be "more or less complete." Barritt would later write that he kept hearing a voice whispering in his "inner ear—'Hello Brian, I hear you OD'ed the Messiah?'" To Tim, Barritt wrote that he said, "I'd hate to be known as the person who got Timothy Leary hooked on smack."

After Liz put the needle into Tim's arm, Barritt wrote that "for the first time in his life Tim Leary slowed down. All his ambition drained away, all his dreams became fulfilled and all he had to do was lie back and dig it." Immediately, Tim analyzed the buzz as a "euphoric downer," which did its work on the first level of his nervous system. When Barritt returned after having been away for a few days, he learned that a stewardess had given Tim a few grams of heroin she had brought back from Beirut. For the next few days, Tim and Barritt used what she had brought and then decided to "knock it on the head [quit]."

In *Flashbacks,* Leary claimed that Barritt could sense the presence of heroin in Tim's house when he was "fifty feet away" and "pestered" him to take it with him as an experiment. After shooting himself up, Barritt did the same for Tim. "When the drug hit my vein," Tim wrote, "I felt the warm flash of euphoria that is worshipped among junkies. No question about it: I felt wonderful for a couple of minutes; for the next half hour I enjoyed a relaxed noodly bliss, a giggly nonchalance about worldly matters. Soon I fell into a heavy sleep."

The next morning, Tim wrote, Barritt was at his door "eager to continue the research." Feeling no desire for more heroin, Tim told him to wait until that night for their next session. "The postponement caused a predictable distress in Brian. To avoid the nagging and fidgeting I gave him half the supply, reserving the remainder for whatever trials I might wish to make at later times." Just before bedtime that night, Tim allowed Barritt to give him an intramuscular injection. "It made me feel mellow and pleasantly somnolent. The third night of the experiment I sniffed some heroin and again felt my cells sigh in satisfaction. On the fourth day Brian had run out of his stash. He became irritable. By the time he got around to requesting a hit from mine, I had already flushed it down the toilet." Barritt contended that the two of them spent a "couple of weeks" engaged in the heroin experiment.

When Charles Slack arrived in Switzerland during the last week in August to interview Tim for his book *Timothy Leary, the Madness of the Sixties, & Me,* the terminally unhip Slack noted that in "dirty white slacks and white sneakers and white sweater with nothing under it" Tim was "shivering" and constantly fidgeting and wiping his lips. His hand shook whenever he held a cigarette. While Slack never saw Tim put a needle in his arm, he was sure that Tim was using heroin. "He had run into this girl in Switzerland who had a pound of heroin and he became a junkie. When I discovered that, I became totally judgmental and totally disappointed because we had always said we would never use downers. We were the up crowd. Even alcohol was not good . . . I thought, 'This is the end.' But then he bounced back from that. Just like he did from everything."

Tim now began referring to Liz Barritt as "Hermoine" from Hermann Hesse's *Steppenwolf*. He saw Brian Barritt as "Pablo," the role Tim himself had played when *Death of the Mind* opened on New York's Lower East Side in 1966. With eerie synchronicity, an American film group interested in making a movie of Hesse's book asked Tim to do a screen test for the role of Haller. By the time the results came back, Tim was no longer available to play the role. Instead, Max von Sydow was cast in the part.

"After Rosemary left," recalled Joanna Harcourt-Smith, "Tim was on heroin for a long time. When I met him, he had just gone through a big heroin detox thing, which at the time involved drinking masses of red wine. It was a way to detox because it would keep you drunk and counteract the effects of withdrawing. According to what both Tim and Dennis Martino told me, Tim was very deeply into it."

In *What Does WoMan Want?*, Tim Leary described Joanna Harcourt-Smith Tamabacopoulos D'Amecourt Leary as "a 21st century fox" who had "boogied naked on the glass table-tops and run hand-in-hand under the crazy moon." The "snow queen of London's Chelsea district and madcap prankster of Europe's jet set," she was often mistaken for "Audrey Hepburn, Brigitte Bardot, or Lauren Bacall's younger sister."

"Her CV," Brian Barritt noted, was "full of famous connections." Born on January 13, 1946, in the Palace Hotel in St. Moritz, Switzerland, Joanna Harcourt-Smith was the daughter of a titled British naval officer whose father had served as Lord Chamberlain to King George V and helped found the Albert and Victoria Museum in London. Her mother, Marysia Ulam, was a beautiful, domineering Jewish aristocrat from Poland who spoke seven languages but never learned how to drive a car or write a check. One of Joanna's relatives was Stanislaw Ulam, the mathematician who helped Edward Teller invent the hydrogen bomb.

A brilliant and precocious child who inhabited a world of fantasy, Joanna claimed that she had been sexually molested at the age of nine by the family chauffeur. When she summoned the courage to tell her mother, Marysia decided that her "fundamentally evil" daughter was telling yet another of her many lies. Joanna slashed her wrists for the first time when she was twelve. On her fourteenth birthday, she lost her virginity in Cairo to the nineteen-year-old son of Egypt's minister of culture. Stealing 20,000 francs from her mother's safe, she ran away with the boy, only to be caught and deported to Lebanon. While attending school at the Ecole Protestante in Beirut, she became a well-known television actress and newscaster. At sixteen, she had an affair with French singing legend Charles Aznavour. Becoming pregnant by him, she aborted his child.

Two years later, she met Michel Hauchard in the casino of the Hotel de Paris in Monte Carlo. Although Hauchard was forty, they began an affair that lasted until after he was released from prison. Pregnant again at twenty, Joanna married a Greek industrialist with whom she had a daughter. When their marriage broke up, she went to live with her mother in Marbella, then moved to America where she married Jean-Claude D'Amecourt, the director of a subcommittee in the House of Representatives. In February 1972, she gave birth to his son. Six months later, while living in "a beautiful house in Marbella," she took "a lot of LSD" and became part of the European hippie jet-set scene.

In that scene, no one was more striking than Tommy Weber. Tall, blond, and handsome, he toured the world with his two young sons, going from one great house to another as a welcome guest. Most recently, he had been in residence at Villa Nellcote, the palatial estate overlooking the bay in Villefrance where Keith Richards and Anita Pallenberg had lived in decadent splendor while down in the basement, the Rolling Stones tried to record the follow-up to *Sticky Fingers,* the album Tim blamed for having helped lead him to heroin.

Although Joanna's husband was still around when she and Weber first met in Marbella, it took them no more than an hour to get together. Scoring some morphine from a friend, Tommy and Joanna decided to visit Keith and Anita, who now lived in Villars-sur-Ollon, not far from where Tim had been arrested by the Swiss police on the day he and Rosemary intended to conceive a child.

During their visit, Richards spent most of his time downstairs playing electric guitar and piano. Upstairs, Anita discovered in Joanna a kindred spirit. As they drank copious amounts of tequila, smoked dope, and snorted coke, Anita told Joanna about this incredible man named Timothy Leary who lived right down the road. As the night wore on and the drugs took hold, Anita, who loved nothing more than to bring people together—if only to see if she could then break them up again—wove her magic spell. She persuaded Joanna that her destiny was to meet this incredibly intelligent and beautiful but ultimately very lonely man who ever since his wife had left him spent all his time hanging out with really stupid chicks, none of whom were at all like Joanna. This was kismet. It was her fate. Ever since Joanna had first read Laura Huxley's *This Timeless Moment,* she had dreamed of finding a man who knew everything about LSD and then becoming so close to him that as he lay dying, she would be the one who gave him the dose of acid that would take him to the next bardo.

Together that night, Anita and Joanna hatched a plan to change the course of history and win freedom for Tim. The Rolling Stones, the world's greatest rock 'n' roll band, would offer to do a quick tour of America with all proceeds going to Senator George McGovern, the Democratic Party candidate in the 1972 presidential election. McGovern would then defeat the hated Richard Nixon in November. As a quid pro quo, or perhaps just an act of mercy, he would pardon Tim. In the hours before dawn, in their chemically altered state, Anita and Joanna agreed that the plan made perfect sense. Even if it failed, Joanna could already see that this would be a new adventure. Joanna and Tommy Weber promptly flew first class to Washington where they actually managed to talk their way into McGovern headquarters and present their idea to his aides, who told them they had come too late. McGovern was already so far behind in the polls that not even the Rolling Stones could help him.

Disappointed, they continued on to New York where Joanna visited her old friend Egon von Furstenberg. While they were there, the phone rang. The caller was Michel Hauchard. He and Joanna arranged to meet for a drink at the King Cole Bar in the St. Regis Hotel, where he showed her the $86,000 check he had just collected from Bantam Books for Tim's manuscript. "Look what I am doing now with your generation's hero," Joanna recalled him telling her. "This guy is worth a lot of money and I own every bit of him." The only way she would ever get to Tim, he told her, was through him. Promising Hauchard she would see him the next day, Joanna flew with Weber to Geneva, rushed to Hauchard's house in

Lausanne, and found his address book which contained five different phone numbers for Tim. After checking in to the Palace Hotel in Lausanne, Joanna began calling Tim. When he finally called her back, Joanna told him she had a message from Hauchard. Intrigued, Tim agreed to meet her. In "Paramour," her unpublished memoir, Joanna wrote that he introduced himself by saying, "You and I have a lot in common. We're both *persona non grata* in several countries. I have a great admiration for a woman who can make a scandal and a statement at the same time." "It comes naturally," she replied.

In his Porsche, Tim took Joanna and Weber to his house to meet Brian and Liz Barritt, and Dennis Martino. "Dennis was small and wiry from years of yoga," Joanna recalled. "Shifty eyes, curly hair, an Italian aquiline nose, sharp cheekbones. He was almost like a monkey. Never still. There was an entourage there and I was just concerned that there was no girlfriend." Joanna had brought two windowpane tabs of Clear Light acid with her and offered one to Tim. As they took them with white wine, she toasted Tim: "Who loves will come with me." Tim replied, "To you, beautiful woman. Just tell me what you want." Like characters in a movie they had both seen many times before, she read her next line perfectly. "Everything," Joanna told him.

After Tim and Joanna had taken yet more acid together, Tim gave Weber $5,000 to go to Amsterdam with his two young sons to put down a deposit on a boat that they planned to sail to Jamaica, where the Rolling Stones would be recording their next album. "Tim just paid him to go away," Joanna recalled. Now that she was finally "with the man who was going to make me somebody in the world," Joanna accompanied Tim to Basel to meet the American producer of the movie based on *Steppenwolf.* "We were always tripping," she remembered. "After we met, Tim and I took acid for forty days solid. Every day."

A week went by. Although the two of them were inseparable, Joanna began getting annoyed because Tim was still not sleeping with her. In the chalet, she came across the copy of *Rolling Stone* with Joe Eszterhas's article about the Brotherhood of Eternal Love bust. "I read that and I understood for the first time why he was a fugitive," she recalled. "Because he didn't explain anything."

With Tim's allotted time in Switzerland rapidly nearing an end, his attorney, Horace Mastronardi, was still trying to get him permanent resident status. After the Brotherhood bust, this was no longer so easy. "Because the indictments had been handed down and there were thirty-six counts of Tim being the mastermind for every bit of hashish smuggled into California from Afghanistan by the Brotherhood," Joanna recalled, "the Swiss were getting nervous and no longer felt this was a case of possession of zero point zero one gram. Even though they were told it was a fabrication, they were saying, 'No more.'"

In *Flashbacks,* Tim wrote that he asked a contact in the CIA to make arrangements for him to go to a country with no extradition treaty with the United States. The contact told Tim that if he went to Austria to work on an anti-heroin documentary, Chancellor Bruno Kreisky might be persuaded to allow him to remain there. There is some question as to who this contact may have been. In "Paramour," Joanna wrote that Dennis Martino was Tim's Austrian connection. Whoever suggested the idea, Tim was more than ready to leave Switzerland. When he learned that Joanna's mother was Polish-Austrian, Tim offered to drive Joanna through the Alps to Vienna, where they would live it up. "And I was glad," Joanna recalled, "because I was sick of the hangers-on and I wanted total possession of this man who incidentally still hadn't fucked me yet." Before they left, Joanna called her mother in Marbella to tell her that she was now with a wonderful man, a psychologist from Harvard named Dr. Timothy Leary. Her mother asked if she could speak with him. Marysia then told Tim that Joanna lived in a dream world where nothing was real. How fortunate that he was an expert in abnormal psychology. If this information disturbed Tim, he did not let it interfere with their travel plans. The next morning, he and Joanna took acid yet again and headed off for St. Moritz in his Porsche. On the way, they stopped in Gstaad to ski. In an ice-filled silver bucket in their luxurious third floor suite in the Palace Hotel, the staff had thoughtfully provided a bottle of Veuve-Clicquot with a note: "Welcome Mr. and Mrs. Leary." After dinner, they returned to their room and he prepared to make love to her at long last.

"It was a full moon," she recalled, "incredibly beautiful, and he had this Samsonite briefcase. From it, he started pulling out *The Tibetan Book of the Dead,* Buddhist beads, an incredibly beautiful tantric ring, and the Crowley tarot deck. He made an altar with candles and set all these things on the altar. The last thing he pulled out were these *Life* magazine pictures of the inside of the brain. And he told me this was where he was going to make love to me." Tim instructed Joanna to look at the pictures so she would know that when he made love to her, he would be touching her in "every precious river and valley of her brain." As she would later write, he told her she was "Lakshmi the goddess who brings wealth and abundance" and he was "Vishnu, the god who dreams the world." Putting the gold ring on her finger to signify their tantric marriage, he took her to bed at last. "I was twenty-six years old and on acid and I was cooked," she recalled. "We went to bed and it wasn't so great."

The next day, the two of them went skiing. Tim had already told Joanna that for him, skiing was "an interesting form of yoga—the faster you go, the less likely you are to get hurt." Tim also wanted to smoke hashish as they went up on the lift. Joanna suggested they eat some before putting on their skis. Tim, obviously a beginner at the sport, could barely keep up with her. All day long he kept falling and getting up again as she took him down the most difficult runs on the Wasserngrat. Touched by his determination and courage, Joanna later wrote that she felt as if they were skiing on "a blinding field of crystallized moonlight in the middle of the day."

On acid yet again, they drove all night from Gstaad to St. Moritz where they stayed with Joanna's old friend, Christina "Putzi" von Opel, the automobile heiress. On Christmas Eve, Andy Warhol, accompanied by "some of his friends of mixed genders" in "tuxedoes, with the women in matching Chanel outfits," turned up at Putzi's chalet. Tim and Warhol, Joanna later wrote, acted like "two terrified roosters, their tailfeathers up and alert, waiting to see which one would outsmart the other." Then they sat down next to each other on the couch. "There are only three real geniuses in America," Tim told Warhol. "You and me, and the third changes all the time." When someone put an old Ricky Nelson record on the turntable, Warhol asked Joanna to dance.

Using back roads to avoid straying into Germany, Tim and Joanna snorted cocaine and smoked hashish to "ballast the LSD" as they drove all night to Vienna, where they breakfasted on espresso, two aquavits, and a couple of quaaludes. They then checked into the Bristol Hotel. "The people who were supposed to make this movie were a horrible commune of hippies," Joanna recalled. "We used them to get more LSD and then we went out to a really nice house in the country." Tim walked through a scene in the film, but soon realized the Wiener Filmkollektiv could not help him obtain permanent resident status in Austria. Instead, they urged him to "go underground in Yugoslavia." Nonetheless, Tim issued a statement on drugs during his stay in Vienna, which he apparently hoped

would help him remain in Austria. In it, he wrote, "I have personally experienced the torments and the attractions of heroin . . . My own life is
fully overflowing with love, enthusiasm, discovery and revelation each
day. I neither want nor need opiate drugs, which some few with nervous
systems perhaps more sensitive than mine may crave." Calling drug addiction "a physical illness," Tim urged all nations to become "civilized
and compassionate in dealing with those who are different from ourselves
and our norms." He went on to say how happy he was to be in Austria,
which "for us personally and I think for the world at large exists as a beacon of compassion and freedom."

A few days after New Year's 1973, Dennis Martino showed up in Vienna with his girlfriend and Tim's daughter. "Susan was eight months
pregnant and dragging her daughter, Dieadra, with her," Joanna recalled.
"David Martino was in India, thinking the radio was talking to him. He
was totally insane and she had just come back from India and she wanted
Dad to rescue her."

Stoked on cocaine supplied by the film commune, Tim was now taking so much LSD on a daily basis that not even Joanna could keep up with
him. She would just lick her tab or simply throw it away. While Tim
might not have noticed that his daughter and Joanna were the same age,
this fact was not lost on Susan. Yet again, she had been relegated to
second-class status in her father's life. "I helped Susan," Joanna recalled,
"but I could not carry on a conversation with her." Susan showed Joanna
a bottle of water that she had brought back with her from the Ganges
River. She then said, "Drink this. It will make all your dreams come true."
Though aware that she was "completely out of my mind by this time,"
Joanna drank it. "Within a few days," she recalled, "I was orange. I could
hardly move." Thinking her condition had to be a result of all the LSD
she had taken, Joanna dragged Tim to the school of medicine in Vienna.
In front of a distinguished professor and his entire class of medical stu-
dents, she stripped to the waist and demanded that he supply a diagnosis.
"Look, class," the professor announced. "A classic case of jaundice due to
hepatitis."

The professor wanted her to go immediately to the hospital, but
Joanna and Tim rushed back to their hotel where, she recalled, "Everything like it always did with Tim sped up like crazy." Dennis Martino
showed up with the news that he had totaled the Porsche. Tim explained
that Joanna had to go to the hospital and that they had no money to pay

for the hotel. Everyone dropped acid and Dennis Martino announced that they should go to Afghanistan. "Hyatullah," he said, "owes you the world."

Hyatullah Tokhi ran a hotel and a rug shop in Kabul. His brother Amanullah had been employed as the maintenance supervisor for the American embassy. Hyatullah and Amanullah Tokhi had become wealthy men by serving as the Brotherhood's primary suppliers of hashish and hash oil in Afghanistan. They had also visited America and, with members of the Brotherhood serving as their hosts, toured Disneyland, Laguna Beach, and the Lion Country Safari. How could such men not offer Tim their help? A plan took shape. According to Joanna, "Dennis said to Tim, 'Hyatullah owes you the world. If you go there, he'll have money. He'll be glad to protect you. Afghanistan has no extradition treaty with the United States.' He sells it and Tim says, 'Putzi von Opel is spending the winter in Ceylon. We'll go to Afghanistan, we'll score money, Joanna will get well, and we'll go to Ceylon and spend the rest of our life on the beach.'"

To Joanna, it all made sense. Counting up their money "like crazy little rats," Tim and Joanna found a flight to Kabul, which left Vienna the next morning. They planned to stop over in Beirut where Joanna still knew everyone who mattered. There they would have a nice dinner with the son of the ex-president and then continue on to Kabul where Dennis would join them. There was one small problem: they could not afford to pay their hotel bill. Piling all her clothing, skis, ski boots, binoculars, and astronomy books on the bed along with her mink coat, Joanna left a note that read, "We have to go. Here's my stuff. And we will pay you." A year and a half later, she made good on her promise.

At the airport, Tim and Joanna boarded an Arianna Airlines flight to Beirut. "All those moments were incredible," she recalled, "because we were still tripping. To get away on an airplane got us more high than anything. Tim hadn't been on a plane since he had left Algeria and so the feeling of freedom was incredible, convincing himself that it was going to work." In Afghanistan, two brothers whom Tim had never met would surely shelter and protect him until he and Joanna could continue on to Ceylon. Together on some beautiful beach without a name, they would bask in the warmth of the sun, and all of Tim's unfinished business would vanish into the clear blue sky like a song.

THIRTY-SEVEN

In Beirut, Tim and Joanna celebrated her twenty-seventh birthday by smoking hashish with a young Lebanese couple whom they had met on the street. By now, Joanna was so sick that Tim literally had to carry her into the elevator of the couple's apartment building overlooking the sea where they all then took green tabs of acid. On the way back to their hotel room, Joanna stopped at a pharmacy to buy a bottle of hair dye. Together, they hopped into the bath. As Joanna began smearing black paste all over Tim's silver hair, Tim laughed as he kissed and caressed her breasts. Moving to the bed, they began making love. Only then did Joanna remember that the dye was supposed to be rinsed out after twenty minutes. By the time she got around to doing this, Tim's hair had turned purple. They both loved the look.

The next day, Joanna continued transforming Tim into the Acid King by dressing him in a shimmering silver shirt and purple satin pants. Joanna, wearing high-heeled platform boots, light blue Levis, a white sweater with a big pink sun on it, and the gold tantric ring Tim had given her in Switzerland, sat between Tim and Dennis Martino on the flight to Kabul. As the plane left Beirut, they all took acid again.

Surrounded by mountains covered in snow, Kabul looked beautiful from the air. Dennis, who had been there many times before, assumed the role of tour guide. He told Tim and Joanna that as soon as they passed through immigration, they should check into the Intercontinental Hotel while he went to Hyatullah's house to inform him that his honored guests had arrived. As Dennis made his way toward the airport window where an Afghani official was stamping passports, Tim and Joanna sat on a bench, feeling like refugees who had just found sanctuary. Suddenly, a short man with a clipped mustache was standing over them. "Are you

Timothy Leary?" he asked. Without waiting for an answer, he grabbed their passports from Tim's hand, gave Tim a card, and stalked out of the terminal. Leaping to his feet, Tim began yelling, "Hey, you! My passport! You stole my passport!" Dennis and a couple of American hippies whom he had just met came over to see if they could help. "Tim was incredibly pale," Joanna recalled, "and he said to me and Dennis, 'I'm going back to America.' He handed Dennis the card the man gave him and it said, 'James Senner, Third Secretary, United States Embassy.' And Dennis said, 'Fuck! You're going back to America.'"

An Afghani woman in uniform then asked to see their passports. Tim told her that a man from the American embassy had just taken them out of his hand and disappeared with them. The woman informed them that if they had no passports or visas, they would be arrested and jailed until they could be deported. Again, Tim tried to explain that their passports had just been stolen. Losing his patience, he began to shout. While several men in trench coats surrounded them, Joanna watched Dennis hurry out of the terminal, hopefully to find them some help.

Given that neither Tim nor Joanna had been admitted to Afghanistan, the fact that the nation had no extradition treaty with the United States did not matter. "It became catch-22 at that moment," Joanna recalled. "We were in no-man's-land." A man in a black leather coat led them to a mud hut outside the terminal where Joanna began to cry. The man informed them that they had been charged with trying to enter Afghanistan without passports and that they would now be taken separately to the men's and women's wings of the prison. Mustering all of her strength, Joanna did what she would later call "a Scarlett O'Hara." "If you do this, I will kill myself. And I won't have to do much. Because I'm dying. And so I will die. My godfather is chairman of the biggest newspaper in England and you will be in so much trouble that you can't even begin to dream of it." And then she fainted. The man decided it would be better not to separate them.

Six soldiers escorted Tim and Joanna into a jeep that headed down a rocky dirt road into what looked like the center of town. The soldiers hustled them from the jeep into another hut where they sat on folding chairs in a room filled with men and women in colorful scarves, all of whom were sitting on the floor. Tim soon realized that they had been brought to the Afghani version of night court. A man in a turban, who turned out to be the district judge, told them they would be sent to the

Plaza Hotel where they would remain under house arrest until the authorities decided what to do with them. Outside, the soldiers loaded them back into the jeep. As they passed a food stall heaped high with glowing tangerines "roughly the same color" as Joanna's skin, one of the soldiers kindly got her a handful to eat on the way.

The Plaza Hotel turned out to be "a rundown adobe building of two uneven floors" with the "z from Plaza missing." Joanna called it, "The Plaza Prison Hotel." With "no one at the front desk and no sign of a telephone anywhere," it was apparent that no one had stayed there for a very long time. They put Tim and Joanna in a "horrible room" on the second floor. "No windows," Joanna would later recall, "three cots, and they have six military men guarding the door. All they give us is chai. Tim is pacing like a lion and I'm lying there and he's saying, 'Oh my God, this is the end. I don't know what's going to happen. I hope they take us back to the United States.'" Tim and Joanna were terrified that the soldiers would decide to take them out and shoot them. Joanna told Tim that they should both take off all their clothes and get into bed. If the guards came for them, they could refuse to get dressed. Together, they climbed naked into bed under a rough gray blanket.

At about six the next evening, Dennis came to visit. Looking "haggard and edgy, unshaven, with dark circles of black under his eyes," he told them Kabul was "crawling with English and American press trying to find out what has happened to you two." Unable to find Hyatullah, Dennis had tried to get an audience with the king only to learn that he was out of town. Other members of the royal court were vacationing in Kandahar. Dennis had an appointment at the American embassy the next day but feared that if he went there, they would arrest him. From the Intercontinental Hotel, he had brought sandwiches, fresh tangerines and oranges, and several packs of cigarettes. He also offered them a joint of green opiated Afghani hash, which they all smoked. Dennis promised to return as soon as he could. One way or another, he swore, he would get them out of there.

The next morning, Tim and Joanna were woken up by two men who identified themselves as members of the king's secret police. They wanted to know why Tim was such an important person in the United States. Tim told them he was a political refugee who had been persecuted for his beliefs and explained that he was hoping the king would welcome him and Joanna as his guests. The men explained that the king might not be on the throne for very much longer and told Tim there was nothing they could do to help him.

On their third day of confinement, a nephew of the king's named Ali, who had gone to school in Berkeley during the sixties, read all of Tim's books, and taken a lot of LSD, came to visit. In order "to ease the boredom of confinement," he offered them some high-grade opium. Ali then interviewed Tim so his uncle could hear his words and "recognize what kind of man you are, then maybe he will give orders to set you free." As Joanna drifted off into an opium dream, she heard Tim say he would not resist going back to the United States so long as he was allowed to take her with him.

The next day, a group of soldiers burst into the room and told Tim and Joanna to come with them to the airport immediately. Clapping her hands in joy, Joanna told Tim that Ali had kept his promise and that they were now going to be allowed to return to Beirut. Equally ecstatic, Tim said, "You see, you see, it works! I told you that Perfect Love conquers all." The two of them were put into a jeep which sped onto a runway at the airport and pulled to a stop at the door of a waiting Pan American 727. "This is not a good sign," said Tim. Before they were allowed to board the plane, a man with a heavy Indian accent, who introduced himself as the airport doctor, gave Joanna a clipboard. On it was a typewritten statement. "I, JOANNA HARCOURT-SMITH, HEREBY RELEASE THE AFGHANI GOVERNMENT FROM ALL RESPONSIBILITY FOR MY PHYSICAL CONDITION IN THE EVENT THAT I DIE ON MY TRIP ORIGINATING FROM KABUL INTERNATIONAL AIRPORT." Tim said Joanna would not sign the paper unless they were given back their passports. As one of the guards prodded Joanna in the back with the muzzle of his gun, the doctor held out his ballpoint pen, clicked it, and said, "Signature and date, please." Joanna dated and signed the statement.

Tim refused steadfastly to enter the plane unless their passports were returned. An Afghani policeman told him the plane was headed to Beirut. Their passports would be returned to them once they were on board. At the top of the stairs leading into the first-class cabin, Tim and Joanna were greeted by a "tanned, bearded man in a suit." "Burke's the name, dope's the game," he said. "I'm here to bring you back to the United States." "Can you imagine an agent saying that?" Joanna recalled. "He thought he was a legend."

They had just met agent Terence Burke, Federal Bureau of Narcotics and Dangerous Drugs, ID card number 107, which put him, he said, just "a single digit away from James Bond." As Joe Eszterhas wrote in *Rolling Stone,* Burke was "suave and swashbuckling, a CIA veteran fluent in Pashtun and Farse [*sic*]" who had "once served as an undercover courier smuggling hashish from India to the United States and then joined the German Interpol to bust the smugglers." Burke was the agent who had first identified Hyatullah and Amanullah Tokhi as the "overlords" of the hashish trade in Afghanistan. Beaming, Burke handed Joanna her British passport with a first-class ticket from Kabul to Los Angeles tucked inside. He then handed Tim his American passport. Inside, every page had been canceled except for the last one on which someone had stamped, "Valid only for return to the United States." In addition to a first-class ticket, Tim had also been issued a special ID card. Next to the entry for "Profession," someone had written "Philosopher." "Because of that," Joanna recalled, "Tim was in heaven. Unbelievable."

Tim continued to insist he could not be taken back to America because there was no extradition treaty between Afghanistan and the United States. Smiling confidently, Burke said, "You're wrong there, Professor. This is an American plane, you're standing on American soil." Sitting right behind Tim and Joanna were two agents in blue suits. Both were armed with .357 Magnums. When the stewardess brought them food, Joanna learned from her that their final destination was Orly Airport in Paris. Joanna was overjoyed. She felt certain she could persuade the French to grant Tim political asylum. An hour later, the pilot announced that due to their late departure from Kabul, Orly was now closed and they would be landing in Frankfurt instead. Tearing pages from her diary, Joanna wrote a desperate message in French and English. "I am Dr. Timothy Leary," the notes read. "I have been kidnapped illegally by American authorities. Please help me when we get to Frankfurt. Alert the press and the police. Do what you can to help me." Telling the agents she needed to use the bathroom, Joanna walked down the aisle and dropped the message on the laps of passengers, most of who were now complaining bitterly in French about the inconvenience of having to land in Frankfurt rather than Paris.

When the plane landed in Frankfurt, Joanna tried to get beyond the transit area by screaming that she needed to see a doctor. A doctor, surrounded by three more armed agents, told Joanna the only thing he could do for her was take her by ambulance to a hospital. Not wanting to be separated from Tim, she refused and the two of them spent the night sleeping on sofas surrounded by agents in a boarded-off Pan Am lounge. "The next morning," Joanna recalled, "I got to call my mother, who went out of her mind. I called my godfather, who at that time owned the *Daily Express* and the *Evening Standard*. This was Max Aitken. I said, 'Timothy says as soon as we get to Heathrow, he's demanding political, philosophical, and spiritual asylum.'"

They then flew to London. At Heathrow, Tim and Joanna were greeted by a horde of immigration officers. As a British subject, Joanna was told that she was now home and could come with them to safety. "And I'm like, 'Never!'" Joanna recalled saying. "'I'm following this man wherever he's going.' Tim was screaming that he wanted political asylum and he had instructed me that I must smile all the way. Every photographer in the world was there, and there's this amazing picture of us smiling our faces off walking through Heathrow. He was absolutely terrified because he knew he was going straight back to the Orange County jail. He was screaming, 'I want to go to Algeria! I want to go to Switzerland! I want to go to Austria! I want to go to Romania!'" Dutifully, English officials said they would ask if Tim could be granted asylum. As Joanna joked with Terence Burke about how funny it would be if they escaped him now, an immigration officer informed Tim it would be impossible for British authorities to consider his request for asylum. Having smoked marijuana with John and Yoko while in England three years earlier, Tim had been put on a blacklist of unwanted and undesirable persons in the United Kingdom. In her unpublished memoir, Joanna later wrote that Tim then said, "A lot of people in high places in the States will be quaking in their shoes when I am on the way home."

That night, on page one, the *Evening Standard* ran a memorable photograph of a tousle-haired Tim, grinning like a circus clown with his mouth wide open and a scarf tied around his neck. By his side, Joanna, in a big lambskin coat thrown open to reveal an amulet hanging from a long string of wooden beads Tim had given her in Gstaad, was smiling so broadly that her eyes had disappeared into slits. In huge black type, the headline read, THE LONDON GIRL AND JAILBREAK PROFESSOR. Atop the same photo in the *Daily Express* the next day was another banner headline:

JOANNA FLIES OUT WITH 'LSD' LEARY. The subhead added, "You Can't Stay Here, Doctor Told."

On the flight to Los Angeles, Tim and Joanna were seated in the upstairs lounge of a Pan Am 747 that had been curtained off for them. As the plane departed, they proceeded to get drunk. When Joanna went downstairs, she walked through first class only to run into Gunther Sachs, the well-known German playboy who was Putzi von Opel's uncle, Brigitte Bardot's former husband, and a close friend of Joanna's sister. Along with another German count with whom he was traveling, Sachs was allowed to come upstairs to visit Tim. "They came up," Joanna recalled, "and Tim did this big number on Gunther asking him to take care of me. From one man to another, he was counting on him . . . Gunther, who was only going to Palm Springs to play golf and hang around with Frank Sinatra, was absolutely delighted. Although I was orange, I was not too ugly. Besides, he had a duty to my family."

Tim, resigned and anxious, then began stuffing airline copies of *Time* and *Newsweek* into his pockets to have something to read while waiting to be processed back into jail. As they flew over America, Tim found a piece of paper on which he wrote, "To whom it may concern. This is to introduce Joanna Harcourt-Smith who is my voice, my love, my life. She is designated to act in my behalf. Please assist her in any way you can to help me get free." He signed it, "Timothy Leary, Amerika, 1973." On Pan Am stationery, Tim jotted a note in which he "lovingly" gave Joanna the "rights to transmit the story of our perfect love." He then gave her his phone book. "Here is the entire counterculture," he told her. "Use it well and get me out." Tim also instructed her to call his old friend Art Kunkin at the *LA Free Press,* who would organize a press conference so Joanna could tell the media about what had just happened to them. "*Faites un scandale,*" Tim told her. As she would later say, "And I knew how to do that very well."

When the plane landed in Los Angeles, Gunther Sachs told Joanna to call him at the Beverly Hills Hotel. Tim and Joanna, with agents in front of them, left the plane holding hands. Agents waiting for Tim cuffed him and pulled him away from her. As they read him his rights, Tim kissed Joanna and told her he loved her and that they would be together soon. The agents then led Joanna to an immigration room. Having burned her green card in Vienna, she had no idea how she was going to get into the country. An hour and a half later, they gave her back her passport and told her she had a permit to enter the United States. In a few weeks, they would issue her another green card.

When Joanna walked out of the transit area, she was confronted by exploding flashbulbs and questions shouted by a horde of journalists holding microphones. "The times have changed," she told the reporters. "And he has come back with solutions to America's problems—the pollution problem, the drug problem." She called Tim "a totally free man. He told me not to worry," she said, "he's happy to be back in California, regardless of the consequences." Grabbing the reporter from the *Daily Express,* Joanna asked if he would drive her to the Beverly Hills Hotel, which he agreed to do.

The story of Tim's capture in Afghanistan and subsequent return to jail in America immediately became headline news around the world. Rosemary Woodruff, who was on the run and hiding out in Sicily, recalled, "I remember seeing the picture of Tim grinning as they took him off the plane after they brought him back to America. It wasn't a smile of resignation. It was the smile of the ego actually eating the personality." Over the years, the Leary smile had become more than an involuntary response to media attention. It was now Tim's trademark, telling the world that nothing had ever really touched him and nothing ever would. In his own mind, he was still completely free.

FOLSOM PRISON BLUES

CALIFORNIA,
JANUARY 1973–MAY 1976

A man who's discovered to be an informer deserves to be hanged or, even worse, to have no one talk to him for if no one talks to you you're better off hanging at the end of a rope.

—Frank McCourt, *Angela's Ashes*

Timothy Leary, booking photo, Orange County jail,
March 18, 1970. *Courtesy of the Futique Trust*

THIRTY-EIGHT

Not having slept for three days and completely orange from hepatitis, Joanna looked a far cry from the elegant clientele who usually checked into the Beverly Hills Hotel. Fortunately, Gunther Sachs and his friend were there to make certain she was given a suite. When she switched on the television, Joanna saw footage of herself addressing the press at LAX earlier in the day on the six o'clock news. The anchorman described her as "Timothy Leary's paramour" and a "disheveled acid freak." It was a judgment with which not even she could quarrel.

Following Tim's instructions to the letter, she called Art Kunkin the next morning. He promised to arrange a press conference that afternoon in the basement of the *LA Free Press*. Then he picked her up at the hotel and took her to visit Tim in the Orange County jail. "This was my first shocking meeting with Tim as a prisoner," she recalled. "I could not talk to him except through glass and he was wearing the orange jumpsuit that prisoners wear. We were both orange, me on the inside and him on the out. In Switzerland, he was very clearly a middle-aged professor. During the trip in Beirut, when I dyed his hair, he got into a kind of defiant rock-star persona. Now he had gone into the prisoner persona, which was more introverted and compliant. He seemed subdued and resigned."

Tim instructed Joanna to tell everyone at the press conference that because they had both been kidnapped in Afghanistan and brought back to the United States against their will, he should be released immediately. "He said, 'Don't worry at all,'" Joanna remembered. "'You make the scandal and I'll be out in a couple of days.'"

In the basement of the *LA Free Press* that afternoon, a very young and fragile-looking Joanna, dressed in black with a colorful silk scarf and wooden prayer beads around her neck, sat behind a brace of microphones.

Art Kunkin was by her side. Although Joanna had no real understanding of the counterculture in America, believing it to be all about dope and music, she very much wanted to become part of it. The counterculture, on the other hand, had absolutely no idea what to make of her. By this point in time, cocaine and quaaludes had replaced marijuana and LSD as the drugs of choice. When he performed onstage, Mick Jagger no longer sported the Uncle Sam hat that he had worn at Altamont. Rather, he looked far more like David Bowie, who personified the new ambisexual glam-rock movement in England. Rennie Davis, a member of the Chicago Eight, had given up on trying to solve the world's problems through political action. Fervently, he was now espousing the teachings of a "perfect" sixteen-year-old guru. While Joanna might have been far more in touch with the new zeitgeist than even she realized at the time, her wired jet-set persona came as a distinct shock to those who remembered the soft-spoken, sloe-eyed Rosemary as Tim's representative.

Joanna recounted in great detail how she and Tim had been brought from Kabul to LA. "And," she recalled, "I told them Tim had told me, 'You can't imprison love.' Which was his big line the first time he was in prison. And that the United States was going to realize they had committed an enormous international mistake and were going to release him." Joanna also told reporters she wanted to speak directly to President Richard Nixon. "I plan to tell him exactly how Timothy taught me to be happy and find perfect love." After the press conference, Kunkin took her to see Tim's lawyer, George Chula. The news Chula gave them was not good. On the escape charges alone, Tim now faced a possible sentence of five to twenty years. The twenty-nine-count drug-smuggling indictment against the Brotherhood of Eternal Love in which Tim had been named as the mastermind was also still pending. Even with the best lawyers and lots of money, Tim faced daunting odds.

Nevertheless, people rallied to the cause. Within a week, Bruce Margolin, a lawyer who offered advice to dopers with legal problems in an *LA Free Press* column called "It's the Law," let his good friend Baba Ram Dass persuade him to visit Tim in prison. "I saw Tim in Santa Ana," Margolin recalled, "and he was not able to pay for anything because he did not have access to funds at that moment. I made it very clear that this was not an issue as far as I was concerned. I could afford to take this on as a pro bono case." Although Margolin knew he would never be able to persuade a jury that Tim had not escaped sixteen months earlier from the California

Men's Colony in San Luis Obispo, he took the case in order to "make sure the public knew Tim was in prison simply for a marijuana offense and nothing of ill will toward society."

When Margolin appeared in court in San Luis Obispo, Judge Richard F. Harris, a cantankerous man who had presided over countless escape trials, warned him that he did not intend to let his courtroom become a circus. Margolin replied that any issues he raised would be legitimate and in good faith. Tim had by now become so notorious that his mere presence in such a proceeding could subvert the entire legal process. Even the manner in which he was brought from the Orange County Jail to San Luis Obispo made news: sitting manacled in a Volkswagen bus protected by a twelve-vehicle police motorcade that inched its way through torrential rain during rush-hour traffic on the freeway in Los Angeles.

In his new cell in solitary confinement at the California Men's Colony, Tim spent most of his time sitting in the lotus position surrounded by "the noise of the swamp." His only companions were two cockroaches. To Joanna, Tim admitted that he was now "at the bottom of the American prison system." He was not allowed to have a typewriter, a tape recorder, a table light, or even a table on which to write. Every time he returned from the visitor's area, he was subjected to an extensive skin search.

Joanna was present on February 10 when Ram Dass and Jack Leary visited Tim. "I felt very distrusting of Joanna," Ram Dass later told John Bryan. "I felt she was very fanatic [sic] and slightly hysterical. More than slightly hysterical. I didn't feel safe with her at all." Jack called her "The Tigress of the Visiting Room." Michael Horowitz, who had been enlisted to help with the case by preparing a detailed summary of Tim's life and a bibliography of his work, summed up the confusion felt about Joanna during this period by saying, "She's great. She's terrible. She's innocent. She's devious." Two days later, Bill Cardoso came to interview Tim for *Rolling Stone*. Cardoso was denied access to Tim in a visiting room where convicted Manson murderer Charles "Tex" Watson sat talking to a female friend, and so he interviewed Joanna. "Nobody in the world," Joanna told Cardoso, "is going to keep Timothy Leary in jail beyond two months and a day from this date." When Cardoso asked Joanna how this would happen, she replied, "By legal means." "And if that fails?" he asked. "We'll simply leave our bodies." With great sincerity, she added, "We believe in miracles."

By this point, Joanna was living in a house in nearby Cayucos with a woman who had once worked as Michael Kennedy's secretary but was now being paid by the Brotherhood to help with the defense. She visited Tim in prison as often as she could. "After a little while," Joanna recalled, "I realized he looked very wobbly. He looked strange. So I asked him what was going on and he told me they had been giving him very high doses of Thorazine. I had no idea why. He was in solitary confinement and he had a twenty-watt bulb. He could hardly write. Margolin had to petition for a sixty-watt bulb. Timothy asked for a pen and they gave him a pencil stub. They were waking him up in the middle of the night and yanking all the furniture out of the cell and coming back and bringing a table and chair and bolting it to the floor." Writing with the pencil stub on the back of an Angela Davis legal brief brought to him by his lawyers, Tim spent the next ten weeks in solitary composing *Neurologic,* a monograph in which he identified the "seven circuits of the human nervous system." Joanna smuggled the manuscript out of prison and then published it in small editions that were sold to raise money for Tim's defense. Michael Horowitz recalled, "Tim gave his instructions through Joanna and we followed them in terms of strategy. She was a European jet-setter, very different from the rest of us. An activist but also an outsider who had to win over the American counterculture. What we didn't realize was that she was dedicated to getting Tim out no matter what, and she would have sacrificed anyone to do that."

One day, Joanna got a call from the American embassy in Amsterdam. After seeing the story about Tim's arrest in the newspapers, Susan Leary, now eight and a half months pregnant with her second child, had beaten her two-year-old daughter almost to death. "They said they had her in a clinic in Amsterdam where she could have her baby," Joanna recalled, "and they wanted to know if they could send her back to me. I went and talked about it to Tim and he arranged for the brother of his wife who had killed herself to take care of Susan and her two children when they flew them back."

Dennis Martino, who had been arrested at the airport in Los Angeles when he returned from Kabul, then got in touch with Joanna from the LA county jail. She went to visit him in a cage on the twelfth floor. "In a conspiratorial voice," she remembered, "he told me he went right to the American Embassy after we were taken in Kabul and the embassy made a deal that they would bring him back to the United States. Of course, he was a fugitive as well because he had violated his parole. So they told him that if he cooperated with the district attorney, he would be set free." Dennis, his eyes burning "with a slightly mad look" as he paced back and forth "like a restless gorilla in a cage," seemed even to Joanna to be raving. Dennis told her how much he hated dope dealers because they were all using Tim to make money. "They carry his picture in their wallet," Joanna remembered Dennis saying, "and when they are busted, the Feds think Tim is the mastermind . . . But none of them will lift a finger to pay his lawyer or get him out of prison. I don't mind busting a few of them, if it can help you and Timothy." Later, Joanna wrote, "I didn't trust him but he was all I had."

Just before Tim's trial began, Joanna outlined the defense strategy to a reporter from the *Berkeley Barb*. First, Tim wanted "the most far-out psychologists in the United States who worked with him at Harvard to come and testify on his state of mind." The second panel of witnesses would be composed of guards from CMC West who would testify that Tim had to escape from prison because his life was in danger. The third panel would include "pop stars and politicians," including Dennis Hopper, George McGovern, Jerry Rubin, and the Rolling Stones. If all else failed, Joanna said she and Tim would go on a hunger strike that would culminate with her visiting Washington to personally deliver a letter from Tim to Richard Nixon. Asked if she actually expected to get in to see the president, Joanna replied, "By that time, I'll probably be so weak, he's gonna have to get out to see me." About the state of her relationship with Tim, she said, "I have no interest in being here without him and he has no interest in living like an animal in a cage. I'm not freaked out or spaced out about the thought of dying. I guess that comes from my relationship with Timothy—I have no more fears."

During his arraignment on February 13, Tim told Judge Harris that he was presenting himself "as a government in exile, an independent political entity." Fearing that the Weathermen or some other radical splinter group might attempt to free Tim, Harris ordered the kind of treatment usually reserved for the most dangerous enemies of the state. Shackled hand and foot, surrounded by twenty guards, Tim was driven each day from the California Men's Colony to the courthouse accompanied by a phalanx of five patrol cars. Everyone who attended the trial had to pass through a metal detector, present all their personal effects for examination, show identification and a Social Security card, and submit to having their picture taken.

Before a jury of eleven women and one man, Tim's escape trial began on March 14, 1973. In a yellow shirt and purple-striped trousers, Tim flashed "the blinding smile which has become his trademark" and pleaded not guilty in a resounding voice. Granted the unusual right to cross-examine witnesses himself, Tim changed into a businesslike dark-blue suit which Joanna's ex-husband Jean-Claude D'Amecourt had worn on their wedding day and sent her for this purpose. Tim added a yellow tie and a pair of sneakers.

Overruling most of Bruce Margolin's objections, Judge Harris kept the trial moving at a rapid clip. "The only thing they needed to prove was that Tim wasn't there at the six o'clock count two years earlier," said Joanna. During the second week of trial, Tim cross-examined special agent Terence Burke. "Dapper with mustache, goatee, and stylishly groomed collar-length hair," as he was described in an article in the *Berkeley Barb,* Burke was accompanied by several armed plainclothes officers from the local sheriff's office who stationed themselves throughout the courtroom while he was on the stand. Burke testified that although he clearly restricted Tim's freedom during the two days of flying between Kabul and Los Angeles, Tim was not actually under arrest until he arrived in California. When she took the stand for the defense, Joanna stated under oath that Burke had offered them hashish and apologized that he did not have any LSD for them. She also said that Burke had tried to get them drunk on champagne. Years later, she confessed, "I lied in a stupid, feeble, idiotic attempt to impugn the government. By then, my head was spinning in such a way that all I could see was to live from one moment to the next. And I was on a tremendous, growing amount of drugs and alcohol." Called back to the stand by the prosecution, Burke categorically denied all her charges.

As much to keep Tim off the witness stand as to save time and money in a case where the verdict seemed a foregone conclusion, the prosecution made an offer before resting their case. In return for a guilty plea, the state would not attempt to arrest Rosemary, Susan, or David Martino, indicating, as Jay Jones wrote in the *Berkeley Barb,* that "some legal action charging them with complicity was in the works." While the offer seemed to be based on information supplied to the government by Dennis Martino, Tim refused to consider it. After the prosecution rested, Margolin informed the jury that he planned to prove Tim had escaped from jail because of threats upon his life and that he acted in a state of "super-consciousness" much the same as a woman who had seen her baby dying and rushed back to the hospital at ninety miles an hour but could later recall nothing about driving there. In part, Margolin's defense was based on the concept that "Huey Newton or somebody had shot a cop in a fight and claimed he was unconscious at the time he pulled the trigger and the court saw that as being a legitimate defense." At one point during the trial, Michael Horowitz picked Huey Newton up at the local airport so the Black Panther leader could testify about conditions inside the California Men's Colony. The defense team, suspecting it might not be in Tim's best interests to have a black revolutionary appear on their client's behalf, decided to send Newton away without letting the jury see him.

After Tim took the stand in his own defense on Tuesday, March 27, he was asked by Margolin to explain precisely what he meant when he wrote in his escape note, "In the uniform of Athens you jailed Socrates. In the uniform of Rome you jailed Jesus Christ and in the livery of Nixon and Reagan you have turned this land into a police state." Tim replied, "My nervous system is in such a state that I live in many reincarnate levels." The judge overruled the prosecutor's objection that this called for a medical conclusion and allowed Tim to add, "My nervous system, as a result of twelve years of disciplined research with drugs and different forms of yoga, allows me to put my mind in different places. My nervous system essentially travels throughout historical time." He went on to explain that "To become 'Timothy Leary' is like getting in a car and turning the key. When I'm behind the wheel of a Chevrolet, I am a Chevrolet. When I am driving a Pontiac on the other hand, I am a Pontiac. Actually we can leave the automobile of our present identity and move throughout our nervous system. I'm not a 'Timothy Leary model' most of the time. I get into this uniform and turn a key on and use the Timothy Leary identity to move through space and time as is necessary to accomplish my mission and my survival." On the day he wrote the escape note, Tim said, "I could just as well have been Socrates or those people who were burned at the stake in the Middle Ages. I was no more Timothy Leary than I was any of these. People in the future will understand what is happening now just as we understand what happened in Salem two hundred years ago." The judge overruled the prosecutor's objections that Tim's answers were "not responsive" and "self-serving."

During cross-examination, the district attorney attempted to establish that since Tim had not taken LSD for several months prior to his escape, he could not possibly have been under the influence of the drug on the night he went over the wall. "I am always under the influence of LSD," Tim answered. "Are you under the influence of LSD now, Doctor?" "Yes," Tim replied. "My brain, I seriously sincerely believe, has been opened up and altered by the many ingestions of LSD and the yoga and the electronic work that I have done on brain expansion." "You're intoxicated right now?" Tim responded, "It's all a mystery to me what is going on."

The next day, Margolin called clinical psychologist Jeffrey Shapiro to the stand. Shapiro testified that he had administered standardized intelligence and creativity tests to Tim on March 10 and that Tim had scored 143 on the IQ test, the "genius level." On the creativity test, Tim "scored higher than anyone I have ever heard of, although his solitary confinement probably lowered the scores." Shapiro was followed on the stand by Michael Kahn, a former colleague from Harvard who now taught at the University of California in Santa Cruz, where Tim's old friend Frank Barron was also a professor. Kahn testified about the scientific validity of Tim's LSD research in connection with the Concord Prison Project. Dr. Walter Houston Clark, now seventy years old, testified that Tim had always been known for his "absolute honesty and truthfulness." He also said Tim was a "law-abiding citizen." The last witness to appear was Dr. Harry Seagal, a practitioner at the Los Angeles Free Clinic, who stated that his recent examination of Dr. Leary had led him to believe Tim was in an LSD-like state on the day of his escape. Seeing himself as a symbol of freedom, Tim had felt compelled to escape, not just for himself but for all those whom he saw in bondage. After presenting final arguments to the jury, the prosecution and defense rested. Three weeks after it began, the trial was over.

After an hour and a half of deliberations on April 3, the jury returned a guilty verdict. "The judge was not mad at Timothy Leary," Margolin would later say, "and in my opinion, he would have given him a concurrent six-month sentence if Tim had not gone to the probation department and told them that if he was given the chance, he would escape again." On April 23, Judge Harris sentenced Tim to another six months to five years in prison for having escaped from the California Men's Colony. Already facing fifteen years of state time for the Laguna bust and ten years of federal time for Laredo, Tim could be seventy-seven years old before he got out of prison again. What Margolin called the "hovering black cloud" in the case was the possibility that Tim "would be declared insane. All I had to do was say, 'I believe my client is unable to understand the consequences of these proceedings' or 'He is unable to cooperate with counsel,' and they would have put him in the funny farm. And he could never have gotten out."

Unlike many of Tim's lawyers, Margolin emerged relatively unscathed from the experience. "Once I finished the trial, I was basically finished with Timothy Leary. Because in part I was warned by Allen Ginsberg to be careful." Ginsberg's advice proved wise. During the trial, Margolin lived for two months in the same house as Joanna, for whom he felt no particular affinity, and Dennis Martino, who, as Margolin said, "turned out later to have been an informant all the way during the trial and even gave information to the prosecution as to what our tactics were for the defense."

After sentencing, the judge allowed Joanna to hug Tim before he was taken back to jail. "Don't worry," Joanna remembered Tim telling her, repeating what had become his new mantra. "I'll be out in a week!" As they stood there together, she recalled, "I saw his eyes becoming more and more empty. As though he was retreating deeper and deeper inside of himself. As if he was erasing the world from his reality. So that all that counted now was his inner life."

Along with other convicts sentenced to do time in the second-oldest penitentiary in the state, Tim rode on a bus with barred windows through the shimmering heat of the Central Valley in May 1973. Inside the ninety-three-year-old stone dungeon that was Folsom Prison, he was stripped and searched, given a tattered gray jumpsuit and oversize cloth slippers, and told to pick out a mattress. Guards with clubs hanging from their wrists escorted him along the bottom tier of 4-A, the prison's adjustment center. Just before Tim got off the bus, one of his fellow cons told him, "Folsom is the annhole of the prison system and 4-A is the bottom of *that*."

As Tim shuffled past the last cell in the row, a prisoner sitting in lotus position on the floor while reading he Bible smiled benevolently at him. The guards led Tim through a metal door into a low dark hallway with three cell doors. They swung one open, motioned him inside, and slammed the door shut behind him. Alone in "the ultimate pit" with a twenty-five-year sentence staring him in the face, any other man might have sunk to his knees and begun to weep in utter despair. "I felt a strange sense of elation," Tim later wrote. "This was it. The indisputable undeniable Dantean bottom."

Even in solitary confinement, Tim was not alone for long. A young blond trusty soon swung open the metal corridor door outside Tim's cell and welcomed him to Folsom by asking if he would like something to smoke. A moment later, he handed Tim a pack of Bugler rolling papers and a white envelope filled with tobacco, a gift from a convict named Charlie who was his nearest neighbor. Charlie also wanted to know if Tim took sugar and cream with his coffee and whether he liked honey. Tim said he did, sent his thanks to Charlie, and rolled himself a cigarette. As Tim watched the smoke curl up through a shaft of sunlight outside his cell, the trusty returned with four paperbacks from Charlie—*The Teachings of the Compassionate Buddha* by E. A. Burtt, *In Search of the Miraculous* by P. D. Ouspensky, *The Teachings of Don Juan* by Carlos Castaneda, and *The Master and the Margarita* by Mikhail Bulgakov. He also gave Tim a cardboard cup of organic honey, a box of graham crackers, and white envelopes filled with coffee, sugar cubes, and powdered cream. Whoever Charlie was, he had welcomed Tim to Folsom in style.

Unable to see one another, prisoners in 4-A communicated by talking through the air shafts. It was not long before Tim heard a voice in the darkness. "This is the bottom of the pit. Nobody gets out of here. It is bliss here." The voice added, "I have been watching your fall, Timothy. LSD is like the invention of the wheel, gunpowder and the Chinese." Tim realized that his next-door neighbor was Charlie Manson. Tim's other neighbor was Geronimo Pratt, a Black Panther who would spend twenty-seven years in jail before his conviction for murder was overturned. "I began to understand," Joanna recalled, "that everything the Bureau of Prisons did was completely calculated. They put them together to inform on one another. And also for manipulation purposes and to blow people's minds."

In August 1969, Manson, then thirty-six years old, had ordered his extended hippie family to slaughter seven innocent people, the actress Sharon Tate among them. Sentenced to death and sent to San Quentin prison, Manson had been transferred to Folsom in October 1972 after the California Supreme Court had declared the death penalty to be unconstitutional, thereby automatically reducing his sentence to life in prison.

"I knew you'd end up here," Manson told Tim. "I've been wanting to talk to you to for a long time, man. Do you know where we really are?" In a voice that Tim found cocky and somewhat patronizing, Manson said, "This is eternity, brother. This is the end of the line. No one ever gets out once they've been here. This is forever."

"Hey," Tim said. "Did you send me the Bugler and the food? Thanks."

"It's my pleasure," Manson replied, his voice so low and assured that it reminded Tim of a fundamentalist minister. "I love everyone and try to share what I have. I've been waiting to talk to you for years. Our lives would never have crossed outside. But now we have plenty of time. We were all your students, you know. You had everyone looking up to you. You could have led the people anywhere you wanted. When I got out of jail in 1965, there were millions of kids cut loose from the old lies just waiting to be told what to do." His voice taking on a slight edge of complaint, Manson added, "And you didn't tell them what to do. That's what I could never figure out. You showed everyone how to create a new head but you never gave them the new head. Why didn't you? I've wanted to ask you that for years."

"That was the point," Tim replied. "I didn't want to impose my realities. The idea is that everybody takes responsibility for his nervous system, creates his own reality. Anything else is brainwashing."

"That was your mistake," said Manson. "No one wants responsibility. Everyone wants to be told what to do, what to believe, what's really true and really real."

"And you've got answers for them?"

"It's all in the Bible, man. Prison gives you time to read the Bible. I figured it all out. Know why everything went wrong? The women. They got scared and forced all these laws and morals on men. What does the Bible say in 'Revelations'? They are the cause of evil. Evil has to be killed. Only a few are to be saved."

Like the psychologist he once was, Tim asked, "How do you feel, Charlie?"

"I feel bad. I got the rawest deal in two thousand years. Sure I laugh at it most of the time. But the pigs got me good. I can't write letters. I can't get visits. They got me completely cut off. They really want to kill me. I can feel it. The murder in their hearts. My trial was a farce. It's stupid. I play out *their* script, act out *their* Bible, take the whole thing on myself—all their feelings of evil and murder, all the sins of mankind, climb on the cross for them. And nobody understands. Nobody understands what I'm doing for them. Do you? Like do you understand about Sirhan Sirhan?"

"I recognize that this is a very Christian country," Tim replied. "And that every convict is forced to play Christ. But to tell you the truth, I don't have much to do with that. I'm an Irish-Catholic pagan. Oldest god game going."

When they talked again the next morning after breakfast, Manson had more questions. He wanted to know what Tim called the moment of truth when you took acid and your entire body dissolved into nothing but vibrations, space and time fused, and it all became just pure energy. Bouncing the question right back at him, Tim asked Manson what he had found there. "Nothing," Manson said. "Like death must be. Isn't that what you found?" Having fielded this question many times before, Tim told Manson this was a trip someone else had laid on him. "It's the moment when you are free from biochemical imprints," he said. "You can take off from there and go anywhere you want. You should have looked for the energy fusion called love." "It's all death," Manson insisted. "It's all love," Tim responded. "I hang on to death," Manson said. "I live by life," Tim replied.

Tim Leary's written account of their dialogue reads as though it was scripted for a movie in which Tim has cast himself as the beneficent being who had given life to the counterculture, while Manson plays the role of Lucifer, the fallen angel who had turned the salvation offered by LSD into yet another source of unremitting evil. Nonetheless Tim did seem to have regarded Charlie Manson as a colleague. "Timothy had long conversations with Manson," Joanna confirmed. "Tim thought he was a very brilliant man but he said that his philosophy was the exact opposite of what he believed. Manson's philosophy was one of vengeful punishing and a Christian God, and Timothy's vision was the Buddhist vision. But he and Manson talked as fellow philosophers. It was *Steppenwolf*."

"They liked each other very much," Wesley Hiler, a prison psychologist who knew them both, told John Bryan. "But they were both on big power trips. They were both megalomaniacs and both felt they were, sort of, Supermen. They exaggerated their uniqueness; they believed in their powers. Yet they were quite different. Leary was not at all psychotic. He was very aware of what was going on, very realistic about everyday life. Manson was not. Manson was definitely deluded, had psychotic delusions, wasn't able to function effectively with people around him. Manson enjoyed being evil."

When Tim left solitary confinement to take his place on the main line at Folsom, he asked a veteran con why Manson was kept in segregation. "He'd get beat up if he came in the yard," the con responded. Tim asked if this was because of Manson's crimes. The con replied that what Manson had done on the street did not matter in here. What really counted, both on the street and in the yard at Folsom, was his size. "He's a runt, you know," the con said. "Can't be over five two." Manson's other problem was that he was "a head fucker, coming on with all that Bible talk. That may scare the squares but in here, it don't cut it. Manson's conned himself into believing his own Bible trip."

Inside Folsom, Tim was soon taken in hand by a well-known jailhouse lawyer with "seventeen show-cause victories to his credit," who moved him to a new cell on the bottom floor of third building and put him to work researching a class-action lawsuit designed to shut the prison down. Tim adapted quickly to the daily rhythm of life in his new home. He slept through breakfast, waking each day around nine-thirty, drank "steaming sweet rich coffee," shaved, and then went to meet his new friends in the yard where they talked "furiously until lunch." After what he described as "a light repast," they stretched out in the sun to smoke and talk with the "many delegations that came to confer and report." After an hour spent lifting weights followed by "a cold shower in water fresh from the American River," everyone enjoyed ice-cream sundaes. "That spring and summer," Tim wrote, "the sky was cloudless and the sun shone for 157 days in a row." When the yard cleared at three, Tim repaired to his cell to read the *San Francisco Chronicle*. After head count and mail delivery, he went to dinner, which was "always a gossipy occasion for dramatic tales: rape in the mattress room, drug busts in the kitchen, heroic crimes, clever capers, daring shoot-outs." At eight-thirty, Tim padded down the cellblock in rubber sandals to stand "under the steaming water, a soapy moment of Lifebuoy buffoonery. Then, with the warm clean bodies of California's most vicious killers all tucked in their beds, one by one we spiraled down the creamy whirlpool of sleep." As others slept, Tim wrote letters on his typewriter and boiled water for "a rich cup of hot chocolate and powdered milk." Climbing into bed, he arranged "the four soft pillows into a comfy pile," turned on his lamp, and browsed "through the dozen wonderful books that had been loaned to me."

Around ten o'clock, he snacked on a hot grilled cheese sandwich, chips, and pickles prepared by his next-door neighbors, "a jolly veteran of forty years federal and state time and his paramour, a willowy soft-skinned 'lady' of thirty." After the older con "removed his dentures and climbed" into the other's bunk, "toothless cries of pleasure filled the air."

Tim Leary's fanciful account of his time in Folsom Prison in *Flashbacks* bore no relationship to the true nature of his situation. "Tim wanted to get out of Folsom," Joanna recalled. "What else could he want? It was the worst place to be." Having moved to San Francisco to continue her campaign, Joanna was now "hanging out in the Bay Area" and going to Michael and Eleanor Kennedy's house "to meet all kinds of well-known people." She was also sleeping with "whomever," such as Owsley Stanley and Abbie Hoffman, while visiting Tim at Folsom once a week. The female guards who would strip search Joanna never failed to make jokes about how afraid they were of getting high on LSD just from touching her clothing. "The whole game," she remembered, "was that I was proving that I loved Timothy by coming back to him no matter who I'd slept with. I would tell Tim about it in detail and it was like a perverse sexual turn-on for him. He got off on this. As a good little French girl, I was very aware that I could keep a man by doing this. And that he was trying to control me sexually by letting me do what I wanted. Just as it was also clear to me that the sexier I dressed when I visited him, the more status he had in prison. So I would search for the skimpiest little thing I could get away with. Dressing for the visit was an absolute sexual ritual and the prison visit itself was simulated sex. It was very sick."

On one of these visits, Joanna brought along Lawrence Ferlinghetti and Allen Ginsberg, both of whom had previously been denied permission to see Tim. Ginsberg, loyal almost to a fault, had just written a broadside in blank verse entitled "Mock-Sestina: The Conspiracy Against Dr. Tim Leary." In it, he linked the emerging Watergate scandal to the government's plans to keep Tim in prison on "trumped up" charges. Asked during a lecture how he felt about Tim, Ginsberg replied, "He's the only man I know that no country in the world will have. So that means he couldn't be wrong."

Ginsberg and Joanna made the long drive from San Francisco to Folsom Prison one Sunday in a two-toned hippie VW bus with Ferlinghetti at the wheel. Along the way, Ginsberg and Ferlinghetti compared Tim to Ezra Pound and Wilhelm Reich, both of whom had also been imprisoned for their beliefs. After they passed through Vallejo, Ginsberg spotted a hamburger joint where they stopped for cheeseburgers with dill pickles and fries. "On the way to Folsom," Joanna recalled, "I watched Ginsberg eat a greasy hamburger with juice running down into his beard and I was absolutely horrified. This graying beard with blood from the meat in it." Having called ahead to ensure that the two poets would be allowed inside with her, Joanna expected to sit with Tim across a table as she had before. Instead, the three of them were made to wait a long time. When they were finally let in, they were escorted to a different part of the visiting room where there was "a glass cage." "We waited some more and Tim came into the cage and his head was shaved and he had blood all over his skull. Very very frightening. He said they had yanked him out of his cell in the early morning and insisted on shaving his head. They shaved it in an extremely clumsy way and he got cut. It was only later that I realized they did it on purpose. They wanted him to look awful in front of his visitors. To show their supremacy over Tim to Ginsberg."

Without preamble, Ginsberg began reciting the heart sutra. Joanna remembered feeling annoyed. "I didn't understand what this man was doing. We had only twenty minutes to visit here! What was he saying?" Ginsberg assured Joanna that this was the most important thing he could do. Then he told her that if Tim was in prison, it was because he had chosen to be there. In fact, there was no real difference between being in jail and being free. In Buddhist terms, Ginsberg was explaining that the void and form were one. When Joanna got angry, Tim did his best to calm her down, explaining that Allen was an old friend who was just trying to be nice. Ginsberg told Tim that Joanna had been "blowing precious money and turning off a lot of otherwise sympathetic people." Looking right at Tim, Joanna defended herself by saying, "Oh, you know, he just hates women." Tim told Ginsberg that Joanna was one of the smartest women on the planet, adding, "I love her. She's doing exactly the right thing." "Later on," Joanna remembered, "Timothy allowed me to hate Allen Ginsberg because he told me, 'He's just an idiot. He hates women.'" (In a conversation with journalist Ken Kelley, Jack Leary confirmed that he had also heard his father say that Ginsberg hated women.) "Tim's rap," Joanna recalled, "was that none of these people were doing anything to help him. They were all derelicts anyway. What he needed was to get out of prison."

In desperate need of money to fund her efforts to get Tim out of jail, Joanna decided she needed footage of Tim inside Folsom to screen at benefits for his defense fund. After prison authorities denied her request to film him in the visiting room, she learned that inmates in California were allowed to give one interview every six months. On the condition that she would have the right to show the film, she authorized a Sacramento television station to send a news crew to interview Tim at Folsom in late July. With the warden, the captain of the guards, and "two members of the goon squad" watching him from behind the camera, Tim told the interviewer that "the best philosophers" often ended up in prison. "Most of the men I model myself after have been lucky if they got away with just being in prison for their ideas." Tim pointed out that everything he had said before the Senate subcommittee in 1966 had happened: "The American Medical Association, the American Psychiatric Association, the American Bar Association, even William F. Buckley—they're all coming around to positions considered radical in the 1960's . . . I've had no more to do with drug usage than Einstein has to do with the Atomic Bomb," he added.

Tim claimed he had "never been legitimately arrested . . . As a matter of fact, I'm in prison right now because I was running for governor of California, and I published position papers on how to gradually eliminate taxes, crime, the drug abuse problem, and so forth." When Tim was asked whether he had suffered any brain damage from his use of LSD, he responded, "People who get to know me seem to think I'm pretty sane. I've written two books in the last few months. My book *Hope Fiend* earned me a quarter of a million dollars advance, so somebody at Bantam Books didn't think it was insane. If I am insane, the government should be happy to let me out and let my insanity be apparent."

Tim gave a virtuoso performance. As prison psychologist Wesley Hiler told John Bryan, "Don't forget that the most successful people in history have been grandiose and that's what gives them the energy and self-confidence to sway multitudes. Leary has all of this and an enormous amount of charisma. But he doesn't have much integrity. He has very little personal conscience." During the interview, Tim wore a pin on his shirt, which he explained was not only "a replica of the remnants of a living organism found on a meteorite" but "proof that life exists somewhere off our planet." In *The Exploration of Outer Space* by astronomer Sir Bernard Lovell, Tim had found "a drawing of the remnant of a living organism found on a meteorite. A nucleic acid molecule. The first signal from extra-terrestial life." Tim named it "Starseed" and made it "the sym-

bol of Psi-Phy" (a play on the term "Sci-Fi"). He encouraged his fellow
prisoners to "etch the design on silver pins and leatherwork handicrafted
in the hobby shop."

In early July, Tim read in *The New York Times* about the discovery by
a Czechoslovakian astronomer named Lubos Kohoutek of a comet that
would become visible around Christmas "with a brilliance greater than
the full moon." For some reason, the media seemed to be ignoring the
story. Could it be there was a conspiracy afoot to hide the fact that the
comet might collide with Earth? Then only the masters of war hidden in
bomb shelters far underground would survive. If only four months remained until what Joanna herself called the "holocaust," then "everyone
should be told." Though even Tim conceded that the comet could "mean
nothing or it can mean everything," he wrote a twenty-four-page monograph entitled *Starseed* which Joanna published and sold. In it, Tim stated,
"It is the time for prophecy. The omens are obvious. The moment of spiritual reckoning approaches. Karmic plague sweeps the globe . . . The
comet Starseed comes at the right time to return light to planet earth.
The structure for the new way is already here. Starseed will turn-on the
new network." Tim concluded, "In the next transmission, we shall describe how the new organization will unite us in joyous communication.
Isn't that what you really want?"

A month later, Tim answered his own question in *Terra II: The
Starseed Transmission*. Portraying Folsom Prison as the modern equivalent
of the Athenian open-air academy where prisoners had nothing to do but
think and exercise, Tim insisted all the information he was about to convey had come to him in a direct transmission from outer space to which
only he and a fellow convict named Lynn Wayne Benner had access.
"THE TIME HAS COME FOR YOU TO ACCEPT THE RESPONSIBIL-
ITY OF IMMORTALITY. IT IS NOT NECESSARY FOR YOU TO DIE."
Identifying the comet as a signal that the time had come for man to leave
planet Earth, Tim offered the world a plan for sending a starship city
through the center of the galaxy to the farthest point of the visible universe to contact and exchange information with higher intelligence. The
project he proposed would unfold in three stages. In the spring of 1974,
an international convocation would work out the technical, economic,
and social blueprints for the voyage. In the fall, the preflight crew would
begin constructing a functional replica of the star-city in the Antarctic.
Before the year 2000, Terra II would be assembled in orbit around the

moon and then launched toward the stars. While the ship would not return within the lifetime of any living terrestrial, messages would be sent
back to inform humanity about the lessons learned from interstellar contacts. The crew for Terra II would be comprised of five thousand of the
most intelligent, brave, creative, entertaining, competent, and beautiful
human beings.

Although Tim never credited it as a source, much of what he proposed came directly from *Blows Against The Empire,* an album recorded
and released by the Jefferson Starship in 1970, which examined "the notion of hijacking a starship and establishing an alternative community of
free souls in space, far away from the spoiled planet." Not that it really
mattered. Locked away in Folsom Prison, Tim Leary had found another
new cause that he hoped would rally people to him just as LSD had once
done. Seeking his freedom in the stars, he fervently believed that the great
comet scheduled to appear in the sky at Christmas would, like the star of
Bethlehem, mark not only the arrival of a superior intelligence from
outer space but his own second coming as well.

THIRTY-NINE

On November 28, 1973, Tim Leary was transferred from Folsom to the far more modern California Medical Facility at Vacaville, a medium-security institution that also housed a licensed, acute-care psychiatric hospital for the criminally insane. "I was not there as a patient," he would later write, "but as a worker on the trusty staff." Tim also suggested that his transfer came about as retribution for his class-action lawsuit demanding the federal government declare the entire California penal system unconstitutional, but the lawsuit itself was thrown out of district court and never refiled. As a nonviolent prisoner with extensive training as a behavioral psychologist, Tim was uniquely qualified to work as a trusty on the hospital staff.

Two days after his arrival in Vacaville, all twenty-nine charges against him in the Brotherhood of Eternal Love case were dropped by Orange County District Attorney Cecil Hicks, who explained that he was no longer willing to waste the county's money prosecuting a fifty-three-year-old convict "who's no spring chicken and who should be out of circulation quite a time." What Hicks did not say was that his case against Tim as the evil mastermind of an international drug ring had always been essentially a media exercise.

Tim's first priority remained to get out of jail. Faced with the real possibility that he might spend the next twenty-five years in jail, he had no choice but to seriously consider the offer Dennis Martino made to him through Joanna. Now living in Orange County with his wife Robin and their son, Orion, Dennis came to visit Joanna regularly in San Francisco. Dennis was having so much fun working with the narcs that he now wanted to become a CIA agent, though he knew his arrest record would probably keep this from ever happening. For months, he had been telling

Donald Strange, his contact at the DEA, that Tim Leary was really a straight guy who, as Joanna would later write, had been "corrupted by the very tools he used to research the mechanics of the human mind."

Whenever Dennis visited Joanna in San Francisco, he brought with him a cornucopia of the finest drugs available—China brown heroin, pure German pharmaceutical cocaine, and hash joints rolled in tobacco. He told Joanna the time had come to forget a revolution that even the most dedicated political radicals knew would not come soon in America. Only the government could free Tim now. "He was always telling me that Tim was never going to get out of prison," she recalled, "because he was the number-one prisoner in the country and Nixon's poster child. I realized it was a totally desperate situation. A complete deadlock between the hippies and the government." Claiming "he was doing all this for Tim and me," Joanna said Dennis told her that the only way Tim was going to get out of jail was "by not taking sides. Tim had to be neither on the side of the hippies nor the government, and he had to prove it." Dutifully, Joanna conveyed this information to Tim before he was moved to Vacaville.

Vacaville was far less secure than Folsom. During visiting sessions, Joanna often smuggled LSD to Tim by mouth-to-mouth contact when they kissed or by taping it inside a yellow notebook. In *Flashbacks,* Leary described a sexual encounter he had there in a hospital janitor-supply room with "Betty, the soft skinned blue-eyed civilian nurse" whose "naked body was moist as a hot octopus. I tried to love her standing but I was too tall. We grappled around giggling and groaning and stumbling over mop buckets . . . We fell against a cardboard crate filled with paper towels, which I tore open." At Vacaville, Tim did fall in love with a female psychiatrist whom prison psychologist Wesley Hiler described as "absolutely gorgeous, both in face and figure . . . She was an M.D. who was taking a psychiatric residence at Vacaville." Hiler, who would later tape record a series of extensive interviews with Tim at Vacaville, told John Bryan, "She fell madly in love with Timothy Leary and so they had a little affair. They weren't able to get together and have sex because of the limitations of the prison environment, but they would hold hands and kiss and do things like that."

At five in the morning on December 12, Tim was handcuffed and placed in a marshal's car so he could be driven to San Francisco where he had been called to testify for the defense in the trial of Tim Scully, Nick Sand, Owsley Stanley, and Michael Randall, all charged with the wholesale manufacture and distribution of LSD and federal income tax evasion. The government's star witness in the trial, which lasted for thirty-nine days, was Billy Hitchcock, Tim's old friend and benefactor from the Millbrook days. Hitchcock, who had been indicted by a federal grand jury in San Francisco for bankrolling America's most proficient LSD chemists so they could supply the Brotherhood with one million hits of Orange Sunshine acid, had agreed to testify against them in return for a five-year suspended sentence and a $20,000 fine. As Tim was driven down an East Bay freeway past the house in the Berkeley hills where he had lived for fifteen years and that now belonged to someone else, he watched the sun rise. Looking up into the eastern sky, Tim saw no trace of the great comet he had predicted would herald the arrival of a superior intelligence from outer space. "It turned out to be an out-a-sight comet," he later wrote.

Joanna, who had already met and "charmed" Richard Hongisto, San Francisco's newly elected very liberal sheriff, was waiting for Tim at the courthouse. Hongisto took Joanna in to see Tim and then left them alone in a room with a long table. "I was dying for Tim to make love to me. And very disappointed that he didn't. And then I told him that I was sick and tired of this business about him getting out next week. And I said, 'You gotta face it, man. You're not getting out of here.'" Fueled by drugs, her frustration soon reached the boiling point. When she visited Tim the next day in the San Francisco county jail, she took the phone and began hitting herself over the head with it. "Blood was pouring down my forehead," she recalled. "I said, 'I'm at the end. I don't know what to do. I've done everything I can.' I was telling him, 'If you're so powerful and you're the LSD guru and all your Eastern philosophies are true and you can choose your own reality, get out of prison! *Get out of prison!*'"

Jolted by Joanna's violent outburst, or perhaps because he had already been thinking in similar terms, Tim told Tim Findley of the *San Francisco Chronicle* that he now found the topic of drugs "boring" and that he was thinking "in terms of getting out of prison—and of leaving the planet." He said that for the past ten months, all his messages had been of "harmony, unity, and reconciliation." Tim then paved the way for what he was about to do by adding, "I consider myself to be the last leading dissenter of that time who is still in prison. Angela, Huey, all the others are out."

Shortly before he was scheduled to testify for Nick Sand, Tim had what John Bryan described as "an extended conference" with United States Attorney John Milano, the federal prosecutor in the case. During the meeting, it became clear that the government would not look kindly on Tim if he appeared as a witness for the defense. Tim told Sand's lawyer that "whatever he has to say at this point would not help his client; it would only hurt him." Without taking the stand or making a decision about cooperating with the government, Tim returned to Vacaville. Sand's lawyer was Michael Kennedy. As Joanna recalled, "The only person Tim was terrified of informing on was Michael Kennedy."

Though *The Village Voice* portrayed the trial as "the story of the acid profiteers," its real significance was that the Department of Justice had decided to implement its continuing war on drugs by using methods previously reserved for high-profile cases involving organized crime figures. These methods included persuading lawyers who had engaged in illegal activities to testify against their own clients and offering immunity to those willing to incriminate their fellow defendants. Wherever Tim looked, people had begun cutting their own deals with the law. As the Watergate hearings unfolded day after day on television, even the most hardened felons in Vacaville watched in fascination as an endless parade of witnesses, many of them lawyers, gave one another up. Tim called Watergate "the last phase of the War between the Generations" and wrote, "One of the many enlightening facets of Watergate is that the whole mess has been created by the lawyers. By the 'whole mess' I refer to the government. A country run by law is being ruined by lawyers."

Although G. Gordon Liddy, one of the leading Watergate conspirators and Tim's former nemesis during the Millbrook days, steadfastly refused to testify against anyone despite the heavy prison sentence levied upon him, his role in the hearings only served to confirm Tim's view of himself as an important historical figure. It also led him to a new definition of what he had learned from a lifetime of taking LSD. "Communication is love. Secrecy, withholding the signal, hoarding, hiding, covering up the light is motivated by shame and fear, symptoms of the inability to love. There is nothing and no way to hide. This is the acid message." Once more, Tim believed in the lesson he had first learned as a boy back in Springfield. Confession *was* good for the soul. This conclusion also suited his own purposes. For only by fully acknowledging all his past errors could Tim Leary now set himself free.

A week after Tim returned to Vacaville following his refusal to testify for Nick Sand, Joanna visited him in prison. "He said to me," she recalled, "'When you get home tonight, send a telegram to the FBI and the DEA saying: Dr. Timothy Leary entirely ready to collaborate with federal agents and federal agencies.'" At first, she believed Tim's offer was "just another scam." Nonetheless, she sent a telegram that night to Don Strange at the Drug Enforcement Division in Los Angeles. She and Tim waited for a response.

On January 2, 1974, in what seemed to be an attempt to prove he had been cooperating for Tim's benefit, Dennis Martino signed a sworn affidavit for Tim's lawyers in San Francisco. He admitted to having worked as an informant for the Bureau of Narcotics and Dangerous Drugs for more than a year. Dennis acknowledged that during Tim's escape trial in San Luis Obispo, it was his job to spy on the defense team, even going so far as to call Joanna from the Orange County district attorney's office so that their conversation could be recorded without her knowledge. Dennis swore that when he asked his superiors if there were many other tapes relating to Leary in their possession, he was told, "There's a library." Dennis's affidavit became part of a legal brief filed with the California Court of Appeals in Los Angeles on February 24, 1974. Eight months earlier during pretrial discovery hearings in the Brotherhood trial, Michael Kennedy had learned that Dennis, Billy Hitchcock, and Charles Rumsey were all cooperating with the government. Attorney Michael Tigar communicated this news in a letter to Rosemary, who was still in hiding. "It is well you are out of the line of fire at this moment," Tigar wrote. "It will be some time before the dust settles."

While Tim waited to hear whether his offer to cooperate would be accepted, Joanna was doing all she could to keep Tim's name before the public. In late November, she showed the film of Tim's Folsom Prison interview to a press conference at Max's Kansas City in Manhattan. In early February, she appeared at a benefit for Tim in the Arlington Street Church in Boston. On March 15, she sold copies of *Terra I* (which contained Martino's affidavit) and *Terra II* as Hawkwind and Man, whom she described in a press release as "two highly evolved British bands on the neurological scale of time," performed before a thousand people in Zellerbach Auditorium in Berkeley in "A Tribute to Dr. Timothy Leary."

Although Tim and Joanna were not married, she had now legally changed her name and was calling herself Joanna Leary. Functioning as Tim's wife, she sent his mother a copy of *Starseed* as a Christmas present. Abigail, now eighty-eight years old and still living with her sister May on Oak Street in Indian Orchard, replied with a handwritten note thanking

Joanna for her thoughtfulness. After reading the book twice, once to herself and then out loud to her sister, Abigail confessed, "I'm afraid we didn't get the message. (we're old with old-age phylosophy [*sic*]) but those who understand . . . this picture of the future surely enjoyed it." Unable to write more because she was "under the weather," she apologized for not being home when Joanna called and hoped that Joanna would enjoy the holiday season. Nowhere in the note did Abigail mention her son. Joanna also sent a copy of the book to Susan. On a rented typewriter, Susan wrote back to thank "Johanna" for her kindness. She was now living in Sandy, Oregon, with her daughter, Dieadra, and her son, Ashley, who had just gotten his first tooth, and was trying to learn how to type well enough to send out letters to bookstores, asking for a job. Her nineteen-line response to Joanna contained so many spelling errors and typos that it could have been written by a child.

In early February, shortly after the newspaper heiress Patty Hearst was kidnapped from her boyfriend's apartment in Berkeley by the Symbionese Liberation Army, Tim sent Joanna to see Randolph Hearst. In return for freedom, Tim offered to supply Hearst with information about the whereabouts of his missing daughter. Since the SLA had been founded within the walls of Vacaville, Tim was convinced he could get in touch with the group's "secret boss," a tough old black con. Tim's plan collapsed when the con refused to talk to him. Meanwhile, after a trip to Europe, Joanna moved with Dennis Martino and Robin Virtel to a cabin on the side of Mount Tamalpais in Marin County. When she learned that her uncle Stanislaw Ulam was a candidate for the prestigious Enrico Fermi Award, she made a "series of phone calls that built finally to vague threats on his life" if he didn't give her money to help free Tim. Joanna abandoned the plan in favor of one with "a kinkier plot."

After being introduced to one of the Bay Area's leading LSD chemists, Joanna convinced him that one of her friends in San Francisco had an uncle who worked at Sandoz Laboratories in Switzerland. Joanna claimed that through her friend she could get him pure ergotamine tartrate, the basic substance from which LSD is made. For $60,000 in cash, Joanna promised to supply five kilos of ergot. She met the chemist in the bar of a downtown hotel, took him upstairs, and introduced him to Robin, who was posing as the friend. Once the money changed hands, Joanna gave the chemist the key to another room in which he would find an aluminum suitcase filled with ergot. When the chemist opened the suitcase, he found a typescript of *Neurologic* and "some prayer paraphernalia and holy bells from the East." In "Paramour," her unpublished memoir, Joanna wrote that she filled the suitcase with a gold tantric ring, Tim's address book, two original unpublished Tim Leary manuscripts, her mother's gold-and-pearl wing earrings made by Cartier before the war, and a letter in which she told the chemist that if she could fool him, then a worse person could do the same and get him busted in the process. Asking his forgiveness, she told him this was a sign that he should quit working as an acid chemist.

With the money they had scammed, Joanna, Dennis, and Robin scored a quarter-ounce of cocaine in Berkeley and checked into a hotel room to celebrate their good fortune. At three in the morning, Joanna drove to the house in Sausalito where Bill Choulos, another of Tim's lawyers, lived, and threw the money down in front of him. His response was that money alone would not get Tim out of jail. When Joanna checked her answering service the next day, she found that the chemist she had ripped off had left her a message. Although he knew he had been robbed, he would do nothing about it. Because they had so much damaging information on him, they were safe. For the next two weeks, Joanna, Dennis, and Robin "snorted and shopped for cameras and jewelry, stereos, and clothes." To create a reason for her sudden wealth, Joanna had her mother visit from Marbella. Joanna and Dennis picked Marysia up in a rented Rolls-Royce and took her to their spacious new home on the slopes of Mount Tamalpais. Marysia stayed for a month and Joanna took her in the Rolls to visit Tim in Vacaville.

During the third week in April, Joanna and Dennis made two trips to Los Angeles to discuss the details of Tim's offer to cooperate with the government. They went to the first meeting, Joanna recalled, "'in a limousine on speedballs. Snorting heroin and cocaine mixed." By now, they were also having sex with each other. At DEA headquarters in Los Angeles, Don Strange greeted Joanna, saying, "So, you are the famous paramour." He told her she would have to attend another meeting with the representatives of other government agencies that were also interested in Tim. Tim was removed from Vacaville Prison and taken by helicopter to the top of a bank building in Los Angeles where, along with Joanna, he met Don Strange, California Assistant Attorney General Jerry Utz, United States Attorney John Milano, and Roger J. La Jeunesse Jr. of the FBI—whom Joanna came to know as "Frenchy." "The government was

in heaven," she recalled. "They were going to roll up the entire underground. I came to the secret meeting dressed as sexy and revealing as I
knew how and I sat down with Tim who was now wearing a seersucker
suit like an Orange County prosecutor."

Don Strange agreed that so far Tim had been "doing very well,"
Joanna recalled. "He had spoken very clearly about his past and they had
a lot more debriefing to do." Strange also told Joanna that Tim wanted to
speak with her. "The second part of my work on getting out of prison,"
Joanna recalled he told her, "is getting a few of those bastards arrested."
When she asked him what he meant, Tim replied, "Those lawyers whose
fault it is that I'm in prison."

FORTY

On the morning of May 25, 1974, in the FBI offices in West Covina, California, before Don Strange, Tom Avdeef of the Orange County district attorney's office, Jerry Utz, and Vern Sidler of the California Department of Corrections, Tim Leary started talking into a tape recorder operated by FBI agent Roger J. La Jeunesse Jr. Each official had his own personal shopping list of questions and concerns, but their common agenda soon became apparent. With all the highest-ranking members of the Brotherhood of Eternal Love behind bars and the leaders of the Weather Underground on the run, Tim could do himself the most good by providing his interrogators with damaging information about his lawyers and the role they had played in his escape from prison. Their real quarry was Michael Kennedy, the attorney who for years had been a thorn in all their sides.

According to the interview transcript contained in Federal Bureau of Investigation file #40-84731, Tim confessed that he had been "led step by step by Kennedy into much of what happened" when he went over the wall at the California Men's Colony in San Luis Obispo, and that "Kennedy definitely wanted to control the escape." When La Jeunesse asked who had financed the escape, Tim said Rosemary had told him Michael Randall from the Brotherhood of Eternal Love had given Kennedy $25,000 to pay for it. He named Michael Standard as the man who supposedly arranged for a passport so Tim could leave the country. Tim said he could now clearly see that "Kennedy actually did not function at all as my lawyer during that period." When Jerry Utz suggested that Kennedy was trying to force Tim to proceed with the plan, Tim agreed. "I can remember Kennedy saying, at one point, Michael Randall and that group won't get you out, the only ones that will get you out are the political people."

On the Friday before the escape, Tim said that Joe Rhine, a lawyer whom Tim identified as being "very much under Kennedy's control," came to visit him with precise instructions as to how he would be picked up outside the prison and told Tim his code name, Nino. Tim confirmed that his account of the escape in *Confessions of a Hope Fiend* was accurate and identified the driver of the getaway car as the brother of a well-known political radical. He named Bernadine Dohrn, Bill Ayers, and Jeff Jones as the Weather Underground leaders who had greeted him at a small state park in northern California and recounted in great detail how they had created a fake ID for him. When Utz asked if Tim had heard from Kennedy or Rhine during this time, Tim said that although there was no telephone at the farmhouse, the Weathermen were phoning Kennedy because he had money for Tim and Rosemary. "We told him to send the money to American Express in Paris. Kennedy was to be kept abreast of what was happening and he was sending love and that sort of thing." Tim then admitted that all this was hearsay, as he himself had never talked to Kennedy on the phone. Later in the interview, when Utz asked whether Kennedy had ever sent money to American Express in Paris, Tim replied, "No. Disillusion number one." Strange asked Tim if there were others who had known about the escape before it happened. Tim named Michael Kennedy's wife, Michael Randall, Michael Standard, and "Bill" Hitchcock. After telling Utz that Rosemary also knew about the escape before it happened, he added, "Incidentally, my daughter, Susan, did not know about the escape, nor did my son." Nor did Dennis Martino or Robin Virtel.

Although he got the dates of his disastrous trip to Cairo and Beirut wrong, Tim named Jennifer Dohrn and Kennedy as "the key to overground connections for the Weathermen." After revealing how he had left Algeria for Switzerland, Tim said, "Kennedy had all of my papers, my house mortgage, matter of fact, Kennedy finally ripped my house off from me," selling it for somewhere around $14,000. "And they paid some money to my kids. I don't know how much."

Tim told his interrogators that an entire "circuit of people . . . were getting a tremendous amount of excitement, interest, and money on my being in prison and actually living off it." Though he still loved Rosemary very much, Tim said that "the cold facts of the matter" were that when he was in prison the first time, "Rosemary was a queen, I was a martyr." Sounding like an embittered con, Tim said the people running his affairs "were better off having me in prison" and "the minute I got out of prison," they all knew "the fun was over."

While he was in prison in Switzerland, Tim said Kennedy had taken charge of his defense fund and raised some $28,000 and then given about $10,000 of it to Rosemary, thereby making him feel certain Kennedy was handling "thousands of dollars in cash" and "I knew that he took a lot of that." Utz then asked a long series of questions concerning the papers Tim had signed giving Kennedy and Rhine the right to sell his house. "When you are in jail, you sign anything," Tim replied. How much money, Utz asked, did Tim think Kennedy took from him? "Uh, I'd say, oh around five thousand dollars." Did Tim think Kennedy absconded with that money? "Yes," he replied, adding that he had no direct knowledge of this. Because he was having trouble with Rosemary at the time and their marriage broke up while he was in prison, she started "working with dope dealers and with Kennedy and Standard," who even now were still standing between the two of them. "I can't get messages to her. I can't tell her what to do because it funnels through Kennedy." Utz asked Tim if Kennedy knew where Rosemary was now. He replied that she was not in the United States but added that he thought Kennedy was lying when he told him that. "Because Kennedy was acting as though the place was bugged."

Utz asked Tim to give a brief summary of his career. He did so, then said, "Present time to the last three or four years, I've no interest in drugs. I see the whole topic [as] boring, trying to make my contribution (unintelligible) that I've had nothing to do with drugs. I've never had anything to do with dope dealings or received any money or had any inside knowledge about dope dealings." Avdeef then jumped in, saying, "Tim, I take exception to that." To which Tim replied, "All right." Tim then told La Jeunesse where Rosemary's parents lived, supplied both her mother's and father's first name, and identified them as being about sixty years old.

At the end of the 140 page single-spaced interview transcript, a parenthetical note indicated that the following statement was made in the middle of the interview but had been placed at the conclusion for clarity. In its entirety, the statement read:

I'd like to discuss my motives briefly in what I'm doing. Number one, I want to get out of prison as quickly as I can. And I believe that telling the total truth is the best way to get out of prison. I don't want to continue in a situation where hiding the truth is keeping me in prison. That doesn't make any sense to me personally or philosophically. Secondly, I feel I have a great deal to contribute constructive, ah, activities in the United States of America. I'd like to use this as step number one in seeing if I can work out a collaborative and an intelligent, an honorable relationship with different government agencies and law enforcement agencies and educational agencies so this does not just turn someone over to get out of prison. It's part of a longer range plan of mine. I'm in full possession of my faculties. I think I can contribute a great deal. I've learned a great deal and I intend to be extremely active in this country in the next few years however the [sic] things turn out. I prefer to work, I'm never going at it illegally ever again, but I would prefer to work constructively and collaboratively with intelligence and law enforcement people that are ready to forget the past and to use my [sic], in the future, because I still have a great deal to say to this country, I believe.

Even as he sat baring his soul to law enforcement officials who believed he could deliver Michael Kennedy into their hands, Tim was getting the details wrong. Among the things he conveniently omitted to say or got wrong was that Kennedy and Rhine had sold his house because Jack Leary had missed three consecutive mortgage payments and a default notice had been served on the property. At the time, Tim had owed his lawyers around $10,000, which he had promised to pay by giving them 15 percent of what then proved to be nonexistent royalties from his books. Tim also forgot to mention that when Michael and Eleanor Kennedy visited him in Switzerland in October 1972, he had spent six hours having dinner with them. At some point during the evening, Kennedy had handed Tim his real passport. In *Aquarius Revisited,* Peter Owen Whitmer reported that Tim received $4,000 from the sale of his house. Jack and Susan Leary were also compensated. Because this was not what Tim's interrogators wanted to hear, he did not tell it to them.

Like Winston Smith at the end of George Orwell's *1984,* Tim might now have really loved Big Brother with all his heart and soul but this did not mean that the feeling was mutual. Although Tim had convinced his confessors that he was willing to give people up in exchange for freedom, his long association with drugs and propensity for saying whatever came into his mind while testifying in court made him less than an ideal witness. To put Michael Kennedy, Joe Rhine, and Michael Standard behind bars, thereby effectively crippling the left-wing legal establishment which had so far stymied nearly all federal prosecutions against the counterculture, the government needed someone to confirm what Tim was saying. "It's a two-part process," explained Kent Russell, the lawyer in Melvin Belli's firm who had prepared the appeal brief published as *Terra II*. "The snitch works with the government and gives them information, which they use to bring charges and indictments against people. If those people plead guilty, then the snitch doesn't have to testify. But if they don't, he does. The basic way that snitches who testify get believed by the jury is through corroboration. That is the key." Bound by attorney-client privilege, Tim's lawyers could not be forced to testify. None of the leading figures from the Brotherhood or the Weather Underground seemed willing to betray one another in exchange for a lighter sentence. "The prosecutors had never seen anything like the Brotherhood," Michael Kennedy recalled. "They brought in some informants from outside and did some infiltration, but nobody ever rolled on anybody else in that organization. Nobody rolled in Weather to my knowledge."

There was only one person who could verify what Tim was now telling the government. Rosemary was not only the linchpin of this case—she was also the missing link. "That was part of the deal," Joanna recalled. "Tim was going to find Rosemary. I was personally in the offices of the DEA with Tim when he made a phone call to Rosemary's mother in Culver City asking her the whereabouts of Rosemary. He was completely charming with the mother and said he absolutely needed to talk to Rosemary. He wanted to know how she was doing and he was really worried about her and that this was the first chance he had to call from prison because in those days, prisoners were not really allowed to make phone calls. All he wanted was a phone number or a location, but she didn't go for it."

Dearest Ro," Rosemary's mother wrote her in Sicily in a letter dated May 20, 1974. "I don't know where to start." Rosemary's mother had received a phone call from Dennis Martino's wife, Robin, who asked if she could talk to Joanna. About to refuse, Rosemary's mother reconsidered. "She said she had $25,000 from Tim for you & had lost John's [Rosemary's

boyfriend] parents' address & wanted to get in touch with you. I told her
I didn't have your address, but could get in touch with you to give it [the
money] to you. Then she said I should call you & see what you wanted to
do. I told her I didn't have a phone no. for you. She said she would call
back later that day." Two days later, Joanna called Rosemary's mother and
said "she had gone to see T. & he said he was concerned about you (ha!)."
By this time, Rosemary's mother had spoken with Joe Rhine who "said he
didn't believe it as he couldn't see either T or J. giving away that amount
of money. So I told him would it be alright [sic] if I referred J. to them.
He said that was a good idea & he would let me know if he heard from
J." When Joanna called again, Rosemary's mother told her to contact
Michael Kennedy. Joanna could give him the money and he would see
that Rosemary got it. Joanna told her "she and T. didn't trust lawyers, but
she was going to see T. the next day again & relay our conversation; that
she was just a go-between. That T. sent his love! and she would call me
again. But I've heard no more from her." Finally, Rosemary's mother
wrote that someone from the State Department had come by and asked
her to identify pictures of Tim and Rosemary in connection with passport fraud committed in the name of "Sylvia Edith McNellis . . . We said
no & that we couldn't positively identify the pictures. He asked us if we
had heard the name Rosemary Bradley & we said yes that was your first
married name. He wanted to know if we had seen you & we said no not
since 1970. I hope this all dies down soon. Let me know if you've heard
anything." "Although it was Joanna who made the call, and not Tim,"
Rosemary recalled, "I knew Tim was actively trying to give me up to
them."

On June 1, 1974, a week after he first sat down in the FBI offices in
West Covina, Tim wrote the most remarkable letter of his life. Eight
pages long, it began, "June 1st, 1974—Chino—Dear Rosemary and John,
The last seventeen months! A period of integration, reconciliation, perfection, mutation, and discovery." Numbering his points as though out-
lining a syllabus for a college course about himself, Tim continued:

1) *I've mastered fear.* Four months of solitary confinement at CMC
East, four at Folsom—the deepest pit of the system—six months on
the main line at Folsom—five months at the dread Vacaville Medical
Facility—living with the most militant blacks, the Nazis, the toughest guards, Manson, David Hilliard, etc.

2) *The old polarities and conflicts of the sixties are over.* All the same people are tired of the old rhetorical fight and hunger for a new reconciliation. It is insane to defend past positions.

3) *It was a mistake in judgement for us to get involved with dope dealers and illegal revolutionaries.* I don't regret it. I feel no guilt. We learn most from our mistakes. Anything that helped us reach this state of perfection is good. But it was weakness that led us to these involvements that caused our exile—fugitive—status. There is nothing wrong with weakness—until one makes a career out of defending past errors, etc.

4) *Truth is the only hope.* Secrecy is a basic despair. While we have been truthful and open about ourselves—we have become involved in a web of secrecy to defend others. You are a fugitive now and in fear because Kennedy and Standard believe they have everything to lose if you tell the truth. I asked Michael Kennedy recently why is Rosemary still a fugitive? He said, "Because people would be badly hurt if she tells what she knows." I said, "So Rosemary is going to play G. Gordon Liddy—to protect Nixon?" Kennedy and Standard are going to have to face the karmic consequences of what they did.

Contrasting his own actions after the bust in Laguna Beach when he "signed a notarized affidavit taking responsibility for your contraband," he asked when Kennedy and Standard would "sign such papers taking responsibility for what they did to place you in exile—fugitive status—" and then continued his list:

7) *Please do not fear the American law or American law enforcement officials.* I've been very involved in confrontations with lawmen, DA's, CDC, narcs, FBI, CIA, sheriffs. The truth of the matter is obvious. Like any other human group, law enforcement people include the mediocre, the unstable, neurotic, etc. However they are as a group more honest, stronger, more dependable and more humane than the other groups we have worked with. For example, record producers, psychiatrists, professors, lawyers, professional liberals, politicians, etc. They are not fun lovers and they are deficient in a sense of humor. But they are for the most part eager to be understood and liked. And they want to be part of anything good that we do and to

share our discoveries and laugh with them. It's the cops who deal
with the worst problems of industrial society and there will be no
solution to earthly problems that does not involve the loving cooperation of the police. What a liberation this discovery is . . .

8) *Dearest Rosemary, I will always love you.* Joanna, who is perfect and
I know that our destiny is linked to yours. We want you to be free.
Joanna and I have devoted all our energies which are unmatchable
to create the situation where you can receive this offer and invitation. Dennis and Robin who were part of the original molecule have
also worked devotedly for our freedom. Believe our financial problems are solved. In this letter, I've outlined where we are now and
where we are going to invite you and John to join us in whatever
love you desire. All we want for you is to be free so your beauty can
shine where and how it will. The Henry Kissinger who can arrange
this truce is—

With the letter, Tim enclosed an FBI business card on which he had
scrawled, "Roger LaJeunesse, known as Frenchy—213-272-6161. He is
FBI, Los Angeles."

"The letter," Rosemary recalled, "did not come to me directly but
was sent by someone whom Tim knew would then get it to me. It was
written by hand without a single cross-out, as though it was meant to be
published. Then, and for a long time afterward, I was very angry at Tim
and very self-righteous . . . I knew it was to get Michael Kennedy." "They
went after Rosemary hard," Kennedy recalled more than twenty years
later. "Hard and heavy. They tortured that woman. Literally, and for
a number of years. I don't think this woman ever broke a law. Unless
we consider smoking dope to be breaking the law, which I don't. They
leaned on Rosemary and Rosemary, who loved Tim to his dying day and
would have done virtually anything in the world for him, had an opportunity because she would have been believed to exchange my freedom for
his. And, as much as she loved him, she chose not to."

Rosemary's stubborn refusal to turn informant forced her to remain
underground long after many of those who had committed far more serious crimes—the leaders of Weather Underground and Eldridge Cleaver
among them—were allowed to resume normal lives. As was so often the
case for someone who got too close to Tim, Rosemary paid a high price.

Not long after receiving Tim's letter, she left Sicily to join her boyfriend John in Colombia. Two years later, she made her way back to America where she lived as Sarah Woodruff on Cape Cod. Although many people there knew who she really was, they did not tell the police. "Being underground," she remembered, "is very schizophrenic. As a fugitive, you are so self-important to yourself and yet you must appear anonymous to everyone else." After spending a year on Cape Cod, Rosemary learned through a lawyer that the federal government might be willing to drop its prosecution of her as a fugitive if the state of California would do the same. Told that her chances of going to jail for having violated probation by leaving the country with Tim were fifty-fifty, she said, "I did not want to trade the life I had for the possibility of going to jail. So I stayed underground for thirteen more years."

"She felt that if she came above ground," Michael Kennedy said, "they would have gotten her for aiding and abetting." Although Kennedy did not represent Rosemary during this period, he encouraged her to surface because in his opinion the only conceivable case against her would require Tim's testimony. "I think what she was concerned with was that he would smear her in some way with the Brotherhood. Smear her with Weather. Smear her with drugs. Smear her in some fashion. She was terrified he would do that and she did not come out. She knew the treachery he was capable of. So she stayed underground."

FORTY-ONE

Dennis Martino and Joanna returned home from Los Angeles on June 4 to find that they had been ripped off. As Joanna later wrote, it was as if someone had backed a truck up to the front door of their isolated, rustic house at 14 St. Jude Street in the hills above Mill Valley and emptied out the entire place: Joanna's fur coat, her jewels, her clothes, and even her expensive new Chanel makeup; Tim's many letters from prison; all the tapes Dennis had made of phone calls in which prison escape plans, blackmail scams, and drug deals had been discussed; Joanna's address book; and Tim's taped interviews with psychologist Wesley Hiler in Vacaville were missing. It did not take Dennis very long to figure out who had done this. Robin, unable to cope with Dennis's obsessive love for Joanna, had recently gone to live with Joanna's coke dealer. The robbery was designed to put money in their pockets and serve as payback for what Dennis and Joanna had done to her.

Joanna promptly called the local police. Within minutes, they were all over the house. After Dennis and Joanna told them what this was about, the cops put a tap on their phone, and the next day listened in as Robin told Joanna she could have her belongings back for $20,000 in cash. Should Joanna make the stupid mistake of calling the police, she would never see Tim's precious prison letters or her fur coat again. Robin agreed to a meeting at noon the next day at a motel not far from the Golden Gate Bridge. In the motel parking lot, Joanna gave her a brown envelope with the money inside. Robin handed Joanna the key to the room where her coke-dealer boyfriend was waiting with everything from the house. As Joanna walked away, four cops grabbed Robin. In the motel room, Joanna persuaded Robin's very wired boyfriend to put his gun down. The police rushed in and arrested him as well.

Robin and her boyfriend were charged with attempted extortion, drug possession, and possession of a dangerous weapon. In Marin County, they were booked on burglary charges to which they eventually pleaded guilty. Now that she had recovered her possessions, Joanna decided to leave the house. "From now on," she wrote, "I would live in hotels with Dennis, until Tim was out of prison." Given the frequency with which Tim began changing prisons, the decision made sense. From Chino, where he had been stashed while being debriefed by the FBI, Tim was transferred to the federal prison at Terminal Island near Long Beach. Soon after the transfer, Joanna phoned George Chula, Tim's lawyer in Orange County, and asked him to take her out to dinner

Described by Joe Eszterhas as "a distinguished, graying man" who dressed with "dignified flair," Chula was short and slight with a dark complexion. Originally from Akron, Ohio, he was very much part of the Orange County legal establishment. He played handball with Judge Byron K. McMillan, went to parties with District Attorney Cecil Hicks, and had cross-examined Neil Purcell many times over the years in drug cases. Above the desk in his den, Chula kept two photographs—one of Tim, the other of Cecil Hicks. "George Chula had a true love and compassion as a lawyer," recalled Neil Purcell. "And he would take the biggest underdogs. This guy would take cases for nothing. He never had much. He didn't drive a very nice car. He didn't have a big fancy office. He worked himself to the point where he had these black circles under his eyes. He would never raise his voice. But in my opinion, he was an excellent attorney. Excellent. He became the Brotherhood attorney because he really felt sorry for those people." In the process, Chula made powerful enemies who wanted him removed as the defense attorney for those busted for drugs in Orange County. Don Strange of the DEA publicly described him as "a Brotherhood stooge." Chula's friends had warned him repeatedly that the narcs were out to get him. For all these reasons, as well as their need to determine whether Tim and Joanna really intended to make good on their promises, the DEA selected Chula as their first target.

In an outfit chosen for her by a female agent and wearing a wire for the first time, Joanna met Chula in a room in the Saddleback Inn in Orange County. With investigators listening in from the next room, Chula pulled a piece of paper from his pocket. "Would you like some cocaine, girl?" Loudly, Joanna replied, "Oh, *cocaina*." Using the edge of a photograph of Tim and Joanna which she had taken that day at the Terminal

Island prison, Chula separated a mound of cocaine into three thick lines. He rolled up a $100 bill and offered it to Joanna. After they did the lines, Joanna told him she would like to keep some for later. Would he be so kind as to fold it into a paper for her? Chula put the cocaine into a bindle and gave it to her.

As they drove to the restaurant in his black Fiat, Chula pulled out a joint, which Joanna got him to admit on tape he had brought back from Mexico. After they sat down in a booth at the restaurant, Joanna excused herself to go to the bathroom and called the narcs in the Saddleback Inn to tell them where she was. When she got up once more to go to the ladies' room, she gave the cocaine bindle to a female officer who was waiting there for her. "I was still getting stoned and drinking," Joanna recalled, "but the agents didn't care. I wrote this line in my book: 'Drugs are legal if you're working for the Feds.'"

During dinner, Joanna did her best to seduce Chula while the agents were "sitting outside in a car taping our conversation." She told him that she needed an ounce of cocaine. "He was thrilled about getting me an ounce and he tells me he will do that as quickly as he can. For Tim. I say some is for me and some is for Tim. That's why I need a big amount. And that it also protects Tim in prison to be able to have coke and distribute it. So he tells me he'll call me in order for us to meet in a few days so he can give me the ounce." After Chula dropped Joanna back at her motel, the feds debriefed her. "I hardly know what I'm talking about," she recalled, "and they are unbelievably excited. Meanwhile, I was visiting Tim every day and telling him word for word what was happening. And he was into it and saying he was going to get out soon and we were going off to a Caribbean island and it would be just the two of us and he was going to protect me and who cares about those bastards."

Four days later, Chula visited Joanna in her room at the Newporter Inn. With narcs again listening in next door, the two of them used cocaine together. Joanna gave Chula $700, which had been supplied to her by the police, and asked him to bring her half an ounce of cocaine. On the night of July 2, as she waited for him to deliver it, Chula, who was very upset, called to say, "I think I shouldn't come but I'm going to anyway." When he showed up half an hour later, he told Joanna that when he got to his coke connection's house by the ocean in Costa Mesa, he decided to walk on the beach before going inside. A young man with a towel around his waist and a walkie-talkie in his hand listening in on the police-band frequency came up to him and said, "I'm the lifeguard on this beach and man, I wonder who you are because four police cars have been following you from where you came from and joking with one another about what a sucker you are." Chula told Joanna that he did not understand what was going on but could not believe she or Tim would be trying to bust him. She reassured him he was just being paranoid because he had been snorting so much coke. Chula then "pulled out joints and cocaine, not the ounce, but the stuff he had on him, a paper folded with a gram inside," Joanna recalled. "We did some drugs and he left me the gram and the joints and then he left. After he was gone, the feds busted into the room. They were incredibly disappointed but they said they had enough to impound his car, which they were very pleased with. I went back to talk to Tim about it and he was very happy and he congratulated me greatly."

"I liked George Chula," said Michael Kennedy. "He was not the most brilliant stunning lawyer around but completely dedicated to his clients and he loved Tim. He was the kind of person, like the Martino brothers, who if Tim asked him to do something, of course he would do it. George enjoyed drugs himself. He smoked marijuana, as everyone did back then, and did some hash. But later on, George got into cocaine."

Having successfully entrapped George Chula for the DEA, Joanna now made good on yet another of Tim's promises to the government—the delivery of all his papers, including the original manuscript of *Confessions of A Hope Fiend,* which Tim claimed would help put Kennedy, Rhine, and Standard behind bars. Two days after Tim's initial interview with the feds, Joanna and Dennis had visited Michael Horowitz, Tim's archivist in San Francisco. As Tim's common-law wife with a signed paper from him giving her full power of attorney, Joanna asked to see all of Tim's papers from the years 1969 and 1970 so she could organize and catalog them. After making Joanna sign a receipt in which she agreed not to let unauthorized people have access to the documents, Horowitz reluctantly allowed her to remove two file drawers of letters and photographs. The next day, Joanna bought two red, white, and blue trunks, placed all the documents inside, and stored them in a locker at the Los Angeles airport. To prove Tim did indeed intend to deliver the goods, she presented Don Strange with a folder containing all of Tim and Rosemary's prison correspondence prior to the escape.

On July 25, the same day that Tim was "making a moving picture for the DEA," Joanna appeared at Horowitz's house with five men who

claimed to be from the Scotch Microcopy Company (the name was selected by one of the agents from the San Francisco telephone book). She
handed Horowitz a note Tim had signed on Terminal Island a week earlier: "These men are helping us microfilm all of my archives from Springfield, Mass. to *Terra II*. Will you please turn over to them all of the files?"
For the next two hours, Horowitz argued that what he was now being
asked to do was improper. Not only were the files confidential, but for all
he knew, Tim might have been under duress when he signed the note.
When Joanna asked Horowitz why he was so paranoid about surrendering the files, he asked, "Aren't these people agents?"

"I was extremely upset," Horowitz recalled, "and I refused to give
them over because I had been protecting them for five years." Telling him
the agents were armed, Joanna said, "Michael, Tim is so desperate now.
Maybe if they get these archives, they'll leave us alone." At the same time
she was "sweet talking" him, Horowitz recalled, "she was also telling me
that these men were not going to leave without the archives. It was in the
afternoon and I had three children in the house and I knew they were
probably going to come back with a warrant." Deciding it made no sense
for him to "go down in a blaze of glory," Horowitz allowed the FBI
agents to load thirty-one boxes containing Tim's archives into the van
parked outside his house. "They drove off and I didn't see the archives
again for another five years. I called key people and told them what happened. Two days later, *The New York Times* ran a story that said the FBI
had seized Timothy Leary's archives and claimed they would now be able
to solve every drug case of the 1960s. I immediately put out a press release
that there was nothing in the archives about drug deals. It was just government propaganda."

Although Horowitz did everything in his power to reassure a jittery
counterculture that no one had anything to fear from the material seized
by the FBI, the government now had unfettered access to every letter Tim
had written not only from prison but also during his time of exile in Algeria and Switzerland. The FBI sent Tim's prison letters to their crypt-
analysis lab so that experts could break the code Tim claimed he had used
to communicate details of his escape to Rosemary and his lawyers. In
Seattle, FBI agents reviewed 21,000 applications for library cards before
they found one issued to William McNellis. Tim's fake library card was
sent to the FBI lab in Washington for handwriting analysis and fingerprint
identification. An extensive search of the basement of the safe house near

Seattle where Tim was sheltered by the Weathermen unearthed two copies of the September 14, 1970, *San Francisco Chronicle* that contained an article about Tim's escape along with various underground newspapers, radical pamphlets, road maps, bank deposit receipts, and a food coupon booklet. All this material was also sent to the FBI labs in Washington, D.C., for processing.

In Chicago, FBI agents tried to match the fingerprints from a receipt Tim had signed at the Sheraton O'Hare with those on his California driver's license. Tracking down everyone who had stayed in sixteen neighboring rooms while Tim was at the Sheraton, agents interviewed salesmen, convention goers, and airline employees, none of whom knew anything about the escape. After reviewing records at the San Francisco Department of Health, FBI agents determined that an application for the birth certificate for William McNellis—who was born on January 14, 1919, and died four years later—had been made on February 1, 1971, by a woman from the Weather Underground who had identified herself as J. C. McNellis.

In interrogation sessions that continued for months, agents repeatedly questioned Tim about his flight from the country. No question seemed too trivial. While the Weathermen were driving him to Seattle, did they pay with cash or use a credit card for gas? Where was the bunk in the camper—in the back or over the cab? How many people could sit around the table in the camper? When the FBI was finally done with him, Tim's file was four feet thick and weighed twenty-three pounds.

While Tim could only give the government what he already knew, Joanna had so impressed the agents with her abilities that they decided to use her to go after bigger game. "Tim told Kennedy and Rhine that I wanted to talk to them," Joanna recalled. "I was wired and they wanted me to get Michael Kennedy to say out loud to me that, yes, he did collaborate in the escape and they wanted me to make him say that he would do it again." Kennedy was far too clever to be entrapped by such an obvious setup and did not even attend the meeting. He sent Rhine who, realizing that Joanna was wearing a wire, did all he could to find out from her what the government was planning next. In this continuing game of cat and mouse, the central targets of the investigation had so far managed to elude their pursuers.

Failing to bag their number-one target, the agents running Tim and Joanna began casting their net wider. Apparently anyone whose politics they did not like was now fair game. "They wanted Jerry Brown," Joanna recalled. "He was running for governor and the California DEA wanted me to entrap him by smoking marijuana with him and having sex with him if I could." Joanna contacted Jerry Brown's campaign headquarters and identified herself as a reporter from the *Daily Express* in England named Sally Bowles (the heroine of Christopher Isherwood's *I Am a Camera,* upon which the musical *Cabaret* was based). She asked if it would be possible for her to interview the candidate. Naturally, they said yes.

Joanna met Jerry Brown in Fresno where he was giving a speech. "I had a real flash with him," she remembered. "I could tell he fancied me. And of course I fancied him too because he had power and he was beautiful. And he asked me if I would like to get on the plane and come with him to Laurel Canyon. When I was in the limousine with him going to the airport, I told him I was really Joanna Leary and I wanted him to do something so Tim could be paroled out of the California prison system into the federal system. When I told him who I was, Jerry freaked out and decided I had better not come with him to Laurel Canyon. I thought it was more important to double-cross the DEA and tell Jerry Brown who I really was. But he came real close to not being governor."

Tim himself was now in transit. At three in the morning on August 2, he was taken by two armed federal agents from his cell on Terminal Island and flown to Minneapolis where he was driven to the federal prison in Sandstone, admitted under an alias, and put in "the hole." At feeding time, a guard told him his name in here was "Charlie Thrush." Joanna was told that Tim was now in a "country club prison like where the Watergate people were in Danbury, Connecticut. A wonderful place where he would be very free and we might be able to have contact visits." Because "we were talking constantly about having a child," Joanna was thrilled by this news. Flying to Minneapolis, she took a taxi to Sandstone in the middle of the night. "In this dump of a town," as she called it, she rented a room above a diner. She visited Tim the next morning and found "a really panicked Tim housed in a maximum-security federal prison, once again in solitary confinement. Inmates were crossing the yard under his tiny window, singing 'Timothy Leary's dead' in a threatening way."

To make matters worse, news of what Tim was doing began to surface in the media. "That same week," Joanna recalled, "there was a blurb in *Newsweek* that said Timothy Leary had now become a federal informant and was being held in a secret location under the name of Charlie

Thrush. I was Virginia Church and he was Charlie Thrush. Because Falls Church, Virginia, is where the Federal Witness Protection Program was. The feds released this to the press. They were turning the heat up max on Tim because he hadn't given them enough. What was really frightening was that when I asked Don Strange of the DEA, he said it was the FBI who leaked the information to get the jump on the DEA and to show they had made this incredible victory. It was the agencies fighting with each other. We thought they were trying to get him killed."

As Tim and Joanna sat in the visiting room at Sandstone on August 9, prison guards took down the portrait of Richard Nixon on the wall and replaced it with one of Gerald Ford. Ironically, Nixon's resignation served only to intensify Tim and Joanna's paranoia. "Now Nixon was gone," Joanna recalled, "but Tim was still in prison. Presidents were falling but he was still in." When Tim charged Joanna with the task of getting him out of Sandstone any way she could, Joanna promised she would go to Washington to talk directly with the new president. That night, because she was "lonely, afraid, terrified," she called Dennis and asked him to join her in Minnesota. With him, Dennis brought cocaine, Thai stick, a gram of Mexican heroin, "and a passionate desire to make love to her."

On August 12, they boarded a plane to Washington. Joanna was still flush with money from the acid-dealer rip-off. "I was walking around with a lot of drugs and never less than $5,000 or $10,000 cash in my bag." Leaving Dennis in the economy section of the plane, she strolled into first class and saw Senator Hubert Humphrey in the first row. Sitting down beside him, she introduced herself and said, "Timothy Leary is in one of your prisons and he's going to get killed and then you're really going to be in a mess." Politely, Humphrey said that although he could not promise Joanna an audience with President Ford, he would make some phone calls and see what he could do to help.

In Washington, Joanna and Dennis checked into the Watergate Hotel and waited for Humphrey's call. Sure enough, the phone rang and an assistant asked Joanna if she could meet with Attorney General William Saxbe at nine-thirty the next morning. Dressed provocatively because she still believed she was "going to seduce Tim out of prison," Joanna was shown into a room at the Department of Justice where twelve men in dark suits sat around a table.

Joanna made her plea: Tim wanted to cooperate with the government but was going to be killed if he was kept in Sandstone Prison very much longer. When she finished, the attorney general of the United States said, according to Joanna, "If I was your father, I'd spank you." "Is that psychosexual enough for you?" she would later say. "This was really the lowest point of the curve. I said to myself, 'I'm fucked. Tim's fucked. We're all fucked.' By now Saxbe was angry at me and lecturing me like 'Little girl, you go home, you've got nothing to do playing with the big boys.'" As she got up to leave, Joanna asked the attorney general to have Tim transferred back to California. Saxbe said, "Well, we'll see what we can do."

In Sandstone, Tim met with federal prosecutor Guy Goodwin, whom Craig Vetter described in *Playboy* as "the notorious witch-hunter of radicals." Goodwin had been the man behind the indictment of Daniel and Philip Berrigan as well as most of the other important government cases against the radical peace movement. "None of the dozen or so highly publicized cases he ran resulted in conviction," Vetter wrote, "but that was never their first purpose. It was more important to Goodwin and his team to gather dossiers on the left and then harass them until they either cooperated or were forced into long costly trials." Goodwin reported directly to Robert C. Mardian, the archconservative chosen by Attorney General John Mitchell in 1970 to revive the Internal Security Division of the Department of Justice, which had been out of business since the McCarthy era.

Described by Michael Drosnin in *New Times* as "a shadowy figure with a passion for anonymity," Goodwin was then a forty-six-year-old former prosecutor from Wichita, Kansas, with "cold, blue eyes staring imperiously over half-frame bifocals" and "a high-pitched voice reminiscent of Truman Capote," who was always "well-pressed and immaculately groomed." One newspaper reporter wrote that Goodwin "waltzed into the courthouse like Loretta Young." Demonstrators in Detroit, protesting a grand jury hearing there, "handed him a gay liberation button."

According to Drosnin, Goodwin had gone after members of the Weather Underground "with the dedication of a fanatic and the success of a Keystone cop." Working with Division 5, the domestic intelligence unit of the FBI and the White House "plumbers," Goodwin and his staff had subpoenaed at least a thousand witnesses to testify before more than a hundred grand juries in forty different states, employing informers whose criminal backgrounds ensured they would be fairly useless as witnesses in court. His unsuccessful prosecutions had "sapped the time, energy, morale, and financial resources of the left." As Drosnin wrote, "Timothy Leary merely joins a long list of informers, themselves prime movers in the alleged conspiracies Goodwin has sought to punish." Senator Edward Kennedy of Massachusetts, the most relentless of Tim's questioners during his appearance before that Senate subcommittee ten years earlier, called Goodwin's operation "a dangerous form of Star Chamber inquisition that is trampling the rights of American citizens from coast to coast." Goodwin, who was trying to indict radical lawyers in the Chicago area for their association with the Weathermen, wanted Tim to appear as a witness before the grand jury there, as well as before one in Los Angeles that was investigating people in the film industry who had helped finance militant organizations. Tim was flown under heavy guard to Chicago, but never testified before the grand jury there. As David Weir wrote in *Rolling Stone,* "The government had a witness who was cooperative but not credible."

Nevertheless, prosecutors began using Tim's name to intimidate those who had once been close to him. On Sunday, August 18, Ed Montgomery reported in a front-page article in the *San Francisco Examiner* that Tim had "blown the whistle" on former colleagues and associates "in hopes of avoiding further prosecution and getting speedy parole." He had, Montgomery wrote, identified a San Francisco attorney "active in the National Lawyers Guild," who, "in league with the members of the Weatherman organization" had engineered his prison escape. A government source told *The New York Times* that Tim was cooperating fully and was in protective custody.

On August 9, the *Berkeley Barb* asked "Has Leary Made a Deal with Feds?" On September 6, the *Barb* answered its own question with a headline that read LEARY THE FINK. In less than a month, the man once revered as a counterculture hero had become its Benedict Arnold.

FORTY-TWO

On September 4, 1974, Tim and Joanna testified against George Chula before the Orange Country grand jury. "Again," Joanna recalled, "I go to the grand jury completely out of my mind on drugs. Totally stoned and trying to justify to myself that those are the bad people and we are the good people." Asked why she was testifying, Joanna told the grand jury, "Because the first year I spent in this country, I met a lot of people who were part of the drug culture . . . I found ninety nine point nine per cent of them to be dishonest, lying people." Asked whether she was offering this testimony to help Tim, she responded, "Sure, but if I didn't like the people I was working with, I wouldn't do it."

Calling himself a psychologist and a philosopher, Tim testified that on January 30, 1973, in the Orange County courthouse, George Chula reached down and pulled up his pant leg and "out of his stocking, he produced a piece of hashish and he handed it to me. I took it and ate it." The next day, Tim said he had met with Chula again in a room where Chula handed him a piece of hashish. Although this "alarmed me very much because I knew the guard was sitting in the glass booth observing what was going on," Tim testified that Chula had said, "It's all right."

Despite Tim's testimony, the grand jury failed to indict Chula on these charges. Instead, they returned indictments for his actions while he was being entrapped by Joanna for the DEA. On September 5, a squad of narcotics agents stormed into Chula's law office, put him in handcuffs, and hauled him off to jail where, as David Weir wrote in *Rolling Stone*, "he was stripped and dressed in prison garb before a judge finally released him." Four months later, Chula was found guilty on a reduced charge of marijuana possession and sentenced to forty-five days in the Orange County jail. "He got off with a slap on the wrist," Michael Kennedy recalled, "because people down there knew that fundamentally he was a decent human being who would never hurt a fly." "They did not disbar him," Neil Purcell remembered, "but he did go to jail. After that, he was broken down. His business started going downhill and he became ill and he didn't represent anybody for a couple of years. He died a few years ago."

On the day after Chula was arrested, a story ran in the *Los Angeles Times* with the headline LEARY, "FORMER KING OF LSD," TELLS RADICALS: "WAR IS OVER." In the article, Tim was quoted as saying that he had come to see "that secrecy and coverup are destructive and dangerous and I wanted to become part of the process of reconciliation and openness that is the spirit of the times." Admitting he had been part of "the polarization of the 1960's—the adopting of adversary positions and rhetorical postures," he explained that it was a "time when the public forum was captured by the crazies of the left and the crazies of the right. I never felt I was a criminal, and I never dealt drugs. I am still a scientist, I feel, and I want to make a contribution." Tim's publicly stated desire to bring about reconciliation in America, however, served to create the opposite effect. As Craig Vetter wrote in *Playboy,* "the paranoia that had been building among Tim's old friends and associates who had known and run with Joanna reached a breaking point."

Ken Kelley had never been close to either Tim or Joanna but he did revere Michael Kennedy for "saving his ass" when he was subpoenaed in his hometown of Detroit to testify before a grand jury investigating the Weather Underground bombing of a women's bathroom in the Capitol building in Washington, D.C., in 1970. Although virtually every prominent left-wing lawyer in America appeared for the defense, it was Kennedy who persuaded a very conservative female judge appointed by Richard Nixon to drop the charges because the federal prosecutor, Guy Goodwin, had failed to stipulate which crimes each of the suspects in the case had committed.

When Kelley moved to California, becoming the editor of the *Berkeley Barb* at the age of twenty-two, he learned what Tim had done to George Chula and got in touch with Michael Kennedy in San Francisco to ask if there was anything he could do to help. Over dinner at Kennedy's house, the attorney showed Kelley a transcript of Tim and Joanna's testimony before the Orange County grand jury. Kelley decided to call a press conference to denounce Tim as a government informant. He and his friend and fellow journalist David Weir formed an ad hoc organization called PILL—People Investigating Leary's Lies.

Because he still considered Allen Ginsberg to be the guiding spirit of the counterculture, Kelley showed him the grand jury transcript to prove that the rumors about Tim were true. Kelley then contacted Jack Leary. Although Michael Kennedy had advised Jack to keep his own counsel on this and told him that "one day you'll talk to your father and you'll spit in his face or whatever you feel like doing," Jack told Kelley that Tim had already done so much damage that he felt the need to point this out and separate himself from it.

With both Ginsberg and Ram Dass now on board, Kelley and Jerry Rubin began circulating a petition condemning the terrible pressure being brought on prisoners everywhere by the government and denouncing Tim for "turning state's evidence and marking innocent people for jail in order to get out of jail himself." Among those who signed the petition were Arthur Miller, Herbert Gold, Philip Berrigan, David Harris, Dick Gregory, Ben Gazzara, William Kunstler, Charles Garry, Michael Kennedy, Judy Collins, and Country Joe McDonald. A press conference was held on September 18 at the St. Francis Hotel, attended by more than a hundred journalists as well as what Vetter described in *Playboy* as "long hairs, people with sitars and babies, arrogant and pushy television crews and up front a table full of faces from a time when Leary's name fit in the same breath with the Beatles and peace and love." Radio station KPFA in Berkeley broadcast it live.

A media event of the first order, the press conference was an authentic flashback to an era that everyone now seemed to know was over. In an ornate ballroom hung with crystal chandeliers, Jerry Rubin joined Kelley at a long table. On the other side of Kelley, Ram Dass and Allen Ginsberg sat beside Jack Leary, now twenty-four years old. Kelley began the proceedings by telling everyone that PILL was lashed together "to dispel the rumors and to condemn the pressure brought by the Government on prisoners to fink on their friends." He compared what was now going on to the McCarthy era and the Rosenberg case, called Guy Goodwin a "swine-ster," and said that although "the fantasies of an acid-addled mythomaniac like Leary are easily impeached in a court of law . . . no one who has had any contact with Leary should be surprised if an FBI agent comes knocking at the door." Rubin, decked out in a green velvet day coat with a bright paisley bow tie and one gold earring, began reading a loose chronology of Tim's activities since he had first been sent to prison two years earlier. Rubin referred to rumors that Tim had made a videotape "in which he named names and pointed the finger at old friends," and noted that one theory now circulating was that "Tim's spirit has been killed but that a phantom Tim lives on, cooperating with his executioners." He also said that "This ghost from the past never had a firm grasp where the truth began and fantasy ended. He used words and sentences for their effect, not for eternal truth." By breaking him and turning him into an agent, Rubin said, the government was consciously trying to spread fear, cynicism, and despair in the hearts of young people. "'See what kind of person your guru Tim Leary is,' they are saying. 'You cannot trust him.' He is trying to give his jail cell to someone else," Rubin concluded. "I feel sick for the death of Tim Leary's soul."

As though to affirm that the spirit of the sixties was still alive and kicking, Paul Krassner heckled Rubin continually during his statement. "Can't you speak without reading from a script?" he called out. Finally, Kelley said, "Shut up, Paul!" Krassner had come to cover the conference as a reporter but he was against the whole idea of it. "I trusted Tim. Even if he was talking, I knew Rosemary was on the lam and only she could corroborate it. I thought Tim was playing the game of his life." The night before the press conference, Krassner had received a call from his friend Gene Schoenfeld, also known as Dr. Hip. "I was sharing a house with a woman who did costumes for plays," Schoenfeld recalled. "So I had this idea. This is really a kangaroo court. I asked her if there were kangaroo costumes and she said yes. I called Paul Krassner and asked him if he wanted to go in a kangaroo costume and he declined. Which was good. Because there was only one available." As Rubin was making his statement, Krassner saw Schoenfeld come hopping out in a kangaroo costume with a pouch and gloves for paws. From the kangaroo's pouch, Schoenfeld pulled a lemon meringue pie, which he intended to smash into Rubin's face. "But it had Saran wrap on it," Krassner remembered. "It was hard to get the Saran wrap off with those kangaroo gloves on. Ken Kelley stopped him before he could do it and pulled off his mask. But Gene did get to say, 'This is a kangaroo court.'"

It was now Ram Dass's turn to speak. Dressed all in white, with his long gray beard trailing down the front of his dhoti, he asked whether Tim was a rascal or a scoundrel. "A rascal," he said, "is only a mischievous, fun-loving prankster who doesn't really hurt anyone. But a scoundrel is malicious and people get hurt." Ram Dass concluded that, sadly, jail had turned Tim into a complete scoundrel.

Bearded, balding, and also in white, Allen Ginsberg looked to John Bryan "like a smaller and more Semitic replica of Ram Dass." The poet began by chanting "Om" for a few minutes. Then he read a statement entitled "Om Ah Hum: 44 Temporary Questions on Dr. Leary." Running the gamut "from serious to bitchy, worried to funny," Ginsberg's gnomic inquiries concerned not only Tim but the state of the nation. "Is he like Zabbathi Zvi," Ginsberg asked, "the False Messiah, accepted by millions of Jews centuries ago who left Europe for the Holy Land, was captured by the Turks on his way, told he'd have his head cut off unless he converted to Islam and so accepted Allah?" Perhaps, he suggested, Tim was "on his way out to outer space in Space Ship Terra II." Ginsberg asked why none of Tim's friends had spoken with him as he was shifted from prison to prison, held incommunicado, and "surrounded by government agents & informers." Voicing a concern shared by many, Ginsberg wondered, "Is Joanna Harcourt Smith his one contact spokes-agent a sex spy, agent provocateuse, double-agent, CIA hysteric; jealous tigress, or what?" He concluded, "Are there any police here at the press conference? America, must I examine my conscience? In the gaspetroleum ballgame are the police winning a meta-physical victory? . . . Will citizens be arrested, indicted, taken to jail for Leary's freedom?" Finally, he wondered, "Doesn't the old cry 'Free Tim Leary' apply now urgent as ever?"

Ginsberg, who admitted to Kelley shortly before the press conference began that he was "in a terrible state of self-doubt," intended his questions to serve as a meditation not only on Tim but on the Watergate crisis, Henry Kissinger's role in the death of Salvador Allende in Chile, and the star chamber proceedings taking place in grand jury rooms all across America. The poet's bravura performance elevated the proceedings, but not everything he said made literal sense or clarified his own position on these issues. Kelley, for one, described Ginsberg's questions as "a cosmic way of waffling."

Ginsberg was never an easy act to follow. When Jack Leary, the next speaker, began in a slow and halting manner to talk about a man whom he never called his father but referred to as "Timothy," what had begun as a media event became the public deconstruction of a life. Jack wore a checkered shirt, wash pants, and a light cloth jacket. Admitting that this was the first time he had ever spoken in public, Jack said he had felt compelled to come forward today because "Timothy is engaged in very dangerous actions which can destroy the lives of his former friends and associates." What surprised him, Jack said, was "that he didn't do this two or three years ago. What died in jail was not his soul, but his self-esteem and public image. Based on my past experience, I know Timothy Leary lies at will when he thinks it will benefit him. He finds lies easier to control than the truth. And he creates fantastic, absurd stories which he gets caught up in, and then cannot distinguish from the truth. Timothy has shown he would inform on anybody he can to get out of jail and it would not surprise me if he would testify about my sister or myself if he could." Jack concluded, "I do not believe by this statement that I am in any way betraying Timothy's trust. Rather, Timothy Leary, by his deceit, is betraying the very meaning of the word trust."

There cannot have been many sons who had ever denounced their fathers in public, but Jack bore, as Kelley would later say, "a lot of scars. A lot of Jackie's friends were dealers who had gotten busted. But he also hated the idea because he had never done anything like this." Before the press conference, Kelley had helped Jack prepare his statement and then rehearsed it with him. "Jack stumbled a lot," Kelley remembered, "and he was reading so there were long painful periods of silence when he was trying to get his bearings. I glared at the whole room daring anybody to interrupt. It took a long time but finally it was over." Outraged, Krassner's "objective pose as a reporter vanished" and he yelled out, "'Judge not, lest ye be stoned.' It was like Communist Russia or something."

The press conference ended in utter chaos. Anthony Russo, who had gone to jail for refusing to testify before a grand jury about Daniel Ellsberg's role in releasing the Pentagon Papers, began making a statement that went on and on. "We were live on KPFA," Kelley recalled, "and he was ranting and raving, making no sense whatsoever, and I think they finally pulled the plug." Kelley felt the press conference had been an unqualified success. "For once, the government was outgunned. Tim was beyond redemption and we told the feds to knock it off. Because if you don't, you're in trouble, not us. Do not indict Michael Kennedy."

"We tried to take Tim out as a witness," Michael Kennedy confirmed. "The kind of thing I would and did do for years in cross-examination. What the press conference said was that I would do this in a trial and the government would be embarrassed because they were placing their credibility in the hands of Timothy Leary." In time, Kennedy's judgment proved to be correct. James Browning, who became the United States Attorney in San Francisco, decided, in Kennedy's words, that he did not want to be embarrassed by the spectacle of Tim testifying in open court and so simply let the statute of limitations on all charges stemming from Tim's escape from prison run out.

The depth of the anger generated by the news that Tim had gone over to the other side seems hard to imagine now. "I'm digesting the news of Herr Doktor Leary, the swine," Abbie Hoffman wrote to his wife, Anita, in a letter dated September 6, 1975. "It's obvious to me he's talking his fucking demented head off to the Gestapo . . . It's not just a question of being a squealer but a question of squealing on people who helped you . . . The curses crowd my mouth . . . I can't imagine anything close except children turning parents in under Nazi Germany."

Nearly every account of the press conference included a statement mistakenly attributed to Kelley. "I was quoted in *The New York Times* and it was *Rolling Stone*'s quote of the month," Kelley recalled. "But it was actually Jerry Rubin who said it. What Jerry said that day was, 'This is the death of the sixties.'" After the press conference ended, Kelley, however, did tell John Bryan, "The 1960's are finally dead. That was just the funeral."

While the organizers of the press conference congratulated themselves for having eliminated Tim as a potential witness against them, the FBI continued to harvest every last scrap of information he gave them. Putting Tim's lawyers in jail had been their original goal. Now the focus shifted to finding a hot trail that would lead the FBI to Bill Ayers, Bernadine Dohrn, and Jeff Jones, fugitives who continued to elude the Justice Department.

On October 24, 1974, Tim was interrogated in the Sacramento offices of the FBI. Three days later, Marshal Art Van Court, who had become Tim's primary handler, brought him to San Francisco so Tim could point out exactly where he had stayed on the night of his escape. With Joanna by his side, Tim tentatively identified two addresses on Sycamore Street as similar to the house where he had been taken by the Weather Underground. The next day, Tim was unable to pinpoint where between Lakehead and Weed in northern California he had met with Ayers, Dohrn, and Jones.

Four days later in the Sacramento offices of the FBI, Tim told the story of his escape yet again. He was shown items seized from the basement of the Weather Underground safe house outside Seattle, and asked about the procedures used by the Weathermen to spirit him out of the country, as well as whether they had ever discussed their contacts in Canada with him. Hoping Tim could identify those who had aided and abetted in his escape, the agents showed him thirty-five photographs, many taken from California driver's licenses or Chicago police files. Though Tim was unable to recognize anyone except as "familiar in a general way" or "resembling" those who had helped him, Tim did positively identify three photographs of the Weathermen's safe house near Monroe, Washington, where he had stayed from September 15 to 21, 1970. On November 12, 1974, Tim was presented with fifty-two documents from his archives. Like a poet being shown his own work by critics who wanted to know what was in his mind when he wrote them, Tim painstakingly explicated his many references to Michael Standard, Joe Rhine, and Michael Kennedy. Though nothing Tim said seemed particularly damning to anyone, he maintained his lawyers had demanded that he fictionalize his account of the escape to protect those involved. All fifty-two documents were then sent "to the FBI Laboratory for extensive analyses."

When Tim was transferred to a rural jail near Sacramento, Joanna went to stay with Art and Marcia Van Court. By now, she could not even go to the supermarket without protection. Although she could "hardly call my mother anymore," she was still "hiding Dennis in my closet . . . He was still working for the DEA but he was not supposed to be around me. They were all charmed by Tim's love for me and they had all taken up the cause of the 'perfect love.' The DEA and the feds were doing this great thing for these lovers so I couldn't be fucking Dennis. But I was."

Tim and Joanna met with federal prosecutor John Milano at the FBI offices in San Francisco. Milano, Joanna recalled, was "supposed to get a federal parole to Tim. Milano came to the meeting late because he got a flat and had to pull a screw out of his tire. He said to Tim, 'You've been screwed. You're never getting out. They're taking the information but they have no intention of releasing you.'" The next time Joanna visited Tim in a little rural jail near Sacramento, she recalled, "I Ic mouths to me, 'Get me a G-U-N.' He says, 'This isn't working, I'm never gonna get out. We've got to do it differently.'" Joanna got a small handgun from "a seedy character" in San Francisco whom she knew "from roaming around there." She also bought two knives and an anatomy book, "To find out where you have to stick someone to kill them," she remembered. "I was going to use the knives to kill Art and Marcia Van Court who had let me into their house and made me food and were the nicest middle-class people I had met in years."

In the motel room Joanna shared with Dennis, he began pressuring her to dump Tim. "He said Tim was just using me," she recalled. "And I'm the most wonderful woman in the world and I should leave with Dennis because he is the real thing and Tim is just a shit. We have a violent argument and I throw Dennis out." In pink kid-leather platform boots, she visited Tim twice in jail "with a gun in my waist and a knife in each boot just in case he was ready to use them on a given day. Because they now trusted me, they didn't use a metal detector on me and I just walked in."

Art Van Court and an FBI agent named Curt from the antiterrorist unit in Chicago drove Tim and Joanna north to find the Weathermen's safe house outside Seattle. Because, according to Joanna, Art Van Court thought Tim was "a hero," Tim was not cuffed. He and Joanna were allowed to sit together in the backseat where they could "neck and kiss and all that stuff. By now, they adored Tim and they wanted him to get out. He had grown a paunch and he looked exactly like them. He would play handball with them at the safe house near Folsom Lake and they just adored him and he was planning on using a gun on them." As they drove through San Francisco, the .357 Magnum, which Curt had taken from his holster and placed on the front seat, fell to the floor and slid backward to Tim's feet. "This was the day we were going to kill them," Joanna recalled. "We were going to kill them and put them in the trunk of the car and then go on." All Tim had to do was reach down and pick up the gun and he could take both agents hostage. In his mind, Tim had screened this movie a million times. He had memorized every line. "I looked at Tim and he picked up this gun and I knew, 'Well, this is it,'" remembered Joanna. "We now had two guns and two knives and one was a big mother gun. Tim was reading the *San Francisco Chronicle* and he wrapped the .357 Magnum in the *Chronicle* and handed it back to Curt. The reason he wrapped it in the *Chronicle* was that he was being tactful with Art Van Court and didn't want him to know Curt had lost his gun to the prisoner. He didn't look at me or say anything and I was thinking, 'Okay, what he's saying is that we're not going to do it.'"

A little while later, the two agents stopped the car by the side of the road to stretch their legs. It was a beautiful fall day in Oregon. Tim and

Joanna went for a short walk in the forest. Doing their best to be discreet, the agents trailed behind. "Are we gonna do it?" Joanna recalled asking him. "Well, have you thought about how this would have to happen?" he said. "No," she replied, "you're the mastermind." "Well," he said, "do you realize that if we kill them and put them in the trunk, then we have to wait for some van to come by? We have to flag them down and then we have to kill them too."

Clearly, Tim had already worked out the entire scenario in his mind. In order to get away with this escape, he and Joanna would, in her words, "have to change cars several times and kill people in the process." Joanna had already rented an apartment in Sacramento under a false name. "I had wigs and everything," she recalled. Yet when Tim asked her, "Do you still want to do it?" Joanna answered, "Well, I guess not." Then she lifted her Instamatic camera and snapped a picture of Tim standing between the two agents. "He had no moral qualms about killing them," she would later say. "He just thought it was not practical. And then Tim showed them the safe house."

Jeff Jones would later say, "I don't see how Tim could have taken federal agents to the safe house outside Seattle because I couldn't have done it. I don't know where that house was. I'm just guessing that he drove around until he spotted a house and said, 'That's it.' We didn't want him to know where that house was. It existed just for him. And when he was gone, the house was gone. I can assure you that we never trusted him on the level that every single thing he touched was eliminated. Everything that was put in place for him was gone when he was gone. To protect ourselves."

A few days after Tim and Joanna decided not to murder Art Van Court and Curt, Joanna had what she described as "this incredible scene with Art Van Court and his wife" to whom she confessed—"with my face in Art Van Court's lap, sobbing"—what had almost happened. "It was just too much. I had to tell somebody. They forgave me. They said, 'We understand.' And they never told anybody. I threw the gun away in the Sacramento River, I got rid of everything."

On January 27, 1975, Tim emerged from the government cocoon to respond to a subpoena to appear before a California prison personnel board hearing at which the professional fate of Vacaville psychologist Wesley Hiler was to be determined. Fired for sharing the audiotapes he had made with Tim with a magazine editor, Hiler was appealing the action on the grounds that his original agreement with Tim included the possibility of publication. Tim, looking tan and well dressed, testified in Hiler's behalf but did the psychologist no good. His firing was upheld and Tim returned once more to government custody.

Joanna, who was now receiving $700 a month from the Federal Witness Protection Program, moved into her own apartment in Sacramento. One day, she was picked up by Art Van Court's deputies and taken to a safe house where Tim, looking, as she would later say, more like a narc than ever, was in the custody of ten or twelve agents. "Tim tells me that Dennis has written a letter to him and addressed it to Jerry Utz, Curt of the FBI, and Don Strange, saying that Tim and I had no intention of really collaborating with them. That we had been telling lies and botching things up intentionally. That I am in fact Dennis's mistress. He goes into detail about the things that I do with him and he writes about the gun incident. He sells us down the river. He does this out of spite and vengeance because he thinks that if I am thrown away, I will go back to him." Even as the agents were "freaking out," they were still "protecting Tim. Their outrage was, 'How could I do this to Tim?' So it was all about how I had betrayed Timothy and Timothy tells me it would be better if I went back to my mother in Spain and stayed there for a while until he tells me to come back."

In what Joanna would later describe as a "terrible, terrible state," she left after having spent three years of her life doing all she could to set Tim free. With no place else to go, she returned to her mother's house in Marbella where she stayed "drunk and Tim called me collect twice a week from a pay phone on the road. They were moving him around and they really felt sorry for him. He was the abandoned lover. The older man, like they all were, with his paunch, and his best friend Dennis had betrayed him too. He was playing that to the max." During these expensive collect calls, Tim continually told Joanna how much he loved her and how she should not worry because he would be getting out soon.

Ken Kesey, Paul Krassner, Wavy Gravy, and others who steadfastly refused to believe that Tim had abandoned them appeared in early February at the "Timothy Leary Wake-Up Celebration" held in the Pauley Ballroom on the campus of the University of California in Berkeley. On the morning of the celebration, Kesey held a press conference. "Leary is an absolute fuckin' ally, his credentials are impeccable. You can't argue with this. We know what Leary is like. He's naive, he's romantic, he's prone to make mistakes, but he is just Timothy Leary . . . We can't lose him." To the thousand people at the celebration that night, Krassner read from the sealed Orange County grand jury transcripts. Quoting Tim's statement that defense lawyers who sponsored illegal activities should also be made to tell the truth, Krassner said, "We're not defending Leary's finkery . . . We're talking about a system whereby people can be broken." At midnight, campus police shut down the event because it had turned into what they called a "drunken dope party." A campus police sergeant later filed a report in which he stated that the Berkeley Free Clinic was tied up all night with "some hostile cases of people freaked out on acid" and that there had been "extensive use of marijuana and other drugs." Although the organizers lost money, they claimed that the celebration had been a success.

On February 24, 1975, Tim called his old friend Jaakov Kohn, editor of *The East Village Other* in New York City. Because Kohn had already been visited by the FBI several times during the past month, he taped the conversation. Tim told Kohn he would soon be getting out of prison. "I've done three years for two joints. That's about enough, huh?" Of Allen Ginsberg, Tim said, "Listen, cool him out, will you? If you see him, tell him that I don't want to see him right now . . . he's using a kind of a Jewish mother blackmail on me that's going to cost a lot of bread. The only reason he's trying to interfere is because he wants to be the first one to interview me and rip me off." Tim also told Kohn he had learned during the past few years that "everybody should tell the truth. I'm very much against cover-ups. After all, that war is over, don't you think?" When Kohn asked him which war he was talking about, Tim replied, "The American civil war of the 1960's."

Four days later, Timothy Leary was officially discharged from the California prison system. Now that he had served two years and eight months of his sentence for the Laguna Beach bust, he could begin serving his ten-year federal sentence for the Laredo bust. Since only President Gerald Ford could reduce this sentence or pardon him, it seemed likely Tim would have to serve at least eighteen months before he could even be considered for parole.

About a month after returning to Marbella, Joanna got a call from Dennis Martino from the airport in Malaga, Spain. He told her he had been in Colombia doing undercover work. With her mother away in Switzerland, Joanna invited Dennis to visit her. Dennis brought "all these tales about being in Colombia and great cocaine and he stays with me while my mother is gone and tells me I should just pack up and run away with him. When my mother comes back, he tells her he wants to marry me. And she just ridicules him to the max." Dennis also told Joanna that he was going to kill himself. "And I have to say," she recalled, "that I told him, 'If you're going to kill yourself, don't do it on my doorstep.'" Completely paranoid by now, Dennis was using coke and drinking. "It was hard to believe his stories because he was just rambling on. When he said he was going to kill himself, I knew he was threatening me. At the same time, he felt like he had painted himself into a hopeless corner. And I said, 'Please don't do this to me.'"

One afternoon after Dennis had moved from her mother's house into a hotel in Marbella, Joanna called to tell him she was going to a party on jet-set billionaire Adnan Khasnoggi's boat but that he could not come with her. By now, Dennis had begun following her everywhere. Telling Dennis that she would see him the next day, Joanna went to the party where someone gave her a couple of quaaludes and she ended up spending the night at someone's house. At around six that evening, Joanna went to Manchu's bar, then the hippest night spot in Marbella. The owner came up and told her the police were looking for her. When Joanna asked why, she was told, "The American who was hanging around you is dead." "So I run back to my mother's house and I tell her and she says, 'I don't want you to betray any emotion. It's a good thing he's dead. Go to the police and turn yourself in. Go to them instead of them looking for you.' She hands me my mink coat and a couple of Valiums and says, 'Chin up. Let's go.'" At the police station, the Guardia Civil showed her Dennis's passport and asked if she knew this man and if he had been visiting her. Joanna answered yes to both questions. They told her that his body had been found at the Hotel La Fonda and that they were doing an autopsy to determine the cause of death. "And then they show me his suitcase and they ask me, 'Was this man a spy? What was he doing?' And they show me the Moog synthesizer he was traveling with to make music on because he was crazy about Pink Floyd. They were incredibly suspicious about the Moog. Like it was the ultimate spy tool."

Later, Joanna identified the body. "The autopsy said that he died of gastritis and peritonitis and a ruptured appendix. I don't believe it. I have Dennis's diary and on the last page, it says, 'Marbella, March 12, 1975,' and 'Loneliness is the raw pattern of self. When we meet again and are introduced as friends, please don't let on that you knew me when I was hungry and it was your world,' and then it says, 'Sooner or later, one of us will know that I really did try to get close to you,' and at the bottom, it says, 'It's all over now, baby blue.' All Dylan lines." Dennis, who had been born on the same day as Bob Dylan, and was, as Joanna recalled, "obsessed with that." When Joanna went to pack up Dennis's things, she found half a bottle of wine and a bottle of Valium that was three-quarters full. "Dennis," she would later say, "could drink and take a lot more Valium than that. If he was killing himself, he wouldn't have left any Valium. He would have taken the whole bottle. I think the chances that he was killed are as high as the chances that he killed himself."

The death of twenty-nine-year-old Dennis Martino under mysterious circumstances in Marbella provided those who still revered Tim with yet more ammunition to use against the woman they believed had set Tim up in Afghanistan. In the spring of 1975, Paul Krassner wrote, "Joanna Harcourt-Smith, espionage agent in the guise of international groupie . . . flies on taxpayer's money to Switzerland, leading Leary by his cock to Afghanistan for her birthday, where he gets abducted." Parodying Allen Ginsberg's questions at the PILL press conference, another critic asked, "Was Mata Hari a totally right-on, completely self-empowered woman who led the way for sisters everywhere to shed the bonds of conventional morality which for so long has kept them barefoot and pregnant or just an unrepentant whore who sold secrets on the side to whoever paid her?"

During the years Tim spent in prison after being brought back from Afghanistan, his former son-in-law, David, Dennis's twin brother, faithfully wrote him letters in which he talked about how much he missed his children and how he intended to reconcile with Susan as soon as he made it as an actor in Hollywood. He asked Tim if John Lennon, Mick Jagger, or Peter Fonda might be interested in using him in a movie. In another letter, David wrote, "Being your son-in-law isn't an easy job and requires a very special person in my view." In 1984, at the age of thirty-eight, David Martino committed suicide by drinking cyanide. What no one seems to have ever known, Tim Leary included, was that it had not been Joanna but David who had gotten Tim arrested in Kabul.

"I busted David Martino in Laguna at 2510 South Coast Highway, the Casa Hotel," Neil Purcell recalled. "It was the kind of place where a lot of dopers would hang out." Smelling the odor of pot coming out of one of the rooms, Purcell "knocked on the door and said we had probable cause that narcotics were being used. Martino opened the door and he just about shit when he saw me. I said, 'Narcotics officers, narcotics investigation,' and we went right on through. Martino started shaking like a leaf. The only thing we had was this marijuana joint that he was smoking because he was expecting somebody. That was why he opened the door. And there were some baggies in there." Purcell searched the room and found "all this correspondence from Leary in Switzerland. We were reading it and we leaned on him. Susan was pregnant or had just had a baby. We started using her. 'You know, Martino, you're going away. You won't see your little daughter until she's twenty-five years old.' Over a fucking joint, he started breaking down and crying and carrying on and we said, 'Look, there's some mention about Leary taking a flight to Afghanistan. When is this taking place?'"

David Martino told Purcell what flight Tim and Joanna would be on from Switzerland to Afghanistan. Purcell then informed Terence Burke. "We led everybody to believe Joanna took him there to get him arrested," Neil Purcell would later say. "But that was how it really was."

FORTY-THREE

Terrified by what the Guardia Civil might do to her if they concluded that she had killed Dennis, Joanna got in touch with the DEA in Los Angeles. They told her not to panic and said that since she was still in the Federal Witness Protection Program, she should fly back to the United States so they could take care of her. Joanna returned to San Diego and went to visit Tim where he was now being jailed along with nine other men "on the high-powered snitch floor" at the newly completed Metropolitan Correctional Center at 808 Union Street, also called the "Cinnamon Stick." "I saw him there," Joanna recalled, "and he seemed to be doing very well. He had this whole little snitch world under control. He was not at all upset about Dennis dying. He was delighted and he told me the same thing my mother had told me. 'This guy was a shit and good riddance.'"

With the five-year statute of limitations relating to Tim's escape due to expire on September 12, 1975, the government began one last desperate push to unearth evidence that would persuade a federal grand jury in San Francisco to return indictments against those Tim claimed had aided and abetted him. On June 26, an FBI agent showed up at the San Francisco bookstore where Tim's archivist Michael Horowitz worked to tell him that Tim just happened to be, as David Weir wrote in *Rolling Stone*, "passing through town." Horowitz agreed to accompany the agent to "a luxurious suite on the fourth floor of the St. Francis Hotel." Tim looked to Horowitz as though he had gained weight. His hair was shorter and he had "a mustache, a blue pin striped suit and a Southern California tan." After Tim introduced Horowitz to his "team," five U.S. marshals and three FBI agents, Tim took his archivist into another room where they talked for an hour. During the conversation, Tim asked for certain letters that he had written before his escape. Assuming the room was bugged,

Horowitz said he didn't know what Tim was talking about and reminded him that he had never told him about his escape. At one point in the conversation, Horowitz told Tim that he was becoming "tedious." Jumping to his feet, Tim gripped Horowitz by the shoulders, looked him in the eyes, and said, "Consider this a visit from another part of the galaxy. I don't know when we'll be passing through here again."

In early July, Tim appeared before the San Francisco grand jury to offer testimony against the Weather Underground and his lawyers. Horowitz realized that he had "to break from Tim and any thought that I was helping the government," so he called a press conference at the St. Francis Hotel in San Francisco on August 6, 1975. Because Horowitz had been granted immunity by the grand jury, he would lose his Fifth Amendment right against self-incrimination and could be jailed if he refused to testify. Attending the press conference were Lawrence Ferlinghetti and Muriel Rukeyser, the head of American PEN, who said that "the cutting off of a writer's files and correspondence reminds one of the old penalty of chopping off a writer's hands." The most emotional statement was made by Paul Harris, Horowitz's lawyer. "If Timothy Leary would read his Irish history, he would know informers are offed, and if he would read his Jewish history, he'd know they aren't even buried in a cemetery." Telegrams of support for Horowitz from Ken Kesey and Allen Ginsberg were read out loud.

When Horowitz finally appeared before the grand jury, he maintained that archivists should "have the same privileged conversation as someone's priest, wife, or attorney. And they didn't know what the hell to do with that. James Browning, who was going to use this as a stepping-stone to run for attorney general of California, denounced me to the grand jury, saying, 'It's people like you who don't cooperate with us who are messing up this country.'" Despite Horowitz's refusal to testify, the grand jury did not indict him.

On August 8, at the Metropolitan Correctional Center in San Diego, Tim was given a new typewriter. The first letter he wrote was to Robert Anton Wilson, concerning Wilson's appearance at Horowitz's press conference: "You mentioned the 'constitution' in your speech. ??? Certainly you realize that the constitution is a set of club rules worked out by slave owners—nd [sic] specifically justifies slavery." Convinced that Rosemary could only find freedom by giving herself up and telling the government everything she knew about the escape, Tim added, "I was sorry to learn (I knew it, of course—) that the people who stage manage [sic] the press-conference are exploiting Rosemary. My friends should really be worrying about her. She is being used rather shamefully."

In an interview published in *Rolling Stone* on September 11, Eldridge Cleaver, still living in exile in France, said that while a lot of his white friends in the movement had criticized him for allowing Timothy Leary to seek refuge in Algeria, "none of them had any idea that he would ultimately go and sing his swan song to the grand jury because this goes beyond the limits of everyone's expectations . . . It never dawned on me that he would cave in like that." When Cleaver was asked why he thought this had happened, he responded, "You have to remember that Leary is doing this without any feelings of guilt because in a certain way, he hates, he feels fronted off by people who were supposedly his converts but who allowed him to remain in prison. They took no action; no one broke him out, no one started defense committees, no movement happened. Tim is an old man and five years in prison is like a death sentence."

In November, Cleaver surrendered to American authorities in Paris and was sent to the Metropolitan Correctional Center in San Diego. "It was there," Joanna recalled, "I met Eldridge and Kathleen. Tim and Eldridge looked like they were getting along very well." Tim's jailer in Algeria was now a prisoner in the cell next to him on a high-security floor where Teamster and Mafia snitches were also housed. Kathleen persuaded Eldridge to phone the Black Panther Party for help. Their refusal to accept his call became, Cleaver later admitted, "huge in my mind. Timothy knew I was a little down about it and he told me I should make a deal with the people he was making a deal with. He wanted to introduce me to them so they could help me." Cleaver faced a possible sentence of eighty-two years in prison on charges of attempted murder of a police officer and assault with a deadly weapon on a police officer stemming from the shootout in Oakland in which Black Panther Bobby Hutton had been killed. He had also violated his parole and engaged in unlawful flight to avoid prosecution. "I talked to Timothy about what was going on between him and them and he told me what they were promising him and what they could do. I wanted to know what they could do for me. If they would talk to the judge and reduce my bail, I would go for that. As far as what did they want from me? It never got that far. I did not want to broach this subject with them. All of that was beyond the pale for me. My pride was the pride of the convict. You don't snitch on anybody and you don't take it in the ass."

On January 22, 1976, Cleaver sent Tim a handwritten note from the Alameda County courthouse jail in Oakland in which he referred to an internal sales memo from Dell Books that predicted there would be increased interest in his book *Soul on Ice* due to his dramatic return from exile. Cleaver added that he now felt like an idea whose time had finally come. Six days later, Tim wrote Cleaver to say that he hoped "you'll be out on the street soon. The underground press is playing you up as sad and lonesome. I don't see you that way at all. There are tens of millions of people who agree with us that the Wars of the 60's are over. Naturally, the old lefties are hostile, but they are hostile towards everything and everyone—including brawling among themselves. Have you followed the insanities of Bill Kinstler [Kunstler]? He is providing a beautiful comic-strip exaggeration of the stupidity of the left. He'll do anything, apparently, to get his name in the media."

Despite all the charges against him, Cleaver never stood trial. His case was plea-bargained and he was sentenced to two thousand hours of community service. Though he had called repeatedly for the violent overthrow of the government, Cleaver spent just nine months behind bars before becoming eligible for bail in August 1976. The leniency shown to Cleaver might have stemmed in part from the dubious nature of the original charges against him. However, the degree of his own cooperation with authorities is not yet known.

Tim, buoyed by the conviction that he would soon be free once more, began corresponding with those whom he considered his peers. He asked literary critic and author Leslie Fiedler if he thought *Gravity's Rainbow* placed Thomas Pynchon in the same epic category as James Joyce. Tim had finished writing *What Does WoMan Want?*, yet another account of his exile in Switzerland, cast this time as a science-fiction novel that took place in the distant future. He had submitted the manuscript to Marc Jaffe at Bantam Books, who had returned it to him. Tim then sent the book to the prominent literary agent Sterling Lord. By October, Tim was writing Neil Freer, an old friend from Millbrook, that "I expect to be out of prison in a few weeks and hope to drop by Woodstock en route to Europe . . . I plan to be in Europe during the winter. To ski. And see people."

In November, Joanna somehow managed to procure a large loan from a Swiss bank in Zurich so that Tim would be able to post bail, if and when the opportunity came his way. In December, Tim wrote the reclusive author Thomas Pynchon, probably in care of his publisher, to let him know the only books besides *Gravity's Rainbow* that he had ever read "over twenty times" were *Ulysses* and *Finnegans Wake*. On January 13, 1976, Tim sent "Beloved Joanna" a note, wishing her happy birthday. "Thank you for three years of miracle and re-creation," he wrote. "Thanks for bringing IT all together—for meaning and fusion. Thank you for strength and devotion. This year we shall be full-filled. I love you, Timothy."

In February, Tim's plans to spend the winter skiing in Europe were derailed when the Federal Parole Board denied his appeal and remanded him to serve two more years before considering his next request. PEN immediately drew up a letter demanding a congressional hearing to investigate whether there was a conspiracy to violate Tim's civil liberties. In reaction to the bad news, Tim unleashed an uncharacteristic fit of public anger in an article entitled "TV and the Outlaw Industry: How Our Paranoias Are Hyped for Fame and Profit," which appeared in the *National Review* on April 16, 1976. That Timothy Leary was now being published by William Buckley, who had always summarily dismissed everything Tim had to say as utter trash, spoke volumes about how the culture had changed. In the article, Tim wrote that since the average American watched five hours of television a day, it was television itself that "creates, manages, and schedules our reality." Because one of the staples of television entertainment was the news, America needed an endless supply of "reality-actors who play parts in the day-time and prime-time shows which define our existence." By committing symbolic crimes, "outlaw martyrs" first come to the attention of the viewing public. Avidly, the public then follows the outlaw through their chase or surrender, arrest, trial and verdict, and then the sale of media rights to their story by their lawyers. "The Outlaw Industry," he wrote, was "managed by lawyers." Moreover, he continued, "The Pop-Music Contribution to the Outlaw Business cannot be over-estimated." Singling out John Lennon, whom he had once revered as a saint and a messenger from God, Tim wrote, "In his admitted compulsion to say-and-do anything to hit the top of the charts, Lennon in one year ripped off a Gubernatorial candidate's slogan (Come Together), the motto of the Militant Blacks (Power To The People, Right On) and the peace movement (Give Peace A Chance). He then banked the proceeds and hired a platoon of who? . . . lawyers . . . to convince the Republican administration that he should be allowed to stay in the American Tax-haven because he was 'harmless.' More successful in skimming the energies of the Outlaw Assembly Line, and much more malevolent is Robert Zimmerman, who first conned onto the media-stage by taking the name of a lyric Welsh poet and chanting plastic protest songs to a barbiturate beat." Tim blamed Bob Dylan for having in-undated the "uneducated, naive nervous systems" of Manson acolytes Sandra Good and Squeaky Fromme with his "sneering hatred and warn-ing contempt amplified electronically and broadcast to create hateful re-alities for millions of adolescent listeners." As a result, both women were "led off to life-imprisonment because they were unlucky enough to have owned record-players in their vulnerable adolescence."

Tim reviled Dylan for recording songs about George Jackson and the convicted murderer and middleweight boxer Rubin "Hurricane" Carter in order to reestablish his own credentials as "the Messiah!" Bob Dylan's "It's All over Now, Baby Blue" had "probably caused more biological and philosophical suicides than any poem in western history . . . the snarling, whining, scorning, mocking" lyrics of "Just Like a Woman," "It Ain't Me, Babe," "Subterranean Homesick Blues," and "It's All Right, Ma" have "systematically converted a generation to neurotic complaint." Tim then borrowed the interrogatory form used by Allen Ginsberg at the PILL press conference to ask:

Did Dylan stand in picket lines? Get his head busted by Company police? March at Selma in the hard rain? Get tear-gassed in Chicago? Sleep in the mud at Woodstock (just down the road from his comfy retreat), lay on a roach-ridden mattress in state prison? Put his body on the line in any real action? Live the fugitive life? Go into exile dur-ing the Nixon-Agnew years? Or put his nervous system on the line in neuronaut exploration? . . . When an entire generation was on the move, swirling into unchartered neurogenetic territory, where was the young millionaire? Protected, dear boy, in the arms of pro-ducer Al Grossman, promoter Bill Graham, Golda Meir, Allen Gins-berg, Joan Baez, and a supporting brigade of Mother figures?

Arriving at what might have been his real point, Tim wrote, "It is no accident that the Weathermen, the most publicized group of Dylan groupies, a bewildered, fugitive band of terrorists now cut-off from their culture and condemned to underground existence, took their name from a depressing 'Dylan' song. One thing is certain as the Uncivil War of the 1960's fades into ancient history—we surely don't need a Weatherman to know which way the wind blows and we've all been blown light-years beyond the rhetoric of violent revolution, haven't we, Bernadine?"

Long before Jerry Rubin would become a businessman obsessed with networking, and many of those who had served with him in the front lines of the revolution began writing memoirs in which they renounced their youthful indiscretions in favor of family values, Timothy Leary had turned his back on the counterculture from which he had once drawn all his fame and power. Better than anyone, Tim knew that unless he could persuade those in power that he really did hate the sixties, he might never get out of jail.

When United States Attorney John Milano appeared before the Federal Parole Board in Washington, D.C., on April 20, 1976, to ask its members to reconsider their recent decision to keep Tim in jail for two more years, he brandished a copy of the current *National Review* with Tim's name on the cover. As Joanna would later put it, "If William Buckley says Tim is okay, then how come they don't think he's rehabilitated?" At six in the morning the next day, Joanna got a phone call from the clerk of the Fifth Circuit Court of Appeals in New Orleans, where Tim was now being represented by a well-connected local lawyer who believed Tim's chances of being granted bail had improved significantly in March when Judge Ben Connally, who had first sentenced Tim in the Laredo bust, died in a hunting accident.

The clerk of the court told Joanna the judge had just signed an order for Tim's release from prison on his own recognizance, with bail to be set pending appeal. "Twenty minutes later," Joanna recalled, "I got a phone call from John Milano in Washington, D.C., saying Tim had just been granted federal parole. After three and half years, on the same day, within an hour of each other, it came from both sides at once."

What seemed like an extraordinary coincidence might have been just that. As Joanna remembered, "Timothy had given them everything he had. Don Strange and other BNDD agents had gone to Washington to testify in front of Senate committees about this great thing they were doing against the Brotherhood and they got their budget increased tremendously and then they opened the DEA. So Tim had served them enormously and I'm sure they also used the information he gave them when the Weathermen finally turned themselves in."

Frantically, Joanna began phoning people. Because of the time difference between Washington, New Orleans, and San Diego, she spent the entire day trying to get the paperwork either from the parole board or the judge to the warden at the Metropolitan Correctional Center so Tim could be released. Tim finally walked out of prison on April 21, 1976. "The media there was enormous." Joanna recalled, "and he lifted me off the ground and grabbed me in an incredible explosion of joy. And he said to them that all he wanted now was to be with me and have a quiet life with his wife."

After they checked into the Valencia Hotel in nearby La Jolla, Tim got "terribly, terribly drunk." The next morning, Tim and Joanna were awakened by two United States marshals who told them that death threats had been made against them. In order to keep them from "ending up on a slab," Tim and Joanna had to disappear into the Witness Protection Program. "Tim said, 'Oh, they're just doing this because they want to keep me a prisoner longer,' and I told him that what we had done was pretty tricky." Pacing back and forth in his hotel room as though he was still in jail, Tim listened as the marshals offered to put him and Joanna in a safe house near Salt Lake City. "I'll go along with it if you put us in Santa Fe," he told them, and the marshals agreed to the deal. Without giving either of them time to say goodbye to anyone, the marshals flew them under false names to Albuquerque.

"They found us an A-frame in the Pecos Wilderness," Joanna recalled, "and said we had to stay there, hidden." When the marshals told Tim that they were going to give them false IDs, he asked that they be issued in the names James and Nora Joyce. With the $700 a month Tim was now being paid by the federal government to be in the Witness Protection Program, he bought a motor scooter. The nearest town was ten miles away.

A month later, *People* magazine sent a reporter and photographer to interview Tim for an article that ran in the June 11, 1976, issue. Tim slipped easily into the public role he would play for the next twenty years of his life. The photograph that accompanied the article showed him clean shaven and barefoot in loose blue jeans with the bottoms turned up and an unbuttoned white shirt with the sleeves rolled up over his elbows.

Grinning as he leaned all the way back in a wicker rocking chair on the wooden deck of the cabin, Tim told the reporter about his brand-new program of space migration, intelligence increase, and life extension for which he had coined the acronym SMI2LE. He not only wanted to live on a space station but planned "to take some of the planet with him." In the middle of the interview, Joanna returned from shopping for groceries and ran "to Leary as though she hadn't seen him in years. They embrace and gaze at each other with intensity—a scene no scriptwriter would dare invent. 'You are a terrific lover,' she says, and kisses him. 'I missed you very much.'"

What was really going on between Tim and Joanna bore little relationship to the portrait painted in the magazine. "Here we were in this cabin in New Mexico," Joanna recalled, "and I had procured acid that I wanted to take with him in order for us to move through the separation and bond again. Tim was still fairly fat, which for him was amazing, and still looking like a narc and he was drinking enormous amounts of alcohol and definitely so was I. The thing that amazed me the most was that he did not want to take LSD. He didn't want to take it. And he was impotent. He didn't say why. At best, he would have minimal partial erections. We spent most of the time buying booze and getting drunk and talking about making this baby. And of course we were having problems doing that." Soon, they began to fight. Looking back on the fights years later, Joanna said, "I would qualify them as drunken fights. He bought a motorbike without a buddy seat so I felt I had now taken the part of the prisoner. Although I never thought about it this way at the time, I suppose it was deep depression from what he'd had to do in order to get out of prison. He was at the bottom. Most everybody had forgotten him. He had no idea how he was going to make a living. When he was not absolutely drunk, he would sit at his typewriter desperately writing things without ever knowing if they were going to be published and anguishing over that. His main contact was Robert Anton Wilson. They would talk on the phone and try to think up ways to get Timothy's message out."

In an interview in the *Berkeley Barb* on June 17, Tim told Wilson, "I did not testify against friends. I didn't testify against what the press called 'the vast drug conspiracy known as the Brotherhood of Eternal Love' since that was a myth that never existed. I didn't testify in any manner that would lead to indictments against the Weatherpeople. When the full details of my actual testimony are known, the Weather Underground might even be grateful to me." Conveniently forgetting George Chula, he added, "The fact is that nobody has been arrested because of me and nobody ever will be." When Wilson asked Tim if he had any concluding thoughts for the readers of the *Berkeley Barb,* he responded, "Yes. As Casey Stengel once said, most men my age are dead already."

Having performed this particular miracle many times before, Tim knew he could rehabilitate himself through the media. But it would require patience and persistence. Wilson's interview was accompanied by two sidebars. In one, Eldridge Cleaver publicly reversed the opinion he had previously expressed in *Rolling Stone.* "I think Leary is a good guy," he said. "A lot of people misunderstood what he's been doing." Cleaver vehemently denied that he himself had snitched on anyone to get out of prison and said of Tim, "He's been before some grand juries and he's testified against some lawyers. But I'm not aware that anybody got busted. He told me that he hasn't gotten anyone indicted or busted." In the other sidebar, various movement figures were asked how they now felt about Tim. Charles Garry, Huey Newton's longtime attorney, said, "A person who gives up his or her principles and starts going down the ladder of being an informer has no future. They all die in oblivion." Morris Kleinschmidt, a radical editor, put it a bit more plainly: "What do I think of Leary's latest writings? I think he's nuts, frankly. He's still a really interesting guy. I think he's still got a contribution to make, but it's certainly not by inviting people aboard a flying saucer."

On June 6, Tim wrote a letter to his mother and Aunt May. Abigail, now ninety years old, was living with her older sister in an assisted-care facility. "I don't know how many papers you get there—but you may know that William Buckley was very helpful in getting my release from prison—and has published articles I've written in his magazine." Tim wrote that he and Joanna were now living near Santa Fe and liking it a lot. "I'm probably going to get a job teaching in a Catholic college here—and we are finding an enthusiastic response from the Catholic people here . . . We plan to be east this summer and would love to come up and see you. Write me, if you wish, at this address and we'll make plans."

In answer to a letter from Tim, William F. Buckley wrote to say that he found the story of Tim's persecution to be appalling. If Tim ever wanted to write about it for *National Review,* Buckley would be interested in seeing it but he did not wish to interrupt Tim's career in the process. Buckley noted how pleased he was by Tim's renewed interest in the

Catholic church and urged Tim to let him know if he was able to find a position with a Catholic teaching institution. Buckley ended his note by sending Tim his best wishes.

On July 2, Tim wrote the chairman of the Psychology Department at the University of New Mexico to ask if there was any chance he might teach there. He now viewed his "political vicissitudes, 1970–76, as a mistaken and unnecessary digression from a life-line which is scientific in its trajectory." Tim included a "brief Professional Summary and Bibliography" and hoped "an appointment can be arranged, at your convenience, to discuss these matters with you."

Still hoping to have a child with Joanna, Tim began going to a doctor who prescribed testosterone and yohimbe to increase his ability to have an erection. When Joanna's mother, who was now planning to live in San Diego, came to visit, they did what Joanna would later call "a complete seduction trip with each other, which was very upsetting to me. Tim always said he was in love with my mother and she was only ten years older than him. She came for a few days and we talked a lot about this baby who was to come. He was upset because it had been three months and I was still not yet pregnant. But he really did not know what to do with himself. He was absolutely desperate about the fact that he had no money except what was being paid him by the government. And he had no idea how to regold his coat of arms."

Unable to find employment at either the University of New Mexico or in Los Alamos, where he had made several new friends in the scientific community, Tim quickly abandoned the wilderness cabin to join Joanna and her mother in San Diego. Defying F. Scott Fitzgerald's notion that there were no second acts in American lives, Tim soon moved to a city that was perfectly suited to his temperament and personality. In the dry hills above Los Angeles, not far from the house beneath the Hollywood sign where Aldous Huxley had died under the influence of LSD, Timothy Leary began the long and arduous process of re-creating himself all over again.

TO LIVE AND DIE IN LA

CALIFORNIA,
JUNE 1976–MAY 31, 1996

Personally, I've been looking forward to dying all my life.

—Timothy Leary, *Design for Dying*

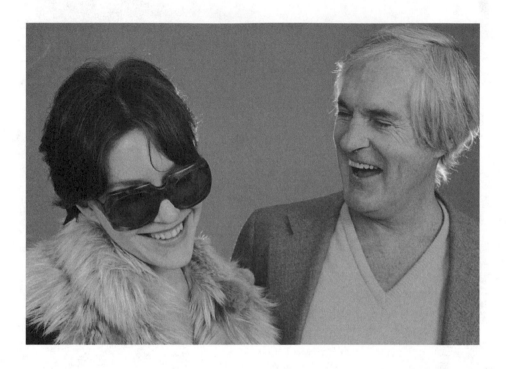

Barbara and Timothy Leary.
© *Roger Ressmeyer/CORBIS*

FORTY-FOUR

Like a struggling young actor determined to find fame and fortune in Hollywood or die trying, Timothy Leary, now fifty-six years old, arrived in Los Angeles in a used Ford Pinto. The sum total of his worldly possessions amounted to not much more than an old typewriter, several manuscripts, and some clothes. Behind him in San Diego, he had left Joanna who had asked him to leave after what she described as "a terrible fight." Joanna was now pregnant with what she felt certain was Tim's baby, although earlier on the day that the child had been conceived, she had also had sex with another man.

Tim began living in Los Angeles in a small house at 8930 Wonderland Drive in Laurel Canyon, where he shared the $725-a-month rent with a young couple who were trying to help him manage his business affairs. Desperate for money, he signed with an agency that began booking him to lecture at universities. On January 11, 1977, he appeared before 1,200 people in the same building on the Berkeley campus where, two years earlier, Ken Kesey and Paul Krassner had held their Wake-Up Celebration in his name.

Two and a half weeks later, a long article entitled "Timothy Leary: Messenger of Evolution" appeared in the *Los Angeles Times*. In it, Tim denied there had ever been a lot of drugs around him while he had been in exile in Switzerland or that he had ever engaged in an orgy. Accompanying the text was a photograph of Tim sitting beside his new girlfriend, a striking young woman with shaggy hair and strong features who gazed at him with love in her eyes.

When she read the article, Joanna, whose mother had only recently died of cancer, tried to commit suicide by slashing her wrists over the newspaper. In February, she gave birth to a son named Marlon at Mercy

Hospital in San Diego. On the birth certificate beside "Father," she wrote, "Does Not Wish To Divulge." "I did that because I was still thinking I could convince Tim to at least show up as the dad. Have a test, find out, and show up. When he came to see me in the hospital, he held the baby and said, 'This is much too cosmic for me.'"

In March, Tim began an extensive lecture tour for which he was paid $2,000 a night. Journalist Nancy Naglin accompanied him and wrote "The Man Who Fell to Earth—Has Tim Leary Turned On His Friends?," which appeared in the March 1977 issue of *Crawdaddy* magazine. Naglin quoted Jack Nicholson as saying of Tim, "He's gone everywhere, done everything, and fucked everybody." In the piece, Tim adamantly denied he had testified against anyone but his lawyers, claimed he had been funneling funds to Rosemary's family so they could hire their own lawyers, and said he had given money to Rosemary's brother so he could fly to Europe to talk to her. Repeating his assertion that he had never advocated drugs, he peddled his new message of space migration.

Two months later, before lecturing at the Santa Cruz Civic Auditorium, on May 26, Tim stopped off at KLRB-FM in Carmel for an interview with radio personality Donna Frantz. She found him extremely charming but noted that he smelled of alcohol. "I've outlasted five directors of the narcotics bureau," he told her. "Jimmy Carter and all those kids running the White House, they were stealing hubcaps and running rock concerts in Atlanta ten years ago. They're all grass smokers." Selling his brand-new vision of outer-space utopia for all he was worth, he added, "I've always been an enemy of gravity. I think high orbit is the place to be."

On October 17, 1978, Abigail Leary died in Springfield at the age of ninety-two. Her last contact with her son had been a Mother's Day letter in which Tim had painted a glowing portrait of his current prospects while describing his daughter, Susan, as "extremely conventional" and his son, Jack, as "a popular figure in Berkeley." Although she had once been her son's foremost champion and protector, Abigail had had no real contact with him in more than a decade. In his writings, Tim Leary made no mention of her death. Nor did he attend her funeral.

In his final letter to her, Tim told his mother that his prime objective now was to get a movie made about his life:

I am living in Hollywood and have become very respectable. The young women and men who run Hollywood—stars, directors, producers are, in a sense, my students from the 60's. I am treated like a celebrity, accorded much respect and have a certain influence on the direction of movies. A big studio is going to make a movie about my life. It will come out in fall-winter 1979—with advertising it will cost over 10 million dollars—and will generate a lot of publicity. Positive for a change. I publish a couple of books a year—and these are selling widely—so after all these years I am finally becoming a respectable success.

Thinking that a biography might serve as a springboard for the movie, Tim asked Ron Bernstein, a New York agent who now represented him, to find a writer for the project. Bernstein offered the job to his client Henry Edwards, a former rock critic for *The New York Times* who had just written the screenplay for Robert Stigwood's film version of the Beatles' *Sgt Pepper's Lonely Hearts Club Band*. Edwards, who had first seen Tim during one of his high priest shows at the Village Gate in the sixties, recalled, "He knocked my socks off by saying, 'Rip up your credit cards and be free.' Tim was a fabulous actor and I was stunned by the power and hilarity of his message. I went out to California to work on the movie and I met Tim while he was living in Laurel Canyon. I was with him the night he met Barbara."

While having dinner with Edwards one night in Oscar's Wine Bar, a restaurant on Sunset Boulevard located across from the Chateau Marmont, Tim went to a pay phone to call Susan. Lindsay Brice, a photographer who would later become one of Tim's closest friends, recounted her version of the event. "Tim asked, 'Is Susan there?' And Barbara, whom he had never met before, walked up to the phone, took the receiver out of his hand, hung it up, and said, 'Forget Susan. I'm here now.' That was how they met." Barbara Chase had a different memory. "I went to call my babysitter to make sure my son, Zach, who was three at the time, was okay and this man was on the phone. I didn't have a clue who he was . . . we started chatting and he knew the people I was with so we all went out, eight of us, for a drink and he asked me out for lunch. By then I knew who he was and I went." Rarely seen in public without dark sunglasses and a long black cigarette holder, Barbara, who wore her dark hair cropped short, bore a striking resemblance to Holly Golightly, as played by Audrey Hepburn in the film version of Truman Capote's *Breakfast At Tiffany's*. Previously married to Richard Chase, an artist who died of AIDS, Barbara

Blum had been born into an Irish Jewish upper-middle-class family in Scarsdale, New York. Her father, a businessman, had died when she was very young. At the age of nineteen, Barbara moved to London where she became part of the film, fashion, and rock 'n' roll scene. After attending Mick and Bianca Jagger's wedding in St. Tropez in May 1971, Barbara went on their honeymoon with them "for about two days" before insisting they drop her off in Cannes. Her younger sister, Tanya Roberts, with whom Barbara had never been particularly close, was an actress best known for her work as one of Charlie's Angels in the television show of the same name. A James Bond girl, Roberts had also posed nude in *Playboy* and starred in B-movie classics like *The Beastmaster* and *Sheena—Queen of the Jungle.*

When Barbara first met Tim, he was "living in this apartment hotel called Le Parc in LA. He was just kind of crashing there. He had no belongings. And he moved in with me in my little apartment. It was so sweet. He came in just one car with a few clothes and some books and papers. The next thing you know, we had a whole house with books and furniture—which was my middle-class upbringing." The attraction between them was intensely physical. As Henry Edwards recalled, "Tim would say to me, 'She knows how to tantalize the neurons into a response that is ecstatic. She is an artist.' She certainly didn't know how to work. She was this woman in dark sunglasses on Rollerblades who could be very controlling about nothing. They were both profoundly middle class."

Edwards often went with Tim to Maxfield Parrish, which Tim described as "the most expensive clothing store in this galactic universe" to shop for white linen pants that Edwards remembered cost $300 or $400 a pair. "Since Tim was addicted to preaching the message of youth, it was important that he look young. I went to the hospital with him when he had what I guess was the first of his three face-lifts. His message was: young is good, old is bad. It was a tough way to live but why did he land in Beverly Hills? Because he was a movie star and he had a concept of himself as a star and a celebrity. Celebrity was very important to him. He preached the message that fame was an aphrodisiac. He said that over and over again. If you stay famous, you can pull women."

Abandoning the idea of a biography, Tim and Edwards decided instead to write a screenplay based on Tim's life. "The deal was that he was cooperating with me and he would help me write whatever I wanted to and if we sold it, I would work out an arrangement with him. We spent an enormous amount of time together and we spent an enormous amount of money. I was as bad as he was." When Tim learned that Edwards did not know how to drive, he and Barbara insisted Edwards learn in their big green Mercedes. "Tim said, 'If you want to learn how to drive, you must learn in the best. Like an admiral sailing the sea,'" Edwards recalled. "I had trouble parking and he said, 'The two white lines are her gorgeous thin inviting legs and your job is take your bumper and touch it in the center, her pleasure zone.'"

Eventually, Edwards completed a 167-page proposal for a film covering Tim's life from 1965 to 1978. "No one," he recalled, "had yet figured out that no one would make a movie about Tim and that he was much hated in that town. Much hated. A lot of people who worked there adored him and were very helpful and gave him money but you were not going to go to a corporation with Tim and get anywhere." David Putnam, then running Columbia Pictures, "had an enormously violent reaction to him." Whenever Timothy Leary's name was mentioned, according to Edwards, Putnam would say that Tim was a social menace. "The fantasy was that Jack Nicholson would do it. I finally ran into Jack Nicholson one day at Maxfield Parrish, which they had closed down for him to shop in, and I said, 'Why didn't you do this?' And he said, 'Well, I get a script, I put it on top of the pile. I get a better one, it goes to position two. When this script went to position four, that was it.' What he was really saying was that he was not going to take that risk. There was no market for it. Tim was a nostalgia figure. There were people who were fascinated by him but it was a cult."

In person, however, Tim could still draw a crowd. When the *Sgt Pepper's Lonely Hearts Club Band* movie premiered in New York City, producer Robert Stigwood flew Tim there on his private jet for the event. "Stigwood thought it was dangerous to have him there," Edwards recalled, "but good publicity. He said, 'He's got crazy eyes but media value.' When Tim and I went to the opening at Radio City Music Hall, thousands of people went berserk for him." Though the movie garnered some of the worst reviews in film history, Tim's presence at the opening gave it a kind of psychedelic authenticity. Describing Tim as "always stoned" during this period, most often on highly potent marijuana brownies that he baked himself, Edwards saw Tim as "running from depression. He didn't want to deal with reality. His drugs of choice were alcohol, tobacco, and marijuana. He ate amazing amounts of marijuana as a hallucinogen."

Not long after Tim and Edwards began working together, Tim sent a long letter to television personality Hugh Downs. Formerly the host of the *Today Show* on NBC, Downs was then appearing on *Over Easy*, a television magazine show produced by KQED, the Public Broadcasting station in San Francisco. "Cocaine is a 'bad drug,'" Tim wrote. "It's so ironic, Hugh. My wife, Barbara, and I are outspoken in our criticism of cocaine. We are quite effective in decreasing cocaine use among our friends." Edwards remembered Tim telling him that he had gone to the actor Tony Curtis's house, and that Curtis had offered him a gram of cocaine in the garage. "Tim snorted the whole gram to show Tony Curtis that he was bigger and better than him. He told me this with this impish grin and then he said, 'But what's wrong with that? For cocaine people, their nose is their pleasure organ.'"

By this point, Tim was actively looking for a new cause. "I don't think Tim was homophobic," Edwards recalled, "but he did not have the most positive feelings about homosexuality because of Ram Dass. Then the gay liberation thing started and it dawned on Tim that he had to be in the vanguard. He told the most heavy-duty gay radical that gayness came out of his genes and acid liberation, and suddenly, out of nowhere, he was on the cover of the *Advocate* describing homosexuality as a genetic mutation, a positive benefit of the race." Tim enlisted Edwards to join him on a bus to Disneyland for the first Gay Night in 1978. "He paraded around Disneyland waving and carrying on like he was Captain Gay," Edwards remembered. "They couldn't believe it. Captain DNA had come to proclaim this tribe part of the future and the evolutionary chain. It was not that he was a con man. He really believed this stuff when it came out of him. Once he said it, it was real."

In the fall of 1978, while Tim and Barbara were visiting New York City, someone gave Tim a few tabs of MDMA (commonly known as Ecstasy), which he was told was the new "love drug." Tim took the drug on an empty stomach. Three hours later, after he and Barbara had "tipsily finished a gourmet five star dinner," which included cocktails, wine, and brandy, Barbara gazed at Tim with what he called the "let's do it, baby look." As he later wrote, "The greatest successes in my life have come from saying yes to Barbara's invitations." Half an hour later, Tim was feeling better than he ever had in his life. Stripping off their clothes, he and Barbara went to bed. "We both understood everything," he later wrote. "All our defenses, protections, and emotional habits were suspended. We realized joyfully how perfect we were designed to be. The only thing to do was caress each other." Starting to come down three hours later, Tim took another hit. He and Barbara then went right on chatting "away like newborn Buddhas from heaven."

Three days later on December 19, 1978, Tim and Barbara were married in Los Angeles at a small ceremony performed by a Universal Life Church minister. Tim would later write that the use of MDMA sometimes resulted in what he called "the instant marriage syndrome." He also noted a report of someone having seen a bumper sticker in Boulder, Colorado, which read DON'T GET MARRIED FOR 6 WEEKS AFTER ECSTASY.

Henry Edwards spent Christmas with Tim and Barbara Leary in LA, eating cooked goose and drinking Cristal. All the while, he was aware that "Tim had enormous problems generating income. He would rant and rave—'I'm not a good provider. I failed. I can't provide.' And then like all problems, it would roll off his back. He would have an emotional moment and then he would get stoned and it would be gone. Still, there was a time when he was so broke that I loaned him $1,500 and he couldn't pay it back." "It was always hand to mouth," Barbara confirmed. "We lived very nicely but every month, it was: 'Okay, are we going to pull this off again next month?' We would be eating at Morton's and Spago four times a week and we had this nice house in Beverly Hills and I liked to buy nice clothes and we had a kid in school."

To support his wife and young stepson in style, Tim found a new agent to represent him for personal appearances. No longer content with lecturing at colleges and universities, Tim's plan was to appear in small clubs in LA as a "stand-up philosopher." In August, the high-powered public relations firm he had hired to hype his shows issued a press release that read, "Timothy Leary Locked in for 7 Perfs at Budd Friedman's Improv." His routine, entitled "How to Joyfully and Profitably Survive the Collapse of Civilization in the Next 10 Years," was intended "to detonate explosive change-charges into the brains of the local music, film, and television community." One reviewer noted that Tim reserved "his harshest barbs for Woody Allen, Filmdom's leading neurotic and most outspoken critic of everything Californian . . . His voice rising the way an evangelist does when preaching about Satan himself, Tim called out, 'Come on, Woody. We know you're small and you think you're ugly, and we know you're ridden with guilt . . . come out to California. Get into

some shorts. Get a suntan. Get your shoes off. Get yourself a convertible. Get a smile on your face. Woody! You've never been high a day in
your life.'"

As though to confirm that no one could ever say the same about him,
Tim and Barbara were arrested on August 28, 1979 by the Beverly Hills
police after a neighbor called to report a woman screaming in their apartment. "There was this Italian girl, who I didn't know, who was always
making so much noise that the couple down below kept threatening to
call the police," Barbara remembered. "They finally called the police on
her on the night that Tim and I had taken, I believe for the first time on
John Lilly's recommendation, ketamine." A powerful anesthetic initially
synthesized for use by veterinarians on farm animals, Special K, as it came
to be known on the street, is a short-acting hallucinogenic that can induce
near-death experiences. "It was just awful," Barbara said, "and I completely lost it. I was freaking out and it was a total death trip for me and I
was not happy. I kept screaming at Timmy, 'I'm dying. I'm dying.'" Responding to a call from the neighbors, police broke into Tim and Barbara's apartment. Calling it "the weirdest scene of my whole life," she
said, "I remember lying there in bed with Timothy thinking I was dying
and then I opened my eyes, and I was in a movie. It took me a long time
to realize that the police were there with a video camera and lights. They
had a whole videotape of me stark naked. They dragged me up and I
started to get sick." Barbara was taken to Cedars-Sinai Medical Center
where she remained for a few hours until the drug wore off. "I was in a
terrible state," she recalled. "God knows what that mug shot looks like. I
should have demanded they retake that shot and have it done by Helmut
Newton." Tim spent some time in jail that night but all charges were
eventually dropped.

Two months later when Tim flew to New York to perform at The
Bottom Line, a publicist booked him on a local television talk show
hosted by Stanley Siegel. Looking very relaxed and Hollywood handsome in an open-collar blue shirt and white pants, Tim settled into a chair
on the set of Siegel's afternoon talk show on November 1, 1979, to hype
his appearance that night. Told beforehand that the interview would not
focus on drugs, Tim was stunned when Siegel reeled off a long list of
drug casualties and demanded, "Any regrets, Tim?" When Siegel announced that he had Art Linkletter on the phone from Columbus, Ohio,
Tim tried to walk off the set. Siegel physically stopped him. Throwing up

his hands in mock surrender, Tim complained, "I'm under arrest here!" As he settled back into his chair, Linkletter said, "Will you take the microphone away from that idiot and just let me talk for a minute?"

Linkletter began by saying he had absolute proof his daughter Diane thought there was nothing wrong with LSD because Tim Leary had claimed it was "God's gift to young people." After Diane committed suicide, Linkletter said of Tim, "I had hoped he would die. I had hoped he would be hung and then I had hoped he would stay in prison for life. Now I'm glad he's out as a pitiful example of an aging hippie, a gruesome example of how drugs ruin a brilliant mind. A third-rate comic in cheap nightclubs with a routine that invites pity—I've seen it on TV—exploited like any ex-convict with a sentimental past." Linkletter went on to say that like so many young kids of that era, his daughter was not a drug addict but an experimenter. For this, he blamed Grace Slick and the Jefferson Airplane as well as people like "Ginsberg the poet and Aldous Huxley in *The Doors of Perception,* all of whom were promoting the glories of drug abuse in what was a drug world." Most of all, Linkletter blamed Tim who as an intellectual, university-based guru had given youngsters a rallying point and a further basis for their experimentation. As Linkletter went on and on, Tim sat there looking bemused and confused. When he finally spoke, Tim offered a halfhearted rebuttal, saying that Linkletter had ridden his daughter's death into the Nixon White House, which he found "ghoulish, just ghoulish," not to mention that Linkletter had also earned his living by making fun of kids on television. *"Art!"* Tim said at one point. "I think it was *you!* Your hypocrisy caused her—" Siegel interrupted him. "I *will* throw you off this show if you don't listen to the questions." Tim fell silent.

After Siegel warmly invited Linkletter to appear on his show whenever he found himself in New York, he asked Tim if he had in fact taken six hundred trips on LSD. "That would be like asking me how many times I've made love," Tim replied. In his own defense, he added, "I think I'm one of the smartest people on the planet today. I'm writing two or three books, I'm giving lectures, I'm very well received—I must be stupid I must be, to be sandbagged this way." Siegel then read a newspaper account of Tim's recent arrest for disturbing the peace while on ketamine with his wife and her five-year-old son present. Siegel demanded to know why, at his age, Tim would need drugs. "Well, that's none of your business," Tim responded. "There are sixty million people who like to smoke

marijuana and it's none of your business or the business of the government to be harassing them." Siegel persisted by asking if it was not the
business of the government to protect itself against people like Tim.
Laughing, Tim replied, "Go back to Iran. You're an ayatollah. What do
you want to do? Cut the hands off people for drinking beer? You have no
right to interfere in the lives of forty-five million people." Tim then wondered why it was that whenever he appeared on television to challenge
the Judeo-Christian ethic, reduce guilt and fear, and encourage people to
thumb their noses at authority, the powers that be could not even let his
voice go out to the people without bringing Art Linkletter into the mix.

When Siegel announced that after the commercial break, his next
segment would feature a former LSD user from Odyssey House, a drug
rehab center, Tim finally decided he'd had enough. Getting to his feet, he
unclipped the microphone from his shirt and walked off the set. "There
goes Dr. Leary," Siegel said. In the New York *Daily News* the next day, Tim
noted, "This kind of thing always happens when a show needs to boost
its ratings."

FORTY-FIVE

Doing his best to function as a loving husband and a doting father, Tim Leary began the new decade by trying his hand at a variety of jobs. He worked briefly as a radio talk-show host on KEZY-AM in Anaheim, continued lecturing on college campuses, and published *The Game of Life,* the fifth volume of his Future History series. Although their financial situation remained perilous, Tim and Barbara entertained constantly. Living next door to former governor Jerry Brown on Wonderland Park Avenue in Laurel Canyon, they created their own literary salon. Alan U. Schwartz, whom Tim had last seen as he sat across from him in a hotel in Geneva initialing every page of *Confessions of A Hope Fiend,* soon became a regular. "It was the height of their social prominence," Schwartz recalled. "They had wonderful parties with writers and actors and very interesting people." Schwartz and his wife regularly joined photographer Helmut Newton and his wife, June, for dinner with Tim and Barbara.

Tim also began writing letters to the editor of the *Los Angeles Times* and the *Los Angeles Herald Examiner.* Using a variety of pseudonyms, he protested his own dismissal as a radio talk-show host, the use of police radar surveillance on California highways, and the advent of free agency in major league baseball. "If Tim was attacking the Catholic Church," Barbara recalled, "he would say, 'I'm an eighty-two-year-old Catholic woman from such-and-such.' If he was attacking the Jews, he would say the same. He knew the letters wouldn't be printed if he wrote 'Timothy Leary.'" One of Tim's letters concerned his outrage at the way the media had reported the shooting of convicted pornographer and *Hustler* publisher Larry Flynt. In March 1978, Flynt was paralyzed for life by a deranged white supremacist and serial murderer who later shot Urban League president Vernon Jordan. In Tim's view, Flynt had been gunned

down for the terrible crime of "activating the self-key of the last demographic group in the U.S. who were shut off from it: the Southern red-
necks." Emphatically, Tim added that Flynt, *was the number-one American
culture hero at the time. He was as important as Kennedy because Kennedy* was
basically a mafioso politician." Yet when *Time* magazine reported the
story, he wrote, "they almost endorsed the act."

It did not take Flynt long to reach out to Tim. "Larry Flynt wanted to
have a meeting with Tim," Henry Edwards recalled, "but before we did
that, we had to be briefed." In a room in the Beverly Hilton Hotel, Tim
and Edwards met with two "ex–CIA agents," who showed them a video
intended to prove beyond a doubt that the government was behind
Flynt's shooting. "It was total nonsense. It was a video of people and faces
and similarities and news stories, assembled material which showed that
this had been a setup by the government. We watched the video and both
Timothy and I knew what it was but Timothy said, 'Oh, I *see*! Oh my God,
this is *conclusive*! Send him my best and my sympathy. I understand.' He
smelled money. We went outside and we got hysterical. And this began
their relationship."

Alan U. Schwartz, now functioning as "kind of" Tim's lawyer, remembered, "Tim had an idea to do a book about Larry Flynt. He was
friendly with him in those days and Flynt was amenable to it. Tim had
done an outline and he said, 'Can we sell it somewhere?' So I took it to a
lot of publishers in New York, including Michael Korda, with whom we
had a meeting. Nobody wanted to touch it." Tim and Barbara, however,
soon began writing an anonymous gossip column entitled "Faces" for
Rebel magazine, owned by Flynt. Over the course of the next few years,
Tim also became a regular contributor to *Hustler* and *Chic*, yet another
Flynt publication. "No one liked *Hustler*," Barbara recalled. "It was that
Larry was standing up for his rights. Timothy was always a great champion of Hugh Hefner too. He thought Hefner was a great American hero
because he opened up sex to the American people. He felt Larry did the
same thing but appealed to a whole other demographic—truck drivers
and blue-collar workers." Tim's need to earn a living was also a factor in
his decision to become Flynt's ally. On March 29, 1982, Prentice Hall published a collection of Tim's writings under the title *Changing My Mind,
Among Others*. "He did it for the money," Henry Edwards recalled. "He
hated that anthology because it was in order and conventional. A linear

book made him crazy. But I liked that book. It was the only one of his books that made sense."

While Tim and Flynt made a very odd couple indeed, Tim took the concept of bizarre show-business partnership to a new level when he abandoned his solo career as a college lecturer to go on the road with G. Gordon Liddy, the man who had put him behind bars more than once at Millbrook. Sentenced to twenty-one and a half years in prison for his role in the Watergate break-in, with another year and a half added for contempt, Liddy had spent fifty-two months in prison, a period he described as "just a little longer than we were in World War II." Unlike Tim, Liddy had never cooperated with the government, refusing to give any information about his fellow White House burglars. After his release, Liddy wrote two successful books and began making appearances on the college lecture circuit. Two weeks after Tim had lectured at the University of Texas in Austin, Liddy appeared there. A bookstore owner who had seen both lectures came up with the bright idea of having Liddy debate Tim in public. "Acting as an entrepreneur," the bookseller "hired a hall," Liddy remembered, "and retained us both to come and debate. It was phenomenally successful. It just took off and we literally ended up doing it on Broadway in New York, being interviewed by Andy Warhol, and then they made a movie of it. We even went to Cannes together. That was how we became friends. We debated each other all over the country." "The essential difference between Tim Leary and G. Gordon Liddy," Paul Krassner wrote in his autobiography, "was that Leary wanted people to use LSD as a vehicle for turning themselves on to a higher consciousness, whereas Liddy wanted to put LSD on the steering wheel of columnist Jack Anderson's car, thereby making a political assassination look like an automobile accident."

Onstage during the debates, Liddy played the role of the straight man, doing his best "to keep some semblance of order" while Tim spun off in a variety of directions. "I was struck by the irony of it," Krassner recalled. "It was all very surrealistic but I thought it was incredible theater. Tim would pace around the stage like he was tracing the outlines of a jigsaw puzzle, and Liddy would stand perfectly ramrod straight and still with the vein in his temple pulsing." "For all of Tim's devotion to the taking of substances which don't put you in the best shape to debate anything," Liddy remembered, "he never once showed up under the

influence of anything. Never did he smoke anything stronger than a tobacco cigarette beforehand. Never did he drink anything stronger than a
Coke until it was over. Whereas when I debated Hunter Thompson, it
was a fiasco. He arrived totally smacked on whiskey of some sort and
then proceeded to try to sober up just before the debate by doing lines of
cocaine in the ladies' room. Onstage, he made no sense at all. Tim was
never that way. He was sober and focused and very professional. There
was no real anger. He never pissed me off and it never got personal. The
greatest expression of anger would be, 'There you go again.' It was more
exasperation than anger. In a sense like a married couple." When they appeared together at the Santa Cruz Civic Auditorium, the headline in the
San Jose *Mercury News* read THE DRUG-AND-THUG SHOW TAKES TO THE ROAD.

Night after night, both men used lines guaranteed to entertain. "I
have to expose you for what you are, Gordon," Tim would say, "a lawyer.
We need people like you. We need to make fun of you." Both men could
think on their feet. When a woman from the audience asked Liddy,
"How's your sex life? And have you ever paid for it?" "Well, madame," he
responded, "how much do you charge?" Like professional wrestlers who
would beat each other to a bloody pulp during the match and then go out
for dinner, Tim and Liddy were constantly together on the road. When
Tim had coffee with Nina Graboi the morning after the Santa Cruz show,
he brought Liddy with him. "I thought he was absolutely charming," she
recalled. "I said to him, 'You know, I should be afraid of you. Eating rats
and doing all these horrible things . . . but I can't.' And he said, 'Don't tell
anybody the truth. This is how I make my living.' Liddy also told me he
liked the people who agreed with Timothy more than he liked the people
who agreed with him. They were more open and receptive."

By the time the Liddy-Leary road show reached Los Angeles, a film
deal was in place. Barbara had contacted Carolyn Pfeiffer, an old friend
from London who along with Shep Gordon, the former manager of Alice
Cooper, and Chris Blackwell, the founder of Island Records, had formed
a film company called Island Alive. Pfeiffer brought in Alan Rudolph, a director who had made several critically acclaimed small-budget films,
among them *Welcome to LA* and *Choose Me*. Although Rudolph had never
made a documentary, he suggested to Liddy and Leary some situations in
which he might want to film them offstage. "I asked Tim if he would be
interviewed on a gun range and he said no," Rudolph recalled. "And I
asked Liddy if he would talk where people were smoking dope and he

said no. As it turned out in the film, Liddy's at a gun range and Tim is doing something up at Esalen. We also had Liddy riding with a motorcycle gang, one or two of whom had known him in prison."

Rudolph shot *Return Engagement* over the course of a single week for less than $200,000. The film opens with Liddy, looking very fit and muscular in jeans and a polo shirt with a large gold medallion hanging from a chain around his neck, singing "America the Beautiful." Tim, older and not nearly so fit, accompanies him on the piano. The former Watergate burglar and the ex–Harvard professor do in fact seem like a happily married couple. Once the actual debate begins, both men appear before a huge American flag right out of *Patton*. Backstage at the Wilshire Ebell Theatre during the filming, stars of all magnitude turned out to be part of the scene. On Tim's side of the aisle, they included Marjoe Gortner, the former boy evangelist; Geraldo Rivera; and Caroline Kennedy. Liddy was supported by Arnold Schwarzenegger, a stalwart Republican and an obvious admirer. "There was always a big party afterward and Tim was lionized by the Hollywood people," Liddy remembered. "The biggest people in Hollywood would sit at his feet. They loved it. I remember a dinner party with Susan Sarandon. After dinner, Tim said with that gleam in his eye, 'All right, Gordon, if I were you, for dessert, I would not have one of those brownies. You see that bowl down there? That's just Famous Amos cookies. That's for you. But the brownies are for the rest of us.'"

Return Engagement is very much Liddy's movie. Onscreen, he is a darker and far more interesting character than Tim, who is pictured doing the same shtick from which he had earned a living for the past quarter of a century. As Tim sits before his brand-new word processor explaining how the computer is altering the process of book publishing, Liddy pushes as much weight as he can handle on a Nautilus machine in a gym while talking about how good it is to feel pain in a fight because this means your opponent is also in pain and the one who can stand the most pain will eventually win.

The most revealing scene in the movie occurs not during the debate but when Tim and Barbara have breakfast with Liddy and his wife at the Chateau Marmont. "We were giving them their calls for the next day," Rudolph recalled, "and I said, 'We're going to have this scene where we're going to have breakfast at the Chateau Marmont. Liddy looked around at me and said, 'She can't make it.' And his wife said, 'Go on, Gordon, tell him why I can't make it.' And he went on like she didn't exist. And his wife said, 'Yes, I can! Go on, Gordon. Tell him. You want to get rid of me.'"

Sporting a bruise below one eye at breakfast, Liddy's wife, who had borne him five children, went on and on as the camera rolled about all the women pursuing her husband, including female reporters who would edge closer to Gordon when they interviewed him on the couch. "They're notorious trollops who'll do anything for a story," Tim notes. Sensing that he cannot win no matter what he says, Liddy says, "I'm pleading not guilty." His wife replies sharply, "You always have. That's why they gave you twenty years." As she goes on talking, Liddy reaches for the jam, smears some on his toast, and drinks more coffee. Completely tuning out his wife, he concentrates his famous powers of attention on the meal before him. All the while, Tim and Barbara are holding hands. Affectionately, Barbara rubs Tim's arm. Once, they even kiss. On their side of the table, there is perfect harmony.

The most dramatic encounter in the film occurs when an ex-Marine gets to his feet during the question-and-answer period of the debate and describes how he was shot in the face with a shotgun at close range by someone who was high on LSD. Now blind, with artificial plastic eyes, he says that although he forgives Tim for what he did to him, he still wants to know, "How do you feel about me? Answer that question." After a long and uncomfortable silence, Tim explains that as a pacifist, he is opposed to violence and has always urged people to act nonviolently. Talking at cross-purposes, neither man communicates with the other. "I hope you can sleep peacefully," the ex-Marine says. Offering Tim his blessing, he bids him good night.

In a review of the debate in the *Los Angeles Times*, entitled "Liddy, Leary Selling A Bad Dose Of Snake Oil," Sylvie Drake wrote, "in spite of the freak-show aspects of this carnival act, it was curiously soporific . . . Who would have thought a con game could be boring?" The film fared only slightly better with the critics. Kevin Thomas of the *Los Angeles Times* called *Return Engagement* not only "well-made" but also "an amusing, provocative, disturbing, and admirably responsible study of this pair of incorrigible showoffs and publicity seekers who seem to have captured the imaginations of so many." In *The New York Times*, Vincent Canby wrote, "The two men are not exactly freaks, but one has the suspicion that they wouldn't be showing off in this way if they could possibly make a living in some other fashion."

Forging a real friendship with the man who had done everything he could to drive him out of Dutchess County was yet another step in Timothy Leary's program of self-repatriation. To be forgiven for what he had done, Tim knew he had to first forgive everyone who had wronged him. By doing so, he made himself seem like a beneficent figure who held no grudges against anyone while transforming those who did into mean-spirited beings unable to rise to a similar level of compassion. His strategy soon began winning him a host of brand-new admirers.

Knowing that the first step in getting a movie made about his life was to have a biography in print, Tim finally stopped trying to inveigle others into collaborating with him and wrote the book on his own. On May 30, 1983, Jeremy Tarcher, a Los Angeles publisher who was married to children's show host Shari Lewis, brought out *Flashbacks*. A year later, a paperback edition appeared. For those too young to have lived through the sixties, *Flashbacks* became the source for all they knew about Tim.

Throughout his life, Tim had saved every scrap of paper that had ever crossed his desk. The archive he had assembled was second to none. The sheer volume of the 465 boxes holding his papers was so overwhelming that at his death, they entirely filled a large two-bedroom apartment in the San Fernando Valley. Tim had always believed that someday his archive would be worth a fortune, to either a private collector or some prestigious university library. Yet when the time came for him to finally set the record straight by writing his own book, he did no research whatsoever. Rather, he seems to have relied on his memory and imagination, and then insisted that what he had written was the historical truth. Even for him, *Flashbacks* ranked as a bravura performance. "When I read *Flashbacks*," Travis Ashbrook, one of the founding members of the Brotherhood of Eternal Love, recalled, "my first question was, 'Tim, why the hell didn't you read your own books before you wrote this one?' He got his time lines wrong. The chronology of it is completely mixed up. Why the hell did he do that? For literary license? Or because he truly didn't remember?"

The reviews that greeted *Flashbacks* accurately reflected how little work Tim had put into it. "He was just horsing around and happened to turn into the Messiah," wrote Herbert Gold in *The New York Times Book Review.* In a review entitled "Tripping & Stumbling" in *The Washington Post,* David Harris, the activist who had married Joan Baez and been sent to prison for resisting the draft during the Vietnam War, described the book as "short on credibility and long on license . . . a story that might have been great reading in the hands of a different author . . . As it is, Leary's autobiographical effort is spotty: too loose in some spots, too tight in others . . . *Flashbacks* unfortunately reads somewhat like Leary wrote it because he was short of money."

Despite the reviews, Tim now had a new product to hawk. As *Flashbacks* was being published, Tim returned to Harvard with Richard Alpert to celebrate the twentieth anniversary of his dismissal from the faculty. Tim's former colleague Brendan Maher, who had returned to Harvard in 1972 after serving as the dean of the faculty at Brandeis, bought tickets for his wife and himself; they were $3 each. "We went to this thing," Maher recalled, "and we were standing in line outside Sanders Theatre. God knows how but thanks to the call of the wild, a large number of people still wearing beads and headbands had emerged from the cellars of Central Square. They hadn't bought tickets but friends who had done so kept letting them fall out of the upper windows. There was a steady stream of tickets falling from the upper windows, which were picked up so the same hundred tickets let in a large number of people." The Mahers, along with another former Leary adversary, Herb Kelman and his wife, finally made their way into a theater jammed to the rafters.

Alpert, wearing a sky-blue Nehru jacket, sat onstage on one side of David McClelland, their former department chairman, while Tim, looking as Maher recalled "slightly out of it" sat on the other. After McClelland introduced them to the overflow crowd, Leary and Alpert began reminiscing. "It was very much, 'Do you remember the old days?'" Maher recalled. "'Oh yes, wasn't it . . . ?' That kind of thing. Then Dick Alpert said to Tim, 'Do you remember the wonderful evening when you were on the balcony of your house and we looked out over the sea as the sun slowly descended into the water and I looked at you and thought of all the times we'd been through and the past and I felt absolutely nothing.' And I thought, 'That's it.' That's what this evening is all about. Absolutely nothing." Kelman, no more enamored of Tim than he had been in 1963, said, "One didn't go there to be enlightened."

Inspired by the recently released movie *My Dinner With Andre*, Alpert had come up with the idea that he and Tim should go with McClelland "to a restaurant in Harvard Square and be videotaped for a documentary," McClelland recalled. "Then Dick called and asked me if they could use my house instead, a big old Victorian in Cambridge. I felt sort of pressured because it couldn't happen unless I said yes. So I agreed. They brought a whole television crew with them and they tore the house apart to put in all their cables and lights and everything." Tim, openly smoking a joint in front of the camera, sat at the dinner table. "See here? I have marijuana. Be sure to get this down. So we can say we're still smoking dope." "My wife thought he was an absolute asshole," McClelland would later say. "To put it mildly. The way he cavorted around in front of the camera. The one thing I did say at that time that got under Tim's skin was, 'Tim, I think we're all passé. I don't think the students are interested in us at all anymore. They've got other things on their minds.' That made him furious. One of the few times I've seen him really angry."

While the sixties might finally have ended at Harvard, they seemed to be alive and well in England. Still viewing Tim as a dangerous force in society, the British Home Office denied him permission to enter the country in September 1983, thereby thwarting his efforts to publicize both *Flashbacks* and *Return Engagement,* which was about to go into theatrical release in Great Britain.

In America, Tim hired the publicity firm of Rodgers & Cowan to coordinate his merchandising efforts for the book. On yet another whirlwind media tour, he flew to New York where he managed to sandwich an interview with *Heavy Metal* magazine between an appearance with Jane Pauley on NBC's *Today Show* and a session with a reporter from *Time* magazine. Michael Simmons of *Heavy Metal* found Tim a "vibrant, charming man . . . He's an unflagging self-promoter. He must have mentioned the title *Flashbacks* twenty-five times in forty-five minutes."

Tim used the two most controversial stories in *Flashbacks* to generate publicity for the book. The first involved his unproven contention that Mary Pinchot Meyer might have used drugs with President John F. Kennedy in the White House and was then murdered by the CIA to keep her from talking about it. The second was his account of a meeting in Los Angeles with Cary Grant, who by the mid-sixties had already used LSD a number of times and, according to Tim, had once wanted to portray him in a movie. After he leaked this item to nationally known gossip columnists, Tim gleefully noted in his own weekly column in *Rebel* magazine, "The ploy worked. Over 1,000 newspapers ran a photo of Cary Grant under screaming headlines: CARY GRANT LSD ENTHUSIAST!! To tell the truth, I was bit worried about how Cary would respond. He was, after all, the

Dean of Beverly Hills society, presiding over charity banquets with Frank Sinatra and Nancy Reagan, the Commander-in-Chief of our Nation's All-out War on Drugs. Obviously, Cary would read my account of his psychedelic past. How would he respond?" Grant responded by openly admitting to *The National Enquirer* that he had taken LSD about a hundred times while participating in a program of psychotherapy supervised by Dr. Oscar Janiger in Los Angeles in 1958. He said that for him the drug had worked as a beneficial form of self-therapy which had opened up his subconscious, thereby enabling him to see all the guilt and misconceptions within. "It's too bad LSD is illegal," Grant told the tabloid, discussing the drug with more candor than Tim had ever done. "It should be controlled. It's the same as taking a shot of brandy, which can do you good. LSD is hallucinogenic, not addictive."

During the following year, Tim devoted much of his time and energy to supporting Larry Flynt. From his wheelchair in a courtroom in LA, Flynt had screamed obscenities at a federal judge while crying "Give me more" after being sentenced to fifteen months in prison for contempt. Flynt had already been fined first $10,000 and then $20,000 a day for refusing to reveal the source of a dubious audiotape in which an informer was heard threatening millionaire automaker John DeLorean to keep him involved in a government drug sting operation. Adding insult to injury, Flynt had appeared in court in a diaper made from the American flag. He had then violated his bail on a charge of desecrating the flag by leaving the state of California. During the contempt hearing, Flynt's lawyer asked the judge for permission to gag his own client. The judge denied the request. Even behind bars, Flynt created new problems for himself. During a jailhouse interview with a reporter from CNN at the federal prison in Butner, North Carolina, Flynt said, "One thing that I will confess to you on tape, and I hope that you are taping it, I have confessed to putting out a contract on President Reagan's life. I want to kill him." Flynt also said he had threatened to kill two federal judges and at least half a dozen federal prison employees. The Secret Service promptly announced that they had begun an investigation into his threats.

Throughout this period, Tim sent Flynt a steady stream of telegrams and letters to let him know he had not been forgotten. "I just cannot believe how they are locking you in," Tim wrote on March 26, 1984. "It's a George Orwell *1984*–plus Kafka nightmare. But I know you are strong enough to handle it. Dear friend—please concentrate on getting out. We all miss you so much and none of us can be free as long as you are chained." Tim wrote again the next day to say that Flynt was the "essence of the American spirit because you are AUTHENTIC!!! . . . A guy that thumbs his nose at authority—which happens to be what USA is all about." On April 9, 1984, Tim wrote Flynt that he and Barbara had just gone to the "hot" party at Spago in Beverly Hills after the Academy Awards. The comedians Cheech and Chong were there along with Jack Nicholson, all of whom sent Flynt their love. Two days later, Tim wrote that although he had no jokes to send, he had just had dinner with Eric Idle of *Monty Python's Flying Circus,* who sat down at Tim's computer to play "The Game of Life," an interactive game that Tim had helped develop. Long before most Americans owned or even knew how to operate a personal computer, Tim had already decided that these miraculous new machines would entirely transform the basic nature of human life. Even though he remained completely computer illiterate and later had to rely on others to perform so simple a task as retrieving his own e-mail, Tim began working with Jeff Scheftel, a UCLA film archivist, to create brand-new forms of interactive software. "He gave me my first computer," Scheftel recalled, "and a notion for a program."

Using film scripts that had already been produced as movies as a model, Scheftel and Tim came up with BOPS, an acronym for "Box Office Prediction Scale." "We would take scripts and evaluate them in terms of how strong the protagonist was," Scheftel remembered, "and how the action turned. We would analyze the various criteria and compare the box office grosses. We were friendly with a number of producers and they would show us new scripts they were considering and we devised a way of rating them in terms of their potential success in the marketplace. It was purely questions and answers and graphs. We wanted them to pay us a fee and get all the other producers involved in it." Although they never marketed this program, the Scheftel Film Aptitude Test was integrated into an interactive software program called *Mind Mirror,* one of the first forays into the gaming market, which, as Scheftel recalled, "came out of Tim's early academic exercises. Basically, it was his thesis from Berkeley transferred onto a computer." *Mind Mirror* was a game in which players created their own psychological profiles by answering questions in which they rated themselves on a variety of personal attributes. Nearly thirty years after *The Interpersonal Diagnosis of Personality* was published, Tim had resurrected The Leary Circle in digital form.

When Larry Flynt sued Tim for the $20,000 he had advanced him to write his unsold biography, their relationship fell apart. Tim transferred his loyalty to Hugh Hefner and became a regular visitor to the Playboy Mansion in Beverly Hills where he met Carrie Leigh. Four months before her twentieth birthday, Leigh had appeared on the cover of the April 1983 issue of *Playboy* and displaced fellow Canadian Shannon Tweed as Hefner's live-in girlfriend. She was introduced to Tim by disco queen and actress Grace Jones, then living with action movie star Dolph Lundgren. Although Hefner had recently suffered a stroke, and in Leigh's words, "was not supposed to do anything that would cause his heart to race," she went up to her dressing room at the Playboy Mansion one night only to see "Timothy Leary and Hef and Barbara [Leary] and Grace [Jones] and they had all these lines of coke set up on these magazines and they were sitting on their knees snorting it up." Ecstasy was then still legal, and Leigh and Hefner took the drug with Tim at a party given by Jones and Lundgren. At the Playboy Mansion, Tim seemed to Leigh like "kind of a voyeur" who "was in a daze" but was "taking it all in and dissecting it inside his head." Because Leigh did not really know who Tim Leary was, she asked Hefner, "Who is this person?" Hefner's response, according to Leigh, was that Tim "was a genius at mixing drugs. That was his main comment about him."

In 1985, Tim and Barbara moved from Laurel Canyon to a house on Sunbrook Drive in Beverly Hills. "Barbara was eager to move to a larger location," Jeff Scheftel recalled, "and that had a lot to do with it. Up there, the social scene grew exponentially. In Laurel Canyon, it was more of an intellectual crowd. Laura Huxley, Norman Spinrad, William Gibson, Robert K. Weiss, David Byrne, Mark Mothersbaugh, Robert Anton Wilson, and Jim Goode, who edited *Rebel* magazine. Up the hill, it was more A-group."

One day, Tim and Barbara had lunch at the Ivy restaurant on Robertson Drive in Beverly Hills with Eric Gardner, a former neighbor from Laurel Canyon who managed music-business celebrities, among them Todd Rundgren and Rolling Stones bassist Bill Wyman. Barbara began asking Gardner for advice and the three of them discussed the possibility of Tim hosting a syndicated radio show. "I gave them the benefit of my knowledge about who the major syndicators were and who to approach and what the sponsorship problems might be," Gardner recalled. At the end of his "little dissertation," Tim and Barbara asked Gardner to represent them in this project. "All the syndicators wanted to do it," Gardner remembered, "but they couldn't find any company willing to sponsor it. Timothy had a lot going against him in terms of making inroads into the commercial world. Everyone loved to have him at their party. Everyone loved to be photographed with him. He was a wonderful slightly dangerous outlaw trophy to have around your pool, especially in Hollywood. But when it came to writing a check and associating with Timothy in any kind of major media project, that was an entirely different story."

Though Tim was a very hard sell in Hollywood, Gardner took a chance on him. While Tim did not earn rock-star money, he did work regularly. Colleges were now paying him $10,000 to $12,000 a night and he sometimes did as many as three or four lectures a week. Gardner also helped find Tim small parts in feature films and television shows. "During my tenure," Gardner recalled, "he did fifteen or twenty cameo roles at ten or twelve grand a pop. Sometimes twenty-five grand a pop." "Tim was in a dozen films," Michael Horowitz confirmed. "He got his Screen Actor's Guild card. In Cheech and Chong's movie *Nice Dreams* he played the head of a mental institution where Cheech and Chong were incarcerated. He started out playing it straight and ended up as a mad scientist. I said, 'Why would you want to play a mad scientist? That's the impression that stupid people have of you.' And he said, 'Don't you get it? That's why I want to play it. I'll up-level them.'"

When Gardner learned that Breyer's Ice Cream had begun using "notorious" public figures –such as Donna Rice, the woman who had helped end Senator Gary Hart's presidential aspirations—to pitch their product in the northeast, he figured Tim would be a natural for their campaign. "But when I called them up and got the ad exec on the phone," Gardner recalled, "he said it was too risky for them. Middle America had been imprinted by things like Art Linkletter publicly blaming Timothy for the suicide of his daughter while tripping."

Had Tim been willing to admit publicly that he had done wrong and then ask for forgiveness, it would have been much easier for Gardner to find him work. Instead, Tim chose, like the professor he had once been, to split semantic hairs. "In the mid-eighties," Gardner recalled, "he sort of revised his personal definition of 'Tune in, turn on, drop out' by saying, 'I wasn't literally saying, "Take drugs." I was saying, "Think for yourself and question authority."'" He became a Libertarian."

FORTY-SIX

On April 1, 1987, Tim attended Andy Warhol's funeral in New York City's St. Patrick's Cathedral, where he ran into his old friend and former screenwriting partner Henry Edwards. The two had been estranged for the past few years because of Tim's failure to pay back the $1,500 Edwards had loaned him while they were working together. Greeting each other joyously, the two men had what Edwards later called "this amazing reunion." After sitting through the service—"which was getting on your knees and doing all these Catholic things I didn't understand"—Edwards gave Tim his extra ticket for the lunch that followed.

"We went to this discotheque for the lunch," Edwards recalled, "and it was star-studded beyond belief. Yoko Ono. Liza Minelli. Every famous person was there having the Andy Warhol funeral lunch. We got food and drinks and sat down at a table and this man came over and sat with us and said, 'Doctor Leary, it's a pleasure to meet you. We share so much in common. My name is Claus von Bulow and you and I are the two most hated people in the world.'" Von Bulow, who had been convicted of murdering his diabetic wife, Sunny, by injecting her with a deadly dose of insulin so he could inherit her fortune and marry his longtime mistress, had only recently been cleared of all wrongdoing in an appeal mounted by Harvard law professor Alan Dershowitz. "Tim was upset," Edwards remembered. "He didn't want to be locked in with this person who had been accused of this tacky murder for money. Tim was someone who was evolving civilization. He was not one of the most hated people in the world. Tim said, 'How nice to meet you' and then he snapped into his outer space evolutionary mode and he transcended Claus."

On any given night in LA, Tim and Barbara could now be found at Spago, Morton's, Le Dome, Helena's, Mr. Chow's, Au Petit Cafe, or The

Flaming Colossus, a former Knights of Columbus lodge at Ninth and Bonnie Brae that had been converted into one of LA's trendiest nightclubs. Tim and Barbara's circle of friends included *Vanity Fair* editor Angela Janklow; Mark Mothersbaugh of the rock band Devo; Dr. Roy Walford, a well-known author and researcher into the biology of aging; as well as others from the worlds of cutting-edge art, film, fashion, and design. Now that he had become social royalty, Tim expected to be treated as such by one and all. Meeting Tim during this period, author and media critic Douglas Rushkoff recalled, "was like taking half a hit of acid. It was dangerous. You had to bring something to the party." Then working for a small fashion magazine called *Exposure*, Rushkoff described himself as "really hungry for the cool Hollywood scene and to go home knowing I had seen Scott Baiao at a party." Rushkoff's first real contact with Tim came when he offered him $1,500 for a piece on computers and consciousness. "It was a really scattered piece," Rushkoff remembered, "so I called him up and asked if I could do an editorial job on it and resubmit it to him. I did a pretty massive rewrite and faxed it over to him and he read it and said, 'Wow, this is great. You're a great writer. It's not what I said but it's great.' After that, we were friends." Concerning Tim and Barbara as a couple, Rushkoff remembered, "I did get a sense when they were together, it was as much a mating of Rolodexes as it was a mating of souls."

In a town where appearance mattered most of all, Tim had never looked better. In a photograph taken by Frederick Ohringer in 1987, he is staring with clear, piercing eyes into the camera, his snow-white hair in perfect harmony with his open-collar white shirt and white pants. His hands thrust deeply into the side pockets of his trousers, he is wearing an expensive V-neck sweater. The air of supreme self-confidence he projects suggests he has earned every one of the wrinkles on his face. In "Timothy Leary, Party Animal," an article that appeared in the *Los Angeles Times* on December 11, 1987, Tim told Dick Roraback, "The Sunset Strip is my turf. It's like the Appian Way, the Boulevard St. Germain. Down there is where I meet old friends, new friends." Reminding Roraback that he was "a philosopher" whose ambition was "to be the MVP of the 20th Century—Most Valuable Philosopher," Tim said he took "all this for granted. Voltaire had his patrons. Aristotle was tutor to Alexander the Great."

In April 1988, a two-page photo spread of Tim and Barbara appeared in *Vanity Fair*. Again dressed in white, Tim smiled at the camera with

improbably perfect teeth while dancing with Barbara who was dressed
entirely in black. Her fingers intertwined with his, Barbara only had eyes
for Tim. In a photograph by Helmut Newton that accompanied the piece,
a very made-up Barbara gazed at herself in a hand mirror while a wizened
and bespectacled Tim leaned over the screen of his word processor. In the
foreground was an open bottle of Corona beer. The article, written by
Ron Rosenbaum, began with an account of Tim holding court at Helena's, the exclusive private dining club funded by Jack Nicholson, who
happened to be there that night with his longtime friend, record executive and movie director Lou Adler. The guests at Tim's table were the actress Joanna Pacula, artist Ed Ruscha, and Gisela Martine Getty, wife of
J. Paul Getty III. Blind and unable to speak as the result of a disabling
stroke, Getty was rolled into the room in his wheelchair "nodding and
smiling to those below like a Caesar in a sedan chair."

In the article, Tim rambled on at length to Rosenbaum about the
socio-demographics of valet parking in Los Angeles and all the little psy-
chodramas that erupted when powerful Hollywood people had to wait
twenty minutes for their cars. Tim noted that he had mastered this particular game. While those who could afford new Rolls-Royces looked on
in envy outside one of the hottest clubs in town, Tim got his old green
"low rent" Mercedes right away because he had done time in Folsom with
the parking attendant. Tim also made a point of demonstrating that his
powers of observation had not waned by accurately identifying the actress Joan Collins from the back even though another of the regulars at
Helena's insisted it was not her.

As they sat together chatting on the back porch of Tim's home on a
sunny day, Rosenbaum pressed Tim to admit there was something amiss
about his claim in *Flashbacks* that he had shared drugs and slept with Marilyn Monroe. Rather than conceding that he had made the story up, Tim
refused with "uncharacteristic reticence" to discuss the affair. In response
to Rosenbaum's questions about prison, Tim insisted that although he
might have cooperated with the authorities to get out of jail, the FBI
knew no one would go to prison "because no jury would believe the testimony of such a spaced-out witness." When Rosenbaum asked Tim
about his current relationship to the drug with which his name would be
linked forevermore, Tim explained that his marriage to Barbara was such
"a high-budget movie" that for "a hard working husband/father" like
himself, LSD had become "an enormous luxury I just can't afford now.

My wife Barbara is very tuned into the exquisite beauty of the surround-ings . . . And so every time we've taken LSD, the next morning she de-cides we have to move to a more expensive house." Laughing, he added, "That's one of the unreported side effects of LSD we never recognized—it doubles your rent."

Ensconced in a house high upon a hill overlooking a city that he be-lieved to be his own, Timothy Leary, now sixty-seven years old, seemed to have gotten away with it all. His personal life had never been so or-dered. His social life had never been more active. To him, it seemed as though the basic laws of karma did not apply.

Even as he played the role of social lion in public, the secret sorrow of Tim's life continued to be his daughter Susan. During interviews, he never brought her name up. Instead, he talked about his goddaughter, the actress Winona Ryder whose father, Michael Horowitz, had long been his friend and archivist, or Uma Thurman, whom he barely knew but to whose mother, Nena, he had once been married. Forty-one years old, Susan Leary Martino had been not only a burden to her father but an abu-sive mother to her daughter, Dieadra, and her son, Ashley. "Clinically," Dieadra Martino recalled, "my mother was a paranoid schizophrenic. I didn't realize that until I got older. But as a kid, I always had negative feel-ings because my mother used to beat the shit out of me. She put me into a coma like three times before I was five years old. She would hit us with the little baseball bat she got when she went with Timmy to see Dodger games. She beat us because she couldn't control her anger. I was in kinder-garten when I was taken away. The next-door neighbors called. And my mother beat up on one of the policemen. She busted his car with the same bat she used to beat us." After the incident, Susan enlisted in the army and Dieadra was sent to a foster home.

Although Tim saw his grandchildren regularly on weekends and at Christmas, taking them to play football in a park in the San Fernando Val-ley or to watch baseball games at Dodger Stadium, he made no attempt to remove them from foster care. "Barbara was the reason that we couldn't live with him," Dieadra remembered. "He wanted us to but he was weak-minded and he let Barbara convince him that having his daugh-ter's two children live with him would fuck up her perfect family life." "The bottom line," Barbara said, "is that Dieadra had a terrible childhood but when she first came in, I tried to love her and be kind to her and it was just impossible. It wasn't like Tim said, 'Let's adopt her and have them live here and bring them up like our children.'" One night when she was eleven, Dieadra visited Tim in his house in Laurel Canyon. "Me, Ashley, and Zach decided we were gonna party," she recalled, "and we were making drinks and eating brownies and we didn't know what was in them. Something caught on fire. The rug, I believe it was. We put it out and tried to hide it but when Barbara and Timmy came back, they went off. Because we were passed out. Timmy wasn't too bad. He kind of laughed at us. 'Oh my goodness, my little children. We should never have left those brownies in the fridge.' But Barbara was furious."

On April 2, 1980, in a desperate attempt to regain custody of her children, Susan took a letter she had written in her shaky, childlike scrawl to a notary public. The letter read, "I, Susan Martino, born Susan Leary, and my brother were sexually molested by my father Timothy Leary when I was a child. It is my belief that the same Timothy Leary has been sexually abusing my daughter." Susan's accusations reflected her illness. "My mom was in the army thinking she would get us back when she got out," Dieadra recalled, "but she didn't." Henry Edwards remembered, "I was there when Susan Leary was arrested for shitting in the washing machines in a Laundromat in the valley. She was wacko. Definitely over the top. But her two little children were amazingly adorable."

Ever since her mother's suicide, Susan had been competing for her father's attention against women who were far more beautiful and poised than she was. "Tim's daughter was a grown woman," Barbara recalled. "Older than me. She could hold a rational conversation but she couldn't behave in a rational manner for any length of time." Traumatized as an adolescent by the bust in Laredo and the ensuing trial, Susan was so intolerant of drug use as an adult that she would walk out of the room if anyone lit up a joint. When Vicki Marshall, Tim's personal assistant, asked him why Susan was sometimes so mean to him, Tim shrugged. "She still blames me for her mother's death."

On December 18, 1988, a week after the article about Tim's return to social prominence appeared in the *Los Angeles Times*, Susan and her boyfriend, Joel Chavira Jr., took Dieadra out to dinner to celebrate her sixteenth birthday. "He was a security guard," Dieadra recalled. "They seemed to have a real relationship and I thought maybe this guy was good for her. My mother seemed happy with him. She used to snuggle up with him and put her arm around him and I had never seen my mother like that." After stopping off to visit Ron and Vicki Marshall just before midnight, Susan and Chavira returned to their apartment in Glendale. As Chavira slept on the sofa in the living room, Susan shot him at close range with a handgun. Chavira woke to the sound of a loud explosion. Feeling blood at the back of his head, he got to his feet with a bullet lodged in the base of his skull and went into the kitchen to confront Susan. Still holding the gun, she accused him of having given her AIDS by being unfaithful. Chavira was hospitalized in critical condition with a fractured skull but survived the attack.

On January 20, 1989, Susan was ordered to stand trial on a charge of attempted murder. "My mother went to jail," Dieadra recalled, "and my grandfather was trying to get her to plead insanity so she didn't have to stay in prison. For a little while, she ended up at Patton State Hospital in San Bernardino County. But then they kicked her out of there, because they found her in the men's area, and sent her back to the Sybil Brand Institute." From Sybil Brand, Susan sent her father a belated birthday present one month to the day after his sixty-ninth birthday on October 22, 1989. "Dear Tim," she wrote in the accompanying letter. "Here is a little bag I made for you with a crochet needle. I know one stitch. I need a little practice but I hope you like the bag. It is for your shaving stuff when you travel maybe if you need one or for putting mail into or for your glove compartment. I hope you find a use for it."

Unable to help his daughter, Tim would often sit in his office late at night writing letters to her. Almost certainly drunk when he scrawled these notes, many of which were written on pages torn from magazines, Tim told her he had given up smoking cigarettes and drinking alcohol. "Oh, Susan," he wrote, "you are my oldest friend and I love you." In another, he said a doctor had told him that he had serious liver and lung problems. "Goodbye dear Susan. Our 40 year friendship is ending. Goodbye." In its entirety, another read, "Dear Susan, you are a terrible daughter." The most poignant letter included a copied promotional photograph of Johnny Depp kissing Winona Ryder. "Dear Susan," Tim wrote. "The picture is my God-daughter Winona Ryder—Susan—why are you not kissing Johnny Depp? Why? Please—get real! Get your act together!" Although Tim addressed and put stamps on the envelopes, he never mailed any of the letters.

With his daughter in jail facing a charge of attempted murder, the dam that Tim had erected to keep himself free from pain began giving way. Behind the public façade of a marriage that had always seemed perfect, deep fissures had developed. Mel Seesholtz, an associate professor of psycho-linguistics at Penn State who was collaborating with Tim on a variety of projects, often stayed with the Learys during this period. "When Barbara would come in," he recalled, "Timothy would jump. Literally. He would jump. He and I would get up early and be in his office talking or reading and she would ring the phone from her bedroom where she basically lived and Timothy would literally jump up and go make her tea and take it to her." "When Barbara would come up the driveway," recalled Vicki Marshall, "Tim would begin to shake."

John Perry Barlow, who had last seen Tim Leary when he brought the Grateful Dead to Millbrook in June 1967, came to Los Angeles to interview Tim for a book on virtual reality. "By this point," Barlow recalled, "I'd been off any kind of mind-altering substances for a long time. The first person I met in the house was Barbara, who said that before I could talk to Tim, I had to eat some of these brownies. I did and then the three of us went on this wild cruise through Los Angeles where we got totally lost and Barbara was screeching at us like a harpy and Tim and I were bucking her authority and laughing like crazy. It was like he had found an ally in me and we were catching up on old times." Calling Barbara "something the devil wears when he is in a particularly sporting mood," Barlow said, "she is also a wonderful human being in an extremely weird way. She was the great love of Tim's life. He said that to me numerous times." As Barlow also recalled, Tim "sort of gave me permission in some weird way to be Barbara's lover."

"Timothy saw himself in many ways as James Joyce," Mel Seesholtz, who had written his master's thesis on *Ulysses* and his Ph.D. on *Finnegans Wake*, remembered. "His physical posture was the same as Joyce. I remember we were in New York one night and we came back to the hotel room and Tim said, 'Hey, Mel, did Joyce manipulate people?' and I told him the story of Joyce and Robert Prezioso, a newspaper reporter whom Joyce maneuvered into having an affair with his wife, Nora. Of course, Nora told Joyce everything so it got a little out of Joyce's control and he ran into Prezioso in the piazza and demolished him verbally. He reduced the man to jelly." As Seesholtz told the story to Tim, he made a gesture with his hands, "sort of like turning a ball right in the middle of my chest," and Tim went "berserk." "He started screaming. 'Never do this! Never do this in front of me!' And then he fell down on his knees, put his arms up into the air, and said, 'Should I worship the Joyce God now?' I was thinking, 'What the fuck are you doing?' Earlier in the evening, Tim had done a riff about how when he died, I should marry Barbara and become Zach's stepfather. The only thing that crossed my mind was, 'Am I supposed to be Prezioso now? Am I Sean to his Shem? Am I Bloom to his Stephen?'"

While sexual fidelity may not have been a major issue in the marriage, Tim's drinking had become a problem. During a visit to their house in March 1989, Seesholtz went to a dinner party with Tim and Barbara at which "Tim got a little drunk and was having a very good time. Tim hated vegetarian food. The drunker he got, the more he kept making snide little comments to the gourmet vegetarian cook, which, of course, Barbara was getting more and more angry about. We left the dinner party to go to the actor Billy Zane's wife's birthday." As Barbara drove his rental car "a million miles an hour up these canyon roads and on Mulholland," Seesholtz felt sure "we were gonna die." Slamming on the brakes, Barbara stopped "at the edge of the cliff." Jumping out of the car, she told Tim that she was leaving him. Then she slammed the door and walked away. "Tim was pretty blitzed," Seesholtz recalled. "We sat there for a minute and he said, 'Hnnh, let's go to the party.' As we walked across Mulholland Drive, he started peeing in the middle of the street. At the party, they were at opposite ends and very distant. Not a word was said between them until we left. The drive home was very quiet."

Seesholtz went to sleep on a pullout bed in Tim's office but was woken up at three in the morning by Barbara, who was shaking him and screaming that Tim had "trashed Zach's room and that I had to stop him. I followed her in there and he hadn't broken anything. The computer was put on the floor. It wasn't thrown. Eventually, we ended up in their bedroom. Barbara was in the fetal position on the floor crying hysterically. Timothy was in bed, reading, out of it, ranting about how he couldn't go to Harry Nilsson's latest child's christening because Harry was in rehab and he was the drug guru and how could he possibly do this?" Seesholtz had returned to his pullout bed in Tim's office when he heard the car start and then pull away. "In the morning," he recalled, "Tim came bounding out and said, 'Barbara left!' Like he was all surprised."

"That was a tough week," Seesholtz recalled. "He was very much lost without her. Especially socially. She pretty much handled all the arrangements. But, like he did with everything, he turned it into a game. We took turns lying to see who could come up with the best lie to explain why Barbara wasn't there." By Wednesday or Thursday, Tim was blaming Seesholtz for Barbara leaving. "She was not big on people staying in the house," Seesholtz remembered, "so it was my fault. I was getting a little frantic and I knew I had to get out of there because this was driving me nuts so I said, 'Tim, if she calls, tell her I left and I'll be gone before she gets back.' Within an hour, she called." When Tim handed Seesholtz the phone, Barbara begged him not to leave because Tim really needed him there right now. On Sunday, she came back to Tim.

Four months later, Tim Leary and Mel Seesholtz had a falling out over $1,000 that Tim wanted Seesholtz to give to him rather than pay in rent to a couple who had already refused to loan Tim and Barbara five times that amount. The disagreement effectively ended their relationship.

On Monday morning, September 3, 1990, jailers at the Sybil Brand Institute found Susan Leary hanging from a shoelace in the one-person cell to which she had been moved two weeks earlier. In August, Susan had been found for the second time to be mentally unfit to stand trial on charges of attempted murder. Her public defender noted that Susan's mental illness had made it difficult for him to help her and that during the past two months, her condition appeared to be deteriorating. She had in fact been planning to kill herself for months. At the beginning of the summer, Susan had sent Tim a letter in which she described in chilling detail exactly how she intended to take her life rather than let herself be sent to a mental hospital. Vicki Marshall began typing the letter for Tim so he could preserve it for his archives, only to get so depressed by its contents that she told him he needed to read it himself. "She was absolutely determined to do it," Marshall recalled. "She got caught once before with a shoelace and put in quarantine and then they let her back in her cell for good behavior. She even learned how to count her heartbeats so she could time how long the guard would be gone. This was such a deliberate act. On the day it happened, Tim called me to say he couldn't come to work with me because Susan had tried to kill herself. Holding my breath, I asked him how she had done it. It was exactly as she had described it in the letter. When I asked him if he had ever read it, he said no."

When she was cut down, Susan's heart was still beating, but she had already suffered so much brain damage that she had to be put on a ventilator in Santa Marta Hospital. "I went down there with Tim," George Milman, a close friend who for many years also served as Tim's lawyer in Los Angeles, recalled, "and she was on life support and they were waiting for the neurologist to come and do the last test and make sure she was brain dead and unplug her." Once the neurologist confirmed that nothing could be done, Milman phoned Dieadra, who needed to sign a written consent form before the doctors could unplug Susan and harvest her organs. "The hardest thing I ever did," Dieadra remembered, "was sign the papers as next of kin."

At 6:00 P.M. on Wednesday, September 5, 1990, Susan Leary Martino, who in three weeks' time would have been forty-three years old, was pronounced dead. Just as her mother had done thirty-five years earlier, she had died by her own hand. In an interview done shortly after Susan's death, Tim described his daughter as "shy and distrustful" with a philosophy far different from his own. As though he was talking about his mother rather than his daughter, he said, "She's a deeply Christian woman who's outspoken against alcohol, smoking, drugs, and flamboyant dressing."

Although Jack Leary had had no real contact with his father in years, he attended the small private memorial service for his sister at Tim's house at which Tim, Dieadra, Paul Krassner, and others spoke. "The saddest I ever saw Tim was at the small memorial for his daughter at his house," recalled Joanne Segal, a family friend. "There was such a giant gap between him and his children. It was so huge that you couldn't even cross it with blame. Because even for blame, there has to be some sort of intimacy."

Among Timothy Leary's papers is a clipping from the *Los Angeles Times* with a headline that reads LEARY'S DAUGHTER DIES AFTER HANGING. At the bottom, he scrawled a final message: "Days of sorrow—miss you dear one. Timmy."

FORTY-SEVEN

In the wake of Susan's death, both Rosemary and Joanna got back in contact with Tim. Although Rosemary had not seen or spoken to him in more than fifteen years, she called from Cape Cod, where she was still living as a fugitive under an assumed name. She spoke to Barbara and left a number where Tim could reach her but he never called back.

A few months before Susan's death, Joanna had begun her own process of reconciliation with Tim by writing a classic twelve-step letter in which she asked him to forgive her for any wrong she might have done him "out of selfishness and ignorance when we were together." She told Tim that he had been the first person she had ever loved and that he had performed "the miraculous operation of opening my heart so that it has never needed to be shut again."

Joanna's life during the intervening years had continued to be chaotic. Declared an unfit mother by a court in San Diego, she had taken her young son to the Caribbean rather than give him up to the man who now claimed to be his father (and with whom she had also had sex on the day the child was conceived). Indicted for kidnapping, with her bail set at $60,000, Joanna agreed to give up the child in return for having all charges dropped and a shared custody agreement. Instead, the man claiming to be the boy's father "disappeared with the child, changed his name, and I didn't see my son again for twelve years. Consequently, I begged Tim, including the promise that I would sign papers that it would not cost him a penny, to please have a paternity test and acknowledge the child because then I could get him back. And he would not do it." Joanna moved to Santa Fe, New Mexico, and began getting sober in 1984. "I had no desire to connect with Tim," she remembered, "because the more pain I accumulated about not seeing my child, the more monstrous he became to me."

A month before Susan died, Tim answered Joanna's note with a letter that could have only been written by an alcoholic in a classic state of denial. "Yes, our relationship was amazing," he told her. "Very few people could understand the incredible friendship and loyalty we developed . . . Yes, you 'committed lots of mistakes' and yes, those events have caused me many 'problems.' But, looking back, at that time of political-social wierdness [sic], who went through more tests, who dealt with the Evil Police-Government powers with more nobility?" As though he had played no part in the process, Tim wrote, "Who did you hurt, in your wicked betrayals? Poor George Chula is the only one who could claim 'real' minor-trivial annoyance—and he understands, and has never complained to me. Your husband from San Diego? I saw him recently at an ABA meeting. He is fine and the wonderful son you gave him is doing well." Pointing out that his comments about her in *Flashbacks* had been loving, he noted, "I was a bit hurt when you never thanked me for them." He then added, "I rarely think about you—but when I do it is with pride and respect and affection."

Two weeks after Susan died, Joanna wrote, "I was deeply touched by the news of Susan's death. In my own way I loved her and felt a poignant sort of empathy with her. I was both angry and sad for several days about the pain some of us go through trying to make sense of our life through personal stories. My thoughts are with you in this moment . . ."

Still grieving for his daughter, Tim joined John Perry Barlow on a speaking tour in Europe. "Being the good Irish boy and a freewheeling agent of God knows what," Barlow said, "Tim went back and forth on Susan. There was so much love and denial of love in him. He viewed love as both a necessity and a weakness. It threatened him to be loved on some level. He was really the most complex, divided human being I've ever met. I knew the man who was in some weird way my master had failed the ultimate test. There I was out on the road with him being his foil with this terrible sense of 'You are the ultimate loser, pal.' "

When Tim returned to Los Angeles, he resumed his celebrity life but nothing was as it had been before. "Tim aged very rapidly the last couple of years we were together," Barbara recalled. "He went from looking like a very healthy older man to really looking like an old man. You can see it in all the photographs. Physically, his body went to pot and of course you could never tell Timothy anything like 'Let's eat or let's do a little exercise. How about a game of tennis?' No way. I would get him to eat on occasion but it was tough. He was living on cigarettes and alcohol and fat."

During the winter of 1992, Eric Gardner booked Tim on a lecture tour in Brazil. Barbara went with him and they stayed with one of the tour organizers in Rio. "They got on the plane," Gardner recalled, "and gleefully flew off to Rio and ensconced themselves in this guy's house and then Timothy went off to do his lectures, some of which were in Brasilia and São Paulo. Barbara stayed in Rio to do some shopping and lie on the beach and this and that. When he came back to Rio to get on the plane to America, Barbara announced she had fallen in love with this guy they were staying with and she wasn't coming back with him." Tim returned alone to Los Angeles. "I think it was devastating for him when she left," remembered Peggy Hitchcock, Tim's old friend and lover from Mill-brook. "Although when I talked to him, he said, 'Peggy, I knew this was going to happen. Because the age difference was so enormous and let's face it, she's a perfect rich man's wife and I'm not a rich man.'" Nonethe-less, Barbara would later say, "Timmy was so brilliant, romantic, and funny. He was, and always will be the love of my life."

With Barbara gone, Tim began reaching out once more to old friends like Jeff Scheftel. "All these new people came around," Scheftel recalled. "A younger group. Definitely a group that Barbara would not have toler-ated for more than five minutes. It seemed to be Timothy's fans. A lot of computer people were up there. He was going out to raves with Zach. He was hanging with Zach's generation in which Zach was becoming a mover and a shaker." Douglas Rushkoff confirmed that it did get "a little desperate after Barbara left. The ratio of real superstars like David Byrne and the movie-star people went down and became fewer in number com-pared to the sweet young struggling-artist people." For the first week or two after Barbara had left, Tim called Vicki Marshall every day when he got up in the morning. By the third week, she found herself calling him. "And the fourth week," she recalled, "I would call him to check in and he would say, 'What do you mean you're checking in? I've got a house full of people here. Bye.'"

Among those who joined the party that summer at Tim's house was RU Sirius (aka Ken Goffman), the editor of a magazine called *Mondo 2000* to which Tim had contributed several pieces that would be collected in his book *Chaos & Cyberculture*. "Right after I quit *Mondo 2000*," Sirius re-membered, "I had a band I called Mondo Vanilli and we went down to LA to run around and get our demo tapes to people. We hung out at Tim's house for a couple of weeks and it was not a good period for him. He basically opened his house to a house party and he was drinking a lot and getting high on anything that was coming around." One night, Sirius and his girlfriend accompanied Tim to a party at the home of Trent Reznor, the lead singer of Nine Inch Nails. "It was the place where Sharon Tate was killed," Sirius recalled. "A bunch of us took Ecstasy and headed up there. It was a great party."

On July 6, 1992, *People* magazine reported the news that "psychedelics guru Timothy Leary, 71, and his fourth wife, Barbara, a filmmaker, have separated after fourteen years of marriage. 'I wish her nothing but the best,' says Leary, who now earns his living as a 'stand-up philosopher' (his term) on the college lecture circuit and in comedy clubs." By the time the blurb appeared, Tim, as he had done so many times before in his life, had already moved on.

Pitching Tim Leary as a "flawed, tragic hero," Eric Gardner began shopping *Flashbacks* to the television networks as a miniseries. For a while, it seemed as though Brandon Tartikoff, head of programming at NBC, was really interested. Eventually, as Gardner recalled, Tartikoff said that after speaking to his sales people, there was no way that sponsors "are going to stand for what will be perceived of as a tacit advocacy of mind-altering drugs." Although Gardner pointed out that NBC had just aired the story of Ted Bundy without considering it "an advocacy of serial killing," NBC passed on the project. So did CBS, HBO, and Showtime. Gardner went to England where he shopped the project to all the ITV networks. "Nobody wanted it," Gardner recalled. He then tried to get it made "offshore" and "have it done as a negative pickup in America. I went to every single major television network in Europe and then I went to Japan. And I couldn't get it made."

After a year and a half, Gardner decided to reconceive the project as a feature film. For two years, nothing happened. Then Interscope Pictures expressed interest. "Ted Field and Robert Cort, who was his partner at the time," Gardner recalled, "got it immediately So we made a deal and signed it In November 1992, and then it took a year to find a writer. Development is a long process." When Bima Stagg, who wrote *Inside,* which had been directed by Arthur Penn, signed on to write the script, Gardner threw a celebratory dinner in his palatial home in the Los

Feliz section of LA. The guests included Ted Field and his girlfriend, Robert Cort, Bima Stagg, her manager, and Scott Kroopf, president of production at Interscope.

"At the beginning," Gardner recalled, "Timothy viewed even Ted Field with great suspicion because he felt his story was going to get Hollywood-ized. Even though for the first time in his life he had the chance to make big money and have his story recorded in a permanent way in pop culture via a feature film and he was also going to be hired as a consultant on the movie, he was still very suspicious at the beginning of the dinner." While Gardner knew Ted Field to be a great liberal, he had had only a few meetings with Bob Cort and did not know him nearly as well. "Timothy and Bob started arguing," Gardner remembered. "Not intensely but they had a couple of disagreements and it turned out that prior to being in the entertainment business, Cort was a field operative for the CIA. When Timothy found that out, he literally got up and embraced Bob and said, 'That's incredible! You were in the CIA! I can't believe it.' And that led into a really great hour or hour and a half on the CIA and LSD and Timothy's downfall at Harvard."

With his story apparently finally headed for the silver screen, Tim tried to create a happy ending for his own life. In December 1992, through her old friend, former Berkeley radical Super Joel, Rosemary arranged to see Tim again. Because she feared that Tim might still turn her in and she could not afford to be seen with him in a place where they might be recognized, they met at the Asian Art Museum in Golden Gate Park in San Francisco. She recalled, "It was twenty years to the day since I'd left him in Switzerland. He was sick and very much aware that his short-term memory was fading. Both of us were so physically altered as to be unrecognizable as who we had once been. But as always when we got together after an escape or when he had gotten out of jail, it was a movie. In Vista-Vision and Technicolor. Wide screen. Tim was so good at creating drama and he so loved to play and was so brilliant at it. He asked me to marry him again that day. I said to him, 'You've never lived with a wife who was menopausal.' And he said, 'Well, they've all left me before then.' I said no. And he said, 'Well then, I'll have to cross you off my list.'"

On March 30, 1994, *The New York Times* reported that a superior court judge in Orange County, California, had dismissed the six-month sentence imposed in 1970 on Rosemary for possession of marijuana. Having lived under an assumed name for twenty-three years, Rosemary was now free to resume some semblance of a normal life. Her aging mother's illness had persuaded Rosemary that, in her words, "It was a time to put an end to all this. I no longer wanted to live with my passport under my pillow, my shoes by the bed, planning escape routes."

With Rosemary off his list, Tim began surrounding himself with good-looking young women, most of whom had not even been born when he had been at the height of his fame. Leslie Meyers was twenty-five and living across the hall from Jerry Rubin in Brentwood when she first met Tim. Rubin, who had just separated from his wife, asked Meyers to put together a party for which he offered to pay. "I had no idea who Jerry was," Meyers recalled. "I thought he was a little Jewish dentist from New York until I went to his apartment and saw all these books with his name on them." Meyers invited Rubin's old friend Anita Hoffman to a party in Rubin's two-bedroom apartment that was attended by three hundred people. Anita brought Tim, who promptly invited Leslie to the party he held every Sunday at his house. The next morning, Rubin called her to ask if he could go with her. Meyers, who was too young to know that Rubin had publicly denounced Tim as a brainwashed traitor, told him, "Jerry, he's *your* friend. Of course you can come."

On the night of Tim's seventy-second birthday in 1993, Meyers took him and his young granddaughter Sarah to Babylon, a restaurant in LA where they were joined by the actor Gary Busey and his girlfriend. Before the meal arrived, Busey left the table to work the room. Tim got up as well. An hour and a half later, Tim and Busey were still walking around the restaurant talking to people they knew. After the meal, Tim told Meyers that there was a Smashing Pumpkins concert at the Palladium to which he really wanted to go. Although Meyers had never heard of the band, she drove Tim there. When someone asked if she had seen Dr. Leary, an "old guy with white hair," Meyers replied, "'He's over there.' In the middle of the mosh pit with all these eighteen-year-olds with no shirt on, Timothy was dancing. It was hilarious. He was having the best time. I thought he was going to get killed. This was like a year and a half before anyone knew who the Smashing Pumpkins were. It was just so Timothy. He was in on everything.

When a band from New York named Helmet opened for Ministry at the Universal Amphitheater in May 1993, Lindsay Brice met Tim backstage. He invited her to a party at his house the next night. When she got there, he asked her, "What do you think of the people here?" When Brice told him they all seemed like good people to her, Tim responded, "I haven't known any of them for more than six months." "These were the Viper Room days," Douglas Rushkoff remembered, referring to the club on the Sunset Strip where the actor River Phoenix died of a drug over- dose on October 31, 1993. "Tim's money was dwindling and he was drinking a lot. I guess you'd call him an alcoholic but even when he was in this heavy drinking phase, there were three to four hours a day when he was the really great lucid fun Tim."

Lindsay Brice and Tim often went to the Viper Room together. Most of their evenings began with her coming up to the house before sunset. Sitting on the patio at Tim's round picnic table, they would have drinks. "I would usually show up with a wedge of brie," she recalled, "and he would always have wine and there would usually be some really bright in- teresting people there. We would have a drink and watch the sun go down and then he would change clothes and off we would go." One night, Tim took her to actor Roddy McDowall's house for dinner. "We went to an art opening first," she remembered, "and we didn't have exact directions and we were late and that was terrible. Stephanie Powers was seated next to Tim and it was a beautiful English dinner party with place cards, the table beautifully set, and two people serving. We had missed cocktails and they were waiting for us to sit down to eat. Stephanie Pow- ers began talking about Kenya and Timothy said something about the Masai and tribal behavior and she told him he was wrong. Then Timothy said, 'I have a joke. A terrible horrible joke. What's the difference between a vagina and a cunt? A vagina is this wonderful warm delicious fabulous thing and the cunt is the thing that has one.'"

A moment later, Tim got to his feet, came around the table, and whis- pered, "Let's get out of here" in Brice's ear. They went to the Three of Clubs, an unmarked Hollywood bar packed with young hipster guys in plaid with goatees, definitely an indie-film crowd. When the two of them walked in, Brice recalled, "It was like the Red Sea parted for Tim to walk straight through to the bar and two seats magically became available and we sat down and Timothy ordered vodka." Later that night, at a coffee house called Insomnia, Tim looked at an exhibition of her photographs. When he learned that her father was dead, he said to Brice, "Your father would be proud of you, wouldn't he? Oh yes." Then he said, "You have me now. I'll be your godfather. I'll host a reception for this show. Let's send out invitations. We'll use my mailing list." Using the phrase "Timothy Leary cordially invites you" a thousand were sent out. The event was attended by a couple of hundred people.

In August 1993, Brice drove Tim, Dieadra, and Tim's granddaughter Sarah to the Los Angeles show on the second annual Lollapalooza tour, featuring Seattle grunge stalwarts Alice In Chains, heavy metal rockers Dinosaur Jr., and Rage Against The Machine. "It was out at some dam in the desert," Brice recalled, "and they had created roads in the sand and Timothy was going to be onstage announcing the bands. I had Dieadra and Sarah in the car. Sarah was eight or nine and Dieadra was pregnant and I had this seventy-year-old man next to me and I was driving fast in my '89 Mustang on this sandy road and I spun out and I sank down in my seat like, 'Oh my God, I'm going to get it now,' and Timothy said, 'Wow! That was fabulous! What spirit.' It was like he was on a Disneyland ride. Then he said, 'Look at the way the light's hitting your knee! That's *fabulous!*' I realized later that he was tripping."

Although Tim had been backstage at the Forum with basketball player and lifelong Deadhead Bill Walton and Tim's stepson, Zach, to see the Grateful Dead, the crowd assembled for this show was a far cry from the blissed-out, newly spawned flower children who followed the Dead. Onstage, Tim spread his arms out wide and announced, "Wow! It's Woodstock! Look, there's Jimi Hendrix!" Brice remembered, "He did this stoner persona. This silly, spaced-out act. The truth was that he was a much sharper, smarter person but he was giving the public what he thought they wanted. I don't think people really got it."

Tim then traveled to six shows on the West Coast leg of the tour, lecturing in one of the festival's tents while Camella Grace, her boyfriend Chris Graves, and his brother Joey Cavella, who had founded a company called RetinaLogic, provided the background visuals. The young media wizards from RetinaLogic soon became regulars at Tim's house, where on any given Sunday the guest list now included Johnny Depp, Winona Ryder, Tom Robbins, and Earl McGrath, the former head of Rolling Stone Records who had become an influential art collector and gallery owner. "You never knew who would be there," Brice recalled "No one had any ego or attitude because Tim was the man. It was like a bunch of cousins getting to know one another. This was granddad's house and we were all cousins and we could hang out. It was congenial and nonthreatening."

Benign as the scene might seem in Tim Leary's house on a Sunday afternoon, the social pace he had been keeping for the previous year would have seriously challenged a man half his age. "I would usually take him home at around two in the morning," Brice remembered, "and then he would stay up all night and work. He liked that. He also did not eat properly. He couldn't be bothered and I think he did a lot of coke to keep his energy up and it made him nuts at times. Out of control. Temper outbursts."

At Christmas, always the worst time of the year for him, Tim finally broke down physically. "He was doing a lot of coke and could not sleep," Vicki Marshall recalled. "He got a prescription for Dalmane from a doctor who loved him and he went through twenty of them in three days. His attorney called him at home and didn't like what he was hearing and when he saw him, he said, 'I'm taking you to the hospital now.'" Severely dehydrated and suffering from pneumonia, Tim was admitted to Cedars-Sinai Hospital. "He was in very bad shape," George Milman recalled. "On the verge of death."

For two days, Tim ran a very high fever. When Leslie Meyers came to visit him, he was being examined by a neurologist brought in by Milman. "Dr. Leary," the neurologist asked, "do you know what day it is?" Tim just looked at him. The neurologist asked another question. "Dr. Leary, do you know where you are? Can you tell me your home address?" Tim stared at him. Finally, he replied, "Do you know who I am? Do you know how many books on neuropsychology I have written? I was a professor at Harvard." On and on and on he went, reciting his entire résumé. Then he said, "So let me tell you something, Doctor. I'm senile and I love it!" "I was on the floor," Meyers recalled. "It was just a scream."

When Vicki Marshall and her husband, Ron, visited Tim in the hospital, she wondered if this would be the last time she would see him. "He was suspicious and paranoid," she remembered, "and he asked us to go to his house and clean up some stuff because he had left pills and drugs around. He also wanted us to bring him sleeping pills because they weren't giving him anything in the hospital. We brought him a couple and then the neurologist came in and started asking him questions and Timmy was toying with him." "Ever have trouble sleeping?" the neurologist asked. "Nah," Tim said. "Ever take any sleep aids?" "Nah." "Any over-the-counter remedies?" "Nah." "How about Dalmane?" Vicki Marshall recalled, "That was exactly what Tim had us bring him and he said, 'Nah.' That was when we realized that we were dealing with something else here. They hadn't pumped Tim's stomach when he came in but a friend of ours who worked in a hospital said, "They're measuring every-thing that comes in and goes out. They're not stupid. They know.'"

Back in their apartment, Ron and Vicki looked up Dalmane in the *Physician's Desk Reference*. "When I read the description of a Dalmane overdose in older people," Vicki recalled, "it was word for word what Tim was experiencing. Especially in older people, an overdose could mimic the symptoms of pneumonia because the person could throw up and then inhale it back into their lungs." When her husband said to Tim, "If you want out of this experience consciously, that's cool. If this is gonna be an unconscious trip, I want off the boat," Tim said, "Well, I don't want out of here."

To those who knew him best, Tim never seemed the same after he came out of the hospital. "He was bored," Vicki recalled, "and I think he was getting ready to go." For the first time in his life, Tim's indiscriminate drug use had caused real damage to the incredible machine that had sus-tained him for so long. Although the long joy ride he had taken through the dry hills above Los Angeles was not yet over, he was now headed in a different direction.

FORTY-EIGHT

Even before Tim Leary had been admitted to the hospital, some of his friends had begun to worry that he could no longer take care of himself. Tony Scott, the British-born director of *Top Gun*, had hired a very capable woman named Denis Berry, the founder of a company called Dial-A-Wife that provided housekeeping services for those too rich and busy to be bothered with the ordinary details of everyday life in LA, to do Tim's shopping and run his errands. After he came out of the hospital, Berry moved in with him. She soon became his social companion as well.

As the two of them were dancing one night in the Viper Room, Berry recalled, "I did this spin and there was this woman wrapped around his neck and it was Aileen Getty." Aileen Getty was the granddaughter of billionaire John Paul Getty, who when he died in 1976 was one of the richest men in the world. She was the daughter of John Paul Getty Jr., whose close personal friends included Mick Jagger and Claus von Bulow. In 1973, her sixteen-year-old brother, John Paul Getty III, had been kidnapped on the streets of Rome and had his ear cut off before being released five months later in return for a ransom of nearly $3,500,000. He then suffered a disabling stroke and had to be carried into clubs where Tim was a regular patron. At eighteen, Aileen Getty had married Christopher Wilding, the son of Elizabeth Taylor and Michael Wilding, by whom she had two sons. In 1985, she was diagnosed as being HIV-positive. "I contracted HIV through unsafe sex when I was married," Getty recalled. Going public with her disease, she lectured widely on the subject and became a member of the board of the American Foundation for AIDS Research. She also used heroin with her young nephew, the actor Balthazar Getty. After an overdose during which she nearly drowned in her bathtub, she remained in a coma for twenty-four hours and was then on life support for five days before recovering. Aileen Getty was thirty-five when she met Tim and had only recently gotten sober. Her first impression of him was how sick he looked. "I thought, 'God, I wonder if he is going to die.' As we went to leave, I asked him how long he thought he had to live. He said about five years and then he asked me the same question. We were pretty much inseparable from that time onward."

On January 17, the Northridge earthquake struck Los Angeles. After barely escaping from her own house, Getty and her two sons moved in with Tim on Sunbrook Drive for a while. On May 10, Tim and Aileen flew to Austin, Texas, where he delivered a lecture on "How to Operate Your Brain." Without having said a word to Aileen about it beforehand, Tim announced their engagement from the stage. Standing next to Al Jourgensen, lead singer of the rock band Ministry at the time, she recalled, "It was the first I'd heard of it. I just grabbed Al's hand and held it tighter and tighter. Then I went and gave Tim a hug and kind of a slap at the same time. Like, you motherfucker, why here?"

Tim made national news during his visit to Texas by getting himself arrested in Austin's Robert Mueller Airport for lighting up a cigarette in the baggage-claim area. "Tim thought smoking in public was going to be the next big one," Douglas Rushkoff recalled. "When he got busted in Austin, he thought it would launch a big thing and the cigarette companies would give him free cigarettes for life. For him, it was all about personal freedom and how totalitarian the society had gotten." Before Tim could be arrested, however, he had to find a policeman. As he would later say, "You can never fucking get busted when you want to!" Searching the airport, Tim located a young cop. Politely, the cop told Tim that if he wanted to smoke, he should just go outside the terminal. While Joey Cavella videotaped the proceedings, Tim lit up to call attention to what he called the "demonization" of smokers. He was detained for an hour in the airport jail. A court hearing was set for May 18, where he faced a $500 fine. Fortunately, the airport police did not search Aileen. "I was carrying coke and I can carry marijuana legally," she recalled. "It was my first arrest and his fiftieth and that night, they ran it on CNN that we got arrested and engaged the same night. It was really great."

"Aileen was so far out and had no rules," Leslie Meyers remembered. "She would do anything, even beyond what Timothy would do, and he found that fun. She wanted to marry him as a joke." Many of those who were close to Tim felt that he and Aileen were merely using each other for publicity. Nonetheless, they wrote out a series of phrases like "Timmy, you are all mine," "I love you to pieces," and "Mrs. Leary, XOX" in what Aileen called their "marriage contract" on the white headboard of Tim's bed. "Timmy kept telling me that she wanted him to marry her," Barbara Leary recalled. "And then he told me he couldn't deal with her anymore. I guess maybe she wanted to be the widow Leary." "She wanted them to die together," Denis Berry remembered. "I later realized it was just kind of foolish talk."

When Tim suffered another bout of pneumonia at the end of 1994, George Milman took him back to Cedars-Sinai Hospital where they gave him a blood test for prostate cancer and discovered that his PSA level was elevated. "They either didn't do the PSA test the first time he was there or they might have told him about it and he ignored it," Milman recalled. "I don't know which. We don't know how long he might have been suffering from it." Graphic evidence that Tim had been living with the disease for some time can be found in photographs taken by Lisa Law, a former member of the Hog Farm commune in New Mexico who directed the documentary *Flashing on the Sixties*. In May 1993, Tim looked old, weathered, and worn but still able to project the undeniable charisma of a star in a brightly colored psychedelic shirt and blue jeans. Nine months later, sporting a brand-new goatee with his hair clipped very short, a gaunt Tim Leary stared into Law's camera. His eyes had sunk so deeply into his face that his nose looked swollen and protuberant. His ears stuck out like those of some ancient Irish elf, a psychedelic gremlin. In less than a year he had aged more than a decade.

Tim, a lifelong baseball fan, had become friendly with John Roseboro, the soft-spoken former catcher for both the Brooklyn and Los Angeles Dodgers. "We both had prostate cancer," Roseboro recalled. "I caught mine early and had it removed. I used to take him to the doctor in Beverly Hills and we were looking at charts and trying to find out what he should do. We discussed the pros and cons of getting rid of the prostate or taking the radiation treatment. He must have already had it for a pretty long time by then because his prostate was inundated to the point where there wasn't much they could do about it. He knew he didn't have too many choices."

Bob Guccione Jr., the publisher of *Spin* magazine, had only known Tim for six months but had already become what he called "a de facto son" to him. While having lunch with Tim at the Bel Air Hotel on January 14, 1995, he noticed that Tim looked a little distracted. "I found out yesterday that I have prostate cancer," Tim told him sadly. Guccione replied, "Oh my God, at least if you catch it early enough, that's okay." "I haven't been to a doctor in years and I finally went and he said it was inoperable," Tim said. Guccione recalled, "I immediately went into denial. He looked great and was not in pain but he wasn't happy about it."

When she heard the news, Rosemary visited Tim in Los Angeles. Although she did not like LA or "the scene at the house," she began doing all she could to help arrange a reconciliation between Tim and his son. "That Jack was a loving father and a good husband somehow paled in Tim's eyes beside the working-class life that he had made for himself. Richard Alpert and I set up a meeting for Jack and Tim, but Tim never showed up. He was just so terribly scared. Then we got him to write Jackie a letter. I helped him quite a bit on it, suggesting he just beg Jack's forgiveness and throw himself at his feet, if need be."

Dated April 12, 1995, the letter began:

> Dearest Jack, Dearest Son, Beautiful Boy, Loving Father . . . I have been sad about our separation and lack of communication. I've hesitated to contact you because I feared your anger and what I felt to be—your contempt. Now I ask you to forgive me for whatever wrongs you feel I have done to you. I am painfully aware that there have been many times I've failed you as a father. And as a friend. My deepest sorrow has been that we could not grieve together after Susan's tragic death . . . Now, is the time—for me, at least—to contact you and ask you to meet so we can talk about important things . . .

Knowing that Guccione had not spoken to his own famous father, the founder and publisher of *Penthouse,* for ten years, Tim showed him a copy of the letter. "There was definitely that wish to reconcile," Guccione recalled. "He gave me a copy of the letter, I think to show me the way to my own reconciliation with my father."

Even as Tim was trying to set his life in order, he remained fixated on the movie based on his life, for he now knew it would be his final legacy to the world. On April 17, 1995, five days after writing to Jack, Tim sent an entirely different kind of letter to Ted Field, the man at Interscope to whom he had entrusted making *Flashbacks* into a feature film. "Dear Ted

Fields," he wrote, misspelling his name before asking if Field was aware of "intricate complex legalities, the scores of legal documents, the comical jibbering which has been exchanged between your 'agents' and my 'agents.' The demands for 'rights'; the obsessively driven lawyering. I am embarrassed that you and I have to be victimized and our friendly collaboration de-humanized by people whom we pay!" Tim wrote that he now fervently wished that "there be no commercial film of FLASH-BACKS," but conceded that as a public figure, he could not stop anyone from making films or writing biographies. "But, let me repeat, I do not want this film made. I just don't want to go along with a system that is notoriously, comically dehumanizing. To me, and, perhaps, to you." Inviting Field to spend "a few pleasant hours discussing the ideas and values in his book," Tim added, "If you have no interest in chatting about our viewpoints about the times and places we have shared . . . well, fuck you." He included his phone and fax numbers and ended the letter "With fond respect from, Timothy Leary."

As always when Tim took the high ground and began fighting on principle, money was involved. Tim had been promised $25,000 to act as a consultant for the film but knew he would not be paid until the project was green-lighted for production. When Eric Gardner had acquired the rights to the book in 1990, he did not pay Tim for the option but rather chose to forgive all the money Tim owed him in unpaid commissions. When Interscope purchased the book and Tim's life rights in 1992, they paid Gardner an option price that still did not equal what Tim owed him. Now that Tim knew he was ill, he began getting, "even for Timothy, a little wacky," Gardner recalled. "We had a series of about twenty phone calls in which he said he wanted to renegotiate our deal. He thought it was unfair I had gotten option money from Interscope and he hadn't gotten any." Out of what he called "reverence and my love for Timothy," Gardner had made all these payments applicable against his own producer's fees, thereby guaranteeing Tim a far bigger payday if the film was made. For hours on end, Gardner listened on the phone as Tim complained about their arrangement. Finally, Gardner agreed to modify the deal. "I guess he knew he was dying," Gardner recalled, "and he didn't care about his estate because he knew all the money that would come into it was going to pay all the taxes he had never paid in his life. There were liens against him in California and New York dating back to 1967."

After Bima Stagg turned in a script that, in Gardner's words, was "clinical, almost an extract of Tim's life," Gardner brought in Randall Johnson, who had written the "brilliant first draft of *The Doors* movie before Oliver Stone bastardized it," to bring more emotion and "interpersonal relations" into the story. A year after Tim's death, Randall Johnson began writing his fourth draft of the script.

Long before Tim ever brought *Flashbacks* to Gardner, Tim's friend Jeff Scheftel had approached him with the idea of making the book into a movie. "Sure, go ahead," Tim had told him. "But they'll never make it while I'm still alive." Scheftel and his partner, Tom Huckabee, sold the project to a small company called RiverRun Productions. "They had worked with Propaganda Films and were major producers of commercials and they allowed Tom and me to write the screenplay together. The year ended and we completed the draft and RiverRun renewed the option. Tim was now making enough money to pay the rapidly increasing bills that came with his new residence and also to take care of some of his debts. He was thrilled." Once Gardner took over the project, Tim told Scheftel that he and Huckabee would still be writing and co-producing the film "because this was your idea." "Gardner would never return my calls," Scheftel recalled. "It was an awkward situation because we only had Timothy's word and he and Barbara had struck another deal with Eric Gardner, to whom they owed money." Eventually, Gardner let his option on *Flashbacks* expire.

To date, no film about Tim's life has yet been made. There are, however, at least three competing projects based on the life of Timothy Leary currently in development. George DiCaprio, at whose wedding Tim presided, hired Michael Horowitz to act as a consultant for a movie based on Tim's life, which would star DiCaprio's son, Leonardo. Darren Aronofsky, who directed *Pi, Requiem for a Dream,* and *The Fountain,* acquired the rights to *Flashbacks* from Timothy Leary's estate to serve as the basis for a script, which is currently in development. Bringing it all full circle, Eric Gardner announced that he would produce a cable television movie based on Tim's life directed by Andy Fickman, who made *Reefer Madness: The Movie Musical* for the Showtime network. As they say in Hollywood, the beat goes on.

Lindsay Brice was staying at Tim's house on August 9, 1995 when a *Washington Post* reporter called to ask Tim for a quote. Grateful Dead lead

guitarist and counterculture icon Jerry Garcia had died in his sleep in
Serenity Knolls, a drug rehab center in Marin County. "That was the first
time I ever saw Timothy cry," Brice recalled. "He was already ill and he
had just gone to an opening of blotter-acid art in San Francisco. A couple
of days after Jerry died, Tim was up watching television at two in the
morning. I went to bed and I could hear him in the next room saying in
kind of a quiet wail, 'Oh God, oh God, oh God.'"

A few weeks later, Tim went public with the news of his impending
death in an article by David Colker entitled "Terminal Man" that appeared in the *Los Angeles Times* on August 28. "How you die is the most
important thing you ever do . . . It's the exit, the final scene of the glorious epic of your life. It's the third act, and you know, everything builds up
to the third act. I've been waiting for this for years." Chain-smoking Ben-
son & Hedges cigarettes as he talked, Tim admitted he had "certain fears
of losing my dignity . . . Having to be diapered, losing whatever is left of
my mental agility. I'm tremendously frightened." Although Tim said he
wanted to die at home with his friends around him, he remained "undecided on many of the details." On one wrist, Tim wore "a metal bracelet
with the name and phone number of a firm specializing in cryonics. On
the other is a bracelet with the name and number of a rival cryonics
firm." Tim said it was "a real possibility" he would take a dose of LSD before he died—"but that too is undecided. I like options . . . You're only as
young as the last time you changed your mind."

On Labor Day weekend, Tim left Los Angeles for what would be his
last extended road trip. With his friend Michael Segal, he went to the Pig-
Nic, the annual rock 'n' roll gathering held by Wavy Gravy and Ken
Kesey and his Merry Pranksters at the Black Oak Ranch in Mendocino,
California. Looking sick and wan and withered, Tim was followed by
camera crews who recorded everything he did for posterity. Holding two
microphones in his wrinkled, liver-spotted hands, Tim stood atop the famous psychedelic bus that Kesey had parked outside the mansion at Millbrook thirty years earlier and told a crowd of tie-dyed, dreadlocked baby
Deadheads that he was not dead. No, no, no. As the Moody Blues had
once sung, he was on the outside looking in and living every day as
though it was his last. Kesey then "canonized" Tim as a psychedelic saint
by firing a three-foot-long cannon in his honor. Draping a cape over
Tim's shoulders, Kesey, now a bear of a man in a white hat and red polo
shirt, placed a wizard's hat on Tim's head and handed him a wand. As

one, all the young hippies for whom this was history in the making began to cheer.

Timothy Leary celebrated his seventy-fifth birthday at home on Saturday night, October 21, 1995. "They had this huge party at the house which was insane," Leslie Meyers recalled. "It must have gone out over the Internet because there were at least eight hundred people up there." When Meyers reached the top of Tim's road, valet parkers told her that they had been full for the past three hours. Meyers got past them by saying she was "Dr. Leary's daughter." She parked behind the catering truck and went to Tim's front door only to discover a huge bouncer guarding it with fifty people waiting to get inside. Repeating the lie that she was Tim's daughter, Meyers walked right past him. "Inside the house," she remembered, "it was insanity. You literally couldn't move. All night long, people were walking up to me asking if I could get other people in. 'I know he's a friend of your dad,' they kept saying." Stars like Tony Curtis, Liza Minelli, and Trent Reznor had turned out to honor Tim. "That was a bash," Douglas Rushkoff recalled. "The great party of parties in Tim's final phase." Those who had known Tim in a previous incarnation were horrified. "It was really depressing," Alan U. Schwartz remembered, "A public spectacle. There were people coming up the driveway who had never met Timothy Leary in their lives but they were going to this party. Hundreds and hundreds of people. Take a snapshot of that and compare it to an intimate dinner with Helmut and June Newton and my wife and I. The quantum leaps of what happens in a life are evident."

On November 1, Denis Berry moved out of Tim's house to return to Santa Cruz. Her departure caused a seismic change in his life. "My leaving destabilized the house," Berry recalled. "I wouldn't have allowed the circus to go on and Tim might not have needed it." Tim added to the chaos by firing Siobhan Cyr, who along with Vicki Marshall had been helping to manage his affairs. Without Berry and Cyr around, the circus kicked into a higher gear. Like a great king throwing open the front gates of his court, Tim began receiving an endless succession of former associates, friends, and lovers, all of whom felt the need to pay their respects. Allen Ginsberg, Ram Dass, William Burroughs, Oscar Janiger, Laura Huxley, and Robert and Nena Thurman all came to visit him. Camella Grace, who had been living in New York with Sean Lennon, flew back to Los Angeles on a ticket Tim had bought for her so she could join Chris Graves and Joey Cavella.

By February 1996, the three of them had moved into Tim's house so they could record his dying with Hi-8 video cameras, scan documents from his archive into digital form, and construct and update Tim's Web site so that people could monitor his condition on a daily basis. The team posed with Tim for photographs taken by Lisa Law. Tim looked gaunt, grizzled, and unshaven, his face a sunken landscape in which his eyes seemed like two dark holes. His long uncombed straggly hair stuck out from his head like a fright wig. Like a child at a costume party, Tim would often walk around the house in a red Chicago Blackhawks ice-hockey jersey with black-and-white trim, the head of a Indian chief on the front, "69" prominently displayed on the back and the sleeves, a pair of oversize eyeglasses perched on the bridge of his nose, and a huge red-and-black mad hatter's top hat.

"After Tim announced his terminal condition," Vicki Marshall recalled, "he was just deluged with offers. Everyone wanted an interview. Everyone wanted to shoot a documentary. He could not go out and speak anymore. He could not write anymore. But he had a real high overhead. Like five grand a month with phones and utilities and a staff to pay. I wanted to make sure that if someone was going to do a documentary, it wasn't going to be about Tim getting thrown out of his house because he couldn't pay the rent. So it was, 'Okay, how much are you offering?' We had to treat it like a business." Canadian filmmaker Paul Davids was the first to begin shooting a documentary. CBS News wanted to do something but would not pay Tim for his time. ABC made an overture. Marshall negotiated with the BBC. "Someone," she remembered, "wanted to give the staff cameras and have us shoot it. I said, 'Oh, now we're going to be working for you guys? No way.'" By this point, Tim had already written what seemed to Douglas Rushkoff like the outline for a book called *Design for Dying*. "I took it to be a proposal," Rushkoff recalled, "and Tim said, 'That's the whole thing. It's done.' It was a hundred-page outline. It wasn't a book." Zach Leary suggested to Rushkoff that they bring in a writer named David Prince to, as Rushkoff remembered, help "expand and flesh out the outline so I could go and make the deal." Eventually, Rushkoff sold the book to HarperCollins for $75,000.

"There was no way to monitor all the deathbed deals," George Milman recalled. "There came a point when I said, 'Timothy, just leave me out of it because it's too aggravating.' Documentaries and a book and electronic rights with RetinaLogic and some other group. Tim wanted to get out of this deal and into that deal. They would give him a paper and he would sign it. A part of me would like to think this was almost a conscious way of mixing things up and showing people how ridiculous and superficial all these deals and contracts were." Trudy Truelove, who had worked as a promoter and booker in Hollywood at a punk club named Sellout, was hired, in her words, "to go up there to Tim's house every day between nine and ten, wake Tim up, give him his coffee, make sure he was okay, get him in the shower, get him dressed, do all his scheduling, answer the phones, and actually book the interviews." Media outlets like the *Los Angeles Times* were never charged, but magazines like *High Times* paid Tim $1,000 an hour for his time. "Tim was so sick and I really wanted to book him as little as possible," Truelove remembered. "But he wanted to continue. He was very adamant about working. He didn't want to be dead weight. It made him feel alive and useful to do interviews." In assembly-line fashion, camera crews from *48 Hours* and *Entertainment Tonight* awaited their turn as Tim talked to a reporter from *People* magazine. "I finally had to stop booking him because he was killing himself," Truelove recalled.

On November 26, 1995, the Sunday *New York Times* ran a long piece on what Tim called "designer dying" accompanied by a photograph of him sitting on the edge of his bed in a psychedelic swirling black-and-white jacket pointing his finger at the camera. "I would say to everybody, do not let the priests and popes and medics tell you what to do." A front-page article in the San Jose *Mercury News* on February 27 detailed Tim's transformation from "1960s drug guru" into "1990s cyberspace geek." In March, *New York* magazine reported that Danny Goldberg, president of Mercury Records, would be releasing a soundtrack CD to accompany a documentary entitled *Timothy Leary Lives*, which was being made by David Silver. Internet users could now log on to Tim's Web site to learn what he had ingested during the previous twenty-four hours. A sample from January read, "3 cups of coffee, 36 cigarettes, 4 glasses of champagne, 1 midnight Brownie, 12 balloons of nitrous oxide, 3 lines of cocaine . . ." In the documentary *Timothy Leary Lives*, Tim sat in bed while being interviewed. By now, his prostate cancer had metastasized into his bones. Sick and thin with his hair uncombed, Tim looked like a deranged homeless person. Sucking on a balloon of nitrous oxide, he said, "I find pain to be extremely interesting. The funny thing about pain is that there is no pleasure as great as when the pain stops."

On February 18, an art dealer brought photographer Dean Chamberlain to Tim's house for the Sunday gathering. Chamberlain proposed doing a portrait of Tim which would takes weeks to set up. Chamberlain worked by opening the shutter of his camera in total darkness and then moving around the room with a flashlight to illuminate specific areas, changing the gels for each new color zone. By doing so, he created a photograph that resembled a painting. When Chamberlain finally shot the photograph on March 5, Tim could no longer walk and was using a wheelchair. Chamberlain sold thirty-five prints for $1,000 each, all of which he gave to Tim. "Suddenly," Chamberlain recalled, "because I had made all this money, I was going to be the hired gun. The product guy. Tim said, 'What are we gonna do now?' I said, 'Tim, I just want to sit here and hang out with you and love you and be with you.' I had to come up with something. So I set up a proper drawing paper in the bedroom and I would sit down and we would do drawings."

With all the traffic in and out of the house, it had become impossible to monitor what visitors were bringing Tim for his pain. "Oscar Janiger brought the first tank of nitrous into the house in December 1995," Vicki Marshall recalled, "and afterward we would get it filled at an automotive supply house. It's actually used for combustion in racing cars. It wasn't very long lasting. You had to have a balloon in your mouth all the time for it to work for pain." By the time Tim sucked on his last balloon, he had gone through eight hundred pounds of nitrous oxide, more than enough to fuel several racing cars. Ironically, Tim's final drug of choice was the pain-killing gas he may have first sampled in his father's dental office in Springfield, Massachusetts, nearly sixty years earlier. He was also taking whatever else he was offered. Lindsay Brice was at the house one night when Tim did heroin. "Did you see me last night?" he asked her the next day. When she said yes, he asked, "Did it frighten you?" "It did because I was afraid you would fall and hit your head or break your hip and the last thing you want is to live out this illness in a wheelchair."

A visitor to the house on March 12 put a morphine patch left over from his mother's bout with cancer on Tim. When Vicki Marshall came to the house the next morning, she found Tim slumped over in bed with a hospice nurse ministering to him. "Tim seriously ODed," Marshall recalled. "Because nobody had taken into consideration that he was already on medication. The hospice nurse said to me, 'It's a good thing his body is not drug-naïve. This patch would have killed anybody else.' We took the patch off him and she threw out all the medications and he was real pissed she had done that." On March 18, the nurse had Tim's pain medication changed. "The hospice people took over his medical care," she remembered, "and they put him on liquid morphine, which was long acting. He started showing off to the kids in the house. He would say, 'Look, I'm going to do morphine,' and squirt some down his throat. He was an absolute child about it." Two days later, Tim fired the hospice nurse because she had found "some morphine he had scored without telling her" and flushed it down the toilet. "Finally," Marshall recalled, "Tim realized he was being a little irrational and he brought her back in." Someone else gave him thirty Dilaudid pills. Only after the hospice people put their own fentanyl patch on Tim did he, as Marshall put it, stop "asking every junkie who came to the house for medication."

All the while, what was surely the strangest Irish wake in history continued. As always, Tim was the ringmaster. "All these Web site kids were there and there was a real cult of Tim going," Rushkoff recalled. "Dean Chamberlain and his wife, Stacy, came in and became true devotees. It was like an ashram. A pop ashram. It got devotional but it was also a professional salon. People would come in and look at the calendar to see who was going to be there when. 'Oh my God. Oliver Stone on Sunday at two. William Burroughs.'" After a life spent preaching to the youth of America, Tim was now being cared for by people who were fifty years younger than him. None were his blood relatives. In accordance with his wishes, everyone went right on partying in a manner that not even his impending death could stop. Two or three times a week, Tim showed up at the Viper Room, usually accompanied by Chris Graves, Camella Grace, or David Prince. "All of a sudden," Mike Vague, who worked there as a deejay, recalled, "the back door would fly open. They'd clear a path and they would be pushing Timothy Leary in a wheelchair and all these people would be nudging one another, saying 'That's Timothy Leary!' Everyone knew this was probably the last time they would see him." Rushkoff, now commuting to the house each week from Palm Springs where he was working on a novel, remembered, "The kids from RetinaLogic were scanning in documents from the archives for Tim's Web site. I would leave on Monday and come back on Friday and they were one document farther down the pile. Life at Tim's was a Viper Room party."

When Denis Berry returned from Santa Cruz in March to visit Tim, she was "aghast at what was going on. I knew he needed to do this, but I couldn't take the confusion. The chaos. I was the one who had gotten his will signed before I moved to Santa Cruz. When I got back, he had changed it thirty-five times." To make certain Tim's earthly possessions would be left in good hands, Denis Berry and Tony Scott's wife, Donna, took Tim in his wheelchair to see his lawyer. "I wouldn't have been comfortable doing it after this point in time," Berry recalled, "because he was too confused. Through all those months, there were certain people and certain things in the will he never changed. His grandchildren were always in the will. Rosemary was always in the will. Zach was not always in the will. He came and went. In the end, the will was pretty much the same as when it had started."

On March 14, two days after Tim overdosed on the borrowed morphine patch, his old friend and colleague Frank Barron brought Jack Leary to Los Angeles for the long-awaited reconciliation. In the movie of Tim's life, this would clearly be the final scene, a touching reunion between an Irish rogue who had done wrong and his only son, whom he still loved deeply. Sitting beside the bed in which his father was dying, the son would somehow find it in his heart to forgive him for everything, thereby enabling him to die a happy man.

Unfortunately, this was also the day that what came to be called the "Harvard reunion" took place on Sunbrook Drive. The reunion was organized by Rick Doblin, founder of the Multidisciplinary Association of Psychedelic Studies. Doblin had found two of the ex-convicts with whom Tim and his graduate students had taken psilocybin inside the walls of Concord Prison thirty-four years ago and made arrangements for them to accompany Gunther Weil to the house. Ralph Metzner, George Litwin, Paul Lee, and Ram Dass were also there. "We were waiting for Jack," a former Harvard graduate student who was there that day remembered, "and he came through the door and sat on the fringe of the group. He didn't sit next to Tim. A lot of the time, he was walking around the house and in the garden. We were all talking and Tim was visiting with other people. He was only there for maybe three or four hours. It was not this great reunion with his father. He was glad he saw him, but he had to get back. He was alone in a room with Tim for a while, but I don't think there was any big thing of 'Dad, I love you.'" "Think what it must have been like for Jack," Rosemary would later say. "All those people, just as at Millbrook, telling Jack how lucky he was to have Tim for a father and how they wished he was their dad. People Jack did not know were telling him what a great man his father really was. And then they let him leave without anyone noticing, offering to call him a taxi, or taking him to the airport."

What for another father and son might have been the defining moment in their lives became instead a muted anticlimax. Jack slipped out the front door as his father sat surrounded by his oldest disciples. Leaving the house on Sunbrook Drive, he returned to the life he had made for himself without any help from his father.

FORTY-NINE

By April, the level of self-deception on Sunbrook Drive had become so grand that many of those in residence truly believed someone would buy the house for them after Tim died so they could continue living there. Though there was no way of knowing who was responsible, Tim's personal memorabilia began disappearing at an alarming rate. His art collection included what Lewis MacAdams of *LA Weekly* called "a gorgeous Ed Ruscha painting of the letters T and L stenciled white against a grid of streetlights." MacAdams also noted that Tim had several works by Kenny Scharf that had been spray-painted on plywood, and a Keith Haring drawing showing tears streaming from the artist's eyes. An "impromptu Casa Leary docent" told MacAdams that Haring had drawn the self-portrait on the day he learned he had AIDS. "It's the only sad painting Keith Haring ever did." Denis Berry and Donna Scott told Tim they were taking his artwork out to be appraised and removed the most valuable pieces from the house. "When we took the stuff out," Berry recalled, "the kids were appalled. They said, 'This is our home. How can you do this? Tim would not have wanted this.' We were constantly fighting with them and feeling like we were being mercenary. It was the adults versus the kids."

The real problems had begun when Tim received a $10,000 advance from Mercury Records for the CD soundtrack and documentary. "In a couple of weeks," Berry remembered, "it was all gone. They had to have cell phones. Tim had to have huge posters for the walls. They painted this. They did that. They bought new computer stuff and film and video equipment for the Web site. We asked them to hold off for a week or two, but they would not listen to us because they had put the money into their account for tax reasons. Tim was dying so it all went to leary.com." "The house became a carnival," Lindsay Brice remembered. "It had always been beige. The walls, the exterior, the carpeting, everything was beige. Suddenly the hallway to his bedroom was upholstered in fake fur. The ceiling was fake fur with little white teddy-bear eyes. The place became very lively and cheerful. It became psychedelic."

With ten or twelve people now on staff, each earning $400 a week, Tim's payroll ballooned to an astronomical $20,000 a month. Berry confronted the staff, and they agreed to a pay cut to $300 a week. Considering that they paid no rent and had no expenses, this did not seem an unreasonable sacrifice. "There would be psychic battles between people," Mike Vague recalled. "'Tim likes me more than he likes you and I can do more than you and Tim wants this and I'm going to direct it and you're going to listen to me.' Everyone got along fine so long as Tim came in and said, 'Knock it off, you and you. You're friends.' And that would be that. But when he stopped doing that, people talked behind one another's backs."

"The media was trying to exploit him for the last story," Trudy Truelove recalled. "Old acquaintances he was never really close to were coming around expecting things like 'you owe me this last interview so I can make money off it.' Janiger wanted files. There was a lot of that going on." Although a parade of stars, including Tim Robbins, Susan Sarandon, Oliver Stone, and Larry Flynt, continued to pass in review before Tim's bed, the kids were the ones who lived with him and did all the dirty work. "They were absolutely up with him all night," Berry confirmed. "They cleaned up his shit. No nurse wanted him. Those kids didn't judge him. They were having just as much fun and they worked hard for their money. They were up with Tim all night and they were loaded all the time because it was there. When people came to see Tim, they brought him the best drugs. That was the way it always was." Trudy Truelove remembered that when she would come to wake Tim up at nine in the morning, "He'd have a balloon and he'd insist I have it with him. 'Tim, I don't want to have a balloon because it's going to fuck me up for the rest of the day.' 'Do it. Do it. Do it.' I'd do it and I'd be fucked up for the rest of the day."

At the end of March, a firm called CryoCare began delivering equipment to the house so that when Tim died, he could be cryogenically preserved. "People were busily—happily—setting up the cryonic bath," Lindsay Brice recalled. "They were thrilled and delighted. But it was grim. There were plastic sheets under a metal structure with a plastic tub for the body to be dipped into. A big sort of Dr. Frankenstein laboratory light to shine down on it. There were tanks for the freezing solution. It was clinical in a horror-movie way. Tim was being interviewed as they did all this behind him and he wouldn't look at it." As soon as Tim had left the room, Camella Grace and others got what Brice later called "every crazy thing they could find" and decorated the ghoulish equipment. They draped a big East German flag someone had given Tim over the bath and put an over-the-head Yoda rubber mask with a cigarette in its mouth inside the tub. A black plastic sculpture of a woman was used for the body. "The people living at the home and some of the rest of us turned it into an art piece," Stacy Valis recalled. "We all started contributing things Tim would need in the afterlife. Booze and cigarettes and *Abbey Road*." When he woke up from his nap, Tim was wheeled back into the room. "They said, 'We've got something to show you,'" Lindsay Brice remembered. "He looked at it and went, 'Oh, it's beautiful. And practical too!'"

On April 18, Tim told a reporter he was "actively exploring killing himself" on the Internet. "I'm very interested in the high tech of dying . . . I have not yet made any decisions. You'll be hearing more soon." In another story, Ken Kesey was quoted as saying that Internet suicide was all that Tim talked about. "I told him, 'Tim, this is your best act yet.' He said, 'Yeah, but what do I do for an encore?'" Kesey said Tim's idea was to die before a camera while at his computer. "I remember when Timmy was talking about killing himself," Dieadra Martino recalled, "and I told him he better not. It's very hard to deal with the fact that both my parents and my grandmother had killed themselves. My parents and *both* my grand-parents? It would just fuck with my head."

With the Internet not yet nearly as commonplace as it has become today, the unfolding drama of Tim's possible online suicide became a continuing melodrama that only those logged on to the Web could follow. Just as he had done thirty years earlier by providing a never-ending series of front-page stories for an alternative press that was in its infancy, Timothy Leary now created content for what was then still called the World Wide Web. As one user breathlessly noted, "The real-time suicide, which I am told is weeks away, will shake the online industry right down to its wires."

While the possibility that Tim would actually kill himself online seemed far-fetched, the list of all the drugs he was now using that was posted on his Web site would have long since have dispatched a lesser man. By the third week in April, Tim was up to fifty cigarettes a day, two marijuana cookies, one joint, and two "Leary biscuits" (butter and a bud of marijuana on a Ritz cracker nuked in a microwave, as Denis Berry described them), in addition to the fentanyl patch, two Dilaudid pain pills, two lines of cocaine, twelve balloons of nitrous oxide, forty-five ccs of ketamine, and DMT, described as "a spicy addition to marijuana."

After taking the DMT, Tim proclaimed, "I'm not going to be sick anymore. I'm going to work in the office tomorrow. We're going to do some projects. Enough of this." Even as Tim was raising other people's consciousness about dying and their freedom to make choices as they did so, Vicki Marshall recalled that "he was in denial about it until about two weeks before the end. I'm convinced he thought he was going to beat it. I remember him saying, 'I'm cured now. I'm not going to die.'"

Though the Web site made no mention of nitrous oxide, Tim's use of the pain-killing gas had now gone beyond all limits known to man. Alone with Tim in his bedroom one night, Stacy Valis and Dean Chamberlain watched Tim begin taking nitrous not from a balloon but directly from the tube which came from the tank. Staying on the nitrous for "many seconds," Tim suddenly slipped back into his wheelchair where he did "this strange twitching with his hands" before passing out. As soon as he regained consciousness, Tim got right back on the tube again. Staring at him "bug-eyed and frightened," Chamberlain realized he had "slightly interrupted Tim's reverie. He looked at me and said, 'If you don't like what you're seeing, get the fuck out of the room.'"

On April 25, Tim went with his extensive entourage to the fiftieth annual banquet of the Los Angeles Advertising Women at the Beverly Hills Hotel. Susan Sarandon had asked him to accept her award as the humanitarian of the year. Camella Grace, who went to the dinner with him, wore a short blue dress, "a dog collar studded with flashing, battery operated lights," and fluffy blue slippers that she had purchased at a garage sale for a dime. Tim also wore a dog collar, and in his swirling black-and-white psychedelic jacket and a bow tie, he was pushed into the event in a wheelchair bedecked with strings of flashing lights. Tim was also accompanied by Trudy Truelove, a very frail Laura Huxley, and Barbara Fouch, the wife of John Roseboro. Inside the banquet hall, some three hundred people were just finishing dinner. Not until Tim was wheeled up to the head table did anyone realize that he was now sitting across from Art Linkletter. Tim was no longer the vibrant, grinning drug guru whom

Linkletter had blamed for the suicide of his daughter. By now, Linkletter must have known that Tim's daughter had also killed herself. Bound together by the worst loss that any parent could imagine, the two men had much in common. If ever there had been a moment for mutual forgiveness or some sort of meaningful communication between them, this was it. Eighty-three years old, Linkletter stared at Tim. "It was such a shock," he later told an interviewer. "I thought it was one of the strangest moments of my life. I was so glad to see him because he is suffering so. It was pretty good evidence about what happens to you when you live that kind of life."

Tim, wheeled onstage by Joey Cavella, began to thank the assembled by saying how touched he was to be there for many reasons and how lucky he felt to be in the presence of his two guests tonight, Laura Huxley and Barbara Fouch. Then his mind began to wander. "Sixty years is a long time," he said. "But I can remember back to the days of 60's." As Tim tried to discuss the contributions that women had made to the culture, his pauses became longer and longer, until it was apparent that he had forgotten why he was there. Calling out to Joey, Tim asked what he should do now. Joey whispered in Tim's ear. Tim started talking about Susan Sarandon but soon had to call for help from Joey again. "Susan," Tim finally said, "we miss you, you're a long way away, but you are in our hearts tonight. Keep telling us what it is to be a human being."

To "polite applause and embarrassed glances all around," Tim was wheeled offstage. In his bedroom on Sunbrook Drive, as his caregivers helped him change into casual clothes and get into bed, Tim suddenly blurted out, "That was horrible, just horrible. In all these years, I've never been at a loss for words." Putting her hand on Tim's shoulder, Trudy Truelove said, "It wasn't that bad. Not as bad as you think." Coming in from the living room, Dean Chamberlain told him, "Tim, that was brilliant. It was the biggest event of the night." Taking Tim's hand, Barbara Fouch said, "Everyone had to take a backseat to you tonight." As yet more praise followed, Tim began feeling better. Someone handed him a nitrous balloon. Then he and his friends headed off to Spago for a late dinner.

In his room late at night, the old man lies in bed. He should be sleeping. Outside his bedroom window, the lights of Los Angeles gleam and glitter. Dreaming with his eyes wide open, his body wracked with pain, though he has taken so many drugs that no one can keep track of them any longer, he cannot sleep. Before him now, eternity looms. Although the old man has intellectually accepted his death and is using it to spread his final message to the world, he cannot come to grips with it on an emotional level.

All the drugs have not brought him peace. The old man knows he has gone so far wrong in his life that for him there will be no absolution or forgiveness. He is not the hero he so badly wanted to be. As though his Catholic upbringing is now all he has left, he asks a friend to take him once more to the church that he renounced so long ago. The friend, doubting that he really meant this, calls the next day. He is told the old man has been talking about nothing else all day long. In a suit and bow tie, he has been sitting in his wheelchair for an hour waiting for his friend to arrive.

With much agony, the old man slowly rises from his wheelchair and gets into a rented convertible for the ride to church. Whenever the car hits a bump, pain radiates like a lightning bolt throughout his entire body. Using his walker, he hobbles alongside his friend into a simple church in West Hollywood. In order not to make a commotion, the two of them sit toward the back.

Although the old man does his best to pay attention, he soon falls asleep. His friend thinks he may have died. Gently reaching for the old man's hand, he is relieved to discover the old man is still alive. When the time comes to take communion, the friend steps forward and does something he has never done before. He takes the wafer in his hand rather than on his tongue, breaks it in half, and shares it with the old man who tells him how important this is for him because he wants to get back in touch with God.

But what not even God can do for the old man is comfort him as he lies in bed late at night, unable to sleep because of the pain. To the woman who cares for him, he often says, "I've been a good boy, haven't I?" As always, the question contains the answer. Unable to weep because he cannot produce real tears, the old man begins sobbing and flailing his arms and legs as he sits naked on his bed. Although he orders the woman to get out of the room and leave him alone, she wraps her body around him. When he is finally able to tell her what he is so upset about, the old man says it is the way he treated his children.

He knows that even if he had the chance to do it all over again, nothing would be different. His son is still alive and the old man could easily pick up the phone and beg his forgiveness, but he will not do it. Except when he can no longer take the pain in the privacy of his own bedroom, he refuses to show his agony to others. By doing so, he would invalidate himself in the eyes of the world. He would invalidate the message of cheery optimism he has always preached. And then everyone would know him for who he really is and always has been, rather than the hero he so badly wanted to be.

Instead, the old man can only lie in bed alone and wait. His dead father will never come home again. His dead mother cannot help him now. His dead wife and his dead daughter are not here when he needs them. Despite all those who surround him during the day, in his bed late at night the old man can only lie and wait for what now seems, even to him, as inevitable as the coming sunrise. From the living hell the old man has made of his life, only death can free him now.

By May, Tim had floated so many different plans in the media about how he intended to die that they began to conflict with one another. Because he had steadfastly refused to dismiss the possibility that he might kill himself online, the people in charge at CryoCare announced that to avoid any possible legal complications, they had decided not to freeze his body after he died. The truth was that Tim had had an argument with a CryoCare representative who showed up in his bedroom accompanied by a photographer for a photo spread in *Wired* magazine. Rather than "be reanimated with someone else's spin," Douglas Rushkoff wrote in *Esquire*, "Tim would rather just die." On May 6, Tim told David Colker of the *Los Angeles Times*, "They have no sense of humor. I was worried I would wake up in 50 years surrounded by people with clipboards." That Tim never really wanted to be preserved for eternity in a chemical bath despite all the years he had talked about it was confirmed by Vicki Marshall. "He used to say, 'Cryonics is the second-stupidest thing I've ever heard of. Being eaten by worms is the first-stupidest.'"

Three days later, wearing a sleeveless jean jacket with patches on it, making him look like an aging biker, Tim was joined by John Perry Barlow, Camella Grace, Trudy Truelove, and a host of others on an expedition to have lunch at the House of Blues on Sunset Boulevard, courtesy of Dan Aykroyd, the surviving member of the original Blues Brothers. Declaring the day to be "Wheelchair Day," Tim's traveling party hopped into wheelchairs and raced one another down Sunset into the club. After lunch, Tim got into the front seat of Barlow's rented Mustang convertible. As they rolled down Sunset Boulevard, a song called appropriately enough "Wheel Chair," a rip-off of "Wild Thing," began blasting from the car's speakers. In the backseat, Camella Grace and Trudy Truelove got to their feet and started to dance.

"They were doing this shoop-shoop thing like prom queens from hell," Barlow recalled, "standing up in the backseat on Sunset Strip. The air was like a negligee and the music was perfect and people were honking their horns in approval. It was one of those great life-affirming moments and Timothy put up his hand to give me a high five and as I looked up at his hand, I saw these flashing lights in the rearview mirror. I thought, 'Oh, Timothy Leary's last bust.' And his first in a while. Because we were packing. We were holding. Big-time."

Fully expecting to be taken away in cuffs, Barlow pulled the car over right in front of the Beverly Hills Hotel, a location that was "kind of perfect. This surfer cop with perfect blow-dry hair came out. Before he had a chance to say anything, I said, 'Officer, I know that what we were doing was wrong but you see my friend here is dying and we're just trying to show him a good time.'" Looking at the cop, Tim nodded with this "sheepish smile on his face like, 'Yeah, it's true. I've been caught at dying.'" The look on the cop's face suddenly changed. "It just totally tweaked and completely undid him," Barlow remembered. "He had never before seen anyone admit that he was dying. He didn't know who Tim was. Just an old dying guy. And he said, 'I'd be lying if I didn't think that what you guys are doing doesn't look like fun. But just because he's dying doesn't mean you girls have to endanger your lives. So get down and buckle your seat belts.'"

On May 10, the day that rumor had it Tim would finally end his life in real time on the Internet, he went live on the Web for an online chat with Ken Kesey. Tim looked unbelievably gaunt. There were angry purple patches of skin on his cheekbones. In his red-and-black Chicago Blackhawk jersey with "69" and his name on the back, he was the face of death. When Kesey said to him, "The sixties ain't over till the Fat Lady gets high," Tim replied, "We're doing it again. The same old fuck-ups but they are ready to go further and further." Wearing a Day-Glo visor on which the American flag glittered, Kesey told Tim the press wanted to hear about his suicide. Struggling to keep his mental focus as he tried to reply, Tim said he wanted to have the option. Everyone should be able to rehearse his own death. Like a sportscaster narrating the event, Kesey asked, "Is he gonna do it?" In answer to his own question, he said, "I don't know." In Tim's honor, Kesey began drinking Bushmills whiskey straight from the bottle. Tim noted it was made from grain. "That's health food." "Irish whiskey," Kesey responded. "Makes you sing and want to bomb the

English." Kesey called Tim his brother and said he wanted to come down and do a trip with him to ease him on his way through death, the way that Aldous Huxley had left this planet. Tim began chanting, "High! High! High! We will get it on and keep it going." Realizing that Tim could only say whatever came into his mind at the moment, Kesey wrapped it up by saying, "Take care, brother. Stay in line." Then he began to sing, "When Irish Eyes Are Smiling." Tim replied, "I'm going to be with you. See you down the line. Stay in touch." Kesey responded by saying that they would meet at Houdini's grave on Halloween.

Not long before Tim died, family friends Gil and Joanne Segal visited him. The only other person in the room was Laura Huxley, who wore a straw hat with flowers on it and a flowing printed dress. In Joanne Segal's words, she was "very pastel looking with translucent skin." As Laura Huxley read from her book about Aldous's death, Tim gazed into her eyes with "as much love as I've ever seen him quietly radiate," Segal recalled. "It was absolutely like two lovers and one of the most touching moments I can ever remember."

As the Moody Blues went back into the studio to record a song called "Timothy Leary Lives" for the Mercury Records documentary soundtrack, Tim continued telling interviewers that, as Aldous Huxley had done, he might yet take a dose of LSD before he died. Unlike Huxley, a camera crew and a photographer happened to be in his bedroom when he said it. When Tim's responses to the *Vanity Fair* questionnaire were published in the magazine's June issue, the last question he was asked was, "What is your motto?" Tim replied, "Dial On, Tune In, Hang Out, Link Up, Escape-Delete."

As Tim neared the end, his notoriously short attention span became infinitesimal. With so little time left, he had no patience for anyone who wasted it. "I don't *want* to make sense," he told one interviewer, making no attempt to hide his annoyance. "If it makes sense to you, with your mind, I'm in trouble." In *Esquire,* Richard Leiby wrote, "If LSD cured addiction, it certainly hadn't worked with Leary, who went from being a lecturing professor of psychology at Harvard before acid to being, at the end of his life, a mean, dissolute drunk."

For those who had opened their hearts to Tim, his every act was a continuing revelation. In the house on Sunbrook Drive, the true believers were still experiencing new truths not only about themselves but about the process of death. The room in which Tim spent his days and nights testified not only to the life he had led but the struggle in which he was now engaged. Long ago, he had ordered the door to be taken off its hinges. Newspapers and magazines lay scattered everywhere. Blood-stained sheets were heaped in a pile. The nightstand was crowded with pill bottles, empty glasses, marijuana roaches, and used nitrous balloons. In the corner, an unused isolation tank hummed. One wall was dominated by a five-by-six-foot blowup of a much younger Tim sitting with Rosemary in front of the bed in which John Lennon and Yoko Ono were recording "Give Peace a Chance." Large round driveway mirrors, which Tim and his admirers had stolen from the driveways of mansions on Benedict Canyon Drive, had been mounted everywhere so he could see everything without having to move his head.

Late one night in mid-May, Tim and Dean Chamberlain sat together drawing in the room. On ketamine enhanced by nitrous oxide, Tim was hunched over his drawing paper struggling for what seemed like an eternity. Periodically, he nodded out, only to suddenly come back to life. At one point, Tim was so disoriented that Chamberlain had to tell him, "We're drawing, Tim." Putting a few more "meandering marks on the drawing," Tim drifted off again. "It was heart-wrenching," Chamberlain remembered. "He wanted so badly to be productive but had so little stamina for concentration. Suddenly, as though calling from this far-off land, he said, 'My optic nerves are singing! I'm blinded by screaming tears! My God, this drawing is blinding me! Its shimmering brilliance is almost too much for me!'"

When Tim looked up from his drawing to stare at Chamberlain through scratched glasses, Chamberlain saw tears in his eyes. "I was simply overwhelmed by my own helplessness," Chamberlain recalled. "I had no guidance to offer. My heart broke. He was on a path alone and so was I. I sensed he had stared into the eyes of death. He had seen something beyond."

With the cryogenics people no longer in the picture, Vicki Marshull and Carol Rosin, a former aerospace executive who had once served as a spokesperson for Werner von Braun, took Tim outside one night to have a serious conversation about what to do with his body after he died. Rosin had already agreed that if Tim ever went into a spasm, she would "administer the drugs that would end it for him." During their talk, Tim told Rosin and Marshall that he wanted to be cremated. When Rosin asked him what she should do with his ashes, he "got right up into my face and pointed at me and said, 'I want you to get me up in space.' I said, 'Oh, okay, I can do that. No problem.' And I had no idea how I was going to do it." Not long after this conversation, Tim told Rosin that the drugs were no longer working. When his old friend Robert Anton Wilson and his wife came to visit, Tim did not recognize them. He stopped eating but continued smoking cigarettes and inhaling nitrous oxide.

At about 5:00 P.M. on May 29, Rosin used a video camera to record the final interview of Tim's life. Wearing a new red T-shirt with a cigarette in his hand, Tim sat with "his little bruised body leaning on the dining-room table and his eyes rolling up in his head so that I thought he was going to die any second while he was talking." Just before Rosin began taping, he gave her a pink balloon and said, "This is my last balloon." When she said, "You don't know this is your last day," he stared at her and said, "No, this is my last balloon. Tomorrow, I leave." She asked if he would mind if she did one last interview with him on tape. Tim said, "I want you to. I want this to be my gift to you." Tim then told her, "My life work has been to empower individuals." After a long pause, he added, "To free herself and himself to grow and be more free. Today, we move into the next place. Use light, enjoy space for individuals." When Rosin asked, ' "What do you want to say to the young people, Timothy?" "Do it with your friends," he answered. "Do what?" "Ride the light into space." Rosin had been in touch with Charles Schaefer, a friend who was the president of a Houston company called Celestis, which sent people's ashes into space. She had shown Tim a three-minute promotional video that depicted the rocket they used burning up as it reentered the earth's atmosphere. "He was jumping up and down in his wheelchair," Rosin recalled, "and shouting, 'Now people will finally know I'm the light.'" Seeing that Tim was fading out on her, Rosin asked, "Timothy, who are we?" "We are the light," he answered. "We are the light bearers." To her question, "What is our purpose?" he responded, "Our purpose is to shine the light on others." Asked what he meant, he replied, "I have sought the light to use light to be in space. Light is the language of the sun and the stars where we will meet again."

On May 31, there were about twenty people keeping a death watch in the house on Sunbrook Drive. Donna Scott, Denis Berry, and Vicki

Marshall had all gone home to change their clothes and rest. Bob Guccione Jr., having driven nonstop from Sacramento to pay his final respects,
got there about seven at night. Outside the house, a private security guard
has been posted to keep away unwanted visitors. Going straight in, Guccione saw people milling around who told him they were all praying for
Tim to die tonight. Guccione was ordered not to talk to Tim or engage
him in any way. "His body is dead," they told him, "but his spirit won't
leave. We just want him to go gently rather than hang on."

Guccione went into Tim's bedroom where chairs had been set up
around the bed. Tim was unconscious and breathing heavily. Someone repeated the message to Guccione that he was not to wake, touch, or try to
talk to Tim. Again, Guccione said that he understood. At that moment,
Tim looked up, beamed, and waved him over. "There was a big laugh in
the room," Guccione recalled. "I went over and sat with him and he held
my arm. Although he was very frail, he gripped it in a vise. If I had
wanted to break out of it, it would have been a struggle. He was literally
holding on for life. He held my arm and he kept saying, 'Yeah, yeah, yeah,
yeah, yeah, yeah.' I think he was trying to say it was okay. Yes, you're here
and that's great and also, 'It's okay.'"

At another point during the vigil, Tim woke up and asked, "Why?"
Fearing he might have been feeling afraid or forsaken, everyone in the
room went silent. Smiling, Tim said, "Why not?" Tim repeated the
phrase, as Douglas Rushkoff wrote in *Esquire*, "fifty times in fifty different
voices. Clowning, loving, tragic, afraid." Christmas lights provided the
only illumination as Tim woke up again at around 9:00 P.M. His stepson,
Zach, sat by the bed holding his hand. Looking at Zach, Tim smiled and
said, "Beautiful." It was the last word he ever uttered.

Just after midnight, Carol Rosin was on one side of the bed. On the
other side was a male hospice nurse. Rosin recalled, "We both sat up at
the same instant. The hospice nurse walked up to Timothy and felt his
pulse and by now people had noticed that he hadn't taken another
breath. He inhaled and then just kind of held it. It didn't come back out.
I ended up with my fingers on the side of his neck and his neck was pulsing hard. I think I put my head on his chest to see if he was breathing.
His pulse just gradually faded. It didn't slow down. It kept beating hard
but it faded until it disappeared and then I said something like, 'Timothy's gone.' According to my watch, it was 12:44 A.M. The room was

thick with his presence and to me, it changed color. I saw this strange pea green brown gold orange and then one by one, people came in to say goodbye."

By the time Guccione reached the body, other people were kissing and holding Tim. "I grabbed him and held his hand and leaned in to kiss his forehead," he recalled, "and it was ice-cold. It was about a minute and a half after he died and that was how quickly he had gone cold. His eyes and mouth were wide open. None of us knew what to do so I went up to the nurse and asked him to come and close his eyes. We had all seen movies where they close the eyes and none of us really wanted to lean forward and touch his corpse and do that." Although the nurse did his best, he could not close Tim's eyes. "Even in death," Guccione remembered, "they couldn't close his eyes or mouth."

Carol Rosin, the last person in the room before the mortuary men came to take away the body, suddenly remembered that she had promised Tim she would take his picture after he died. Six months earlier, she had put a camera behind the dresser for this purpose. "I had totally forgotten about it until I could practically hear him telling me to take this picture," Rosin recalled. "So I did. I'm not even sure why he told me." Before the mortuary men did their work, Donna Scott cut snippets of Tim's hair, which she gave to a few people.

Dressed in white and covered with a red blanket with an orange flower in his hands so large that the petals reached his face, Tim was rolled down the hallway from his bedroom. By now, the living room was packed. Everyone stood in silence until they were told it was time to say their final goodbyes. One by one, they approached the body to touch and kiss Tim and whisper their last words in his ear.

After Tim was cremated, his ashes were put into an urn and distributed in small amounts to those closest to him before he died. Dean Chamberlain and Stacy Valis put their share in a little shrine to Tim in their home. Nearly a year later, seven grams of Tim's ashes, contained in a small glass pharmaceutical vial with a black screw-top cap, were sent into space on a Pegasus rocket launched from Grand Canary in the Canary Islands. The rocket also carried seven grams of the mortal remains of twenty-four other people, among them Gene Roddenberry, the creator of *Star Trek;* Princeton physicist Gerard O'Neill; Todd Hawley, co-founder of the International Space University; and Kraft Eriche, a German scientist who worked at Rockwell Aviation.

A self-proclaimed cheerleader for change who himself had never been able to change, Timothy Leary had finally achieved his heart's desire. In death, as he could never be in life, he was not only free but soaring through the heavens at which he had gazed so often in wonder during his most improbable life.

Timothy Leary, January 1996, four months before his death at
the age of seventy-five. *Photo courtesy of AP Photo/Walt Weis*

ACKNOWLEDGMENTS

So few people believed in this book that I would like to thank those who did. First and foremost, my deepest gratitude goes to James H. Silberman, with whom I have had the great pleasure of working for nearly thirty years. He rescued this project from oblivion, steadfastly kept the faith as I completed it, and then did yeoman service trimming the manuscript. Without him, this book would have never made it into print.

Thank you to all the good people at Harcourt who were patient enough to wait. André Bernard read it first and said yes. Tim Bent, whose brilliant hand is on every page of this book, is as fine an editor as I have ever known. I want to thank him for making himself available to me whenever I needed him and for only losing his patience with me once. Thanks as well to Sloane Miller for putting up with me on the phone and to Marilyn Mazur for her help with the manuscript. David Hough helped me navigate the rough shoals surrounding the physical production of this book with cunning ease and great élan.

I would, of course, like to thank everyone whom I interviewed. I am most especially grateful to the men who were Timothy Leary's class-mates at West Point so long ago. The late John Beach, Tim's roommate, was especially helpful to me in re-creating this period. I would also like to thank Sally Olmstead Barnes for her letter about the Leary family in Springfield.

The late Merv Freedman was an astonishing source of information no one else could have provided concerning Timothy Leary's years at Berkeley. I am only sorry that he did not live long enough to read the manuscript. The same is true for the late Frank Barron, who knew Tim for most of his adult life and did his best to help me refine my view of the man. My thanks also go to Charles Adams for writing me about his recollections of Tim and Marianne in Berkeley. I am also indebted to Brendan Maher at Harvard, who was kind enough to send me clippings from his own files on Timothy Leary.

Robert Altman, who took some of the finest photographs of Tim and Rosemary and was her great friend, helped put me in touch with many of Tim's friends and associates. Michael Horowitz, Tim's longtime archivist, retrieved innumerable magazine articles and out-of-print books for me from the Leary archives as well as his own extensive collection. Vicki Marshall not only lent me her personally inscribed Timothy Leary first editions but also survived three days of finding and copying documents in the Leary archives. Denis Berry, who along with Donna Scott, serves as the director of the Futique Trust that administers Timothy Leary's archives, has made it possible for me to quote from Tim's letters and books. All this material remains the property of the Futique trust and cannot be used without express written permission. My heartfelt thanks to her for all the support and endless good cheer. Michael Segal provided me with videotapes and much information. Thanks to Professor David Winter of the University of Michigan for his help in obtaining permission to quote from the letters and memos of David McClelland.

Rob McCloud sent me an article from *Rolling Stone* magazine that I could find nowhere else. Stanley Siegel provided me with a video copy of Tim Leary's appearance on the *Stanley Siegel* Show. Thanks to Bill Day for making me a copy of it. Paul Swanson gave me a copy of *Timothy Leary's Last Trip.* Thanks to Sam Minsky for helping me find someone to explain the Leary Circle and to Rick Frye for lending me his copy of *Storming Heaven.* Art Kunkin provided me with copies of *The LA Free Press.* Thanks to Alan Douglas for *Jail Notes* and *You Can Be Anyone You Want To This Time Around.* Thanks to Bill Gelin for *The Man Who Turned on the World,* the late Nina Graboi for *One Foot in the Future,* Robert Forte for *Outside, Looking In,* Mary Della Cioppa for personal photographs, Frances Raeside for *Timothy Leary, the Madness of the Sixties, and Me,* and Joanna Harcourt-Smith for her unpublished memoir, *Paramour.* I should also like to thank Erica Silverman, who did the original deal.

A special thank-you to Peter Owen Whitmer, without whose help I could never have documented Tim's early life in Springfield. His psychobiography of Timothy Leary provided me with access to sources who would otherwise have never made their way into this book. I truly appreciate his kind and open-hearted cooperation. Thanks to Rogers Masson for trying to make transcribing the interviews a digital process. If I have failed to mention anyone by name who extended a helping hand to me during the past ten years, please forgive the omission and know that I am grateful to you as well.

For staying with me on the endless journey that writing this book became, I would like to thank my wife, Donna; my son, Sandy (who as my only research assistant photocopied underground newspapers for me and was shocked by their content); and my daughter, Anna. Finally, this book would never have been possible without Rosemary Woodruff, who not only opened her address book to me but her heart as well. We first met on a sunny terrace in Algeria in 1970 and then did not see one another again for nearly thirty years. Although I have dedicated this book to my daughter, it belongs to Rosemary as well. Not for all that she went through but for who she was.

A NOTE ON SOURCES

I met Timothy Leary in October 1970 when, as the associate editor of the London bureau of *Rolling Stone* magazine, I was sent to interview him in Algeria after his dramatic escape from prison in San Luis Obispo. Arriving in Algiers without a visa, just as he had done before me, I managed to talk my way into the country and find my way to the Black Panther Embassy in El Biar. There, Eldridge Cleaver directed me to the beachside hotel in El Djamila where Leary was then living with Rosemary.

As we sat talking in the sunshine on the little patio outside his hotel room, Tim seemed completely lucid but nothing he said made any sense to me. Although the man had only just aligned himself with forces advocating armed revolution in America, he seemed to have no grasp whatsoever of political reality. I had already interviewed and written about Weathermen who were doing hard time in prison for crimes against the state. In terms of what was happening on the street back then, Tim's wholesale endorsement of violent action seemed not only ill considered and completely cavalier but also downright dangerous.

All the same, I reported the story and it ran some weeks later in *Rolling Stone* under the headline TIM LEARY, OR BOMB FOR THE BUDDHA. Although Dennis Martino also had been present during the interview, he did not make much of an impression on me. The same was not true of Rosemary. Although she did not say much, she seemed far more present and in touch with basic reality than Tim. When I returned to London, I provided Tim's phone numbers and contact information in Algiers to Michael Zwerin, whose "Outside" column in the *Village Voice* I had faithfully read each week while attending college in New York City. For good reason, the story he filed garnered far more attention than my own.

Some months later while Tim was in Switzerland, I contacted him by phone about the possibility of doing another interview. He warmly invited me to come see him, saying, "You'll teach us about journalism and we'll teach you about acid." I decided not to take him up on his offer. I did not speak to him again until shortly before his death when I called and asked if I could see him. I had no real understanding of the media circus then swirling around him but his response led me to believe that there was little to gain by trying to insinuate myself into his circle at that point in his life.

Due in no small part to all the inaccuracies, chronological errors, and outright lies that I discovered in his own writings, I made a point of trying to read everything ever written about Timothy Leary as I researched this book. In a time when Amazon.com was not yet the resource for out-of-print material that it has since become, this involved a time-consuming search for books that existed primarily in private collections or could only be procured through interlibrary loan.

For those who might want to read more about Timothy Leary, I would, of course, recommend *Flashbacks*. As flawed and inaccurate as it can often be, there are sections in which I believe Tim is telling the real story insofar as I could substantiate it through other sources. I would also recommend *Changing My Mind, Among Others* and, if only for Ralph Metzner's introduction, the republished version of *Psychedelic Prayers. Confessions of a Hope Fiend*, long out of print, is also worth finding.

Be Here Now by Ram Dass remains a counterculture classic in its own right and Richard Alpert's account of his transformation from Harvard professor to Western guru still rings true. John Bryan's *Whatever Happened to Timothy Leary?*, currently out of print, is a valuable source of information about Tim's life up to the point when the book was published in 1980. *Storming Heaven* by Jay Stevens and *Acid Dreams: The CIA, LSD, and the Sixties Rebellion* by Martin A. Lee and Bruce Shlain remain the definitive works on the acid pioneers. There is also much to recommend in Michael Hollingshead's *The Man Who Turned On the World*, that "man" not being Timothy Leary but rather Jesus Christ. Charles Slack's book, *Timothy Leary, the Madness of the Sixties, and Me* is poignant and honest. So, too, is Jonah Raskin's *Out of the Whale*, only part of which deals with Leary.

No one needs me to recommend Tom Wolfe's *The Electric Kool-Aid Acid Test* but no book has better captured the utter madness and complete abandon of those times. *The Doors of Perception* by Aldous Huxley, *The Joyous Cosmology* by Alan Watts, and *The Psychedelic Experience* by Timothy Leary, Ralph Metzner, and Richard Alpert remain seminal works in the field.

As I was laboring to complete this project, someone told me, "Those who love Timothy Leary will hate your book. And those who hated him will never read it." With that thought in mind, I'd like to salute all those who have made it this far in the text.

BOOKS AND MONOGRAPHS BY TIMOTHY LEARY

Author's note: Although most of this list appears at the beginning of *Flashbacks,* the fourth and fifth items on it have to my knowledge never been published. Nor could I find them in Timothy Leary's archives, which is not to say that they do not exist in some form or another.

The Dimensions of Intelligence (MS. thesis, Washington State University, 1946)

The Social Dimensions of Personality (Ph.D. thesis, University of California, 1950)

The Interpersonal Diagnosis of Personality (John Wiley, 1957)

The Multi-Level Assessment of Personality (Psychological Consulting Service, 1957)

The Existential Transaction (Psychological Consulting Service, 1960)

The Psychedelic Experience (with Ralph Metzner and Richard Alpert, University Books, 1964)

The Psychedelic Reader (ed. with Gunther Weil, University Books, 1965)

Psychedelic Prayers from the Tao Te-Ching (University Books, 1967)

High Priest (New American Library-World, 1968)

Politics of Ecstasy (Putnam, 1968)

Jail Notes (an Alan Douglas Book/World-Evergreen, 1971)

Confessions of a Hope Fiend (Bantam, 1973)

Neurologic (with Joanna Leary, Starseed, 1973)

Starseed: A Psy-Phi Comet Tale (Starseed, 1973)

The Curse of the Oval Room (Starseed, 1974)

Terra II (with Joanna Leary and L. W. Benner, Starseed, 1974)

Communications with Higher Intelligence (ed., Spit In The Ocean, 1977)

Changing My Mind, Among Others (Prentice-Hall, 1982)

Flashbacks (Jeremy P. Tarcher/Putnam, 1983)

Design For Dying (with R. U. Sirius, HarperEdge, 1997)

Future History Series (Peace Press)
Vol. I: *What Does WoMan Want?* (1976)
Vol. II: *Exo-Psychology* (1977)
Vol. III: *Neuropolitics* (1977)
Vol. IV: *Intelligence Agents* (1979)
Vol. V: *The Game of Life* (1979)

ENDNOTES

ONE

"To him, they seemed 'urban, urbane, well-to-do' ...": Timothy Leary, "1920–1930, Springfield, Massachusetts," *Flashbacks: An Autobiography* (Los Angeles: J. P. Tarcher, Inc., 1983).

"A watchmaker by trade ...": "Veteran Jeweler, 92, Passes Away," *The Springfield Daily Republican*, December 27, 1933.

"At the age of seventy-five, Dennis liked to embarrass ...": interview with Sally Olmstead Barnes, November 7, 1997.

"It was on the top floor of his house ...": Leary, "1920–1930, Springfield, Massachusetts," *Flashbacks*.

"By then, Sarah had already given birth ...": interview by Peter Owen Whitmer with Phil and Anita Shea, 1983.

"The star of the family was Frances ...": *The Springfield Daily Republican*, June 11, 1898.

"Despite his overwhelming love for theater ...": interview with Sally Olmstead Barnes, November 7, 1997.

"Two years older than Tote ...": "Arthur L. Leary, Well Known in Business Life Is Dead at 45," *The Springfield Daily Republican*, April 29, 1931.

"Years later, Tim Leary would write ...": Leary, "1932, Springfield, Massachusetts," *Flashbacks*.

"Tim also learned from Arthur ...": interview with Peter Owen Whitmer, April 14, 1997.

"Invented the same year Tim was born ...": Frank Bauer, *At the Crossroads, Springfield, Massachusetts, 1636–1975* (Springfield, MA: U.S.A. Bicentennial Committee of Springfield, Inc., 1975).

"Sally Olmstead Barnes, Frances Leary's granddaughter ...": letter from Sally Olmstead Barnes, February 10, 1997.

"A parochial power broker with connections ...": Leary, "1920–1930, Springfield, Massachusetts," *Flashbacks*.

"One of his closest friends was ...": interview with Peter Owen Whitmer, April 14, 1997.

"Among the Catholic elite in New England ...": Peter Owen Whitmer, "The Legend of a Mind: A Psychobiography of Timothy Leary" (unpublished, 1975).

"With the help of his uncle ...": interview by Peter Owen Whitmer with Phil and Anita Shea, 1983.

"At the bottom of the obit ...": document, Tote Leary's papers.

"On April 23, 1917, he was invited ...": ibid.

"On January 7, 1918, Tote Leary married Abigail Ferris ...": Whitmer, "The Legend of a Mind," 63.

"Although any union between a Leary son ...": interview with Frank Barron, November 4, 1997; interview with Sally Olmstead Barnes, November 7, 1997; and interview with Rosemary Woodruff Leary, November 6, 1997.

"When Abigail, by far the livelier . . .": Leary, "1920–1930, Springfield, Massachusetts," *Flashbacks*; and Whitmer, "The Legend of a Mind."

"On July 13, 1918, with World War I soon to end . . .": document, Timothy Leary Archives.

"At the academy, he drove a Packard . . .": Leary, "1920–1930, Springfield, Massachusetts," *Flashbacks*.

"Once Abigail gave birth to a son . . .": Whitmer, "The Legend of a Mind."

"His departure from West Point . . .": interview with Peter Owen Whitmer, November 21, 1997.

"On the general's seventy-sixth birthday . . .": letter from MacArthur, Tote Leary's papers.

"His army days behind him . . .": Whitmer, "The Legend of a Mind."

"He and Abigail read a lot . . .": interview by Peter Owen Whitmer with Phil and Anita Shea, 1983.

"When his sister Frances shocked the family . . .": Leary, "1920–1930, Springfield, Massachusetts," *Flashbacks*.

"More than once, Phil Shea . . .": interview by Peter Owen Whitmer with Phil and Anita Shea, 1983.

"Drunk after church one Sunday afternoon . . .": Whitmer, "The Legend of a Mind."

"Coming home drunk one night . . .": Leary, "1932, Springfield, Massachusetts," *Flashbacks*.

"Awakened by his weeping mother . . .": ibid.

"Their influence became so stultifying . . .": Leary, "1932–1935, Springfield, Massachusetts," *Flashbacks*.

"Massachusetts, the state that once produced . . .": *The WPA Guide to Massachusetts* (Boston: Houghton Mifflin, 1937),

"In order to pay his drinking debts . . .": interview with Sally Olmstead Barnes, November 5, 1996.

"Despite the grim reality of their situation . . .": Leary, "1923–1935, Springfield, Massachusetts," *Flashbacks*.

"On the day after Christmas in 1933 . . .": ibid.

"In a single night, he lost every cent . . .": ibid.

"All told, it amounted to around $60,000 . . .": interview with Peter Owen Whitmer, November 21, 1997.

"Rather than leave the money directly to her . . .": interview with Sally Olmstead Barnes, November 7, 1997.

"Dennis also left Sara the houses . . .": interview by Peter Owen Whitmer with Phil and Anita Shea, 1983.

"Abigail raised such a fuss . . .": interview with Peter Owen Whitmer, November 21, 1997.

"No longer able to pay the taxes . . .": interview with Sally Olmstead Barnes, November 7, 1997.

"Like the Ferris home in nearby Indian Orchard . . .": interview with Peter Owen Whitmer, April 14, 1997.

"Looking for what she called 'funny business' . . .": Timothy Leary, *Chaos & Cyberculture* (Berkeley, CA: Ronin Publishing, 1994).

"With the smell of floor polish in his nose . . .": Whitmer, "The Legend of a Mind."

"On the other side of the latticed screen . . .": Leary, *Chaos & Cyberculture*; and Leary, *Flashbacks*.

"Even as his great-uncle utters . . .": Leary, *Flashbacks*.

"What about the Montgomery Ward catalog . . .": Leary, *Chaos & Cyberculture*.

"A single vivid image of her . . .": Leary, *Flashbacks*.

"Years later, Tim Leary will write . . .": ibid.

"Instead of listening in school this past week . . .": Timothy Leary, *What Does WoMan Want?* (Los Angeles: 88 Books, 1976).

"Father Michael adjusts his hearing aid . . .": interview with Peter Owen Whitmer, November 21, 1997.

"At long last, he tells the boy . . .": Leary, *Chaos & Cyberculture*.

TWO

"Had Abigail Leary truly wanted her only son . . .": interview with Larry Gormally, November 5, 1997.

"Alumni of Harvard, Yale, and Princeton . . .": interview with Peter Owen Whitmer, November 21, 1997.

"Among its graduates were William Manchester . . .": Peter O. Whitmer with Bruce VanWygarden, *Aquarius Revisited* (New York: Macmillan Publishing Company, 1987).

"Manchester, who attended Classical High . . .": interview with Peter Owen Whitmer, January 7, 1998.

"Lucia Gallup, who sat next to Tim . . .": interview with Lucia Gallup, October 9, 1997.

"Tim also had his own monogrammed stationery . . .": interview with Peter Owen Whitmer, November 21, 1997.

"At Christmas, he sent out preprinted holiday cards . . .": document, Timothy Leary Archives.

"During his freshman and sophomore years . . .": Timothy Leary, "1936–1938, Springfield, Massachusetts," *Flashbacks: An Autobiography* (Los Angeles: J. P. Tarcher, Inc., 1983).

"Despite scoring 127 on the Terman IQ Test . . .": Whitmer, *Aquarius Revisited*; and document, Timothy Leary Archives.

"The turning point in his high-school career . . .": Leary, "1936–1938, Springfield, Massachusetts," *Flashbacks.*

"In his autobiography, Leary calls the girl 'Rosalind' . . .": ibid.

"In a memo to himself, written at the age of seventy-four . . .": document, July 23, 1994, Timothy Leary Archives.

"With Rosalind's help, Tim transformed himself . . .": Leary, "1936–1938, Springfield, Massachusetts," *Flashbacks.*

"Tim's photograph appeared on the front page . . .": *The Classical Recorder,* June 4, 1937, Timothy Leary Archives.

"At seventeen, the boy who had once lived exclusively . . .": document, Timothy Leary Archives.

"He was so busy with extracurricular activities . . .": interview with Lucia Gallup, October 9, 1997.

"The accompanying rush of feelings . . .": Leary, "1936–1938, Springfield, Massachusetts," *Flashbacks.*

"Although William Manchester's grades . . .": interview with Peter Owen Whitmer, November 21, 1997.

"It was Hill's custom to welcome . . .": Leary, "1936–1938, Springfield, Massachusetts," *Flashbacks.*

"Although Kant phrases the concept . . .": William L. Reese, *Dictionary of Philosophy and Religion* (Atlantic Highlands, New Jersey: Humanities Press, 1980).

"While escorting adult visitors around the school . . .": Leary, "1936–1938, Springfield, Massachusetts," *Flashbacks.*

"Tim, who by this time was already engaging in . . .": Peter Owen Whitmer, "The Legend of a Mind: A Psychobiography of Timothy Leary" (unpublished, 1975).

"Pointing out that Tim had skipped school . . .": Leary, "1936–1938, Springfield, Massachusetts," *Flashbacks.*

"On June 14, 1938, when Timothy Francis Leary . . .": ibid.

"Much like Boston College, Notre Dame . . .": interview with Larry Gormally, November 5, 1997.

"At one time, a third of all the priests . . .": The Catholic University of America, *New Catholic Encyclopedia* (Washington, D.C.: McGraw-Hill, 1967).

"A Democrat elected to the Massachusetts . . .": *Biographical Directory of the American Congress 1774–1971* (Washington, D.C.: U.S. Government Printing Office, 1971).

"In his will, Father Michael bequeathed . . .": interview with Peter Owen Whitmer, April 14, 1997.

"Although the exact nature of the relationship . . .": interview with Peter Owen Whitmer, January 7, 1998.

"Walsh never married . . .": Dorothy G. Wayman, *David I. Walsh: Citizen-Patriot* (Milwaukee, WI: The Bruce Publishing Company, 1952).

"In the spring of 1942, a scandal would nearly . . .": ibid.

"A year later, Walsh interceded . . .": Nigel Hamilton, *J.F.K: Reckless Youth* (New York: Random House, 1992).

"Tim would spend a year at Holy Cross . . .": Leary, "1936–1938, Springfield, Massachusetts," *Flashbacks.*

"In return, Tim would then be expected . . .": interview with Peter Owen Whitmer, November 21, 1997.

"In 1938, Holy Cross was still run . . .": Leary, "1936–1938, Springfield, Massachusetts," *Flashbacks.*

"Along with 20,000 others . . .": *The WPA Guide to Massachusetts*; and *Holy Cross AA News*, September 24, 1938, Timothy Leary Archives.

"In class, Tim was required . . .": Leary, "1936–1938, Springfield, Massachusetts," *Flashbacks.*

"His plans included writing . . .": letter from Timothy Leary, September 28, 1938, Timothy Leary Archives.

"He even joined the Sodality of the Blessed Mary . . .": letter from Timothy Leary, October 8, 1938, Timothy Leary Archives.

"To prove to his mother just how well . . .": letter from Timothy Leary, October 9, 1938, Timothy Leary Archives.

"Attached to one letter home . . .": letter from Timothy Leary, September 26, 1938, Timothy Leary Archives.

"He reported having an awful cold . . .": Undated letter from Timothy Leary, September, 1938, Timothy Leary Archives.

"This was not easy because meals . . .": letter from Timothy Leary, October 8, 1938, Timothy Leary Archives.

"He worried about the college laundry . . .": Undated letter from Timothy Leary, Timothy Leary Archives.

"His fellow classmates seemed awfully thick . . .": letter from Timothy Leary, September 28, 1938, Timothy Leary Archives.

"Yet when one of his professors . . .": "Mr. Dawson and Holy Cross College—An Apology by Timothy Leary," Timothy Leary Archives.

"Tim won enough money from running . . .": Leary, "1936–1938, Springfield, Massachusetts," *Flashbacks.*

"In a note written in pencil to Tim . . .": document, Timothy Leary Archives.

"His archives contain a pamphlet . . .": document, Timothy Leary Archives.

"After achieving what he would later describe . . .": Leary, "1936–1938, Springfield, Massachusetts," *Flashbacks.*

"Because another qualified candidate . . .": interview with Peter Owen Whitmer, April 14, 1997.

"Believing there was no reason . . .": Leary, "1936–1938, Springfield, Massachusetts," *Flashbacks.*

"Ignoring notes sent to him . . .": document, Timothy Leary Archives.

"He broke the front window . . .": Whitmer, "The Legend of a Mind."

"In the words of one of his friends . . .": Whitmer, "The Legend of a Mind."

"At wit's end, Abigail wrote . . .": document, Timothy Leary Archives.

"Tim's third-quarter grades . . .": document, Timothy Leary Archives.

"He did, however, intercept the letter . . .": handwritten notation, document, Timothy Leary Archives.

THREE

"At dinner last night with his mother . . .": letter from Abigail Leary, June 29, 1941, Timothy Leary Archives.

"Now they are all either Mister Dumbcrow . . .": Timothy Leary, "August, 1940, West Point, New York," *Flashbacks: An Autobiography* (Los Angeles: J. P. Tarcher, Inc., 1983).

"Never mind whether the shouted orders . . .": ibid.

"Nazi soldiers are occupying the Channel Islands . . .": Robert Taylor, "The Young Manhood of Timothy Leary," *The Boston Globe Sunday Magazine,* November 29, 1970.

"After assessing the situation . . .": R. Ernest Dupuy, *Men of West Point: The First 150 Years of the United States Military Academy* (New York: William Sloane Associates, 1951)

"Young ladies of refinement . . .": Theodore J. Crackel, *The Illustrated History of West Point* (New York: H. N. Abrams in association with the United States Military Academy Class of 1940, 1991).

"While the cadets recline . . .": Dupuy, *Men of West Point.*

"The outcry against ending summer camp . . .": Crackel, *The Illustrated History of West Point.*

"Before him, the Hudson River reflects . . .": Taylor, "The Young Manhood of Timothy Leary."

"Beast Barracks: three months of basic training . . .": ibid.

"As Tim sat with his back stiff as a board . . .": Leary, "August, 1940, West Point, New York," *Flashbacks.*

"When Tim failed to do this . . .": document, July 6, 1940, Timothy Leary Archives.

"Far from regretting the loss . . .": Leary, "August, 1940, West Point, New York," *Flashbacks.*

"Like all the other plebes who made it . . .": ibid.

"As the summer air crackled . . .": Crackel, *The Illustrated History of West Point.*

"'My dear cadet,' Abigail wrote . . .": letter from Abigail Leary, August 27, 1940, Timothy Leary Archives.

"On September 4, Aunt Mae wrote . . .": letter from Mae Ferris, September 4, 1940, Timothy Leary Archives.

"On October 10, Father George G. Murdock . . .": letter from Father Murdock, October 10, 1940, Timothy Leary Archives.

"Tim would later write, 'During the gray autumn' . . .": Leary, "August, 1940, West Point, New York," *Flashbacks.*

"On October 22, Tim wrote his mother . . .": letter to Abigail Leary, October 22, 1940, Timothy Leary Archives.

"She noted that a special dinner . . .": document, Timothy Leary Archives.

"'Timothy, my angel,' she calls him . . .": letter from Rosamund Larson, October 23, 1940, Timothy Leary Archives.

"On October 28, Tim wrote Abigail . . .": letter to Abigail Leary, October 28, 1940, Timothy Leary Archives.

"His other roommate, John Blair Beach . . .": obituary, John Blair Beach, *San Francisco Chronicle,* March 11, 1999.

"Three days before the big game . . .": letter from Richards Vidmer, October 27, 1940, Timothy Leary Archives.

"Though plebes had to remain in their rooms . . .": e-mails from John Beach, January 12, 1999, and January 6, 1999.

"The two of them ended up in an all-night tavern . . .": interview with Thomas Lawson, January 12, 1999.

"Even though Tim got away with it . . .": interview with John Beach, January 5, 1999.

"In his autobiography, Tim Leary supplied . . .": Leary, "August, 1940, West Point, New York," *Flashbacks.*

"For a short while, Tim had taken the Point . . .": e-mail from John Beach, January 6, 1999.

"Asked nearly sixty years later . . .": interview with John Beach, January 5, 1999.

FOUR

"At halftime, the entire corps . . .": Robert Taylor, "The Young Manhood of Timothy Leary," *The Boston Globe Sunday Magazine,* November 29, 1970.

"'Dear Mother,' Tim wrote on November 5, 1940 . . .": letter to Abigail Leary, November 5, 1940, Timothy Leary Archives.

"On November 19, 1940, Tim wrote Abigail . . .": letter to Abigail Leary, November 19, 1940, Timothy Leary Archives.

"After Army closed out a dismal . . .": letter from Timothy Leary, December 4, 1940, Timothy Leary Archives.

"Writing to Abigail on December 6 . . .": letter from Timothy Leary, December 6, 1940, Timothy Leary Archives.

"On December 9, Tim wrote Abigail . . .": letter from Timothy Leary, December 9, 1940, Timothy Leary Archives.

"On the same day, a handwritten notice . . .": document, Timothy Leary Archives.

"In a letter to her the next day . . .": letter from Timothy Leary, December 10, 1940, Timothy Leary Archives.

"Tim also did not tell his mother . . .": Timothy Leary, "August 1940, West Point, New York," *Flashbacks: An Autobiography* (Los Angeles: J. P. Tarcher, Inc., 1983).

"Feeling no pain, he smoked a cigarette . . .": Peter O. Whitmer with Bruce VanWygarden, *Aquarius Revisited* (New York: Macmillan Publishing Company, 1987).

"First Classman Wilson Reed . . .": interview with Wilson Reed, January 11, 1999.

"Thomas Lawson, a first classman . . .": interview with Thomas Lawson, January 12, 1999.

"'It was the most god-awful rotgut' . . .": interview with Wilson Reed, January 11, 1999.

"Described by Lawson, his roommate . . .": interview with Thomas Lawson, January 12, 1999.

"Although John Beach remembered Stilson . . .": interview with John Beach, January 5, 1999; and interview with Bert Rosenbaum, January 11, 1999.

"Joe Reed recalled, 'We each did our duty' . . .": interview with Wilson Reed, January 11, 1999.

"Bert Rosenbaum, who remembered . . .": interview with Bert Rosenbaum, January 11, 1999.

"In Tim's version of the story . . .": Leary, "November 1940, West Point, New York," *Flashbacks.*

"'Mr. Leary didn't,' Reed recalled . . .": interview with Wilson Reed, January 11, 1999.

"'At that time,' Lawson would later say . . .": interview with Thomas Lawson, January 12, 1999.

"Confirming this sequence of events . . .": interview with Wilson Reed, January 11, 1999.

"Stilson later told Beach . . .": interview with John Beach, January 5, 1999.

"'He was so drunk the night before' . . .": interview with Bert Rosenbaum, January 11, 1999.

"'Normally,' Lawson would later say . . .": interview with Thomas Lawson, January 12, 1999.

"'I wouldn't have minded leaving West Point' . . .": Leary, "November 1940, West Point, New York," *Flashbacks.*

"By the next morning . . .": ibid.

"In 1807, just five years after the academy . . .": Theodore J. Crackel, *The Illustrated History of West Point* (New York: H. N. Abrams in association with the United States Military Academy Class of 1940, 1991).

"General Benjamin O. Davis Jr. . . .": Bradley Graham, "Long Retired Black General Gets Fourth Star," *The Washington Post,* December 10, 1998.

"Even after being commissioned . . .": interview with Thomas Lawson, January 12, 1999.

"The two black plebes who entered the academy . . .": Leary, "November 1940, West Point, New York," *Flashbacks.*

"Even after he had moved across the hall . . .": interview with John Beach, January 5, 1999.

"Never mentioning his own heroic actions . . .": ibid.

"On December 22, Tim wrote to his mother . . .": letter from Timothy Leary, December 22, 1940, Timothy Leary Archives.

"Beach confirmed that although . . .": interview with John Beach, January 5, 1999.

"In a letter to his mother on December 29 . . .": letter from Timothy Leary, December 29, 1940, Timothy Leary Archives.

"Although plebes were not allowed . . .": e-mail from John Beach, January 16, 1999.

"In early February, Tim finally presented . . .": Leary, "February 1941, West Point, New York," *Flashbacks*.

"In a letter he sent to John Beach . . .": interview with John Beach, January 5, 1999.

"Years later, Tim Leary told Peter Owen Whitmer . . .": Whitmer, *Aquarius Revisited*.

"Thomas Lawson, who did not testify . . .": interview with Thomas Lawson, January 12, 1999.

"At every formation, cadet officers swarmed . . .": Leary, "February 1941, West Point, New York," *Flashbacks*.

"Acting as what Beach called a 'kangaroo court' . . .": interview with John Beach, January 5, 1999.

" 'I resolved to stick it out' . . .": Leary, "February 1941, West Point, New York," *Flashbacks*.

"In a letter he sent to Tim's mother . . .": document, Timothy Leary Archives.

FIVE

"Throughout her life, Abigail had always . . .": letter from Abigail Leary, July 11, 1941, Timothy Leary Archives.

"On February 15, she wrote . . .": letter from Abigail Leary, February 15, 1941, Timothy Leary Archives.

"In response, Tim sent his mother . . .": letter to Abigail Leary, undated, Timothy Leary Archives.

"After spending the weekend at West Point . . .": letter from Abigail Leary, February 24, 1941, Timothy Leary Archives.

"On February 28, Tim wrote an untitled . . .": Peter O. Whitmer with Bruce VanWygarden, *Aquarius Revisited* (New York: Macmillan Publishing Company, 1987).

"A week later, in block letters . . .": letter to Abigail Leary, March 3, 1941, Timothy Leary Archives.

"On March 8, Abigail wrote her son . . .": letter from Abigail Leary, March 8, 1941, Timothy Leary Archives.

"On April 1, Tim wrote Abigail about . . .": letter to Abigail Leary, April 1, 1941, Timothy Leary Archives.

"On April 6, Tim wrote that he wished . . .": letter from Timothy Leary, April 6, 1941, Timothy Leary Archives.

"That same day, Tim received a letter . . .": letter, April, 1941, Timothy Leary Archives.

"On April 11, Father Murdock wrote to thank . . .": letter from Father Murdock to Abigail Leary, April 11, 1941, Timothy Leary Archives.

"What Father Murdock neglected to tell . . .": interview with John Beach, January 5, 1999.

"Reacting to what must have been . . .": letter from Abigail Leary, April 16, 1941, Timothy Leary Archives.

"On April 19, Tim replied with a rare typed . . .": letter to Abigail Leary, April 19, 1941, Timothy Leary Archives.

"On the same day she received Tim's letter . . .": letter from Abigail Leary, April 19, 1941, Timothy Leary Archives.

"She also wrote Father Murdock . . .": letter from Abigail Leary, April 19, 1941, Timothy Leary Archives.

"Captain Caraway wrote to say . . .": letter from Captain Paul Caraway to Abigail Leary, April 22, 1941, Timothy Leary Archives.

"The most remarkable response came . . .": letter from John Morton to Abigail Leary, April 23, 1941, Timothy Leary Archives.

"After the weekend, the superintendent wrote . . .": letter from Brigadier General R. L. Eichelberger to Abigail Leary, April 30, 1941, Timothy Leary Archives.

" 'Hell, you're not licked yet' . . .": letter from Abigail Leary, May 20, 1941, Timothy Leary Archives.

"Bert Rosenbaum remembered him having . . .": interview with Bert Rosenbaum, January 11, 1999.

"On May 26, with just fourteen days . . .": letter to Abigail Leary, May 26, 1941, Timothy Leary Archives.

"Afterward, she wrote to say . . .": letter from Abigail Leary, June 1, 1941, Timothy Leary Archives.

"On June 10, Abigail wrote . . .": letter from Abigail Leary, June 10, 1941, Timothy Leary Archives.

"On Wednesday, June 11, graduation day . . .": letter from Abigail Leary, June 11, 1941, Timothy Leary Archives.

"With all the plebes standing . . .": interview with Thomas Lawson, January 12, 1999.

"As Leary would write in his autobiography . . .": Timothy Leary, "February 1941, West Point, New York," *Flashbacks: An Autobiography* (Los Angeles: J. P. Tarcher, Inc., 1983).

"Thomas Lawson, the first classman . . .": interview with Thomas Lawson, January 12, 1999.

"On June 12, the day after . . .": letters from Abigail Leary, June 12, 1941, and June 15, 1941, Timothy Leary Archives.

"Living by himself in a tent . . .": Leary, "February 1941, West Point, New York," *Flashbacks.*

" 'Apparently, he did talk to members' . . .": interview with John Beach, January 5, 1999.

"In longhand, he wrote out his letter . . .": letter from Timothy Leary, undated, Timothy Leary Archives.

"On July 31, Abigail wrote to tell Tim . . .": letter from Abigail Leary, July 31, 1941, Timothy Leary Archives.

"In an undated letter, Tim replied . . .": letter from Timothy Leary, undated, Timothy Leary Archives.

"In his autobiography, Leary would write . . .": Leary, "February 1941, West Point, New York," *Flashbacks.*

"Thomas Lawson, whose father flew . . .": interview with Thomas Lawson, January 12, 1999.

SIX

"On a hot August afternoon . . .": Timothy Leary, "August 1941, Indian Orchard, Massachusetts," *Flashbacks: An Autobiography* (Los Angeles: J. P. Tarcher, Inc., 1983).

"A pleasant-looking balding professor . . .": interview with Peter Owen Whitmer, June 3, 1999.

" 'By the semester's end I was the amazed recipient' . . .": Leary, "August 1941, Indian Orchard, Massachusetts," *Flashbacks.*

"Peter Owen Whitmer, a psychologist . . .": interview with Peter Owen Whitmer, November 21, 1997.

"Unlike Holy Cross or West Point , , ,": Leary, "August 1941, Indian Orchard, Massachusetts," *Flashbacks.*

"In a list entitled 'Women Teachers' . . .": document, July 23, 1994, Timothy Leary Archives.

" 'The expulsion was more than an academic setback' . . .": Leary, "Fall, 1942, Tuscaloosa, Alabama," *Flashbacks.*

"From the Theta Chi house there . . .": letter to Abigail Leary, December 2, 1942, Timothy Leary Archives.

"While his enrollment in the ROTC program . . .": Leary, "January 1943, Fort Eustis, Virginia," *Flashbacks.*

"On March 8, 1944, Tim wrote Father Murdock . . .": document, Timothy Leary Archives.

"Staffed by former commercial airlines personnel . . .": Leary, "January 1943, Fort Eustis, Virginia," *Flashbacks.*

"The two met in Buffalo, New York . . .": ibid.

"Nonetheless, on July 15, 1944 . . .": document, Timothy Leary Archives.

"Promoted to corporal, Tim reported . . .": Leary, "January 1943, Fort Eustis, Virginia," *Flashbacks.*

"At lunch, the staff gathered . . .": ibid.

"Marianne's strict German Catholic parents . . .": ibid.

"Nancy Adams, who would become Marianne's . . .": interview with Nancy Adams, May 28, 1997.

"Nancy Adams recalled, 'She once told me' . . .": ibid.

"Marianne attended Marylhurst College . . .": Marianne Busch's college transcript, Timothy Leary Archives.

"After graduating with honors in June . . .": letter of recommendation for Marianne Busch, Oregon City Woolen Mills, May 14, 1942, Timothy Leary Archives.

"While studying there for her master's . . .": interview with Peter Owen Whitmer, June 3, 1999; and interview with Dewey Graham, June 4, 1999.

"As Tim Leary would later write . . .": Leary, "January 1943, Fort Eustis, Virginia," *Flashbacks.*

"On April 12, 1945 (the date Leary cited . . .)": ibid.; and interview with Peter Owen Whitmer, June 3, 1999.

"'There's a classic story about Marianne's parents' . . .": interview with Peter Owen Whitmer, November 21, 1997.

"On their honeymoon night . . .": Leary, "January 1943, Fort Eustis, Virginia," *Flashbacks.*

"Taking his case on appeal . . .": letter to Timothy Leary, October 4, 1944, Timothy Leary Archives.

"On August 23, 1945, he is awarded . . .": diploma, University of Alabama, Timothy Leary Archives.

"On January 19, 1946, Sergeant Timothy Leary . . .": discharge papers, Timothy Leary Archives.

"During their time together . . .": Leary, "January 1943, Fort Eustis, Virginia," *Flashbacks.*

"In 1977, he retitled the thesis . . .": Michael Horowitz, Karen Walls, and Billy Smith, *An Annotated Bibliography of Timothy Leary* (Hamden, Connecticut: Archon Books, 1988).

"'It was a dragnet master's thesis' . . .": interview with Peter Owen Whitmer, November 21, 1997.

"In September 1947, Tim was accepted . . .": Leary, "January 1943, Fort Eustis, Virginia," *Flashbacks.*

SEVEN

"As Tim and Marianne drove over . . .": Timothy Leary, "January 1943, Fort Eustis, Virginia," *Flashbacks: An Autobiography* (Los Angeles: J. P. Tarcher, Inc., 1983).

"With the war over and the economy . . .": letter from Charles Adams, June 1, 1997.

"Six or seven years older . . .": Leary, "January 1943, Fort Eustis, Virginia," *Flashbacks.*

"Much as World War I had introduced . . .": interview with Merv Freedman, February 20, 1997.

"'On April 1, 1946,' Ernest R. Hilgard writes . . .": Ernest R. Hilgard, *Psychology in America: A Historical Survey* (Orlando, FL: Harcourt Brace Jovanovich, 1987).

"'Clinical psychology was burgeoning' . . .": interview with Merv Freedman, February 20, 1997.

"Tim enrolled as a doctoral candidate . . .": Leary, "January 1943, Fort Eustis, Virginia," *Flashbacks*; and interview with Merv Freedman, February 20, 1997.

"Tim stayed by Marianne's side . . .": Leary, "1947, Berkeley, California," *Flashbacks.*

"On September 29, 1947, a delighted Abigail . . .": letter from Abigail Leary, September 29, 1947, Timothy Leary Archives.

"'After Marianne and Susan came home' . . .": Leary, "1947, Berkeley, California," *Flashbacks.*

"'She was not depressed' . . .": interview with Nancy Adams, May 28, 1997.

"'I never heard that Marianne had trouble' . . .": interview with Helen Lane Valdez, May 20, 1997.

"Merv Freedman, a decorated army vereran . . .": interview with Merv Freedman, February 20, 1997.

"'We named him John Busch Leary' . . .": Leary, "1947, Berkeley, California," *Flashbacks*.

"'When Jackie was born' . . .": interview with Merv Freedman, February 20, 1997.

"Mary Della Cioppa,Tim's second wife . . .": interview with Mary Della Cioppa, June 2, 1997.

"'Tim came by the AVC clubhouse' . . .": interview with Helen Lane Valdez, May 20, 1997.

"Others involved in the AVC . . .": Leary, "1947, Berkeley, California," *Flashbacks*.

"'The class Tim was in at Berkeley' . . .": interview with Peter Owen Whitmer, November 21, 1997.

"Nonetheless, in his autobiography . . .": Leary, "1947, Berkeley, California," *Flashbacks*.

"In an eloquent letter of resignation . . .": Robert Coles, *Erik H. Erikson: The Growth of His Own Work* (Boston: Little, Brown and Company, 1970).

"'I found myself trapped once again' . . .": Leary, "1947, Berkeley, California," *Flashbacks*.

"'We both had a strong interest in literature' . . .": interview with Frank Barron, January 30, 1997.

"As Arthur Koestler, with whom Tim would interact . . .": Arthur Koestler, *The Ghost in the Machine* (New York: The Macmillan Company, 1967).

"'Two things were grabbing hold' . . .": interview with Frank Barron, January 30, 1997.

"'I wanted psychology to be an objective discipline' . . .": Leary, "1947, Berkeley, California," *Flashbacks*.

"The thesis was based on . . .": summary of the dissertation, September 1950, Timothy Leary Archives.

"Right from the start . . .": John Bryan, *Whatever Happened to Timothy Leary?* (San Francisco: Renaissance Press, 1980).

"There was some irony in this . . .": interview with Peter Owen Whitmer, January 7, 1998.

"Gerald Kasin, a mechanical engineer . . .": interview with Gerald Kasin, August 19, 1997.

"'After Hiroshima,' Tim Leary would later write . . .": Leary, "1947, Berkeley, California," *Flashbacks*.

"Costing $40,000 . . .": Bryan, *Whatever Happened to Timothy Leary?*

"'I helped them move into the house' . . .": interview with Merv Freedman, February 20, 1997.

"'The whole enterprise was animated' . . .": letter from Charles Adams, June 1, 1997.

"For two months, the Learys lived . . .": postcard from Marianne Leary, December 12, 1953, Timothy Leary Archives.

"In a letter to Nancy Adams . . .": letter from Marianne Leary, February 13, 1954, Timothy Leary Archives.

"'When Tim came back from Europe' . . .": interview with Merv Freedman, February 20, 1997.

EIGHT

"In *What Does WoMan Want?*, a thinly disguised . . .": Timothy Leary, *What Does WoMan Want?* (Los Angeles: 88 Books, 1976).

"'We would then stagger back' . . .": interview with Anne Apfelbaum, May 26, 1997.

"Peter Owen Whitmer recounts a story . . .": interview with Peter Owen Whitmer, January 7, 1998.

"'It was just a terribly lively gay time' . . .": interview with Mary Della Cioppa, June 2, 1997.

"'No one lives like this anymore' ": interview with Anne Apfelbaum, May 26, 1997.

"'Every weekend Marianne and I went to parties' . . .": Timothy Leary, "1953 Berkeley, California," *Flashbacks: An Autobiography* (Los Angeles: J. P. Tarcher, Inc., 1983).

"By this point, Tim had already begun . . .": ibid.

"'Frank Barron sent me to him' . . .": interview with Mary Della Cioppa, June 2, 1997.

"Described by Merv Freedman as . . .": interview with Merv Freedman, February 20, 1997; and interview with Mary Della Cioppa, June 2, 1997.

"Edith Kasin, a clinical psychologist . . .": interview with Edith Kasin, August 19, 1997.

"'When Tim and Mary started having an affair' . . .": interview with Anne Apfelbaum, May 26, 1997.

"'Lust is such a powerful thing' . . .": Leary, "1953, Berkeley, California," *Flashbacks*.

"'Marianne was very dependent on Tim' . . .": interview with Merv Freedman, February 20, 1997.

"'I think she was desperate to make a connection' . . .": interview with Anne Apfelbaum, May 26, 1997.

"Freedman recalled, 'Tim encouraged her' . . .": interview with Merv Freedman, February 20, 1997.

"Apfelbaum added, 'Tim would kind of say' . . .": interview with Anne Apfelbaum, May 26, 1997.

"Nancy Adams, who was not a member . . .": interview with Nancy Adams, May 28, 1997.

"Mary Della Cioppa remembered Marianne running . . .": interview with Mary Della Cioppa, June 2, 1997.

"Peter Owen Whitmer remembered one story . . .": interview with Peter Owen Whitmer, March 20, 1997.

"When Merv Freedman returned to Berkeley . . .": interview with Merv Freedman, February 20, 1997.

"In *Flashbacks*, Leary would write . . .": Leary, "October 21, 1955, Berkeley, California," *Flashbacks*.

"Tim 'thoughtlessly' suggested . . .": ibid.

"'He was going to send Marianne and the children' . . .": interview with Mary Della Cioppa, June 2, 1997.

"During the afternoon of October 21 . . .": interview with Nancy Adams, May 28, 1997.

"'I, like most men, feel inadequate' . . .": letter from Charles Adams, June 1, 1997.

"'No, I can't,' she told him . . .": interview with Mary Della Cioppa, June 2, 1997.

"In his autobiography, Leary maintained . . .": Leary, "October 22, 1955, Berkeley, California," *Flashbacks*.

"Tim rode with Marianne's body . . .": ibid.

"At 9:28 am, she was pronounced dead . . .": "Psychologist's Wife Found Dead in Car," *San Francisco Chronicle*, October 23, 1955.

"'She was punishing herself' . . .": interview with Merv Freedman, February 20, 1997.

"'My darling, I cannot live without' . . .": John Bryan, *Whatever Happened to Timothy Leary?* (San Francisco: Renaissance Press, 1980).

"As an adult, Jack Leary would claim . . .": interview with Jack Leary, April 22, 1997.

"'Everyone would have been better off' . . .": interview with Merv Freedman, February 20, 1997.

"Shortly afterward, Tim told Nancy . . .": interview with Nancy Adams, May 28, 1997.

"In his autobiography, Leary wrote . . .": Leary, "1953, Berkeley, California," *Flashbacks*.

"'Leary told police he and his wife had stayed up' . . .": "Psychologist's Wife Found Dead in Car."

"Year later, Tim would tell Joanna . . .": interview with Joanna Harcourt-Smith, January 3, 1997.

NINE

"Later that Saturday morning . . .": interview with Helen Lane Valdez, May 20, 1997.

"At 10:30 am, an hour after he returned . . .": letter to the Busch family, September 10, 1956, Timothy Leary Archives.

"At two that afternoon . . .": Leary, ""1953, Berkeley, California," *Flashbacks*.

"'When they told Jackie his mother was dead' . . .": interview with Anne Apfelbaum, May 26, 1997.

"'Was Tim upset on the day of the suicide' . . .": interview with Nancy Adams, May 28, 1997.

"'In terms of how Tim reacted to the suicide' . . .": interview with Merv Freedman, February 20, 1997.

"'You could see in part he was blaming himself' . . .": interview with Nancy Adams, May 28, 1997.

"At the airport, Barron told Mary . . .": interview with Mary Della Cioppa, June 2, 1997.

"'That is to say' . . .": interview with Anne Apfelbaum, May 26, 1997.

"When Tim got off the train . . .": letter from Timothy Leary, September 10, 1956, Timothy Leary Archives.

" 'I am told that one of Marianne's sisters' . . .": interview with Merv Freedman, February 20, 1997.

"On October 29, 1955, Mr. and Mrs. Armand L. Bengle . . .": document, Timothy Leary Archives.

"Later, John Busch went to Berkeley . . .": letter to the Busch family, September 10, 1956, Timothy Leary Archives.

" 'The following week was pretty disjointed' . . .": interview with Helen Lane Valdez, May 20, 1997.

" 'She was humorless and rigid' . . .": interview with Mary Della Cioppa, June 2, 1997.

"Nancy Adams would later say . . .": interview with Nancy Adams, May 28, 1997.

" 'But in less than six months' . . .": interview with Anne Apfelbaum, May 26, 1997.

"Susan was so grateful . . .": interview with Mary Della Cioppa, June 2, 1997.

"Tim's fluctuating moods . . .": Peter Owen Whitmer, "The Legend of a Mind: A Psychobiography of Timothy Leary" (unpublished, 1975).

"Believing himself 'the world's best father' . . .": interview with Mary Della Cioppa, June 2, 1997.

" 'Before Marianne's suicide' . . .": interview with Nancy Adams, May 28, 1997.

" 'After Marianne died' . . .": interview with Edith Kasin, August 19, 1997.

"Even before their mother's death . . .": interview with Mary Della Cioppa, June 2, 1997.

"In his introduction to An Annotated Bibliography . . .": Michael Horowitz, Karen Walls, and Billy Smith, *An Annotated Bibliography of Timothy Leary* (Hamden, Connecticut: Archon Books, 1988).

"In layman's terms, the book posited . . .": John Bryan, *Whatever Happened to Timothy Leary?* (San Francisco: Renaissance Press, 1980).

" 'This book is a masterpiece' . . .": interview with Richard Varnes, February 10, 1997.

"Rolf LaForge did not copyright . . .": interview by Peter Owen Whitmer with Rolf LaForge, March 7, 1974.

" 'Tim wrote about the whole interpersonal enterprise' . . .": interview with Merv Freedman, February 20, 1997.

"According to Peter Owen Whitmer . . .": Whitmer, "The Legend of a Mind."

"Whitmer added, 'The book caused tremendous' . . .": interview with Peter Owen Whitmer, January 7, 1998.

"As Varnes said, 'At the time' . . .": interview with Richard Varnes, February 10, 1997.

" 'I had suggested to Tim that since Marianne' . . .": interview with Mary Della Ciopppa, May 29, 1997.

"Although nearly a quarter of a century . . .": interview with Merv Freedman, February 20, 1997.

"In what he liked to refer to as . . .": Timothy Leary, *What Does WoMan Want?* (Los Angeles: 88 Books, 1976).

"In 1942, he was part of a convoy . . .": document, Timothy Leary Archives.

"On February 14, 1956, General Douglas MacArthur . . .": document, Timothy Leary Archives.

" 'Tote was living in a hotel in lower Manhattan' . . .": interview by Peter Owen Whitmer with Phil and Anita Shea, 1983.

"In longhand, Tim wrote his father . . .": letter to Tote Leary, undated, Timothy Leary Archives.

"From Berkeley on September 10, 1956 . . .": letter to Tote Leary, September 10, 1956, Timothy Leary Archives.

"Two months later, Tim wrote . . .": letter to Tote Leary, November 14, 1956, Timothy Leary Archives.

"On December 1, 1956, after returning . . .": letter to Tote Leary, December 1, 1956, Timothy Leary Archives.

"Peter Owen Whitmer would later say . . .": interview with Peter Owen Whitmer, November 21, 1997.

"Tim did not attend the service . . .": ibid.

" 'Tim didn't know how he felt' . . .": interview with Mary Della Cioppa, June 2, 1997.

" 'Coffey lived with his wife and three children' . . .": ibid.

" 'I didn't pick up on anything' . . .": interview with Edith Kasin, August 19, 1997.

"In a letter to the author discussing this subject . . .": letter, July 2, 1997.

" 'Tim was not trading sexual favors' . . .": interview, February 20, 1997.

" 'When Hubert was arrested' . . .": interview with Mary Della Cioppa, June 2, 1997.

" 'When I came in to the clinic' . . .": interview with Anne Apfelbaum, May 26, 1997.

"Merv Freedman would later say . . .": interview with Merv Freedman, February 20, 1997.

" 'I gave him that nose he had' . . .": interview with Mary Della Cioppa, June 2, 1997.

"A friend who went with Tim to Mexico . . .": Whitmer, "Legend of a Mind."

"Tim punched Mary in the face . . .": interview with Mary Della Cioppa, June 2, 1997.

"On the back of a stunning . . .": photograph, Timothy Leary Archives.

"Mary Della Cioppa later said . . .": interview with Mary Della Cioppa, June 2, 1997.

"Moreover, as Helen Lane Valdez admitted . . .": interview with Helen Lane Valdez, May 20, 1997.

" 'Before Marianne's suicide' . . .": interview with Merv Freedman, February 20, 1997.

"On June 30, 1958, Tim wrote Susan . . .": letter to Susan Leary, June 30, 1958, Timothy Leary Archives.

"In Torremolinos on the Costa del Sol . . .": Leary, "Spring, 1959, Florence, Italy," *Flashbacks.*

TEN

"He had brought along a trunk . . .": Timothy Leary, "Trip 1: Death of the Mind: Abysmal Prelude," *High Priest* (New York: New American Library in association with the World Publishing Company, 1968; Berkeley, CA: Ronin Publishing, Inc., 1995).

"He soon began to experience . . .": ibid.

"Jackie had been given a puppy . . .": ibid.

" 'Each hair was a burning rod' . . .": ibid.

" 'I sat in the darkness' . . .": ibid.

"The third went to a colleague . . .": ibid.

" 'For the first time since my thirty-fifth birthday' . . .": Timothy Leary, "Spring 1959, Florence, Italy," *Flashbacks: An Autobiography* (Los Angeles: J. P. Tarcher, Inc., 1983).

"Barron read the manuscript . . .": interview with Frank Barron, January 30, 1997.

"While in Florence, Barron told Tim . . .": Leary, "Spring 1959, Florence, Italy," *Flashbacks.*

" 'Frank Barron,' David McClelland recalled . . .": interview with David McClelland, February 5, 1997.

"A 'tall, elegant, mustachioed' man . . .": David Cohen, *Psychologists on Psychology* (New York: Taplinger Publishing Company, 1977).

" 'I had admired his work as a psychologist' . . .": interview with David McClelland, February 5, 1997.

" 'Nobody was snowing David McClelland' . . .": interview with Frank Barron, January 30, 1997.

"As soon as he had enrolled Jack and Susan . . .": Leary, "January 1960, Cambridge, Massachusetts," *Flashbacks.*

" 'Mother and Aunt Mae came trotting' . . .": Leary, "February 1960, Indian Orchard, Massachusetts," *Flashbacks.*

"As she walked Tim out to the car later . . .": ibid.

"On cue, Susan and Jackie stood . . .": John Bryan, *Whatever Happened to Timothy Leary?* (San Francisco: Renaissance Press, 1980).

"Having come to Cambridge to resurrect . . .": Leary, "January 1960, Cambridge, Massachusetts," *Flashbacks.*

"Declaring himself to be basically sympathetic . . .": letter from David McClelland, May 3, 1960, Timothy Leary Archives.

" 'I was an assistant professor at Harvard' . . .": interview with Charles Slack, March 20, 1997.

"Neil Friedman, a former graduate student . . .": interview with Neil Friedman, April 22, 1997.

"One night as Tim and Slack . . .": Charles Slack, *Timothy Leary, the Madness of the Sixties, and Me* (New York: Peter H. Wyden, 1974).

"Slack asked whether Tim had ever had sex . . .": interview with Charles Slack, March 20, 1997.

"Each evening when the kids were in bed . . .": Leary, "January 1960, Cambridge, Massachusetts," *Flashbacks.*

" 'I was the Jewish boy on the way up' . . .": interview with Richard Alpert, October 28, 1996.

"Brought up in a 'Jewish anxiety-ridden' . . .": Ram Dass, *Be Here Now* (San Cristobal, NM: Lama Foundation, 1971.

"Alpert taught courses in human motivation . . .": ibid.

"Adored by children . . .": Leary, "January 1960, Cambridge, Massachusetts," *Flashbacks.*

"The son of George Alpert . . .": Bryan, *Whatever Happened to Timothy Leary?*

"He owned a Mercedes-Benz . . .": Ram Dass, *Be Here Now.*

"In the face of this feeling of malaise . . .": ibid.

" 'After I took the psilocybin' . . .": interview with Richard Alpert, October 28, 1996.

"Alpert would be Huck Finn . . .": Leary, "January 1960, Cambridge, Massachusetts," *Flashbacks.*

"As soon as the academic year ended . . .": Peter O. Whitmer with Bruce VanWygarden, *Aquarius Revisited* (New York: Macmillan Publishing Company, 1987).

"Buying a used Ford so old . . .": Bryan, *Whatever Happened to Timothy Leary?*

"Tim and Jackie then headed for Cuernavaca . . .": Leary, "Summer 1960, Cuernavaca, Mexico," *Flashbacks.*

"Down the highway from the villa . . .": Leary, "Trip 2: The Sacred Mushrooms of Mexico," *High Priest.*

"Ten miles away in Tepoztlán . . .": Jay Stevens, *Storming Heaven: LSD and the American Dream* (New York: Atlantic Monthly Press, 1987).

"A 'few cornfields away' . . .": Leary, "Trip 2: The Sacred Mushrooms of Mexico," *High Priest.*

" 'I was a middle-aged man' . . .": Bryan, *Whatever Happened to Timothy Leary?*

"More specifically, Tim's sexuality . . .": Timothy Leary, *Chaos & Cyberculture* (Berkeley, CA: Ronin Publishing, 1994).

"In Casa del Moros, a rambling . . .": Leary, "Summer 1960, Cuernavaca, Mexico," *Flashbacks.*

"In reality, he was an East German refugee . . .": Whitmer, *Aquarius Revisited.*

"Learning that these mushrooms still grew . . .": Leary, "Trip 2: The Sacred Mushrooms of Mexico," *High Priest*; and interview by Peter Owen Whitmer, November 16, 1973.

"Around noon on August 9, 1960 . . .": Stevens, *Storming Heaven: LSD and the American Dream.*

"After being 'pushed out of history's notice' . . .": Leary, "Summer 1960, Cuernavaca, Mexico," *Flashbacks.*

"Soon after, the poet Robert Graves . . .": Stevens, *Storming Heaven: LSD and the American Dream.*

"Tim picked up a mushroom . . .": Leary, "Trip 2: The Sacred Mushrooms of Mexico," *High Priest.*

"The mushrooms tasted . . .": Leary, "Summer 1960, Cuernavaca, Mexico," *Flashbacks.*

"Feeling as though he was on nitrous oxide . . .": Leary, "Trip 2: The Sacred Mushrooms of Mexico," *High Priest.*

"It was like swimming on a moonless night . . .": ibid.

"In sharp focus . . .": ibid.

"When Richard Alpert arrived . . .": Ram Dass, *Be Here Now.*

"A few months after that . . .": Stevens, *Storming Heaven: LSD and the American Dream.*

"In *High Priest,* Tim's first autobiography . . .": Leary, "Trip 2: The Sacred Mushrooms of Mexico," *High Priest.*

"By then, as Jay Stevens noted . . .": Stevens, *Storming Heaven: LSD and the American Dream.*

"Peter Owen Whitmer recalled . . .": interview with Peter Whitmer, March 20, 1997.

"'During that meeting with McClelland' . . .": Leary, "Summer 1960, Cuernavaca, Mexico," *Flashbacks.*

"'He was very excited because' . . .": interview with David McClelland, Feburary 5, 1997.

"When Tim talked about his experiences . . .": Leary, "Summer 1960, Cuernavaca, Mexico," *Flashbacks.*

ELEVEN

"Returning to Harvard for the new school year . . .": Timothy Leary, "Trip 4: The Dark Paradox," *High Priest* (New York: New American Library in association with the World Publishing Company, 1968; Berkeley, CA: Ronin Publishing, Inc., 1995).

"The day Tim checked in for the fall semester . . .": Timothy Leary, "Fall 1960, Cambridge, Massachusetts," *Flashbacks: An Autobiography* (Los Angeles: J. P. Tarcher, Inc., 1983).

"'I went to Tim and tried to relate' . . .": interview with George Litwin, March 24, 1997.

"It was at Sandoz Laboratories . . .": Martin A. Lee and Bruce Shlain, *Acid Dreams: The CIA, LSD, and the Sixties Rebellion* (New York: Grove Press, Inc., 1985).

"Following Litwin's lead, Tim dictated a letter . . .": Leary, "Fall 1960, Cambridge, Massachusetts," *Flashbacks.*

"'It was all there' . . .": Leary, "Trip 4: The Dark Paradox," *High Priest.*

"Expecting to lay back . . .": Aldous Huxley, *The Doors of Perception* and *Heaven and Hell* (New York: Harper and Row, 1954).

"Even so, as he would later write . . .": Sybille Bedford, *Aldous Huxley: A Biography* (New York: Alfred A. Knopf/Harper and Row, 1974).

"On October 3, 1960, Tim wrote Huxley . . .": letter to Aldous Huxley, October 3, 1960, Timothy Leary Archives.

"'What kind?' Huxley asked . . .": Leary, "Trip 4: The Dark Paradox," *High Priest.*

"'We clicked along agreeably' . . .": Leary, "Fall 1960, Cambridge, Massachusetts," *Flashbacks.*

"(After thirteen years, one third . . .": Lee and Shlain, *Acid Dreams.*

"Although this practice unnerved . . .": Leary, "Trip 4: The Dark Paradox," *High Priest.*

"By then, Tim was in what . . .": ibid.

"'You've got those pills' . . .": ibid.

"'I knew he was right' . . .": ibid.

"'Sure,' Charlie replied with a grin . . .": ibid.

"'I thought of upstairs' . . .": ibid.

"In the hallway, O'Donnell drew away . . .": ibid.

"'I'll tell you why you can't go' . . .": ibid.

"'Timothy called me,' George Litwin recalled . . .": interview with George Litwin, March 24, 1997.

"As votes were still being counted . . .": Humphry Osmond with John A. Osmundsen and Jerome Agel, *Understanding Understanding* (New York: Harper and Row, 1974).

"Fourteen years later, Osmond would write . . .": ibid.

TWELVE

"On November 15, Tim Leary responded . . .": letter to David McClelland, November 15, 1960, Timothy Leary Archives.

"Ginsberg had already taken peyote . . .": interview with Allen Ginsberg, January 20, 1997.

"**Having come to Boston to address . . .**": Jane Kramer, *Allen Ginsberg in America* (New York: Random House, 1968).

"**One week later, Tim knocked . . .**": ibid.

"**'They were sharing flats' . . .**": interview with Jeanne DiPrima, July 9, 1997.

"**'Leary had this big beautiful house' . . .**": Kramer, *Allen Ginsberg in America.*

"**For his part, Tim was delighted . . .**": Timothy Leary, "December 1960, Trip 6: The Blueprint to Turn on the World: Ecstatic Politics," *High Priest* (New York: New American Library in association with the World Publishing Company, 1968; Berkeley, CA: Ronin Publishing, Inc., 1995).

"**At 9:00 am, Jackie and a friend . . .**": ibid.

"**Summoned by the great horns . . .**": Leary, "December 1960, Trip 6: The Blueprint to Turn on the World: Ecstatic Politics," *High Priest.*

"**By Monday afternoon, rumors about . . .**": Leary, "December 1960, Trip 6: The Blueprint to Turn on the World: Ecstatic Politics," *High Priest.*

"**During lunch one day at the Faculty Club . . .**": interview with Huston Smith, February 19, 1997.

"**Making good on his promise . . .**": interview with Allen Ginsberg, January 20, 1997.

"**With Olson in the fold, Tim wrote Arthur Koestler . . .**": document, Timothy Leary Archives.

"**Described by his own biographer . . .**": Mark Mazower, review of *The Homeless Mind, The New York Times Book Review,* January 2, 2000.

"**A few days before he arrived . . .**": Timothy Leary, "Getting High on Toil and Suffering," *Flashbacks: An Autobiography* (Los Angeles: J. P. Tarcher, Inc., 1983).

"**At Harvard, Tim took Koestler . . .**": ibid.

"**He told his host he would stick with alcohol . . .**": ibid.

"**'I was too much an Irish Catholic' . . .**": Leary, "Trip 7: You Have to Go out of Your Mind to Use Your Head," *High Priest.*

"**Tim arrived at Ginsberg's 'terminally dingy' . . .**": Leary, "Literary Elites and Black Hope," *Flashbacks.*

"**In the kitchen, Jack Kerouac . . .**": "The Set and Setting," Timothy Leary Archives.

"**Not only did they share the experience . . .**": Leary, "Literary Elites and Black Hope," *Flashbacks.*

"**As these were 'the days of naturalistic research' . . .**": "The Set and Setting," Timothy Leary Archives.

"**As though the session were just another drunken . . .**": ibid.

"**In an entirely different frame of mind . . .**": Leary, "Literary Elites and Black Hope," *Flashbacks.*

"**Later, Leary wrote that he had told him . . .**": "The Set and Setting," Timothy Leary Archives.

"**'Kerouac was drinking a bit' . . .**": interview with Allen Ginsberg, January 20, 1997.

"**Mainly, I felt like a floating Khan . . .**": "The Set and Setting," Timothy Leary Archives.

"**Three months later, Kerouac wrote . . .**": Robert Forte, editor, *Timothy Leary: Outside Looking In* (Rochester, VT: Park Street Press, 1999).

"**'Throughout the night Kerouac remained' . . .**": Leary, "Literary Elites and Black Hope," *Flashbacks.*

THIRTEEN

"**In a letter written in 1959 . . .**": Paul Mariana, *Lost Puritan: A Life of Robert Lowell* (New York, London: W. W. Norton & Co., 1994).

"**'We went to Robert Lowell' . . .**": interview with Allen Ginsberg, January 20, 1997.

"**'Lowell,' Leary would later write . . .**": Timothy Leary, "Literary Elites and Black Hope," *Flashbacks: An Autobiography* (Los Angeles: J. P. Tarcher, Inc., 1983).

"**Tim, Ginsberg, and Orlovsky then headed . . .**": ibid.

"**Barney Rosset recalled, 'I didn't know' . . .**": interview with Barney Rosset, November 19, 1996.

"**Oblivious to everything . . .**": Leary, "Literary Elites and Black Hope," *Flashbacks.*

"As Ginsberg would later recall . . .": interview with Allen Ginsberg, January 20, 1997.

" 'The next day I went to Grove Press' . . .": interview with Barney Rosset, November 19, 1996.

"At Allen's flat we tallied up the score . . .": Leary, "Literary Elites and Black Hope," *Flashbacks.*

"In February, Ginsberg wrote Tim . . .": Timothy Leary, "December 1960, Trip 6: The Blueprint to Turn on the World: Ecstatic Politics," *High Priest* (New York: New American Library in association with the World Publishing Company, 1968; Berkeley, CA: Ronin Publishing, Inc., 1995).

" 'What really flipped me out' . . .": interview with Barney Rosset, November 19, 1996.

"The rules of the research project . . .": document, Timothy Leary Archives.

"Never shy when it came . . .": Leary, "January 1961, Trip 7: You Have to Go out of Your Mind to Use Your Head," *High Priest.*

"As soon as she arrived . . .": Leary, "Literary Elites and Black Hope," *Flashbacks.*

" 'She would call me from his place' . . .": interview with Barney Rosset, November 19, 1996.

"In January 1961, Allen Ginsberg wrote . . .": letter from Allen Ginsberg, January 1961, reprinted in *Esquire* (July 1968).

" 'I delivered it to his house' . . .": interview with Allen Ginsberg, January 20, 1997.

"Assessing his own role . . .": ibid.

" 'Why not start right now' . . .": Leary, "Trip 8: The Random Spinning of the Mind Must Be Centered by Prayer," *High Priest.*

"Going into the living room . . .": Ram Dass, *Be Here Now* (San Cristobal, NM: Lama Foundation, 1971).

"Looking up, he saw his parents . . .": ibid.

" 'Pretty soon,' Alpert would later write . . .": ibid.

" 'They were like psychedelic mom and dad' . . .": interview with Gunther Weil, October 26, 1996.

"Confirming this, Alpert would later say . . .": interview with Richard Alpert, October 28, 1996.

"Each graduate assumed a different role . . .": interview with George Litwin, March 24, 1997.

" 'Ralph was the German Oxford academic' . . .": interview with Gunther Weil, October 26, 1996.

" 'Prison work is considered' . . .": Leary, "Trip 9: The Sacred Mushroom Goes to Jail," *High Priest.*

"Frank Barron, who went with him . . .": interview with Frank Barron, January 20, 1997.

"Presnell told Tim that with prisoners . . .": interview by Peter Owen Whitmer with Dr. Madison Presnell, October 11, 1973.

"As Tim would later write, Presnell . . .": Leary, "Trip 9: The Sacred Mushroom Goes to Jail," *High Priest.*

"Tim's first reaction to Metzner . . .": ibid.

"While Susan sat upstairs . . .": interview by Peter Owen Whitmer with Dr. Madison Presnell, October 11, 1973.

FOURTEEN

"Around a table in a dreary room . . .": Timothy Leary, "Trip 9: The Sacred Mushroom Goes to Jail," *High Priest* (New York: New American Library in association with the World Publishing Company, 1968; Berkeley, CA: Ronin Publishing, Inc., 1995).

"Nonetheless, on March 27, 1961 . . .": ibid.

"When Tim asked why . . .": ibid.

" 'Gunther was silly and acting like a hipster' . . .": ibid.

" 'It was a horror trip' . . .": inteview with Ralph Metzner, October 29, 1996.

" 'I felt at home in prison' . . .": Leary, "Trip 9: The Sacred Mushroom Goes to Jail," *High Priest.*

"One of them was Jimmy Carrigan . . .": interview with Gunther Weil, October 26, 1996.

" 'We never had any violence with them' . . .": interview with Ralph Metzner, October 29, 1996.

"For Weil, the sessions were . . .": interview with Gunther Weil, October 26, 1996.

"When the first prisoner involved . . .": Leary, "Trip 9: The Sacred Mushroom Goes to Jail," *High Priest.*

"'Everyone in the Massachusetts correctional' . . .": ibid.

"Metzner actually went so far . . .": letter from Ralph Metzner to Robert F. Kennedy, July 18, 1962, Timothy Leary Archives.

"'We sat in our offices at Harvard' . . .": Leary, "Trip 9: The Sacred Mushroom Goes to Jail," *High Priest.*

"Years later, Richard Alpert would explain . . .": interview with Richard Alpert, October 28, 1996.

"Two years after the inception . . ." Rick Doblin, "Dr. Leary's Concord Prison Experiment: A 34-Year Follow-Up Study," *Journal of Psychoactive Drugs* 30, 4 (October–December 1998).

"In an article about the Concord Prison Project . . .": Leary, "Trip 9: The Sacred Mushroom Goes to Jail," *High Priest.*

"In 1998, thirty-five years later . . .": Doblin, "Dr. Leary's Concord Prison Experiment."

"In an article published along with Doblin's report . . .": Ralph Metzner, "Reflections on the Concord Prison Project and the Follow-Up Study," *Journal of Psychoactive Drugs* 30, 4 (October–December 1998).

"As for the original data for the Concord . . .": interview by Peter Owen Whitmer with Dr. Madison Presnell, October 11, 1973.

FIFTEEN

"Using his incredible energy . . .": letter from Timothy Leary, January 1, 1961, Timothy Leary Archives.

"In February, Aldous Huxley wrote . . .": letter from Aldous Huxley, February 6, 1961, Timothy Leary Archives.

"'There were two schools of thought' . . .": interview with Dr. Oscar Janiger, October 25, 1996.

"'Did I tell you that Dean Josiah Bartlett' . . .": letter to Alan Watts, February 23, 1961, Timothy Leary Archives.

"Inspired by the spiritual change . . .": Alan Watts, *In My Own Way* (New York: Pantheon, 1972).

"In time, he would acknowledge . . .": ibid.

"'Hope you can come' . . .": letter to Aldous Huxley, March 3, 1961, Timothy Leary Archives.

"'At this point,' he wrote . . .": letter to David McClelland, March 7, 1961, Timothy Leary Archives.

"As the academic year ended . . .": document, Timothy Leary Archives.

"Allen Ginsberg had urged him . . .": Timothy Leary, "Trip 11," *High Priest* (New York: New American Library in association with the World Publishing Company, 1968; Berkeley, CA: Ronin Publishing, Inc., 1995).

"Ten years earlier while drunk . . .": Richard Severo, obituary for William Burroughs, *The New York Times,* August 4, 1997.

"Although Burroughs had recently written . . .": Leary, "Trip 11," *High Priest.*

"Soon everyone was in . . .": ibid.

"'One of them got caught in bad visions' . . .": ibid.

"Harry Murray, whom Tim Leary would later call . . ."; Timothy Leary, *Changing My Mind, Among Others* (Englewood Cliffs, NJ: Prentice Hall, Inc., 1982).

"Murray began the conference . . .": ibid.

"In the afternoon, Huxley discussed . . .": interview with Herbert Kelman, February 15, 1997.

"As Tim left the session . . .": Leary, *Changing My Mind, Among Others.*

"After thanking Frank Barron . . .": Peter Owen Whitmer with Bruce VanWygarden, *Aquarius Revisited* (New York: Macmillan Publishing Company, 1987).

"'The overall reaction I had' . . .": interview with Herbert Kelman, February 15, 1997.

"Tim Leary would later write . . .": Leary, *Changing My Mind, Among Others.*

"As George Litwin recalled . . .": interview with George Litwin, March 24, 1997.

"Having come to turn her on . . .": Judith Thurman, *Isak Dinesen: The Life of a Storyteller* (New York: St. Martin's Press, 1982).

"Dinesen, then seventy-five . . .": Parmenia Migel, *Titania: The Biography of Isak Dinesen* (New York: Random House, 1967).

"Susan Leary later recalled . . .": interview with Susan Leary, undated transcript, Timothy Leary Archives.

"After he left Tim's house . . .": Leary, "Trip 11," *High Priest.*

"'Bill had the idea' . . .": interview with Allen Ginsberg, January 20, 1997.

SIXTEEN

"'Dr. Leary,' he said . . .": Timothy Leary, "Trip 12," *High Priest* (New York: New American Library in association with the World Publishing Company, 1968; Berkeley, CA: Ronin Publishing, Inc., 1995).

"Huxley suggested that he find . . .": Michael Hollingshead, *The Man Who Turned on the World* (London: Blond & Briggs Ltd, 1973).

"'I was in my office at six or six-thirty' . . .": interview with George Litwin, March 24, 1997.

"Tim then phoned a mutual friend . . .": Leary, "Trip 12," *High Priest.*

"'He moved in as a kind of majordomo' . . .": interview with George Litwin, March 24, 1997.

"Although Hollingshead loved psilocybin . . .": Leary, "Trip 12," *High Priest.*

"In *High Priest*, he wrote . . .": ibid.

"In *What Does WoMan Want?*, calling her 'Flora Lu' . . .": Timothy Leary, *What Does WoMan Want?* (Los Angeles: 88 Books, 1976).

"Compared to what Tim had experienced . . .": Leary, "Trip 12," *High Priest.*

"'They could tell we had been beyond' . . .": ibid.

"Seeing Hollingshead as some sort of . . .": ibid.

"'Hollingshead was a major shift' . . .": interview with Gunther Weil, October 26, 1996.

"Ralph Metzner, who was not a fan . . .": interview with Ralph Metzner, October 29, 1996.

"'Hollingshead?' asked Richard Alpert . . .": interview with Richard Alpert, October 28, 1996

"The role he played . . .": Leary, "Trip 12," *High Priest.*

"'I took acid a week after I started at Harvard . . .": interview with Gunther Weil, October 26, 1996.

"'Everyone was sleeping with everyone' . . .": interview, January 27, 1997.

"In his biography . . .": *John Bryan, Whatever Happened to Timothy Leary?* (San Francisco: Renaissance Press, 1980).

"When asked whether LSD turned . . .": interview with Frank Barron, January 30, 1997.

"The meeting was set up by a mutual friend . . .": interview with Peggy Hitchcock, December 2, 1996.

"After Flo introduced Tim . . .": Leary, *What Does WoMan Want?*

"'He started talking to me about' . . .": interview with Charles Slack, March 20, 1997.

"Tim dismissed the book . . .": Leary, *What Does WoMan Want?*

SEVENTEEN

"'There was an in-group' . . .": interview with Brendan Maher, February 5, 1997.

"'During that fall,' Herbert Kelman remembered . . .": interview with Herbert Kelman, February 15, 1997.

"Maher recalled that he learned . . .": interview with Brendan Maher, February 5, 1997.

"David McClelland also began hearing . . .": interview with David McClelland, February 5, 1997.

"'I began to realize,' McClelland later told . . .": Jay Stevens, *Storming Heaven: LSD and the American Dream* (New York: Atlantic Monthly Press, 1987).

"In a memo entitled . . .": ibid.

"Proposing several modifications . . .": memo from Richard Alpert, Timothy Leary Archives.

"On February 20, 1962, The Harvard Crimson . . .": Stevens, *Storming Heaven: LSD and the American Dream.*

"Alpert and Leary quickly sent a letter . . .": Andrew Weil, "The Strange Case of the Harvard Drug Scandal," *Look* (November 5, 1963).

"'Let's define the drugs' . . .": memo from David McClelland, February 21, 1962, Timothy Leary Archives.

"'I was really the one' . . .": interview with Neil Freidman, April 22, 1997.

"'Whether or not the students took drugs' . . .": interview with Herbert Kelman, February 15, 1997.

"When Kelman walked into the meeting . . .": ibid.

"Calling the meeting to order . . .": undated transcript, Timothy Leary Archives.

"McClelland decried . . .": ibid.

"'I wish I could treat this as' . . .": Robert E. Smith, "Psychologists Disagree on Psilocybin Research," *The Harvard Crimson,* March 15, 1962.

"Calling his colleagues 'false messiahs' . . .": Timothy Leary, *Bulletin of the Massachusetts Pscyhological Association* (1964).

"'Tim's normal reaction to criticism' . . .": interview with David McClelland, February 5, 1997.

"'As usual,' Kelman recalled . . .": interview with Herbert Kelman, February 15, 1997.

"'I worked my way through the recent literature' . . .": interview with Brendan Maher, February 5, 1997.

"Later, in Flashbacks, Leary would describe . . .": Timothy Leary, "Spring 1962," *Flashbacks: An Autobiography* (Los Angeles: J. P. Tarcher, 1983).

"Maher recalled, 'It was downhill' . . .": interview with Brendan Maher, February 5, 1997.

"'At this point,' Leary wrote . . .": Leary, "Spring 1962, Harvard," *Flashbacks.*

"'Alpert said he was going to arrange' . . .": interview with Brendan Maher, February 5, 1997.

"Still, according to Tim . . .": Leary, "Spring 1962, Harvard," *Flashbacks.*

"Previously, Weil had asked Tim . . .": Andrew Weil, *The Natural Mind* (Boston: Houghton Mifflin Company, 1972).

"Describing his trips many years later . . .": Robert Forte, editor, *Timothy Leary: Outside Looking In* (Rochester, VT: Park Street Press, 1999).

"As Peter Owen Whitmer wrote . . .": Peter Owen Whitmer with Bruce VanWygarden, *Aquarius Revisited* (New York: Macmillan Publishing Company, 1987).

"Under the headline . . .": Smith, "Psychologists Disagree on Psilocybin Research."

"The next day, Anthony G. Greenwald . . .": letter, *The Harvard Crimson,* March 16, 1962.

"Even Elliot Perkins . . .": letter, *The Harvard Crimson,* March 17, 1962.

"On March 16, 1962, however . . .": "Hallucination Drug Fought at Harvard—350 Students Take Pills," *Boston Herald,* March 16, 1962.

"On March 28, The Harvard Crimson reported . . .": *The Harvard Crimson,* March 28, 1962.

"'Inspector O'Connell was proud . . .": Leary, "Spring 1962, Harvard," *Flashbacks.*

"David McClelland recalled . . .": interview with David McClelland, February 5, 1997.

"'When it became known on campus' . . .": Timothy Leary, *Changing My Mind, Among Others* (Englewood Cliffs, NJ: Prentice Hall, Inc., 1982).

"Through Smith and Walter Houston Clark . . .": Timothy Leary, "Trip 14," *High Priest* (New York: New American Library in association with the World Publishing Company, 1968; Berkeley, CA: Ronin Publishing, Inc., 1995).

"Sounding like a small-town Irish parish priest . . .": ibid.

"Finally Pahnke agreed . . .": ibid.

"Tim would later write that he told Pahnke . . .": ibid.

"Michael Hollingshead, who was there . . .": Michael Hollingshead, *The Man Who Turned on the World* (London: Blond & Briggs Ltd, 1973).

"Rick Doblin, who conducted a follow-up study . . .": interview with Rick Doblin, April 21, 1997.

"'The door opened,' Smith recalled . . .": interview with Huston Smith, February 19, 1997.

"'Everybody I spoke with' . . .": interview with Rick Doblin, April 21, 1997.

"After the experiment . . .": interview with Susan Leary, undated transcript, Timothy Leary Archives.

"'Our eyes met and we grinned' . . .": Leary, "Trip 14," *High Priest*.

"'For Leary,' Michael Hollingshead would later write . . .": Hollingshead, *The Man Who Turned on the World*.

EIGHTEEN

"The hotel's full-color brochure . . .": document, Timothy Leary Archives.

"Since virtually no one stayed at Hotel Catalina . . .": Timothy Leary, "Psychedelic Summer Camp," *Flashbacks: An Autobiography* (Los Angeles: J. P. Tarcher, 1983).

"'Timothy and Richard decided they would like' . . .": interview with Peggy Hitchcock, December 2, 1996.

"Leary described 'Pretty Peggy Hitchcock' . . .": Leary, "Ambushes by the Harvard Squares," *Flashbacks*.

"group fantasy": interview, January 27, 1997.

"In *Flashbacks*, Leary wrote that . . .": Leary, "Islands In The Sun," *Flashbacks*.

"'They had all the graduate students' . . .": interview with Peggy Hitchcock, December 2, 1996.

"As Tim Leary would later describe it . . .": Leary, "Psychedelic Summer Camp," *Flashbacks*.

"'It was very different' . . .": interview with Ralph Metzner, October 29, 1996.

"'It was totally innocent' . . .": interview, January 27, 1997.

"As Tim stood on the top terrace . . .": Leary, "Psychedelic Summer Camp," *Flashbacks*.

"Years later, Susan Leary remembered . . .": interview with Susan Leary, undated transcript, Timothy Leary Archives.

"'The fact that they were standing' . . .": Leary, "Psychedelic Summer Camp," *Flashbacks*.

"Although he could see . . .": Stephen Talty, "The Straight Dope," *Playboy* (November 2003).

"He pulled his best players . . .": Leary, "Psychedelic Summer Camp," *Flashbacks*.

"Tim and his two children moved . . .": Leary, "Farewell to Harvard," *Flashbacks*.

"'It was a fairly big house' . . .": interview with Peggy Hitchcock, December 2, 1996.

"Influenced by Hermann Hesse's *Steppenwolf* . . .": Leary, "Farewell to Harvard," *Flashbacks*.

"Metzner would later say . . .": interview with Ralph Metzner, October 29, 1996.

"'It was meant to be a sister community' . . .": interview, January 27, 1997.

"George Litwin would later say . . .": interview with George Litwin, March 24, 1997.

"Tim told the press that the BIG family . . .": *Boston Herald*, February 27, 1963.

"'With us,' Tim said . . .": "BIG Family Pledges BIG Home Battle," *Record-American*, February 28, 1963.

"Years later, Susan would say . . .": interview with Susan Leary, undated transcript, Timothy Leary Archives.

"a Harvard graduate student remembered feeling that . . .": interview, January 27, 1997

"On October 16, members of the executive . . .": letter from Robert Bales, December 4, 1962, reprinted in *The Harvard Crimson*, December 12, 1962.

"A week later, Tim told a meeting . . .": *The Harvard Crimson*, October 22, 1962.

"'We agreed,' Tim would later write . . .": Leary, *Flashbacks*.

"'In this, the third year of our research' . . .": Leary, "Farewell to Harvard," *Flashbacks*.

"In the opening paragraph . . .": Fred Hechinger, "Use of Mind-Distorting Drugs Rising at Harvard, Dean Says," *The New York Times,* December 11, 1962.

"Three days later, the *Times* reported . . .": Fred Hechinger, *The New York Times,* December 14, 1962.

"On December 26, Aldous Huxley . . .": Grover Smith, editor, *The Letters of Aldous Huxley* (New York: Harper and Row, 1969).

"An impressive-sounding . . .": Statement of Purpose of the International Federation for Internal Freedom, courtesy W. B. Maher, Harvard University.

"The aim of the organization . . .": Leary, "Farewell to Harvard," *Flashbacks*.

"'Within a few weeks,' Tim Leary would write . . .": ibid.

"Originally located in the Charles River Park . . .": interview with Gunther Weil, November 14, 1996.

"His sessions reports. . . .": Documents, Timothy Leary Archives.

". . . the world's largest,": Leary, *Flashbacks*.

"On January 30, 1963, Brendan Maher . . .": letter from Brendan Maher, January 30, 1963, Timothy Leary Archives.

"Injecting DMT took him . . .": Timothy Leary Session Report, December 10, 1962, Timothy Leary Archives.

"With Brunnel's help, Tim planned . . .": Leary, *Flashbacks*.

"'Since IFIF was non-profit' . . .": ibid.

"On April 15, 1963, Maher wrote Tim . . .": letter from Brendan Maher, April 15, 1963, Timothy Leary Archives.

"Maher recalled, 'In the spring' . . .": interview with Brendan Maher, February 5, 1997.

"'The part I remember most vividly' . . .": interview with David McClelland, February 5, 1997.

"'In that capacity,' Maher would later say . . .": interview with Brendan Maher, February 5, 1997.

"In May, 'loaded with IFIF money' . . .": Leary, "Farewell to Harvard," *Flashbacks*.

"On May 6, the Harvard Corporation . . .": document, Timothy Leary Archives.

"In response to a letter from Walter Houston Clark . . .": letter from William Bentinck-Smith to Walter Houston Clark, February 9, 1967, Timothy Leary Archives.

"'One afternoon,' Leary later wrote . . .": Leary, "Farewell to Harvard," *Flashbacks*.

"'I gave him $3,000 when he went to Mexico' . . .": interview with Richard Alpert, October 28, 1996.

"'The Harvard firing was painful' . . .": Leary, "Farewell to Harvard," *Flashbacks*.

"'Alpert wanted to stay' . . .": interview with Brendan Maher, February 5, 1997.

"On May 28, an unsigned editorial . . .": editorial, *The Harvard Crimson,* May 28, 1963.

"On May 29, *The New York Times* reported . . .": *New York Times,* May 29, 1963.

"Andrew Weil quoted an unnamed . . .": *The Harvard Crimson,* May 29, 1963.

"In an undated letter on Harvard University . . .": letter from Richard Alpert, undated, Timothy Leary Archives.

"'My Dear Brendan,' Tim wrote . . .": letter to Brendan Maher, May 13, 1963, courtesy W. B. Maher, Harvard University.

"As you know, I was first suspicious . . .": letter from David McClelland, June 10, 1963, Timothy Leary Archives.

NINETEEN

"'Within a few days,' Tim would later write . . .": Timothy Leary, "Earthly Paradise," *Flashbacks: An Autobiography* (Los Angeles: J. P. Tarcher, 1983).

"On May 29, a front-page headline . . .": George Dusheck, "Paradise in Mexico," *San Francisco Call-Bulletin,* May 29, 1963.

"After attending a meeting Tim held in Palo Alto . . .": Robert S. DeRopp, *The Warrior's Way* (New York: Delacorte Press/Seymour Lawrence, 1979).

"When Tim invited famed diarist . . ." Anaïs Nin, *The Diary of Anais Nin, 1947–55, Volume V* (New York: Harcourt Brace Jovanovich, Inc., 1974).

"What Tim did not know . . .": John Kobler, "The Dangerous Magic of LSD," *The Saturday Evening Post* (November 2, 1963).

" 'Why?' Leary wrote in *Flashbacks* . . .": Leary, "Earthly Paradise," *Flashbacks.*

"Tim flew to Mexico City . . .": ibid.

"Referring to the mutilated corpse . . .": "Harvard Ousting Aide in Drug Case," *The New York Times,* June 15, 1963.

"Expelled from Harvard and Mexico . . .": Leary, "Islands in the Sun," *Flashbacks.*

" 'Dominica was straight out of Joseph Conrad' . . .": Jaakov Kohn, "In the Beginning: An Interview with Gunther Weil," *The East Village Other,* February 21, 1969.

"Two policemen escorted him . . .": Leary, "Islands in the Sun," *Flashbacks.*

" 'When we got to the island' . . .": John Bryan, *Whatever Happened to Timothy Leary?* (San Francisco: Renaissance Press, 1980).

" 'The group came back in pieces' . . .": ibid.

"As Tim Leary would later write . . .": Leary, *Flashbacks.*

" 'They kept getting thrown out of everywhere' . . .": interview with Peggy Hitchcock, December 2, 1996.

"Under rows of maple trees . . .": Michael Hollingshead, *The Man Who Turned on the World* (London: Blond & Briggs Ltd, 1973).

"Known locally as the 'Alte House' . . .": Leary, "September 1963, Millbrook, New York," *Flashbacks.*

"Built in 1936 for half a million dollars . . .": Bryan, *Whatever Happened to Timothy Leary?*

"A successful stockbroker at Lehman Brothers . . .": Martin A. Lee and Bruce Shlain, *Acid Dreams: The CIA, LSD, and the Sixties Rebellion* (New York: Grove Press, Inc., 1985).

"According to Aymon de Roussy de Sales . . .": interview with Aymon de Roussy de Sales, November 19, 1996.

"Tim and his extended family . . .": Leary, "September 1963, Millbrook, New York," *Flashbacks.*

"Although Tim and Metzner wrote . . .": Timothy Leary and Ralph Metzner, "Hermann Hesse: Poet of the Interior Journey," *Psychedelic Review* 1, no. 2 (Fall 1963).

"Tim was now romantically involved . . .": Hollingshead, *The Man Who Turned on the World.*

"Described by Aymon de Roussy de Sales . . .": interview with Aymon de Roussy de Sales, November 19, 1996.

"Of their time together . . .": interview with Peggy Hitchcock, December 2, 1996.

"On October 18, Tim Leary spoke by phone . . .": memo, Timothy Leary Archives.

"In Los Angeles on November 20 . . .": Timothy Leary, *Chaos & Cyberculture* (Berkeley, CA: Ronin Publishing, 1994).

"As he said goodbye to Aldous . . .": Leary, "September 1963, Millbrook, New York," *Flashbacks.*

" 'Light and free,' she would later recall . . .": Laura Archera Huxley, *This Timeless Moment: A Personal View of Aldous Huxley* (New York: Farrar, Straus and Giroux, 1968).

"Described by Peggy Hitchcock as . . .": interview with Peggy Hitchcock, December 2, 1996.

"*Newsweek* went so far as to report . . .": Bryan, *Whatever Happened to Timothy Leary?*

"By December, when the Sunday *New York Times* . . .": "Psychic-Drug Drug Testers Living in Retreat," *The New York Times,* December 15, 1963.

"Neil Freer, then living with his wife . . .": interview with Neil Freer, October 19, 1996.

"Even her dental bills were sent to him . . .": document, June 15, 1963, Timothy Leary Archives.

" 'I soldiered through' . . .": interview with Gunther Weil, November 14, 1996.

"Not yet thirty at the time . . .": interview with George Litwin, March 24, 1997.

"After completing his Ph.D. . . .": interview, January 27, 1997.

"'Millbrook was a beautiful environment' . . .": interview with Ralph Metzner, October 29, 1996.

"A handout given to guests . . .": "How to Play Transpersonative Living: A Visitor's Guide, Millbrook, New York, January 1964," Timothy Leary Archives.

"'It was Harvard all over again' . . .": interview with Ralph Metzner, October 29, 1996.

"'A big thing there was' . . .": interview with Kim Ferguson Exon, November 13, 1996.

"'The most extreme one' . . .": interview with Ralph Metzner, October 29, 1996.

"On the day they met in the kitchen . . .": Timothy Leary, "The Magical Mystery Trip," *Evergreen Review* (July 1968).

"When the fire burnd down . . .": Meditation House logbook, Timothy Leary Archives.

"Describing the moment in *Flashbacks* . . .": Leary, "Winter 1963–1964, Millbrook, New York," *Flashbacks*.

"Tim spent the night totally beyond his mind . . .": Ibid.

"'I always had this desire to have children' . . .": interview with Peggy Hitchcock, December 2, 1996.

"'Richard Alpert was protective of Jack' . . .": interview with Kim Ferguson Exon, November 13, 1996.

TWENTY

"Five feet nine inches tall, Nena von Schlebrugge . . .": Ford Modeling Agency catalog, Timothy Leary Archives.

"However, for $60 an hour . . .": John Bryan, *Whatever Happened to Timothy Leary?* (San Francisco: Renaissance Press, 1980).

"'Nena was very removed' . . .": interview with Darlene DeSedle, February 11, 1997.

"'At that time,' according to Aurora . . .": interview with Aurora Hitchcock, April 10, 1997.

"As Tim Leary would later write in *Flashbacks* . . .": Timothy Leary, "Summer 1964, Millbrook, New York," *Flashbacks: An Autobiography* (Los Angeles: J. P. Tarcher, 1983).

"'Hindsight is always twenty-twenty' . . .": interview with Peggy Hitchcock, December 2, 1996.

"The book was dedicated . . .": Timothy Leary, Ralph Metzner, and Richard Alpert, *The Psychedelic Experience: A Manual Based on the Tibetan Book of the Dead* (London: Academy Editions, 1971).

"(Originally entitled 'The Void' . . .": Martin A. Lee and Bruce Shlain, *Acid Dreams: The CIA, LSD, and the Sixties Rebellion* (New York: Grove Press, Inc., 1985).

"In a ritual guaranteed to send fear . . .": Leary, Metzner, and Alpert, *The Psychedelic Experience*.

"'I got a message on acid' . . .": Lee and Shlain, *Acid Dreams*.

"After tripping their way . . .": Tom Wolfe, *The Electric Kool-Aid Acid Test* (New York: Farrar, Straus and Giroux, 1968).

"'I remember when we finally went up' . . .": interview with Allen Ginsberg, January 20, 1997.

"'Tim was on retreat' . . .": interview with Peggy Hitchcock, December 2, 1996.

"As Tom Wolfe later wrote . . ." Wolfe, *The Electric Kool-Aid Acid Test*.

"After so much hard traveling . . .": ibid.

"In *Flashbacks*, Leary claimed not to have . . . Leary, "Summer 1964, Millbrook New York," *Flashbacks*.

"'What happened,' Alpert recalled . . .": interview with Richard Alpert, October 28, 1996.

"'I want you to get me three yards' . . .": interview with Darlene DeSedle, February 11, 1997.

"In Tim's words, the documentary . . .": Leary, "Summer 1964, Millbrook, New York," *Flashbacks*.

"Although the invitations sent out . . .": document, Timothy Leary Archives.

"Aurora Hitchcock had on . . .": interview with Darlene DeSedle, February 11, 1997.

"In the auditorium at Cooper Union . . .": Jay Stevens, *Storming Heaven: LSD and the American Dream* (New York: Atlantic Monthly Press, 1987).

"'Tim's lecture that night influenced the socks' . . .": interview with Tom Robbins, November 22, 1996.

"With Alpert as his best man . . .": Leary, "Summer 1964, Millbrook, New York," *Flashbacks.*

"'There was a ceremony in the church' . . .": interview with Jack Leary, April 24, 1997.

"Gradually it dawned on Darlene . . .": interview with Darlene DeSedle, February 11, 1997.

"While Charlie Mingus and Maynard Ferguson . . .": Michael Hollingshead, *The Man Who Turned on the World* (London: Blond & Briggs Ltd, 1973).

"The happy couple cut a wedding cake . . ." Bryan, *Whatever Happened to Timothy Leary?*

"Before he left, Tim wrote Metzner . . .": Stevens, *Storming Heaven.*

TWENTY-ONE

"In a photograph taken on their honeymoon . . .": Ralph Metzner, introduction to Timothy Leary, *Psychedelic Prayers* (Berkeley, CA: Ronin Publishing, 1997).

"As Ralph Metzner would write . . .": ibid.

"Although both he and Nena had traveled . . .": Timothy Leary, "Himalayan Honeymoon," *Flashbacks: An Autobiography* (Los Angeles: J. P. Tarcher, 1983).

"'I sat with him and he had a difficult trip' . . .": interview with Ralph Metzner, October 29, 1996.

"By demonstrating the correspondences . . .": Leary, "Himalayan Honeymoon," *Flashbacks.*

"'I feel these meditations on psychedelic' . . .": Metzner introduction, Leary, *Psychedelic Prayers.*

"'Often we nibbled a morsel of temple ball' . . .": Leary, "Himalayan Honeymoon," *Flashbacks.*

"With Metzner, Tim and Nena visited . . .": Metzner introduction, Leary, *Psychedelic Prayers.*

"With Metzner gone, Tim returned . . .": Leary, "Wisest Man in India," *Flashbacks.*

"Metzner believed that in Krishna Prem . . .": Metzner introduction, Leary, *Psychedelic Prayers.*

"Before leaving, he and Nena took LSD . . .": Leary, "Wisest Man in India," *Flashbacks.*

"At the front door of the big house . . .": Metzner introduction, Leary, *Psychedelic Prayers.*

"'In my absence,' as Leary wrote in *Flashbacks* . . .": Leary, "Dissipative Structures," *Flashbacks.*

"'Dick Alpert said this guy was so wonderful' . . .": interview with Ralph Metzner, October 29, 1996.

"Charles Slack, who was an occasional visitor . . .": interview with Charles Slack, March 20, 1997.

"During Tim's stay in India . . .": Michael Hollingshead, *The Man Who Turned on the World* (London: Blond & Briggs Ltd, 1973).

"One day, in order to cure Alpert's cold . . .": ibid.

"Deciding he needed to call his ex-wife . . .": interview with Paul Krassner, October 21, 1996.

"Krassner went on to give LSD to Lenny Bruce . . .": Martin A. Lee and Bruce Shlain, *Acid Dreams: The CIA, LSD, and the Sixties Rebellion* (New York: Grove Press, Inc., 1985).

"Concerning his first visit to Millbrook . . .": Paul Krassner, "Dr. Leary—or, How I Learned to Transcend Ego and Expand My Consciousness," *The Realist* no. 55 (December 1963–January 1964).

"Tripping in the woods one day . . .": Hollingshead, *The Man Who Turned on the World.*

"'We finally were just drinking it' . . .": Ram Dass, *Be Here Now* (San Cristobal, New Mexico: Lama Foundation, 1971).

"One day during a trip . . .": Lee and Shlain, *Acid Dreams.*

"Now nineteen, Susan was learning how to bake . . .": Hollingshead, *The Man Who Turned on the World.*

"On February 16, 1965, Jack Leary was interviewed . . .": document, Timothy Leary Archives.

"'We always said they came back' . . .": John Bryan, *Whatever Happened to Timothy Leary?* (San Francisco: Renaissance Press, 1980).

"Tim found what he would later describe . . .": Leary, "Dissipative Structures," *Flashbacks.*

"Alpert's memory of this . . .": interview with Richard Alpert, October 28, 1996.

"In the version Jack told John Bryan . . .": Bryan, *Whatever Happened to Timothy Leary?*

"'I was sort of the guardian' . . .": interview with Richard Alpert, October 28, 1996.

"At the time Alpert's response . . .": Bryan, *Whatever Happened to Timothy Leary?*

"Despite rumors to the contrary . . .": interview with Richard Alpert, October 28, 1996.

"After having 'hung in there' . . .": Bryan, *Whatever Happened to Timothy Leary?*

"Tim Leary would later write in *Flashbacks* . . .": Leary, "Dissipative Structures," *Flashbacks.*

"'They threw me out of Millbrook' . . .": interview with Richard Alpert, October 28, 1996.

"Hollingshead and Metzner, who never . . .": Metzner introduction, Leary, *Psychedelic Prayers.*

TWENTY-TWO

"Wearing tight jeans bound by a silver chain . . .": Timothy Leary, "Dissipative Structures," *Flashbacks: An Autobiography* (Los Angeles: J. P. Tarcher, 1983).

"'I knew he liked me' . . .": interview with Rosemary Woodruff Leary, September 25, 1996.

"This was the Maha Yantra . . .": Leary, "Dissipative Structures," *Flashbacks.*

"As Ralph Metzner wrote . . .": Ralph Metzner, introduction to Timothy Leary, *Psychedelic Prayers* (Berkeley, CA: Ronin Publishing, 1997).

"'What a wonderful mother you will be' . . .": interview with Rosemary Woodruff Leary, September 25, 1996.

"Operating out of the newly founded . . .": Michael Hollingshead, *The Man Who Turned on the World* (London: Blond & Briggs Ltd, 1973).

"The master plan called for . . .": ibid.

"'By 1965,' Rosemary recalled . . .": interview with Rosemary Woodruff Leary, September 25, 1996.

"In what seems even now . . .": letter to Richard Alpert, October 12, 1965, Timothy Leary Archives.

"After Thanksgiving, strangers dressed . . .": Leary, "Busted at Laredo," *Flashbacks.*

"He set off with Rosemary . . .": ibid.

"Before leaving the estate, Tim buried . . .": Timothy Leary, "Episode and Postscript," *Playboy* (December 1969).

"By the time they arrived in Laredo . . .": interview with Rosemary Woodruff Leary, September 25, 1996.

"Nearly a decade earlier, Allen Ginsberg . . .": Allen Ginsberg, *Howl and Other Poems* (San Francisco: City Lights Books, 1956).

"With a warm, welcoming smile . . .": Leary, "Episode and Postscript."

"'Stay right here' . . .": ibid.

"For perhaps the very first time in Tim's life . . .": ibid.

"'It will all be different *mañana*' . . .": ibid.

"Shoving aside Tim's typewriter . . .": interview with Rosemary Woodruff Leary, September 25, 1996.

"Instead of spending the night . . .": Leary, "Episode and Postscript."

"'I was saying, '*Tim!*' . . .": interview with Rosemary Woodruff Leary, September 25, 1996.

"Just to make sure . . .": Leary, "Episode and Postscript."

"'I remember bright lights' . . .": interview with Rosemary Woodruff Leary, September 25, 1996.

"'What is this seed I found' . . .": Leary, "Episode and Postscript."

"'Have you ever been in the situation' . . .": interview with Rosemary Woodruff Leary, September 25, 1996.

"Under the glare of the naked lightbulbs . . .": Leary, "Episode and Postscript."

"'I was in the cell with Susan' . . .": interview with Rosemary Woodruff Leary, September 25, 1996.

"'Metal on metal is the worst sound' . . .": Leary, "Episode and Postscript."

"The next morning, Tim and Jack . . .": ibid.

"As Rosemary recalled . . .": interview with Rosemary Woodruff Leary, September 25, 1996.

"'The Government's most pressing reason' . . ." Leary, "Episode and Postscript."

"For two months . . .": ibid; and Leary, "The Peat Moss Caper," *Flashbacks.*

"In a statement Tim read to the court . . .": document, Timothy Leary Archives.

"'My second counsel was' . . .": Leary, "The Peat Moss Caper," *Flashbacks.*

"Despite the size of his legal team . . .": handwritten notes, Timothy Leary Archives.

"Years later, Alpert would say . . .": interview with Richard Alpert, October 28, 1996.

"His eloquent opening statement . . .": document, Timothy Leary Archives.

"'The jury trial was pointless' . . .": Leary, "Episode and Postscript."

"Miss Helen Loftis, who performed the search . . .": *Del Rio News-Herald,* March 1966.

"To support Tim's claim . . .": Leary, "Episode and Postscript."

"'Someone had to stay at Millbrook' . . .": interview with Rosemary Woodruff Leary, September 25, 1996.

"Returning to court after the lunch recess . . .": Tom Green, "Dr. Leary Discloses Marihuana Supplier," *Laredo Times,* March 1966.

"Although it was only half an ounce . . .": Leary, "The Peat Moss Caper," *Flashbacks.*

"On the same day in San Francisco . . .": *The New York Times,* March 11, 1966.

"As the door to the jury room swung shut . . .": Leary, "Episode and Postscript."

"As the UPI wire service report . . .": *The New York Times,* March 13, 1966.

"Rosemary would later say, 'I remember' . . .": interview with Rosemary Woodruff Leary, September 25, 1996.

"Tim would later write, 'The sentence caused' . . .": Leary, "Episode and Postscript."

"Smugly, *Time* magazine noted . . .": "The Silver Snuffbox," *Time* (March 18, 1966).

"In the *New York Herald-Tribune,* Seymour Krim . . .": "Dr. Leary's Defense: A Swinging Beginning," Seymour Krim, *New York Herald-Tribune,* April 6, 1966.

"In a letter to the editor . . .": Howard J. Haas, M.D., letter to the editor, *The New York Times,* March 17, 1966.

"An editorial in *El Tiempo* . . .": editorial, *El Tiempo,* March 16, 1966.

"In Greenwich Village on March 13, 1966 . . .": William Insra, *New York Herald-Tribune,* March 13, 1966.

"Two days later, Tim held a news conference . . .": Sidney E. Zion, *The New York Times,* March 16, 1966.

"Two days later, *The New York Times* ran . . .": "Specious Marijuana Defense," *The New York Times,* March 18, 1966.

"In a remarkable photograph . . .": *Life* (March 25, 1966).

"'The picture is accurate' . . .": interview with Rosemary Woodruff Leary, September 25, 1996.

"'She had always been a dutiful conforming child' . . .": Leary, "The Peat Moss Caper," *Flashbacks.*

TWENTY-THREE

"On March 27, 1966, Richard Alpert . . .": letter from Richard Alpert, March 27, 1966, Timothy Leary Archives.

"On April 3, an impressive three-quarter-page ad . . .": advertisement, *The New York Times,* April 3, 1966.

"Working out of an office in the United Nations . . .": Nina Graboi, *One Foot in the Future* (Santa Cruz, CA: Aerial Press, 1991).

"On April 16, Billy Hitchcock wrote . . .": letter from William M. Hitchcock, April 16, 1966, Timothy Leary Archives.

"Tim Leary would later write . . .": Timothy Leary, "The Peat Moss Caper," *Flashbacks: An Autobiography* (Los Angeles: J. P. Tarcher, 1983).

"'The next step was for me to accept' . . .": Timothy Leary, "Episode and Postscript," *Playboy* (December 1969).

"'So now Tim is on his way' . . .": interview with Rosemary Woodruff Leary, September 25, 1996.

"Labeling the phenomenon . . .": "An Epidemic of Acid Heads," *Time* (March 11, 1966).

"On March 25, 1966, the cover of *Life* . . .": *Life* (March 25, 1966).

"On March 30, Dr. Louria . . .": *The New York Times*, March 30, 1966.

"On April 7, a five-year-old girl . . .": *The New York Times*, April 7, 1966.

"A day later, the girl was reported . . .": *The New York Times*, April 8, 1966.

"When police came to arrest him . . .": Jay Stevens, *Storming Heaven: LSD and the American Dream* (New York: Atlantic Monthly Press, 1987).

"On April 14, Brooklyn District Attorney . . .": *The New York Times*, April 14, 1966.

"Most of the recommendations so far . . .": letter from Ralph Metzner, April 14, 1966, Timothy Leary Archives.

"On April 16, Koota called for . . .": *The New York Times*, April 16, 1966.

"On April 19, Koota met with New York City . . .": *The New York Times*, April 19, 1966.

"On April 25, Koota discussed a probe . . .": *The New York Times*, April 25, 1966.

"On April 26, Dr. Harry Gideonese . . .": *The New York Times*, April 26, 1966.

"On April 27, the American Medical Association's . . .": *The New York Times*, April 27, 1966.

"On April 29, the New York State Senate . . .": *The New York Times*, April 29, 1966.

"'He seemed ill at ease that Saturday' . . .": Marya Mannes, "The Raid on Castalia," *The Reporter*, May 19, 1966.

"Tim, clad in jeans and a light-blue shirt . . .": ibid.

"'That night,' Bowden would later recall . . .": interview with Michael Bowen, January 21, 1997.

"Once he realized there were no naked women . . .": G. Gordon Liddy, "The Great Dutchess County Dope Raid," *True* (June 1975).

"When the movies ended . . .": Leary, "The Peat Moss Caper," *Flashbacks*.

"'On the night of the raid' . . .": interview with Rosemary Woodruff Leary, September 24, 1996.

"In his memoir of that night . . .": Liddy, "The Great Dutchess County Dope Raid."

"'Millbrook was in a sense a public nuisance' . . .": interview with G. Gordon Liddy, December 9, 1996.

"'Pants!' Liddy would later write . . .": Liddy, "The Great Dutchess County Dope Raid."

"'I remember Liddy as this dark' . . .": interview with Rosemary Woodruff Leary, September 24, 1996.

"In the bedroom, Rosemary was clinging . . .": Liddy, "The Great Dutchess County Dope Raid."

"'So they got the peat moss' . . .": interview with Rosemary Woodruff Leary, September 24, 1996.

"'I needed some money' . . .": interview with Michael Bowen, January 21, 1997.

"'This raid,' Leary told Liddy . . .": Liddy, "The Great Dutchess County Dope Raid."

"'As they were taking him away' . . .": interview with Rosemary Woodruff Leary, September 24, 1996.

"'By Sunday noon,' Tim would later write . . ." Leary, "The Peat Moss Caper," *Flashbacks*.

"'Tim's reaction to all of this' . . .": interview with Rosemary Woodruff Leary, September 24, 1996.

"lsd psychologist arrested again . . ." "LSD Psychologist Arrested Again," *The New York Times*, April 18, 1966.

"The banner front-page headline . . .": "Raid Mansion, Seize LSD Prof," *Daily News*, April 18, 1966.

"Two weeks later, a new print ad . . .": document, May 10, 1966, Timothy Leary Archives.

"'At some point,' Rosemary recalled . . .": interview with Rosemary Woodruff Leary, September 24, 1996.

"Speaking to a thousand people . . .": Timothy Leary Defense Fund News Release, April 22, 1966, Timothy Leary Archives.

"Astonishingly, Tim urged his audience . . .": Bernard Weinraub, *The New York Times,* April 22, 1966.

"An editorial in *Life* . . .": editorial, *Life* (April 29, 1966).

"Although she later called it . . .": interview with Rosemary Woodruff Leary, July 17, 2000.

"In a statement that could only have been . . .": document, Timothy Leary Archives.

"'There were several options' . . .": interview with Rosemary Woodruff Leary, September 24, 1996.

"'He totally shattered Rosemary's life' . . .": interview with Michael Kennedy, November 18, 1996.

"On May 9, Alexandra K. Rewis . . ." letter from Alexandra K. Rewis, May 9, 1966, Timothy Leary Archives.

"'Oh, no,' Susan told her . . .": Marya Mannes, "Young People and LSD: A Talk with Susan Leary," *McCalls* (July 1966).

"On May 9, Senator Robert F. Kennedy . . .": *The New York Times,* May 9, 1966.

"Before Kennedy could convene . . .": Martin A. Lee and Bruce Shlain, *Acid Dreams: The CIA, LSD, and the Sixties Rebellion* (New York: Grove Press, Inc., 1985).

"Wearing his professorial-looking suit . . .": John Bryan, *Whatever Happened to Timothy Leary?* (San Francisco: Renaissance Press, 1980); and Lee and Shlain, *Acid Dreams.*

"Perian, looking harassed, told Tim . . .": Leary, "The Peat Moss Caper," *Flashbacks.*

"Beginning his testimony by praising . . .": transcript, "Statement of Timothy Leary LSD Experimenter, Testifying on Behalf of the Castalia Foundation of Millbrook, New York," Special Subcommittee on Narcotics of the Senate Judiciary Committee hearing, Eighty-ninth Congress.

"Tim failed to mention that his own driver's license . . .": letter from Timothy Leary to Department of Motor Vehicles, May 2, 1966, Timothy Leary Archives.

"All the same, he continued by stating . . .": transcript, "Statement of Timothy Leary LSD Experimenter."

"In *Changing My Mind, Among Others,* Tim would . . .": Timothy Leary, *Changing My Mind, Among Others* (Englewood Cliffs, NJ: Prentice Hall, Inc., 1982).

"In his autobiography, Tim added . . .": Leary, "The Peat Moss Caper," *Flashbacks.*

"The best proof of how successful . . .": "Leary Sees Crisis in the Use of LSD," *The New York Times,* May 14, 1966.

"'His appearance before the subcommittee' . . .": interview with Rosemary Woodruff Leary, July 17, 2000.

"'I saw it on television' . . .": interview with Rosemary Woodruff Leary, September 24, 1996.

TWENTY-FOUR

"Tim Leary would later write that after . . .": Timothy Leary, *Changing My Mind, Among Others* (Englewood Cliffs, NJ: Prentice Hall, Inc., 1982).

"'It is our belief,' Kleps told the subcommittee . . .": Art Kleps, *Millbrook: The True Story of the Early Years of the Psychedelic Revolution* (Oakland, CA: Bench Press, 1977).

"To protect Tim from reporters . . .": Nina Graboi, *One Foot in the Future* (Santa Cruz, CA: Aerial Press, 1991).

"The cover sheet that accompanied . . .": statement by Timothy Leary, May 26, 1966, Timothy Leary Archives.

"They told Tim that Ted Kennedy's older brother . . .": Leary, *Changing My Mind, Among Others.*

"Tim Leary would later write that it . . .": ibid.

"Concerning such projects, Robert Kennedy . . .": Martin A. Lee and Bruce Shlain, *Acid Dreams: The CIA, LSD, and the Sixties Rebellion* (New York: Grove Press, Inc., 1985).

"He was now calling for the establishment . . .": statement by Timothy Leary, May 26, 1966, Timothy Leary Archives.

"The headline in *The Washington Post* . . .": "Leary Proposes a Ban on LSD Except in 'Psychedelic Centers,'" *The Washington Post*, May 27, 1966.

"After Tim's statement was read . . .": Senate subcommittee transcript, May 26, 1966, Timothy Leary Archives.

"In *lsd*, a book published in 1966 . . .": Richard Alpert, Sidney Cohen, and Lawrence Schiller, *lsd* (New York: The New American Library, 1966).

"In the past few months, Cohen testified . . .": Senate subcommittee transcript, May 26, 1966, Timothy Leary Archives.

"In a dark gray suit he had bought . . .": Jane Kramer, *Allen Ginsberg in America* (New York: Random House, 1969).

"Unwilling to spend any more time in a cell . . .": interview with Rosemary Woodruff Leary, September 24, 1996.

"While all this was going on . . .": document, Timothy Leary Archives.

"Richard Baker, then thirty . . .": David Chadwick, *Crooked Cucumber: The Life and Zen Teachings of Shunryu Suzuki* (New York: Broadway Books, 1999).

"'The conference was supposed to be in Berkeley' . . .": interview with Paul Lee, January 22, 1997.

"In an article published in the *Journal of Philosophy* . . .": Huston Smith, "Do Drugs Have Religious Import?," *Journal of Philosophy* 61 (1964): 517–30.

"At the LSD Conference in San Francisco . . .": interview with Paul Lee, January 22, 1997.

"On Friday night, Tim spoke in a hall . . .": Timothy Leary, "The Molecular Revolution," *The Politics of Ecstasy* (New York: G. P. Putnam's Sons, 1968).

"During lunch at the Plaza Hotel . . .": Timothy Leary, "Altered States," *Flashbacks: An Autobiography* (Los Angeles: J. P. Tarcher, 1983).

"'I called it "Drugs on Campus"' . . .": interview with Merv Freedman, March 6, 1997.

"'The inspiration for it came from' . . .": letter from Merv Freedman, May 5, 1997.

"In 1968, *Mad* magazine . . .": *Mad* (April 1968).

"After Tim made an appearance in Seattle . . .": interview with Tom Robbins, November 22, 1996.

TWENTY-FIVE

"Deeply in debt, he spent the summer . . .": Castalia Foundation Millbrook Summer School Application, 1966, Timothy Leary Archives.

"'By this time,' Rosemary Woodruff recalled . . .": interview with Rosemary Woodruff Leary, September 24, 1996.

"Using slide projectors modified with fans . . .": interview with Rudi Stern, December 3, 1996.

"When Haller began freaking out . . .": Timothy Leary, "Altered States," *Flashbacks: An Autobiography* (Los Angeles: J. P. Tarcher, 1983); and Gene Gaffney, UPI Report, September 21, 1966.

"Onstage, Haller moved toward . . .": interview with Rosemary Woodruff Leary, September 24, 1996.

"Reminding Haller that he had . . .": Gaffney, UPI Report.

"At the end . . .": interview with Rudi Stern, December 3, 1996.

"The next day, *The New York Times* . . .": "Dr. Leary Holds First Service of New Life Formed Before 2,400," *The New York Times*, September 21, 1966.

"She observed that most of the audience . . .": Diana Trilling, "Celebrating with Dr. Leary," *Encounter* no. 6 (June 1967).

"On September 23, 1966, Judge Raymond C. Baratta . . .": *Boston Herald*, September 24, 1966.

"'Noel Tepper, a local guy' . . .": interview with G. Gordon Liddy, December 9, 1996.

"The motion to drop the cases . . .": *Boston Herald*, September 24, 1966.

"'Impressario Leary, high priest' . . .": Eleanore Lester, "'Taking a Trip' With Leary," *The New York Times*, December 4, 1966.

"Describing in minute detail . . .": interview with Timothy Leary, *Playboy* (September 1966).

"Robert Anton Wilson, a science-fiction writer . . .": interview with Robert Anton Wilson, October 8, 1996.

"'It isn't like twenty thousand orgasms' . . .": interview with Owsley Stanley, March 18, 1997.

"Robert Masters, the LSD researcher . . .": John Bryan, *Whatever Happened to Timothy Leary?* (San Francisco: Renaissance Press, 1980).

"When Tim republished the interview . . .": Timothy Leary, "She Comes in Colors," author's note, *The Politics of Ecstasy* (New York: G. P. Putnam's Sons, 1968).

"When Tim was invited to Toronto . . .": Leary, "Altered States," *Flashbacks*.

"Jean McCready, Tim's secretary . . .": interview with Jean McCready, November 30, 1996.

"In a memoir entitled . . .": Diane DiPrima, "The Holidays at Millbrook—1966," in Cynthia Palmer and Michael Horowitz, editors, *Shaman Woman, Mainline Lady* (New York: Quill, 1982).

"'There were times when I would be' . . .": interview with Jean McCready, November 30, 1996.

"Kim Ferguson Exon, who grew up at Millbrook . . .": interview with Kim Ferguson Exon, November 13, 1996.

"Jeanne DiPrima, who on Thanksgiving Day . . .": interview with Jeanne DiPrima, July 9, 1997.

"'Jack and Susan Leary were a really sad' . . .": interview with Jean McCready, November 30, 1996.

"'Jackie Leary occupied the top turret' . . .": interview with Jeanne DiPrima, July 9, 1997.

"Concerning his father, Jack . . .": interview with Jack Leary, April 24, 1997.

"A decade later, Jack would tell . . .": interview with Jack Leary by Ken Kelley, September 1974.

"Jeanne DiPrima recalled . . .": interview with Jeanne DiPrima, July 9, 1997.

"'There was a lot of animosity to me' . . .": interview with Jack Leary by Ken Kelley, September 1974.

"'On the weekends' . . .": interview with Jeanne DiPrima, July 9, 1997.

TWENTY-SIX

"As soon as Thanksgiving weekend was over . . .": "LSD 'Preacher' Unable to 'Pray'," *Rochester Times-Union*, December 1, 1966.

"A week later, he dined with Humphry Osmond . . .": letters to Humphry Osmond, November 14 and 28, 1966, Timothy Leary Archives.

"Your letter addressed to Dad . . .": letter from Charles N. Fansler Jr., December 9, 1966, Timothy Leary Archives.

"As Tim Leary would later write . . .": Timothy Leary, "Episode and Postscript," *Playboy* (December 1969).

"When he was arrested while driving . . .": Timothy Leary, "Altered States," *Flashbacks: An Autobiography* (Los Angeles: J. P. Tarcher, 1983).

"Dear Law Enforcement Agent . . .": letter from Noel Tepper, undated, Timothy Leary Archives.

"Tim characterized the constant . . .": Leary, "Episode and Postscript."

"'California sunshine makes all seeds grow' . . .": letter from Michael Bowen, November 1, 1966, Timothy Leary Archives.

"After touring San Francisco's . . .": Donovan Bess, "LSD Missionary Has Plans Here," *San Francisco Chronicle*, December 13, 1966.

"On January 5, 1967, Tim conducted . . .": "A Non-Profit Religion, says LSD Prophet," *Chicago Daily News*, January 6, 1967.

"*Playboy* editor Robert Anton Wilson wrote . . .": Robert Anton Wilson, *Cosmic Trigger* (Phoenix, AZ: Falcon Press, 1986).

"'They called it' . . .": interview with Michael Bowen, January 21, 1997.

"In 1956, John Starr Cooke . . .": Martin A. Lee and Bruce Shlain, *Acid Dreams: The CIA, LSD, and the Sixties Rebellion* (New York: Grove Press, Inc., 1985).

"'Big bell-shaped flowers' . . .": interview with Michael Bowen, January 21, 1997.

"Imprinted with these instructions . . .": Lee and Shlain, *Acid Dreams.*

"(Having just synthesized . . .": interview with Owsley Stanley, March 18, 1997.

"Allen Ginsberg, Gary Snyder . . .": Jane Kramer, *Allen Ginsberg in America* (New York: Random House, 1969).

"'The only way out' . . .": John Bryan, *Whatever Happened to Timothy Leary?* (San Francisco: Renaissance Press, 1980).

"Jerry Rubin, who had bailed out . . .": Kramer, *Allen Ginsberg in America.*

"'Jerry Rubin was up there shouting' . . .": interview with Michael Bowen, January 21, 1997.

"Shortly before Suzuki-roshi . . .": Kramer, *Allen Ginsberg in America.*

"Having first taken LSD . . .": Marty Jezer, *Abbie Hoffman: American Rebel* (New Brunswick, NJ: Rutgers University Press, 1992).

"Paul Krassner, who first introduced . . .": interview with Paul Krassner, October 21, 1996.

"Allen Cohen, editor of the *San Francisco Oracle* . . .": Lee and Shlain, *Acid Dreams.*

"After he took acid, Abbie Hoffman . . .": Abbie Hoffman, *Soon to Be a Major Motion Picture* (New York: Grosset & Dunlap, Inc., 1980).

"Owsley Stanley would later recall . . .": interview with Owsley Stanley, March 18, 1997.

"Tim later described his appearance . . .": Leary, "Altered States," *Flashbacks.*

"He omitted mentioning . . .": Bryan, *Whatever Happened to Timothy Leary?*

"From the stage, Tim told the crowd . . .": Leary, "Altered States," *Flashbacks.*

"'Tim did his lecture and people threw' . . .": interview with Rosemary Woodruff Leary, September 24, 1996.

"'Everything he said was very provocative' . . .": interview with Owsley Stanley, March 18, 1997.

"Stern would later recall . . .": interview with Rudi Stern, December 3, 1996.

"Tim Leary would later write . . .": Leary, *Changing My Mind, Among Others.*

"'I began to see the game player' . . .": interview with Rudi Stern, December 3, 1996.

"'Tim Leary,' Owsley Stanley remembered . . .": interview with Owsley Stanley, March 18, 1997.

"Timothy, why are you doing this?": Leary, *Changing My Mind, Among Others.*

"'This is an ugly, hateful Iron Age newspaper' . . .": Bryan, *Whatever Happened to Timothy Leary?*

"The next day in the *San Francisco Chronicle* . . .": ibid.

"In a scathing cover piece . . .": Warren Hinckle, "A Social History of the Hippies," *Ramparts* (March 1967).

"'We bombed in San Francisco' . . .": interview with Rosemary Woodruff Leary, September 24, 1996.

"Although Tim swore that he was now . . .": Bryan, *Whatever Happened to Timothy Leary?*

"On February 14, 1967, he was arrested . . .": *San Francisco Chronicle,* February 15, 1967.

"Two remarkable photographs . . .": *Albany Times-Union,* April 9, 1967.

"On May 1, Susan sent an extraordinary . . .": letter from Susan Leary, May 1, 1967, Timothy Leary Archives.

"'Susan was very protective of Tim' . . .": interview with Rosemary Woodruff Leary, September 25, 1996.

"Art Kleps would later write that to . . .": Art Kleps, *Millbrook: The True Story of the Early Years of the Psychedelic Revolution* (Oakland, CA: Bench Press, 1977).

"'She felt bad about everything' . . .": interview with Rosemary Woodruff Leary, September 25, 1996.

TWENTY-SEVEN

"On May 18, 1967, in big black type . . .": "300 Back Formation of 'Anti-LSD Group'; Leary Calls Move 'Whipped-Up Hysteria,'" *Millbrook Round Table,* May 18, 1967.

"Ten days later, an ad hoc committee . . .": *Millbrook Round Table,* May 25, 1967.

"When the Grateful Dead came . . .": John W. Scott, Mike Dolgushkin, and Stu Nixon, *DeadBase, Jr.* (Hanover, NH: DeadBase, 1995).

" 'This was the week that the Six-Day War' . . .": interview with John Perry Barlow, December 2, 1996.

"As part of a series of articles about drugs . . .": *Boston Record-American,* June 16, 1967.

"On a busy Saturday in July 1967 . . .": John Bryan, *Whatever Happened to Timothy Leary?* (San Francisco: Renaissance Press, 1980).

"Art Kleps's wife, Wendy . . .": Art Kleps, *Millbrook: The True Story of the Early Years of the Psychedelic Revolution* (Oakland, CA: Bench Press, 1977).

"Some of Jack Leary's friends . . .": Bryan, *Whatever Happened to Timothy Leary?*

" 'It was like this king had arrived' . . .": interview with Darlene DeSedle, February 11, 1997.

"When he returned to Millbrook . . .": Timothy Leary, "Emergence of the Drug Culture," *Flashbacks: An Autobiography* (Los Angeles: J. P. Tarcher, 1983).

"In their tepee . . .": Timothy Leary with Robert Anton Wilson and George A. Koopman, *Neuropolitics: The Sociobiology of Human Metamorphosis* (Los Angeles: Peace Press, 1977).

"Together, Tim and Rosemary devoted . . .": Leary, "The Magical Mystery Trip," *Evergreen Review* (July 1968).

"Before the year was out . . .": Bryan, *Whatever Happened to Timothy Leary?*

"All summer long, Chester Anderson . . .": ibid.

" 'Publishing arm of the Diggers' . . .": The Digger Archives, www.diggers.org.

"As the 'two LSD shamans' . . .": Emmet Grogan, *Ringolevio: A Life Played for Keeps* (Boston-Toronto: Little, Brown & Company, 1972).

"Beneath a front-page headline . . .": "Eldridge Warns Bennet Students . . . Tim Leary Still 'Off Limits,'" *Millbrook Round Table,* September 28, 1967.

"Tim, however, continued advising people . . .": interview with Gordon Ball, April 14, 1997.

"Two weeks later, Tim issued a memo . . .": document, Timothy Leary Archives.

"Four days later, the *Millbrook Round Table* . . .": "Hitchcock Tightens 'Estate' Regulations," *Millbrook Round Table,* November 9, 1967.

"As his mother, Abigail, now in her seventies . . .": letter from Abigail Leary to Susan Leary, October 18, 1967, Timothy Leary Archives.

" 'You're illuminated' . . .": Timothy Leary, "Drop Out or Cop Out," *The Politics of Ecstasy* (New York: G. P. Putnam's Sons, 1968).

"Owsley Stanley would later confirm . . .": interview with Owsley Stanley, March 18, 1997.

"As he was talking to his son . . .": Leary, "Drop Out or Cop Out," *The Politics of Ecstasy.*

" 'His shiny, hairless head' . . .": Leary, "Emergence of the Drug Culture," *Flashbacks.*

"Earlier in the summer . . .": Kleps, *Millbrook.*

"Rosemary left Millbrook for Berkeley . . .": interview with Rosemary Woodruff Leary, October 20, 2000.

"Tim, in a 'distraught condition' . . .": Kleps, *Millbrook.*

"When Metzner confessed to Rosemary . . .": interview with Rosemary Woodruff Leary, October 20, 2000.

"She got the thirty-seventh hexagram . . .": *The I Ching or Book of Changes,* Bollingen Series IIX (Princeton, NJ: Princeton University Press, 1967).

" 'Our first Hollywood production' . . .": Leary, "Emergence of the Drug Culture," *Flashbacks.*

" 'Tim was on mescaline' . . .": interview with Rosemary Woodruff Leary, September 24, 1966.

"On Thanksgiving night, Jack Leary . . .": news clip, undated, Timothy Leary Archives.

"'They had us in the dining room' . . .": interview with Jean McCready, November 30, 1996.

"'Put it in a vial' . . .": Kleps, *Millbrook*.

"The next day, Jack's hair . . .": "Cheerful Leary Released in $2500 Bond," *Poughkeepsie Journal*, December 13, 1967.

"Then he said, 'Merry Christmas' . . .": "Overstepping Reasonable Bounds," *Poughkeepsie Journal*, December 11, 1967.

"'To engender a little positive publicity' . . .": Kleps, *Millbrook*.

"On the license application . . .": document, Timothy Leary Archives.

"In a wedding photograph . . .": *New York Post*, December 13, 1967.

"On the day after the wedding . . .": "Overstepping Reasonable Bounds," *Poughkeepsie Journal*, December 13, 1967.

"Armed with arrest warrants . . .": *Poughkeepsie Journal*, January 6, 1968.

"On February 20, 1968, *The New York Times* . . .": *The New York Times*, February 20, 1968.

"Kleps would later write that Tim . . .": Kleps, *Millbrook*.

"'The claim was that Bill Haines' . . .": interview with Rosemary Woodruff Leary, September 24, 1966.

"When Tim returned to Millbrook . . .": Kleps, *Millbrook*.

"Collecting $14,000 as his settlement . . .": Bryan, *Whatever Happened to Timothy Leary?*

"'It ended as it had begun' . . .": Kleps, *Millbrook*.

"'They actually had an amphibious vehicle' . . .": interview with Marshall McNeil, May 6, 1997.

"Long after she had left the estate . . .": interview with Jean McCready, November 30, 1996.

"Nearly thirty years later . . .": interview with Rosemary Woodruff Leary, September 24, 1996.

"Rudi Stern recalled . . .": interview with Rudi Stern, December 3, 1996.

TWENTY-EIGHT

"Though small in stature . . .": interview with Travis Ashbrook, June 5, 1997.

"In 1966, knowing nothing about LSD . . .": Elliot Almond, "Hippie Haven — Brotherhood of Eternal Love, 'Psychedelic Evangelists' Or Street-Smart Drug Dealers?," *Los Angeles Times*, 1989.

"'John had a religious experience' . . .": interview with Travis Ashbrook, June 5, 1997.

"California's Franchise Tax Board . . .": Almond, "Hippie Haven."

"'We all liked it' . . .": interview with Travis Ashbrook, June 5, 1997.

"At 670 South Coast Highway . . .": Timothy Leary, "Brotherhood of Eternal Love," *Flashbacks: An Autobiography* (Los Angeles: J. P. Tarcher, 1983).

"Rosemary, who first visited Mystic Arts . . .": interview with Rosemary Woodruff Leary, September 24, 1996.

"In *Flashbacks*, Tim would describe Griggs as . . .": Leary, "Brotherhood of Eternal Love," *Flashbacks*.

"Although Leary would later recall his time . . .": interview with Stew Albert, November 15, 1996.

"'We were getting high with him' . . .": interview with Travis Ashbrook, June 5, 1997.

"'I remember us being on our honeymoon' . . .": interview with Rosemary Woodruff Leary, March 11, 1997.

"Tim defined the political struggle . . .": Timothy Leary, "How Merry Jerry's Yip Stopped the War," *Berkeley Barb* (May 31–June 6, 1968).

"He seemed, as Tim later described him . . .": ibid.

"Tim asked him to 'rustle up a cow' . . .": ibid.

"In his acknowledgments . . .": Timothy Leary, *High Priest* (New York: New American Library in association with the World Publishing Company, 1968; Berkeley, CA: Ronin Publishing, Inc., 1995).

"Although the cheery optimism . . .": document, Timothy Leary Archives.

"'An era had ended' . . .": Leary, "How Merry Jerry's Yip Stopped the War."

"'A new model is needed' . . .": ibid.

"'These kids won't play the game fairly' . . .": ibid.

"Deciding that he and Rosemary no longer . . .": Leary, "Brotherhood of Eternal Love," *Flashbacks.*

"On Friday, April 26, Charles Slack . . .": Charles Slack, *Timothy Leary, the Madness of the Sixties, and Me* (New York: Peter H. Wyden, 1974).

"'I kept telling Helen Gurley Brown' . . .": interview with Charles Slack, March 20, 1997.

"Seeing that the line outside the Village Gate . . .": Slack, *Timothy Leary, the Madness of the Sixties, and Me.*

"'We flew first class' . . .": interview with Charles Slack, March 20, 1997.

"When Slack asked Tim whether . . .": Slack, *Timothy Leary, the Madness of the Sixties, and Me.*

"'I didn't know if it was facetious conversation' . . .": interview with Charles Slack, March 20, 1997.

"'It was obvious that Bobby' . . .": Leary, "Brotherhood of Eternal Love," *Flashbacks.*

"With Hubert Humphrey now virtually guaranteed . . .": document, undated, Timothy Leary Archives.

"Tim predicted that with LBJ . . .": Leary, "Brotherhood of Eternal Love," *Flashbacks.*

"The Motherfuckers, a former street gang . . .": Stew Albert, "Free Timothy Leary," *The Georgia Straight* (April 1–9, 1970).

"'Their haven lay in a spectacularly beautiful' . . .": Leary, "Brotherhood of Eternal Love," *Flashbacks.*

"'We told him, 'You just stay up here' . . .": interview with Travis Ashbrook, June 5, 1997.

"Anita Hoffman, who with her husband . . .": interview with Anita Hoffman, October 29, 1996.

"A long-haired hippie gave them . . .": interview with Rosemary Woodruff Leary, September 24, 1996.

"When Tim learned what was going on . . .": Leary, "Brotherhood of Eternal Love," *Flashbacks.*

"In a footnote in *Flashbacks* . . .": Leary, *Flashbacks.*

"In a *Rolling Stone* interview, Ray Thomas . . .": as quoted by Leary, *Flashbacks.*

"Because Hubert Humphrey had been gaining . . .": Leary, "Brotherhood of Eternal Love," *Flashbacks.*

TWENTY-NINE

"'The thing I liked about Abbie' . . .": Leary, *Changing My Mind, Among Others.*

"Most of the material . . .": Michael Horowitz, editor's note, in Timothy Leary, *The Politics of Ecstasy* (New York: G. P. Putnam's Sons, 1968; Berkeley, CA: Ronin Publishing, Inc, 1990).

"In a review of the book in *The Village Voice* . . .": Allen Ginsberg, "'Christmas on Earth'—Remarks on Leary's *Politics of Ecstasy,*" *The Village Voice* (December 12, 1968).

"On the same day that Ginsberg's . . .": Timothy Leary, "Episode and Postscript," *Playboy* (December 1969).

"With his college appearances . . .": Timothy Leary, "Cultural Evolution Versus Political Revolution," *Flashbacks: An Autobiography* (Los Angeles: J. P. Tarcher, 1983).

"Suffering from cabin fever . . .": Leary, "Brotherhood of Eternal Love," *Flashbacks.*

"'People were always pressing things on us' . . .": interview with Rosemary Woodruff Leary, September 24, 1996.

"With just fifty-five minutes left . . .": Joe Eszterhas, "The Strange Case of the Hippie Mafia," *Rolling Stone* (December 7, 1972).

"Jack later told Tim's biographer . . .": John Bryan, *Whatever Happened to Timothy Leary?* (San Francisco: Renaissance Press, 1980).

"'They were facing me' . . .": interview with Neil Purcell, July 18, 2001.

"'There was a window of opportunity' . . .": interview with Rosemary Woodruff Leary, September 24, 1996.

"'I got out and came right up to the window' . . .": interview with Neil Purcell, July 18, 2001.

"Twenty-eight years old, Purcell . . .": Eszterhas, "The Strange Case of the Hippie Mafia."

"With Tim's license in his hand . . .": interview with Neil Purcell, July 18, 2001.

"'Tim got out to talk to him' . . .": interview with Rosemary Woodruff Leary, September 24, 1996.

"Jack Leary told John Bryan . . .": Bryan, *Whatever Happened to Timothy Leary?*

"'She kind of clenched it up' . . .": interview with Neil Purcell, July 18, 2001.

"'Some bottle went thunk' . . .": interview with Rosemary Woodruff Leary, September 24, 1996.

"Looking into the hat . . .": interview with Neil Purcell, July 18, 2001.

"'Everyone around the courthouse' . . .": Leary, "Brotherhood of Eternal Love," *Flashbacks.*

"On 'routine patrol,' Purcell saw Tim . . .": Eszterhas, "The Strange Case of the Hippie Mafia."

"'It is all part of the insanity' . . .": letter to Abigail Leary and Mary Ferris, January 30, 1969, Timothy Leary Archives.

"On March 18, Tim again wrote . . .": letter to Abigail Leary and Mary Ferris, March 18, 1969, Timothy Leary Archives.

"On the day Jack was scheduled . . .": document, Timothy Leary Archives.

"On May 6, Jack Leary appeared . . .": Bryan, *Whatever Happened to Timothy Leary?*

"'I said I would come and pick up the mail' . . .": interview with Michael Bowen, January 21, 1997.

THIRTY

"They would then both . . .": Timothy Leary, "Episode and Postscript," *Playboy* (December 1969).

"This was not particularly hard . . .": Martin A. Lee and Bruce Shlain, *Acid Dreams: The CIA, LSD, and the Sixties Rebellion* (New York: Grove Press, Inc., 1985).

"Some evenings, half a dozen . . .": Michael Hollingshead, *The Man Who Turned on the World* (London: Blond & Briggs Ltd, 1973).

"Since cars from the city . . .": Leary, "Episode and Postscript."

"'Overall,' wrote Michael Aldrich . . .": Michael Aldrich, "High Court Frees High Priest," *The East Village Other,* June 25, 1969.

"Nonetheless, he called this . . .": John Bryan, *Whatever Happened to Timothy Leary?* (San Francisco: Renaissance Press, 1980).

"Asked how he felt, Tim said . . .": Leary, "Episode and Postscript."

"Carol Randall, then married to John Griggs . . .": interview with Carol Randall, October 26, 1996.

"'In that same space of time' . . .": interview with Rosemary Woodruff Leary, September 24, 1996.

"Travis Ashbrook would later say . . .": interview with Travis Ashbrook, June 5, 1997.

"Tim would later write that the reporters . . .": Timothy Leary, "Cultural Evolution Versus Political Revolution," *Flashbacks: An Autobiography* (Los Angeles: J. P. Tarcher, 1983).

"'My statisticians and poll experts' . . .": Timothy Leary, *Changing My Mind, Among Others* (Englewood Cliffs, NJ: Prentice Hall, Inc., 1982).

"By his side sat Rosemary . . .": Dial Torgerson, *Los Angeles Times,* May 20, 1969.

"The most newsworthy plank . . .": Leary, "Episode and Postscript."

"'It promised to be great theatre' . . .": Leary, *Changing My Mind, Among Others.*

"In one campaign poster . . .": Bryan, *Whatever Happened to Timothy Leary?*

"'Tim appointed me campaign manager' . . .": interview with Art Kunkin, November 11, 1996.

"' "Come together" was mine' . . .": interview with Rosemary Woodruff Leary, September 24, 1996.

"'I believe I have a great deal to say' . . .": Jaakov Kohn, "Come Together, Join the Party," *The East Village Other,* June 4, 1969.

"After Owsley Stanley was sentenced . . .": Lee and Bruce, *Acid Dreams.*

"'Open your eyes, Tim' . . .": Jerry Applebaum, "Leary Campaign Has Its Drawbacks," *Los Angeles Free Press* (July 18, 1969).

"As Douglas later put it . . .": interview with Alan Douglas, February 10, 1997.

"As he sat across the table from Tim . . .": Leary, "Cultural Evolution Versus Political Revolution," *Flashbacks*.

"Accompanied by Jann Wenner . . .": ibid.

"'It was a promotion' . . .": interview with Alan Douglas, February 10, 1997.

"The day after the session . . .": Leary, "Cultural Evolution Versus Political Revolution," *Flashbacks*.

"'The Bed-In was totally a media event' . . .": interview with Rosemary Woodruff Leary, September 24, 1996.

"In Tim's words . . .": Leary, "Cultural Evolution Versus Political Revolution," *Flashbacks*.

"Tripping on LSD, he and Rosemary . . .": Timothy Leary, *Jail Notes* (New York: Grove Press, Inc., 1970).

"As he stood near the pond . . .": Joe Eszterhas, "The Strange Case of the Hippie Mafia," *Rolling Stone* (December 7, 1972).

"Travis Ashbrook was driving with his wife . . .": interview with Travis Ashbrook, June 5, 1997.

"Thirty minutes after being admitted . . .": *Los Angeles Times*, August 6, 1969.

"In *Flashbacks*, Leary mistakenly wrote . . .": Leary, "Cultural Evolution Versus Political Revolution," *Flashbacks*.

"'It wasn't psilocybin laced with strychnine' . . .": interview with Travis Ashbrook, June 5, 1997.

"On the front door, pig . . .": Marilyn Bardsley, The Crime Library, www.crimelibrary.com/manson/.

THIRTY-ONE

"She was recovering in a Berkeley hospital . . .": *Laguna Beach Daily Pilot*, September 26, 1969.

"On September 24, a full-page photograph . . .": Timothy Leary, "Deal for Real," *The East Village Other*, September 24, 1969.

"Long before her autopsy was completed . . .": Art Linkletter, "Linkletter Girl's Death Laid to LSD," *Los Angeles Times*-Post Service, date unknown.

"The day his daughter died . . .": Urban Legends Reference Pages: Horrors (The Scarlet Linkletter), www.snopes2.com/horrors/drugs/linklttr.htm.

"In a book entitled *Drugs at My Door Step* . . .": Art Linkletter, *Drugs at My Door Step* (Waco, TX: Word Incorporated, 1973).

"Concerning Tim, he said . . .": ibid.

"He made seventy speeches a year . . .": "Art Linkletter," Biography.com, http://search.biography.com/cig-bin/.

"Though Tim wanted to address the massive crowd . . .": interview with Rosemary Woodruff Leary, September 24, 1996.

"'The drive to Altamont was to become' . . .": Timothy Leary, "Cultural Evolution Versus Political Revolution," *Flashbacks: An Autobiography* (Los Angeles: J. P. Tarcher, 1983).

"'I remember standing on a transformer onstage' . . .": interview with Rosemary Woodruff Leary, September 24, 1996.

"'The Hells Angels riot' . . .": Leary, "Cultural Evolution Versus Political Revolution," *Flashbacks*.

"'Altamont,' Tim told the *Berkeley Barb* . . .": John Bryan, *Whatever Happened to Timothy Leary?* (San Francisco: Renaissance Press, 1980).

"Two years earlier . . .": Timothy Leary, *High Priest* (New York: New American Library in association with the World Publishing Company, 1968; Berkeley, CA: Ronin Publishing, Inc., 1995).

"In *Flashbacks*, Leary would write . . .": Leary, "Cultural Evolution Versus Political Revolution," *Flashbacks*.

"'Because he wasn't even in Chicago' . . .": interview with Stew Albert, November 15, 1996.

"When Tim was asked by defense attorney . . .": Chicago 8 Conspiracy Trial transcript, Timothy Leary Archive.

"'If I had taken the stand' . . .": Leary, "Cultural Evolution Versus Political Revolution," *Flashbacks.*

"Faced with a maximum sentence . . .": *The Boston Globe,* January 21, 1970.

"Confidently telling reporters . . .": Bryan, *Whatever Happened to Timothy Leary?*

"In addition, the film would feature . . .": Timothy Leary, *Changing My Mind, Among Others* (Englewood Cliffs, NJ: Prentice Hall, Inc., 1982).

"After four days of voir dire . . .": Clint Erney, "Leary Marijuana Possession Jury Assembled After 4 Days," *The Register,* February 6, 1970.

"In notoriously conservative . . .": Don Smith, "Courthouse Is a Stage—Timothy Leary Playing His Role as High Priest to Hilt," *Los Angeles Times,* October 27, 1969.

"'I was the one really on trial' . . .": interview with Neil Purcell, July 18, 2001.

"'It was Officer Purcell who was on his hands' . . .": Gene Cowles, "Strange Happenings—Leary Pre-Trial Hearing—Color It Psychedelic," *Laguna Beach Daily Pilot,* date unknown.

"Purcell was astonished that . . .": interview with Neil Purcell, July 18, 2001.

"When Jack replied that he was . . .": Cowles, "Strange Happenings," *Laguna Beach Daily Pilot.*

"'In the course of that trial' . . .": interview with Neil Purcell, July 18, 2001.

"'If I fought my case and won' . . .": Leary, "Cultural Evolution Versus Political Revolution," *Flashbacks.*

"'They have attempted' . . .": "Attorneys Concede Two Learys Guilty," *The Register,* February 19, 1970.

"While they were gone . . .": Clint Erney, "Leary Given 1–10 Years in Prison," *The Register,* March 17, 1970.

"In an attempt to keep Tim . . .": letter from David McClelland to Michael Standard, reprinted in the *Los Angeles Free Press,* date unknown.

"'I think his conduct over the past years' . . .": Bryan, *Whatever Happened to Timothy Leary?*

"'These are the times' . . .": "Rosemary Wept," *Berkeley Barb* (March 6–12, 1970).

"Commenting on the verdict . . .": Chet Flippo, "Ten Years in Texas for Tim Leary," *Rolling Stone* (April 2, 1970).

"With sentencing in Orange County . . .": Bob Hayes, "Top Court," *Berkeley Barb* (May 1, 1970).

"On the sunny little patio . . .": Bob Hayes, "Holding Together," *Berkeley Barb* (March 6–12, 1970).

"In her presentencing report . . .": Orange County Probation Department, Pre-Sentencing Report, March 11, 1970, Timothy Leary Archives.

"'Love cannot be imprisoned' . . .": "Leary's Wife Draws 6 Months in OC Jail," *The Register,* March 12, 1970.

"The gallery was so crowded . . .": Erney, "Leary Given 1–10 Years in Prison."

"Neil Purcell recalled . . .": interview with Neil Purcell, July 18, 2001.

"'They laid it all on Tim' . . .": interview with Rosemary Woodruff Leary, September 24, 1996.

"'That's why the judge wouldn't give us bail' . . .": Steven V. Roberts, "Leary Goes to Prison on Coast to Start Term of 1 to 10 Years," *The New York Times,* March 22, 1970.

THIRTY-TWO

"After being transferred . . .": Timothy Leary, "Twenty-four Steps to Freedom," *Flashbacks: An Autobiography* (Los Angeles: J. P. Tarcher, 1983).

"As Rosemary recalled . . .": interview with Rosemary Woodruff Leary, September 24, 1996.

"On the intelligence test . . .": Timothy Leary, *Confessions of a Hope Fiend* (New York: Bantam Books, 1973).

"'I was in the California Youth Authority' . . .": interview with Jack Leary, April 22, 1997.

"Concerning Tim's state of mind . . .": John Bryan, *Whatever Happened to Timothy Leary?* (San Francisco: Renaissance Press, 1980).

"The best choice by far . . .": Leary, *Confessions of a Hope Fiend.*

"Addressing her as . . .": Timothy Leary, Prison Letters, 1970, Timothy Leary Archives.

"In early April, a photograph of Tim . . .": "Message from Leary," *The East Village Other,* April 1970.

"'I gave him my word' . . .": interview with Rosemary Woodruff Leary, March 4, 1997.

"In one, he wrote . . .": document, Timothy Leary Archives.

"Although one gray-haired prisoner . . .": Timothy Leary, *Jail Notes* (New York: Grove Press Inc., 1970).

"Making sure he was always well supplied . . .": Timothy Leary, Prison Letters, 1970, Timothy Leary Archives.

"'She was living in her car' . . .": interview with Anne Apfelbaum, May 26, 1997.

"Tim became his assistant . . .": Leary, *Confessions of a Hope Fiend.*

"Rosemary had organized it . . .": interview with Rosemary Woodruff Leary, March 11, 1997.

"'Acid was flowing like water' . . .": interview with Anita Hoffman, October 29, 1996.

"Rosemary had invited a variety . . .": interview with Rosemary Woodruff Leary, March 11, 1997.

"Earlier in the day as policemen had stood . . .": interview with Larry Sloman, November 14, 1996.

"'Allen mentioned something about' . . .": interview with Anita Hoffman, October 29, 1996.

"'This was just after Kent State' . . .": interview with Rosemary Woodruff Leary, March 11, 1997.

"Entirely open, with no cells . . .": Timothy Leary, Prison Letters, 1970, Timothy Leary Archives.

"Three days later, Orange County . . .": "Keep Leary in Jail, D.A. Tells Justice," *Los Angeles Herald Examiner,* May 18, 1970.

"Justice Douglas, citing a 1966 case . . .": United Press clipping, undated, Timothy Leary Archives.

"Although Joseph Rhine, another of Tim's . . .": Gerald Pearlman, "The Radicalization of Timothy Leary: An interview with Joseph Rhine," *Psychedelic Review* (1971).

"In early June, he wrote Rosemary . . .": Timothy Leary, Prison Letters, 1970, Timothy Leary Archives.

"Tim, identifying himself . . .": Michael Grieg, "Poetic Brief—Leary's Plea—Very Free Verse," *San Francisco Chronicle,* October 7, 1970.

"'He was coming up with some' . . .": interview with Rosemary Woodruff Leary, March 4, 1997.

"'He could tolerate almost anything' . . .": interview with Michael Kennedy, November 18, 1996.

"In *Flashbacks,* Leary supplied another reason . . .": Leary, "Twenty-four Steps to Freedom," *Flashbacks.*

"'I bought into the need for him to escape' . . .": interview with Rosemary Woodruff Leary, March 4, 1997.

"'Michael Randall and myself put the money up' . . .": interview with Travis Ashbrook, June 5, 1997.

"When Weatherman Bernadine Dohrn . . .": Leary, *Confessions of a Hope Fiend;* and Martin A. Lee and Bruce Shlain, *Acid Dreams: The CIA, LSD, and the Sixties Rebellion* (New York: Grove Press, Inc., 1985).

"'We weren't following Tim's story' . . .": interview with Jeff Jones, January 25, 1997.

"To the question of why the Weathermen . . .": interview with Jeff Jones, January 25, 1997.

"John Bryan wrote that what was called . . .": Bryan, *Whatever Happened to Timothy Leary?*

"'I was there' . . .": interview with Michael Kennedy, November 18, 1996.

"'The only person who knew how he got out' . . .": interview with Rosemary Woodruff Leary, March 4, 1997.

"IN THE NAME OF THE FATHER . . .": document, Timothy Leary Archives.

"When the eight-thirty whistle sounded . . .": Leary, "Twenty-four Steps to Freedom," *Flashbacks.*

"He described Dohrn as wearing . . .": Leary, *Confessions of a Hope Fiend.*

"In what Leary later described as . . .": Leary, "Twenty-four Steps to Freedom," *Flashbacks.*

" 'I insisted we stop at Cost Plus' . . .": interview with Rosemary Woodruff Leary, March 4, 1997.

"The communique, signed by Dohrn . . .": document, Timothy Leary Archives.

" 'It's a merger of dope and dynamite' . . .": Leo Laurence, *Berkeley Barb* (September 18, 1970).

"When J. Edgar Hoover was asked . . .": Charles W. Slack, *Timothy Leary, the Madness of the Sixties, and Me* (New York: Peter H. Wyden, 1974).

"Robert Anton Wilson recalled . . .": interview with Robert Anton Wilson, October 8, 1996.

"Travis Ashbrook, who helped bankroll . . .": interview with Travis Ashbrook, June 5, 1997.

"Succinctly, Baba Ram Dass . . .": Bryan, *Whatever Happened to Timothy Leary?*

THIRTY-THREE

"He peered into the bathroom mirror . . .": Timothy Leary, *Confessions of a Hope Fiend* (New York: Bantam Books, 1973).

" 'Tim was quite shocked' . . .": interview with Jeff Jones, January 25, 1997.

" 'Tim's head was shaved' . . .": interview with Rosemary Woodruff Leary, March 4, 1997.

" 'The first hit of Algiers' . . .": Leary, *Confessions of a Hope Fiend.*

"As soon as the news of Tim's escape . . .": interview with Paul Krassner, October 21, 1996.

" 'If a fugitive colony could be established' . . .": Abbie Hoffman, *Soon to Be a Major Motion Picture* (New York: Grosset & Dunlap, Inc., 1980).

"Described by Albert as looking . . .": interview with Stew Albert, November 15, 1996.

" 'Inter-racial harmony' . . .": Leary, *Confessions of a Hope Fiend.*

" 'There he was' . . .": interview with Rosemary Woodruff Leary, March 4, 1997.

" 'I was to try and explain the Third World' . . .": interview with Stew Albert, November 15, 1996.

"The case that Cleaver intended to make . . .": Hoffman, *Soon to Be a Major Motion Picture.*

" 'When the Algerian Government gave Leary' . . .": interview with Stew Albert, November 15, 1996.

"Always adept at selling himself . . .": Leary, *Confessions of a Hope Fiend.*

"We had a lot in common. . . ." Leary, *Confessions of a Hope Fiend.*

THIRTY-FOUR

"What mattered most to both Tim . . .": interview with Richard Castrodale, October 1970.

" 'Beloved Brother,' he wrote Allen Ginsberg . . .": letter to Allen Ginsberg, October 10, 1979, Timothy Leary Archives.

"Before he got behind the wheel . . .": Jonah Raskin, *Out of the Whale* (New York: Links Books, 1974).

" 'We were driving through' . . .": interview with Anita Hoffman, October 29, 1996.

"Seeing an Arab sitting on the hotel steps . . .": Raskin, *Out of the Whale.*

"Anita Hoffman realized that Tim . . .": interview with Anita Hoffman, October 29, 1996.

"Feeling that LSD was for 'affluent rebels' . . .": Raskin, *Out of the Whale.*

" 'We hardly ever saw Kathleen' . . .": interview with Martin Kenner, November 18, 1996.

"Anita Hoffman, who had come . . .": interview with Jennifer Dohrn by Bruce Soloway, KPFA or WBAI, date unknown.

"Much of what they felt . . .": Tom Wolfe, *Radical Chic & Mau-Mauing the Flak Catchers* (New York: Farrar, Straus and Giroux, 1970).

"When Anita accompanied her fellow delegates . . .": interview with Anita Hoffman, October 29, 1996.

"Cleaver, in his own defense . . .": interview with Eldridge Cleaver, November 1, 1996.

"Suspecting a plot to kill him . . .": "Fugitive: Cleaver Killed Panther," Associated Press, February 25, 2001.

" 'I've heard this before' . . .": interview with Eldridge Cleaver, November 1, 1996.

"When Albert asked Cleaver . . .": Stew Albert, *Who the Hell Is Stew Albert?* (Los Angeles: Red Hen Press, 2004).

"'We weren't under any misconception' . . .": interview with Rosemary Woodruff Leary, March 4, 1997.

"Cleaver, who had taken acid once . . .": interview with Eldridge Cleaver, October 22, 1996.

"'Leary was very offended by that' . . .": interview with Stew Albert, November 8, 2004.

"'Algeria,' Cleaver recalled . . .": interview with Eldridge Cleaver, October 22, 1996.

"'Eldridge huddled with the FLN' . . .": Timothy Leary, *Confessions of a Hope Fiend* (New York: Bantam Books, 1973).

"'The idea,' Stew Albert remembered . . .": interview with Stew Albert, November 15, 1996.

"Although Leary would later write . . .": Leary, *Confessions of a Hope Fiend.*

"In Beirut, an al-Fatah spokesman . . .": *Newsweek* (November 9, 1970).

"'The problem,' Jennifer Dohrn would say . . .": interview with Jennifer Dohrn by Bruce Soloway.

"'Do you really want to have your press conference' . . .": Leary, *Confessions of a Hope Fiend.*

"He managed to utter . . .": *Newsweek* (November 9, 1970).

"The Lebanese government . . .": Leary, *Confessions of a Hope Fiend.*

"One Egyptian airport official said . . .": *Newsweek* (November 9, 1970).

"'From this point on' . . .": interview with Jennifer Dohrn by Bruce Soloway.

"Kenner, who by this point . . .": interview with Martin Kenner, November 18, 1996.

"Later, Dohrn reported . . .": interview with Jennifer Dohrn by Bruce Soloway.

"'Eldridge was full of shit' . . .": interview with Martin Kenner, November 18, 1996.

"'The attitude of the Panthers changed' . . .": Leary, *Confessions of a Hope Fiend.*

THIRTY-FIVE

"Ken Kesey, who had been . . .": Ken Kesey, "An Open Letter to Timothy Leary," *The Marijuana Review* 1, no. 6 (January–June 1971).

"'We don't believe Ken Kesey wrote it' . . .": Robert Greenfield, "Tim Leary: Or, Bomb for Buddha," *Rolling Stone* (December 2, 1970).

"Identifying himself with revolutionary heroes . . .": Timothy Leary, "An Open Letter to Allen Ginsberg on the Seventh Liberation," *The Marijuana Review* 1, no. 6 (January–June 1971).

"On January 5, 1971, during a live phone interview . . .": Timothy Leary interviewed by Jaakov Kohn and Alex Bennet, "Hedonic Isolationism," *The East Village Other,* January 12, 1971.

"For the infraction of 'sitting unarmed' . . .": Timothy Leary, *Confessions of a Hope Fiend* (New York: Bantam Books, 1973).

"'Tim and Rosemary went down south' . . .": interview with Eldridge Cleaver, October 22, 1996.

"Although Tim now viewed Algiers . . .": Leary, *Confessions of a Hope Fiend.*

"'It was a high-rise' . . .": interview with Rosemary Woodruff Leary, March 4, 1997.

"'Implying that I was holding out' . . .": Leary, *Confessions of a Hope Fiend.*

"'At this point, we felt the first flicker' . . .": interview with Rosemary Woodruff Leary, March 4, 1997.

"On the day before their dinner party . . .": Leary, *Confessions of a Hope Fiend.*

"'He organized a party' . . .": interview with Eldridge Cleaver, October 22, 1996.

"'I am not going to argue with you' . . .": Leary, *Confessions of a Hope Fiend.*

"'They put us in the center of the floor' . . .": interview with Rosemary Woodruff Leary, March 4, 1997.

"'We took his pack of cigarettes' . . .": interview with Eldridge Cleaver, October 22, 1996.

"Tim then wrote a 'civil rights message' . . .": Leary, *Confessions of a Hope Fiend.*

"'It was straight out of Kafka' . . .": interview with Rosemary Woodruff Leary, March 4, 1997.

"In a taped statement that Cleaver released . . .": Norman Spinrad, "Leary Busted," *Los Angeles Free Press* (February 5–11, 1971).

" 'If E. C. [Eldridge Cleaver] could persuade' . . .": Leary, *Confessions of a Hope Fiend.*

"After selected clips from their conversation . . .": "Leary Urges Young: Quit Drugs, Revolt," *The Boston Globe,* February 20, 1971.

"Cleaver did everything he could . . .": John Bryan, *Whatever Happened to Timothy Leary?* (San Francisco: Renaissance Press, 1980).

" 'He was also supposed to be part' . . .": interview with Rosemary Woodruff Leary, March 4, 1997.

" 'We did not want to enter Switzerland' . . .": Leary, *Confessions of a Hope Fiend.*

" 'It was a setup' . . .": interview with Eldridge Cleaver, November 1, 1996.

" 'He was a silver-haired man' . . .": interview with Rosemary Woodruff Leary, March 4, 1997.

" 'He was as tall as a giant' . . .": Leary, *Confessions of a Hope Fiend.*

"Dick Diver, the hero of F. Scott Fitzgerald's . . .": F. Scott Fitzgerald, *Tender Is the Night* (New York: Scribner's, 1934).

" 'So there we were in Switzerland' . . .": interview with Rosemary Woodruff Leary, March 11, 1997.

" 'A French Resistance hero of sorts' . . .": Joanna Harcourt-Smith, "Paramour" (unpublished); and interview with Joanna Harcourt-Smith, December 7, 1996.

"Hauchard portrayed himself as completely . . .": Timothy Leary, "Landlocked in the Alps," *Flashbacks: An Autobiography* (Los Angeles: J. P. Tarcher, 1983).

" 'I would leave Tim behind' . . .": interview with Rosemary Woodruff Leary, March 11, 1997.

"Wrapping himself in the blankets . . .": Leary, "Landlocked in the Alps," *Flashbacks.*

" 'I remember Allen Ginsberg organizing' . . .": interview with Rosemary Woodruff Leary, March 11, 1997.

"In it, he wrote that the criminal . . .": Allen Ginsberg, "Declaration of Independence for Dr. Timothy Leary," *Los Angeles Free Press* (July 16, 1971).

"Urging the Swiss to grant . . .": Michael Horowitz, *Apologia for Timothy Leary* (San Francisco: Fitz Hugh Ludlow Library: 1974).

" 'So there was a lot of pressure' . . .": interview with Rosemary Woodruff Leary, March 11, 1997.

"While Mastronardi busied himself . . .": Leary, "Landlocked in the Alps," *Flashbacks.*

" 'It was in prison in Switzerland' . . .": interview with Rosemary Woodruff Leary, March 11, 1997.

"Suggesting they use the same strategy . . .": Leary, "Landlocked in the Alps," *Flashbacks.*

" 'When Tim came out' . . .": interview with Rosemary Woodruff Leary, March 11, 1997.

" 'It was a fantastic moment' . . .": Fitz Hugh Ludlow [pseudonym for Michael Horowitz], "Historic Meet—Tim & Dr. LSD," *Berkeley Barb* (September 24–30, 1971).

"In his book, *LSD: My Problem Child* . . .": Albert Hofmann, *LSD: My Problem Child* (New York: McGraw-Hill, 1980).

"His 'absence during her last two fertile times' . . .": Leary, "Landlocked in the Alps," *Flashbacks.*

" 'Initially,' she recalled . . .": interview with Rosemary Woodruff Leary, March 11, 1997.

" 'Events moved with prearranged precision' . . .": Leary, "Landlocked in the Alps," *Flashbacks.*

" 'Younger than me and quite attractive' , ,": interview with Rosemary Woodruff Leary, March 11, 1997.

THIRTY-SIX

" 'I'm sure,' Rosemary recalled . . .": interview with Rosemary Woodruff Leary, March 11, 1997.

"When Jack Leary called his father . . .": interview with Dieadra Martino, November 10, 1996.

" 'Dennis,' Rosemary recalled . . .": interview with Rosemary Woodruff Leary, March 11, 1997.

"From Kabul, Dennis brought . . .": Brian Barritt, *The Road of Excess: A Psychedelic Autobiography* (London: PSI Publishing, 1998).

"Together, they stood where Aleister Crowley . . .": ibid.

"'Eventually,' Tim later wrote . . .": Timothy Leary, "Landlocked in the Alps," *Flashbacks: An Autobiography* (Los Angeles: J. P. Tarcher, 1983).

"Barritt was then informed . . .": Barritt, *The Road of Excess.*

"'This was right after Clifford Irving's hoax' . . .": interview with Alan U. Schwartz, September 25, 1997.

"The next day, Schwartz . . .": Barritt, *The Road of Excess.*

"When Schwartz realized that Tim . . .": interview with Alan U. Schwartz, September 25, 1997.

"'When *Confessions of a Hope Fiend* came out' . . .": interview with Rosemary Woodruff Leary, March 11, 1997.

"In what seemed like an attempt . . .": document, Timothy Leary Archives; and "To Whom It May Concern," document, Timothy Leary Archives.

"'We had a reconciliation of love' . . .": interview with Rosemary Woodruff Leary, March 11, 1997.

"In its entirety, the note read . . .": Rosemary Woodruff Leary, *Rolling Stone,* date unknown.

"'Our backgrounds fuse' . . .": Barritt, *The Road of Excess.*

"When Tim and a small circle of friends . . .": ibid.

"He told Kahn that Barritt . . .": Kenneth Kahn, "Dr. Timothy Leary: Blowing the Conditioned Mind," *Los Angeles Free Press* (August 18, 1972).

"On Sunday, August 6, 1972 . . .": Joe Eszterhas, "The Strange Case of the Hippie Mafia," *Rolling Stone* (December 7, 1972).

"One of the more remarkable conclusions . . .": ibid.

"As a *Los Angeles Times* reporter noted . . .": Evan Maxwell, "Dream of Universal Love Shattered by Drugs," *Los Angeles Times,* February 20, 1973.

"Barritt would later write . . .": Barritt, *The Road of Excess.*

"In *Flashbacks,* Tim would later write . . .": Leary, "Captured in Kabul," *Flashbacks.*

"In an outline for a book . . .": "Outline for Contributions by T. L. to a Book by J. L. & T. L.," undated, Timothy Leary Archives.

"He wrote that after visiting . . .": Barritt, *The Road of Excess.*

"In *Flashbacks,* Leary claimed that Barritt . . .": Leary, "Captured in Kabul," *Flashbacks.*

"Barritt contended that the two of them . . .": Barritt, *The Road of Excess.*

"When Charles Slack arrived . . .": Charles W. Slack, *Timothy Leary, the Madness of the Sixties, and Me* (New York: Peter H. Wyden, 1974).

"'He had run into this girl' . . .": interview with Charles Slack, March 20, 1997.

"'After Rosemary left' . . .": interview with Joanna Harcourt-Smith, December 7, 1996.

"In *What Does WoMan Want?,* Leary described . . .": Timothy Leary, *What Does WoMan Want?* (Los Angeles: 88 Books, 1976).

"'Her CV,' Brian Barritt noted . . .": Barritt, *The Road of Excess.*

"When she summoned the courage . . .": Joanna Harcourt-Smith, "Paramour" (unpublished).

"Six months later, while living in . . .": interview with Joanna Harcourt-Smith, December 7, 1996.

"'Look what I am doing now' . . .": ibid.

"In 'Paramour,' her unpublished memoir . . .": Harcourt-Smith, "Paramour."

"'Dennis was small and wiry' . . .": interview with Joanna Harcourt-Smith, December 7, 1996.

"As they took them with white wine . . .": Harcourt-Smith, "Paramour."

"'Tim just paid him to go away' . . .": interview with Joanna Harcourt-Smith, December 7, 1996.

"In *Flashbacks,* Leary wrote that he asked . . .": Leary, "Captured in Kabul," *Flashbacks.*

"In 'Paramour,' Joanna wrote that Dennis . . .": Harcourt-Smith, "Paramour."

"'And I was glad' . . .": interview with Joanna Harcourt-Smith, December 7, 1996.

"Tim instructed Joanna to look . . .": Harcourt-Smith, "Paramour."

"'I was twenty-six years old' . . .": interview with Joanna Harcourt-Smith, December 7, 1996.

"Tim had already told Joanna . . .": Harcourt-Smith, "Paramour."

"Using back roads to avoid . . .": interview with Joanna Harcourt-Smith, December 7, 1996.

"In it, he wrote . . .": document, Timothy Leary Archives.

" 'Susan was eight months pregnant' . . .": interview with Joanna Harcourt-Smith, December 7, 1996.

"She then said, as Joanna would later write . . .": Harcourt-Smith, "Paramour."

"The professor wanted her to go . . .": interview with Joanna Harcourt-Smith, December 7, 1996.

THIRTY-SEVEN

"Leaping to his feet, Tim began yelling . . .": Joanna Harcourt-Smith, "Paramour" (unpublished).

" 'Tim was incredibly pale' . . .": interview with Joanna Harcourt-Smith, December 7, 1996.

"As they passed a food stall . . .": Harcourt-Smith, "Paramour."

"Joanna called it . . .": interview with Joanna Harcourt-Smith, December 7, 1996

"With 'no one at the front desk' . . .": Harcourt-Smith, "Paramour."

"They put Tim and Joanna . . .": interview with Joanna Harcourt-Smith, December 7, 1996.

"Looking 'haggard and edgy' . . .": Harcourt-Smith, "Paramour."

"At the top of the stairs . . .": interview with Joanna Harcourt-Smith, December 7, 1996.

"They had just met agent . . .": Joe Eszterhas, "The Strange Case of the Hippie Mafia," *Rolling Stone* (December 7, 1972).

" 'Because of that' . . .": interview with Joanna Harcourt-Smith, December 7, 1996.

"Smiling confidently, Burke said . . .": Harcourt-Smith, "Paramour."

" 'The next morning' . . .": interview with Joanna Harcourt-Smith, December 7, 1996.

"Having smoked marijuana with John and Yoko . . .": Harcourt-Smith, "Paramour."

" 'They come up' . . .": interview with Joanna Harcourt-Smith, December 7, 1996.

"As they flew over America . . .": Harcourt-Smith, "Paramour."

" 'Here is the entire counterculture' . . .": interview with Joanna Harcourt-Smith, December 7, 1996.

"Rosemary Woodruff Leary, who was on the run . . .": interview with Rosemary Woodruff Leary, March 11, 1997.

THIRTY-EIGHT

"The anchorman described her as . . .": interview with Joanna Harcourt-Smith, December 11, 1996.

" 'I plan to tell him exactly how' . . .": Arthur Kunkin, "The Capture of Tim Leary," *Los Angeles Free Press* (January 26–February 4, 1973).

" 'I saw Tim in Santa Ana' . . .": interview with Bruce Margolin, October 21, 1996.

"In his new cell in solitary . . .": Bill Cardoso, "Tim Leary and the Long Arm of the Law," *Rolling Stone* (March 15, 1973).

"To Joanna, Tim admitted . . .": letter from Joanna Harcourt-Smith to the *Los Angeles Free Press*, undated, Timothy Leary Archives.

" 'I felt very distrusting of Joanna' . . .": John Bryan, *Whatever Happened to Timothy Leary?* (San Francisco: Renaissance Press, 1980).

" 'Nobody in the world' . . .": Cardoso, "Tim Leary and the Long Arm of the Law."

" 'After a little while' . . .": interview with Joanna Harcourt-Smith, December 11, 1996.

"Writing with the pencil stub . . .": Timothy Leary, *Neurologic* (San Francisco: privately printed and published by Joanna Harcourt-Smith, May 1973).

"Michael Horowitz recalled . . .": interview with Michael Horowitz, March 3, 1997.

" 'They said they had her in a clinic' . . .": interview with Joanna Harcourt-Smith, December 11, 1996.

"Dennis, eyes burning . . .": Joanna Harcourt-Smith, "Paramour" (unpublished).

"First, Tim wanted 'the most far-out' . . .": Kathie Streem, "Leary's Lover Vows—'Fast To Death,' " *Berkeley Barb* (March 9–15, 1973).

"During his arraignment on February 13 . . .": Cardoso, "Tim Leary and the Long Arm of the Law."

"In a yellow shirt and purple-striped trousers . . .": Jay Jones, "Leary on Trial—Refuses DA's Deal," *Berkeley Barb* (March 15–March 29, 1973).

" 'The only thing they needed to prove' . . .": interview with Joanna Harcourt-Smith, December 11, 1996.

" 'Dapper with mustache, goatee' . . .": Jones, "Leary on Trial—Refuses DA's Deal."

"Years later, she confessed . . .": interview with Joanna Harcourt-Smith, December 11, 1996.

"In return for a guilty plea . . .": Jones, "Leary on Trial—Refuses DA's Deal."

"In part, Margolin's defense . . .": interview with Bruce Margolin, October 21, 1996.

"Tim replied, 'My nervous system' . . .": Timothy Leary, *Changing My Mind, Among Others* (Englewood Cliffs, NJ: Prentice Hall, Inc., 1982).

" 'To become "Timothy Leary" ' . . .": Jay Jones, "Leary on Stand—Escape Details Told," *Berkeley Barb* (March 30–April 7, 1973).

" 'I get into this uniform' . . .": Bryan, *Whatever Happened to Timothy Leary?*

" 'I am always under the influence of LSD' . . .": Dale Brozosky, "Disturbed from a Yogic State of Concentration," *Los Angeles Free Press* (April 6, 1973).

"Shapiro testified that he had administered . . .": Jones, "Leary on Stand—Escape Details Told."

"Dr. Walter Houston Clark . . .": Brozosky, "Disturbed from a Yogic State of Concentration."

" 'The judge was not mad at Timothy' . . .": interview with Bruce Margolin, October 21, 1996.

"After sentencing, the judge allowed Joanna . . .": interview with Joanna Harcourt-Smith, December 11, 1996.

"Just before Tim got off the bus . . .": Timothy Leary, "Folsom Prison," *Flashbacks: An Autobiography* (Los Angeles: J. P. Tarcher, 1983).

" 'This is the bottom of the pit' . . .": Bryan, *Whatever Happened to Timothy Leary?*

" 'I began to understand' . . .": interview with Joanna Harcourt-Smith, December 11, 1996.

" 'I knew you'd end up here' . . .": Leary, "Folsom Prison," *Flashbacks.*

" 'Hey,' Tim said . . .": Timothy Leary with Robert Anton Wilson and George A. Koopman, *Neuropolitics: The Sociobiology of Human Metamorphosis* (Los Angeles: Peace Press, 1977).

" 'It's all death' . . .": Bryan, *Whatever Happened to Timothy Leary?*

" 'Timothy had long conversations' . . .": interview with Joanna Harcourt-Smith, December 11, 1996.

" 'They liked each other' . . .": Bryan, *Whatever Happened to Timothy Leary?*

" 'He'd get beat up' . . .": Leary, *Neuropolitics.*

"He slept through breakfast . . .": Leary, "Folsom Prison," *Flashbacks.*

" 'Tim wanted to get out of Folsom' . . .": interview with Joanna Harcourt-Smith, December 11, 1996.

"In it, he linked the emerging Watergate . . .": "Mock-Sestina: The Conspiracy Against Dr. Tim Leary," Allen Ginsberg (Rallying Point, date unknown).

"Asked during a lecture how he felt . . .": Gordon Ball, editor, *Allen Verbatim: Lectures on Poetry, Politics, Consciousness* (New York: McGraw Hill Book Company, 1974).

" 'On the way to Folsom' . . .": interview with Joanna Harcourt-Smith, December 11, 1996.

"Ginsberg told Tim that Joanna . . .": Craig Vetter, "Bring Me the Head of Timothy Leary," *Playboy* (September 1975).

"Tim told Ginsberg that Joanna . . .": interview with Joanna Harcourt-Smith, December 11, 1996.

"(In a conversation with the journalist . . .": interview with Jack Leary by Ken Kelley, September 1974.

" 'Tim's rap' . . .": interview with Joanna Harcourt-Smith, December 11, 1996.

" 'Most of the men I model myself after' . . .": Leary, *Changing My Mind, Among Others.*

"As prison psychologist Wesley Hiler . . .": Bryan, *Whatever Happened to Timothy Leary?*

"During the interview, Tim wore . . .": Leary, *Changing My Mind, Among Others.*

"In *The Exploration of Outer Space* . . .": Timothy Leary, *Starseed* (San Francisco: Level Press, 1973).

"In early July, Tim read . . .": ibid.

"A month later, Tim answered . . .": Timothy Leary, Lynn Wayne Benner, Joanna Leary, *Terra II: The Starseed Transmission* (San Francisco: Guanine, The Network, 1974).

"Although Tim never credited it . . .": Jeff Tamarkin, *Got a Revolution: The Turbulent Flight of the Jefferson Airplane* (New York: Atria Books, 2003).

THIRTY-NINE

"'I was not there as a patient' . . .": Timothy Leary, "Folsom Prison," *Flashbacks: An Autobiography* (Los Angeles: J. P. Tarcher, 1983).

"Two days after his arrival in Vacaville . . .": John Bryan, *Whatever Happened to Timothy Leary?* (San Francisco: Renaissance Press, 1980).

"For months, he had been telling . . .": Joanna Harcourt-Smith, "Paramour" (unpublished).

"'He was always telling me that Tim' . . .": interview with Joanna Harcourt-Smith, December 11, 1996.

"In *Flashbacks,* Leary described . . .": Leary, "Escape Plot," *Flashbacks.*

"At Vacaville, Tim fell in love . . .": Bryan, *Whatever Happened to Timothy Leary?*

"'It turned out to be an out-a-sight comet' . . .": Timothy Leary with Robert Anton Wilson and George A. Koopman, *Neuropolitics: The Sociobiology of Human Metamorphosis* (Los Angeles: Peace Press, 1977).

"Joanna, who had already met . . .": interview with Joanna Harcourt-Smith, December 11, 1996.

"Jolted by Joanna's violent outburst . . .": Tim Findley, "What Leary's Mind Is Up To," *San Francisco Chronicle,* December 14, 1973.

"Shortly before he was scheduled . . .": Bryan, *Whatever Happened to Timothy Leary?*

"As Joanna recalled . . .": interview with Joanna Harcourt-Smith, December 11, 1996.

"Though *The Village Voice* portrayed the trial . . .": Mary Jo Worth, "The Story of the Acid Profiteers," *The Village Voice* (August 22, 1974).

"Tim called Watergate . . .": Leary, *Neuropolitics.*

"'Communication is love' . . .": ibid.

"'He said to me' . . .": interview with Joanna Harcourt-Smith, December 11, 1996.

"Dennis swore that when he asked . . .": *The People vs. Dr. Timothy Francis Leary* B-26358, San Francisco, Grace County, 1974.

"'It is well you are out of the line of fire' . . .": letter to Rosemary Woodruff Leary from Michael Tigar, April 28, 1973, Timothy Leary Archives.

"On March 10, she sold copies . . .": press release, Joanna Leary, March, 1974.

"After reading the book twice . . .": letter to Joanna Leary from Abigail Leary, December 3, 1973.

"On a rented typewriter . . .": letter to Joanna Leary from Susan Martino, February 9, 1974.

"Since the SLA was founded . . .": Bryan, *Whatever Happened to Timothy Leary?*

"When she learned that her uncle . . .": Craig Vetter, "Bring Me the Head of Timothy Leary," *Playboy* (September 1975).

"In 'Paramour,' her unpublished memoir . . .": Harcourt-Smith, "Paramour."

"For the next two weeks . . .": ibid.

"They went to the first meeting . . .": interview with Joanna Harcourt-Smith, December 11, 1996.

"At DEA headquarters in Los Angeles . . .": Harcourt-Smith, "Paramour."

"The government was in heaven . . .": interview with Joanna Harcourt-Smith, December 11, 1996.

FORTY

"According to the interview transcript . . .": United States Department of Justice, Federal Bureau of Investigation, Report of SA Kurk I. Klosser, Bureau File #40-84731, Title: Timothy Francis Leary, Jr. CG 4-66, interview transcription, Timothy Leary Archives.

"'It's a two-part process' . . .": interview with Kent Russell, February 10, 1997.

"'The prosecutors had never seen anything' . . .": interview with Michael Kennedy, November 18, 1996.

"'That was part of the deal' . . .": interview with Joanna Harcourt-Smith, December 11, 1996.

"'Dearest Ro' . . .": letter to Rosemary Woodruff Leary, May 20, 1974.

"'Although it was Joanna who made the call' . . .": interview with Rosemary Woodruff Leary, March 11, 1997.

"On June 1, 1974, a week after he first sat down . . .": letter to Rosemary Woodruff Leary, June 1, 1974.

"'The letter,' Rosemary recalled . . .": interview with Rosemary Woodruff Leary, March 11, 1997.

"'They went after Rosemary hard' . . .": interview with Michael Kennedy, November 18, 1996.

"'Being underground' . . .": interview with Rosemary Woodruff Leary, March 11, 1997.

"'She felt that if she came above ground' . . .": interview with Michael Kennedy, November 18, 1996.

FORTY-ONE

"As Joanna later wrote . . .": Joanna Harcourt-Smith, "Paramour" (unpublished).

"Described by Joe Eszterhas as . . .": Joe Eszterhas, "The Strange Case of the Hippie Mafia," *Rolling Stone* (December 7, 1972).

"'George Chula had a true love' . . .": interview with Neil Purcell, July 18, 2001.

"Don Strange of the DEA . . .": Eszterhas, "The Strange Case of the Hippie Mafia."

"'Would you like some cocaine' . . .": Craig Vetter, "Bring Me the Head of Timothy Leary," *Playboy* (September 1975).

"'I was still getting stoned and drinking' . . .": interview with Joanna Harcourt-Smith, December 11, 1996.

"'I liked George Chula' . . .": interview with Michael Kennedy, November 18, 1966.

"On July 25, the same day that Tim was . . .": Matters Pertaining to "Leary Archives," Federal Bureau of Investigation File #SC100-3667, October 25, 1974.

"She handed Horowitz a note . . .": Rasa Gustaitis, "Is Tim Leary's Joanna a Narc?," *New Times* (October 18, 1974).

"'I was extremely upset' . . .": interview with Michael Horowitz, March 3, 1997.

"When the FBI was finally done with him . . .": Peter O. Whitmer with Bruce VanWygarden, *Aquarius Revisited* (New York: Macmillan Publishing Company, 1987).

"'Tim told Kennedy and Rhine' . . .": interview with Joanna Harcourt-Smith, December 11, 1996.

"With him, Dennis brought . . .": Harcourt-Smith, "Paramour."

"'I was walking around with a lot of drugs' . . .": interview with Joanna Harcourt-Smith, December 11, 1996.

"In Sandstone, Tim met with federal prosecutor . . .": Vetter, "Bring Me the Head of Timothy Leary."

"Described by Michael Drosnin . . .": Michael Drosnin, "Nixon's Radical Chaser Bags a Whopper," *New Times* (October 18, 1974).

"As David Weir wrote . . .": David Weir, "Tim Leary: Soul in Hock," *Rolling Stone* (August 28, 1975).

FORTY-TWO

"'Again,' Joanna recalled . . .": interview with Joanna Harcourt-Smith, December 11, 1996.

"Asked why she was testifying . . .": Craig Vetter, "Bring Me the Head of Timothy Leary," *Playboy* (September 1975).

"Calling himself a psychologist . . .": David Weir, "Tim Leary: Soul in Hock," *Rolling Stone* (August 28, 1975).

"'He got off with a slap on the wrist' . . .": interview with Michael Kennedy, November 18, 1996.

"'They did not disbar him' . . .": interview with Neil Purcell, July 18, 2001.

"On the day after Chula was arrested . . .": Evan Maxwell, "Leary, 'Former King of LSD,' Tells Radicals: 'War Is Over,'" *Los Angeles Times*, September 6, 1974.

"As Craig Vetter wrote . . .": Vetter, "Bring Me the Head of Timothy Leary."

"Ken Kelley had never been close . . .": interview with Ken Kelley, October 30, 1996.

"Although Michael Kennedy had advised . . .": interview with Michael Kennedy, November 18, 1996.

"With both Ginsberg . . .": John Bryan, *Whatever Happened to Timothy Leary?* (San Francisco: Renaissance Press, 1980).

"A press conference was held . . .": Vetter, "Bring Me the Head of Timothy Leary."

"He also said that . . .": Bryan, *Whatever Happened to Timothy Leary?*

"'Can't you speak without reading' . . .": interview with Ken Kelley, October 30, 1996.

"'I trusted Tim' . . .": interview with Paul Krassner, October 21, 1996.

"'I was sharing a house with a woman' . . .": interview with Eugene Schoenfeld, October 29, 1996.

"'But it had Saran wrap on it' . . .": interview with Paul Krassner, October 21, 1996.

"'A rascal,' he said . . .": Bryan, *Whatever Happened to Timothy Leary?*

"Running the gamut . . .": Vetter, "Bring Me the Head of Timothy Leary."

"'Is he like Zabbathi Zvi' . . .": "Ginsberg Asks 44 Questions About Leary," *Berkeley Barb* (September 20–26, 1974).

"Ginsberg, who admitted to Kelley . . .": interview with Ken Kelley, October 30, 1996.

"Admitting that this was the first time . . .": Bryan, *Whatever Happened to Timothy Leary?*

"There cannot have been many sons . . .": interview with Ken Kelley, October 30, 1996.

"Outraged, Krassner's 'objective pose' . . .": interview with Paul Krassner, October 21, 1996.

"'We were live on KPFA' . . .": interview with Ken Kelley, October 30, 1996.

"'We tried to take Tim out as a witness' . . .": interview with Michael Kennedy, November 18, 1996.

"'I'm digesting the news of Herr Doktor Leary' . . .": Abbie and Anita Hoffman, *To America with Love: Letters from the Underground* (New York: Stonehill, 1976).

"'I was quoted in *The New York Times*' . . .": interview with Ken Kelley, October 30, 1996.

"After the press conference . . .": Bryan, *Whatever Happened to Timothy Leary?*

"On October 24, 1974, Tim was interrogated . . .": Federal Bureau of Investigation File #SC100-3667, Timothy Leary Archives.

"Although she could 'hardly call' . . .": interview with Joanna Harcourt-Smith, December 11, 1996.

"Jeff Jones would later say . . .": interview with Jeff Jones, January 25, 1997.

"A few days after Tim and Joanna decided . . .": interview with Joanna Harcourt-Smith, December 11, 1996.

"'Leary is an absolute fuckin' ally' . . .": Steve Long, "In Search of Tim Leary," *Berkeley Barb* (February 14–20, 1975).

"'I've done three years for two joints' . . .": Steve Long, "Leary Mysteries Dissolving," *Berkeley Barb* (March 14–20, 1975).

"He told her he had been in Colombia , , ,": interview with Joanna Harcourt-Smith, December 11, 1996.

"In the spring of 1975 . . .": Paul Krassner, "The Love Song of Timothy Leary," *Arcade* (Spring 1975).

"Parodying Allen Ginsberg's questions . . .": "444 Unanswered Questions About Timothy Leary (with apologies to Allen Ginsberg)," author, source, and date unknown.

"He asked Tim if John Lennon . . .": letters from David Martino, May 7, 1974, and December 6, 1975, Timothy Leary Archives.

"'I busted David Martino in Laguna ' . . .": interview with Neil Purcell, July 18, 2001.

FORTY-THREE

"Joanna returned to San Diego . . .": interview with Joanna Harcourt-Smith, December 11, 1996.

"On June 26, an FBI agent . . .": David Weir, "Tim Leary: Soul in Hock," *Rolling Stone* (August 28, 1975).

"Horowitz realized that he had . . .": interview with Michael Horowitz, March 3, 1997.

"Attending the press conference . . .": Steve Long, "Dr. Timothy Leary and the San Francisco Grand Jury," *Los Angeles Free Press* (September 1975).

"When Horowitz finally appeared . . .": interview with Michael Horowitz, March 3, 1997.

"The first letter he wrote . . .": letter to Robert Anton Wilson, August 8, 1975, Timothy Leary Archives.

"In an interview published in . . .": interview with Eldridge Cleaver, *Rolling Stone* (September 11, 1975).

" 'It was there,' Joanna recalled . . .": interview with Joanna Harcourt-Smith, December 11, 1996.

"Their refusal to accept his call . . .": interview with Eldridge Cleaver, November 1, 1996.

"On January 22, 1976, Cleaver sent . . .": letter from Eldridge Cleaver, January 22, 1976, Timothy Leary Archives.

"Six days later . . .": letter to Eldridge Cleaver, January 28, 1976, Timothy Leary Archives.

"By October, Tim was writing . . .": letter to Neil Freer, October 4, 1975, Timothy Leary Archives.

"In December, Tim wrote the reclusive author . . .": letter to Thomas Pynchon, December 5, 1975, Timothy Leary Archives.

"On January 13, 1976, Tim sent . . .": letter to Joanna Harcourt-Smith, January 13, 1976.

"As Joanna would later put it . . .": interview with Joanna Harcourt-Smith, December 11, 1996.

"A month later, *People* magazine . . .": John Riley, "Tim Leary Is Free, Demonstrably in Love and Making Extraterrestial Plans," *People* (June 11, 1976).

" 'Here we were in this cabin' . . .": interview with Joanna Harcourt-Smith, December 11, 1996.

"In an interview in the *Berkeley Barb* . . .": Robert Anton Wilson, "Leary Trades Drugs for Space Colonies," *Berkeley Barb* (June 17, 1976).

" 'I don't know how many papers you get' . . .": letter to Abigail Leary, June 6, 1976, Timothy Leary Archives.

"In answer to a letter from Tim . . .": letter from William Buckley Jr., June 22, 1976, Timothy Leary Archives.

"On July 2, Tim wrote the chairman . . .": letter, July 2, 1976, Timothy Leary Archives.

"When Joanna's mother . . .": interview with Joanna Harcourt-Smith, December 11, 1996.

FORTY-FOUR

"Behind him in San Diego . . .": interview with Joanna Harcourt-Smith, December 11, 1996.

"Two and a half weeks later . . .": William Overend, "Timothy Leary: Messenger of Evolution," *Los Angeles Times*, January 30, 1977.

" 'I did that because I was still' . . .": interview with Joanna Harcourt-Smith, December 11, 1996.

" 'I've outlasted five directors' . . .": interview with Timothy Leary by Donna Frantz, KLRB-FM, May 26, 1977.

"Her last contact with her son . . .": letter to Abigail Leary, Mother's Day 1978, Timothy Leary Archives.

"Edwards, who had first seen Tim . . .": interview with Henry Edwards, April 29, 1997.

"Lindsay Brice, a photographer . . .": interview with Lindsay Brice, February 10, 1997.

" 'I went to call my babysitter' . . .": interview with Barbara Chase Leary, November 20, 1996.

"As Henry Edwards recalled . . .": interview with Henry Edwards, April 29, 1997.

" 'Cocaine is a "bad drug" ' . . .": letter to Hugh Downs, July 3, 1979, Timothy Leary Archives.

"Edwards remembered Leary telling him . . .": interview with Henry Edwards, April 29, 1997.

"In the fall of 1978 . . .": Timothy Leary, *Chaos & Cyberculture* (Berkeley, CA: Ronin Publishing, 1994).

"All the while, he was aware that . . .": interview with Henry Edwards, April 29, 1997.

"'It was always hand to mouth' . . .": interview with Barbara Chase Leary, November 20, 1996.

"In August, the high-powered public relations firm . . .": press release, 1979, Timothy Leary Archives.

"One reviewer noted that Leary . . .": Larry Eichel, "Look Who's a Stand-Up Comedian," *San Francisco Examiner,* August 29, 1979.

"'There was this Italian girl' . . .": interview with Barbara Chase Leary, November 20, 1996.

"Two months later when Tim flew to New York . . .": Videotape, The Stanley Siegel Show, November 1, 1979

FORTY-FIVE

"'It was the height of their social' . . .": interview with Alan U. Schwartz, September 25, 1997.

"'If Tim was attacking the Catholic Church' . . .": interview with Barbara Chase Leary, November 20, 1996.

"One of Tim's letters concerned his outrage . . .": "Letter to the Editor," undated, Timothy Leary Archives.

"'Larry Flynt wanted to have a meeting' . . .": interview with Henry Edwards, April 30, 1997.

"Alan Schwartz, now functioning as Tim's . . .": interview with Alan U. Schwartz, September 25, 1997.

"'No one liked *Hustler*' . . .": interview with Barbara Chase Leary, November 20, 1996.

"'He did it for the money' . . .": interview with Henry Edwards, April 30, 1997.

"Sentenced to twenty-one and a half years . . .": interview with G. Gordon Liddy, December 9, 1996.

"'The essential difference between Tim' . . .": Paul Krassner, *Confessions of a Raving, Unconfined Nut: Misadventures in the Counter-Culture* (New York: Simon & Schuster, 1993).

"Onstage during the debates . . .": interview with G. Gordon Liddy, December 9, 1996.

"'I was struck by the irony of it' . . .": interview with Paul Krassner, October 21, 1996.

"'For all of Tim's devotion' . . .": interview with G. Gordon Liddy, December 9, 1996.

"When they appeared together . . .": David Rosenthal, "The Drug-and-Thug Show Takes to the Road," *The Mercury News,* May 3, 1982.

"Night after night, both men used lines . . .": ibid.

"'I thought he was absolutely charming' . . .": interview with Nina Graboi, October 8, 1996.

"'I asked Tim if he would be' . . .": interview with Alan Rudolph, January 14, 1997.

"'There was always a big party' . . .": interview with G. Gordon Liddy, December 9, 1996.

"'We were giving them their calls' . . .": interview with Alan Rudolph, January 14, 1997.

"In a review of the debate . . .": Sylvie Drake, "Liddy, Leary Selling a Bad Dose of Snake Oil," *Los Angeles Times,* July 13, 1982.

"Kevin Thomas of the *Los Angeles* . . .": Kevin Thomas, "'Return Engagement' for Liddy, Leary," *Los Angeles Times,* November 27, 1983

"In *The New York Times* . . .": Vincent Canby, "Film: Liddy and Leary in 'Return Engagement,'" *The New York Times,* November 23, 1983.

"'When I read *Flashbacks*' . . .": interview with Travis Ashbrook, June 5, 1997.

"'He was just horsing around' . . .": Herbert Gold, *The New York Times Book Review,* date unknown.

"In a review entitled . . .": David Harris, "Tripping & Stumbling," *The Washington Post,* June 10, 1983.

"'We went to this thing' . . .": interview with Brendan Maher, February 5, 1997.

"Kelman, no more enamored of Tim . . .": interview with Herbert Kelman, February 15, 1997.

"Inspired by the recently released movie . . .": interview with David McClelland, February 5, 1997.

"Michael Simmons of *Heavy Metal* . . .": Michael Simmons, "Cheerleader for Change: The Timothy Leary Interview," *Heavy Metal* (October 1983).

"After he leaked this item . . .": Timothy Leary, "Rebel Hero of the Week," *Rebel* (December 21, 1983).

" 'It's too bad LSD is illegal' . . .": "Cary Grant Talks About His Drug Use & How He Wants Another Child," *The National Enquirer,* December 21, 1983 (?).

"From his wheelchair in a courtroom . . .": John Kendall, "Flynt Sentenced to 15 Months in Prison," *Los Angeles Times,* date unknown.

"During a jailhouse interview . . .": Paul Wilner, "Secret Service Probes Flynt's Televised Threat to Kill Reagan," *Los Angeles Herald Examiner,* March 16, 1984.

" 'I just cannot believe how' . . .": letter to Larry Flynt, March 26, 1984, Timothy Leary Archives.

"Tim wrote again the next day . . .": letter to Larry Flynt, March 27, 1984, Timothy Leary Archives.

"On April 9, 1984, Tim wrote Flynt . . .": letter to Larry Flynt, April 9, 1984, Timothy Leary Archives.

" 'He gave me my first computer' . . .": interview with Jeff Scheftel, April 25, 1997.

"Although Hefner had recently suffered . . .": interview with Carrie Leigh, February 11, 1997.

" 'Barbara wanted to move' . . .": interview with Jeff Scheftel, April 25, 1997.

" 'I gave them the benefit of my knowledge' . . .": interview with Eric Gardner, April 10, 1997.

" 'Tim was in a dozen films' . . .": interview with Michael Horowitz, February 19, 1997.

" 'But when I called them up' . . .": interview with Eric Gardner, April 10, 1997.

FORTY-SIX

"Greeting each other joyously . . .": interview with Henry Edwards, April 29, 1997.

"Meeting Tim during this period . . .": interview with Douglas Rushkoff, March 18, 1997.

"In April 1988, a two-page photo . . .": Ron Rosebaum, "Back in the High Life," *Vanity Fair* (April 1988).

" 'Clinically,' Dieadra Martino . . .": interview with Dieadra Martino, November 10, 1996.

" 'The bottom line' . . .": interview with Barbara Chase Leary, November 20, 1996.

" 'Me, Ashley, and Zach decided' . . .": interview with Dieadra Martino, November 10, 1996.

"The letter read, 'I, Susan Martino' . . .": document, Timothy Leary Archives.

" 'My mom was in the army' . . .": interview with Dieadra Martino, November 10, 1996.

"Henry Edwards remembered . . .": interview with Henry Edwards, April 29, 1997.

" 'Tim's daughter was a grown woman' . . .": interview with Barbara Chase Leary, November 20, 1996.

"When Vicki Marshall, Tim's personal assistant . . .": interview with Vicki Marshall, July 9, 2002.

" 'He was a security guard' . . .": interview with Dieadra Martino, November 10, 1996.

" 'Dear Tim,' she wrote . . .": document, Timothy Leary Archives.

" 'Oh, Susan,' he wrote . . .": documents, Timothy Leary Archives.

" 'When Barbara would come in' . . .": interview with Mel Seesholtz, February 17, 1997.

" 'When Barbara would come up the driveway' . . .": interview with Vicki Marshall, October 20, 1996.

" 'By this point' . . .": interview with John Perry Barlow, December 2, 1996.

" 'Timothy saw himself in many ways' . . .": interview with Mel Seesholtz, February 17, 1997.

" 'She was absolutely determined to do it' . . .": interview with Vicki Marshall, July 9, 2002.

" 'I went down there with Tim ' . . .": interview with George Milman, February 12, 1997.

" 'The hardest thing I ever did' . . .": interview with Dieadra Martino, November 10, 1996.

"In an interview done shortly after . . .": Terry Spencer, "Leary Daughter Dies After Jail-Cell Hanging," *Los Angeles Daily News,* September 7, 1990.

" 'The saddest I ever saw Tim' . . .": interview with Joanne Segel, April 29, 1997.

FORTY-SEVEN

"A few months before Susan's death . . .": letter from Joanna Harcourt-Smith, undated, Timothy Leary Archives.

"'Yes, our relationship was amazing' . . .": letter to Joanna Harcourt-Smith, July 8, 1990, Timothy Leary Archives.

"'I was deeply touched by the news' . . .": letter from Joanna Harcourt-Smith, September 21, 1990, Timothy Leary Archives.

"'Being the good Irish boy' . . .": interview with John Perry Barlow, December 2, 1996.

"'Tim aged very rapidly' . . .": interview with Barbara Chase Leary, November 20, 1996.

"'They got on the plane' . . .": interview with Eric Gardner, April 10, 1997.

"'I think it was devastating for him' . . .": interview with Peggy Hitchcock, December 2, 1996.

"Timmy was so brilliant, romantic, and funny..." E-mail from Barbara Leary, December 16, 2005.

"'All these new people came' . . .": interview with Jeff Scheftel, April 25, 1997.

"Douglas Rushkoff confirmed that it . . .": interview with Douglas Rushkoff, March 18, 1997.

"'And the fourth week' . . .": interview with Vicki Marshall, October 20, 1996.

"'Right after I quit *Mondo 2000*' . . .": interview with RU Sirius, April 23, 1997.

"On July 6, 1992, *People* magazine reported . . .": Toby Kahn, "Passages," *People* (July 6, 1992).

"Eventually, in Gardner's words . . .": interview with Eric Gardner, April 10, 1997.

"She recalled, 'It was twenty years to the day' . . .": interview with Rosemary Woodruff Leary, March 11, 1997.

"On March 30, 1994, *The New York Times* reported . . .": "Chronicle: One of Timothy Leary's Former Wives Comes in from the Cold," *The New York Times*, March 30, 1994.

"'I had no idea who Tim was' . . .": interview with Leslie Meyers, November 10, 1996.

"When she got there . . .": interview with Lindsay Brice, February 10, 1997.

"'These were the Viper Room days' . . .": interview with Douglas Rushkoff, March 18, 1997.

"'I would usually show up with a wedge of brie' . . .": interview with Lindsay Brice, February 10, 1997.

"'He was doing a lot of coke' . . .": interview with Vicki Marshall, October 20, 1996.

"'He was in very bad shape' . . .": interview with George Milman, February 12, 1997.

"When Leslie Meyers came to visit him . . .": interview with Leslie Meyers, November 10, 1996.

"'He was suspicious and paranoid' . . .": interview with Vicki Marshall, October 20, 1996.

FORTY-EIGHT

"As the two of them were dancing . . .": interview with Denis Berry, April 9, 1997.

"'I contracted HIV' . . .": interview with Aileen Getty, October 22, 1996.

"'Tim thought smoking in public' . . .": interview with Douglas Rushkoff, March 18, 1997.

"As he would later say . . .": Lewis MacAdams, "Tune In, Turn On, Drop Dead," *LA Weekly* (May 17–23, 1996).

"'Aileen was so far out and had no rules' . . .": interview with Leslie Meyers, November 10, 1996.

"'Timmy kept telling me that she wanted' . . .": interview with Barbara Chase Leary, November 20, 1996.

"'She wanted them to die together' . . .": interview with Denis Berry, April 9, 1997.

"'They either didn't do the PSA test' . . .": interview with George Milman, February 12, 1997.

"'We both had prostate cancer' . . .": interview with John Roseboro, April 25, 1997.

"Bob Guccione Jr., the publisher of *Spin* . . .": interview with Bob Guccione Jr., January 4, 1996.

"Although she did not like LA . . .": interview with Rosemary Woodruff Leary, March 11, 1997.

"Dated April 12, 1995, the letter began . . .": letter to Jack Leary, April 12, 1995, Timothy Leary Archives.

"'There was definitely that wish to reconcile'...": interview with Bob Guccione Jr., January 4, 1996.

"'Dear Ted Fields'...": letter to Ted Field, April 17, 1995, Timothy Leary Archives.

"Now that Tim knew he was ill...": interview with Eric Gardner, April 10, 1997.

"'Sure, go ahead'...": interview with Jeff Scheftel, April 25, 1997.

"'That was the first time I ever saw Timothy cry'...": interview with Lindsay Brice, February 10, 1997.

"A few weeks later, Tim went public...": David Colker, "Terminal Man," *Los Angeles Times,* August 28, 1995.

"'They had this huge party'...": interview with Leslie Meyers, November 10, 1996.

"'That was a bash'...": interview with Douglas Rushkoff, March 18, 1997.

"'It was really depressing'...": interview with Alan U. Schwartz, September 25, 1997.

"'My leaving destabilized the house'...": interview with Denis Berry, April 9, 1997.

"'After Tim announced his terminal condition'...": interview with Vicki Marshall, October 20, 1996.

"'I took it to be a proposal'...": interview with Douglas Rushkoff, March 18, 1997.

"'There was no way to monitor'...": interview with George Milman, February 12, 1997.

"Trudy Truelove, who had worked...": interview with Trudy Truelove, February 11, 1997.

"On November 26, 1995, the Sunday...": Laura Mansnerus, "At Death's Door, the Message Is Tune In, Turn On, Drop In," *The New York Times,* November 26, 1995.

"A front-page article...": Pamela Kramer, "Designer Dying," *The Mercury News,* February 27, 1966.

"In March, *New York* magazine reported...": Beth Landman and Deborah Mitchell, "Tune In, Turn On, Drop Out," *New York* (March 18, 1996).

"Sucking on a balloon of nitrous oxide...": *Timothy Leary Lives,* produced by David Silver.

"'Suddenly,' Chamberlain recalled...": interview with Dean Chamberlain, February 10, 1997.

"'Oscar Janiger brought the first tank'...": interview with Vicki Marshall, October 20, 1996.

"'Did you see me last night'...": interview with Lindsay Brice, February 10, 1997.

"'Tim seriously ODed'...": interview with Vicki Marshall, October 20, 1996.

"'All these Web-site kids were there'...": interview with Douglas Rushkoff, March 18, 1997.

"'All of a sudden'...": interview with Mike Vague, February 11, 1997.

"Rushkoff, now commuting to the house...": interview with Douglas Rushkoff, March 18, 1997.

"When Denis Berry returned from Santa Cruz...": interview with Denis Berry, April 9, 1997.

"'We were waiting for Jack'...": interview, January 27, 1997.

"'Think what it must have been like for Jack'...": interview with Rosemary Woodruff Leary, March 11, 1997.

FORTY-NINE

"Tim's art collection included...": Lewis MacAdams, "Tune In, Turn On, Drop Dead," *LA Weekly* (May 17–23, 1996).

"'When we took the stuff out'...": interview with Denis Berry, April 9, 1997.

"'The house became a carnival'...": interview with Lindsay Brice, February 10, 1997.

"'There would be psychic battles'...": interview with Mike Vague, February 11, 1997.

"'The media was trying to exploit him'...": interview with Trudy Truelove, February 11, 1997.

"'They were absolutely up with him'...": interview with Denis Berry, April 9, 1997.

"Trudy Truelove remembered that when...": interview with Trudy Truelove, February 11, 1997.

"'People were busily—happily—setting up'...": interview with Lindsay Brice, February 10, 1997.

"'We turned it into an art piece'...": interview with Stacy Valis, February 10, 1997.

"'They said, "We've got something to show you"'...": interview with Lindsay Brice, February 10, 1997.

"On April 18, Tim told a reporter . . .": Leary talks of logging off while he's logged on," *The Mercury News,* April 19, 1996.

" 'I remember when Timmy was talking about' . . .": interview with Dieadra Martino, November 10, 1996.

"As one user breathlessly noted . . .": David Hyman, sent to the author by Chip Hall, Release Software Corp., chip@releasesoft.com, April 14, 1996.

"By the third week in April . . .": leary.com, April 14–21, 1996.

"Even as he was raising other people's . . .": interview with Vicki Marshall, October 20, 1996.

"Alone with Tim in his bedrooom . . .": interview with Dean Chamberlain, February 10, 1997.

"Camella Grace, who went to the dinner . . .": "The Final Trip," David Colker, *Los Angeles Times,* June 3, 1996.

" 'It was such a shock' . . .": ibid.

"In his bedroom on Sunbrook Drive . . .": ibid.

"Putting her hand on Tim's shoulder . . .": interview with Trudy Truelove, February 11, 1997.

"Coming in from the living room . . .": interview with Dean Chamberlain, February 10, 1997.

"Rather than 'be reanimated' . . .": Douglas Rushkoff, "Leary's Last Trip," *Esquire* (August 1996).

"On May 6, Tim told . . .": David Colker, "Leary Severs Ties to Cryonics Advocates," *Los Angeles Times,* May 7, 1996.

" 'He used to say' . . .": interview with Vicki Marshall, October 20, 1996.

" 'They were doing this shoop-shoop thing' . . .": interview with John Perry Barlow, December 2, 1996.

"When Kesey said to him . . .": *Timothy Leary's Last Trip,* documentary, A. J. Catoline and O. B Babbs.

"The only other person in the room . . .": interview with Joanne Segel, April 29, 1997.

"When Tim's responses . . .": "VF Questionnaire," *Vanity Fair* (June 1996).

" 'I don't *want* to make sense' . . .": Lewis MacAdams, "Tune In, Turn On, Drop Dead," *LA Weekly* (May 17–23, 1996).

"In *Esquire,* Richard Leiby wrote . . .": Richard Leiby, "The Magical Mystery Cure," *Esquire* (September 1997).

"At one point, Tim was so out of it . . .": interview with Dean Chamberlain, February 10, 1997.

"Rosin had already agreed . . .": interview with Carol Rosin, May 19, 1997.

" 'There was a big laugh in the room' . . .": interview with Bob Guccione Jr., January 4, 1996.

"Tim repeated the phrase . . .": Rushkoff, "Leary's Last Trip."

"Rosin recalled . . .": interview with Carol Rosin, May 19, 1997.

" 'I grabbed him and held his hand' . . .": interview with Bob Guccione Jr., January 4, 1996.

" 'I had totally forgotten about it' . . .": interview with Carol Rosin, May 19, 1997.

INDEX